D0560930

THE COURT OF THE LION

THE COURT OF THE LION

A Novel of the
T'ANG DYNASTY

ELEANOR
COONEY

DANIEL
ALTIERI

WILLIAM MORROW AND COMPANY INC.
NEW YORK

Excerpts from the following works are used with permission:

The Background of the Rebellion of An Lu-Shan, by E. G. Pulleybank. New York: Oxford University Press, 1966. Reprinted from *London Oriental Series*, Vol. 4. Copyright 1955 by Oxford University Press.

Chinese Eunuchs: The Structure of Intimate Politics, by Taisuke Mitamura. Tokyo: Charles E. Tuttle Company, 1970. Translated by Charles A. Pomeroy.

The Divine Woman: Dragon Ladies and Rain Maidens in T'ang Literature, by Edward H. Schafer. San Francisco: North Point Press. Contains Tu Fu's ode on the Temple of the Consort. Copyright © 1980 by Edward H. Schafer.

Great Ages of Man: Ancient China, by Edward H. Schafer and the editors of Time-Life Books. Copyright © 1967 by Time-Life Books.

Shore of Pearls: Hainan Island in Early Times, by Edward H. Schafer. London: University of California Press. Copyright © 1969 by the Regents of the University of California.

Tu Fu: China's Greatest Poet, by William Hung. Cambridge, Mass.: Harvard University Press. Copyright 1952 by the President and Fellows of Harvard College. Renewed 1980 by William Hung.

Translations of the following poems are copyrighted © 1989 by Daniel Altieri: "Poems of the Heart" by Juan Chi, "Shih Ching" ("Book of Odes"), "A Poem" by Shen Yueh, "Poem in the Old Style" by Li Po, "Admonitions," and "Thatched Hut" and "Pretty Women" by Tu Fu.

The authors also gratefully acknowledge use of:

China: A Short Cultural History, by C. P. Fitzgerald. London: Cresset Press Ltd., 1969.

Harem Favorites of an Illustrious Celestial, by Howard S. Levy. Taiwan: Chung-T'ai Printing Company, 1958.

"Les Grands Fonctionnaires des Provinces en Chine sous la dynastie des T'ang," by Robert des Rotours. *Toung-Pao 25*, 1927.

"The Rise of the Eunuchs in the T'ang Dynasty," by John K. Rideout. *Asia Minor* (new series) I, I, 1949.

Library of Congress Cataloging-in-Publication Data

Cooney, Eleanor.
   The court of the lion : a novel of the T'ang Dynasty / Eleanor
Cooney, Daniel Altieri.
      p.   cm.
   Bibliography: p.
   ISBN 0-87795-902-1
   1. China—History—T'ang dynasty, 618–907—Fiction.   2. T'ang
Hsüan-tsung, Emperor of China, 685–762—Fiction.   I. Altieri,
Daniel.   II. Title.
PS3551.L792C68   1988
813'.54—dc19

                                                                            88-10914
                                                                            CIP

Printed in the United States of America

First Edition

1 2 3 4 5 6 7 8 9 10

BOOK DESIGN BY LINEY LI

To Gwendda
who first pointed us down the Silk Road
and
To our parents

ACKNOWLEDGMENTS

SPECIAL thanks to our friends and supporters: Loxy Devin, Leslie Houser, Helen Flake, Duckworth Steinbeck, Terryl Burns, Mary Simon, Fane Jones, Bill Jones, Donna Jones, Norris Crawford, Linnis Vignone, Fritz Cramblitt, Lawrence Ray, Richard Gale, Nicholas McCumber, Dr. Torsten Jacobson, Jim Larsen, Edward Piersen, Corrine Petteys, Linn Bottorf, Lee Edmundson, Barbara Fortune, Charles Delimur, Phyllis White, Michael McCowan, Lettie Cowden, Margaret Mary O'Rourke, and Linda Freedman.

Special thanks are also in order to Frederick Walker, M.D., for his help with medical, pathological, and forensic questions and to William Hand, D.V.M., for his knowledge and assistance in many matters involving Oriental pharmacology, for his eccentric brilliance, and for sharing our appreciation of the bizarre.

Special thanks to our good friends Barbara and Hugh Dawson for helping to open China to us.

Special thanks to Marcelee Gralapp and Sharon Gralapp, the Boulder Public Library Foundation, and The Colorado Council on the Arts and Humanities.

And to Robert Gottlieb of the William Morris Agency, for being our agent and much, much more; to Al Zuckerman of Writer's House, and our sincerest thanks to Liza Dawson, Ann Harris, and Eden Collinsworth.

For technical support in the preparation of this manuscript, additional thanks to Susan Hayes of Software Toolworks, Sherman Oaks, CA, for Software Country's *The Book of Change: I Ching;* and to Allen Bomberger at Poor Person Software, Palo Alto, CA, and to Brenda Bennett and her colleagues at the New Micropro in San Rafael, CA. Also, regarding matters of computers and technical assistance, our special thanks are extended to Kathi and Jeff Edwards of Computer Solution, and thanks to Kaypro Computers, and to our friends at the R.O.P. Computer Labs (Mendocino

County's Regional Occupation Program) and our friend Bill Nesting at High Tech Research of Redding, CA, for his special help and hardware add-ons.

And last but not least, our thanks to the magnificent Northern California coast, for being home, and to the people fighting to protect it from the oil industry; and to our many other friends, both bipedal and quadrupedal.

CONTENTS

List of
MAIN HISTORICAL CHARACTERS
with Pronunciation Guide

The Romanization system used for Chinese names and words in this book is a combination of the Wade-Giles system and the old Yale Romanization system. The modern pinyin phoneticization system, though used in all present-day scholarly works, has been avoided here in order to present Chinese words in the form that we feel is more familiar and recognizable to Western readers.

The names below are those of real people who actually lived in T'ang China. It is suggested that the reader say the names out loud a few times to familiarize himself with the pronunciation of the various syllables.

AN CHING-HSU (on-ching-súe): elder son of An Lu-shan.

AN LU-SHAN (on-lew-sháhn): former captive slave risen to position of respect and high rank in the Chinese military, fated to become the Emperor's adopted "son."

A PU-SSU (ah-pū-sŝū—final syllable with a sybillant "s"): a northern tribal cavalry officer who first serves under An Lu-shan but later rebels against the general's bloodthirsty insanity.

CHANG CHIU-LING (jhang-joe-líng): poet and statesman, banished to the island of Hainan by Li Lin-fu.

EMPRESS WANG (wahng): the Emperor's barren wife, banished for using witchcraft in an attempt to conceive.

GENERAL FENG (fung): a general with close ties to the imperial family. An Lu-shan's first escort into Chang-an. An imperial family tutor and trainer who has become close to several crown princes. Club-footed.

KAO LI-SHIH (gow-lee-shér—first syllable rhymes with "cow," last syllable rhymes with "purr"): the chief palace eunuch and the Emperor's close friend.

LADY OF HAN (hahn) and **LADY OF CHIN** (jhin): two more sisters of the Precious Consort.

LADY OF KUO ("awe" with a hard "gw" preceding): the Precious Consort's elder sister, who also became a palace favorite.

LADY WU (woo): the Emperor's consort at the beginning of the story; second in rank only to the Empress Wang.

LI CHU-ERH (lee-chew-a͏́re): An Lu-shan's eunuch servant.

LI LIN-FU (lee-lin-fo͏́o): the Emperor's chief minister, feared and respected by all.

LI PO (lee-baw): famous T'ang poet, occasional government minister. But generally a reclusive and scandalous person of great literary merit and friend of the other great poet-scholar minister Tu Fu.

LI SHIH-CHIH (lee-sher-jhe͏́r—second and third syllables rhyme with "purr"): Chinese general and man of letters who originally saved An Lu-shan from a criminal's death but who later was forced into being his enemy.

LU PEI (loo-ba͏́y): an apprentice eunuch under Kao Li-shih.

MINGHUANG (ming-wahng); also called **HSUAN-TSUNG** (swan-sung): Emperor of T'ang China.

MING WU: elderly female practitioner of Dark Taoism, reputed to be an immortal.

NIU HSIEN-KO (nyo-syen-g͏́e—last syllable rhymes with French "le"): Li Lin-fu's right-hand man and assistant chief minister.

YANG KUEI-FEI (yahng gway-fay); later known as **Precious Consort**: former Taoist nun who became the Emperor's lover and focal point of his life.

YANG KUO-CHUNG (yahng-gwuh-chu͏́ng): cousin of the Yang sisters and lover of the Lady of Kuo.

FOREWORD

Our story opens in A.D. *738 (by Western calendrical reckoning), the twenty-fifth year of the K'ai Yuan reign period, at the court of T'ang Minghuang, Brilliant Emperor of the T'ang. The locale is the bureaucratic city and imperial palace of Ta Ming, rising above the great capital city of Ch'ang-an in the province of Shensi on the fertile plain at the elbow of the Wei River.*

It is a period of both artistic and technical cultivation and economic and agrarian stability, with an ever-widening merchant and middle class, and national borders that reach from the great fertile steppes of central Asia to the humid jungles of Annam (Vietnam). Commerce and communication have been greatly expanded and the negative effects of drought and flood ameliorated by granaries, canals, locks, and levies. Under this benevolent regime, the peasant foundation of the empire has enjoyed some relief from the harshness of highly unfair taxation and land practices. An educated class of civil servants slowly replaces the entrenched ruling aristocracies, and China enjoys the benefits of a single strong central government. But it is also a time when the prosperity, peace, and uninvaded sovereignty of the Chinese empire hang in a delicate balance. Great forces mount against the realm from both within and without. The Tibetans push at the borders of the distant west; the nomadic Mongolian cavalries of the Hsi and Khitan (barbarian neighbors) are stacked against the north. The historical ages-old secessionist tendencies of China's own northern territories also threaten the empire from within.

The Emperor T'ang Minghuang is loved as a wise and humane ruler and a great patron of the arts, painting, and the Golden Age of Poetries. He has done much to alleviate the suffering of the common man, reducing the ungainly number of huge landholdings, feudal lords, and princes and instituting egalitarian land reforms. But he has lost the will to deal with pressing military realities, and after only twelve years on the throne has allowed the six armies of the interior realm to grow weak while only the northern military governors strengthen their commanderies.

Underlying the social, political, and military realities of the T'ang dynasty was another reality. According to Chinese philosophy of the time, there existed an invisible, intangible world influencing the empirical world of human events. Despite the emphasis placed by rational Confucianism on logic, order, and decorum in determining the fates of men, and though superstition and magic were continually assaulted by the government, most Chinese people saw the world as a delicate interplay and balance of primal forces—yin and yang.

The stability of the natural and man-made worlds was dependent on the constant harmony of these two principles. Yang, the male principle, is fiery, bright, and overt. It is associated with the dragon that glides through the water and the intense sun and flaming pearl that penetrates the clouds. It is open, forceful, violent. Yin, the female principle, is dark, covert, mysterious. It is associated with water, cloud, and shadow. In the natural world, a drought would be considered an overabundance of yang: *floods and heavy rains, an excess of* yin. *In the political world, too much* yang *could result in violent upheaval and use of force; an imbalance of* yin *means dangerous female influence: subterfuge, scandal, clannish conspiracies among matriarchs, consorts, and empresses that would result in mysterious assassinations.*

Somewhere in the vastness of China rest the bones of every person in this story.

BOOK ONE

KAN YU*

ENCOUNTERING
SORROWS

*Title of a cycle of twelve poems by the eighth-century statesman and poet Chang Chiu-ling. The veiled purpose of these poems was to warn others of the dangers of men in criminal collusion. He spoke specifically of the chief minister Li Lin-fu.

1

Nights of Sorcery

It is alleged that the Lady Wu (Wu Hui-fei, Favoured Consort) was visited by the ghosts of the princes whom she had wronged. She became seriously ill and, despite the efforts of diviners to save her, . . . died a violent death.

—Howard Levy

Chinese historiographers have tended to emphasize natural disasters closely preceding troubles in the human sphere, in the belief that they constituted warnings from Heaven. We therefore hear a good deal in our sources about various calamities which befell China . . . before the outbreak of the rebellion. The greatest of these was a period of continuous rain in the capital province of Kuan-chung, and . . . around Loyang. . . . Such an excess of *yin* over *yang* was later, and perhaps even at the time, taken as a sign of the dominance exerted over the emperor by his favourite [consorts] and [their families].

—Edwin Pulleyblank

NOVEMBER 15

Her plump fingers arranged the jewelry on the table.

"You will receive the rest of it after it is done," she said. The fingers that picked up the jewels for consideration were lean and weathered. Expertly, they turned and hefted the offerings, then laid them down again. The hand lay alongside the glittering array; thumb and forefinger caressed one another thoughtfully. Then the blunt nails tapped the tabletop gently. The Consort Most Favored Lady Wu waited, her own hands fluttering from her throat to her lap, where they intertwined for a moment before sliding into her sleeves.

"The blood that you ask me to spill is costly," the aristocratic voice said quietly. "We are not speaking of cows and chickens, are we? What you show me here would pay for perhaps one minor harem woman or two officials below the ninth grade. But a princeling . . ." The voice was polite, but she sensed contempt just below the surface, and impatience. She lifted another box onto the table and opened it. She also laid out a note for one million in copper cash.

The assassin considered for a moment, then sighed.

"The young ones, you understand, are more difficult. I prefer to kill them while they sleep. If it is done correctly, they proceed directly from sleep into death, without passing through this world. There are not many who possess this skill; I consider it to be the highest expression of my art. I offer you this service, but it entails extra expense . . ."

"How much for this . . . service?"

"For another fifty thousand taels of silver, I will send him into the other world as gently as a mother rocking her baby to sleep. Your own sleep will be as untroubled."

Lady Wu exhaled sharply.

"Of course," he said, shrugging, "it is not necessary. I can treat him as an adult."

The assassin raised his eyes to Lady Wu's. "With adults, it is another art form entirely, one that I enjoy as well, but for a different reason. It would be wasteful to deny some of my subjects the opportunity to contemplate the face of death; I must admit that there is a bit of the thespian in me. There are so many different ways to portray death!" he said with enthusiasm. He looked at her as if deciding which sort of death he would tailor for her. Habit, she supposed. She felt naked in his presence, sensing his familiarity, like a physician's, with the human anatomy.

"I . . . I will pay you the extra," she said hastily.

"Ah, Lady Wu, you are so kind," he replied, gathering the money and jewelry. "So kind."

DECEMBER 1

"The dead speak to him," one court lady had said to another. The consort Lady Wu pulled tight the quilt around her shoulders as she contemplated these words. She was alone in her quarters in the palace. She sat, wrapped in quilts, on her chaise. It was late—more than halfway between the time when the sun had set and when it would rise again.

Breathing had become difficult for Lady Wu of late. She thought consciously about each breath, forcing her chest to expand to take air in, then squeezing it out again. Often she sat for several hours, thinking only of breathing, afraid that she might forget.

An investigation had been ordered by the Emperor into the death of Prince Ying. A physician had been called in, a man who made a study of forensic science. A corpse, the physician had claimed, could "speak"—it could tell him every detail of the individual's death. The man was traveling from the eastern capital of Loyang, a journey of several days. Somewhere in the palace, the dead prince lay packed in snow and ice, waiting.

Lady Wu waited, too. Since the moment that the elegant hands had gathered the jewels and money from the polished tabletop, she had felt as if she were suspended over an abyss. The prince's death, the assassin had assured her, would appear to be self-inflicted. But she had not anticipated the magician-physician who held conversations with corpses. She imagined the skills of the two men pitted against one another. The assassin's skill was all that stood between a verdict of murder and one of suicide.

The man's credentials were impeccable. Many was the time that he had expedited the departure of a soul from this world in the service of the consort Lady Wu's uncle. Uncle had always referred to the process as "untying a knot"; necessary, occasionally, in order to insure the smooth accomplishment of his aims. He went about the task with the same calm as if he were ordering a new piece of furniture for the house or arranging for a family trip to the mountains. Certainly his sleep was not interrupted, and he continued to eat his food with his usual enjoyment and to train his little birds to sing.

She remembered a round, fluffy bird sitting on Uncle's index finger with its little chest puffed out as it sang, tilting its head to one side as it imitated Uncle's whistled songs. The memory of Uncle's bird brought her another image. She had often watched her sons feed living rodents to their pet snake. The reptile would ignore its quarry, for hours and sometimes days until its appetite was finally aroused. The mouse, oblivious, would nibble on bits of grain or preen its whiskers and fur as the snake glided nearer. The mouse, she thought, was absurd in its complacency as death approached, its twitching nose and beady black eyes failing to warn it. Now she felt like a fat, ignorant rodent in her nest, unable to sense the approach of the enemy. The air thickened around her.

The murder of the prince had not been her idea. Or had it? Her mind was confused. Several months before, the consort Lady Wu had been engaged in a determined effort to refine herself. She had been trying to eradicate a stubborn image that had taken hold in her mind, very different from the image of the doomed rodent, but no less disturbing. It was hardly fitting that an emperor's consort and mother of six princes should think of herself as a large, dumb animal; the thought that anyone else might possibly perceive her as a brood mare or a sow had alarmed her.

True, she gave birth every spring, the same time of year when the Emperor's mares dropped their foals. Her waist had thickened after numerous pregnancies. Perpetual gestation had become her main occupation; it had been years since she had practiced any of the arts painstakingly taught her as a girl.

Recently, the childless Empress Wang had taken her own life. The extent to which the Empress was mourned at court had made a strong impression on Lady Wu. The Empress had possessed another form of femininity, unencumbered by fecundity, quite different from Lady Wu's. People spoke in sad tones of the Empress's elegance, refinement, artistry, and slender silhouette. If I were to die, Lady Wu had thought, what would they talk about? That was when the unwelcome picture of herself as lactating beast had intruded.

She had applied herself to the practice of her calligraphy, set aside years ago, and had even composed some poetry. She labored long and hard, and was rewarded for her efforts with stiff, self-conscious brushstrokes, thick in places where the bristles should only caress the parchment, and with occasional dark blobs of ink where there should have been nothing. She had turned to another womanly art, that of flower arranging. She ordered fresh flowers sent to her quarters in the Hall of Consorts every day. The flowers were often unresponsive to her touch as well; they sagged, bunched together, and drooped sullenly. With practice, though, she found that she could put them in fairly graceful poses as long as she kept her arrangements symmetrical.

Just when she had begun to tire of flower arranging, a remarkable thing happened. The flowers began telling her stories. She noticed, among the peonies, lilies, and pear blossoms delivered to her, imposters—made of silk—that had never existed in nature. Tiny characters, which at first glance resembled the natural patterns of spots inside a tiger lily, invited her to look closely at the stamens of the flowers. She saw that they were actually tightly rolled bits of paper.

When she unrolled the papers, she discovered an artistic hand forming words that she might have written herself, as if one of her fondest secret fantasies had come to life. The papers addressed her as "Empress Wu" and told elaborate tales about the beloved "Empress."

The first story had gripped her attention. It portrayed the "Empress" Wu cleverly uncovering an assassination plot against the Emperor, courageously warning him at great danger to herself. In another tale, she argued in a ladylike but firmly persuasive manner with the Emperor in favor of the abolishment of the death penalty in the realm. Her humaneness made her beloved by her subjects, and the Emperor thanked her for her guidance.

But her favorite stories had been the ones that showed her as an old, old lady, a dowager empress and widow, and mother of the new Emperor. In one story, her son Mao, though grieving deeply for his deceased father, accepted the Mandate of Heaven and succeeded him on the throne. Following the precedent set by his father, the new Emperor regularly consulted the Empress Wu, knowing her guidance and wisdom to be indispensable. In another tale, it was a tradition for the old lady to appear regularly at a spring festival, the crowd clamoring eagerly for a glimpse of her frail, bent form, always seeking assurance that she had lived through yet another winter. And she had wept sympathetically as she read another which told the story of the sad spring when the old lady failed to appear. With her people, she had mourned her own death and the death of the era she personified.

The unidentified teller of these tales did not concern himself with chronology. She had scarcely had time to recover from her sorrow over the death of the elderly queen mother when the flower tales took a giant leap backward in time. The consort Lady Wu, not yet an empress, was depicted taking decisive action, fulfilling her destiny as a descendant of the fearless Wu clan. Understanding that she was fated to be empress and her son Mao to be crown prince, the Lady Wu of the stories was shown putting aside detrimental sentimentality and setting about to do what was right and necessary. It was here that the teller of the tales showed his true artistry. Lady Wu, holding the small scroll in her plump fingers, her lips silently forming the words as she read, had felt her pulse quicken as she read about a woman, a noble creature, with a mystic grasp of what it meant to be an agent of death.

With monklike discipline, the assassin Lady Wu of the flower scrolls grieved for her victim. There must be grief. Without grief, the life of the one sacrificed is rendered valueless; it would be a valueless act to take a valueless life. She allowed her grief to exist, but carefully contained it so that it did not spread beyond its allotted area. Undisciplined grief, she knew, would weaken her and interfere with her purpose. Instead, she drew nourishment from her grief. Sorrow for the untimely death of Crown Prince Ying became an expression of regret that in an imperfect universe, human beings must assume responsibilities more suited to the gods.

The Consort Wu who held the scroll in her hands was filled with sympathy and admiration. She read again the touching story of the old lady appearing on a flower-decked balcony before her happy, grateful subjects. She could see the ancient Empress's skin, translucent with age, on the hand she raised to the crowd. She could feel the sun warming the old bones and she looked out through the dim eyes over the city in its haze of colors. Next to her stood her emperor-son, Mao, tender and solicitous.

The Consort Wu had carefully wrapped the scrolls in a bit of silk and lovingly placed them in a drawer. It was clear now: the key to the future depicted in the flower-scrolls was the death of the crown prince, Ying, Emperor Minghuang's son by a long-deceased concubine.

Wu's own son Mao, it was known, was the Emperor's next favorite; he would be named crown prince, she was sure. And since Wang had taken her own life, there was no empress. With Mao as crown prince, Lady Wu saw her own succession taking place easily, naturally . . .

The assassin had been very costly, and it had not occurred to her that she could pay more than one hundred thousand taels of silver and then have nothing to show for it. The death of the Prince was meant to purchase the crown for Mao. Surely one receives the goods for which one has paid . . . but what she thought she had bought from the universe had not come to her.

Mao had failed to recognize his opportunity. He had wept piteously for days after his half-brother had been found dead, and had declared that he would sooner slit his own throat than succeed Ying as crown prince. And though he could not have had knowledge of his mother's complicity in the death, he regarded her with fear and suspicion, refusing to speak to her. And the twelve-year-old had conferred for hours, it was said, with his father, the Emperor. When the child emerged from Minghuang's quarters, he was calmer and happier than he had been since the death of Ying. The Emperor had excused him from the responsibility of assuming the crown.

The fearless Lady Wu of the flower-scrolls also failed to materialize. One morning as she was dipping her hands into her washbasin, she saw the face of Prince Ying smiling up at her through the water. She had smashed the basin on the floor. And on three consecutive nights, she had awakened in the dark with the conviction that a large, heavy animal lay next to her on the bed. She had felt the warmth of its body and heard its breathing. She had lain, terrified to move, until dawn.

She had never known pure fear before. It was a sick feeling that traveled to the tips of her fingers and made her eyes water.

She waited as the investigation began. Her fear and guilt, she knew, gave off an odor—and the finely tuned senses of the investigators would follow that odor inexorably to her door.

Now, one night shortly before the scheduled arrival of the magician-physician who talked with the dead, she sat wrapped in quilts. The silence around her was deep. She was awake but fighting drowsiness, afraid that if she slept, she would stop breathing, and afraid to lie down on her bed lest she receive another visit from the animal. She awaited someone she had summoned through the secret palace network. It was another risk, she knew, but she could not simply sit like snake food. She wanted protection.

She concentrated on her breathing. In, out, in. Occasionally her head lolled; she woke in panic. She reestablished the purposeful rhythm of her breathing, fixing her eyes on a sliver of moonlight showing through the shutters.

Across the room, her empty bed was visible in the low lamplit shadows. She looked at the smooth surface, imagining the silky covers touching her skin. It was a temptation. Her head nodded onto her breast.

A sound pulled her head up. She listened. Had it come from outside, or from directly under her chair? It had been either a loud cry in the distance, or a very soft sigh in the room where she sat.

She strained her ears, her body tense. The sound did not repeat itself. Slowly, her grip on the arms of her chaise relaxed. She rearranged the quilts and shifted slightly to a more comfortable position. After a time, she dozed again.

An animal sound, a hissing groan, woke her abruptly, coming from directly behind her head. She leapt from the chaise and looked in the direction from which the sound had come. Nothing. The sound came again, this time from the bed. In the instant that she turned, the sound translated itself from animal to human. Someone sat on her bed, arms raised as if stretching after a night's sleep, yawning long and deep.

Lady Wu backed up, reaching behind herself for support. The figure, finished with its yawn and stretch, watched her. It rose and walked toward her. It was a short silhouette, not much more than child-sized. Lady Wu's breath came in shallow gasps. She found that the wall was behind her, preventing her from backing any further. A musty, smokey odor entered her nostrils. In the shadows, the head of her visitor tilted inquisitively to one side.

"They will not connect you with the death," a woman's voice said.

"Ming Wu," said Lady Wu softly, recognizing now the seldom-seen shamaness and practitioner of Dark Taoism for whom she had sent. In the pale light she saw her necklace of little glittering bottles and small white bones. Lady Wu sat down, the strength gone from her legs. She rested her head in her hands while waiting for her heart to slow down.

"A crown prince!" said the old lady in an admiring tone. "You are new to this, are you not? Up until now you have occupied yourself with bringing princelings into the world, and not with ushering them out." Lady Wu stood then, and turned up the oil lamp to see the face of the witch-woman about whom she had heard for years. Wrinkled like a dried fig it was, with slits for eyes and a broad, insolent grin with one tooth winking. Lady Wu drew back. "A crown prince!" the old lady repeated.

"I need protection," Lady Wu began. "They have started an investigation. It is important that their search and their findings do not lead to me. My sons—"

"You are a paragon of unselfishness, girl," the old woman interrupted, mimicking Lady Wu's tone. "But I told you: They will not connect you with the death. Ming Wu can promise you that." She looked steadily at the younger woman, her broad grin fading. "The verdict will be suicide." Her face was now solemn.

"Suicide!" said Lady Wu joyfully. "Then I have nothing to fear!" Ming Wu's hand came up then, and grasped Lady Wu's chin firmly.

"I did not say that," the old woman replied, turning Lady Wu's head first one way, then the other. Lady Wu was too amazed to object or resist. The hand was warm and dry, the touch authoritative. "No," the old woman said. "You were not made for this, girl. It is in your family, but it has passed you by." Lady Wu pulled her head back then, grabbing the woman's wrist as she did so.

"Nonsense!" she said. "Don't touch me." She let go of the wrist immediately, disturbed by the feel of the bones under the dry skin.

"But I will draw you a circle of protection, since that is what you want," said the old woman. "Sit," she commanded. Lady Wu sank to the chaise.

An hour passed, during which time Ming Wu moved so slowly around Lady Wu's chaise that the motion was imperceptible. Lady Wu found herself unable to focus her attention. She fought to stay awake; each time she shook the drowsiness off, she saw that the witch-woman had moved further around the imaginary circle, though Lady Wu never saw her move. Finally, she could not fight it anymore. She allowed her eyes to close and let go of everything.

A woman's voice in her ear brought her halfway to the surface. In Lady Wu's mind, a picture formed of a young woman with black hair and a handsome, masculine face.

"The circle is complete," she said. "No one will ever mention the death of the prince to you. But Lady Wu . . ." At the sound of her name, Lady Wu summoned her attention for a moment. "There is one whom I cannot keep out of the circle, and from whom you are never free. That one is yourself, Lady Wu."

She slept. When she awoke in the morning, she was in her bed. There was no sign that Ming Wu had been there.

DECEMBER 7

Ming Wu had been right. The official verdict was suicide, and the Emperor had issued a statement to that effect. And not a word was spoken to Lady Wu about the matter. Though the entire palace was occupied with gossip, hearsay, and speculation, the talk flowed around her like water around a rock. No one asked her what she thought. No investigator questioned her. Ying's name was never mentioned in her presence. The subject simply ceased to exist in her vicinity. Her breathing improved; the air she took in seemed lighter. She started to forget about the necessity to breathe, often for hours at a time. At night, she lay down in her bed again. The animal left her alone, and her sleep was dreamless.

She began her flower arranging again. The Prince's death and her role in it hardened inside her until it felt like a small rock. The rock shrank and became harder as it burrowed deeper inside her and she enveloped it with her thick, soft flesh.

She remembered the hag's hand gripping her chin that night, appraising her as if she were a donkey being considered for purchase. It's a wonder she didn't peel my lips back and look at my teeth, thought Lady Wu. Not born to it. It's in your family, but passed you by. She snorted derisively to think of it now. I am my uncle's true niece. What must be done, must be done. As for the child Mao and his headstrong refusal to accept the gift I have purchased for him . . . there is still time for that. He will soon see the right course. I will bide my time; let his wounds heal first. Passed me by. Pheh!

The circle drawn by Ming Wu faded from her memory. She chose instead to take credit herself for the fact that she had not been implicated in the death. It is my calm, and my implacable resolve, she told herself. Had I not inherited these traits from Uncle, then I would have acquired them on my own. She began to see herself in the company of the great empresses and palace ladies of the past who, unafraid, took decisive action. Why, she had even heard of an empress, also named Wu, who had killed one of her own babies. The idea held a strange fascination. It was a type of killing that stood by itself. She toyed with the notion as she arranged a stand of orchids. She looked at the flowers she was trying to put together artfully. They stared back at her, sullen and recalcitrant in their refusal to stand as she wanted them to. They drooped ungracefully.

She had never noticed how ugly they were. Their textures were fleshy; their convoluted shapes resembled obscene body parts with lurid, inappropriate coloration. In the Emperor's menagerie were many different kinds of tropical monkeys. At certain times of the year, the creatures' sexual parts took on coloration like these orchids and swelled out of their normal proportions. She had seen the females thrusting their hindquarters against the mesh of their cages, screeching lustily; the males responded with strange dances, hurling themselves from the walls in their frustration. The orchids in front of her made her think of those monkeys. The smell of the flowers was unpleasant, too. She tried again to balance the setting. It was clumsy and ugly. These are not flowers, she thought angrily, jerking them out of the bowl. She crumpled and squashed the blossoms and twisted and broke the stems, then threw the mass on the floor, grinding them into the carpet with her foot until all that was left was a pulpy mass. She stared at it, shaking.

Late that afternoon, Prince Mao paid his mother a visit. She was surprised; for several weeks he had treated her as if he could see through her. But the visit was what she had hoped for.

Entering her room, he didn't speak at first. He looked at her; she looked back, saying nothing either, and then returned to her needlework, watching him with her peripheral vision. He walked around the room, picking up objects, examining them, and putting them down again. She was relieved. This was what he used to do as a very young child. He liked to fondle his mother's treasures; he'd had the air of a connoisseur since he was old enough to stand up and grasp things. And he invariably chose, without any prompting from her, the finest objects, the ones most finely made or rare and exotic. And it had never been necessary to take them out of his hands; he never broke or dropped them.

Watching him now, she feigned unconcern, though her fingers trembled slightly holding the needle. He has come back, she thought exultantly. The boy approached her chair and picked up one end of the long piece of silk she was stitching.

"Competent, but uninspired," he said. She raised her head in surprise. What was this? "Your work has a plodding quality," he continued. "You learn the rudiments of a craft, and, with practice, are able to turn out acceptable examples. But never, never will you take even one small step into the realm of light."

"Light?" she asked, incredulous.

"Light. Inspiration. Art," he answered, dropping the piece of silk. He stood, waiting for a reply. She looked at her twelve-year-old son. There was no doubt that he was an intelligent child, with literary promise and a good, rational sense. But he was, in most ways, still a child, not inclined to hold forth on adult abstractions. This was strange. She decided to humor him. Obviously, he had been listening to grown-up conversation and was taking some first tentative steps.

"What is art, then?" she asked him patiently.

"It is a realm of magic. It sits atop the ordinary world, invisible to it." He leaned toward her. "Invisible!" he said emphatically. She drew back.

"I . . . I do my best," she said. "I think that some of my work does not entirely lack grace . . ."

"But how you toil! When you arrange blossoms in a bowl, you strain like a plow horse. Your work with ink and brush resembles the muddy footsteps peasants leave behind them in the fields at planting time," he concluded with a satisfied air. The words stung Lady Wu with their incisiveness. There it was, the idea of herself as some sort of large animal; strong, stupid, hardworking. She couldn't tolerate being compared to peasants and workhorses. But her astonishment at the phrases coming from the child standing before her outweighed the personal insult they carried.

"I am sorry that my efforts do not meet your high standards, Master Mao," she replied. When she pronounced his name, he raised his brows and gave her a look that she had never seen before on his face: veiled, conspiratorial, mocking.

"But it should be effortless," he continued. "An empress, for instance, can be a work of art in herself, without ever lifting a brush or a needle. Her

mere existence—her voice, the expression of her eyes, her essence. Her silhouette," he added.

An empress.

Lady Wu had not allowed herself to think much about the late Empress
Wang. The Empress, after being deposed and exiled by the Emperor for the
practice of Dark Taoism, had slid a knife into her own heart—an act that had
shocked the palace. Lady Wu had thought it a masculine thing to do, brutal
and strange.

She had not connected her own actions with the death.

Two of her sons, while playing boys' games of stealth, had seen something one afternoon which she had felt it her duty to report to the Emperor.
Two months later, the Empress Wang was dead. Lady Wu's mind had not
permitted her to contemplate the sequence of events that had led to the Empress's final despair. But now she saw, with perfect clarity, a straight line
which started with herself speaking in discreet tones to the Emperor, telling
him what the children had seen that afternoon. The line led directly to the
Empress, alone in her family shrine in Szechuan with a knife.

The boy was watching Lady Wu.

"She was much too thin!" Lady Wu blurted.

"Who was too thin?" the boy asked.

"That was why she couldn't bear sons," Lady Wu went on. It is not my
fault that she is dead! I was doing my duty!" She rose from her chair, dropping
the needlework on the floor. "Obviously, her life-force was weak. She barely
had enough for herself! A bag of bones!"

"A bag of bones," the boy mused. "Let us see . . . it has been several
months now. They say that the skin first dries, then stretches thinner and
thinner until the bones begin to show through here and there. It is a slow
process, but the bones eventually cleanse themselves of the flesh . . ."

"Stop!" she shouted.

"And emerge," he continued, "clean and beautiful. It is a pity they must
be hidden away in the darkness."

Lady Wu looked at the boy. This was an impossible conversation to be
having with her son. Preposterous. She was shaking violently.

"Are you cold?" he asked in a soft voice. She was, in fact, perspiring
profusely. The room was filled with bright afternoon sunlight. Brass, freshly
polished, gleamed. Her son's skin, young and smooth, was flawless in the
light. The dark and bright colors of rugs and furnishings flowed against the
richness of finished wood. There was no refuge. This was far worse than any
night terror she had experienced. At night, one could light a lamp and dispel
a bad dream. Awake, in full daylight, there was nowhere to go, no lamp to
light.

"Are you cold?" he repeated, his hair black and shiny in the light. He was close to her now. He took her hands. His own hands were icy. She dropped them. An image, one that she had had to repeatedly push away, now entered her mind with full clarity. She saw Ying, the murdered prince, packed in snow and ice, lying in a dark cellar.

She saw the still face, the mouth slightly open, the white teeth glinting in the frozen flesh. The frozen mouth that could never speak. She saw the protest on the frozen lips that could never tell what had happened that put him in that cellar.

Until now. She saw that the boy in front of her had Mao's face—but the eyes were those of Prince Ying. He smiled a sad, rueful smile. Transfixed, she stared into the eyes of the murdered prince. As she did, he moved his eyes, looking beyond her over her shoulder. She heard the thin cry of an infant coming from the corner of the room behind her. Slowly, slowly, she turned. A woman was seated on the chaise holding a newborn in her arms. The woman raised her head. Lady Wu pressed her hands to her chest to contain her hammering heart. It was the Empress Wang. She looked at Lady Wu with the same sad smile as the prince.

"You see," said the Empress, "we would rather not be dead."

Four Months Earlier: AUGUST 7

Prince Li Mao, twelve-year-old son of the Emperor Minghuang, Brilliant Divine Ruler of the T'ang, crawled on his belly on the gritty stone floor of a balcony overlooking the Empress Wang's private courtyard. He and his younger brother, Prince Li Chi, had gained access to the balcony through an unused wing of the palace. Now he moved toward an opening in the carved grillwork affording him a clear view. He moved up from underneath so that only his eyes and the top of his sleek black topknot showed. It was early evening. The light was fading, and the grillwork cast long, distorted shadows.

Below them was the carp pond. Opposite, on a level with them, were the Empress's rooms and her own balcony; she was probably resting; the day had been very hot. The boy saw no sign of life. Below, in the pond, the object of their predatory stealth meditated in the murky water. A giant carp, a fine specimen already showing signs of turning. The boy noted with excitement the gauzy shreds of skin and scales that waved just behind the head. In a few months, he knew, the shreds of skin would grow into wings as the carp metamorphosed into a dragon. The boy had slung over his shoulder a net and a water bag. Their intention was to slip over the railing, climb down to the courtyard, capture the giant, ancient fish in their bag, and remove him to an old well they knew behind the eunuch's quarters. They would keep a lid on the well to prevent him from flying out as his wings grew. He would be theirs.

But no one must see them. Prince Mao turned toward his brother. He saw by the younger boy's dubious expression that his courage was deserting him.

"Are you a girl? An infant?" he whispered to the child. "I can do it alone if I must. But remember: He'll belong to *me!*"

"I'll come," the young one said, though it was plain that he yearned to crawl back into the shadows.

"All right," whispered Mao. He turned to the peephole in preparation for the move. He froze and put his hand over Li Chi's mouth.

A figure had appeared on the Empress's balcony. It was an elderly woman, short and dressed in tattered black clothing. She had many small objects hanging on her person; though the light was poor, the boys could see bones, charms, talismans, bird claws, and little glittering bottles about her neck and waist. She leaned casually on the Empress's railing as if she were quite at home.

Mao's grip on his young brother tightened. He felt the child's heart racing like his own.

"Ming Wu!" he breathed, recognizing the legendary witch-woman who, it was said, lived somewhere in hidden unused rooms on the palace grounds. So she was flesh and blood after all. His young brother's eyes bulged with fear over his covered mouth. They had both heard the stories about her—that she could fly at night, change into all manner of animal, be in two places at one time, and, worst of all, that she could see through stone. They held themselves still as the old woman's glance surveyed the courtyard.

She looked down at the carp in their quiet pond. She spoke to someone inside the room, gesturing, and then dropped something into the water. She contemplated the fish as they fed; then, to the boys' amazement, spat from the Empress's balcony into the midst of the roiling fish. She spoke again toward the door, then spat once more into the water. She smiled.

The boys dared not to move, sure that the witch-woman's eye was already on them as they crouched in the shadows. They were astonished a moment later when the Empress herself, in a loose white silk robe, stepped out onto the balcony and stood next to the witch. They conversed quietly, the old woman giving the Empress something to wear on a waist belt. Presently, both women disappeared into the room.

Mao's grip on his brother's mouth and body relaxed. Pointing in the direction they'd come from, he indicated to the boy that he'd slit his throat ear to ear if he made a sound or blundered in any way.

They ran through rooms, halls, and passageways to the north wing of the palace. They were out of breath as they rushed into their mother's chambers. There she reclined, nursing the new child, born only two months ago. Lady Wu regarded her sons with curiosity; they were both filthy with dust from the unused rooms they had crawled through, and streaked with sweat from the heat and hard running. Their eyes glistened with the thrill of the discovery.

"Mother," Prince Mao began, panting.

"Stop," she ordered him. "Compose yourself. Take three deep breaths. Be sure that what you're about to say is worthwhile." She shifted the baby from one swollen breast to the other. In her free hand she held a large fan which she used on the infant as it nursed, eyes shut, brow smooth and untroubled.

The boys had flung themselves upon the rug.

"Mother," Prince Mao began again, "we have seen Ming Wu." The fan ceased its motion. "She was standing on the Empress's balcony. The Empress stood right next to her, and they talked. She was old and ugly, and she was spitting . . ." Lady Wu interrupted her son.

"Tell me the whole story," she said, leaning forward attentively. "Tell me everything you saw."

AUGUST 7

It was a hot summer evening. The rooms of the palace were quiet. Most of its inhabitants lay still, drowsing in the muggy heat, trying not to move. In a room on a courtyard the Empress Wang lay on her bed, her beautiful face strained and her body wet with perspiration. Acrid smoke hung in the air along with a faint odor of burning hair.

"Must you be singing under your breath?" she said, exhaling, to the figure bent over her naked belly. The old woman looked up from her work and smiled. She had a solitary tooth. The humming ceased.

"Ah, God, that hurts me," said the Empress in a low voice.

"Good, good, good," replied the old woman. "Now hold yourself still, girl."

The shamaness held a slender stalk of burning matter over the tender ivory skin just above the black pubic hair. The tip of the stalk was held just far enough from the skin so that the fine hairs sizzled and the flesh reddened. There was a pattern of angry red marks inscribed on the area below the navel. From time to time she blew on the tip of the stick, causing it to glow, and brought the stalk down again. The humming started again. The Empress's breath came out between clenched teeth.

"Now listen to me, girl," the old lady said to the Empress. "The next time you do the clouds and rain thing with your old man, have some of this waiting for him inside your body." She indicated a substance in a bottle, and for emphasis added an obscene gesture, her index finger moving back and forth in the circled thumb and forefinger of her other hand. "Be sure to put it all the way in, unless you want a female infant. Then you will be calling me back to kill it, and it's a long walk for me." The Empress covered her body and sat up, slightly dizzy. She was annoyed by this; but she was a desperate woman who was engaging the enemy—which was her barrenness.

After the Empress's rival, the fecund Consort Wu, had given birth to her sixth child and fourth son, the Empress had felt a hollowness that could not be assuaged. The sons popped out of Wu the way piglets popped out of a sow. Every year at approximately the same time she could be seen lolling on her cushions, fat, rosy, and ready to burst. There was a certain smug complacency about her demeanor as the servants fanned her or fed her dainty tidbits of fruit and candy. And she always gave up walking entirely as the time for confinement approached; Wang had to endure the distasteful sight of Wu's sedan chair being carried here and there, the protruding belly of its occupant always draped ostentatiously with bright blue or turquoise silk. And soon another pink, squalling man-child would be presented to the Emperor; Wu had done so well that he did not even resent the occasional girl held up for his approval. With as many heirs as he had, a girl could be regarded as a pretty plaything, a pet, to be married off expediently to another royal clan. What luxury, Wang thought, while I must watch the seasons roll by, year after year, with my body as flat and taut as a child's. A vision of Wu lying on her side with twenty naked, squirming infants sucking at as many nipples came into Wang's mind. The sow!

The Empress was in her fortieth year, and time was running away from her. It was her deepest wish to give the Emperor an heir. Just one, and she would be satisfied. The Emperor had told her often that her childlessness was of no concern to him. "Let others do that particular job," he had joked. "You should be grateful to be spared." Small comfort. A man could not understand. She wished to be related to him by blood through the person of a living heir, and she wanted to know all of it, from the first faint swelling to the moment when a young man would walk into her chambers and greet his mother.

When she was younger, she had fantasized about birth. She imagined an enormous boy, born with a full head of black hair and howling. With the passage of years the vision had dwindled, though it still clung to life. The boy was now small and so wizened that at first it would be thought dead. But then it would open its eyes, take a breath, and look at her.

The old woman had raised the shade and now stood out on the balcony that overlooked the Empress's private courtyard. The Empress lay back on her bed and closed her eyes. The shamaness looked at the courtyard below in the amber light of the setting sun. Heat rose from the white masonry. Clusters of bamboo stood motionless in elongated shadows of statuary and stone. The old woman hummed to herself, her spotted hand resting on the railing. The long, dry trilling of cicadas answered back and forth in the leaden air.

The shamaness leaned on her arms and looked down into the large ornamental pond below. Giant carp hung in the still water. Only the fin-tips undulated slightly; no muck from the bottom was stirred as the fish communed. She drew a small piece of dried meat from her pocket and put it into her mouth, gumming it. Then she leaned so that she was directly over the pond, and spat the meat toward the smooth water. As soon as it hit, the surface churned with mouths, scales, and fins; the piece of meat disappeared. Now the fish milled about greedily, nipping at one another, the water murky. The old woman smiled; this time she simply spat, watching with pleasure as the fish attacked the surface where the gob hit.

"You should come and watch your precious darlings, girl," she called over her shoulder to the Empress. She spat again. This time the carp ignored it. "Carp do not become dragons. They are vermin, like rats—and smart like rats. If there is not enough to eat, they start on each other." She pointed. "That big one with the broken fin and his skin hanging in shreds. One of the others must have tried to take a bite out of him. He's as long as my arm. I would guess him a hundred years old." The Empress rose up onto an elbow and watched the old woman on the balcony in the twilight. She rose, holding the hair from her loosened coiffure up from her neck. She went out and stood alongside the woman, whose head barely came up to the Empress's shoulder. She gazed down into the water. The old lady spat again, and the Empress turned away, disgusted by her own interest.

"They are fish, that is all," she said. "Please go away."

The old woman stood for a time, ignoring the Empress's order, looking down at the *tai-hu* stones in the courtyard, their involuted contours resembling strange faces. She was humming softly; presently she withdrew her hands from the railing.

"There is one more thing, girl," she said still looking at the stones. The Empress turned to look at her. The woman produced a small bag from the folds of her dirty black clothing. She opened the drawstring top and fished inside with her finger. She drew out a long braided cord to which was attached a small disk of wood; she held the disk in her palm for the Empress to look at.

"Wear this. If you do, you'll have a son, and be worthy of comparison with your predecessor."

She reached around the Empress, tying the cord around the younger woman's waist. "Like so. This is the single most important thing. The rest of it," she said, indicating the discarded moxa sticks lying on the railing, "is child's play without this. Otherwise, all you'll have to show for my work here today will be your singed hairs." The Empress looked closely at the *pi-*

disk in the fading light. Inscribed on it were the characters for heaven and earth, and other characters, the sight of which sent a shock through her. It was the Emperor's ineffable name and the secret signs of his horoscope, known only to a few and forbidden to be uttered.

"How . . . !" she began.

"Your brother told me, of course," the old woman answered. "Hmm, I can see that you don't approve," she said, peering at the Empress's face. She shrugged and reached as if to untie the amulet.

"No!" The Empress pushed her hands away. The woman smiled.

"Smart girl. Now do as Ming Wu says. Wear it into the bedchamber, and that fat little prince with the black hair will be tugging at your breast in a year's time." The Empress tightened her hand around the amulet.

"Now you must leave," she told the old woman. She snapped her fingers, and a servant silently appeared in the chamber to escort the shamaness in secret from the Empress's apartments. On her way out the door, the old woman poked a stick of dried cow dung into the Empress's ornate oil lamp and lit her pipe with it. She sucked at the pipe until she was sure it was lit, producing clouds of foul-smelling smoke which lingered long after her departure.

Alone, the Empress opened her hand and reluctantly looked at the amulet. "I am very tired," she said softly. The sight of the amulet caused a strange combination of emotions to rush through her. Hope and fear went together often enough; but in contemplating the action she'd taken this evening, she felt something else: a sense of ultimate decisiveness. Infant or no infant, her life was about to change forever.

She stretched out on her bed. The day's heat remained after the sun had set. She drifted into her private area of contemplation. Here, she could luxuriate at will in the fantasy that had sustained her for years, but which had grown threadbare of late. Tonight, the fetus-infant who opened his eyes and looked at his mother had ample life-force pulsing through his; he spoke his father's taboo name. All traces of feebleness had vanished. She let him turn and open his eyes again and again as she moved into sleep.

AUGUST 10

The summer heat often made the Emperor passive. Unlike many of his predecessors, he was lean and wiry, shunning the royal tradition of excess poundage. Now in his late fifties, he retained the sexual vigor of youth. But sometimes, when it was hot like this, he lay on his back and allowed her to entertain him as she saw fit. She was skillful; over the years she had made it her business to compensate for her lack of fertility. There will be artistry in my touch, she thought, even if there is to be no issue. He will not forget me.

Tonight he lay with his eyes half closed. She ran her cool hands over his body, making him hard without a direct touch, teasing a bit, holding back. She watched with satisfaction as his "old man" stood up stiffly and a drop or two of pearly liquid appeared.

"He is all yours," the Emperor said, smiling slyly at her as he stretched languidly.

She wore her lightest silk robe, the amulet concealed underneath at her waist as the old woman had instructed her. Without removing the robe, she sat upon him, allowing him to enter slowly, slowly. She was aware of her lightness; she knew she could rest her full weight upon him without discomfort. She made a game of holding his arms down, as if she were actually strong enough to pin him. He responded to the fantasy, struggling against her grip, then giving up. The game served her purpose well. Uppermost in her mind was the objective of preventing him from discovering the amulet about her waist. She knew that this was the most dangerous territory she'd ever ventured into; she'd nearly discarded the wooden disk earlier. Looking down at his face as he lay beneath her, she felt her deception acutely. Her attention was focused entirely upon obtaining his seed and keeping his hands away from her waist at the same time, all the while feigning passion. This is what it means, she thought remotely, to be a woman.

If I can only bring him to the moment of *chu-lai* so that he will sleep and I can slip away, she thought. She was working hard tonight, keeping pace with him, attentively following his rhythm, encouraging him to finish quickly.

But he would not. Time and time again they approached the climax, she straining every muscle, and then he'd pause just short of orgasm. She'd wait a bit, then start again, attempting to vary her thrusts and motion, coaxing him along, moving faster and faster, thinking surely he must do it now, surely he must give it up. The heat—how can he continue this way? She was soaked with sweat and growing tired. The Emperor was a man of experience, with perfect control. If he was in the mood, he might continue this way for hours. Usually this was the thing she prized above all else—his ability to postpone his own pleasure, taking greater pleasure in bringing her to the pinnacle of response. It is a sin, she thought, to deceive him when he is working for my pleasure. But there is to be none in it for me tonight. Let him take it, she thought, let him take it now so that this may be over.

She was putting on a good performance, but she could not fool him. He sensed her detachment. Knowing she was not really with him, he allowed himself to finish, tensing his body, catching her in the midst of a run of short, quick thrusts. She felt the gentle pulsating that told her it was over, and thrust down upon him to take in every drop deeply. They separated and lay still. Presently, a eunuch silently entered the chamber and began to fan them with cool air. She waited until the Emperor slept, then stole out quietly to her own quarters.

The Emperor had been disappointed that he'd been unable to arouse her, and this made her sorry. Next time, she thought, I'll have no trouble going with him wherever he wishes to lead me. But now his life-force was inside her, and the words of Ming Wu went around and around in her mind. Fat little prince with black hair . . . As she drifted, she endeavored to feel the presence of this new prince. She felt a slight burning sensation between her legs, but that was all. Tomorrow, she thought, I shall destroy the wretched amulet. Wearing that shaman charm into the Emperor's bedchamber is as close as I've ever come to lying to him. The first and last time.

AUGUST 14

The Emperor sat long into the evening. The decision he faced was nearly impossible. Why had she done it? Worse, why did Lady Wu inform him of Wang's activities with the witch? Wang had wept when he called her in to question her, but she had not lied or tried to evade the truth. The presence in the Emperor's quarters of the hag Ming Wu with her charms and mumbo jumbo was an offense in itself; he had demanded to know everything that had transpired. And she had told him. To think that she would attempt to influence royal lineage through barbaric magic—it was shocking. At least she did not compound the offense by lying. She is honorable, he thought. She does not lie.

And what of her obsession with giving him an heir? Let Wu give him sons. Let *her* be eternally swollen. He was not starved for male descendants. The Empress's predecessor, Lady Yang, had done well, and there were others in the harem who produced an occasional boy. All told, he had thirteen sons and fifteen daughters. He expected that there would be more, but this was not a demand he'd placed on the delicate Wang. He had told her many times that her childlessness meant nothing to him. Her position, her brother's, her father's, the sinecures of the entire Hotung family branch—none of them were in any way threatened by her barrenness.

He owed the family much. The Wang clan's loyalty had been the backbone of his long struggle as the heir apparent. During the Emperor's first year on the throne twelve years ago, Wang's brother Shou-i had risked his life more than once protecting him and his father, Jui-tsung, from assassination attempts by agents of Father's ambitious sister, the Princess T'ai Ping. And when he was a young man, the Wangs had aided him in avenging the death of his uncle, the Emperor Chung-tsung, murdered by Uncle's own wife, the ambitious Empress Wei. The coups had been long and bloody, and the Wangs had stayed by his side.

Why did she feel she had to produce? It was unnecessary. Besides, her barrenness was a comely condition. She was so slender, so light when she sat on his lap. He had clothes commissioned especially for her, using the finest seamstresses in the harem. She was the very silhouette of an empress in her tight bodices and wing shoulders, her waist so narrow that he could nearly put his hands around it. Why compromise that waist? Wu was pretty, but she was a cow . . . not an empress.

By employing Dark Taoistic magic, Wang had refuted the just Confucian code, which he had been trying to establish in the empire. It was an integral part of his life's work to turn people away from irrational, superstitious practices which could only foster chaos, confusion, and neglect. Order, logic, filial propriety, and respect were the keys to a peaceful, prosperous empire. There was no other way. News of the Empress's transgression had, of course, leaked out, leaving him no choice but to act. An empress's behavior had to be exemplary in every way. Obedience and tranquility were absolute requirements. And her twin brother had fostered the scheme and obtained the services of the witch. Now the world was waiting, watching him. To ignore this unfortunate incident, or to gloss it over, would be seen as a flaw which could be seized upon later. The peace of his K'ai Yuan reign period was still relatively new, untested, unstable. There were still factions that watched and waited for some weakness or lack of will. He would rest firm in his resolve to keep his mandate to rule. The Empress had broken that mandate; it made her a traitor, and traitors could not go unpunished.

How tenuous was this pinnacle of power, this being the Emperor, the Son of Heaven. And how far it removed him from the ordinary world of men. Sentimentality and remorse were emotions unaffordable to him. There was no room for mercy if it might culminate in dissipation; no allowance for personal indulgence if it violated an ethic.

He loved the Wangs. If love could be measured in loyalty, then it could be said that they loved him. The elder Wang, father of the Empress and her twin brother Shou-i, had graciously accepted honorific titles but had asked for little else—never enfeoffments or strings of cash.

Had the Empress misunderstood his little jokes? Had she inferred other than what he meant when he called her his "beautiful boy" and such? Her slender frame inspired him to say these things; it must have seemed to her that he was complaining obliquely about her lack of issue. He rested his head in his hands. He was sure of that now. Words! What damage they could do. Words that he spoke as a mere man were heard by those around him, even those close to him, as the words of an emperor. There were no jokes; every phrase was burdened. He had lost the freedom to speak as men speak every day in the streets, on horses, in canal boats, shops, teahouses, and pleasure parks . . . as men spoke to each other, to their wives and children. When he spoke, it was a decree; when he wrote, it was an edict. There was none of the simple banter between human beings. The Son of Heaven was not, it seemed, a human being. He was mortal, pained, alone, but not a human being. And now he faced the edict he must issue.

The situation called for punishment, but out of respect for her and his infrangible ties with the Wang clan he would temper his anger. Picking up his brush and working quickly, he wrote his words. His body ached from sitting in one position for many hours. He lay down, though he knew there would be no sleep.

He was still awake when long shafts of sunlight came through the shutters. He watched as a thousand specks traveled from dark to light and then to dark again, entering into existence and disappearing. Like lives, he thought.

He looked without appetite at the tray of fruit, pastries, and tea that had been brought in earlier. There was always a kitchen staff on duty to respond to his insomniac requests. No matter what hour, they were ready to peel, slice, and brine fruit, or to steam and fry sweet dumplings, apples, and pears. Tea or hot, thick, fruity liquors would appear on a silver tray within minutes of a word from him. He had had his eunuch, Kao Li-shih, awakened to join him, but the delicacies remained untouched.

The eunuch, still half-asleep, yawned and rubbed the night's crust from his eyes as he looked over the Emperor's shoulder at the final draft of the edict. It was terse, good archaic prose; simple and mercifully redemptive. The Wangs would be retired on pensions. Shou-i, the brother, was to be banished to Silla, the far northeastern peninsula across the Yellow Sea. The Empress would be reduced to a commoner, though made comfortable. The final lines protected her well-meaning intent; the family was in no way blacklisted.

"You realize, of course," said the Emperor to his eunuch, "that historians will distort this. Their tendency will be to glorify me as the victor and disparage the Wangs as the vanquished." He looked gloomily at his brushstrokes. "How will this make her look in a hundred years?"

The Emperor did not move from his morning couch, but stayed there until the afternoon shadows lengthened across the tiles. Kao Li-shih remained with him, though no request had been made for him to do so. The muscles of the Emperor's face were strained under the sagging contours of the flesh. There was exhaustion there that went beyond that of long, sleepless nights, as if he had in him a deep well of fatigue. At best, it was superficially covered up from day to day, but now the eunuch could see it plainly as the Emperor lay in the afternoon sunlight. And he felt it. What the Emperor felt, the eunuch felt—the acute sense of loss, betrayal, and remorse under which the Emperor labored. Tiny beads of sweat had formed on the eunuch's soft, feminine brow as he waited.

"You know," Kao Li-shih began, "that it is better that you don't see them. I fear it would weaken your resolve. It is better done and finished." The Emperor opened his eyes. The drum tower rolled the fourth watch; fresh tea and pastries were brought in and the morning's untouched plates removed.

The servant leaned over the Emperor and took the dried writing brush out of his hand, where it had been since early morning. Grasping the wrists, he pulled the monarch to a sitting position. In place of the brush, he put a pair of rosewood and silver inlay chopsticks, wrapping the fingers of the unresponsive hand around them. He pointed to the jellied fruit and warm rice cakes and motioned with his index and middle fingers, mimicking the act of directing food into his mouth.

"Eat something now," he ordered his master. "It's done. The edict has been sent down. It's finished—their lives have been arranged for them. There is no more to do."

"And what of the elder Wang?' asked the Emperor. "He is innocent of these matters. Why should he suffer for the bad judgment of his children?" Kao Li-shih sat and faced the Emperor. He took a bite of food, chewing carefully as he chose his words.

"The elder Wang died at the family home in Szechuan. His younger brother was with him. I had delayed telling you. The missive reached us by envoy late last night. He has been buried with all the honors of his office, his loyalty to the imperial family intact." He paused. "He will never know."

The eunuch watched his master's face as the burden of anxiety lifted and was swiftly replaced by grief. The Emperor exhaled softly. He extended his chopsticks then and took a morsel of food.

"Death . . . my old friend," he laughed sadly.

2

The Flower Fables

Kao Li-shih was shrewd, perceptive and astutely aware of everything around him. He was robust and very strong [by Chinese measure], just over six feet tall. By nature he was respectful, cautious and very secretive, . . . highly capable of carrying out the imperial will. He was totally devoted to the protection of the Emperor Minghuang; . . . [and this devotion frequently elicited from the Emperor the words:] "with Kao Li-shih watching over me, my rest and sleep are most peaceful." His covertness was held in awe, his artful skills of subtlety and secrecy earned him the praise and flattery of others. . . . He was entrusted into the honored inner gates of government, attracting many close followers who sought his kindness and favors.

—*from* Hsin T'ang Shu (New T'ang History),
translated by Daniel Altieri

Chang Chiu-ling, the hero of the literati . . . was a literatus of the purest kind . . . a vigorous and conscious defender of his class and an inveterate enemy of those who sought advancement by other means . . . to such an extent that his attitudes often seem narrow and intransigent.

—*Edwin Pulleyblank*

Chang Chiu-ling, the southern literatus, was espousing the interests of the southern merchants. . . . The old aristocracy had been largely ousted in favour of the literati recruited by the examination system and . . . coming from the east and south.

—*Edwin Pulleyblank*

DECEMBER 10

Kao Li-shih, chief eunuch to the Emperor Minghuang, walked down a long empty hallway. With him were two younger eunuchs, both tall and powerfully built, one of whom carried a tray of food and a kettle of hot water. The hall was musty, the carpeted floor thick with dust. They passed windows tightly shuttered so that only cracks of light showed here and there.

They came to a massive door. The young eunuch not holding the tray took a key from his sleeve and released the padlock that held it shut. After they had passed through, the eunuch locked the door behind them. They continued down the hall. Coming to another locked door, they repeated the procedure. When they came to a third door, they stopped. Quietly, carefully, the young eunuch released the padlock and gently pushed the door open.

The room was sparsely furnished. Against one wall was a small desk and a chair. Against another wall was a large bed. The floor was bare. On the bed lay a sleeping woman, her arms bound to her torso with heavy cloth that had been wound around her chest. As the three entered the room, another young eunuch seated in a chair near the bed was stirring the brazier that heated the room in this remote, unused wing of the palace.

They shut the door softly behind them. Kao Li-shih raised his eyebrows in a silent question; the eunuch in the chair responded with an expression that told Kao Li-shih that nothing had changed. The woman on the bed stirred and moaned. She opened her eyes and looked at the eunuchs. She lay quietly. The eunuch holding the tray approached the bed.

"Good morning, Most Favored Consort Lady Wu," he said. Kao Li-shih watched as the other two moved up close behind him as if ready to assist. "It is time to eat," he continued, "but first you shall have a bath and fresh clothing." Kao Li-shih watched with interest as the two eunuchs raised her to a sitting position.

"I must speak to the Emperor," she said.

"The Emperor has gone to Loyang," the first eunuch replied. "He will not return for some time." They began to unwind the cloth strips that bound her arms.

"Then I must go there and find him," she said, trying to rise from the bed. Gently, they held her down. She looked around at each of the eunuchs. "I must speak to my father," she implored. Now she sat quietly as they removed the last of the bindings from her arms.

"You see," she said, "I must tell him that I did not commit suicide. He believes that I took my own life, and he blames himself." Tears began to roll down her face. "But I was murdered while I slept. Murdered!"

"Lady Wu," the eunuch said, ignoring her words, "there is hot water in readiness, and pastries from the kitchens. And your hair is badly tangled. I shall comb it for you."

"He believes that I killed myself because I dreaded the responsibility of succeeding him. He thinks that he is to blame!" she said in an anguished voice. "He is not to blame!"

"If you will stand now, Lady Wu, we will give you fresh clothing," the eunuch said firmly as he and another pulled her to her feet. They had not let go of her arms since the bindings had been removed.

Cautiously, they began to pull at one of her sleeves. It was necessary to release the arm momentarily in order to remove it from the sleeve. In the instant that the arm was not being held, it came up with great force as if she meant to knock the attending eunuch unconscious with a blow to the underside of his chin. Deftly, he pulled his head back and caught her arm with his free hand.

Kao Li-shih watched as the eunuch went through their practiced motions of bathing and dressing Lady Wu, who continued to sob and mutter. After they had dressed her, Kao Li-shih nodded to the eunuch guarding the door, who indicated that he was alert and the door was locked. Kao Li-shih spoke to the tallest young eunuch, who held Lady Wu's arms.

"Let her go," he said quietly. They released their grip and stepped back. She stood for a moment, looked around at her captors, then walked quickly to the door and faced the eunuch who stood guard. She spoke in a whisper. "It is vital that I speak to my father," she said intently, conspiratorially. The eunuch watched her warily. "Open the door," she ordered. He looked back at her, saying nothing. Then he howled in pain. Lady Wu had sunk her teeth into his arm. The others rushed forward to disengage her, gently pushing her jaws apart. The bitten man had restrained himself from striking her or retaliating in any way. As they pulled her back toward the bed, she repeated her message:

"Murdered while I slept! A child! A crown prince! My father must be told!"

"This is how it is during her every waking moment," one of the attending eunuchs said to Kao Li-shih. He shrugged apologetically. "All of us have a wound or two, bites, scratches. But we keep her fed and clean, and see that she comes to no harm and, mostly, that she does not escape." They held her firmly now and rewound the cloth strips about her arms.

"I commend you," said Kao Li-shih. "You are doing what needs to be done, sad and difficult as it is. Remember," he admonished them, "you are not to speak of any of this. Her words, the talk of murder, must never reach the Emperor's ears, directly or indirectly. You understand?"

"Perfectly," the young eunuch replied.

:: ::

The Emperor Minghuang had risen to power in the midst of adversity. When he was
a young prince, his uncle, the Emperor Chung-tsung, was murdered by his own wife.
The Empress Wei had conspired with several of her paramours in a bid for the throne.
But the young prince avenged the death of his uncle by killing the Empress and her
lovers.

Chung-tsung's brother, the young prince's father, succeeded the murdered Emperor. But he was a self-effacing man, and within two years announced his abdication
in favor of his son. Just as Minghuang was preparing to ascend the throne, he met
with another dangerous and determined adversary, also a female—his aunt, the Princess
T'ai Ping, sister of the murdered Chung-tsung. She had influenced five of the highest
ministers of state, apparently determined to become the second female Emperor of China.
Had not Minghuang had all her partisans slain, she may well have done it. She herself
was granted the privilege of taking her own life.

Minghuang prevailed and took his place as the Son of Heaven. For twelve years
his reign was distinguished by humaneness and vision. His land reforms resulted in
abundant harvests, stimulating the economy. He lifted some of the burden from the
common people through moderation of the tax system. And he recognized oppression
in another of its forms: there can be no rational, orderly society, he thought, when
people struggle under the burden of superstition—irrational beliefs, fear of the supernatural. Thus he forbade the practice of magic, especially the sort known as Dark
Taoism, the use of which had proliferated in the last one hundred years. His hope was
to bring the rational teachings of Confucius to the realm.

The "mandate to rule" was not just a phrase to him; it was quite real. When
he was a young crown prince fending off the advances of those who would claim the
mandate for themselves, he thought it a simple matter—he was meant to rule; there
could be no interference. When he ascended the throne, he knew about the frailties of
human beings, their greed and other innumerable unsavory tendencies. But he had a
certain faith in the universe and felt that he had been born to his position for a reason.
The mandate, he believed, was his without question. As time went on and the empire
thrived under his rule the evidence was everywhere around him that the mandate
belonged to him.

But gradually, the mandate became a philosophic riddle to the Emperor: Clearly,
it was real—but what did that mean for him as a man? The banishment of the Empress
marked the beginning of a deep decline for him. With her death two months later,
followed shortly thereafter by the death of the crown prince and then the madness of
Lady Wu, the question became an acutely agonizing one.

DECEMBER 11

Kao Li-shih, chief eunuch to the Emperor Minghuang, watched his sleeping master. The Emperor's mouth was slightly open, and the whites of his eyes showed between his lids. His breathing was soft and shallow. It was the middle of the day, and the Emperor lay fully clothed on the large bed in his palace apartments. The eunuch sat in a chair at the head of the bed.

He watched the Emperor's face for any sign that he was dreaming. It is unfair, thought the eunuch, that his sorrows should pursue him while he sleeps. When he is awake, I can do what I can to protect him; when he sleeps, I am ten thousand miles away.

Of late, Kao Li-shih had sat with the Emperor for several hours after he fell asleep. If the eunuch saw agitation on his face or heard it in muttered fragments of words, he placed his hands on the Emperor's shoulders and gave him a firm shake. If I thought that he was dreaming about the crown prince, thought the eunuch, what would I do? Dreams often restore the dead to life, making them whole again, reversing time. For the duration of the dream, the sorrow has never existed. The eunuch knew the hollow feeling left when a sublime dream-joy vanished; the feeling of waking in the gray morning light as the empirical facts of this world quickly arranged themselves. Would I let him converse with Ying, see him alive and well, only to let him open his eyes later to discover it was an illusion?

For now, the eunuch was satisfied that sleep brought oblivion. The features were slack, the eyes motionless.

Kao Li-shih held a piece of paper in his long hands. It is obvious, he thought, that it was a poet who wrote this "Memorial to the Throne." The effort to speak in official court language was plain to see. But the writer's natural inclination toward flamboyant metaphor showed through here and there, in such phrases as "birds of prey . . . feathered in gold and turquoise," their beaks and claws "stained with blood." The scholar and poet-minister Chang Chiu-ling, the author of the Memorial, was referring to individuals of high rank in the court who would, in his opinion, do whatever was necessary, including murder, to advance themselves or a cause.

: :

The verdict in the death of the Emperor's beloved crown prince had been suicide. Kao Li-shih had been present during the examination of the body. The physician had traveled a long distance, arriving with a retinue of assistant physicians. He had conducted the examination as if he were lecturing a group of students—which, in a sense, he was. For all those in attendance— Kao Li-shih; a few court physicians; and two high ministers, both members of the imperial cabinet—the science of forensics was new. The man's enthusiasm for knowledge had affected them all. They had each known Prince Ying in life, but under the spell of the physician's words, their interest had become, briefly, academic.

The prince, said the physician, had died as a result of poisoning. He demonstrated to the assembled group certain changes in the vessels of the viscera, in the "triple burner" and the downwardly disseminating yang organs, which indicated that the poison had been consumed over a period of at least a week. And it was clear, he said, that the injury was self-inflicted. Why, they had asked, do you say that? Because this particular poison, he had replied, leaves a distinctive metallic taste in the mouth. It is not, therefore, the sort of poison one would administer surreptitiously to another. It is a suicide poison. Taken in small doses, one is guaranteed an easy, painless death. And how was the body found? he had asked. Lying peacefully in bed, as if asleep.

Fascinating. When the physician delivered his verdict, no one had dissented. For the Emperor, it had meant a descent into self-blame, punishing himself daily, hourly. Kao Li-shih had been disturbed by the Emperor's readiness to embrace the responsibility for Ying's death. It was as if he had finally found a way to blame himself for the entire universe of matter which continually disposed itself into configurations of pain.

And now the scholar-minister Chang Chiu-ling sought with his Memorial to dredge up once more the possibility of murder. Kao Li-shih had thought that the official verdict would lay to rest any further such talk.

The eunuch stood up and stretched his limbs and looked at the Emperor's sleeping face. It has been twenty years now, he thought, and all of it has merely been training for this moment. The purpose of my life is to serve and protect you. At the age of twenty, I could not have understood that my tasks would be at cross purposes to one another. But, he thought, tucking the document into his sleeve, I shall do my best. So far, only Master Chang Chiu-ling and myself know about this damnable piece of paper.

He left the Emperor's quarters, ducking his head, as was his habit, to avoid hitting it on the doorframe.

Kao Li-shih proceeded north from the imperial apartments via the narrow waiting halls, devoid now of any ministers or officials awaiting private audiences during the period of mourning. He walked out into a small side courtyard of twisted trees and decorative mosaic paths. He followed a path that wound down the hillside and through a gate in the blue-tiled Wall of Nine Dragons and continued down the steep drop to the north wall of the palace city. He left the path and entered the well-garrisoned wildness of Tungchien Park, crossed through uncultivated groves of trees, his boots sinking deep into the crusty snow, and approached the rear courtyard of the Hall of Consorts, its palaces surrounded by woods and walls.

Kao Li-shih pushed open the heavy door to the harem quarters, entering the warm, moist atmosphere of steam redolent with perfume. Women's voices and laughter, echoing in the vast bathing room, carried down the corridor.

The eunuch passed through an atrium where women, in attitudes of repose among colorful silk cushions, snoozed, played games, and groomed themselves like so many cats. Small children and babies with glistening black hair and fat arms and legs, all imperial offspring, wandered here and there or played in small groups under the women's eyes. As the tall eunuch passed through, the children turned their round faces up toward him.

The tiled bathing room was hot, the air thick with steam. Naked women, their flesh rosy from the hot water, dangled their legs in the pool or floated on its surface with languid strokes. Around the pool, they rubbed scented oil onto one another's shoulders and wrung out their long hair. Odors of perfume and sweat rose with the vapor to the guilded squares of the ceiling. The ornamental carvings of the screens and woodwork were filled with overt sexual symbolism; Kao Li-shih the eunuch stood in his long brocade robe against a tracery of cranes, *ling-chih* mushrooms, scudding clouds, vulvate peaches, double gourds, and the swollen head of the aged and lusty immortal Lu Tung Pin. The women's laughter and conversation continued unabated; they ignored the eunuch. Another robed figure stood on the other side of the pool.

Kao Li-shih raised a long jeweled finger in a discreet signal. The younger eunuch Lu Pei, an apprentice, responded immediately to his master's gesture, leaving his post and circling around the pool to Kao Li-shih's side. Kao Li-shih saw the unspoken question on the apprentice's face.

"I have just come from his quarters. I administered twice his usual dosage of sleeping powders, but it took him nearly two hours to drift off. I have never seen a man so fatigued, yet unable to sleep. His limbs jerk this way and that, and his eyelids tremble." Kao Li-shih rubbed the ridges of bone above his eyes. "I would not have thought it possible, after the death of the prince, for him to absorb any more grief. I thought he had reached his capacity, but I was wrong."

"Lady Wu," remarked the young eunuch.

"Lady Wu, mother of six of the Emperor's sons," said Kao Li-shih, "is at this moment confined to a room in an unused wing of the palace. Three very large, strong young eunuchs, not unlike yourself, Apprentice, are with her night and day. They feed her as if she were an infant, spooning the food into her mouth. Most of the time her arms are bound to her sides, and her long fingernails have been trimmed down to the fingertips; it is necessary, occasionally, to loose the bindings so that she may be bathed and put into fresh clothing. None of her three attendants wish to lose an eye or suffer any lacerations."

"She is strong, then," commented Lu Pei. "That is particularly ominous in these cases. The ghosts are in combat in her body?"

"Oh, yes," answered Kao Li-shih. "She is strong. But with the strength of madness. She strains, at every moment that she is not asleep, to break her bonds, escape from her room, and go straight to the Emperor." As they talked, the two eunuchs moved to an outer hallway where the air was cooler.

"It would be unthinkable," said Kao Li-shih, "to allow her to speak to the Emperor. I would kill her myself if it were necessary in order to stop her." The young eunuch, his eyes full of curiosity, waited politely for his master to elaborate. Restraint, thought Kao Li-shih, is a valuable asset.

"The Emperor, as you no doubt know, struggled for years as a crown prince against subterfuge in the court. The Mandate of Heaven, it seemed, the divine right to rule, was a reward that went to the one most willing and able to shed blood—often that of one's closest relatives—and to manipulate the will of others. The years of struggle affected him deeply. Have you ever contemplated the meaning of the 'mandate of rule'? I do not think that a day of the Emperor's life goes by that he does not become entangled in the question implied by those words."

The two eunuchs walked slowly side by side, their voices low, in the long outer hallway surrounding the bathing room.

"It seems plain to me," the apprentice answered thoughtfully. A mandate is something that must be done. It implies that there is no choice."

"No choice!" said Kao Li-shih. We are getting close to the heart of the matter. You have been at the palace how long?"

"One month and a half," answered Lu Pei.

"Then you have no doubt heard stories about the Empress."

"I have. The women are fond of speculating. But I discount much of what they say. A few facts emerge that I choose to believe: she was beautiful, the women mourned her, and the Emperor blamed himself for her death. The rest of it—the talk of witchcraft—well, I don't know. I do know how stories, especially those told by the women, can grow limbs, like trees."

"You have correctly chosen the truth. Yes, she was beautiful, with bones like a bird's. The Emperor could nearly span her waist with his hands. To him, and to everyone else, she was the very picture of an empress. Imagine —he used to design clothing for her, choosing the fabrics and seamstresses himself. She was one of his works of art."

"The women say that the Empress was barren," said the apprentice. Kao Li-shih sighed.

"An empty vessel, as she herself put it. And as the years went by, her disappointment grew. The Emperor is surrounded by women, as you know. There are, all told, one hundred and twenty-two who may produce offspring for him. The consort Lady Wu has been by far the most prolific. She produced six sons in less than eight years." The apprentice shook his head incredulously.

The two eunuchs arrived at an alcove that afforded them a clear view of the pool and the bathers. They sat on a carved stone bench, a brazier at their feet. "It is a shame," Kao Li-shih continued, "that the Empress did not appreciate the advantage that she had in the Emperor's eyes precisely because of her barrenness. 'Wu is pretty,' he told me once, 'but she is a cow, not an empress.' " Kao Li-shih shrugged. "I could not help but agree. Wu suffered from an excess of femaleness, whereas Wang was exquisitely feminine."

"I think," said the apprentice, "that I understand the distinction. But men and women do not always understand one another," he added reflectively. Kao Li-shih regarded the young eunuch. His stature and proportions were those of a normal young man; only his complete lack of beard and the carefully modulated contralto voice suggested that he was a eunuch. Obviously, he had been cut not so long ago, after he had reached young manhood—unlike Kao Li-shih, who had been cut at the age of nine and a half. My apprentice has probably had an experience or two, thought Kao Li-shih, which I, as a Pure-from-Birth, can only know as a page from a book.

"It was several months ago that Lady Wu gave birth to her sixth son. The Empress, it seemed, could stand it no longer. Have you heard of Ming Wu?" Kao Li-shih asked the apprentice.

"I have heard that there is a shamaness who lives underneath the palace, who has been there for a thousand years, who can see through stone, and who is seen when she wants to be seen, among other powers. It is my surmise that she exists primarily in the fevered imaginations of the naive," answered Lu Pei. "Or if she does exist, she is merely a strange old woman who stimulates those fevered imaginations," he added.

"You are wise to withhold your ready belief, Apprentice. But I can tell you—she does exist. And there are unused, forgotten parts of the palace where she may very well make her home, though I could not say how long she has been there. But it often seems as if she is seen only when it suits her." Kao Li-shih paused for a moment. "Though there may have been an exception," he said. "If she had wanted to be seen during the incident about which I shall now tell you, then we might be forced to concede that she can see through stone. If, on the other hand, the eyes that saw her were invisible to her, then stone is as opaque for her as it is for you and me. In any event, she was seen, and it was the beginning of the Emperor's sorrows." The apprentice was now leaning forward attentively, but endeavoring to keep his curiosity at the level of polite interest. I will reward him, thought Kao Li-shih.

"The Empress Wang and Lady Wu were not fond of one another. Such disharmony among wives is not good. From what I have told you, one would conclude that only the Empress had justification for dislike: Lady Wu's fecundity was a hardship for the Empress to bear. It would seem that Lady Wu was in a position to be magnanimous toward the poor Empress." Kao Li-shih picked up an iron rod and stirred the embers in the brazier. The apprentice looked thoughtfully at the floor as his master unfolded his story.

"On the day in question," Kao Li-shih continued, "shortly after Lady Wu had given birth, two of her other numerous offspring—having been told by their mother, no doubt, to be her eyes and ears around the palace—ran to her to tell her that they had seen Ming Wu and the Empress standing together on the Empress's balcony. There is nothing like a woman's sure instinct for another woman's motivations. Lady Wu, I am sure, wasted no time in guessing the reason for the presence of the shamaness in the Empress's quarters." Kao Li-shih looked at Lu Pei and waited.

"A fertility ritual!" the apprentice exclaimed.

"Correct," answered Kao Li-shih. "Your powers of reason are excellent. But part of a eunuch's job is to have the ability to think as both man and woman." Kao Li-shih smiled. "You still have a preponderance of yang in you. You need a more thorough acquaintance with the yin aspect."

"I am learning," the apprentice replied, "but much of it is still a mystery to me."

"You have my sympathies. But it is my job to teach you—perhaps I can provide you with some valuable insight as well. In any event, from what the Emperor told me, it appears that Lady Wu did not go immediately to the Emperor with the information." He waited for the apprentice to respond. The younger eunuch's brows were knitted.

"Perhaps," said Lu Pei, "she was vacillating, unsure whether she should go to the Emperor. I cannot see what reason she would have for causing such serious trouble for the Empress."

"Pretend that you are Lady Wu," Kao Li-shih said. "Suppose that you are aware of the unfavorable comparison of your person to the Empress's. Your only advantage has been your ability to produce heirs—and the irony is that you have done too well. Your waist is wide and soft. Your breasts are pendulous. Your artistic and conversational skills have grown accordingly flabby. When you find out that the Empress has been visited by Ming Wu, and that most likely she has called upon the powers of Dark Taoism to give her an heir, you recognize that both a threat and an opportunity have been placed in your lap . . . especially if you wait for several days," he said significantly. "And I can assure you," he added, "that she was not vacillating."

"I can see the opportunity for Lady Wu that you speak of. To have caught the Empress at such clandestine activities, knowing the Emperor's dislike of magic; . . . if I were she, as you have hypothetically suggested, I would have wasted no time in taking my information to the Imperial Father. The threat, as I see it, would be that the Empress might actually conceive, and produce, at long last, an heir. Then I—Lady Wu—would lose my only advantage. Yes, I would have gone to the Emperor as quickly as I could."

"A few days would make all the difference, would it not?" Kao Li-shih answered. "You are right. By waiting, Lady Wu risked an occurrence she certainly didn't want—the Empress conceiving. But it was a calculated risk. Consider this: knowing the Emperor's vehemence concerning Dark Taoism, she understood that he would take deep offense at the Empress's actions—bringing a shamaness into the palace and, worse, attempting to influence royal lineage through such magic." He paused. "But think of how the Empress's crime would be compounded if she had already lain with the Emperor in his bed," Kao Li-shih finished. A look of comprehension came onto the young eunuch's face.

"Of course," he said quietly. "If the Emperor had found out about the ritual right away, then there was the possibility that he might forgive her, and nothing would have come of it. So Lady Wu waited, knowing that the consequences for the Empress would be far more dire . . ."

"Exactly," said Kao Li-shih.

"But if there was no solid evidence except the word of two children . . ." the apprentice began. He thought a moment. "Couldn't the Empress simply have denied it all? Wouldn't the Emperor have believed her?"

"He would have," answered Kao Li-shih, looking in the direction of the bathers for a moment. A nude woman, her back to the two eunuchs, stood in their line of vision wringing out her hair. "But Lady Wu calculated correctly one more thing. The Empress was incapable of lying. Lady Wu knew this; she knew that if the Emperor questioned her, Empress Wang would tell the truth." He paused, remembering. "And that is exactly what happened."

"And so the Emperor banished her," said the apprentice. "The women still discuss it at length. They wonder how, if he loved her, he could have done it."

"Because of the mandate," answered Kao Li-shih. "It left him no choice. The Empress defied his effort to banish superstition. For her to set such an example, to bring the witch into the palace, left him no choice. You see, word of her transgression found its way out of the palace, into the city, and onto the lips of every merchant, food vendor, and street sweeper, and their wives, uncles, and children." Kao Li-shih recalled the Emperor's helpless anger. "His natural inclination was to forgive her, as any decent man would do to his wife. He wanted to extend that charitable impulse to her, but he couldn't. He had to make an example of her to the watching eyes of the empire."

"Because of the mandate," said the apprentice.

"It was at this time that he saw what this mandate, this being an Emperor, meant for his human desires. It was as if he, as a man, did not even exist."

Kao Li-shih read the apprentice's thought then. "Yes, you and I are compromised as well; but our limitations are clear. For the Emperor, it was a realization that came relatively late. In any case, he tempered his punishment of the Empress. He reduced her status to that of commoner, made sure that she would be provided for, and banished her to her ancestral home in Szechuan. She went, but within three months she took her own life."

"The women say that she threw herself upon a sword in a pagan ritual," said the young apprentice.

"They also say that she eviscerated herself in a cemetery. There is no end to their imaginations. No," answered Kao Li-shih, "the Empress was a dignified woman. Her suicide was a proper one. She knelt before the Buddha in her family shrine, and slipped a fine, very sharp Khitan dagger into her heart."

"They also say," the apprentice said, "that she had been . . . bleeding. I mean . . . moon's blood. You know . . ." he said, trying to maintain decorum while speaking of the deceased Empress.

This young man is still unaccustomed to a eunuch's familiarity with all things female. That awkwardness will fade with time, thought Kao Li-shih.

"Moon's blood or the blood of a lost birth: we will never know which it was. The only one who knew was the Empress herself," answered Kao Li-shih. "I need not tell you of the Emperor's sorrow. The mandate, it seemed, had exacted its price from him. With the death of the Empress, he began to lose his will to rule. With the death of the crown prince, I believe he died a bit himself. And now, with the ignominious madness of Lady Wu, I believe he sees his life and everything connected with it as a sacrifice on the altar of this mysterious thing called the Mandate of Heaven. It is painful for me to witness it."

"You mentioned a message," the apprentice said, "that Lady Wu wants to deliver to the Emperor."

"It is unspeakable," answered Kao Li-shih. "Abominable. You are aware, no doubt, of the controversy surrounding the death of the prince. Was it murder, or suicide? From the beginning the Emperor rejected the possibility of murder. I think he couldn't bear a recurrence of the plotting, subterfuge, and backstabbing that he experienced as a crown prince. Suicide, however, fitted better into his view of a universe punishing him for being the recipient of the mandate to rule. When the official verdict of suicide was passed, he embraced it, took it to heart as the final blow. He can blame himself for the boy's death. He has gone to bed never, it seems, to rise again. He eschews all responsibilities of government. He does not go to the morning audience, but lies in bed, feeding off the sorrow, helpless to shake it off. And Lady Wu, if you please, if released from her cell, will rush straight to his bedchamber, open her mouth, and, with the voice of the dead prince, cry, 'Murder!' "

"Do you mean to say that she is possessed by a *guei?*" asked the apprentice quietly, one eyebrow slightly raised.

"The Lady Wu that we knew has ceased to exist. Now when she speaks, she says that she is Ying, returned from the dead to tell his emperor-father the truth about his death," Kao Li-shih replied.

"A hungry ghost," said the apprentice.

"Or a woman gone totally mad," said Kao Li-shih. "Whichever it is, she must be prevented from reaching him. I cannot allow him to see the Consort Wu, mother of six of his sons, in such a grotesque condition. I am equally adamant that he not hear his dead son telling him that it was murder. It is all too odious; he is fragile now, and I fear he could shatter."

"But what if it was murder?" asked Lu Pei.

Kao Li-shih sighed. "It is interesting that you should raise the question," he replied. "A memorial, a written statement intended for the throne, has come into my hands from one Chang Chiu-ling." The younger eunuch smiled at the mention of the poet-minister's name. "I know; we are all tempted to smile when we think of Master Chang. It is more difficult when one is face to face with him, believe me. His protruding beak and scrawny neck force me to think of a great scavenging bird."

"His mother must have been frightened by a vulture when he was in the womb," the apprentice added.

"Or perhaps his father was a vulture," Kao Li-shih joked. "I believe that Master Chang hatched from an egg on some high crag and then flapped down to the city, deciding that the court needed a vulture-poet to rattle his beak from time to time. But he is a statesman as well, and he has placed in my hands a carefully composed document, stating his belief that Prince Ying died by the hand of an assassin. He wanted me to deliver it to the Emperor. I told him he was mad if he thought that I would intrude on the Emperor's grief and confusion with such a document without solid evidence to support it.

"Already Master Chang's poems, full of subtle innuendo, travel the capital," Kao Li-shih continued. "I pointed out to him that if there were any truth to his suspicions, a far better approach would be to allow the guilty party to think that we are in unanimous agreement on the suicide verdict of the investigating Ta Li Shih office. Then his, her, or their guard may be let down. I told him that I would take the document, read it carefully, commit it to memory, and then treat it as if it were a private correspondence between thieves or a "Peach Garden" oath sworn in blood by rebels. I promised him that I would burn it, and all traces of it, from our lips and minds." Lu Pei nodded in understanding.

"And if Master Chang has evidence to support his statement . . . ?"

"Yes," answered Kao Li-shih. "We come back to our question. What if, after all, it was murder? My first duty, uppermost in my mind and heart, is protecting Emperor Minghuang. I have done it for twenty years. In the beginning it seemed plain enough; an enemy of the Emperor was also an enemy of the T'ang, and vice versa. Now, consider my dilemma. If evidence turns up that contradicts the word of the forensic physician and the Ta Li Shih, if we indeed have a murder on our hands, then clearly there is at large an enemy of Minghuang and the state. It would be my duty to expose the murderer." He looked at the younger eunuch. "But the Emperor's state of mind now is brittle, fragile. I fear—no, I know—that the knowledge that once again plotting and killing are taking place within the Constellation Gates would kill him." Kao Li-shih sat in silence for a moment. "So, my young apprentice, tell me: How do I protect my Emperor?"

The two sat on the stone bench not speaking for some time. Kao Li-shih could plainly see the consternation on the younger eunuch's face as he considered the riddle put before him. He may as well learn early, the elder eunuch thought, what is expected of our race. We are servants and not servants at the same time. We learn to maintain an even balance of obedience and will. We are confined, yet move freely. Kao Li-shih bent and stirred the coals in the brazier with a slender iron rod.

Outside, the icy wind made the heavy wooden shutters rattle behind the thick winter quilts fastened tightly over them. Though the harem sanctum— the Palaces of the Great Within and the Palaces of Auspicious Prosperity— were shielded at the center of the palace complex, Ch'ang-an's winter could be felt through these inner walls. The quilts bulged and buckled at the windows.

Kao Li-shih drew from his sleeve the rolled-up memorial from the poet-statesman. Opening it, he read a bit, then turned to the apprentice.

"Our poet is fond of indulging in *yin-yu* [veiled speech]. At this very moment his poems circulate through the court and the capital. The 'kingfisher' is among us, he says. An entire court of ministers are looking around at their colleagues with anxiety and suspicion, wondering who this feathered egg-robber might be, while the poet himself flaps overhead, the 'lone goose,' the scorned hero of his own contrived literary conceit. How apt that he has chosen this metaphor; our scrawny scavenger bird sees the court as a giant aviary where crows and finches, hawks and chickens strut and scratch about, peck, and steal one another's nests." As he spoke, Kao Li-shih carefully touched the edge of Chang Chiu-ling's memorial to the glowing embers. "In this document, he has attempted to speak the official language of the statesman. But he cannot help himself; no matter what dialect he speaks, it becomes metaphor and innuendo."

The heat caused the loosely rolled parchment to open gradually. Kao Li-shih and Lu Pei watched as the fire ate up the words in fragments:

. . . they realize that virtuous men are being granted advancement . . .
unworthy men, themselves fearful that the way is vanishing before
them, are panicking . . . together raising a tumult, devoting their attentions to slander and death . . . desire to mislead Your Majesty and
his humble servants . . . seek to obstruct good men . . . If this is not
stopped early, then I fear that in the end those who bring about calamities now will bring ultimate destruction to this court . . . they
utter. . . .

When the last of it was consumed, Kao Li-shih stirred the ashes, breaking
up the burnt pieces that still retained their shape. Satisfied, he stood. He looked
at his apprentice, who continued to look pensively at the brazier. Enough for
one day, thought Kao Li-shih.

"Come," he said to the apprentice. "There are other matters in which
you may assist me."

They left the alcove and reentered the bathing room. "I have thought,"
he said to Lu Pei, "that after the funeral of the crown prince, two days hence,
I would make a present to the Emperor. In the past I've been successful at
choosing women for him. The right one, you know, is like the right medicine
administered at the right moment." The apprentice looked at his hands as Kao
Li-shih spoke. He does have memories, the elder eunuch thought. He still sees
the women through his own eyes; I can only see them if I look through the
Emperor's eyes.

"Come." He signaled to Lu Pei to follow. They entered the small room
where the harem records were kept. "There have been some new arrivals.
Before we look at them, we will examine the records. We will check their
training and origins, and see which of them are likely to be menstruating
during the fortnight following the funeral." He opened a heavy volume that
lay on a table. "Since the death of the Empress, my job has been more difficult.
As the Emperor sinks deeper into his lassitude, he makes fewer and fewer
requests for women to be sent to him. It is a shame. The harem ladies, you
know, speak highly among themselves of the Emperor's virtuosity."

"Another of his artistic pursuits set aside," remarked the apprentice.

"Indeed," replied Kao Li-shih.

Morning, DECEMBER 13

A cortege of pipers, drummers, and chimes passed the colorful row of court
mourners—third-level officials and upward. The somber parade plodded
toward the bowed gates of the Residences of the Ten Princes where, in the
courtyard, an altar of heavenly worship had been set up. Kao Li-shih breathed

the thick sweet odors of incense carried on the cold winter air; heavy vapors of death and purification settled on the slow processional.

The sun glinted on the yellow gilding of Ying's casket and the sealed burial tablets. Below the concentric rises of the altar, on an outer terrace with low railings, according to the unerring prescriptions of the *Book of Rites,* the ritual stone chimes, drums, and bells of the funeral orchestra awaited the arrival of the Imperial Patriarch. Powdery snow blew around the musicians' feet. A breeze snapped the tunnel of banners inscribed with the standards of the deceased prince.

The chief eunuch, his view unimpeded due to his height, stood behind the forest of gold, blue, turquoise, and lavender robes and watched as the protocol of cleansing began. The blue-and-gold litter of the Emperor approached the altar stairs. Kao Li-shih himself had prepared his master for today's sad event, helping him perform the ritual cleansing and purification of soul and body; the eunuch hoped that the father's grief would go into the tomb with the son.

As he watched for the figure of the Emperor to emerge from the carriage, a hand touched his shoulder. He turned to find the thin face of the minister Chang Chiu-ling looking up at him, the muscles of the jaw twitching anxiously. He spoke in a subdued voice.

"A word, Master Kao?" The eunuch turned back toward the ceremony briefly, saw that the Emperor was on his way up the altar stairs, walking steadily and without assistance. Signaling the minister to follow, Kao Li-shih led him away from the solemnities. They stepped with care over patches of ice and drifted snow and descended a long, narrow stone staircase that led into a secluded garden grotto of rock and pine. The funeral music started in the distance; melancholy strains, at once a tune full of resignation and an admonishment to the living to have hope in the midst of sorrow, carried on the cold wind. Kao Li-shih turned and faced Chang Chiu-ling. He said nothing, but raised his eyebrows to the minister in a signal to unburden himself.

"I find the times of ceremony the best for private conversation," the minister began. "Often it is in the times of greatest observation that we are least observed. At this moment all eyes are drawn to the gold casket and the bowed head of our Emperor." He paused, his reddish eyes dropping momentarily from the eunuch's face to the ground. He looked up again. "Naturally, it is about these sad circumstances that we must speak."

Poet, thought Kao Li-shih, your self-importance is embarrassing. Long before he had ever met Chang Chiu-ling, Kao Li-shih had detected in his poetry certain tendencies. He is forever in search of the precious metaphor, the conceit, no matter what the price. He waited to hear what the minister had to say.

"I commend your insight and your intercession in preventing the delivery of my importunate memorial to the Son of Heaven," the minister said. "But as you know, my only wish is to contribute to the safety of honest, principled men."

"A complicated task, is it not?" answered the eunuch. "But moving hastily, allowing our suspicions and fears, our imaginations, to overcome our better judgment, Master Chang . . . surely you know how dangerous this can be." The minister's gaunt face reddened at the reproach.

"Tell me, then, Master Kao. How do we rid the government of its enemies? How do we protect ourselves? I fear they have already gone too far."

"And who are 'they,' Master Chang? Are they already insidiously planted within the court, or are 'they' some factions or diverse individuals who wish to erode the House of Li from the fringes? Already your poetry, with its talk of kingfishers and such, has inspired a climate of innuendo and suspicion. There is not a junior assistant or prefectural magistrate among us who will not experience a measure of censure because of it," the eunuch said sternly, feeling his anger rising. The scrawny little man stood before him and received the strong words with dignity. "If," Kao Li-shih continued then, almost feeling pity for him, "I repeat, if there are dangerous 'birds' among us, perhaps we ought not to fluff their feathers or stir up their nests so soon. To protect ourselves, Master Chang, we lie in wait. We develop patience; we attack nothing with such ardor that we are stretching our bows before we have shaped our arrows." There, thought the eunuch; I speak to him in his own metaphorical tongue.

The minister turned toward an ornamental balustrade. His gloved hands gripped the rail, moving, Kao Li-shih thought, like talons on a tree branch. The minister's face was positively flushed now.

"Your mistake, Brilliant Councillor," Kao Li-shih continued, was not in attempting to bring your grave suspicions to the Emperor's attention. Your error was in bringing it without clear evidence." Then, to console the man a bit, he added, "You understand, of course, the weight your words would carry?"

The minister turned then, transferring a talon from the railing to Kao Li-shih's arm, and pressed his raptorial face close to the eunuch's. Kao Li-shih stiffened, but willed himself not to draw back. He imagined how poorly the man would fare in a real conspiracy.

"That arrow you spoke of," the minister said, dropping his voice. "I have it."

Kao Li-shih raised a skeptical eyebrow. "The evidence. The proof of conspiracy," the minister explained.

"I am listening," Kao Li-shih answered, surprised at the minister's forth-rightness.

Still gripping Kao Li-shih's arm, the minister spoke. "There is a girl, a household servant, a handmaiden to the harem. Her family has served mine in Chu-chiang for many years. Quite unwittingly, she brought to my apartments notes . . . of the strangest kind, on oddly shaped scraps of silk . . ."

"Notes?" Kao Li-shih interrupted. More poetic fancy, possibly?

"Yes. She cannot, of course, read—she thought she was simply decorating herself."

"She decorated herself and came to your apartments?" asked Kao Li-shih with mock reproval in his voice.

"They were stories, inventions, Master Kao."

"I am afraid I do not understand. How could she 'decorate herself' with stories, inventions as you call them; and how could they imply a murderous conspiracy?"

"You will have to see them for yourself, Master Kao," replied Chang Chiu-ling. "I think that you will understand then. And there is an insidious touch to all of this which causes my skin to prickle." He leaned closer to Kao Li-shih, his breath warm on the eunuch's chin. Kao Li-shih pulled his fur collar up higher as if shielding his face from the cold.

"You see," the minister continued in a whisper, "she found the notes in cleverly crafted silk flowers in the Hall of Consorts." Kao Li-shih felt a small ripple of alarm at this. He looked at the man who stood before him. No, this was not some feverish literary invention. The fear around the minister's eyes made it plain that, for once, he was not speaking metaphorically, as if he and everyone around him were characters in one of his poems. "It is important that we meet, Master Kao—alone, and discreetly," said the minister. "I will turn the notes over to you."

Kao Li-shih was exasperated. "Why did you not bring them with you now?"

"I had not decided, until I saw the wretched posture of the Emperor, that I would take this step. And I had to know, Master Kao, that you were willing to consider and would not do to them what I am sure you did to my memorial," the minister answered, summoning his dignity. "I know that my credibility has suffered somewhat in your eyes," he added. The music was moving now as the musicians left the altar terrace to follow the casket on the processional to the tomb in the family's Chao-ling mausoleum north of the city. Kao Li-shih sighed.

"Poet-Minister," he said, "you were correct to bring your news to me and to no one else. We will meet where our presence will go unnoticed. In the early morning, before the first watch is called, beneath the northeast portal of the Ch'eng Tien Gate. It is utterly deserted there before the officials file through for morning audience; the expansiveness of the courtyards will ensure that no one approaches or overhears us without our knowledge. Tomorrow?"

"Tomorrow," replied the minister. He bowed very slightly to the eunuch, then turned and left the grotto by a different staircase. Watching the receding figure, Kao Li-shih noted the careful steps and the thin shoulders. No, he thought; the minister does not resemble a vulture so much as he does an ibis, stepping delicately among tufts of marsh grass with a tender frog in its beak.

The eunuch began to mount the stone staircase. Flowers with hidden writings in them in the Hall of Consorts. This is not, if true, the work of an amateur. My Emperor, you only think that your favorite son took his own life because he feared the responsibility of being an emperor someday and having to send men to war.

He reached the top of the staircase and moved toward his position behind a row of ministers. How am I to protect you?

Pre-dawn, DECEMBER 14

The poet-minister Chang Chiu-ling moved along the broad main boulevard of the city. In the hour before dawn on this bitter cold morning, the street was not quite deserted. The minister, walking as close to the buildings as he could for maximum invisibility, took comfort in the occasional ox cart creaking by in the snow, lantern swinging.

Chang Chiu-ling stopped to rest. With each step it was necessary to break through a layer of ice on top of the deep snow, and his feet in their deerskin boots ached from the cold and the sharp edges of ice. His chest burned with exertion. The route he had chosen meant he had to walk twice as far as he usually would from his office to the Ch'eng Tien Gate, for he wished to avoid walking the great empty length of the central courtyard. Upon emerging from his building, he had left the enclosed complex of the Chancellery and Secretariat by one of the northernmost gates and followed the streets of the city south. He would follow the perimeter of the bureaucratic complex and then enter it again by the Vermilion Sparrow Gate. Then he need only cross the central courtyard's width to find himself at the Ch'eng Tien Gate. His heart pounded. He had added many thousands of steps to his journey, to be sure, but he preferred the relative security of the streets.

His hand enclosed the soft leather pouch hanging from his belt. He had a long way to go still, but he estimated that he could reach the Vermilion Sparrow Gate before he would have to stop to rest again. He closed his eyes and leaned against the wall for a brief moment as he gathered his strength. My scholarly way of life seems to have diverted my life-force from my muscles to my brain, he thought. How soft I've become! His legs trembled, but he forced himself to raise his foot from its hole in the snow and take the next step. Impossible to be stealthy under these circumstances, he thought, the reverberations of his feet breaking the ice echoing in the still air as he labored forward. Someone passed him, walking in the opposite direction, carrying a small candle lantern. He could discern a large bundle, a load of some sort, on the pedestrian's back. A farmer or tradesman on his way to market or to barter at some wealthy home in the city. Just to make sure, he watched over his shoulder as the figure plodded away from him. He started again.

It had seemed much simpler when he had made the arrangement with the eunuch. Meet before dawn, give him the flowers, and be done with it. Now, the darkness and cold were sapping him. How much farther to the accursed gate? Another figure approached and passed without a word. He stepped up his own pace, legs aching with the effort, until he had to stop to catch his breath, in spite of his promise to himself. In the split second after the reverberation of his last footfall, he thought he heard a matching sound twenty or thirty paces behind. An echo? He could not be sure. He began moving faster. Surely the noise of his footsteps would wake the entire city. It filled his ears. The faster he moved, the more footsteps and echoes mingled. The sound pushed him forward in a mounting panic of motion until he felt sure that someone now ran twenty paces behind him, matching him step for step. Chest burning and heart battering at his throat, he forced himself through the hard snow until he recognized, in the first dim light, the marble balustrade of the Vermilion Sparrow Gate. He dreaded the dash he would have to make across the open courtyard, but then he would be at the Ch'eng Tien Gate and in the company of Kao Li-shih. No one would dare to interfere with the individual closest to the Emperor. He would be safe. With his last strength he gripped the cold marble railing and began climbing the steep, icy staircase that would take him to the level of the courtyard. He pulled himself up the slippery steps. He was almost there; just a few feet up the stairs to the open space beyond. But his heart was about to burst. He would have to stop. He dropped to the stairs to catch his breath, lungs aching as they took in deep draughts of cold air. A gentle breeze dried the icy sweat on his face. There were no sounds, no footsteps. His breathing and pounding heart gradually slowed. I am a fool, he thought, a scared rabbit, running from the sound of my own footsteps. He thought with longing of comfortable rooms, warm couches, books, his writing desk. His hand felt for the leather pouch on his belt. Soon he would deliver it to Kao Li-shih and be done. This, too, he reminded himself, is a scholar's work.

"Master Chang." The contralto voice of a eunuch broke abruptly into the scholar's thoughts. "Master Chang, is that you . . . ?"

Chang jumped with involuntary shock. Kao Li-shih? Here? He had been given to understand . . .

"Master Chang," said the voice, moving nearer. "Where are you, Poet?" the familiar voice asked.

"I am down here, Master Kao, on the stairs," Chang heard his own voice, sounding like a child's, calling out in response. "I am quite exhausted. And I am confused. Were we not to meet at the Ch'eng Tien? I am glad . . ."

"Forgive me! My eyelids are quite nearly frozen, Master Chang. I have been waiting for you up here for some time. I had become very worried." A large figure loomed out of the darkness on the stairs above him. Chang Chiu-ling rejoiced. A most welcome sight. There could be no mistaking that massive frame. The man dropped slowly and gracefully from step to step with the chief eunuch's characteristic ease. Chang Chiu-ling did not move. He knew he could rest now. He was safe and thankful.

At that moment, behind him and far below, other footsteps sounded on the terrace and began to climb the stairs. Chang paid them little attention and looked hard at the face of the approaching man. He could make out nothing of Kao Li-shih's familiar features; the eunuch's ermine collar was pulled up high against the cold.

"Master Kao, it is good to see you again," Chang Chiu-ling said. "But I was given to understand that our meeting would be kept quite discreet—that we would be alone." The large man said nothing; he was now only a few steps above him, silent. Why does he not answer? An unpleasant taste was rising in the back of Chang Chiu-ling's mouth.

"Poet . . . Poet . . . ," a low voice came from the stairs below. He tried to rise but found his legs weak and useless. No, he thought. This cannot be happening.

"We have come for your purse!" the low voice continued.

"Master Kao!" Chang cried. "Who are these men?" No answer came from the large man who now stood on the step just above Chang. "I cannot go through with this, Master Kao, if we . . ."

"Master Chang . . ." the low voice behind him spoke again. "We want your purse and nothing else from you . . . not your words."

"Eunuch . . . what is this? Tell me . . . what is this?" Chang looked up into the hidden face, his eyes wide, pleading like a child. The large man said nothing. Chang could now hear that one's loud breathing in the still air. The small hairs on his neck bristled. This was not Kao Li-shih; this was a stranger. When the stranger did speak, it was as if he, too, recognized that the deception was over. His voice was gutteral, unrecognizable to the poet.

"Master Chang, untie the purse from your waist. Don't turn around."

Dawn, DECEMBER 14

Mornings before dawn were the coldest time of winter. The foggy grime of coal and charcoal smoke that habitually hung over the city had cleared during the bitter night, and the stars were large and unobscured as Kao Li-shih approached the entrance to the imperial city. He showed the imperial seal to the constable guarding the tall studded gate that led to the wide courtyard and the adjoining maze of alleys and avenues, which at this hour would be uncluttered by the traffic of the ministries' business. The guard, recognizing the chief eunuch, bowed and waved him through without even glancing at the seal.

Kao Li-shih walked south toward the Ch'eng Tien Gate. He entered the wide avenues between the central wings of the Chancellery and Secretariat compounds, the tier-hipped roofs of their buildings rising in ridged steps to towering heights of four and five stories. The silhouette of lofty, sweeping eaves and crenellated walls were visible against the clear starry sky. Kao Li-shih kept his eyes slightly raised as he walked; the ground appeared in a ghostly image just underneath his line of vision, and he was able to negotiate without carrying a lantern.

Ahead, he could see the outline of the Ch'eng Tien Gate with its graceful bracketed eaves. Kao Li-shih began to climb the marble stairs to the gate watchtower which overlooked the Orchid Terrace of government and the fortress mansions of the harem and the imperial family. His feet crunched on the brittle snow. The inside of his nose burned with the bitter air. He paused to listen: nothing.

If I know the minister Chang Chiu-ling, thought Kao Li-shih, he has been here for at least an hour already and awaits me at the top. My footsteps will alert him to my arrival. I can take the accursed flowers, whatever they may be, and resume my night's sleep before the sun is up. Then, by the light of morning, when my judgment is clear, I shall read these "inventions." What could they possibly say? The minister successfully conveyed his concern to me, without uttering a single quote. I hope against hope that I will not have to rip the scabs from the Emperor's wounds with news of murder.

Reaching the top, Kao Li-shih stood for a moment, listening, his heart beating hard from the exertion. There was a slight wind, but no other sound. He sensed, to his surprise, that the minister was not there. He was quite alone. He chose a sheltered spot in one of the gate's arched passages and waited.

The cold crept through the soles of Kao Li-shih's heavy boots. The wind had died down; the still air carried with perfect clarity the pre-dawn cry of the muezzin from the Arab quarter of the vast city beyond the walls of the palace complex. The eunuch contemplated the long empty sound. There is, he thought, a note of sorrow in all religion.

He stamped his feet. His toes were becoming numb. Despite his nervous anticipation of the meeting with the minister, Kao Li-shih found himself feeling drowsy. He had risen several hours before his customary time, and now the first flush of purposeful energy was wearing off. His bones ached, and his fatigue allowed the cold to penetrate his thick clothing too easily. He noticed that the huge courtyard was becoming visible. The snow was reflecting the first light of dawn before any light was visible on the horizon.

Poet-Minister, thought Kao Li-shih, this is indeed ironic. Many is the time when I have crossed a room or stepped discreetly behind a post in order to avoid an impending contact with you. It is not easy for me, since I am a head taller than everyone else, to disappear into a crowd—but I have slipped from your view many times. And now I stand here, in this deathly cold, having left a warm bed, eagerly craning my neck for a glimpse of you. Compounding this irony is the fact that the message you say you're bringing could cause even more grief and trouble than we have already had at the palace.

The cold was moving up into the eunuch's legs. The entire courtyard was now plainly visible stretching into the distance. Not a footprint could be seen on the even carpet of snow aside from the eunuch's own. A thin sliver of gray now showed on the horizon, and the stars were fading. He waited.

Kao Li-shih knew that the man he awaited could not count unreliability among his faults. True, he was often enthralled by the sound of his own speech and the importance of his message, too obviously savoring his own choice of a word or phrase. True, too, that he leaned too close when he talked to one, too self-absorbed to notice the little particles of spittle that flew from his mouth to land on one's face or clothing.

But poetic pretension and an officious manner, Kao Li-shih knew, in no way indicated a lack of punctuality or inability to keep an appointment. The eunuch knew, as did everyone, of Chang Chiu-ling's strict adherence to the progression of daily time in official city watches—the pounding of the drum towers. His life was ruled by sundials and the rigid movements of the water clock in the imperial orrery. Kao Li-shih knew that the minister, after agreeing to the meeting, would not have returned to his home in the Pu-cheng quarter of the city. Rather, he would have remained awake in his office until the time of the rendezvous—especially when so pressed by his own sense of urgency. Why, then, was he not here?

The body, Kao Li-shih reflected, often knows the truth first. His stiff, tired limbs, aching from the cold and from standing still, were whispering a message: The poet is not going to come. Let us give him more time, his mind responded. He had never known him to fail to keep his word; it was not in the man.

The dawn light had become a soft, diffuse gray. The great buildings around the square began to reveal themselves. Far away on the horizon, the drum and bell towers and the Big and Little Wild Goose Temples were silhouetted against the sky. Kao Li-shih mentally went over his words to Chang Chiu-ling. No, there could be no mistake.

His teeth were chattering as he rubbed his weary eyes. Poet, I am beginning to believe in your kingfisher. You must be in his claws now. Otherwise, you would be here. And he would not have intercepted you unless your poems had attracted his attention—and the death of the prince was something other than suicide.

Murder. The mysterious flowers Chang Chiu-ling had spoken of may or may not have provided evidence of murder; if they had, I would then have been obligated to go to the Emperor. Your absence here this morning, Poet, is stronger evidence—but completely intangible. I am empty-handed.

Prince Ying had been barely seventeen. A tender age, to be sure, to end one's own life. The prince's funeral had not been the first funeral for Kao Li-shih. The ceremony had vividly resurrected for Kao Li-shih another funeral, long ago, of another young boy. He recalled the ritual mourning garments, the slippers of white hemp, the body laid out in brocades, the coffin draped in red silk, the mourner's sad songs. Buddhist monks and holy men in saffron robes, Taoist shamans and shamankas in black had chanted while the women wailed—his mother most of all. And Kao Li-shih remembered thinking, as a child of nine, that the prayers, the burning of enigmatic inscriptions, the ritual, were to make his brother well again—that he would presently sit up and take a piece of fruit from the offering dish. For the moment the brittle cold of the bleak courtyard receded in importance before unpleasant and unwanted memories of the past. Perhaps, Kao Li-shih thought, it was this frozen paralysis and the sense of helplessness consuming him this morning that now brought it all back to him; the stinging cold, the waiting, the thin, imminent line of light on the horizon that threatened to remove the one comfort of this unpleasant situation, the stark privacy of nighttime. He felt a gelid exhaustion creeping in every bone and joint of his body; with it came the depression that he was so vulnerable to and the rush of bad thoughts that usually followed.

Memories. In all of them, loss was implicit: Kao Li-shih was unable to help himself as he recalled, in perfect visceral detail, the wretched time when he was a child, when the suddenness of his brother's death had left him unprepared for what was to come, and when the meaning of that untimely death for his own life was not to become clear for some time. Standing there in the bitter dawn waiting desperately for the poet, a confused, cold, ominous feeling grew in him. He did not fight it now, but gave himself over with perverse satisfaction to total lurid recollection.

The memory rose now of the day when his brother had first complained of pains in the hollow below his ribs. It was most unusual because Elder Brother rarely complained of anything. As a baby, Elder Brother had never cried, his mother used to say, when he stumbled and scraped his elbows and knees. When the first pains came, he only grimaced and accepted them. They seemed to go away for a while. But then, a few days later, when he screamed for the first time, he set the entire household into a panic. What could make Elder Brother scream so? Everyone came running. But then his screams of agony died down that afternoon, and all that issued from his throat for the rest of that day and the next were low, terrible moans.

The family called in physicians for the lungs, stomach, spleen, bowels, and liver, but nothing seemed to help. As an adult, Kao Li-shih had little faith in physicians. His lack of trust, he was sure, had its origins in that distant past. Quite early in life he had reached the conclusion that the body is too much a mystery for the minds of men.

Elder Brother's pulses were read and reread continually—sluggish and hollow, racing and scattered, and finally, floating and weak. All that night he tossed and writhed, groaning and perspiring. The next day he was dead, found lying in his bed by a servant, his face turned wistfully upward—eyes open, staring at the gauzy canopy overhead as if watching something invisible to the eyes of the living. The child Kao Li-shih had been nearest to Elder Brother's room and was the first to run in when the servant called out. To this day he had not forgotten the odd thoughts that entered his head at that moment, alone in the room with the mound of insentient flesh that had been his brother. He remembered examining the corpse's face and thinking that, although Brother's eyes were dead and could no longer see, his spirit—the one that stayed with the earthly remains—could look to the ends of the universe. Brother was really seeing much more than the linen canopy of his bed and the wooden ceiling; he was seeing far beyond that. He was seeing now into those magic secret worlds reserved only for the Taoist magicians, the Tantric mystics, the few. It had occurred to him while he was looking at the staring eyes that Elder Brother had indeed become one of them.

The servants wailed with grief, but his father said nothing. And his mother, usually given to crying at just about anything, merely stood in the doorway, her face expressionless, as they bore the body of her firstborn out. Her eyes seemed as dead as Elder Brother's; they stared out blankly as if they were communing with something far past the limits of their vision. Or as if, the child Kao Li-shih had thought, she viewed the whole event with a detached, strangely courteous, vicarious interest—it was happening, but not to her. It was not until days later that she broke. Her piteous sobs had drowned out the chanting of the professional funeral mourners; for the young Kao Li-shih, her cries had been the most terrible sounds he would ever hear. At the funeral, he had resolutely cupped his palms tightly over his ears. But Father wouldn't allow any such displays and kept pulling the child's hands away.

Today, at Ying's funeral, Kao Li-shih had felt the same despair. But he no longer tried to block out the sounds. With age came pragmatism and, with it, a sense of realism that told him how foolish it was to waste his vital energies trying to hide from the unpleasant truth—unless you were a master of the art of self-deception. Only then might you spare yourself the pain.

Sometime during his brother's funeral it had come to him: it simply did not matter what he, Kao Li-shih, wanted at all. His brother was not going to sit up and take the fruit offerings from the dish. Neither was his mother's grief about to go away, nor would her wailing and crying stop. His brother was dead. And despite all that the saffron-robed Buddhists would later tell him, Kao Li-shih knew that he would never speak or laugh or play with his brother again. And that was that. The feeling of finality had pressed against him until it seemed to pass inside, into his flesh and then into his bones, where it stayed and became part of his being.

It so consumed him that when his father told him that he would be taking his elder brother's place in promised "service," the words had no effect. He was numbed to everything. He was a stone, he used to say to himself. A small, hard, polished stone, as oblivious to warm sun and fragrant breezes as he was to snow, rain, and bitter wind. He would dream a stone's dreams, he used to tell himself, and think a stone's thoughts.

The days after his brother's death piled inconsequentially upon one another. He moved through them, the sky changing from dark to light and back again while hardly a thought moved in his guarded mind. Then one day when he was nearly nine years old, his father had come quietly into the room where he slept.

He woke the boy with a gentle hand on the shoulder; Kao Li-shih had stirred from dreamless sleep to look into father's carefully veiled eyes. He spoke very gently to the child; under his arm he carried a parcel. In later years Kao Li-shih would often wonder what his father could possibly have been feeling when he walked into the child's room that morning so many years ago. He had tried to imagine it, but he had never been able to. There must have been some guilt, though. What else could account for the unusual gentleness he had shown to the boy as he helped him rise and dress?

Father seemed embarrassed, and, in the next moment, lowered his eyes and silently picked him up and raised him out of the bed and onto his feet. Then, hastily, he pulled a robe down over him and eased his arms into a small red quilted jacket. It was cold, even in that southern province, sometime at the end of autumn.

"Take this." Father had given him the parcel, which turned out to be a bundle of clothing.

"Father?" the boy had asked, fear and uncertainty taking shape like ghosts in his heart. He could still taste that moment; it was as real to him now as it had been forty years ago. "I don't want to go anywhere." He remembered resisting, trying to sit down on the cold wooden floor. "Where is my mother?" Did he really offer that resistance to his father? Or was this only the way he remembered it now? Yes, he must have done it. The memory was real.

And he was absolutely sure of what his father had said next: "You know what you have to do." He remembered the eyes, and the hands that dressed him rapidly and perfunctorily, then herded him across the floor. "What you and I must do is of no concern to the women, boy. They would not understand it. It goes back to my father and his father." The words came softly, crowding one another, Father's voice low and conspiratorial. "It is a matter of the honor and the obligations of this House of Feng. It our duty now. It is not something that concerns a woman. It is *not* a world of women." And then came the words that had put the first direct sword of fear into his young heart, mysterious and meaningless though they were. "You will understand all of this after it is done."

He had asked a weak question then, in some vain hope of deflecting Father's purpose. Should he say good-bye to his mother, his grandmother and grandfather, his aunts? But that was the last that his father said. He did not answer, but hurried him out into the early morning courtyard and into the carriage before anyone else in the household was awake. He kept trying to read something in his father's eyes, but his father kept them carefully averted as he climbed behind him into the carriage.

That was when the veil that had settled over the child months before lifted with horrible suddenness. His father had become a complete stranger. And now that stranger was pushing him brutally out into the world beyond that small measure of land, his father's grounds, that was just about everything he had ever known. And he knew then where he was to be taken.

Kao Li-shih could remember the sound of his own screams, but they had never been uttered out loud. He had not broken the silence inside the jolting carriage, but inside his head, long, terrible, phantom screams sounded. He knew what was going to happen to him, because Brother had told him.

Elder Brother used to brag about the prestige that would come from being an imperial eunuch. That was where Elder Brother was going to be sent, he had told his little brother. Not just into the house of a mere rich man, but to the palace. Think of where I am going to go, he would say; think of the things I am going to see. And Elder Brother even used to brag about the operation that he was going to undergo in order to enter his wonderful new life, knowing, in a cruel, taunting, older brother way how much it upset Little Brother.

Once he had stolen a knife from the kitchen and sneaked back into his little brother's room. While the young one watched, transfixed and against his will, Elder Brother had dropped his trousers. Taking hold of his penis and his bag of eggs, he held the knife menacingly close, as if he were about to slice them off himself. He actually touched the skin with the blade, his face grimacing in mock pain, until Little Brother begged him to stop.

That cold morning in the wagon, Kao Li-shih had wet his pants. Father, in his haste to get him out of the house, had not even allowed him the few seconds he needed to pass his morning water, and with his fear, he had no longer been able to hold it. Forever after, the memory of that fear for Kao Li-shih was inextricably linked to the smell and feel of warm, piss-soaked legs gradually turning cold and clammy. He had crouched in his soaked trousers, possessed by shame and fear, while his father rode with his eyes resolutely turned away from his son's, never once looking at him during the entire trip.

The wagon rumbled onto cobblestones, then turned into a narrow alley. The child made no attempt to move, holding himself perfectly still until the wagon jolted to a stop. Then he tried to crouch even lower between the seats, pressing his head down between his knees in the desperate hope that if he made himself infinitely small he might somehow be forgotten.

Weary of remembering, Kao Li-shih stamped his feet. The cold had bitten through the tips of his boots so that his toes ached as if he had dropped a heavy stone on them. He welcomed the pain, wishing for any kind of distraction to stop the flow of memory. But memories, he knew, bad ones in particular, had a way of following each other like the links of a chain. Once the process of recall had begun, there would be no escaping. Already he had moved from the death of his brother to the morning his father woke him to the strange and terrible ride in the carriage and his father's unseeing eyes and face like a stranger's. Next, of course, would come the alley, its smells and darkness . . .

Kao Li-shih shook his head and brought his shoulders up high so that the warm fur of his collar hugged his neck. He stamped his feet again and rubbed his hands together hard against the creeping cold and the memories, but they were moving into place now and would not be stopped.

There was another image that the passage of forty years could not soften: his first sight of the surgeon's sign which hung over the doorframe, an ancient carved glyph of a penis and scrotum traced delicately in gold leaf beneath the threatening form of a blade . . .

Even though the boy had had no choice in the answer to the surgeon's ritual question, his father had not even allowed him the dignity of responding himself.

"Will you or will you not regret what the blade is about to do?" Under moral law, the surgeon was required to utter these words before the knife did its irreversible work. It mattered little whether a particular castration was part of the barely legal and involuntary slave trade, or the conscious act of a free man—or a young boy with no say in the matter at all—the question still had to be asked.

"He will not!" his father answered stiffly before leaving the room.

But Kao Li-shih harbored no hatred toward his father, nor the surgeon who cut him, nor the official of Lingnan Province whose quota to the court was undoubtedly filled that day. He had come to understand, at great expense to soul and energy, that this act committed against his body was destiny. It was a matter of inviolate tradition—honor, as his father had put it. He, Kao Li-shih, was simply a small bit of the grease that lubricated the myriad wheels of state: a magistrate in Lingnan had been promised the eldest son of the Feng family; promised that the boy be cut and sent up into service with the Nei-sheng department of the imperial house, the inner chambers. And he, Kao Li-shih, was merely a payment for a long-ago favor in an ancient line of favors once granted his family—a favor performed so long ago that no doubt there had been no one left alive at the time he was cut who even remembered what it was. And so it went: the debts of fathers always passed to their sons.

He had never traced to its source his life's fate which eventually tied him to the Emperor of China. Whatever that original favor had been for which his future manhood had been exchanged, he would never know—nor did he want to. It was irrelevant, in any case. What was plain was that he had been fated from birth to be by the Emperor's side, and the universe had chosen a certain mechanism to achieve that end. He was here now to suffer with him his sorrow at the death of his Empress and, now, his son . . . and he was also fated, so it seemed, to stand here in this cold morning while the knowledge of murder grew more certain by the hour.

After he had recovered from the surgery, he had been sent to Loyang. The first several months in the eastern capital were shattering and traumatic for the nine-year-old Pure-from-Birth eunuch. He was relegated to serve his apprenticeship in the custody of the eunuchs of the inner chambers of the imperial household of the Emperor Chung-tsung. He was now the adopted son of his sponsor at court, the old eunuch Kao Yen-fu and his wife, and was known as Li-shih from the home of Kao.

But there was little time to adjust to his new world, because after those first few months of his entrance into the grand palace in the great eastern capital of Loyang, he found himself in the midst of war. Not a war of nations, but a hellish siege waged by a brutal and merciless woman—Chung-tsung's wife, the Empress Wei. It was a time of murders in broad daylight, of ambushes and knifings in hallways. But for Kao Li-shih, there was an emotion even more acute than the fear that was everywhere during the dreadful days of Aunt Wei's thirsty pursuit of power: It was the shame he felt when he understood what he was and what he would inevitably become. He would not grow into manhood like other boys; he would only grow into one of those strange creatures he had seen and heard running in hysteria like old women down the long corridors of the palace. And though he was barely ten years old, humiliation had overwhelmed him. How could a grown man move as they did or talk as they did? It seemed that they waddled when they ran, and they were always in a panic, their shrill, reedy voices rising and echoing. Because he was so young, he was easily infected by their fear. Not that there was no reason for it—the danger was quite real.

Old Kao Yen-fu, his adopted father, the one eunuch who was a source of strength to him and who, in their few short months together, had opened the boy's heart to the world of ancient poesies and ritual music, was murdered attempting to protect Emperor Chung-tsung. He was clubbed over the head and dumped ignominiously into the dark icy water of the canal that ran outside the palace walls. Once again young Kao Li-shih found himself in a carriage —this time with a nineteen-year-old prince and two guard-escorts; they were racing, flying headlong through the narrow alleys and over the steep bridges that crisscrossed the maze of Loyang's rivers and canals. While their driver beat the team with the fury of a madman, the boys were thrown together by the violent lurching and swaying. The escorts, their voices barely heard above the rumbling of the wheels and the frenzied rhythm of the horses' hooves on the stones, shouted for the two boys to keep their heads low. The wheels bounced off the ground and the carriage shuddered as if it were about to fly apart, swinging wildly this way and that, groaning under the strain. They flew down narrow wall-locked alleys and rose suddenly and breathlessly to the summit of one steep bridge after another in their path. Inside, the young Kao Li-shih had braced himself, eyes squeezed shut, certain that at any moment they would topple over the railing and he would go the way of his good "father" Kao Yen-fu—drowned in the brackish filthy black of the canal, pulled under by the weight of horses yoked in strangulated panic, the fragmented livery of wood and iron slipping heavily beneath the cold, oily surface, the screams of the attendants and the prince the last sounds he would ever hear . . .

That morning a thousand eunuchs fled the halls of the palace. And those officials loyal to Emperor Chung-tsung also knew their fate: Some escaped with their families, some without; others learned firsthand the plain truth that the Emperor's wife, the Empress Wei, was as brutal as Grandmother Wu before her. That morning the Emperor of the T'ang, Uncle Chung-tsung, was found murdered, splendidly regaled in the blue phoenix robes of divine state, his arms and legs bound and his head forced down into a cauldron of boiling water so that his face was cooked away from his bones. As if merely for good measure, many of the eunuchs of the Nei-sheng, the Emperor's inner household, were similarly dispatched. And so the others fled—and the visiting crown prince was hurried into a waiting carriage with a little nine-year-old, a Pure-from-Birth still untrained in imperial service, retrieved from his hiding place beneath the couches in the great hall to attend the prince's needs because there was no one else left.

Outside the city, they were met by escorts, members of the faction once loyal to Emperor Chung-tsung. From there, Crown Prince Li Lung-chi and his child-eunuch, young Kao Li-shih, fled by carriage across hundreds of arid li to the western capital in Ch'ang-an. North of the city, on the great P'enya Road, they were received by the Dragon Militant Militia and the young crown prince's father, Jui-tsung, an incompetent dullard who was forced to mount the throne in opposition to the ruthless forces of Aunt Wei—a throne he was no more suited to fill than would be the stumpy bear he so much resembled.

And even with Wei dead, it was far from over. For Crown Prince Li Lung-chi's slow-witted hulk of a father, there was the threat of his own sister, the Princess T'ai Ping; she came close to killing him, but, in truth, she was far more interested in doing away with the son, her nephew the crown prince.

Kao Li-shih grew up fast. In his twelfth year, his cunning and wisdom were already well known. And many times in the next few years he was to save the life of the brilliant, incandescent Prince Li Lung-chi, now his inseparable friend and soon to be, by virtue of the abdication of his father, the Brilliant Emperor Minghuang of China. And so it was that Kao Li-shih, quite as much through the fearsome machinations of women as through the vagaries of fate, became the personal ally of the most compassionate, wise, and sensitive ruler that the empire had ever known.

And so here I stand, he thought. The high spot where he waited afforded him a clear view over the symmetrical golden tiled roofs of the bureaucratic city, now catching the sun's rays. Beyond, he could see the Ch'eng Tien's mirror image, the Vermilion Sparrow Gate, which opened on to the city's broad main boulevard. Out there, in the endless maze of low *hu-tung* roofs and neatly bordering trees, men had to struggle every day. But there was no mystery as to the nature of the enemy: conscription, taxes, cold, hunger. Brutal; but clear, predictable.

From the plaza below came a shout and the crack of a whip. Commerce was beginning. A cart of freshly dressed game lumbered through the bureaucratic city toward the imperial kitchens. Kao Li-shih watched the driver of the cart, who was dressed in thick quilts, his breath forming clouds as he shouted at his laboring oxen. How, the eunuch speculated, would that man handle these politics of ultimate destiny? Come up here, fellow, thought Kao Li-shih. I will drive your cart to the kitchens, haggle with the eunuchs over the price of the meat, and then return to your house on the edge of the city, though I fear your wife will be in for a disappointment. You, in the meantime, will return to the palace with the intuitive knowledge that the crown prince was murdered; but you'll be empty-handed, without a shred of tangible evidence. What will you do?

Let me give you some advice. The Emperor's heart is broken. I would prefer that you refrain from talk of murder unless you have proof. Since you don't have it, but only know it in your heart, then you must keep your knowledge to yourself—but double your vigilance.

The kingfisher. Kao Li-shih rubbed his weary eyes and imagined a kingfisher diving toward the calm surface of a lake. A small commotion, then the bird flew upward, a silvery fish twisting and writhing in its grip. Poor poet. In the eunuch's mental picture, the sun sparkled on the water as the bird climbed skyward, his feathers of iridescent blue-purple catching the light. Why had he not thought of it before?

Blue-purple. Kao Li-shih's eyes flew open. Blue-purple. The poet, in his metaphor, was referring not only to the predatory nature of the bird, but to his color. He exhaled softly. So it is you!

Oh, how I would have preferred to find a clever amateur behind it all, a concubine or a minor official with ambition. No, your signature is present, so subtle that it nearly escaped me. Notes in flowers, a no doubt costly, imported assassin capable of out-thinking the forensic physicians from Loyang . . . and now a vanished poet-minister.

The orange orb of the sun now showed over the city rooftops in the east. In the plaza below, early morning commercial traffic and those on official business left their tracks in the fresh snow. Kao Li-shih bade a silent farewell to Chang Chiu-ling, whose homely face he doubted he would ever see again. He started down the marble staircase, ashamed of his relief—in spite of his curiosity—that the poet had not been able to bring him the mysterious flowers. Without proof he could not—no, he thought, let us be honest—he would not have to go to the Emperor and tell him that he had been the victim of a conspiracy. Now that the identity of the kingfisher was clear to Kao Li-shih, he silently thanked the poet for not appearing. The kingfisher. There are not many men who would care to oppose that one openly. But now that I know who you are, I will have the luxury of protecting the Emperor at my own discretion. I have no doubt that I can be more effective that way in any case. I must remember, the next time I am holding forth to the apprentice on the effects of yin and yang, to explain that the yin imbalance does not always come from women. In a man the danger can be far more subtle.

Kao Li-shih hurried down the steps and started across the snowy expanse. If I were in the habit of writing poetry—which I am not, thank the gods—I would not have chosen the kingfisher as my metaphor. I would have used a more apt comparison from the animal world. I will be vigilant. I will look under ever rock and in every crevice for you . . . Lizard!

3

Illusions

The Brilliant Emperor made the irretrievable mistake of appointing a brilliant crook as minister of state. Prime Minister Li Lin-fu was not a well-lettered man . . . What he lacked in proficiency with the written word, he more than made up, however, with his usual oral eloquence . . . he was a man whose words were steeped in fragrant honey, but whose intentions always contained a murderous dagger.

—*William Hung*

[Li Lin-fu] belonged to the highest ranks of the Kuan-chung aristocracy. He entered official life through hereditary privilege and was no friend of the literary gentry. He possessed qualities which were much rarer among the Chinese of those days than . . . the ability to compose in the balanced style. He had a passion for order and system . . . and arts frequently associated with mathematics.

—*Edwin Pulleyblank*

The clashes between Chang Chiu-ling and Li Lin-fu have been dramatized by the historians, for in them was rightly seen a turning point in the reign of Hsuan-tsung [Minghuang]. Chang was desperately fighting to maintain the position of the literati (the southern literatus).

From [the appointment of Li Lin-fu] in 736 until his death in 752, Li Lin-fu was virtual dictator. Niu Hsien-k'o was completely subservient to him and never ventured to interfere.

—*Edwin Pulleyblank*

Pre-dawn, DECEMBER 14—The Chancellery

"The possession of the Consort Wu's body by a *guei* is not just hearsay. We cannot deny the evidence of our senses. We have witnessed things in her behavior, Councillor, which . . ."

"Your common soldiering background, General Niu, has betrayed you," interrupted Chief Minister Li Lin-fu. "Indeed, it has stayed with you. Perhaps Master Chang Chiu-ling was right about you when he opposed your promotion." He stared at the man standing in front of him in the narrow rectangular office. He maintained an expressionless face, allowing his irritable impatience to build as he appraised his assistant. "Am I right? Do you give me any evidence of a command of reason or logic? I am surprised that the Son of Heaven accepted the arguments for your appointment to this office and my side. I had thought, for a while, that I had reason to think otherwise, but . . ."

"Then I must deny what I saw and heard myself?" asked General Niu Hsien-ko apologetically. "The consort displays the mannerisms of the boy in her voice and speech. Can this not be construed as proof, Councillor?"

"Proof, yes, of the narrow scope of your vision, General," the chief minister said sharply. He ran his hands along the gilt edge of the tabletop in front of him, noting with satisfaction his assistant's increasing discomfort and confusion. The man opened his mouth, thought better of it, apparently, and shut it again. Then he attempted to arrange his features into an intelligent, thoughtful expression. In vain, my friend, in vain, thought Li Lin-fu, carefully restraining the impulse to squash him like an insect. Li Lin-fu made a beckoning gesture. "Let me ask a favor of you, Master Niu," he said then. "Step to the window. I want you to look at something and then describe to me what you see. Defer to my wishes, for a moment, if you will. Push those shutters open," he directed. "Raise the winter quilts . . . not too far, please; this cold night air causes me some irritation. It is a burden I bear—this predisposition to catarrh. And, of course, we have little use for the Cold Palace," he joked. General Niu rewarded Li Lin-fu's wit with a guarded look which told the chief minister that not only was the allusion lost on his subordinate, but his ignorance was so complete that he looked suspiciously toward his master in an effort to determine whether he had been insulted, threatened, or complimented. It is tempting, my friend, to show you exactly what it means, Li Lin-fu reflected. Though I don't suppose I would be justified in exiling you merely for being somewhat dull.

He gestured, indicating that Niu should turn his attention to the window. "What I want you to look at should be—let me see; it is past the third watch—quite low and close to the horizon by now. Can you see a large tower beyond the trees?"

"Yes, Councillor, of course. Above the Grand Harmony Hall, I detect the silhouette of the peak of the Vermilion Phoenix Tower."

"Good. If I am not mistaken," Li Lin-fu said, still seated and not looking at the window at all, "a familiar star now appears to rest almost on the tip of that Phoenix Tower spire."

"Yes . . ." Niu said, and fell silent. He is being careful, noted Li Lin-fu.

"What does its position tell you?" Li Lin-fu asked.

"Well . . ." Niu began reluctantly, "as a soldier, I became quite adept at determining the time by the positions of the stars. This star has made its usual trek across the sky . . . I would judge that we are close to the fourth watch," he concluded.

"You are correct that we are close to the fourth watch," Li Lin-fu replied. "But you have made a grave error in judgment about the other."

"The other?" asked Niu.

"Close the window, please. This winter air is brutal. It is unfortunate that I cannot spare the time to winter in a milder climate—perhaps Lingnan. But with the responsibilities of the Chancellery and the Secretariat, and the troubles with the Ministries of Finance and Defense also falling on the shoulders of the wearer of the Ssu-k'ung robe, I find myself to be overtaxed, Master Niu, but unable to take my leave, even temporarily." The chief minister coughed lightly and cleared his throat. "Especially if I'm not to let these matters fall into the hands of an inexperienced class of scholar-bureaucrats." Niu said nothing, but waited. "You tell me, General, that the star has moved across the heavens," Li Lin-fu said. "How do you know this?"

"Because it is nearer to the tower now than it was an hour ago," Niu said warily.

"And that is enough to tell you that the star has moved, Master Niu?"

"Certainly, Councillor," Niu said with dignity. "That is the simplest deduction. It has moved, and all the other stars as well. There is a fixed relation between heavenly bodies."

"What other brilliant deductions do you make when reading the sky, General?"

"Well . . . I am embarrassed to speak on something about which I know so little . . . but there are those who examine the heavens through a sighting tube. They have found that the canopy overhead moves according to a strict pattern, quite predictable, and corresponding to the seasons." He hesitated. "There are, however, celestial occurrences that are not predictable: shooting stars, red skies, darkening of the sun or moon. These irregularities in the orderly sequence attract our attention. They are portents—if read correctly, they can tell us our fate."

"There is nothing comparable to the assurance of the ignorant," the chief minister remarked. His assistant did not react, but stood, waiting. He knows that he is about to be taught something, Li Lin-fu thought, annoyed that any of his actions should be predictable to Niu.

Moving his hands to the sides of his desk, he said, "Do you know the work of our reknowned court astronomer Nankung Yueh?" As he spoke, he folded back the false top of his desk, revealing a strangely marked inlay wheel. Each segment bore a recessed jade and mother-of-pearl ideogram—ancient ritualistic characters, boldly curvilinear like the markings of the prehistoric diviner's tortoise shell. With a flick of his finger, the chief minister caused the wheel to rotate with masterful smoothness. With a touch of his hand, it stopped. In the center, covering the hub, rested a stationary square of cinnabar enamel. Four intersecting lines of gold wire divided the large square into nine small squares of equal size. Each was marked with a red numeral from one to nine. "He has been influenced considerably by the ideas that flow to us from the Persians," he continued. General Niu's eyes were fixed on the mysterious wheel. "They have a long and commendable record with things of this sort." The chief minister looked up at his assistant. "You see, it is not just spices and silk that pass through the Jade Gate." He closed the lid to the desktop. "Have you paid a visit to the observatory on Mount Li? No? Of course not. But I would highly recommend it, Master Niu. Highly! Surrounded by such an impressive display of instruments—armillary spheres, sundials, astrolabes, alidades, and a most complex orrery of brass, marble, and glass—perhaps the astronomer can teach you what I have not been able to."

Li Lin-fu felt a familiar, pleasurable sensation. Circumstances were in collusion. His carefully contained anger at the failure of his plans was being released gradually, in measured amounts. It nourished his mind, speeding his thoughts, allowing him to reach nimbly into his vast storehouse of knowledge. A wealth of parables, ready for construction, presented themselves simultaneously for any point which he wished to illustrate. His mind felt like a fine machine of precisely honed, shining, interlocking parts made of precious metal. And the man before him would listen all the way through until he, Li Lin-fu, had obtained satisfaction.

"Master Yueh has even improved upon the work of Chang Heng, who was observing the heavens six hundred years ago. He has perfected his predecessor's armillary sphere." Li Lin-fu closed his eyes, savoring in a voluptuous way the miraculous device. With one hand he indicated an imaginary sphere; with the other hand he made a fist and rotated it inside the curve of his hand. "One sphere turns precisely inside the other. Let it suffice to say that the engine is driven by a perpetual flow of water and a rather complex system of gears. Do you know what he has learned?"

"No, Councillor, nor would I presume to guess," the general replied.

"Master Yueh has discovered that the positions of the heavenly bodies represented by his device correspond to our observations of the heavens only when the spheres turn in relation to each other. Neither is static or fixed in regards to the other, but . . . constantly in motion," he finished. Niu furrowed his brow. Li Lin-fu anticipated with pleasure his imminent demonstration to General Niu of the latter's faulty, incomplete processes of thought. He felt the words forming into perfect progressions of illustrative logic and arranging themselves just behind his eyes and at the root of his tongue. "Do you suppose that I am merely digressing, Master Niu? That I am capriciously leaping from topic to topic and have decided, suddenly, to lecture you on the latest advances in the science of astronomy?" Niu bore an uncertain expression, as if he thought that this was indeed a possibility. "No," the chief minister continued. "I do have a purpose, and it is directly related to the topic we were discussing earlier." He looked at Niu and tilted his head questioningly. "Can you recall?"

"I believe we were discussing the possession of the Consort Wu," the general replied with dignity.

"Our astronomer's spheres imply an important principle. They suggest that it is not only the heavens that adjust their constellations for the earth, but the earth that adjusts its own position for the heavens. To put it quite bluntly, Master Niu, it seems that the earth moves." Li Lin-fu noted with satisfaction a look of superstitious peasant shock which appeared fleetingly on Niu's face. "Returning to your observation of the morning star," Li Lin-fu continued. "If the earth moves, then so does the Vermilion Phoenix Tower. And so does the building we stand in. *Therefore* we have no choice but to discard your statement that the star has 'made its usual trek across the sky' as a fallacy. Because, General, indications are that it is *we* who stand in a different relation to the star, so that it only *appears* to have moved in relation to us. This, in turn, implies a parallel which is applicable to other realms as well. Master Niu: the lesson here is that there are *no* fixed points of observation. Everything is in motion, thereby altering the position of everything else. If this is true in the solid world of empirical matter, then how could it be less true in the world of thought, already so shadowy, insubstantial, and fleeting?" He spread his hands in supplication as he looked imploringly at his assistant.

"I am not sure . . ." Niu began hesitantly. The chief minister continued as if his subordinate had not spoken.

"It should be sufficient to understand that you can make no judgments from one simple point of vantage, my ambitious peasant." Li Lin-fu folded his hands and fixed Niu with a steady gaze. "The astronomer Master Yueh relies solely on observation and reobservation; he makes judgments and then corrects those judgments by constantly testing them. What does not fit into a scientific syllogism is not simply tossed away. Rather, it is reapplied to create a new theory of larger scope. He knows that our petty needs and beliefs do not play a role in celestial mechanics. There are *no* portents in the heavens, auspicious or inauspicious. By freeing himself of suppositions, of preconceptions, he frees himself of the blindness of *superstition*. This is a lesson that may carry over into *this office*. Do you understand me?"

"Yes, Councillor."

"Our preconceptions are a product of our inability to perceive and reason, Master Niu. We do not feel the earth move, but men of science are finding that it indeed moves. Therefore, it is our responsibility to hunt down and destroy other preconceptions . . . or *misconceptions.*' Li Lin-fu pronounced the last word with ominous emphasis.

"And what . . . misconceptions might those be, Councillor?" Niu asked with caution. Now, thought Li Lin-fu, I will tell him.

"You have assisted in perpetrating certain dangerous rumors, General. Rumors that indulge the girlish fears of young eunuchs. Rumors that support their nearly perpetual hysteria, and that play into their ignorant and childish superstitions." He paused. Niu shifted uneasily. "You have reported that the Consort Wu is possessed by the *guei* of the deceased prince. Not only have you given credence to young attendants who tell you that they have watched her mimic Ying's gestures and rant in his voice, but it is quite apparent to me that you believe them. I am forced to conclude that you share their fragile judgments and womanish logic. If you insist on following these predispositions of yours, I *could* arrange it for you to join their stable." Niu's hand moved involuntarily in a protective gesture to his lower abdomen.

"I hope that you are jesting, Councillor," Niu said, aghast.

"Are any of these topics conducive to levity, my friend?"

"Councillor . . . my only intention was to serve you well, to report what I had heard and seen of the most favored Lady Wu since her . . ."

"Since her what?" Li Lin-fu snapped. "What is it she suffers from? Possession? Is that what you believe, fool?"

"Should I not believe that?"

"It is not my wish, Master Niu, to tell you what you *should* believe. I would prefer to be able to rely on your mental processes. Think: if it were believed that she is possessed by the boy's spirit, then the voice that speaks through her would be credible and dangerous—a witness to certain actions that could be construed as a crime against the throne."

"Then I must not assert that . . . ?"

"Assert what you wish!" Li Lin-fu replied vehemently. "You are *free* to do so. But understand that there will be penalties for those who spread innuendo that might serve to confuse our Imperial Father's ears; that might prejudice him against certain of his most faithful servants in government. Tell me: do you wish to serve this office with superstition? Do you wish to bring lies before the Son of Heaven?" Niu's eyes widened. He drew himself up.

"Councillor! I am not a liar!"

"No one is until he has committed his first falsehood. Now hear me: the Consort Wu is quite mad. Her words must bear no weight. Her voice is *not* the voice of the Crown Prince Ying. Her words must be given no credibility. She is lost to phantoms of her own creation. She has taken on the voice and mannerisms of Ying because of her own desperate guilt. There is no unappeased spirit, no hungry ghost . . . Yes, she is possessed, my ambitious soldier—but by *sickness* only. Ghosts and demons are not involved. You are to cease referring to her in any conversation, under any circumstances. I have no doubt that the details of her behavior are fascinating topics for gossip, but if you are interested in serving this office, and me, you will not hear any of it, or repeat it, or think of it! Am I clear?"

"Yes, Councillor."

"The matter is over. Lady Wu will be of little help to us politically. We have failed in our attempt to enlist the support of her family in achieving our goals at this court. I had thought that she was made of stronger stuff—I am quite disgusted, General. We have obviously encountered, in both her and the boy Mao, a weak branch of the family." He tapped his desktop impatiently. And such care he had put into the plan! He pulled open a drawer in the desk and removed a soft leather pouch. He opened the flap and shook it. Delicate white silk flowers spilled onto the polished wood. "But you have done well in apprehending Master Chang Chiu-ling, General. He is a prize specimen of the sort of young literati who are gradually gaining control, influencing important policies." He picked up one of the flowers. "Tell me, General, what prompted you to choose this morning to stop him in his path and bring him to me? You have been following him as a matter of routine for several weeks since the appearance of his so-called poetry in the city, and especially since his recent conversations with the 'eunuch empress.' "

"Councillor, we know his habits well now," replied Niu, not without some pride in his voice. "After he was seen walking from the funeral yesterday with the eunuch Kao Li-shih, and since we were unable to place ourselves within earshot, we doubled our vigilance. And last evening, instead of returning to his home in the city as he usually does, he stayed in his office. We saw the lights burning all night. When he emerged just before dawn, we decided to let him travel some distance until we were sure that no one was about. We felt certain that he was on his way to a rendezvous. We apprehended him at the critical moment—when no one could see him from his building which he had left, and before he was within hearing or seeing distance of whoever it was he would have met."

"I commend your instinct, General," said Li Lin-fu. It was true. The man had proven himself, capturing the poet just at the moment when he bore on his person the potentially incriminating flowers. He held one up and twirled it. "Pretty, aren't they? I surprise myself at times," he said, holding the delicate blossom up to the side of his head, then tucking it behind his ear. Aware of the grotesque effect of a beautiful flower adorning his sparse hair and bony face, he assumed an effeminate posture and womanish gesticulations. Niu smiled appreciatively, visibly relieved at his superior's turn of humor. "Do you think I could join the Academy of Letters?" Li Lin-fu mocked in girlish tones. "I shall write lovely, lyrical poems advising our Imperial Father how to deal with the northern barbarians who threaten the empire. We shall *bathe* them and dress them in fragrant *silks*. Then they'll behave themselves, won't they Master Niu? They'll stop being so nasty!" Immensely pleased with his own humor, he made a loose-wristed gesture. "Or perhaps we can just read them some poetry as they go to sleep at night in their foul-smelling skin tents," he continued, enjoying the ease with which he caused General Niu to meta-morphose. He watched his assistant. Just look at him, thought Li Lin-fu. A moment ago he was in abject fear of losing his balls; now he grins and laughs like a fool at my jokes. He has just the right combination of ignorance and a rudimentary desire to learn—but unburdened by education or the dissipating effect of brilliance. He is perfect for his position. Li Lin-fu also appreciated the man's ability to absorb insults good-naturedly. Leaving the flower behind his ear, the chief minister abruptly ceased the charade.

"General Niu, I am going to allow you the privilege of interrogating Master Chang Chiu-ling yourself."

"I?" said Niu, surprised and pleased.

"Yes. I wish to observe your technique, to test what you have learned." Turning to the window, he partly lifted the heavy quilt. The sky was gray, the snow-covered roofs of the great city stark in the cold dawn. "You are to escort him to my residence, where you are to await my instructions as to which room we shall use for the questioning. Keep him blindfolded, naturally, and his ears plugged. I will be there by the late morning watch, when the questioning will begin. I shall place myself behind a partition; he will think that he is alone with you. You are to determine how he got the flowers, what he intended to do with them, and how much he knows, though I can assure you that we were never in any danger." He looked toward the door. "I must rest before the physician arrives to torment me. Go now." General Niu made a perfunctory bow.

"I am most appreciative, Councillor," he said.

Alone in his office, Li Lin-fu examined his handiwork: white tiger lilies, petals of silk stretched over delicate wire frames. Upon casual observation, the flowers looked real. But Li Lin-fu had correctly foreseen that Lady Wu would discover the imposters among the real ones. He carefully spread the petals. The pattern of spots radiating from the center of the flowers looked to be nothing more than natural markings—until one held the blossom close to the eye. The "spots" were tiny characters, words enticing one to unroll the paper stamens and read the stories within. He shook his head incredulously. A superb plan. He held one of the little scrolls up to the lamplight.

Though unable to read the characters, his eye told him that it had been a careful, artistic hand that had held the brush. The hand, in fact, belonged to one of his daughters. Of his twenty-five children, fourteen were girls. He had carefully selected three of them; by the age of five, each girl had begun to learn the unfathomably vast written Chinese language. Their childhoods had been entirely devoted to the study of reading and writing. By the time they had attained their twelfth years or so, the children were ready to serve as their father's hands and eyes when it came to any matter in which utmost discretion was necessary. What could be safer than a young daughter, docile and cloistered, who knew nothing of politics and palace affairs? He had dictated the flower-petal stories to the girl; she had happily written them down, her only desire being to please her father and perform perfectly and obediently.

The written language had eluded Li Lin-fu; the world of radicals, strokes, and bells, compendiums, lexicons, *fan-chieh* phonetics, and rescensions were beyond his grasp. The effort to learn how to read and write had caused him nothing but rage and frustration. The characters undulated like snakes before his eyes, reversing themselves, moving around on the page and speaking gibberish to him where they spoke eloquently to others. Literacy was an impenetrable wall, books a closed universe.

But he had not been entirely deterred. Through native intelligence and sheer will, he had found his own secret key to the hidden world. He had developed a mathematical formula which, applied to a written page, revealed to him enough of the page's contents to enable him to form an approximate interpretation. With practice he had learned to perform the calculation mentally in the same amount of time it would take to read the page. Though the finer nuances of meaning escaped him, his technique worked well enough so that he had been able to conceal his deficiency from all but a few readers and scribes retained by him; these assistants were well aware of the price they would pay for revealing the secret.

And for his special projects, such as this one, there were his little daughters. He dropped the flower onto his desk. It had been such a masterful plan, and it had worked perfectly—up to a critical point. It started with a thirteen-year-old girl, her head bent in concentration over her writing desk as she took down Father's words; it ended with the death of the seventeen-year-old crown prince. Perfect! Li Lin-fu had accomplished the removal of Ying with little risk to himself. It was Lady Wu who arranged for—and even paid—the assassin. The chief minister had only had to suggest to her a course of action at the right time, in the right way, and the path was clear for Mao to assume the crown, help make his mother an empress, and aid in the establishment of powerful solidarity with the Wu clan. It struck Li Lin-fu as ironic that the most difficult and potentially dangerous part of the plan, the actual death of the boy, had been accomplished with relative ease—and the part that Li Lin-fu had thought would follow logically had been fouled. It infuriated him to think that a headstrong child of twelve had called a halt to the beautiful unfolding of a plan, carefully calculated, the sole aim of which was to restore fangs, fire, and strength to the empire.

I have proven my own theory, thought Li Lin-fu. Who could doubt the compelling danger of literature? With a few simple tales, carefully timed and artfully placed, I caused a woman to become a murderess. It is a fortunate thing that I am firmly committed to preserving the empire and not to exploiting it for my own glory.

Thinking about the seductive powers of literature, he saw an inherent flaw in his plan. He had taken the risk of sending the flowers to Lady Wu because he had calculated that she would be wise and destroy them. He had been wrong. Obviously, she had become enamored of the talking flowers and had kept them; he imagined her state of mind, waiting for the appearance of the next silk lily that would whisper in her ear a story about the great "Empress" Wu. He was certain that she had indulged in a fantasy about the flowers—that they were, in some sense, real, and that they carried an urgent message to her from the source of all things. I am sorry, Lady Wu, he thought; it *was* an urgent message, but making you an empress was of only secondary importance.

He swept the flowers into a drawer. Well and good, he thought. It is useless to rail against the boy Mao or his mother for her weakness and insanity. Obviously, my calculations were imperfect or incomplete. The fault lies with me. I shall review the numbers, which do not lie, and find my error. Then I will know whether I should have chosen another plan altogether or have taken a different approach in the one I chose. I *will* find the way. And with the questioning of the poet-minister, this business will be finished.

He turned in his chair to a shelf above his head and pulled down a sheaf of papers tightly bound in thread and parchment. They were the recent poems of the minister Chang Chiu-ling. He collected the works of all the young poets currently in vogue in the capitals—those whose work might allude traitorously to himself. He saved copies of the gazettes and newspapers that circulated in the capital city of Ch'ang-an; his agents and readers brought him everything that might contain clues to the prevailing political climate.

He leafed through the printed pages of the young minister's twelve-poem cycle *Encountering Sorrows*. He counted. Five characters to a line; four, five, or six couplets to a poem. The poems, his readers informed him, adhered to the strict parallel prosody and semantics of the "ancient-style." He had little patience with such irrelevancies and would wave his readers on irritably. Get to the point!! Tell me what I need to know! What is dangerous about these words? What old aristocratic families might be lining up against me, and what young scholar-officials, their identities hidden ludicrously in pretty images and clever tricks of language, are placing obstacles in my path? Am I, Li Lin-fu, mentioned, either directly, obliquely, or metaphorically? I must ask one of my readers, he thought, to scan these lines for any mention of flowers—and any "flower" radicals deceitfully embraced within the characters of the poems. He closed the overleaf, annoyed at the old, familiar feeling, upon sight of a page of writing, of being shut out.

It was well into morning now. Li Lin-fu went to the window, partly lifted the winter quilt and opened the shutter. He looked out over the steep pitch of the lower-level roof. Below that roof, the heavy masonry wall dropped to the rocky incline of the cliffs of Dragon Head Hill. Beyond high, thick walls and a natural moat, rose the wild, uncultivated tree line of the Tungchien Park. He had commandeered this outpost at the rear of the Chancellery, a portion of the imperial city abandoned for nearly a half century or longer, as some said, since the renaming and rebuilding of the palace complex during the short-lived Chou dynasty of Grandmother Wu. The Chancellery buildings had been avoided, others said, because they digressed from the auspicious north-south geomantic axis of the heavenly constellation of Tzu-wei; they were insidiously out of balance with the perpendicular order of the imperial city. But, then, standard geomancy was of little concern to the chief minister. Li Lin-fu thought of these official apartments as a second throne room—a fortress from which he could administer policies of financial and military centralization. Li Lin-fu knew his role; there were lessons to be learned from history.

He had an ancient model—"the Minister of Iron," Li-tsu, who had guided the first emperor of a united China a millennium ago. Li Lin-fu frequently had the sections dealing with Li-tsu read to him from the early histories. Like that ancient councillor of Chin, Li Lin-fu sought to prevent the fissures that weaken a strong central imperial power. The present danger, Li Lin-fu saw plainly, was the dissipation of power. Influence was shifting slowly, almost imperceptibly, away from certain established families. The House of Li, of which the chief minister was a member, and the House of Wu, one of the ruling families of the previous dynasty, were two such old families accustomed to power. It had been Li Lin-fu's hope that an alliance with Lady Wu's family would serve to counteract a destructive trend.

As it was now, any family who could afford it could send a son to the capital for the annual civil service entrance examinations; the government was, supposedly, accessible to any young man who could pass. The examinations were rigorous, he knew, and the emphasis was on literacy. It was not enough to simply give an intelligent answer to a question pertaining to governmental theory—taxes, land distribution, commerce, etcetera; it was necessary that the answers to these questions be couched in specific poetic or literary forms. The luxury of word-painting, he supposed, had its place—in tearooms or ladies' salons. But in matters of government, it was not merely irrelevant—it was a clear danger.

In the last one hundred years the numbers of these scholar-officials had swollen from only seven thousand to a sluggish, wordy bureaucracy of tens of thousands. And the worst of them, the ones from "outside the passes," especially from the landed families of the rich southeast, had little comprehension of political reality. Most of these educated fools, thought Li Lin-fu, would prefer to take tea with the enemies that line the northern border of China. They would rather pay them off with the silken spoils of luxury, buy the peace with tribute and appeasement, when the only fair treatment of these barbarians would be to drive them back beyond the wall until every tribal warrior, born and unborn, tastes his own blood. The first emperor of a united China had understood that. And so do I. And that emperor of a thousand years ago had understood, too, how to build a wall. He had burned books and mixed the ashes in the limestone mortar of the wall. Then he had the scholars buried up to their necks in construction sand—and lopped off all those divergent, confusing ideas.

: :

A polite scratching at the door informed him that the physician had arrived. Li Lin-fu replaced the bound papers on their shelf and called out for the man to enter.

The chief minister balanced two small, bitter pills on his tongue and raised a steaming bowl of hot pepper wine to his lips. It was part of the continuing "jade screen treatment" for the "pernicious cold influences that have settled deep into the lungs . . ." as the physician poetically phrased it. Li Lin-fu considered the irony of the diagnosis: a tendency to weakness of the protective *chi*. He, who was always surrounded by guards.

The physician's talk rambled as he attended to the chief minister this morning.

". . . a weakness that has allowed gradual injury to your *chi* flow . . . an interruption in its smooth exchange . . . and an effectively dissipating disharmony to the lungs, Councillor. A disturbance that has affected the dissemination of water vapor, causing you certain problems of profuse perspirations during sleep and following—"

"Cease, Physician," Li Lin-fu interrupted. "Enough." He was growing impatient, his thoughts jumping ahead to the impending interrogation. He thought of the poet waiting in the windowless room. "I suspect you will tell me, *again,* that it is also manifested in my kidneys, in this problem of frequent urination. I needn't hear it again. Once is quite sufficient. Remove the needles."

"But Grand Councillor . . . I have not completed the great abyss meridian . . . simply another moment," the physician said as he struggled with a small bowl of astringent and the slender gold needles in Li Lin-fu's scrawny sunken chest.

"Physician, *now.* I cannot move and I must. The midmorning watch has already been sounded and I have business. It is best that you leave quickly. We will continue the treatment tonight . . . at *your* convenience."

"The one alone is not effective treatment against these colds in the chest, Councillor," the physician admonished as he removed the needles. He indicated the stone bowl of pungent paste waiting on the desk, a poultice which was to be rubbed onto the skin and allowed to dry.

"I will continue with the pills, Physician, and I'll pay especially close attention to the color of my piss." Li Lin-fu smiled, enjoying the vulgarity. "Close my robes, and hurry. The Buddhists say that three *kalpas* have passed since the earth began; I hope you will not take another."

"Yes, Councillor," said the harried physician.

"Good. Now take your things and go," he said as the physician fumbled hastily with the needles, bowls, bottles, and the rest of his equipment. Before the man had finished, Li Lin-fu stood to allow the attendants who accompanied the physician to dress him. They prepared him for the cold, covering his chest with a quilted sleeveless jacket, followed by two more layers of underclothing. Over these went the outer garment, a robe of iridescent blue-purple. Finally, a heavy floor-length cape with a fur collar was lifted onto his shoulders. He left his office to meet his escorts.

Six large men awaited him in the reception hall. The eldest, a man in his late fifties, dropped to his knees upon catching sight of the chief minister. The others, lined up behind him, remained motionless. Li Lin-fu's chief of deputies and of internal securities leaned onto his hands from his kneeling position, brought his chest and forehead to the glossy black floor, then straightened to his feet, all in one continuous motion. The effort caused him a slight shortness of breath and a reddening of the face. This simplified version of the usually more complex kowtow, in which obedience and respect were expressed by multiple repetitions of the act, had come to mark Li Lin-fu's office. He insisted that only those who were to address him directly should humble themselves, and then to make it brief. He could not tolerate delay and cumbersome ritual.

"Lord Grand Councillor," said the man, "it is time to leave. All is in readiness."

With three deputies in front and three behind, Li Lin-fu started down the long hallway. The escorts matched his anxious pace, their lacquered leather armor creaking, the hems of their coats chasing dust into bands of light coming through the narrow windows.

The three deputies preceding him reached the circular stairwell. Li Lin-fu followed, maintaining a good six paces between himself and the men. He glanced out a narrow window in the stairwell.

"Stop!" he ordered. The steady tramping of feet ceased abruptly. Looking down, he saw that the top of the carriage canopy with horses and men waiting to transport him was visible. He counted. He spoke to the lead escort. "The color of the canopy is incorrect for the third day of the week. Every color has a numerical value. That one is wrong. And the horses and constabulary are wrong as well. I want an odd number for the canopy—yellow. And there are four horses. Remove one to make it three. And I want twenty men—eleven in front, nine in the rear." He thought for a moment. "Plus seven behind the nine." The deputy turned without comment or hesitation, to carry out the chief minister's orders.

They did not ask questions. These men had served Li Lin-fu's father in the capital province of Kuanchung; they received salaries five times the *hu* of grain of a ninth rank official. They did not read or imagine beyond the day. Their rewards were good. They knew that their place was not to be ambitious, but to serve—only. They were free to respond to him. He heard them now, in the courtyard below, repeating his orders, hurrying the old stablemen with shouts as they unharnessed the horses and ran to the Chancellery stables to change the colors and standards of office.

Quickly, he reviewed the numbers he had chosen, added them up in varying combinations, and squared them. Satisfied, he continued his descent of the staircase. Now Master Chang waits, thought Li Lin-fu. He sits alone in the fifth numeral in the center of the earth in the center of heaven.

Li Lin-fu entered the small dark space through a hidden doorway and seated himself behind a jade partition. The milky stone, sometimes called "crystallized dragon semen," was carved in an intricate pattern that allowed the chief minister a clear view of the room beyond while giving him the security of concealment in the dappled shadows behind the screen. The windowless room he looked out on was lit with oil lamps; their soft glow showed faintly through the translucent green of the jade.

Li Lin-fu enjoyed the feeling of disembodiment such invisibility gave him. It was pleasant to watch a man who was unaware that he was being watched. For some time he observed Minister Chang Chiu-ling, who thought he was alone in the richly furnished little room. The poet-minister sat, head resting in his hands, thumbs gently massaging the temples. He did not look around him. Is this man capable, Li Lin-fu asked himself, of leading a coup against me at court? We shall see what this southerner is made of.

General Niu Hsien-ko entered the room then, carrying a basin of steaming water and a cloth. Chang Chiu-ling raised his eyes, looked briefly at the general, then resumed rubbing his head. Niu dipped the cloth in the hot water, wrung it out, and offered it to the poet.

"A nasty blow, Master Chang," the general said with sympathy. The poet took the cloth without answering and applied it to the bloodied area on the back of his head. He winced, but held the cloth in place. He tilted his head back and shut his eyes. Yes, thought Li Lin-fu from his hidden point of observation, I imagine you have a bit of a headache, Poet. Chang Chiu-ling still did not speak.

Niu tried again. "Who might have wished you harm, Master Chang?"

The poet opened his eyes then and gave Niu a long look. Then he spoke. "Master Niu, I only remember being struck from behind. I have no notion as to the identity of my assailant or assailants."

"Our deputies found you, Master Chang, lying in a pool of your own blood."

"I am most grateful," replied Chang. "It could have been much worse for me." He slumped in his chair. "General, I do not feel at all well. Please take me back to the Chancellery!"

"Minister! We cannot take you back in your present condition. It would be most irresponsible of us. You are far safer here, with us," said Niu kindly.

"Then take me to my home in the city," the minister said, the cloth still pressed to the back of his head.

"Minister, someone is stalking you. You will agree, I'm sure, that there have been too many unusual events of late. Even your home would be dangerous for you now. You were overtaken right under the noses of the Imperial City Constabulary. But our deputies were the first to spot you. They chased after the ones who struck you, but they were too late."

"Then there were several who assailed me?"

"So I am told, Minister. I did not witness the unfortunate attack myself."

Chang Chiu-ling did not answer immediately. He sat pensively, not looking at General Niu, who stood watching him. Li Lin-fu noted with irritation that the general's stance at this moment was more like a soldier on guard duty than an officer conversing with a minister. This was wrong, of course; it would convey a subtle message to Chang Chiu-ling that he was being held prisoner, not just cloistered for his own protection. Nothing is harder to eradicate, thought Li Lin-fu as he looked at the general, than the peasant mentality. And indeed, Chang's next words confirmed that he knew the true state of affairs.

"I recall being transported some distance, General, though I was barely conscious." He looked steadily at Niu. "Where am I, General?" he asked pointedly.

"Where you are, Master Chang, is not important at this time. It should be sufficient that you, a high minister of the realm, are safe."

"But I gather that I am not *free* at this point . . . ?"

"Free to do what?" Niu replied. "Free to leave and provide hidden assassins the opportunity to finish what they have begun?"

"Free to find out exactly where I am and to leave your company, General," Chang Chiu-ling replied.

"It would not be advisable for you to go at this moment, Master Chang."

"Then I am being held against my wishes, though I have acknowledged my gratitude to this office."

"Only, as I have said, momentarily, and for your own safety," Niu said beseechingly. "Surely you, of all people, so close to the heart of the imperial administration, understand that there have been too many strange and unaccountable things . . ."

"Why may I not just walk out of here?" Chang interrupted sharply. Behind the jade partition, Li Lin-fu issued a mental command to Niu. It is you who are supposed to be asking the questions, fool. Maintain the upper hand.

"You would be unable to find your way out of here, Master Chang."

"And there are guards, are there not?"

"Yes, but only for your own protection. Unfortunately, these have become dangerous times."

"Indeed they have, General Niu." Chang Chiu-ling stood then. "Please call in the guards."

"I cannot do that, Master Chang."

"General, I outrank you by two grades. Call them in here," Chang ordered. Li Lin-fu watched with interest. General Niu was like a well-trained dog. When he heard a command, no matter from whom, every fiber of his musculature twitched with the compulsion to obey. Li Lin-fu smiled. It *is* amusing; the general is also aware of my presence behind the screen, ordering him silently *not* to call in the guards.

Finally Niu answered. "I cannot, Minister."

Chang Chiu-ling sat down again, picked up the cloth, and reapplied it to the back of his head. Niu stood as if unable to think of anything to say. It was Chang who spoke first.

"The guards are not members of the palace constabulary, then. Which means that I *am* being held prisoner, as if I were a criminal."

"There are *no* criminals here, Master Chang, I assure you. There is, simply, no need for such measures as calling in the guards."

"Then I wish to know which chapter and article of the *T'ang-lu shu-i* [legal code] has been invoked for my restraint for, as you call it, my *protection?*"

"Master Chang," Niu said, "I do not understand your fear in my presence. I am in the service of the imperial government, a humble servant of the Son of Heaven; obedient, as you are, to that supreme authority. The reason you are here now is so that you may share any knowledge you may have that could help us to discover the identity of these enemies who have trespassed against the sanctity of the celestial gates. I know that you and I have had our differences, Master Chang, and that you once opposed my appointment, but please remember that we have saved your life," he said firmly. That is better, thought Li Lin-fu. Now take control. "Our main concern," Niu continued, "is with anything that might prove of interest to our Imperial Father. Minister," Niu said then, turning firmly toward Chang Chiu-ling, "were you not carrying something when you were assaulted?" Chang Chiu-ling did not answer. He resumed rubbing his temples. "As I stated, Minister," Niu continued, "our deputies of internal security had almost reached you when you were struck. A pity they did not reach you sooner—you might have been spared. We are very concerned about the incident, not only because a high minister was assaulted on official ground, but because you had, apparently, something they wanted. The men tell me that they witnessed a struggle for a small package, or purse, that was torn rather forcibly from you," he said, pointing to the dangling shreds on the poet's belt. "We know it was not your money they were interested in; they left that with you. They struck you, left you for dead, and fled with the pouch," he finished, and waited for a response. The starting signal of the game, thought Li Lin-fu. Niu's words are the equivalent of a formal announcement that the players are now in position and the match will begin. The poet recognizes this moment, too. Who could be interested in cards, or racing animals, when there are games such as this to be had? He waited for the poet's counter to this opening move. Perversely, he found himself siding with the poet insofar as the match of wits went.

The poet sat, head hanging, still saying nothing. Niu spoke again, his voice kind.

"Please tell me what was in the pouch, Master Chang, and who might be interested in it. Perhaps we could be of assistance; we shall certainly be indulgent to the extent that this office and our circumstances allow."

Chang Chiu-ling heaved a great sigh then and raised his eyes to Niu's.

"General," he said quietly, "I deeply appreciate the opportunity you are extending me. Your sense of protocol is impeccable. You are allowing me the benefit of the doubt here in a most gentlemanly way." Niu listened, slightly confused. "Your delicate approach," Chang continued, "allows us to discuss the vitally important issue of the pouch in an offhand manner. Civilization is a glorious thing, is it not, General? Here we sit, the product of centuries of conversational refinement. You ask me, in a most nonchalant way, about some sort of . . . 'pouch,' which may or may not have been attached to my belt and which may or may not have been the object of a struggle. It is an art we are practicing, General; and I know that I have the prerogative of responding in terms of this art. 'Pouch?' I might say; 'I am not sure that I recall . . .' or, '. . . the pouch was empty; the thieves mistook me for someone else . . .' You have given me the latitude for many varied responses. But, as a poet, though a poor one, I am burdened by an excess of ability to understand veiled speech. Now correct me if I am wrong, General. Your office has the pouch in its possession, and you are fully aware of its contents." He removed the cloth from his neck, looked for a moment at the blood, then returned his gaze to General Niu. "White silk flowers, with delicate writing on them," the poet said, enunciating clearly.

Li Lin-fu was disappointed. Was the game to end so quickly? He had hoped for a confession, but not before more entertainment than this. The chief minister in his secret place watched General Niu, who was plainly taken aback. Poor Niu, thought Li Lin-fu; you were enjoying your role of authority and comradely concern, but the poet has just stripped it from you with a few words. But Niu paused for only a moment before answering.

"Master Chang, you are correct. I have seen the flowers myself." He said no more, apparently allowing the poet to take further initiative.

"Then you know, surely, what I had planned to do with them," said Chang. He had covered his face with his hands. He had the attitude of a man completely broken. Li Lin-fu had seen the posture before, usually in men about to make a confession.

"Perhaps," said Niu, "you had best tell us." Chang Chiu-ling took his hands from his face. Li Lin-fu was surprised to see the minister's gaunt cheeks streaked with tears. What was this?

"Master Niu," said the poet-minister, "I am deeply ashamed." He reached for Niu's sleeve, clung to it, and then dropped to his knees on the floor. "I am mortified to be revealed for the lowly creature that I am," he moaned. "You have turned over a rock, and look at what is revealed, writhing in the light! It is I." He gave himself up to weeping then, still clinging to Niu's sleeve.

"Master Chang, please . . ." said Niu, flustered, as he pulled his sleeve from the minister's grasp.

Li Lin-fu recognized that the moment of confession was imminent. But this had been far too easy. And the tears! These literati are obviously poor subjects for interrogation. See how easily he has caved in, and Niu has not so much as laid a glove on the man or even alluded to any possible damage to the poet's tender hide. Li Lin-fu was disgusted. This was a poor object lesson for Niu as well. How was he to learn the art of interrogation if the subject immediately began to whimper?

"General, I beg of you," Chang Chiu-ling said. "Please . . ." Well, Li Lin-fu thought, at least we shall soon have it. He cannot deny, now, his knowledge or his conspiracy with the eunuch. "Please . . . keep my shameful secret. I still await *his* decision," the poet begged with imploring eyes. General Niu's mouth hung slightly open in amazement, perplexity showing plainly on his face.

"*Whose* decision, Master Chang?" asked Niu, his brow wrinkled. He had lost entirely his tone of interrogator; he was now simply a man who had lost the thread of a conversation, asking a question in hopes of again joining the discussion. Whose decision, indeed? Li Lin-fu asked silently. Mine? And how could he expect *this* office to conceal treachery aimed directly at it?

"Our Imperial Father's decision," answered Chang. "You know, when you live with a deceit for a long time, you gradually begin to believe it. Am I not a pathetic creature? I have actually *felt* the satisfaction of creation upon reading the tales! I have believed it, General Niu, I have felt it! Oh, I am in deeper peril than I could have imagined," he said, covering his face again. Niu, forgetting himself, turned a confused face in the direction of his hidden master and stared, slack-jawed, as if awaiting instructions. No, no, no! Don't look at me, imbecile! Li Lin-fu thought angrily. But Chang Chiu-ling, his head hanging, had not noticed.

"I am not asking for your complicity, General," the poet continued. I am only asking that you ignore my indiscretion. In a reciprocal universe, you can be sure that I will receive my punishment eventually, so you needn't concern yourself. I have charted my course. I am only asking that you let me follow it." Again he grabbed the general's sleeve. "It must go no further than your ears alone! Do you understand?" Niu nodded a reply to what appeared to be the request of an insane man. "Before I tell you the rest, which my conscience sorely impels me to do, you must swear your allegiance in a 'Peach-Blossom' oath. Do you swear?" Chang demanded of Niu.

"Yes, yes," Niu said. "I do comply. Now please continue, Minister."

"I made a discovery, General, and I yielded to temptation. It is as simple as that." Chang wiped his nose on his sleeve, sat up, and took a long breath. "The flowers, Master Niu. They are masterfully executed, as I'm sure you did not fail to notice. But their exquisite form is no match for what is within them: a magnificent miniature hand, comprising fragments of literature; wondrous tales, full of rich and beautiful prose . . . I have not seen their equal nor read anything of such quality since the great prose poetry of the giants of the Han."

"Master Chang," asked Niu, "*where* were these flowers found?" Good, thought Li Lin-fu; at least he has thought to ask a relevant question.

"A chambermaid found them, General, in a rarely opened desk drawer in the Hall of Consorts."

"A chambermaid, Master Chang?"

"Yes. She visited me fairly often . . . A most pleasant, willing, and submissive little woman, though not, of course, the sort with whom one discusses ideas or literature . . . She could not even write her own name, naturally. But pretty . . . very pleasing . . ."

"She brought you the flowers, Minister?"

"Yes. But not in the way that you might suppose. Those flowers came to me adorning her pretty head! Imagine it, Niu. You are bending over your woman's shoulder, breathing her fragrance, admiring the light playing on the gloss of her black hair. She has decorated herself for your pleasure. White tiger lilies are pinned to her coiffure! For a moment, the chambermaid is an empress. But wait! You get close to the flowers, and what do you see? Writing! I requested that she give me the flowers from her hair as a gift, a remembrance. She, not knowing how to read, happily turned them over to me, thinking that my interest in them was confined simply to the fact that they had adorned her head. I read the tales later that night, General, and decided that they were a gift to me from the gods." He stopped and gave Niu a long, significant look. "I know who wrote them."

Li Lin-fu leaned forward in his hidden space. General Niu turned and looked sharply at the poet.

"Who, Minister?" he asked.

"It was our deceased Empress Wang," Chang replied.

"The Empress?" Niu asked, confused again.

"No doubt. No one else had such a double mastery of poetics and calligraphy as she. No one spent as much time in pursuit of strange tales and fables in the imperial libraries . . . She was excited by everything: the Jataka tales of the Buddha, the stories of the kings of the underworld, the fairy consorts of the rivers Lo and Hsiang, and the immortals . . . Everything! And this eclecticism showed in the brilliance and originality of these tales . . . full of enchantment, spells, and the magical life of noble ladies and legendary princes and queens of the Golden Age, and how those ladies were embraced by a fertile rainbow dragon and gave birth to kings." He paused in wonderment. "From the evidence of my incomplete fragments, the Empress Wang seems to have dedicated them to the Emperor's grandmother!"

"I am sorry, Master Chang," Niu began. "I'm afraid I don't . . ."

"*The Empress Wu,* General! She makes continual reference to the Empress Wu, Emperor Minghuang's grandmother. I imagine that she wished to dedicate them to her imperial husband in memory of that great lady." He leaned forward now, all traces of remorse and shame gone. He was the literary man again, expounding a theory with single-minded enthusiasm. Li Lin-fu smiled in the shadows as he listened. Poet, he thought; I did not give you enough credit.

"My theory," Chang continued, "is that Wang wrote them when she was still a young girl in training—a budding and beautiful favored consort. These works have the stamp of a mind not yet burdened by the cares of adulthood. A child's—or a childlike—imagination is everywhere evident in them." He wiped his nose again and smiled, as if lost in pleasant thoughts of these fables.

"Master Chang," Niu asked, "why should this discovery bring such fear and emotion to you?"

"Because I have kept their discovery a secret. If the Emperor heard of their existence, he would, naturally, wish to take possession of them himself, to hold them up as works of his deceased Empress's merit before the consorts and concubines, the members of the Six Palaces. And since he so sadly decreed his Empress's posthumous reinstatement, he would most likely wish them sealed and buried with her as proof of her nobility and superiority. So you can see, Master Niu, that my secret and illegal possession of these rare literary gems could bring me censure, a loss of sinecure, perhaps even blacklisting. But since the Emperor did not know about them, and does not still, I am quite safe." He looked at Niu humbly. "And I can, I pray, trust you to keep my secret."

"Your secret is safe with this office," Niu responded. "But . . . why are these works so important to you? Why do you keep them?"

"I feel considerably relieved, Master Niu. This has been a burden, eating at me like worms in a book. There is more. In answer to your question, I must respond with a most difficult truth. May I have some tea?" Niu rose and left the room briefly to give the order for tea to an attendant.

Li Lin-fu watched Chang Chiu-ling intently for any sign that the poet might be aware that he was being observed. Chang glanced up at the ceiling, then rubbed his eyes. He pulled a rumpled handkerchief from his sleeve, wiped his nose, then stuffed the cloth back into the sleeve. Niu returned with the tea. The minister took it, blew on it, sipped loudly, and put the bowl down while Niu waited for him to speak.

"I am not the creative mind some would have you think, General," Chang began. "I am, in truth, something of an inferior artist, one who showed promise in his youth, but whose wellspring has dried to a trickle. A 'worn-out horse' is the literary term, I believe." Niu's face showed sudden comprehension.

"And with these 'literary gems,' as you call them, you hoped to . . ."

"Yes, Master Niu. With some careful and skilled reworking—you see, if nothing else, I am a good pedant—these tales might have earned me the fame that has, thus far, eluded me. I had hoped to use them so that I may be granted a prestigious place in the T'ang's highest literary circles—the Academy of Talents or even, if I do not presume too much, the great Han Lin Academy of Letters. Now do you understand?"

"These positions would be, I assume, the crowning glory of your life's accomplishments?"

"Yes, General. That is the sorry circumstance." He took another sip of tea and gazed sadly at the floor. Niu sat quietly too, as if trying to comprehend such aspirations.

"Minister, I understand what you have told me here. But why have there been . . . rumors of secret meetings between you and our August Father's chief eunuch?" Why, indeed, thought Li Lin-fu.

"It had been my hope that Master Kao Li-shih might intercede for me in matters of appointment if he found my new literary ventures worthy of bringing to the attention of so great an arbiter of taste as our Emperor Ming-huang." Chang sighed. "But the eunuch, as you know, is as protective of the Emperor as a mother tigress and has thus far resisted my entreaties. He told me that my timing could not possibly be worse, considering the Emperor's state of mind. Kao Li-shih is the one closest to the Emperor, as you know. Thinking only of my own interests, I persisted. The eunuch asked me why I thought that the Emperor would take even one look at my work when he refuses to attend to the smallest official document. Or even," he added, "to get out of bed at all. He has withdrawn, Kao told me, since the suicide of Ying and the death of the Empress, from everything."

"And this morning, Minister?" Niu asked.

"My insatiable ambition, General. I was attempting to intercept Master Kao at the early morning audience. This time I was going to give him the flowers—my hope was that the artistry of the silk tiger lilies themselves would break down his resistance and that he would consent to show them to Emperor Minghuang. I see clearly now, though, the grave imposition I would have been inflicting on our Emperor." Chang's face was glistening with sweat now. "I can only be grateful to the fates and to this office for stopping me," he finished, putting his face in his hands.

In his hidden alcove, Li Lin-fu rose silently from his seat. Poet, he thought as he left through the small door to the rear, the match goes to you. On his way out, he signaled to a guard.

"Tell Niu I've sent for him. And remove the poet from the interview chamber. It is over."

Li Lin-fu had no doubt that effete scholars plagiarized for their own advancement, pilfering words and ideas from one another. But the poet Chang

Chiu-ling had, he was sure, demonstrated nothing but his resourcefulness and originality today. His reward, thought Li Lin-fu, will be his life. Not only had he shown courage, but in his bid to save himself, he disclosed a piece of information invaluable to Li Lin-fu. As he climbed the stairs to a small office, he envisioned obstructions dissolving. Here is my answer. It was before me all the time.

While waiting for Niu, Li Lin-fu thought about the Emperor's grandmother and Lady Wu's namesake, the great Empress Wu. Since you conjured her ghost, Poet, then it shall be she who looks over my shoulder when I decide your fate. You cannot possibly remain at court. Even if I believed that you are only a self-interested scholar, a 'worn-out horse' using stolen tales to advance your career, I could not allow you to stay. Even if I destroy the flowers, you still carry the words in your mind. You are as dangerous as a plagiarist as you are as a conspirator: in either case, your aim is to carry these words to the Emperor. As a conspirator, you deserve only death; as a plagiarist, you deserve to be removed from court and sent far away, where your ambitions will have no more consequence than a branch falling from a tree on a mountaintop.

Niu entered the office with an uneasy expression, as if expecting to be berated by his superior. Instead, Li Lin-fu asked, "Do you know about the Empress Wu, General? I am most grateful to the poet for reminding me of her."

"I know only that she was the wife of our Emperor's grandfather and that she killed many people," Niu answered.

"She was not an empress, General, in the sense that we know. She became a female emperor. She ruled for fifteen years just as if she were a man, renaming the dynasty, even, to Chou. One hundred and nine people went to their deaths as she accomplished her succession. The first, General, was her own three-day-old daughter, born when she was only a consort. She strangled the infant in order to incriminate the woman who was then empress; it was her first step. She went on to kill twenty-two others in her immediate household, including, later, two of her sons. As she gained power, she found it necessary to kill off fifty princes and, later, at least thirty-six ministers and generals. And when she was empress, she had her male harem. The 'Stork Institute' saw to it that other of her voracious appetites were also satisfied. Yes, it is true that she killed people as though she were swatting flies. I recall another incident when twenty-five scholars ended their illustrious careers with their heads on spikes at the palace gates. They had dared to question her authority to rule. But not everyone with whom she disagreed died immediately. You have heard, no doubt, of the 'Shore of Pearls'?"

"The island of Hainan," Niu answered, still uneasy.

"One thousand miles to the south," said Li Lin-fu, is the coast of Lingnan on the China Sea. It is very hot there, General. And there is abundant life such as is always found in the tropical climes; a fascinating variety of insects, serpents, and plants which inhabitants of temperate zones cannot even imagine. Think of the contrast, General, between such life-forms and those of the far north, where nature must practice economy. Plants and animals existing under rigid conditions have no time for any sort of experimental frivolity. Colors are subdued, practical. But in the tropics, it is different. There, with the excess of heat, light, and moisture, we find out what nature really yearns to do. We see her true mind. I've heard that the trees are laden with the most delectable-looking fruit. Some varieties are good and will nourish you, while others . . . one bite and you will die in agony. Poison, General. Nature dearly loves to put poison in things that jump, crawl, and grow. And she loves to decorate them in the most brilliant colors and let them multiply in feverish profusion. It is no wonder that the Empress Wu had an affinity for the tropics. I don't believe that she ever visited there herself, but I know that the island of Hainan received many 'guests,' courtesy of Her Highness. Those who were troublesome to her soon forgot any court business as they occupied themselves with their immediate surroundings. There are people there, too, if you can call them that: an indigenous race of savages scarcely distinguishable from the monkeys who scream and chatter in the treetops." Niu had listened to Li Lin-fu's description of Hainan with an ever more dubious expression.

"Chief Minister," he said, his voice shaking slightly, "I am aware that I did not, perhaps, distinguish myself in the interrogation room just now, but it is my wish to remain in your service here—"

"No, General," Li Lin-fu interrupted. "Not you. Not as yet, anyway. No; I want you to make arrangements for Minister Chang Chiu-ling. Tell him that he is departing immediately for his new position as cultural emissary to the island of Hainan. Tell him that he is not to worry any more about an appointment to the Han Lin Academy of Letters. And tell him that soon he shall see flowers that will make him forget forever his white tiger lilies." Niu, relieved, made a slight bow and prepared to leave.

"General," said Li Lin-fu. Niu stopped and turned. "You put it well. You did not distinguish yourself in the interrogation room. But we were successful nonetheless. I *have* the information I need."

"Then I am very fortunate, Councillor," Niu answered.

"Very," Li Lin-fu concurred.

: :

By early afternoon, Li Lin-fu lay in a darkened room. He knew Emperor Minghuang, a few miles away, also lay in a room with the blinds drawn. In the evening, Li Lin-fu would rise. But the Emperor would call for more sleeping powders and sink deeper into his troubled dreams. He would sleep through the night. In the morning he would ignore the eunuch's commands to rise. Li Lin-fu pictured Kao Li-shih shaking the Emperor, then pulling him up by the wrists to a sitting position. The Emperor would see the light creeping in around the blinds and remember that his favorite son was dead.

Let me sleep, he would say.

In another part of the palace, the high ministers would be standing at the morning audience. In their hands would be papers—memorials, drafts, proposals. They would talk among themselves, arguing matters of government and policy. They would grow impatient, and cast occasional glances toward the empty throne where the *jui-i* scepter lay.

The poet, while fighting for his life, had extemporized in the interrogation room. But Li Lin-fu recognized the part of the story that was true: a sleeping emperor; an emperor paralyzed by grief, indifferent to affairs of state.

To think that he, Li Lin-fu, had nearly consigned his efforts with Lady Wu to the dung heap. Forging a tie with the Wu clan would have been a useful thing, without a doubt. But he had not foreseen that the death of Ying would give him such an immediate advantage in tending to urgent business that the Emperor had been neglecting for years. Your grief, my Emperor, has freed me at last. Like flowers in a garden, your sorrow and ennui will be cultivated. While you sleep, I will work.

Li Lin-fu thought of his frequent differences with the Emperor over matters of policy concerning the north. Conscription was the only means, in Li Lin-fu's opinion, to build the armies guarding the northern borders. A good source was the many migrant families caught each year not registering with the military Censorate for tax purposes. Forced conscription of these families ensured manpower for the armies and workers for the many jobs that had to be done to maintain a military colony. The Emperor, susceptible to the persuasive arguments of scholar-bureaucrats at court, favored a more lenient policy toward these families, allowing them to settle and pay off their tax debts. The Emperor was susceptible, too, to those arguing for decreased military spending and appeasement of the Khitan. There is no appeasing barbarians! Four hundred years ago China had been divided because of tribal forces pushing down from the north. During the Sui dynasty, the period of unification, the intruders had been pushed back and the borders reestablished. That division must not happen again. Li Lin-fu did not intend to stand by and allow the T'ang to be weakened because some misguided intellectuals could not see the plain necessity in front of their faces. China will not be secure until every Khitan and every Hsi left alive is driven back so far that he will never find his way again.

Li Lin-fu prepared to sleep. P'inglu, Fanyang, and Hotung, the three adjacent extreme northern provinces of China, were like a door left standing open. Anyone could enter as he pleased.

A cold wasteland, where every living thing huddled close to the ground in the monotonous landscape of endless dry brown hills, rocks, and stunted trees. And the faces of the people there were dried to old leather by the wind that never stopped.

4

Enter a Barbarian

An Lu-shan is not worthy of the hare's death [*i.e.*, a death to be pitied]. . . . An Lu-shan's nature is cruel and fierce and his countenance a rebellious one. . . .

—*Chang Chiu-ling, from* Tz'u-chih T'ung-chien
(The Comprehensive Mirror of Government),
translated by Daniel Altieri

Thereupon [An Lu-shan] became a reconnaissance officer. From earlier days An Lu-shan was acquainted with the hills and rivers, springs and wells. Once with three or five horsemen under him he captured several tens of Khitan. Every time he was given more and more troops, he would double the number of enemy caught. . . .

. . . When he grew up he was a vicious thief, cruel, full of wiles, and clever at reading men's thoughts. He understood nine barbarian languages. He became a middleman for the barbarians in the frontier markets.

—*from* An Lu-shan Shih-chi (Biography of An Lu-shan),
translated by Edwin Pulleyblank

These [northern] establishments for the defense of the frontier entailed armed forces of 490,000 men and 80,000 horses. . . . Mobility was of supreme importance to the army. . . . [Therefore], attention [was paid] to the acquisition and breeding of good mounts.

—*William Hung*

THE lights of the camp appeared as a ghostly shimmer of orange under the low, thick clouds. An Lu-shan raised his massive hand, signaling the children to stop. In the fading light of dusk he could see their pale, attentive faces. He spoke the last words he would utter to them before the attack.

"Remember. Be the garden snake that gently parts the grasses," he admonished in a soft voice. He looked around the half circle of twenty-six faces. He detected no uncertainty; he saw a trained unit, ready to respond to him. He turned in the direction of the lights and began moving toward the slight incline which led to the rim of the gorge. The children followed noiselessly, their feet wrapped in soft leather.

Preceding the children, An Lu-shan reached the rocky ledge and raised his hand again for them to stop. Flattening himself against the stones and dry grass, he moved to the edge and peered down. It was perfect, better than he could have wished.

The Khitan camp was spread out below in the shelter of a narrow canyon. Campfires scattered here and there lay between rows of tents and skin yurts. Judging by the size of the camp, An Lu-shan estimated that there were approximately one hundred men and boys. Gruff voices and hoarse laughter rose from the canyon floor. A group of boys dared each other in games of strength. Some men looked on, teasing and admonishing. Others lay by the fires, eating, dozing, and talking quietly. An Lu-shan knew with certainty the sounds of a camp at rest, off its guard. The wind carried the odors of cooking smoke to his nostrils; there were other scents which spoke to him of a long day's travel, men fatigued.

But another odor, redolent and unmistakable, caused a surge of sensual anticipatory pleasure in An Lu-shan. His eyes traveled from the tents and campfires to the western area of the small canyon. There, a makeshift fence had been made of piled brush, forming a corral. Standing quietly, at ease and drowsy, were what An Lu-shan guessed to be as many as a hundred Ferghanian cavalry horses boxed at the end of the gorge. Horses of iron. The finest, strongest, and swiftest of war animals.

The corral, he saw, was between steep walls—but not so steep that agile children couldn't scale them. To the extreme west was a narrow cleft where the canyon walls came together. The opening, not more than a few yards wide, was probably filled with brush too, though the light was not good enough for him to be certain.

He looked back toward the camp, which was slowly being enveloped by darkness. Here and there a shower of bright embers floated upward as wood was thrown on a fire. An Lu-shan listened to the voices. Fragments of words and phrases in the gutteral Khitan tongue reached his ears over the sounds of the wind. Complaints, boasts, jokes. Men at rest after a hard day of travel. An Lu-shan knew the Khitan, understood their nature. He had correctly predicted their motives and movements. Forage for livestock and horses was hard to find along the nomads' northern route at this time of year, so they would herd their horses toward the marshy bottomlands to the south-west near the river. There, many such companies of Khitan tribesmen would draw together and secure themselves in an invincible army of men and horses. But An Lu-shan knew that small herding parties such as this one were apt to box their horses in this area of small accessible canyons. It made it easy to keep the herd together—but mostly, it provided relief from the constant wind. Looking at the camp below him, An Lu-shan knew that the wind affected all men the same way. Khitan, Sogdian, Hsi, Hsiung-nu, or the Chinese people—the Han—it mattered little. You only wanted to get away from it. During the day, when you rode, there was no escaping it. It buffeted you and filled your face with grit. The horses simply flattened their ears and dropped their heads and plodded resignedly. For men, it meant wrapping yourself so that only a slit for your eyes was left, and even that was not enough. The wind drowned out any talk, so you just rode in silence, mile after torturous mile. When you found a canyon like this, you could build a fire, relax, talk, sleep . . . even if it made you, perhaps, more vulnerable to attack. But An Lu-shan knew that these men expected no attack. They were north of the areas usually patrolled by the Chinese; and lately, the Chinese policy had been to defend the borders only, not to send scouting parties north in any aggressive action. No, these fellows expect a night like any other. They drink, roll up in their blankets by the fire, and nod off as they watch the flames.

An Lu-shan withdrew his head from the rim of the canyon. He turned back toward the children and caught a sharp scent; it was just right. Stealth, determination, and a touch of fear. There was just enough light left for them to see his signals. They moved fluidly in response to the motions of his hands and the soft hissing, clicking, or whistling noises he made, positioning them-selves just so. An Lu-shan paid attention to the slight shifts in the wind around him. He gave another signal. Five children broke the ranks and moved along the rim toward the horses; when they had gone far enough, he made another soft sound with his tongue. Hearing it, the boys began their descent toward the horses in the corral. With lightness and grace they lowered themselves from cleft to cleft along the rocky face, hand over hand, ledge to root, like monkeys, careful that no bits of debris preceded them. Out of range of the dying fires, their faces darkened with dirt and their arms and legs swaddled in dark clothing, the boys were no more than shifting shadows on the canyon wall. When they alighted on the ground, there were nervous mutterings from some of the horses. An Lu-shan imagined the experienced hands of the boys touching the horses, soothing them, as they moved, using the animals as cover, toward the line of piled brush. In pouches on their backs they carried skins of flammable naphtha. An Lu-shan and the rest of the children waited in tense silence until the five completed their task and ascended the canyon wall again. An Lu-shan reflected that these boys, the eldest among them no more than twelve, were as brave as any men he knew. But as I have planned it, he thought, there will be no actual fighting, no risk to their lives.

Now they must wait. They had used the light of the fading dusk to their advantage; the last traces of light on the western horizon would have to disappear before they could begin. Though the darkness in the canyon was nearly complete except for the fires, he did not want their silhouettes to be visible against the sky. The waiting, he knew, was by far the hardest thing for the little ones.

A bit later An Lu-shan's ears tensed. The horses were shifting about. Something was making them restless; they grumbled and whinnied, pressing against one another in their close confines. The wind was simply pausing, gathering strength. An Lu-shan was exultant. A devil wind! Were not the gods with him now?

But he must hurry. The still air around him could change at any moment to howling fury. His timing must be perfect. Moving back from the rim of the canyon, he pulled the leather pouch from his back and untied the flap in one motion. He pulled out a heavy, warm bundle. With a soft whistle he summoned the eldest boy of the group, his son An Ching-hsu, who was never more than a few feet from his side. They began to unwrap the bundle. Length after length of hide came off, until a ceramic box the size of a man's head lay on the ground. The boy removed from his own pouch another bundle: scraps of dry tinder. Using a piece of leather to protect his hand, An Lu-shan opened the ceramic box. Embers from his campfire of that afternoon, packed in ashes, glowed in the darkness. The boy sprinkled the dry tinder onto the embers, carefully shielding it, ready for the wind which could start at any time. The boy blew gently. The embers glowed. A ribbon of flame rose in the tinder.

Feeling behind his back, An Lu-shan removed three arrows from his quiver. They were long and sleek, with iron tips. Just above the tip on each one was a tightly wrapped wad of cloth; An Lu-shan tested the wads in the dark for tightness. The children, he knew, would be in their positions, bows ready, their strange arrows, with bulbous iron devices fixed behind spiked metal wings, poised; their signal had been the small flame that the boy had cultivated.

An Lu-shan crept back to his position on the rim of the gorge. The camp was quiet. The fires had died down, but still cast enough light for him to see well enough. He drew his Sogdian bow and fixed his eyes on his target. The boy held one of the wrapped arrows to the flame; the naphtha-soaked rags ignited instantly. Immediately the boy transferred the arrow to his father's hand. There was no time to lose. An Lu-shan rose to his feet, eyes still trained below, and pulled the string of the heavy carved bow to its limit.

At the moment that he released the arrow, a powerful gust tore through the canyon. The arrow, blown off course, fell several yards to the side of the line of brush, hitting the earth in the corral. It missed the animals but lodged itself firmly in the ground where it burned like a torch. A hissing curse escaped An Lu-shan's lips. The animals raised an alarm, scattering from the flame in their midst, whinnying in fright. An Lu-shan held out his hand, grazing An Ching-hsu's shoulder roughly. Instantly, another flame arrow was placed in his hand. Still cursing, he drew his bow, beseeching the wind to allow him another shot. Then he saw in the dim light a man running from the nearest tent toward the horses and the mysterious flame. All right, my friend, muttered An Lu-shan; you shall help me now. He moved his aim from the pile of brush to the running man, who, miraculously, had not yet shouted. An Lu-shan waited until the man was at the brush pile and pulling it apart with his hands to get through. He released the arrow. This time his shot was true. The arrow entered the man's neck; he faltered for a moment before toppling. The burning arrow embedded in his body crackled peacefully for a few seconds in the midst of the brush. An Lu-shan gave a sharp whistle then.

The children lined along the rim rose to a well-practiced archer's kneel. Instead of aiming downward, they raised their oddly shaped arrows upward in an angle above the horizon. The naphtha-soaked brush below caught fire and roared. At the same moment the first volley of arrows flew in staggered precision. They rose, and on their downward arc, piercing, undulating screams filled the night sky. Before the first volley was spent, the second volley flew from the children's bows. Screams combined with throaty howls. Men emerged from tents, torn from sleep, their terrified faces illuminated by the raging brush. Some covered their heads and zigzagged like rabbits as the terrible sounds flew over their heads. Not soldiers, An Lu-shan guessed, but mere outriders, herdsmen. The soldiers among them grabbed for weapons in the confusion—a spear, a long sword, a bow without arrows, arrows without bows, empty sword sheaths. One man held a captured Chinese breastplate over his head as he ran.

Each child had thirty or more arrows; shooting in timed sequence, they could make the ceiling of horrible, eerie sounds last for some time. The arrows fell to earth on the opposite rim of the canyon. Then the wind chose to come to life again, fanning the brush fire below fiercely, swirling and scattering burning debris in all directions. An Lu-shan could see some of the men running toward the panicked horses. The herd charged first this way and then the other. But the men were driven back by the heat and flames, unable to get to the horses. The animals had found the narrow exit to the rear of their corral, the brush cleared away earlier by the boys. The herd was squeezing through, two and three abreast. Waiting for them were four older boys on herding ponies; the frightened horses would be rounded up and driven south until their fear had been run out of them.

The wind was now buffeting the walls of the canyon around the camp. Tents wobbled and collapsed. The wind rattled the loose flaps of the yurts, their tight skins wrinkling and stretching. The scattering brush started fires here and there which quickly blazed out of control. Overhead, the volleys still flew from the children's bows; the frightened vortex of sound now multiplied as if a thousand hungry ghosts had fallen from above the earth to descend on the camp below.

"Yes!" An Lu-shan cried out in the Khitan tongue, knowing he could not be heard above the noise. "We are hungry ghosts! We are angry wind demons, we are ancestors of the dead!" He laughed exultantly. "I and these children!" He seized a flaming arrow and whirled it around his head. Then, in Chinese, he shouted, "I am Lo Hsuan, god of fire! Here is my beard!"

Among the voices below, he heard orders being shouted. But it was too late. Some among them had no doubt recognized the deception, but all order was gone now as the majority of men and boys fled in superstitious terror of vengeful demons. The Khitan scrambled, in a fevered nightmare, away from the camp, toward the open grasslands, and up the far rocky walls. An Lu-shan knew that not a one of them would dare return to the campsite before daylight.

The battle was won without fighting. The children had been ready. An Lu-shan reveled in the unity of their allegiance and the simple victory. He dropped his bow and picked up two of the children near him, raised them to the sky, then hugged them to his large chest. "My little masters," he cried, "the victory is yours!" One of the boys laughed; the other wept with the release of his fear.

They had ridden all night, putting a safe distance between themselves and any Khitan courageous enough to give chase, though An Lu-shan was certain that not even a pack animal had been left in last night's attack.

It was midmorning. They had slowed their pace considerably, knowing they were back in Chinese-patrolled territory and within hours of reaching home, the *t'un-t'ien* military colony. An Lu-shan had allowed a rest stop of several hours around dawn; the power of recovery of the animals they had captured was truly astounding, but he did not wish to overtax them. When we arrive, he thought, these animals are not going to be exhausted and plodding. He was so close now to making real the picture that had been in his head for many weeks. Details of the picture varied at different times, but always, in the center of it, was himself.

Lulled now by the peaceful rhythm of the horse beneath him and in need of sleep himself, the picture came to him easily, vividly, in one of his favorite versions. As if through someone else's eyes, he looked out through the entry flap of an officer's tent at a commotion in the distance. It was always a brilliant sunny day in this picture. A huge dust cloud. Children shouting, dogs barking, people dropping their work and running to see. The dust cloud formed itself into horses. Magnificent horses, as far as the eye could see. In the middle, at the front, astride the largest horse, the whites of its eyes, the incarnadine brilliance of the flared nostrils revealing its fiery spirit, rode Master An Lu-shan: Master An, former slave, captive of the Chinese, riding victorious into the camp. In the picture, he saw his own face, smiling, black-bearded. He saw the picture through a Chinese officer's eyes.

He dwelled on the pleasant image as he rode. The wind this morning was comparatively light. People would be out and about in the camp today. They would be there to watch him return; the picture would soon be real— but he would not be watching himself from inside a tent. He had counted one hundred and twelve horses, plus several pregnant mares. Not a major victory, he knew, for the northern defense of P'inglu Province, but bound to make a fine impression, draw attention his way. Not a life lost; children doing the job of men, trained and responsive to his command. Prized horses, and to-morrow's soldiers. His soldiers.

In the five years since his capture by the Chinese he had shaken off his slave status and become a free man, useful and respected in his job as overseer of the nonmilitary part of the settlement. It was he who arranged for living quarters, food, and work distribution for the families of the conscripted men. There were hundreds of jobs that had to be done so that the settlement could support itself: management of prisoners and livestock; production of food, clothing, and weapons for the soldiers; construction of dwellings. Because of him, that part of the camp was running with exceptional smoothness; his pride and joy had been the iron-working hut he had brought into being. Now the colony could make many more of its own weapons and did not have to rely so heavily on the military caravans of the central government to the south. And his ability to organize the children—they worked like adults for him, eager only to please. The Chinese officers, he knew, had been watching him with approval. They know that I am indispensable, he told himself often; I have proven it with the families and the children. Now they will see that I am indispensable as a military strategist as well. They cannot waste my skill any longer. Let the eunuchs learn from me how to manage the colony. I can teach them.

He glanced behind him. The children rode, two and three to a horse, in a long string behind him. Some of the boys slept, the littler ones leaning back against older boys or slumped forward against the ponies' necks. Directly behind him rode his sons; the elder, An Ching-hsu, supported the younger,

An Ching-tsung, who slept, mouth slightly open, eyes shielded with a cloth from the sun and wind. Further behind, in a long line two and three horses wide, was the herd of prize horses. His booty. Behind and to the side of the herd rode the older boys, experienced herdsmen.

In the sleeping child behind him, he saw himself. A child, riding the caravan, the ancient, eternal procession of animals, goods, and people making its endless trek from the lands in the distant west through the vast northlands.

Once, before the caravan, he had had a family. In the furthest recesses of memory, back nearly before time began, he had sat on a woman's lap, reaching up to pat her face with pudgy hands. Her eyes looked into his. A mother's eyes, infinite with love. As a baby, before he had any words at all, he had recognized what was in those eyes and reached for it. He remembered a bright garden, flowers, and the splashing of water on rocks as he sat on the pretty woman's lap.

A few years later men had come. He knew now that they had been Kushan soldiers. His father lay dead, their house was burning. His mother, weak and wounded, had fled with him and some other relatives. They had struggled overland then, a long way, on yak and camel. It was bitter cold, and he grew thin. His mother grew weaker and slipped farther and farther from him in delerium, until her eyes no longer saw him. They tied her to a sledge and continued the journey.

One day they saw, from what must have been a hundred li away, a cloud of dust stretching forever on the horizon in the enormous landscape of rocky hills and high frozen lakes. The men in the group had become jubilant; he was afraid. He had heard the stories that came out of these forsaken deserts: phantom winds, monsters, moving boulders. The mass of dust, he was sure, was a cloud of ghosts.

As they grew closer, his fear was replaced with astonishment. The cloud on the horizon became a snake undulating as far as he could see in either direction. Closer still, he saw that the snake was alive, made of people and animals. The sounds traveled to them across the buffeting winds: the bold sparkle of bells; then the barking of dogs; drums and flutes mingled with the braying of camels and the shouting and singing of human voices. And when they were close enough to hear the creaking of the cart wheels and the metallic jangle of utensils and weapons, the smells came to him, to stay forever. The acrid stink of camels. Untanned leather, greasy smoke, rancid butter, and incense, whose exotic aroma had made him think of colors. And there must have been a thousand camels, yaks, and men, carts and sledges, raising the dust that blew into their faces, stung their eyes, and filled their throats.

They had found the caravan that traveled the great Silk Road. They would join it now and be safe. But when they untied his mother from the sledge, they found that she was dead.

He had tried to get to her, but the caravan masters put themselves between him and the corpse. But as they wrapped her thin, still fluid form in cloth, he had seen. For just a moment her face had appeared in the folds of the cloth. Her eyes were sunken, but still open and not so long from having seen; the pale skin tight across the high cheeks; the long silky black hair matted with dust. He had let out a long wail of loneliness when he saw her.

And then a very tall man with strange oval eyes, a hooked nose, and hair and beard almost the color of fire came and told him that she would be taken care of. He must go with the others now, the men said, and leave his mother. He pointed. Those people will give you shoes and something to eat and drink. They seemed kind, but he hung back, unnoticed, then followed at a distance the men who took his mother. He watched the linen-wrapped form being passed from hand to hand along the caravan; then he saw someone shake coins from a small purse into another's ready palm.

Then they took the body a distance from the others, behind some rocks. They noticed him and chased him away. But he came back. This time they grabbed him and shoved him hard back toward the road while he screamed and fought. But he had seen them, unwrapping the body, then smiling their brown rotten-toothed smiles as the first man pressed down upon her.

The caravan, and the settlements and cities along its route, became life for the orphan for many years after that. The caravan, journeying from customhouse to customhouse, goods increasing in price with each middleman they passed through, became mother, father, and brother for him, and sustenance. By the time he was sixteen or so, he was the leader of a band of youths, orphans like himself, whose business it was to waylay stragglers and late joiners, separating them from the caravan and its guard of dogs and outriders: it meant food, clothing, and money to be had immediately; and goods to be taken to the next city along the route and sold or traded. Gold, jade, pomegranates, exotic birds and dancing horses, Roman glass—An Lu-shan had had his hands on all of these things at one time or another and had learned their value and the art of trade as well as that of thievery. Looking at these things, he had felt that he was seeing the world that lay beyond the windy, desolate nowhere. He remembered unrolling a bolt of fabric that had come from the far west, thinking that it would just be silk, every variety of which he had already seen. He had stared in dumb shock at the beauty of the cloth when it was laid out. It *was* silk, with threads of gold running through it—but iridescent plumage from tropical birds had been woven into the fabric as well. He did not understand the emotions that had rushed through him at that moment; but he knew that he had to have more of the world than bits and pieces, artifacts. He had hidden the cloth from the others; he still had it to this day.

:: :

An Lu-shan negotiated the rocky path through the settlement. The bases of the hills surrounding the camp resembled a forest of giant tree stumps; a low, oppressive snow sky severed them halfway up. Skin yurts and mud-brick hovels were clustered behind crumbling fortifications. The camp's monotonous maze of skin and tile roofs was broken occasionally by crude drum towers, their rough brick and stucco walls stained with soot and perforated by narrow windows. But no sentries or crossbowmen manned the towers during the day; Chinese policy had relaxed considerably lately. Streams of cooking smoke rose up and flattened against the ceiling of clouds.

Word of the routing of the Khitan and the capture of the horses had spread through the camp. None of it had come from An Lu-shan's own lips; he knew that the children would take care of that for him. He was enjoying the opportunity to exercise false modesty: "The children did it all," he had said humbly several times. But under his breath he repeated titles conferred on him by the camp population. "Sogdian Hero" and "Barbarian Friend" were two that had reached his ears. And he had walked by the corral where the Ferghanian horses were quartered with scarcely a glance in their direction. Now he moved down the path, his feet and legs wrapped, in northern nomad style, with skins and furs. On his upper body he wore the Chinese Army-issue military quilts. He was quite conscious of the effect of the combined costumes.

The youngest children, too small to even hope to accompany Master An on one of his forays, swarmed around him in their smokey-smelling rags. Several followed him, mimicking his walk; others ran past him, trying to catch his eye or tugging at his quilts. He kept his eyes straight ahead, as if he could not see them. One child ran ahead and kneeled in the snow on tiny knees and cold little pink hands; as An Lu-shan drew near, the child bucked, pretending to be a wild horse. The others took up the game instantly. One snapped at his heels like a crusty old camp watchdog grown sour from abuse and neglect. The rest set up a chorus of brays, howls, and whinnies that they had heard their older siblings learning to master.

He stopped suddenly; they became quiet in the same instant. He allowed a hungry look to spread across his face as he slowly tugged at his black beard. Then he lunged, catching up the youngest child, and held him aloft.

"Who am I?" he growled.

"A giant hairy man of the north!" said a girl.

"A shaman bear!" several shouted at once.

"I am very hungry," he intoned menacingly. He brought the child toward him, then took hold of the end of a rag from the child's leggings with his teeth and began to chew slowly. The little one screamed and struggled, fear and laughter mixing. The circle of porcelain faces around him, cheeks pink with cold, were contorted with delight.

The merriment in the midst of the post's somber dreariness affected the adults laboring nearby, carrying stones and blocks of ice or brewing vats of hot rancid-butter tea. They smiled in An Lu-shan's direction. The child in his hands struggled between two urges. In the midst of a peal of laughter, his little face crumpled and he gave in to tears. Without hesitating, An Lu-shan opened the front of his jacket and brought the child to his fat, hairy chest—quite unlike the chests of the children's fathers and uncles, he knew. Surreptitiously, he slipped the "nipple" of a hidden skin flask into the child's mouth. The crying stopped immediately as the boy "nursed." The children gaped as drops of yellowish fermented mare's milk trickled down An Lu-shan's chest. Koomiss, he knew, was not something the children would be familiar with, being a delicacy horded by the adults for themselves. Two toothless old men lowered their brush-filled barrows and laughed appreciatively, their shriveled faces turned up in great smiles.

"Master An is nursing!" a girl cried as they pushed and crowded for a closer look.

"Are you a magician?" another girl asked.

"No," he said, cradling the child carefully so that the nipple was hidden from view. "But I am a Sogdian. In Sogdia, the winds are so furious that sometimes . . ."—he paused, putting on a sad face—"the little mothers blow away. You see, they are too light."

"Do the mothers blow away when the babies are in them?" a girl asked with concern.

"No, no—they are far too heavy then. It is only after the baby is out and they are light again that they must be careful not to let the wind get them. They must carry heavy stones in their clothing to weigh them down. But alas, sometimes a woman will forget and go outside without her stones. Then do you know who must feed the infants?" he asked. They shook their heads. The adults listened attentively as well. "Heaven has provided our menfolk with great suckling tits, too, . . . and covered them with hair to keep the milk warm against the cold winds."

"Master An," a child asked, "may we taste it?" He lowered the child he'd been holding to the ground and closed his jacket.

"No, I am sorry. I must conserve. I haven't much milk left, because I have no wife with children any more. Heaven does not fritter away a Sogdian tribesman's great gifts . . . and neither must we. You understand that, do you not?" They nodded as if they did.

But you are only Chinese, he thought; you can never hope to understand the mysteries of the barbarian north. He resumed his walk, the children now following quietly, as if they might still catch an imagined glimpse of his pendulous breasts. He headed toward the long, low tent. Smoke issuing from its chimneys told him that work was already underway. He calculated that there would be no more than three days in which to accomplish a great deal of work. Perhaps no more than two.

: :

"Children!" An Lu-shan addressed the group in the metal-working hut. "A great man is on his way at this very moment to see us! The aristocrat General Li Shih-chih travels north from Ying-chou. He wants to see our demon arrows, but we had to use every last one when your brothers chased away the barbarian Khitan. We must work very hard so that we will have enough arrows to put on a demonstration for him."

The children stood close to the narrow tile flues which rose from the coal-fired *kangs*. Not only did the flues carry smoke through the vents in the high-peaked roof, but An Lu-shan had redesigned them so that they effectively circulated heat throughout the long tent. The sturdy skin walls, reinforced with an interior thatchwork of limbs and lined with thick felt, rippled in the high winds.

At the far end of the tent, two older girls maintained a forge while a smith hammered and shaped the metal "screamers" and the spiked wings which controlled the flight of the arrows and fed air into the devices. The two girls, faces sweaty and flushed, pushed and pulled the plunger that fanned the furnace. Each had hold of a handle protruding out of opposite sides of a slate box at the rear of the oven; the clanging of the smith's hammer and the rushing of the air in the furnace bellows filled the tent. An Lu-shan shouted over the noise.

"It was easy to scare away the Khitan. But today we will make arrows which would make them burrow into the ground in terror!" The children, pleased with the fantastic image, set to work.

He watched closely as the first group labored with short bunches of cane and bamboo tubing. They bound the tubes carefully in the traditional uneven bundles of the *sheng* flute pipes. The small, supple fingers inserted tiny reeds with meticulous care at just the right angle for the desired pitch. Then, using iron awls, they made holes evenly along the length of the pipes. When they had several pipes finished, they blew through them. Others, fashioning wings for the arrows, looked up in startled pleasure at the musical, wailing sound. An Lu-shan picked up a cooled-down bulbous metal noisemaker. While the children blew through the reed pipes, he blew into the device cupped in his hands. The combined sounds of the musical pipes over the demonic growl he produced caused everyone to stop work momentarily. For several minutes they continued the strange concert to the accompaniment of the wind and a few wild dogs. He lowered the device and smiled.

"What will those barbarians think, eh?"

"Desert spirits," said a boy, "luring them into their caves with music!"

"We'll be desert spirits!" said another.

"We will even, perhaps, frighten General Li Shih-chih a little bit!" An Lu-shan joked. He knew what their response would be.

"No, Master An," a boy replied seriously. "It is not possible to frighten a Chinese general. It cannot be done."

"But we shall try, shall we not?" An Lu-shan asked.

"Yes!" they shouted happily. Returning to his work, An Lu-shan reflected. Frighten a Chinese general? Difficult, yes . . . but not impossible. His own stomach tightened . . . in fear? He was thinking of General Li Shih-chih. Once again An Lu-shan's fate rested in this man's hands—the same man who, five years before, had interceded and saved him from a thief's death by decapitation.

: :

General Li Shih-chih probably does not remember the wretched thief, one among several, whose face he looked into on that day. An Lu-shan had had to walk with his fellow prisoners for several days with his arms pinned painfully behind him. His captors, a Chinese border patrol, had treated him as if he were already a dead man. The soldiers rode horses while the prisoners walked. At night they ate and drank, ignoring the bound men who stared with raw hatred and hunger. One of the men had died from thirst along the way; An Lu-shan had survived by drawing on deep resources, both mental and physical.

He and eight of his men had been captured one night in an ignominious manner. During his years on the trade routes, he had come to think of himself not as a thief, but as a businessman with an unerring eye for quality goods and a knack for gleaning only the best. He had found that the selection of goods increased in quality and value according to their proximity to the Jade Gate, the point where the Silk Road entered China. By the time individual traders reached that point, their stocks would have been upgraded gradually along the route. For An Lu-shan, a judicious choice in the selection of his victims could result in an abundant harvest. He could then move back along the trade route and sell the goods or trade them for other, more enticing merchandise. Robbers were often robbed; An Lu-shan, knowing too well the ways of thieves along the road, never was. Thus he had risen to the top rank of two professions, thief and trader. In his mind, he had come to regard the thieving part of it as a form of currency with which he, as a trader, purchased his goods.

The crime for which he had been captured had, ironically, nothing to do with anything remotely resembling Persian silk or Roman glass. There had been a famine that year in the northern territories after a particularly harsh winter. The tribes had been unable to drive livestock through the passes, and people were suffering from prolonged hunger. But a nearby Chinese military colony was importing abundant livestock from the south. An Lu-shan knew this because he could smell the animals on the wind at night: sheep, thousands of them. To get to them meant actually entering Chinese territory.

An Lu-shan had taken a band of eight men. His plan had been for each man to smother a sheep and carry it on his back. Eight sheep would provide meat for as many families for a week. They had been successful, until a sheep being carried on one of the men's shoulders revived, taking a deep breath and bleating piteously, waking several guards. Cursing, they had had to drop the animals and run. Three men escaped; five of them, An Lu-shan among them, had been cornered and captured.

An Lu-shan had said nothing. He did not want the Chinese to know that he understood their language. The soldiers spoke freely in front of him, and to his amazement, he heard them referring to himself and the other captives as spies. It seemed that they believed that An Lu-shan and his men had entered the military colony on the pretext of stealing sheep and that their true intent had been to learn the lay of the camp, gain free access, and carry military secrets back to the north. Spies! He was a trader, a businessman, and, for now, a livestock thief. He had no interest in anything military.

And so they had been forced to embark on the long march to the camp of the military investigator, who was under jurisdiction of the military governor of Fanyang. During the march An Lu-shan had had time to contemplate. So they think I am a spy, an infiltrator. He pictured himself learning secrets and carrying them back through dangerous territory. I could be those things. In fact, I would be very skillful, would I not? He recalled the masterful stealth with which he and his men, under his direction, had entered the camp without waking the guards. It had been his impeccable instinct which had guided them through the maze of the camp to where the animals were quartered. How had he known where to put his feet from one moment to the next? Had the accursed sheep not bleated when it did, no one would have known they had been there. He saw that he was, in fact, a military strategist. He soon forgot that it had been, after all, only sheep he was after that night; by the time he and the other men shuffled into the camp, starved and exhausted, he had become, in his mind, a spy.

But he had no wish to be decapitated for it. Such was the likely punishment awaiting him either as a thief or as a spy. Arriving at the camp, they found that there was to be a hearing of sorts, followed by swift execution. They were brought before the then military investigator, Li Shih-chih. The men had to stand in a line, weary, hungry, and frightened, as Li Shih-chih looked each man in the eyes and asked him to describe the crime for which he had been apprehended. Several of the men had refused to speak at all and only stared back at the investigator sullenly. Others begged for mercy or mumbled unintelligibly. As Li Shih-chih moved down the line toward him, An Lu-shan summoned all the authority that was in him. The military investigator finally stood before An Lu-shan.

"What is your name?" he had asked in the barbarian tongue as he studied An Lu-shan's heavily bearded face.

"My Chinese name is An Lu-shan," he had answered in Chinese, returning the man's look of direct interest.

"What is your crime, An Lu-shan?" Li Shih-chih asked, now speaking Chinese, also.

"I have a great fondness for roast mutton, Your Excellency; so much so that I am driven to extreme and dangerous action in order to procure it." He held the investigator's eyes as he spoke. Li Shih-chih smiled faintly as he looked at An Lu-shan.

"Do you know what the penalty is for theft of military property?"

"I do not think that you will be holding a feast in my honor," An Lu-shan replied.

"The penalty for thievery and spying is the same," Li Shih-chih said, "though a choice is offered. You may choose one of two deaths: by beating or by decapitation."

An Lu-shan paused before answering. "In either case, Your Excellency, the loss would be yours." Li Shih-chih raised his eyebrows slightly at this. An Lu-shan continued boldly. "Does the military investigator wish to destroy the two barbarians, the Hsi and the Khitan? If you kill me, you would be killing a brave soldier."

The guards standing nearby exchanged looks which said plainly that they considered this one to be as good as dead. Li Shih-chih looked at An Lu-shan without saying anything. Then he turned and walked slowly back down the line of men, making an occasional gesture with his right hand, immediately after which a guard would roughly pull a man from the line. The unfortunates were hauled to the center of the compound and forced to kneel. Li Shih-chih returned to An Lu-shan and stood before him.

"What is your choice, An Lu-shan?"

Without hesitation, An Lu-shan replied, "For them, I choose decapitation. For myself, I choose to be beaten to death, for it is slower, and I wish to remain in this world as long as I can."

Again a faint smile played at the corners of Li Shih-chih's mouth. Looking at the man, An Lu-shan marveled at the smoothness of his skin and the cleanliness of his clothes, teeth, and fingernails. Such examples of civilized refinement were a rare sight on the frontier. For a moment An Lu-shan imagined rooms, buildings, cities full of such people—calm, clean, well-fed, richly clothed, their hair smooth and glossy. Li Shih-chih regarded An Lu-shan for another moment, then turned toward the condemned men and gave another signal. One of the guards drew his long sword from its sheath and approached the first prisoner. Then Li Shih-chih gave another terse order to the guard standing near An Lu-shan, who stiffened as the guard drew his sword and came toward him. But the guard merely gave him an incredulous look and proceeded to cut the ropes that bound his hands and feet. He was free. Li Shih-chih beckoned to An Lu-shan.

"Come," he said. "You will be given something to eat, and we will discuss your new duties."

He was to start as a slave. His work would be lowly, his status nonexistent. He was to do what was assigned to him, and he was to be grateful to have been allowed to keep his head attached to his shoulders.

But there was one more bit of audacity with which he'd had to approach Li Shih-chih. In the settlement he had left, where he had intended to return with the sheep, two small sons awaited him. Nine years before, An Lu-shan had taken a wife, a woman whose dark eyes had stopped him in the midst of a consultation with her father, a trader.

For a few years he had lived the role of a householder, until his wife died giving birth to their second son. The two children, aged nine and four at the time of An Lu-shan's capture, had become accustomed to the nomadic life of their father and were learning from him how to procure a livelihood in the settlements and rugged landscape through which the trade routes traveled. An Lu-shan asked Li Shih-chih if the two children could be brought to the camp where he was to be a slave.

The investigator had thought for a moment; then he replied that the children would be allowed to join him, but that feeding and sheltering them was to be entirely An Lu-shan's concern. He was to provide for them out of his own rations and whatever else he could make come his way. There are already many mouths to feed, he had said.

The boys and some of his belongings had been brought to him, riding the next convoy that arrived from the direction of the larger permanent military installation, Tu-hu Fu. And for the last five years the camp had been their home. The children mixed freely with the children of the military families, and they would be growing up Chinese had An Lu-shan not taken care to teach them the language and hunting and stalking skills of the "barbarian" north.

An Lu-shan's menial slave status had lasted only a year or so; the Chinese had soon recognized that they could not afford to waste his abilities. He knew instinctively that he should not, at first, attract attention to himself, but should go about his tasks quietly. His appearance, he knew, was quite enough to cause him to stand out. To the Chinese, a beard was a few stringy wisps on the chin. His face with its luxuriant growth of black hair was a source of fascination to them. That and his size set him apart from them, though his eyes and theirs were the same. During the first year, he had observed his captors closely. The Chinese were unlike other people he had encountered. They talked much more than tribal people. As his mastery of their language grew, he found that they relished long conversations about intangible things. They speculated endlessly, weaving great invisible nets with their words, then dropping them the way children do when they have grown weary of a game. But at the same time, they were orderly, practical. He became aware of the vastness of the empire behind them; with awe, he watched the seemingly limitless supply of men, animals, food, and weapons that flowed into the military colony. What sort of world lay in the distant south? He could only imagine it. He saw envoys, high-ranking officers, and members of the investigative military Censorate ride into the camp for important conferences. He had listened peripherally to conversations. The subject almost constantly on their minds and tongues was tribal insurgence along the border.

The attack on the Khitan camp and the capture of the horses had been a year in the planning. Though all children in the colony were expected to work, it had been his innovation to organize them. His close daily contact with the children had made it easy to train them for the excursion into enemy territory. They had not known themselves until a month or so before the attack what it was they were being trained to do; when they learned, they had, of course, enjoyed keeping the secret. And An Lu-shan had timed it so that the raid would come just before a scheduled visit to the camp by Li Shih-chih, who had since been promoted to the rank of assistant military governor and no longer had his headquarters there. If Li Shih-chih does not remember the prisoner who spoke out so presumptuously, he will be reminded shortly, An Lu-shan thought as he prepared himself. First there was to be the demonstration, by the children, of the screaming arrows; then An Lu-shan was to attend a private meeting with the man. It was easy for An Lu-shan to conjure the whizz of the sword blade, followed by the soft, heavy thud of a man's head hitting the ground. He had heard it enough times in his travels. Yes, he thought as he recalled the sound, I spoke. What had I to lose? What was it that had caused the military investigator to refrain from that small gesture of the hand as I stood before him that day? A few words, that is all. A few well-chosen words.

An Lu-shan had seen countless men die in a hundred different ways, and decapitation was by far the worst. Not because it was painful; if the swordsman was skillful, it was the quickest way to die. But it was the insult, the ultimate degradation. A body without a head, a head without a body. A decapitation always drew an interested crowd. An Lu-shan knew the peculiar fascination with which each person watching imagined his own head rolling in the dirt, saw his own body swaying for a moment, headless, as if perplexed. And when the head was picked up by the hair and carried away, all eyes followed. And some, he knew, imagined themselves standing before the Ten Kings of Hell in judgment, carrying their heads under their arms, the insult continuing even after death, their earthly bodies severed and mutilated, unfit for the grave. An Lu-shan had saved himself from that with a few well-chosen words. And now, five years later, he would again stand before Li Shih-chih and determine his fate with words.

In his quarters, An Lu-shan opened a hide trunk. He rubbed his hands. Then he lifted garments and inspected them, one by one. An embroidered Persian jacket, a treasure purloined on the Silk Road long ago. Its gold threads flashed as he put it on. After a moment he pulled it off. No; he will perceive me as an ambitious fool. He folded it carefully and replaced it in the trunk. He pulled out a heavy sheepskin garment, a sleeveless tunic worn by northern tribal warriors to protect them from the wind while allowing freedom of motion for the arms. He put it on and considered the effect his appearance would have on the general. He wanted Li Shih-chih to understand that he had more knowledge of these northern nomadic tribes than anyone on this side of the border. But, he thought, I must be careful that he knows where my allegiance lies. It would not be well for him to look at me and see a tribal barbarian. If he is going to put me in command of my own troops, then he must trust me completely. He pulled the tunic over his head. I do not wish to look absurd, either. I must not resemble a slave or a farmer. He must perceive me as a soldier . . . of humble rank but ripe for promotion. He selected a new quilted military jacket, unsoiled and untorn. Though his tent shuddered in the bitter cold gusts of wind, he was uncomfortably damp with sweat as he opened the flap and stepped outside.

: :

The screaming of the arrows echoed in his ears as he walked toward the military governor's tent. The demonstration had been executed with hardly a flaw, and An Lu-shan had gloated, delighted with the huge crowd of spectators. The whole camp, it seemed, had wanted to see for themselves just what it was that had driven the Khitan from their tents in such holy terror. He had managed a few discreet glances in the direction of Military Governor Li Shih-chih during the spectacle. The man's face had shown keen interest, causing An Lu-shan to feel certain that he was showing Li Shih-chih something he had not seen before.

His sweat had dried during the demonstration, but as he approached the military governor's tent, he found that his palms were becoming damp. He paused for a moment, wiped his hands on his coat, and lifted the entry flap.

: :

Five years before, he had been as good as dead when he conversed with Li Shih-chih. Now he sat on Li Shih-chih's cushions holding a bowl of tea. Li Shih-chih had changed little since the last time An Lu-shan had seen him. He was a bit leaner, that was all; and he looked at An Lu-shan with much the same expression as when they had first met. And again he asked questions.

"How old were the children that you took when you raided the Khitan camp, An Lu-shan?"

"None older than thirteen, Your Excellency. The youngest was seven," An Lu-shan replied.

"My impression," said Li Shih-chih, "is that you planned this expedition for quite some time. You have painstakingly built a powerful reputation for yourself at this colony. By risking the lives of children, you risked the new life you have made here since your capture. You also created a risk for me. You are aware, no doubt, that I would have been indirectly responsible if there had been any deaths. What if it had all gone wrong?" he asked, without rancor.

An Lu-shan shook his head. "There was never any possibility of it going wrong. By using children instead of men, I left myself no alternative."

"Good," Li Shih-chih replied. "Because I need not tell you that if the Khitan had killed any of the children and failed to kill you, then I would have seen to it personally that my error of five years ago was rectified. And this time you would not have had a choice," he added.

"Of course. You were the one who intervened when my wretched head was about to roll in the dirt. But by making a risk for you," An Lu-shan said slyly, "I also made a possible gain for you. I know that you understand the nature of risk. When you changed my status from dead man to slave, you took a risk. When I took the children out and exposed them to danger, I took a risk. When one takes a risk, one must think: I will lose everything or gain ten times what I had."

Li Shih-chih put his bowl down, leaned back on his cushions, and regarded An Lu-shan. "When I saved you from the executioner, An Lu-shan, it was not because my heart was soft or that I thought you innocent of the charges. I could see that you were clearly the most dangerous man in that little group." He shrugged. "I thought of killing you and freeing the others. What did I stand to gain by saving you from the executioner?" he asked.

An Lu-shan smiled. "I *am* dangerous, Your Excellency, to the Hsi and the Khitan." He leaned forward intently. "I have shown you what I can do with a few children," he said, and paused. "Let me show you what I can do with many thousands of men."

Li Shih-chih stood and walked to the tent flap. He lifted it and looked out toward the dry hills to the north. "The Khitan have been moving about lately. They are restless. We have come to expect skirmishes, small encroachments on Chinese territory; but lately it seems as if they are consolidating their forces. I do not like it; furthermore, the allegiance of some of our own people in these remote territories—Hopei and Fanyang Provinces in particular—is questionable. There are antagonisms, old rivalries between them and their rulers in Ch'ang-an. In addition to the constant threat of invasion, we have also to deal with the possibility of secession." He turned to An Lu-shan. "We cannot push back the barbarian invaders without the undivided loyalty of our people in the northern provinces."

An Lu-shan nodded thoughtfully. "I have been among the people you speak of. I would venture to say that I understand them." He framed his next sentence carefully. "They are not without some resentment toward those who are sent from the southern capital to rule them," he said, shrugging his shoulders. "Though they are Chinese, they still feel that southerners are . . . foreigners who have come from far away to impose foreign rule upon them. Some of them do not even speak true Chinese, but retain their strange dialects. They are like little nations," he finished, pleased with his assessment. Li Shih-chih was studying him.

"I have heard that you speak several tongues yourself. How many?" he asked with curiosity.

"Eleven," An Lu-shan replied modestly, "plus a grasp of the northern Chinese dialects," he said, fondling a fringed pillow. He could feel Li Shih-chih looking hard at him, though he did not lift his own gaze. He had become uncomfortably warm again and felt the sweat beading on his forehead.

"An Lu-shan, you are a man of many worlds," said Li Shih-chih finally. "Where does *your* allegiance lie?" he asked pointedly.

An Lu-shan was ready for this question. "Your Excellency, I have lived among the Chinese for five years. Before that, I moved among all manner of tribal peoples and countries beyond the Chinese borders," he said, and paused, as if thinking out his next words. "I have had ample opportunity to compare. Suppose I had joined the Khitan. I could then spend the rest of my life being cold, dirty, and ignorant, fighting a losing battle against the greatest empire on earth." He looked at Li Shih-chih. "I would have to be a fool," he said simply.

Li Shih-chih smiled. "If you were to do battle against the Hsi or the Khitan—with men instead of children—what would your tactics be?"

Again An Lu-shan was ready. He drew a long breath. "There would be more similarities than differences, Excellency. The expedition with the children was a demonstration of what can be accomplished through mobility, scouting, and strange surprises," he said, giving Li Shih-chih a crafty look. He paused for a moment, then recited from memory: " '. . . Immobilize an invader by capturing his baggage, food, and mounts while they are grazing. Scorch the earth, block the springs, and understand the moods of Heaven and Earth—and make them serve you. Don't join in actual combat unless strategy, numbers, and odds are in your favor. Seek the confidence of all peoples along the way: Discover what they have been promised by your adversary, and promise them more. Find out what their historical divisions and antagonisms are, and exploit these rifts. Make their hopes your hopes, their allegiances, your allegiances, and then they will be faithful to you. And again, never engage in battle until you know for certain that you *will* win!' " he finished and watched Li Shih-chih for his reaction.

"*The Classic of War,*" he said, impressed. "So you are widely read, as well," he said, half jokingly.

"I read not at all!" An Lu-shan answered proudly, thumping his chest. "Nor can I write. But that does not stop me from learning from books! But I speak from my own experience as well. In the north there is no other way to fight the enemy on his own territory."

Li Shih-chih thought for a moment before speaking. Then he looked at the Sogdian. "You are a foreigner, An Lu-shan, and a strange, savage, and wily one at that. I am not accustomed to rewarding such men for their audacity and insubordination, but I seem to be making a habit of it in your case. You are obviously a highly intelligent and talented man, and I must trust my own instinct of five years ago when I decided to spare your 'wretched head,' as you so aptly put it." He paused. "I shall be arguing in favor of a military commission for you when I meet with my superior, the military governor Chang Shou-kuei." An Lu-shan's face split in a wide grin. "Have you, in your travels, passed through Fanyang Province?" Li Shih-chih asked.

"To be sure!" An Lu-shan answered with enthusiasm.

"Then you would be willing to take up residence there?" Li Shih-chih asked.

"Willing?" An Lu-shan replied, and put on a fierce face. "I would be that much closer to the Hsi and the Khitan," he said menacingly.

Li Shih-chih stood. "After I leave here, I will be visiting two more military colonies before reporting to Chang Shou-kuei," he said as An Lu-shan quickly rose to his feet. "I believe that our talk will be mostly a formality; he has implicit faith in my judgment." He looked An Lu-shan up and down. "I remember my admonition to you that procuring food for yourself and your children would be your own concern," he said. "I can see that you had no difficulty. It looks as though you ate their food as well as your own. Tell me, are they mere skeletons?"

"No, no, Excellency! They are strapping boys!" An Lu-shan replied, flattered by Li Shih-chih's compliment. "And fine hunters as well. They are invaluable to me. I have taught them everything I know," he added, giving the officer a look fraught with significance.

Li Shih-chih nodded thoughtfully. "Do they enjoy roast mutton?"

"Roast mutton?" An Lu-shan asked, puzzled for a moment. Then he remembered his own remark when he had stood in the line of condemned men five years ago. "Roast mutton!" he laughed. "Roast mutton! Oh, Excellency, that is fine. Fine indeed. Yes! They have inherited their father's taste for this delicacy. I see to it that they have all they can possibly eat!"

Li Shih-chih went to the tent flap and opened it. "You will know before two weeks have passed," he said, looking at the Sogdian for a long moment before dismissing him.

An Lu-shan walked away from the tent, trying to contain his exultation. His heart pounded heavily. As was usual when An Lu-shan walked through the camp, a small band of children materialized around his ankles, chattering and shouting. He scooped one up and held it aloft, and looked at the small face framed against the white sky. The cheeks were red with cold and grimy with dirt and the remains of a recent meal. The child's nose was running, too . . . but the eyes were bright and clear.

" You!" he said to the delighted child. "I could wash your face and dress you in silks and no one could distinguish you from a princeling!" The child squirmed in An Lu-shan's grasp as he was lowered toward the bearded face. An Lu-shan gave the child a conspiratorial grin. "Want to come with me?" he whispered. "To see the great cities and palaces in the south? Because I promise you, that is where I am going to go."

5

Grandmother's Ghost

Avoiding the split, I have left the cabinet.
Enjoying the unmingled, I sip the cup.
I shall inquire of my usual guests:
How many will come today?

—*Li Shih-chih*

Many of the guests that usually came to share [Tu Fu's—poet and minister under Minghuang] wine and food fell away for fear of Li Lin-fu. . . . Li Lin-fu's displeasure was, however, not to be regarded in jest [for many ministers succumbed] to execution or suicide.

—*William Hung*

HEAVY carts were a ubiquitous part of the congested commerce of the city streets. They lumbered along, no more noticeable than the unnumbered souls who swarmed around them in the endless river of millions of nameless lives.

The great wheels jounced and crashed in muddy ruts, groaning and creaking, their axles coated in thick smelly black grease. Huge loads fixed under tarpaulins with ropes and thick oaken boughs swayed outlandishly. When heavy rains turned the streets to deep mud, the wheels of the carts could become mired. The drivers would lash the oxen as the wheels sank deeper; sometimes, the beasts could pull a cart from the mud as their masters screamed and cursed them. But sometimes the precarious balance was lost, and a cart would topple, the massive load pinning a child or an old person who could not move so quickly. The shouts and crying would attract a great crowd of curious people.

They would drop their loads, emerge from shops and stop their business to stare. For a moment, the unfortunate drama would draw the attention of the people in the street. For the spectators, the small scene before them was a few moments wherein they could contemplate the riddle of fortune. One man, or woman or child, writhed under a heavy wheel, or perhaps a load of bricks, while another stood and watched. Why? Life on the streets was a great sheet of suffering and pain, far removed from the heights of the pure, unnamable, indistinguishable, unsuffering Tao of the eternal cosmos.

For one immeasurably small moment, the entire universe would concentrate all its frenetic energy on one immeasurably small place. Then, just as arbitrarily, it would lift its head and turn, screwing its eyes on some other small and futile struggle and it would all be forgotten. That was the way it always was.

The sedan chairs of the rich and powerful would often push quickly by in these instances, their occupants wishing to avoid unpleasant brushes with the common brutalities. But a magistrate would be obliged to stop. It was innate to the Confucian code that he lived by. And it was hoped that such compassion was innate to the man's own inner moral directive, too—one could ask for no less in one's officers. Some philosophers described human nature as essentially good, but it was never certain whether they believed what they expressed. Others said that most men would not pluck a single hair from their forearms to save the world. In any case, the civil authorities would be summoned, and in the confusion and suffering someone would attempt to unravel the fault and the liabilities.

The apprentice eunuch Lu Pei, passing through a narrow alley in the Orchid Terrace of government, was surprised to see two tall carts coming his way over the cobblestones. It was strange. He saw the carts in the streets so frequently that they may as well have been invisible; to see them here, in the complex of alleys and courtyards connecting the imperial government buildings, was incongruous. Accompanying the carts were guards, brusquely clearing the way and shouting to the drivers to move with more alacrity. The eunuch shrank into the recess of a doorway as the carts passed. As they creaked by, with only a foot or so to spare, Lu Pei was surprised at the number of guards escorting the strange processional. There were more in the rear that he had not seen at first. They ignored him completely, their gruff voices loud in the enclosed space between the high walls. He counted. Twenty-six guards! At this close range, he was struck by the appearance of these men. What did they remind him of? Often he had seen bands of criminals being led through the streets to some place of corvée labor. These fellows guarding the carts had the same demeanor. Their language was crude; a few had distinct scars or missing teeth. What could those carts be carrying that would require the protection of twenty-six ruffians? And where were they going?

He forgot his original purpose in being out on the Orchid Terrace grounds.

He would follow; but he would keep his distance; something was out of place. No use in drawing attention to himself. He waited in the shelter of the doorway until they had nearly reached the next corner before setting out after them, maintaining a distance of about one hundred paces between himself and the last cart. My master Kao Li-shih would, he thought confidently, do exactly the same.

The wagons moved at a steady pace, slowing only occasionally to negotiate the narrow alleys and the tiled ascents between the Chancellery and Secretariat compounds. As the processional moved out into a wide avenue, Lu Pei saw that a high decorative footbridge lay ahead. Paralleling the route of the ox carts, the bridge rose in a gradual curve to a walkway atop a two-story building and continued down on the other side of the building. There would be a clear view from the top. He ran as fast as he could to catch up so that he could look directly down on the carts and perhaps get a clue. When he reached the apex of the bridge's curve, he ducked down and peered through the square "thunder" pattern of the decorative balustrade.

There was nothing to identify whatever lay under the dark blankets. The carts swayed as they passed under where he crouched. They were moving faster now, the lead guards shouting orders to the drivers, who whipped the already straining oxen. Lu Pei ran ahead to where the bridge settled onto the crenellated top of a low wall. Ahead of the ox carts, he could see a blind corner and a crowd of Ch'ang-an's merchants returning from their morning bartering of coal, lamp oil, inks, and papers to the vast offices of government.

It must have been a good morning, because the crowd was in high spirits. Orders and profits had obviously gone well. The merchants, some on foot and some in small donkey carts, talked and laughed. The alley they moved along was perpendicular to the wide street where the mysterious ox carts were traveling. Lu Pei's eyes moved back and forth from the ox carts to the merchants. The merchants approached the corner at a leisurely pace; the ox carts, while farther away from the corner, were gaining speed and closing the distance rapidly. He could see that each group was oblivious to the other's presence.

He opened his mouth to shout a warning to the lead ox cart. But something made him desist. Something told him that if he held his counsel, he would find out what was under those tarpaulins. He knew that if he waited only a moment longer, it would be too late no matter what he did. He held his breath. The merchants, their donkeys, wagons, and wheelbarrows would emerge innocently from the inconspicuous side alley in a matter of moments.

What would Master Kao have done in these circumstances? He had only to ask himself that to know what he should do. He settled back quietly and watched.

From where Lu Pei crouched there was a clear view of one of the many decorative canals that crisscrossed the government grounds. The carts' path was now parallel to it, and a low marble railing was all that stood between the roadway and a drop down to the water.

In the next moment, Lu Pei found himself sympathizing with the animals. If I were an ox pulling a cart, he thought, and even though the heavy wooden yoke lying across my shoulders would serve as a constant reminder of my bondage and servitude, my first impulse would be to save myself. He saw that the animals below him were trying to do just that as the noisy crowd of men and donkeys emerged from the alleyway. The oxen pulling the lead cart had been urged to such a speed by now that the cart they pulled was being propelled along by its own momentum. Faced with an obstruction in their path, and with the awesome weight of the rolling wagon behind them, and sharing, it seemed, only one mind between the two of them, the oxen did not try to stop, but veered sharply toward the low canal railing. At the same moment, the merchants and their animals checked themselves and scattered backward. The top-heavy load on the ox cart shifted, tipping the cart so that the outer wheel lifted up off the ground and the cart was slammed hard against the marble railing. In the confusion of shouts, brays, and bellows that followed, Lu Pei's eyes beheld a most wonderful occurrence.

The massive load under the blanket had slid with the impact and now hung out over the water. A corner of the tarpaulin was coming out from under the ropes that bound it. Sliding slowly out and dropping down into the murky brown canal water below were identical enamel boxes, as wide and high as the length of a man's arm. Lu Pei had not seen anything quite like them before.

The tops were hinged and fastened with locks, and in the center of each top was a narrow slot. Memorizing their size and color and what he could make out of the floral embellishments as the boxes emerged and fell, Lu Pei turned and left his post. The carts, the gang of thugs, the strange boxes. Down below, the lead guard shouted orders as the men tried to right the cart and drive away curious spectators. He did not wait to watch the rest; he had seen something, though he didn't know what. He must find Kao Li-shih.

: :

Kao Li-shih sat at his writing desk, his brush poised over a clean piece of paper. He shut his eyes in concentration, recalling the exact configuration of the key he had seen that afternoon dangling from the belt of the Chancellery chief of internal securities. The old man usually kept the key carefully hidden from sight under a fold of his quilts, but today Kao Li-shih had watched him having a conversation with an officer of the guards. Whenever he wished to make an emphatic point, the old man gesticulated in an imperious manner with his right arm—and peeking out from the folds of his clothing was a large brass key. Kao Li-shih had watched for a long time, waiting for the flash of the key over and over until he had memorized its shape. He touched his brush to the paper and made an outline. Yes, he thought, that is exactly right. He turned the paper so that he could look at his drawing from all angles and check it against his mental picture. He stopped turning the paper and looked hard at what was before him as a smile of recognition spread across his face.

He had wondered that there was only one key dangling from the old man's belt. He knew that there were two doors to unlock to get where he wanted to go; he also knew that no two doors had the same lock. The simple answer to the riddle now lay before him on the paper. He stood up. The imperial foundry could make a key for him from his sketch in one afternoon, with no questions asked.

Kao Li-shih's presence on the Secretariat and Chancellery grounds was not unusual at any hour. But gaining access to the building when the day's business was done and the closely guarded figure of the chief minister had been escorted out was another matter entirely. However, he knew the floor plan of the chief minister's office-fortress, having obtained a drawing from a eunuch employed there, so there would be no fumbling around, no trial and error. With careful, purposeful movement, he could avoid being seen.

He needed to get through the two massive studded doors at the entry to the building. What he was looking for would be found upstairs. When Lu Pei had come to him that day and described the incident of the ox carts, he had thought it interesting, a little strange, perhaps. But he had not attached much importance to it until he heard that one of the iron and porcelain boxes described by the apprentice was now affixed to the wall near the entry to Li Lin-fu's offices. He had reflected then upon Lu Pei's impression of the guards. Thugs, he had said. It all fitted. Chief Minister Li Lin-fu's personal bodyguards and most of the men in his private security contingent were known to be less than gentlemen. He seemed to like to surround himself with men who could no more read or write than a monkey could; Kao Li-shih supposed that their allegiance to Li Lin-fu came from their gratitude at being spared a criminal's life of hard labor, or a criminal's death by execution. They formed an elite corps around him, responsive to his every order and accountable only to him. That the boxes had been escorted by such men and were now appearing in the Chancellery had alarmed Kao Li-shih. This was not the first time he had heard of boxes like these. If his surmise was right, they would soon start appearing everywhere in the offices of government.

The grounds around the Chancellery building were quiet. It was twilight; there was enough light so that he could see without being seen. Removing the newly made key from his sleeve, he inserted it into the thin metal slot on the outer door's armored plate. He twisted it and felt the reassuring submission of the perfectly lined levers in the lock to the teeth of the key, allowing the passage of the key through the immovable bars. There was a metallic clang and the thick iron bolt jumped back into the timbers. He pushed the door open. There was a dark, narrow passage a few feet long, with a second door at the end. He entered, shutting the first door behind him. He stood in the total blackness. Now was the test of his theory of the locks. Approaching the door, he felt for the slot. Taking the key, he turned it upside down from the way he had put it in the first lock, slipped it in, and turned. Smoothly, yieldingly, the lock gave way.

There was nothing that compared with the feeling of solving a problem by perceiving another man's logic. Your penchant for order and mathematical balance has betrayed you, Kao Li-shih thought; the riddle was simple, perfect, balanced, logical, ingenious—and obvious. It was exactly what one should expect of Li Lin-Fu. Held one way, the angular piece of metal mimicked the written character "*shang*," which meant "the first of two volumes." Turned the other way, the key duplicated the opposite of "*shang*," its mirror image and linguistic mate, "*hsia*," "the second of two volumes." Kao Li-shih had recognized the riddle the moment that he completed his drawing of the key from memory and turned it about. Congratulating himself, he pushed the door open and stepped into the hallway. Ahead lay the circular stairwell that led to the chief minister's private sanctuary above.

He stood for a moment to listen. The silence around him was total. He had never actually visited these offices before, but many years ago, when the building was still empty, he had observed the office-fortress's dark, abandoned windows from the top of the Vermilion Phoenix Tower on the other side of the imperial city. It had seemed wild and ghostly then, with tall, twisting, moss-covered pines reaching up its sloping walls. Now that Li Lin-Fu had taken over the huge building and made it his domain, it retained the same atmosphere, on the interior as well.

The stairwell was cold and dark, and the climb tiring. Either it is the weight of my winter robes, he thought, or the lack of sufficient sleep with which I am afflicted lately. He was winded by the time he stepped out onto the chief minister's floor.

When his footsteps ceased, there were no noises but the heavy sound of his own breathing and a slight clicking and scratching from somewhere beyond the inner stairwell walls. Kao Li-shih drew his breath in and held it, startled for a moment by a scurrying sound nearby. But he realized that it was nothing other than the frantic sounds of rats. He recognized the noises that echoed up the chimney shafts, the massive brick *kangs* that brought the coal fire warmth up from below. He released his breath and continued. With the basement now empty, the keepers of the Chancellery furnaces gone for the night, the vermin would lose their shyness and scramble and bicker for the precious warm space around the embers. Rats and men, Kao Li-shih thought, are brothers under the skin. He stopped and listened carefully again. Satisfied that the only sounds were those that carried up from the basement, he continued toward the offices of the chief minister. He paused to light a small candle lantern from a flickering oil lamp at the top of the stairs. With the bobbing of the lantern, a small circle of light stretched and shrank his shadow against the cold bare stone.

Ahead, he could discern the door to the chief minister's offices. To the right of the door was an ornate table on which rested a large rectangular shape. As he drew nearer, he could see the hinges and the lock, then the cloisonné flowers and grasses adorning the surface. He stood over it and moved the candle about. It was just as Lu Pei had described. The designs were rendered in bright purple and turquoise—the colors of the chief minister's office. On the top, in the center, was a narrow slot. Kao Li-shih shook his head with sorrow. It was as he had feared. Over half a century before, boxes just like this had dotted the offices of government. They were the invention of the Emperor's grandmother, the Empress Wu. Through the decorative slots went scraps of bamboo, paper, or silk; on these scraps appeared names. The boxes provided anonymity: Anyone could become an "advisor to the state" simply by dropping into the box a name—a colleague, a rival, an enemy. The presence of a name in one of the boxes was enough to suggest that an individual's ethics or loyalty were questionable. No doubt Li Lin-fu further emulated the Empress with a network of hirelings who at any time could put together "evidences of treason" against anyone. Any official could be deemed "counterproductive" to the state at any time. The inevitable result of this system of arbitrary incrimination would be black-listings, forced confessions, banishments. And like Grandmother Wu's imperial reign of terror fifty years before, the presence of the boxes would insure an atmosphere rife with suspicion and intimidation.

He hefted the small brass lock. It was really only a token lock; he knew that he could pull the hasp out with one solid jerk of his wrist if he wished. He pulled tentatively, then let go. As much as he wished to examine the contents of the box, his innate sense of caution made him desist. If this box is a legacy of Grandmother Wu, he thought, then I shall find that fact out soon enough without letting Master Li Lin-fu know that someone is watching. He held the candle aloft. The workmanship was beautiful. Kao Li-shih appreciated the irony, considering the box's purpose. It would be characteristic of both the Empress and the chief minister to remember not to neglect details. Kao Li-shih thought of the disappearance of the poet-minister. That, he suspected, was just the beginning.

: :

The apprentice eunuch Lu Pei marveled at the strangeness of fate. He, the son of a minor governmental cleric of a distant province, stood alone and unattended in the residential quarters of the Son of Heaven. Kao Li-shih had left him where he was standing and had gone to confer with the Emperor. They were several rooms away from him now, and he could hear their voices, though the words were indistinct.

Carefully, he filled his lungs. This was the Emperor's air he was breathing. He let it out slowly, delicately, as he looked around him. The room he was in was one he had seen from the garden outside. He recalled looking up and seeing this wing of the Emperor's apartments resting high atop slender pillars rising out of the ground which tumbled steeply to the ravine below. From where he had stood, the windows had looked black and opaque; whatever lay behind them as remote and inaccessible as a dream. Now he was behind those windows.

Lu Pei had accompanied Kao Li-shih past the imperial guards and into the Emperor's inner sanctum of the Phoenix waiting chamber in the Hall of a Hundred Flowers. From there they had passed down a long corridor and into the lesser Han-yuan hall throne room, a small chamber set aside for private audiences. It was here that Kao Li-shih had left the young apprentice. The room he stood in was perfect. Light from the open blinds struck the walls and flooded the floor, picking out the rich colors. He had seen beautiful rooms before, but he thought he saw more sensitivity in the placement of objects— stands, vases, day couches, kneeling pads—than he had seen anywhere before. The harmony of color and form made him think of the refinement of the soul that Kao Li-shih had spoken of once when he was discussing the Emperor. Kao Li-shih had been trying to convey to Lu Pei something of the pain of loss such a man might feel. Lu Pei thought of the dead Empress; as he did so, the beauty of the room became fragile, tenuous. He thought that for just a moment he felt a shadow of the Emperor's grief, but the feeling passed as quickly as it had come. His gaze fell on a row of teakwood chairs with backs that had inserts of *bai-yun* marble, the natural markings in the thin slices of stone creating a near perfect sequence of black-and-white snow scenes. As he stared in awe at this cooperative effort between man and nature, he felt something pushing against his leg. He looked down and into the circular amber eyes of the largest cat he had ever seen. Its fur was long and gray, its face flat and impudent. It looked at him for a moment, then rose from its haunches and padded ahead of him through a doorway. He listened. The voices were still far down the hallway, in a room, to the best of his judgment, to the right of a pair of mother-of-pearl and jade inlay screens. It was obvious that he would disturb no one in his wanderings if he kept to the rooms on this side of the screens. As the cat walked away from him, he noticed that clinging to the underside of its tail and the fluffy backs of its legs was what looked like wood shavings and sawdust. The cat flicked its tail grandly, oblivious to the debris. Well, he thought, I cannot go wrong by following a cat, can I? Especially such a creature as this. Kao Li-shih had told him about the Emperor's cats. They were gifts of a peace-keeping emissary sent from the treacherous Tibetan court. The animals had been blessed by priests, so it was said, in mountains farther west and even higher than the sacred roots of Tien Shan. Lu Pei followed the cat into an adjoining room and stared, aghast.

The room that he and the cat entered was in chaos. Rugs had been rolled up and carelessly bunched against the walls. Scrolls lay piled up in heaps here and there; two tall teakwood stands supported neglected, dusty multihued vases with dead flowers drooping in them. Three heavy window quilts hung loosely along the far wall. Tentatively, he approached and lifted one a few inches. Below was a ravine leading to the garden. A brackish carp pond reflected the late morning sunlight; weeds grew stiffly around the statuary. He heard a musical tinkling. Looking around, he saw two more cats just like the first. One lolled on the bare floor; the other, perched on a high ornamental stand, licked and groomed itself. Its collar of hammered brass had tiny decorative bells on it. The tinkling stopped as it looked at him. Like the first cat, these two were also covered with bits and pieces of wood. And, he now noticed, sawdust filled the corners of the room like drifted snow.

The cat on the stand jumped down, landing with a thud. It walked over to him and looked up, its paws kneading in anticipation. He stooped and stroked the big head and tickled under the chin; the cat contorted itself into a posture of ecstasy as it received his touch. Lu Pei shook his head in consternation at the chaos, the sawdust, the furniture hastily shoved aside. What did it mean?

His attention was caught by an irregular mass draped in silk in one corner of the room. He approached it gingerly. He looked around the silent, empty room to make completely certain that no one was watching, then knelt down and lifted the silk. He caught his breath.

He found himself looking down into a miniature world carved in cork, with cliffs, rivers, groves of trees, walls, temples, and tiny bridges complete with minute rails and balustrades. It descended, by hills and ravines, from level to level, complete, contained, perfect. So lifelike was it that he felt if he were to lean too far, he might plunge headlong, shrinking to an appropriate size as he fell in. The scale was such that even the tiniest fly would seem the size of a water buffalo. It was as if he were a *hsien*—an immortal—floating in the clouds, supported by nothing more than the ether around him. The tiny world he looked down on was in the process of emerging alive from an inanimate piece of cork. Small metal carving tools lay nearby. And on the floor all around the unfinished work were curls and shavings of the soft wood, the same as that which he had seen in the cats' fur.

Incredulous, he raised the silk a few more inches. He had heard about men who devoted their lives to maddening precision like this. It was difficult for Lu Pei to put himself in the place of such artists. He thought of monks he'd been told about who wrote whole sutras in the thin brush outlines of a waterfall. He tried to imagine such patience and devotion, to the exclusion of everything else. He could not. He thought of his own fickle, wandering attention, bored and fidgeting after an hour at calligraphy, casting about for some distraction.

What he had stumbled on was, he knew, the hobby of an emperor. Reverentially, he lowered the silk, trying to arrange it just as it was. Imagine, he thought, hands such as mine touching the personal possessions of the Son of Heaven. As he left, he was careful to brush away any footprints he may have put in the dust on the floor. Two of the cats rose to their feet and padded after him as he backed into the room where Kao Li-shih had first left him. He paused. He could hear the murmur of the Emperor's and the chief eunuch's voices. He stood quietly and listened. Now the voice of Kao Li-shih was clearly distinguishable; the other, that of the Emperor, was soft, barely audible. He waited.

: :

Kao Li-shih held his exasperation in check behind a mask of polite attention as the Son of Heaven spoke.

"From what you say, the boxes placed around the Chancellery can only improve the appearance of those offices. I have heard that the halls and rooms there are exceptionally dank, dark, and forbidding. Cloisonné, you said? From what artisan's factory, I wonder."

"I do not think," Kao Li-shih replied, "that Master Li Lin-fu is concerned with the aesthetics of his offices." The Emperor was seated at a table, the embroidered sleeves of his robe carelessly rolled up over his bony forearms. Around him were sheets of paper and pots of ink in different colors; the eunuch noted that the fingernails of the Son of Heaven were black with ink. Crumpled bits of paper lay on the floor around his feet.

"I presume that you see something other than beauty when you look at these boxes," he said to Kao Li-shih. The hand holding the brush was poised over a clean sheet as he spoke; then it moved with speed and precision, the brushstrokes forming large, bold characters. In places, the bristles seemed to barely touch the page. Small spatters and stray droplets accompanying each stroke did not detract in the least.

Kao Li-shih considered for a moment before answering: "I would not mind them at all if they hadn't had their precedent."

The Emperor smiled at this. "So you think Grandmother Wu is looking over the shoulder of Master Li Lin-fu? If I told you what she really used the boxes for, you would find it difficult to see our chief minister emulating her."

He held up a sheet he had just finished, considered it, then tossed it onto a pile. "It was her peculiar pleasure," he continued, "to know who was sleeping with whom. I believe she had designed her boxes to be irresistibly beautiful, the way flowers are to insects. Yes, names went into the boxes. But her interest in those names was mostly prurient. She had quite an appetite, you know."

"I have no doubt," Kao Li-shih replied. "But I think that affairs and liaisons in the court were only a small part of what she learned from the boxes. And I think it will be the same for Li Lin-fu. We are talking about the power of innuendo. It takes away men's initiative to know that someone hiding under cover of anonymity can suggest that one is ambitious, treacherous, incompetent, self-serving, or even just lazy." Kao Li-shih stood well back from the table as the Emperor's brush flew.

"I find it hard to believe," the Emperor answered, "that worthwhile men could be even remotely affected by such a threat. Perhaps only ambitious, treacherous, incompetent, self-serving lazy ones have anything to fear from such a system, and rightly so. I am learning control through letting go of control, do you not think?" he said, holding up a painted character for Kao Li-shih to look at. Indeed, the strokes showed a power and spontaneity that only came with release.

Kao Li-shih rubbed his forehead. "Excellent work, as usual," he said as the Emperor set the paper aside and prepared a fresh one. "But I disagree. Honest men can be intimidated, too. We are not all paragons of courage, as you know. People fear for their families . . ." With these last words, the Emperor's attention seemed to be caught for the first time. He looked up at Kao Li-shih with an expression of genuine surprise on his face.

"Fear for their families?" he said. Kao Li-shih immediately regretted the reference. "What danger does Master Li Lin-fu pose to men's families?" he asked.

"I meant only that he is taking matters into his hands that are . . . perhaps . . . not appropriate to his position," Kao Li-shih said, knowing how weak and insupportable such a statement sounded without evidence behind it. Damn! Your own son, he thought, watching the Emperor's face. I cannot say it! "Think of the presumption," he went on. "The last person to use such a device was the Empress, your grandmother. The mere act of placing the boxes tells me who he thinks he is!"

"Some said of my grandmother that she drank a cup of blood instead of tea in the morning," said the Emperor, bending to his work once more. "Master Li Lin-fu is odd, I'll admit, but I scarcely think he can be compared to my 'dear' grandmother Empress Wu. No doubt he is collecting some sort of statistical information with the boxes. You know how he likes to count things, and arrange numbers, and divine the covert workings of the universe from his equations. His systems are known only to him, but if he finds them a satisfactory metaphor, then so be it. Nonsense! He is my valuable servant." He paused. "I depend on him."

"That is another thing. He is becoming accustomed to taking your place at the morning audience. Your repeated absence is becoming the topic of loose talk. We understand your grief and share it—but all mourning must eventually be put aside." The Emperor looked up from his work and smiled.

"Tell me, does he actually sit on the throne?"

"Of course not," Kao Li-shih answered somewhat irritably. "He speaks from behind the jade screen."

"Then both you and he know that it is only a symbolic act. He understands my philosophy—what I want for the empire," he said with an imploring look. Putting down his brush, he rested his head in both hands and raised his eyes to Kao Li-shih. "I am not ready, Kao Li-shih. I am not ready. I must heal."

Kao Li-shih sighed. "Then at least examine official materials. I will bring them to you myself. You must keep your hand in!"

"I have not been entirely inattentive," the Emperor began.

Kao Li-shih knew what he was going to say and shook his head. "With all due respect, Honorable Master, I do not consider an edict commanding all counties in the empire to establish altars to the 'Sire of the Wind' and the 'Master of the Rain' to be 'legislation.' I respect the proper worship and sacrifice to Heaven and Earth . . . but I consider it ironic that you are encouraging people to indulge in superstitious practices, after—" He cut himself off, but the Emperor supplied the words for him.

". . . After I banished my empress for that very reason," he said quietly. He picked up his brush again and began making long, slow, thoughtful strokes on the paper in front of him. "The concept of yin and yang, Kao Li-shih, transcends superstition. An imbalance occurs first in people's minds and then can manifest itself in the natural world. You know of the flooding and violent windstorms in the eastern provinces. If people feel they are appeasing the forces—"

Kao Li-shih interrupted him. "Tell me. Do you remember who wrote these words in hallowed *vermilion* ink?" He closed his eyes and began to recite from memory: " '. . . Day and night I am in terror, overlooking the abyss. When can I ever cease to meditate earnestly upon the Way and to seek for good government even asleep and in my dreams? I follow men's desires and ever concern myself with the masses of the people. I bend myself to my tasks . . .' " He looked at the Emperor. "You wrote them, Master, in the tenth year of the K'ai Yuan reign period, when you instated an amnesty for men who had run off their land attempting to escape military service. And in the same decree your very words were: 'If the longer there is peace, the more one relaxes, then the defenses of the country will fall into ever greater disorder.' " He spoke the words slowly, enunciating as if to someone slow or deaf. "And then you wrote the Decree of the thirteenth year of the K'ai Yuan. You said, 'I have been late for my meals, dressed before dawn, and never dared to take my ease.' You said, further, that you would not stop until 'the wandering beggars had all returned to work the lands of their families.' And you didn't! You said you were 'deeply distressed and had sent out commissioners to show mercy to the registered families who had run away.' This is the Emperor I remember. A man who *governed,* who knew every minute detail of what concerned his empire." He paused. "This is so unlike you," Kao Li-shih said quietly. "We are here discussing intangibles, while you let control of your government slip from your hands. I am most unhappy," he said, shaking his head.

"The universe is as much intangible as it is tangible," the Emperor said.

"Yes, and it is as much tangible as intangible," Kao Li-shih retorted. "But this is a futile conversation, is it not?"

"Kao Li-shih," said the Emperor patiently, "Li Lin-fu is a good servant. That is all. He is also a distant member of my family. His presence, the work he is doing, has allowed me to rest. You talk to me about the boxes. I am not worried about boxes! The graineries are full; there is peace in this realm! What more would you have? This is the work I must do now," he said, indicating the brushes and papers in front of him. "My painting master, Wu Tao-hsuan, tells me that I am getting near something. He has me practice every day. He told me that when I start to see 'bones' in my work, when my strokes 'live,' that the life-force will be flowing through me again. We spoke of control through relinquishment. The same principle exists in government. What we don't do is as important as what we do. I can afford it, Kao Li-shih."

No, Kao Li-shih thought; you cannot afford it. Looking at the fragile cheer of the man, his paints and brushes around him, symbols of hope, Kao Li-shih knew that he could not tell him what he knew about the strange flowers, the missing poet-minister, the madness of the Consort Wu, and the death of his favorite son. Your trusted servant Li Lin-fu is a murderer, he wanted to say, but I have no proof. To Kao Li-shih, knowing what he knew, the presence of the boxes was insidious; from the Emperor's point of view, they were innocuous, an eccentric's private business. I must sound like a lunatic, he thought with frustration.

"At morning audience tomorrow," he said quietly to the Emperor, "perhaps you could try."

The Emperor responded with a shrug and bent to his work. "Perhaps, Kao Li-shih. Perhaps," he said.

Kao Li-shih waited for a moment, thought of nothing more to say, and took his leave.

: :

Early morning sunlight flamed on the gold tiled rooftops of the imperial city. Kao Li-shih climbed the wide stairs of the Grand Harmony Hall, Lu Pei at his side. The chief eunuch had not slept well; he had spent the night mentally repeating and amending his conversation of the day before with the Emperor. If I made any impression at all on him, Kao Li-shih thought, then he will be here this morning. If he is not here, I have failed miserably. His head ached as he and the apprentice passed the brass-and-gold lions that guarded the raised terrace before the audience hall. Most of the men here this morning are no doubt suffering from some physical complaint, he reflected. That magistrate's teeth are probably bothering him; the stiff joints of the old councillor being helped up the stairs are obviously uppermost in the poor man's mind. Many was the time that Kao Li-shih had stood in the midst of a ceremonial or ritual event and thought of the sore backs, flat feet, piles, and shortness of breath beneath the magnificent robes. His own fatigue and ill humor this morning made him especially conscious of the little afflictions he knew were all around him.

They entered the vast Grand Harmony Hall, already resounding with the thunder of drums and the deep tolling of bronze bells, and took a place toward the rear. Officials had lined up in accordance to their rank. The banners of the offices had been unfurled, and the dragon carpet had been unrolled down past the multiple *jian* of pillars. Kao Li-shih's eyes moved along the carpet's gold, blue, and vermilion length as it traveled along the central nave to the steps of the imperial dais with its phoenix throne.

The throne was empty. Where the Emperor should have sat rested a jade scepter, lying across the armrests. Kao Li-shih muttered a small oath under his breath.

"So," he said softly to Lu Pei. "We are gathered here again to speak to a piece of stone. A stone that miraculously talks back to us. I ask you: What do we need an emperor for at all if we have this wonderful magic rock?" Lu Pei shook his head in consternation. The boy was clearly still awed by the pomp around them. The silk robes of rich embroidered textures and colors —gold, purple, lavender, turquoise, blue, and green—made a dazzling prism in the center of the hall. The golden crane braziers sent up their plumes of scented smoke. But Kao Li-shih had seen too many such ceremonial procedures over twenty years to be much impressed; the smoke irritated his eyes and made his head throb, and the formal rituals seemed tiresome and laborious. Not only that: They obstruct, rather than expedite, good government, he thought bitterly. Especially lately.

Kao Li-shih studied the rows of ministers. He wished that he had been more attentive in recent weeks, had been more observant of the faces. Was anyone missing? If the boxes were any indication, then there should be some disappearances. It was difficult to say, though. Legitimate personnel changes did happen. He would expect a man like Li Lin-fu to work his changes subtly, gradually. He would never appear to be overtly ambitious, would be careful not to appear to be usurping power. Kao Li-shih thought of Chang Chiu-ling's disappearance on that cold morning. There had been, a few days later, a letter of transfer, along with a contrived story about the poet's aging father's decline in Lingnan. The Emperor had accepted it, paid little attention to it. And Kao Li-shih had had to struggle with himself to keep from divulging the whole sorry tale. With Master Li Lin-fu, it seemed as if one could never determine what was happening until it had already happened. Now, looking around him, his imagination ran away with him. There were upper-grade officials, those above the third grade, and members of the royal family, faces completely familiar to him and whose absence he would notice immediately. But the others . . . trying to recall not just one face, but many faces that you never took particular notice of, and in a crowd that changed all the time anyway . . . it was futile. The audience was beginning. He gave up and turned his attention toward the empty Phoenix Throne.

There was nothing unusual about the requests and grievances brought forward by ministers and magistrates this morning. Kao Li-shih listened to the voice answering them from behind the screen. The tone was easy and gracious as it acceded to various bureaucratic requests: minor improvements in the locks along the upper Wei River, aid to a small afflicted village in distant Chiangsu, corvée labor for needed improvements to the Kuanchung granaries, a slight raise in salary for all metropolitan ministers above the seventh grade. You certainly know how to ingratiate yourself, Kao Li-shih thought as the voice droned on.

It was unusually warm that morning, and the sunlight flared hypnotically on the gilded surfaces of the dragon pillars. The beautiful weather, Kao Li-shih thought with annoyance, is also conspiring to impart a sense of well-being to the assembled officials and confidence in these sham proceedings. Bathed in this light, he thought as he observed the colored robes and broad spans of multihued carpet, almost anything would seem right and purposeful. His left temple throbbed gently and he drowsed a bit in the warmth as the voices receded. It would be over soon. This afternoon, he thought, I will pay a visit to the Emperor; if I can distract him for a few moments from his playthings, I will tell him the business that was carried out here this morning.

Presently he saw that the last minister had taken his place and no one else responded to the call to come forth if he had business to put before the throne. In the rustling pause that followed the call, he waited for the dismissal.

Instead, he was brought to attention by the distinctive ring of the audience chimes that always announced the reading of an edict from the throne. The chimes sounded a second and then a third time, for the magic number three, representing the triumvirate of the universe: heaven, earth, and man. To Kao Li-shih, the chimes had an incongruous playful sound. He was wide awake now, and listening. This was the first edict to be read since Li Lin-fu had quietly taken the Emperor's place at morning audience.

It was not the chief minister's voice that they heard next, but that of one of his readers.

Kao Li-shih nudged Lu Pei. "He doesn't know how to read," he whispered. "A little secret I found out about."

The boy gave him an incredulous look, and they both addressed their attention to the edict.

It began with a complex, lengthy introduction not unlike the unmetered lines before the body of a prose poem. The meaning of the words was difficult to follow, but Kao Li-shih gathered that the topic was the problem of barbarian military pressures in the northern provinces. Familiar phrases struck his ear now and again; all at once he recognized the source—they were from the writings of Li-tzu, the fearsome Minister of Iron of the Chin dynasty, whose bloodbath policies had forced China into unity a millennium ago.

Just as suddenly as Kao Li-shih's recognition had come, he lost it for a moment as the words and phrases shifted. Now they were listening to anecdotes from the long-winded histories of the Three Kingdoms. Hidden somewhere in this bulky, meandering treatise, he was sure, would be something of importance. He would not allow his attention to wander through sheer boredom—as his and everyone else's was no doubt meant to do. He would listen to every stultifying word.

Almost imperceptibly, the text of the edict slipped into official language. By now many of the listeners were shuffling impatiently. Those who weren't, including Kao Li-shih, began to exchange looks as the obscure meaning of the words became evident.

Alarmed, Kao Li-shih motioned to the boy to remain where he was, and left his own place to move behind the ranks of officials and make his way toward the front as the reader droned on: ". . . furthermore, the Censorate body of the military affairs investigators is already deeply mired in corruption and inefficiency. The country is experiencing the plight of the man with the severed arm . . . The arm can no longer respond to the mind that wills its movement and the living body travels farther from the unliving arm . . . Whereas the members of the Censorate body can no longer fully comprehend the military events that shift like the wind with such suddenness along the distant northern garrisons . . ."

Kao Li-shih moved silently and discreetly to a position close behind the reader, who continued, unaware of the proximity of the tall eunuch: ". . . in *fu-ping* militia units and among the *hsing-chun* expeditionary army stations, and the *t'un-t'ien* military agricultural colonies, that it is right that we command the vice president of the Ministry of War and the censor in attendance to combine their offices and to utilize the members of the Censorate body of the military affairs investigators . . ." Kao Li-shih was now practically looking over the man's shoulder as he read.

". . . to concentrate on a commission for encouraging agricultural prosperity and self-sufficiency in the northern military colonies; that the formation of such a commission will regain military prowess . . ."

The man finished, and lowered the paper, rolling it up. The audience hall was filled with whispers and rustles. Before the reader could complete the act of rolling the edict, Kao Li-shih's long arm appeared over his shoulder and gently but firmly grasped the document. Taken completely by surprise, the reader turned and looked up into the smooth face of the Emperor's eunuch. Astonished, he opened his mouth to object, but Kao Li-shih spoke first.

"You read very well, my friend. The Emperor wishes to know your name and give you a commendation," he said quietly, pulling the paper from the man's hand. He held the reader's eyes with his own and tucked the document into his sleeve. "The ceremony is not yet over," he told the confused man and directed a look toward the jade screen. "Your master requires further service of you." The reader's head snapped back obediently toward the hidden place where Li Lin-fu sat. In that moment Kao Li-shih took his leave, disappearing behind the ranks of ministers, leaving Li Lin-fu's servant waiting for an imaginary command.

In a few seconds he was at Lu Pei's side and beckoning him to follow. They left the hall before anybody else, and Kao Li-shih, once in the open air, cursed out loud.

"It is too bloody much, Lu Pei. It is not enough that we have lost our balls. Now he wants to take away the last remnants of our effectiveness," he said, hurrying down the steps.

"I am afraid," Lu Pei said, running to keep up with him, "that I understood very little of that."

"You are not alone," Kao Li-shih answered. "I would estimate that fewer than one-tenth of those present this morning comprehended the full import of the 'edict.' Gods! Right under our noses!"

"Begging your pardon, Master Kao; but what does it have to do with us?" The two eunuchs were now walking briskly in the direction of the imperial living quarters.

"The Censorate, Lu Pei. Its job is to oversee the actions of the military, to make sure they obey the legal and ethical standards of the empire, and to investigate policy and expenditure—especially in remote outposts, far from the centers of government. Military men tend to forget that they are part of the empire, Lu Pei, and do whatever they damned well please. They need to be watched. Do you know who most of the censors are?" Lu Pei shook his head. "Eunuchs, my apprentice. Like us. There is a vast army of keen, sharp-eyed eunuchs filling these positions in the northern military outposts."

"But they are not losing their jobs, Master Kao. From what I could gather, their responsibilities will merely increase. Something about a commission to ensure agricultural prosperity . . ."

"Oh, yes," Kao Li-shih replied. "They will be very, very busy indeed. They will be counting sheep and cattle, keeping records of the countless diseases and injuries livestock are heir to, deciding whether Mr. Lo has exceeded his *mou* of land allocated to him and is encroaching on Mr. Chu's land, and listening to the complaints and arguments of farmers and settling their family squabbles." He walked in angry silence. "In effect, service on the Censorate will be reduced to an honorific position. It will be so slow as to be nearly imperceptible. It may take years, but it *will* happen. I can assure you, 'agricultural prosperity' is at the bottom of Li Lin-fu's list of priorities. What he wants," he said to Lu Pei, who hurried along beside him, "is to assume the duties of the Ministry of Defense. It is obvious. And he wants the watchdogs, who might object to some of his actions, out of the way, busy elsewhere. It is dictatorship! And if the Emperor refuses to recognize it, then he will proceed unimpeded. As he has already!"

They turned into a walkway paralleling long, low buildings of endless shuttered rooms. Lu Pei asked no more questions as Kao Li-shih increased his stride and muttered to himself. They passed the Pavilion of the Hundred Flowers and the Tower of Diligent Rule. The residential palace of Ta Ming stretched out around them into ten thousand rooms—the auspicious number of the myriad things of creation.

Lu Pei accompanied Kao Li-shih through the same entryway that they had used yesterday. Kao Li-shih left him with a terse order to wait there, and stalked away toward what Lu Pei now knew were the Emperor's private sleeping quarters. Once again he found himself standing alone in the magnificent Han-yuan throne room. And lolling on a tabletop was one of the huge gray cats, gazing expectantly at him.

Kao Li-shih walked quickly through the Emperor's rooms. He was nowhere about. His painting table sat forlornly empty; passing through the room where he and the Emperor often took morning tea, he sniffed the air. No odor of food; no sign that anyone had sat there recently. He came to the door of the sleeping room. It was shut. Is it possible, Kao Li-shih thought, that he still sleeps? The sun was high in the sky by now; light streamed through the greased-paper panes of the windows.

The old servant who habitually tended to the Emperor's personal needs sat dozing on a pile of cushions outside the door, his head hanging forward.

Kao Li-shih nudged the old man, who woke with a start and scrambled to his feet when he saw Kao Li-shih.

"A thousand pardons," he began obsequiously, "but I was simply taking a small rest . . ." Kao Li-shih waved away whatever else the old man was going to say, and gestured toward the door.

"Is he ill?" he asked.

"No, no, no!" the old man protested. "Never more fit. He is the picture of glowing health, our Immortal Ruler . . ." Kao Li-shih pushed past the man, opening the door to the sleeping room. He paused at the threshold. The room was in complete darkness. The air was stale, with a pungent remnant of scented smoke. The sound of deep, slow breathing came from the direction of the bed. Kao Li-shih moved toward the window, stumbling over pieces of furniture, and found the heavy quilt. He untied the strings that held it in place, and pulled it away.

A shaft of light hit the bed, revealing a motionless form under the covers. Kao Li-shih released a long, slow breath. Here is my emperor, he thought with disgust.

He jerked the silk bed quilt back. The Emperor lay naked, curled up like a baby in the womb, his deep sleep undisturbed. Kao Li-shih shook him harshly by the shoulder. He moaned and curled up more tightly.

"Master!" Kao Li-shih said firmly. The Emperor turned his head in the direction of the voice. The eyes opened halfway, tried to focus, then gave up the effort, rolling back up into the sockets. Kao Li-shih shook harder. "It is time to wake up." He pulled him to a sitting position then, produced the paper from his sleeve, and rattled it in the Emperor's face. "Your 'faithful servant' Li Lin-fu has been busy while you slept," he said. "If you can remember how to read, then I recommend that you address your attention to this!" The eyes came into focus then and looked at Kao Li-shih with recognition.

For a moment, the two men stared intently at one another. Then the Emperor's hand rose and pushed the proferred paper away.

"Go away," the Emperor said. "Let me sleep."

"I will let you sleep all you want . . . after you read this!" Kao Li-shih said, thrusting the paper forward again. The Emperor's face contorted with anger then.

"Go away, Kao Li-shih! What in hell do I pay you for? Leave me alone!" He looked around for a moment; then the eyelids descended, the mouth fell open, and he slumped over onto the pillows. He was sound asleep again. Kao Li-shih shook him. There was no response.

Kao Li-shih gave up. But his attention was caught by a small tray on a table next to the bed platform. There was a silver cup with some sort of sticky residue in it, and a dish of white powder. Kao Li-shih put his finger in the powder and tasted it; it was bitter and chalky. He tasted the sticky substance in the cup: plum wine, with the same bitter aftertaste.

A sleeping potion. He looked at the unconscious Emperor. Is this the same man who used to be dressed before the sun was up, reading sheafs of official documents, planning legislation? He replaced Li Lin-fu's edict in his sleeve and gently pulled the covers back up over the still form. Well, Master, he thought; I hope your dreams are pleasanter than mine.

: :

Lu Pei stepped aside as Kao Li-shih swirled past him. One look at the older eunuch's face told the boy that things had not gone well. He hurried behind his master as they left the chamber and entered the outer hallway. Kao Li-shih turned abruptly and thrust his hand under Lu Pei's nose.

"Do you know what this is?" The tip and nail of the small finger was covered with white powder.

"Ehh!" Lu Pei grimaced. "It's foul . . . musty smelling."

"Extract of thorn apple. If you ever have trouble sleeping, tell me. I will get you some of this."

"I gather," said Lu Pei carefully, "that he did not look at the document."

"No! He is looking only at the insides of his own eyelids at the moment and is not about to look any farther," Kao Li-shih answered, then touched the fingertip to his tongue. "A very strong concentration. It was only the force of my anger that enabled me to rouse him at all. It's obvious that he means to sleep through everything."

Several hours later Kao Li-shih sat, deep in thought, in the harem records office, searching his memory for each and every recollection of the chief minister. In the old days, before Li Lin-fu had ascended to his high office, Kao Li-shih had seen him much more frequently. In fact, thinking about it now, he was not sure he could remember when he had actually laid eyes on him last. It is truly amazing, Kao Li-shih thought. A prince is dead; an emperor's consort has descended into madness; a young minister has vanished as if he had never been born; Grandmother Wu's ghost is resurrected through the damnable boxes, and now, with utter nonchalance, the members of the Censorate have been turned into farmhands. His work is everywhere . . . but my adversary is invisible. He has literally dropped from sight. He travels in covered litters, never by the same route, seemingly. He is a disembodied voice behind a screen, a phantom working his will on the tangible world.

And what of Chang Chiu-ling? His disappearance is, in a way, my own fault. The man was stretching himself way beyond his limits . . . and I had taken it merely for histrionics, or poetic license, or some such balderdash. The day of the funeral, when he spoke to me in the grotto. I recall the first inkling that he had something serious to show me. Why didn't I send him an escort from the Flying Dragon Eunuch Elite? It is odd, Kao Li-shih reflected, how well Chang Chiu-ling was suited for the role he played in this little drama. He was a southerner, an intellectual with no credentials to his name but his high grades on the civil service examinations and some little local fame, like his father, for his improvements to roads in the south around Canton. Years ago, the Chancellery offices, particularly the office of the chief minister, were involved in scandal and infighting . . . and the adversaries were divided along clear lines: the old moneyed and landed aristocracy of Kuanchung, the north and west, versus the young, idealistic literati—bright, but often naive, scholars—from southern families. It was as if it was fated for Chang Chiu-ling to place himself directly in the path of the chief minister—though I doubt that the poor man had any perception of the ancient pattern he was fulfilling. An obscure son of an obscure family; I should have known that he didn't have a chance. He simply didn't have the backing at court to take on such an opponent.

But Li Lin-fu had always been a sly one. Before he was appointed to the chief ministry, several of his colleagues had been caught up in the scandals and infighting and had been degraded. But not Li Lin-fu. If ever he participated, no one ever knew. His method of advancing himself was always quiet and adroit. Every time one looked around, it seemed, he had moved from one high office to another, gradually exerting his influence over critical government bodies. First the Department of Punishment, then the Censorate, and then the Civil Office Ministry of Appointments. The latter move, Kao Li-shih reflected, was perhaps the least noticed and most important. It meant, in some cases, that young literati who had passed their civil service exams and were looking for an appointment had yet another test to pass—the approval of Li Lin-fu. If, for some reason, he didn't like you or your family, your chances for advancement could be seriously hindered. Or if you already had a job but fell from grace somehow, you might find yourself reappointed to some faraway, rustic province. And only rarely did the Emperor review Li Lin-fu's choices, so complete was his trust in him . . . and his reliance on him.

It was true that Li Lin-fu was a fine administrator whose work was invaluable to the Emperor. Whatever he turned his attention to had a way of turning to gold: his economic and social reforms on coinage, land reallocation, the private breeding of war horses, migrant family registration . . . and music. Oh yes, that was a clever move, Kao Li-shih thought, recalling the day several years before when Li Lin-fu had conferred with the Emperor on a mutual project—the reestablishment of the ancient Yueh-fu Music Bureau for the purpose of gathering folk melodies and transcribing the lyrics. It had been Li Lin-fu who had suggested to the Emperor that the music was a way to understand the problems and pleasures of the people. Kao Li-shih could remember the exact words Li Lin-fu had reportedly spoken to the Emperor: "You can learn a great deal by listening to those songs, the way a physician learns by listening to the body's many pulses." Music—one of the Emperor's great loves. Li Lin-fu could not have chosen a better, more thorough way to ingratiate himself.

Charm. The man had actually had it, homely as he was. There was a time when Li Lin-fu used his own considerable musical skills to charm the Emperor and his guests at private dinner parties, playing with the female musicians of the Pear Garden Orchestra. It was as if he was aware of the effect created by his ugly little self among the beautiful young women: a toad among tiger lilies. Kao Li-shih corrected himself: a lizard. And he was never drunk; even at the end of the evening when everyone else was bloated with food and wine, his fingers moved nimbly as a crane over the strings, his prowess unimpaired. And even the drunkest guest, listening with half-closed eyes through his alcoholic haze, could not fail to notice Li Lin-fu's mastery of both registers and the rendering of perfect counterpoint harmonies. Notes struck like water flowing over the rocks, they'd say, often just before passing into unconsciousness and being carried away by their servants. Li Lin-fu would dismiss their compliments, saying that it was nothing, that music was married to mathematics, as if his performance was nothing more than a clever parlor trick.

Which it probably was. Kao Li-shih had heard of Li Lin-fu's theory that there was a mathematical key to everything. What if he has found it?

The thought was profoundly disturbing to Kao Li-shih. Looking at the chief minister's quiet, determined ascension, one could be nearly convinced. Here is a man who is the embodiment of autonomy. Everyone knows that he hated his father, giving him and his grandfather no credit at all for his own advantageous position. Instead, he chooses to thank the auspicious numbers of the date of his birth for his wealth and political fortune. Once, several years before, he demonstrated to his distant cousin, the Emperor, how his birth numbers were divisible by the prime factor of the "magic square," whatever that may be. And though he despises the literati, he has no great love for the old aristocratic families, either. It was well known that he frequently snubbed some of them at court, eschewing their frivolity, their games, their effete pursuits—the squandering of their energies on enormous estates and all-night polo games. Restoring them to power, then, is a matter of expedience to Li Lin-fu—the better of two evils. He is not doing it because he loves them. His own enormous house, Kao Li-shih reflected, is not a luxury—it is a fortress. Obviously, he considers the safety of his person, at any expense, to be necessary for the empire.

Kao Li-shih sat up, startled, as the first clear vision of his adversary came to him: single-minded, to the exclusion of all else, the preservation of the empire his only goal. Personal glory was irrelevant, meaningless to this man.

And he would pursue his end through his own eccentric science, known only to himself, accountable to no one but himself.

Urgency seized him. He thought of the Emperor, unconscious under the pile of quilts, drifting through dreams, paralyzed with grief. *I could shake him until his bones rattle, and it would be as effective as caressing him with fluff from baby birds. I am frightened for him, and for all of us. A murderer has quietly slipped into the Emperor's vacant chair. Oh, it is bad.* Rumors fly about that the Emperor himself is in danger, that there are factions at court that resent his inattention and the growing dictatorship of Li Lin-fu. *And I, it seems, am the only one cognizant of the full extent of the damage and danger . . . except, of course, for poor Chang Chiu-ling, wherever he may be.*

What are the possibilities? Am I capable of opposing Li Lin-fu alone? I think not. The only one who can stop him now is the Emperor himself. He thought, for the thousandth time, of approaching him with the facts of Ying's death. *Murder, Honorable Master. Your favorite son is dead because you happen to be an Emperor.* Kao Li-shih let out a long, resigned breath, and for the thousandth time, rejected the thought. *His grip on life itself is too tenuous. I might lose him altogether.*

He needs new life in him. The sight of my ugly face hovering over him, scolding, berating, or pleading, is not going to be sufficient to wake him up. If anything, it will increase his resistance. Ah, if only the Empress could come back to us. Almost longingly, he thought about her voice, eyes, teeth. He recalled the dry rustle of her exquisite clothing; even her scent. He used to be able to detect it in a room she had just left; he imagined he could smell it now. He knew that he was feeling the Emperor's own desire, conjuring it from the past.

Love. It brings them back from the edge of death, from what I have heard. It makes them whole again. Songs and poetry were rife with testimonials to its healing power. *But the Emperor seems to be beyond its reach; he has no interest at all in any of the harem women—says his "old man" is as limp as a drowned snake. Who, then? What woman is going to come and work this miracle and wake him up before it is too late?* Kao Li-shih was interrupted by Lu Pei quietly opening the door and entering the room. In the moment that his eyes met the apprentice's, inspiration hit.

"Grand Verity," he said aloud.

"Pardon me?" said Lu Pei politely as he shut the door behind him.

"That is her name."

"*Her* name?"

"It has been two years. I had nearly forgotten!" Kao Li-shih leaned forward as the apprentice lifted his eyebrows appreciatively. "Lu Pei, we are going to try to wake the dead."

6

Admonitions

Although Hsuan-tsung coveted Yang Yu-huan, he was undoubtedly aware of the political repercussions which might ensue if he openly took her away from his son. He therefore resorted to the expedient of having her first renounce her marital ties and become a Taoist nun. . . . [It is alleged in the rescript ordaining Yang Yu-huan as a Taoist nun] she was clothed in Taoist robes and given the religious name of T'ai-chen—Grand Verity.

—Howard Levy

. . . humble, submissive, respectful and reverential. . . . A husband is Heaven, and Heaven cannot be disdained. Fullfil your duties with dignity; think before you act. This shall gain you honor and glory, for a husband is Heaven, and Heaven must be honored.

—from The Admonitions of the Instructress to
the Court Ladies, *translated by Daniel Altieri*

It is known and well recognized that ladies prefer gossip, fussing and primping . . . and political intrigues to moral improvement.

—Anonymous Chinese, fifth century,
translated by Daniel Altieri

THE nun Grand Verity looked at her face in a mirror propped on a table. She turned, raising a small hand mirror and positioning it in such a way that she could see her profile in the larger mirror. Turning further, she observed the back of her head. Her hair was done in a sleek knot. She looked for a long time at the arrangement of shining coils, then turned so that her profile came slowly into view again. She stared, transfixed, at the perfection of the line of forehead, nose, and chin. Drawing her lips back, she exposed small, even white teeth and observed how the planes of the lips changed prettily as she did so. She let the lips relax into an expression of solemnity and admired the symmetry of her face from various angles. Tears welled in her eyes. Such a waste.

Her decision was made. She would lose her mind if she continued to wait, without knowing why or for how long. She would run away. Her life would be hard, but she had come to the point where she had to do something to break the alternating cycle of languishing melancholy and burning impatience. She gave a small snort of derision. Both of those emotions, the Instructress warned from yellowed parchment, would erode a woman's desirability just as surely as jealousy, disobedience, or a bad disposition. Today, all of these emotions threatened to consume her.

She had just been told by the abbot that she would probably remain in the nunnery for another year, possibly two. A year! Thinking of it, her heart sank like a stone dropped down an old well and her tears overflowed. She picked up the mirror. Even in the midst of her grief, she could not resist watching the drops run down her perfect cheeks.

She had already been cloistered in the Taoist nunnery for two years, mind and body subject to rigorous training. What was left to learn? The time seemed insurmountable. She was now seventeen years old. She would be an old lady by the time she was released and taken to the palace. And even then, she was not altogether certain what awaited her there. It would not be the first time she had been there; she sustained herself with memories of her one visit. It had been a son of the Emperor who had brought her. It had been part of a strange interlude in her life, an interlude that was still going on to this day.

She had led an unruffled existence until two years ago. Her father had died, and she and her mother and brothers and sisters had gone to live with their uncle, a minor census official in Szechuan. They were neither rich nor poor, but closer to rich than poor. They had lived very well, and Uncle took a lot of pleasure in telling the children their family history, reminding them that the Yangs had been nobility a century ago. She was the fifth eldest of eight children. Her three older sisters and she were a small family unto themselves, close in age and temperament. A favorite childhood game of the sisters had been to act out little dramas adapted from historical and mythological stories. Uncle's influence was plain to see, for they tended to choose stories involving queens and empresses. These great ladies had a variety of fates in the sisters' dramas: Sometimes they wound up as fallen women, locked in ignominious matrimony to a crude, barbaric peasant, half man and half animal, or perhaps a demon from hell. Sometimes they ascended to lofty places in the clouds atop mountains to live forever as immortals with princes and emperors. But always they were different from the common folk: whether they rose or fell, they consistently started as royalty, or at least nobility. The game was played no other way!

Over the years, the sisters became quite used to the idea that they were displaced royalty. And the future, which they talked about all the time when they were younger, was a wonderful land where the Yang sisters occupied their rightful place. Grand Verity was the only one of them who had not been married yet. Her three older sisters had acquired and discarded husbands already; Eldest Sister had been divorced twice. None of the husbands had been quite sufficiently aristocratic—they had been high-grade officials, rich merchants, and minor noblemen. The sisters had a way of gaining their freedom plus wealth and holdings when they tired of these men, who were usually much older than themselves. Grand Verity suspected that the gentlemen were simply worn out and found it easier to capitulate than to oppose the strong-willed sisters. And now the three were residing with relatives in the capital city of Ch'ang-an, husbandless, well-to-do, and waiting . . . for her. Two years before, an event had occurred that the sisters thought would be the key to their lost kingdom.

A son of the Emperor Minghuang, Prince Ying, had come to Szechuan on a military tour of duty. The prince had come with his mentor, the eunuch General Feng, to Uncle's home on some sort of business connected with the census, something to do with conscription and troop quotas. She had been introduced, and the prince's eyes had followed her about the room whenever she was in his presence, causing her to look in a mirror later, trying to see herself through his eyes.

Arrangements had been made. When the military entourage left Szechuan for the capital, she found that she was to accompany them. When her sisters heard the news, they smothered her with kisses and laughed with joy.

One day during the journey, the prince spoke to her for the first time. He asked her questions about herself, and then asked her if she was ready to be a prince's consort. She had smiled and replied that even if he were a commoner, she'd be his. "I am honored," he had replied, "but the prince for whom you are intended is not I. I chose you for my younger brother." Her smile had faded. His younger brother? How much younger? Ying himself was barely fifteen, her own age at the time. "Well," Ying had reflected, "he is eleven now, but becoming a man very fast! In only two or three years he will be one!"

She'd fought to conceal her disappointment while he went on to explain that he had procured her for his brother because the boy was a favorite of his and showed particular promise, and that he, Ying, wanted to play a role in initiating him into manhood. Trying to reassure her, he told her that the boy was at least as handsome as he was and would probably grow to be much taller. She was to be the bride of a little boy. This was far worse than being wedded to an old man. For the rest of the journey she had fretted in secret until, in her mind's eye, her intended had become practically an infant barely able to walk and still peeing in his pants. When she finally met the boy, however, she had been relieved. He was almost as tall as she, and was indeed close to becoming a man. But he had looked at her with a boy's ambivalence. It was obvious that he was of an age when females were possibly of some budding interest to him, but the feeling confused him and he resented it. Given a choice, he would prefer games of war with his brothers and games of the hunt with old Feng. She had felt more than a little absurd; she, a full-grown woman of fifteen, being presented for approval to a barely pubescent boy. But she was also relieved: if he had shown any more interest, she would probably have had to bed him and initiate him into manhood. It would scarcely have been the fulfillment of her secret erotic fantasies, entertained since early adolescence, of her first time with a man—groping with an ignorant boy as inexperienced as herself. She was grateful to be spared.

So she had reconciled herself to marrying the boy Mao after two or three years, and expected to be put in the harem and to live at the palace in the meantime. She was an accomplished musician and a natural dancer, and knew that these were assets. She felt quite at home in the palace. And why shouldn't she? It was altogether fitting for her to be here. Besides, she told herself, the boy *was* comely, and in a few years the difference in their ages would disappear. He would make an attractive husband one day, and marriage to a prince . . . one could only do better by marrying the Emperor himself. She would wait. And her sisters would wait, too.

But things took an unpredictable turn. As was customary, she was to be presented to the prince's father, the Emperor. She had heard much about Minghuang, the man who ruled China. She was not at all afraid to meet him, though the women who prepared her for the meeting seemed to think she should be. It will simply be a case of royalty meeting royalty, she had thought; I may not, strictly speaking, hold a title at the moment, but I *am* a member of the Yang family. Two centuries before, during the Sui dynasty, the Yangs had been mightily influential at court: high officials, advisors to emperors. The first T'ang emperor, Kao-tsu, had benefited from association with the Yangs . . . No, she had no fear. She was eager to see the face of the Son of Heaven.

She had been taken before him in the usual manner—approaching on her knees with her eyes downcast. She had been told not to look directly at his face, but to keep her gaze cast toward the floor. As she approached, the tips of his slippered feet came into view. She raised her eyes just a bit more until she could see his knees and his hand resting on the arm of the chair. It had surprised her how much the hand looked like a working man's hand. It did not have the limp, useless look of hands she had seen on so many men of nobility. At the top of her vision was a blur—his face. She had been unable to resist the impulse. She raised her eyes and looked at the face of the Son of Heaven . . . and found his eyes looking directly into hers. She did not drop her gaze immediately. Girl and emperor had held each other's gaze for about four heartbeats. Neither looked away. She saw, in those moments, a man neither young nor old, but intelligent and tired. And his face was familiar without resembling anyone she knew. She had been surprised by his lack of corpulence. Emperors, she had learned from childhood, habitually clothed themselves in rich, luxurious layers of fat. This man was nearly gaunt. Next to him stood a very tall eunuch with a face like a mask. The Emperor made a barely noticeable gesture with his right hand, causing the eunuch to bend down so that his ear was level with the Emperor's mouth. The eunuch listened for a moment, then straightened and regarded her. She dropped her gaze and backed away politely, still sensing the two men looking at her.

That evening, she had been told that she would not be marrying the prince. She cursed her own brazenness in looking the Emperor in the eye. Obviously, her violation of protocol had cost her the betrothal; no doubt that was what the Emperor and the tall one had discussed when they were looking at her. Why, why, why, she berated herself, can't you ever do as you're told? You have ruined it. Your willfulness and disobedience have ruined it not only for you, but for the entire family. Facing Uncle and Mother would be difficult, but it would be a trifle compared to facing her three sisters, who had dispatched her on her journey with threats against her life should she fail. Having Little Sister installed at court, they knew, was the answer to their fondest hopes, for it would follow as naturally as night follows day that they would be right behind her as she entered the illustrious inner circle. She had recalled the night when she learned that she was to leave the family and join the prince's entourage. She and her sisters had been awake until dawn, hugging themselves with glee, creating fantastic pictures of their new life at the palace. Eldest Sister, recently divorced from husband number two, had assured the others that this was the natural culmination of things. That the Yang sisters should go to court was predestined, she had told them—unavoidable, preordained, as inevitable an occurrence as the fact of a million farmers throughout China rising before dawn to hitch their oxen to plows. Inevitable, perhaps . . . but that did not prevent Eldest Sister from adding that Grand Verity may as well drown herself if she let the opportunity go by. With a heavy heart, she resigned herself to being sent, with forfeiture of the bride-price, back to her family in Szechuan.

But it didn't happen that way. Instead of being taken home, she was taken a few miles from the palace to a Taoist nunnery. The only answer she received to her questions was that she was to be educated there. For what, she was not told. That had been two years ago. For two months she waited. Her quarters were comfortable, and a lady's maid had accompanied her to see to her needs. She spent her days walking in the gardens, napping, playing music, secretly practicing her reading—Father had taught all his daughters to read—and simply waiting. It would be several weeks, she was told, until her sisters could visit her.

She was not too lonely, though. There were many older ladies living at the nunnery who had fascinating stories to tell. Some of them were retired concubines and harem women who had come there to live after leaving the palace, and one lady in particular became her friend. She had spent more than twenty years as a concubine in the harem of Emperor Kao-tsung, Minghuang's grandfather. She had fallen in love, she said, with a certain high official and had asked the Emperor's leave to marry. Permission had been granted, and she had spent several idyllic years with the nobleman. When he died, he no longer had any family to take care of her, so she had come to the nunnery to live out her days in comfort and seclusion.

She had listened very carefully to Grand Verity's story. She made her repeat the part where she was taken before the Emperor, wanting every detail of the encounter. The girl had been alarmed at the way the old lady sat and thought about it. My offense, she told herself, must have been more grave than I thought. Am I to spend my life cloistered here for my offense? I will kill myself, or run away. They will never hold me. But the old lady had given her an admiring look.

"My dear, it is plain to me what happened and why you are here. It is quite simple. The Emperor wants you for himself."

"But I was betrothed to the prince!"

"Not any longer," the old lady had replied. "They told you the marriage was off. By putting you here, your Imperial Father has annulled the betrothal in a graceful manner. After some time has elapsed, you will, I am sure, be taken back to the palace. By then few will remember or care that you were to marry the prince."

"But how long will I wait?" she had asked in alarm.

"Not so very long. A few years, four at the most," was the reply. Not so very long! The girl nearly despaired. It was well and good for an old lady to think of three or four years as "not so very long"; she was nearly seventy, and time was an altogether different thing for her; a year to her was like a month to Grand Verity.

Grand Verity thought about the old lady's words: "He wants you for himself." She had asked her friend to tell her what that meant.

"You may not believe me now, but you will find yourself mostly in the company of women. The Emperor has hundreds of women in his harem here . . . and another harem in Loyang. You will be lucky if you go to his bed more than once or twice a year. You will probably find yourself hungry for love, as I was . . . and the way you hear about it in the *ch'u*—the 'songs.' Those songs are not mere fiction," she had said emphatically. "Many a harem woman finds herself with nothing but time on her hands, and perhaps a yearning for a certain man whom she cannot have because she is a member of the harem. I was lucky," she said reflectively. "The Emperor let me go, to a man I loved, before my looks were entirely gone. If you wish to avoid being lonely, this is my advice: You will either have to be one of his particular favorites or one of the ones he is indifferent to." She looked at the girl. "From what you have told me, it seems that he took a fancy to you," she said thoughtfully, then added quickly, "but that does not necessarily mean any-thing. He may not even remember you when you return. He may have chosen you the way he might, on a whim, pick out a particularly lovely piece of porcelain that caught his eye for a few moments. It is everything in your life, but only a very small event in his."

"The old Emperor let you go," the girl said, "but you knew him, did you not?" She wanted details.

"Yes," the old lady answered, "I knew him and bore a daughter for him. In one sense, I 'knew' the Emperor, but in another sense, I didn't know him at all. It was not until I had left the palace to be with my husband that I found out what it was to really know a man." She looked at the girl. "It was the years with my husband that I choose to remember when I am going to sleep at night . . . not my years in the harem." She looked dreamily out the window then. "It is almost a game. I try to see if I can remember something about my husband that I have not yet recalled . . ."

The old lady's words had thrown the girl into a turmoil. So it was likely that she would return to the palace, and not be held prisoner here, or sent back to her family. Probably she was to be one of the Emperor's women. But it sounded as if she would be swallowed up in the great crowd of females there, just one more of too many. Marrying the child-prince would have been vastly better! And she could expect a life of docility and obedience, and waiting and waiting and waiting . . . First there would be a wait here of several years, while she was "educated," and then she would go on to an entire lifetime of waiting. She asked her friend just what this "education" was going to be. The old lady looked surprised.

"You mean you have not guessed?" She would reveal no more, but told her to be patient.

: :

When her sisters were able to visit her, she fell into their arms and told them what the old lady had said. In Grand Verity's mind, it was all a loss. Instead of being a wife of the prince, she would be a minor harem woman. It was hardly the grand return to royalty that she had pictured for herself and her family. She was bitterly disappointed. But Elder Sister had smiled and taken the girl's chin in her hand.

"It is better than we could have dreamed," she said, her eyes shining.

Grand Verity and the other two sisters looked at one another and then at Elder Sister. She always seemed to know something that the rest of them didn't.

She told them a story. Nine hundred years ago, in the Han dynasty, a slave girl had become an empress, she said, simply by charming the Emperor Liu Ch'e. And not only did the girl become an empress, Sister intoned with significance, but her brother came to court and was made a general. Another family member became the Emperor's chief advisor. Within a few decades, the Empress's family were controlling the empire. It is all in the power of the personality, Sister said. Some women have only their training. Others have the magic gift. Don't be intimidated by the rules, she had said; remember that none of them apply to you. Later, Grand Verity had recalled the old lady's words: "Be one of his favorites," she had said, "or one he is indifferent to."

For another three months she had taken daily music lessons. At first she merely kept rhythm on a set of chimes; then she received instruction on the sixteen-string *chin*. There was no talk during musical practice, so she found herself concentrating on the music in a way she was unaccustomed to. It became speech, and, when she played with the rest of the orchestra, she imagined that she and the other musicians were holding conversations.

One morning she was taken from her room by an old nun and shown to a garden grotto. She was left alone then, with the admonition to wait.

Presently a plump middle-aged man whom she did not recognize entered the grotto. He smiled at her, then sat down on the ornate stone bench. Until now she had seen only other women here. He said nothing, but looked at her in a kindly manner. She returned the look politely, then dropped her gaze, unsure of what was expected of her. Perhaps this was to be a lesson in proper comportment. I will show him that I need no training. While her eyes were downcast in the direction of his lap, he threw back the front of his robe, exposing his portly nakedness. Then he reached for her hand and placed it on his "old man," lying flaccid on his thigh.

Though her instinct was to draw her hand back, she politely let it rest where it was, until he placed his fingers around her own and squeezed. He did it again, then nodded at her. She gave a tentative squeeze without his assistance, and he nodded again, telling her to continue. It was exactly the way it was when a music teacher was happy with her for repeating a lesson properly.

As she squeezed, she felt a return pressure under her hand, as if a small live animal were moving in her palm. She watched as the penis grew larger under her touch. So this was how it happened. She had seen much sexually explicit artwork and the male organs of babies and little boys, but this was the first time she had seen or touched a man's penis. Holding it in her hand, she was astonished at its miraculous growth and hardening. It had nearly doubled in size.

After a minute or two, the man took her hand away, closed his robe, stood, and left the grotto.

That night, she had been unable to sleep. What happened that day, she was sure, was the beginning of her mysterious "education." So her initiation to love was not to be with a virgin boy *or* an emperor, but with a man whose name she didn't know, whose attitude was as impersonal as if he'd been giving her a lesson in calligraphy. She felt her early fantasies about love receding further than ever. Given the choice, she told herself, she'd have taken the inexperienced child over this man. She didn't like his air of too much knowledge while she had so little. Not that she and her sisters hadn't discussed the topic, down to every possible detail. But she knew that only experience really meant anything. She anticipated the "training" with mingled dread and curiosity.

Within a few days she was escorted from her quarters and taken to a luxurious bedchamber, where she was left alone but for a servant who sat wordlessly in an alcove.

She waited for perhaps fifteen minutes. She tried to allay her nervousness by imagining that she was Eldest Sister. What would *she* do in this particular situation? Probably make the man fall madly in love with her and renounce his vows, she thought, as the door opened.

The portly man entered, gave her a pleasant smile of greeting, but still did not speak. He sat on the bed and invited her with a gesture to do the same. Again he opened his robe, and this time he indicated to her that she was to remove her own clothing. She hesitated for a moment; then boldness overtook her as curiosity got the upper hand. She undid her robe, took it off, and put it neatly aside.

He did not touch her, but merely looked at her, his eyes moving slowly over her body. As he was doing so, she was amazed to see his penis grow hard, rising stiffly until its own weightiness caused it to lean to one side. She had not touched it at all. Another lesson.

She never found out his name. Over the next year, she was his student, learning from him every possible sexual act between man and woman, and every method that existed to please a man. Her teacher was a master of control. He had even simulated impotence in order to teach her how to remedy it with grace and artistry.

It was all artistry. He had amazed her with his ability to act a role. One day when he came to her, she was shocked to see his eyes, usually placid and benign, blazing with anger. She had believed it completely and assumed that she was the cause. He had even broken a vase, swatting it from a table with the back of his hand. Then, as suddenly and unexpectedly as it started, it was over. It had been an act. At different times, he had been angry, indifferent, ardent, sad, or distracted. He was very good at it. It was all part of her education—but such a consummate actor was he that she had a difficult time remembering that he was playing a role. She learned to respond appropriately to these moods. Her training emphasized careful concealment of her emotions. The face and body, he taught her, are instruments of expression. At every moment, their wish is to reveal the innermost emotions. Only constant, carefully applied opposition and training will insure that they are not revealed and that proper emotions are shown instead. "Correct your character as with an axe, embellish it as with a chisel," read *The Admonitions of the Instructress to the Court Ladies,* the centuries-old text delineating the art of womanly virtue. She learned to be happy, sad, coy, vexed, or petulant on command.

As her training progressed, she became increasingly cognizant of the paradox of her present life. Docility and obedience were taught at every step. A lady, said the instructress, must be humble, yielding, respectful, and reverential. "Fulfill your duties calmly and respectfully," wrote the instructress, "reflect before you act. This shall win you honor and glory." She thought of her moment in front of the Emperor. She had not been acting or concealing her emotions in any way; she had behaved in a most impudent and unladylike manner by looking him in the eye. But if her friend's interpretation was correct, he was not so utterly repulsed. He desired me, she thought, . . . enough to take me away from his own son.

It had been Eldest Sister who soothed her fears when she was sure that her fate would be to become just another harem woman, anonymous and languishing. "He chose you," she had said, "*because* you looked him in the eye. Remember that, especially when they are filling you up with the instructress's words." All the training, the relentless removal of character "flaws," . . . her sister saw it as merely a stepping stone, the acquired virtues as weapons in a clever woman's arsenal.

What, she asked herself, did she know of men? What do they *really* want a woman to be? The way the instructress puts it, she thought, it is as if danger lurks at every turn where a woman's thoughts and utterances are concerned. It seems that if we are to make ourselves fit companions for men, then we must go to great pains to transform ourselves as completely as a tarantula turning into a songbird; or a rat into a swan; or a frog into a kitten. Looking at femaleness through the eyes of the instructress, she saw the yin and yang principles carried to their utter extremes. Yin was dark; yang was full sunlight, like a summer afternoon. And yin was wet, like a damp, dark cellar, a cave where things grow that thrive on darkness and moisture. Yin was like turning over a stone and watching the wriggling things that flee the light. Those were a woman's thoughts and emotions: mushrooms, cobwebs, mildew, and pale, slimy living things. What were a man's thoughts? She did not know. She did not know what the Emperor was thinking when he looked at her that day. Was he looking into her female mind? Could he see all those dark things? She had her moments when she doubted Eldest Sister's words. Maybe he was looking into my mind, she thought, and what he saw there made him decide to send me here, to be transformed.

She vacillated. Sometimes, thinking of the Emperor and her future, she saw herself like her Eldest Sister—audacious, willful, capable of wrapping the Son of Heaven around her finger, and the *Admonitions* be damned. But there were other moments when she imagined actually coming face to face again with the ruler of China. Was there any reason at all to think that he would even remember her, let alone take particular notice of her? When this frame of mind was upon her, she would weep bitterly. I am merely going to be an addition to his collection, a pretty thing that will increase his wealth a bit. I will sit on a shelf, like the beautiful pieces of artistic bric-a-brac all around Uncle's house. As a little girl she used to occasionally squeeze out actual tears of sorrow for these inanimate objects gathering dust, sitting in their nooks and cabinets. Now I will be like them, she thought. But a vase will last hundreds of years, if no one drops it. Women grow old . . . as I am doing right now.

Time! Gods, how she struggled against the slowness of time and the stultifying pace of life. The image of her face in the mirror blurred as fresh tears filled her eyes. Two years was eternity. They put her away, like a specimen in a menagerie, and expected her to just sit and wait. She threw the mirror down and heard with satisfaction the crack of the ivory handle on the hard wooden floor. How did she know that they would ever let her out at all? No. She would wait no longer.

Her sisters visited her from time to time. Their visits sometimes had the quality of boosting her morale, as if they were afraid she might drown herself or run away when her impatience overwhelmed her. She knew that she would be incapable of doing any damage to her person, simply out of respect for her own beauty. But I am quite capable, she had thought many times while looking at her face in the mirror, of running away.

According to her calculations, her sisters were due to visit in about two weeks' time. When they come next, they will find me gone, she thought. I will do what I must: I will find a rich scholar-nobleman or even a merchant —never mind his status—a man of means who will be able to give me all his attention.

She began to gather her belongings. She would slip out in the early, early morning. She had relatives in the city, and she would get to them. She flung open the lid of a trunk and began pulling out clothing. But she stopped, her hands full. No, that wouldn't do. They'd turn her back. Very well . . . If I must, I will find a madam of an expensive brothel and join. I certainly have the skills now. I should bring the top price. What madam could refuse me, she thought bitterly, with my qualifications? I shall earn my own money. She resumed stuffing a large hamper, throwing in jewelry, shoes, combs, undergarments, and whatever else she could grab. She pulled out an ivory-inlay hairbrush, a gift from her brother. She stopped and looked at it. Idiot, she told herself. What was she thinking? Yang Chien, her very own brother, had a house in the city. He was the eldest, an extremely rich man who was not even slightly interested in participating in the restoration of the Yangs to nobility. He didn't care a fig whether Youngest Sister, Grand Verity, was married to a rug merchant or an emperor. If she were to announce to him that she had plans to marry a pig farmer, he would laugh and give her his blessing. He laughed like a buddha at everything. She had been annoyed with him when she was first on her way to the palace, the way he had shaken his head and given one of those enigmatic little smiles of his, as if he were enjoying some small, private joke that she and the rest of them weren't privy to. He would, she was sure, give her the same smile when she turned up on his doorstep . . . but he would not humiliate her, turn her away, or send her back to her family. Perhaps, she thought, I will simply become a maiden lady in the home of my brother, and all men be damned! She finished packing her two hampers and looked around the room. She'd leave what she couldn't carry. The world is full of pretty things and treasures; I can replace all of it.

When would she actually go? She listened, trying to hear if it was still raining in the courtyard outside her quarters. Water dripped against stone, quietly and persistently. She felt drowsy. She would sleep, and if the rain had stopped when she woke, she would be on her way. She turned her lamp down, wrapped herself in her quilt, and closed her eyes.

The next thing she was aware of was someone gently tugging the quilt and a voice in her ear. It was her handmaiden, whispering urgently and softly.

"The three ladies are here to see you," the woman said. "They wish me to tell you . . ."

"We wish her to tell you that you are a little fool and that we are going to pluck out every hair on your exquisite head!" a voice interrupted. Grand Verity sat up, astonished. Eldest Sister, standing just behind the servant, held disdainfully aloft one of the baskets Grand Verity had packed with her belongings the night before. Behind Eldest were Middle and Younger Sisters. Sunlight streamed through the open windows; the rain was gone. She had overslept.

"And perhaps we shall cut off your nose as well, my darling," Eldest Sister added. "Bald and noseless, you won't dare venture outside."

"But if she is bald and noseless," said Middle Sister, "then the Emperor will, if she is lucky, put her to work mucking out his stables."

"Then we are agreed," said Younger Sister, "we shall not maim her permanently. Her hair will grow back; her nose might not."

The three older sisters of Grand Verity moved into a semicircle in front of the girl's bed as the servant retreated. Grand Verity should have known that Eldest Sister would divine that she was planning something and pay her a surprise visit. The sight of them, resplendent in the morning light, had a way of restoring her equanimity. Her hastily stuffed baskets looked a trifle absurd now, her plans to run to Brother ridiculous. She smiled. The odor of gardenias and jasmine wafted on the air.

"You smell like prostitutes trying to pass as princesses," she said by way of greeting, sitting up and arranging the pillows behind her. Eldest and Middle Sisters sat on the bed, and Younger Sister drew a low footstool up close.

"It is a magic scent we purchased from an old lady," Eldest Sister said, opening one of Grand Verity's baskets to inspect the contents. "She assured us that it smells like flowers only to wealthy men. To poor men it smells like a fish left out too long." She smiled at Grand Verity. "To men of moderate means . . ."

". . . it smells like a bowl of stew!" said Younger Sister.

"And tell me all about the strange rags you are wearing," Grand Verity said.

"Rags!" Middle Sister exclaimed with feigned shock. "She has been locked up so long that she does not recognize high fashion when she sees it." Indeed, there was truth to that. They were positively exotic, the wing shoulders of their gowns rising nearly to their earlobes. And the gowns were unlike anything she had seen before. They were heavily embroidered and had a distinctly foreign look to them, with elaborate sashes and multiple layers. And their hair! It was swept upward and arranged in structures that looked as if engineers, rather than hairdressers, had done the work. Under her arm Middle Sister held the tiniest dog that Grand Verity had ever seen, so small that she did not notice it until it squirmed and protruded its head, with bulging eyes and flattened nose, from Sister's sleeve. It growled at her when she extended her hand.

"Lovely creature," she said. "What is it? A tamed rat?"

"Be careful not to insult me. He is very loyal."

"The rags, as you call them, came to us from Persia. It happens to be what fashionable nomads are wearing, so of course, we wear it too!" said Younger Sister. They all laughed, easily and spontaneously. For Grand Verity, seeing her sisters was truly the proverbial breath of fresh air. Here, in the nunnery, the atmosphere was subdued, quiet, with a preponderance of older women and monks and nuns. Sometimes she went days without any real conversation. And colors, while not exactly drab, were predictable. When her sisters entered a room, they filled it with their fragrance and vivid colors, the musical tinkling of their ornaments and jewelry, their laughing voices and flashing eyes. It was very, very good to be with them again.

Eldest Sister, finished with her inspection of the basket, put it on the floor.

"Our poor baby was packing to run away, wasn't she?" Her tone changed from her earlier one of playful banter. She took Grand Verity's chin in her hand. "Don't think we are not aware of your frustration and impatience," she said kindly. The sympathetic way that she spoke caused the tears to rise in Grand Verity's eyes.

"I am a prisoner," she said. "I am wasting away. I am not even sure why I am here." Her sisters leaned closer to her, surrounding her.

"It seems that way to you now," said Younger Sister. "A time will come when you will be grateful for the time spent here."

"I know you don't believe us, but it's true," said Middle Sister, stroking Grand Verity's hair.

"But what am I *doing* here?" Grand Verity pleaded.

"We know how hard it is to be on the inside, waiting. Time becomes your jailer," said Eldest Sister. "Time has a different meaning for us than it does for you."

Grand Verity studied Eldest Sister's face. It was like admiring her own in a magic mirror that endowed her with certain qualities. The four Yang sisters were acknowledged beauties; youngest and eldest, it was generally agreed, the most so. Eldest's face was like her own, but with a touch of masculinity. Not physically—Eldest's features were small and delicate—but there was something in her face that made it plain that she valued her own opinions, the way men did.

"You have experienced a lapse of faith, obviously," Eldest Sister continued, gesturing toward the basket resting on the floor. "Don't you remember what I told you?"

"Two years," said Grand Verity. "I was told that I could expect to wait two more years. I can't stand it. I can't, I can't, I can't!" she wailed. "I wish I had the courage to kill myself."

Eldest Sister seized both her hands and spoke firmly. "Listen to me. The future that waits for you while you are waiting here is worth ten more years, at least. I promise that!" she said with emphasis. "I myself would wait for twenty years if the Emperor had chosen me."

"And where were you planning to go?" asked Middle Sister.

"What does it matter? I was going to dress as a man and join the army. I was going to be an old hag living in the streets of Ch'ang-an, sleeping under bridges and begging for my food. I was going to be sold into slavery or married off to a barbarian chieftan. What difference would it make?" she said petulantly.

Her sisters exchanged looks.

"I suppose we must tell her, if only to stem the tide of this terrible sarcasm," said Eldest Sister. "It hurts my ears."

"Two months," said Younger Sister.

Two months? Grand Verity had no idea what they were talking about. She looked around at their faces. She should have been more observant. It was plain to her now that they had been holding something back. They looked positively smug now with some secret knowledge.

"All right," she said. "Tell me immediately. Now!"

Eldest Sister pulled her head down with both hands and whispered in her ear. "I have heard a rumor, Little Sister. The waiting is over," she said, giving the girl a tantalizing look.

"Over?" she said, still not comprehending.

"Expect a visit from the Emperor's eunuch, the one called Kao Li-shih."

"The tall one. I remember him clearly," said Grand Verity. "But you couldn't be right. The abbot told me just yesterday that I could expect to wait two more years!"

"She doubts us!" Eldest said to Middle and Younger Sisters. "Very well, let's be on our way," she said, and made as if to rise to her feet. Grand Verity pulled her back down.

"No! I'll listen, I'll listen. But how . . . ?"

"Eldest Sister knows ladies at the palace. Ladies at the palace know the eunuchs . . ." Middle Sister began and shrugged.

Younger Sister leaned forward then. "The Emperor," she said solemnly, "can't get it up."

The sisters dissolved with laughter. Grand Verity looked around quickly. Were they having fun with her?

"Please!" she said. "Stop tormenting me! What is this about?" she demanded.

"You were once afraid that you would be put in the harem and forgotten," said Eldest Sister. "From what I have heard, the Emperor has been showing as much interest in the harem women as his eunuch might."

"Oh, that is wonderful," said Grand Verity. "I'll be taken to the palace and be as useless as a musician playing to the deaf. You have cheered me immensely."

"Do you still not understand?" said Eldest Sister. "In the two years since you have been here, his Empress died, his consort went mad, and his favorite son killed himself. He is a shattered man. He sleeps all day and stays awake all night."

"Better and better," remarked Grand Verity unhappily.

"Don't you see the opportunity? You are not simply going to the palace to get fat while you await your turn with the Son of Heaven. You are being brought there for a purpose. You have been chosen."

The girl gave her sister a dubious look. Eldest Sister caressed her face and held it as if it were a rare work of art.

"You, my dear child, are going to give him the kiss of life. It is that simple," Eldest Sister said with finality, and looked at Grand Verity with raised brows.

"If you run away now," said Middle Sister, "you can be sure that we will come after you with a net and haul you back."

"It is better than we could have planned it ourselves," said Younger Sister.

"Which tells me what has been obvious all along. We are all going to court. It was meant to be. Only the gods could have made a plan like this!" Eldest Sister said exultantly.

Ah, but Eldest Sister was a compelling talker, thought Grand Verity. She could make you believe anything. She felt a wave of excitement now. Was it possible?

"And we will be right there to help you with your task!" said Younger Sister.

"We won't be in the bedchamber with you," said Middle Sister, "unless, of course, you ask us!"

"The Emperor loves to play," said Eldest Sister. "At least, he did in the old days. We know what he likes! Music, sport, games of chance, and beautiful women!" Indeed, Eldest Sister was known for her abilities on horseback. She could ride as well as any man and played a fierce game of polo.

"It is you who should be going to the Emperor," Grand Verity said to her. "You are much more suited."

"No, no, no!" she objected. "Remember? *You* were chosen. I have no intention of interfering with destiny. Besides, we don't necessarily need emperors or even princes! Some noble husbands, with land and titles, will be sufficient." She paused. "Besides, there is a certain somebody who will make a very attractive addition to our little family group at court. And I do so want to see him again," she said coyly.

" 'The Fox'!" Grand Verity cried. Young Yang Kuo-chung, their handsome first cousin; gambler, charmer, entrepreneur. Eldest Sister, they all knew, had had her fling with him a few years ago when he came to Szechuan looking for their branch of the family. Oh, he was delectable, there was no denying it. Grand Verity had been too young for him to take particular notice of her, but she had certainly noticed him. "But where is he?" she asked Eldest Sister.

"From what I gather, he is in the north, doing some horse-trading with the military outposts for his friend the governor of Szechuan. He's getting rich," she said reflectively. "But I think that he is getting tired of hard saddles and sleeping in tents. If I know him, he'll be ripe for some sweet-smelling silks and possibly an appointment from the Emperor. An official position for him could certainly do no harm to us."

"You mean the sweet-smelling silks that lie next to your own sweet-smelling skin, don't you?" said Middle Sister to Eldest. More laughter.

"It doesn't bother you much that you *might* be committing incest with your half-brother, does it?" said Younger Sister.

"If the rumor is true," said Eldest Sister, "that our late father and the mother of the Fox had a little love affair and produced a beautiful boy, then it only explains why he is so perfect for me. I send my thanks to Father, just in case it is true."

"Is she not a brazen hussy?" said Middle Sister.

"A bad woman," agreed Younger Sister.

They made it all sound so easy. Grand Verity knew now that they were right. She could feel it, too. Her time here was almost over.

: :

When they had gone, she tried to imagine her task. She had been taught well, but would it be enough? There would be a lot of formality surrounding her advent at court—little dinners with the Emperor, social functions. But she knew it all came down to one thing: could she make the Son of Heaven's "old man" stand up by itself? For the first time, she was grateful to her tutor, the fat monk. He had left no stone unturned in her "education." Little waves of apprehension rippled in her stomach. But he was somebody else. He was not an emperor.

7

The Mapmaker

Since the dual principles of the universe add up to storm and rain,
A hundred mountain gullies pour down torrential streams.

—*Tu Fu, translated by William Hung*

An Lu-shan this scoundrel . . . of mixed foreign blood had won some
advantages over the barbarians of the Northeast mainly through treachery. . . .

—*William Hung*

AN Lu-shan, commissioner for foot and horse of the P'inglu army, felt an
idea moving in his mind. Light rain spattered the sides of the tent. Before him
on the table was a map. He turned up his oil lamp as the last light faded
outside, and took a long drink of wine. He looked at the brownish squiggle
on the map and thought about the Shira Muren River. For the last fortnight,
rain had fallen on P'inglu, swelling the small streams and rivers in the area of
the camp. The big river in the north, well into Khitan territory, would be
running high and fast now, too. It was a natural barrier between the Chinese
and the Khitan. No one crossed the river except in drier seasons, and even
then it had to be done with care. On the other side of the river, he knew, the
Khitan felt safe. No Chinese would dare to cross for many more months.

He took another long pull of his wine. He thought about the Khitan
camps and villages. He pictured people going about their business, relaxed,
their guard down, hunting falcons resting on arms where bows should be. He
imagined the ragged children playing their games, the greasy smoke rising
from the fires, women gossiping or singing as they worked, men tending the

horses and getting drunk. Then, with equal clarity, he pictured the relaxed, happy faces going white with terror. He saw panic and pandemonium as the people scattered. A few brave ones would make a stand, but they would fall easily. He could feel, just as if it were happening, the twang of his bowstring as he released it, heard the arrow enter human flesh. The hooves of the horse underneath him pounding the earth . . . It was he, An Lu-shan, riding. The Khitan fell away before him. He watched face after face as surprise turned to shock and then terror as the unexpected visitor and his army swept down upon them. He opened his eyes and took another drink. He fairly ached to get at them. He wanted to see it and feel it just as he had imagined it.

He saw other things, too. He imagined a big room, richly appointed, with a huge table in it. The room was in a great building, rising up out of the center of a city. The city was the capital Ch'ang-an as he saw it in his carefully cultivated fantasies: countless thousands of people in beautiful clothes, rooftops glinting gold in the sun as far as the eye could see. In his imagined room, men with clean hands and hair and silk robes clucked and shook their heads in amazement. The name on their lips was that of An Lu-shan, the famous barbarian general from the north. There was nothing, it seemed, that he couldn't do. He was accomplishing the impossible, they said, as they sipped tea from dainty cups. How does he do it? they asked one another. Does he fly? Can he walk through stone? The Hsi and the Khitan will be pushed off the edge of the earth soon, if he continues what he is doing. How fortunate we are that he is on our side! said one to another. He is saving the empire! We must bring him here; we must honor him. What are his favorite foods? Their talk stopped abruptly as a door opened. They all turned their heads.

An enormous man with full black beard and a luxurious suit of ornamental armor entered the room. Their faces registered apprehension, unsureness, then relaxed again as he smiled benevolently at the officials. I am An Lu-shan, he said. I have come.

Outside, the wind picked up, throwing gusts of rain against the hides of the tent. An Lu-shan filled his mouth with the sweet wine, held it in his cheeks for a moment, then let it slide down his throat all at once. He shifted in his seat and smelled the redolence of his own body. He pulled toward himself a bowl of greasy stew, now gone cold, and took a large mouthful, washing it down with more wine. He thought about his career so far. Li Shih-chih, now the military governor of P'inglu, was pleased with his protégé and had told him so by promoting him again . . . from the rank of mere general to his present status. An Lu-shan had gained recognition as an able leader and clever strategist, had led several successful small campaigns, and had the respect of his men. An Lu-shan was happy with all of this . . . but he was far from satisfied. He looked at the remains of his stew. It was well and good to be recognized here in this desolate territory, to be held in awe by soldiers and farmers. But he knew from experience that if one wanted to be noticed in high places, one must practically defy the laws of nature. One must do something daring, impossible, audacious; and bring back booty, or victory . . . or both.

He thought again about the Shira Muren River. There *is* a way across. On the map in front of him were marks made by the official cartographer. The marks showed the nearest crossing point that would be accessible when the waters had gone down at the end of the rainy season. The problem now, of course, was the deep, swift current. Strong horses might be able to make headway against the current, but men—the infantry—would not. However, he was thinking about something he had seen once, as a boy: A small caravan he'd been riding with had come to a river, swollen by heavy rains. The boy An Lu-Shan had watched with fascination as one of the men, an unusually skillful rider, had taken a heavy rope and tied it to a tree. Taking the rope on his shoulder, he then urged his horse into the water, forcing the animal across the river. On the other side, he secured the rope firmly to another tree. He had created a hand bridge. Those men on foot had been able to pull themselves across, while the horses with their riders swam across just inside the rope, forming a barrier between the men and the swift current. It had worked. An Lu-shan had no trouble envisioning the same process on a larger scale: a wider river, more ropes, more men and horses—many hundreds more, a thousand, two thousand—and a surprise attack. He pushed the cold stew away from him and studied the map. The crossing point marked by the cartographer was a good one, no doubt. But it was many miles up the river, and the army, once across, would have to backtrack for several days in order to align themselves with the Khitan encampments he wanted to take. He took another long drink of wine, and thought.

His mind drifted back to the big capital city in the south. News travels fast, almost with the speed of thought. They would hear about the stunning victory within days, he knew. And you realize, do you not, he asked himself, that bad news travels even faster. If you fail, they will find out about it before you have time to take your next breath. The Chinese were known for their swift, exacting retribution. How would you like to be a common foot soldier, An Lu-shan? he asked himself. Or a slave again? Or—he laid a loving, protective hand over his groin—the unthinkable: a eunuch. There was, he thought as he addressed himself to the map, no room for failure.

: :

The high cliff walls reflected the light of the rising moon. Below, the raging muddy river was obscured by almost total blackness. Guided by its roar, An

Lu-shan's forward party stepped out onto a promontory of wet grassy earth. Small trees and bushes caught in the floods brushed and snagged along the rocks as the water rushed over the banks. The moonlight revealed a narrow cleft in the cliffs of the opposite shore. The fissure would allow them passage through the river canyon on the other side—passage without another two days' journey upriver on this side, then two days downriver on the other. At the spot indicated on the map by the cartographer, the river flattened, its temper not yet fired by the streams that gorged it downriver. But in reaching that point and circling back, many days would be wasted. The more time spent traveling, the greater the risk of being seen by sentinels. Only complete surprise would do.

Their shouts were barely audible above the sounds of the swollen Shira Muren. An Lu-shan's soft leather boots were soaked as he walked along the muddy shore accompanied by his eunuch and his eldest son. They stood on either side of him now as his lieutenants and lieutenants major brought up the first contingent of P'inglu's infantry. Behind them, nearly two thousand men—foot soldiers and horsemen—waited for the signal to descend to the shore. The rising moon, now just above the narrow cleft in the rocky cliffs opposite, cast a band of light revealing the flooding river's rounded swells, solid and gray in the half-light. Trees, brush, and sod bobbed in and out of the slender line of light, like phantom tangles of bones, flesh, and hair. An Lu-shan studied the river, judging the distance to the opposite shore. Several officers came and stood nearby. They exchanged looks in the moonlight, then turned their eyes back to the raging river.

"Master An." The elder lieutenant was the first to speak, shouting above the noise of the water. He was a thick man with tight, close eyes and sinking jowls, a man An Lu-shan could trust—A Pu-ssu, a Juchen cavalry officer from the distant north. He was a tribal chieftain who had won prestige in small preemptory expeditions for the Chinese. He had fought for the T'ang against the Muslims out beyond Tunhuang; and now Li Shih-chih had appointed him to serve under An Lu-shan. ". . . then you are certain about the crossing place, General An?" he shouted. "This is where the cartographer's office has placed it? Then he means to put us in a watery grave, does he not, General?" A Pu-ssu gestured toward the dark water. The ribbing of his lacquered leather helmet shone like a beetle's back in the light of the rising moon. The other officers stood, silently supporting him in his confrontation. For a long while An Lu-shan said nothing.

"This is where the cartographer has, himself, placed our point of crossing, A Pu-ssu. Do we question the orders of the military governor's office? His maps are correct. There is nothing for ten li either west or east with such access through the cliffs. Tell me, Lieutenant, have your cavalry officers seen a better place that I did not see?" An Lu-shan turned and glared at his silent officers. They dared not speak. "Are there any among you, my officers, who have seen such a place and not told me? You are free to now." He waited.

His officers turned toward each other or stood with closed mouths..

"Speak!" he commanded. "Speak!" he roared again; and then he pointed. "Do you see how perfectly the dragon's back is cracked?" he asked, gesturing to the high fissure in the mountain and opening his palm as if offering it to them like a string of fat ponies. "That passage in the stone across the river will save us several days. The Khitan will be surprised; every damnable one of them will piss on his foot. And all we must do is cross to it—forge a little water that lies between us and those cliffs. That is all!"

An Lu-shan could see A Pu-ssu's pronounced neck muscles tighten in anxious response. The officer said nothing for a while as he looked at the river. Then he spoke.

"No one should cross until the rains have passed," he said tersely.

"Look up in the sky, Lieutenant! Tell me what you are looking at! Eh? Are you looking at rain? Do you feel any rain on your hands or face or have you been too long in the damned desert with the Arabs and Jews to know what it is? I say the rain *is* over." An Lu-shan looked past A Pu-ssu to the others, challenging them to contradict him. "Do you agree?"

The others kept silent. But as he turned and left them, he heard them speaking among themselves. He sensed their treachery and rebelliousness. He would not have it! He retraced his steps until he stood near them again. Their talk ceased.

"Eunuch . . . Master Li!" he shouted toward the figure slightly behind him and to his left. "What words do you have for this crossing place?" An Lu-shan waited for his eunuch, Li Chu-erh, to respond.

"Very few, Master An . . ." The young eunuch's tone was clearly reserved. That always irritated An Lu-shan.

"Few? Few?" he mocked. "So you have few words. That is unusual." He looked to the officers. He made games of testing the eunuch. Li Chu-erh never broke, and though at times that annoyed him, he thought it an admirable trait.

The eunuch lowered his head as if pondering the question deeply, then spoke. "Perhaps only . . . one, Master," he said.

" 'Only one, Master,' " An Lu-shan taunted Li Chu-erh and turned toward the officers, smiling from one to another of them. "And what is this single, great pronouncement of yours, Master Li Chu-erh?" He took a special pleasure in the slow, mocking recitation of the eunuch's name. "I am certain we shall all be interested in hearing your expert military counsel," he added.

"If I am free to give it . . ." the servant responded.

"You are. In fact, Eunuch, I command you to do so."

The others stirred.

"Then I have little choice. In your words, I am commanded . . . to tell you . . ." Li Chu-erh did not look around but looked only at the general. He paused, then finished, "that the word is . . . insane, Master An."

"And that is your pronouncement . . . a military pronouncement from my 'tailless' commandant," the general scoffed.

Undaunted, the eunuch continued: "You will throw away the lives of many of your soldiers . . . They won't live to see battle. If common sense and military judgment are one and the same, General An, then that is my—"

Before Li Chu-erh had completed his sentence, An Lu-shan brought the broad side of his sword down on the eunuch's left shoulder with violent speed. The resilient metal resounded with a sharp crack as the force of the blow unbalanced An Lu-shan. He stumbled back as the eunuch dropped to his knees in the wet grass.

"And that is my judgment . . . Servant!"

Caught by surprise, the officers said nothing, but backed slowly off the small spit of land. An Lu-shan stood, sword in hand, over the eunuch. They know better than to get in my way, he thought, and raised the sword again to deliver another blow.

"Father . . . Father . . . !" his elder son cried, grabbing An Lu-shan's free arm. "Don't hit him!" An Lu-shan easily broke the grip of the wiry fourteen-year-old and pushed him down on top of the eunuch, who was trying to scramble to his feet. An Lu-shan cast a sharp glance toward the officers, a clear warning not to interfere. They drew back.

"Father, don't hurt me. Please don't hurt me!"

The son raised an arm to ward off his father's sword. The eunuch struggled to his knees, his clothing tangled in the brush. The sight of the two cringing figures fired An Lu-shan's wrath.

"You give me no choice! You have made a dangerous and treasonous example of yourself! It is most unfilial behavior!" he shouted, raising the heavy sword high again. As it came down, a sudden turn of his wrist brought the flat side of the weapon's cold metal hard against the child's outer arm.

An Ching-hsu did not scream or cry, but whimpered and covered his head with his arms defensively. An Lu-shan studied with disdain the huddled figure of his son in the moonlight.

"You have shown disrespect for your father!" An Lu-shan huffed, bending to gather a handful of the boy's jacket in his meaty fist and pulling him toward him. "And that is not an example to be made before my officers! I tell Li Shih-chih that I take you with me to teach you military propriety. Should I tell him a lie?" he said, giving the boy a shake.

The child said nothing, but merely stared back at his father.

"Then . . . should I tell him a lie?" An Lu-shan repeated, raising his free hand as if about to strike him on the cheek. "I will not tolerate insubordination!" With that, he flung the boy back down on the ground. "Do I need to strike you again and again until you understand? I do not enjoy beating you, but you give me no choice!" He knelt then and took a handful of An Ching-hsu's hair, pulling the head up so that the boy was forced to look at his father. Even in the dim light, the expression of sullen hatred was plain to see. An Lu-shan felt the rage boiling up inside him again—rage at anyone, anything that would dare to defy him, hold him back. Slowly, cruelly, he started to pull the boy to his feet by the hair.

"Master An . . . leave him." It was A Pu-ssu, speaking from just behind him.

The sound of his lieutenant's voice cleared An Lu-shan's head. He remembered the vast army of men and horses standing behind him, waiting for his command. For a moment, he stood quietly, still holding the boy up by the hair. Then he let go, pushing him away in disgust. An Ching-hsu scrambled toward the eunuch, who pulled him to a safe distance from An Lu-shan. An Lu-shan walked back toward the officers.

He would not discuss it further. This was where the troops would cross. The river was swollen everywhere, and to go farther up to the actual crossing point marked by the cartographer would destroy their advantage of time and surprise. An Lu-shan knew that this loss of time would prove a greater risk than mere water. An Lu-shan had crossed the river here before. He would lose a few men to the extreme cold, but that was all. He had already weighed the possible losses against the advantage he would gain.

Only two sets of eyes other than his own had seen the officially marked map—those of his eunuch and the boy An Ching-hsu. The fool without balls had come dangerously close to revealing An Lu-shan's private decision to change the crossing point. But An Lu-shan was satisfied that he would keep his mouth shut now that he had been given a taste of how his master would deal with treachery; and the same went for the whimpering boy. Let either of them dare!

An Lu-shan gave the signal to begin the difficult crossing. There were no more protests. The eunuch and the boy stood resignedly to the side. The grassy slopes of the river bank, now lit to silver by the rising moon, burst into life and activity. And the moon held no threat, if not ringed with rainbows. Only the black toad and the hare could witness the place of his crossing from their pearly perches on the moon . . . and they wouldn't talk. An Lu-shan enjoyed the thought of this silent witness. He returned his gaze to the horses and men that now filled the spaces along the banks.

He knew that neither his enemy nor his superiors—the commandant Li

Shih-chih and the military governor Chang Shou-kuei—would expect the daring speed of his premature crossing. And now they were blessed by such perfect light.

An Lu-shan turned to the river, and his officers joined him. He knew that the soldiers must be kept in constant motion—they must be busied before fear had a chance with them.

Orders were shouted as horses and men were organized. The commotion vied with the roar of the river. Great bags of coiled rope were brought forward and laid on the banks where An Lu-shan ordered. He inspected them in the dim light. On top of the piles, jagged metal spikes, hooks, and fastening links gleamed. He would need four of his strongest horses and best riders.

He chose—as he always chose for the most difficult tasks—quickly. With his tightly closed fist carried aloft on a slightly crooked arm, he pointed at four men as he went down a line of about twenty of his best. The chosen ones came forward without hesitation, knowing that the task ahead would not be as bad as incurring the wrath of the Sogdian general. Obedient soldiers, moving to carry out commands almost as quickly as he could think them . . . that was the military machine as it should be.

While he saw to the task of tying the loose ends of four heavy coils of rope to as many stout trees, the four honored soldiers led their horses to the grassy promontory in front of the anchor trees. One of the men began to remove his weighty lacquered leather armor.

"Leave it on, Lieutenant." An Lu-shan's voice halted him in midaction. "Leave it on." An Lu-shan imagined that he saw, in the moonlight, a brief flash of fire from the man's eyes. He ignored it; he would make the brave officer an example for the others. An Lu-shan shouted to him: "If you sink with your armor on, then so shall we all sink! But at least we will be forewarned of our fates!"

There was only the briefest of pauses as the man took in the words, then shrugged the breastplate back into place. An Lu-shan saw the men exchange looks among themselves, though the light was too dim for him to read their expressions. They mounted their uneasy horses, each man carrying a coil of rope with him and hooking the cruel metal spikes to his belt.

With the river roaring and the horses stepping about nervously, An Lu-shan spoke to the mounted men.

"You know what you must do," he shouted. "You will get across if you don't allow a thought into your minds. Give yourselves up to your horses! They know how to do it!" And giving them no further time to think about it, he brought his hand down hard on the rump of the first horse. "Go!" he shouted.

The horsemen squeezed their knees and jabbed their heels against the animals' well-muscled flanks; the horses wheeled and turned, jostling their riders together, stubbornly refusing the prospect of the noisy river. An Lu-shan pulled out his leather riding whip and flailed the horses from behind, urging them forward with shouts and blows. The lead rider pulled his right rein, yanking the animal's head hard against his thigh. The horse's protests were futile as the soldier kicked his heels hard against the horse's haunches. With nowhere else to go, the horse stumbled forward into the water. One by one the others followed, driving their horses into the river. Splashing, snorting, and whinnying, the animals heaved themselves in frightened arches through the waves that rolled over their hindquarters. The riders screamed and cursed, their free hands lashing cruel leather thongs violently across the horses' necks and jaws. The beasts lunged in a desperate struggle to escape their tormentors, thrashing and bobbing toward the center of the river.

At the top of his voice, An Lu-shan shouted at the riders, though he knew they would not hear him: "Move, you fools! Move forward!" He could see that the water was running very, very swiftly in the center; he began to fear that all four of the horses would lose their footing in the deep swells, the water filling their nostrils and mouths. Then a shout went up from the men gathered on the riverbank straining their eyes in the dim light. Two horses had spun about in the current. The animals now faced upstream, their riders receiving the full brutality of the water. Then one of the horses began to spin round and round, completely out of control; a soldier, somersaulting from the animal's back, was caught in the flailing legs of his mount.

"He is lost!" cried A Pu-ssu.

"There he is!" another officer shouted as they saw the rider's drowned body bob to the surface downstream and catch in a tangled mass of foaming roots and brush, a flash of wet lacquered leather and gleaming metallic escutcheon—it was the lieutenant who had started to remove his armor before entering the raging water. An Lu-shan heard his own words again: we will be forewarned of our fates.

The man was gone. A reasonable price to pay to anchor the lines. And now the ones still left beat their horses in a mad frenzy. The riderless horse was the first to escape the river, moving back toward the bank it had started from and flinging itself out on its knees. It stood then, not moving, head hanging with exhaustion.

An Lu-shan and his officers could not see the progress of the three others as they moved beyond the center of the river and into the darkness, and soon the water drowned out their cries. He could only wait. The crowd of men gathered on the bank became very quiet, straining their ears for a sound. For a long time they heard only the voice of the river as their eyes and ears vainly tried to discern a sign.

Then one of the great ropes moved like a heavy serpent stirring, and, miraculously, it stretched taut and hung dripping just above the water. His men cheered. One, at least, had made it across. Soon the two remaining ropes were stretched, too. He ordered a group of ten men to pull on the ropes with all their strength, to test them. They held. They pulled in the one loose rope which trailed downstream in the current; An Lu-shan bade a silent farewell to his lieutenant from whose hands the rope had been pulled by the angry river. This was it. He gave the order to cross.

Confused lines of men, horses, and supplies wound toward the banks. Snaking rivers of foot soldiers, barely visible now as the moon sank behind a thick patch of clouds, moved and halted erratically as An Lu-shan stood by, his officers shouting orders. The first full line of mounted soldiers lashed their horses into the water just upstream of the outer rope line. They were to take the full weight of the current pushing them against the rope. The foot soldiers would pass within the lines of rope in two or three columns, taking what they could of stores and weapons tied onto their shoulders and shielded from the river's full force by the tight line of horses next to them. This was his plan. They would vanquish the water; it would not be the other way around. The enemy, the Khitan, never let water stop them. They always moved across it almost magically, putting raging rivers behind them, frustrating the advances of the Chinese border patrols. He would show them now that An Lu-shan could do the same. The first column of men walked toward the river.

Half the men were across now, minus some casualties. The men on the bank had relaxed somewhat, now that they saw that it was not impossible. He even heard some wry jokes here and there as the third wave of men was preparing itself; An Lu-shan himself would be leading it. Behind him stood the long line of foot soldiers ready to do as he told them. Hefting his bundle onto his back, he gave them the signal to follow, and waded into the water. It swirled, icy and swift, around his legs. It was the runoff from mountain snows, and the rushing weight of it pushed hard against him, a mindless force that could drag him down and kill him indifferently. It smelled of mud and cold and fear and death; as it penetrated his armor and clothing at chest level, the image of his fallen lieutenant bobbed to the surface of his mind; rolling, turning, submerging, rising, a dead thing that had lost its power to resist the water's will.

Grabbing hold of the rope, he pulled deeper into the stream. Without this lifeline, the river would easily have swept him away. An Lu-shan pulled hand over hand, the rough fiber tearing at the flesh of his palms. The water foamed around his neck and chin now; he could feel the river bottom beneath his toes. It was deeper than he had anticipated. It could not get any deeper; this was their limit. He could hear the others behind him, their shouts and cries carrying over the water's din. We are just voices and heads now, he thought, fighting our way through this death water in the dark. There must be a part of Hell that is just like this.

These are brave men who would follow me into this river, he thought. He shouted above the water for their benefit.

"It is nothing . . . nothing at all . . . All the fine ladies of the cities bathe in rivers like this! They do not smell of rancid fat like your women! They do not smell like goats! Now you . . ." He stopped as his mouth filled with water and he spat it out. "Now you can have the fine women for yourselves but for the price of some fine pea soap!"

"Then I hope they are waiting for us on the other side, General!" came an answering shout just behind him.

An Lu-shan pulled himself along the rope with all his strength; to his right the horses also struggled, their strength barely adequate. He could see the panicked flashes of wet, dappled hides. He felt his aching hands slipping as the water in the center of the river pushed against the side of his face with full force, pulling his helmet from his head. As the helmet filled with water and dragged against the current, the band tightened around his neck. He felt a surge of panic now; he could not take even one hand from the line to free himself of the choking leather strap. He fought to keep mouth and nose above the cold black water. In the next moment An Lu-shan was struck a hard blow to the head by a heavy, flailing leg as a man tumbled over him, ripping his ear and breaking the leather strap from around his neck with excruciating swiftness. The choking was gone; so was the man who had freed him, his body disappearing in the dark river.

He could see the opposite bank now, the moon shining on wet rocks, the bedraggled men and horses assembling on the shore. He and the men he led were nearly halfway across. So far An Lu-shan had counted nineteen men lost to the water, and three horses. Acceptable losses, he thought.

The bodies were swept downstream to become tangled in branches, snagged on sharp rocks. Better to cull the weak ones now. Only the best, the strongest, will get across the river. With me. An unexpectedly violent wave of water washed over his head then, filling his mouth, eyes, and nostrils. Gasping for breath, he turned to look behind, to see if those near him were still breathing. There was enough moonlight to see the eyes of the man behind him—wide with fear. He turned to see what it was that the man was looking at.

It was impossible.

They were rushing headlong toward a large island in the center of the river. It couldn't be! Yet his perceptions told him that they were moving upstream at a high rate of speed. All at once, he understood. The island was coming toward them, looming thick and black, ragged patches of moonlight showing through the broken pattern of branches. A massive pile of broken trees and earth bore down on them, torn loose from the flooded banks upriver. An Lu-shan could not judge its exact size, but it looked as if a mountain were filling the river gorge, blocking out everything. Around him, the fearful shouts and screams of the men were faint against the renewed roar of water as the moving island created a high, dangerous new current. It was making its progress down the river in lurches: moving, stopping, moving again.

Barely keeping his head above the water, he struggled to see. The infernal thing was not moving now. It had lodged itself and hung upstream from them by fifty feet or so. He hung on to the rope with all his strength, the fibers digging deeply into his hands. He screamed at the men behind him to keep moving forward, to get out of the way before the thing decided to move again. To his right, riders lashed their panicked horses. High screams pierced the deafening noise. It had moved! The mass slipped from its tenuous moorings and bore down on the line of helpless men and horses. It moved diagonally for a short distance, then came to a halt again. Hand over hand, he pulled himself hard through the water. Either I will die here in this river, he thought, and never see Ch'ang-an, or I will get my carcass to the other side. There was no time to even look behind him. Soon his shoulders were above the water, then his chest, then his waist. He stumbled, slipping on a smooth rock, regained his footing, slipped again, and finally dragged himself out of the water on his knees. It was not until he tried to stand and found his legs quaking violently from the cold and exertion that he realized the extent of the drain on his strength. He crawled onto a flat rock. Horses and riders were emerging too, the animals slipping and stumbling, their hooves clattering on the rocks. Several men emerged right behind him and lay gasping on the ground. But there were no more. And the horses coming out of the river, eyes white with fear and their long manes plastered to the bulging sinews of their necks, were riderless.

"Where are the rest?" he shouted at the men.

The nearest one, a boy of about eighteen, replied in ragged sobs: "They have gone back. They have turned around."

"Gone back!" he said incredulously. "That is the worst thing they could do!" He stood then and shouted out into the darkness and noise. "You are ordered to come this way! There is no turning back! Do you hear me? You will all be executed! Every one of you!" He waited. There was, of course, no reply.

"They cannot hear you, General," said a voice near him. They are trying to save themselves." He turned. It was A Pu-ssu, soaked and exhausted.

"They *will* hear me!" He turned back to the river and shouted again, so loud that the sound of his own voice filled his head and rattled his ears.

"Save your strength, General! See to your men here!" said A Pu-ssu, seizing An Lu-shan's arm. An Lu-shan shook off the restraining hand and peered out over the water. He could just make out, now less than fifty feet from where the first rope was stretched, the outline of the monstrous clump of debris where it hung.

With a bilious surge of stomach and heart, An Lu-shan saw it move then, beginning to turn in a stately manner before lurching, rocking as it picked up speed, the current carrying it diagonally forward—in the direction of the men who had turned back. And now, as if from far, far away, from somewhere in Hell, the collective wails of the doomed men reached An Lu-shan's ears—a thin, faint sound, quickly drowned out by the excited shouts of the men gathered on the riverbank. The heavy ropes tied to the trees, the lifelines which had brought them across, snapped like strings as the thing in the river moved by, huge, black, and oblivious to the men and beasts it smashed and dragged under. An Lu-shan stared, stupefied, at the ropes trailing in the water, as men shouted and ran to and fro on the bank. There were no more voices coming from the river. The only sound that met their ears was the drone of the water.

"Perhaps your choice was not so blessed."

An Lu-shan turned and encountered A Pu-ssu. He hadn't realized that the officer was standing right behind him.

"My choice . . . ?"

"The choice of a crossing place, . . ." said A Pu-ssu, hesitating for effect, "General."

An Lu-shan felt blood rush to his face.

"*My* choice?" he said angrily. "It is the cartographer's stupidity that is responsible. He is an incompetent bungler! He will be beheaded!"

"Of course, General. That is what I meant," said A Pu-ssu with false deference. "And now we must conduct our raid against the Khitan with only slightly more than half of the troops and horses."

It was true. The first two waves that had crossed before An Lu-shan were about half the total force; most of the ones he had been leading had been drowned and crushed, and the rest, the ones remaining on the opposite side, were stranded, with no way to get across. An Lu-shan felt actual rage against the cartographer, as if it had not been entirely his own decision to cross here. He wished the man were here now so that he could throttle the life out of him. Instead, he grabbed A Pu-ssu's shoulders.

"The rest of them must come across!" he said furiously. "We will send riders across with more ropes. We will start over!" A Pu-ssu shook off An Lu-shan's hands.

"Are you never satisfied, General? We do not know how many hundreds of men and horses have been drowned, and you are ready to kill the rest of them! No, I think not. The ones on the other side will refuse to come across. And they will be completely within their rights to make a report to the

Censorate about this entire expedition! If I were on the other side with them, that is what I would order them to do! And that is what Lieutenant Min Ssu will probably do! Take my advice, General, and leave it alone!" The two men stood staring at one another. They both shook with the cold and with their anger.

Then An Lu-shan spoke in a quieter voice: "I have quite enough men on this side to do what must be done. Let the others do what they will." With that, he turned away from A Pu-ssu.

A Pu-ssu spat on the ground behind An Lu-shan, but the general ignored it. He was done with him for now. If I were to respond, it would only be to kill him, An Lu-shan thought, and he is too valuable to me now.

Sodden armor creaking, An Lu-shan climbed down off the rock. Raggedly, the men were beginning to organize themselves. Some were quieting the horses, others gathered stray bits of equipment and weapons. Though they had brought terra-cotta jars, sealed with wax and containing lamp oil, flint, and tinder, there would be no fires tonight. Too risky. Near the strip of sour muddy shore beneath tall, craggy walls, bits of canvas, wood, rope, and a helmet or two rolled fluidly in the dark water.

An Lu-shan imagined the sun rising in the morning, the first rays glinting off the bodies of his drowned men and horses. The picture in his mind was brutally clear. Some were snagged in tree branches and piled like logs against rocks; some floated serenely, many miles down, where the water finally quieted itself, its rage spent.

: :

The knife was very sharp. He had honed it himself. He held his left thumb over a small rhinocerous horn cup, and took a long drink of wine. For no reason that he particularly understood, he thought of his mother and raised the cup of wine in silent salute to her memory. Setting the cup down, he picked up the knife.

The thick crimson drops hit the flared, polished white surface, running smoothly down like spring runoff in a mountain ravine. He was thoroughly familiar with the ease with which blood flowed; he had seen it many, many times. It was life . . . and death. He had made a lot of blood flow; this time, it was his own.

In three days, magnificent carriages and noble steeds with silver trappings and colored plumage would arrive, bringing envoys and the eunuch military investigators from the capital and from Military Governor Li Shih-chih. He would be ready for them when they arrived.

An Lu-shan, commissioner for foot and horse of P'inglu Province, sitting at a low table inside his tent, collected half of a small cup of his own blood and bandaged the thumb with a strip of cloth.

With a shallow circular motion, he moved a small pestle in the bottom of the cup, turning minute amounts of fish glue and powdered alum into the thickening blood. The mixture congealed into smelly pea-sized lumps. He sniffed it. Perfect. Like fish left lying about for too long. The odor, he knew, would fade completely as the mixture dried. Next, he sprinkled in a bit of water, some lampblack, and some charcoal powder. Again he turned the pestle until a thick paste rested at the bottom. To this he added a few pinches of other substances, one of them—strangely perfumed—collected, he was told by a merchant, at tremendous expense and danger from the inner cavities of a sea dragon. One could seldom believe merchants, he thought as he pulled the drawstring of the small leather pouch that held the perfumed substance; their talk was only to raise the price of their goods. Talk for profit could never be trusted. He scraped the contents of the cup into a shallow stone bowl. Grasping the bowl with iron tongs, he passed it over the glowing coal embers of a brazier until the mixture congealed. The proportions were right; the mixture magically formed itself into a ball. He blew on it gently, admiring its perfection.

With a pair of chopsticks, An Lu-shan lifted the hardened lump off the bottom of the stone bowl and dipped it into a cup of cold water. He pulled it out, raised it close to his eyes, and smiled. The texture of the reddish-brown lump was perfect: flawless, uncracked, and silky like the cool center of a lump of coal stone; smooth and liquid-looking like the crystal center of milky jade. Dragon semen, he'd heard a geomancer call it once. Someday, he thought, I would like to see a dragon ejaculate. He took another drink.

It looked perfect; now to see if it would be perfect drawn across the rough surface of military map parchment. He ground a tiny bit of his newly manufactured "boat" into a marble inkstone, added a touch of water until the ink was of the proper consistency. He dipped his brush and gently drew it across the paper. He watched as the thin, graceful line dried. On his worktable, in a column of sunlight from the open tent flap, he placed the sample alongside the official military cartographer's map. From every angle the counterfeited ink was undetectable. He raised his cup again. To you, Mother, he thought.

The blood was a trick, one of a thousand he had learned during his former life. It was how the color of the inks and seals that coded official documents was matched: Chinese invoices, border passes, bills of lading, military dispatches. Useful knowledge for the wise entrepreneur traveling the Silk Road. And like countless other tricks and sleights of hand he had learned from clever wandering monks and greedy merchants, he knew it would be useful in some way, someday.

Where had he learned this trick? He tried to remember. He thought back to those distant times. Had it been in the narrow, dusty streets of Kokand? Or Aqsu, Kashgar, Khotan, or Miran? Had it been from the hand of a Persian, a Kushan, a Parthian, a Greek, or a Jew? Had An Lu-shan cultivated someone's friendship in some distant, dim oasis merely in order to discover the logistics of his movements, the number of his traveling companions and what treasures they carried—what rare gems, precious metals, spices, and aphrodisiacs they hid under a deceptive load of common merchandise? And, having discovered by what route they would rejoin the main caravan, through which mountain passes they would reroute to avoid either the robbers they had been warned of or the "winds of the dead"—inimical spirits that would lure travelers with strange music and drums—did he and his cohorts then separate them from their valuables, ambushing them with firesticks, stones, and stolen crossbows? Or did An Lu-shan and his comrades, deciding the risk was too great, choose not to attack?

And to which one of those masters of alchemy, forgery, or sleight of hand had he drawn sufficiently close to smell the wine on his breath? And with whom had he shared the remains of that same wine, feasting on his bread and fruit in a narrow alley? Whose weathered, calloused hands had he studied so closely as he learned his special tricks, only to rob and perhaps kill him outside the cool sanctuary of the oasis? At times it all ran together in his memory. But there were some episodes in his past that stood out as clearly and distinctly as the pale blue eyes he had seen once in a black man's face.

Like the memory of the one-armed monk in the Buddhist oasis at Tun-huang. It was when he was still a very young boy being passed from family to family along the northern roads of Hohsi Province. While the man told him stories, the young An Lu-shan sat looking at the odd fleshy stump. The monk, noticing the child staring at the place where the limb used to be, told him that he had severed his own arm to give it to his master for the secrets of a sutra. The arm, he explained to the young orphan, was only a meaningless part of the illusory material dream—part of a form that would pass away. He was a mendicant, living by the alms he collected by enlightening others to the images and meanings inherent in the thousand Buddha caves and grottoes that surrounded them in the red-yellow sandstone cliffs. And, with his single hand, the monk demonstrated for the young An Lu-shan tricks in the sand with small sticks and coins that seemed nothing less than impossible magic. He had waved away the child's disbelief, telling him that it was not the tricks done with his visible hand that should amaze the boy, but rather, the real magic, done with the hand that was not there. And the monk had smiled. That smile had frightened him and stayed in his dreams for a long time after that. So had the brown, wrinkled face and the shiny, hairless, oddly marked scalp. And the hand—the awful, odious ghost hand—had for years after that lurked in dark places, waiting to grab at his ankles or cover his mouth while he slept. The tricks done with the hand that is not there, he mused. I did not appreciate the monk's words then, thought An Lu-shan as he prepared to begin his forgery. But I do now.

The punitive expedition against the Khitan north of the Shira Muren River in the vast Na-lu Mountains region had been successful. The northern tribe's losses had been heavy, and they had been warned: the Chinese forces of P'inglu Province had a new leader and an aggressive new stance. The looks of shock on the enemies' faces had far exceeded An Lu-shan's expectations; he had even had the pleasure of skewering on his sword a man that he recognized—a chieftain he'd fought with over a woman a long time ago.

Yes, the expedition had been a success, but An Lu-shan's losses of men, horses, and equipment to the water had attracted attention. And the ones left on the opposite side of the river after the ropes were broken by the cursed moving chunk of earth had returned to camp with lurid stories on their lips of the cries of the doomed men and their own narrow escape from death.

He spread the cartographer's map out before him. He had much work to do. A duplicate must be made, identical to the original in every respect but one: the officially sanctioned crossing point. He must change it to look as if the place where he and his men crossed had been chosen by the cartographer and not by An Lu-shan. He would lie only because they were forcing him to lie. It was not enough, apparently, that he win border skirmishes with masterful strategy, striking fear into the enemies' hearts and driving them back from China's borders. In three days' time he would have to entertain a delegation of eunuch investigators and make a full account of the recent campaign. It was damned foolishness, he thought, that he had to answer to these she-men who had never lifted a sword. He imagined them screaming like women at the prospect of riding into combat; afraid they'd tear their clothes or break their fingernails. I'd like to see any one of them put so much as a toe into that river, he thought, as he selected a blank piece of parchment the same size as the map.

It will have to be perfect. They are probably not stupid and unimaginative like my eunuch, Chu-erh, he thought. They will be difficult to deceive. Like women, they have an uncanny sense of another's deceits.

Carefully, he wet his brush with the newly made ink. He tried to remember if he had ever actually met Li Shih-chih's cartographer. Once, he thought. He remembered a very thin fellow seated at a table in a military field tent, bent over his papers and instruments. An Lu-shan was not entirely without regret at what he was about to do to this undoubtedly worthy man, though it was made somewhat easier by the fact that he could not clearly recall his face. Friend, thought An Lu-shan, raising his wine cup and mentally addressing the cartographer, consider yourself honored. You are about to join the others who sacrificed themselves for the success of my mission. I will simply think of you as having drowned in the river that night.

He worked for a long time. To steady his hand, he drank wine. His work was good. Very good, he thought, when he was at last nearly finished. It was warm; the kind of early spring day that sucked the chill from the air and touched the rolling blue Mongolian grass with light. The kind of day that made the rivers run dangerously high with the runoff of melted snow. He muttered to himself, rehearsing what he would say to the Censorate. Certainly I thought of choosing a crossing point much further upriver, Your Excellencies. But I did not want to go against the judgment of the learned cartographer. Who am I to be so presumptuous as to . . . as to . . . His head nodded onto the table in the warm afternoon sunlight. A small nap and I will put the finishing touches on my work, he thought, lumbering toward his cot. Just a small rest.

A faint rustling woke him. He had slept deeply; his face felt hot and creased. Opening his eyes, he saw the backs of the bare legs of his son An Ching-hsu in front of his face. The child had crept in while he slept and was now looking at the map lying on the table. Stealthily, An Lu-shan reached out and closed his hand around the boy's left leg. The child jolted in terror.

"May I assist you in some way?" asked An Lu-shan.

The boy, frozen, did not answer for a moment. Then he spoke: "You will never get away with it, Father. You must be mad to think it."

He is a brave child, An Lu-shan thought, but impertinent . . . and developing a habit, lately, of impeding my plans. He gave the leg a threatening little shake.

"And what would you advise me to do?" he asked the child.

"Perhaps . . ." he began tentatively, "it would be best to tell the investigators of an attempt to save time . . . to . . . to tell them of your desire to cross to the chasm." An Ching-hsu kept his eyes forward as he spoke. An Lu-shan did not answer, but waited to see what else he would say. "It is only that Master Chu-erh tells me that the eunuchs from the Censorate are . . ."

"I will tell you what they are . . . They are without balls!" An Lu-shan interrupted harshly. He felt the boy stiffen again. "When Master Chu-erh was a boy of nine, he was sly and deceitful—like all Mongolian children. He was hard to manage—the way you have become," he said, letting go of the boy's leg and rolling to his feet.

An Ching-hsu backed slowly toward the open flap of the tent as his father moved toward him menacingly.

"Did you know that it was I who made him what he is now?" he asked the boy. "That I was forced to take my blade to him? *I* cut him. He became, after that, a most faithful servant to me along the trade routes. And he has remained faithful to me, and much of him is still a man. He has not regretted my actions. He is not at all a dandy like the others from Fukien who sing and cry like self-seeking women. A Persian, a physician I met once, told me it all has to do with when the child is cut. How old are you?"

The frightened boy did not speak but continued to back away.

An Lu-shan did not expect a reply from his son; instead, he answered his own question. "You are fourteen, if I remember correctly, and"—he eyed the boy appraisingly—". . . should I add the year in the womb, as is customary with these Chinese, then you are almost fifteen."

The boy had, by now, backed all the way out of the tent and was moving toward a small hill behind him, eyes intent on his father.

An Lu-shan smiled wickedly and pulled his long sword from its sheath. "Lift your skirts!"

An Ching-hsu yelped in terror. By now there were tears running down his cheeks. He moved slowly backward in the bright sunshine. Men working nearby turned their heads to watch the scene.

An Lu-shan did little to discourage them. "Do you want to see a boy become a girl?" he yelled out to anyone who could hear.

"Father . . . I only meant to help you! Father . . ."

The boy began to climb up the small hill behind him. It was clear that he really believed that An Lu-shan would cut him and leave him to die or live the rest of his life a eunuch. The child had, An Lu-shan knew, seen his father's fury and the suddenness with which he could draw blood when angry. There would be no reason to doubt him. Enjoying the game, An Lu-shan advanced a few more steps, brandishing the blade with a hungry look in his eyes as the boy scrambled farther up the hill, stumbling and dislodging small rocks, eyes huge with fear, arms raised imploringly.

"Father," he said in an urgent whisper so that no one nearby would hear, "it is only that the eunuch told me that the investigators would be shrewd, that they are grand and smart and that some of them have come from Ch'ang-an and that they . . ."

An Lu-shan stopped. "Ch'ang-an!" he said, turning the magic name over in his mind like a pearl in the calloused fingers of a fisherman. He lowered his sword. "They are coming from Ch'ang-an, to see me!" he said exultantly, picturing in his mind for the thousandth time the city of his imagination. Then he noticed the cowering boy, poised for flight, on the hillock in front of him. He gave a growl and a perfunctory wave of the sword to tell him he was through with him for now. An Ching-hsu ran. An Lu-shan knew that there was no danger of his telling anyone about the map . . . not after this masterful performance with the sword. He laughed to himself and put it back in its sheath. They learn early to protect their precious nuggets, he thought, going back into his tent to finish his work. My guests are coming a long, long way to see me, he thought, his heart jumping in his chest.

: :

Several days later, word was brought to him. The delegation, having arrived the day before, was refreshed and rested and wished to see him at his earliest convenience.

I will look at it only one more time, he thought, unrolling the wide, heavy, water-stained parchment. I will look at it as if I were a member of the delegation. If I look at it with my own eyes, I will find flaws that will take away my nerve.

It was perfect. Artistry, in fact. The Shira Muren River coiled like a snake across the paper, the edges of which were frayed, rumpled, and authentically touched with grime. Here and there, the ink was smeared, as it would be by stray raindrops. And there, at the second bend in the river, was the crossing point—clearly indicated and signed with the cartographer's official seal. He admired the map for a moment more, then rolled it up again. He cast a long look out of his tent. The low hills rolled away like waves, churned by the rolling shadows of the clouds. Miles of nothing but miles of nothing. A light breeze carried a mixture of perfume and the smell of sweaty horses to him. It was time to go.

Before him was a long corridor of multicolored tents and handsomely carved lintels and ridgepoles. To An Lu-shan, it looked like the foreign marketplaces in Ch'ang-an's western wards. That he had never been there was not important; he saw them in his mind. Stories from his childhood combined with the memories of beautiful garden cities along the trade route gave substance to his imagination.

Several hundred paces ahead of him, Li Chu-erh bullied a flock of women who scurried before the eunuch like farmyard hens scattering to make way for the general as he strode toward a makeshift courtyard formed by the tents of the visiting delegation.

8

The Constellation Gates

The prime minister [Li Lin-fu] espoused especially his rapid advancement because An had the admirable qualification of being a complete illiterate.

—*William Hung*

There are . . . stories to show the great respect which An had for Li Lin-fu. It is said that whenever An spoke to the dictator he would sweat profusely with anxiety.

—*Edwin Pulleyblank*

THEIR smell was the first thing he noticed, even before he could see them. *It is a good thing for Li Chu-erh that he does not drench himself in perfume,* An Lu-shan thought as he followed his eunuch toward the tent where the delegation was waiting. *I would not tolerate it.*

Before they entered, Chu-erh stood back deferentially to let his master be first. Their eyes met for a moment. An Lu-shan gave a barely perceptible nod; the youth gave an even slighter one in acknowledgment. The counterfeit map was not going to be the only expression of An Lu-shan's artistry today. He lifted the flap and went in.

There were four of them. It was plain that they were as curious about him as he was about them. There was the briefest of pauses as they assessed him before bowing with a fragrant rustle of silk. Underneath his armor, An Lu-shan felt prickles of warmth, and he knew that his forehead was beaded with sweat. In response to their bows, he merely lowered his head a little, and stood back as the formal greetings were exchanged. Li Chu-erh addressed them, explaining that he would serve as interpreter for his master, whose Chinese was—he shrugged politely—limited.

From his vantage of feigned ignorance, An Lu-shan studied the half-men as they went through the contortions of ritual. When they bowed, their long, spidery arms dropped loosely along their knees. He listened closely to their voices. One of them sounded like any man; another had a voice like an adolescent boy, like Chu-erh's. The other two had contralto voices that sounded sometimes male, sometimes female.

The combination of their strange voices and obvious authority, exuded with every word and gesture, unnerved An Lu-shan. Damn, but they were hard to read. Their eyes revealed nothing, and the smiles on their faces were formal and mirthless.

The rituals seemed interminable to An Lu-shan—the talking, bowing, and posturing preposterous as he stood in his full armor sweating, by now, like a pig. Chu-erh was doing a good job—perhaps too good, An Lu-shan thought as he listened.

"My master relies on me like a crippled man on his crutch, a blind man on the eyes of his friends. I am his link with polite society and the government who rules his hand," he told them, causing them to exchange knowing smiles and look inquisitively at An Lu-shan. One of them, a scrawny fellow with a boy's voice, tilted his head to one side and looked directly at An Lu-shan.

"A fascinating specimen," he said to his colleagues. Then he said to Chu-erh, "Tell him we are most delighted to meet the brave Sogdian who does not know the meaning of the word danger."

They took seats around the table and began to talk among themselves. An Lu-shan kept a set expression on his face, such as he had seen on the faces of rustic chieftains. It was a face that would make them think that he couldn't understand their words. But as they talked, he found it increasingly difficult to maintain that face.

"It is a wonder that any horse could carry him," said a short man with a homely countenance and masculine voice.

"A colossal brute, isn't he?" answered another, the tallest of the lot, with round, girlish features, his contralto taking on a womanish tone as he said it.

As if he needed a translation, An Lu-shan turned to Chu-erh.

"They are impressed by your fatness," said An Lu-shan's servant in gutteral Sogdian. "They say you are large and fierce."

"Tell them," he answered in the same tongue, "that I wish to see what is under their robes." He smiled at Li Chu-erh's consternation as the young eunuch, flushing, turned to the delegates. He hesitated for only a moment before speaking.

"My master wishes you to know that he eats a lot so that he will have strength to fight the Hsi and the Khitan," he improvised.

The short one who had made the joke about the horse spoke again: "This one may prove a bit tricky," he said, eyeing An Lu-shan critically.

An Lu-shan, in turn, studied the speaker. He was thicker than the other three, with a low, wide forehead and small, deep-set eyes. As he turned to speak again, An Lu-shan noticed that his nose protruded no farther than his brow. A very dangerous type, he thought.

". . . When word was brought of the barbarian's success," the short one was saying, "I had my doubts. The question I asked was, at what cost is this success bought? Now that I am actually looking at him, I ask the question with considerably more urgency."

A low murmur of assent went around the table.

"I gather you do not trust him," the tall one said in a dry, understated way from the end of the table. To An Lu-shan, he was by far the strangest of them all, with his girl's head atop his long, lean body.

"It is not a matter of trust! If this humble servant of the government may be allowed to continue!" the small, thick man said. He and An Lu-shan looked at one another with intense interest as the others waited deferentially for him to finish.

I have my opinions about you as well, thought An Lu-shan as the eunuch's tiny eyes rested unblinkingly on him. I am beginning to be able to read you. You are a hard master, indeed. An Lu-shan saw intense jealousies and obsessive resentments in those eyes, and a tendency toward sulking, fits of nerves, and vindictive retaliations. No doubt your colleagues are used to your displays of temper, An Lu-shan thought as the man resumed speaking. You look like a toad.

"He is most competent in the field of battle and with the strategies of the art of war . . . but my impression is one of arrogance and impulsiveness," he said, looking toward the general.

Tall Girl-Face at the end of the table shook his head impatiently. "I don't doubt any of it," he said. "But his personality is not a matter for discussion. We must assess the evidence, not the look in his eye or the line of his mouth . . . though I concede that it is most tempting," he added, looking at An Lu-shan and tilting his head to one side.

An Lu-shan glared back at him.

"Therefore, gentlemen, it is to more solid evidence that we must address ourselves," Girl-Face continued. "I believe that there is a map . . . ?" he said with raised eyebrows, looking at Li Chu-erh.

An Lu-shan's eunuch looked at his master. "They wish to see the map," he said tonelessly, in Sogdian.

"The moment I have been waiting for!" An Lu-shan replied, placing the rolled parchment on the table. At the same moment that he put the map on the table, An Lu-shan noticed Girl-Face exchanging looks with the Toad, who said nothing more, but looked down at his hands and stretched out his fingers in a slow, feminine gesture.

An Lu-shan's map lay on the table, reflected in the polished black surface. He was proud of the table and the chairs that went with it. It was all part of a shipment of furniture, bound for officers' quarters in another outpost, that he had seen in the course of an inspection and appropriated for himself: teak and rosewood, silk cushions with designs of lotus, hibiscus, plums, conjugal ducks, clouds, and leaves—all could hold him spellbound for hours, sitting alone, running his rough hands along the flowing supple coolness of the curves of the legs, the strange curls of the carvings, and the icy softness of the silks. The four eunuchs appeared to take no notice of his splendid acquisitions, as if such things were so familiar to them that they didn't see them at all. He eyed them with a strange mixture of feelings: their jadedness irritated him, as if they were bored by everything. You useless bitches, he thought; I'd like to have you under my command for just a week along the frontier. *I'd* wake you up. But he was envious at the same time—of the lives they must lead, surrounded so by the beauty of China that they were actually glutted on it. I, too, will have my fill, he thought, watching their effete gestures as they prepared to look at the "evidence." An Lu-shan waited, affecting the stiff formality of an officer at inspection.

Li Chu-erh was speaking to the delegation briskly as he unrolled the map and weighted the corners down with a small statue, a knife, and empty sword scabbards. "My master apologizes for his lack of fluency in the mother tongue, but he wishes me to tell you that he is afraid that he is too much a barbarian, a . . ."

The eunuch turned to An Lu-shan with a questioning face.

"Watch your tongue, Old Woman," An Lu-shan said irritably in Sogdian.

". . . too much a peasant," Chu-erh continued, "to make an attempt at speech—which could only be crude and rudimentary—in your noble presence. He catches a word here and there, you understand, but not enough to follow these proceedings or to unravel the directions in which complex arguments might travel . . ." Chu-erh finished arranging the map, shrugged, and stepped back. "He wishes only to tell you that he regrets the unnecessary losses, but that he was acting on instructions from the cartographer's office . . ."

With an iron will, An Lu-shan maintained his facial expression as the eunuch investigators turned their attention to the map.

He watched the Toad's little eyes most carefully as they scrutinized the parchment. The heavy paper began to roll itself up again, pushing the weights toward the center.

Chu-erh quickly moved forward to flatten the map and add extra weight. "Look at the course of the river as it is drawn on the map before us," he said.

"And if you would be so kind, follow my finger along the curve here." He pointed to where the Shira Muren undulated across the paper. Around it were small clusters of characters written in brownish-red ink, and stacks of tiny numbers in neatly configured columns: the measure of distances in li scaled to the calibrations of a military caliper.

"I believe that this is where the error lies," Chu-erh said, indicating two wide loops in the river's course and bringing his finger down on the one representing the curve of the river closest to the camp. "You see the cartographer's mark here."

All the investigators, leaning closely over the map, grunted their acknowledgments—with the exception, An Lu-shan noted, of Toad, who said nothing at all, but stared fixedly at the parchment.

Raising his arms in a broad gesture, An Lu-shan spoke, in the northern tongue, from his corner of the tent. He felt as if he were being roasted alive inside his armor. He was almost as wet as when he had crawled out of the river that night.

"My master wishes to tell you that the cartographer must have become confused because of the snakiness of the river's course. He must have placed his mark here instead of . . . up here," Chu-erh said, moving his finger to the other loop. "An obvious mistake on his part. The general does not know this portion of the Shira Muren. It is an area that was somewhat unfamiliar to him when he was transferred here as P'inglu's commissioner of foot and horse . . ." Chu-erh paused, listening, as An Lu-shan spoke again. "Had he been acquainted with the other crossing point, he would have known that the map was in error," Chu-erh finished.

Another low murmur went around the table.

Then Tall Girl-Face spoke. "It is unfortunate that the general was so reliant on the accuracy of the cartographer," he said.

"Indeed it is," Li Chu-erh responded with an obsequious bow of the head.

The Toad raised his eyes from the map finally and looked in An Lu-shan's direction. "It is unfortunate that we are so reliant on the accuracy of the general," he said, rising to his feet, his words matching Girl-Face's like the singsong of parallel couplets.

"It is obvious that what we have is a regrettable error," said Girl-Face, "considering the abundance of water this spring from the snows that fell during the winter. The extent of the error must be evaluated by the extent of the losses. What were the figures again?" he asked his colleagues.

"More than four hundred and fifty men, and about fifty horses," the scrawny one said evenly.

Girl-Face nodded thoughtfully. "And that, in turn, must be weighed against the gains of General An Lu-shan's offensive raid," he said. "In any case, I believe we have a matter that must be taken up with the cartographer and the stone-block makers in his office. Are we in agreement?"

Chu-erh turned to An Lu-shan. "They are filled with admiration for your prowess in winning the battle with so few men," he said in Sogdian. "But the cartographer will have to answer for his stupidity."

An Lu-shan grinned broadly. "Thank the fine ladies very much for me. And then I want to get out of this stinking armor."

Later, An Lu-shan stood in the open door-flap of his tent and let the cool breeze dry the sweat from his body. When he and Chu-erh had finally peeled the armor off him, they had found that he was indeed soaked to the skin in his own sweat. As the eunuch pulled the pieces from him, An Lu-shan had felt the way a serpent must feel when it hatches from its egg.

: :

". . . the unexpected attack has probably broken the back of any Khitan offensive that may have been planned for the spring. The defeat comes at a critical time for the warlord King K'o-t'u-kan and his followers, effectively eroding his prestige. It should be noted that An Lu-shan accomplished the victory with roughly half his forces, taking full advantage of the element of surprise. . . . His abilities are astonishing. . . ."

Chief Minister Li Lin-fu put his hand on his daughter's shoulder. Her thin, high little voice left off reading the letter from Military Governor Li Shih-chih of the Fanyang and P'inglu regions as she turned her face upward, awaiting Father's instructions.

"Go back to the part about the river crossing, my dear. I would like to hear it one more time."

The girl's shiny head bent again to the page. Li Lin-fu walked thoughtfully to the window, open wide to admit the warm spring breeze. The child began to read again:

". . . to accomplish his objective, it was necessary to cross the Shira Muren River at an inauspicious time. The water was swift and high, the rains having only recently ceased. . . . Official reports indicate that General An Lu-shan compelled an entirely reluctant army of men and horses to enter the turbulent waters. . . . Overcoming their natural resistance by sheer force of will, he caused them to go where their own sense told them not to go. . . ."

Li Lin-fu, by now behind his daughter again, touched her shoulder once more. "Now let me hear about the disaster . . . the part that begins with 'the frightful chunk of earth . . .'?" With pleasurable anticipation, he crossed back to the window and idly counted starlings he saw landing in a tree in the garden.

> ". . . the frightful chunk of earth appeared as if from Hell. . . . Grow-ing out of the darkness, it swept down the river to devour hapless men and horses . . . the men on the shore tortured by the cries of their companions, unable to help them. . . . Losses were very heavy . . . though when the final tally was taken, casualties due to actual fighting were practically nil, so complete was the element of surprise. . . ."

Li Lin Fu let the child read on through the account, and waited for the section where the cartographer was mentioned. He watched the starlings in the tree below take off all at once, as though they had but one mind.

> ". . . it has been determined that the accident was a result of an in-judicious choice of a crossing point. . . . At the place where General An Lu-shan crossed, the river had been fed by a tributary, thus inten-sifying its fury. . . . Another crossing point lay two days' journey upriver, at a point where the waters were lower and comparatively calmer. . . . An investigation indicates that the fault lay with the official cartographer, Tu Chen, whose error resulted in the unjustifiable loss of men and horses. . . . The man has been appropriately punished for his carelessness . . . a Censorate council sentenced him to loss of his position and castration. . . ."

The flock of starlings had moved to a nearby roof, where they formed a line along the top and sat preening their feathers and looking around them. Li Lin-Fu's daughter continued to read, but he did not listen particularly to the part of the letter dealing with technical details of troop quotas, training programs, and objectives in the continuing effort to solidify defense of the frontier. He waited until the barbarian's name came up to bring his attention into focus.

> ". . . An Lu-shan shows not only uncanny tactical skill, but has other distinct advantages over his highly trained Chinese counterparts. His ability to function as a diplomat among the tribal peoples in our own northern areas could prove to be of immense value. . . . The importance of gaining the loyalty of territories where secessionism is a continuing problem cannot be overstressed, as you well know. . . . This An Lu-shan is a rough sort of fellow who spent a good part of his life living among just such people. To them, he seems less an

outsider than officials from the T'ang . . . they feel he is one of them, and respond to his authority readily and cooperatively. . . . He cannot, of course, read or write, but compensates with his considerable native cleverness. He speaks, we are told, eleven different languages. . . . I commend him to you with certain reservations: There is a ruthless, unstoppable quality to him, and I would not stake my life on his truthfulness . . . but his potential value in the defense of the north should be plain for you to see—"

Li Lin-Fu repeated words to himself mentally: cannot read or write, a rough fellow, a ruthless quality, eleven languages. He interrupted the girl, who stopped reading in midsentence, and caressed her small, lovely face. "Thank you, little one. Now let Father think for a bit. He will require further assistance from you. Have you your writing brush and ink in readiness?"

"Yes, Father," the girl replied, her face dimpling with pleasure. Her nimble little hands reached for a fresh sheet of paper, which she lovingly flattened and weighted down. Li Lin-fu went to the window and took a deep breath of the warm spring air. At last, it was dry. All winter he had fought against the insidious moisture entering his lungs with each breath. He could feel the cold and damp which had settled deep in his chest finally loosening its grip. It had been months since he had felt warm. Without turning, he began to dictate his reply to Li Shih-chih:

"I am most grateful for your informative letter concerning the formidable barbarian general An Lu-shan. I ask only one more favor of you now: Please extend to him my most cordial invitation to come, at his earliest convenience, to Ch'ang-an. I wish to meet him."

Li Lin-fu walked around behind where the girl sat so that he could watch her work. Her brush moved quickly over the page, the characters appearing on the paper as if they were alive. Watching her hand, he shook his head in admiration. It was a perfect hand, fully formed like an adult's in its definition and purposefulness, but child-sized, miniature. He caressed the back of her head as the brush flew to the concluding character of the letter.

She looked up at him.

"Just one more letter, Little One. Are you tired?"

"No, Father, not at all." She blotted the letter to Li Shih-chih, set it aside, and prepared a fresh piece of paper. Li Lin-fu looked up at the ceiling while he gathered his thoughts. Something in Li Shih-chih's letter had inspired him. He had come to trust his intuition over the years, even though it was often as much a mystery to himself as it might be to someone else. He laughed a bit, appreciating the strangeness of what he was about to ask. Strange, perhaps, but it could certainly do no harm . . . and he had learned from long experience that it was never, never too early to plan for the future. Carefully, he framed his words, and began.

Absurd though they seemed, the breathing exercises prescribed by the physician seemed to be having a positive effect. The coughing fits which had wracked him all winter had been absent for nearly a week now. He stood at the open window, alternately closing first one nostril and then the other as he filled his lungs with the sweet air and expelled it slowly, slowly, as if blowing a long note on a flute. He listened to his own words as Daughter read back to him the letter to his chief of internal securities. He smiled at the way these important men's words sounded coming back to him in a female child's voice. But he was careful not to let her see the smile, lest she think he made fun of her.

> ". . . You are to arrange for my agents in Hopei to depart im-
> mediately for P'inglu. . . . If they travel steadily, they will reach the
> Great Wall in less than two days and, once beyond that, the military
> outpost of Ying-chou in another day. This is what I require: that they
> find out all pertinent facts concerning the barbarian general known as
> An Lu-shan—age, disposition, origin, peculiarities of personality, tac-
> tics in dealing with subordinates, religious or superstitious leanings,
> idiosyncratic likes and dislikes. I also require that agents be dispatched
> to look into the matter of the recent punitive castration of one Tu
> Chen, former cartographer to Military Governor Li Shih-chih. Find
> the man, interview him, obtain from him the facts, as he sees them,
> of the river crossing and the erroneous map. And you are authorized
> to offer him the sum of fifty thousand taels of silver for the purchase
> of the *bao-tse*,* which are to be brought then directly and discreetly to
> me by special courier . . ."

The little girl finished reading the letter by pronouncing her father's name and title. He turned from the window. It is really quite remarkable, he thought, that such an ugly, fish-faced fellow as myself could produce such consistently exquisite daughters. He smiled at her.

"You will have to refresh my memory, my dear," he said to her. "Who was your mother?"

::

At the T'ung-kuan Pass, one hundred li east of the city of Ch'ang-an, An Lu-shan and his small retinue of fifty mounted soldiers, exhausted and filthy from

*Dried testicles.

two weeks' hard traveling, paused for a rest. It was early afternoon, and hot. Each day was hotter than the last as they moved south and spring turned to summer. The road was dry as they approached the two tall wooden watch-towers on either side of the pass, and the dust rose behind them. Atop the tower on the right, An Lu-shan could see the first beacon lamp. At dusk, this and the nine others at ten-li intervals between here and Ch'ang-an would light the way for travelers approaching the great city. He was almost there.

He was just about to put his foot to the ground when a shout from the forward ranks made him turn. Instinctively, his hand went to his sword. In the next moment, the hand dropped to his side as he stared.

His practiced eye counted quickly. About two hundred horsemen were sweeping toward them, riding in formation, the sunlight flashing off the golden standards they carried. An Lu-shan and his men stood dumbly where they were as they were surrounded in a single precision maneuver, horses and men streaming around them like winter runoff around rocks. The realization hit An Lu-shan: This was an official escort, sent to accompany them on the last leg of the journey. His chest swelled. This was as it should be.

A heavy-set, burly man, as big at least as An Lu-shan, detached him-self from the group, and without hesitation approached the general and swung down from his saddle. He walked with a staff and an odd, rolling limp caused by a deformed foot. He came close and smiled with large yellow horse-teeth.

"Greetings, An Lu-shan!" the man said, startling the general by speaking in perfect ancient Kushan. "I am Feng. General Feng, of the Sixth Army of the Interior Realm! When you have rested a bit, we will ride with you the rest of the way!"

An Lu-shan pondered as he rode. When word had arrived three weeks before from the Chancellery and the Ministry of War that he was to depart for the capital, he had chosen fifty of his finest horsemen. Originally, the plan had been to exchange tired horses for fresh ones at the military commanderies along the way; for the first leg of the journey southwest from P'inglu Province, he had stuck to that plan. But as the journey progressed, he had grown impatient and had begun to bypass every other commandery. Shortcuts, many of them over difficult mountain terrain, had cut much time and many li from the journey—but the strain showed on the men who had slept half as much as usual and on the horses pushed twice as far. To be early, to arrive before he was expected, was his objective. But now they were met by this escort from the capital. He looked around him. Men and horses were as fresh as if they had just set out that day. Somehow, he had been outguessed. He looked at Feng, riding alongside him.

Feng's face under the elaborately carved iron helmet was pleasantly ugly.

He was powerfully built, but some sixth sense suggested to An Lu-shan that he was a eunuch. If so, he was not at all like the Censorate investigators—the eunuchs from Fukien with the unmistakable girlishness of those cut at an early age and sold into service. An Lu-shan had heard about another kind—men who chose to have themselves cut, much later in life, and buy, with their precious *bao-tse,* a place in high service to the empire, especially the military. If Feng is one of these, he thought, then he is a different creature entirely from the men-women of the Censorate. He admired the rare, elaborate work of the gilded iron-plate armor encasing the huge barrel chest. Is this, he asked himself, how they outfit all their officers? It was not difficult to see himself in such a grand suit of armor.

His eyes traveled down to the general's foot. Enormous and misshapen, it was encased in an intricately decorated deerskin boot, the whole lower leg resting in a strangely contrived stirrup that brought the foot higher and closer to the horse's shoulder than the normal foot on the other side. As An Lu-shan deferentially averted his eyes, Feng turned toward him, smiling.

"Do not be concerned about staring at my foot, General," he said cheerfully. "It is my mark, and I am proud of it. Feel free to satisfy your curiosity."

An Lu-shan liked his manner. He felt at ease.

"Oh, I have seen far worse in my travels, Feng. I saw a man once with two heads! The small one was like a baby's and slept most of the time. Sometimes it would yawn and smack its lips. The man talked to it, told it stories."

Feng laughed, throwing his head back and displaying all his teeth. "Indeed, that puts my poor foot to shame. But at court, it is sufficiently grotesque to gain respect for its owner." He turned to An Lu-shan. "They say that my name is well-known throughout the empire. I do not suppose you have heard of the 'infamous' Feng, have you, General?"

"I am sorry," An Lu-shan replied. "In the northern provinces, we hear little besides the howling of the wind."

Feng shook his head sympathetically. "You have come a great, great distance. I do not envy you. It makes me think back to the Tibetan expeditions. Too much time traveling for too little fighting! A nasty enemy but far too elusive. Life is different for men like us, An Lu-shan. We are not family men of the plow and the hoe. To us, distances are part of our lives. They are unavoidable obstacles, to be crossed when they must be . . . like rivers."

Like rivers? An Lu-shan looked at Feng. What did he know? A clever one, obviously, to be able to speak the Kushan tongue so well.

"Your time was excellent, General," Feng continued. "We have heard much about your strength and endurance, but your speed was truly amazing. A trip of no less than fifteen hundred li! And that is the buyer's estimate, not the seller's."

An Lu-shan shrugged modestly. "It was not difficult, Feng. It was not like riding into enemy territory."

"Oh, but yours was a difficult route, General."

"How do you know my route, Feng?"

"We know a man's route as much by the places he does not pass through as by the ones he does pass through, An Lu-shan. The empire is like a woman," he shouted in great merriment as the pounding of the hooves grew louder. "The closer one strokes to her gate, the more sensitive she becomes!"

They were picking up their pace now. To the north were low, yellow sandstone hills. There were dwellings carved in the sides of these hills, and the inhabitants poured from them when they heard the dust and commotion of the riders. And further down the road, between Wu-tsun and Hsun Chiang-hsi, people flocked along the borders of the fields. Unafraid, they did not run as they might have in other times. A long, stable peace had no doubt worn down that instinct. Chickens and babies in their arms, women and children joined the men in the fields to stare and wave at the procession of horse soldiers.

"These soldiers," An Lu-shan shouted to Feng in the Kushan tongue. "Are they the ones who have tracked me so astutely?" Feng laughed.

"These fools are not soldiers, An. They could not track a dog by its droppings, let alone a man of the north like yourself."

"Not soldiers, Feng? I don't understand."

"You have been dealing too long with conscripted bandits and murderers at your northern commanderies to know the sweet disciplined face of a young Chinese soldier. Sons, An Lu-shan. Sons!"

"Even the worst criminal is a son, Feng, . . . of somebody!"

"These are not sons. No woman would claim them from her womb. And no man would claim he slept with any woman who did!" Feng declared loudly. "Look around you at those faces. The ten lords of Hell, An Lu-shan, and the bastard's egg of a turtle," he finished, switching to Chinese without a pause. "These are not members of the Sixth Army of the Interior Realm, or even the Fourth . . . these are the 'elite' Chancellery guards," he said, grimacing cheerfully. "They are the stinking bloody afterbirths of pigs and dogs. Morons and thugs! Like ourselves, An Lu-shan, they belong to Chief Minister Li Lin-fu, not to our Divine Son of Heaven!" Laughing, Feng dug his heels into his horse's sides.

The dust rose around them as they galloped. Li Lin-fu. The man that An Lu-shan was to meet when he got to Ch'ang-an. This was the important official who had sent for him, chief minister and president of the Ministry of War. Pigs? Dogs? Bloody stinking afterbirths? It was all very strange to An Lu-shan. And what did Feng mean—that they "belonged" to this Li Lin-fu? He felt elated and confused, victorious and apprehensive as he rode along. He was becoming increasingly aware that he was far, far from his own territory.

An Lu-shan watched the general galloping beside him, his strange twisted foot hugging the horse's side. Morons and thugs. He decided not to ask any more questions, but to let Feng reveal his meaning as he saw fit. I like him, An Lu-shan thought. I do not think he is trying to deceive me or make a fool of me. My instinct tells me that this is one I should know. I may need him in this new world I am about to enter.

Feng turned toward him then. "We will camp tonight at the village of Chintui-ch'eng. They are expecting us and will have food and drink prepared. Tomorrow you will be bathed and refreshed at the hot springs garden at Mount Li Shan before you are taken into *His* presence."

"Thank you, Feng," An Lu-shan replied. "I am badly in need of a bath." He smiled, aware of his weary, sweaty, dust-caked appearance.

::

The forested mound of Mount Li Shan rose abruptly out of the flat fertile plains northeast of Ch'ang-an. A great green hump, its top lost in humid mist, marked the geomantic magic of the ancient thermal springs. An Lu-shan and Feng rode alone along a narrow paved road, lined with even columns of perfectly manicured evergreens, leading from the village of Lin-tong to the gates of the hot springs. The Chancellery entourage had broken off their escort and ridden away, and An Lu-shan's men remained at the barracks outside of Lin-tong, where they would have the cool water of the river for bathing and plenty of food. Their horses would be cared for. The sons of T'ang, Feng explained, lavished attention on their horses, the backbone of their empire. The T'ang emperors practically worshiped them, he said. Minghuang, continuing the tradition of his forebears, had commissioned great carvings of prize stallions and magnificent paintings by the renowned master Han Kan. Listening to Feng as they rode, An Lu-shan reflected that he seemed to know something about everything. He felt comfortable with him and adopted a policy of listening rather than talking.

Soon they were riding through the gates of the hot springs. He took a deep breath. The garden cities he had seen along the Silk Road crumbled to ashes in his mind as his eyes tried to take in what lay around him. He saw pavilions with lofty, sweeping eaves rising above delicate red and gold pillars. Carved marble balustrades topped gently curving bridges; ornate aquatic fountainheads of carp, dragons, and turtles lined reflecting pools filled with lotus and hyacinths. Rockeries, mosaic paths, and staircases wound in and out among the huge boulders and towering trees of the mountain's base, climbing in terraced steps up the steep wooded slopes. It was strange. He looked at what he thought were uncultivated hillsides of woods and rocks. But then the light would change, and he would find that he was looking at walkways and pavilions, hidden and undulating, weaving among the ridges and following the natural lines of rock formations. He had trouble focusing his eyes, not sure at any time what he was looking at.

"Do you like to be jerked off, General?" Feng's voice startled him out of his contemplation of paradise.

An Lu-shan looked at his new friend and threw back his head to laugh incredulously.

"There are women here from the palace harems who will bathe you in scented pea soaps and perfumed oils and take quite fine care of you!" Feng said with a lascivious grin. "They are here to take care of guests—special ambassadors and military leaders, like ourselves! Training makes the difference, An Lu-shan. Leave nothing to chance! Their hands are soft and fine, like the rest of their bodies, and they are free to make you happy. Almost free, anyway. They belong to our Imperial Father's harem, so they won't do the "clouds and rain" thing, but they'll do anything else you want when they bathe you. You will like being jerked off by those soft, nimble hands. I myself find it most enjoyable!" An Lu-shan gave him a quick look. Feng understood instantly. "I may have given them my 'bag of eggs' for promotion, An Lu-shan. But I did not give them my 'old man.' Only a fool does that." An Lu-shan nodded, thinking about it. "I can still find pleasure with the women," Feng said. "Though perhaps you don't care for that sort of thing. Perhaps," he shrugged, "you are mindful of the warning of the ancients that too much of it will cause you to lose your powers entirely!"

"I am greatly afraid of it, Feng!" An Lu-shan replied, still laughing. "It is with the most terrible fear and trembling that I will let the fine ladies touch me with their little hands."

"I thought so," said Feng, as a groom approached carrying a step stool. "You see, An Lu-shan? they will not even let you climb off your horse by yourself! You are a guest of the imperial city . . . and you are the guest of Li Lin-fu!"

: :

Feng had been right. Experience made all the difference. Twice she had made him come. An Lu-shan had never experienced such a sweet-smelling, silky woman before. The last woman's hand that had been on his 'old man' had been almost as calloused and leathery as his own and had done the job as if she were milking a goat. He smiled. He'd never seen so much hot water in one place, either. He was clean and refreshed down to the smallest fold on his great, fat body and had a relaxed, empty feeling in his groin. And after the hot bath she had rubbed and pummeled the weariness from his limbs. She had even decorated his head with flowers when she was finished.

Now Feng and An Lu-shan strolled the grounds of the hot springs in fresh clothing, the warm breeze drying their hair. Curious children followed them, but ran away laughing with delighted terror if An Lu-shan tried to reach for one of them. They would gather their courage and come close again, then dart away shrieking if he even looked at them.

Feng shrugged. "It is your face and beard," he said. "They probably think you are a demon-slayer out of some fable they have heard. I am uglier, but they are used to me."

"Who are these children, Feng?" An Lu-shan asked.

These were not like the ragged little beggars he was accustomed to. They were clean, pretty children, dressed in silks. Feng picked one up.

"These, my friend, are the children of the Ten Mansions. Some are children of the Emperor, some are children of the Emperor's children who are grown. They are all royalty," he said looking at the solemn face of the princeling he held. "I am sure he has lost count of them, there are so many. But he has his particular favorites. I instructed two of them—Ying, the crown prince, and his brother Mao."

An Lu-shan raised his brows. This was impressive.

"I taught them what I could at their tender ages about horsemanship, falconry, and something of the arts of combat." He put the child down. "I even took them on their first hunt. I wish you could have seen it, An Lu-shan. It was a spectacle. Imagine the drummers and beaters stirring the brush, pounding out noise to rival heaven's thunder. Then come the little ones, the jealously guarded royal lineage of the House of Li. All around them are lancers and archers. Ying's bow is so heavy he can barely carry it, and Mao is dragging a lance twice as long as he is. They are on the trail of their first tiger. And Ying brought down his prey that day, An Lu-shan, . . . though not without some help, of course. Ying accompanied me, a few years later, on a tour of duty in Szechuan. Rode over three hundred li with me, far past the post station at Ma-wei, without a complaint. And when we got there, he even bargained for the beautiful niece of a Censorate official—and brought her home for his little brother. Think of it!" He slapped his leg enthusiastically. They walked in silence for a few paces. Feng shook his head sadly. "So much promise in the boy. Such grieving at his death."

"His death?" An Lu-shan asked, surprised.

"Suicide, General. And barely seventeen years old. Can you fancy it?"

An Lu-shan couldn't. It was difficult enough for him to understand grown men killing themselves. He had tried to imagine plunging a knife into his innards, blowing out his own flame. Letting go of one's life intentionally! Unthinkable! But a youth, a mere boy? He shook his head.

Pensively, the two men continued walking, An Lu-shan keeping a slow pace to accommodate Feng's laborious limp. They were approaching a cluster of half-completed buildings. Pillars held up empty air; walls ended abruptly in space, stacks of roofing tiles standing against them. Scattered about were pieces of elegantly carved lattice trim. Piles of stone and marble and hewn wood lay here and there, and bamboo scaffolding stood abandoned, birds perched on the top rungs preening their feathers. They followed a stone path leading into the area of unfinished construction. Sitting in the tall grass were wooden crates. An Lu-shan stopped to examine one, pulling apart the loose dovetail joints. He pulled out a handful of rotting straw, revealing beautiful ceramic tiles, colors blazing in the sunlight. Another crate held porcelain beasts for the eaves of buildings: monkeys, dragons, snakes. Golden acroteria ornaments lay half unpacked, as if the workers simply walked away in the middle of the job. A bronze fountainhead in the shape of a carp lay in the tall weeds which grew everywhere among the abandoned boxes. An Lu-shan looked questioningly to Feng, who was turning a small statue over in the grass with his staff.

"Look around you, An Lu-shan," said Feng. "Ying took more than his own life when he poisoned himself."

"I don't understand, Feng."

"We are standing in the ruins of an emperor's vision, An Lu-shan," said Feng, waving the staff. "You see, Minghuang is an artist. It had been his plan to restore these hot springs to their former splendor, the way they were fifteen hundred years ago in the time of the Chou emperors. It was his pride, his great project! He studied paintings, maps, literature, and even poetic descriptions from that time, trying to get every detail perfect. Oh, you should have seen it! There were artisans and architects, sculptors, woodcarvers, painters, and builders crawling all over the place. Arguments! Art experts and historians called in by the Emperor as consultants screaming at each other over some small detail of authenticity, and the Emperor in the midst of it all, directing, arbitrating, making drawings, talking to common laborers. A happy man," he said, shaking his head. "Or at least a busy one. But now . . . I have not laid eyes on him for months, An Lu-shan."

"He grieves for the prince?"

"The prince and his empress not long before that. Another suicide." Feng looked at An Lu-shan, his habitually laugh-lined face sad and solemn. An Lu-shan shook his head. Feng flipped a piece of latticework over with the tip of his stick. "Of course, he keeps the workers, the artisans and all, on a retainer so that they may continue to feed their families. But it has all stopped, An Lu-shan. It is like death. His interest died with Ying and the Empress. Already the weeds and the water begin to claim the work. Such a shame, such a shame." Feng heaved himself down on a crate and began to massage his club foot, obviously tired from the walk. "He's a good foot, An Lu-shan. He does his best, but he hurts sometimes. I take care of him," he said, holding it tenderly, gazing beyond An Lu-shan toward the spacious grounds.

An Lu-shan watched the general working on his foot and contemplated what he had just learned about the Emperor. Just one day ago, he marveled, I was a saddle-weary soldier completing a long journey. I did not know Feng, I had never set foot on these enchanted grounds. I knew nothing about the Son of Heaven. Now I sit here, my hair full of flowers, while someone who actually knows him tells me intimate stories about the man who rules China. As An Lu-shan looked at him, the expression on Feng's face changed abruptly from dreamy contemplation to focused attention. He was looking at something behind and beyond An Lu-shan. An Lu-shan's hand moved reflexively toward a sword that wasn't there.

"What is it, Feng?" he said quietly, but as he said it he saw a look of radiant pleasure come on to the general's face. Slowly, he turned.

Deer. A big white-tailed buck and two dainty does moved delicately and tentatively into the open not thirty feet away. They stepped among the Emperor's discarded treasures, raising their heads, ears spread, and gazed with soft brown eyes in the direction of the two men. Then three other creatures stepped out and joined the deer; smaller, exotic, with strange curly horns and striped coats.

"Gazelle," whispered Feng ecstatically. "The Emperor's favorites, imported at great cost for his retreats and sanctuaries. So shy you almost never see them. But see how tame they are! It is because they have made friends with the deer, who are unafraid because no one hunts them here, and they know it."

"Beautiful creatures," An Lu-shan agreed in a soft voice, privately thinking of how they would taste, roasted and juicy. Not here, An Lu-shan, he admonished himself. Not the Emperor's gazelles.

They watched the animals graze. They came so close that An Lu-shan could hear their jaws grinding and their little hooves rustling the tender grass with each step. All at once the animals' heads rose in unison and they looked back toward one of the ruined buildings. In the next moment they were gone, bounding noisily through a thicket of trees, alarm spreading among them as if they had one mind.

Feng laughed. "They hear what we cannot," he said, resuming his foot-rub again. "I wish I had great spreading ears like theirs, so I could hear the enemy approaching before he even knows where I am!"

An Lu-shan stood and stretched. Gods, but he was weary. He yawned, enjoying his fatigue the way one does when one knows that a long, comfortable sleep is coming soon.

"I will walk a bit, Feng, while you rest," he said. "Then perhaps you will show me where I might let my tired carcass sleep for a while."

Feng waved his staff as if offering An Lu-shan the entire grounds. "I will be right here, An Lu-shan. We are in no hurry today."

An Lu-shan left Feng and walked toward the ruined building. He could see that restoration had begun on it and wanted to see how far it had progressed. When he was out of sight of Feng, he left the path and walked through the tall grass toward a crate in the shade of a wall. He could see that the top was partly open. It was too tantalizing. Gently, he lifted the boards and pushed the straw aside. On the very top was a treasure he would have claimed for himself immediately had he found it on the Silk Road. Carefully, he lifted the smooth porcelain curving figure of a celestial dragon. Claws and whiskers and a lashing tail embraced a flaming golden pearl. He turned it slowly in his hands. Multicolored glazes swirled and dripped down to its translucent, feathery tail. He rubbed it with his sleeve. Did he dare? He saw himself taking this treasure, this emperor's dragon, back up north with him. He saw himself showing it, and telling them about this place, this day. It was small enough to conceal in his loose sleeve. He slipped it in and replaced the top of the crate after loosening the straw so that no trace of an impression remained.

His mind filling with the pleasant prospect of the story he would tell, he moved back toward the path and in the direction of the ruined building. As he got closer, he saw that very little had been done to this one. He climbed the four or five steps that led to the entryway, and went inside.

It looked as if no one had been there for a thousand years. The roof was gone. Open to the sky was what had once been a splendid pool, now partially caved in and filled with rocks. He walked to the edge. Hot water still bubbled out of the earth, trickling from lime-encrusted spouts and leaving a trail of color over the rocks. He started to stoop, to feel the temperature of the water, when a sound stopped him with his hand poised over the spout.

It was a low growl. It had not come from behind, but from in front of him. He raised his eyes to a pile of rubble partially in shadow in the far corner of the room.

How could he not have seen it? Crouched there among the fallen rocks, its spotted coat blending into the shadows, was a leopard. Its flat yellow eyes looked directly into his as another growl escaped its slightly open jaws. Lying under the leopard, its neck twisted grotesquely, was one of the Emperor's gazelle. Its slender front leg jerked spasmodically. It was still alive. Don't run, he told himself. Don't run. For long, languid moments there was no sound except his own breathing and the gurgling water. An Lu-shan straightened gradually; as he did, the porcelain dragon slipped from his sleeve, smashing to bits on the stone floor. At the sound, the cat, with the gazelle's neck in its mouth, took one mighty leap upward to the top of the wall and was gone. An Lu-shan hurried outside. He saw a flash of spotted coat disappearing behind a row of pillars.

He looked around him at the green, tranquil landscape. How could such a place harbor a predatory devil like that? It was like some demon from Hell invading Paradise. There had been little time for fear; he had been too completely astonished. Now he stood, the universe reverberating from the sight he had just seen. The yellow eyes had looked at him from another world, an animal world. He had felt the absolute, uncompromising purity of purpose behind those animal eyes, had seen it in its teeth, claws, whiskers, and the awesome power of its body as it leapt to the top of the wall. He felt the aftermath now of the fear juice; his knees wobbled, his heart pounded. He remembered the dragon. Damn! He went back inside. Only a section of the tail was intact. He decided to keep it. The rest I will have to bury somewhere, he thought, looking with regret at the shattered pieces of the Emperor's treasure. He picked them all up carefully.

Stepping outside again, he paused. There was no sign of the cat. He moved back along the walkway, looking for a suitable place to bury the pieces where they would never be noticed. He avoided going into the woods around the buildings; best to stay out in the open with the animal lurking about. To his right he saw an open pavilion; just beyond it was a rocky garden. Perfect. He walked through the pavilion, picking up a sharp stone he found there. He was about to step out into the garden when he stopped. Twenty paces away, a young, beautiful woman squatted on the ground. In front of her lay the gazelle. In her hand she held a sharp knife; with it, she was cutting long thin strips of meat from the carcass and eating them. He could smell the blood. He watched her, transfixed. He could see the muscles of her jaws working. Her face was as smooth and white as unpainted porcelain; her long, black shiny hair fell over her knees and tattered black clothing and almost touched the ground. Around her neck and dangling from her waist were bird claws, talismans, bits of bone and shiny glass, clinking and jingling with every move. Chewing, she looked up, directly at him. Her deep, dark eyes fixed him in a way that reminded An Lu-shan of an animal accustomed to men—unafraid, indifferent. Still looking at him, she raised another strip to her mouth and ate it. Then she smiled at him, mouth full, blood on her lips and teeth.

It was the strangest thing he had ever seen. To make sure that he was not asleep and having an odd dream, he looked around him. The path through the tall grass was there, the ruins, the rotting red wooden pillars tilting against the outline of the distant trees, the pool collapsed with rock, the sound of water and birds, the heavy smell of sulphur, the broken pieces of porcelain in his hands. He tested the air. A strange smell hung there faintly—burning grass or weeds? He watched her for a while before withdrawing. She ignored him and went on eating. He wanted to call to Feng; he could not.

: :

The afternoon burst into heat and the sun rode in and out of thick white clouds as the ceiling of heaven hung low. The close air along the narrow streets was heavy and fetid, full of the smell of too many people who could not escape.

Shopkeepers unrolled awnings, stretching them out on thin bamboo posts, extending them until they almost shaded the blazing paving stones of the street. Umbrellas lined the bridges, providing a bit of shade for the traveling peddlers underneath.

There was little commerce today, except in the teahouses and at the boiled ice-water establishments. Many shopkeepers, defeated by the heat, had given up and gone home. In the trees and bushes and brown grass, ten thousand insects fanned their legs and wings, their whirring filling the still air.

The poor stayed off the streets if they could. If they were close to any water, they would roll up their trousers; and if they were fortunate enough to own sandals or boots, they would remove them and wade, or just sit on a bank or a low wall with the water up to their knees. But there was little escape from the heat. One thing that was certain was summer in Ch'ang-an. The rich sought the coolness of whatever water they could find, taking iced drinks and chilled and sectioned fruits in sauces of cold, sugared brine on the canopied decks of pleasure barges with beautiful swan- and carp-shaped prows. For the rich or the poor, the heat was the same—but most of the rich, at least, were exempt from the oppressive closeness of the city.

Others of the wealthy classes sought the cool refuge of the public gardens of the Serpentine and Xing Ying parks, and there they would meet the poor. Then the only difference between them would be the circumstances and particulars of their outings. The rich, followed by their attendants, would have more elaborate picnics: a finer selection of drinks, rare fruit juices from the south—Fukien, Lingnan, Kuangchou, Annam, and the isle of Hainan—and assorted delicacies and sweetmeats whose arrangements, colors, textures, descriptions, and names would make them think of mountains, snow, and icy streams in winter.

It was not uncommon on these days of mutual discomfort that families of the rich would share their bounty with families of the poor. Often bargains would be struck for exchanges of food for labor and service at some future date. Sometimes terms of the trade were set down by the poor: there were cases of the rich being robbed, sometimes brutally, along the quiet paths of the parks and rockeries. But the authorities wished to play these incidents down—few reports of such barbarism appeared in the daily gazettes.

For the more daring, there was escape into the wild coolness of the forest parks north of the imperial city and palace grounds. Much of this land was walled off, but through the magnanimity of earlier emperors, portions of it had been opened to the public. And there, at certain times of the year, they could hunt for squirrel, quail, wild pigeon and duck, and sometimes a roebuck. The woods north of the Palace of Grand Enlightenment were stocked with all kinds of birds, but hunting was still a rare privilege. The great forests of central China had long ago succumbed to the demand for charcoal. Hunting was not what it once was. And those who did not reside in the tropical jungles of the south, the Huang Shan Mountains, and the great piny slopes of the far north and west could only imagine the once great sport as it appeared in ancient painted friezes and murals of archers and wild boars, bears, and great horned deer.

But the educated found a new sport in these thickly wooded hills north of the city: a love of the past. Taking advantage of the hot day as an excuse, they would escape the city to explore the ancient ruins of the Han dynasty capital, overgrown and embraced by the leafy coolness of vines and broadleaf trees. Crumbling towers lay like split melons, and walls were barely recognizable, appearing as mounds of grassy, weed-covered earth. The ruins were alive with ground squirrels, foxes, rabbits, peacocks, garden snakes, and scurrying hens. The ground, once littered with magnificent bronze bells and carved stele, had been picked clean by wealthy collectors. Those who could afford the transport had removed so many of these pieces of the past that laws of preservation had had to be enacted. But the laws were largely ineffectual; the looting continued. Ancient works of art and worship now sat forlorn in private gardens and grand, empty halls, topics of idle conversation.

Even in the midst of Ch'ang-an's summer heat, there were a privileged few who shivered with cold. Some of the very rich and lazy, it was said, sat in innovative cool rain rooms, basking in frigid air. Well water from deep in the earth, icy even on the hottest summer day, would be pumped onto a tin rooftop. As the air in the room chilled, treadle-operated fans pushed it across in cool blasts.

The palace had one such room; some gardens of the very rich had rain rooms, too. But those who made use of these rooms on the hottest days complained that it made them too cold. They said that it turned their skin blue, driving the warming *chi* from the body so that their bones ached and they shook all over. It was hard to say, they remarked, which was worse: the heat or the cold.

Li Lin-fu, though it was well within his means, did not use such a room. Nor did he stay at his estate in the rolling grasslands south of the city. He worked all of every summer day in his office at the high fortress Chancellery. The servants had put dark cloth over the open windows to turn back the heat; he had had them taken down. Wrapped in dark robes, he sat soaking up the heat and sweating profusely in the broad streams of sunlight that poured into the room. It was the only time he was truly comfortable. It was his theory that the heat could drive out the excess yin, the patterns of excess cold and cold blockage and the damp, pernicious influences and mucus that had contaminated his lungs. His physician rebuked this theory—mainly, Li Lin-fu knew, because the man disliked attending him in the heat. He spared the physician as much as he could because he liked him, but his officers received no such deferential treatment. He hoped the heat would dissipate the poison in his lungs; he knew it would challenge the patience and the loyalty of his officers.

On this day, as Li Lin-fu worked at his desk, General Niu Hsien-ko stood in a hot shaft of light. The room buzzed with flies; the mosquito gauze had been pulled off the window along with the cloth shades. Outside, the Vermilion Phoenix Tower was nearly obscured by a shimmering haze.

Li Lin-fu wiped his brow and was pleased to note that Niu was glistening with sweat, blinking it out of his eyes from time to time. He looked acutely miserable.

"General, it is not advisable to fight it. Uninhibited sweating is good for your body. It removes the poisons that settle in the five vessels, without disturbing the outer enveloping *chi*. Although the physician might argue against this theory, one has only to look at the filth on this rag. My physician associates the sweating of summer with damp pernicious influences. He sees such dampness as not elicited by the dryness of the air, but as a dampness capable of blocking the spleen's raising of the pure into the blood and *chi*. The poor man has it quite wrong. Don't you think so, Niu?" The chief minister raised the soiled silk rag with which he had wiped his face and examined the grime on it. "Some of this is surely only the dust in the air, the usual dirt that settles on our skin; but much of it, I'm sure you'll agree, comes from inside. These toxins impede the flow of . . ." He stopped, and smiled ingratiatingly. "Enough! Enough, General Niu! If you do not stop me from rambling on these topics, then who will?"

"But, Councillor I . . ."

"But you, my assistant, do not have the presence of mind to simply tell your councillor to shut up when I have rambled too long on one of my theories, and you have much to tell me about our visitor from the northern provinces, this General An Lu-shan. You must be writhing with impatience, General! It would not do for me to be improperly prepared for the man, who will be arriving here in only a few hours! Now," he said, assuming an attentive air, "tell me something else about him, something I don't already know. Tell me about Sogdians. You've served as an in-absentia military governor in those regions, as have I. The difference is that you have traveled up there, whereas I always thought it best to avoid the unnecessary burden."

Niu opened his mouth as if to speak, but the chief minister interrupted him.

"Give me something other than the same ordinary facts. We don't learn anything about a man from a simple list of his appointments and titles. We live in a world, General Niu, where titles, sinecures, and principalities heaped upon a man are too often not commensurate with his worth. Look at you!

You were once a military governor before coming to me." Li Lin-fu smiled. "Look at all the worthless old nobles that fill our halls every morning. Do you understand me?"

"I believe so, Councillor," Niu replied.

"After a while," Li Lin-fu continued, "the number of titles after a man's name become no more meaningful than the number of tiny sparrows fried in a hot oil cauldron by a vendor on a winter day. Duke of this, archduke of that, president of this, vice magistrate of that . . . and it goes on and on. General, I want to know something about the man."

"An Lu-shan is a Sogdian," said Niu. "His family fled the Kushan massacres . . ."

"Ah! Now we are getting somewhere, General. What do you know about Sogdians? If you do not understand, I will give you an example: We base much of our military policy on a certain kind of knowledge . . . knowledge not only of an enemy's movements and troop strengths, but of his beliefs and superstitions and of the character of his people. Are they courageous? Or would they rather hide than fight? Do they ambush us, or meet us in the open? What are their beliefs about an afterlife? Do their gods punish them for cowardice? You see, those are the things we have always tried to know before we take on anyone—whether Tibetan, Juchen, Sogdian, Hsi, Khitan . . . any tribe, any nation. We as the Han people—the people of ancient China proper—have certain characteristics that we are born with."

Niu Hsien-ko could no longer stand the heat.

"May I, Councillor?" he asked.

"Be comfortable, General, by all means!" Niu grasped the front of his outer tunic and pulled it over his head. The sweat fell in small droplets from his chin to the hot stone of the Chancellery office floor. He looked out the window as if gathering his thoughts.

From outside, beyond the walls of the imperial city compound, the stench of the Ch'ang-an summer invaded the room. Not far away in the streets of the city, the sound of cymbals clashing—ching-che, ching-che—made the peculiar, unmistakable rhythm that announced the coming of the night-soil wagon. The filth of the city, its wastes, brought the tired earth of the farms back to life. And now the sky darkened with the sword-iron threat of a thunderstorm. The rain would turn the filth to muck and the alleys to mud, and the culverts would overflow with it. The air grew thick and motionless. Then came the breeze.

The crack and rustle of leaves flickering silver and the rush of pine bows brushing against the high sloping walls of the building filled the room. A gust of cool air scattered papers on the chief minister's desk, and then the dragon spoke as a tremendous crack of thunder split the sky. A few first drops spattered heavily against the windowsill. Spits of rain hissed against the burning flag-stones of the courtyard; then heaven broke open. Red and gold, the imperial city shone sleek with water . . .

"Then you are asking me to tell you about the character of a Sogdian, Councillor?" the general responded, at last.

"Precisely! For example, . . . are the Sogdians more superstitious as a people than other northern barbarian nations?"

Niu thought for a moment before answering: "They are considerably less superstitious, Grand Councillor, and, generally, quite a bit harder to trick."

"What else, General Niu?"

"They are very open with their intentions and quite forceful. I remember that they were also very forceful with their women and especially their children." He shrugged. "At times they could be most brutal."

Li Lin-fu tapped the table impatiently. "General Niu, I beg you. Something that might help me."

"Well . . . they are not afraid of the Chinese military organization. They were difficult to question, Councillor. If we tried to attempt an inventory of their livestock or of their families . . . they appeared to be open and honest with us, but they maintained a very elusive side. If we were to ask one of them, for instance, how many people constituted his household, he might respond with: 'As many wives and children and old parents as I have.' "

"And they were quite correct," said Li Lin-fu. "It takes no great intelligence to determine that, General Niu."

"Also . . . after many of the Sogdian families had fled south into Chinese territory, we began to see an increase in actions directed against the Chinese authorities along the northern border provinces . . ."

"And these incidents mainly involved the Sogdian populations?" Li Lin-fu asked, watching the water dripping off the roof tiles above the window.

The rain had stopped. It was still hot, but the air had cleared. The sun was starting to break through, and a wispy shred of rainbow light hung against the deep blue-gray of the leaden sky.

"No. And that was the strange thing. Somehow the Sogdians had incited the local populations into incidents against us."

"But the northeast border peoples, Chinese or tribal, General Niu, have always hated their T'ang overlords. Hopei Province has long had dangerous secessionist tendencies against this court, has always been an especially dangerous prospect for this ruling house, ripe for rebellion against us. They resent us for usurping the power of their own ruling houses. In certain ways they are as dangerous as the barbarian Khitan and Hsi. This certainly is nothing new." Li Lin-fu looked at Niu expectantly.

Niu wiped his tired face. Outside, the sun had broken through the clouds completely. The two men listened to the pattering of water dripping from the eaves. They heard the far-away rhythm of the cymbals; the night-soil wagon had resumed its rounds.

"There is one other thing, Grand Councillor," Niu began hesitantly, "but . . ."

"But what, General Niu?"

"But I was reluctant to bring it up in your presence earlier."

Li Lin-fu waited.

"There is a rumor . . . Perhaps it is nothing more than a rumor. It is about An Lu-shan." He wiped nervously at his forehead and chin. "But I . . ."

"But you thought you must tell me, General Niu. And you were not wrong," Li Lin-fu coaxed.

"It is, quite simply, a rumor being spread among the troops in the north. The guards who rode with Feng to meet An Lu-shan got drunk by the river with An Lu-shan's men last night, when Feng and the barbarian went together to the imperial hot springs at Lin-tong village . . . and the northerners told the men a most amazing tale about their chief . . . I am certain there is little truth to it. A tale for women . . ."

"I am sure that the men would appreciate being compared to women. And I am not surprised that such stories would prove fascinating to you, General Niu. In any case, continue . . ."

"It is not something that can be proven, Councillor. That is why I hesitated to trouble you with it. But they are saying that An Lu-shan's mother was of mixed barbarian blood and that she was a shamaness. They are saying that she had either no sons or no sons left after the Kushan conflicts; I don't know. But the poor woman was frightened of having no heirs, so she prayed out of desperation to a king of Hell."

Li Lin-fu detected a slight tremor in Niu's voice as he said the words. His face was flushed, too—either from the heat or from embarrassment at his own foolishness. Or perhaps, Li Lin-fu observed, he is foolish enough to be genuinely frightened by the story.

"And what was the result of these bargains with the 'underworld'?" asked Li Lin-fu, with the barest hint of mockery in his own voice. He went to the window to listen to the songbirds emerging after the rain. I will give the poor fool a chance to compose himself, he thought.

"The god supposedly visited with her at night. And she had a son—An Lu-shan. His was a breech birth. And on that night astrologers reported seeing a red comet pass overhead, and the beam of a star of evil magic lit the midwife's tent with red light . . ." Niu stopped.

Li Lin-fu understood now the significance of the tale. These were all signs that pointed to an excess of yang, an imbalance with dire consequences to those of a superstitious turn of mind. It was no wonder that the story was spreading among the troops.

"But there is a little more to the story, Councillor, if I may . . ."

"Then finish it, General, but do it quickly. My patience has begun to wear thin with these fairy tales." Li Lin-fu did not turn from the window but put his hands firmly on the sill and leaned out, taking a long draught of the cleared air.

"Only, Councillor, that the soldiers said that the reason General An could so convincingly mimic the sounds of wild beasts to deceive the enemy was that the beasts howled and chattered around his tent the night he was born. Their voices were the first sounds he heard," Niu finished, fidgeting uneasily under Li Lin-fu's gaze.

"It is all very interesting, General Niu. But it is interesting to me for a very different reason than it is to you. The fact that the stories of this nonsense take root in the camps tells me that the soldiers and the neighboring populations hold this man in great esteem and fear. That in itself is more interesting than all the myths in China . . . because you have just told me more about the man than I could have hoped for. Sometimes I underestimate you, General. The same way I underestimated our departed poet, Master Chang Chiu-ling." Li Lin-fu took another breath and was seized by a coughing fit. Niu stood by, embarrassed, while his master hacked and then spat out the window.

"Then you don't think that there is anything to these tales, Councillor —that they are only . . . nonsense?"

"You have asked the wrong person, General Niu," said Li Lin-fu, holding up his hand between coughs. "Do I look like a shaman or a necromancer to you?"

::

A ring of artificial hills separated the city of Ch'ang-an from the endless vale of farmland and sprawling suburban estates surrounding the city. Fifty feet wide at the base and some thirty feet from ground to top, the mounds of earth and stone obscured all but the tallest buildings from view for anyone looking at the city from a distance. The hills in summer were covered with grasses, flowers, and vines.

The hills had been built from earth and stone more than eight hundred and fifty years before the T'ang, during the Han dynasty. Seven hundred years later, during the short-lived and tiresomely ambitious period of the Sui dynasty, when forced labor and great public works projects drained government coffers and exhausted the available manpower with park and canal projects, an imperial decree regarding the city walls was enacted. All registered citizens of Ch'ang-an who were not yet working, including women and children and the old who were not infirm, became "volunteers for the state." It was a way of pressing citizens into corvée labor without taking them from their homes. For the "volunteers," it was another burden on top of all the rest.

Each day they "tithed" time from their household chores, carrying cuttings and prunings to the walls and planting them. It was done so that, to an enemy approaching, the walls would look like natural hills, the city hiding safely behind them. And, indeed, that was the effect, though there were no enemies to deceive; there had been none within the borders of China for centuries. Thus Ch'ang-an, the garden city of China, came to be surrounded by lush foliage and flowers, enemies or no. It was beautiful. But like all public works projects, it was done at too great an expense.

From inside the city the effect of these walls was both elegant and strange. The visual splendor of Lin-tong's purple hills, some thirty li northeast, came to belong to the city. At the center of town, the distant hills seemed to be nothing more than the continuation of the city's infinite boundaries; it was as though those hills and the even larger mountains beyond them, seventy-five to a hundred li from the city, were only at the far perimeters of Ch'ang-an's parks. The city went on forever. Or so it seemed.

:: :

As Feng and An Lu-shan approached the city's P'ing Kang Gate—the great eastern gate—An Lu-shan looked back over his shoulder at the Lin-tong hills, hazy in the morning light. The hot springs lay like a secret memory in their bluish-purple shadow. The long, straight road they had traveled since leaving there vanished in the distance behind them.

They rode full out, hooves pounding, stones flying. First Feng's horse would lead, then An Lu-shan's. Feng's huge stallion foamed at the bit and its nostrils flared blood red. An Lu-shan could see the animal's massive muscles outlined in glistening sweat on the white, salty shoulders. He could hear the horse's rhythmic breathing above his own mount's as Feng rode past him, nearly unseating him with a playful swipe of his arm. They raced for half a li until it was evident that the horses had had enough, that they would kill themselves with the strain in the blind and frenzied effort to please. The generals reined them in, bouncing, breaking their gaits gradually to a walk.

An Lu-shan wiped the sticky dust and sweat from his face. He saw that his hand was red with the fine spray of mud kicked up from the ground by the horses. The great eastern gate of the city, topped with massive crenellated battlements, was now only a few hundred yards in front of them. Ahead, he heard the beating of the drums. Feng had told him that the drums announced the lifting of the morning curfew, and he had planned their arrival to coincide. The city was now open to the great flood of human traffic—on foot, in carts, on barges or donkeys' backs.

The day would be hot. Slowing down from the gallop, An Lu-shan found that his blood continued to race as if they were still riding at top speed. His face felt hot—but from the inside, not from the temperature of the air. The slight giddy dizziness he attributed to last night's wine; he had no memory of finding his way into the beautiful private chamber where he had awakened that morning with the small, skillful hands of the concubine moving over his body. As soon as his eyes had opened, she held out a steaming bowl of hot liquid. "This will return your head to its normal size," she had said sympathetically as he tried to sit up and winced with pain. And indeed, within a few minutes of drinking it he felt strong and clear, the throbbing in his temples gone. "It is a special kind of tea," she had said, "for banishing the wine demon." He had smiled at her as if she were a goddess of mercy.

What else could he do but get drunk last night? After he had seen the leopard and then the young woman at her strange repast in the garden, he had sat by himself for a good while. He knew he should find Feng, warn him of the danger. But he just wanted to sit very still. By the time he did force himself to return, he had lost the desire to talk about the incident. He had found Feng sitting contentedly in the sun, tossing small rocks to amuse himself. It was not until later, after they had eaten and were well into their third pitcher of wine, that An Lu-shan had mentioned the incident to Feng. The cat was from the Emperor's menagerie, probably, Feng had said without a lot of concern. No doubt it had been caught and put back in its pen by now. As for the woman . . . well, these gardens were meant to be open to the people, though hunting of the Emperor's gazelle . . . that was strictly forbidden. There are some wild people, he said, who live in the woods like wild animals. Maybe she is one of those. Or, he had laughed, maybe you saw Li Shan Lao Ma. Who? An Lu-shan had asked. The witch-woman of the hot springs, Feng had said. An immortal, a daughter of the gods. A hag, a thousand years old. But this one was young, you say? Maybe she is a concubine who decided to live in the woods and eat raw flesh and never comb her hair. Feng had reached out and grabbed a woman standing nearby, and pulled her down into his lap. Eh? Are any of your sisters missing? Did one grow tired of scented silk and warm water? The girl had laughed. Sing for Master An, he had said. Sing him one of the songs about the legendary Li-shan Lao Ma. And they had continued to drink and sing until . . . An Lu-shan remembered nothing else until he woke up the next morning and the woman gave him the tea.

So it was not surprising that he should feel a bit dizzy or that his blood should fill his head. But it was strange. His head felt as if it were too large and too small at the same time. It made him want to laugh. And he felt words piling up. He knew that if he opened his mouth, a river of words would come out. The horses were walking now as Feng and An Lu-shan mingled with the stream of people heading toward the gate to the city. An Lu-shan looked sideways at Feng. The man's ugly face was relaxed and rested, as if he had drunk only mother's milk the night before.

"Tell me about the man I am going to meet today, Feng."

Feng thought for a moment before answering. "I will tell you this," he said pleasantly. "This is not just another investigator who awaits your arrival, An Lu-shan. It is our own Master Li Lin-fu, chief minister, bearer of the Ssu-k'ung robe . . ." He paused. ". . . also known affectionately as the Lizard." He is the man to whom you are solely responsible, and to whom I am solely responsible—to whom even my superior on the Tibetan campaigns, my drunken commander Ko-shu Han is responsible. Indeed," he said with a shrug, "to whom the rats in the granaries and the fleas on the rats are responsible. No one's power or prestige is sufficient to avoid his touch!"

"And the Emperor . . . ?" An Lu-shan asked.

"And the Emperor . . . precisely," Feng responded.

An Lu-shan was not certain he understood. "Then what is this Li Lin-fu?" An Lu-shan asked angrily. "What does he expect of me? I am only a soldier!" A guilty picture of himself sitting in his tent, forging the cartographer's map, presented itself. What if it is ever discovered? What if this Li Lin-fu somehow knows about it?

"Only a soldier, An Lu-shan?" said Feng. "I doubt that!"

"No price is too high to pay to win against the Hsi and the Khitan. He must understand that. The old border defenses, the old northern militias, have grown weak, Feng. They have grown lax while these Chinese sit down here pissing in their warm-water pools, thinking themselves safe. They should see it! They'd piss in their silk drawers if they did!" An Lu-shan ranted. He knew he was talking too much, but he could not help himself. "I wish I could show them the face of just one Khitan warrior thirsty for blood!"

Feng smiled at this.

"Rats and lizards! You talk about rats and lizards! Any silk-drawers Chinese would jump into a pit full of them rather than face just one devil of a blood-drinking Khitan! I tell you, Feng, they care nothing for their own lives. By the gods, if we had an army of them, China would have nothing to fear! No price is too high, I tell you, if we can drive them back even ten paces! You tell that to your Li Lin-fu!" he finished, breathing hard, face flushed.

"I don't think," Feng said, "that you will find any disagreement on this topic with Master Li Lin-fu. You wanted to know what kind of a man he is? I'll tell you. Even your blood-drinking, suicidal, devil of a Khitan would crap in his drawers if he had to sit down to tea with Master Li Lin-fu." An Lu-shan was seized by laughter.

"But Feng!" he said. "His drawers are already full of crap! How would he be able to tell the difference?"

Feng threw back his head and laughed exultantly. "By the weight, An Lu-shan, by the weight!"

They were laughing hard, tears starting from their eyes. An Lu-shan noticed that the neck of his horse, his own hands on the reins, and the ground under them seemed to be falling away. His laughter filled his ears, and the top of his head seemed to be floating several feet above him. He shook his head as the spasms of laughter subsided, as if he could shake the strange feeling out of his ears and nose. The image of his head as a hollow gourd with dried-up seeds rolling around in it brought on a fresh surge of mirth. Feng, as if he saw it too, laughed with him. People nearby looked curiously at them. Who could blame them, An Lu-shan thought, wiping his streaming eyes and nose. Two huge madmen, laughing like fools.

"None of you understand!" he shouted to the crowd, thumping his chest and startling his horse. "*I* understand!" People moved back, shaking their heads and muttering among themselves.

"I understand too, Fat Man!" yelled one fellow in the crowd. "You're not the only one!" They were nearly at the gate now and had to slow down as the crowd funneled through.

"I will impart only one small bit of advice to you, An Lu-shan," said Feng. "Anything more would only hinder you. There is a line from an ancient poem, by a poet named Ju-an Chi. It is over five hundred years old, written when the Han dynasty crumbled from too many ambitious generals. He said '. . . the ghosts wailed the night men learned to speak!' When the poet wrote those words, it was as if he had already met our chief minister. They tell me that you have the senses and cunning of a wild animal. If that is so, then use them! When you are sitting before the Lizard, you must listen with more than your ears. You must listen the way a superstitious old woman listens to ghosts at the well."

They were at the gate now, passing under the arches. And then they entered Ch'ang-an.

Before An Lu-shan was a broad boulevard lined with white cement walls, overhanging balconies on two- and three-story buildings, gates and doorposts of brightly painted wood. Distant towers reached to the sky over an endless expanse of low, squat rooftops, shop awnings, and umbrellas. And stretching to infinity, surging in every direction, occupying every bit of ground, was humanity. An Lu-shan would not have thought there could be this many people in the entire world. They walked, rode, and were carried; they moved in and out, around and among each other, eating, shouting, selling, herding animals, carrying loads. From his vantage point astride his horse, An Lu-shan looked out over the undulating sea of heads stretching beyond the limits of his perception. He tried to comprehend what he was seeing, but he couldn't. For a brief moment he felt the fear that the little child had felt long ago, glimpsing, for the first time, the Silk Road caravan winding forever in endless li of dust, noise, and stink. Too big, too expansive, as if size were a devil itself. The smells of smoke, food, and garbage made his head and body tingle with old memories of other cities, other times. He felt like a child now as forgotten emotions rushed through him, tumbling over each other, illogical, irrelevant, contradictory. The horses pranced nervously, surrounded by the jostling crowd.

Feng turned around, smiling, to face him. "You are not the only warrior here, Lu-shan," he shouted.

They entered the main boulevard. As they plunged into the current of people and animals, carriages and carts, An Lu-shan felt the way he had felt on the night he waded into the river.

He kept the broad figure of Feng in sight as they made their way along the street. They could move no faster than the people around them. He saw that the main boulevard was fed by innumerable smaller streets and alleys; looking down those alleys as they passed by, he could see that they, too, intersected with other streets, and on and on and on. Even in this crowd of every imaginable type of human being, he drew some attention.

"Hey, Jew!" somebody yelled.

He looked down and saw a man holding a six-year-old child.

"Jew!" The man was addressing An Lu-shan and waving his free arm as he pushed through the crowd toward the general's horse.

As they got close, An Lu-shan saw that the child's eyes were milky white, staring. It was blind. "I am not a Jew, sir!" he shouted back to the man. "I am a Sogdian!"

"Let him feel your beard, Jew!" said the man, thrusting the child up toward An Lu-shan.

The child was a puny, skinny thing, and An Lu-shan could not tell whether it was a girl or a boy. Like a monkey, it seized An Lu-shan's leg and scurried up to his face, where its little hands grabbed hold of An Lu-shan's beard. The horse pranced in a circle, snorting, with the man holding on to one of the stirrups and laughing, as An Lu-shan stared transfixed into the child's sightless, clouded eyes. A radiant smile broke across its face as it tugged on the beard as if trying to pull it out by the roots. With one hand on the reins, An Lu-shan tried to control the horse; with the other hand, he pulled, trying to disengage the hands from his beard. Hairs ripped out of his skin and he thrust the child back down to the man. He spurred his horse through the crowd, hearing the man still calling behind him "Hey, Jew!" His face stung and his eyes watered. A crazy man and a little demon, he thought. My first acquaintances.

Then he realized that he had lost Feng. He stood up in the stirrups, scanning the crowd. No Feng anywhere. This was very bad. I do not know which way to go or whom to ask, he thought, panicking. Damn, but it is hotter today than it was yesterday. He was covered with sweat and growing angry. I'll miss my meeting with Li Lin-fu. Calm yourself, he thought sternly. Think.

A strategy occurred to him. He would leave the main thoroughfare and find a smaller street, less crowded, and move parallel to the large street until he felt he would be ahead of Feng, then cut over and find him. Pulling on the horse's bit, he guided the animal to the left and into the narrow confines of an alley. The relief was almost immediate; it was much quieter here. He looked around. On either side were tall white concrete walls containing tightly closed wooden gates. People moved here and there, but were not packed together like animals. He paused to breathe for a moment, the sights, sounds, and smells still echoing through his hot, dizzy head. The air had grown still and heavy, but now a sudden breeze whipped up paper and debris, swirling it around the horse's legs. Thunder rolled overhead, and he felt spatters of rain. The deluge quickly gathered momentum; within minutes, the gutters on either side of the alley were rushing with brown filth, and the cobblestones were slick under the horse's hooves. An Lu-shan took his helmet off and allowed the cool water to fall on his head and run down into his clothing as he rode. Li Lin-fu. He said the name softly to himself. I must find my way through this city of seething millions and find one man. He pictured a very dignified lizard sitting at a desk, wearing a silk robe, rings on his long green fingers, waiting for General An Lu-shan. He whipped his horse. He must find Feng.

The rain depleted itself quickly. Steam rose from the ground, breath of the dragon given up by the earth, as the sun broke through the clouds.

He passed colorful, richly carved gates recessed into the high alley walls. What could possibly lie behind them? Did they all belong to the Emperor? Were there beautiful women and grand pleasure parks behind these walls, as there were at the hot springs?

Just as he was thinking this, a loud scraping sound, wood against stone, made his horse shy to one side. As if in answer to his question, a set of thick, studded gates was being pushed open to his left. Before he could see anything, he heard noises—hooves, someone shouting orders, talking, laughter, running feet. Another voice. A woman's, yelling loudly, more laughter. He smelled horses in the rain-washed air, rich and pungent, mixed with smells of silks and oils. The gates opened fully, and people and animals poured out into the alleyway. He moved to the side; he would let them go by.

There were two magnificent carriages with satin curtains, each pulled by two gaily caparisoned horses draped in colored silks, manes done up in feathers, tails braided. There were outriders—handsome young men with gleeming black hair scooped into hard topknots. One was wearing a great wide-brimmed horsehair hat. Another had a sleek hooded falcon on his wrist.

As the carriages came up behind him, a lusty, bawdy, perfumed odor reached him. Unmistakable. Women! And a faint whiff of something else: the vaguely acid, pissy smell of household eunuch servants. From behind the satin curtains he heard women's voices laughing and singing, taunting one another with childhood rhymes. The curtains flapped and rippled with each bounce and sway of the carriages over the rough broken pavement of the back street.

The laughter and songs of the girls—he was sure that they were very young—stopped as the party drew parallel to him. Two female heads thrust themselves out between the curtains of the first carriage. They were beautiful, more beautiful even than his attendants at the hot springs. The faces were bone white, like porcelain, with only a hint of rouge on the cheeks. The eyes were made up deep and black, a thin painted eyebrow curving gracefully up toward a thick pile of hair adorned with jewels and pulled high off the forehead. He stared.

They stared back at him for one astonished moment, then turned to each other with the wicked look that children have before they laugh at an adult. They put their hands to their mouths and giggled, pulling their beautiful heads back inside the curtains. His face flushed hot. Yes, he thought, feeling his wet, bedraggled beard, I am sure I am quite a sight to you. He caught, for an instant, an image of himself through their eyes: a monster, a demon, a clown. Their husbands will no doubt scold and reprimand them for looking at him outside the confines of their carriage, showing their faces so shamelessly like that. Those young men were their husbands, surely. He wondered that they did not stop the coaches right then and there to punish the women. He expected it at any moment. But the topknotted young dandies took no notice and continued to talk and laugh among themselves, giving him the same impertinent look as they rode by.

They were moving toward the intersection; they turned and went in the direction in which he had intended to go. Very well, he thought, digging his heels into his horse's sides. You are a curiosity to me, just as I am to you. He followed.

The two carriages entered the street with the horsemen riding several paces ahead. This street was just as crowded as the one where he had lost Feng; he doubted that his progress here would be any quicker. Cursing, he guided his nervous animal through the throngs in order to get closer to the carriage; the outriders were effectively clearing a pathway through the crowd. If he stayed close, he would move faster. That damned crazy man and his blind little monkey-child, he thought. What kind of idiotic world is this? Because of them, I will miss my meeting with the chief minister of the empire, the chancellor of the Ministry of War. He seethed with fury and frustration as he fought his way through the mob like a fish battling its way upstream. And as if to add to his rage, the females behind the satin curtains of the lead carriage continued to sing loudly and gaily. Occasionally one would stick her pretty head out between the curtains for a look around, ignoring completely the entreaties of beggars. The topknotted young men on horseback threatened with their riding crops any unfortunates who got too close, leaning down to deal out whacks across the legs here and there.

He drew closer to the second carriage. The outriders were watching him—as if he were some sort of street beggar or criminal! If they had any idea who it is they are looking at, he thought, they might be a trifle less arrogant. I could cut them down in seconds if I wanted to, even without weapons. Whatever it is you are guarding in that carriage could be mine for the taking, he muttered to himself, and, in his mind, saw them lying in the street, their beautiful silks smeared with dirt and blood, while he, An Lu-shan, pulled open the decorative fretwork shutters covering the satin curtains . . .

But this was not a trade route, a rocky, hellish, lawless trail between way stations. One did not do these things in the grandest city of the grandest land on earth; one could not. There were rules and order. And yet still he saw the men in the dirt and the beautiful young thing in that first carriage with the soft round face and the white cool smooth porcelain skin . . . He was Commissioner for Foot and Horse for the northern province of P'inglu and much of Fanyang . . . and soon he would be their greatest military leader and they would all know who he was. And this man, Li Lin-fu, would know who he was too.

An Lu-shan craned his neck anxiously, scanning the mass of people as he would an army. He had to find a way back to the other street or he would never find Feng. You could spend your life wandering through this cursed city and never find your way. Then something caught his eye. Far ahead, almost where the parallel lines of the boulevard's curbs seemed to join together, he discerned the figure of a large man on horseback looming above the crowd. He recognized the shoulders, the stance. Feng! He was moving down the street, making his way slowly but definitely in An Lu-shan's direction. He is a good soldier, An Lu-shan thought, to have figured out my strategy. Relief flooded through him. Feng would spot him soon.

He was close enough to the carriage, almost beside it, to hear the sound of muffled feminine laughter, coming from inside, and another sound . . . a man! He and the carriages were traveling steadily along the boulevard. He kept one eye on the figure of Feng in the distance, advancing steadily, and the other eye on the fantastic, unbelievable panorama of life in Ch'ang-an.

They passed brightly colored awnings of bazaars and shops. He saw gracefully arching bridges spanning canals, the littered muddy water solid with long freight barges. Innkeepers swept steps; shopkeepers set out signs, sacks, and crates. In motion everywhere were wheelbarrows, carts, oxen, and donkeys; porters and household servants rushed about in frenzied morning business. Tramps, pickpockets, and market thieves—invisible to everyone but me, An Lu-shan thought wryly—moved through the crowd at their own leisurely pace. I can spot a thief the way the blue pheasant can spot the choicest ginseng plant, he thought, watching them move from stall to stall. Even with his back turned, he could see them creeping the way cats creep around a birdhouse. The more cautiously they moved, the more obvious they were to him: first a melon here, then fried dough or honeyed bananas and gingered plums there. The younger stole toys: colorful lanterns and pennants on sticks, small snakes of folded paper-and-string that moved like living serpents, painted fans and musical bells. He watched as one young fellow made off with an enameled cricket cage with a live occupant while the merchant and bystanders were distracted by a spinning, singing top. But the older ones always stole food— and that was the difference, An Lu-shan thought, between the winged dream of youth and the dull stone pragmatism of age.

He saw city workers—slaves, convicts?—washing debris off the streets and into the canals with a powerful flushing spray of water from enormous wheeled drums with movable handles and long tubes of bamboo that directed the water like archers' arrows. He had never seen so much strange and new, nor anything as grand as the buildings or as endless and wide as the avenues. He focused his vision on the distance: Feng was drawing nearer. He knew he was too far away for recognition, unless Feng's eyesight was as good as his own, but he stood in the saddle and waved his arm vigorously. He had been seen. Feng was waving back. They had found each other. He would stay where he was and be entertained while he waited.

The carriages were stopping, too. They drew up outside a long sheltered bazaar. The outriders cleared the crowds near the two carriages and placed small stools under their doors. As if taking the placing of the steps as a signal, the people in the market formed a wide circle to observe their honored guests. They pointed and talked among themselves as the young girls from the first coach stepped down. The girls' manner changed noticeably from the moment their feet touched the market pavement; they moved quickly and waited expectantly and obediently outside the closed doors of the other carriage. They waited, An Lu-shan was sure, for their husbands; obviously, he had been wrong about those silk-trousers on horseback. The crowd seemed to know what to expect. They pushed and shoved for a better look and stood on the tips of their toes, laughing and chattering.

Ducking his head to avoid the low awnings, he moved to a position where he would have a clear view into the second carriage when the doors opened.

They did not merely open; they flew apart. Laughter and squeals emanated from within. With a flash of purple silk, a woman emerged part way. He saw tousled black hair and heavily rouged cheeks . . . then someone pulled her back inside. More squeals and scuffling, the carriage rocking.

The two girls waiting outside looked at each other, covered their mouths, and giggled. The door was flung open again, and Purple Gown pushed her way out, hair falling in limp strands across her forehead. Behind her, he saw the sheen of bright, embroidered silks—expensive ones, he assessed instantaneously—a heap of pillows, and—the blood rushed to his groin—a glimpse of a man's naked flesh, robes hiked up, "old man" red, hard, and glistening against a background of dark shiny quilts. The door slammed shut.

Stupidly incredulous, An Lu-shan stared at Purple Gown as she held out a slender ivory hand to an attendant and climbed gracefully down, just as if she were the very picture of virtue and respectability.

The two girls bowed and escorted her into the bazaar; the crowd parted, but closed behind them, following closely.

Purple Gown now moved down the broad arcade of the open market with her two attendants following. Without a glance, they passed a group of acrobats putting on a display of martial arts. She appeared bored with the scene as two sweaty men, stripped to the waist, grunted and shouted; they revolved slowly while wicked iron implements, segmented and linked with chain, twirled dangerously fast in their hands—first under their feet and then over their shoulders—filling the air with a murderous humming. The two men engaged each other in perfect agreement of the moment in their deadly dance.

An Lu-shan had seen this sort of thing before. In the streets of Kashgar when he was a child he had seen two foolish old monks play like this, and, even then, he had wondered how all this dance and show could be a match for sheer strength. Now Purple Gown moved unconcernedly by another performer; this man spun a horizontal row of circular-toothed blades with a long flexible pole. To do it, he had to reach between a set of heavy wooden bars, also horizontal, fitted with cruel iron spikes. The object, An Lu-shan saw, was to keep the row of ten blades spinning simultaneously. His timing had to be perfect. A lapse in the rhythm would cause the springy pole to snag on the teeth of a whirling blade, sending the man's naked arms violently against the toothed bar. The fool was already bleeding profusely, but the ten blades were now spinning like wagon wheels and the crowd that had gathered there was urging him on with great enjoyment and the anticipation that comes from that certain animal taste for another's blood.

But it was Purple Gown An Lu-shan was interested in, not the sight of idiots disemboweling themselves and each other. He had seen enough of that in his life. His eyes followed her as she moved beyond the acrobats. What was a woman like Purple Gown doing in such a market as this? Was the man in the carriage her husband? She was a great beauty, no soured peasant wife or household servant forced into the market by her chores. Obsessively, he watched her. She had the air of one who knew exactly where she was going. She walked directly to a brightly colored stall full of large bamboo cages of exotic birds.

Her attendants had gone ahead of her to fetch the proprietor, a dry, brittle old man with stooped shoulders who rushed out the instant he saw who was coming. His walk belied his age. He was typical, An Lu-shan thought, of merchants whose avarice preserved them against the advance of their years. He'd seen a thousand old men just like him—too greedy to pass their wealth on, too busy to die.

The old man greeted Purple Gown with a low, stiff, obsequious bow; then he smiled and waved his hands about excitedly. The woman nodded her head in the direction of first this and then that cage. She waved away a lacquered one proffered by the shopkeeper. The old man called his assistant. Cages, birds squawking within, hung suspended from wheeled racks. The assistant rolled them this way and that as everything in the shop was shown to Purple Gown. As she walked here and there, her skirts and brightly colored shawls swirled and shaped the air around her. The old man took her arm then to guide her toward a curtained doorway; with an acquisitive smile no doubt meant to whet her appetite for the wonders that lay beyond, he prepared to pull the curtain back. An Lu-shan was familiar with the ploy; show the patron the standard stock first and save the most exotic specimens for last.

". . . Your Jealous One does not want you to choose the birds without him!" a strange little voice called loudly from the carriage. "The feathers must set off the opals of his beautiful eyes . . . They must have beautiful voices and sing in the bedroom as the turtles move with candles on their backs! They must love your tiny knight as you do . . ."

An Lu-shan turned to look as the doors opened. A man's square and handsome face poked out; the head was topped with thick, shiny black braids. His eyes were dark and painted. As he spoke, the rest of his body emerged, and General An Lu-shan's mouth dropped open with shock.

He was a dwarf. His head was the size of any man's, but his body was stumpy and as small as a child's. But the bulge in the front of his little silk trousers assured An Lu-shan that this was no child. An Lu-shan looked at the bulge and recalled tales from the Silk Road of the unappeasable little men from the seraglios of Persia. The dwarf pushed his way through the people, running to Purple Gown on his absurd little legs and embracing her around the hips with his little arms, burying his man-face in her lower belly, singing to her as he did, his high little voice carrying over the crowd noises to An Lu-shan's ears:

> "I long for the time when she comes—*(hsi)*
> we approach the garden stairs that shine and glisten with
>   dew.
> We are anxious to part no more—*(hsi)*
> so endlessly we talk of love—
> our eyes drink of each other but our thirst is never slaked,
> and we look at one another—*(hsi)*
> and at last our hungers must be fed . . ."

While he sang in his child-man voice, his stubby fingers massaged the soft silk-covered flesh of her behind.

"My little horny fool . . . my erotic toy . . . ," Purple Gown said, smiling down at him, her hands tenderly stroking the hair of his braided topknot. "You are in rut. What must I do with you?"

"Buy me the colorful birds that speak, my lady. Give them your voice . . . that I might never be without you," he implored in his squeaky voice, looking up at her with the eyes of a mooning child. Taking his hand, she walked, shopkeeper scuttling behind, toward the curtained room. They moved out of range of An Lu-shan's hearing, but his eyes never left them until they disappeared behind the curtain.

An Lu-shan sat on his horse and stared stupidly at the drapery as it fell shut. Where was he? He could feel the great seething city all around him, a world richly strange and incomprehensible, contrived . . . no, carved . . . out of complexities he did not yet understand. But he would! He shook his head as a lurid picture of the rampant little dwarf lying between Purple Gown's thighs bloomed in his mind. He laughed. He threw his head back and looked at the hazy sky and laughed and laughed. I am here! I am in Ch'ang-an! He felt as if his mind would overflow its banks, like a river in spring.

"General An Lu-shan?" The sound of Feng's voice snapped him to attention. At the same moment, a loud squawking came from behind the curtain. He did not turn around right away, but decided to have a bit of fun with Feng by feigning unconcern that they had nearly lost each other in this city of millions. He continued to watch the curtain.

"She will be coming out at any moment," he said to Feng. "You have never seen anyone like her."

"On the contrary," Feng replied. "I know her well. I am glad that you have enjoyed our great city of Ch'ang-an this morning."

"It is a fine village," he said, still facing the bazaar. ". . . We have many such villages like it, where the paths of sheep herders cross."

"And where the paths of Silk Road thieves cross . . . ?" said Feng.

"And the paths of thieves if they crossed . . . but thieves do not cross paths. They are too wary of one another's skill."

"It is well for a thief to be wary," said an unfamiliar voice. An Lu-shan turned, startled, the small hairs of his neck bristling. He faced a beardless horseman, a eunuch by appearances, broad in the chest and shoulders like Feng, and wearing similar armor. From a distance, indistinguishable from Feng. But it was not Feng.

"Where is Feng?" It was all he could think to say. He cursed his slowness.

"Feng is not your Chancellery escort, General. He is a military man and closely tied to the royal family, but his job ended at the gates. He has returned to his duties, and I have assumed mine. I am to see that you arrive safely and comfortably at the Chancellery suites in time to prepare for the late morning repast," the large eunuch said.

An Lu-shan felt strange and flushed as he had earlier. He had forgotten this odd feeling for the time being, absorbed as he had been in the city unfolding before him. But now the feeling of unreality was upon him again. He had heard the voice of Feng coming from this man. Or had An Lu-shan imagined it? Spoken words reverberated mockingly in his head, distances became confused, and he realized that he did not know if he had been in the streets for hours or minutes. He stifled an insane urge to giggle like a woman in the face of this stranger. He saw now that things had not been right all along since entering the city. His concentration, he saw now, had been focusing, fastening onto this or that detail so that everything else was pushed aside. His mind was being attracted to things, fixing on them the way minute chips of iron fix to a lodestone. He saw more and less at the same time, and somehow none of it was under his control. It was as though he were ill and possessed, and the root of his tongue itched with the urge to talk with someone . . . to talk more and more. He stared at the eunuch before him. The eunuch wheeled his horse around.

"Follow me, General An," he said, spurring his horse into the crowd. As An Lu-shan urged his horse away from the bazaar and followed the man out into the street, he saw that he was not only being led, but followed as well.

Horsemen rode out into the main boulevard from side streets and alleys, steadily gathering in numbers and momentum behind him. It was like the day at the T'ung-kuan Pass when he was first greeted by General Feng and the others. The others? Their faces were familiar. These were the same thugs and ruffians—those motherless sons—closing around him. They had surprised him once more. They stepped up their pace, the streets clearing ahead of them with amazing swiftness. He rode again to the pounding of hooves, the squeak of leather, and the jangle of metal weaponry. He eyed the two riders flanking him. They wore uniforms he hadn't seen before, as if honoring some decorum of the city: a long purple robe, and shins and chests encased in shiny black lacquered-leather plates. Two minute Chinese characters were emblazoned in a small gold circle on each of their right shoulders. They did not talk among themselves or look at anything around them, but rode with a fierce demeanor through the streets of the great city.

: :

Li Lin-fu was pleased. His plans had gone well. The barbarian was to be delivered to him shortly, and if his calculations were correct, with a certain amount of his reticence diminished. All was in readiness. He opened the shutters of his office window wider to let the hot air in.

He had not wished to waste time in finding out just who this An Lu-shan was. If the barbarian was to serve the chief minister—to be his hand in the defense of the north—then Li Lin-fu had to know immediately if the man was going to be responsive to him. He sighed. These tribal people are often so stubborn, so difficult to read, their faces like closed doors. Masks of pride and suspicion. When he was younger, Li Lin-fu might have had more patience, been willing to take more time in peeling back the layers, finding out what lay behind a pair of slit eyes. But time was wasting. The Hsi and the Khitan were unlikely to wait while Li Lin-fu went through the social niceties dictated by etiquette. If An Lu-shan was to be effective and useful, then Li Lin-fu was obliged to find out who he was and establish the upper hand swiftly, surely, and without question. That was why he had arranged to have an extract of the cordyceps mushroom added to the barbarian's morning tea. The mushroom's essence had a magical effect: it was often used to make men tell the truth. Not that he expected An Lu-shan to be susceptible in the manner of ordinary men; information he had gathered about him indicated that he was not an ordinary man. But it would perhaps cause him to be honest in ways beyond his control. A polite scratching at the door interrupted his thoughts.

The door opened, and his chief of internal securities entered, arms weighted down by heavy furs. Li Lin-fu sighed again. His was a life of sacrifice, there could be little doubt. *For the empire, I will do nearly anything that is required of me,* he thought, holding his arms out and allowing himself to be dressed in his winter clothing. *Even risk my health.* He grimaced at the thought of what he was about to do. It would be like some bad dream of stepping from a summer day into the heart of winter.

: :

An Lu-shan thought that he had finally taken leave of his senses. All day he had struggled to get hold of the strange feeling in his feverish head; but now, he thought that it had got the better of him at last.

The room they brought him to was as cold as a cave. Droplets of water clung to the stone walls, and air as chill as an early spring wind in Mongolia blew on his face and ruffled his hair. Water drummed overhead. The sound was like sitting in a chieftain's miserable hut during a winter rain. Before him, sitting in a chair behind a table, was a man whom An Lu-shan could have broken in two with one hand in combat. Nothing showed but his ugly head; the rest of his body was swathed in furs as if the streets outside were not blazing with heat. He even wore gloves. Chief Minister Li Lin-fu stood and bowed perfunctorily. An Lu-shan was irritated to feel, despite the cold, sweat starting to pop out on his forehead. He returned the bow. Li Lin-fu indicated the chair, and An Lu-shan sat. Li Lin-fu looked at him for a few moments before speaking.

"You have traveled a long way, An Lu-shan. The empire is most grateful to you."

"It was not difficult, Your Excellency," An Lu-shan replied. "I go where I am needed."

"I know you do," Li Lin-fu replied. "That is why I extended the invitation to you. It seems that you are unstoppable. At least," he said with a shrug, "a bit of water can't stop you! It seems that for each of us, one of the elements is a particular enemy." He stopped talking for a moment and coughed a few times. "Water, interestingly, is mine. It decided a long time ago that it would kill me, An Lu-shan. It has settled in my chest and sends out pernicious vapors." Tilting his head, he looked at An Lu-shan. "What would your enemy be?" he asked. "Fire?"

An Lu-shan thought of the night he and the children raided the Khitan encampment with the flame-arrows. "Not fire, Excellency," he said. "Though it was fire that drove me from my home as a child, I can only regard it as a friend, since it meant that I would eventually arrive here. As for earth and air . . . well . . . again, I can only say that they have served me well."

"You are at home in the elements, I know," said Li Lin-fu, "whereas I must protect myself. I have thought about what you must have experienced the night you took your army across the river," he said, clapping his gloved hands. A servant entered and set down a tray of steaming hot tea. An Lu-shan shifted slightly in his seat, on guard. "Surrounded by water," Li Lin-fu continued, pouring two bowls and offering one to An Lu-shan. The bowl was absurdly small and dainty, seeming to An Lu-shan not much larger or thicker than an eggshell. An Lu-shan took it carefully in his large fingers and raised it to his mouth, then quickly lowered it. The tea was undrinkably hot. He watched as Li Lin-fu drank his entire bowl without hesitating, then looked expectantly at An Lu-shan, who distinctly felt a droplet of sweat roll out from the hair of his scalp and down the side of his face. Damn! I am sweating more in this ice chamber than I did out in the street with the sun blazing down on me, he thought, resisting the urge to wipe his face with his hand.

"The men's fear was more disturbing to me, Your Excellency. I knew we could get across. Not all of them knew it."

"But you convinced them," Li Lin-fu said. "You knew, after all, that it was an officially sanctioned crossing point, that the men were not being asked to do the impossible. At least, according to your map, it was an official crossing point," he said, taking his eyes from An Lu-shan's face and busying himself with pouring another bowl of tea.

An Lu-shan looked at Li Lin-fu, preposterously dressed in his heavy furs, ugly face averted. Now he understood why Feng had referred to him as "the Lizard"; it was not simply his appearance, though the shape of the head—and the way the odd, fleshy eyelids flicked—strongly suggested one. The resemblance lay in his manner. Cold, amoral—like a reptile. An Lu-shan felt as if they were not two men, but two different kinds of animals. An Lu-shan was often able to "see" things in a stranger's face and demeanor, and know something about that person's past. And now he experienced that feeling more powerfully than he had at almost any previous time. It was plain that the man sitting in front of him had done things he could scarcely imagine, things so dire as to make his alteration of the map resemble nothing but child's play. He found with horror that he had the urge to confide. I could tell him, he thought. I could tell him about making the ink, about selecting the parchment, about sitting in front of the eunuchs. With a mighty effort of his will, he refrained. But it cost him. The sweat fairly rolled off his face now.

"Yes," he answered simply. "That is what the map said." He could resist it no longer; he brought his hand up and wiped the moisture from his forehead. Li Lin-fu looked at him as if nothing were amiss.

"Are you fond of music, General?" he asked abruptly, standing up as if about to take his leave. "I hope you are, because I have arranged for you to make an appearance in honor of your promotion to military governor of P'inglu."

An Lu-shan stood, stunned.

But Li Lin-fu did not give him time to open his mouth. "My assistant Niu will help you with the details. Welcome, An Lu-shan." With that, he turned and left An Lu-shan standing in the strange room.

Military governor of P'inglu. Had he heard correctly? That was the position held by Li Shih-chih, the man who had saved him from execution years ago.

The drumming of water gradually ceased, as if some mechanism had been shut down. An Lu-shan was thoroughly chilled, and he thought with yearning of the heat rising from the paving stones of the city. He, too, left the room.

:: :

Li Lin-fu congratulated himself as he returned to his hot, comfortable office. I am a genius, he thought. My mind is so resourceful that I never know what it is going to present me with next. They are wrong when they say I have no humor! I am the most fun-loving fellow in the empire!

The plan had come to him seemingly from nowhere as he had sat in the wretched rain room with the barbarian, watching the man sweat. Li Lin-fu, looking at the water pouring off the man, had felt like a gatherer of statistics measuring rainfall. It told him everything he needed to know about the barbarian An Lu-shan. But the plan presented itself like a gift from Heaven. This man, this great, hulking, sweating, fire-breathing hairy brute, is just what they need at court, he remembered thinking as the man spoke in his crude Chinese. Wouldn't he be grand at a formal dinner? One does not need much imagination to know what sort of table manners he has. Especially when he gets drunk. He imagined the consternation and offended dignity of the effete court ladies and gentlemen as An Lu-shan committed some lewd act or gross social blunder. That was when the idea had come to Li Lin-fu. As clearly as if it were happening in front of him, he saw An Lu-shan presented to the court as a percussionist—which would take a minimum of skill—in the Emperor's Pear Garden Orchestra, all the members of which were beautiful young women.

Li Lin-fu was sitting at his desk, shaking his head with delight, when General Niu scratched at the door and entered.

"You have met the barbarian, Excellency?" he asked tentatively, approaching the desk.

"He is perfect, General Niu. I could not have fashioned a better commander for the north even if I were a god!"

:: :

The mysterious letter would make no more sense to him now than it had the first three times he read it, but he would try once more. It was the least he could do.

The man shocks me by sending me a letter from the grave, but gives me no clue as to its meaning. Like the old days, Kao Li-shih thought. It was too easy to conjure the scrawny figure of the poet-minister as he had last seen him—standing too close, burning with the intensity of the message he had to deliver, but disguising it, obscuring it. It was too easy to recall the odious feeling of the man's breath on his face as he leaned closer.

Kao Li-shih removed the papers from their hiding place deep inside a trunk under a neat pile of winter quilts. He carefully unfolded the pages one more time and spread them out on his desk so he could see all the text at once.

The letter had arrived as mysteriously as Chang Chiu-ling had departed. Two evenings ago there had been a knock on the outer door of his apartments, and his creaky servant had risen and opened it. Someone pushed his way in. The old servant had immediately become two times as obsequious as was usual, causing Kao Li-shih to look to see who it was.

From his writing desk behind the silk screen, Kao Li-shih could see the visitor in the waiting hall—a tall, important-looking eunuch, his formal robes trimmed with ermine and gold. The man said nothing for a while and peered impolitely past the servant and into Kao Li-shih's inner chambers. The servant requested the man's calling card politely, either pretending that it wasn't at all past visiting hours for his master or forgetting the time completely.

The man in the waiting hall still said nothing, but continued to peer into the rooms, exuding annoyance, while waiting. He must have seen my silhouette cast by the oil lamps onto the screen, Kao Li-shih had thought, because when the man finally spoke, he spoke only to that part of the room where Kao Li-shih sat.

As the old servant moved the lantern around the entranceway, Kao Li-shih, looking through a small tear in the screen kept unrepaired for just such a purpose, now clearly recognized the face of the captain of the inner chambers—who was also an officer in the secret order of the Flying Dragon Eunuch Elite. The servant kept speaking, and the visitor finally deigned to answer.

"May I have your calling card . . . my master will set an appointment for you . . . ," the old man mumbled.

"What I need to say, old fool, does not need a calling card. Are you so blind you no longer recognize me? I have something from very far away for Master Kao." The visitor's tone was forceful and arrogant.

Move aside, old fart, Kao Li-shih had nearly said. You are senile, your sea of marrow has dried up. You don't even recognize the captain of the eunuch guards. But he didn't say it, because the old man was faithful and devoted, if a bit too much so.

"Let him in," Kao Li-shih finally shouted. "He is an old friend."

The man closed the door behind him and crossed over to the desk, handing Kao Li-shih the letter from Hai-nan, the "Shore of Pearls"—a letter from a dead man.

::

Kao Li-shih studied the pages of the mysterious letter under the light of his oil lamp. He had examined them under all kinds of light at different times of the day . . . but there was nothing more to be had from them. Perhaps it was a trick, but if so, it was the cleverest he had ever seen. The letter was in verse unmistakably characteristic of the poet-minister. And the hand was his as well—a very difficult thing to fake.

The parchment was the most curious thing about the letter. He had never seen anything like it. It was obvious to Kao Li-shih that Chang's adversaries planned everything down to the last detail of his jungle isolation, even making certain that he was without paper and ink. But they underestimated his sheer will and resourcefulness, Kao Li-shih thought, as indeed we all had. Kao Li-shih was reminded of the tale of the monk imprisoned in a cave who transcribed the Diamond sutra using his skin for parchment, his bones for quills, and his blood for ink. But Chang Chiu-ling at least was not living in a bare cave. He had plants and animals around him.

He turned the small stack of parchment papers over slowly in his hand. The surface was dry, brittle, and lumpy. It appeared to be the clever creation of a man who was given nothing to write on or with. A cruel joke to play on him, but Master Chang seems to have found a way. Evidently, Kao Li-shih imagined, where poor Chang is in the jungle there is simply no bark or bamboo to make even the crudest writing surface. And in any case, whatever bark he found would simply not stand up to the test of all those miserable thousands of li of travel. Nor would it stand up to the manner in which it most likely had to be transported—secretly, inside things, folded and refolded. It is amazing that any of this is still readable. He brought the printed surface of the top sheet up close to his eyes. Some sort of berry juice, or blood, for the ink. In fact, Kao Li-shih thought, it is a miracle that any of it made it past the damned jungle agents at Yai and Ch'ang-hua, most of whom by now would be in Li Linfu's employ. He shook his head. And to think that he had always thought of Master Chang as the most impractical man he had ever known . . .

Kao Li-shih tried to picture the poor poet, no doubt delirious with tropical fever and working under the most primitive of conditions, rediscovering the invention of paper. Of course, he hadn't the proper pulp fibers, or anything resembling them. And no alum. What about the sizing glue for the surface? Kao Li-shih found the image of the man experimenting with fishheads and lizards and sap from the trees most distressing. He pictured the poor man half-naked and scrambling about on all fours grabbing at scurrying little things, and getting bitten. This one is too sticky and won't dry, and that one dries too brittle. And then there would have been the problem of the drying racks, woven from reeds, and the problem of where to put them so the infernal tropical insects wouldn't swarm all over the wet "paper"—a sodden, pulpy mass that must have smelled like dung before it dried. But then, he thought, what else did the poor poet have to do with his time?

This time Kao Li-shih decided to chant the verse slowly and out loud.

Perhaps hearing the prosody would make a difference. If I were more of a scholar, he thought, I might attempt to "hang the bells" of the characters in another order—maybe the last character in each lone. With a feeling of futility, he read:

Verse 1

"Butterflies drink the turtle's tears, and
  in the Cold Palace a thousand dragons fly.
The vapors of Heaven lie low.
Dark and blue the malarial clouds drive the rain
  and thicken the air.
A rent of lightning and a crack of thunder.
The jungle seethes in mist.

Verse 2

"I am two weeks on my back
  sweating and . . . [indecipherable] tossing and turning.
They tell me that the native Li people have brought me water,
  and an elixir of herbs to make me well.
I do not remember.
Only now am I beginning to stand and walk,
And it is not over yet . . . [indecipherable].

Verse 3

"These natives kept me dry in a hut of plaited leaves,
  between fitful sleep and wakeful stupor,
from my window a flickered flame of yellow and crimson wings,
  weaving baskets of hanging nests.
A darting of serpents here and there,
  red and striped and gold,
green and white and shimmered with silver,
  everywhere seen and never seen . . . [indecipherable]
in and out of my dreams.
The cries and howls are songs without tune.

Verse 4

"I am chilled to the bone,
  as night comes without the beat of the curfew drums.
This noise, an endless cacophony of too much life
  out of too much death,
penetrates my skull until . . . [indecipherable].
Black gibbon and langur,

Civet and giant squirrels bound through the trees,
leaping up in frightened flight.
And under the mottled canopy of light and shadow
deer—muntjac, thamin, sambar—
wild boar and badger and mongoose,
the great bear and clouded leopard run before
the flashing scales of the wicked pangolin lizard.
Spotted snake-eagles and spine-tailed swifts,
red minivets and black drongos, green bulbuls and yellow wagtails,
and serpents of diamonds and rubies nod to the old woman in
    black.
But all of this is nothing to the other side of my eyes."

". . . the other side of my eyes"? Kao Li-shih read it over twice.

Verse 5

"The old witch-woman came to me again this night in tattered
    black robes,
with bottles and claws and talismans and coins around her waist.
She asked me many times before,
And I had always refused. . . .

Verse 6

"She said she would keep coming until I agreed
And that it would not do to refuse her indefinitely.
I went with her and saw things that I should not have seen,
and having been done . . . I do not know what I can undo.
She told me that the end of things I saw were only the
beginning of things I could not see . . . [indecipherable].
Down long corridors and into darkened rooms and the brittle . . .
[Indecipherable] bones crunching underfoot
I saw a great man, large and strong and round with a great head
    and thick black beard."

Not Chinese, I suppose, Kao Li-shih said to himself. But I imagine that he
means more than that here.

"He was walking with another among the ruins.
The other misshapen only on the outside,
carried too much of the world upon his gnarled foot.
Beside them, the deer and gazelle grazed the tall grass.
I saw the bearded one through the witch's eyes,
from high atop the ruins.

As I looked closely at that face,
the toothless hag asked me what I saw.
I told her that his appearance was strange,
and that he was new to these Constellation Gates.
She blew smoke from her pipe.
She laughed and drew her old wrinkled face up like a corpse,
and told me that I was wrong.

Verse 7

"The old hag told me that that one had been here many times
    before.
And that he would be here many times again,
time and time without end.
He is no stranger. He is you!
He is your baby, you have nurtured him.
He is your princely son."

Kao Li-shih squinted and brought the smeared section of the page close to his
eyes.

Verse 8

"The old woman was gone.
The mist lay low on the forest floor that night when I awoke.
The trees around my clearing sighed and whispered,
like an orchestra of ten thousand *hsiao* and *sheng*.
The stars were bright,
the square of earth tossed up against that panoply of light.
Monkeys chattered and howled,
and told of things I could not know.
The days drifted into the nights,
countless and effortless, indistinguishable
as the wind is from the air.
For jungles are without time.
And the ghosts still fight for my body,
the evil now outnumber the good,
and I fear that I shall fall prey to them.
But the old woman never returns."

Kao Li-shih sighed and lowered the paper, rubbing his tired eyes. It was
tempting to dismiss the letter as the pathetic rantings of a delirious poet exiled
to the jungle. He looked again at the paper. The trouble, the grief he went
through to get this to me . . . He could feel the urgency, the poor poet's

fevered sense of purpose. The last time I was tempted to dismiss you, Kao Li-shih thought, I misjudged you and did you a great wrong. But damn you! Why can't you say it in plain language? What are you saying, Poet?

He thought about sending a reply in similar cryptic verse. He would tell Chang about an emperor still sleeping, unable and unwilling to get out of bed; lost, entranced, absorbed in trivial hobbies while the Lizard sidles nearer and nearer. He is under the throne . . . no, he is perched on the arm. No . . . he has moved imperceptibly onto the seat. Kao Li-shih smiled at his own impromptu doggerel. I could have been a poet-minister, too, he thought, carefully folding Chang's brittle paper and putting it away, feeling, as he did so, as if he were stifling the man's voice.

9

Rainbow Chemise, Feathered Skirt

Stately and solemn—the Temple of the Hsiang Consort.
Spring, and dark blue water by vacant walls.
Insects trace characters in the moss on her jade girdle.
Swallows dance in the dust on her halcyon canopy.

—*Tu Fu, translated by Edward H. Schafer*

In this particular month, the Taoist nun from the Yang clan arrived from the palace of Grand Verity to be instated as the Precious Consort in the Phoenix Garden. She was attended as if she were an empress; the musical piece "Rainbow Chemise, Feathered Skirt" was played during her presentation to the Emperor.

—*Yo Shih, translated by Daniel Altieri*

"LOVE, Kao Li-shih?" The Emperor shook his head. "I am no more capable of it than you are." He leaned to one side with a small piece of food in his hand and watched pensively as one of his huge cats nibbled daintily at the morsel.

Emperor and eunuch were in the imperial bedchamber; the Emperor was sprawled among the cushions, along with two comfortably nestling cats, while Kao Li-shih sat on a chair facing him. Plates of food and bits of paper lay strewn about on the silk bed covers. It was very late; the sun would rise in only an hour or so. The Emperor had taken to going many days and nights without any sleep at all, then sleeping for the same amount of time, waking only occasionally to eat or attend to nature's call. Kao Li-shih rubbed his weary eyes.

"Would you lower a bucket into a well that you knew contained only sand and rocks?" the Emperor sighed, letting the cat lick his hand. The animal's tongue, long and pink, extended from its mouth with dextrous fluidity, exploring with great thoroughness between the Son of Heaven's fingers.

Watching him, Kao Li-shih was inclined to think that the Emperor was right, that the idea was absurd. "Will you at least look at her?" he asked.

Again, the Emperor sighed. "If I must, Kao Li-shih. If I must. I don't suppose it will cost me any great effort to look at a beautiful woman." He paused, thinking. "I do not clearly recall her. What did she look like?"

Kao Li-shih's heart sank. He had thought that the girl had made more of an impression on the Emperor, who had, after all, gone to a fair amount of trouble to gracefully dissolve the betrothal to Prince Mao and place the girl in the nunnery. Kao Li-shih knew that he must proceed carefully. A certain amount of care was required here. Talking the girl up too much would only arouse the Emperor's resistance; on the other hand, he wanted to be sure that the Emperor took notice of her arrival. He shrugged.

"I have seen her, not long ago. She has unusual eyes. She is a musician. And," he added, "she has excelled, I was told, at her training. I should think that you might be curious to see the effects of her two years of study."

"Two years?" the Emperor said. "Mao must be close to thirteen now. Perhaps I will make a gift of her to him after all. Has he expressed an interest in visiting the harem yet?"

Kao Li-shih's heart sank another notch. "Yes, he has. But . . ."

"Kao Li-shih, don't think I do not appreciate your efforts," the Emperor interrupted. "But you must understand. I am used up. Empty. Dead inside. I have long looked forward to being old and being finished with all of that. It has happened at last."

"You are barely sixty. That is scarcely a venerable age," Kao Li-shih said drily.

"Add twenty or so extra years for my grief and fatigue, and you will have my true age," the Emperor said, settling back among the cushions. "You and I are much alike now. I have an 'old man,' and you don't, but it's just something for me to piss through. And it suits me, Kao Li-shih. It suits me. I feel the same way in my mind as well."

"Self-pity," said Kao Li-shih.

The Emperor looked at the eunuch. "I am sorry, Kao Li-shih. Of course I will look at her. I may be half dead, but I am not blind." He looked toward the window. It was still black night. Insects flew blindly around the lamps. "Will you have breakfast with me?"

"I am delighted," said the eunuch, standing and stretching his weary limbs, "but I must go and sleep for an hour or two first."

::

The girl looked out the window of the carriage as it bounced along the rocky road leading from the nunnery. Kao Li-shih studied her face. After his pre-dawn conversation with the Emperor, he had very nearly tossed his idea onto the dung heap. He had felt the Emperor's ennui and lassitude as if it had been his own. He had felt tired, hollow inside, drained of purpose, and knew that he was experiencing exactly what the Emperor was feeling. Indeed, his master had been right. This must be how it feels, he had thought, to be very, very old. But he had gone ahead. The arrangements had already been made to remove the girl and bring her to the palace; besides, he had been curious to see how the "Emperor" inside himself would react to her.

She turned from the window and looked at him. Yes, he remembered that bold look now. He recalled the bride-to-be of Prince Mao on her knees before the Emperor, regarding him as if he were some sort of interesting animal. Looking at her now, Kao Li-shih saw something in the shape of her face. He felt a rush of emotion, an odd combination of hunger and satisfaction at the same time. The look on her face was nearly impertinent. He could only hope that the Emperor would still be able to see whatever it was he had seen that day, and not be indifferent or, worse, irritated. He could not really know the extent of the Emperor's fatigue, how far it might have sunk into his soul.

"You can look at *me* that way," he said to her. "It does not matter. But I would advise you to look more in the direction of the Son of Heaven's feet than his countenance." She continued to look at him for a moment before returning her gaze to the passing landscape.

"Your name is Kao Li-shih. You were standing next to the Emperor when I was presented to him more than two years ago. He whispered something to you. Ever since, I have wondered what he said." She turned her eyes back toward him.

Kao Li-shih realized that she had accomplished two things with those sentences: she had effectively reminded him that they both knew that she had looked the Emperor in the eye once before and had lived to tell the tale; and she had challenged him to reveal to her the Emperor's words.

"He told me that such an impertinent girl should be put to work in the imperial kitchens gutting chickens."

"Is that why I am being returned to the palace?" she asked innocently. "To gut chickens? If so, I am ready. I have been well trained."

I don't know, Kao Li-shih thought. I have my doubts. The Emperor is a tolerant man, but in his present state of mind I don't know how much patience he has.

For the rest of the ride, he tried to discern whether he was feeling his own fatigue and doubts or those whose source was the Emperor himself.

She was looking steadily out the window now. He allowed his eyes to move downward. He shook his head. The girl had gained a bit of weight during her stay in the nunnery; one could call her plump without fear of exaggeration. Not fat like poor Consort Wu by any means, but she did not present the reed-slim silhouette of the Empress, either. Well, my girl, he thought, if the Emperor shows even the faintest interest in you, then I shall see to it that you will spend a few weeks away from dainty cakes and candied fruits before he sees you again.

No sooner had he thought this than she produced a sweet from her sleeve and popped it into her mouth. Impatiently, he held his hand out to her. "Give those to me," he said irritably.

::

Grand Verity could not sleep. She sat up in the strange new bed. Oil lamps burned softly in the corners of the room; she could hear the faint snores of her handmaiden, sleeping behind a screen.

She felt as if she would never sleep again. An odd feeling, because sleep had become her main means of escape during her long wait at the nunnery. She had got into the habit of going to bed as early as possible and staying there in the morning as long as she could. And in the afternoons, when time took on a particularly flat, stale quality, she again sought refuge in her bed. Afternoon sleep was the best escape, when her dreams became especially peculiar and vivid. When she woke from day sleep, she always felt heavy and groggy, and sometimes she didn't know who she was, or where, or why.

The way she felt now was exactly the opposite. No dream could possibly equal the reality that she occupied. Her mind was clear and alert; her head felt like one of the clear quartz stones she had seen in Uncle's collection. She felt as if she could see in the dark. She threw the covers aside and walked soundlessly across the carpeted floor to the window. The snores came steadily from behind the screen. She pulled the gauze netting up and looked out at the city below.

The palace city, high atop the Dragon Head Hill, sat above the imperial city complex and the rest of the city of Ch'ang-an. Below, Grand Verity could see the dark outlines of roofs. Some of the buildings in the imperial city were huge, and she could see windows here and there fully lit, and moving figures inside the rooms. The business of governing the empire did not, evidently, cease simply because the sun went down.

Below and beyond, in the city proper, faint twinkling lights from distant street lanterns defined long avenues stretching, it seemed to her, to infinity. Though the day had been hot, the night air coming through the window, rising up from the city and carrying mystery, promise, uncertainty, and suspense, was cool. It chilled her skin, making goose bumps under the thin silk of her nightdress. She hugged herself in the darkness and thought about to-morrow, when she would be brought before the Emperor for the second time in her life.

She wished that her Eldest Sister were here. She wished that her sister could take her place, just for a while. The behavior toward her of the eunuch Kao Li-shih was strange. She knew that it had been he who had arranged for her release from the nunnery. Yet his attitude toward her was so stern, almost unfriendly—as if she posed some sort of threat to the Emperor; as if he had to protect the Son of Heaven from her bad manners. He had now arranged it so that she and the Emperor would not meet directly at first; she was to be one of several dancers in a performance tomorrow. She would only be able to get fleeting glimpses of him, while he would be able to study her at his leisure. She tried to remember what he looked like, but could only conjure up an indefinite blur where his face should be. The hands, short-nailed and veined, were a lot easier to remember. She could clearly recall the hand lifting from the arm of the chair to signal the eunuch, the eunuch bending down to listen. With a great effort she was able to give the Emperor a face, but it was not his own—it was a composite of faces of older male relatives—and she was able to hold the image of the substitute face only briefly before it dissolved. She yawned and shivered, and realized that she was suddenly very tired. Before returning to her bed, she put her head out the window as far as she could and looked down the wall below her. She was very, very far from the ground. She held her head where it was for a few moments, feeling the sleeping palace all around her and the vast city stretching below, its lights blending at the horizon with the stars in the black sky. She pulled her head back in, replaced the gauze, and moved soundlessly back to the bed. Climbing in and pulling the covers up to her chin, she thought again of Eldest Sister. Even you, she thought, speaking to the image in her mind, would be a trifle anxious, maybe just a little bit nervous. The thought was strangely comforting, and she began to drift, the Emperor's formless face trying again to assume features in her mind.

: :

Once again, she found herself in a carriage with Kao Li-shih, but this time the road was smooth, and the wheels sang in the soft dust. He was taking her to a hot springs resort not far from the city; she felt him glancing at her now and again, but the feeling was different from that of their first ride together. His attitude toward her had softened somewhat since the dance performance. She knew she had done well, though she was just one of many dancers, singers, poets, and musicians who took part in the hours-long event.

She had been taken to an enormous hall called the Pavilion of Diligent Rule that looked out over the sprawling beauty of the grand Phoenix Garden.

Inside the hall, there was room for a vast number of people to sit, and a large open stage area for the performers. Excitement hung in the air; one of the other dancers had told her that this was the first performance to be held in a long, long, time.

It had been exhilarating, terrifying. She had participated in many performances in her time, but had never seen so much strange and new. Most of the music she had never heard before, and the singing that accompanied it was in language unintelligible to her. Dancers leapt and whirled to the singing voices and a chorus of drums; the sounds of exotic, unfamiliar instruments blended with familiar ones. One of the other waiting performers had whispered to her that this music came from the far distant west, farther than anyone could imagine, where China ended and the land of the Brahmins began. Fascinated, she had watched the dancers moving to the syncopated rhythms of the drums. Where did they get their endurance? How could they leap so high and turn in midair like that, arms and legs flying, with never a misstep or a foot in the face of another dancer? And there had been poems—some humorous and satirical, some mooningly amorous—and pantomimes done to music. One particularly exciting piece was an entire polo game acted out. Though there were no actual horses, the performers moved as if they were indeed riding phantom mounts—and she swore she could hear galloping hoofbeats as they moved. And the audience took sides, cheering teams of "players" on as if there really were wagers to be won, scores to be settled. In an exciting drum dance, two giant lotuses on the stage opened up and gave birth to two beautiful young girls in tight foreign-looking costumes. The dance was plainly sexual. As the girls writhed and undulated to the dizzying drums, they cast hungry, heavy-lidded looks at the audience, caressing their own bodies and finally, as the dance ended, ripping their tight shirts down to reveal their breasts, the nipples painted bright red.

Grand Verity had watched the court ladies and gentlemen who comprised the audience. Their eyes glittered with drink and self-satisfaction; they responded to the performers with shouts and whoops or sat quietly watchful, whichever was appropriate. She could not find anyone who could be the Emperor anywhere in the crowd, though she could plainly see Kao Li-shih, standing solemnly in the rear.

When her own turn came to perform, she summoned all her concentration and moved through a piece taught to her during her stay at the nunnery by a teacher sent from the palace. The name of the dance, "Rainbow Chemise, Feathered Skirt," became real for her when she was given a garment of white feathers to wear for the performance, the most sumptuously beautiful piece of clothing she had ever seen. She pretended, for the time that the dance lasted, that she was a mythic white crane assuming human form and performing a dance of gratitude for the human mortal who had returned her stolen feathers to her. She had been concerned that her dance would seem too tame, too pallid after all the colorful, ostentatious jumping and whirling to drums. But the hall had fallen into attentive silence as she danced. Well, she had thought as the music of the entirely female orchestra carried her through the complex motions, they are well-bred and know how to be polite to a newcomer. For that I am grateful.

And then she had completely forgotten her own dance as she watched, incredulously, the piece that followed. Young girls—dark-eyed and dark-haired beauties—did an impossible dance of grace and agility atop rolling wooden balls slightly larger than a man's fist. The balls made a loud rumble on the floor, a drone that sounded steadily beneath the music and singing as the dancers' feet kept each and every ball moving. As they twirled and skipped on their moving carpet, they never faltered, and their faces were as calm, relaxed, and smiling as if they were doing no more than wading through a brook in a garden. She had looked carefully to see if perhaps it was a trick or an illusion; she saw that it was not when the dance ended and the girls bent in a swooping motion and held a ball up in each hand for the audience to see. She scanned the crowd again for the Emperor. Is he so jaded, she asked herself, that all of this is tiresome to him, and not worth his time and trouble?

In the confines of the carriage rolling along the smooth, dusty road, she turned to Kao Li-shih.

"Does the Emperor not care for displays of music and dancing?"

"He cares for them very much," the eunuch replied. "He especially enjoyed this one," he added.

"He was there?" she said, surprised.

"He was there," said Kao Li-shih.

She thought hard. Her memory could not be that bad. Even though she could not clearly recall his face, she should have been able to distinguish him from the rest of the people there. And an emperor would surely have a special place to sit. He would not just be another member of the audience, would he?

"It has been a very, very long time since he has been to a performance," said Kao Li-shih. "In order to prevail upon him to go, I had to agree to certain conditions," he said enigmatically. "Be assured that he was there. And," he added, a kindly tone in his voice, "be assured that he especially enjoyed your performance. That particular piece is one of his . . . favorites. Our journey to the hot springs today has come about because you danced so well." He turned back to the window. "He has not been to the hot springs for a long, long time, either."

Grand Verity studied Kao Li-shih's profile. She sensed that he was quite a bit more than a servant to the Emperor; one could feel the complete attentiveness of the eunuch to the Emperor's life, to the exclusion of nearly everything else. But there was nothing slavish in his manner. He was no lackey, no groveling bootlicker. It was plain that he had chosen as his life's work to look after the man who was the Emperor, but he had sacrificed none of his integrity in doing it. He was almost . . . she hesitated to say it, even to herself . . . a wife. That was it! It had been difficult to put a name to it. With the exception of the sexual aspect, he was a wife to the Emperor. A male wife. Well, she corrected herself, he is certainly male in his heart, I can see that. An unwelcome image flitted through her mind of a eunuch's mutilated anatomy. They lost everything, she knew, and had to squat like women to pee. Through some kind of horrid little lead tube implanted in their bodies. Looking at the dignified Kao Li-shih, whom she was now beginning to like, she forced the picture from her mind. She did not like to think that way about someone who deserved her respect. She sometimes felt as if her thoughts could be overheard, like whispers. Returning her mind to the subject at hand, she realized what he had just implied about the Emperor not having been to the hot springs.

"Do you mean that he is going to be there too?"

"Of course," Kao Li-shih replied with a small conspiratorial smile.

I think, she said to herself, that I understand. For now, he likes to watch me without being watched himself. She was grateful to Kao Li-shih. He had given her a helpful clue without betraying the Emperor's confidence.

As the carriage rolled into the hot springs grounds, she felt the air around them change. This was a magic place, enclosed within its own aura, separate from the rest of the world, geomantically perfect. Gnarled trees, arched bridges, and low buildings with graceful curving roofs were reflected in pools of still water. A faint whiff of sulphur carried on the breeze. She found herself wishing more keenly than ever for her sisters; here, come to life before her eyes, was the mythic landscape of their childhood games.

She was escorted from the carriage to her quarters. Here, the dreamlike atmosphere intensified. She had an entire wing of a building to herself; it was unlike any house she had ever been in before. The walls, instead of being solid, were of graceful, carved stone grillwork, so that the rooms, even the bedchamber, were open to the outside air. The feeling was that there was no boundary between the interior of the house and the surrounding gardens. The feeling of being either inside or outside, usually so defined with regular houses, was missing. From her doorway she had a view of a small lake. Twin pavilions cast their images on its silvery surface; one was at the edge of the lake, the other sat in the center, connected to the first by a stone walkway leading magically out over the water. Around the lake, the mountainous terrain rose and fell; she could make out the roofs and walls of buildings and pavilions nestled here and there on different levels, their architecture blending harmoniously with the contours of hills, rocks, and woods. Vapor from countless pools of boiling water bubbling up out of the earth rose in wisps everywhere and diffused the sunlight; pockets of it hung in the clefts between rocks so that the solid ground appeared to be dissolving into ethereal matter. Looming in the east, so that the entire hot springs compound seemed to be sheltered under its benevolent eye, was a huge blue-purple mountain—Mount Li Shan, Kao Li-shih had told her—its top disappearing into another world above the clouds. The mountain looked enormous and much farther away than it actually was; she knew that this was an illusion, a trick played on her eyes by the mist that hung in front of the mountain, lightening its color so that it seemed to be many more li distant. She brought her gaze back to the buildings, the pavilions, the room she stood in.

It was impossible to imagine that such a place could have been built by human hands. It felt as if it had been there from the beginning of time, forming itself from the stuff of dreams, growing the way plants do out of the rocks and earth. She knew what went into the construction of buildings. She remembered when her family had added a wing to the house in Szechuan. There had been piles of raw, overturned earth where the men had dug. Heaps of wood and stones lay everywhere; men stirred a great vat of mortar, built walls stone by stone, sawed wood, and pounded the joints of beams into place. The ground was muddy and barren, scarred by footprints and the tracks of wheelbarrows and littered with scrap. And when the work on the new wing was completed, the gardeners had come in, laying sod and putting plants into the ground so that overnight all traces of the painstaking construction process disappeared, making the building look as if it had been there for a hundred years. Watching this had made her wish for buildings that just *were*. That was the way she and her sisters had imagined the celestial domiciles of the mythic characters they used to impersonate in their little dramas. Ascending to lands in the clouds atop mountains, they would take up residence in palaces that had not needed to be built, that were not the products of mere human construction, but which were simply there; had always been, and would always be. These buildings around her now were old, she knew; so old that they may as well be those mythic buildings she had wished for.

Her handmaiden and the lady's maid were busily unpacking her hampers and arranging her clothing and jewelry. She sat on the huge bed and thought. Her childhood games were taking on new meaning. When she and her sisters had played, they had believed in their roles while still retaining their own identities. It was a game and not a game at the same time. Now she thought hard about what it might mean to actually be one of those characters they had invented. Was she not in reality becoming one now? There was no longer any separation between her "true" self and the great ladies whose lives she had acted out in inspired fantasy. She looked around the room. It was beautiful. There was ornately carved furniture, the wood glowing reddish and polished. The bed she sat on was covered in blue-green silk embroidered with scudding clouds; a porcelain vase on a low table was the bluest blue she had ever seen.

She leaned closer and looked at its finely crackled surface. This was not, of course, the first time she had seen fine rooms and elegant appointments; but a new feeling had come over her now. Something of the magic of the hot springs imbued the things in the room with a strange life-force she usually didn't see in inanimate objects. There was, in all this beauty, a waiting, seductive quality . . . and, as with the buildings, that same feeling—that they were alive in some way, that they couldn't have come into being through the mere efforts of men's hands. This was the world she had been looking for since childhood. How terrible, how unthinkable it would be to lose it now . . . after coming so close. She touched the cold, brilliant surface of the blue vase and thought about her sisters, waiting . . . for her. She felt the old apprehension, the fear of failure that felt a little like falling. Yes, she thought, he liked the way I danced. But there will have to be more, much more. I must seduce him. But how?

Somewhere on the grounds, she knew, was the Emperor. She thought of him watching her, from some discreet vantage point, as she danced. Spying, really. He will, she knew, be watching again. Then, like a bird alighting on a windowsill, an idea came to her.

When she and her sisters used to play, they made up elaborate plots, building on traditional tales and legends. Inventing stories and speech had always come easily to her. She rose from the bed. Though it had been many years since she and her sisters had last played, she felt the old impulse coming over her. But it was different now. There would be no part of her that remained detached; whether it was because it had ceased to be a game or because she had moved further into the game than ever before she could not tell. She spoke to the handmaiden.

"Tell one of the servants to take a message to Kao Li-shih. Tell him I should like to bathe in one of the hot pools when the sun is going down, and ask him which one is the best."

Her clothing had been unpacked and laid into fragrant wooden chests. Lifting the lid of one, she removed a bundle wrapped in silk, carried it to the bed, and opened it. The white feathers of the cape she had worn in the dance rustled enticingly as she spread the garment out. It had been given to her as a gift after the performance, a reward for doing well. She smiled to herself, thinking of how Eldest Sister would surely approve of the little drama that was now taking form in her mind. No, she thought; there will be no languishing anonymity in the harem for me.

::

The Flying Rosy Cloud Pavilion stood to the west of the Nine Dragon Lake. Two of the hot springs harem ladies accompanied Grand Verity along the stone path that wound through the gardens around the lake's perimeter. The

pink and orange sunset was reflected on the black water; large birds flew down
and skimmed the surface, uttering desolate cries. The air was soft the way it
is only in the early morning or early evening. The women carried hampers
of clothing and food, and one of them carried an oblong object wrapped in
cloth. And though it was still fairly light and they weren't needed yet, there
were several ornate candle lanterns.

The Flying Rosy Cloud Pavilion was open on all four sides, with the
front looking out over the lake. On the three remaining sides were topiary
gardens. Trees sculpted into fantastic animal shapes loomed in the fading light,
creating cover around the pavilion. The ladies led Grand Verity up a small
staircase and into the pavilion, in the center of which was a pool, steam rising
gently from the surface. Hot water gurgled from a terra-cotta pipe at one end
of the pool; at the other end, a small spillway directed the overflow down a
rocky streambed which wended its way to the lake. One corner of the pavilion
had been furnished comfortably with divans and carpets. As the ladies went
about hanging the lanterns and setting out the food, Grand Verity knelt at the
edge of the pool and felt the water; its heat caused a small shiver of excitement
to run up her arm. She stood and looked around her. Neither she nor any of
her sisters could have invented a more perfect setting.

Though there was still a fair amount of light, she had the ladies light the
lanterns. Around her shoulders was a loose cape. Stepping into the shadows
where she knew she couldn't be seen, she undid the strings at her chin and
allowed the cape to fall to the ground. Underneath, she wore another garment.
She smoothed the white feathers and waited, listening.

: :

Kao Li-shih and the Emperor stood very still in the shelter of a tree whose
low branches curved toward the ground and up again like an elephant's tusks.
Through the branches they had a clear view of the open, southerly side of the
Flying Rosy Cloud Pavilion. They had been there for the better part of an
hour. The Emperor carried a small flask of wine, and he and Kao Li-shih
passed it back and forth, though the Emperor took considerably more than
the eunuch did.

The Emperor was animated. Kao Li-shih had forgotten that his master
had the capacity for animation, so long had it been since he had seen him like
this. He watched his glittering eyes as the Son of Heaven took another swallow
of wine. On any other evening at this time, Kao Li-shih thought, he would
be at his painting table, getting ready for another night of solitary slashing
and scribbling with his infernal brushes, or he might be in bed still, waiting
for the sun to go down completely before even bringing his head out from
under the covers.

Watching his master, the eunuch was amazed at what one could still learn about a person after having known him for many years. He had never known the Emperor to take pleasure in such clandestine observation. He had hidden himself at the dance performance, and now they hid among the trees. Though Kao Li-shih had had to bully and scold him to get him to attend the performance and had had to agree to the absurdity of the Emperor secreting himself among the musicians, the Son of Heaven had at least roused himself from his torpor and gone. The dance performance had been Kao Li-shih's idea, and he had had to arrange it in the Emperor's name, but the expedition to the hot springs had been the Emperor's own idea. And the girl! She was clever, and responsive. When the message had arrived from her, informing Kao Li-shih that she wished to bathe, he knew that she had entered into a conspiracy with him so subtle, so tacit as to be practically nonexistent. She had not forced him to divulge the Emperor's secrets. She was making his job that much easier—and for that, he was grateful. And now here they stood, like adolescent boys peering through a window into a lady's dressing chamber.

All of this was strange—but at the very least it was life, activity, purpose. The Emperor's eyes looked eagerly in the direction of the approach to the Flying Rosy Cloud Pavilion.

"I have heard that there are men who never touch a woman, but who can obtain satisfaction merely from watching them," the Emperor said in a low voice. "Perhaps I have become one of those men."

Kao Li-shih considered for a moment and reached for the flask. "Actually, there are eunuchs who make a habit of just that practice. The women do not think of them as men in any way at all, and ignore them. They do not know that the eyes watching them are fully masculine." He took a drink. "Though watching, of course, is all they can do. And I remember the case of the servant who pretended to be a eunuch. An insignificant little man. No one paid him much attention. He 'became' a eunuch, and spent all his time in the harem, watching the women bathe."

The Emperor turned to Kao Li-shih and looked at him curiously. "And what about you?" he asked.

Kao Li-shih was just taking a breath to answer, to tell him that he might as well ask a horse what it's like to fly, when the Emperor put a hand on his arm and stiffened, attentive.

Female voices were moving through the woods. As they drew nearer, the Emperor stepped back a few paces, pulling Kao Li-shih with him. They had a clear view into the pavilion from where they stood, while they themselves were hidden in the protective shelter of the low tree branches.

There were three women: first, one of the harem ladies, then Grand Verity, wearing a bulky cape that covered her from shoulder to toe; then another harem lady. The ladies were laden down with baskets, but Grand Verity carried nothing. The Emperor's hand stayed where it was on Kao Li-shih's arm; it was plain that he had forgotten it, so intently was he watching the girl, who walked to the edge of the pool, tested the water, and then moved out of their line of vision. The Emperor's hand dropped from Kao Li-shih's arm. They waited, saying not a word.

When the lanterns were lit and the food laid out on a low table in the corner, one of the women seated herself on the carpet and unwrapped a musical instrument. It was a five-string *chin*. She took a few moments to tune it, the notes carrying clearly to the hiding place of the Emperor and Kao Li-shih. Then she began to play.

Kao Li-shih could hear the Emperor draw his breath in. The woman was playing a slow, simplified version of the "Rainbow Chemise, Feathered Skirt" song. Then he heard the Emperor gasp with delight. Grand Verity was walking out from the shadows—where she had disappeared—wearing the magnificent white feather garment from the dance performance. She began to do the dance, but it was a slow, languid version, in time with the instrumental accompaniment.

She had done the dance well before, but this was real artistry. She had incorporated into the choreography an uncanny and slightly unsettling impression of a large water bird—the strange, delicately ponderous lifting of the feet, the undulations of the neck, the clipped, almost jerky movements of the head, the eyes staring, unblinking and devoid of emotion. The slowness of the music allowed her to exaggerate these effects until she seemed scarcely human. Kao Li-shih could see the Emperor's head shaking slightly as he made small noises of admiration.

The clear notes of the *chin* were joined by a chorus of frogs nearby. The tempo of the music began to increase gradually. As it did, the dancer began to whirl, first slowly, then faster and faster. All at once the garment was undone and slipping from her shoulders. With a single smooth motion of her arm, she removed the white feather cape and threw it into the shadows. At the same moment, the Emperor released a long sigh of pleasure: She had been wearing nothing at all beneath the feathers. Nude, she continued to turn, but slower and slower now, until she stopped, knelt, and gazed at her reflection in the pool, as if wondering at her magical transformation from bird to woman. Then she continued the dance, but all traces of her bird nature were gone. She was human now.

I was wrong about her being fat, Kao Li-shih thought as she turned slowly around and around. Her breasts were large, but not at all pendulous, and though her hips were rounded and substantial, her waist and limbs were dainty. He felt his own pulse quickening and looked hopefully toward the Emperor, whose breath was now slow and nearly labored as he leaned forward, taking in her every motion.

She stood by the pool now, arms raised over her head as if imploring the clouds or the gods or the sky. Then she brought her arms down and carefully descended the stone staircase that led down into the steaming water. The music subsided to a gentle background song. The dance was over; now she simply went through the motions of a woman bathing who thinks she is alone and unwatched. She stood waist-deep in the water, skin flushed pink in the lantern-light, combed her hair with her fingers, and rubbed the pea soap into her skin. The look on her face was thoughtful and melancholy.

Standing next to the eunuch, the Emperor was beginning to undo his clothing, yanking hastily at his sash and kicking off his shoes.

"I was wrong, Kao Li-shih," he whispered, pulling his long tunic over his head. "I am not one of those men who are content to watch. Not as yet, anyway. Gods, but she is beautiful!" He ripped the garment in his impatience to be rid of it, flailing his arm up and down in an effort to make a stubborn sleeve release its grip on him. "She is acting out the myth of the Hsiang consort, Kao Li-shih," he whispered urgently. "She is a goddess waiting for a mortal man to come to her. If I do not go now, I am no better than a piece of dog dung, and not worthy of her!" He left the close confines of his hiding place then, removing bits of clothing as he went, until he was stark naked, and climbed the few steps to the Flying Rosy Cloud Pavilion. Kao Li-shih was shocked to see how emaciated the Emperor had become. His ribs and backbone were clearly visible, and his skin had an unhealthy pallor. Pathetic sight though he was, he was moving with a purpose and energy Kao Li-shih had not seen for a long, long time. And to think that he had been, at one time, worried that the girl's impudence might repel the Emperor.

The eunuch watched his master approach the pool. The girl did not change her expression or demeanor at all as the Emperor joined her in the water; though her back was to him, Kao Li-shih was certain that she was aware of his presence. It was not until the Emperor had come up behind her in the water and embraced her, putting both hands on her breasts, that she even acknowledged that she was not alone. Kao Li-shih looked down at the flask in his hand. Raising it, he took a another drink.

Grand Verity heard a disturbance in the water behind her. Instead of turning, she continued to wring out her hair, though her heart jumped nervously. When a pair of arms slid around her and hands came up to her breasts, she looked down. She recognized those hands. They were the same ones she had seen resting on the arms of the throne over two years ago. A mouth caressed her neck, a man's aroused body pressed from behind. The hands exerted gentle pressure as a voice whispered in her ear. It sounded like a quote from a poem, though she didn't recognize it: " 'I thought I must be in a dream, at Y'ang-t'ai . . .' "

::

Hoofbeats shook the earth as the horses carrying the Emperor and the woman raced down the field. Wielding the polo mallet with a mighty stroke, the Emperor hit the ball squarely, sending it flying ahead of him. He whooped with delight. Kao Li-shih could scarcely believe that this was the same man who had winced and put his head under his pillow at the sight of daylight just a week ago. On the sidelines, the Precious Consort, as Grand Verity was newly named, sat demurely and smiled when either of the opposing players scored. This was to be expected. One of the players, the Emperor, was her lover; the other, the woman on horseback, was her eldest sister.

This sister was a remarkable female. Kao Li-shih had seen women on horses before, but none of them had actually been riding. Rather, they sat sedately atop a horse and were led. This one, dressed in men's riding satins and tunic, was astride one of the Emperor's best horses. She bent herself low over its neck while she dug her heels into its sides, making the animal completely an instrument of her will, controlling it with one hand and holding the mallet in the other.

As if two Yang females, the Precious Consort and this horsewoman, were not sufficient, on either side of the consort sat yet another sister. Surrounded by food, flowers, and musical instruments, these two additional ones behaved as if they were royalty visiting from some imaginary foreign court. Every step they took was accompanied by the nearly deafening clatter of their jewelry; it was scarcely possible to breathe the air that they passed through, so laden was it with their flowery perfume, which emanated from the folds of their elaborate clothing with each motion they made. And when they spoke, their eyes and hands accompanied their voices with ostentatious looks and gestures. The sisters were in complicity with one another no matter what they said or did. The four women together formed a circle of femaleness around the Emperor; they teased, they giggled, they conspired, they insulted him and each other, and he absorbed it like parched earth when the rain finally comes.

The sisters had materialized a mere two days after the girl had done her amazing dance by the hot pool. Left alone in his hiding place in the trees, Kao Li-shih had continued to drink the wine in the Emperor's flask until he was quite uncharacteristically drunk. Though he was accustomed to feeling shadows of the Emperor's emotions, this had been one place where the eunuch could not follow. The Emperor had stayed in the pool for a very long time, exploring the girl's body with his hands and talking to her in a voice too soft for Kao Li-shih to hear clearly.

Kao Li-shih had done something he had done only once or twice before in his life. He allowed the wine to run in his veins, allowed the loneliness he kept impeccably at bay to rise in him. Like wavelets lapping the shore of a pond, the loneliness had washed gently against his mind and soul as he watched the man and woman in the pool. He thought of nothing in particular, called on no memories, painful or otherwise. He simply sat in his solitude and watched as their motions in the water fused and became rhythmic. So slow, so languid. Sometimes their faces looked like the faces of sleepers; moments later, they looked like the faces of people in pain or intense sorrow, then like people sharing jokes and secrets.

The two women who had accompanied Grand Verity eventually slipped away. When the Emperor appeared to be about to diminish his *ching* for the second time, Kao Li-shih had lifted the empty flask in salutation. My master, he thought, it appears that there are still a few shreds of life left in you. Quietly, the eunuch had risen from his seat and, feeling ahead of him in the dark for small branches that might hit his eyes, found his way out of the enclosure and made his way toward the path that would take him to his quarters.

A scant day later, Grand Verity's name was changed along with her status. Kao Li-shih had seen for himself that the Emperor was pleased with Grand Verity, but this promotion was altogether astonishing. When the Empress had been alive, the Emperor had done her the honor of keeping the rank just below hers vacant, so that she might enjoy the luxury of removal from other women. Grand Verity now occupied that sacredly empty position of precious consort; Kao Li-shih had uttered a silent apology to the ghost of the Empress, glad that he could at least offer the assurance that the Emperor had told him that as long as he lived, no other woman would become empress.

Pieces of earth and grass, torn up by the horses as the Emperor and elder sister made a sharp turn, were sprayed in the direction of the spectators. Precious Consort and her sisters, laughing and shouting, picked the pieces up and threw them back at the players. The elder sister had gained the advantage, cutting in from the left, surprising the Emperor, and driving the ball back in the opposite direction. When she scored, the women on the sidelines broke into unrestrained exultation. The Emperor rode at them as if he meant to trample them for their impudence, brandishing his mallet and pulling his horse to one side at the last moment. Kao Li-shih wondered at the women's behavior. Was there no limit to their insolence? They seemed to make a game of flouting every possible social convention; now they smiled and clapped their hands at the Emperor's defeat. The eunuch shook his head incredulously. It appears that I have much to learn about human nature. That a woman could take the ball away from the Son of Heaven is quite extraordinary enough; that the other women would dare to show pleasure when it happened is further cause for disbelief. And when one considers the possible consequences if she wins the game, he reflected, then reason and logic have lost all meaning.

There was a wager riding on the outcome of the match. Precious Consort had tantalized the Emperor by telling him of her extraordinary sister who could play polo like a man. She had mentioned also that the woman was beautiful and witty, and had gone on to enumerate other talents. The Emperor, of course, had gone for the bait and told Precious Consort to send for her immediately, that they would have a game. She will probably beat you, Precious Consort had said. The Emperor had laughed. Impossible. A woman beat me at polo? But I would love to see her try! And if she wins? Well, the Emperor had said, if she wins, then I will give *her* a title, too.

And so the match had been arranged. But the sister hadn't shown up alone: She was not one, but three. And as a man who is drunk falls down among his silk cushions, the Emperor had let himself collapse into the sweet-smelling, eye-flashing, silk-rustling, audaciously female presence of the Yang sisters.

Kao Li-shih had thought that he understood the feminine mind thoroughly. What would *he* have done if he were a woman who had been allowed to play polo against the Emperor of China? The answer was plain: I would play, he thought, but I would understand at the beginning of the match that the Emperor would be the victor. What other possible outcome could there be? And I would certainly know that even though I had been promised a title if I won, the real way to win would be to lose—knowing that I would receive the reward anyway. To win against him would be an unthinkable insult. He watched as the elder sister wheeled her horse around and took off after the Emperor, who had recovered the ball and had sent it back down the field. Her set, almost grim expression as she spurred the animal in pursuit of her quarry made it clear that she fully intended to win if she could—and she needed to score only once more in order to do it. The players were well matched: Though the Emperor had the natural masculine advantage, the woman was considerably younger, with a mastery of her horse equal to any man's.

And she understood the importance of strategy. The Emperor had had to veer off his straight course in order to get at the ball to hit it again. The woman did not try to reach it at the same time as her opponent; seeing that he had to lose a few precious moments retrieving the ball, she urged her horse downfield. When the Emperor made his hit, she had already moved into position. Once again, she intercepted and sent the ball flying in the opposite direction. It sailed, as if it knew exactly where to go, all the way down the field and between the goal sticks. She had won the match. Her sisters jumped to their feet and began to hurl flowers onto the field in her direction—flowers that should only have been thrown at the Emperor.

Uneasily, Kao Li-shih watched the Emperor circle around the field a time or two to let his horse cool off. The eunuch caught Precious Consort's eye and tried to tell her by his expression to show a little less exuberance. But it was in vain. The women were too completely occupied to pay any attention.

And now the Emperor was approaching. Kao Li-shih did not like the face the Emperor was wearing; it reminded him too much of the face of fatigue and sorrow that he had worn until just a short time ago.

Precious Consort noticed it too. She rushed over to the horse's side as the Emperor drew up. He slid down off his mount, leaned tiredly against the animal and buried his face in its side. Precious Consort seized his arms and tried to turn him around, a worried expression on her own face.

"You cannot be sad!" she said with alarm. "We will play again! But this time *I* will ride, and you can watch me fall off the horse!"

He turned then, the sad expression entirely gone from his face, and grabbed her, laughing. Kao Li-shih breathed again. He had been jesting! Incredulous, the eunuch tried to remember the last time the Emperor had indulged in levity of any kind. For that matter, he thought, when was the last time that *I* smiled? Or anyone at court? The women were now crowding around the consort and the Emperor while he playfully pulled the pins from her hair and she struggled to stop him. The elder sister rode up then, and a groom hurried to help her down from the horse.

"You!" said the Emperor. "I am very angry! What if word gets out that a lady beat me at polo? Obviously, you care nothing for the empire!" But he was smiling as he said it.

She shrugged. "And obviously, you are too old to play," she said. "I was doing my best to let you win, but it did me no good." An ingenuous look came onto her face then. "Don't we have a little wager to settle?"

The Emperor tipped his head to one side as if he didn't know what she was talking about. "I am a confused old man! I do not always remember my own words. I'm sure you understand—I simply cannot be held responsible for everything I say!"

The women closed around him then, imploring, scolding, tickling, poking. Kao Li-shih had thought that his incredulity had been stretched to the limit, but this . . . !

"Is it titles you want?" said the Emperor, weak with laughter. "Very well! Titles you shall have! You," he said, pointing to the younger of the two other sisters, "shall be the Lady of the Bottom of the Frog Pond. And you," he said, pointing to the other, "shall be the Lady of Discarded Broken Furniture. And you." He paused thoughtfully, looking at the elder sister. "You shall have vast holdings. You shall be the Lady of the One Thousand Hairs on a Grasshopper's Leg."

::

He conversed with her while he made love. For Precious Consort, this was something entirely new. At the nunnery, the monk had never said anything at all that was not of an instructional nature, and then it was terse. The Emperor asked her questions and told her stories even in the midst of the "clouds and rain" thing.

It was very late at night, the same day as the polo match. Precious Consort and the Emperor lay in the huge bed in his quarters at the hot springs. After Elder Sister's victory, they had all traveled out to the hot springs to celebrate. He had, of course, been joking about the titles; the Yang sisters were now officially restored to nobility, with Middle and Younger sisters becoming the Lady of Chin and the Lady of Han; Elder Sister was now the Lady of Kuo. The Emperor had scarcely been able to contain his delight upon learning that all the sisters were musicians. He had called forth the Pear Garden Orchestra, and he and the sisters joined them and they played and sang far into the night in one of the open-air pavilions. The steam rose from the pool and the sweet wine flowed as the Emperor demonstrated his mastery of so many instruments.

And they had invented a game. When the Emperor was quite drunk and everyone was naked in the hot water, the sisters had challenged him to blindfold himself. Let us test your powers of observation, they said. Let us see if you can tell one of us from the other just by feeling our bodies. He had enthusiastically tied a sash around his eyes, and the sisters moved about in the water so that he didn't know where any of them were. They were free to elude him until he actually got his hands on one; then she had to hold still while he decided, through his sense of touch, whether he had the Lady of Han, the Lady of Chin, or the Lady of Kuo. Or even Precious Consort herself, whose contours should have been familiar to him. They splashed and squealed while the Son of Heaven, with the sodden piece of silk tied around his head, lunged to take hold of a foot or an arm in the steaming water. He was wrong as many times as he was right, and they were soon quite thoroughly exhausted with laughter and the effort to disguise their voices so as not to give him any clues as he carefully studied with his fingers a hand, a shoulder, a breast, a dainty leg, or a belly.

"Did I not tell you," he said to her now in the big bed, the silk covers whispering in time with their motions, "that the dance you did on that first night, and the music, are my own special work?"

"No," she answered. "Kao Li-shih only said that it had particular meaning for you." They lay on their sides, facing each other. She was nearly asleep, and let her hands run slowly up and down the smooth, dry skin of his back. It was odd. She could scarcely recall her education at the nunnery. So many little tricks, techniques. They seemed irrelevant. He moved inside her slowly, gently.

"I wrote the song. The dance I arranged, working with a consultant." He paused. "I was playing that night, too." She roused herself and opened her eyes.

"Where were you?" she asked.

"Have you not guessed?" he answered. "I was with the drummers. I was in costume, with a bit of makeup. I looked like a very undistinguished middle-aged musician." He paused. "Which is, of course, what I am."

"No," she said, "you are hardly undistinguished as a musician. You are the best wether-drum player I have ever heard. As for your appearance . . . I suppose I must concede that you were undistinguished that night. I certainly never saw you."

"But I saw you," he said slyly.

"I learned the dance at the nunnery. Someone came out from the palace to teach it to me." She thought a moment. "I was taught many things there, you know."

"I know what they didn't teach you."

"There is nothing they neglected to teach me."

"They taught you what was in their power to teach, but there is one thing that is beyond their ability. Who was your tutor?"

"I never found out his name. He was a monk. He was fat." She did not like thinking about him. Not now, when she was here with the Emperor like this. The Emperor was laughing softly.

"I know who he is. No, I don't think he could have taught you everything. There is something I would dearly love to teach you. I hope I will be able to."

She was not altogether certain what he meant, but she felt an odd thrill, a deep, dark ripple of excitement in the center of her body.

As if he was aware of what she felt, he moved against her appreciatively. "Yes," he said. "The omens and portents are good. I am a good teacher, but some things are beyond my control."

"What do you mean?" she asked, feeling little arrows of anticipation.

"It is the one thing in all the world that can't be counterfeited. There can be no pretending, and it cares nothing for whether I am an emperor, a thief, or the driver of a night-soil wagon." He heaved a sigh. "It is very difficult to achieve." He had stopped moving now, but remained inside her body. "Tell me, did you love the fat monk?"

"Certainly not!" she answered. The very idea was a joke. It was repulsive, preposterous.

"In order for me to teach you this thing, you and I are going to have to achieve the impossible. You are going to have to love me, and I am going to have to love you. But it is going to have to be exactly equal: one cannot love more, or less, than the other."

She was silent for a while, thinking about the possibility of love. Going through her "lessons" with the monk, she had felt nothing at all but weariness and impatience. And nothing he had done was for her pleasure. He had taught her to make cries and moans of feigned ecstasy, telling her that it would give more pleasure to her partner if she did them convincingly. She had tried it only once with the Emperor, out of habit, but he had put his hand over her mouth and said he would rather listen to the braying of a donkey. I am a musician, he had said; false notes cannot escape me and they hurt my ears. A woman's pleasure, the Emperor had said, is deeper than a man's. Let me show you. And he had "played" her body like one of his musical instruments, drawing the sounds out of her almost against her will. How did he know these things? He had smiled enigmatically and said that it was purely selfish on his part, that he enjoyed it. Was this love? On top of everything else— coming to the palace, bringing her sisters, entering a world that exceeded their wildest flights of fancy—was she also going to have love? And what was this thing he talked about now? We will have to love each other exactly the same, he had said.

"Do we love each other?" she asked.

"The signs look very good," he answered. "We will know soon."

Wine and hot water had made them both tired. Bodies still joined, they drifted into sleep. She dreamed that there was a thunderstorm and it rained small animals, and she looked at her own face in a puddle of water and was surprised to see a man's face looking back at her.

:: :

Early in the morning, Kao Li-shih found the Emperor in the ruins of a par- ticularly ancient pavilion. He had set up a small portable writing table and was busily making ink sketches. The eunuch approached and looked over his master's shoulder.

"I believe that this was the site of the very oldest building on these grounds," the Emperor said. "I think that this would be the ideal location for the lotus pools. From references I have come across in studying the Chou histories, the first pool to be built here was in the shape of a lotus. I would like to re-create it, Kao Li-shih, and present it as a gift to my consort. This sketch is my idea for a decorative mosaic motif," he said, holding up a piece of parchment, "and this is a sketch for the shape of the pool itself. What do you think?" Kao Li-shih studied the drawings.

"They are very fine. I hope that we can still obtain the services of Shao- lao, the mosaic artist from Lung-chuan. He is one of the few who could do justice to your ideas," he said, carefully disguising his elation. To see the Emperor making plans, resuming his activities . . . Did he dare believe it?

"The pool will have improved pipes and a way to recirculate the water, of course," the Emperor continued. "An archaeological restoration does not have to include outmoded systems. Ceramic, I believe, is more durable than terra-cotta." He took a critical look at his sketch. "The lotus, Kao Li-shih, is the symbol of purity and rebirth."

Appropriate enough, the eunuch thought.

Then he thought of the papers . . . the papers he had taken from the chief minister's reader months ago—the decree, so insidiously and audaciously insinuated into the daily business at the morning audience, that threatened to eventually strip the Censorate of its powers of vigilance. He remembered the Emperor's drugged eyes, looking at him from so far away when he had tried to make him read the papers, to be cognizant of the threat in their midst.

He had kept those papers, thinking that perhaps a day would come when the Emperor would look at them and see for himself that Li Lin-fu was something other than a faithful servant. Already, there were indications that the responsibilities of the powerful eunuch elite were gradually being shunted into useless, token jobs meant only to divert their attention.

"Master," Kao Li-shih said tentatively. "If I may, I would like to call on you later with some official business. There are some papers that need your attention. The Censorate—"

The Emperor interrupted him with a wave of his hand. "Please, Kao Li-shih! Words like 'official business' and 'Censorate' give me a headache. They smell bad! They are dreary!"

"But Master—"

"Please!" the Emperor implored. "Let me be! Surely I have responsible servants whose job it is to tend to these things! I am a man recently risen from his sickbed. I am in the midst of a glorious dream. I beg you not to come to me with words like that," he said firmly, turning back to his work.

Kao Li-shih stood for a moment, astonished. Then he turned and left the Emperor to his sketching. Preposterous. Ridiculous. He strode through the ruins, his temper rising. I was right, he thought, when I calculated that the power of love would bring him back from the dead. What I could not foresee, or know, is that love is a devouring monster itself. He thinks he has left his sickbed? He has simply gone from one to another.

He stopped and looked out across the lake. Everything was so peaceful, so beautiful. He took a deep breath and pushed the worried feeling back. No. It is simply that my timing was wrong. I chose the wrong moment. He thought of the papers that he had been keeping for these many months. I will keep them longer, as long as is necessary, he thought, stepping onto a stone path that led through a garden of bamboo, twisted and cultivated into strange, graceful shapes. At least, the eunuch reflected, he has put his sorrow behind him.

BOOK TWO

LI REN HSING*

PRETTY WOMEN MEANDERING

*The title of a ballad in the ancient *yueh-fu* style by the renowned eighth-century statesman, literary genius, and chronicler of the reign of Minghuang, Tu Fu. Often referred to as China's greatest poet, Tu Fu was, as late as the nineteenth century, more widely read in China and published in more editions there than Milton, Donne, Shakespeare, Spenser, and the Old Testament *combined* were in the West. Tu Fu's *Ballad of Pretty Women Meandering* pictures in great detail a luxurious spring outing by the three elder Yang Sisters—the ladies of Han, Chin, and Kuo—and their powerful cousin, Yang Kuo-chung. The openly incestuous relationship with the lady of Kuo is veiled in the metaphors of plants—"willow catkins" and "white frogbit"—in the latter part of the ballad. Stylistically, this work represents a somewhat tongue-in-cheek return to an early, didactic poetic form, the *yueh-fu*—known by both its question-and-answer format in the fourth and fifth couplets and by its subtle purpose to "inform" and "warn" an emperor of the dangerous conditions that had come to surround him—in this case, licentiousness and the distracting excesses of concubines and consorts.

10

A General's Debut

Grossly fat, with a simple ingenuous manner which concealed a shrewd cunning, [An Lu-shan] ingratiated himself by flattering the Emperor and amusing him with clumsy gaffs and clownery. His pretence of simple uncouth barbarism, and ignorance of etiquette became one of the standing jokes of the gay Court, particularly amusing to the favourite, Yang Kuei-fei. . . . The Emperor, who regarded the Turk [An Lu-shan] as a good-natured buffoon, accorded him high favours to please his mistress. An Lu-shan was allowed to visit the consort in the inner palace, an unheard of privilege, and even took part in private dinner parties at which only the Emperor and Yang Kuei-fei were present.

—C. P. Fitzgerald

Though [An Lu-shan] was sharply suspicious and cunning at heart, he had a disarming appearance of innocent simplicity . . . with a protruding and hanging belly, said to weigh alone at least four hundred pounds. He was delighted to have men laugh and women giggle at him and was never slow to join in general hilarity. . . . He induced the Yang sisters . . . to adopt him as a brother. . . .

—William Hung

At gay fetes and festivals the uncouth general submitted to ridiculous and even indecent practical jokes at the hands of the ladies of the palace. The Emperor, completely under the sway of Yang Kuei-fei, made no objection, and, indeed, was highly amused.

—C. P. Fitzgerald

... and in 745 [the emperor] publicly made [Yang Kuei-fei] his favorite concubine. This woman ... was said to have been plump and beautiful, gifted in music, and endowed with an unusual perspicacity, which she used expertly to capture the love of the emperor. She was soon regarded by everyone in the palace as empress, and her three talented and pretty elder sisters, Mrs. P'ei, Mrs. Ts'ui and Mrs. Liu frequented the palace as sisters-in-law and also as favorites of the emperor and were ennobled as the *Lady of Kuo,* the *Lady of Han,* and the *Lady of Ch'in* respectively.

—*William Hung*

By imperial decree, each and every month, on the same day, the [Yang sisters] received a stipend of some ten thousand strings of cash for the procurement of exotic and expensive cosmetics. But the Lady of Kuo's beauty was perfect, and she would not succumb to the use of cosmetics to adorn her face. Instead, she preferred to go about, daily, plain and unpowdered and unornamented. Thus the famous Tu Fu said, of her, in a poem: "[The Lady of Kuo] disliked and rejected cosmetics, refusing to defile her face with them. She chose, instead, to merely lightly pencil in her mothbrows before attending to affairs of court.

—*Morohashi Tetsuji, translated by Daniel Altieri*

AN Lu-shan wondered if this was some sort of rite of initiation that all newcomers had to endure, or whether it was an elaborate joke designed specifically for him and at his expense. When he had received the order, he had not wished to appear an inexperienced provincial, and had reacted as though what he heard was perfectly natural, possibly something that he expected. Later, he fretted. Had his feigned nonchalance only made him look that much more like a bumpkin and a fool? Were the chief minister and the lackey General Niu snickering about it at this very moment?

It was early morning a few days after his extraordinary meeting with Chief Minister Li Lin-fu. Raising himself up from his pillow, he swung his legs over and put his feet on the floor. His head throbbed and his limbs ached as they had every morning since his arrival, only today it was worse. He had to get drunk every night if he was to sleep at all; the closed air of the city and the too-soft bed in his quarters had kept him growling and sleepless until dawn on the first night. With wine, he had been able to sink into stuporous slumber on the second and third nights. But this last night, thanks to Li Lin-fu's "invitation," no amount of wine could give him respite. His brain had seethed until light seeped in around the blinds as doubt, anger, and uncertainty tumbled around and around in his skull. When the birds began twittering outside, his whole being felt like a great, raw saddle blister. And now, no sooner had his feet touched the floor than a servant appeared proffering a tray of steaming tea and pastries. He glared at the man and rudely waved him away, but catching a whiff of the fragrant steam, changed his mind and called him back. The servant responded to his commands as if he were an extension of An Lu-shan's own being. They move about like ghosts, An Lu-shan thought as he watched the man. They make no sound when they walk, as if they had no flesh or blood, or even lives of their own. A wicked urge seized him as the servant brought the tray to him again. He reached for the food, then pretended to change his mind and even more rudely dismissed him. The man had nearly reached the door, bowing politely, when An Lu-shan growled for him to come back. He would do this all day long if I chose to keep the game up, An Lu-shan thought. At no time did the man show the slightest impatience or exasperation; he merely responded to the contradictory commands with perfect obedience. Finally An Lu-shan accepted the tray and got rid of him, shaking his head with disbelief as he moved his bulk from the bed to a chair.

When the servant had evaporated back into the shadows, the general returned to his problem. He thought of the many tests of manhood that he had both witnessed and endured in the north. The challenges ranged from feats of strength and bravery to endurance of extreme pain; all were meant to prove one's right to belong. Obviously, he was being called on here to prove his right to belong. But instead of wrestling a man until he pinned him, or allowing heavy rocks to be piled on his chest, he would have to do something far more difficult. The sniveling little weasel Niu, the one with the eyes that looked everywhere but at your own when he spoke, had informed him that he, An Lu-shan, would perform, courtesy of the chief minister, as a musician several nights hence with something called the Pear Garden Orchestra. He knew nothing at all about music. He had wondered at first if perhaps the chief minister had been misinformed, but recalling the strange feeling in the air during their first interview, rejected the idea. Li Lin-fu was aware of everything, including, no doubt, the fact that An Lu-shan had as much musical ability as an ox.

He brooded on his predicament as he had all night long. Either this was a legitimate ritual of some sort, an "honor" being bestowed on him, or an attempt to make him look ridiculous. Though his instinct warned him that it was the latter, he knew that he might be wrong—and to refuse would be to risk a breach of protocol. Besides, he thought, if it *is* a joke, then I should show my willingness to participate so I won't look like one of those solemn, humorless rustics you see so often in the north, with an exaggerated sense of dignity that only reveals how suspicious and ignorant they are. But following on the heels of that possibility was another even more annoying and subtle one: Perhaps the order to perform in the Pear Garden Orchestra was something so patently absurd that no one in his right mind would take it seriously—and to go ahead with it would be to reveal his unsureness of what he was doing. Don't ever let Li Lin-fu know, he warned himself, that you are uneasy or unsure of yourself.

He turned the possibilities over and over in his weary mind without getting closer to any kind of resolve. He understood that he was, in some obscure way, being challenged. An Lu-shan had never shrunk from a challenge in his life. It infuriated him that the nature of this challenge, its size, shape, and smell, eluded him. How could he know how to respond? He didn't know the tribal rules in this damnable place. He slammed his fist down on the dainty little table in front of him, upsetting the procelain teapot and spilling hot tea onto his lap. Cursing, he knocked the chair over as he quickly stood up. The hot liquid had barely enough time to soak through his clothing when the ghost-servant materialized, and in what seemed to be one effortless motion, pulled the fabric of An Lu-shan's trousers away from his legs so that he wouldn't be burned, deftly righted the teapot and the chair, and mopped up the spilled tea from the table. There was nothing in the man's face that showed the slightest reaction to his master's outburst—not a trace of shock, interest, curiosity, or reproval. The spectacle of the servant down on his knees removing the spilled tea from the carpet brought a sudden insight to An Lu-shan, as if a door had opened for just a moment on a room he had never seen before. *This whole world that he now inhabited was completely dependent on creatures such as this one.* The servant was, in a way, his key to understanding that world. That he had his own thoughts and opinions An Lu-shan did not doubt; but to look at him one would think that his mind had been wiped clean of every thought except the comfort and convenience of his superiors. It went beyond obedience: They had taken a human, the most willful and contrary of living things, and turned him into something else entirely. It was pure alchemy! Magic! One could only have respect for a society capable of such a transformation, and for the infinitely complex layers of manners and attitudes, building on one another over centuries, that required for their very existence that such creatures be fashioned from human material. Big, sweating, stupid, stinking oaf though you are, he told himself, you *will* learn. You will move as deftly through these gilded halls, kissing the hands of fine ladies and nibbling on roasted sparrows, as any "silk-trousers" ever has. You spent your life traveling the rough roads of the north, making the ways and tongues of a hundred different tribes your own. Well, you can shut up and stop your whining now. It was your fondest wish to get to this place, and now, by your own will, you are here. This is merely another tribe. You will make its ways your own, and teach them a few things they never dreamt of as well. He yawned mightily.

And, he told himself, you will start immediately. As it happened, he was to attend a court dinner party that very evening. He yawned again, stood, and moved back toward the bed. Court dinner, tribal feast—was there really any difference?

: :

He was drunk, but not just on wine. He was surrounded. Their voices made his head dizzy, their flashing jewelry dazzled his eyes, and their scent mingling with the aroma of the food made his "old man" stir in his trousers. In the privacy of the darkness under the tablecloth, he lovingly caressed himself, while the other hand raised cup after cup of wine to his mouth. On his left sat the Lady of Chin and her sister the Lady of Han; on his right, making his memory of Purple Gown in the streets of the city wither like last week's dream, sat another sister, the Lady of Kuo. She was speaking to him, but he was letting comprehension go by. He was watching her mouth, and listening to the music of her voice, but not to the meaning of her words. She had finished what she was saying and was looking at him with her head tilted in a way that meant that she expected him to answer. He turned to his left and gave his most endearing smile to her two sisters.

"I cannot understand what she is saying." He shrugged. "She is too beautiful."

"Well, you are not so easy to understand, either," replied the Lady of Chin.

"But not for that exact reason," added the Lady of Han, laughing.

"I was asking you," came the Lady of Kuo's voice from his right, "about the land where you came from."

He turned back to her. "I can listen to you if I keep my eyes shut," he joked. He paused before he spoke again, making an effort of will to control his thickening tongue. "Where I come from, a stone hut would be a palace, a stinking skin a fine robe, and I am the handsomest of men. And the smartest."

"Where we come from," she answered with a charming smile, "we are ugly old hags, ignorant and uncultured. Barely fit to be serving women."

"You could never know," he said, shaking his head, "what an ugly woman is until you have been where I have been."

"I would like to see the world through your eyes," she said thoughtfully. "I wish I could sit where you are sitting and look at myself sitting here talking to you." She glanced around the table at the twenty or so other guests, who appeared to take no particular notice of the stranger in their midst. "I wish I could see all of this through your eyes," she said in a discreet voice to An Lushan. His hand underneath the tablecloth ceased its motion, embarrassed, as if she were not only looking through his eyes but occupying his other senses as well.

"I wish you could, too, madam," he said, leaning toward her. "Then you would know how much there is for me to learn." The Lady of Kuo was looking past him at her sisters. He knew that he was the center of the attention of all three, and was basking in it. He wanted more of everything; more wine, more food, and especially, more of their attention. On an impulse, he leaned closer, dropping his voice and putting on a sad expression. "I am faced with a problem. Being a newcomer, I do not know whom to trust." Her reaction, a discreet and conspiratorial attentiveness, was gratifying. She said nothing, but waited for him to speak. He took a deep breath, and spoke the puzzling words out loud for the first time since the "invitation" had come to him. "The Pear Garden Orchestra," he said simply, and waited. Her brow wrinkled just a bit in consternation.

"What about the Pear Garden Orchestra?" she asked. Obviously, he would have to tell her more. He had hoped that the name alone, and her reaction to it, would tell him what he wanted to know. He took another drink of wine before forming his words.

"I am to play in the Pear Garden Orchestra."

Her reaction seemed to confirm his worst fears. Her eyes widened and her mouth fell open just a bit before an expression of incredulous mirth spread across her features.

"Say it again slowly," she said. "I want to be sure I am not misunderstanding you. Your Chinese is very good, but it is . . . rough. You say you are to play *in* the Pear Garden Orchestra?"

"That is exactly correct, madam," he said, summoning his dignity. "The order has come to me from my sponsor, Li Lin-Fu." He glanced anxiously to his left. Her two sisters had not heard her, but he could tell from their faces that they knew she had uncovered something interesting, and they were waiting. She, meanwhile, held her forehead lightly in her hand and laughed softly.

"Oh, my poor fellow!" she said.

"What is it?" he said with alarm. It must be something far worse than he had dreamt. "I should not have told you!"

"No, no," she said quickly. "Your luck and your instincts brought you to exactly the right person. You could not have done better than to tell me."

"Madam, please!" he said. "What is this Pear Garden Orchestra? I am not a musician! I will make a fool of myself!"

"You lack some other attributes as well," she replied, smiling. Then she leaned so close that he could smell her glossy hair as she whispered in his ear.

"The Pear Garden is composed entirely of ladies. Young, beautiful ladies." His face flushed as the realization hit him. It *was* a joke, a ridiculous joke, to be played at his expense and in front of the entire court, possibly even the Emperor himself. So this was how they amused themselves! He thought of Li Lin-fu's scrawny neck, and his hands twitched with the desire to wring it. The Lady of Kuo touched his arm reassuringly. "You have nothing to worry about. I understand their joke completely, and I know how to turn it back on them and make you the clear victor."

"Madam, I . . ."

"Didn't I tell you that you found the right person? You must trust me!"

Looking at her face, the objections he was about to voice died on his tongue. He had had to trust people in far more dangerous and compromising situations and with less time to decide; his instinct, as she put it, rarely led him wrong. He heaved a great, long sigh of relief and acquiescence. Her two sisters could stand it no longer; they were leaning in from the left behind him now while she imparted the information to them in a soft, rapid feminine whisper that he really could not understand. The conference behind his back was completed in a flurry of gasps and incredulous giggles while he smiled and raised his wine cup to some of the other faces around the table who were taking an interest in the spectacle of the barbarian general and the three beauties in their mysterious collusion. Feeling a light touch on his arm again, he turned back to the Lady of Kuo.

"My sisters and I are musicians. We will prepare you for your 'debut,' " she said in a serious tone. "And we will train you in everything else you need to know. We will consider it a privilege."

An Lu-shan recalled his image of himself dressed in silk and supping daintily on songbirds. Yes, he would do that, and more! He threw his head back and laughed aloud. He gazed around him with drunken disbelief at the three gorgeous, flower-scented creatures in their flashing garments, conferring vigorously at this very moment about his destiny, who had been brought to him by sweet fate. He remembered old Feng's words to him as they were approaching the gates of the city—that Ch'ang-an was like a woman. He thought of himself following Purple Gown through the streets during his very first hour in the city; and now, he was to put himself in the little white hands of these three sisters in order to prepare himself to play in an all-female or-chestra! Ch'ang-an wasn't *like* a woman, it *was* a woman! But this was "woman" as he had never experienced her before. If Ch'ang-an was a woman like Purple Gown and the Lady of Kuo, the Lady of Han, and the Lady of Chin, then the north was a woman who smelled like a goat, with seams of grime in the leathery skin of her face, stringy, greasy, tangled hair plastered to her head, and black and yellow teeth worn to the gums. Except, he admonished himself, raising his cup in silent salute, for you, Mother. For the thousandth time, the baby on the pretty woman's lap in the garden reached for that face, that beautiful face. He drained the cup and lowered it as his mother's face faded back into the secret place in his mind where it resided, safe from time, where it would wait until the next time he should call it forth. His other hand crept secretly back under the tablecloth to resume its fond caresses as he laughed again, quietly and privately, to himself. A woman! Ch'ang-an is a woman!

That night, he slept soundly for the first time since his arrival in the city.

: :

When he awoke, he experienced a moment of incredulity. He, An Lu-shan, entrusting his fate to women! He must have been quite drunk indeed. What strange spells this city cast on him! He doubted very much that he would hear any more from the Lady of Kuo and her sisters. At least he now knew what this Pear Garden Orchestra was. He would, of course, politely decline the "invitation" to perform; the joke was over. Women's talk was not something one gave credit to, he thought, heaving himself up from the bed and taking the lid off the chamberpot. If a woman looks you straight in the eye and makes a promise or a judgment, he reflected, leaning with one hand against the wall in front of him and watching the pot fill, she cannot be taken any more seriously than if she were a trained monkey. Giving his "old man" a few shakes, he watched the last drops fall into the yellow froth and thought about the Lady of Kuo's translucent skin and intoxicating fragrance. Now, that was something he could take seriously. He toppled back into the bed. Promises of help were one thing; her flesh was another thing altogether. He imagined the dark, secret places of her body, and knew that he would be able to put his nose and tongue anywhere at all and it would smell like a flower garden, like some delicious food. The thought caused a ripple of arousal in his groin. Not like the sweaty, stinking encounters he had known in his life, under hides stiff with filth in a back alley with his trousers down around his knees and his bare ass exposed to the cold wind. No, not like that at all, he thought, grappling with the unfamiliar imagined sensations of silk, soft beds, and smooth, clean, scented woman-flesh. Drifting back into sleep, he resolved that he would experience it. The woman, Ch'ang-an, who had lured him through the streets, who had surrounded him at the dinner, who was everywhere in every exquisite court female, impossible, tantalizing, unattainable, would sometime, somehow, open her legs to him.

The letter arrived on his tea tray later that same morning. He could not read it, but he picked it up and examined it. The parchment was as light as a bug's wing. When he opened it, he came fully awake. That smell. It was the smell of the Lady of Kuo's hair. He turned the paper over, felt it between his fingers, weighed it in his hand. So. Either she had written with some excuse in order to back out in a ladylike way, or—was it possible?—she had meant what she said last night. He shouted for the servant.

"Bring me someone who can read!" he ordered.

"I will have to fetch one of the eunuchs," the man said.

"Just be quick about it," An Lu-shan said impatiently. A eunuch, he thought with disgust. Let's hope he doesn't smell of piss.

The tiny, frail old man the servant finally brought back did not smell of piss so much as he smelled old, like damp cloth folded and stored in a dark place. He held the piece of paper as if it were a sacred document and read aloud in a cracked, contralto singsong that made An Lu-shan grind his teeth with irritation. But the message was altogether gratifying, if strange:

> "The Lady of Kuo, the Lady of Han, and the Lady of Chin urgently request the presence of the handsome, fierce, hairy, talented, fat warrior of the north, An Lu-shan, at a music lesson today where he will learn to strike the tiny stone chimes like a finch singing in a golden cage, like the *yama* cricket alone on a leaf on a tree deep in a valley between two mountains, like a smooth stone sitting under a waterfall for a thousand years . . ."

The letter went on to say that if he would consent to bestow this honor on them, he would be called for right after the third watch and brought to them.

A woman of honor. She had kept her word. But could he trust her judgment? He had certainly believed in it last night. But last night he was drunk. Very, very drunk. But, he thought, you do yourself a dishonor. What difference does it make how drunk you were? Your own judgment of men's minds and characters has rarely failed you. Men's minds. What of women's minds? Thinking of women's minds was like contemplating a journey to a foreign country. He recalled in detail the Lady of Kuo's face. She was, without a doubt, a woman; but had he not felt . . . different when he was talking with her? All at once some part of his mind slammed its fist down, just the way he had done when he upset the tea table yesterday morning. Fool! You hold in your hands a letter, reeking of her perfume, written in her own hand, inviting you to join her and her sisters in a music lesson somewhere in the palace, in a room your feeble imagination could not even have begun to conjure before you came here, and you sit and question? Yes, you have seen ignorant, solemn rustics in your life, but none so thick-headed and suspicious as yourself.

"You," he said to the moldy-smelling old eunuch standing nearby in an attitude of abject servility. "Can you write as well as read?"

"But, of course!" the man replied with an obsequious dip of his homely head.

"Then fetch what you need, and come back here."

: :

"Sister, you are quite mad," the Lady of Han said with a sly smile. "He will never agree to it. You could sooner induce an ox to sing." Inclining her ear toward her instrument, she tightened each string with one hand while plucking with the other, making minute adjustments to her exact satisfaction.

"But just think of it," said the Lady of Kuo imploringly. "Now that I've pictured it, I don't think I'll be able to stand not actually seeing it."

Her sister sighed sympathetically. "I know," she said, gazing into the distance, contemplating the strange, wonderful idea as if it had already manifested itself before them. "I'm sure I shan't sleep a wink, or enjoy a bite of food, until I see it, too. It's a cruel universe that would deny us."

"Cruel and capricious," agreed the Lady of Kuo, walking thoughtfully back and forth. "The key to it is to make him understand that the joke is not on him, but on them. If we can do that . . ."

"If *you* can do that, Sister," corrected the Lady of Chin from her window seat on the other side of the room.

"Well, you can help me, can't you?" the Lady of Kuo said to both her sisters. "You want to see it just as much as I do, am I not right?" Assent was plain on both their faces. The three sisters looked at each other for a moment or two before collapsing with laughter. It was the Lady of Kuo who dried her eyes first and became serious. "They deserve to have a joke played on them. He is, in his own way, a real aristocrat. He has simply never had an opportunity to know his true nature. He is fine indeed!"

"Where has he been? What has he seen?" asked the Lady of Chin. "We must take him with us on a ride through the city. I want everyone to see us with him."

"That countenance—he is like some hairy, smiling demon. And so huge and fat!" said the Lady of Han. "I wonder about his . . ."

"Don't even *think* of it," the Lady of Kuo interrupted with mock reproval.

" 'It'?" said the Lady of Chin. "I wouldn't be surprised if he has more than one!"

"With snake's heads!" added the Lady of Han.

"We shall have to draw lots to see which of us will find out," her sister replied.

"Ladies, ladies, ladies! Please!" said the Lady of Kuo, her hands over her ears. "How easily you digress! We were discussing something else entirely. This is not helping me at all!"

"My advice, Sister, is this," said the Lady of Chin seriously. "Simply start with the music lesson. Implementing your idea will, I believe, follow naturally. When will he be here?"

"Within the hour. Is everything in readiness?"

The Lady of Chin held aloft a set of delicate stone chimes. She struck a single note. It rang prettily in the air.

"Everything is in readiness, Sister," she said. "The stones await their master musician!"

::

An Lu-shan was very proud of himself. He had just learned that he was not, after all, devoid of musical ability. The sisters had found out the exact pieces that were going to be played on the night of his "performance," and had taken him through them over and over. He had felt foolish and out of sorts in the beginning, but soon found that these women were not merely indulging in some form of feminine frivolity, but were very able teachers. They played slowly at first, bringing him to each of his musical cues until he no longer needed a signal from them. He found that he was quickly able to recognize the phrases leading up to "his" moment, and when he struck the chimes, he did not feel that he was breaking the music's continuity.

And now, as if in some miraculous dream, he found himself in the perfumed interior of a carriage not unlike the one that had carried Purple Gown when he had been lured helplessly through the Ch'ang-an streets like a fish snagged on a line. As they rode, they pulled the curtains aside from time to time to observe the great crowd of people in the streets or to watch for some intriguing display of goods. They were taking him, they had said, to the marketplace to get him some beautiful new clothes. Next to him sat the Lady of Han; opposite them sat the Lady of Kuo and the Lady of Chin. He smiled, thinking of Purple Gown's lusty pet dwarf. Is that, he asked himself, what I am?

"You know," the Lady of Kuo was saying, "that you have the heart and soul of a musician. You should let us tutor you beyond the preparation for this silly little event."

"She is right," said the Lady of Han. "You have what is called an 'ear.'"
When she said that, he remembered something.

"I have made music before," he said enigmatically. "I made music that caused men to run for their lives, for their very souls." He was thinking of the screaming arrows, and saw again in his mind's eye the beautiful sight of the Khitan scattering into the night in superstitious terror while his "music" played over their heads. And it was because of that "music" that he was here now, in this sweet-smelling carriage with these creatures, on his way to shop for silks in the greatest city in the empire. An idea came to him then. "You have taught me; now you will have to allow me to return the favor. I will give *you* a music lesson."

They spent the afternoon in the marketplace. Wherever they went, the merchants bowed and groveled and rushed to and fro, arms laden with shining, brilliantly colored bolts of silk or ornaments for the hair or little embroidered slippers. Ivory hairbrushes with silver inlay, tiny tinkling bells of hammered gold, silk pouches filled with the fragrant dried petals of flowers, headdresses made from the plumage of tropical birds; the sisters moved through the profusion of goods with a purposeful, practical air, choosing this and rejecting that with scarcely a backward glance. Though he did his best to hide it, An Lu-shan was impressed. At one merchant's establishment where they stopped, the owner rushed forth as soon as he saw the carriage, telling the women that he had something new, something the likes of which they had never seen before, and why did they even waste their time going to anyone else in the entire city, when they knew that they could rely on him, their devoted, faithful, watchful, and tasteful servant?

"Please," the Lady of Kuo said to the man, "show us something new. We have with us a visitor from far away. We are frightfully embarrassed to show him all these uninteresting, commonplace things! What must he think?" she said, turning imploringly to An Lu-shan, who, understanding her joke, assumed a serious, bored manner.

"Whatever it is you have," he said to the merchant, "it had best be very good indeed!" Only a small flicker of uncertainty crossed the man's face before he begged them to be seated, had a boy serve them some tea, and bustled off to get this wondrous thing he had boasted about.

While he was gone, the Lady of Han leaned toward her sister. "You devil! You don't care for anyone's feelings at all, do you?" she whispered. "Did you see the poor man's face? He is in mortal terror now that his offering will look drab to us!"

"Don't worry, don't worry," the Lady of Kuo said, laughing. "It is what he wants me to say! He would be disappointed if I said anything else! Besides, it's true, isn't it? We don't want An Lu-shan to be disappointed!"

"An Lu-shan," said the Lady of Chin, "she's a bitch, this one. A sweet talker, a tongue like honey, but a bitch."

Far from taking offense, the Lady of Kuo inclined her head graciously toward her sister. "Thank you, my darling, for speaking the truth."

An Lu-shan drank it all up like wine, and was laughing with them when the proprietor came back up the stairs from his basement storeroom, cradling a bundle in his arms so lovingly that one would think that he carried within it a hair from the Buddha's head. With elaborate and important flourishes, he laid the roll of rough silk on the carpet, and tenderly opened it. Inside was a layer of fine white paper. He grasped the corners of the paper, looked around once to be sure his audience was attentively in suspense, then slowly peeled it back.

In spite of themselves, all three sisters let out little gasps of astonishment, turning the merchant's face into the very picture of smug satisfaction. Even An Lu-shan was unable to conceal his awe.

It was a jacket. It was made of the strangest fabric he had ever seen; he was reminded of the silk, woven with bird feathers, that he had appropiated from a trader on the Silk Road. But it was something else—something he had never seen before. The surface was iridescent and velvety at the same time, with impossibly complex patterns of swirls, spots, and stripes in opalescent hues of green, blue, and black. An Lu-shan and the sisters stared.

"Butterfly wings," the merchant said quietly. "Sewn by little girls, with the finest thread and the tiniest of stitches, onto silk." He shrugged. "It is so fragile that it can be worn only once, and then it must be thrown away. It is very, very expensive."

The Lady of Kuo stood and pulled An Lu-shan to his feet.

"Can you get enough to make a coat for this gentleman?" she asked. The merchant looked dubiously at An Lu-shan's tremendous belly and chest. He circled around, clucking his tongue. An Lu-shan cooperatively lifted his arms while the man measured his circumference by wrapping a piece of string around him and marking it.

"I can do it, but it will be . . . costly, madam."

"Good," said the Lady of Kuo. "I would like enough for three coats for him. And enough for my sisters and me as well."

Feverishly, the man wrote down the order in a ledger.

"Perhaps," he said, "I can interest you in some other things as well."

"No doubt," said the Lady of Kuo.

An Lu-shan was still standing when the Lady of Han picked up a length of blue silk and playfully draped it over his shoulders and wrapped it around him, tying it with a sash of deeper blue woven with metallic gold. Pleased, she stepped back to admire him.

"Is he not gorgeous?" she asked her sisters and the merchant, who stood with his mouth agape. The Lady of Kuo then stepped up behind him and placed a lady's hair ornament on his head. A cascade of glittering silver beads hung tinkling on one side of his head; the Lady of Chin stood in front of him, eyes shining with mischief, and dabbed a bit of scented white powder onto his face. Enjoying the fun, An Lu-shan took several mincing steps across the floor, imitating the walk of the daintiest court ladies. The three sisters laughed happily.

"He is too beautiful!" said the Lady of Kuo. "We could not be seen with him in public like this! No one would even look at us!"

"I am the Lady of Dog Tail," he said in a high, singsong falsetto, a near-perfect impression of the exaggerated feminine speech one often heard at court. "I want all your husbands brought to me immediately! I am very hungry!"

The merchant, nervous at first, had relaxed and apparently decided that it was all right to join in the fun. He smiled hesitantly, looking around him, then laughed along with the women.

An Lu-shan could well imagine how preposterous he looked. A giant, ugly bearded lady, dressed in exquisite silks. Thoroughly enjoying himself and inspired by his appreciative audience, he picked up one of the porcelain tea bowls, made as if to raise it to his lips with an effete gesture, and crushed it into fragments in his hand. He looked at the pieces and pretended to burst into tears. "Oh, gracious me!" he wailed. "This is what happens to all my husbands!"

The sisters crowded around him, adding jewelry, sashes, bangles and other female knickknacks to his costume, laughing and squealing with delight.

"My feet!" he cried. "What is a lady to do with her feet?" Sadly he indicated his large leather military shoes protruding incongrously from beneath the hem of his "gown."

"Wait!" exclaimed the merchant, rushing toward his storeroom. "I think I have just the thing!" He returned with the biggest pair of ladies' embroidered "cloud-toe" silk slippers any of them had ever seen. He held the shoes out and looked at them sorrowfully. "They are from Persia. It is a very sad story, but one that has ended. I used to have a regular customer, a very wealthy Ch'ang-an businessman, who had a daughter who was a giantess. She had fallen on her head when she was a baby, and by the time she was seven years old she was as tall as a grown woman; when she was fifteen, she was three heads taller than the tallest man. Her father loved her and did everything he could to help her forget her size. He built special rooms onto his house just for her, with tall ceilings and large-size furniture. A normal person would appear no taller than a child in her quarters; a grown man's feet would dangle above the floor if he sat in one of her chairs. And he built high, high walls around a private garden for her, so that she could walk there in privacy, free from jeers and prying eyes, and stare into the reflecting pools and pretend that she was not a monster." He shrugged, turning the slippers over. "And clothing . . . He had the most feminine, fashionable things made for her. These shoes were one of many pairs that he ordered through me."

They all stared in silence at the slippers, their laughter of a few minutes ago forgotten. The Lady of Kuo spoke first.

"What happened to her?"

"She is dead." He shrugged again. "She was nineteen years old. Her health was always poor, and one day she just died. The slippers arrived a few days after her death. I kept them as a remembrance and a curiosity."

For a few more moments, no one spoke, but looked at the shoes, each thinking about the lonely giantess walking in her garden.

"Well," said An Lu-shan finally, anxious to revive the mood of levity, "there is another lady in need of these slippers now." Removing his boots, he slipped his feet into the giantess's shoes. They were too large, even for him, but he stuffed a bit of cloth into the toes to make them snug. "They are perfect. Do you still think I am beautiful?" he said coquettishly, turning around in front of the sisters, who were now looking at one another with conspiratorial smiles.

"Tell him," the Lady of Han said to the Lady of Kuo.

"Yes," agreed the Lady of Chin. "Tell him now."

The Lady of Kuo looked at him, considering. "An Lu-shan," she said. "I want you to wear those slippers the night of the concert."

Wear ladies' slippers? He did not understand. But then they would hardly be noticeable, so why not?

"I will wear them if you want me to." He was finding it difficult not to agree to anything she said.

"And," she said, pausing significantly, "I want you to wear the robe, the sash, the jewelry, and the face powder as well."

He looked at her uncomprehendingly.

"And the hair ornament," added the Lady of Chin.

"You are madwomen, obviously," he said shaking his head and laughing. "You want me to dress in women's clothes and appear before the court?"

"An Lu-shan, think!" she said, seizing his arm. "The chief minister and his people are trying to play a joke on you! Do you remember what I said last night? That I knew how to turn their joke back on them and make you the clear victor?" Her eyes were shining with deviltry now. "This is the way!"

"But they—the people at court—will think I am an insane fool! What if the Emperor is there? What if it makes him angry?"

"An Lu-shan, think of it," said the Lady of Chin. "Li Lin-fu and his people are trying to embarrass you. They thought they could have a good laugh by putting you, a newcomer, in an awkward position."

"If you appear with the Pear Garden Orchestra dressed in ladies' clothes, you will have turned everything around," said the Lady of Kuo. "You will have shown your courage and humor. Your resourcefulness. You will earn the respect of the court, I guarantee it. And," she added emphatically, tapping his chest lightly with her finger, "*You* will be the winner."

He thought about it. He was beginning to see it. He had been a jokester in his time and knew the value of a good prank. He recalled the strange room where he had met Li Lin-Fu for the first time, where it was as cold as a tomb even though it was the middle of summer. Li Lin-fu had gained the upper hand that day with an elaborate joke whose intent was deadly serious. No doubt his idea of putting An Lu-shan in a female orchestra was an extension of that same joke, and had the same intent behind it. How delicious it would be to come out, as the Lady of Kuo so aptly put it, the winner. It *was* his favorite word.

"You are as effective a talker as I have seen anywhere in my travels," he said to her. "You could probably convince a fish to climb a tree."

"Or an ox to sing," said the Lady of Han as she looked at her sister admiringly.

: :

The next few days before the night of his "performance" were passed pleasantly in the company of the sisters. He was introduced to the ladies of the Pear Garden Orchestra, who were told of the plan and sworn to secrecy by the Lady of Kuo. The musicians giggled and whispered among themselves, but appeared to like the idea, and agreed to go along with the joke. The sisters held a tea party for An Lu-shan and the musicians so that they could get to know one another. Sitting among the twenty or so beautiful young women while they taught him endless absurd little details of comportment, etiquette, and table manners gave him a most pleasant, heady feeling. He had never imagined that there could be so many different ways to pour tea and raise it to one's lips, to eat from a plate of food, or to greet someone whose rank was inferior, equal, or superior to one's own. They carried on mock conversations with him, pretending to be so-and-so's wife, daughter, or mother, and taught him little discursive tricks designed to smooth over breakdowns or awkward moments in social chatter. He proved to be an able and willing student. At other times in his life he would have been disgusted with such effete frivolity, but somehow he was in a different mood today and found it exotic and intriguing. There was, after all, shrewd strategy involved, and it appealed to him. Of course, he told himself as he smiled at the delicate flower who now sat before him giggling while she raised and lowered his hand for him, showing him the proper way to propose a toast with one's wine cup, you are intoxicated by all this femaleness and not in your right mind.

Then came the fitting for his "gown," which the sisters were having made from the blue silk in which they had swaddled him on their trip into the city. Two seamstresses—also initiated into the secret and duly admonished—measured, snipped, and marked while the sisters looked on with ill-concealed mirth. He told them that their jealousy was showing, that because a lady more beautiful than they had shown up at court they had to resort to casting aspersions on her grace, delicacy, and charm. They retorted that, quite to the contrary, they would be making a public abdication, and were only trying to enhance her already perfect beauty for the occasion, though they knew that they would soon be out in the cold, discarded and forgotten, because of it. The banter passed back and forth between the barbarian general and the aristocratic ladies as easily as it ever had between An Lu-shan and his compatriots. He wished old club-footed Feng could see him now, standing in the private apartments of the Yang sisters, laughing and joking with casual ease and being fitted for a gown. After this, he thought, perhaps I will finally learn that life is a dream, a mystery, ever changing, and what it brings can never be predicted.

He made good his promise to give the sisters a "music lesson" too. On the day after the tea party, he invited them to accompany him to one of the many open parks on the palace grounds. When he had made his journey to Ch'ang-an from the north, he had brought with him some of his screaming arrows—not because he had anticipated having to use them, but because he had made them himself and they had been vital to his rise from obscurity and servitude. He wanted to bring something powerful and mysterious, some token of what he was, something the Chinese would never have seen before, that would enhance the formidable person of An Lu-shan, the general from the north.

So far, he had not had an opportunity to show his arrows. When the idea had come to him in the carriage, he recognized it for what it was—pure inspiration, the secret reason fate had made him carry the heavy, cumbersome load concealed in blankets and lashed to his horse. He knew he had found the right audience in these women.

And the sisters rewarded him. They gave him their full attention as he brought the first arrow out, handed it around for them to examine, and with a solemn and mysterious air fitted it into his bow and aimed the arrow up so it would make a high arc before falling back to the earth. He pulled the bowstring taut and held it there, poised, for a few significant moments so that the sisters would be in suspense just that much longer and so they could admire his powerful arm and hand before he released the arrow.

The howling groan that cut the clear sky was superbly incongruous against the landscaped tranquility of the park. The sound was like the lament of a remorseful ghost contemplating eternity; the sisters stood, transfixed, as the last echoes reverberated in the bright air. He selected another arrow with a smaller, differently shaped tip. This time the sound was like the thin wail of a dying child or a wounded animal.

"Music to freeze the heart!" said the Lady of Kuo admiringly. "Like voices without souls! May I?" she asked, indicating the bow.

He showed her how to fit the arrow into place. He did not expect her to be able to pull the bowstring back far enough to send the arrow into the air with the necessary force to make it sing—but she surprised him with the sureness and strength with which she sent it flying. The scream it made caused all the sisters to laugh and shout exultantly as they watched it reach the apex of its arc and fall toward the earth at the end of the garden, where it stuck, quivering, into the ground.

"It's more than music!" said the Lady of Chin. "It's like the essence of a poem in one sound!"

"No," the Lady of Han said thoughtfully, "it's like your worst nightmares and all your regrets and fears being sent away from you forcibly!"

"The Khitan thought their worst nightmares were falling out of the sky to pursue them to the ends of the earth," An Lu-shan said with satisfaction. "These arrows of mine brought me here. Were it not for them, I would not be standing before you today," he added with dramatic emphasis.

He told them the story of the raid on the encampment—the trained children responding fluidly to his every command, the devil wind, the fires, the Khitan running as if their own doomed souls were on their heels thirsty for retribution. He described the fat, beautiful horses, and the triumphant return to the military colony with nary a life lost nor even a finger scratched. The sisters listened, rapt, absorbing every word, turning the arrows over in their hands as if they were treasures from the other side of the world. It made him feel as if he, too, were listening with their ears, and he was inspired to embellish and embroider the story, especially the part where he found himself face to face for the second time with Li Shih-chih. His promotion from captured slave to general made the women gaze at him with thoughtful, admiring eyes; the story of the river crossing, the dark, rushing water, the moving clump of earth and rocks that was death itself, the screams of the drowning men, caused their eyes to cloud over with vicarious fear. So swept along was he with the momentum of his vivid narrative that he barely stopped himself in time from describing the forgery of the map. It was very, very tempting; he knew that the Lady of Kuo, especially, would appreciate his nerve, cunning, and audacity in pulling off that particular little coup, saving his balls and probably his neck and changing his life forever. He took a deep breath, looking at their eager faces waiting for him to go on, but some prudent part of his mind said, Fool, shut your bragging mouth before you ruin everything. You do not tell military secrets, upon which your life depends, to a flock of women. He shook his head in amazement at what he had been about to do. Then he smiled. He had to give them credit. No one, man or woman, with the exception of Chief Minister Li Lin-fu, had caused An Lu-shan to even toy with the idea of divulging one of his vital secrets.

He shrugged, skipped over the map episode, and told them about the long journey down from the north, his meeting with Feng, the encounter with the leopard, and the strange, unnerving vision of the young woman in the garden with blood dripping from her mouth. At this part of the story, the sisters looked at one another with wonderment.

"It sounds as if An Lu-shan caught a glimpse of Li Shan Lao Ma," the Lady of Kuo said, and the sisters laughed. Li Shan Lao Ma. That was the name Feng had uttered that evening at the hot springs when An Lu-shan had got drunk enough to tell him of his bizarre experience.

"No, no," the Lady of Han said. "Li Shan Lao Ma is ancient, a crone with a face like a skull."

"I heard that she sometimes appears as a little girl, crying!" said the Lady of Chin.

"Just don't let any strange young women without proper credentials seduce you at the hot springs, An Lu-shan," said the Lady of Kuo jokingly, "or you might suddenly open your eyes to find your body joined in the heat of passion to a hag who should have been dead hundreds of years ago!" More laughter.

An Lu-shan laughed, too. Then he told them about his first trip into the city, about his throbbing, feverish head, and about Purple Gown and her lusty dwarf. At this, the sisters again looked at one another.

"We know her!" cried the Lady of Han. "Was she also accompanied by two young girls? And a couple of handsome young men?"

"That would depend on what one means by 'handsome,' " An Lu-shan said a bit peevishly, remembering their absurd topknots and dandy clothes.

"You encountered one of the most exclusive courtesans in the entire city, An Lu-shan," said the Lady of Kuo. "The richest men in Ch'ang-an must make appointments months in advance to visit her. You caught her going on one of her shopping trips." The Lady of Kuo picked up the bow again. "Let me shoot one more of your magic arrows," she said.

The afternoon sun was beginning to sink, elongating their shadows. Looking at the dark shapes cast on the clipped grass, An Lu-shan saw four fantastic creatures moving about, with impossibly long, slender bodies and tiny heads. He selected another arrow for the Lady of Kuo to shoot. The one he chose was weighted in such a way that it would whirl as it flew, making an undulating cry, mournful as the end of time. He watched his shadow as it presented the Lady of Kuo's shadow with the arrow. He felt a familiar, faint ripple of anticipation as he remembered for the fortieth time that day that tonight was the night.

::

He held himself still as they put the finishing touches on him, an elaborate wig and white powder. He had expected them to be dissolving in laughter, with himself the object of a hundred jokes, but their laughter had died out. They had gradually become quiet and pensive as the clothes and makeup went on; by the time a mirror was held up for him, they were positively solemn.

He could see why. The figure looking back at him was not clownishly absurd, as he had expected, but dignified in an exotic, massive, formidable way. The wig, with its tinkling hairpieces, and the incongruous beard and white makeup made him look like the monarch of some faraway, unknown kingdom. For a moment he admired himself, looking into his own eyes as if he were meeting the stranger in the mirror for the first time. Which in truth, he reflected, he was.

"For this evening, your name will be Cherry Blossom," the Lady of Kuo joked, breaking the spell. He looked at her and smiled coquettishly.

"If the Emperor ever saw me like this, you would soon have to call me 'Empress' Cherry Blossom."

"What a chapter to add to your tale," she said. "From captured slave to general to empress."

: :

This was not possible. How could he have got into such a ridiculous predicament? He cursed, feeling beads of sweat forming on his forehead. It was one thing to play, and talk, and dress up—but he was finding that it was an altogether different thing to stand there in his outlandish ladies' clothes, waiting to walk out in front of a room full of guests and act out an absurd joke.

He pulled aside the curtain in the doorway to the great room they called the Pavilion of the Hundred Flowers. What he saw gave him a sick feeling in his belly. There were at least a hundred people seated at low tables; servants carrying huge trays of food and drink moved among the guests, court ladies and gentlemen whose talk and laughter filled the room to its gilded ceiling. The tables and comfortable-looking couches surrounded a raised stage area on three sides; a dais on the fourth side was occupied by what appeared to An Lu-shan to be an official of some importance. A small party of women sat with him; to An Lu-shan's surprise, he recognized the Lady of Chin and the Lady of Han, but the third woman he did not know. There was no sign of his sponsor, the one who had instigated it all, Chief Minister Li Lin-fu.

Replacing the curtain, he drank from the cup of strange-tasting, peppery wine the Lady of Kuo had brought him. The only way he would be able to get through this would be to get drunk.

The Lady of Kuo appeared before him with a tiny brush in her hand to touch up his lip paint.

"You must look your very best tonight, 'Empress' Cherry Blossom," she whispered conspiratorially. He guessed her meaning right away. Panic gripped him.

"Do you mean to tell me that the Emperor is going to be watching?" he said, aghast, as the realization hit him. The man, the "official" on the dais!

She looked genuinely surprised at his reaction. "Of course the Emperor is here! The Pear Garden Orchestra is one of his pet projects! I thought you would realize that you were going to be playing for him!"

"The joke has gone far enough," he said, reaching for his wig, his courage abandoning him. "I have no intention of insulting the Son of Heaven and making a fool of myself." With the speed of a cat, the Lady of Kuo's hand shot up and detained the hand about to rip the wig from his head.

"Insulting him? Are you mad? He will love it!!"

"I doubt that! He will probably have my pretty head lopped off!"

"No, no, no!" she said vehemently. "I am trying to tell you. Please listen to me! I *know* the man!"

"I suppose you and he are good friends," he said with sarcasm.

"As a matter of fact, An Lu-shan, we are the best of friends. My little sister is his Precious Consort. She is but one rank away from being empress!"

Now he understood who the third woman was! The one sitting with the sisters!

She paused, looking at his face, obviously trying to think of something to say that would convince him. "Did you know that I beat him at polo? Did he banish or behead me?" she implored, as if inviting him to look to see if her head was sewn on.

Nearby, the other musicians were watching them, smiling and whispering.

"He is not some vindictive chieftain, An Lu-shan. He is not some inflexible potentate jealous every moment of his royalty," she exclaimed. "Yes, he is the Son of Heaven; but I can assure you that the man under those robes is a good-natured sort who loves a joke. He is a man, An Lu-shan! Like you!"

He doubted that the Son of Heaven was a man like himself, but once again he found the Lady of Kuo's persuasiveness difficult to resist. He was appalled at the fear crawling up and down his arms and legs. It exceeded anything he had felt before going into battle, leading a raid, or even facing the river that night. He thought of the frightened men and horses plunging in, his will an implacable force driving them to do the impossible. And now here he stood, in his absurd wig and gown, feeling the same fear his soldiers had felt that night. Like those men choosing the dark, swift, icy water over General An Lu-shan's wrath, he knew that he had no choice but to go out, sit with the ladies, and play his delicate little stone chimes for the Emperor of China. He had to laugh, in spite of his trepidation. They say that it is a reciprocal universe. Before me stands the fiercest commander I have ever met—the Lady of Kuo. She is showing me no more mercy than I showed my men on the riverbank that night. And he knew that he would do anything to avoid her wrath, or even her disapproval.

She was glaring at him fearsomely now, the little paintbrush poised while she looked for flaws in his makeup. He shrugged.

"You have won," he said to her. "You will get no more argument from me. I am going." She gave him a brilliant smile as she dabbed his face with the brush.

"You will not regret it."

: :

"Women's clothes, General Niu?" said Chief Minister Li Lin-fu in a matter-of-fact way, as if he had been expecting it.

"Yes, Councillor, and very fine clothes, too. Very expensive-looking fabric. Well made."

"And very fashionable, too, no doubt!" Li Lin-fu said with only a faint trace of sarcasm.

"Well," Niu began doubtfully, "I am certainly no expert on ladies' fashions, but—"

"Really!" Li Lin-fu cut him off. "The only reason I hired you at all was because I believed you to be an up-to-the-minute source of expertise in the capricious, shifting world of what smart court ladies are wearing!"

Niu did not finish what he was going to say, but stood with patient resignation, waiting for whatever was coming next. Li Lin-fu looked down at the table for a moment and shut his eyes in exasperation before looking up at his assistant again.

"Please go on, General," he said in an evenly controlled tone. "I did not mean to interrupt you."

Chief Minister Li Lin-fu had a growing sense of things developing in ways he had not planned. His vexation was occurring on several different levels. First, he was irritated with the thing itself—that his joke, the culmination of which he had been anticipating with such pleasure, had turned into something else in its actualization. And that led to another related but larger annoyance: He did not like the coy way the universe had defied his calculation of cause and effect, impudently throwing back in his face a ludicrous and distasteful development.

An Lu-shan, the uncouth barbarian, the crude, unlettered provincial with the hairy face and strange speech, was being lionized at court as the great social success of the season—and he, Li Lin-fu, had unwittingly set it all in motion. When word had been brought to him of An Lu-shan's frolicking and fraternizing with the Yang females, he had thought it curious but not entirely unlikely. For many of these upper-class women, it was, he knew, an acceptable social affectation to have daring sexual liaisons with improbable partners—the odder, more inappropriate, or exotic, the better. Li Lin-fu had accepted that perhaps all three of the women had taken on the barbarian as their playmate, and he had not been particularly concerned. Nevertheless, he had seen to it that they were watched whenever possible.

He had known about the foray into the city, but had not attributed too much importance to it. Such an expedition would be consistent with a natural social compulsion to put their conquest on public display. He knew about the little archery lesson in the garden as well; he discerned from Niu's wide-eyed description of the noise from An Lu-shan's arrows that the barbarian had invented a weapon worthy of the chief minister himself, and he had granted An Lu-shan a certain begrudging admiration. That he was spending a lot of time with the women in their private apartments was a fact well-known to Li Lin-fu. But now, Niu was standing before him, reporting on the performance earlier that evening of the Pear Garden Orchestra in the Pavilion of the Hundred Flowers. And from what he was telling the chief minister, it would seem that something very important had escaped Li Lin-fu's attention: The females had, apparently, taken it upon themselves to tutor the general, or rather the commissioner for foot and horse, in the womanly arts and in music. That, combined with some crude attractiveness in his personality invisible to Li Lin-fu, was winning him favor with the frivolously playful highborns.

Niu appeared to be choosing his words carefully; Li Lin-fu put a forbearing expression on his face and waited, one finger lightly tapping the table.

"The orchestra played for quite a while after dinner, and Commissioner An Lu-shan did his part very well indeed," Niu said.

"Did he now!" said Li Lin-fu. "What a talented fellow he is, eh?"

"The guests were very appreciative of him, especially the Emperor," Niu said, and paused, obviously not happy about going any further.

"Go on, General," Li Lin-fu said in a gentle, dangerous tone. "Please."

Niu heaved a sigh, shrugged and plunged ahead.

"There is not much more to tell. Afterward, the commissioner was taken to meet the Emperor."

"And was the commissioner still wearing his stunning gown and wig?"

"Yes. And makeup."

"And were the Yang females with the Emperor?"

"Yes. All four of them. They, the Emperor and Commissioner An Lu-shan conversed for a while. It was all very jolly and high-spirited." He stopped again and chewed on the inside of his lip.

"General, please!" said Li Lin-fu. "Am I to read your mind? What happened next?"

"Commissioner An Lu-shan went to the harem later," Niu said reluctantly.

Li Lin-fu said nothing for a full minute while Niu stood miserably before him, as if he himself had issued the invitation to Commissioner An Lu-shan, and shown him to the very door behind which the women of the Emperor's harem resided. Finally Li Lin-fu spoke, his voice polite and quiet.

"Thank you, Niu. You have been most helpful. You may leave now."

After Niu had hastily retreated and shut the door behind him, Li Lin-fu continued to sit at his desk and look at the spot where Niu had been standing.

This was not what he had planned at all. He would have to think things through very, very carefully. An Lu-shan had moved beyond mere cavorting with the Yang sisters. In a matter of days, he had exercised his brutish charm in such a way that he was suddenly on intimate terms with the Emperor himself. He had put on a successful buffoon's performance for the court. They love that sort of thing, Li Lin-fu thought with annoyance; it had simply not occurred to him that the barbarian, fresh from the northern wastes, would have the sophistication necessary to pull such a thing off, or that he would have attracted mentors such as the Yang sisters to show him how to do it. When the original inspiration had hit Li Lin-fu to put An Lu-shan in the Pear Garden Orchestra, he had certainly pictured a room full of laughing faces; what he had not pictured was the barbarian clowning and playing up to their laughter and winning their applause and approval. He thought of the sisters giggling with infuriating, smug satisfaction at their antic, at Li Lin-fu himself! Effete dolts, he thought. Playing their silly little court games while the very empire is threatened! Feeling his anger rising, he stopped, told himself that this would not help at all in assessing what had happened, shut his eyes, and gathered his thoughts.

He must make an effort to separate his irritation at having his joke thrown back in his face from other, more important considerations. Li Lin-fu had taken great care to establish his authority with An Lu-shan; at stake was the barbarian's value to the empire as a military leader in the north. His ability to do Li Lin-fu's bidding, to be his servant and emissary, was crucial and must not be impeded. There was no other reason for him to be here at all.

On the one hand, too much independence on An Lu-shan's part presented obvious dangers. But there is, he reflected, another possibility. Acceptance at court could be beneficial to his morale and solidify his allegiance to the empire, motivating him to do the job for which Li Lin-fu had procured him. The question, Li Lin-fu thought as he idly lined up small ornamental objects on his desk, is whether An Lu-shan's capacity for dissolution and self-aggrandizement exceeds his will, his ability, or his desire to serve. Care and vigilance, Li Lin-fu, he said to himself with a sigh and a shake of his head, care and vigilance. Your hands, as usual, are full.

Preparing to leave his office, Li Lin-fu mused that, at that very moment, the barbarian probably had *his* meaty hands on the white flesh of one of the Emperor's women. Li Lin-fu let his imagination take him into the room where the distasteful coupling was no doubt taking place. That mountain of fat, he thought, allowing a series of pleasantly obscene images to form in his mind. It will be a wonder if she will be able to find his "old man" at all.

: :

He had made her take off every bit of clothing and stand perfectly still while he circled around her. He arranged her limbs in interesting poses, which she obligingly held while he looked at her from every angle. He had never had the chance to examine a woman's naked body this way before. He had always had to satisfy himself with glimpses and fragments. Either it was too cold, or he was in a hurry, or the light was poor, or the woman in question refused to do more than hike up her musty-smelling clothes and get it over with. His wife had never let him see her body at all, insisting on total darkness. Once, a long time ago, in some forsaken settlement along the trade routes, a prostitute had been willing to indulge him by removing her clothes and lolling on a bed while he held a lamp and looked at her. But she had been enormously fat, with breasts and belly so pendulous that she was simply a lump of flesh without a definable shape. The creature before him now was small and comely, just the perfect plumpness, and clean and sweet-smelling.

He would never, ever question the judgment of the Lady of Kuo again. He would never make a single move or decision without consulting her. He would be her slave; her wish would be his command, he vowed, laughing incredulously, raising the wine pitcher to his lips, not bothering to pour the wine into a cup, and letting his eyes move languidly over the pink, rosy flesh of the girl smiling prettily at him, her arms raised over her head and one little foot resting on a chair.

She was his reward. A personal gift from the Emperor himself to An Lu-shan. Take your choice, the gaunt man with the sad eyes and smiling face had said to An Lu-shan with a munificent gesture. There are hundreds of women in the harem; perhaps there is one who will suit your fancy.

After the Lady of Kuo had forced him into the river, so to speak, he had performed as a musician with the utmost seriousness and dignity. The audience had laughed in a pleasant way, not jeeringly, as he struck the absurd little chimes. And afterward, the Lady of Kuo descended on him, telling him that the Emperor wanted to meet him. Give me time to get out of these ridiculous clothes, he had said. No, no, she said, stopping him, pulling on his arm, and once more he did as she said. And he was taken before the Son of Heaven; he, An Lu-shan, in his ladies' clothes, wig, and makeup. And the Emperor had received him, smiling with pleasure, complimenting him on his wonderful joke. You are An Lu-shan, he had said. I am most happy to meet you. You are as fine an actor and musician as you are a general. And next to him was the fourth sister. She looked almost exactly like the Lady of Kuo, but younger, smaller. The same look in her eye. She regarded him boldly; he knew by the look that he had already been thoroughly discussed among the sisters. Her eyes on him, she spoke to the Emperor. Wouldn't he be splendid, she said to the Son of Heaven, in the role of Kao Mei in our festival next spring? Yes, indeed, the Emperor had said. An Lu-shan could see by the way he looked at this youngest Yang sister that this man, this Emperor, would burrow ten li into the ground with his bare hands if the girl requested it of him. Do you think you could act the role of a god of fertility? the Emperor had asked him.

Of course, it would be most unpleasant for you, because you would have to drink a lot of wine, and make love to a lot of beautiful young women, and wear flowers in your hair, and see our city dressed in flowers while the citizens celebrate the passing of another winter. You probably do not, he said with a shrug and a friendly smile, wish to do it. And An Lu-shan had laughed, at ease in the presence of the Son of Heaven. And then the Emperor had told him that he could make a choice from the harem. And all the sisters looked at one another and at him with impudent, knowing looks. Just that easily had he found himself a member of their inner circle.

And then this. He was pleasantly drunk now, fresh from a hot bath, a silk robe hanging loosely on his fat body.

"Come here," he said to the girl. She came and stood before him. He pulled her onto his lap, facing him, her legs straddling his own, her hands on his shoulders. He looked up at her face. Her features were delicate and childlike. Her nostrils were especially small. He reached up and tentatively began to put the tip of his little finger into her nose; she tolerated it for a few seconds, then pushed his hand away, laughing. With a questioning look he reached toward her ear and tried to put his finger in it. She writhed and giggled as he tried one ear and then the other. She let him put his finger into her mouth, biting it ever so gently and caressing it with her tongue. Withdrawing the finger from her mouth, he moved it down her neck, between her breasts, and down to her navel. He paid only a brief visit there before slowly moving downward to explore. He fixed her eyes with his own. "I think," he said, "that there is another place for me to put my finger." She shifted her position just enough to make it easy for him, and did not object when he slid the sly finger up into her body. He clenched his teeth at the rush of urgent response in his groin. Withdrawing the finger, he lifted the girl in his lap by her armpits and brought her down hard onto his stiff organ, making her suck her breath in. He shut his eyes as he moved her up and down. The woman, Ch'ang-an, would be his. Was his already. He would spread her legs and drive himself deep, deep into her tender flesh. His breathing came harsh and fast. Her soft, scented flesh, her smooth, silky, slippery flesh. He would drive deep, and spend himself, and come back for more. And more. She was his, now.

: :

The Lady of Kuo invited him to tea the next day to talk about their triumph. Though it was plain that she was pleased with the way things had turned out, there was something subdued in her manner. She did not speak with her usual animation, and often looked out the window with a pensive expression.

Inspiration seized him. She knew about his visit to the harem; she had been standing right there when the Emperor made his offer. It was obvious what was wrong. She was jealous! She was thinking of him with the girl, and abhorring it.

He would have to reassure her. The girl was nothing, a plaything. Why, most of the time, he had been pretending that the girl, whose name he didn't even know, was the Lady of Kuo herself. He felt that he knew a lot now about these mysterious creatures, women. He was feeling generous and relaxed after his night of satiation; he was ready now to give her what she needed and wanted. It was logical that she should be his prize; everything that had happened to him since he came here seemed to be leading to it. He leaned toward her and took her hand in one of his and let the other hand rest heavily on her knee. She looked at him as if startled out of reverie.

"I am yours, you know," he said, looking into her eyes. An image of the naked girl in his lap flitted through his mind as he said it. He allowed the hand on her knee the gentlest of squeezes; he felt a quick sexual thrill as he marveled that it was her flesh, under her gown, that he was feeling.

"An Lu-shan, I am sorry," she said, standing abruptly, displacing his hand. "If I seem distracted, it is because I am anxious. I am waiting for somebody. My cousin, Yang Kuo-chung." She paused.

The naked girl in his mind evaporated. He had never seen the Lady of Kuo even slightly flustered before.

"I wrote to him a long time ago, and have not yet received a reply. He is supposed to come to the capital to see me and to join the court," she said. "I had been hoping for a letter today, but none came, and I am quite desolate."

An Lu-shan, acute awareness of his blunder racing to the tips of his fingers, spoke quickly to cover his awkwardness.

"Where is he?"

She looked at him, eyes beginning to fill with tears.

"Somewhere in the north. Trading on the Silk Road."

"Well," he said, trying to assume a thoughtful, sympathetic air. "Well. If he knows his business, then he is probably quite alive and healthy. And if he has received your letter, if he is any kind of man at all, then he is on his way down here to see you. I guarantee it, madam," he said. "And if he doesn't come, he's a damned fool," he said with feeling.

She didn't reply, but her eyes were filled so that the tears, while not yet escaping and spilling down her face, glistened and trembled on the rims. The sight of those small sparkling pools, the liquid manifestation of her inner grief, made him see the extent to which he had overreached. He felt foolish, importunate, a grotesque buffoon. His cheeks burned with embarrassment. It is certainly not for you that those exquisite tears are about to slide down her cheeks and splash to the floor, he told himself. Not for you, you fat fool.

Those delicious little drops, which I would love to taste with my tongue, come forth for someone named Yang Kuo-chung. What sort of man, he wondered fervently as he prepared to take his leave, is this cousin, this Yang Kuo-chung, who makes rain fall from the eyes of the Lady of Kuo?

He thought about it for the rest of the day. By nightfall he was thoroughly familiar in his mind with this man, this Yang Kuo-chung, having forged a portrait of him composed of bits and pieces of his jealousy and resentment. And he did not like him at all.

That night he dreamed about the harem girl, that he had entered her body and was moving back and forth in ecstatic lust. Thrusting hard, on the brink of orgasm, he looked at her face and found that she was not the harem girl at all, but the giantess whose slippers he had worn.

11

The Virile Fox

[In his early years] Yang Kuo-chung was fond of drinking and gambling, and, being an adventurer without self-restraint, had borrowed heavily from many people. . . . Having no good connections by marriage, he eventually resorted to joining the army in Shu [Szechuan] . . . where he made important acquaintances . . . and acquired, much to his pleasure, enormous wealth in commodities. . . .

[Later, at court, Yang Kuo-chung] relied heavily upon the kindnesses and favors of superiors, seizing any opportunity to advance himself. . . .

[During that early period, the dictator] Li Lin-fu charmed and beguiled Kuo-chung into doing anything he wanted him to, . . . but while Li Lin-fu obstinately and continually obstructed [Yang Kuo-chung's] advancements, he was secretly guiding him from behind the scenes. Thus it was that Yang Kuo-chung rose quickly, being [at first] an unscrupulous and reckless ["playboy"], avoiding nothing, afraid of nothing. Yang Kuo-chung took up a [highly visible] and public, scandalous affair with [his second cousin?] the Lady of Kuo County [much] to the Emperor Minghuang's . . . pleasure. Yang Kuo-chung cleverly made use of his loyal inner circle of supporters to keep well informed. The Emperor regarded his talents well, appointing him to various boards and commissionerships of Finance and Revenue. But Yang Kuo-chung did not tarry long in any single appointment; rather, he acquired numerous titles and considerable prestige—and this rise in power began to anger the Chief Minister Li Lin-fu.

—*from* Hsin T'ang Shu (New T'ang History),
translated by Daniel Altieri

Kuo-chung's own father was only a minor official. . . . As a young man Kuo-chung was unscholarly and given to drunkenness and loose living. He was despised by family and neighbors and in resentment took up a military career in Szechuan. There he presumably met his second cousin, the future Kuei-fei. . . . He is accused of having seduced another of his cousins [later titled the Lady of Kuo] there. . . . He obtained the patronage of a wealthy man of the province, Hsien-yu. . . .

—Edwin Pulleyblank

Yang Kuo-chung—a poorly educated, vagabonding, but handsome, eloquent, and clever rascal, a paramour of the . . . Lady of Kuo— started at first as His Majesty's gambling companion, then became the Secretary of the Bureau of Public Finance with a growing number, until over forty, of concurrent positions.

—William Hung

Who is this late horseman who arrives leisurely sitting upon his saddle . . . ? Look how the onlookers all shrink back as he dismounts stepping onto the elegant flower-brocaded cushions of silk. . . . Beware, beware! Do not place your hands upon him, lest he scorch them. Do not approach the minister [Yang Kuo-chung] too closely or he might berate you.

—Tu Fu, translated by Daniel Altieri

Kuo-chung had illicit relations with the [Lady of] Kuo County and did not mind being criticized as the "virile fox." Every time they entered the court, they rode side by side on the road and did not bother to pull down their curtains.

—Hsin T'ang Shu, *translated by Howard S. Levy*

BY the light of a sputtering oil lamp, he read the letter that had arrived two days ago.

My dearest cousin: I know that your great and good friend in Szechuan, the honorable Hsien-yu, will see that this letter reaches you . . .

The perfume that wafted up from the delicate paper was hers; it had survived the journey, and now entered his nostrils and went directly to where erotic memories of her resided in his brain. He held the letter to his nose and inhaled deeply, as he had already done at least a dozen times.

> . . . No matter where your duties have taken you my thoughts were there. There is an ancient *yueh-fu* ballad that reads, ". . . would that I were a pale moonbeam that I might speed to thee in light. . . ." Indeed, these should be my words! I hear legends about you, my most celebrated and handsome cousin. There are many stories that have passed to these most indiscreet and undeserving ears. Tales of the Fox have even reached the divine ears of our August Imperial Father. He searches for a man worthy of his gaming prowess; he awaits your challenge. He tells us that he grows restless for a good game of polo, double-sixes, and tiles, so long has it been. Especially polo—he is desperate to relive the matches of his youth. And I tell you, dear cousin, he is quite adamant about finding a worthy gambling partner; dice, sticks, stones, and tiles, everything—he hungers for them all. And I have no doubt that such a man as you . . .

The wind was now blowing so ferociously that tiny whirlwinds of grit danced inside the tent where the walls met the ground.

"Do you hear her words, my little friend?" he whispered to the still form next to him under the heavy blankets. "The Yangs have returned! They are restored to their rightful place! The Yangs return to play!"

He received no response and expected none, because he knew that the girl was deeply asleep. She stirred a little and groaned, but did not awaken. He reached over, gently lifted a corner of the blanket, and looked at her tightly closed, sleeping face.

"Rest, poor thing," Yang Kuo-chung whispered to the child. "Get all the rest you can. I'll not be asking anything further of you, and the next ogre may demand a lot more than I. Children should sleep at night . . . but then I forget that for you, childhood ended long ago . . . that in fact, you never were a child. Your time in this world is, perhaps, already half over. I would be surprised if this sort of life would see you much past twenty-four; truly, I should be surprised if you made it even that far." He lowered the blanket. "So you are probably now well past middle age."

He could hear the horses outside jostle against each other in the wind, muttering and stepping about. Gravel and debris hissed against the side of the tent. Men, talking in low voices, walked by. The wind. Always, the wind. As if she heard it in her sleep, the girl rolled over and lay on her back.

Folding the letter carefully, he put it away in his pack. He looked at the child, who snored, mouth ajar.

"Look at you," he said. "Already you have the teeth of an old woman. You should have bright, sparkling pearls fixed to your young skull."

She sighed deeply, and muttered an unintelligible phrase.

"Are you dreaming? Good! A child should dream. And what else, after all, do you have, eh? It is the only time that things are good and pleasant for you, am I right?" Without quite touching her, he traced the innocent line of her brow with his forefinger. "I will give you a dream," he said. "Listen closely. Now, let me see . . . in this dream, you are the child you've never been . . . It is the Festival of the Weaving Star. You unroll your weaving out on the flagstone under the stars with all the other little girls . . . You set the candles out like the white river of the Milky Way, and you carry a little gold box with the spinning spider inside it and wait for your herdboy . . . He comes with cowbells, and steps over the river to take you away . . . that, child, is what a little girl's dream should be."

She shifted, moaned, and rolled over so that her back was to him again.

"And now," he continued, "you are riding on the waves of a great lake on the most beautiful pleasure barge you could imagine—like one of those magnificent golden miniatures they sell at the Dragon Boat Festivals. And this barge has terraces and pavilions and brightly colored lanterns all around and many beautiful ladies—in this dream, you are yourself, but a lady . . . and there is music on this barge; can't you hear it? The soft plucking of the strings and the flutes—so sweet, those breathy lilting flutes, and so mysterious! But all this music of men is nothing compared to the music of nature. Listen! The blue water laps against the golden hull . . . A spring breeze rustles the treetops on the shore. And look—the water lilies ride the ripples like painted flowers on a silk banner . . ." He paused as the sound of harsh male laughter carried from another part of the camp.

"You are not far from the shore," he whispered. "You can smell the rich sweetness of the jasmine blossoms. You can see the playful white fairies as they tumble and skim their milkweed seeds across the lake." The child's eyes opened then, but Yang Kuo-chung could see that she was still asleep, far, far away from him.

"This is unfair," he said. "Forgive me. That is *my* sweet dream, of Ch'ang-an in spring. The beauty of the Chia-cheng—a covered road of eighteen li from the grand halls of the Ta Ming palace to the splendors of Serpentine Lake and Indian Lotus Park. A covered pleasure road where it can never rain or snow. How could it be your dream? How selfish of me. I am sure that any lakes you have seen in your short life have been gray and frozen. No water lilies, no dragon boats with beautiful lanterns. No festivals," he said sadly. "It is good that you are not awake to hear me tease you. But I wish it could be your dream, too." He lay back and stared at the walls of the tent rippling with every gust of wind. "How could I take you there? Your masters wait for you in their tents. If I tried to steal you, to save you from all of this, your family and village would hunt me down. And even my skills as a horseman would be worth nothing on these broken-down old beasts. They would catch me and kill me, or worse—and I would never see Ch'ang-an or my dear Lady of Kuo again. So you understand. Besides," he said softly, shaking his head, "it would not do. It just would not do."

Unable to resist, he reached for his pack and took out the fragile parchment one more time. I must not be wasteful, he thought. I must conserve the fragrance so that it will last until I reach Ch'ang-an and can at last bury my nose in her hair, her skin, her silk underclothes. He held the paper under his nose and closed his eyes. Already the fragile scent was fading.

: :

Yang Kuo-chung rolled a few belongings up in a heavy quilt, tied it securely, and lashed it to his pack pony. What did not fit easily into his saddlebags he threw on the ground. It could all be replaced. When he had awakened this morning from sweet dreams of Ch'ang-an and the Lady of Kuo, he knew this would be the day that he would leave, and now he burned with impatience to be on his way.

Around him, peasants were scavenging his discards. Bright bits of cloth, polished knives, utensils, and little treasures he had no further use for flashed in the sun against the brown earth. He tossed a generous leather pouch containing several *liang* of silver ingots to someone standing next to him. The man who caught it had been his friend, companion, and colleague in his business dealings throughout the north. He was the biggest man Yang Kuo-chung had ever seen, with arms thicker than a normal man's thighs and hands that could span the distance of a horse's face from eye to chin.

"Here, my friend, this is yours. See that Hsien-yu and the governor of Szechuan get their horses." He untied another small purse from his belt and threw it as well. "And that will ensure that you have plenty to pay your outriders. I promised my clients horses in fine condition. You will see to it. I can trust you, my old gambling partner. And there is something else that needs tending to: Look in your tent," he said, tugging at a strap on the horse's belly.

"You leave us so soon, Fox?"

"I have not left this forsaken place soon enough," Yang Kuo-chung answered, heaving the heavy saddlebags over the pack pony's back.

"And what have you left in my tent?"

"The girl and the gaming trunk. See that she gets back to her father's village. I have paid off that whoring slavemaster. If he lays one finger on her before you can bring her back, kill him. But do it as these damned northerners do."

"And what way is that, Fox?" he asked, a knowing smile on his face.

"Cut the hand he touches the girl with first . . . with that."

He tossed his friend a small, wicked Ordos dagger; the man snatched it from the air, blade first, in his calloused palm.

"Then I should kill him by his own law!" the other said.

"Precisely!" Yang Kuo-chung smiled, pulling tight a strap around the pony's belly. He swung himself up into the saddle and took a last look at the camp: clusters of tents, ponies huddled against the wind, the charred remains of fires. It looked especially bleak to him now that the vision of Ch'ang-an burned brightly in his head. He looked back toward the corral and the prize herd of horses. My work, he thought, is done.

The wind picked up, throwing grit in their faces. The big man tucked the dagger into his belt and walked Yang Kuo-chung and the horse and pack pony to the perimeter of the camp.

"We shall miss you, Master Yang. I can't take all the fools up here for their gold without you."

"Perhaps not all of them." He laughed. "But enough so that you will not starve! You will get along quite well without me. When you have delivered the horses to Hsien-yu, come to the capital. I will take care of you there."

The man shook his head. "I am more suited to this rocky wilderness, and it to me. But thank you."

"If you change your mind, you know where to find me," said Yang Kuo-chung, turning his horse's head toward the road that went south.

His animals started down a slight incline, stepping carefully. No sooner did he have his back to the camp than Yang Kuo-chung's thoughts turned to the future. If he pushed himself and killed the horses beneath him, he might reach Ch'ang-an and the Palace of Grand Enlightenment in two weeks—with luck. He was ready. Heavens, but he was ready.

The camp had barely begun to recede behind him when he thought he heard a scream. He stopped and listened, thinking that the wind was playing a trick on his ears. He was about to ride on when he heard it again. This time there was no mistaking it. A pale, thin, translucent scream carrying on the wind. A child's scream.

Cutting the pack pony free of his horse with a swift slice of his knife, he wheeled around and galloped back up the hill, a terrible fear in his heart. As he approached the camp, he saw running figures. There were shouts, confusion.

He urged his horse forward. The tent . . . the tent where he had left the child. Men were clustered around it. He leapt from his horse and ran, shoving through the crowd. He stopped when he saw the broad back of his friend, Ordos dagger in hand, standing over the kneeling figure of the who-remaster. The man on the ground was looking in astonishment at his own two hands, severed from his wrists, lying on the ground. The fingers jerked spasmodically—the red bloody legs of enormous insects. Blood spurted from the wrist stumps. The man had just opened his mouth and begun to let out a howl when the giant, with a single blow, cracked his neck and silenced him forever.

The giant looked up then and saw Yang Kuo-chung.

"By his own law," he said, breathing hard, turning the body over with his foot. With his eyes, he told Yang Kuo-chung to look inside the tent.

Yang Kuo-chung found the frail form of the girl wrapped in a coarse woolen blanket, a dark, wet stain spreading in the area of her heart. He dropped to his knees next to her. The soft brown eyes were open, the features set in an expression of agony. He put his head in his hands, shut his eyes, then forced himself to look again at her face.

"It is my fault," he whispered to the dead girl. "My fault entirely. I was in such a hurry. Thinking of pleasures, of myself. I should not have left you alone for even a moment with that man so near. I am sorry. So sorry." He reached over, tried to smooth the pain off her face, and pulled the eyelids shut over the staring eyes. "So sorry," he whispered.

He was aware of his friend standing in the doorway to the tent. He stayed with her for a minute or two more before covering her face and rising to his feet. His friend's eyes met his.

"He killed her for no reason except that she did not belong to him anymore," the giant said.

"He was a wretched animal. We should have killed him long ago," Yang Kuo-chung said quietly.

He was on his way again after seeing to the burial of the child. There would be no retribution for his friend; every man who had witnessed the execution of the whoremonger had agreed that he deserved the death he received many times over. Yang Kuo-chung had offered to ride with the giant until they were out of this territory, just in case the dead man had relatives or cronies, but his offer was refused. It is not necessary, his friend had said; let them try to lay a hand on me. Let them try.

The mood of pleasant anticipation with which he had set out that morning was gone; in its place was a heavy feeling of fatigue and introspection. He could not get rid of the girl's eyes in his mind. It was a child he had been looking at—but no child looked back at him. He had seen death in many forms, but could never reconcile himself to the death of children. He had been only a child himself, barely six years old, the first time he had seen a dead child, and the memory, unwelcome and unasked for, forced itself on him now.

The baby's lips had been blue and encrusted with pine needles; blue, shiny, and swollen like the *yin* flowers—the mushrooms that grew deep in the sour, brackish piney soil of the ancient garden of his uncle's house in the hills of western Szechuan. A tiny, wizened thing, it looked a million years old to the child Yang Kuo-chung who had accidentally uncovered it while playing; before running to the house to tell the grown-ups, he had looked for a long time into the blank open eyes of the newborn infant, eyes that had never seen anything at all.

His father had never taken him back to Uncle's house, and nobody ever talked about what happened. And he had been admonished against even thinking of it himself, as if a child's memory could be wiped clean, with a few words from an adult, the way a servant's broom wiped clean the bricks of the garden path. And he had tried not to think of it, so much so that he had made himself secretly ill. The memory had frozen itself into a boyhood terror that he might ever think about, dream about, or see those swollen mushroom lips again.

And though he had been a mere child, with no knowledge of the world, he had understood perfectly, with a precocious knowledge that preceded experience, what had happened, fitting the pieces together from fragments of adult conversation.

His aunts had provided him with most of the information, warbling like canaries for months following the incident. A poor cleaning maid, it seemed, had hidden the shamefaced dishonor of her act under the loose folds of her clothes. When her day had come, she had dropped the child, ignominiously, like a monkey giving birth, smothered it, and wrapped it in a tattered rug that no one would miss. Then she had hidden it in a far grove of pines in a remote part of the garden for the wild dogs and crows to dispose of. And no one would ever have known had not a bold little nephew come from far away that very same day . . .

And now he had seen those swollen lips again on the face of a child, one he had tried, but not quite hard enough, to save. He knew that it would take time, distance, and a lot of weary riding to put this fresh memory in abeyance.

: :

He stank, and wanted a bath more than anything in the world. His horse stank, too, poor animal. Not the sweet horse smell that he loved and that was tied up with pleasant memories of hunting, gaming, and sociability, but a tired, unpleasant smell that reminded him of the odor of birch leaves rotting on an ancient Szechuan forest floor. It was a smell that made him think of autumn and too many wasted years, too much distance, and too much time laboring on the salty backs of tired, unnamed beasts. Watching the muscles work in the shoulders of his horse, he had to force himself to not count its steps, or try to calculate how many more steps would deliver him to the capital of Ch'ang-an and to the palace, or how many were already behind him on the journey. He had been traveling for eleven days and knew, at least, that the number of steps behind him was far greater than the number in front of him. To think that a fragment of perfumed paper had made its way across all this vast distance, found him, and offered what he considered to be the perfect reward for his work of the last several years!

Not only was she offering him access to her own impossibly delectable person, a place he had been before, briefly, and where he wished to return, but she was laying as bait the possibility of financial commissionerships, position, and the promise of taking his natural place in the celestial inner circle.

There had been little to do during the long ride except let his imagination run free. He was especially looking forward to informing his parents in a nonchalant way of where their "wastrel" son had wound up. Was he dead on the floor of some brothel, a knife quivering in his back and his purse ransacked? Was he drowned in a canal in a dubious part of some city, floating face down in the first light of the morning sun while children poked at his unfortunate corpse with long sticks? Was he wandering the streets, sightless eyes rolled up into his head and his hand held out supplicatingly to passers-by, asking them with slobbering mouth to help a poor man buy his cheap wine, a man once so full of promise and the pride and hope of his mother and father but now a mere shell of humanity? How, he asked himself, had he ever escaped any of these dire eventualities, when both his parents had assured him that such was the very best he could hope for unless he applied every bit of his being to the pursuit of scholarship, the triennial examinations, and a resulting high government position or even the recognition of any lowly civil position, at that? Honored Mother and Father, one imaginary letter began, my friend the August Emperor of China sends his warmest greetings and hopes that you are well and healthy . . .

He put back his head and laughed, savoring the image of their consternation, astonishment, and mixed feelings of pride and affronted authority. He could scarcely wait. Had he not been, after all, their shining hope for the return of prestige to their branch of the family? And had they not been dreadfully disappointed when it became obvious that he preferred the wineshops and brothels of the cities to the hushed study rooms of the academies? There had been passionate arguments. You are shamefully dissipating your youth and talents, his father would rage and his mother beseech tearfully. Can't you understand, he would say patiently, over and over, that I am receiving the best possible education a young man could hope for? You think I am merely philandering, when in fact I am meeting people: brilliant poets; adventurers; entrepreneurs; and yes, even scholars and officials. I have found more education and refinement in my forays into the crowded, bawdy wards of cities than I could ever find in the dry, stale, cloistered world of books and study.

What, after all, was the purpose of an "education"? From what his father had told him at least a thousand times, it was apparent finally, when all the talk had died down, that the purpose was to be able to earn a good living. What, he had asked his father, was the difference between a rich merchant and a prestigious scholar-official? Both could accumulate the same wealth and comfort. And the merchant, he had told his father, might even be able to pass on his wealth without the official's habit of acquiring, over the years, the land of every poor tenant farmer around him just to support his expanding, non-earning family.

Yang Kuo-chung's father's eyes had blazed with wrath at that pronouncement, and he had said in a quiet, dangerous voice that if the young master felt that way, then perhaps he had best make other living arrangements. His mother declared that the family had truly lost its greatness, that its vitality had become scattered, dissipated, that with the loss of its fortune, with bankruptcy, there had come an equivalent moral bankruptcy. And she had looked at him with tearful eyes that clearly saw in him the personification of that bankruptcy: his drunkenness, his lack, as she saw it, of fiber and will, his refusal to conform.

Exasperated, he had told them that he was exactly what he was made to be and, in his own way, was conforming. Was he not a Yang, and were the Yangs not supposed to blaze their own trails in high places? And what about you, Mother? Are you not a grandniece of the man who was chief minister under Emperor T'ai-tsung? And wasn't your own sister a notorious favorite of the Empress Wu? Were the Yangs not direct descendents of the royal family of the last dynasty—were they not members of the Sui? That particular foolish bit of self-aggrandizement, his father had said, belonged to his brother—Yang Kuo-chung's uncle—and those members of the family who chose to indulge in a connection that was dubious at best and an outright lie at the worst. Those daughters of his brother—Father's nieces—certainly believed themselves to be long lost queens; perhaps Yang Kuo-chung would be happier if he went and joined that branch of the family, since he was obviously more suited to them, and they to him.

Throughout his childhood, this errant side of the family had always been held up for him as an example of conceit, vanity, and all that was illusory, shallow, weak, and devoid of substance. Thus a secret admiration was nourished in him over the years for the "other" Yangs. And when he was a young man of twenty-two, he finally got the opportunity to go to that part of Szechuan where they lived and to meet them.

He had gone there to take up a military career. His parents had long ago bade farewell to their hopes that he would eventually come to his senses and pursue the scholarly life, and were at least relieved that he would be earning a good living as something other than a thief or whoremonger, careers they

had considered likely for him. It had not taken him long to find these other
Yangs, and when he did, it was like waking up from a long, hazy half-sleep.
At last, he understood who he was. Things he had been saying to his father
for years that always left him with a sick, oppressive feeling of opposition and
bitterness seemed, in this other household, to simply be good sense, talk
flowing freely between rational, reasonable people. He was home!

Speaking with Uncle, he found that ideas which until then had only been
half-formed became clear, complete, and obvious. Of course there were many
roads, not just one, Uncle agreed with him, but only a traveler could know
that. Ease and sociability were the most important and visible traits of the
Confucian gentleman, were they not? There was much to be said for an ability
to move among the rich and powerful. Just as some men spent their lives
cultivating their prosody or their knowledge of politics or history, so a certain
type of gentleman might carefully cultivate his ability to move in rarified
circles. And Uncle understood exactly how that very same hunger for experience which could lead a man to the upper limits of society might also require
him to explore its depths. For each minister, millionaire, or emperor you sit
with, Uncle had said, you must share a cup with a thief, a drunkard, a beggar,
or even a murderer. You must know all of life, he had said, pouring more
wine for the young man. Yes, it is good to know how to read, but that does
not mean that you must spend your life locked away with books. Study? There
is one thing worth studying, he had said: the Confucian classics. Their tenets
are the grease that allow the gears of this world of fools to turn smoothly.
This world, Uncle had said with emphasis. Confucius himself did not waste
his time worrying about the metaphysical. He left the worrying about such
things as ghosts, spirits, and the ethereal plains of existence to others, addressing himself to the immediate problems: order and harmony in a difficult
world.

And the daughters, his cousins—the "long lost queens." Father, he had
thought, you don't know how accurate you were when you said that. There
had been four of them, the youngest not much more than a child and the
eldest only a few years younger than himself. They were all beautiful, but the
eldest was the one he couldn't stop looking at; he remembered feeling as if he
had met himself in female form. And it did not take long for them to claim
each other in a delicious, illicit love affair that lasted for the duration of his
visit. The notion of incest heightened their passion; one night, Eldest Cousin
caused in him a nearly unendurable paroxysm of desire by whispering in his
ear that there was a rumor, a deep family secret, a possibility that they were
more than cousins—that her father might also be *his* father. The only one who
knows for certain, she had said, is your mother. His mother! The irony of it
had delighted him and made him think very differently about his mother and
her attitude of staid propriety. Oh, Mother, he had thought, if you knew that

I know . . . and it would explain a lot of things, including his affinity with these "other" Yangs, and Uncle in particular.

He had gone on then to pursue his service for the military governor in another part of Szechuan. Fortified and inspired by his recent encounter with his relatives, he had decided he would try, once and for all, from a safe distance, to explain who and what he was to Mother and Father. He was still very young and thought that this was something he had to do: he had paid a great prose writer to compose an apologia to his family in which he attempted to express and justify his position. The thought of this clumsy effort of youth still embarrassed him. So be it! That was then!

Not that everything in the letter had been entirely absurd. It had been passed around, he knew, among the members of his immediate family, from his parents to his gossipy and critical aunties, and there had been plenty in it to show that he was a long, long way from being a total disgrace to them. He told them he was studying military organization and horses, and had been given several minor posts, including that of advising the military governor and his wealthy ally Hsien-yu on the purchase and training of war horses. I am becoming quite a shrewd businessman and equestrian in the process, he had told his family. You would be proud of what I have learned along the way and of the posts I am filling without passing any examinations. I am, after all, a Yang, he had said to them, no matter how much time has made you forget it.

And to make his point in the most tangible way possible, he had sent them money, something he had been been able to do for many years now as his fortune increased. It had not taken long for his talents to be recognized; in addition to his duties as official connoisseur of horseflesh, he often functioned as courier and delegate to the great capital city of Ch'ang-an. And he had acquired wealthy patrons, there and in Szechuan, who paid him handsome commissions to move along the Silk Road in search of business, goods, deals, horses, and breeding stock. By the time he was finished with his military duties, he was already an established entrepreneur much in demand along the borders of the northern frontier provinces of Fanyang, Hopei, and P'inglu. And his contacts and military connections had afforded him a handsome private income as a middleman in the supplying, transporting, and routing of military stores. And he had friends in high places in the north, too. One of the men he saw regularly in his travels was Li Shih-chih, who had served in many important posts in these northern military governments. It was from this close friend that Yang Kuo-chung had learned inside details of the sensitive and often dangerously unstable political realities of these border areas where some of his most lucrative trading with military installations was done. At first his interest had been purely selfish—he wanted to know the risks to himself and his thriving business. But his acquaintance with Li Shih-chih—whose loyalty to the empire was intense and whose knowledge was considerable—had awakened in him an interest in government that did not center entirely on his own future prospects. He had come to understand that the empire did not merely exist—that it required passionate vigilance to keep it from vanishing like a dream.

Yes, he had done well, and was often able to send his family extra gifts of money beyond what he gave them regularly. He did not mention to them that one of the things he had learned in his travels was that he was a talented, dangerous gambler, and that his legendary skills with the dice, the sticks, and the tiles were often the source of tidy sums with which his mother and aunties could buy themselves gifts of fancy clothes and expensive baubles. There was no need to tell them. He was satisfied just knowing it himself. He liked to contemplate his mother showing off an exotic new hair ornament sitting on her head and never knowing that the money to buy it had been won in a game from a man who had, perhaps, lost most of his teeth in drunken fights, whose knife tucked in his belt quite probably had traces of dried human blood on it, and whose stock and trade might well be the acquisition and sale of stolen merchandise, including, occasionally, young boys and girls. Telling her, he thought with a smile, would spoil the pleasant irony.

After eleven days of travel, he was beginning to notice a change in the landscape. He could rest in the shade of trees now, real trees—the thick, green leafy trees of the T'ang, not stunted bushes worn down by the wind. Gradually, the contours of the land were becoming softer and greener. The wind no longer buffeted him monotonously hour after hour; he was passing through increasing numbers of cultivated fields. He had not realized how thirsty he was for civilization until the north had begun to physically recede. Gods, but he had been up there for a long time without any respite. He did some counting in his mind and was astonished to realize that for nearly three and a half years he had not left the three provinces of Fanyang, Hopei, and P'inglu. It had been more than four years since his last visit to Ch'ang-an. When the letter from Eldest Cousin had arrived, he had allowed himself to think that the universe had a grand plan for his life after all.

Baby Cousin. It was all because of Baby Cousin. He could not remember her very clearly; she had been too young for him to take much notice of her when he had gone to visit her family. The little girl who had followed her older sisters and cousin around, doing her best to get their attention, was now an emperor's consort, and her sisters were titled ladies and had received enormous amounts of money and property within the city. He knew that there were husbands to go along with the titles—but that was of no concern to him. The "husbands" were, more than likely, creaky old men, insignificant vestiges of the sisters' new rank, and he doubted that he would ever lay eyes on any of them. Eldest Cousin had a new name now: She was the Lady of Kuo. How absolutely beautiful that name sounded to him when he said it out loud. Kuo!

He wondered what he would look like to her. Had the distances stretching out and out, the years of sleeping in smelly hide tents with rocks for his pillow and riding the bony backs of plodding horses in the damnable winds transformed him into something hideous without his being aware of it? He laughed. Maybe she will be shocked by my appearance. I think that I am still the handsome young man who was her lover, but in reality I am horrible to look at and crazy from the wind. A poor, pathetic wind-crazed madman. Here I am, my love. I have ridden halfway across the earth to share your bed and to take my pick of important, well-paying jobs. Where is the Emperor? I want to meet him. But first, take your clothes off.

There were times, he reflected, when he was convinced that the wind *had* affected his sanity. In the north, it was common knowledge that it could make you crazy. He had heard that in some of those dangerous and bothersome non-Chinese nations north of the border, there was a different set of laws for those times when the wind blew hardest. To kill another when the air was calm could earn you cruel and violent retribution by the family of the victim—death by torture, perhaps, or castration. But it was a different matter to murder during those times when the wind ripped incessantly down from the passes of the Na-lu Mountains and rattled your soul. Then, murder, while not altogether pardonable, was an understandable thing—and you might lose only a hand or your tongue. What else but the wind could have made him take the girl, the caravaner's whore-child, whose father had sold her to buy food or, more probably, liquor? He had rubbed himself raw in her tight little body, which had scarcely been ready to receive a man, her little tits so unripe that he could hardly get them into his mouth. And afterward, the sense of waste and uselessness, and a loneliness he couldn't explain or understand . . .

He thought of her, so far away now, lying under the pile of rocks they had put on her grave to discourage scavenging animals. For just a moment, he fancied that her ghost, light as a puff of smoke and just as transitory, sat behind him in his saddle. I want to see the dragon boats and the milkweed fairies, said the ghost, so I came with you. But she was not there at all, he knew; whatever remained of her had been left far, far behind. He had left the wind behind, too.

::

Yang Kuo-chung was riding hard, but the harder he rode, the more the ball seemed to elude him. He wasn't really awake yet; a thin veil of morning still dulled his senses. Wake up, he told himself. Wake up!

Thick tufts of grass grabbed at the flexible bamboo mallet that always seemed about to snap in his hand. Damn this place; the grass was too tall here. This was hard, unmanicured ground, not like the fields back at the palace. Hooves pounded, clumps of dirt, grass, and stones flew into the riders' faces, and still he could not get at the ball, a tiny sphere of willow root that had nearly cost him his life several times. Digging his legs deep into the horse's sides, he turned and pivoted, reins stretched tight across the animal's neck until the bit nearly lifted from the mouth. A hard squeeze of his left calf and he turned the beast around in time to meet the Emperor's challenge. The flanks of the two horses slammed together, and he felt pain as his shin met the Emperor's long outer stirrup. Aah!! Fool, he told himself, go!!

Again he drew a bead on the ball, a straight line ahead, and squeezed with his knees. At the same time Minghuang pushed himself hard against the high leather and brocade cantle of his saddle. The two horses galloped neck and neck down the field. The Emperor's horse gave the Fox a good chase, but was not fast enough! His chest low to the withers, Yang Kuo-chung dropped his shoulders and raised the mallet behind him, his eye never leaving the skittering white ball that danced ahead of them to the left. He squeezed from the right, and his horse, so highly trained that it could not help but obey his command, almost lost its footing . . .

Yang Kuo-chung had never played this hard. It was he and the Lady of Kuo pitted against the Son of Heaven and old General Feng. The field had come down to just the four of them this morning—a very personal game, like the games of the Emperor's youth when only a few family members played against each other. Who would believe these old men could have such energy? Only four on the field and the ball was never at rest, the net bags always alive.

This old, club-footed Feng is fast for such a big bastard. This man, only a few years older than the Emperor, was the same one who had taught the game to Minghuang when he was still a crown prince. What a teacher he must have been! And the two of them had been teammates for nearly forty years. They knew each other's moves as if they were the same person. Well, thought Yang Kuo-chung, the Lady of Kuo and I do not do so badly ourselves, though we have been playing together for only a month. There she was now, closing in on Feng's blind side. He knew what she was going to do.

She blocked Feng's move and stepped on the ball, backing her mallet on it, and Yang Kuo-chung was behind her to receive her gift. But again he and Minghuang found themselves on a collision course. The Emperor's stallion panicked, and the Fox's horse shied and reared. Ride her neck, he told himself; throw your weight down on her crest, hands to her neck, let up on the reins. The Fox had reacted in time and brought his mare down—but too slow, he told himself. You nearly pulled her over backwards with you. They recovered and spun to see the Emperor struggling with his mount. Yang Kuo-chung sucked in his breath as he saw the old man's tail slip to the rim of the cantle.

He shuddered. He could feel the Emperor's pain! Mounted attendants flew to the center of the field and rode to Minghuang's side, but the Emperor waved them away, grimacing for only a moment and then recovering.

Yang Kuo-chung released his breath; as strong a rider as the old man was, he could not stop himself from worrying about him. It was no wonder that the eunuch Kao Li-shih hardly ever showed his face at these events. I'll hear about the old fool's death soon enough, Yang Kuo-chung had heard the eunuch say more than once. I'll not let it spoil my breakfast.

Yang Kuo-chung turned around to ride the block against Feng. The old eunuch general was going for the Lady of Kuo. Good! She will keep him busy. General Feng is slowing a bit at this time of his life, but he still rides a good block, thought the Fox. Minghuang could slip by with the ball, and now it traveled along the Fox's weaker side . . . but it was plain that the Emperor could do nothing with the ball yet, neither pass nor ride his shot. Not yet! Get on him! Yang Kuo-chung, seeing his opportunity, came up hard from behind and took the ball from the Emperor. But he knew it was not yet firmly in his grasp—he was vulnerable, and Minghuang might retrieve it on his good side.

The sleep that had been hanging over him earlier vanished. I am awake now, he thought—completely awake—and changed his mallet hand with the speed of a Steppe horseman or a Persian. No one could change hands the way he did! He leaned his good shoulder across the withers. Now he rode to the willow on his strong side—but the Lady of Kuo could not help him. Feng was blocking her.

The old soldier still had it in him. It was obvious that he had lost nothing of the horsemanship he had once taught to a crown prince. He would not let the lady interfere, obstructing her by pivoting his horse around, this way and that, precise turns on the forehand. The old eunuch rode too well; she was trapped. "The Fox" knew that he would have to take the ball down the field himself. It was a long way, and the Emperor was still on him and closing . . .

With a lightning move, the Emperor dipped low over the side of his horse toward the ground and leaned into the ball; his mallet was on it before Yang Kuo-chung could stop him. He had taken the ball from the Fox with surprising speed. And indeed he was surprised! He had, as usual, underestimated Minghuang's equestrian skills, which by all rights should have been seriously impaired by time. But the Emperor had stayed in practice, obviously, and he was light and lean.

Yang Kuo-chung did not usually take pleasure in an opponent's escape from him, but now he watched with perverse pleasure as the old man circled around to protect his gain, hooting a cry of victory like a common soldier. The path to the goal was clear now. But there was a danger! The Lady of Kuo and her gaily caparisoned horse had broken through the general's defense.

She's too fast for the old soldier, Yang Kuo-chung thought, but she may be too late to help me. The Yangs had scored many times recently against the Emperor and loyal old Feng, but perhaps not this time! He watched as the Emperor tapped the ball into place for his goal shot, raced to follow it, and raised his mallet for the final shot that would carry it into the bag between the festively colored posts . . . a light tap, not too hard . . . The ball was rolling toward home now, gently, uninterrupted. Yang Kuo-chung hesitated for half a heartbeat. Do I let the Emperor have this one game, which he will if I wait even a moment longer? He dug his heels into his horse. I am a legend, thanks to the sisters. I must live up to it. Watch the Fox become a darting kestrel.

Though the ball was as good as gone between the goalposts, Yang Kuo-chung changed direction, caught up to it, stopped it, and in the same motion hit it backwards down the field with vicious speed toward the Lady of Kuo . . . gone! The Emperor shouted with surprise and admiration at his opponent's skill. Old Feng was just as surprised to find that the Lady of Kuo had craftily escaped him, her horse springing forward with the speed of a launched arrow, and was moving on a tangent toward the approaching ball, which was quickly in her possession and rolling ahead of her down the field toward the opposite goal, coaxed along by occasional light taps of her mallet. Yang Kuo-chung, exultant with the sweet anticipation of victory, watched her. Was there, anywhere, the Fox asked himself, a woman like her? A Yang through and through, she extracted such obedience from her horse, achieved such perfect oneness and unity with the animal. He felt a distinct erotic thrill as she soared on horseback like the gentle flight of an *apsaras*—a Buddhist angel—and the old general, so fast before, seemed somehow trapped in a weightier universe, lumbering behind with the ponderous gravity of an old cow. They would never catch her, never stop the goal and the final point that would win the game. Polo, it seemed, was a game for the young, and today it belonged to these two Yangs. As it had on every other day. The Emperor, Yang Kuo-chung knew, would be unhappy if they "let" him win. He wanted a real game and, if he won, as he nearly did today, a real victory. He was proud of the Yangs—that they could beat him and could ride better than the best of his elite corps. They were a part of him now.

: :

Grooms and attendants with footstools, a supervising official of the stables, and several maids-in-waiting for the Lady of Kuo assisted in the dismounting. Large fans, bright with painted golden phoenixes and dragons, and two large fringed umbrellas sheltered the Son of Heaven's polo party as they strolled toward the colorful party tents waiting for them, spreading languorously into the leafy shade of trees at the fringes of the Indian Lotus Playing Field. Thin translucent silk mosquito screens covered with delicate floral designs were swiftly erected in place around the open-sided tents; they rippled softly with the merciful breeze that rushed through the park. For an instant, the breeze increased—warm and sunlit sweet—and the whispering air bent rustling paths in the late summer grasses, as if some invisible creature walked there; the crowns of the trees gently swayed and hissed. The tent sides fluttered in leafy clusters of light and shadow. Grooms walked the sweating horses down, soothing the animals' occasional nervous shying at the snapping of the brightly colored imperial banners.

In the main tent, the three sisters of the Lady of Kuo lolled on a large cushioned dais, waiting for the players. The Emperor eased himself down to the cushions near them and shut his eyes for a moment. Precious Consort fanned him playfully.

"She played her best game of polo, yet, don't you think?" he asked them, eyes still shut, accepting the cool perfumey breeze of the consort's silk fan. "Applaud your noble sister, ladies."

"She was magnificent," said the Lady of Chin; "it is a shame that she does not play an equal game of tiles."

The Lady of Kuo heard this just as she came into the tent and directed toward her sister a dangerous look.

"Darling Sister, you should learn that the greatest virtue in the world of statecraft and games is to hold one's tongue and assess one's own weaknesses," she said, sinking to the cushions and pulling Yang Kuo-chung down with her.

"A Yang female hold her tongue? Impossible, Dear Cousin," said "the Fox." "And I am certain our Brilliant Emperor would agree. Surely you do not wish for your sister what you would not demand of yourself." He put his head in her lap and gazed up at her. How beautiful she was, how refreshed by the air and the delectable vigor of the game—the skin of her face like a pearl, uncaked with rouge and powder, lightly streaked with sweat. Before him, for a moment, the child he had seen so many years ago!

The Emperor opened his eyes and smiled with pleasure.

"I am so happy that you reminded me," he said. "It makes my loss today so much easier to bear. You see how quickly an aging man forgets? It was but a day ago that *she* lost to *me* at tiles! And there was a wager attached, was there not?" he said innocently, looking around him. He put his hand to his forehead. "Let me think. It is coming back now. I think that you promised me, if you should lose, that you would sweep a certain alley in the city in preparation for the relocation of the citizens who live there to clean, new homes on the Street of Good Harmony. What is happening to my memory? How could I have forgotten something so wonderful?"

Stewards arrived, their presence announcing the small army of kitchen servants to follow. They entered, carrying silver and jade trays laden with sweetmeats, diced fruit, and nuts arranged in delicate patterns of peacocks and carp. Cloisonné pitchers of iced drinks with floating bouquets of bright red and yellow flowers were set on the low tables with the food.

"In fact," Minghuang continued, spearing a piece of fruit, "it was just this morning as I was putting my brush to another page of commentaries for the *Classic of Filial Piety*—you see, I mean to finish my exegesis for posterity now that Master Li Lin-fu has freed so much of my time—that I discovered my memory to have failed me again. If it weren't for our good scholars of the imperial library archives, I fear I should have put words into Master Kung Tzu's mouth that were never uttered in that ancient state of Lu . . . But my wager with our Lady of Kuo was simple, and since she produced no hands of *pung* or *chao* or *kung* during our final set at tiles then I fear . . ."

"She sweeps the street!" the Precious Consort said with glee. "And we all get to watch her!"

"And we shall have a party!" said the Lady of Chin.

"I shall order carts and labor to assist the people who are moving, and the imperial kitchens will prepare refreshment for them. And . . ." the Emperor said, looking at the Precious Consort with a sly smile, "so that our dear Lady of Kuo won't sulk, we will pay her for her work. The alley in the other direction shall be hers, to redesign and expand her garden as she wills it. And so that her sisters won't sulk, I shall bestow the cash and the artisans to expand *their* mansions as well. And all because you, my dear Kuo, showed me such superb horsemanship today. There is really nothing I appreciate more in this world, and I thank you."

"And what about the broom I shall use? You cannot expect me to use anything but the most superior broom."

"The handle will be inlaid with ivory and gold. The straw will be the stiff hairs from an elephant's tail—balanced like the finest writing brush."

The sisters were applauding as if the expansions and remodelings were something they hadn't expected.

"The extra money will be useful," said the Lady of Han with a sigh. "Maintaining and nourishing our old husbands is so expensive."

"Our *doddering* old husbands," added the Lady of Chin.

"What colossal ingratitude," the Lady of Kuo said to her sisters.

"Would you have preferred strapping brutes who would make demands on you?" the Emperor asked them. "It can be arranged, if that is what you prefer. Of course, you will probably lose your titles and your position, but . . ." He shrugged.

"You know, I have looked into the future and seen something strange," said the Precious Consort. "I have seen my sisters as old, old ladies, trembling old blue-veined archduchesses. They are all married to young men who want only their money and titles. Every once in a while, one of the old ladies politely and humbly asks her young husband, whom she knows is very busy with young, beautiful women, to please do her a small favor, to come to her in the dark one time, with his eyes shut . . ."

The ladies of Chin and Han looked at each other and smiled; the Lady of Kuo laughed.

"Is that how it is for you, sisters?" she asked them. "*My* old husband avoids me entirely; at times I am sure that he does not even know who I am." She and Yang Kuo-chung looked intently into each other's eyes as she spoke, little smiles on their lips.

"Well," said the Lady of Han coyly, "I have noticed that my husband is not as old as he once was."

"As for my husband," said the Lady of Chin, "well . . . how shall I put it? If age is wisdom, then he is very, very wise indeed. I had always been told that a husband is Heaven. If it is true, then the canopy of Heaven is wearing thin and becoming so brittle that the stars may tumble out the way jewels do from an old brooch."

"But we want to know, Sister, if you are shaking his jewels," said the Precious Consort.

"Yes," said Yang Kuo-chung. "Are you, so to speak, stirring the dragon in its misty lair?"

"You'll just have to ask him yourself, Cousin, will you not?" she replied.

"Why, you little unhousebroken pet!" Kuo exclaimed.

"Be gentle with your old husbands, in any case," said the Emperor. "I had nothing in mind but political expediency when I arranged the marriages. Less gossip from the old families, you know. If I had simply brought you in and given you titles, they would have accused me of creating new aristocracies. As it is, I am simply marrying off some of the old dying ones. We have Kao Li-shih to thank for the suggestion. If one of the effects of my work is to keep the old worthies who are your husbands in this world a bit longer because they have, perhaps, rediscovered some old pleasures, then I am glad. They have served me well, and I am happy that they might have one last taste of their youth. And here is one ancient, doddering, half-dead old man who knows that it is possible."

"But little did you know that you were bestowing—or should I say unleashing—the three Queen Yangs upon the nation," Yang Kuo-chung said. "I think that my first duty as Minister of Finance—a position I will fill only until the proper person comes along—will be to establish a permanent beneficial building fund for my cousins, since each one of them is constantly vying for the distinction of having the most magnificent mansion in Ch'ang-an. Each one of them will spare no expense in tearing down her house if she but hears

a rumor that a neighbor's property may be more grand. And then the artisans
will be at it again. Day and night." He accepted a piece of fruit into his mouth
from the Lady of Kuo's hand. "At least," he said, "these architects and artisans
are assured of work to feed their families—eternal sinecures with the Yangs."
The Emperor laughed and shook his head with pleasure as he remembered
something.

"I have a little surprise for you," he said. "Just yesterday, a new folk
song was recorded in the registers of our beloved Yueh-fu Music Bureau. A
peasant song."

The Emperor hummed softly to himself and then began to chant:

> "To have a son will make you sad . . .
> Only a 'Yang' will make you glad.
> Our August Father reveres that name . . .
> With it you may paint a rich doorframe."

"That is a song that I have never heard," the Lady of Kuo said, pleased.

"Of course you haven't," said Yang Kuo-chung. "Unless you've been
out working in the fields, singing along with the peasant farmers. Now there's
something I'd love to see."

"And I would love no less to see *you* up to your knees in mud behind
an ox-drawn plow," the Lady of Kuo said pleasantly.

"I know when she can sing it!" said the Lady of Chin happily. "Tomorrow, when she sweeps the alley!"

"Hush, Little Wart!" the Lady of Kuo retorted.

"That song sounds a bit like treason, doesn't it?" said Yang Kuo-chung.
"A secret society. These Yangs have come to overthrow the prosperous and
peaceful House of T'ang . . ."

They all laughed, except for the Lady of Kuo, who was reaching over
to give her sister a dig in the ribs. She spilled peach nectar from her cup onto
her arm as she did it, and Yang Kuo-chung picked the arm up as if it were a
delicate wing of a roast fowl and began to lick the thick sweet liquid from her
skin.

"And I imagine," he continued, still holding her arm, "that the official
chroniclers, the historians of our dynasty, will speak of the 'Rebellion of the
Imperial Wife's Sisters' as they do the 'Rebellion of the Yellow Turbans.' They
will give it some silly, long-winded name, and these brigands will come to
be known by the costumes they wore—phoenix gowns with winged shoulders
and brightly sashed waists, overjackets of blue satin, with gold and ivory
hairpins dangling above their pretty rouged cheeks. They must have been,

according to these historians, at something of a disadvantage when it came to infantry combat, their skirts tangling between their legs and all."

"You are so damnably foolish, my drunken cousin," the Lady of Kuo said affectionately.

"And the armies of the Emperor were never surprised," Yang Kuo-chung continued. "The barking of the little dogs in the rebels' sleeves and the squawking of the colorful parrots on their shoulders always announced their presence. Plenty of warning, you see, not to mention the jingling of their jewelry and . . ."

"And do not worry," Minghuang said. "The sisters' war chariots were much too slow for the great armies of the T'ang, gilded as they were with golden birds and dragons and pulled by miniature ponies with braided manes and tails and rolling on tiny wheels . . . They were quickly routed by the swift cavalries of the Brilliant Emperor."

They laughed and raised their cups to the "rebellion." The Lady of Kuo raised her cup high, drank, and then poured the rest of the sticky peach nectar onto Yang Kuo-chung's arm.

"I hope you are as good at licking with your tongue from your own arm as you are at wagging it with all your foolish talk, Cousin."

Yang Kuo-chung laughed and writhed away from her, but it was too late. Before he could escape, the Lady of Han and the Lady of Chin also poured their cups on him.

The Lady of Chin began to sing, and the others soon joined in: "To have a son will make you sad . . . Only a 'Yang' will make you glad. . . ."

The Emperor laughed until the tears stood in his eyes. Then he sat up and waved his arm. Someone was approaching. Yang Kuo-chung followed the Emperor's gaze and was not at all happy to see a massive figure on horseback at the other end of the field approaching the tent under the trees.

"It is An Lu-shan," said the Emperor happily.

The women, too, began calling and waving, and he could see the general raise a fat arm in a return greeting. Well, thought Yang Kuo-chung; for me, this little party is over. He stood and brushed grass and debris from his legs.

"Pardon me, my wonderful friends, but I think I will start riding back to the palace. I am hot, sweaty, and sticky, and soon there will be ants crawling all over me. I think I will go and have a bath."

The Lady of Kuo gave him a disappointed look.

He caressed her chin. "I will come and visit you tonight, if you will have me." He signaled to his groom to bring him his horse.

On his way back to his quarters he encountered Kao Li-shih, who seemed surprised to see him. The two greeted each other pleasantly.

"I hope you can reassure me that the Emperor survived the game without splitting open his skull or fracturing his limbs," the eunuch said drily.

Yang Kuo-chung laughed. "He is unscathed but for a bump on the tailbone, which I think I felt even more than he did," he replied, rubbing his own lower back sympathetically as they walked down an open hallway.

"That is why I do not care to witness these matches," Kao Li-shih said with distaste. "It is far too painful for me. I stay away if it is possible for me to tactfully do so. But who, may I ask, was the victor?"

"The Lady of Kuo and I won the match," Yang Kuo-chung replied. "But we did not have an easy time of it. Old Feng and the Emperor presented us with a serious challenge. And it was the lady who scored the winning point, taking the ball between the goalposts at the final possible moment. It was close. Very, very close."

Kao Li-shih raised his eyebrows.

"Do you mean to tell me," he said, his voice serious but his eyes smiling, "that you did not defer to the Emperor?"

Yang Kuo-chung hesitated only a moment, then smiled in return.

"Do you mean did we not 'give' him the game? No, we did not," he said, shaking his head. "It occurred to me. And I had the perfect opportunity to gracefully let the ball get away. It was already on its way down to the other end of the field. In a matter of seconds, Feng and the Emperor would have scored the winning point. That was when I gave serious consideration to holding myself back. But"—he shrugged—"I didn't. I took the ball from them and gave it to the Lady of Kuo."

Yang Kuo-chung and the eunuch walked in silence for a few moments.

"I admit that part of it was simply that I cannot stand to lose. But there was another reason. I thought that to hand him the game would be to dishonor him as a man. When people undertake to play a game, there is an unspoken agreement that all participants are well matched. To give him the game, to let him win, would be . . . how shall I say it? . . . condescending, insulting. It would be the same as telling him that he is something other than a man and a worthy opponent. It would be lying to him. And somehow, as I watched him ride and play in earnest, I felt that the man did not need to be lied to." He looked questioningly at Kao Li-shih. "You know him far better than I do. I hope I did the right thing."

Kao Li-shih stopped walking and gave him a frank, encouraging look.

"You did. It is how I have always treated him. It is how I now wish more people would treat him. The first time I saw the Lady of Kuo beat him, I worried. A woman beating the Emperor at polo? But then I came to understand that he respected her for it—not only for her skill, but for her honesty. And he will respect you for it too, I promise."

They began to walk again.

"But where are the others? You seem to have returned alone. Surely the party has not broken up so soon. Did I not see Master An Lu-shan riding out to join the festivities only a short time ago?"

"The party, as far as I know, is still going on, and will go on for many more hours. But I am afraid," he said, encouraged by some subtle signal in the tone of Kao Li-shih's voice, "that it ended for me as soon as Master An's silhouette appeared on the horizon. And since I have no wish to spoil the Emperor's enjoyment, I thought it best for me to withdraw."

Kao Li-shih held up his hand.

"Say no more, Master Yang. That is the other reason that I prefer to be absent. If I am not there, then no one need see my face set in a false mask of tolerance and good humor. It is a dreadful strain, and I am afraid that as I grow older, the disguise becomes thinner and thinner. Therefore, I think it best not to be seen at all."

Yang Kuo-chung looked at the eunuch. "So, Master Kao. It is difficult for you, too. I am glad to learn that. I feared that I was the lone malcontent."

"No, Master Yang," Kao Li-shih replied. "You are not alone."

: :

Two nights after the polo game, Yang Kuo-chung and the Lady of Kuo attended a concert of the Pear Garden Orchestra. Yang Kuo-chung admired the twenty or so exquisite women who turned their instruments to play for the Emperor. Even for an Emperor, thought the Fox, it is extraordinary that such a bouquet could be gathered of beautiful female creatures who are also master musicians. The party of listeners in the open air pavilion talked quietly in the late summer twilight as stray practice notes sounded on the flutes. Delicate fingers tuned the stringed *chins* and *bi-pas* to the hollow, haunting registers of the *hsuan* and *sheng* pipes and the elegant tones of the twenty-five-string lute. There was a pause as the orchestra leader nodded her head at the attentive musicians.

In unison they began, bursting into a strong, bright Kuchan rhythm. Yang Kuo-chung looked around at the others in the pavilion. The Emperor looked particularly pleased and relaxed this evening, but Baby Cousin, the Precious Consort, seemed a trifle withdrawn. She was not caressing some part of the Emperor's anatomy, as she usually did, or whispering in his ear. She looked, to Yang Kuo-chung, distinctly pensive this evening.

People in the audience were laughing at something. Yang Kuo-chung turned back toward the musicians. The fat General An Lu-shan, wearing a lady's dress, was tiptoeing in from behind and climbing the low platform where the musicians sat. He made his way to an empty spot among them; though there were some smiles, the women continued to play as if they were quite accustomed to the huge bearded "lady" in their midst. An Lu-shan carefully rearranged his gown in an exaggeratedly feminine fashion as he prepared to sit. He fluffed it out and, before sitting, dipped his enormous bulk in a delicate curtsy to the Son of Heaven, who laughed and smiled with a welcoming gesture of his hand. While the musicians played around him, An Lu-shan acted out a buffoonish little pantomime. He pretended to fuss with his hair ornaments; he picked up his chimes and glanced around him as if apologizing for being late, then tilted his head with a worried look on his face, trying to determine where the others were in their music and where he should come in with the chimes. On cue, the musicians all paused for just a moment, and An Lu-shan sounded his chimes with a dainty flourish of his great hairy hand. The audience, the Emperor especially, found this screamingly funny, and tossed coins and flowers at An Lu-shan, who put his arms protectively over his head as if they were tossing rocks at him. Then the music resumed . . . delicate fingers to the lutes and *chins,* lips to the reeds and porcelain pipes . . . the same lilting folk melody, but now faster and jauntier. Yang Kuo-chung watched the Emperor turn, laughing, to the Precious Consort, who forced a little smile in return.

Well, Baby Cousin, thought the Fox, I don't find it particularly amusing either, though I suspect we have different reasons. He was irritated to hear the Lady of Kuo next to him laughing enthusiastically along with the others.

"So there's the fool who is all the rage among you idle ladies," he said to her.

"He's cute, Cousin, and very talented . . . see how well he plays the stone chimes, the wooden clappers, and the drums. He's made wonderful progress."

"Any lout can bash rocks together, my cousin. I'm just surprised that he's learned to do it without a head between them," Yang Kuo-chung said with a polite smile. She looked at him with exasperation.

"Incorrigible."

"I should say quite the same of your friend."

"You're jealous of him, then."

"I should think not."

"It's just that he has the seriousness of a child imitating an adult. Learning his music with such concentration. He follows my instructions very closely, you know. He is quite charming and appealing, as you would discover if you would take the time to know him."

"I would not have the time if I lived six lifetimes, my dear Lady of Kuo. I'm afraid I find him quite unappetizing." She gave him a look she might give a recalcitrant child and turned her attention back to the scene in front of them.

When the music was finished, and after the applause and the bows, the harem orchestra members put down their instruments and crossed single file, talking and giggling, to the Emperor's day couch on tiny steps. They arranged themselves obediently on the pillows at his feet, still whispering and laughing.

On a silver tray on a small tea table in front of the Emperor was a pile of miniature silk purses. Each was beautifully brocaded with the gold and blue imperial phoenix. Minghuang gave each of them a purse, starting with the oldest in the strict order of their rank and age among the household wives. He complimented them separately on their beauty and on the progress of their musical talents. One at a time, they rose and thanked him and he whispered secrets in their ears. Some of them blushed and giggled, and Yang Kuo-chung imagined that in the weeks ahead they would each elaborate on what the Emperor had told them, embroidering on his special message to her, until she became in her own mind the "Imperial Father's favorite." They'd bicker and laugh, he also imagined, trying always to cover up the frustrations of their secluded, cloistered lives. Looking at the poignant beauty of these women, he felt sorry. Such a waste. Yang Kuo-chung observed Precious Consort studying the harem musicians as they opened their purses. He knew what each woman was looking for—a wafer-thin jade coin which would indicate that she had won that night with the Emperor. And though Precious Consort looked with a penetrating eye, the women gave her no clue. Whoever had discovered the jade coin with the scudding cloud and vulvate mushroom and peach design was not revealing it. So that is what is bothering Baby Cousin tonight, thought the Fox. She is not covering her jealousy very well; it is easy to see it in her eyes and in the set of her mouth. He glanced at the Lady of Kuo's profile and tried to imagine his own feelings if she were to show interest in some other man. No, he thought; I would not like it very much. Not very much at all. But Baby Cousin and I are in very different positions.

Now An Lu-shan was joining the women on the cushions around the Emperor's feet. How far, thought Yang Kuo-chung, is this grotesque satire going to be carried? There was one purse left on the table. The Emperor picked it up, held it in his hand as if weighing it, and then, grinning, tossed it at An Lu-shan, who snatched it from the air. While the scandalized women tittered and covered their mouths, the barbarian opened his purse with exaggerated slowness and reached his thick fingers inside. He felt around with a worried expression, as if he couldn't find anything in there; then girlish delight spread across his heavy features as he drew out a coin and held it up for everyone to see. It was all a joke, of course; Yang Kuo-chung knew that one of the ladies had received the real coin and would be going to the Emperor's bedchamber that night; but he did not enjoy thinking, even in fun, about such a repellant coupling as the Emperor and the huge bearded woman.

"I hope that my meager talents will please you tonight, my Imperial Father," An Lu-shan said in a falsetto voice while bowing his great stupid form nearly to the ground.

"I am sure that they will disgust me, my porcine concubine . . . and I am in fear, as well—for my life depends solely on the mounting position that you choose."

People laughed while Yang Kuo-chung shuddered with distaste and reached for his wine cup.

"Then you don't think he's cute, Cousin?" the Lady of Kuo goaded, nudging him in the side.

Now An Lu-shan was on his feet and doing a silly little dance. Precious Consort was smiling faintly now. I know what you are wishing, Baby Cousin, thought the Fox; you are wishing that An Lu-shan was your only rival for the Emperor's favors.

Yang Kuo-chung turned to the Lady of Kuo. "Kittens and children are cute. I don't find Sogdians cute, my beautiful cousin, and I doubt that I ever will. In fact, I don't even find Sogdian children cute, now that you have raised the issue."

"Well, he is a very good friend of mine, and I hope you can bring yourself to be polite to him."

"For whose sake? Yours or his?"

She thought about it for a moment before answering.

"Mostly for mine."

"In that case, I will make a gentlemanly effort."

"Thank you. Because he is coming toward us now," she said, dipping her head in greeting.

It was too late for Yang Kuo-chung to escape. He turned his head just as An Lu-shan heaved himself down on the cushions next to the Lady of Kuo. From this proximity, Yang Kuo-chung could see that the barbarian was flushed and more than a little bit drunk. He was smiling broadly at her, obviously expecting more praise and compliments on his "performance."

"Am I your prize student?" he said to her.

"You show a lot of promise," she said, "but you are far too eager for attention to be a serious musician," she said, smiling.

"I cannot help it if I am so beautiful that they can't take their eyes off me!" An Lu-shan said ingenuously.

Then he leaned forward and looked around the Lady of Kuo at Yang Kuo-chung. He took a drink from his wine cup and gave the Fox a quick, subtle looking-over calculated to escape the attention of the Lady of Kuo. But not my attention, the Fox noted to himself. He nodded his head in greeting to the barbarian.

"This one has avoided me since he got here," An Lu-shan said to the Lady of Kuo with a puzzled little lift of his eyebrows.

"He is the sort of man who likes to observe, first," she said. "Then, when he becomes your friend, it is for life."

"He is handsome," said An Lu-shan. "It is plain now why there was never any hope for me. If I were a woman . . ." he said suggestively, letting his absurd hair ornaments tinkle and his eyes flutter, much to the Lady of Kuo's amusement. If you were a woman, thought the Fox, I might just lose my appetite forever.

"Aren't you a woman?" Yang Kuo-chung said pleasantly. "We all thought you were a shy and blushing new member of the Emperor's household. Young and sweet and untouched by any man."

An Lu-shan put his head back and roared in a most unladylike way, displaying his great red mouth and large molars.

"You are right on that last count," he said to the Fox, and took another drink. "I hear you are a gambler. Do you play double sixes?" His "feminine" demeanor was entirely gone now as he looked directly into Yang Kuo-chung's eyes, licking stray drops of wine from the hair around his mouth.

"I enjoy the game," the Fox answered, returning his look. "And I like a good wager."

"Then we must play sometime!" An Lu-shan declared, banging the table with his fist. "Only we won't play for money." He gave the Lady of Kuo a sidelong glance and a mischievous smile.

"How flattering!" she said. "It is every woman's dream to have men waging bets over her, as if she were a prize horse."

An Lu-shan gazed at her.

"Is she not the most beautiful creature you have ever laid eyes on?"

"Without a doubt," Yang Kuo-chung answered. "The most beautiful. Ever."

"For now, I must content myself with just looking at her. Until I win that wager!" said An Lu-shan, giving Yang Kuo-chung a leering smile.

The thoughts behind the unpleasant smile were quite plain to Yang Kuo-chung, and he felt himself bristling with anger. It was as if the man were peering through the window of their bedchamber. Who is this rude oaf who invades my privacy? He sensed the barbarian watching for some outward sign of resentment from Yang Kuo-chung. He would be damned if he would give him the slightest satisfaction.

He smiled back at An Lu-shan. "Until you win," he said, and raised his cup.

An Lu-shan leaned close to the Lady of Kuo and spoke in her ear, his eyes still on Yang Kuo-chung. "And when I do, I will teach you as much as you have taught me."

She laughed, apparently not offended by his crude suggestion.

"You will find out what love is really all about," he said, letting his paw rest on her knee.

Yang Kuo-chung felt hot blood rising to his face, but willed himself to keep his composure.

"I will teach you things that no dandy silk-trousers ever could. Secrets!" An Lu-shan grinned.

Yang Kuo-chung said nothing, but contemplated behind his set mask of indifference a truth that he had stumbled over for the thousandth time, one that he always forgot until it was staring him rudely in the face just as the barbarian general before him was doing now. There is always, no matter how perfect any situation may seem, a defect. It was necessary, a part of nature, woven into the very fabric of things, inevitable. Some part of it had to be wrong. It usually took longer for these defects to show themselves; he was grateful, at least, that this one had shown up so soon.

"I'm sure," he said to An Lu-shan, "that you are full of secrets."

An Lu-shan took his hand from the Lady of Kuo's knee, laughed, and drank more wine.

"He knows me," the barbarian said to her coquettishly.

: :

"Why do you play such absurd games with him?" Yang Kuo-chung demanded. The Lady of Kuo was removing the pins that had kept her hair in an impossible architectural structure all evening. He lay on the bed; she sat near an open window letting the cool night air bathe her skin.

"At least you recognize that they are only games," she said. "That is all they are. Just games."

"And you think they are harmless."

She turned and looked at him fiercely. "Of course they are harmless! He, too, knows that it is all nothing but fun and amusement!"

Yang Kuo-chung sat up and rearranged the pillows behind him. "I know that it is the fashion among you women to have as a plaything some exotic creature. It makes you feel daring and intrepid, and you like the little whiff of danger inherent in it, and the admiring looks of your peers. 'See what *I* have found,' you say."

"He enjoys it as much as we do," she said sharply.

"But you expect *him* to recognize the boundaries of the game as you do! Do you think that An Lu-shan is some obedient pet, some trained bear? Maybe it *is* a game to him. But why are you so sure that you and he are playing the same game?" Yang Kuo-chung leaned forward emphatically. "How do you know what kind of games he really likes to play?"

Exasperated, she put her comb down. "This is absurd," she said. "I cannot believe that you could be jealous of him!"

"I admit that I am not happy to see his hand resting on your leg. And I certainly cannot bear the thought of that mountain of lard lying on top of you. And I don't enjoy watching him whisper obscene suggestions in your ear. But I am not *jealous*," he said with feeling, "because I don't believe that you mean to go any further than the game-playing with him. But it is horrible and grotesque to me to see this little mock flirtation going on. It means one thing to you, but it means something entirely different to him. Doesn't it bother you that his mind is teeming with pictures of himself *having* you in every way possible? Do you enjoy knowing that your 'pet' is thinking such thoughts about you? What makes you think that you can toy with a man like that? Because it is the fashion?"

"Really," she said. "It is *your* imagination that is running wild. He has been an excellent student, musically and in other respects. He came here knowing nothing of civilized ways, and I offered to teach him. He is grateful. He likes to joke and play—but that is all! The rivalries of men never cease to amaze me," she said, turning to the window. "They are formed out of almost nothing. Monsters that you fashion out of a suggestion here, a jealousy there, a suspicion over there—and then you breathe life into them and believe in their reality!"

"Do you see the rivalry as only coming from me?" he asked, keeping his voice calm. "Did you not see the pleasure he took in flaunting his audacity in my face? And he insulted me! You heard him call me a dandy, a 'silk-trousers.' "

"He meant it as no insult!" she declared. "He was acknowledging the difference between you and him. It was a joke, a harmless joke! And this subject is becoming most tedious!" She was standing now, hands on her hips, looking down at him. Her hair was loose and her eyes were angry.

Maybe she was right. Maybe he was going too far. Not that he could ever find An Lu-shan anything but odious; he could never take a liking to him or find his boorish antics hilarious the way everybody else seemed to. And not that he didn't believe that the man despised him, saw him as an enemy, for being who and what he was. But perhaps the real danger lay in making more of it than he should. Pride and a short temper were, he knew, two of his worst shortcomings, and his probable downfall. He sighed. He did not want her angry, or tired of him, or thinking that he was a hothead. He took her hand and gently pulled. She resisted a little, and he pulled a little harder. He smiled; she tried not to. He looked sad. Then she did smile and allowed herself to topple over onto him.

"You're such a damned fool," she said.

"I know it, I know it," he said, burrowing his face into her hair. "Are you planning on leaving me now, tonight, while I sleep?"

"Not tonight. It would be too much trouble."

"Then I have a surprise for tomorrow," he said mysteriously.

She gave him an inquisitive look. "All right," she said. "I'll wait until tomorrow night to leave you."

::

Yang Kuo-chung rolled the thick stem of the *hung-hsun* lovingly between the thumb and forefinger of his right hand. Many centuries ago the fabled Emperor Han Wu-ti had praised the shimmering luxuriance of the mushroom's velvety red cap. According to the legends, they had grown up mysteriously in the dank, blessed earth of an imperial construction site. At the moment of the auspicious discovery, Han Wu-ti had halted all work, calling in shamans and necromancers to offer up the appropriate prayers to the spirits of the sacred mushroom—the *ling-chih*. Geomancers had swarmed over the site, spinning their compasses over the branches and stems, the elements and directions, and pointing their divining rods this way and that around the magical spot.

So this was the wicked fruit of the magicians, the Lady of Kuo said with a crafty smile that he found provocative and sensual. He passed the beautiful faded crimson mushroom with the white speckles to her and said to look at it closely. He told her that she was looking at a doorway to magic. He knew that she was willing to go through that door, a place where the barriers between the real and the unreal were not so definite. A place where anything could happen, and would if you were willing to believe it. She was his erotic Grand Queen Mother of the West—his Hsi Wang Mu.

She told him stories her father (and perhaps my father, he thought) had told her when she and her sisters and brother were children. During his early days with the Censorate office, he had traveled to the distant province of Fukien to register families living there, and there he had encountered a strange mountain tribe who worshiped a god called "Mani" and who ate the sacred mushrooms. They even drank their own urine after the kidney's yin had recycled the stored *chi* and the yang organs had thoroughly processed the potent fluids that then flowed down through the bladder. Yang Kuo-chung smiled at her when she told him this. He said that he could well imagine drinking hers, but not his own. In fact, he said, whether she had eaten mushrooms or not, the prospect was quite pleasant to him. She slapped his arm, hard.

Now she was looking at the mushroom she had heard about since child-hood. She turned it around slowly in her hands, letting the light caress it, catch it this way and that. Yang Kuo-chung watched as her eyes shone with excitement and curiosity. She did not see him smile at her. He was touched by the way the infinite magic of the universe was manifest in her. It was something few women could express; she was his equal.

The appearance of the fungus was not what she had expected, she told him. It was not the shiny lacquer-surfaced mushroom so often mistaken for the fabled *ling-chih*. It was a soft, smooth red-and-white, like a sun-faded piece of silk. This was the real thing, Yang Kuo-chung told her: the legendary soma of India; the *ling-chih* of the ancient historian Pan Ku. The magician he had got them from had assured him of it and had allowed Yang Kuo-chung to sample a small amount. The inebriation he had experienced far exceeded that from wine, he told her. Perhaps the legends were true that the Fukien tribes had found the elusive magical fungus in China in the coastal mountains where they lived. Her father would not have been, after all, so very far from those fantastic isles, Tsu and Peng-lai, of the Eastern Sea—and it was known that they grew there.

He told her how he had come to possess these particular mushrooms. While traveling the Silk Road, he had won them from an old wizard in a game of double sixes: When it got down to the final stakes, it was either the wizard's nubile young bride or these precious treasures. Yang Kuo-chung had chosen the mushrooms. In the proper fruit brines and soups, they were quite tasty, the magician had told him. And their effect, when consumed in moderate portions, was nothing short of miraculous and inspiring. But the old wizard had also warned him that these mushrooms were particularly potent.

They had been picked, the man had claimed, from the lush, piney slopes of hills with particularly strong yin confluences and to the east of a rocky prominence—a powerful green dragon, so the geomancers would say. Taken in too great an amount, the old man had admonished, the excessive yin power of these mushrooms would have a disastrously disturbing effect upon the harmony of the five yin organs. These organs would become unable to regulate and store the essential *chi* and spirit, altering the "sea of marrow"—the brain—and thereby upsetting the sensitivity of eyes and ears and disturbing the equilibrium. Quite simply put, you would hallucinate. Yang Kuo-chung was told that the power of the mushroom enabled you to see things that were not there—or perhaps things that were not meant to be seen. That was the danger of excess. Yang Kuo-chung knew there were dangers, but the adventure was simply too tempting to ignore. He had never believed in elixirs of immortality—he felt too strongly that there was a karmic purpose to a finite span of life. But he did believe in the mushroom's potent magic.

It will be a great adventure for us, he said to her, and saw on her face the same daring curiosity and hunger for experience that he knew was plain on his own. Shall we, he asked? They looked at each other and laughed.

He took the mushroom away from her, tore a small section from the gill, and dropped the piece into a silver bowl. He began to prepare the juice as the wizard had instructed him, a broth that would draw out the deep, hidden yin.

::

They ate the mushrooms that morning in the Lady of Kuo's apartments, dipping them in the brine of the breakfast fruits and drinking the broth the mushrooms had sat in. They agreed that they were, in fact, quite tasty.

They laughed and played, and the time passed and the room became gently illuminated. Tiles and inlays flamed with color, and they noticed shimmering halos of gold and blue surrounding objects. The red colors stood out the most, like the fiery reflection of the sun on the rippling water of a pond when the day is dying. They lost themselves, transfixed by the blaze of the pillows and the vibrating colors of walls, lattices, rugs, and ornaments.

They ordered wine from the aging eunuch steward of the inner chambers. They could hear the old man muttering his disapproval to the servants in the hall; it was too early in the day for wine, he said. And when he came into the room bearing the tray, his face set in a neutral expression, they heard an echo of what he had said in the hall—but the man's mouth was shut. They looked at each other and laughed with astonishment. Time was wrong, twisted! Had it ever been correct? As the wine was being poured, they laughed again and felt as if they were swimming in the deep bright amber pools in their cups. Now the room sparkled with the soft crystal of the wind chimes. Tender shafts of light stretched through the shutters and onyxed in fine tinkling shards of dust along the polished floor. "It is time to go out," Yang Kuo-chung said. They stepped out onto the balcony.

The trees of the courtyard and distant park inhaled with the wind. The air! They could *see* it, blowing in soft, labored puffs across the landscape. And then they seemed to have the thought simultaneously: a kite! We have to fly a kite! And the kite would be like the *bonze,* the priest who could ride a dragon or rest his head on a sleeping lion. It would float their souls where their bodies could not go.

The servants brought the most beautiful and elaborate silk kite in the Lady of Kuo's collection. She owned no paper kites! The youngest servant, still a child, sent it aloft in the windy courtyard. The air was so thick and soft and warm that it seemed possible to climb up into it oneself. There were four separate cords controlling the multitiered kite, and a fifth one, a mysterious red string.

The kite climbed straight up. It spun, the tails following in perfect concentrics, the swirling ink circles of a master calligrapher. Up again. The trees, excited by the new presence in the sky, breathed more rapidly now. The warm velvet-blossomed air smothered them in sweet perfume. It inhaled! And from above, the kite hissed. Alive! It lashed its tails and snapped. It rose again with angry speed. It sped upward, whining in the split sky. The Lady of Kuo wanted Yang Kuo-chung to take the wires of the kite, but he refused. He preferred to watch, telling her he lacked the elegant skill.

She took the wires from the servant. The cords tugged at her hands and the kites dove. She jerked the strings and the four tails spun again in even tighter circles. The sky exhaled. The trees held their breath. Silence! Then the kite tails snapped and buzzed like the lashing tails of a giant insect in the hot, blue, fragrant light. She gave him a significant look, then, and pulled hard on the mysterious red cord . . .

He stared at the sky. A small bamboo box at the base of the first tier of the kite popped open. For a long time the box simply followed the kite as it disappeared over the trees and then shot up again. Then the box burst open, like some strange airborne egg, the sides collapsing outward. Color bloomed in the sky and became butterflies. A million thin translucent paper wraiths fluttered over the garden and trees. Yang Kuo-chung, enraptured, extended his vision and captured the apparitions falling as congealed light and air. And then he thought of horses. Horses!

::

It could only be the mushrooms, he thought, as they clattered out of the stables. Such ideas would never occur to a man still in full command of his senses. He laughed at that thought. No . . . it is when the mushroom is *not* in me that I am deprived of my senses. He felt as if a thin, dulling layer of habit and complacency had been stripped from his eyes, ears, nerves, and skin. He tingled and vibrated, as if the doors to his mind had been thrown wide open. A mysterious thought occurred to him: rooms without doors or windows. The mushrooms put doors where there had been none before. As many rooms as there were in the palace, there were that many again in the mind, times ten thousand. And some of them had no doors at all. Until now! The Lady of Kuo told him that the six-hundred-year-old verses of the *Wen-hsin Tiao-lung* spoke about inspiration and how it leapt out at you suddenly, like a tiger! Yang Kuo-chung had never attempted to decipher anything so arcane as a treatise on literature, but this image he understood. A tiger! A perfect comparison. This morning, inspiration had leapt out at him like a tiger: They would ride through the halls of government—through the audience hall in full morning session. The Lady of Kuo accepted the inspiration without hesitation, lashing her animal and challenging him to follow.

They rode their horses over the cobblestones of the Orchid Terrace, kicking up chips of stone, then up the wide marble stairs. A few old ministers and their servants looked at them with mild curiosity; others were startled and ran for cover. The mushrooms opened the door. They sprang onto the first tier of wide marble stairs of the Grand Harmony Hall and pushed up, horses laboring mightily beneath them, past the posturing bronzes of giant lions, past the crouching dogs, thousand-year-old turtles, slender cranes, and golden deer that flanked the final flight of stairs. They rode through the clouds of sweet yellow smoke together, hooves ringing deafeningly across the sacred polished floors of the audience hall. He had never known such a satisfying sound in his life. It penetrated to his bones. And as he watched the sparks fly from the stones beneath Kuo's horse, she was Tien-mu, the mother of lightning, and he was Lei-kung, lord of thunder, passing through the clouds together. A god and goddess of hideous form—wings, beaks, and talons of owls—in flight through the sky.

Then someone stepped out in front of them, waving his arms for them to stop. Yang Kuo-chung pulled hard on the reins to avoid running into the man. His horse reared and spun, its hooves sliding out from under it on the slippery marble. Then he was down, landing hard on his back, his feet flying against the great brass drum at the end of the hall. As a tremendous boom rang out, he saw the glimmering coffered ceiling of wooden lace of red and gold, tiles and pillars of dragons and stars, waves, clouds, and pearls and a sea of rustling robes and astonished faces. Then the back of his head hit the floor with a thud.

He awoke to her face, pale with anxiety, looking down at him. His head was in her lap. Her hair hung in loose, damp strands about her forehead. When his eyes opened, she laughed with relief. He found himself admiring her pearly teeth and full lips, and wondering for a moment if he was dead.

Six servants from the inner household staff fanned them. A cold towel with a block of ice from the cool palace basements was held against the top of his head.

"We were worried for a bit, Stupid Cousin," she said.

He moaned and squeezed his temples between his hands. He made no effort to rise.

"Your topknot saved you from cracking your skull like an egg."

: :

He had received an unexpected letter that morning. Not only was it unexpected, but it had been tampered with—opened, examined, and resealed. In the top right-hand corner the seal of the office of the military governor in P'inglu Province—his good friend Li Shih-chih—was still visible. But the other original ten postal seals were gone, and there had been no effort to remove the obvious row of circular impressions on the paper left by the missing seals.

The letter was folded inside a thick inner envelope, the kind used for important documents and missives demanding secrecy. But whatever confidentiality Li Shih-chih had intended had been violated. What was this?

Yang Kuo-chung was not accustomed to feeling uneasy about such things. He had always been able to draw privacy and discretion around himself effortlessly, especially where the imperial mails were concerned. But it seemed as if those days were gone. Long-distance missives were no longer secure in the postal system, which, until he received this letter, had seemed foolproof. Each well-garrisoned postal station would affix its own individual nearly unforgeable wax seal alongside the others on the fold. Each seal would be dated with a numerical code indicating the cycle of stems and branches and hours. Since no wax seal could be properly duplicated, and a break on any of the dated seals would indicate the approximate region and time in which the letter was violated, investigations by the imperial authorities were swift and efficient. The perpetrators were more frequently than not captured, usually named as spies, and hung without trial on the same day. And so it had continued to be even after the death penalty had been practically eliminated. Yang Kuo-chung had always felt confident with this knowledge—until now.

But the extraordinary thing about this particular case was the audacity: No attempt had been made to hide the act; no effort, even, to forge the seals. This was disturbing. The trespasser who did not think it necessary to cover his trail was far more dangerous than the one who took pains. A wicked smile is always more insidious than a covert look. The missing seals were simply replaced by a single stamp—two tiny characters, Ssu-k'ung, emblazoned on a purple background—the stamp of the office of Chief Minister Li Lin-fu.

Yang Kuo-chung had been able to read some of the letter, but found most of it puzzling. He realized that if he was to understand every nuance, he would have to ask for the assistance of someone with better literary skills than his own whom he could trust. He had been tempted to take Kao Li-shih, the Emperor's eunuch, into his confidence. He liked him and felt that he was discrete and trustworthy, but he didn't know him well enough yet—and so held back. He could think of only one other person. And he had reservations about this person for only one reason—which was that the name of An Lu-shan appeared toward the end of the letter. The Lady of Kuo was very fond of An Lu-shan.

He had the letter in the inner pocket of his jacket. The Lady of Kuo stood over him, sponging the sweat and dirt from his forehead after a polo match. They were resting in the shade of a tent near the imperial playing fields. She had remarked on how poorly he had played that day, which indeed he had. His head still hurt from his fall in the audience hall the week before, and he was preoccupied with the letter in his pocket.

"Your riding was an amateur display, at best," she said, dragging the ivory-handled boar-bristle brush painfully through his tangled hair. She started to rebraid his topknot. "Next time, perhaps you should play against the imperial children."

"Perhaps I will," he said absently.

Children. Children's games. When does that exact moment occur when you give them up? Games that had been so important, that had consumed so much of your time and energy. You grow up, and one day you look back and realize that you have left them behind. No more "tease the crane" or "jackstones." No more hobbyhorses or false mustaches. Your hands are no longer busy with the intricacies of "cat's cradle." You don't recall exactly when you stopped, but you surely did.

Usually, her remarks about his riding would provoke him to defend himself, to prove he was as good as he had ever been. Today, he didn't care. Discreetly, he felt the letter through the fabric of his jacket. He might not be able to recall his final game of "jackstones," but he would always remember the day the letter with the missing seals arrived. He felt that he was being thrust rudely, headlong, into some new kind of awareness.

He looked around them. They were quite alone. The nearest tent was well out of earshot. He signaled the steward waiting nearby to leave them, then drew the letter from his pocket.

As soon as she saw it, the Lady of Kuo stopped brushing his hair. "Don't cover it with your arm," she said. "Let me see it."

There was, he reflected, no going back now. Once her curiosity had been aroused, that was it. He would have to trust her—no matter what the letter said about An Lu-shan. He sighed and put it in her hand.

"It was already opened once, before it was in my hands," he said.

"It is from your friend Li Shih-chih, isn't it?"

"How did you know that?"

"Who else from P'inglu?" she said, pointing to the stamp of the governor's office in the corner.

"Then I guess I would do well to try to hide nothing from you this morning."

"No doubt the best course of action," she said, and opened the letter.

"It is not Li Shih-chih's seal of office for much longer. He is in his last month of service there. He has been replaced. And do you know by whom?" He watched her read, saw her brow wrinkle as she took in the meaning of the words. "Your adorable fat man," he said.

"I know about his promotion," she said, looking up from the letter. "It is no secret. And it was certainly not my idea, Cousin." She continued to read.

"It is difficult to say *whose* idea it was. But that is why I need your help. I need you to read it aloud to me. I trust your accuracy with the characters better than my own—and I trust your discretion," he said unsmilingly, searching her face.

"Do you trust me?" she asked with equal seriousness.

He looked at her. "Yes," he said simply.

She began to read the letter:

"My dearest friend, Yang Kuo-chung:

"I hope that this missive finds you in a better set of circumstances than I. I am a very frightened man. But I am frightened more for the innocent members of my family, my staff, and their families than I am for myself, although I can say that fear for myself is also growing daily. These are strange and disturbing times, yet I still cannot say what it is that so frightens me. I have endeavored to conceal it from the others, but each day my act of deceit where family and friends are concerned, especially my wife, grows more difficult to maintain. I sense deputies and agents of another among my own staff. But I am certain of nothing. I suspect everyone and no one.

"As you have probably already heard, I have been replaced as military governor of the P'inglu region. The maintenance of my household is not in question, as I have been provided with a generous pension. But I feel that there is something more insidious at work here. Fanyang and Hopei Provinces have gone the same way as P'inglu. Increasingly, appointments to the military governorships in these northern frontier province territories is going to those of non-Chinese origins—unlettered barbarians—because, perhaps, it is felt that they can better understand the nature of the enemy—northern tribal peoples. That is one explanation. I do not believe it.

"With the removal of the investigative military Censorate from any real role of importance, military affairs can be managed without the righteous interference of honest inspectors. This is a dangerous trend. The body of government must always be diligent in exercising limits upon itself. Our military leaders must not be free to make decisions without the strict and abiding counsel of moral leaders. In this respect our eunuch investigators have served us well. Until now. They too are finding their ranks reduced and themselves less than useful, their pride quieted by bribes and their sense of worth and noble purpose corrupted by fat pensions from the Ministry of War. Should any of these well-meaning Censorate inspectors continue, out of habit, to be diligent in their sense of duty, should any of them undertake to look into the delegation of military authority, to inspect the practicality and actions of military leaders in the colonies, or to look into their ramifications for the local populace, to count the stores, to examine the merit of any expensive campaigns, the hardship and plight of soldiers and their families, then they will themselves be hounded by scandalous lies and have all they can do to fight charges of treason and the ever-present threat of blacklisting that confronts them and their families.

"This is the situation as I am leaving it. I can stay here with my family no longer. But before I leave you, there is one more matter. I have discovered much about this An Lu-shan that should be of considerable interest to you . . ."

The Lady of Kuo turned the sheet over and stopped reading. Then she turned the other pages over again one by one. She looked from back to front. She turned the outer envelope up and looked underneath it.

"Why don't you keep reading, Cousin?"

"This is very strange . . ."

"What?"

"The letter ends. I mean the part from Li Shih-chih ends here. See!" She turned the page over for him to examine. "But there is more on another page in another hand. A very delicate, feminine calligraphy starting here . . . My instincts tell me it is a very practiced female hand." She held it up to him. "Don't you agree? I didn't know that there were any lettered *women* on Li Shih-chih's staff."

"Let me see that." He took the bottom page out of her hand and looked closely at the last sheet of handwriting. She was right. It was definitely somebody else writing, and definitely female, two facts that had escaped his attention the first time he had tried to read the letter. Even the paper was different. Again, no attempt had been made to hide anything.

"Read the rest of it," he said, giving it back to her.

She resumed:

> "Master An Lu-shan is a most worthy addition to the critical northern defenses of the T'ang against the ever-present danger of the Mongol tribal nations—Hsi, the Khitan, the Turks. He is a rallying point for our faithful Uighur allies. He is an inspiration of courage and fortitude, a soldier to lead us to everlasting peace and stability in the service of our Divine Son of Heaven. Ten thousand years to the Emperor Ming-huang and the glorious T'ang and to his loyal servant, Military Governor-General An Lu-shan."

"That's it, Cousin?" he asked.

"That's it, Cousin." She looked at him. "Well—you see, our An Lu-shan is not so bad as you have supposed."

"How can you be so foolish?" he exclaimed. "This is a pile of dung. The last part of this note did not come from Li Shih-chih or anyone remotely connected with his office. I know my friend Li Shih-chih too well. Your fat buffoon, I would wager, has friends in high places."

"Minghuang . . . ?"

"No. He is too busy playing, indulging himself, reconstructing his pleasure palaces with the funds I so nobly scrape off the taxes and pass through the Ministry of Finance. Besides, the Son of Heaven does not operate in this fashion. There are others at the pinnacle of power, my naive cousin. This letter was intercepted. Li Shih-chih obviously had something very important to tell us about the barbarian general. He had learned something of crucial importance; this was, no doubt, to be his parting message to us. Those words were taken out, but the person who did it left the first part of this letter intact as a warning to any of us who might get too curious. And look who sends us that warning, my love." He showed her the seal. "None other than Chief Minister Li Lin-fu."

"But the note, the handwriting at the end, is so pure, so clean and simple—as if it were the writing of a . . ." She stopped and shook her head. "My idea is too foolish."

"No, Cousin! Say it! Maybe I am having the same thoughts!"

"It just seems to me, my dear Fox, that although the calligraphy has a delicate sense of rhythm and flow . . . that somehow, there is no spirit behind the brush, no power or . . ."

"Or sophistication, wisdom, form . . . li. That's the word you were looking for isn't it? Li." Yang Kuo-chung didn't wait for her answer. "It looks as if it were executed by a child," he said. "That's what you are thinking, isn't it? The soft little hand of a female child."

"A child," she agreed. Now the Lady of Kuo seemed to find her own idea difficult to believe. Incredulously, she said it again. "The hand of a child . . . ?"

::

Yang Kuo-chung, president of the Ministry of Finance, sat in his office. The rich fragrance of new sandalwood cupboards filled his nostrils, and the bright silks of the new cushions he had ordered were beautiful in the late morning light. But the satisfaction he should have felt eluded him. If ever there was a time to compose a letter to his family justifying his existence, this was it. Now he really had something to tell them. And to write the letter, he could have, if he desired them, the talents of all the great and famous members of the Han Lin Academy of Letters from which to choose his composer. Compared to the first crude, embarrassing attempt of his youth, it would be a masterpiece.

But somehow he was not as interested in rubbing his parents' noses in his success as he once had been. He had seen to it that they received ample pensions, and that was sufficient personal vindication. The only time his old feelings roused themselves at all was when he thought about his mother's sisters. Father and Uncle, he knew, had aged and were considerably faded, but that bickering clutch of aunties never seemed to get any older. All he had to do was close his eyes and he could recall with perfect fidelity their shrill, nagging voices, worse than any eunuch falsetto, gaining strength, not losing it, as they advanced into old age.

What was it about old women? The old men became bent and weak, but the women just got shriller and tougher with time. Women, he speculated, must be nature's way of protecting the wizened men after their strength and virility were gone. It seemed as if what was essential to the greater physical strength of men was more immediately vulnerable to age and deterioration. How many tales had he heard as a boy from the storytellers about some crone, carrying twice the weight from the well on her shoulders as she ever did in her youth, coming upon the ghost, the weak unfixed apparition, of her departed husband? The husband long dead, turned to dust and shadow, and *she* still doing the chores . . . Is that how it would be, he mused, with the Lady of Kuo and himself? Well, my aunties, if I ever do write a letter, it will be for *your* benefit alone.

Yes, he had secured a prestigious position in the high government in true Yang style, stepping over the usual protocol, the Emperor giving him the appointment as a gift, an award, in honor of his gambling skills, his "way" with money; and yes, his office had just been redone to his specifications, with thick, new rugs, lacquered furniture, carved lattices, and scrolls and vases handpicked by himself and Kuo in the finest markets of the city. But his pleasure was hollow. Like an unwelcome cloud passing in front of the sun on a warm day, the letter from Li Shih-chih had cast a chilly gray shadow over things.

It had been weeks since the letter had actually been written. For all he knew, his friend was exiled—or worse—by now. If his report on the political climate was accurate, and Yang Kuo-chung knew Li Shih-chih to be reliable and levelheaded, then the chances were good that something terrible had already happened to him. And with the Censorate so deteriorated, the members so in fear for their lives that they slunk for cover at the slightest noise, then how would anyone ever know?

And the violation of the letter and the replacement of the text had been a clear message intended personally for Yang Kuo-chung. It was an open declaration of hostility from the office of the chief minister, and a little demonstration of Li Lin-fu's immunity to the law. His power. And Yang Kuo-chung had learned from Kao Li-shih why the Lizard was so unfriendly. It seemed that it had been years since the Emperor had made an important appointment himself without consulting his chief minister or, more often, leaving the choice entirely up to him. Li Lin-fu probably had someone in line for the job, someone handpicked by him, answerable to him. But most likely, Kao Li-shih had said, it was the principle that had made him angry. He was used to having his own way.

Innocently, unwittingly, Yang Kuo-chung had been transformed into the enemy of this autocratic and evidently dangerous man. A man who broke postal seals—a crime that would earn anyone else the removal of his head—with impunity. A man who let certain parts of Li Shih-chih's letter speak for themselves as a tacit warning, and who removed other parts, vital information about An Lu-shan, because it didn't suit him to have too much known about the barbarian. "His" barbarian; he was making that amply clear, too. And Yang Kuo-chung detected a dark humor in the message, too—the text he had substituted, the obviously fake homage to An Lu-shan, presented mysteriously in the handwriting of a child. Figure out this riddle if you can, the message sneered. This should give you an idea of who you are up against.

What had Li Shih-chih wanted to tell him about An Lu-shan? It was infuriating not to know. Frustrating and infuriating. He was certain that whatever it was, it was quite different from the insipid tribute in little girl's handwriting. He snorted with disgust to think of how the fat one had everybody flummoxed. Especially the Emperor. This very morning, Yang Kuo-chung had heard news that had appalled him.

There was to be an imperial commission: a portrait, to be executed by the greatest of the figure painters, Han Kan. A portrait of General An Lu-shan. The Lady of Kuo had told him the details, and he could scarcely believe his ears.

The silk, she said, had been chosen, and its surface sized. The scroll painting would measure nearly ten feet when fully unrolled and would commemorate, in one stroke, several grand events. For one, the foaling of an auspiciously marked mare in the imperial stables coincided with the Emperor's decree of the renaming of the royal reign period to *Tien Pao*—Heavenly Jewel. The new title for the reign period—some thirty years after Minghuang had established his first—was to mark the beginning of a period of unbroken peace with the barbarians in the north and their submission and supposed allegiance to the T'ang.

And, of course, at the center of this grand effort of the empire and of the Ministry of War, and hence at the center of the painting, would be the great Sogdian general An Lu-shan—now raised to military governor of the vast P'inglu region, replacing the loyal and honest Li Shih-chih. Gods! It was one effrontery after another! The whole thing would have been merely an absurd joke if it were not so frightening.

An Lu-shan was to be depicted sitting proudly astride a magnificent dappled stallion. His bulk, which already exceeded the ample roundness of a prosperous magistrate, was to be further exaggerated with intricate representations of leather, lacquer, sharkskin, cinnabar, and colorful silks and topped with an arrogant blaze of lacquered gold and silver escutcheons—a kind of idealization of grand armor representing the warrior's acts of appeasement more than his acts of war. The costume would make him look more like a giant insect than a brave warrior, Yang Kuo-chung thought.

And the painting would be accompanied by lengthy colophons, executed by a famous calligrapher, telling the legends of the dragon horses: how dragons came out of an icy lake in faraway Kucha and changed form in order to couple with mares of a noble breed. The offsprings from these unions, so the colophons would note, were very spirited stallions. They would further describe how these horses were worthy of and suitable for the military governor and general An Lu-shan, who was himself born of yang and fire, red skies and comets. And finally, the colophons would further extol the virtues of General An Lu-shan by telling us how the nation's eight hundred thousand imperial horses and its cavalry should look to General An's example and his inspiration.

The rest of the scroll would be occupied with the figures of barbarian Hsi and Khitan chieftains, who, with their officers and grooms, would all be paying homage. The whole thing was, in Yang Kuo-chung's opinion, dreadful rubbish. He took Li Shih-chih's letter from under a piece of polished stone on his desk, opened it and smoothed the paper, and read again his friend's last words: ". . . But before I leave you, there is one more matter. I have discovered much about this An Lu-shan that should be of considerable interest to you . . ."

Yang Kuo-chung sat at his desk and thought about the north and the many friends and connections he had there—friends in common with Li Shih-chih. There had to be a way to get through to one of them, to find out . . . The postal system, obviously, was out of the question. How, then? He sat until the afternoon sun hit his eyes at an uncomfortable angle, forcing him to move.

Three days later, a message was brought to his office by a eunuch he had not met before. It was an invitation to a dinner at a private home in the city. Your attendance, the man said pointedly, would be greatly appreciated. One of the guests will be the eldest son of your friend Li Shih-chih.

::

Yang Kuo-chung lay naked and covered in sweat, the bedclothes pushed into damp rumpled heaps around him. He must have been kicking and thrashing in his sleep. He had been running from something in his dreams, something he hadn't been able to see. It moved behind him, never getting any closer, but always there, invisible and breathing hard. And then he flew out of his dream like a rock thrown through a thin paper screen. He thought he had screamed, but the Lady of Kuo still slept deeply at his side. This was the third night it had happened. This would be his last night in these apartments, he decided. Even in the daytime he was beginning to feel uncomfortable at the hot springs. He no longer found any pleasure in this place. Something had soured his taste for it—the lingering mists, the mountain, the sulphured air. Something about it had gone wrong; in any case, it was too far from the Ministry of Finance offices.

There was another thing. The stars were simply too large and bright. There was no comforting gauze of soot and light between him and the firmament the way there was in the city. Here, it was all clear emptiness between him and the sky. Why did he find it disturbing in this place? It had never bothered him in the north, where the sky was ten times as vast and the night even blacker.

It would have been better, he thought now, if some great being of creation—the Hindus, Brahmins, and Taoists all had their figurative inventions, vaporous and translucent—had erected a protective canopy between earth and the stars. No more celestial portents to confuse, perplex, tantalize, and mislead the human race. Too much rampant numinosity . . .

There were ghosts here. Not the common ancestral variety that came to follow you like haranguing relatives, harassing you, mocking and scorning the daily moral poverty of your life. Not that kind, which were always with us.

The ghosts here were older, more alien. They came, he imagined, from inside the earth, up through the rocks and fissures of the hot springs. Primal, inhuman spirits looking for an opportunity to displace you and take possession of the grounds again.

He would leave tomorrow. He felt better, having made that simple decision. In the morning he would have the servants pack the few bits of personal possessions that would follow him back to his apartments at the palace. Damn the hot springs. He did not love it the way his cousins did. Baby Cousin's enthusiasm was nothing short of unbridled exuberance. To her, the grounds and buildings were the dream palaces of a child's fantasies; to him they were unpleasant, crumbled, haunted ruins. They were, in a word, tainted.

With summer all but gone and the city no longer shimmering with heat, there was no real reason to stay here. But then why did he need an excuse at all? He gave the sleeping Lady of Kuo a gentle nudge. She mumbled and rolled over.

Now he was cold, nearly shivering. The temperature had dropped and his body had dried quickly. He pulled a soft linen robe over himself and brought the bed quilts up to his waist. He pushed the mosquito netting away from his side of the canopied bed, leaned over, and pushed the window shutters out. Now that he was already gone, now that he had severed the spell that held him here, he felt free to look out.

The stars had vanished, obscured behind a thick white fog that had settled on the Nine Dragon Lake. He could still see the vaguely comforting outlines of familiar rooftops illuminated by the final crescent of the moon: the Mansion for Viewing Phoenixes, the Hall of Cock Fighting, the Delightful Spring Pavilion, the Flying Rosy Cloud Pavilion. He smiled. He couldn't feel his "ghosts" anymore. Was it because it was nearly morning, or simply that he was leaving? He thought about calling for his servant to light the reading lamp and bring him his letter chest. Instead, he lit the lamp himself and reached over and shook the Lady of Kuo. She struggled to open her eyes.

"Heavens, not again!" she said, fogged with sleep. "This is the third time you've awakened me with these nightmares. Don't you believe in letting me sleep?"

"Sit down next to me, please." Yang Kuo-chung swung his feet onto the floor and patted the cushions near him.

Reluctantly, she rolled out from under the covers and sat on the side of the bed with him, wrapping a quilt around herself. Her lips and cheeks were pale, her mothbrows smudged and undefined, and her hair hung in a thick braid. She was attentive, though tired and perhaps, he thought, just a little bit disgusted. But her voice was patient.

"What is it now, Cousin?"

"I was bothered again," he said.

"By your dreams?"

"Yes. And other things. I am leaving this place tomorrow. Will you leave your sisters here and come back to the imperial city with me?"

She thought about it, perplexed. "Perhaps. But what is this?"

"There is something wrong with this place. Can't you feel it?"

"Only nervousness from too little sleep."

"No. There is sincerely something wrong with this place. Minghuang should apply himself to his restorations in the eastern wards, his Hsing-ching palaces, and your mansions. He should give this place up, leave it to the ground squirrels and the deer and . . ."

"And what, Cousin? The ghosts?"

"Whatever. If you wish to bring it up again. It is an overwhelmingly powerful feeling. I'm not ordinarily superstitious but . . ."

"You are indeed becoming an old soothsayer. The burdens of office, Cousin?" she asked, smiling.

"There is something else I wanted to tell you about your devoted music student."

Her smile faded. "Well, I am awake now," she said. "What do you have to tell me?" She moved closer and covered his hand with her own.

"I found out what was in the missing part of the letter," he said, looking intently at her.

Her eyes became alert.

"I told you that men like our General An Lu-shan do not practice music for the sake of music," he said. "Have you ever traveled along the northern frontiers?"

"Never," she replied. "And why would I ever wish to travel in that hellish place?"

"I don't know. An imperial pilgrimage, a *fengshan*, may someday take you there. Had you been there, you would already understand what I am about to say. It is simply that the civilized world is like an old silk table covering . . ."

"Oh, this should be most inspiring, Master Yang. Do go on, please."

"The center of the cloth is fine and the fabric strong. That is the world that you know. But around the edges, it is becoming frayed and tattered. That is the world of the north. The world at the center, the world that you know, is intact now, but . . ."

"But fragile and vulnerable and ultimately threatened by the same corrosion . . ."

"There. You learn fast."

"I listen to you a great deal. I have learned to mimic."

"I suppose I should be flattered. But you will not listen to me when I talk to you about An Lu-shan."

"Military Governor An Lu-shan, now," the Lady of Kuo emphasized. "He is proud of his appointments—that he achieved them by honest work and loyal campaigns rather than by books and bribery."

"You have become quite his defender."

"And he tells Sisters and myself a very sad tale of his deliverance from death to a new life with the help of your trusted friend Li Shih-chih. And he told us how Kushan soldiers invaded his village when he was a little child, and he had to flee with the remnants of his family into Chinese territory, and how they found the Silk Road caravans and about his mother's awful death . . ."

"And did he tell you the specific facts? The details of how he was saved from the ignominy of a murdering criminal's execution?"

"He told us that he was merely a thief, and only out of desperation," she said. "He stole sheep and military provisions for his starving children. That was all. Under the T'ang code of *tzu-shou* he gave a voluntary confession and made good the stolen merchandise."

"Just a thief? Voluntary confession? Is that what he tells you? I am indeed as touched as the compassionate Maitreya." He looked at her for a few moments and put his hands on her shoulders. "Listen to me, very closely. I told you that I found out what was in the letter. Li Shih-chih's eldest son is in the city. I met with him several nights ago. His father has vanished, and he does not know where he is. But the last time father and son saw each other, Li Shih-chih told him what he knew about An Lu-shan." He saw that he had her attention, and went ahead. "For years the authorities in the northern provinces had hunted a notorious band of brigands—thieves and cutthroats who had terrorized the trade routes for years. They killed anyone standing between themselves and whatever loot they wanted; and sometimes, it seems, they killed just for the sport of it—defenseless donkey drivers, even. There had not been such a dreadful scourge on our peaceful roads for nearly one hundred and fifty years. Did you know," he asked, though of course there was no way she could have known, "that the carnage ended when An Lu-shan was captured for stealing a sheep? That seems to me to be more than a coincidence."

"That's because you are suspicious by nature, Cousin," she said, beginning to rise from the bed. "But I think you have gone too far, now."

"Have I?" He took her arm and sat her back down. "Two months ago, a thief was captured in P'inglu. He, too, was trying to steal military provisions. And he told the whole story, my love. It seems that he had heard of the success of one An Lu-shan . . . and he was unable, though it cost him his head, to resist boasting that the very same An Lu-shan had once been the leader of a band of brigands of which he, too, had been a member. Many years had gone by, but his memory for places and details was very good. And his description of the An Lu-shan that he once knew left little doubt that his former leader —petty thief, cutthroat, highwayman—is none other than our brave commissioner for foot and horse, military governor, grand and glorious defender of the empire, and prize music student of the Lady of Kuo, An Lu-shan."

She looked at him, the skepticism plain on her face. "I know nothing about the things you are telling me. This does not sound like irrefutable evidence to me, nor does it sound like the man I know. What I *do* know is that I have had nothing but good feelings about him. So have my sisters— and so has the Emperor."

"I am quite sure that your feelings about him have been nothing but good, my dear cousin. And I am sure that he has had equally good feelings toward you . . . and perhaps that is not all. I am certain he is feeling other things between his legs and wishes to pull your skirts up over your head . . ."

She turned and stared at him for a moment, then slapped him hard across the face. He did not flinch, but the sting of her hand lingered. Though he knew better, he continued. He felt irritated, raw, stretched out against himself. He didn't know what it was, but it was easy to take it out on her. He attacked her again, feeling her own pain as a balm against his own. Why was he doing this?

". . . and are *you* feeling worthy to present 'pillow and mat' to him, my dear Lady of Kuo? To teach him something aside from music and makeup?"

"Cousin, you are a damned and presumptuous fool," she said in a dangerous voice.

"Or maybe I am speaking the truth, eh?" he challenged her. "Go back to sleep. We will join the carriages in the morning, then?"

"Thank you, Master Yang, for offering to get me away from here to someplace where I might sleep at night." She patted his knee and looked at him as if she were going to kiss him. Then she hit him again—harder this time, with the full force of her fury.

She rose from the bed, threw the quilt aside, and called for her hand-maiden to remove the toiletries and hairpins that rested on the bedside stand. She asked to be escorted to her own apartments in the far wing, and left without looking back at him, her maid struggling with the ties on her robe. He knew that she didn't care whether her robe was wide open—she would have walked naked out of that room. She was angry, far angrier than he had ever seen her, and he was the cause of it.

He sat there, still feeling the perverse querulousness that had goaded him to say something he knew perfectly well to be ridiculous. He did not know why he had said it. He did not believe that there was anything between the Lady of Kuo and the barbarian. In fact, he did not know why he did anything of late.

He did not go back to sleep. He could not; his blood was surging and boiling. He looked around him. It was this place! He was sorry for the words that had come out of his mouth, but he had been unable to stop them. She had been patient with him, up to a point, patient the way a filial child is with an aged and confused parent. He did not deserve her, he felt, but like that same filial child, she stayed by him. Until now, perhaps.

What had he done? She would, he knew, still be angry with him in the morning. She would brood on the insult, and with good reason. He knew better than to go after her and pursue the matter. Don't do it, some infinitely wise and restrained part of him warned, unless you're hungry for disaster.

What would he do with the rest of his ill-spent night, his last night on the grounds for a good long time? A letter? He looked at his writing chest without interest. And to whom would he write, in any case? His old friends at the governor's office in Szechuan? Why? They could not help him with any of this.

The rest of the news brought by Li Shih-chih's son had been discouraging. Shortly after Li Shih-chih had been relieved of his position as military governor in the north, the son had left on a tour of duty in another part of the province. When he returned a few weeks later, his father had simply disappeared. The young man had traveled to Ch'ang-an because he knew that his father had had an appointment with the Ministry of War there—an appointment he had not kept. No word had been sent—no message, nothing. For a man of letters like Li Shih-chih to not write or communicate was profoundly disturbing. And the rest of the family and the household staff, the son said, had also vanished. There were no clues, no traces. They were just gone. When he failed to find his father and family in the capital, he had sought out Yang Kuo-chung. My father had told me, he said, to find you if things turned bad.

Since there was no hope of sleep, he decided that with the first light of dawn he would take a walk outside.

The mist had begun to break up when he stepped outside. It was early dawn, and though a few stars still hung in the pale sky, they did not bother him. He was quite alone.

He crossed over the steeply arched marble bridge to the other side of the Nine Dragon Lake. From there he followed the trail that led to the ancient palace restorations and eventually to the base of Mount Li Shan. The grass was high and wet with dew and hung heavily over the path, making it nearly invisible in the dim light. Through the mist he could just make out the staggered outlines of pillars and buildings ahead—shadowy eaves raised skyward like pleading fingertips.

The black perimeter of the woods was alive with the chirping and singing of awakening birds. Something in the grass, startled by his approaching feet, darted off. Ahead he heard the hoot of an owl and then saw the heavy flapping of large silent wings disappearing deep into the thick canopy of trees at the base of the mountain. From the ridge far above came the hoarse cries of crows that haunted the decayed remains of the king of Chou's beacon tower.

As he walked further, Yang Kuo-chung smelled the distinct rotten-egg odor of a warm sulphur spring before he could hear it trickling over the rocks. He climbed a few steps that led into the roofless remains of a once grand hall, surrounded by pillars and half-walls of latticed concrete and tile. He nearly stumbled into a crumbling lotus-shaped pool of fieldstone, mortar, and brick, snagging his sandal on the sharp remains of a copper spout. He caught himself just in time. He stared down into the ruined pool and saw, for only a moment, an image of his body sprawled there, neck broken, sightless eyes turned toward the sky. He would have to pay more attention to where he walked, he told himself—the ruins were ghosts, too. The whole place was just like this jagged hole that he had almost fallen into.

Wasn't that really it? Wasn't all of the hot springs a dangerous, primal sinkhole hiding behind a seductive facade of decaying history? It lured you in, and then swallowed you up.

There was not one inch of the place that was not infected. Yang Kuo-chung felt certain now that he was one of its victims. It had made him a prisoner of his own childish sullenness and temper, had rendered him unable to control himself. Even the restoration of these exquisite tiled lotus baths for the Precious Consort and her sisters would not change the insidious atmosphere here. New tiles and mortar, colorful glazes and inlay would only be a thin covering for what he felt to be some vile, unmerciful purpose at the core of its being.

A being. That was it, of course. Why hadn't he realized it sooner? It was as if the whole hot springs was a *being*. His dreams had been trying to tell him that. Something breathing but never getting any closer. The being, he perceived now, was everywhere on the hallowed grounds, in the ancient palaces, the baths. It never got any closer because he was right there in the middle of it; it was already on top of him like the "sitting ghosts" of frightening childhood stories. They sat on the chests of sinful people as they lay in bed, squeezing the air from their lungs and hissing like vipers. And now he understood just what these "sitting ghosts" really were: they were yourself.

He stood up, annoyed with himself for succumbing to these thoughts. Thoughts that border on superstitious nonsense, he warned himself. But something *was* wrong. Something had made him lash out at the Lady of Kuo. He had been on edge, troubled, for weeks now. He felt that he was losing his equanimity. And it was not just because of the disturbing news reaching him from the north—there was something else, and he couldn't deny what he felt: it was the hot springs.

Not that all of his bad feelings about the place had such intangible sources. At Precious Consort's "suggestion," the Emperor had begun work again on this far too expensive project. It had annoyed him to see so much money slipping quietly from the public tax coffers into the imperial funds—money that could be better spent. There was very little he could do about it; Li Lin-fu had seen to that. The money was there, no doubt, to keep the Emperor preoccupied and out of the chief minister's way. There were plenty of pleasure palaces here, already restored and sumptuously magnificent. It was sinful that there should be more. It was not that he was opposed to high living. Done right, high living could, he believed, be an instrument to cultivate the higher sensibilities. It was the right of every ascended being. But the extent and the cost of it here was simply criminal. It was too much, that was all.

He wanted to get back into the meadow again, back onto the path. He moved quickly to the other side of the hall past two more identical pools and the remains of low retaining walls and down the rear steps and onto the grass.

He went toward the distant border of trees and into the wide open area that spread out at the base of the mountain. Not too far from the path there were deer and gazelle grazing in the tall wet grass, ghostlike in the early morning mist. He watched them for a while, phantoms moving in the silvery white fog light, the delicate heads on long graceful necks rising up from their foraging now and again to listen, poised in silence. Maybe, he thought, they *were* ghosts. He was a ghost to himself, now.

Maybe, he thought, these "ghosts" that seemed to be everywhere here were only his own guilt, come to sit on his chest and squeeze the breath out of him. But he couldn't wait to leave. He would go in the morning, as planned, and just hope that the Lady of Kuo would forgive him.

He continued down the path with no particular idea in mind of where he was. Something caught his eye then—something that anyone who didn't have his eyes would have missed. He bent down, lifting his robe from his knees, and pushed the high grass away from the slender white polished skull of a gazelle. Here and there bits of leathered flesh and hair still clung to it. And then he saw, in the dirt down among the roots of the grass, bits of shiny red, blue, and green. He dug around for more of it. They appeared to be pieces of a statue or ornament.

To his delight and amazement, he found intact the multicolored *san-tsai* whiskered head of a porcelain five-clawed celestial dragon. Then he uncovered the great fluked tail and the flaming pearl embraced in the coiled serpentine body. It was, even shattered, as perfect and exquisite a work of Kaolin porcelain as he had ever seen—a superbly rendered imperial dragon dropped, no doubt, from some artisan's crate. A gem from the great kilns, broken and forgotten here.

Then a wonderful idea came to him. He would take the pieces, clean them, and put them back together. He would present the mended dragon to the Lady of Kuo as a reconciliation gift. What could be more perfect, more appropriate? A shattered dragon restored to life. The sun began to warm his back now as he carefully excavated the ground with a stick. It would be no good unless he found every last piece.

12

Generals Depart

Though outwardly Li Lin-fu had quelled all opposition, he had not been able to prevent those who had been his instruments from conceiving ambitions of their own. There was . . . above all Yang Kuo-chung. The latter in particular, though outwardly obsequious, was secure in the emperor's favour and beginning to conduct secret intrigues against his rival.

—*Edwin Pulleyblank*

With the death of Niu Hsien-ko, Yang Kuo-chung rose quickly to fill the vacuum.

—*Anonymous Chinese (ninth century)*

FROM his quarters at the hot springs, Kao Li-shih could hear laughter. The Emperor and An Lu-shan were having another of their all-night drinking and gaming parties. They were far away from him, across a small lake, but in the still night air their voices carried clearly over the water. They were having a friendly argument about horses. The Ferghanian pony, An Lu-shan was saying, is by far the king of horses—fast, hardy, responsive, faithful to its master. Compared to the animals bred in my own stables here from a rich Arab bloodline begun by my grandfather using Khuttal and Tukharan breeds, your Ferghanian ponies are just mutts, the Emperor declared. Better than no horses at all, I concede, but mutts. Is that so? An Lu-shan challenged the Emperor. When I return from the north, I shall bring with me a pair of horses: a mare and a stallion. When you see these horses, you'll start a whole new line and name it after me in my honor, that's how grateful you'll be. An Lu-shan, said the Emperor, laughing, I don't need a horse that can carry the weight of two men. Your jealousy is showing, An Lu-shan replied; you know that a woman prefers a man with plenty of fat on him, that she can lie on like a soft couch. When they lie on *you,* they get poked by your bones. Is that what they've told you? asked the Emperor. That's what they all say, said An Lu-shan. Then perhaps I'd best adopt your eating habits, An Lu-shan. Will you teach me how to pad my poor old bones for the ladies?

And so on. Kao Li-shih was accustomed to the repartee. Their friendship, since the night of the performance several weeks before, had become thick. Between the Precious Consort and An Lu-shan, the Emperor was never alone at all anymore. Sometimes it would be the three of them, making plans for the latest restoration at the hot springs or how they would dress An Lu-shan to play the roles of various deities in traditional festivals that the Emperor and consort wanted to revive. Sometimes it would be all four of the sisters, the Emperor, and An Lu-shan; or the sisters, Yang Kuo-chung, and the Emperor; but never, Kao Li-shih had observed, did any of these groupings include both Yang Kuo-chung and An Lu-shan—at least not for more than a few minutes. Obviously, closer acquaintance and the passage of time was doing nothing to soften Master Yang's feelings toward the barbarian.

If anything, those feelings had worsened; it was obvious to Kao Li-shih that there was more involved than Yang Kuo-chung's mere personal distaste for An Lu-shan. There was now mutual bad feeling of some kind between the handsome Yang cousin and the general; that it had something to do with the affections of the Lady of Kuo he did not doubt. Whatever it was, Kao Li-shih knew where his own allegiance lay.

He had grown quite fond of Yang Kuo-chung, who was unfailingly pleasant and polite to him. The young man had depth to him, and Kao Li-shih appreciated the honest, straightforward way he treated the Emperor: like a friend or an equal, without a trace of fawning or overblown gratitude for favors granted. Instead, he gave the impression of a man fully aware that although fortune had for some reason singled him out for special treatment, and he was enjoying it to its fullest advantage, it had not gone to his head or blinded him to the realities of life outside his comfortable world. He had talked with Kao Li-shih about his travels in the north and his experiences and observations. His thought processes were sound and shrewd, his perspective clear and balanced. He understood the world in a way that few rich, handsome, pampered young men could.

The eunuch listened to the barbarian's hoarse laughter coming from the open pavilion where he and the Emperor were playing their third game of double sixes. His laugh always got louder and more overbearing around this time of night; Kao Li-shih knew, just from the sound of it, how much wine the general had consumed. Now the laugh had taken on a particular braying quality that was infinitely irritating to the eunuch; he stepped from the window and pulled the curtain, though he knew it would do little to protect his ears from the sound.

He was not the only one who had noticed how An Lu-shan's laugh changed. He had discussed the topic with Li Chu-erh, the general's own eunuch, who had recently been sent down from the north to join his master in the city and who knew him better than anyone. When it gets that sound to it, like a donkey in the mating season, he had said, then I get out my rags and buckets, because I can be sure that in the morning there will be a pool of whatever he had for dinner the night before either on the bed or on the floor for me to clean up.

The Emperor evidently was not bothered by An Lu-shan's laugh; he seemed, in fact, to go out of his way to elicit it. Nor did he notice the disdain the barbarian showed to Kao Li-shih himself, the way he wrinkled his nose as if he were smelling something bad. Of course, there was no reason why the Emperor should notice it, because An Lu-shan was always careful to do it when the Emperor wasn't looking. And the times when he spoke to Kao Li-shih as if he were a servant were the times when the Emperor was either absorbed in what the consort was saying or was not there at all.

Kao Li-shih sighed. But your happiness, he told himself, is not, after all, what is important. An Lu-shan worked hard to make the Emperor happy, and for that Kao Li-shih could only be grateful. The barbarian had an amazing range of acting abilities which he applied with a fierce attentiveness to the Emperor's needs. If the Emperor told a story, An Lu-shan listened with care and responded appropriately, with rage, sorrow, regret, or joy. If the Emperor talked about *his* sorrows or regrets, An Lu-shan behaved as if they were practically his own. But never, Kao Li-shih observed, was there a trace of insincerity or obsequiousness in any of this; he always managed to convey an interest that was genuine, a sympathy that was uncontrived. And he was good at things the Emperor loved to do: riding, gaming, hunting. They spent hours consulting on this or that restoration at the hot springs, and the barbarian showed remarkable acumen when it came to appointments, architecture, and decor. Kao Li-shih knew that the man could not read and write as well as a three-year-old child, but somehow he had acquired knowledge of a fairly refined sort and had sufficient wit to charm the Emperor with it. His greatest specialty, though, was acting the buffoon, making the Emperor and the sisters laugh until the tears rolled down their faces.

But Yang Kuo-chung didn't laugh, and neither did Kao Li-shih. I suppose, thought Kao Li-shih, that we are just a pair of spoilsports. But both of us have good reasons to keep our mouths shut. Master Yang finds everything else in his world quite pleasant, thanks to the Emperor, and no doubt does not want to seem ungrateful by complaining about the Emperor's pet oaf. And I? The Emperor's happiness is worth much more to me than my own, which is of little consequence. Besides, he thought, it will not be very much longer before Commissioner General An Lu-shan returns to his hide tents and cold winds to assume his new and important duties. No doubt he is a very effective military man, and what he is showing us here are the very traits that make him one. I, for one, will be relieved to have him leave and exercise his talents on the poor devils who must serve under him.

Kao Li-shih picked up the well-worn sheaf of documents he had taken from Li Lin-fu's reader that day long ago in the morning audience. At least some progress was being made here; the Emperor had agreed to examine the papers and hear what Kao Li-shih had to say.

Master Yang Kuo-chung had been most helpful to Kao Li-shih in this matter. Kao Li-shih was growing to trust him and had shown him the papers, relating to him the travesty of Li Lin-fu sitting behind the screen intoning in the Emperor's place while systematically and deviously draining the Censorate's power. To Kao Li-shih's great satisfaction, Yang Kuo-chung had been disturbed and visibly concerned to learn that such a thing was going on under the Emperor's oblivious nose. He had told Kao Li-shih that he would do what he could; perhaps, he had said, all that is needed is a fresh voice, Master Kao. And so he had broached the subject of the documents to the Emperor, and mentioned Kao Li-shih's wish to discuss them. Apparently, he had done it in a skillful, tactful manner: The Emperor had listened and said that he would hear the eunuch out.

But, Kao Li-shih thought, I will wait until the fat one has departed for the north. I do not want any interference from him.

As he was thinking on these things, An Lu-shan's laugh came across the water, long and loud, followed by the sound of something shattering on the stone floor of the pavilion. Shaking his head with distaste, Kao Li-shih rolled up the documents and carefully replaced them in his desk. It was very late. If he went to sleep now, he might be rested enough to present a civil face to An Lu-shan and the Emperor in the morning.

: :

"I hate him, Lu Pei. I am growing to hate him more every day," Li Chu-erh, An Lu-shan's eunuch, was saying to the apprentice.

"It is not necessary to love your master, Chu-erh," Lu Pei replied. "Nor does he have to love you."

Well, thought Kao Li-shih, approaching the sunny place on the rocks behind a ruin where the two sat talking, those are certainly profound words. But what exactly do they mean?

The two younger eunuchs were nearly the same age and had quickly become friends. Both had accompanied this most recent expedition to the hot springs, so Kao Li-shih knew he would be able to find them together this

morning. He came up quietly, not exactly eavesdropping or sneaking up on
them, but postponing until the last moment interrupting the candor of their
conversation.

"Love him? Don't make me laugh," said Chu-erh in his strange accent.
"After you have cleaned up someone's vomit there is no possibility of even a
shred of respect, let alone love," he said bitterly.

Lu Pei did not reply; it was obvious that he had never had to do anything
like that in the line of duty. Kao Li-shih smiled, recalling the braying laugh
of the night before and what he had once heard Chu-erh say about the rags
and buckets. There is a level where some men are completely predictable, is
there not?

"And look," Chu-erh went on, "at the scars on my legs. He has whipped
me plenty of times when I didn't move fast enough or when he wanted me
to keep my mouth shut about something."

An Lu-shan administered whippings to his eunuch? Kao Li-shih stopped
where he was and listened. Chu-erh was speaking freely to his contemporary
in a way he would not with Kao Li-shih.

"I always know when he's got something on his conscience," said Chu-
erh, "because he takes it out on me or one of his sons. But mostly me, because
he despises our kind."

"That is not unusual," said Lu Pei. "I think it has something to do with
their fears."

How true, thought Kao Li-shih.

"You should have seen him that night by the river. He was like a madman. He called me a 'tailless dog' in front of the soldiers and officers, jeered
at me, and gave both me and his son a beating before he forced his army into
the water."

"It sounds as if his conscience was smarting badly that night," remarked
Lu Pei.

Right again, thought Kao Li-shih. A short silence followed, as if Chu-
erh were weighing something that he badly wanted to say, but could not quite
bring himself to do it. He is holding something back, thought Kao Li-shih.
Something about that famous river crossing of which we have all heard so
much.

"He makes me sick!" Chu-erh said, slicing the air in front of himself
with a stick, lopping the heads off a stand of wildflowers with vehement
emphasis. "This morning I found him sleeping in his own vomit. I thought
I would puke, too. If he thinks that I am going to spend the next ten years
of my life with him while he conquers the Khitan and becomes the big hero,
he is crazy. I will find a way to get away from him."

Ten years conquering the Khitan? What was this? Kao Li-shih knew that
An Lu-shan was to be a military commander of some importance in the north,

serving Li Lin-fu, whose policy of fierce protection of the borders was well-known. But Kao Li-shih had heard nothing about the initiation of warlike action against the tribal nations beyond those borders. At that moment, he allowed the two younger eunuchs to hear his approaching footsteps on the rocky path. As he expected, Chu-erh stopped talking abruptly, turning to look at Kao Li-shih with a fearful, suspicious look. *He does not yet know that our kind are a tribe, a brotherhood,* Kao Li-shih noted, putting a smile on his face to reassure the youth.

"Tell him that it's all right, Lu Pei," Kao Li-shih said, finding a comfortable place to sit on the rocks.

"Master Kao Li-shih can be trusted with anything you say," said the apprentice simply. "Talking to him is like talking to yourself or to me."

It was obvious that Chu-erh was not at all used to trusting anyone older who seemed to have authority. He looked at the ground and began digging a small hole with the stick in his hand.

"You and Master An Lu-shan will be returning to the north shortly, will you not?" asked Kao Li-shih.

"Yes. I am not very happy about going," said Chu-erh, filling the little hole up and tamping the earth with the stick. "I knew him when I was just a ragged little captured child of the enemy and he was not much more than a paroled prisoner, doing any job around the camp that he could to get food for himself and his sons. He was harsh and full of self-importance then. What will he be like now?"

"He is the Commissioner for Foot and Horse and, now, Military Governor of P'inglu Province, is he not?" asked Kao Li-shih. "And new provincial territories are added to his 'domain' every day."

"Yes," said Chu-erh, and paused, digging furiously again with the stick. "He is. But he will be doing a bit more than overseeing the conscription and training of soldiers."

Kao Li-shih said nothing, but waited. Lu Pei, to his credit, said nothing either.

"An Lu-shan and Chief Minister Li Lin-fu have been having many secret talks. They forget sometimes that I am not deaf and blind or an idiot," he said, jabbing the ground hard with the stick.

"Is he to lead a campaign against the Khitan?" Kao Li-shih asked, with no particular emphasis, and concealing his surprise. There was no way the youth could know how rare a thing it was to lay eyes on the elusive chief minister.

"And against the Mongolian Hsi nation, as well. He is going to expand the Chinese Empire," said Chu-erh simply, staring at the ground.

Kao Li-shih and Lu Pei exchanged incredulous looks.

"And how," asked Kao Li-shih, "is he going to accomplish this feat?"

"I heard him and Li Lin-fu talking about it. He wants him to cross the Shira Muren River and drive the Khitan all the way back to the Na-lu Mountains, and declare all of it part of the Chinese Empire. Li Lin-fu said he'd get him all the men and supplies that he would need to do it. He said that the armies of the realm get too much money that they don't really need and that he'd see to it that some of that money would be put to better use."

"The six imperial armies of the realm!" said Kao Li-shih with alarm. "This campaign of expansion is to be at their expense!"

"They made a deal. An Lu-shan will have ten years to do it in and everything—all the men and power—he will need, but in exchange he must deliver directly to Li Lin-fu almost an army of captured Hsi and Khitan prisoners within two years. The chief minister says that bringing these thousands of prisoners to the court will be a demonstration of the rightness of his policies in the north. He is to begin right away. That's why we will be leaving soon." Chu-erh sat glumly, staring at the ground. "If he finds out that I have said anything about it before he's actually begun, he'll kill me. He certainly cannot do much more to mutilate me; killing me is all that's left."

Kao Li-shih looked at Li Chu-erh. Was he understanding him correctly?

"Do you mean to tell us that An Lu-shan was your 'surgeon'?"

Chu-erh nodded. Kao Li-shih and Lu Pei looked at each other again. Though neither of them had had much choice about becoming eunuchs—Kao Li-shih because he had been only a child and Lu Pei because of economic necessity—the job had at least been done at the hands of skilled practitioners. There had been pain, but there had also been reassurance and speedy recovery. Fear had been kept to a minimum. What had happened to Chu-erh had obviously been some horrendous punishment, carried out under appalling conditions. Kao Li-shih doubted that An Lu-shan had been trained by a physician to do what he had done to Chu-erh. And Kao Li-shih understood Chu-erh's perverse bondage to his master; given the conditions of his life, his extreme youth and dependency, he had little choice, once the deed had been done, but to be virtually a slave to An Lu-shan. Once you have been cut, Kao Li-shih knew, you are branded; your options few. Kao Li-shih could only imagine the confusion of conflicting emotions, ranging from loyalty to hatred, in Chu-erh's mind. On the one hand, An Lu-shan was his provider, the one person who kept him from being a total outcast; on the other hand, he was the monster who had mutilated and humiliated him, and he reminded him of it over and over again.

And this, thought Kao Li-shih, was the man into whose hands Chief Minister Li Lin-fu was putting unprecedented power—the man who was going to be given vast armies for the purpose of extending the borders of the Chinese empire. But there was something even worse than this: The decision had not come from the Emperor, but from one of his officials. Which was, after all, what Li Lin-fu was. A high-ranking one, to be sure, but just an official none-theless. Not an emperor—a fact that he seemed to be forgetting.

He turned his attention back to Chu-erh, still jabbing sullenly at the ground.

"Don't worry," he said to him. "An Lu-shan will never know what you've told us. And perhaps I can help you to feel less unhappy about your life for the next couple of years."

Chu-erh looked up with an expression of curiosity.

"Stay with An Lu-shan," he said, watching the young eunuch's face lapse back into an expression of disgust, "just for a while longer. Be loyal, be silent, and be observant. Watch everything he does, memorize it, and imagine your-self telling all of it to me and Lu Pei the next time you come down from the north. If he beats you, say nothing, but remember it. If he mistreats his men, or misuses his rank, or cheats or lies, or confides in you anything concerning his plans, say nothing. But remember it, every word."

"That won't be difficult," said Chu-erh. "I'll simply add it to what I already know."

"I don't doubt that you've seen a lot already," said Kao Li-shih, and Chu-erh nodded, averting his eyes. "Don't fear. I'm not going to press you for any more details now. I know that you are worried that you have said too much already. I want you to know that there are unique privileges, compen-sations if you will, that come from being what you, I, and Lu Pei are."

The youth said nothing, but made a small noise that clearly conveyed his disbelief.

"Have you heard of the Censorate?" Kao Li-shih asked.

"Yes," he answered. "My master and I encountered them in the north." He hesitated. "They investigated him after the river crossing." His fidgeting increased while he said these words, and when he was finished, his eyes flicked anxiously from Kao Li-shih's face to Lu Pei's and back to the ground again.

"I told you I'm not going to press you for any more information now," Kao Li-shih reassured him. "I mention the Censorate only so you can appre-ciate who they are. They are, as you must know, all eunuchs. They have a long tradition of being the eyes and ears of the empire, especially in the faraway military outposts, where some high-ranking officers feel that they are beyond the jurisdiction of the court. And while I cannot make you an official member of the Censorate, we can agree among ourselves that you are an informal emissary of the court in that same tradition. Your loyalty will be to the court, to the Son of Heaven, to the great T'ang itself! But it must be a secret for now."

He could see from Chu-erh's face that these words, purposely chosen for their ringing impact, were making an impression. He pressed on.

"What I *can* do, officially, right here and now, is to make you a member of the Flying Dragon Eunuch Elite."

"The what?" said Chu-erh, intrigued now.

"The Flying Dragon Eunuch Elite. We are a brotherhood of eunuchs. We exist for two main purposes: protecting the Emperor, and protecting each other. When you go north with An Lu-shan, you will be carrying with you the knowledge that you are one of us. We will have the ceremony tonight."

There was, in reality, no particular ceremony attached to being initiated into the Flying Dragons, just a simple oath of loyalty. But Kao Li-shih felt that, in this case, an impressive little ceremony would do no harm and would have the effect of making it more real for this youth. It would give him something definite to carry with him on his journey. Kao Li-shih looked at him sympathetically. Such a hard, hard life he's had. And now this journey back to the north with his master, a dangerous, brutal, unpredictable man whose sense of self-importance would be grotesquely inflated. And not only that; An Lu-shan was now heavily obligated—materially, financially, legally, and psychologically—to his sponsor, Li Lin-fu. It will go hard on those around An Lu-shan as this thing is carried out. Very, very hard—especially on this one here.

"We will meet later this evening," he said to the two younger eunuchs. "I must go now, and think."

: :

"Kao Li-shih, I owe it to you to listen to your opinion. I am glad and grateful that you concern yourself with the safety of the empire. I should always hear what you have to say."

The Emperor sat naked on the edge of a hot pool, his thin legs stretched out into the water. In front of him, her arms resting on his thighs and the back of her head cradled on his belly, the Precious Consort floated, eyes half closed, humming a tune softly while the Emperor played with her long black hair.

"Then I urgently and respectfully request that you look into a certain matter. Tell me; has your chief minister consulted you concerning An Lu-shan's duties?" Kao Li-shih stood over the two naked people, feeling like a scolding parent.

"Of course he has, Kao Li-shih!" said the Emperor patiently. "An Lu-shan will be doing what he has been commissioned to do. He will be masterminding the revived policy of vigorous defense of the northern borders. He will be overseeing the conscription of new men. He will be in charge of feeding them, arming them, training them, and mobilizing them. And he will be acting as an emissary of the T'ang court to the citizens who are so far away that they don't fully realize that they are Chinese. And I believe that he is perfect for the job."

"He may be," Kao Li-shih said, "but that does not change the fact that your chief minister, as is his habit now, is taking it upon himself to make decisions only you should be making. He tells you he is strengthening the borders. But I have found out that he means something very different by that than what you may think!"

"But he does mean to strengthen the empire!" said the Emperor. "At the heart of everything he does is that one irrefutable fact!"

"I have found something out. I want you to consider it very carefully. But . . ." He stopped, and indicated the Precious Consort.

The Emperor shook his head. "She can be trusted, Kao Li-shih. Whatever you are going to say, say it."

Kao Li-shih went ahead. The Emperor was in a receptive mood today, and if he had to speak in front of the woman, so be it.

"Border protection, to Li Lin-fu, means border expansion. He and An Lu-shan have devised a plan. An Lu-shan will be undertaking a massive, aggressive, warlike movement into Khitan territory. We are not talking about a few li across the border—we are talking about hundreds. And subjugating all the people therein. He is talking about taking ten years to accomplish this thing! Ten years! That can only mean something huge and inconceivably expensive. Your chief minister has decided that the best place to get the money to fund this war of aggression on the Khitan is by bleeding the armies of the interior! Slowly at first, so that no one will notice, but in time decreasing their strength until they are too weak to fight even a harem uprising! They will be useless, because their very lifeblood will have gone into An Lu-shan's invincible army in the north! Li Lin-fu has decided, on his own, to make this sacrifice to his obsession with the north. Did he tell you any of this?" Kao Li-shih demanded.

Precious Consort was no longer humming her tune. She had separated herself from the Emperor's legs and had moved out into the water a short distance from the two men, where she busied herself washing her hair.

"He told me he was doing what was necessary. That is all I need to know. He is not usurping my authority, Kao Li-shih, because I have already used my authority to place the entire northern military question in his hands! *I* gave him that power, and he is using it! And look at what he has done already! He recognized the potential in An Lu-shan, who was only a very minor commander in the north, brought him here, took a close, hard look at him, and decided that he was the right man. And I . . . I have gained a true friend in An Lu-shan. He *is* my friend, Kao Li-shih; what he does up there, he does for me. He cannot help it!"

"But there is a principle here that is being abused! It is irrelevant that Li Lin-fu is your trusted servant or that An Lu-shan is your best friend!"

"I did not say 'best' friend, Kao Li-shih; I still reserve that position for you," the Emperor interrupted.

"Thank you," the eunuch said with an appreciative nod. "Let me rephrase that. It is irrelevant that An Lu-shan is a friend to you. It is simply wrong that these two men should have such free and unlimited power! And at the expense of the interior armies! I do not like it. I just do not like it."

"Kao Li-shih, Kao Li-shih," said the Emperor, shaking his head. "Then it is *I* you do not trust, since I chose Li Lin-fu for his job."

"But you didn't really choose him. You just think you did. He chose himself!" Kao Li-shih paused, frustration rising. "Do you remember that I spoke to you about the Censorate?"

"Yes. I thought that's what we were going to discuss today."

"We are discussing it, ultimately. Soon, thanks to Li Lin-fu, the Censorate will be unable to do its job. A perfect example of the sort of thing the Censorate keeps an eye on is what we have been discussing here today! It does not matter that you trust Li Lin-fu and An Lu-shan. That is well and good. But you know that the principles of good government require that somebody watch them! If they are doing a fair and honest job, above reproach, then they should not mind being watched! *Why* has Li Lin-fu taken steps to take those eyes off himself?"

"Is that what he is doing? I got the impression that he was merely expanding the duties of the Censorate to other areas."

"Oh, please!" cried Kao Li-shih in exasperation. "How can they properly supervise military spending and see to it that high-ranking officers do not abuse their power if they are settling squabbles between neighbors and husbands and wives and keeping track of how many goats and pigs get eaten by wolves or poached by petty thieves or have choked on a piece of wire?"

The Emperor said nothing for a moment, as if thinking on Kao Li-shih's words. The eunuch watched him with a faint stir of hope. Am I, he thought, at last seeing a tiny crack in the Emperor's apathy? Am I, perhaps, just possibly, reaching him? The consort had moved to the other side of the pool, where she sat quietly listening, no longer keeping up the pretense of feminine indifference.

"All right, Kao Li-shih. Give me those papers you've been waving in my face for so long. Let us come to terms. If you will trust my judgment as far as leaving things as they are with Li Lin-fu and An Lu-shan, then I will see to it that my chief minister's directive is overridden as far as the Censorate goes. Their duties will be what they have always been. Your logic is impeccable there. Indeed, there is no reason why anything the commissioner does in the north under the command of Li Lin-fu should not stand the light of day. Indeed, it will ultimately serve to show *you* that their activities are above reproach."

Kao Li-shih breathed a long sigh of gratitude as he pulled the worn roll of documents from his sleeve. He had not been able to impart to the Emperor his alarm about the ten-year war on the Khitan, but he had, at least, accomplished this much.

"I hope so. I fervently hope so."

: :

Two days later, Kao Li-shih was startled by a knock on his door at his quarters back at the palace. It was well past the middle of the night. He himself had been unable to sleep, and he had thought that he was the only one awake in the entire world. He was further startled to open the door and find young Master Yang Kuo-chung on the other side. There was a slight odor of alcohol about him, but nothing in his manner to indicate that he was drunk. His eyes glittered as he asked in a low voice if he could come in. He was breathing hard, as if he had hurried to get to Kao Li-shih's quarters.

"I have a bit of news that may interest you," he said, closing the door behind him. "Are we alone?"

"Quite," answered Kao Li-shih. "Please come in and sit down. I have been awake all night and have some hot tea in readiness."

"First," said Yang Kuo-chung, "let me tell you that I know about An Lu-shan's war against the Khitan, and how he and Li Lin-fu worked it out between them. I know about the threat to the armies of the interior, and I know that the Emperor was never consulted. I also know your feelings on the matter, and share them."

"How do you know these things, Master Yang?" Kao Li-shih asked cautiously.

"My little cousin, Yang Kuei-fei, the Precious Consort."

Kao Li-shih was irritated, but had to concede that Yang Kuo-chung was the next person Kao Li-shih was going to talk to about the matter.

"I know," said Yang Kuo-chung. "You are thinking that she went off in an irresponsible female way babbling secrets. In fact, she gave much thought to the matter. She has not told her sisters, or anyone else, but she decided to tell me. You would be surprised at her discretion and the soundness of her judgment." He gratefully took the bowl of tea proffered by Kao Li-shih, then smiled. "But of course, whether her judgment was sound in telling me remains to be seen, does it not, Kao Li-shih?"

"Suffice it to say that I am eager to hear what you have to say, Master Yang," Kao Li-shih said, and waited.

Yang Kuo-chung drank down his entire bowl of tea, put it on the table, then leaned forward and spoke.

"Niu Hsien-ko is dead."

"What!" Kao Li-shih exclaimed. "When? How?" Li Lin-fu's own right-hand man! This was significant news indeed!

"It happened not more than an hour ago. His horse threw him. He landed head first on the pavement. His neck snapped like a twig, and his ghost bid his carcass a hasty farewell."

"And how did you find out about it?"

"By being in the right place at the right time, Master Kao," said Yang Kuo-chung with a smile. "I seem to have a knack for it. I was returning to the palace after meeting with some business friends of mine in the city. We stayed out rather later than we had planned, nearly until dawn, well past the fifth drum beat, attending a most delightful little party given by a well-to-do lady friend of mine on a pleasure barge on the canal. I had the choice of staying in the city as a guest or returning to the palace to get a few hours sleep before the sun came up. I made the right choice. As I was approaching the Ch'eng Tien Gate, I came upon a band of drunks carrying a corpse on a board and cursing one another in loud voices, each of them fearing that he would be blamed for the death of the unfortunate they were dragging, and dropping, and clumsily rolling back onto the board, which was too narrow. There was enough light from the lamps at the gate for me to see all of this. I was curious, and when I approached, I must have surprised them, because they dropped him again so that the poor fellow was lying face down in the street. They all just fell back stupidly while I pulled the corpse's head up by the hair to look at the face. There is absolutely no doubt who it was, even in the poor light."

"And how did you find out the circumstances of his death?" Kao Li-shih asked eagerly.

"It was plain that the neck was broken. I could feel it when I lifted the head. I have encountered it before in hanged men, petty criminals, in the north. There is no mistaking it. And the top of the head was gashed, with the scalp partly torn away. When I asked them how it had happened, they all began talking at once. Soon it became evident that poor Niu had been drinking all night and had tried to impress his friends with his horsemanship by making the beast jump over walls and across drainage ditches. It seems that his horse, sagacious animal, decided after some time that it had had quite enough of this entertainment and stopped just short of a particular wall which it wisely ad-judged to be too high. Niu was airborne like a spirit released from its earthly fetters for one short moment before his head came into contact with the stone pavement on the other side of the wall. And that is how it happened."

He poured himself another bowl of tea and shook his head.

"It is interesting how completely one is transformed into a liability when one suddenly, unexpectedly becomes a corpse. His friends were discussing several different methods for the disposition of the body, including weighting it with stones and sinking it in the canal. They pleaded with me not to go to Li Lin-fu with my knowledge of the death. I assured them that they needn't worry, that Li Lin-fu and I were not in the habit of exchanging information. What struck me was their fear that they would be punished for what was, after all, a result of Niu's own stupidity. And their stupidity was evident, too; they had abandoned their horses in the confusion, thinking they would make less noise if they carried him themselves on foot, but the sound of their shouting and arguing could be heard, I'm sure, on the other side of the city. An ignorant, fearful, suspicious lot."

"So perfectly typical," put in Kao Li-shih, "of Li Lin-fu's men. Thugs and fools."

"When I left them I could not resist having a bit of fun at their expense. I warned them not to do anything undignified with the corpse, unless they themselves wanted to suffer the same indignity in the nether world. I wish you could have seen the frightened looks they gave each other. In the end, they just left him propped up by the gate and fled."

"Where he will be found in the morning," said Kao Li-shih.

"Yes. Although I was having fun with them, there was another reason why I didn't want the body sunk, or buried, or otherwise done away with. It is important that he be found dead, so that there is no question about his fate. You see, Kao Li-shih, his death creates a vacancy. And I want his job!"

Kao Li-shih was dumbfounded, but he listened to what Yang Kuo-chung had to say.

"I am eminently qualified," added Yang Kuo-chung. "I have spent many years in the north. I know the people, the territory, the politics of even the smallest border skirmish. I would not consistently agree with everything Li Lin-fu decided to do, and I can assure you, I am far less inclined to pour money and power in unlimited quantities onto our friend An Lu-shan. I do not like what I see happening; I could be a temperate influence. And," he said intently, "I am not afraid of Li Lin-fu."

Kao Li-shih shook his head doubtfully. "I can see that you are not afraid. But you don't know what I know about Li Lin-fu."

"I don't care what he's done. I am not afraid! I want that job, Kao Li-shih. I cannot help but think that Fate put me at those gates so that I would see the corpse of General Niu before anyone else did! At this moment, there is no assistant to Li Lin-fu!"

Looking at Yang Kuo-chung, whose eyes had a penetrating seriousness as he was speaking, Kao Li-shih realized that what he was saying made perfect sense. He felt a growing excitement. This could be an astounding piece of luck!

"You are right," he said thoughtfully. "Officially, Niu was the lieutenant chief minister, though in actuality he was nothing more than a flunky and a yes-man for Li Lin-fu. There has not been a functioning lieutenant chief minister in years. Li Lin-fu has always put someone in the job who would do exactly as he said, who would never have an opinion of his own or raise a single question on an issue. In effect, it is an office that has been nonexistent."

"Until now," said Yang Kuo-chung with a conspiratorial smile. At that moment, Kao Li-shih made his decision.

"Until now," agreed Kao Li-shih. "But Master Yang, there are some things I must tell you about the chief minister. You say you are not afraid, and I believe you; but I could not in good conscience allow you to go through with this without telling you these things." The murdered prince. The disappearance of the poet minister Chang Chiu-ling. The mysterious flowers. The terrible secret Kao Li-shih had carried for so long. The time had come; Yang Kuo-chung would be the first person Kao Li-shih had ever told. Then he rose to his feet as an urgent realization hit him. "But time is of the essence. In all likelihood Li Lin-fu does not yet know that his man is dead! There is only one person, other than the chief minister himself, who can appoint you to the office."

Yang Kuo-chung stood then, too. "I know. The Emperor."

"We will drag him out of bed if necessary. But we must hurry!" Then he put his hand on Yang Kuo-chung's arm. "There is no time now to tell you the whole story, but know this: Li Lin-fu is a murderer. And he is well on his way to becoming a dictator. He will stop at nothing."

For a brief moment Yang Kuo-chung stood and absorbed Kao Li-shih's words. Then he opened the door. "I know some things about him too," he said. "But I told you, Kao Li-shih; I am not afraid."

The next moment they were out the door and hurrying down the corridor, a small lantern swinging in Kao Li-shih's hand. Soon they were almost running. Kao Li-shih felt a growing, palpable urgency nipping at their heels as they trotted along, robes flying.

It was the presence of Li Lin-fu he was feeling. Li Lin-fu, who always, somehow, knew everything a few days, hours, or minutes before anyone else did; it was as if the man's senses had an uncanny ability to be everywhere, all the time. As if he could hear your thoughts. But now, this one time, was it possible that he and Yang Kuo-chung were a step ahead of him? Could such a thing happen? If they were, he knew it was only by a few heartbeats. Passing windows, their quick footsteps muffled in the soft-carpeted hallways and on the backstairs, Kao Li-shih saw that the dark of night was still intact. Darkness, he felt, would protect their advantage as long as it held out. If they could just get to the Emperor before even the smallest sliver of gray touched the horizon.

A glance at Yang Kuo-chung's face in the lantern light as he grimly hurried along next to him told Kao Li-shih that his companion was feeling exactly the same thing. And Kao Li-shih saw something else there, too. This young man, this handsome, wealthy, privileged young man with a fondness for sport, gambling, and frivolity, who need never lift a finger or take any responsible action if he chose not to, was in a state of metamorphosis. There was something in him that no amount of play and indulgence could keep down. Something that was coming of age right before Kao Li-shih's eyes. He was choosing another path—one far more difficult, one that did not favor comfort and ease. Something was wrong in the government, in the life of the empire, and like a responsible man, Yang Kuo-chung knew that he must do what he could to right that wrong, even if it was detrimental to his personal contentment and posed a clear danger. By taking this job, he would, in effect, be placing himself in direct opposition to Li Lin-fu. That took more than ordinary courage.

No, thought Kao Li-shih as he looked at Yang Kuo-chung's stern expression; he has, for this moment, forgotten about the Lady of Kuo's skin, his latest wager with the Emperor, the fine new horse he recently acquired, collecting useless titles, and turning a tidy profit from the sale of goods.

Breathing hard, they climbed a last staircase and turned down the long, wide corridor leading to the imperial quarters. The guards at the door fell back without a word when they recognized the eunuch and the Emperor's close friend who accompanied him. Entering the first chamber in the Emperor's apartments, Kao Li-shih hastily lit a wall lamp. He rummaged through a small writing desk for ink, paper, and brushes. Then he turned to Yang Kuo-chung.

"Follow me," he said in a low voice.

Soon they were at the very threshold of the room where the Emperor and most assuredly the Precious Consort lay dreaming, limbs entwined. Softly, Kao Li-shih pushed the door open on the breathing darkness within. As he did, he no longer felt the shade of Li Lin-fu pressing them from behind. He knew, as he approached the bed to wake the Emperor, that they had won this race. He even allowed himself the luxury of a short pause as he stood over the bed.

Silently, he implored the Emperor to give this crucial appointment to Yang Kuo-chung. The man was one of the Emperor's favorites, he knew: that, and the fact that he had finally relented on the matter of the Censorate, gave Kao Li-shih hope that they had not run through the dark palace in vain, that he would see the logic of what they were about to present to him and act on it. He listened, just for a moment, to the breathing of the two sleeping lovers before reaching for the Emperor's shoulder.

: :

The sun was just rising when Yang Kuo-chung returned at last to his own apartments. Though he had been awake the entire night, the fatigue he should have felt was not there; it had been entirely burned away by the intense feeling of purpose coursing through him.

He stripped off his wrinkled, tired clothing and tossed it away. He filled the wash basin, splashed his neck and body and dipped his head for a moment into the cold water. He seized a rough towel, rubbed his skin and hair dry, and put on fresh clothing. He was ravenously hungry; he decided he would allow himself time to eat, and called a servant.

While he ate, he thought. The first thing he would do would be to gather every bit of information he could pertaining to military spending in the territories comprising An Lu-shan's jurisdiction. He must thoroughly acquaint himself with the situation as it stood now. Where did the money come from, where did it go, and exactly who was accountable for it? He would, he was sure, need this knowledge for future comparison. Then he would acquire a knowledge of the rates of increase or decrease over the last few decades. Or centuries, even. There was nothing to stop him from looking as far back as he could. He would examine historical records. Surely he would be able to find a precedent, something that had occurred in the past that would serve to instruct him in the present. There were hundreds of sources dating back more than a thousand years. I am one up on you, An Lu-shan, thought Yang Kuo-chung; I can read—at least, quite a bit better than you can. You no doubt think that you are the first of your kind; but I will find out all about you by looking at the past, which no doubt contains in it somewhere your future. If it is there, I will find it. And the same goes for you, chief minister.

He devoured a last handful of fruit pastries, drank a hot bowl of tea, and rose from his desk. He would begin immediately.

He was halfway down the staircase when he remembered. He stopped, exasperated. He had made a date yesterday with the Lady of Kuo; they were to meet this morning to go riding. He could scarcely believe the difference between how he had felt one short day ago and how he felt at this moment. Yesterday, for the first time in several weeks, he had put unpleasant things out of his mind and had been thinking most of the day about the pleasant prospect of the outing—what horse he would take, places they would visit, a course he'd been wanting to challenge the Lady of Kuo to ride. He had utterly forgotten it. And now, he remembered the exact moment that the forgetting took place: when he had lifted the head of the corpse in the street and saw the dead face of Niu Hsien-ko.

He contemplated sending her a message, but quickly rejected the idea. She deserved to know from him, firsthand. She was, after all, above everything else, his ally.

: :

"So you and the chief eunuch went to the Emperor's bedchamber, ripped the covers off him, and demanded that he give you a job?" the Lady of Kuo said, looking in the mirror, carefully drawing a graceful arch on her brow.

"Two jobs," answered Yang Kuo-chung. "Not only did he appoint me to the position of lieutenant chief minister, but he made me a member of the Censorate as well. It was Kao Li-shih's idea."

"The Censorate?" She lowered her brush and looked at his reflection in the mirror. "Oh, dear. And just when we were discovering what love is all about."

"Don't worry, my darling," he laughed. "It may be true that the majority of the Censorate are eunuchs, but I don't think the Imperial Father will require me to make that sacrifice."

"He'd better not," she said, resuming her brow-painting. "Or he will have to answer to me." Then she put her joking manner aside and turned toward him with a serious face. "You are quite sure you know what you are doing?" she said. "It seems obvious that Chief Minister Li Lin-fu is not the sort of man to whom one assumes an opposing position without being very, very skillful, careful, and protected by magic."

"I am to be his assistant, not his enemy!" Yang Kuo-chung said reassuringly.

"Oh, stop," she said. "Do you think you are talking to some dumb little harem girl? Did I not see the stamp of his office on the letter from Li Shih-chih? Am I to think that your intention is to be just a replacement for the poor dead bootlicking General Niu?"

"Of course not," Yang Kuo-chung said quietly.

"There would be absolutely no point in your taking the job unless you intended something entirely different. And you have made it quite clear what you think of Commissioner An Lu-shan. You are doing it to make things less easy for him and the chief minister. And that, my love, makes you the enemy of a dangerous man." She put her brow-brush on the table and looked sadly into the mirror. "You will be killed, and it will be my fault. I brought you here." Tears rose in her eyes.

Yang Kuo-chung jumped to his feet and took her shoulders in his hands.

"I will not be killed!" he said, and kissed her neck; but as he said it, a shadow flickered across the back of his mind. Li Lin-fu is a murderer, Kao Li-shih had said. A murderer.

"I should have known that this would happen. I have always admired your brains as well as your comeliness. I don't know what made me think that you would be content to spend your days playing."

"With you, I almost could," he said with sincerity. "But things are wrong. I smell something rotten. I cannot just stand by, frittering away my life and doing nothing!"

"I know, I know, I know," she said sadly. "But you must understand what I am feeling. I know when something has started, has been set in motion. It's as if everything has shifted minutely, almost imperceptibly—but I can feel it." She had painted but one brow; she sat and looked at her reflection now without any apparent interest in finishing the job.

Yang Kuo-chung stood behind her, helpless. As usual, she had penetrated to the heart of the matter. She was not even leaving him a way to pretend, to offer her reassurance. And he itched with impatience to be out the door, down the stairs, and beginning the work he had to do. He knew she could feel that, too. There was simply no way to sweet-talk a woman such as this. He lifted her hair and kissed her neck again.

"I will come back tonight," he whispered. "But I must, I absolutely must, go now."

She did not reply. She sighed, picked up her brush, and began painting the other eyebrow.

: :

He passed through the Ch'eng Tien Gate, leaving the palace city behind him, and entered the bureaucratic city compound. As soon as he passed through the gate, the disturbed atmosphere of his thoughts since his conversation with the Lady of Kuo cleared. Around him rose the tall buildings housing the countless offices, thousands of bureaucrats, and one billion pieces of paper required to govern an empire. Walking briskly through here today was different from all the other times he had passed through on his way to or from the palace city: Now, he was truly a part of it. He was seeing with different eyes. There was much to be done, and he knew where he would begin.

First, he would pay a visit to the Chancellery office. It was only fitting that the new lieutenant chief minister should introduce himself. He had never met his new immediate superior, the Lizard. A singularly unattractive sobriquet, he thought. I wonder what sort of name he will be giving to me, his new right-hand man? Does he even know yet? Well, he reflected; all of this will be known soon. Very soon. Yes. An early morning visit to the Chancellery is definitely in order.

Then, he would proceed to the office of the Ministry of Finance and set his minions to work obtaining the records he needed to study. Though he had not yet done anything of great importance with that first position bestowed on him by the Emperor, he had actually begun to acquaint himself with the complexities of how money moved through the millions of hands of the people comprising the empire. Up until this moment, his interest had been more or less philosophical, detached. He had thought a lot about the strange phenomenon of money—everyone mysteriously agreeing that certain pieces of paper and metal had a precise value, and allowing it to be the regulator of their existences. Someone has to be rich and someone has to be poor in order for there to be the many-layered, complex society that was the stage for our human lives. And what put people exactly where they were and said just how far and when they would move? Money. And though people were unable to agree on a million other things, there was a massive, strange, collusive agreement about money—what it was, how you got it, what its value was.

Well, now he would be doing a lot more than just thinking about it. If money was the empire's lifeblood, then he would acquire an understanding of it as if he were the empire's physician. As lieutenant chief minister, president of the Ministry of Finance, *and* as a member of the Censorate investigating military matters, he would make military spending in the north his special area of attention. If An Lu-shan thinks he has an uninterrupted river of money and supplies and men flowing in his direction, thought Yang Kuo-chung with pleasure, then he will soon find out differently. Even if I prove to be but a small irritant, a stone in the hoof, then I will have been useful.

Arriving at the Chancellery, he approached the guards at the main door, expecting to be asked some questions, and prepared to show them the official seal given to him by the Emperor before sunrise that morning. But their manner made it plain that they were expecting him. They stepped aside immediately, letting him pass without a word through two massive sets of doors.

Inside the fortresslike walls, the halls were quite deserted. Letting his curiosity and his instinct guide him, he walked a long way without meeting anyone. When he came to a stone staircase, he began to climb. Inside these thick walls of stone, the atmosphere was as chill and gloomy as a late afternoon in midwinter, though in fact it was a beautiful morning in autumn. The windowless spiral staircase, lit by oil lamps as if it were the middle of the night, took him up several stories before he found a door that would open. He stepped out into a long hallway with a stone floor. Shafts of sunlight from narrow windows lightened the gloom considerably here. He went to the first window and looked out. He caught his breath, astonished at how far above the ground he was.

Far below were the tops of the trees growing in thick, uncultivated profusion in the forest that was Tung Chien Park. He felt as if he were looking down from the sky itself. In the unimaginably distant past, before men had built anything on this site, a high, steep hill, with a sheer cliff-face on the west, rose up from the flat land around it. The city of Ch'ang-an had been built on the flat ground; the bureaucratic city, the palace city, and the palace itself, in ascending order, eventually occupied the small mountain. The Chancellery building, occupying the extreme northwestern corner of the bureaucratic city complex, was perched on the very edge of the cliff, the building's west wall a continuation of the sheer cliff wall below it. One could walk in from level ground on the eastern side of the building, as Yang Kuo-chung had done, walk to the other side, and, looking out a window, find oneself gazing down, down. He had climbed at least four stories, so the effect was positively dizzying. From where he was, he could see not a single human soul, though he knew he was in the middle of the greatest city in the empire. He enjoyed the odd feeling of remoteness for a few moments, the wall dropping away below, the tangled forest, the distant clouds on the horizon, the huge sky, before pulling his head back into the cool stone interior.

He listened. Had he heard a door being shut? He continued walking. He came to a set of double doors; next to the doors, on a small table, sat a beautiful and curious-looking cloisonné box. He got a distinct feeling of having arrived at his destination; he would be willing to wager that this was Chief Minister Li Lin-fu's office. He turned his attention to the box.

The top was a hinged lid held shut by a small brass lock, and in the middle of the lid was a slot. Stuck in the slot was a rolled up piece of paper. Most curious, he thought, examining the unusual workmanship of the cloisonné. He stared at the piece of paper protruding invitingly from the slot. He could not resist for long. Looking around, though he knew he was quite alone, he plucked it from the slot and unrolled it, experiencing only a small jolt at the sight of his own name at the top. He found he could read most of the letter easily. In the same delicate, childish, feminine hand that had appeared in the violated letter from Li Shih-chih, it read:

> Master Yang Kuo-chung: We congratulate you on your appointment to the position of lieutenant chief minister. We look forward to a long and fruitful partnership. Though we are sorrowful at the untimely death of General Niu, we are pleased to have him replaced by a man of intelligence and vitality. We regret that other matters requiring our urgent attention prevent us from meeting you immediately. We *will* meet soon. There is much work to do.

Holding the paper in his hands, he felt the way he imagined an animal must feel at the moment when it realizes that the hunter's eye is on it and the bow is drawn. This was the second time Master Li Lin-fu had communicated with him in this oblique, but very effective, way. Oh, but this was a masterpiece, without a doubt. On the surface was a simple message of welcome and congratulations; beneath that surface was another message, subtle, the real one. It was anything but simple, and it said something entirely different. It said: I already know that the Emperor gave you the appointment. You may have beaten me to the knowledge of Niu's death, but don't be overconfident, because it was only by the breadth of a flea. And I know enough about you to be able to correctly predict that you would come to the Chancellery first thing today, climb the stairs exactly as you did, find the box, and read the paper.

He rolled the paper up and tried to put it back exactly as he had found it, though he knew it wasn't possible. Li Lin-fu was probably miles from here, but his presence was a palpable thing. Or perhaps he was close by. For a moment, Yang Kuo-chung entertained the idea that the chief minister was directly on the other side of the door, listening to the rustle of the paper being unrolled. He thought of himself and Kao Li-shih running through the halls of the palace, racing a phantom. He shook his head in grim appreciation. The man certainly knows how to make himself felt, does he not?

But there was still another message conveyed by the letter from Li Lin-fu, one that gave Yang Kuo-chung a certain satisfaction despite the disconcerting knowledge that his movements and behavior had been so easily forseeable. It said: I am angry that I was beaten, angry enough that I do not want to meet you face to face.

Yang Kuo-chung turned back toward the stairs, wondering as he did if that, too, was predicted by Li Lin-fu. Going down the stone staircase, the noise of his footsteps echoing around him, he thought of things Kao Li-shih had said when talking about Li Lin-fu. Dictator. Murderer.

Li Lin-fu was right, thought Yang Kuo-chung. There is much work to do.

13

Peaches of the Immortals

The wicked prime minister [Li Lin-fu] was [forever] plotting the fall of prominent men. . . .

By the spring of 747, [countless upright ministers of state, including] Li Shih-chih, and Li Shih-chih's son were all dead by execution or suicide.

—*William Hung*

According to the T'ang historians, the eunuchs were kept in their proper place until the abdication of Empress Wu in 705. In the reign of Chung-tsung, 705–710, they suddenly pullulated, and acquired in the reign of [Minghuang] Hsuan-tsung a political influence, which subsequent reigns served only to increase. . . . If the numbers of higher ranking eunuchs from the reign of Hsuan-tsung onward seems disproportionately large, it should be remembered that the organization developed, if not actually created by Kao Li-shih, [certainly followed his example and], from at least the year 730, formed a channel through which all state business had to pass. . . . Chief ministers could only approach the Emperor through his eunuch.

—*J. K. Rideout*

Among them [eunuchs] are some who were brought as captives from foreign areas and who were later made eunuchs; others were born in China and were cut by their own parents so that they could offer them in service to the ruler and thereby obtain his favor.

—*Translated from an anonymous French source (nineteenth century?)*

Little men—dwarfs and pygmies—both native and exotic; were as fascinating to the Chinese of T'ang as to other medieval peoples. But the vogue for them seems to have been more pronounced in T'ang than under earlier Chinese dynasties. . . . they did have their dwarfs, who were entertainers, dancers, and musicians.

—*Edward Schafer*

But Li Lin-fu was also the man most afraid of other men in the empire. Having unjustly brought about the death of countless human beings, he was apprehensive of revenge. His magnificent mansion in Chang-an was a veritable fortress with reinforced walls, secret chambers, and underground communications. None of his numerous concubines, twenty-five sons, and twenty-five daughters knew in which room he might choose to sleep at night.

—*William Hung*

The fee for the [voluntary castration] operation was six taels (about $84) and the specialist remained responsible for his patient until he was completely healed. Since most of the clients were quite poor and could not pay immediately, they would make arrangements to pay for their operations out of future salaries. . . . Several apprentices worked under the specialist to learn techniques, thus the profession became traditional.

In preparing for the operation, the abdomen and upper thighs of the patient were tightly bound with white strings or bandages. After the parts to be cut off were washed three times in hot pepper-water, the patient was seated in a semireclining position on a heated, couchlike affair known as a *k'ang* and his waist and legs were held firmly by the assistants. The specialist, with a small, slightly curved blade in his hand, then faced the prospective eunuch and confirmed his intention by asking "*Hou huei pu hou huei?*" (Will you regret it or not?) If the man showed the slightest uncertainty, the operation was not performed. If the man gave his consent, the knife flashed and a new eunuch was made. Both the scrotum and the penis were cut off and either solder or a plug was inserted into the urethra, after which the wound was covered with paper that had been soaked in cold water and carefully bound up. Assistants would then walk the eunuch around the room for two or three hours before allowing him to lie down.

The new eunuch was not permitted to drink water for three days after the operation and he suffered from extreme thirst as well as from his wound. The plug was removed after three days, and if urine gushed out, they knew that the operation had been a success and congratulations were exchanged. If no urine appeared, no one could save the man from an agonizing death. However this method of operation was [statistically, very] successful. . . . The severed parts . . . known as *pao*, or "treasure," [were] then placed on a high shelf. This [shelf] was called *kao sheng*, or "high position," and it is said to have been symbolical of the original owner attaining a high position. . . .

—Taisuke Mitamura, translated by Charles A. Pomeroy

LITTLE Daughter had become familiar with the signs that meant Father was angry. She studied his face. The indications were there in abundance: a barely perceptible throbbing of the flesh of his temples, a little dance of the skin around his left eye. She decided that he was angrier than usual this morning. Though she wanted to giggle, she did not. His head, she was thinking, looked as if it were about to pop with whatever was in there.

He had begun the day as glum and sulky as a spoiled little child in the nursery. And though she was aware of a great many adult things that the other children were not privy to, and had a good idea of what was bothering him, she did not like to see him being morose and preoccupied. She was, after all, a child, and he was her father. And her father was perfect. It was the death of General Niu that was making him act like this, and it was mysterious to her. Though she herself had been very fond of "Uncle" Niu—he had always been generous with the children, spending time with them and telling them stories and bringing them presents—she had always thought that Father didn't like him at all. The way Father acted toward Niu, she had assumed that he found him stupid, annoying, and a trial to his patience. Now he was acting as if he had lost a brother. Adults were, she decided, strange creatures.

Yes, he was affected. She could see that plainly. And it was getting worse. In the last several hours she had watched his tic grow to a worrisome intensity. The entire side of his face—not just the skin around his eye—twitched and fluttered absurdly. It was disgusting and comical to her. He didn't seem to notice her studying his face. And that was good, because try as she would, she couldn't take her eyes off him. Now his head seemed about to burst like a well-woman's bag too full of water.

Just as she was making that comparison, her father slammed a narrow, bony fist down hard on the tabletop. Then, clenching his teeth tightly, he raised both hands to the sides of his face and embraced his cheeks in a tenuous moment of composure.

I must not, he thought, allow myself to become so angry; anger is an enemy to the body's external, protective chi; it is damaging to the flow of energy through the vessels of the body. He had told Daughter about this danger to one's health many times: Do not get angry; do not let anger consume you. And now he must control this damaging anger; he must inhale and exhale slowly, follow the breathing prescriptions of the physician.

She held herself perfectly still while her father held his breath in. Several seconds passed in silence. She watched with interest, not moving. Then with surprising suddenness, he brought both fists hard against the tabletop again. He flung a heavy stack of papers onto the terrazzo floor. She stepped back out of the way. This was interesting. She had seen him angry, but never like this. As he rose from his desk, violently overturning the stool behind him, he shot both arms out and knocked over the vases that were perched on slender stands on either side of the desk. They crashed to the floor spraying shards of multicolored porcelain across the room. The noise!

In the midst of his rage, a part of his mind wondered if she was frightened. Well, there was no reason to spare her. Though she was his precious jewel, his flower, she was also the confidante of his every mood and feeling. She must learn.

He would not shield her any longer from this thing that ate away at him. It was following him everywhere now, growing proportionately, it seemed, to the "wasting disease" of his chest that had had him in its grip even throughout the summer. He felt as if these things were swallowing him. No, there was no reason to hide it from her. If she was to understand this world of men, then she must see it all. He raised his eyes to hers. She was watching him calmly, interestedly, with no trace of fear on her young face.

"Do you know what they are doing to your father?" he shouted at last, tearing a thick stack of parchment from the desk and hurling it to the floor. "Do you have any idea?" He turned to the rosewood shelves behind him and knocked to the floor, one after another, a row of potted plants and figurines of porcelain and jade. "Could you have any idea of . . ." He broke off, unable to continue, seized by a violent paroxysm of coughing.

"Father," she said solicitously, taking a step toward him. "Father . . . ?"

He waved her away. He coughed and coughed. It was like fire. His eyes watered, his brains rattled. She stepped back and watched him. Finally he was able to take a deep breath.

"Do you know," he said quietly, "that they have been attempting to make a fool of me, to give away our borders to the enemy? Our burdensome Censorate, full of foolish old aunties, persists again and again in interfering with my policies of strength and sanity in the north. I had done my best to get rid of them, but like a festering sore, they are back. That they have reestablished a meddling Censorate bureaucracy that investigates and confuses all our military affairs, that confounds all our loyal and illiterate generals with words and books and reports and quotas is bad enough. But that they are also attempting to pull the pillars down on us . . ." He paused, feeling another coughing spell coming on. With an effort of will, he fought it off. Raising both fists, he continued as calmly as he could. "They attempt to undo everything I have done in the north to protect their perfumed lives from hordes of foul-smelling nomads . . ." His fists crashed down on the desktop again. "Those lettered fools . . ." he shouted, and stopped himself.

Beads of sweat formed on his forehead. What are you doing? he asked himself. You are allowing them to drain your strength, and they aren't even here! You are playing into their hands shamefully. He sat down heavily. Remember who you are, he said to himself. You will take care of them, *your* way. He smiled. Already, a wonderful idea was coming. How could he have doubted himself, even for a moment? He shook his head. They nearly got to you, old fellow. They nearly got to you.

"The literati at court, Father?" Daughter was saying. He looked at her. She listened to him and often seemed to understand. It never ceased to amaze him. She had absorbed quite a bit of him. And had become like him in many ways, he thought.

"You see, don't you, how they *all* seek to work against your father's efforts? Not only the literati at court, but our chief eunuch, Kao Li-shih, who meddles by putting ideas in the Emperor's ear and pushes for appointments for this pretty boy—this self-absorbed, silly young polo player." He considered for a moment. "The sisters are a good distraction for him . . . but this *cousin* is turning out to be something else altogether."

"Yang Kuo-chung?" she asked. "The man who has replaced General Niu Hsien-ko, Father?"

"That is the one, my dear." He knew she had heard him speak about this man many times—the arrogant young imperial favorite. "He may assume the position—in name only—of my subordinate in the Chancellery. But he will *never* achieve Niu's stature. He is too smart, and that does not help him. There is no one who can replace General Niu—a man of total loyalty and unquestioning principles. There is no one else! And we are all the weaker and less secure because our good general now rots in the grave, eaten by the same indiscriminate worms that digested the corpulent mass of my stupid father . . ." He stopped himself. "But you see, my dear, your father is just being a crazy old man, rambling . . . an affliction of age and too many cares." He paused and smiled kindly at her.

He had, she could see, calmed considerably. He touched her smooth cheek, and she picked up her brush. When he touched her face that way, it usually meant that he wanted her to write something for him.

"Take up your brush again for just a moment," he said. "A few ideas are forming in my head. I should like to get them down before they, too, are lost." He absently stroked the top of her head, then righted the stool and sat down, composed once again, at his disheveled desk. Out of storm and chaos, he thought, comes clear reason.

His daughter took her place at her writing desk. She lifted her eyes expectantly.

Of his forty children, he thought, looking at her serious expression, she was the only one who might someday share the secrets of his rooms—the only one who might someday know in which of the many chambers of his vast estate he would choose to sleep on any given night. He might tell her behind which secret panel and which revolving wall, through which tunnel, through what pavilion and garden he would pass that evening. This was something he told no one, not even his chief of internal securities. It was his responsibility to keep his enemies from finding him. And somewhere at the core of this secret, undeclared even to himself, was, perhaps, the desire to hide from and elude the final shadow: Even Death itself might become confused and lost, unable to find him, in the maze of corridors.

Li Lin-fu had already told her many things that he would not tell anyone else. She was accustomed to keeping his secrets. And he knew that these secrets were as safe with her as if he had never told them at all. She knew even more about him than his most trusted servants, certainly more than any of his wives. He felt that she truly loved him, too. It was significant that she was so pretty and he was so ugly. In his mind, they represented the duality of opposites: she was so different, and yet an absolute part of him. Perfect. Unformed and forming in his image.

"Father . . . what else can I write for you this evening?"

His equanimity had returned. He spoke slowly and clearly, anger gone from his voice. His heart no longer leapt in his throat; his pulse was no longer 'floating.' He would need his usual calm and resolve to deal with the problems that mounted against him. He thought of how forces at the court aligned against him and how the Censorate would now watch his every military move in the north. And how they would watch An Lu-shan. And he thought of how he must reward those loyal to him and the nation. He thought how he must gain new allies at court, even if it meant alliances with certain select members of the literati class that he so detested.

His thoughts kept returning to the recently reformed Censorate; those investigating eunuchs were an obstacle to him. The solution, obviously, was to discredit them, and he knew just how he would do that. Stay calm, he told himself, and all obstacles will fall away before you. But first, a few other details.

"Some notes, Little One, that you can read to me later. Remind me to inform the vice president and the secretary of the Ministry of Civil Appointments to make special note of those candidates for position who hold to the proper political view in their triennial essays. Such talents should not be wasted in the provinces. These young men should be awarded for their merit. It should be understood that mine is not a war against the lettered. Those who understand the necessity of a strong and aggressive military policy in the north and west, those who have praised our recent victories against the Tibetans and the Hsi and Khitan . . . I must reward those men of letters who understand why I choose the men that I do who are neither literati nor Chinese to serve me in the north as military governors—such men as Kao Hsien-chih and even Ko-shu Han, our debauched and drunken carouser, but a great general. And these exceptional men of letters must be ones who understand why I have chosen, especially, this An Lu-shan to guard the borders at P'inglu and Hopei Provinces.

"Remind me to have my agents review those exam booklets, my little flower. To look for talent. We must recognize, early on, who our supporters are. It seems I must ally myself with some, at least, of these ambitious word-smiths, if their thinking is correct. Times are changing. The numbers forecast change all the time. Only a fool could ignore that fact. Such obvious intelligence among the new literati should be justly rewarded in higher grades and civil appointments in the capitals. Perhaps there is even room for the commissioning of a new award for literacy in military politics—the Kuan Ti Award, or something similar. But I am getting a bit ahead of myself, my dear. Don't write too much just now. Just notes, to remind us. We will think about all of this later . . . perhaps, after the evening repast, depending on how we are feeling."

Daughter raised her slender wrist from the porcelain support and washed her brush. She swirled the soft tip in water, making a billowy, inky cloud, then delicately shaped the clean fox fur bristles with her lips. She rested the large bamboo brush on a small ceramic pillow, lining it up with the other brushes, then blotted the wet ink on the page with a fresh piece of felt. She looked up at her father. He was his old self again. That made her happy.

Of all the children, he thought, there were none he disliked. It would be impossible. They were the perfectly ordered household, and he was proud of that. His daughters were not being prepared for marriage—they did not practice all those foolish arts of weaving and managing the household chores and decorating themselves for prideful, dominating husbands. Li Lin-fu had little desire to play the alliance game, little desire to see his children married off to other families of the useless Kuanchung nobility. If any of them did choose marriage, and two or three of his older daughters had, he would let them go. But it was not a big problem. Most of the girls were happy to stay with him and their family. They liked being useful to him and were glad to avoid the unpleasant fate of being sent off to bear the jealous scrutiny of mothers-in-law and wives—all those cackling hens that filled most houses. None of that for his children, unless they really wanted it. They could stay here and be loyal and obedient to him, and learn to love what he loved—music and numbers. The prime factors, the magic square, the triangle of rod numerals, the planets and stars and the universal algorithms they provided. All of this was a clean mirror reflection of his paternal guidance, his stern reason, and his love and compassion for them and of their filial piety for him. It was the pure simplicity of his legacy . . .

He looked at Daughter. His pride.

"Tell the household staff," he said, "to gather all the children into the Garden of Supplicating Branches. They are to prepare to play their music and to join me for the midday repast. It will be good for us to be together. It has been a long while, and I have been very busy. But now that our building plans are under way, I am able to make the time."

She rose from her desk.

"Yes, Father."

Li Lin-fu called for the little girl's handmaiden. He always insisted on an escort for her. He knew that she would much rather wander back alone through the long twisting corridors, exploring on her own. And there was so much to see; so much was changing all the time. Especially now with the mystifying construction project at the center of the estate.

But then he had already decided to reward her curiosity later. He would take her on a grand tour of the new addition.

:: ::

The perfect harmony of yin and yang was, he was willing to admit, as essential to the builder's art as anything was. Too much moisture, and the ground would be unfirm, slippery, with a tendency to erode, the whole affair dangerous and unstable. Too much heat and sun, and the ground might be hard and packed, resistant to digging and the laying of foundations. Too much dryness, and the natural patterns of drainage would not reveal themselves. But those were really the only considerations necessary in choosing a building site, aside from purely aesthetic ones.

He had allowed the geomancers to choose the beginning date for his master building project, but that was all he allowed them to do. He had looked at the numbers himself, privately, and by some coincidence, he and the geomancers had come up with the same date, and so they had begun.

He was not at all inclined to admit to the accuracy of these "magicians," with their irrational doctrines of terrain, their fears of disturbing the earthly dragons, their channeling of *chi,* and their deflection of bad *feng-shui.* The site had been chosen, prepared, graded, and excavated without the aid of geomancers or any of the usual geomantic considerations—to hell with the shapes of the hills and hollows, the irrelevant considerations of the contours of the land. To hell with their rods and sticks and spinning compasses that had no basis in the incontestable accuracy of the numbers . . .

Nine and One were the auspicious numbers produced by his own calculations. He had been pleased. Nine always connoted fullness, and One signified beginnings. And so the first day of the ninth month was the proper time of autumn to begin his project. And now it was the tenth month, and the work was proceeding smoothly.

Completed, it would be the fruition of years of painstaking planning and designing, and the ultimate fortress of security—a system of moving, revolving chambers, a wing whose rooms and corridors mysteriously rearranged themselves from day to day and night to night, hopelessly confounding and driving to madness anyone who tried to find his way to where the chief minister lay sleeping or sat working. No one could enter it, and no one could leave it without the mathematical key to the puzzle of the rooms. Finally, he believed, he would have created a completely sacrosanct inner region of perfect privacy and safety.

The configuration of the building was based on Heaven's ultimate concept, mathematical perfection, known by many names: the plan of the Nine Mansions, the concept of the Magic Square, the ancient tortoise-shell Lo Document. He had designed and redesigned working models—revolving wheels and segmented squares—and had played with them at his desk at the Chancellery offices for years. And not once during those years did poor, faithful General Niu question their purpose. He truly missed his loyal assistant.

When the mechanical design was perfected, the chief minister had initiated the formidable construction project. He knew that even Heaven could not have translated the potent concept more succinctly into architecture. And thinking of the forces gathering against him at court, the timing could not have been better.

The workers, drafters, surveyors, masons, timber carvers, and even the chemists who distilled the liquid mercury on which the rooms and the governing gears and levers would float were all brought to the estate in shifts, and were only allowed to work for a few days on the project before they were replaced. None of them would know the others' purposes or the schedule of their plans. Nor, most important, would any of them ever receive enough information to formulate what the final design might be. Li Lin-fu would summon the different shifts at odd and random hours. But the mercuric chemists he always brought in during the dark, buried hour of the tiger . . .

:: :

"Tonight I am going to give you a treat, my dear," he said to Daughter. "No other member of our family has been allowed back here since your father began all of this work."

He took her hand, and they walked away from the family compound. They proceeded over an arched bridge and down a long open corridor that skirted the lawns where the family's ancestral temples once stood. Over the years, the chief minister had converted the temples to other uses. An eerie light from beyond the perimeter of the garden walls illuminated strange, colorful scenes painted on the overhead brackets and lintels of the corridor. On each of the horizontal supports, real and mythical battles entwined around the insignia of the royal House of Li and the emblems of the Ssu-k'ung office. In the odd glow, the depictions of war seemed to flicker with the flames of battle—vigorously painted bowmen and rearing horses burst into life against a veil of layered hills, wiry trees, and dotted brush. Nature was clearly sub-servient to man in all the paintings that adorned the chief minister's architecture.

"Father, where is all the light coming from?" she asked.

"From the construction site. Your father has created day out of night."

"It's exciting, Father!"

"And there is so little to see yet, compared to what there *will* be," Li Lin-fu said, squeezing her hand.

The chief minister and his daughter left the cover of the long open corridor and passed through an arched gate toward the source of the light. They entered a huge, brightly lit clearing. Trees had been removed along with a substantial piece of earth—a small hill had been cut away and the ground leveled. Dozens of bullock carts and stacks of brick and unfinished lumber covered the landscape. The foggy breath of men moving to and fro was plainly visible in long shafts of light.

Surrounding the construction site were giant lanterns containing enormous candles. Behind and angled slightly above each of the candle lanterns were large polished metal dishes that served as reflectors to increase the light. As they walked around the circular excavation, her father told her that in order to change night into day, he had had to buy nearly all the wax in Ch'ang-an, getting nearly every precious pound of it from the barge merchants before their products ever made it to the warehouses. But it was a good thing, he explained with a smile, because otherwise, the idle rich would waste the candle wax in lighting their estates for foolish all-night parties and various games and equestrian challenges. They would, he told her, though he did not expect her to believe such excess, even light entire fields for midnight archery contests.

What he could not explain to Daughter just yet was that, above all, this project was an experiment in power, a test of a theory. He believed that it was possible to compensate for the natural frailty and mortality of his body by employing certain principles. The unique design of his building would, he believed, draw in and amplify the protective *chi* around him. Vital work that must be done to guarantee the security of the empire would, he projected, take many years yet—possibly decades. He could not entrust the job to anybody else. If he was, therefore, to do his work for the empire, then he must rely on his intellect and the mathematical order of the universe to extend his years and keep him functioning and vigorous.

He would employ those same forces that turn the earth and the stars. He would parallel and reflect the geometric and mathematical structure of the universe in his own inner fortress. It would function as a shield against forces, seen and unseen, man-made or not, that might seek to destroy him.

Within the constants of his theories, the direction of the lines of *chi* crisscrossing the earth changed with the seasons and the movement of the stars. Only a moveable structure could realign itself to the shifting lines of force, and only a structure with the correct shape could collect and magnify those lines of force. His building was designed to do both.

The eight-sided structure would move around a central axis, always facing the same line of force. He must give credit where it was due. The geomantic diviners had not been completely wrong. They had invented the eight-sided mirror which was often hung on houses to deflect negative energies—bad *feng-shui*. Their principle was correct insofar as the eight sides went—the eight trigrams of the universal octagon—but they misunderstood it and were actually using it backwards. It was so simple, it made him laugh. The eight sides must *receive* the natural lines of force, the *chi*—*not* turn it away. They should act as lenses, not mirrors.

The forces he wished to attract were, he understood, tied inexorably to the wave-theories of the rise and fall of yin and yang. He further understood that these forces always adhered along planes, like the six sides of a snowflake. Therefore, by combining the six-faceted crystalline circle, like the snowflake, with the eight-faceted trigrams of Heaven and Earth, a building could become a focusing agent of absolute power.

It had never been understood before. It was a secret that had been waiting for all time for Li Lin-fu to divine. He had arrived at his understanding not through magic, or geomancy, or any other such balderdash, but through mathematics—the clean, absolute purity of numbers—and an understanding of natural forces.

The chief minister's eight-sided building would revolve around a square at the center. A complex system of trains and gears driven by a waterwheel in the Pa Stream would turn the structure—which would float on a frictionless sea of liquid mercury—rotating its faceted sides toward the exact seasonal alignment of power. And it, in turn, would rotate its master, who would be seated at its center in the Room of Five within the potent square based on the plan of the Nine Mansions.

And, of course, a building whose floor plan changed with the fluidity of thought offered another extremely practical advantage: The inside of the house would be a constantly redefinable maze. He contemplated with pleasure the fate awaiting any unwelcome guest who accomplished the impossible and gained entrance. His first stealthy footstep would trip off sensitive triggers, setting the machinery in motion. The building would turn so gently that the "guest" would not feel it or be aware of it. Where there had been a door, there would now be a solid wall. Sealed in, he would eventually suffocate— but slowly, so that he would have plenty of time to contemplate the riddle. Or, if he had been unfortunate enough to be in a hallway when the machinery began to move, he might find his bones splintering between the shifting walls. You are most welcome, Li Lin-fu mentally addressed the imaginary intruder, to my home. He smiled, then remembered Daughter standing quietly by his side, watching the amazing spectacle.

He told her to be careful and to stay close to him. It was dangerous, what with trenches and sinkholes, slivers and spikes everywhere. And the traffic—high-wheeled carts, horses, and oxen—for construction work continued long into the nights. In the darkness, even with the lantern light, they would not be able to see her. Nighttime work, he explained, had special hazards: the flickering flames caused shadows to shift, sometimes confusing the animals. There was just too much going on for a child's safety.

These enormous high-wheeled ox-drawn trucks carried long rough-hewn timbers, heavy stacks of bricks, bags of lime and building stone, and marble, slate, and terrazzo past the doorpost guards every evening. They would begin rumbling through the gates and over the flagstone terraces shortly after the evening repast and would continue creaking and clattering through the gates well into the night.

The girl started, and clutched at his hand. Something had flown overhead. Then several somethings, squealing, flapping, and diving. They seemed to grow right out of the air, until the autumn stars winked on and off with scores of little black flying creatures. Then there were a hundred, then a thousand of them dancing in the air. Some of the workers ran, waving their picks and shovels over their heads, while others laughed at the ones who ran and struggled to swivel the hot reflectors up toward the sky.

"Father!" she cried. "What are those things?"

"Bats." He let go of her hand. "Nothing but bats." Li Lin-fu reflected that to the superstitious, meanings always seemed to reveal themselves in sudden symbols—a meteor, a rainbow, a flying fish . . . or bats.

As the creatures passed through the beams of light, he saw glimpses of their tiny red eyes and furry little fox-faces, their stretched leathery wings like kite silk over a frame. They looked like something out of Hell, but they were only flesh and blood creatures, harmless, probably afraid themselves of the light and the shouting of the men.

"Father, what do they mean?" she asked as some of the workers still ran about and others continued to laugh. "Aren't they supposed to mean good luck? How could they, when they look like little demons?"

"They signify nothing but the infinite imagination of nature," he answered. "Though here, for me, they are indeed an omen of good luck! But not the sort that some superstitious peasant would have you think, my dear. Their presence means that there are caverns beneath us—caverns that might go far into the earth; caverns that may ultimately be very useful to your father's plans."

::

His daughter sat by his side watching intently as he inscribed circles and squares and rows of numbers on a piece of parchment with a thick brush. Then he drew a wild spray of lines connecting the enigmatic geometric forms. His brush flew; he was heedless of the black ink spattering onto his robes and even his face. He coughed and rubbed his chest, and she saw sweat on his forehead. She brought a dampened cloth, which she had in readiness, up to his face and wiped the ink and sweat away.

"Father," she said, looking at the page of symbols and numbers, "I want to learn everything that you know. Everything." He put his brush down and looked at her. Was it possible, he asked himself, that this girl-child was to be his successor? There was not a single one of his sons whom he would even consider. He had long accustomed himself to the idea that he would do his work so thoroughly that the empire would be secure for centuries after his death. But it would not be a bad thing to leave behind someone he had personally trained who was also devoted and faithful to him. She was certainly eager to learn. He had an idea then.

"I will teach you my numbers some day soon," he said fondly. "But there is something else I can show you right now. Do you see the small ceramic box on your father's desk?" He saw with satisfaction the pleased, expectant look that came onto her face when she was about to be let into her father's confidence.

"Yes, Father. It looks like a miniature copy of the Empress Wu's information boxes."

"You are right. Would you like to see the principle of the boxes in action? The chief of the household staff will collect 'suggestions' that we put in these boxes throughout the estate. There are boxes for the gardening staff, for the nursery, for the chambers of your father's wives, for the kitchen staff and so forth."

"I have seen them in the halls," she said.

"Well, then, this will be an exercise in government for you. Now think. Have you any complaints about any of the servants in our house? Efficiency, honesty?"

"I don't know . . ." She hesitated.

"Perhaps one of your tutors? Now think carefully." Li Lin-fu waited patiently after these last words. He wanted to give her time to think.

"Well, maybe there is one. Maybe."

"Yes? Go on."

"She steals and she has a nasty mouth. She is bitter toward the little ones. She resents them, I suppose."

"She steals? You say she steals? What does she steal from us, my dear?"

"She has made us promise to never tell . . . She said she would twist our arms and spit in our food, and . . . and . . . lock us in dark closets and in the linen chests with the bedroom quilts."

"Ahh!! You wouldn't like her to do that, would you?" Li Lin-fu said. "But you need hide nothing from your father. You know that, don't you?"

"She takes little bracelets and rings and tiny hair ornaments from the girls' quarters and trinkets and toys from the nursery. I know she sells them. I followed her one day. She was talking to a merchant at the door and handing him some things in a handkerchief."

"Then put her name and what she does on a slip of paper and drop it in the box," he instructed her. The girl hesitated for a moment over a sheet of paper, then picked up her brush and began to write slowly. As she wrote, her speed and intensity increased until she was attacking the paper furiously. Li Lin-fu watched with approval as the child released all her resentment toward the servant. She blotted the page, folded it, and dropped it in the narrow slot in the top of the hinged box.

"And you are free to invite others in the house to do the same. Perhaps some of your sisters would like to say something about the woman. You needn't worry," Li Lin-fu assured her. "She won't find out who did this, and she won't bother you again. She will be working somewhere else from now on."

His daughter looked at him. She said nothing.

And so it would be, he thought, with those members of the Censorate . . . And soon, also, Daughter will have her first actual lesson in the politics of words.

::

On the evening of her dismissal from the well-paying inner-household staff, a young woman stood on the roof of the highest pavilion in the garden. This one had always been her favorite. Its magnificent stupa *spire atop seven gold-tiled tiers seemed to scratch the very canopy of heaven. It was the most beautiful thing she had ever seen.*

Her crime, the theft and sale of trinkets from one of the wealthiest (and, certainly, most powerful) households in Ch'ang-an, had been discovered. She had tried to explain that she did not do it for herself, but so that she could send money to her parents, who were both old and sick. It made no difference. Loss of her job and censure were to be her punishment, and she knew that word of what she had done would get to her family. The disgrace was more than she could endure. She would not endure it. The breeze ruffled her hair. The ground was so far down she felt as if she were floating above the earth.

The pavilion had entered her dreams often and made her think how beautiful the Magical Isles and the Heaven of the immortals must be—the gardens of the Grand Queen Mother of the West's peach trees, whose crimson and yellow fruit ripened only every five hundred years, surrounded by palaces of crystal and emerald, pavilions of jade and nephrite, halls of silver and alabaster and many-hued translucent marbles . . . and, above it all, the gold-scaled hulls of grand dragon boats floating in the white clouds . . .

Why should she stay here and suffer for her transgressions? She would fly, instead, to the immortals—and to the peaches she had never tasted . . .

: :

The next morning the gardeners discovered the broken body of a young woman among the ornamental stones in the Garden of Supplicating Branches.

That same morning, Daughter learned, as did all the other children, of the fate of the servant girl. She must have taken the spooky, winding, cobwebbed brick stairs to the highest level of father's To Catch the Moon Pavilion. No one ever went up there. It was haunted, the gardeners said. Owls nested there. But once on top, Li Lin-fu's daughter imagined, the girl must have seen, spread out before her in endless rectangles of starlit rooftops, wild gardens of rambling paths and rockeries, arching bridges over meandering brooks, and haunting groves of pine and bamboo; everything that she could never have, because of her crime. And that night, from the seventh level, she did the unthinkable and stepped out onto the clear-starred autumn air . . .

: :

It was autumn of the second year of the Tien Pao reign period. Everywhere, the cold slate floors of the bureaucratic halls hissed with the rustle of a thousand slippers. A sea of fragrant silk robes echoed the colors of the forest leaves. The word was out.

The scandal was on the tongue of every minister in the capital. The Censorate was under investigation for minor infractions, gross violations of propriety, fraud, and, most of all, bribery. Bribery—that was a strange one, they all said. Why should simple acts of bribery—the grease that turned the axles of provincial government—be examined? Bribery was a timeless, tacitly agreed-upon mainstay of Chinese officialdom, an unofficial protocol; but it was now under investigation. Never did one fat magistrate dine as a visitor of another without a bribe in his napkin. It was unthinkable. Bribery was the calling card of government. Now every tongue wagged with the news that the eunuchs of the Censorate were under investigation, and bribery was the major charge. And what of the president of the investigative military Censorate, this brash young Yang Kuo-chung? they were all asking in the same breath. Gossip, rumor, and conjecture were everywhere. The officers of an imperial appointee were under investigation.

: :

He was pleased with himself. It had gone as well as he could have hoped, if not better. Grandmother's ghost had responded to his invocations. All he had had to do was set things in motion, plant the seeds of innuendo here and there, and wait for the boxes to fill with insinuating evidence. It is fascinating, he thought, how quickly men will respond to an opportunity to incriminate a colleague, especially if anonymity is guaranteed. Merely make a suggestion, and they will rush to give it life, substance, and form.

The Chief of Internal Securities knelt on the floor before Li Lin-fu's dais, waiting, while the physician fluttered and fussed about the chief minister. A peculiarly noxious mixture was being prepared this morning; the man had ground a brownish powder to fine dust with his mortar, then added water to a mixture of herbs. Mixing it all together, he flattened the resultant dough on waxy parchment with a heavy porcelain roller. Now he was cutting it into little pills, which he then lifted with a pair of bamboo tweezers onto an embossed circular silver dish trimmed with jade. On the dish he also placed a bowl of tepid tea.

A servant applied hot, steaming, pungent-smelling rags to Li Lin-fu's chest. The chief minister coughed and spat a thick knot of phlegm into a brass urn near his feet.

"Excellent," said the physician. "It is loosening its grip."

He held the plate of pills and tea under the chief minister's nose. Li Lin-fu grimaced with disgust at the foul odor, but the physician made no effort to withdraw the plate. He held it closer until Li Lin-fu could no longer stand it and backed away from the stench. He coughed again, covering his mouth and nose with one hand and pointing a finger at the plate with the other. When he recovered his breath, he spoke.

"*Heavens*, Old Meddler! Have the cats shat in your poisons today? What is that foul smell? What are you torturing me with this time?"

"A mixture, Grand Councillor," the physician answered.

"I can see *that*. But of what?"

"It is the strongest combination against your particular weakness. Taken in the auspicious mixing of *three*, it should prove most effective. There is *hsi hsin*, a rare species of wild ginger, effective against mucus blockage in nose and head colds. It is a particularly powerful emetic and diuretic. Then there is *t'ien men tung*, which accounts for the unpleasant asparagus smell; like *pei mu*, it softens dry hard coughs but also serves to strengthen the lungs. Then there is *huang ch'i*, which works to induce as well as dispel perspiration and fortifies the three "warmers" as well as the spleen, which is affected by the internal dampness. It is all there in a base of fish oils. I believe it is the ultimate medicine against this illness. It is a most highly praised mixture mentioned repeatedly throughout the thirty volumes of Sun Szu-miao's *A Thousand Golden Remedies* and throughout the fifty volumes comprising his commission's works on pathology. I am quite certain that we shall drive it out, Grand Councillor. I hope that it will be an effective combination against the pernicious influences that have settled so deep into your lungs, and now spleen and kidneys as well."

"Nobody hopes it more than I," Li Lin-fu said. "Especially since I am the one who must eat it. Would you care to join me?"

The physician smiled forbearingly.

"That is most amusing, Councillor. But if you would, please, eat it quickly . . . It loses its potency shortly after mixing. The Persians have discovered the remedy to be quite effective . . ."

"The Persians, you say . . . ! Then let *them* eat it. They have their murdering ar-Rahman, their Allah, to save them from the stink. But what choice do you give me? Should somebody else eat them for me and accrue the benefits?" He grinned at the physician, thinking that the old man was an agreeable if somewhat ponderous product of his own single-mindedness, the pleasant embodiment of harmless stubbornness, a man with a single obsessive compulsion that left no room for malice, or anything else—least of all humor. It was admirable and comforting! Li Lin-fu pinched his nostrils shut and pushed the round gluey pills into his mouth and washed them down with the tea. He smiled. "When are you going to ask me to eat human flesh?"

"My heavens, Grand Councillor!" the stunned physician exclaimed. "Why would I ask you to do that?"

"Then you haven't read *all* the treatises, Physician. Don't you know that Ch'en Ts'ang-ch'i in his *Digest of Medicinal Remedies* suggests the ingesting of human flesh for such pernicious influences of the lungs as mine?"

"Definitely not, Grand Councillor," said the old man, shocked. "And I shall not abide by such a prescription at all!"

"Ah, it is indeed heartening. You are such a man of principle. Do you mean that you would not even prescribe such sweet infant's flesh—'two-legged mutton'—as our conquests in the north might supply, if it would do me good?" Li Lin-fu teased.

"Not by the farthest stretch . . ."

"And that is how little you care of my life. A choice between me and a barbarian infant?" Li Lin-fu said seriously, trying not to smile.

"Councillor!" the old man scolded him.

"Physician, Physician," Li Lin-fu laughed and shook his head. "I am merely being humorous, having a bit of fun."

"Humorous, Councillor? I hardly think . . ."

"That's the problem with too many of our literate officials—men of letters in general. They have no humor. How are we to live in this miserable world without some humor?" He paused and rubbed his chest. "I can think of one exception . . . a man of letters with true humor. Our bawdy and . . ."

He chose his next word with care. ". . . *rustic* poet Li Po. Now *he* has humor. Scathing at times, but plentiful."

"I find him merely crude, Councillor," the physician said with disapproval.

"I *like* crudity, Physician. In proper amounts it defines a man's personality. Don't you think that I am a rather crude fellow myself?"

The old man was making an effort to frame a diplomatic answer to that question when Li Lin-fu abruptly changed the topic.

"What of the boxes?" he said to his Chief of Internal Securities, still waiting patiently on his knees.

"We have missed no one," the man answered. "The Ta Li Shih has opened up investigations of the accused eunuch officers of the Censorate."

"Good. We do not want such flagrant violations against the state to go unpunished. It would be bad for the morale of honest Confucian officials. You do understand?"

"Indeed, Councillor!"

: :

The office of the Ta Li Shih had left the day of the hearings to be announced at Li Lin-fu's discretion. And Li Lin-fu had decided to consult the mathematics of the stars to determine that date. In his miniature observatory on the roof of the newly added seventh story of his office fortress, he looked at the sky.

Beside him on the viewing platform stood a gnomon taller than two men, strangely calibrated, designed to measure the length of the solar shadow. And perched nearly twenty-five feet above the rooftop was the intricately ornate star observation platform on which he made highly accurate calculations of meridian transits. It was on this perch that the chief minister also consulted the planisphere and laid the sighting tube along the correct axis of the rotating torquetum. It was under a particularly clear autumn sky on this star tower that evening, two hundred and forty-five feet above the forest floor of the Tungchien Park, that he made his grand miscalculation and never knew it.

A fit of coughing seized him just as he had the delicate instruments precisely adjusted. It racked his body and blurred his vision. His senses, those fragile links to reality, were momentarily severed by the pain. Though his condition had worsened that autumn, he continued to think of it as simply a shadow that moved along the contours. It would pass, eventually, leaving no damage or disturbance behind.

When the paroxysm finally used itself up, he readdressed himself to the portion of the sky he had been watching, and continued gathering data for his calculations. What he did not realize was that the violent convulsion had thrown the instruments minutely out of alignment, causing him to mistake a planet in motion for a star. Thus, his calculations determining the date of the Censorate hearing were based on a star that had, in fact, not moved at all, and a planet that had.

The star might just as well have moved. From six different provinces, from innumerable magistry offices, the boxes continued to yield up their uncompromising evidence against the eunuch officers of Yang Kuo-chung's Censorate, and damning evidence it was. The investigators of the military Censorate were named individually, and the exact dates and descriptions of their transgressions were cited.

: :

It was like dreaming that you are drowning, then waking up to find that it is real. Filthy, muddy water pours into your mouth and nose and into your lungs as you try to claw your way up the dank, hellish, slippery, algaed walls of the well.

The letters, the notes, the anonymous scraps of paper and silk that bore the particular evidence against Yang Kuo-chung's officers in the Censorate were like that black water and the inside of that well. How could his men defend themselves? How do you say where you were or what you did on days that should never have mattered in your life at all? How do you go back and reclaim time for which there is no accounting? He did not know how he could protect his officers from even the pettiest of the recriminations and libel that built around them. And how should he instruct them?

Were they expected to plead *tzu-shou*—make voluntary confessions? And having pleaded to dubious crimes, minor and petty infractions at best, what kind of censure would these officers have to endure? Yang Kuo-chung knew that his aides would be unable to help their officers. These were the thoughts he grappled with when a light tapping on the door to his office startled him out of his thoughts and nearly out of his chair.

It was Kao Li-shih, who did not wait to be invited in but entered the room quickly and purposefully.

"I realize that it is very early, Master Yang," Kao Li-shih said before Yang Kuo-chung had a chance to speak. "I should apologize for coming unannounced. But I saw the oil lamps from outside." He paused. "Useless poets tell us that autumn is the Ministry of Punishments. It's all quite fitting, isn't it?"

"Your metaphors are not so well appreciated this morning. But join me for tea," Yang Kuo-chung said, pouring another bowl.

"Thank you," Kao Li-shih said, accepting the bowl. "It was quite cold out there this morning," he remarked. "An early frost, perhaps." He took the hot bowl of green tea up to his lips and blew on it, then set it back down without drinking and rubbed his hands together over the rising steam.

"Master Kao, somehow I do not think that you came all the way from the palace to this office for a stroll and a discussion of the weather," Yang Kuo-chung said, waiting.

"You are quite right! Such exercise in this cold is not good for the body. It is not something I would do unnecessarily." He drank the hot tea slowly, thoughtfully. "There is one consolation to all of this, Master Yang. It is my opinion that Li Lin-fu is no longer as subtle as he once was. My instinct tells me that he has acted somewhat hastily. Compared to things he has done in the past, this present action is almost clumsy. Certainly not up to his usual standards." Kao Li-shih was thinking of the murder of Crown Prince Ying, undoubtedly Li Lin-fu's most masterfully conceived and executed plan, and knew that Yang Kuo-chung understood what he meant. He had told Yang Kuo-chung about the flowers, the "suicide," the madness of Consort Wu, and the disappearance of Chang Chiu-ling. He had almost felt guilty for waiting until after the young man's appointment to the lieutenant chief ministership to tell him, but he had not wanted to risk scaring him away. "It is my opinion that he may be slipping. But then he may cover this by simply being more brutal."

"And what will be the outcome of this nonsensical attack on the Censorate, Kao Li-shih?"

"I am sure you realize that it is timed perfectly to coincide with your various investigations into General An Lu-shan's northern military build-ups, campaigns, stores, and expenditures in P'inglu and Hopei."

"It is, indeed, a clear warning to me, Master Kao, to keep my nose out of our chief minister's pet military projects." Yang Kuo-chung raised a thick sheaf of paper containing the names of minor Censorate officers, dates, and an incomprehensible array of figures. He dropped it back on the desk. "What do I tell them? These are minor civil officers—eunuchs of the lowest grade. Even my aides whose ranks are higher would have little recourse. But these . . . ?"

"You feel that they will be defenseless against accusations that have no basis in fact. You are right! But insofar as these are minor infractions at best, a simple voluntary confession would be all that would be required under law."

"And they should confess to something they haven't done or have no knowledge of doing?" Yang Kuo-chung asked, incredulous.

"It is the most prudent way, for now. You are dealing with Li Lin-fu. It is *his* government. That is the most obvious fact of our lives." Kao Li-shih shrugged and took another sip of tea. "But that could change," he said enigmatically.

"Change?" Yang Kuo-chung asked. "How? When?"

Kao Li-shih unfolded his long body from the low stool where he had been sitting. He looked down at the Fox at his desk.

"First, let me give you some cautionary advice. Hold your tongue at the hearings, contrived though they will be. You will not be the brash young imperial favorite there. And tell your aides to hold theirs as well. Let the minor officials fend for themselves. Their voluntary confessions will bring a slight censure to the department, a momentary loss of prestige, and that is all. It will simply slow your investigators down in the north for a while. Let it pass, hold back, and regroup your forces. I have seen much of this before—the boxes; the banishments of good, honest officials; the plottings. My advice is to hold fast. By attacking the minor officials under you, he is merely warning you for now. Let him think that you are intimidated, and he will soon turn his attention away from you."

"But what did you mean about the situation changing?" Yang Kuo-chung asked again.

Kao Li-shih walked toward the door.

"I told you that I think that he is slipping," he said. "I believe that it is his health. I have heard rumors that a physician visits him nearly every day. He is putting up a fight against something, and I believe he is feeling, shall we say, the limitations of his life span. Of course, he is a master at hiding all news about himself. He is never even seen anymore, and I think it is because his illness, whatever it is, is written plainly on his face. And he does not want to be thought of as mortal like the rest of us. And indeed, it is difficult to think of him that way. But remember, Yang Kuo-chung, . . . he *is* mortal." He opened the door. "Thank you for the tea, Master Yang."

After the eunuch had gone, Yang Kuo-chung thought about what he had said. It made good sense, though it was abhorrent to him to acquiesce to lies. But maybe Kao Li-shih was right. Fighting back, retaliating, could be a mistake at this moment. Let him think that I am cowed, and perhaps things will not be so bad for the accused eunuch officials. A slight censure, a momentary loss of prestige, Kao Li-shih had said, but no lasting damage. And perhaps Li Lin-fu will do us a favor and succumb to whatever illness is gnawing at his vitals.

He sighed. He was grateful to Kao Li-shih for giving him perspective and sound advice; he had been wondering what he had got himself into, and had even found himself yearning, if only for a moment or two, for the empty north, the cold, rocky ground to sleep on, and the wind. He felt a little bit better and set about making a list of the accused eunuchs—who they were and what their jobs had been for the last several years. He would at least be prepared.

::

Yang Kuo-chung was still at his desk in the Censorate offices hours later when a loud knocking again jarred him from his thoughts. He had closed the heavy

wooden outer door against any further interruptions and had barred it with
an iron bolt as he went through sensitive records of the business of the Censorate. He ignored the knocking, not wanting to be disturbed. There was
another knock, harder this time, then silence. He looked up, waited, and when
no more knocking came, was satisfied that whoever it was had gone away.
He returned his attention to the papers in front of him. He had lost his place
in a difficult document he had been reading, and had to start all over again.
One good thing about this job, he thought, is that my reading ability is
improving.

This time it was not a knock, but hammering that rattled the delicately
carved spandrel above the entranceway. Be very still, he told himself. Let
them think the office is empty. Why had they not left? It should have been
clear to them that there was no one inside. There was a pause, then more
hammering. He returned stubbornly to the papers, flipping through the immense stack of expenditure ledgers for the outlying P'inglu and Hopei military
encampments. He would take the eunuch's advice. Weather the censures out.
Minor penalties, fines, small setbacks . . .

The intermittent hammering was now persistent. He could not concentrate with all the noise. And now the decorative pottery and porcelain on the
shelves danced with each of the jolts. A heavy piece crashed to the floor. He
stood up from his chair. What *was* this??

A tremendous shudder that shook the room made him drop his papers
and grab the corners of his desk. As if in a dream, he watched the wall opposite
where he stood bulge and crack with the next blow. Cabinets toppled forward,
scattering papers and books. A booming voice came from behind the wall.

"Master Yang!" it said. How did they know he was in here? Had they
been following the eunuch? Not likely. Kao Li-shih was too clever for them.
Then he realized it! Damn! Barring the door had been a mistake, a giveaway.
He was the only one who could be inside. The heavy voice came again.

"The offices of the Censorate are officially under siege for crimes against
the military security of the empire by orders of the Chief of Internal Securities
for the Chancellery! Can you explain why the door was barred?"

The blows began again. He turned and steadied the free-standing shelf
behind him, mind racing. Were they waiting at the rear exit? He snatched up
a sheaf of papers, started to reach for a dagger inside a hidden sliding drawer
in his desk, but changed his mind. Surely it would not come to *that*.

"You are ordered to relinquish this space and everything in it!" the voice
commanded. "All records and ledgers are now the property of the Chancellery
office!"

The pounding began anew. Yang Kuo-chung did not wait to hear the
rest or to see the faces behind the shattering walls. He made for the rear exit,
turning one last time to see the wall behind him bursting into a shower of

shining wooden fragments like the lacy foam of an ocean wave—ebony, rose-wood, purple sandalwood, teak—and twinkling flakes of mother-of-pearl and mica inlay scattering along the black stone floor and flying through the air. A piece struck him sharply on the shoulder. He did not turn around again. He ran out of the office by the back stairwell, fleeing from the sound of tables and chests being thrown over, sliding panels and drawers ripped open, shelves torn down from the walls, and the unmistakable yawning and cracking of splintering woodwork.

He took the cold winding brick stairs six and seven at a time. He stopped for a moment at the bottom to listen and to catch his breath. From behind and far above there still echoed the sounds of the office being pulled apart, but no one appeared to be following him. He tucked the sheaf of papers under his robes. Why hadn't he taken the dagger and concealed it in his sleeve? What had stopped him? He knew. Even when the very walls were being broken down, something in him denied it all, had said that these things were not supposed to happen here. Gods! Was this life here making him lose his nerve and his instincts? He would not have been so slow to act in the north!

Keep running, you fool, he told himself. These thugs, these miscreants, wouldn't treat an imperial favorite any differently than they would a scabby alley dog. Move!

Imperial favorite? What a meaningless bit of nomenclature that was at this moment. At least his superior deserved the legends that surrounded *him*. As he ran, hugging the rescued sheaf of papers to him, he recalled Kao Li-shih's words: *. . . he may be slipping. But then he may cover this by simply being more brutal.*

Yang Kuo-chung left the Chancellery wing and started north across the Orchid Terrace.

::

He hammered at the doors of Kao Li-shih's apartments.

"Kao Li-shih! Kao Li-shih!" he shouted at the top of his lungs. He pressed his ear to the door. He heard nothing at first, but then thought he heard groans and the sound of slippers crossing the wooden floor. He hammered and called again, and waited for a small eternity, breathing hard. Then the door opened slowly and a wizened face peered out—an ancient man, only half awake and clutching his night robes, came out into the hall. Asleep in the afternoon? Yang Kuo-chung did not try to fathom it.

"Where is Kao Li-shih?" he demanded of the old servant.

"He is not here," the man said in a thin old voice. "He is with the Imperial Father. He has been residing in his rooms in the imperial chambers."

"When will he return?"

The retainer shook his head; he did not know. Yang Kuo-chung could see that the old man did not look at him too closely, trying to be polite, no doubt, by averting his eyes. He knew he must have presented quite a sight to the man—disheveled, perspiring, and without even his outer jacket, which he had not had time to put on. Despite the outside cold, the Fox could feel that his face was flushed and his ears hot. He stood for a moment, undecided, while the servant waited politely and discreetly. Well, he would have to do something quickly. He removed the sheaf of papers from under his robes and thrust them toward the servant.

"These are all that is left. But they are the most important. Don't ask me to explain. Just take them, hide them, and give them to Master Kao when he returns."

The servant took the papers, but Yang Kuo-chung could see a confused and worried furrow on the old man's brow. As the Fox rushed away from Kao Li-shih's apartments, he could still see that look in his mind's eye. It would probably stay on the old retainer's face a long time.

Yang Kuo-chung ran across the final stretch of courtyard toward Lin-te Hall. It loomed ahead of him, an imposing, forbidding structure, the outline of its lofty, angular eaves against the sky heightening his sense of futility and foreboding. The building, deep within the Ta Ming Palace grounds, was multitiered and castellated and flanked by high crenellated towers. Its appearance to Yang Kuo-chung as he ran toward it was that of a fortress—not a hall of resolution and harmony. As he ran, he couldn't help feeling the way a small rodent must feel when it runs across open terrain under the moving shadow of a bird of prey.

He leapt up the three flights of outside stairs with all the speed that was left in him and made for the enclosed safety of the winding brick stairwell. He was burrowed, for the moment, like the little animal who reaches cover. Chest heaving, lungs pained, he reached the top of the stairs outside the hearings chamber on the Lin-te's upper floor. Exhausted, he placed his hands on his knees and leaned against the curved wall sucking in deep draughts of the damp, musty air. He had run the entire distance from the imperial city to the center of the palace complex, and now he felt as if he were about to collapse. But the bird did not have him yet!

He ascended the final stairs, the last spiral of the stairwell, to the floor above. Close to the last stair "the Fox" ducked into a recess in the wall for a moment. He was still breathing hard—they would hear him too soon. From here he could see that the chamber doors were closed and heavily guarded. It was as he had feared—the "hearings" had already begun.

His heart almost stopped as a hideous scream from behind the doors filled the cavernous space of the outer hall. The sound hung in the air, frozen, reverberating, like the last note of a great bell. He remained in the stairwell passage, shocked into immobility, his eyes fixed on the magnificent tiger incense burner that stood sentinel beside the stairs that led into the hearings chamber. What was happening inside had gone beyond his worst imaginings. Government was collapsing in on itself like a burning hut of bamboo. All order had given way. Autumn was the Ministry of Punishments. Autumn was the west and metal and signified by the tiger. And that day the tiger—in the guise of a chief minister—had bared its bloody claws; the great fanged mouth breathed spiraled plumes of frozen white smoke; white was the color of autumn and death, and white was no color at all . . .

Fury now rose inside him; if he was indeed the prey, then his pursuer would learn who it was that he stalked. He had to get into that room. He thought about the giant who had been his friend in the north, who had broken the neck of the whoremonger with a single blow. How he wished he were here now to help him get by these Chancellery thugs and goons blocking his way.

But no murderer's hands would drop twitching onto the bloodstained ground that day unless he did it himself. He was alone. If he tried to get help, who would listen to him? These were mere "hearings." Who would believe his urgent rantings? Only Kao Li-shih, but he did not know where to find him. And there was no time! This murderer, this chief minister, was free to do as he wished behind the deceitful jade partitions of his Ssu-k'ung office! Free behind his mockery of the law! Another dreadful scream pierced the air. He stepped out of his hiding place.

Though Yang Kuo-chung was the second most powerful man in the Chinese bureaucracy, he understood that without an emperor, his position amounted to nothing. He stood in the center of the hallway facing the guards before moving toward them, looking at them with utter scorn. They returned nothing but an intractable silence, their jaws firmly clenched against any response. They are well trained, he thought.

"Perhaps you are all too stupid to know who I am, but that will not excuse you. Now let me pass!" His voice sounded strange and dangerous in his own head. He made an attempt to enter the chamber; the guards formed a line between him and the doors. "Why am I not permitted inside the hearings chamber?" he demanded, his blood rising. "Am I not the highest member of this branch of the Censorate body? I demand an answer from you, now!"

"We have our orders, Master Yang," one of the men replied. "No one is to be admitted."

None of the others spoke, moved, or looked at him. He stared at them for a while, then turned around and took a few steps as if he were going to leave. When he did, the guards moved back into their original positions. Another scream, followed by a long moan, came from behind the door. He turned then and rushed at the doors. His hand was nearly on the long brass latch when three of the guards grabbed him from the front and two others pinned his arms behind him.

"I will have you all arrested for resisting an appointee of our Imperial Father!" he shouted. His voice boomed around him, echoing in the hall. "Let me pass or you will all be dead men! The chief minister is not the only one who can see to your banishments! Remember that!" The guards were unmoved by his threats. They fastened themselves to him even tighter than before and began to drag him away from the chamber doors.

Struggling violently to shake them loose, he nearly stumbled, his leather boots sliding along the polished terrazzo of the floor. Don't fall, don't let them get on top of you, he told himself. There were more screams. They took him to the top of the stairs and let go of him. Were they going to push him? He didn't wait to find out.

With sudden, brutal jabs of his foot he kicked the two guards who had pinned his arms. They clutched at their stomachs, letting out howls of pain; one of them writhed on the floor. He spun around, his knee flying into the groin of one of the three left. As the man doubled and dropped, Yang Kuo-chung dodged the other two and with an enormous effort lifted a heavy tripod incense burner. For a brief second he held the massive iron ornament even with his shoulders, the tremendous weight stretching every tendon and muscle, his pulses pounding. Then he threw it, hitting one of the guards in the chest. The burner knocked the man down, hit the floor, and rolled down the hall, reverberating like thunder as it did. The last guard, seeing that he was alone with Yang Kuo-chung, looked at him for a moment and then turned and ran down the stairs.

Yang Kuo-chung raced for the hearings chamber, lifted the latch, pushed one of the thick wooden doors inward and slammed it behind him, finding himself in an antechamber. But he must think quickly. The guard who had run was shouting for reinforcements. They would be clattering up the stairs at any moment. He would have to find a way to bar the doors, and quickly.

A piece of decorative metal? An iron bar? He turned to the *lien-tse* blinds on the towering windows. Thick metal rods secured the bottoms of each of the heavy rolled blinds against the winds at this height. One of them would be perfect. He moved to the nearest window and pulled hard at the metal weight. It would not give. He stopped and listened. It had grown quiet in the next room; the screaming had stopped. They would hear him, but it was a chance he would have to take. The guards outside were a greater danger.

He seized the slatted blind. He would have to rip the entire cursed thing down. He tugged and twisted, trying to pull it loose from its moorings at the ceiling. More guards had reached the hallway outside now. He could hear the cries of pain from the ones he had disabled, and he heard shouts and orders and scuffling as the others moved toward the massive doors. He jerked on the blind. The first tear appeared far above near the intricate bracketed corbeling on the ceiling. Then another tear. He let out a yell and pulled with all his might. Let them hear him! They would know soon enough that he was here! The slats began to splinter and shards of wood rained down. Then the entire ten feet of blind collapsed onto him like a giant snake that had dropped from a tree.

He wedged the iron bar with the blind trailing behind it in the latches of the door just as they started to move. He stepped back. On the other side, the guards pounded and shouted, but the door held. He turned then and opened the door to the hearings chamber itself. He halted and stared.

The room was empty. It was as if there had never been anyone in there at all. No officials, no torturers, no tortured. Whoever had been here had gone.

He stood in the middle of the room a long time staring up at the judges' platform, the tables draped with rich crimson-purple silk cloth, and then down at the kneeling pads at his feet. He bent over and examined them closely. There were no indentations, not a sign that anyone had knelt before the inquisitors' platform.

When he first came to the doors of the hearings chamber, moments before, he had heard cries, screams of pain. He did not know where the victims, his Censorate officers, had been taken in such a hurry, but he had *heard* them. They had been tortured. He imagined them admitting to anything simply to avoid any more pain. Minor censures, Kao Li-shih had said. Minor censures for minor officials. Embarrassments! Simple punitive measures to slow the work of the investigative Censorate in the north, and that was all! But he had heard the screams of pain, the cries of honored servants of the Censorate. Where was the law? Where was the sanity of an enlightened emperor now? Gone. Asleep, unwakable, unreachable, unbelieving. Locked away far beyond the Hsuan-wu Gates, at play in his Pavilion of the Hundred Flowers. And if these eunuch officials were not dead yet, they probably would be soon, after confessing to crimes they never committed.

Under *tzu-shou*, the act of confessing should save their lives—but how could he expect Li Lin-fu to honor the law? This man made his own rules. The aides and officials and all those connected with them would be blacklisted, banished out beyond the Cold Palace, beyond the gates of Hell. Beyond all reason of justice. Their crimes would be made to look inexcusable, traitorous to the state, a conspiracy against the military security of the north, attacks against the royal House of Li.

The stories of the poet-minister and others who had disappeared were real. Kao Li-shih had told him, and now he knew that he spoke the truth. And there was nothing he could do. He was powerless. He shuddered at the memory of those cries.

They had made him see his existence too clearly. His own life—the playboy turned high official—was a sham. All the messages from Li Lin-fu had said the same thing—that he, Yang Kuo-chung, was out of his league. At that moment, it appeared to be the truth. His life, his "work," had all the purpose and meaning of the motions of the rotating silhouette of a mythological hero-figure in a heat-driven lantern.

Where had his officials been taken? Had they disappeared into covered carriages? Were they dead? Near death? With them went the papers, the investigating body's records of northern affairs, everything from the offices of the aides. All confiscated when the eunuchs had disappeared two days ago—everything except what Yang Kuo-chung had hidden in his own apartments or brought to Kao Li-shih's chambers that morning.

Yang Kuo-chung stood alone in the empty hearings chamber, feeling like a child again, helpless, enraged at things beyond his understanding, the overwhelming will of another. But there were no answers here, and he knew he couldn't risk staying any longer.

Once outside, he began to run. It was not because anyone was chasing him; he just had to run. It was as if the decisions for his own body were no longer his. And overhead the clouds were moving fast, fleecy knots and wispy strands spreading across the great curved expanse of cobalt blue . . .

::

"A party . . . a party!" The dwarf ran around in small tight circles, his stubby arms flapping like the wings of a flightless bird. "A party for your tiny knight. My lady is going to have a party for me! A grand party with all of our girls and lavish tables of colorful delicacies and musicians and dancing . . ." He ran in the other direction now, bouncing over the cushioned divans and clinging like a monkey to the heavy brocaded curtains. "I shall be dressed up in the finest silks and satins and wrapped in ten thousand liang of glimmering golden chains and bracelets! I shall wear the makeup of the peacock and the eyebrows of the moon moth upon my handsome face! And all the eastern markets and all of the P'ing-kang and Ch'ung-jen wards shall sing praises to my beauty!" He jumped down from the curtains and ran over to her. He rubbed himself against her leg and looked at her face adoringly. "And I shall decorate my 'boner'—which already grows, my lady!—with oils and feathers!" He laughed and scampered away.

And as she watched him capering about the splendid room, she could see by the bulge in his satin trousers that he spoke the truth. She smiled fondly. He was her perpetual child, but permanently aroused with the insatiable appetite of a stallion. She spoke to him while her handmaidens combed and braided the shining length of her hair.

"My little dildo," she said. She had as many names for him as suited her moods. After she bought him she never gave him a real name, and he had never told her what his name had been, as if he had no past. Besides, pets do not have names they can remember, he once said.

"Do you know who will be our guests of honor at the party?" she said to him. "You could not guess if I gave you all the hours you spent fondling yourself."

"Only to keep it hard for you," he said, running back to her and resting his head in her lap. "A harbor silts where no ship docks!" The outrageous child-man preened the feathers of his helmet.

"Yes. And I am most grateful, Little One," she said patiently. "But can you guess who is coming, then?" She held her fingers out for manicuring and spoke in a dignified tone of voice. "It is a very great person."

"The Queen Mother of the West!" he cried, jumping up and down, "and her coterie of smooth-assed little boys whom she brings so I might teach them how to fuck. And bugger them, too!" he chortled. "The rabbit in the moon and the princesses of the Magic Isles!" he shouted, and tore around the room again.

"No, my horny little fool. It is even better than that and a far greater honor than all the peculiar immortals of your perverse dreams."

"I cannot guess at all, my lady," he said with despair. "I must confess. The one with the big head is right! My mind is indeed weakened from all the jism that flows from my tiny little loins." His big eyes looked up at her pleadingly. "I cannot guess at all," he said, pretending to wipe tears from his eyes with the hem of her skirts. Then he lifted the skirts to her knees.

She pulled her hand away from the servant girl who had begun to paint her nails, and swatted him affectionately. He let go of her skirts and cast his eyes sulkily toward the floor. She stroked his head.

"If you will be quiet, then I shall tell you." She placed her hand back in the servant girl's. "A different color on each of the nails, today, don't you think?" she said pleasantly to the girl. "Something special. We have received a most magnificent letter and more taels of silver and strings of cash than we have ever seen. With such funds we could break all the sumptuary laws of the city and build a mansion to rival those of the fabulous Yangs. But we are to hold a party with it, and the rest is for us to keep and do with as we like. Perhaps we shall rebuild our house and redesign our gardens as the Yang sisters are forever doing. Or . . ." she said dreamily, "*travel!* Yes, travel, like a princess and prince, from one grand palace to another . . ."

"And *who* is it from, my lady?" The dwarf implored impatiently, pressing his hardness against her knees. "Such suspense. Such suspense. I cannot bear another moment. I cannot wait to hear!"

She smiled down at him.

"It comes from the great munificence of our chief minister of state. He wishes, he tells us, to entertain very important men of another race—ambassadors of some other country not nearly so grand as our own. He does not want them to judge our great nation from the poverty of our imperial lodges—he refuses to have them put up there. They are to join us in our beautiful pavilions, be entertained by us, and rest here in our beds. It is a parting gesture he wishes to make for them, he said, before they are sent on business to some islands in the southern seas. So much money, Little One, from our Imperial Father's chief minister! More money than you have ever seen."

He fondled her legs through her skirts.

"We shall have such fun," he said, stroking her arms and kissing the white flesh with his lips. "Such fun! I shall begin to order the cooks to their work now . . . Duck and pheasant and quail and roebuck and eel and cakes and anise and . . . *peaches,* my lady! I shall make it *my* job to find peaches!" His square, handsome face beamed with enthusiasm. "Peaches in autumn!"

: :

There are times, Li Lin-fu reflected happily, when only the very finest that money can buy will do. And it is a truly satisfying thing to have spent a great deal of money and to have received in return full value for the amount spent. Too often, he thought, it turns out the other way, and one feels cheated.

The professional mourners had been very expensive indeed, but they had done their jobs masterfully. It was an art—he had not realized it until now, but that is what it was. As a musician himself, he could appreciate it. Their wails and shrieks of pain behind the studded doors of the hearings chamber had been utterly real—so much so that he, Li Lin-fu, waiting in a nearby antechamber, had thought for a moment that a mistake had been made and that the mourners were actually being tortured. No, it was simply that he had paid for and received the very best—not mere funeral singers, but ones whose wails could summon the ghosts of the dead! He sincerely hoped that the young lieutenant chief minister, president of the Ministry of Finance, and head of the Censorate, Yang Kuo-chung, had enjoyed the performance as much as he himself had.

He smiled. Just as professional mourning was an art, so was torture. What a dreadful word, he thought. How crude in its implications. Oh, yes, these Censorate aides were going to be tortured, but by nothing so unimaginative and commonplace as, say, hot needles under the fingernails or being strung up by their arms twisted behind their backs until they screamed out anything they thought you wanted to hear. He had, in his time, experimented with physical torture. It was interesting up to a point, and useful in certain cases where quick results were desired, but on the whole, it was unsatisfying and woefully predictable. He preferred to exercise his imagination—his art.

He pulled aside the curtain of the carriage he rode in. They were very nearly at their destination.

The Censorate's highest grade eunuch aides were on their way to a grand event deep in the eastern market in the unlikely and endless alleyways south of the Hsing-ching palaces. The lavish carriages, the grand procession of state, slid past the evening's lanternlit throngs, shops, and bazaars, winding past li after li of high white-washed walls, gaily decorated doorposts, and balconied wineshops and brothels of the notorious P'ing-kang ward.

The crowds parted before the proud assemblage of archers, pipers, pennant bearers and lancers, gold-and-blue phoenix phaetons and satin-shuttered carriages, and two hundred armed outriders. Li Lin-fu had created the spectacle for the benefit of the people in the street, for the ten eunuch "ambassadors," and for his own traveling protection. From behind his blinds, he watched as balconies quickly filled with people scrambling for a good view of the entourage. Children squealed with delight, tossing handfuls of rocks and dust. Older children climbed the walls and shouted threats to the horsemen like menacing ambushers. It was a grand time.

Not far off the main boulevard, the procession stopped at the gates of Madame Li's establishment. The small army dismounted and stationed themselves outside the gaily festooned palace of entertainment. The high wooden gates opened and the carriages rumbled into the cobbled courtyard. The buildings were outlined with lanterns, and a light breeze rustled the purple banners, put up in honor of the office of the Ssu-k'ung, as the party entered the reception hall.

At a cue from the dwarf, the music began. Striking rhythms, bold melodies, and the laughter of young women filled the pavilions. The evening was beginning on a note of promise, Li Lin-fu mused pleasantly as the bearers raised his gilded chair.

:: ::

"They have arrived! They have arrived!" The child-man's voice called out as he scurried about among the servants and caterers and musicians. "This is indeed the grandest day of our wretched little life!" He swirled around, displaying himself, ridiculous in a miniature lacquered-armor breastplate and broad sequined cape. Violent rainbows of ostrich and peacock feathers adorned his cap, his large dark almond eyes were outlined with turquoise, and his cheeks were heavily rouged. Today he was the Prince of the Flying Thunder Owls, the King of Carp, the Tortoise-headed River God, Master of the Undersea Dominions and Rover of the Endless Subterranean Palaces, and Fei Wei, the four-winged dragon of fertility. He was everything and staggered by the weight of his own beauty and importance. When he opened his parasol, the world would be plunged into darkness, and when he played his guitar, its notes, in accordance with the elements, ruled the winds.

Li Lin-fu was delighted with the little man. He had never known the deformed to give so much pleasure. Perhaps his children would find it entertaining to have such a one at home, he thought.

Li Lin-fu was seated at the head of a long table with Madame Li next to him. The ten eunuch aides were seated along both sides of the table. They did not speak, and their faces were expressionless as Madame Li's banquet hall began to fill with her girls, who passed in a line to the head of the table and knelt before their honored guests. Li Lin-fu presented the first ten females with small purses of silver coins. The ones who followed were given gifts by his attendants—colorful bolts of silk, tiny gems wrapped in handkerchiefs, and jade and ivory ornaments for their hair. They thanked the chief minister with effusive and endless repetitions of gratitude until the dwarf shooed them brusquely away.

As the wine steward brought in the serving tray and poured the first cup for each of the honored guests, the tiny knight climbed onto the table, stood solemnly before Li Lin-fu, and kowtowed three times. He then rose on his stumpy legs, the top of his head reaching just barely above the heads of the seated guests, and reached down and raised a "three-color" phoenix-headed wine ewer to his forehead. Then he lowered it below his waist before raising it again, the signal for his guests to begin to drink.

The ten eunuchs cast questioning looks at one another, searching for a clue. Li Lin-fu merely smiled at them and raised his cup.

"Drink, gentlemen," he said congenially. "To the health and long life of everyone here, and to the health of the empire!" Their cups rose, but spiritlessly, raggedly, their unhappy faces tense with uncertainty. The evening, Li Lin-fu thought, promised to be one of his finest. He raised his cup again. "And to your health, especially," he said to the tiny knight who still stood before him on the table.

"I thank you from the bottom of my little heart!" the dwarf piped, bowing again. "For our guests, we have spared no costs! But then, we have spent no coin," he giggled. "Our grand and generous councillor of state has seen to all the bills. To his Royal Dignity and his honorable guests!" He raised the ewer to the small orchestral ensemble and they began to play again, this time tunes and rhythms from the fathomless distances of central Asia. The dwarf whirled about to the music, his high-pitched voice rising above the sound of the orchestra. "Sixteen-string *chins* and Assyrian angle harps and Persian harps and tiny wether drums and chimes and cymbals and flutes and pipes—the *hsuan*, the *sheng*, the *hsiao*—give drunkenness to our souls! Exotic wines from the western markets—'mare's teat,' Turfan grape wine and millet wines with pepper and pomegranate flowers and ginger and anise and sassafras and saffron and honey give drunkenness to our bodies! Let the food commence!" He put the wine ewer back on its tray, swept up his glittering cape and leapt down and scrambled under the table.

: :

Madame Li watched her ten guests with fascination. It had been unmistakable from the first moment they entered the hall: the slightly stooped postures and gangly limbs; the odd, fleshy smoothness of their faces; the carefully controlled contralto voices. But why were they being entertained here, of all places? She had seen many strange things in her day, but "bobtail dogs" in a brothel? Never. And these were Fukien aunties, the sort who—she shuddered to think of it—had *everything* cut off to secure government positions. There would be nothing, nothing at all, that they could do with her girls, the finest in Ch'ang-an. And it was plain that the guests were not in a good frame of mind; they had been, in fact, distinctly uneasy when they arrived, though they appeared to be relaxing somewhat. Why were they here? The dwarf, she could see, was asking himself the same questions. He peered out from under the table, first here, then there, casting curious looks at each of the seated officials. He is probably trying to look under their robes, she thought with amusement.

At least Master Li Lin-fu's use of the word "race" in the letter read by her capable and literate steward now made sense. Indeed, she thought; they are, though definitely Chinese, of another "race"—the race of eunuchs. She looked at Li Lin-fu, smiling, eating, and drinking. What could his purpose be? She wanted to ask him, but thinking of the money he had lavished on her, she desisted. He has paid for a party, she thought, ten times over, and a party he shall get. Perhaps the mysterious purpose will reveal itself later. Hers was not, after all, to ask . . . She felt a set of little arms embrace her legs beneath the table. Her tiny knight, at least, was having a grand time.

: :

With the food came the entertainers. Madame Li had done well, Li Lin-fu thought, with the money he had paid her. And the dwarf's forays into the exotic foreign markets of West Ch'ang-an had been most productive. It was a rare thing for Li Lin-fu to allow himself the indulgence of the medicinal benefits of entertainment. Tonight he would enjoy himself, and put work and problems out of his mind. It was *his* night. His and, obviously, the dwarf's!

The first trays of food had been brought to the tables. There were multicolored porcelain soup bowls filled with delicate broths of river fish and gingered pork. The chopsticks were of carved rosewood and ivory inlay. Repoussé silver and carved translucent jade platters were piled high with fragrant sweetmeats, nuts, candied fruit, and sweet doughy pastries filled with berry jellies, sesame, and soy paste; sliced pheasant, quail, and lamb with dark sauces of garlic and star anise; steamed peas and peppers arranged to resemble bouquets of exotic tropical flora and fauna—specifically, the miraculous flowers and birds of tropical Lingnan and the isle of Hainan. That had been the chief minister's request in his letter to Madame Li. And the dwarf had spared no energy in his hunt through the western wards to find the foreign ingredients and the talent to prepare them.

The eunuchs were eating. At first, several of them had shown no interest in the food, but merely sat with blank, tense expressions. A few of them had hesitantly accepted food, but Li Lin-fu noticed that they only took food from platters that he himself had already been served from. Surely they do not think I would do anything so crude and clumsy as poisoning them, he thought, and made a show of eating the food and swallowing it. Eventually even the stubbornest among them gave in and began to help themselves. He knew that they were hungry; they had received only tea and an occasional biscuit during their two days of confinement. Li Lin-fu signaled the wine steward. Make sure their cups are never empty, he told the man, and smiled at his guests. There was a commotion. The dwarf was out from under the table and climbing onto a chair next to Madame Li.

"For the amusement of our guests," he shouted, "I have searched the entire city for the rarest, the finest, the most astonishing and mind-boggling acts that will make you think you are in a dream"—he laughed and flourished his cape—"which you are! Let the entertainment begin!"

A bounding troupe of acrobats entered the hall with an array of balancing rods, hoops, barrels, rolling spheres, feathered arrows and fiery lances, and a menagerie of tiny monkeys in glittering costumes. One of the creatures ran straight for the dwarf and jumped in his lap.

"My lady has brought lovers for her little man!" the dwarf exclaimed. "But alas, they are too small for me—I would split them in half in the throes of our sweet monkey passion!" He howled with delight at his joke, and thrusting his pelvis, pretended to be copulating with the monkey. This drew one or two faint smiles from the eunuchs and an appreciative guffaw from the chief minister. Madame Li, also laughing, slapped the dwarf on his little rump. He dropped the monkey and climbed into her lap, putting his arms around her neck. "Forgive me," he said. "I did not mean to make you jealous! You know that I am insatiable!" The eunuchs were now glancing at one another, laughing in spite of themselves. The wine was doing its job, Li Lin-fu noted with approval, dissolving their reticence. They knew by now that the food and drink was not poisoned, and though they were surely still uneasy about their fates, they had decided to relax and enjoy the spectacle. Several of them, it appeared, had made the decision to go ahead and get very drunk, and were keeping the wine stewards busy. Li Lin-fu approved. That was the brave, manly thing to do under such circumstances. He was glad that he had already made the decision to spare their lives, though there was no way they could know it.

The juggling and balancing acts continued throughout the dinner, which went on hour after hour, course after course; and the skill of the performers, their seeming ability to defy all natural laws, had a disorienting effect on the senses which, combined with the intoxicating effects of the wine, created an atmosphere that was, just as the dwarf had promised, like a dream. The tiny monkeys danced on platters atop impossibly balanced poles. Jugglers threw flaming batons into the air with bloodcurdling yells, and acrobats vaulted, sprang, and somersaulted over one another. Each astounding maneuver was punctuated by a strident clash of the brass cymbals and a tune on the stone chimes.

In the middle of the acrobatic acts came the strangest performance of them of all: a female contortionist, clad in a skin-tight suit of serpent scales. Her body truly possessed the qualities of a snake—she could turn and twist her limbs in every direction, tying her arms and legs in impossible knots. But as if these feats or her sensuously glistening appearance alone were not enough, she stood in the center of the room where everyone could see her clearly and turned her head completely around like a wagon wheel on an axle. A hush fell over the tables for a moment, and then the entire hall burst into wild ululations of disgust and amusement. Madly pleased with himself, with his powers to bring forth the strange, the freakish, the dwarf jumped up and down and howled, banging his wine cup jubilantly on the edge of the table.

Li Lin-fu was as interested in the spectacle of the eunuchs as he was in the exotic acts. He felt that he had succeeded in putting them in a state of utter confusion, a perfect limbo. They could have little knowledge of what had actually befallen the offices of the Censorate. They had been cleverly taken away, simply removed, without explanation or violence, surreptitiously and one at a time, before the destruction began. There had never been any "hearing"; they had not even been informally questioned. They never saw a thing; they had no idea what to expect. Their senses were clearly numbed by now. Li Lin-fu could scarcely contain his curiosity. What would all of this possibly mean to them? What sense would they make of it? A banquet? A party? *Women?* He studied their faces. Did a single one of them, he wondered, have an inkling of what was in store for them? He could not be sure, and he enjoyed the guessing game. That quiet one at the end of the table, perhaps? No, he looked as if he might be ready to pass out. The slightly arrogant one who has refused to look me in the eye all evening? Yes, perhaps. Well, he will find out soon enough, if he has not already guessed.

Li Lin-fu was enjoying himself hugely. He realized how hard he had been working lately. How rarely do I take the time anymore, he thought, to revitalize myself through pure pleasure. And none of this had actually cost him even a coin. Another thing the eunuchs could not possibly know was that they were paying for the party themselves. The money had been confiscated out of the Censorate's reserves of funds for operations and for salaries —their salaries! What would they think if they knew that their money, their livelihood, the salaries of high-ranking eunuch officials, had been channeled into the purse of the wealthiest brothel-keeper in all of Ch'ang-an? Li Lin-fu savored the irony—eunuchs' money finding its way to a brothel!

The dwarf jumped onto the table then, spreading out his cape like a set of wings to get the attention of the guests.

"Your humble and conscientious servant," he piped as the crowd gradually quieted, "left no stone unturned, no avenue unexplored, no skirt unlifted . . ." He paused while his audience laughed. ". . . in his relentless search for the finest in delicacies and entertainment. And if I were to drop dead now at your feet, I could go to my reward a satisfied, happy, and fulfilled dwarf knowing that I gave you the best in the world. Peaches, my friends! We shall have for our dessert peaches—the rarest, freshest, largest, sweetest, juiciest, most magical erotic fruit that can be had in these final autumn days before winter!" A murmur of delight and approval went through the room, but he held up his stumpy arms once more, commanding silence. "But first," he said significantly, turning slowly in a complete circle, "the magicians." He leapt from the table.

Magicians? The smile faded from Li Lin-fu's face. He had certainly not asked for magicians. He detested magicians. Who had put the little monster up to this? There had been no mention of bringing magicians to these festivities. This was not what he wanted at all. He did not want the atmosphere they brought. Monks, illusionists, magicians, shamans, necromancers, gomcheu— witches all of them, exhaling the same fetid, illogical air. Smug in their "mysteries" and "knowledge." Full of deceit, illusion, artifice, mirages—having you believe that they enjoy some exclusive connection with invisible, unknown worlds. Li Lin-fu's chest constricted unpleasantly. He could feel a coughing fit coming. Not here, he told himself, his iron will moving into place. Not here. He shut his eyes and breathed deeply. As he did, an unpleasant image of the grave of his father rose to the surface of his mind. Go back where you came from, he snarled at it and opened his eyes. The desire to cough had passed. He turned and smiled pleasantly at Madame Li and joined in the applause for the dwarf. Somehow, he would sit through this.

Bowls of fresh, soft, fragrant peaches arrived, and so did three strange men, all dressed in the black robes of Taoists. One of them was very tall and thin and slightly stooped from age, the top of his head covered in fragile wisps of golden white hair that spilled over his forehead like snow on a mountaintop. A narrow fringe of wispy beard hung from his chin like icicles. The two others were considerably younger: One was short, soft, and round, with the disturbingly comfortable face of a carved wooden smiling god of prosperity; his teeth were oddly gapped, and thick wild tufts of black hair adorned his large skull. The other was slight and almost childlike, with thin, red lips that reminded Li Lin-fu of the skin of a worm; large, dark eyes very far apart; and a tiny, flat nose that nearly disappeared into his face. To Li Lin-fu, this one looked like something fetal and unformed, dropped too soon from its mother. But the oldest, the ancient white-haired one, looked as if he had not been born of a woman at all, but had existed as an old man for all eternity.

And as they lowered themselves to crosslegged postures on thick cushions at the center of the hall, Li Lin-fu observed something all three had in common, despite their diverse faces and bodies: hands of unearthly and exquisite delicacy, like the carved limestone or ivory hands of a Hindu or Buddhist deity; fingers of disturbing beauty, poised, it seemed, in long, frozen *mudras*. Li Lin-fu did not like this. He could see that the little dwarf had become even more gleeful than before.

He found that the dwarf's antics were no longer charming or amusing. He felt irritated and slightly disgusted now with the ugly, disproportionate little creature who scurried around among the magicians, bringing them tea and cakes and platters of candied fruit. With small gestures of their perfect icon hands, the magicians refused everything but a single ewer of honey-golden wine and three brass goblets decorated with low reliefs depicting ancient Han dynasty hunting scenes. For a long while they sat nearly motionless on their pillows, moving only occasionally to sip at their wine. They looked straight ahead, saying nothing. Li Lin-fu hated their arrogance and unreadability.

With the platters of peaches arrived the highly skilled dessert caterers whose art it was to carve the ripe red fruits before each of the guests. Using deft movements of tiny serrated kitchen knives and curved picks, they caused the round fruits to blossom into tropical flowers with spiraling petals still tightly closed, like buds. Then each "flower" was bathed in a central Asian "dew" of thick fermented mare's milk; to this was added a colorful and aromatic cinnamon and rosehip wine. The guests applauded the elegant effort. Even the ten Censorate eunuchs, forgetting the excruciating uncertainty of the evening, nodded a special commendation to their hostess and to the tiny knight who now returned to her side. Peaches were the ultimate statement—the final course of a banquet of six hours and one hundred and twenty different dishes.

Madame Li's party would not soon be forgotten, Li Lin-fu thought, including what was coming later. Word of everything that happened here tonight, he knew, would spread throughout the city like a raging fire in the crowded tenements of the southwest. That was good. But these magicians . . . ?

Standing on his stool, the dwarf raised a pair of silver chopsticks over his head. He motioned for the percussionists in the orchestra to strike the brass cymbals and the wooden clappers.

"The peaches must be eaten in a special way," he announced in his jubilant and squeaky little voice, "otherwise our Grand Queen Mother of the West—Hsi Wang Mu—will be displeased. She will not deliver her sexual blessings upon us. Our virility and femininity will disappear like smoke before a winter wind!" The dwarf cast a quick glance at the eunuchs. "With the heavy end of your chopsticks strike the center the way our owl-god of thunder strikes his drums. Like so!" He demonstrated, striking the center of the flower-bud peach in front of him. The carved fruit fell open like a blossom presenting itself to the sun. "You see! How simple and delicious!" The tables applauded him; the girls laughed with delight. "Master Li Lin-fu—our Divine Son of Heaven's Grand Councillor of State—must be the first," the dwarf continued. "We humbly beseech him to lead the way in our dessert just as he helps our Great Imperial Father lead the nation in ten thousand years of peace and prosperity!"

Li Lin-fu made the expected ritual gesture of decline and humility, then smiled to the room and raised the heavy end of his chopsticks in preparation to strike the "blow." At that moment, the old magician turned his head, looked Li Lin-fu directly in the eye, and smiled radiantly. Li Lin-fu paused for only a short moment, then brought his chopstick down. But the stick made a ringing sound as it hit. Li Lin-fu looked down. The plate was empty. The bowl which had sat on the plate until a moment ago and the fruit in it had disappeared. The room became abruptly silent. All eyes followed Li Lin-fu's. On his floor cushion some twenty feet away, the old magician still sat motionless. He had not moved. The other two had not changed their positions, either. Then the old white-haired magician nudged the jolly round-faced one at his side. That one spoke, showing his widely gapped teethed.

"My master wishes some tea to follow his dessert. He is, unfortunately, mute and requires us to speak for him. But he wishes to thank our grand and noble chief minister for sharing his sweet repast."

There was no laughter. All eyes in the room traveled from the old magician to Li Lin-fu. The chief minister was expressionless. The old magician took an audible deep breath, causing everyone to look back in his direction. The man opened the front of his robe and, as the hushed room watched him intently, exposed the naked wrinkled flesh of his ancient belly. With one slender, ageless, ivory hand, he appeared to be reaching into his abdomen, the hand and arm vanishing for a moment up past the thin forearm. With a sudden jerking motion, the hand came out, a coil of intestine wrapped around the wrist. In the hand was the jade-and-gold dessert plate, and on the plate was the untouched peach-flower in cream and wine. A collective gasp issued from everyone in the room. The magician quickly tucked the bit of intestine back inside his body and closed the hole, leaving no mark and no blood. He held the plate toward Li Lin-fu and bowed his head graciously.

"My master wishes to inform you that he is done with dessert," the round, cheerful God-Face continued, "and wishes to return it to our grand councillor."

Li Lin-fu accepted the steward's return of the dish. The peach-flower was closed, the thick sauce on top undisturbed. The room was waiting for the chief minister's reaction. The illusion had been perfect—so perfect that it enraged Li Lin-fu, but he was careful to conceal it. He nodded graciously to the master illusionist, thinking that such a man should just as well be put to death, then raised his bony hands and began to clap.

Wild applause broke out. The dwarf went mad with joy, leaping from his chair to the table, somersaulting, slapping his knees, and laughing ludicrously. Li Lin-fu turned to the ten eunuchs, who shook their heads, laughed, and muttered among themselves.

"That was a masterful trick, was it not? Since all your eyes were fooled equally, it was not just for my benefit." Detestable apparition-mongers, the chief minister thought.

"You have heard our grand councillor," the tiny knight exclaimed. "The illusion was for the enjoyment of all!" He signaled the orchestra. Music began again, and conversation resumed as the guests began to eat their desserts at last. Li Lin-fu looked at his own peach-flower. He did not believe that it had ever been inside the stomach of the old magician, but he had as much appetite for it as if it had.

Li Lin-fu studied the three illusionists. The old one was now leaning toward round God-Face and tapping that one's wrist. God-Face lowered his head as if listening, eyes closed. Then his head jerked up and he smiled when the old man finished tapping his wrist, and they both looked in Li Lin-fu's direction.

Li Lin-fu recognized it for what it was. He had heard tales of men who could go into trances and "hear" the unspoken words of others, but he had refused to believe these things. And until now, he had refused to even admit the detestable idea into his consciousness. He waited. God-Face was going to speak again. The room fell quiet when the man raised his arm.

"Our humble master wishes to inform you, Grand Councillor, that although the entertainment was for the benefit of all, it was not an illusion."

"Oh, this is going to be good! So very good!" the tiny knight cried out from the tabletop. "We are going to hear things we ought not to hear at all. And I like that, very much!"

"Hush, Dwarf!" Madame Li said, grabbing at the jewelry around his ankles. But he shook off her hand and pranced around the table, upsetting plates and cups with his whirling cape and feathered plumes.

"Illusions are the appearance of things that are not," the magician's spokesman continued. "What you have seen is only the tiniest peek at all the things that are—the mere top of the ocean, the underside of the cloud, the shining face of the moon. But"—he paused—"my master bows to you," he said to the chief minister. "He says that you are indeed the grandest magician of them all, Master Li Lin-fu—we all bow to you—because," he said, making a gesture that took in the room, the food, the music, the guests, himself, and his comrades, "you make a party appear where there is *none.*"

"Oh, this is better than I could have hoped!" the dwarf shouted as the room applauded again and the music began.

"Have the 'magicians' dismissed, please!" Li Lin-fu whispered, leaning toward Madame Li. "And thank our little friend for such a stimulating choice of entertainment. Although, you will excuse me, Madame Li—this is not to impugn your gracious hospitality—but many such illusionists, such apparition-mongers, were banned from China, sent back across the Tibetan frontier years ago under direct imperial order. I do not suppose that you would remember that." Startled by his words, she signaled the three "performers" to leave. They rose and bowed in unison to the head of the table, politely backing away from the chief minister as they left the room. Seeing her worried look, he reassured her. "There is, of course, no infraction here, Madame Li. It is quite likely that anything can be found in the western markets: Brahmin, common Hindu, Tantric, Vedic, Manichaean, and Muslim magicians. You may even find small secret houses of Persian hemp smokers so lost in the potent hallucinations of their drug that they roll the final embers, the glowing balls of ash upon their tongues to light their next pipeful—without feeling any pain. No, there are far too many holes through which anything can slip. We can not root it all out. One could, I do not doubt, find in small, hidden booksellers' stalls down darkened dead-end alleys outlawed volumes of western magic—the Persian necromanican, the Moghrebi books of magic. Anything! And our little friend—your tiny knight, as you so aptly call him—has his stubby fingers on the pulses of this city, no doubt, as a worthy physician peruses the many pulses of the body. He, I am certain, with his most unusual powers, could find anyone . . . *anything,* that might be invisible to the rest of us."

She smiled, politely deferring to Li Lin-fu.

As Li Lin-fu talked, the dwarf swirled on the open floor to the rhythms of a Uighur folk melody, imitating, so he said, a "wind-tossed" autumn leaf. Li Lin-fu observed that the little man was harmlessly caught up with himself for the moment and the girls of the house were joining him in the dance pantomime. The eunuchs, Li Lin-fu could see, were quite drunk.

"Such men were banned for a good reason," Li Lin-fu said to Madame Li. "They tended to breed a certain sense of . . . unrest among the common people."

"Councillor, you will excuse me for my . . . ignorance," Madame Li said, apologetically. "But what little I know of the matters of government and of social philosophies—ethics, if you will—come from the lips of our distinguished clientele. This is not an issue which is discussed a great deal. But where is the harm with such 'illusionists'? I fail to see it. Life is so mean and squalid for most of the rabble of the streets. Such adventures, fantasies, could only brighten their lives, their thoughts, even for a few moments, could they not?"

"If you will allow me to explain, in my all too clumsy fashion, Madame Li," Li Lin-fu replied in a polite, firm tone. "Illusion, magic—call it what you will—is perceived differently by each set of eyes that witnesses it. Those of us fortunate enough to be touched by the enlightened Confucian wisdom of our state have little to fear. We understand that they are merely games of pretending. Think of tales told by a corner storyteller to children. He conjures wonderlands, magical demons and beasts, and the golden peaches of immortality. *We* know that such things cannot exist. But does a child? Does he have such powers of discrimination yet? And even when we are older and should know better, are the barriers so clear? The borders between what is real and what is not, even for those of us who have refined our thinking? For the ignorant, then, who are like children in their thinking, madam, it is all the more dangerous; such frivolous games can become quite real—and deadly." Li Lin-fu took another drink and looked around the room. He was feeling his wine himself, now; his tongue was loose and eloquent. The dwarf was still whirling to the music, jewelry and feathers a blur of color. "Children," Li Lin-fu continued, "struggle only with the ghosts of their childhood fears. But men struggle daily with the ghosts of their own mortality. And they are willing to accept any weapons in this battle. And that is the inherent danger—the power of "illusionists," madam. What power could the state have over such men were they to be let loose, without restriction, on the masses? The irrational is often more attractive, more . . . *appealing* than the rational, offering as it does the false hope of cheating the laws of nature." He took another drink, warming to his subject. Madame Li was an attentive listener, and he was in fine form tonight.

"I love the tricks of magic as much as the next man," he said. "It is when magic becomes entangled with politics that I fear. Is there anything more dangerous than a Muslim dying for his ar-Rahman—his Allah—and his foolish camphor-scented gardens of Paradise? We Chinese are only going to the Great Perhaps, but the Muslim knows beyond any doubt that he is going to his Paradise, especially if he dies in battle; therefore, he has no fear. Our recent military setbacks along the Talus River are proof enough of that. No, illusion is far too dangerous a beast to be set free again. I have even proposed the dismantling of many of the Buddhist monastic institutions that perpetuate their own unique brand of superstition and escape our state tax roles." He smiled at his hostess, knowing that he had completely won her over with his charm and the acuity of his argument. The steward filled his cup again. He made eye contact with his chief guard. Not a signal just yet, but a discreet indication to be ready, that the time was drawing near.

He turned back to his hostess. "How many men ask for their fantasies to be acted out here in your establishment, Madame Li?" he continued. "And though most of these fantasies are assuredly quite harmless, sexual in nature only, the idea is certainly nothing new to you. Irrationality, fantasy . . . illusion. Holes through which men try to escape things that cannot be escaped. Confucius told us to leave the questions of the supernatural out of our daily lives, madam. We are accountable only to the real world, the world of men and things and ideas. But it is the plight of ignorant and discontented men to be susceptible to illusions of all kinds, not just the supernatural. And they will get along very well until someone, some "illusionist," if you will, comes along and plants ideas in the brackish soil of their minds. And do you know what sprouts there, like so much fungus in a dark cellar? Unrest, madam. Rebellions for false causes. All of it is great trouble for governments. What may seem like small fissures can grow until the peace of the very empire is threatened!" He certainly had her attention now, as well as that of one of the eunuch officials, who was not laughing along with his fellows, but listening with a grave expression. Li Lin-fu leaned forward and spoke intently to his small audience. "And now that the great T'ang must pursue a course of unimpeded military security, such men who spread false rumors, who seek to undermine our stability, must be put in their place."

Li Lin-fu finished talking just as the music ended. The audience applauded the efforts of the dancers and cheered and laughed and raised their wine cups to the tiny knight. The dancing had given the dwarf a considerable erection. He pranced about, shamelessly displaying the bulge in his trousers to the Censorate eunuchs who now laughed, all but one of them, wildly, contagiously, unconsciously. Drunkenly.

"And in all of this, Madame Li, your task is no less important than mine. As the keeper of such a grand establishment, your job is to quell certain of men's needs; mine is simply to quell their ambitions.

"But we were speaking of illusion. At this moment some of our guests may be gazing enviously upon your little friend's 'turtle.' Maybe, like the ignorant followers of a fakir, they are wishing for something they cannot have." The chief minister signaled his constables, who discreetly took their positions around the room.

"And if they are not wishing for it already, then in a short while they will be. They will be wishing that they could reverse the barter they once made. They will wish that they could give back their badges of imperial privilege and all their positions in the inner circles of government for the return of the 'triumvirate' of their manhood." He glanced at the one eunuch who was listening to him; the man's face was a mask of apprehension. You, Li Lin-fu said in his mind, have guessed the nature of my little surprise, haven't you?

Li Lin-fu stood. His own exit was to be the final signal to his constables. He took Madame Li's hand and bowed deeply. "You have been a most gracious hostess," he said, ignoring her perplexed expression at his impending sudden departure. "You gave us a party which will undoubtedly be recorded by historians and poets. They will call it Madame Li's great 'Flowers of Hainan Banquet.' "

He turned then, and with the guards who immediately closed ranks around him, left the room.

14

Ice and Tears

The fierce and brilliant world of Hainan, surrounded by blank, primordial waters, provided little that the Chinese imagination could grasp. Mirroring no familiar conception, it could paralyze the minds even of cultivated men. Or if some comprehensible content could be discerned, it was likely to be a loathsome and deadly vision—a scene as unlike the good homelands far to the north as possible . . .

But is it possible that an opposite image was sometimes created by the island in the minds of sensitive men? . . . We have already noted the hesitant optimism of . . . Su Shih [eleventh century exiled poet and statesman]. . . .

He left his thoughts in a poem . . . He dozed off, and dreamed of a phantasmagoria of high mountains and valleys, alive with weird monsters and sounding with strange music. Awakening to find himself in a rain storm, he (as he says) "playfully made these verses."

—*Edward Schafer*

I sit chanting . . . an old fellow chatting with Heaven;

. . .

I chant and whistle—to bring the winds of heaven to me!
A thousand mountains—active with scaly, armored things,
Myriad valleys, drunk with mouth organs and bells!

. . .

An urgent poem will set the dragon horde running!

. . .

We should marvel that Tung-p'o [Su Shih]
   grows old—His face decays, but his language is still artful.

—*Su Shih, translated by Edward Schafer*

For food—no meat;
For excursions—no friends;
For dwellings—no houses;
For diseases—no physicians;
For winter—no charcoal;
For summer—no cold springs . . .

—Su Shih, translated by Edward Schafer

My drink has been salty and my food rancid, and I have felt the oppression and violence of typhoons and [malarial] fogs . . .

—Su Shih, translated by Edward Schafer

Ancient records give us the name of Li Shan Lao Ma as that of a female immortal. Dwelling somewhere on the borders between the feudal States of Yin and Chou, there lived the woman of Mount Li, who once served as a ruler. Speculation has it that she was a mortal possessing extraordinary abilities. She won the support of the feudal lords, receiving lasting praise, and became a legend. And hearsay and rumor about her did not fade but, rather, continued for a long time, extending even beyond the T'ang and Sung periods (seventh to twelfth centuries). Thereupon she came to be venerated as an immortal, known only as the Old Woman or "the Old Mother."

By the time of the T'ang dynasty, Li Shan Lao Ma had already been encountered many times . . . [It is even said that] the legendary Yellow Emperor [of the third millennium B.C.] received from the old woman of Li Shan an amulet imbued with divine powers against evil and covered with secret inscriptions, and, this charm was said to have already been in his possession for some one thousand and eighty years [before that].

—Chi Hsien Chuan (Collected Annals of the Immortals), *translated
by Daniel Altieri*

ICE. Cold, clear ice. He wanted to stretch his hot, feverish body onto it. Flakes of snow, dry with the cold, danced across the surface. Around him, the frozen winter landscape lay silent. The ice was so clear it was black, with long white frozen lines descending into its depths. Flattening himself, he spread his arms and legs out and pressed his face against the ice. So cold. So clean. Let the clean, pure, deep cold absorb the festering, sweltering heat from my body. Freeze my sweat. Freeze the stink of my rotting flesh and its excrescences. He gazed down into the ice, wishing he could descend into it. He thought he could see creatures moving down there. Creatures that actually lived in the ice, moving through it as if it were water or air. Ice creatures. He envied them with all his being. Why can't I be one of them? Why can't I live in such a dark, cold, pleasant world? He cried, letting his tears flow onto the ice and freeze. Then an idea came to him. If I cry enough tears, they will freeze around me, until I am surrounded by ice.

Something large was moving down there. A dark shape rotating. Alarm went through him. He tried to lift his face from the ice but could not—he was frozen to it by his tears. The dark shape was turning, turning, moving toward him. He did not know what it was, but he knew absolutely that he did not want to look at it or be seen by it. He pulled, and his flesh began to tear. The thing stopped its movement just inches away from him. Look at me, it said in his mind. I was murdered. Look at me.

It was a face. The face of Prince Ying. The eyes were open and pleading, but the mouth did not move. The mouth was terrible; the lips were frozen slightly open so that the teeth glinted through. Dead teeth. He looked into the eyes that looked up at him from the cold black ice. A dreadful sorrow welled up in him, and he cried anew. There is nothing I can do for you, he said to the prince with his mind. Look at me, the prince said again. It is so cold here. He tried again to pull his face away, anything to get away from the pain and sorrow he saw in those eyes. Anything. He pulled with all his strength. His flesh ripped. Under the ice, the prince cried, louder and longer. Don't leave me. It pierced his soul.

He woke to the sound of his own voice wailing from his mouth. There was no ice, no cold, no prince. Just the sweltering jungle night, his bed of rags and leaves, and his body soaked in dream sweat.

Staring into the darkness, breathing hard, the poet-minister Chang Chiu-ling let the face of Ying recede for the hundredth time. The sorrow hung on him for a while, but gradually loosened its grip and faded away too. He imagined the face and the sorrow dwelling in the same dark place, waiting to come out again. As always, he felt the dreadful disappointment that there was, after all, no ice, no cold. Frantically, before it evaporated completely, he tried to grab at the illusion. Now his tears were real; this time, they weren't for the murdered prince, but for the beautiful, delicious cold, murdered each time he awoke from the dream.

Sitting up now, he cradled his head and tried to recall winter days in Ch'ang-an. Snow. What did it feel like? He was not at all sure that he had ever actually seen or touched it. With all his strength, he tried to imagine walking in the snow on a frozen winter night in a park in the city. He put a cold white moon in the sky to help his imagination, and concentrated mightily. He was able to recall perfectly the way snow creaked underfoot when the air was especially bitter. But when he reached his hand down to touch the snow, it was . . . warm. Disgusted, as if he had put his fingers on a piece of excrement, he gave it up, and fell back down on the bed and let his mind drift back into the shifting chaos of images fed by the one thousand chattering, clicking, rustling, screeching noises of the tropical night. The fever was on him and had been for days. Until it passed, there would be little rest. He shivered, he sweated, his teeth rattled. Reaching out in the dark, he found the gourd, raised his head enough to take a long drink of the fiery, bitter liquor in it, and let his head fall again.

He made no effort to control the weird, obscene, ridiculous, frightening pictures that bloomed in his mind like diseased flowers. Do what you will, he challenged them. I don't care anymore. Come and get me. He let great, hairy insect legs caress his face, opened his mouth and let green, poisonous juice from their bodies pour. Huge pink spotted frogs copulated in profusion, with smiling, smirking faces, singing in high soprano voices, while centipedes with wicked spiked legs walked delicately up his nose and into his ears. Eat my brain, he said to them, laughing. Eat my tongue. He stretched his jaws wide to receive them. Crawl up into my head and pick my skull clean. Eat. They were all eating now. The frogs, the centipedes, the hairy black insects with dry, rustling wings. That was the jungle. Everything eating everything else, all the time. It was all he could hear everywhere around him. The chewing and munching of mouths, teeth, mandibles, slippery wet lips. But his laughing stopped now. He was afraid, and the tears flowed from his burning eyes. No, please, he begged. No, no, no. But it was too late; he knew what was coming, and he knew he would be powerless to stop it.

The mantis had come, turning her black, shiny head inquisitively from side to side. She saw him, as he knew she would, and her forelegs, gleaming and hairy, shot out and seized him, impaling him with their pointed tips, and raised him delicately to her churning mouthparts. He wept helplessly as she turned him this way and that in her horrible embrace and then began eating his head, which he knew was no longer flesh and bone but chitinous material with a greenish jelly inside. The crunching of her powerful mandibles drowned out everything but his pathetic moans as she ate, and ate, and ate.

And the poet slept again, sinking deeper, moving down through delirium and into his dreams, where gradually it became quieter, colder, quieter. Soon, he was stretched out on the black, silent ice once more, the mantis and other creatures gone, the terrible noises gone, absorbed into the noiseless depths of the icy world. He looked down into the ice with longing, wishing he could descend into it, to join the beings that lived down there. He cried.

: :

The poet-minister Chang Chiu-ling pulled aside the tattered reed curtain in the door of his hut and looked out on the day. He had had a very bad night, tormented by horrible creatures whenever he shut his eyes. Even worse, he had dreamt of the murdered prince three times. Each time the face looked up at him through the ice, he had been taken completely by surprise. In spite of the dreams and the fever, he felt a little better this morning, though weak and dizzy, than he had for many days. He looked down into the ravine toward the hut of his nearest neighbor and strained his eyes for the little curl of smoke that let him know that another living soul still breathed and walked about. Not that he and the man, a former low-ranking magistrate, had a great love for one another; often weeks at a time would go by without the two exchanging a word. But he needed to know that he was not completely alone. The smoke was there, drifting up among the tangled trees. He settled down on his haunches and looked around.

He was ravenously hungry. He had eaten nothing during the last few days; whenever the fever had him in its grip, he would forget that there was even such a thing as food. The only sustenance he had taken was the bitter, evil-tasting liquor he got from the natives. Now his stomach felt like a burning hole of emptiness. Lowering the curtain, he turned toward the ragged collection of baskets where he kept his meager stores of fruit and dried monkey meat. He pulled the top off the first one. Empty! So was the one next to it. Seizing the third and last, he turned it upside down, but the only thing that plopped to the ground was a small lizard. His hand shot out to grab it, but it was too fast for him, scuttling between his feet and out the door.

He sat and stared for a few minutes, then hurled the empty baskets across the tiny room. He had been robbed! Robbed while he lay helpless! Someone had crept in here, no doubt grinning with amusement at the sight of the poet raving in his delirium, and helped himself. Tears of rage sprang to his eyes. He knew, without a doubt, who had done this, and who would now pay.

He picked up a rock and started down the steep hill that led to his neighbor's house, tripping and stumbling as he went. He had to stop every few minutes to rest, hanging onto a tree trunk or vine. Whether he was awake or asleep, somebody or something was always seeking to torment him. There was no rest, ever. That son of a goat down the hill could get all the food he wanted, but obviously he found the taste of stolen food more to his liking. He pictured the man standing over him, munching on the food from Chang Chiu-ling's baskets, watching him writhe, moan, and sweat. Sliding and scrambling, he reached the bottom of the hill. He crouched for a moment, catching his breath, and then, still bending low out of sight, ran toward his neighbor's hut.

The man was nowhere to be seen, but Chang Chiu-ling knew by the smoke drifting out through the hole in the roof that he was in there. Still holding the rock, he crept stealthily forward until he was within range. His mouth hung slightly open so that the furious pumping of his heart was clearly audible in his throat. It was a hollow sound, blind and meaningless. He stood then, and hurled the rock with all his strength.

A perfect shot. It hit the side of the hut and went right through the straw matting, landing with a thud inside. A loud cursing immediately followed. Chang Chiu-ling dove for cover, then looked all around him for another good rock. Fighting to contain his gleeful laughter, he raised his head above the vegetation just enough to have a look at his handiwork.

The curtain in the doorway was flung aside. His neighbor emerged, tall, gaunt, and tangle-haired, holding the rock, eyes blazing with wrath.

"Filthy dog of a poet!" he shouted. "Show me your ugly face! Let me wring your skinny neck for you and end your misery!"

By way of an answer, Chang Chiu-ling hurled the only weapon he'd been able to find, a plant pulled from the ground with a large clod of earth attached. It hit the man squarely in the chest, knocking him over. While his adversary was on the ground, the poet broke from his cover, standing up suddenly in the tall weeds.

"Eat dirt, Magistrate!" he yelled, hurling another chunk of earth, hitting his target on the head this time. "Come dine with me! Here is a sample of what will be on the menu tonight, thanks to your voracious greed!" The neighbor sat up, outraged.

"You pathetic fool!" he shouted. "Do you think that I need to rob your miserable hut to fill my stomach? Are you hungry?" he challenged the poet. "I said, are you hungry?" He was on his feet now, ducking inside his hut. In a moment he reappeared, holding a large lizard by the tail. Against his will, the poet began to salivate at the sight. The lizard was already beheaded, gutted, and cooked. The magistrate held it aloft, swinging it gently back and forth. "I asked you a question, Poet. Are you hungry?"

Raising the lizard to his lips, he took a bite, tearing the meat from the carcass with exaggerated slowness and emphasis, and chewing with his mouth open. "Better than the finest roast fowl to be had in Ch'ang-an!" he said, mouth full of meat, nimbly ducking a small rock that whizzed by his head. "Delicious!"

"First you rob a sick man," Chang Chiu-ling shouted bitterly, "then you torture him. You are not human!"

"Ah, but I am, Poet. I am. It is because I am human that I have the ability to torture," he said, and took another bite. At that moment, the universe narrowed to one small point for Chang Chiu-ling, and that was the smoked lizard in the magistrate's hand. He sobbed out loud, sinking back down into the grass, his energy spent. The man stopped eating, looked at him with an expression of pity and disgust, wiped his mouth on his ragged sleeve, and flung the lizard in Chang Chiu-ling's direction. It sailed end over end in a high arc, landing a few feet away from where the poet lay. "I have just lost my appetite," the magistrate declared, turning his back on the poet and reentering the hut.

For a moment or two, Chang Chiu-ling lay and looked at the sky, though he had heard the lizard land heavily nearby. His tears ran down the sides of his face and collected in his ears. Then he turned and looked at the lizard lying stiffly on the ground. Two large bites had been taken out of one of the haunches; he imagined that he could see traces of the man's saliva around the edge of the wound. But the flesh looked tender, pale, and delicious. He lunged for the lizard as his stomach contracted painfully.

He retreated, scrambling back up the hill, holding the lizard in his mouth so that his hands would be free, sucking on the flesh as he went. When he reached his own hut, he squatted on the ground and ate.

He cleaned the delicate bones thoroughly, licking them and chewing off every bit of edible flesh. On the ground in front of him marched a column of ants, industriously carrying away minute scraps that fell while he ate. An idea was coming to him. The idea for his next poem. He began to shake with laughter. Oh, it was too wonderful! It would be on everyone's lips at court! It would be handed down through the generations, whispered by lovers in the midst of an embrace a thousand years from now! He laughed until the tears were rolling once again in their well-worn gullies down his face.

He stuck out his tongue to taste the tears. He had a theory. Tears of grief tasted different from tears of laughter. He wanted to collect the tears in little crystal cups and pass them around a table of ladies and gentlemen so that they could sip them and discern for themselves that there were two distinct flavors. He would prove that it was so. He sat very still, concentrating. But these tears . . . they were different! They tasted distinctly neither of grief nor joy! Well, he asked himself, what am I feeling? He was not sure at all. The tears were flowing copiously now, but he could not have said whether they came from joy or grief. They welled up from inside him like a spring whose source is the vast, infinite center of the earth.

: :

He had worked for many days on the poem. It was time to show it to his friend . . . his great friend, the magistrate who lived down the hill. A fine man—generous, honest, and a connoisseur of good poetry. He would make the poem a gift, to repay him for his generosity. He thought about the delicious smoked lizard the man had given him to eat after his bout with the fever, when he was too weak to go out and forage for himself after his own food stores had been plundered, undoubtedly by natives, while he lay helpless. It unnerved him the way they crept about on their obscene naked feet, quiet as cats, sneaking up on a person so that he wouldn't know they were there until they were standing looking over his shoulder. More than once he had been shocked to feel warm breath on his neck and, turning, had found one of them grinning at him with stained teeth. They were like children . . . large, pubescent children. He shuddered. They were a sly, amoral lot, with no more sense of right and wrong than the lizards, snakes, and eels that they hunted and dined upon. A civilized man, Chang Chiu-ling thought as he carefully rolled up the fragile parchment that he had made with his own hands, has an obligation to uphold civilization—no matter what remote jungle he must live in, and regardless of whether his audience is composed of other gentlemen, naked savages, or a three-eyed spider upside down on the wall.

He raked his fingers through his matted hair, carefully tied a woven grass strand around the rolled-up parchment, and ducked out of the hut. He looked down the ravine for the reassuring wisp of smoke . . . and stopped where he was. He stared, bewildered, at the hole in the roof below; it was blank, still, and smokeless. He stood stupidly for a moment or two, unsure of what to do in the face of this unexpected wrinkle in his plan.

Then he smiled. He knew what his friend was doing. Too modest to accept a gift, the man was pretending he wasn't at home. Well, the poet-minister muttered to himself, he is wrong if he thinks Chang Chiu-ling gives up so easily. He started down the hill, but found that his legs had become weak and rubbery from the three days of sitting on them while he worked on the poem. His knees buckled on the steep part of the path, causing him to stumble and pitch headlong. He tumbled down, grabbing at the vegetation as he went, and landed in a heap at the bottom. He squeezed his eyes tightly shut. No more tears, he sternly told himself. No more.

Carefully straightening out the rolled-up parchment, which had been squashed and rumpled in the fall, he stood and moved slowly toward the hut of the magistrate. Everything was very still; the reed curtain in the doorway hung motionless, his footsteps the only sound in his ears as he approached. He began singing a little song, an improvised rendition of his poem hummed unintelligibly under his breath. The sound reassured him as he approached the silent hut; he'll hear me, the poet thought, and know I'm coming. He stood just outside the curtained doorway and sang louder, then stopped and waited for a response.

There was none. He stood very still, listening hard for any sound from within. Probably his friend was playing a joke on him by pretending not to hear him. He strained his ears. Even the tiniest noise would not escape his notice.

Then he heard it. A nearly infinitesimal sound; it could have been the rustle of a sleeve, or it could have been the release of a breath. A gradual smile spread across his face. There it was again! Slowly, his hand came up and into position in front of the doorway; then all at once, he yanked the curtain aside and jumped into the hut with a yell. He stood there, poised, still smiling, the sound of his cry echoing in his ears, and stared into the darkness.

It was as he thought. The magistrate was most certainly at home—though there was little light inside the hut, the poet could make out the shape, on the sleeping-mat on the floor, of his friend. The man certainly had control! He had not jumped or flinched or made even the smallest motion when the poet had leapt suddenly into the hut. He waited patiently for the magistrate to give up the game, sit up, smile, and laugh; then, he would present him with the poem. He wanted very badly to laugh out loud, but he suppressed his hilarity, though it moved inside him like an incipient earthquake. He knew that his friend was doing exactly the same thing; what an effort it must be for him to lie there, mirth straining for escape in every limb and muscle, and not twitch so much as an eyelid or a corner of his mouth!

Chang Chiu-ling could take it no longer. The dam burst, the laughter erupting from his nose and mouth in torrents of howls and snorts. And now he heard the laughter of the magistrate joining his own. Oh, it was fine to laugh together, with a friend, over a good joke! Was there really anything in life more worthwhile? There was not. He laughed and laughed, letting the tears flow, letting it all flow out of him in gathering and subsiding spasms that shook his entire body. The magistrate's laughter danced just above his own, matching his in its cadence, rising and falling in perfect rhythm. And still the man hadn't moved. What a magician! He lay there, laughing and laughing along with the poet, eyes still closed, face turned slightly toward the wall, mouth unmoving. I have always, the poet reflected, had nothing but the finest friends, the most ingenious men around me, and this is proof!

Unable to stand any longer, the poet-minister sank to his knees, doubled over, and let his forehead rest on the floor as he laughed, weakly now, his strength almost spent. Slowly, like a mountain stream swollen in spring that dries up in the heat of August, their laughter tapered into nothingness. The poet remained with his forehead on the ground, letting his breathing return to normal, enjoying the blissful feeling flowing through his veins in the aftermath of mirth. Presently he raised his head and stared hard at his friend on the bed.

He still had not moved. The poet raised himself painfully to his feet and went to the doorway, then pushed the curtain aside and secured it so that some light would enter the gloomy interior of the hut. He walked over to the bed and looked again at the magistrate's face. He had not been able, in the dim light, to read the expression on the man's face, and the message in it for him. Obviously, the magistrate had been waiting for Chang Chiu-ling to get some light into the hut and take a close look at his face.

"I am sorry," he apologized to his friend. "How stupid of me. How despicably clumsy I am, and lacking in subtlety, to make you wait! And you have been infinitely patient. I will look at your face now, carefully, in a way worthy of your artistry." He moved close, bending over the bed, straining to see the man's face, which was turned toward the wall and so was partly still in shadow.

He read his friend's thoughts then. Obligingly, he reached over and turned the head so that the feeble shaft of light fell full on it.

"That is much better," he said, settling on his haunches to study the features of the magistrate. He smiled, tipping his own head to one side. The eyes, he saw now, were not completely closed, but peeped out at him through the slightest of cracks beneath the heavy lids, and holding an expression of prankish craftiness, looked directly into his own eyes. The mouth, too, was slightly open. Inspiration leapt at Chang Chiu-ling then. There was a word on those lips! He was sure of it! The magistrate had formed a word, then stopped either right in the middle of the word or at the end of it and held his mouth just as the word had shaped it. And he, Chang Chiu-ling, was to guess that word! That was, of course, why the magistrate had had to laugh without moving any part of his face.

"Oh, my poor friend," he said. "You have had to work awfully hard this morning because of my dreary thickheadedness. I am sorry. You must understand, I have not been well at all these past weeks. Not well at all. Normally, I am the most perspicacious of men, but my illness has made me slow, stupid, plodding. But look! I will pull myself together through sheer will! I will not disappoint you, my friend." He leaned close then and whispered, just in case any inquisitive ears might be pressed against the outside of the hut. "I will guess the word, but I shall not say it loud. Do not fear."

Putting a finger to his lips, he knit his brow in concentration, addressing his attention to the magistrate's mouth. Just as wind moving over rocks shapes them as the centuries go by, so words and their intent leave a shape on men's lips.

He removed the finger he had pressed to his mouth, and carefully tried to hold his lips in the exact same shape as the magistrate's, then let his voice out slowly and softly so that he would hear the mysterious word.

What he heard jolted him. He had not expected the word to be a name, and certainly not that name. He tried again, to make sure he was not making a mistake. He took a breath, shaped his lips, and let his voice out.

"Li Lin-fu," he heard his mouth say. It frightened him badly. He looked at the magistrate with bewilderment. Why would his friend bring that loathsome name up? Was he playing some sort of unpleasant game with the poet? He felt betrayed. Only moments ago, they had been laughing together, and now he was being forced to think about the dreadful personage who had taken him from his pleasant little life in Ch'ang-an and put him in a sweating, diseased hell-hole to spend his days watching his precious life-essence flow from him, break up into a million tiny inconsequential streams, and disappear into the dark, indifferent earth. He felt the tears rising behind his eyes.

Then he heard the magistrate's voice. News, it said. Soon there will be news. From Ch'ang-an.

The poet looked sharply at the man on the bed to make sure he wasn't lying or having fun with him. The magistrate was still looking at him through his nearly closed lids, and as he had laughed before without moving his lips, he now spoke to the poet the same way.

You heard me, he said. You wonder why I am speaking the name of Li Lin-fu? Do you think I enjoy speaking his name any more than you do? Who do you think sent *me* here? And all the other poor ragged ghosts that make up our wretched tribe? We are all hungry, Poet. Hungry for any little scrap that comes our way. And Master Li Lin-fu will soon be increasing our number . . .

Chang Chiu-ling crouched over the bed, quivering with excitement.

"Who!" he cried. "Who is coming? What are their names?" The magistrate did not answer the poet, but merely looked at him in a way that made the poet think he was done with talking forever. "Who is coming?" he shouted at the unmoving face. "Damn you! Answer me!" He seized the thin shoulders and shook hard. The magistrate still did not answer, but allowed a thin trickle of blood to roll out of one of his nostrils. The poet stopped shaking him then, realizing what he had to do before the magistrate would tell him who was coming, and when. He made a great effort to quell his anger and excitement and appear composed. Gently, he laid the shoulders back on the bed and straightened the threadbare clothing.

"I will make you some food, and prepare something for you to drink, and when you are comfortable, I will read you my poem." He looked modestly down toward the ground, not wanting the magistrate to see his pleasure in his accomplishment. "It is not a very good poem, or a very skillful or astute poem, and I do not wish to bore you or waste your time with it, but . . ."

He stopped then, seeing plainly on the magistrate's face an expression of pained impatience with his false self-effacement. "Well," he said, scrambling toward the corner where the magistrate kept his food, "it is actually a rather good poem, but it requires considerable intelligence in he who reads it or hears it . . ."

It was difficult work getting the magistrate up off the bed and arranged comfortably in a sitting position. He refused to hold his head up properly, but kept allowing it to sag forward onto his chest or loll to the side, pulling his upper torso with it. The poet appreciated the joke, but since he had been ill, his strength was easily taxed. Finally he tied a cloth around the magistrate's head and secured it to the wall behind him. He arranged the hands in the lap and stepped back to make sure that the man looked comfortable.

The magistrate was about to say something. His mouth was opening slowly, thoughtfully. The poet waited anxiously, hoping that he would hear, perhaps, the names of those who were coming. But the magistrate was going to keep him waiting, it seemed. He did not speak, but let his mouth hang open. Another word. The poet was going to have to guess another word. He was growing impatient with these games, but concealed his feelings and set the food out before the magistrate. A bowl of fish broth. A piece of lizard meat. A dried eel. Then he sat down opposite his friend, who now had an introspective look in his eyes that was entirely incongruous with the open mouth that looked as if it was about to shout something terrible at the poet.

Ignoring the magistrate's obscure expression, Chang Chiu-ling lovingly unrolled the parchment, cleared his throat, and began to read:

THE FABLE OF THE ANT

"Was not, in Search of Truth, the Statesman Chu Yuan, buried
   deep.
In Longings unfulfilled, a watery grave to sleep.

"And do They not all honor him with Dragon Boats?
But I . . .
Have thrown myself into the Ice and turned my Head to Stone
And fixed here on the ground, am now as much of crystal as
   of bone . . .
Eternal as a tomb of Ancient Kings; my eyes turned toward
   the sky.
Unlike that nobler Chu Yuan, I alone can never die!
But still my Head I see . . .
And cannot help but sobbing, think . . .
How shall they honor Me?

"Such tears, in Joy or Grief, I cannot know . . .
But like runoff from a winter's snow . . .

Cascading down my cheeks they flow.
And, oh! Alas! Such tears I Weep . . .
In stone-bound rivulets narrow and steep.

"On Pilgrimage came the King of Ants,
His Vassals, Lords and Ladies All . . .
To the glorious founts of my marble *Ears*.
To sup and drink and then Debate . . . this Flavor of my
    Tears.

" 'Tis Joy,' says one Philosopher Ant on spikey legs of six,
'For Joy is sweet and grief is sour and this is singular and
    rich . . .'

"Then these are tears of joy, indeed, all tasting, they agreed,
    delicately conversing . . . , politely, drinking, sipping . . .
    gentlehearted in their greed . . .

"But there was one among them much wiser than the rest . . .
He reared on two black, shining legs, his abdomen gaily
    dressed.
He preened a bit, and brushed and combed and groomed his
    pointy beard . . .
And with a taste quite calmly said, '. . . it is just as I feared!'

"For this, though sweet, can never be a tear of Joy, you see . . .
For Joy can bring but sorrow and grief but Pleasantry.
'Tis grief you taste for grief is sweet . . .
Ten thousand soldiers pounding feet.
The wail of mothers losing sons,
Of wars, of times, of lives undone.
But sweet is grief; its cleansing sheds
The lonely sobs for empty beds.
' "But Joy is sour!" how can you say?
For grief has such a price to pay?
The cost is ever sweeter here
The price of sorrow ever dear.
All rose and cheered his talents deft
And honored him that day . . .
Ants raised their cups and cheerily left . . .
All sobbing went away.

Now nobles gone, their Kings and Queens; philosophers'
    words all said . . .
This verse, now spent, I shall rename 'The Fable of My
    Head.' "

The poet gazed modestly at the floor, waiting for the praise which he knew would be forthcoming. He waited until his neck grew stiff. My friend must be formulating a very careful critical appraisal of my work, he thought.

When the pain in his neck became unbearable, the poet finally raised his eyes. He was disappointed to see that the magistrate was not going to say anything about the poem. His mouth had not moved at all, and the poet could see that the mysterious word, or name, was still on those lips. He sighed, and settled himself into a comfortable position.

"All right, my friend," he said to the magistrate. "I am a patient man. I will wait for you to choose the moment to speak."

For the rest of that day, the night following, and the entire day after that, the poet waited for the magistrate to speak. He had tried a thousand times to guess the word, or name, that his friend was going to say, but it eluded him.

Toward evening of the second day, a new expression had come onto the magistrate's face. His lips were curling back over his teeth in a mirthless smile, and he appeared to be taking a deep, deep breath. His whole aspect was one of such urgency that the poet could barely tolerate the suspense. He wept, he ranted, he sat perfectly still, he offered more and more food until there was none left in the hut. He whispered entreaties in the magistrate's ear, he told him jokes, he read the poem over and over. But the magistrate still did not speak. He continued to smile, ever wider, and to grow larger with every passing hour.

By the evening of the third day, the poet knew that he could no longer stay awake. Afraid that if he slept, the magistrate would speak, he fought it. He sang as loud as he could, and forced himself to walk around in a tight circle inside the hut. When he sat, he rocked back and forth and slapped his own face, and sang and sang and sang. Poems, obscene stories, love letters he had written as a youth; he put them all into songs. But sleep eventually claimed him, folding her big dark wings around him, pushing him down into his dreams, which were, as usual, waiting for him. Before long he was sprawled on the black ice, and soon after that he was looking into the eyes of the murdered prince. Then the magistrate's voice cut through the poet's dream with perfect clarity, the only sound in a silent, frozen world. Again, it was a name.

"Ming Wu," he said.

When the poet heard that name, he began to cry.

: :

It had taken three men to carry the gentleman from the hut. It had been the singing that had attracted them. At first, they had sat, fascinated, in the forest at the edge of the clearing, and listened. People arrived, walking silently so as not to disturb the singer, listened for a while, and exchanged looks of incredulity. Though they could not understand the words to the amazing songs, they knew whether a song was sad or happy, funny or angry, by the way it was sung.

The singing had gone on for almost an entire night, but when it turned into crying and screaming, some of the people listening decided that something must be done. A quick conference was held and several of the men were chosen to enter the hut. They took weapons with them, in case of trouble, and made their way quietly to the door.

Telling the story later of what they had found when they went inside, the men were practically all speaking at once, so great was their eagerness to make sure no detail was left out. This was by far one of the very best gentlemen stories to be told yet. The people from the far north who came to the Shore of Pearls were expected to do odd things and often went mad, but as far as anyone could recall, nothing quite like this had ever happened. One of the village elders finally held up his hand and implored everyone to be quiet and let just one man speak.

We smelled it before we saw it, the man who was chosen to speak told the group. When we lifted the flap in the doorway it hit us in our faces like a breath from Hell. One gentleman was on the floor crying, and the other one was sitting up, as dead as he could be, all bloated up like a pig's carcass left lying in the sun. And laid out in front of the dead one was a feast, all kinds of food. The gentleman on the floor had been trying to make the dead one eat. We could tell by the food sitting in his mouth and spilled down the front of his clothes. We tried to explain to the gentleman on the floor that it was unhealthy to be in closed quarters with a dead person and that he was not being fair to the man's spirit by trying to detain it when it would obviously want to get as far away from that smelly, ugly corpse as possible. It is doubtful that he understood what we were saying, because when we carried him out of the hut we could not tell whether he was laughing or crying. We decided that he must have been suffering from the fever, and took him to his own hut up the hill, and left two of the old women with him to take care of him until the fever should pass. Then we went back and looked again at the corpse sitting up in front of the food. We took the food away so that the man's spirit would have nothing there to detain it any longer, apologized for the inconvenience, opened the doorflap so that it could leave, and then set fire to the hut.

The people laughed and shouted at the amazing story. It made them recall other strange things done by gentlemen from the north. One older man remembered the time, years and years ago, when a gentleman declared that he was the King of the North and that his subjects were awaiting his return, then waded into the sea and drowned himself.

What about the one, said another man, who held a big wedding feast, and it turned out that the bride was to be his dog?

And somebody asked the question that was always asked when the gentlemen were being discussed: where do they come from, and why do they come here?

Well, said one of the men, I heard that the place they come from is carved entirely of stone, that there are no birds, plants, or animals of any kind, and the people are so numerous that they must stand shoulder to shoulder in great rooms unless they are lying down to sleep.

Here is my idea about them, said another man. I do not think that these gentlemen are awake. I think that they wandered out of their beds when they were asleep, walked here, and now they think they are dreaming, and that we, and our island, and everything on it are part of their dream.

There is one thing of which we can be certain, said another, and that is that however they came here, they are being rewarded for doing something wonderful.

There was no dissent among the people on that point.

And, said the same man, a new one arrived just this morning. When the gentleman's fever has gone down, we will bring this new one to him. It will help him to have one of his own kind to talk to now that the other one is dead. And who is to know? Perhaps they knew each other in that crowded stone place where they come from.

: :

When the poet awoke, he knew he was returning from somewhere far, far away. He focused his eyes and saw a eunuch's face, vaguely familiar to him, and entertained the thought that he had returned somehow to Ch'ang-an.

But he knew that he had not. His mind was very clear; so clear that everything that had happened in the last several days came back to him in vivid, lurid detail. He closed his eyes and groaned softly. I was insane, he thought. Completely insane. For a moment he wondered if the face looking anxiously down at him was not just another materialization out of his dreams and sickness. He raised himself up on an elbow and looked long and hard at his visitor. He did not seem to be made of fever and memories, but of more substantial stuff: bone, hair, skin, a bit of grime. He lay back down.

"I know you," he said to the man, who smiled in a relieved way.

"I am glad," said the eunuch. "I was afraid you were going to die, and then there would be nobody in this forsaken world who knew me."

"I also knew that you were coming," said the poet.

The eunuch looked surprised.

"Not you in particular, but I knew somebody was coming. Somebody whose fate had been decided by Chief Minister Li Lin-fu."

"But how could you know?" the eunuch asked.

"A dead man told me," the poet answered, and laughed weakly. Seeing the confusion on the eunuch's face, he stopped laughing. He did not want the poor man to think he was crazy. "I am sorry. Though you are somebody I have known, I do not remember your name."

"My name is Hsueh A-to. I was a Censorate official. You are Chang Chiu-ling. I remember when you received your 'appointment' as cultural emissary to the indigenous people of Hainan."

"Is that what people were told?" said Chang Chiu-ling. "That is a very, very excellent joke. Yes; as you can see, I am a most important, effective, well-respected, and fulfilled man here." He gestured around the miserable hut. "Well paid, too." The poet sat up, then pulled himself to his feet. He swayed for a moment as a wave of dizziness passed over him. "Hsueh A-to," he said. "You are welcome. We will eat, and drink, and you will tell me everything, everything. I am starved, you understand, in every way."

"Starved for food, too?" asked the eunuch doubtfully. "It seems that there would be plenty to eat on such an island."

"You are right. There is food in abundance. But such is the food here that I am ill to my soul because of it. Eels, my friend. Snakes. Earthworms. Broiled bats. Lizards. Newborn rats. And such is my abject state that I have developed a taste for all of it. Can you understand what I am saying? It is loathsome, and I eat it, all of it! It is stuck between my teeth, moving through my guts, and I eat and eat, and am disgusted and never satisfied." He moved toward the food baskets, knowing that they had been replenished while he slept. He had been aware, during occasional moments of lucidity, of people moving around in his hut, bringing food, staring down at him, talking. "I am hungry all the time. For real food, for news from home, for some evidence that I did not dream my life in Ch'ang-an."

"I, for one," said the eunuch, "wish that the last part of my life in Ch'ang-an had been a dream. Since it was not, I am glad to be on this island. I would go and live on the bottom of the sea if I could."

The poet looked at the eunuch with sympathy.

"Something very unpleasant happened to you there, did it not, my friend? It has been some time since Master Li Lin-fu has sent any more 'cultural emissaries' here; obviously, things have been happening. We will drink, and you will tell me everything. Everything."

::

"Torture. I have learned that it is not always what you expect it to be," said the eunuch, pouring himself another cup.

They were both drunk. Chang Chiu-ling could not imagine ever desiring to be otherwise. They sat outside the poet's hut; it was late twilight, but no lamps had been lit. There were no features to their faces and no colors around them. The two men talked, just able to discern each other's outlines; two voices in a darkened world, intimate and anonymous at the same time. The sounds of the jungle night were beginning.

"I had always believed that where there was torture, there would be screams," the eunuch said. "My colleagues and I were most assuredly tortured, but there was no sound at all except the silence of our dreadful humiliation."

Chang Chiu-ling said nothing, but recalled the interrogation session with General Niu when he had battled for his life, knowing that the invisible eyes of Li Lin-fu watched him from some hidden place.

What a tale the eunuch had told him this night. From the moment long ago when the poet had been removed from the interrogation chamber, having no clue as to whether he would live or die, the world of the imperial court had ceased to exist for him. There had been the long, long journey in the closed carriage , blindfolded, ropes chafing his wrists and ankles. They had drugged him so that he slipped in and out of consciousness, his mouth dry and stuffed with rags except when some bitter-tasting liquid was forced down his throat. Though he was hardly aware of anything but the ceaseless jolting and bumping of the carriage, deep in his mind he knew, by the gradual heat that overtook them, that they were moving south. It had been the dead of winter when they left Ch'ang-an; by the time the carriage finally stopped, after traveling for an eternity, he could smell the sea and felt the tropical sun blazing down.

He knew nothing of what had happened in the world he had been forced to leave behind years before; nothing of what had happened to the evidence of murder that he had tried to convey to Kao Li-shih, nothing of the fate of the Emperor whose favorite son had been murdered by one of his highest ministers. Remembering the evil flowers filled with strange, seductive tales, he shuddered with amazement that he had ever been so daring and presumptuous as to think that he could bring the man who made them to justice. Foolish poet, he said to himself. Mad poet.

The story the eunuch told him now was every bit as fantastic as the flower tales. An emperor curdling in his own grief and turning the reins of power over to the man who murdered his crown prince. Kao Li-shih raging at the Emperor for his inattention. And then the advent of the Yangs—the Precious Consort, the three sisters, the dashing and autocratic Yang Kuo-chung. The all-consuming love affair of the Emperor and the consort, the pleasurable excesses. And all the while, Li Lin-fu the Lizard working quietly in the background; rendering the Censorate powerless, bringing the strange barbarian An Lu-shan down from the north and turning him loose on the court. The incongruous friendship between this hairy foreigner and the Son of Heaven! It sounded like a tale written by a drunken madman! And then the death of Niu, and the swift and mysterious appointment of this Yang playboy to the position of lieutenant chief minister! Not only had the Emperor made Yang Kuo-chung Li Lin-fu's assistant, but he breathed life back into the Censorate and put this same young man at the head of it. Apparently, the Son of Heaven had not sought the permission of his chief minister in doing any of this, and Li Lin-fu was not pleased. Not pleased at all.

"And this," said the eunuch, "was where my grief began. Li Lin-fu set out to retaliate against Yang Kuo-chung by discrediting the entire Censorate. We, the eunuch members of the Censorate, were abducted, accused of crimes we did not commit, and tortured in the most dreadful, perverted way you could imagine.

"He gave a party," the eunuch said, and took a long drink, "at the most expensive whorehouse in the city." He paused, staring into the dark.

Chang Chiu-ling shuddered. He could have guessed the rest of it, could have stopped the man from going on and known the entire story, but he didn't. He let the eunuch speak. He wanted to hear it.

"The women, the choicest and most beautiful courtesans in the city, did not know that the ten honored guests of the chief minister were, each and every one, eunuchs. Tailless dogs. I believe that these women were not even aware of the existence of such creatures.

"It was an elaborate party that went on for many hours. You must understand our state of mind. We are unused to parties, frivolity. A eunuch's life is a sober one. When he submits to the knife, certain things become irrelevant. Not only were we in a situation we were entirely unaccustomed to, but we were in shock; we were prisoners who expected at any moment to meet our deaths. We were plied with food and drink, and every stage of the party seemed designed to detach us further and further from our lives. Magicians. Music. Women dancing suggestively." He heaved a sigh. "You could not know what goes on in a eunuch's mind when he is confronted with sexuality. Whether he is a Pure-from-Birth or not. You cannot know the thoughts of someone who must live forever outside of it. Oh, this was one of Li Lin-fu's masterpieces. Not only were we frightened for our very lives, but we were being mocked and tormented at the same time. And all the while he was so gracious, so solicitous, so full of pleasure. He feeds on torment, Poet, like a fat leech on blood. And he slowly put another fear in us, one that might be difficult for you to understand.

"Do you know what a eunuch's body looks like, Poet? Do you know what is done to us? What we become?"

There was silence. Yes, the poet thought, I know. You are left with scars and a little lead urethra to piss through. You are not even as well-equipped as a woman. But Chang Chiu-ling said nothing. He waited for the eunuch to continue.

"A eunuch allows no one to see his body. No one, do you understand? Not even another eunuch, not a physician, no one. He tends to it alone and keeps it covered at all times, even when he bathes, because he cannot stand to look at it himself. And think of this, Poet," the eunuch said, his voice becoming soft. "Imagine yourself a eunuch. Everywhere you go, you are aware of the grotesque pictures occurring in the minds of people around you. None of them ever speak it out loud, but they would give almost anything to lift your robes. They want to see, Poet! They want to look! And in the meantime, they allow their imaginations to satisfy their curiosity. Can you guess, Poet, what a eunuch dreads most in all the world?"

"He dreads," said the poet slowly, "having a woman see his body." He knew by the short silence that followed that he had guessed correctly. He thought of the eunuchs at the party, threatened with death on one side and humiliation of the worst kind on the other. He could think of nothing sadder.

It had grown completely dark by now. The poet and the eunuch had become only voices in the blackness. Enhanced by the total night around them, a vivid picture of everything Hsueh A-to was telling Chang Chiu-ling took form in his brain, as if he were in the eunuch's head, experiencing his memories. He could hear him drinking more wine.

"You must understand," the eunuch said at last. "I was very drunk. I was filled with dread, so I drank, and drank, and drank. We were taken to rooms by Li Lin-fu's men. Do not think that I did not put up a fight when I saw several of the women come in. 'He is a virgin,' one of the thugs told the women. 'That is why he is afraid. Show him there is nothing to be afraid of,' and they laughed horribly. The room was in semidarkness, with only a candle burning. While the men held me down, the women began to undress me. They undressed themselves, too, and brushed their breasts across my face, and spread their legs and sat on me. I struggled. The women laughed, and tickled me, and thought it was the most amusing thing they'd ever seen. Then one of them coyly began moving her fingers down my belly and put her hand in the place where she expected to find something. She was shocked to find only empty air. 'Are you a woman?' she demanded of me, and her sisters put their hands there, too. They looked at my face, and at each other. Then they tore at my clothes. One of the men lit the lamps then, as if he knew what was coming.

"The men laughed and shouted, Poet, and the women shrieked in indignation and disgust. Drunk as I was, I burned with shame and rage, and hoped that Li Lin-fu would do me the favor of putting me to death. But he did not. I found out later that several of my colleagues committed suicide, so terrible was their shame."

"Why did you not . . . ?" Chang Chiu-ling asked.

"Because I am a coward. That same night, we began a long journey. I knew I would never see Ch'ang-an again, and that was satisfactory to me. Li Lin-fu had won."

They sat and listened to the night for a long time, each of them contemplating the adversary who had put them both on this island, broken men. Who, Chang Chiu-ling wondered, is Li Lin-fu? Yes, I know he is the chief minister and a man of arcane science, and that he is small and ugly and has cold green liquid running in his veins instead of blood, but: *Who is he?* How did he acquire such intimate knowledge of the workings of men's hearts and minds? That is what it is, of course. He *knows* you, without even having met you, and from that knows exactly what to do to you. When he sent the tiger lilies to the poor Consort Wu, it was because he knew her. When he had me interrogated, it was because he knew me. And when he conceived his dreadful party for the eunuchs, he knew them, too.

Chang Chiu-ling contemplated this young, handsome, daredevil Yang Kuo-chung that Hsueh A-to had told him about. I hope you are very wise or lucky, or a magician, said the poet, addressing the man he had never met. Does Li Lin-fu know you, too?

He wondered if Li Lin-fu was ever visited in his dreams by Ying. Why, why, why, he wondered, does the murdered prince come to *me* almost every night? To remind me of my failure? How many times, Prince, have you looked up at me through the ice and told me you were murdered? I know you were murdered. I was the *only* one who knew it, aside from the chief minister, the wretched Consort Wu, and whatever professional killer she undoubtedly hired to do the job. I do not know if Kao Li-shih ever fathomed the truth. When you look at me the way you do and cry that you were murdered, I always think that *I* am the one who did it. It is not fair, Prince, because I am the one who tried to tell them what happened to you. I tried to tell your father the Emperor that you did not take your own life. And I died trying. Look at me! Am I not a dead man, as dead as you are? I tried, but I was doomed from the moment I found those flowers. And so was the Consort Wu. Li Lin-fu left her no choice when he selected her to carry out his work. From the moment the tiger lilies bloomed in his mind, she was his captive. And so, it turned out, was I, because fate decreed that I would be the one who would try to carry those flowers to Kao Li-shih. Please, Prince. Please don't come to me that way anymore. I cannot bear the weight of that sorrow, don't you understand? I tried. I tried. Please, please go away.

Someone was shaking him hard in the darkness.

"Master Chang! You are crying," said the eunuch's voice gently. "Are you awake?"

"I am drunk, Master Hsueh. I am drunk, I am dreaming, I am mad, I am dead, I am alive, I am awake and in Hell." He pulled himself to his feet. It was full night now, and the concert of the jungle fairly roared around them. He listened for a moment to the sound of five thousand tiny frogs, ten thousand insects, one thousand mournful night birds calling, seven hundred bats squealing, and one hundred monkeys crying and chortling. He cocked his head. He also heard distinctly the sound of five hundred dry snake bellies rustling as they slid around tree trunks. "I am awake and in Hell," he repeated, and groped in the dark for the entrance to his hut.

He remembered his guest.

"You are welcome, Hsueh A-to, to sleep here. Tomorrow we will see about building you a fine house. A mansion, if you wish. We can have anything we want here."

::

He must have been mistaken. He was not on the island of Hainan after all, but in the palace in Ch'ang-an. He was in a long, empty hallway, and though it was quite dark, he knew which direction he should go in, and began walking purposefully. He passed closed doors and knew that there were people lying motionless in beds behind those doors.

He walked a long way—around corners, down stairs and up again, down corridors, feeling as silent and stealthy as a cat in the darkness. Or a ghost. How glad and relieved he was that it had all been a mistake and that he was not on the island! There were people he must contact, must speak to, who needed to know that he was here. And so much work to catch up on.

He found the door he was seeking. He pushed it open and was surprised to see, in the soft light, a woman sitting in a chair, wrapped in quilts. He felt her fear, which filled the room, as if it were something alive. He moved closer and was surprised to see that the woman was the Consort Wu, eyes shut, shaking violently. Looking at her, he understood that she was ruined, that there would be no solace for her, ever.

"Everything changes when you become a murderer," said a voice. He nodded his head sadly. "There is no going back."

There was an old woman standing next to him. He knew that she was Ming Wu, a witch who had lived for thousands of years.

"But watch," she said, and flew in a circle around himself and the woman in the chair. Her feet did not touch the ground, and she left a faint phosphorescent trail in the darkness. Around and around she went, faster and faster, until there was a circle of glowing, greenish light surrounding them.

"The circle means that she will never be caught," said Ming Wu. "She will never be called a murderer. She is protected from implication in the crime. But that is all she is protected from."

"Wait!" he cried. You have put the circle around me, too! I am inside it!" Ming Wu was moving so fast now that he couldn't see her.

"I am sorry," she answered, "but it cannot be helped."

He broke through the circle then and ran out the door, but found opaque night beyond the threshold. His shin hit a piece of low furniture hidden in the dark; he cursed, tried to step over it, and smashed his forehead against something hard with knobs on it. He felt his foot going through thin wood, the splintered ends digging into his flesh. Arms extended, he groped in the blackness and found hard, sharp corners of large objects. Trying to avoid them, he walked forward, but took no more than a few steps before painfully banging his knee on the edge of a table. I am in a storeroom, he thought. I am destroying the Emperor's valuable property. He is going to be very angry.

Then he was awake. The room full of invisible furniture was gone, and so was the palace. There was the gray dawn, his aching head and dry mouth, and his stiff, tired body.

And the memory of the witch-woman putting a circle around the murderess, and himself inside the circle. He stared at the faint light showing through the cracks in the walls of his hut. He felt more lost, more desolate than ever before. If it was true that the witch had cast a spell so that the Consort Wu's crime would never come to light, then what would such a spell mean for him, the carrier of the evidence? It would mean that he had always been doomed. He contemplated the troublesome riddle of fate. At what point in his wretched life did he start moving toward that moment at the Ch'eng Tien Gate when the cold and horrible realization came to him that the man descending the stairs was not Kao Li-shih, but a stranger? Had his life ever meant anything at all, or had it, from the moment of his conception, been merely a series of futile events whose design was to put him in that place at that time? How far back did it go? Into the lives of his parents, his grandparents, all of his ancestors back to the beginning of time?

And what of the witch? Is a witch a creature of free will, or is she some instrument of fate herself? What is a spell, a curse?

He sat up and held his head in his hands. He knew the truth now. This island had always been waiting for him. This hut, this pile of rags he slept on, were the inevitable reward for his life's work, the culmination of everything he had ever done. He reached for the wine gourd. Before he drank, he raised it in a silent salute to the eunuch, who lay unconscious and curled up in a tight ball in the corner. Your life was very different from mine, and yet everything *you* ever did was fated to put you here, too. We are brothers.

He rolled over and prepared to sleep. He thought about Kao Li-shih and wondered if any of his letters had ever reached him. Kao Li-shih, my old friend, you work so hard for the Emperor. By now you know that even our best-intentioned acts can bring about strange results. The Emperor's love affair . . . Hsueh A-to said that it was you, Kao Li-shih, who brought the girl to the Emperor with hopes of reviving him, and it worked—too well.

As he drifted off, he began to compose his next letter to Kao Li-shih. Tell the Emperor for me . . . tell him that if fate somehow required the sacrifice of my miserable life in order to bring about this miracle of love in his, then so be it . . . I am most happy to have been of service . . . most happy . . .

13

Festival of Lanterns

While the cause of the lover's quarrel is nowhere stated, I [Howard S. Levy] think that it arose over the issue of the emperor's having relations with other women in the harem. Consort Yang [Kuei-fei] probably did not mind if the emperor had an occasional affair with her sisters, but his frequenting the company of women of other clans [i.e., the consort Plum Blossom] posed a direct threat to the influence which she and her relatives were able to enjoy. . . . [Yang Kuei-fei] was a woman of unusual courage who gambled with her life in order to strengthen her emotional hold on the emperor. She did this in the correct belief that Hsuan Tsung's utter dependence on her would ensure her triumphant return to the [palace].

—*Howard S. Levy*

[The Festival of Lanterns of the Chinese] is probably the only event of mankind that would be visible to beings living on the moon. At the same time every year, somewhere in the central and eastern areas of the great landmass we know as China, flickering trails of manmade light would begin to appear. These traces of light would become so dominant against our planet's dark side that they might seem to these exotic beings to be Volcanic fissures in the earth itself.

—*Anonymous eighteenth-century French historian, from* Encyclopédie du Phénomène, *translated by Eleanor Cooney*

"**O**UCH!" Precious Consort yelped. "What do you think you are doing? Combing a horse's tail?"

"I'm sorry, Consort. It's just that it gets so tangled when you dance," Hung-t'ao apologized, pulling the comb through the long silky hair.

The yanking on Precious Consort's scalp was bringing her already irritable mood to the surface.

"She was there today," she said suddenly. "Ow!"

"I'm sorry, Consort . . . who?"

"Stop being so sorry and watch what you're doing. You know perfectly well *who*." She held her head still as the servant got through a particularly stubborn knot. "She was there this morning at the Music Hall of Pure Origins when I performed *her* 'Dance of the Frightened Swan.' I'm sure you could see her. I spotted her myself from the platform. She was in the last row, spying on me; waiting for me to miss a beat, but I didn't, the poor sow."

"Do you mean Consort Chiang?" Hung-t'ao said carefully.

"None other," said the consort archly. "*Her.* Chiang Mei-fei . . . our little 'Plum Blossom.' Our *fat* little Plum Blossom. She doesn't perform the dance he had commissioned for her anywhere near as well as *I* do. She is simply too fat to be a dancer. By the time she is finished, she is drenched in sweat."

"You dance it a hundred times better, Precious Consort." Hung-t'ao said soothingly, with the tone of someone accustomed to knowing what to say and when.

"I dance *everything* better." She sat in silence for a moment. "Besides, her udders are too large, don't you think?"

The attendant giggled. The consort smiled at this, too. They knew each other well. The girl had been with her since her days in the nunnery. The consort knew the girl understood her completely, having seen the full range of her moods, from sunny cheer to sullen temper tantrums. She felt a comfortable alliance with the servant and knew she could completely relax, drop all decorum, and be herself in front of her.

"I'm quite serious," the consort continued. "She's too fleshy all over. A more appropriate name for her version of 'The Frightened Swan' dance would be 'The Astonished Porker.' "

They both laughed very hard at this, Hung-t'ao covering her mouth with glee.

"Why," the consort said, serious again, "does my imperial husband spend so much time with her? She is hardly his ideal of . . . fragile femininity."

"She left the performance early," Hung-t'ao added.

"Well, my sisters always make a point of leaving early when Consort "Plum" performs. Usually right in the middle of her most 'graceful' and 'delicate' moments."

"Your magnificent sisters cannot help but be noticed wherever they come and go," Hung-t'ao said, reaching for fresh gauze to dab at the cosmetic on her mistress's forehead.

"He is spending a great deal more time with her lately," the consort said, brooding. "I had hoped it would be over by now."

"I don't follow our Imperial Father's activities closely enough to know," the girl said diplomatically.

"Oh, nonsense . . . my Imperial *Husband*'s activities," the consort corrected. "And you know everything that he does better than I do. It was you who told me that he hides her in closets when I am about to surprise them . . ."

"Oh, Precious Consort . . . please," the Hung-t'ao beseeched. "If he knew that I . . ."

"Why do you worry so, girl? What passes between us goes no further. You are just an extra set of eyes that I have not told him about because he abhors magic and superstition," the consort said reassuringly.

There was a long period of silence. The girl continued her efforts with her mistress's hair and makeup while the consort fell to brooding again.

"What does she give him that I can't?" she said suddenly, slamming a hairbrush down on the table, making Hung-t'ao jump. "If he wants variety, he has my sisters!"

The attendant did not answer immediately, but grew thoughtful.

"I will wash your hair, now, Precious Consort, and scent it with gardenias and musk oil, his favorites," she said at last. "And I think that tonight would be a good time for you to visit him." She continued her work quietly for a few moments, then looked at her mistress's face in the mirror. "Unannounced would be best, Precious Consort!" she added.

: :

The Precious Consort's handmaidens and seamstresses had fussed for hours with her hair, makeup, and clothes, as if it were an act of love. Which it is, Precious Consort reminded herself. She took a last appraising look in the polished mirror.

Her lips were sensuously rouged, her cheeks subtly highlighted. Green mothbrows lifted her eyes, so it seemed, in an expression of perpetually delighted anticipation. A delicate touch of crimson on her forehead set off the auburn highlights of her hair, which was piled high in front and brought up in swirling knots on the side.

She had chosen a beautiful combination of jade and silver ornaments and—specially—the rhinocerous-horn combs Minghuang had given her. She wore a purple overjacket with cherry-branch designs in brocaded satin and high-winged shoulders, cinched waist, and full puffed sleeves in the fashionable

Kuchan style. Underneath was a flowing gown of dark blue silk. The iridescent turquoise of her eye makeup brought the colors of her face into perfect harmony with the rest.

Hung-t'ao accompanied her along the path until they saw the imperial standards adorned with feathers outside the Emperor's rear hot springs apartments.

"Leave me now, unless you want him to know that you have put me up to all of this," the consort whispered. "Let me walk the final corridor alone. And although I told him that I was not coming tonight, he will not suspect your 'role.' " She paused to unveil the subtlety of her plan. "He had recommended that I work tonight on my poetries since we would be dining with our eccentric master Li Po tomorrow. I told him that I would have something ready for the poet's critique. But"—she paused, finger to her lips—"I will tell him that I have suddenly run out of inspiration, that our meager language does not provide us with enough adjectives to describe a heavily laden branch of *Plum Blossoms* in spring." They both giggled at that. "I shall merely say that I came for some help, not wishing to be embarrassed before such an honorary immortal of the wine cups as Li Po! Now go!" she said, giving the girl a gentle push.

She walked the final hundred yards through the corridors to the Emperor's door. She had become quite resolved as to what she had to do. Hung-t'ao had let her know, without actually saying it, that Minghuang would be having another of his all-too-frequent trysts with the loathsome Plum Blossom. It was an outright slap in the face; this bitch now occupied evenings that had until recently been the exclusive domain of the Precious Consort. She wanted it out with him, tonight. Was she his favorite, or was she not? What exactly did her title mean, and everything that had passed between them?

Two imperial attendants leapt to attention at the sight of the Precious Consort.

"Precious Consort!" one of them said nervously. "The Son of Heaven is not . . . he is not . . . expecting anyone this evening!" the man stammered. The other raced for the door of the imperial apartment.

So now he even posts guards to warn him of my coming, she thought. He makes alliances against me with lowly guards. Am I such a shrew? She pushed past the first attendant and went straight for the door. The attendant who had run inside came out now to block the outer doorway, his face flushed with alarm.

"He is busy with . . . *reworking* the pages of a . . . draft . . . to be presented at . . . audience . . . He wishes no disturbances!"

This one is a bit better at handling deceit, she thought. He speaks forcefully, but look at how flustered he is.

"Audience? Tomorrow? So now I am a disturbance!" She lowered her eyes for a moment, then looked up. "Well, then. Perhaps I may be of some assistance to him, instead. As a dutiful wife, you see. He works too late, sometimes. By himself."

She began to move through the doorway. The second attendant raised his arms as if to stop her. She froze him with a look.

"Don't put your hands on me," she warned.

He offered no more resistance, but stepped aside, dropping his arm resignedly.

She passed through the reception foyer and toward the closed doors of the inner chambers. Two of the Emperor's big Tibetan cats batted at the sashes of her gown as she walked by, their bells jingling. They want affection, she thought; no doubt they've been ignored this evening.

She adored the cats and, under normal circumstances, would have stopped to play—but tonight she had no time for anything. She raised her hems and gently pushed the larger one away with the soft outer side of her slipper. "Shoo, shoo, Pussy, not now! Mother has other things on her mind."

The cats took that as an invitation to play. One of them rolled enticingly on the floor in front of her. She scooped it up and cradled it in her arms; the other now crouched in front of her, head lowered and hindquarters ready to spring in mock attack.

"So you are trying to stop me, too, are you? Well, it won't work." She put the first cat down and bent briefly to stroke the other's long, soft fur. "No one can stop me," she whispered to the animals.

Precious Consort approached the inner door very quietly. She held her breath in and listened. There were definitely two voices—the Emperor's, unmistakable. The other, very soft, barely audible—female. Hers! There was a rustle, slippers along the tiles, movement, a squeaking of screens sliding open and closing again. More low talk, hurried and anxious.

"My Imperial Husband is busy?" Precious Consort called out loudly through the door. There was no answer for a moment.

"I am preparing a draft, my dear," the Emperor said finally. "It is almost done. The papers are scattered over the floor and the ink is wet. I have barred the door against the cats. They are far too playful in the evening; they would destroy everything before my secretaries could transcribe it, sporting with some small beast all over these pages . . ." Minghuang stopped.

She thought now that she could hear the faintest whisper of that other voice. A plan? An escape?

"I will wait on the couch outside and play with the cats; they no doubt feel neglected tonight. We are content to wait, my Imperial Husband, until the pages dry and you can collect them. Perhaps I can read them with you and help you to arrange them for their best literary impact . . . my poetry has grown stale this evening. Perhaps I might be fortunate enough to get some inspiration from you."

She waited, but there was no response from inside. No more movement; no squeaking of screens. Nothing . . . until she heard a faint whisper. She pressed her ear to the door.

Then the whisper rose into clarity, all pretense dropped.

Why? Plum Blossom's voice asked, plaintively, querulously. Be quiet, the Emperor answered. Do you want Consort Yang to hear you? How long will it go on like this, my Imperial Father? Plum Blossom demanded. How long? Never mind how long, he said. What would you have me do? she pleaded. I would have you out of here, now. That is what I would have you do and *will* have you do, he said, his voice exasperated. And do you fear her disposition so much that . . . That is an impertinent question from you, Consort Plum Blossom, he interrupted. I fear no woman's wrath. Not yours, not Consort Yang's.

Oh, doesn't he, now, the Precious Consort thought from her post outside the door. Then what is all the fuss in there about?

It is disharmony among jealous wives that so displeases me, the Emperor said then. Precious Consort smiled as she heard the girl start to cry. Oh, heavens! Servant, take her back . . . These women all begin to sound like quacking ducks, Minghuang said with disgust.

It was too much for the Precious Consort; she was unable to hold her tongue any longer.

"Tell her that I request that you send her to me," she shouted through the door.

"And *who* is that?" the Emperor answered, surprised, as if he expected her to be far down the hall.

"Why, it is only your other little 'duckling,' of course! My Dear Husband, tell her that 'mother-fowl' wishes to bathe with her tonight at the springs . . . I would like it if we could 'paddle' around together . . ."

"That fat slave!" Precious Consort heard Plum Blossom shout out as she was hurried down the rear stairs. Hot blood rushed to Precious Consort's face. How dare she call *me* fat, the cow!

"Then you *have* been spying on me!" Minghuang yelled from behind the door . . .

"And you *have* been lying to me, Husband. But I came tonight to discuss the virtues of prosody with you, and instead . . ."

"And instead, I find you spying on me!" he shouted, enraged. "You, who are supposed to be working on your poetry!"

"To what end, my Imperial Husband? Will you have me nominated to the Han Lin Academy of Letters when you are through with me? Shall I be the first female academician? From nun to wife to consort to academician! What great fortune!" she said.

"Remember your place, Wife!" He was now up against the other side of the door, his voice muffled but close. His lips must have been nearly pressed to the thick wooden door, she thought.

"But I no longer know what that place is. You had promised me weeks ago that Plum Blossom would be transferred any day back to the halls of the 'Exalted Male Aspect' in Loyang. We are still waiting."

"Oh, she will be sent back there, I promise you that," he said, ". . . if only to give my poor ears a rest. I cannot stand the bickering between you two. But it is no business of yours what I choose to do."

"Indeed, it is not, my Husband," she said with mock humility. "But how do you like the first couplet of my poem for Master Li Po? It will be in *chueh-chu* quatrains, I believe. It starts:

> "Alas, the Peach awakens the appetite . . .
> but My Lord chooses to eat the Plum, instead . . ."

The door swung open. He would weaken, she knew, but she hadn't expected it to be so sudden or abrupt. Their eyes met, and he looked away. She studied him, an old man naked but for his dressing gown; then her eyes left him, and she looked into the room behind him. They continued to stand there. It must be far more awkward and uncomfortable for him than for me, she thought. The room was in disarray. Dishes with half-eaten fruit, nuts, and pastries were scattered about; the bedclothes were in a tangle. He gave her a long look and moved aside.

"Are you going to come in, or do we just stand here like fools all evening?" Minghuang asked. The two cats raced into the room just as she was pulling the door closed behind her.

"The *papers* have all been put away, I trust," Precious Consort asked. "I cannot keep your long-haired pets out. They are too fast for me." She bent over and picked up a woman's slipper that peeked out from under the Emperor's canopied bed. She held it away from her as if she were holding a dead rat by the tail. "Poor thing," she said. "Her feet will be cold."

He snatched it from her.

Their eyes met again. This time he did not look away. He was still looking into her eyes as he walked to the window shutters, pushed them open, and flung the slipper out into the pond below.

"Is that what you wish me to do, my Precious Consort?"

"I do not presume to ask the Son of Heaven to do what he does not *want* to do, my Husband," she said. "That would indeed be a foolish and presumptuous mistake." She said it as if she meant it.

He sat down tiredly on the edge of his bed and motioned for her to come over to him. His robe fell open as he sat, revealing his narrow, round-bellied torso. She walked over to the bed and stood facing him. He reached out and placed his hands on the satin hips of her gown.

"What is all of this about?" he asked softly. "You know that you are my principal wife. You know that you are in no danger of being replaced." He looked up at her, his hands caressing her hips and buttocks. "It is you that has awakened so much in me," he said. "Minor forays into the harem have never bothered you before. Why now?"

"If you will forgive me, my Husband . . . but Consort Plum Blossom hardly seems a 'minor foray.' That is not her design. A woman knows these things."

"And a woman knows how to follow me around . . . doesn't she?" he said without malice, as if he didn't expect an answer. His thumbs moved closer together, massaging her inner thighs, causing a little thrill to ripple through her. He could feel, she knew, the delicate curly texture of the hair of her "gate" under the silken fabric of her gown. She glanced discreetly at his lap. She had got here in time, she thought; his evening must not have been consummated yet. His "old man" was beginning to rise.

"You once told me, not so long ago, my Husband, that there were few women so loved by the others in your palace as myself. You told me that no woman had been as loved and accepted as I since your departed Empress Wang. Such news filled my heart in ways I cannot tell you. And I would not mind your Plum Blossom," the Precious Consort lied delicately, gazing at his face, "if she did not spread such rumors and hatred of me. I can feel coldness spreading among women who once adored me. I have even tried that much harder to be the loving consort that they first looked to. But it is almost impossible now, with *her*," the consort pleaded. She knew she had him now. "It is not *I* disturbing the harmony of your household; *she* is the jealous one, Husband—she will not be satisfied with a little of your time . . ."

"All right," he said at last. "I promise you that she will be sent back to Loyang next week. The staff will begin the preparations for her trip tomorrow." He withdrew his hands from her hips. "Certainly something is causing us disharmony. She is needed anyway as a dancing instructor at our music academy in the eastern capital," he said to recover his prestige.

"She is indeed a fine dancer," the consort said, picking up his hands and putting them back on her hips. "My handmaiden Hung-t'ao has made that remark on many occasions, and I have had to agree."

The Emperor laughed and shook his head.

"It will be written in the histories that Emperor Minghuang was known for his weakness, his susceptibility to females. *Impertinent* females. It was, they will say, his downfall." He embraced her around the hips and then slid his hands up and down the backs of her legs. "I am glad that you take such care with your clothing and cosmetics when you sit down to work on your poetry," he remarked.

She laughed. "It is a great aid to my inspiration," she said, and sat down on his lap.

: :

"Kao Li-shih," said the Precious Consort one day soon after the Emperor had promised to send Plum Blossom back to Loyang. "You knew the Empress Wang, did you not?"

The Consort and the eunuch were in the Emperor's private sitting room, waiting for him to come and join them for the evening meal. Kao Li-shih looked at her for a moment before answering.

"Yes," he said. "I knew her."

"How well did you know her?" the consort asked.

Kao Li-shih smiled ruefully. "Women are extraordinary creatures," he said. "You are even capable of being jealous of the dead."

"I am not jealous of her!" she protested. "I just want to know what she was like. He loved her, didn't he?"

She looked at him in a way meant to let him know that she wanted the truth, not circumspection meant to mollify her. He heaved a sigh of acquiescence. He knows me too well by now, she thought, to try to slip out of my grasp. She waited.

"He loved her so much," Kao Li-shih said finally, looking steadily at the consort, "that when she died, I feared that it would soon be over for him as well."

"And it is true that he lost all interest in females for a long time afterward?"

"Until you came along. And I had a very difficult time indeed convincing him to even look at you after I got you out of the nunnery."

"What did she look like?" the consort persisted.

"There is a painting of her, Consort. The Emperor keeps it rolled up and hidden in some secret place. Perhaps he will allow you to look at it."

"Maybe you can find it for me," she suggested, but he shook his head.

"I'm afraid I have no wish to paw through his personal belongings in order to satisfy your feminine inquisitiveness. You will have to get at it yourself. Though my advice, Consort, is to desist for the time being. And I am sure I have made a grievous error that I am going to regret for the rest of my life by even mentioning that such a painting exists."

"If you tell me what she looked like," the consort said coyly, "then I won't have to ask him about the painting."

"I know that I am only adding fuel to the raging fire of your jealousy . . . but she was beautiful, very slender, and older than you are."

The consort thought about that.

"But she was barren," the consort said. "That is what the women tell me."

"Yes," Kao Li-shih said sadly. "She was barren."

"And that is why she killed herself?"

"It is much more complicated than that, Consort. And now, I think we had best change the topic, because I hear the Emperor coming."

The conversation, far from satisfying the Precious Consort, left her with a hundred more questions. When the Emperor entered the room, his face kind and so genuinely glad to see her, the need to know pressed her urgently. Who had this woman been whose death nearly killed him, too? Does he love me as much as he loved her? How did she kill herself? But the biggest question, the one that sometimes kept her awake at night, was one that there was no answer to: Suppose, she asked herself, the Empress hadn't died, but he had met me anyway. Would he still have loved me? Would he have loved me more than he did her?

She smiled and extended her hand to him.

: :

If she did not ask the question soon, it would be too late. He would be asleep. His breathing was already growing shallow and regular; he might even be asleep now. She moved a little. He shifted his weight, resting an arm heavily across her belly. He hummed a little tune in her ear. He was still awake.

"Father," she said, using the pet name she reserved for rare moments.

"Are you speaking to me?" he said from far away. She gathered her nerve. A better opportunity than this would not come along soon. The mood tonight had been exceptionally fine—humorous, fond, forgiving. Everything in his manner had said what he had not quite put into words yet: You are the one woman I could not live without.

"What happened to the Empress?" she said.

He did not move or react in any way. She wondered if he had fallen asleep after all. Just when she decided he had, and was relieved that she would not have to worry about her question anymore tonight, he spoke.

"Even a dead woman cannot escape your scrutiny."

"That is what Kao Li-shih said to me. That I was jealous of her. But it is not true. It is just that I feel . . . left out. There are so many years of your life from which I am excluded."

He laughed softly. At least he was not angry.

"But you were only a child or not yet born during much of my life."

"That is not my fault!" she said. "You loved a woman before you loved me. Something terrible happened. You sent her away, and then she killed herself. Can you blame me for wanting to know? Put yourself in my place, if you can!"

He rolled over, removing his arm from across her stomach. He lay separate from her now, on his back. She could feel him staring at the ceiling.

"All right," he said, after a long time. "I will tell you what I know. I don't think that she would object." He paused. "Mind you, she took the answers to certain questions to the grave with her. There are things that I will never know myself. You know, I am sure, that she was trying to conceive a child, an heir."

He stopped, and did not speak for a while. Precious Consort waited, shivering slightly in the dark.

"When she died, she had been bleeding. We will never know if she had conceived and lost the infant, or never conceived at all. In either case, it was enough to make her take her own life. But I will tell you the story from the beginning.

"Perhaps you know, too, that years ago certain magic practices and their perpetrators were banned in the empire . . . and that it was to one of these forbidden shamans that my Empress, in her desperation, turned . . ."

: :

The Empress Wang had begun to smell the air of home. Six days of jolting and bumping in the carriage on the the narrow mountainous Chienmenkuan Pass into Szechuan had carried her far from the exotic smells of the palace and the air that wafted in from the city. Food, perfume, incense, smoke, and humanity; a mix of olfactory messages had been her daily fare for years. The night air coming through the open window of the carriage carried an odor of sun-baked pine needles; the message went straight to the center of her brain: home.

She took deep lungfuls of the eloquent air, trying to divine its message about the future. It spoke to her of many things, but said nothing of her fate; alone, banished, exiled . . . She shifted her position to relieve her stiff neck. It was useless. There was no comfort, only exhaustion. She slipped in and out of a light doze, unsatisfied, unrested. Her sleep was broken into confused half-dreams that kept rhythm with the wheels rumbling under the floor.

It had been more than two months since the edict of the Wang family's banishment had been passed. She had not seen the Emperor Minghuang since the morning he'd called her in for questioning. His equanimity had frightened her; he had been a stranger to her at that moment. She had been moved within days to her hot springs apartments many li from the palace; there she'd waited for the heat of summer to wane a bit before starting the long overland journey to the family home in northern Szechuan. She had passed the days making music and playing games—chess, cards of the four kings, liupo, double sixes, tiles, and stones—with harem women and various court ladies sent there to keep her company. Poetry and calligraphy had also occupied her when her own thoughts did not; at night, it became her habit to read by the light of her oil lamp, occasionally watching the various insects that, attracted by the light, became mired in the hot residue of the lamp. She could see their tiny black eyes and delicate wings as they struggled and died, looking dignified and resigned at the end.

While she waited out the long, late summer days, something had happened that had never happened before. Two complete lunar cycles had come and gone, and she'd seen no blood.

She told no one and walked as lightly and delicately as she could, as if to hold things in place. Oh, the irony! She was incredulous at the workings of the universe with its odd sense of humor. So be it; I'm with child—and soon I will be a commoner. What other jokes will be played on me? Will the child be born with a tail, six fingers, or an eye in the middle of its forehead to remind me of my transgression?

The knowledge which, at any previous time in her life, would unquestionably have meant a public announcement and rejoicing was now carried quietly. She was not sure that she wanted to come face to face with this child of hers. Is it my son, the prince whose face I've seen for years in dreams, or some intruder who found his way through the use of magic? Or perhaps . . . she laughed bitterly when another possibility came to her. It will be a girl. Just another flower for the Emperor to add to his bouquet, and I will die giving birth to her.

But if it is the "fat little prince" promised by Ming Wu . . . , who am I? We'll return together, she thought. I'll wait, and return with my little son. The Emperor is not a hard-hearted man. I know the anguish it causes him to deal harshly with people . . . He will take me back. I will be the Empress again, but I must wait. My son and I will return.

Her two months of relative isolation at the hot springs had been spent contemplating her strange predicament. She dreamed a lot. Sometimes she was the Empress again, resplendent and forgiven, sitting on the knee of the Son of Heaven while he put his tongue in her ear and thanked her for the finest son of all, the true heir—the crown prince. In another dream, she'd found herself in unfamiliar hallways of the vast palace, unable to follow instructions given her by servants. She had become lost and found herself back where she'd started. And there was a recurring dream in which she lived in small, dark rooms underneath the palace, hearing footsteps and voices over her head. She was very old and had only one tooth. Her skin was old burnt leather and her clothes were musty. The floors of her rooms crackled with small, white animal bones as she walked. The voices above her occasionally spoke about the beautiful Empress Wang; she remembered vaguely that it was herself they spoke of, but she had a different calling now and couldn't be bothered. Her "child" lived down there with her, an entity that shifted from being human to looking like a small dog and then a monkey. She knew the voices upstairs would disapprove of her child, so she kept it down in the dark rooms with her . . .

She had embarked for Szechuan late in September. It was not as hot as mid-summer, but the journey was still uncomfortable. She and her small entourage traveled by night to avoid the heat and stopped to rest during the day at inns and imperial travel lodges along the well-traveled post road. When she stopped, people she encountered—proprietors, other guests, traveling officials—all treated her as if she were still the Empress and always would be. Their deference and courtliness were impeccable, conveying to her that she was the Empress taking a journey to her father's shrine as any filial child would do. No reference was ever made, directly or obliquely, to the edict and banishment, word of which had spread with the speed of thought throughout the empire.

: :

The deer lifted their graceful heads and watched her livery as it rolled by. Their large ears stood out attentively while their jaws worked from side to side, the mild brown eyes following the motion of the carriage. In one instant they looked poised for flight; in the next, the heads were lowered and grazing resumed.

The carriage wound through the woods on the drive that led to her childhood home. She had awakened that morning feeling thirsty and with an ache on one side of her head. When she had first stood up from her bed in the lodge she had experienced a curious weighty sensation in her abdomen. All of it had passed now, and she merely felt dull. The palace and its realities seemed remote as the atmosphere of home enveloped her.

Her father's old retainer stood in the sunshine. He bowed deeply when he saw her, the narrow slits of his ancient eyes conveying affection, sadness, sympathy, and greeting. Briskly, he ordered the servants to their task of removing Wang's belongings from the coaches and seeing to her comfort. The apartments she had had as a child were prepared for her again. She wanted rest and, tomorrow, an evening walk and an interval of solitude with the spirit of her father at the family's ancestral temple.

: :

The child Wang awoke in her little bed in her father's home in Szechuan. She drowsed happily as the sun streamed through the latticed shutters. A maidservant entered and raised the blinds, and smiled at the half-sleeping child. From her bed, Wang could see across the courtyard. Her uncle's shutters were not yet open for his morning tea with Father. Small tame yellow finches fluttered on her sill, anticipating the sweet crumbs the girl would give them from her breakfast.

In the corridor outside her chamber she heard female voices and the comforting sound of her great-great-grandmother's slow, shuffling steps, accompanied by her chattering maidservants.

She loved this summer house, so far west, wooded, and wild. She came here every year to her father's home. He'd been sent to this distant post when she was an infant. In the winter she and her brother, grandmothers, and mother stayed at the other family house far away to the east and south along the hot and humid Li River until Father called for them. The cold winter air, he declared, was bad for a child's lungs.

Here, she and her brother could play without restriction in the fields and forests, where a child could spend an entire day out-of-doors without seeing an adult. They could creep up on the deer who grazed on the slopes; the creatures tolerated the children up to a distance where the animal's liquid eyes could be seen as they gazed with curiosity at the boy and girl . . . And once, even, they thought they saw the elusive black and white bear; they had held their breaths as a startling set of black-masked eyes looked at them through the dense forest of bamboo before disappearing . . .

Today, she thought as she drowsed in the summer morning sunshine, I'll go and wake up brother and we'll climb into the hills to look for the spring we heard about from the servants. Their game this summer was to build tiny shrines in hidden places, decorating them elaborately with rocks and plants and strings and bits of silk and broken pottery. Anyone happening by would not notice one of their shrines; only if you were told to expect it would you see it. They spent hours in the cool forest, squatting at the base of a tree, building miniscule walkways in the tangled web of roots, and landscaping with moss and sticks. The miniature worlds they created gave them great satisfaction, their heads almost touching as they bent over their work with total absorption.

We'll find the spring and build a shrine with a waterfall. We'll divert water into a little pool and build a bridge across it. I must go wake him. He likes to sleep late on these summer mornings. She tried to open her eyes, but found the lids to be so heavy that she couldn't lift them. Maybe I've slept too long, she thought. Maybe he's already up and gone for the day without me. I must wake up. She strained with all her might against her eyelids, but was able only to open them part way. Close to her face, she could see the brocade pillowcase where her head rested. She could feel the position of her body, but was unable to move her limbs. Struggling to open her eyes, she glimpsed her hand on the pillow. It lay alongside her face. She was surprised to see that the nails were long and manicured. And the position of the bed seemed to be wrong; the window that looked across to her uncle's quarters was not there. Instead, an embroidered tapestry blocked her view. Oh, the frustration! Brother will be up and away without me; I can't bear the idea.

With a mighty effort she lifted her eyelids a little, but found herself sinking back down after another glimpse of the strange immobile hand next to her face on the pillow. I must hurry, she thought as she sank.

She awoke, bursting cleanly through the layer of sleep into full consciousness. The disappointment was simultaneous; there was no child's summer day in Szechuan, no shrine to build, no seven-year-old brother. She was an empress, nearly forty years old, and the fatigue of living descended on her swiftly, displacing the child's anticipation. Already the day was hot. She kicked off the coverlet and lay naked. The light streamed into the rooms she had known as a child. But it was pale and washed of color now. Thin, pellucid, as if even the sky, too, had somehow faded with time . . .

∷

A sedan chair had been offered to carry her from the house to the shrine, but she had waved it away, telling them that even an empress preferred to walk sometimes. Stepping out into the house's main courtyard in the early evening, she experienced a feeling familiar to travelers who return to a childhood place. The winding stone paths and twisted trees were intact, exactly as she had left them, but they had a strangely shrunken, diminished quality. The ornate carved grillwork, a source of great magic to her when she was a child, was merely cut stone. Looking up to the screened windows of her uncle's quarters above the west side of the courtyard, she felt a lack inside her. Once, those windows had meant warmth and life; looking at them now, their light lien-tse *blinds of plaited bamboo rolled shut, she thought of the grieved old man, mourning his brother, who now moved behind them.*

Crossing the courtyard, she entered a covered walkway and passed the circular door to the library, pausing to sniff the odor of oil and varnish of the rich rosewood lattice. She stepped outside again into another courtyard, passed through a free-standing crescent-shaped door with the inscription "yu shen yueh ti"—*place of the moon's good friendship—carved above. Then a narrow pathway led mysteriously under the graceful arch of an overhead corridor, down a few steep stairs, through another small courtyard, and to the outside through a moongate whose inscription in flaking gold characters read* "chu ching tao yu"—*the bamboo path is the way to mystery.*

She followed the path in the moonlight toward the wooded hillside beyond the garden. Tai-hu stones, shaped by nature but cultivated by men and placed on ornate pedestals, showed their convoluted shapes in strong relief. She stopped walking. There was a slight pulling sensation in her pelvic region. Her face in the pale light was thoughtful. She continued, starting up the stone staircase toward a small pavilion not visible from the house. Soon she saw the sweeping tiled roof with upward curves at the four corners, the venerable pillars and carved rails nearly obscured by the late summer growth of vines and weeds. She entered and stood, listening to dry leaves skittering on the stone floor. A hollow sound. She was breathing hard from the climb. The air was tinged with autumn.

She stood still. She felt a downward grab and pull. The pulling increased as if something were moving slowly and deliberately through her. It became a downward dragging which concentrated in point of intensity in the lowest part of her abdomen. The feeling held for a minute or two and then relaxed its grip; as she let her breath out she felt a warm liquid rush.

The moonlight in the pavilion was very bright. She lifted the front part of her gown and looked at the insides of her thighs; long dark streaks of blood crisscrossed on the white skin. Droplets glistened on the stone floor. Carefully holding the gown away from her body to avoid staining the silk, she left the pavilion.

She descended the stone staircase, followed the path down the hillside and back into the garden, and approached the house. She passed through the moongate and ascended the small staircase that led underneath the arched overhead corridor. Crossing the courtyard, she paused. She lifted her gown and brought the skirt of her chemise up to her teeth. She bit through the outer hem, then ripped a large piece of fabric from the garment. She wadded it, and placed it between her legs to absorb the blood before entering the house.

She stepped inside. It was dark and quiet. She stood for a moment, trying to recall the location of something, then turned decisively toward the library. Her hands passed along the walls until they found the carved circular doorway; without hesitation she found the latch and swung the door open. The air of the room was warm and musty; objects and furniture were clearly discernible in the moonlight coming through the gauze mosquito netting over the open windows. To her left stood an ornate wooden chest, its polished brass fittings glinting. On the right side of the room was a small table with sliding drawers.

She went to the table and pulled out the right-hand drawer. She found a key under a silk cushion. She closed the drawer, crossed to the chest, fitted the key into the small brass padlock, snapped it open, and lifted the lid of the chest. An exotic array of collected knives and swords and daggers lay in the chest. She picked up a short Sillan sword with a wide blade and held it by its rhinoceros horn handle, the silver inlay cool to the touch. She replaced the sword in the chest. An Arabian scimitar with a wicked curved blade, then a yataghan knife. Too long. She rejected both. She lifted a Khitan dagger, designed to be hidden in one's boot. The blade was short, but serviceable. She tested it with her thumb. She put it in her sleeve and shut and locked the chest. She left the house.

She came to a small clearing on the slope of a hill a quarter of a mile to the west of and below the house. Black marble steles stood grouped together, one for each deceased family member occupying the semispherical vault on the edge of the clearing.

This place had been chosen by the geomancer for its beauty and potency; it faced south, the vault sheltered by the low rise of auspiciously shaped hills. A small stream ran all year in a narrow cleft between soft grassy knolls. The clearing commanded a sweeping view of the valley below; Wang could see the river in the distance, its snaky curves between the black spikes of pines silvery in the moonlight.

She passed a small shrine where oil lamps flickered and followed the path which led among the steles. Her hand passed over carved characters that spoke of a person's life and accomplishments. She thought of the dark, heavy density of the marble as a repository for a life. A life is a flimsy, translucent thing, which will disperse itself into nothingness; this black rock draws life into itself like a magnet and holds it there. The stones were as tall as human figures. They were her ancestors, standing attentively around her in the moonlit clearing. These departed ones are very polite, she thought. There is no need for laborious explanations. They don't weep, scold, or admonish. They have no wish to interfere, though the postures of some of them—huddled, talking, now, in low whispers—tell me they are a little bit sad. So am I.

She felt a gentle squeezing, like a hand wringing out a rag to extract the last few drops. She found a grassy place among the stones, removed the wadded piece of silk from under her gown and looked at it in the pale light. There was blood and dark scraps of embryonic matter. With the dagger, she dug a small hole. She placed the cloth in the hole and covered it with dirt. *In her mind, a young man kissed his mother good-bye and strode out of her chamber, shutting the door firmly behind him.*

She turned and left the area where the steles stood and ascended the path toward the family shrine. Approaching the steps of the miniature temple, she recalled the secret shrines she and Brother used to build in the summer before their seventh birthday. *This could be one of them, she thought. I am a tiny shrew standing here on the steps of a shrine built by children in the roots of a giant pine. The children are at home sleeping and don't know that I come here at night to meditate. Or perhaps I'll just build my nest in here, and fill it with twigs and bits of fur.*

Oil lamps cast a soft glow inside the shrine, showing gilded Buddhist statues in their niches. She took a stick of incense from its holder, lit it from the oil lamp, and used the flame to light the small candles and joss sticks on the altar. She blew the flame out on the stick and inhaled deeply the sweet smoke to purify her breath. The candlelight revealed a tablet eulogizing her father:

> The Honorable Wang Jen-chiao, Lord Great Chamberlain and Duke
> of Pin Principality, was gentle and good, merciful and forgiving. In his service
> to the government he was liberal and easy, manifesting love of the people. At
> the court, he spoke with sternness and an upright countenance. There are none
> who could come up to his virtue. But he alone died early.

She recognized the imperial seal; the tablet was sent down from the Emperor himself.

As the incense smoke curled and drifted gracefully upward, she burned the votive paper charms for her father. She chose characters to burn that would petition for rank and protection in the afterlife for him, that his earthly domain might be carried over. She concentrated on an image of his face in her mind, sitting still for a long while.

She rose and went to stand in the open door, watching the moon as it sank close to the horizon. She recited an ancient verse by Ju-an Chi, speaking the words softly to herself:

> Etch upon your breast
> Every moment of sunset's time.
> Adjust your sleeves, unsheath a slender sword,
> And lift your eyes to the fleeing clouds.

> Among them a dark stork
> Raises its head and shakes its beak.
> Darting aloft, disappearing into the void,
> Forever silent, never to be heard again.
> It is no friend to the cuckoos and the crows
> That circle round the court.

She removed the knife from her sleeve and wiped the dirt from it. Her heart was beating fast. She turned and went back inside. She faced the small statue of Buddha Amitabha, who sat as he had sat for centuries, eyes veiled, lips faintly amused, delicate fingers upraised in a mudra of compassion.

I know all things, he said to her in the silence. She held the knife in the flat of her hand, like an offering. I know this, too, he said. He smiled, and waited.

"Amitabha," she said. "Amitabha, Amitabha, Amitabha, Amitabha, Amitabha," she chanted the name that would deliver her to the Western Paradise. Her voice became a low, urgent whisper. She closed her eyes. "Amitabha, Amitabha, Amitabha, Amitabha, Amitabha . . ."

The blade was poised over the flesh between two ribs in her chest. In her dark rooms under the palace, an old woman muttered and shook her head, pacing nervously over the white bones.

"Amitabha, Amitabha, Ami . . ." The blade surprised her with its impatience; her eyes flew open against her will, wanting to see this world one last time.

On the day Chi-mao in autumn of the seventh month and the twenty-fifth year of the K'ai Yuan reign period,* the Emperor sent down an edict, saying:

My Empress of the Wang clan was not blessed by the Mandate of Heaven. She was extravagant and insincere. She planned and fomented treason and provoked the court with her associates. It was apparent that she fluctuated in her heart and contained an evil that might have been avoided. How could she be reverent and obedient to the ancestral temple and be a maternal woman exemplary to the entire empire? I deem it necessary to depose her to [the status of] commoner and to confine her tranquilly to a life in retirement. She has been guilty toward the [imperial] family and disgraced the ancient kings, but this has still been done reluctantly for the great cause of our nation.

: :

---

*August 14, 737.

". . . and so you see," the Emperor said to the Precious Consort, shifting his position in the bed, "that I must bear the knowledge that she died because I sent her away. And I had to send her away for no other reason than that I am an emperor. Ordinary men are allowed to forgive their wives, but that was a luxury not allowed me." He moved again so that he was leaning on one elbow looking down at her in the semidarkness.

For the first time, she thought that she understood something of the dark, secret, sad side of him that he usually kept hidden from her. She thought of those mysterious wasted years that Kao Li-shih often referred to, when the Emperor had been in a deep pit of despair. She had never really believed or understood, until now. Her own life seemed shallow and frivolous by comparison, and ridiculously short. He had been alive so much longer than she and had had to carry such a heavy burden. What could she possibly know of what he really felt or thought? And though the Emperor had just finished divulging intimate details from his past to her, things he had never mentioned before or had refused to talk about, even though he had let her that much further into his life, she felt more left out than ever.

Five years the Empress had been dead. For five years, there had been no empress at all. A thought crept into her mind; to be sure, it was not the first time she had contemplated the idea of herself as an empress, but it had always occupied a distant realm somewhere in the future.

He had told her that he loved her above all other women. The next step was logical, inescapable. As if he had read her thoughts, he spoke.

"And when she died, I made a vow that there would be no other empress as long as I lived."

Early Evening, Third Day of the Festival of Lanterns New Year Celebration

Flames licked the sky in one of the nameless, numberless back lanes of the great city's western slums. Old man Su raised a crockery jar to his lips and drank deeply, standing at a distance that afforded him a view without scorching his worn clothing. The heat of the fire felt good on this cold night. The pockets of his coat sagged with the weight of his loot.

Thatching, dampened in the recent storms, had smoldered since early that morning, the third and final day of the lantern festivities. The wind carried sparks from fireworks and lamp displays; the flimsy wooden structures of the southwestern wards, where thousands lived in ignominious squalor, were the favorite stopping places of wayward bits of fiery debris blowing in from the thronging avenues. It was an inherent law of the universe that disaster always sought out the poor.

By late evening the fire had sprung with such ferocity that the row of hovels had seemed to explode at once. The light was reflected in open tiled culverts where rivers of sewage ran sluggishly; the skeletal frameworks of crowded shanties stood out starkly as the fire raged. Old Su raised his jar in salutation as the framework gave way, collapsing gracefully in upon itself. There were screams; he saw a running figure, clothing aflame, leap and then roll on the ground. Fire, he thought, is a thorough cleanser. Tonight it will consume some of the filth and the lives of a few sleeping infants, drunkards, and old ones, hastening them on their journey through this world. In the fevered pitch of this final eve of drunkenness and boisterousness, it would scarcely be noticed. That's not the way *I'm* going to die, old Su thought. Not by fire. I am hardly so stupid as that. My death will be a happy, drunk, painless one, and I will leave my bloated corpse bobbing with the rest of the debris in the canal where I will have stumbled. Ha! But I shall be long gone. It will be someone else's problem to deal with what I have left behind. Ha!

There was activity ahead on the Lane of the Ten Worthies. Old man Su was not one to join a crowd, but he had ways of moving on the periphery so that he could observe while still remaining virtually invisible. He was one inconspicuous old man in a city of millions, and he was a veteran of over fifty of these annual festivals when the entire city seemed to take leave of its senses. For three nights each year, anything at all could happen as people surged through the streets, the lights exploding above their heads. Curfews were lifted as the citizens of Ch'ang-an reveled in the birth of the new year and the tales of the blessed Buddha. The morning sun often rose on scenes of devastation, and the authorities had to make regular rounds to remove those who had passed out in the streets and alleyways.

The scorched odor of *huo yao** hung in the air after the bright white flashes that threw their illumination indiscriminately on every type of human dwelling, be it hovel or palace. Now old Su made his way along the narrow street, the flashes of light revealing the architecture of poverty. Here, in the long, narrow, ill-smelling alleys between two squat, blue-tiled minarets and not far from the exotic, rambling Arab markets, lives were crammed together in a grim economy of space. No breadth of tree or grass, no span of crisp, white-washed wall or recessed fretwork broke up the dingy facades of wood, bamboo, and burlap. There were small fires burning here and there in the street, with groups of people warming themselves, drinking, and eating. Eating delicacies, no less! The city's gentry was generous tonight; there was good food everywhere. Tonight the poor did not have to feed on the dogs and cats and rats that ran wild in the alleys, nor would their palates be limited this night to the meager and colorless state doles of rice and millet from the

*Gunpowder

granaries. A crowd was forming a bit further down the street. Old Su moved closer, attracted by shouts and excited voices.

Light cast from lanterns held high on long poles revealed flashes of brilliantly colored clothing. Turquoise, bright red, and shimmering gold contrasted with the dingy tones of brown and gray worn by the denizens of these streets. Like moths to the flame, the drab ones were drawn to the bright ones. Old Su smiled. Certain things never change, he thought. Deeming the spectacle worthy of his attention, he moved into the crowd near its edge.

Four slender young women, their dress bearing the clear, certain mark of unbridled opulence and the unmistakable crease from the back of a sedan chair, accompanied a tall, fiery, and arrogantly handsome young man. The man's thick, shiny black hair was pulled in a topknot and crowned with the starched silk cap of some high official rank or other. Whoever he was, he must be very important, very powerful. But he glided through the crowds without the identifying presence or protection of servants or guards. Old Su supposed that even the great sometimes wanted their anonymity. Someone remarked that the clothing of the women was strange, but in the great capital city so much passed in and out of fashion, drawing from areas as far north as the Ferghanian steppes and as far south as the jungles of Champa, that the remark had little meaning. The subtler nuances of couture were lost on the wretches who watched the group in awe. A lengthening waistcoat, perhaps, or the extension of a sleeve and added height to a winged shoulder, an extra dart in the bodice, new shadings to the eyes and cheeks, or new treatments to the coiffure—decorated sidebuns, a higher wave above the forehead like a great tidal bore on some distant southern estuary; new elaborate ornaments of gold and silver—none of this had a great deal of meaning to the eyes of those from these backroads of subsistence-level poverty. And whether the exotic, alien creatures were from the wealthy merchant class or true aristocracy was a distinction that escaped most of those who watched them picking their way among rubble and bonfires as the crowd parted deferentially. They were simply the *rich*. Ha! But nothing is lost on me, old Su thought.

The youngest girl, little more than a child, had a large, brightly colored bird on her shoulder. It squawked and fluttered with each deep boom of the official fireworks in distant Xing Ying Park, but it never left its perch. Some strange and fancy fetish, no doubt, from some far-off malaria-riddled colony. One could see so many strange new things in the city, but rarely in streets such as these.

The four had been carried from their magnificent carriages in sedan chairs into the Lane of the Ten Worthies. They had not ventured very far, their faces aglow with the lights of their hand-held lanterns. They could hear the sounds of the streetwise drunken rabble around them—laughter, gruff voices, the sound of breaking jars. The youngest, wide-eyed and fearful, reminded her companions again that this was not a good section of town as she raised a nervous hand to the talons on her shoulder. There were bound to be all manner of tramps and rude, drunken youths about. Besides, it smelled so awful. Yang Chou was never so crowded as this; maybe she did not like the capital after all. But it would never have done to refuse the invitation to visit her beautiful and famous cousins, these important relatives of the Hung Nung clan. And one of them, the Precious Consort, was now practically an empress. Mother had positively demanded that she accept the invitation. But Mother didn't know about these forays into the slums that were so fashionable these days. Certainly it had been different when Mother had been a girl. Cautious, she hung back.

Then Eldest Cousin, taking hold of the little one's wrist, motioned to the others and said, "Come on, come on, Child—it's certainly not as horrible as Hell!" He turned to the other women in the party and gave a knowing wink. "Especially on a night of Buddhist festival. Haven't you read the Sutra of Compassion and Mercy, Little Cousin? A family could eat for months on the cost of just one of your hairpins or you earrings. Look at that brooch! The burden of some poor wretch's soul could be lightened on this plane of suffering with a bit of wine and some food for his stomach."

The young girl's face was a study in worry and anxiety as her distaste for the squalor around her and her reluctance to part with her jewelry and ornaments vied with her transparent fear of the Hell that might await her in the hereafter if she were to fail to seize this opportunity. Amused by her consternation, the handsome man tugged at the sleeve of his female companion in demonstration.

"I don't suppose you want hungry ghosts pulling at your clothing with empty rice bowls and wine cups," he said gleefully. "Or think of the little children who, but for a few copper coins, could be carrying lanterns tonight. Would you deprive them of the innocent joys of childhood? Perhaps you'd like to scrabble around in Hell yourself with no lantern to light your way," he intoned meaningfully to the girl, conjuring up the popular heterodox image of Hell. The Lady of Kuo looked at Yang Kuo-chung sharply. Wasn't he going a bit far in teasing the child? But her sisters laughed, joining in the playful torment of the girl; they refused to drop the game.

"The child is afraid to walk down a dark corridor in her own house," the Lady of Han said. "Think of her in the endless dark corridors of Hell, where the things waiting for her in the blackness will be more than figments of her imagination. I hear that little gibbering demons like to grab at your ankles!"

"And they get tangled in your hair and ride on your back," the Lady of Chin added for emphasis, "chattering their endless nonsense rhymes in your ear with their foul-smelling breath!"

Real fear showed in the girl's eyes now. And the look on Yang Kuo-chung's face was evidence that now he, too, thought they had all carried the joke too far for the sake of a little fun. Sounds from the fire in the side street off the Lane of the Ten Worthies reached them. The civil authorities were arriving, and the foreman was shouting orders to his men and attempting to clear the alley so that they could get in. The red glow could be seen over the tops of the squat buildings. Without warning, the girl bolted, running toward the scene of destruction. A coterie from the crowd, delighted and curious at her strange behavior, broke off and followed her, shouting to one another.

She had taken her companions by surprise. They ran after her. They were used to giving coins to the poor on festival nights, to bringing caskets of wine and baked mooncakes and scented lantern oils to anonymous impoverished doorsteps, descending into the dark slums in their finery. It was all part of the grand game, the wondrous ambience of these festive city nights. They would rejoice in the sense of adventure as they pulled each other along the tight, fetid alleys, daring one another to go further. It was the girl's first such excursion, and they had found her reactions most amusing as the carriages and then the litters carried them deeper and deeper into the poorest sections of the city. But she was a nervous, imaginative child, and now they all feared that her initiation had been too much. What would the sisters say to the girl's mother and father if something were to happen to her? They hurried after her. There was no telling what the foolish thing might do.

When they caught up to her, she had pushed her way into the cul-de-sac to the perimeter of the crowd enjoying the spectacle. Water drums had been brought in, their solid wooden wheels creaking agonizingly as they rolled over the rutted lane. The steady sound of the lever-driven pistons mixed with the rhythmic gushes of sluggish brown water as the men trained the wide bamboo nozzles sealed with pitch on the smoldering ruins. Charred doorposts rising from the rubble—the agonized heads of phantom serpents—hissed and steamed. The blackened water flowed into the sewage culvert; tongues of flame shot up here and there in the pile. The strained, sweaty faces of the men operating the pump reflected their exhaustion and nonstop work; if the entire city were to be kept from burning, they had to work continuously during the festival nights. Laughter and jeers of drunken encouragement came from some of the onlookers when they saw the richly attired girl staring incredulously at the scene before her.

A weeping woman rocked to and fro on her haunches. Nuns of the Merciful Order of the Kuan-yin salved and bandaged the hands of a naked baby who sat nearby, its mouth rectangular as it screamed. The burnt corpse of another small child lay on the ground before the woman.

The girl turned to her companions who had drawn up behind her.

"Come away now; this is far too dangerous for a child!" Yang Kuo-chung implored her, taking her arm. In response, Little Cousin ripped the coin purse from his belt, tearing the silken strands. Emptying it into her hand, she threw the copper coins at the weeping woman. Glittering in the firelight, they rained down on the woman's head and fell into the mud around her. The woman took no notice, but continued her rocking and moaning as youths and beggars from the crowd surged around her scuffling for the coins. The enormous bird on the girl's shoulder stretched its wings nervously as it shifted about.

"What is the matter with her?" The child cried out to her cousins, pointing to the bereft woman. "Does she want more? Is that it?"

"Enough is enough, Cousin!" The Lady of Kuo scolded. "Look at what you've started!" She looked at her sisters. "At what we've all started!" She indicated the free-for-all as people fought for the money. "We're leaving right now!"

"No!" the girl cried, shrugging their restraining hands from her. Before her was a dream-real glimpse of the promised Buddhist Hell. She would pay now for the hungry ghosts who pushed and shoved in the blackened mud in the fiery iconography of the living scroll before her. She removed her earrings and ornate hairpins. She fumbled with the catch of her elaborate silver-inlay belt and slid it out from the loops in her jacket. Drunken youths grazed her sides, jostling and jeering. A rude hand seized the magnificent brooch on the front of her embroidered jacket. The silk puckered and tore. A fist smashed into the face of the thief as someone endeavored to restrain him: it was Yang Kuo-chung. The bird had had too much; he spread his great wings and flapped up to the railing of a balcony overhead. The girl dodged the scuffling bodies around her, eluded Yang Kuo-chung, who was now distracted, and ran closer to the ruins.

Her loosened hair had come down around her shoulders. She pushed the shiny black strands aside. Surely this was the test, she thought, as she moved in. Had not their Divine Emperor decreed that there should be hospitals, orphanages, and kitchens for the poor? Had he not said that this human tragedy was the test of the moral fiber of an empire? And had not the followers of the compassionate Maitreya assumed these noble and difficult tasks for the state? Nuns and priests? And weren't we all nuns and priests witnessing for the all-merciful Future Buddha . . . ? She rolled the hairpins, jewels, and belt into a ball in her fist, hefting them for a moment as if to gauge their weight in future penitence. She held her breath and closed her eyes, the images of a thousand merciful *lohans** before her. Then with a long underhand throw, she sent her treasures upward. They climbed for a moment, then cascaded back to earth, shimmering as the crowd closed in on them. Lifting her skirts above the mud

*Earthly saints

and debris, she turned and ran back to her cousins. Yang Kuo-chung had already rushed forward to grab her. The group hurried away toward the waiting servants who would carry them far from the burning shacks, the wailing woman, the dead infant, and the Lane of the Ten Worthies.

Old man Su thought it odd when this high-born group rounded the corner. They were moving quickly, almost running; the tall handsome man had dropped some paces behind the women and drew a mean little dagger between them and the pursuing crowd of the poor—the beggars and thieves and rabble. Old man Su didn't think people like these rich could possibly know how to run. Or how to fight! But this noble was different—fierce, quick, deadly, as certain, it seemed, of the streets as of the great halls he must walk through every day. Old Su stepped back as they approached, then presented himself as they rushed by, their fragrant garments rustling sumptuously. Smiling with his black and yellow teeth, he held up both hands imploringly while muttering a Buddhist blessing. Two of the women ignored him and the child only ran that much quicker. But the oldest of the three women, under the watchful, impatient eye of the man with the dagger, paused for a moment, and tore off a few hair ornaments and jade bracelets and a small silk coin purse. Without touching the upturned palms, she dropped everything into old Su's hands, leaving a perfumed wake which lingered for a second or two.

The smile on old man Su's face was gone as soon as they had passed. He pocketed the coins and jewels and raised his jar for a long drink, wiping his mouth with his sleeve. He continued down the street and entered the shadows.

Old man Su had thought himself quite fortunate. What he could not have known was that the Yangs always left a trail of jewels wherever they went. One had only to follow them. But this night, in these dark alleys, without their gay processions of brightly colored horses and carriages and attendants, how could anyone know who they were?

::

A million colored, flickering lights, framed in the tiled square of the Cinnabar Phoenix Gate, spread below the majestic palace heights of Dragon Head Hill like an explosion at the center of the universe. Great rivers of translucent colored lights five hundred feet wide converged in hazy, twinkling luminosity on the city's horizon eighteen li south of the palace. The northern extremes of the capital, the bureaucratic complexes, wealthy residential wards and the Hsing-ching Palaces between the eastern and western markets were ablaze with a solid rippling sheet of lantern-light, a clustered mass of three million individual flames, stars of the centrifugal arms of the endless rivers of the Milky Way. Throughout Ch'ang-an's entire length and breadth, and to the fields and suburbs beyond, these lines of sparkling fires reached without interruption. The roof lines of the great urban structures—mansions, monasteries, nunneries, multitiered temples, bell towers, drum towers, pagodas, dagobas, watchtowers, observatories, gates, and walled ramparts were strung with lights, their ordered architectural outlines delineated by strings of glowing color.

Far away, close to the Big Wild Goose Temple, a volley of explosions shook the magical night air; torrents of light sprayed the sky, whirling, blasting and shuddering with the pyrotechnic beauty of "fire trees," "flame flowers," and "peach blossoms." For fractions of seconds, repetitious miles of urban squares, alleys, gates, and courtyard houses in the far suburbs were illuminated by the fireworks, flashing visible as tilelike grids. Volleys at the southern Gate of Luminous Virtue were answered by a brilliant retort that lit the treetops; reds, yellows, oranges, and blues were reflected in the glassy waters of the Indian Lotus Pond and Serpentine Lake.

Finally an angry explosion and ear-splitting reverberation came from the palatial heights of Dragon Head Hill. With a bursting of fireballs flashing above the gold-tiled roofs of the imperial and palace cities, the grand processional began. The sound was deafening, the momentary paroxysms of light blinding. The enormous studded doors of the Cinnabar Phoenix Gate opened. The great displays of light announced the emergence of the Son of Heaven. Amidst thunder and light, Heaven's representative on earth would descend the heights of the palace hill. Four million faces turned upward.

A parade of imperial livery, a column of ornate floats, cavalry, lancers, drummers, and pipers emerged from the gates of the Forbidden City. The vast retinue descended the steep incline of the Dragon Head. A blue terrazzo road undulated downward like a serpent through a stone forest of obelisks. The final three hundred yards were guarded by the watchful stone eyes of the inhabitants of the Spirit Way. Potent marmoreal figures, in imitation of their ancient Han dynasty predecessors, lined the wondrous path: chimera, serpents, rhinoceroses, turtles, hippopotamuses, elephants, ostriches, and horses were staggered along the road's gracefully sweeping curves. Then came the bodhisattvas, somber court ministers, and fearsome warriors in armors of hide and chain mail. Demon slayers with fierce expressions and bannered tridents raged at the cultivated slopes beyond the city, their enigmatic countenances of stone reflecting the conundrum of the T'ang. The huge wheels of the imperial floats ran in deep stone grooves, their great greased axles straddling but never touching the taboo path carved with whiskered celestial dragons and flaming pearls. The walkway of the Son of Heaven was reserved for his feet alone.

The assemblage of wheeled architecture lumbered down like a city descending from the clouds. Straining teams of muscular attendants and stalwart oxen pulled back on taut ropes as the entourage was brought down the hill to the safety of the level plain. Atop the grandest float rode the Emperor T'ang Minghuang in perfect serenity beneath a canopy of carved lattice. The grand wagons rumbled out into the humanity-packed squares and entered the city through the Red Bird Gate. Troops cleared the main thoroughfare of Ch'ang-an, the Avenue of the Vermilion Sparrow, which bisected the city and was five hundred feet wide from shoulder to shoulder, stretching out into the distant suburbs. Tonight, aflame with lanterns, it was reserved for the Emperor. The masses of Ch'ang-an, city of eternal peace and, equally, eternal commerce, had turned out to see him. But tonight, he did not ride alone. Speculation flew. Was he about to take a new empress? The figure of a woman, her posture one of poise and confidence, could be seen at his side.

This Precious Consort, the youngest of the glamorous Yang sisters, was the only woman to ride at his side on state occasions since the banishment of his queen. And this new one was a consort of the highest rank. Rumors and questions spread like the proverbial wildfire through the crowds that evening. Would the Son of Heaven take another queen? The word was that she rarely left his side. But then, how could anyone know? Despite a few brief glimpses of the imperial carriages along the covered road to the Hsing-ching Palaces and even rarer glimpses of the lofty pair as they rode out in processional outings with the Yang sisters to the Indian Lotus Park or the hot springs, there was no other evidence. The lives of the Divine were private. But it was noteworthy and significant, people agreed, that during this most important of celebrations in the great western capital the girl sat where only the Empress, dead for five years now, had sat before.

That night, atop the imperial float, amidst the flood of light and swaying of the canopy, the Precious Consort had been unusually quiet, reticent, almost diffident, dealing with doubts and speculations of her own. Until recently she had been quite certain of the power of the spell she was weaving. She had been everything that she had set out to be with him: seductive, mysterious, an insolent child, a wise woman; presumptuous at times, but always beguiling. There had been no secrets, no need to hold anything back. She had let her life flow into his, had tried to feel everything that he felt—even that immense, unfocused, ungraspable loneliness that he alone, as an emperor, must know.

Her sisters could not have known all that would be hers when they had been triumphantly anticipating her instatement at the palace. How could they? The only possible exception would be Eldest Sister, whose eyes had told her everything that day in the nunnery when her own patience had grown so thin and she was about to run away to Brother's: her unspoken words told her to have patience, for with the greatest union would come the greatest . . . ? But Eldest Sister had never finished that thought, never quite formulated it, just left it floating with all the other pure feelings and essences somewhere out there in the universe. It didn't matter! That day, the Taoist nun Grand Verity had understood what her eldest sister meant, and so it had been. There was nothing that was not shared between the consort and her imperial husband. She had taken it all in, absorbed it and made it hers, took all of him in, too . . . but now she wondered. Had *he* done the same . . . ?

Minghuang had lavished his attentions upon her immediately. They had rejoiced in their mutual love of play, music, and the dance. He had even *composed* for her! The entire six palaces of the harem had treated her like a grand queen mother because of a few words from him. And now she rode in the grand processional, at his side. The last one to sit where she was sitting was the Empress Wang. Soon, it would be necessary to speak with him. The matter of this child Plum Blossom needed to be cleared up, done away with. It stood in the way of everything. Besides, it was intolerable.

At first she had been willing to put up with his occasional excursions into the harem. She had been taught in the nunnery school about the intricacies of the male's passions. Picture separate rooms in a house, the instructor had told her. You are in one room, and perhaps another female will occupy a different one. If your own room is comfortable and well-appointed, and he visits you there often, then you should not speculate on the other rooms where he may venture. But Plum Blossom was lolling, to Precious Consort's mind, in a room far too grand and frequently visited for her own liking. But the worst part of it, the part that gnawed at her contentment all the time now, was that he had not kept his promise. He had said weeks ago that the creature would be sent back to Loyang. He had not done it, and what was worse, he had invited Plum Blossom to his bedchamber twice since he had made the promise. She meant to express her dissatisfaction in no uncertain terms. All that remained now was to choose the moment, and it would be done. She had resolved to speak.

The ability to set firm goals made it possible for her to do these things; she had had this facility since she was very young. She remembered the time when they were little children and her sisters had dared her to touch a garden snake. She could still taste that moment of apprehension as she watched their kitten play on the grass, feinting with the creature. The kitten reflected her own feelings: Its eyes were big and black with caution, but it could not resist the snake and extended a curious paw while its whole body, tense and taut like a bow, was prepared to spring backward if necessary. She had decided then that if the kitten actually touched the small yellow and orange serpent that she would have to touch it, too. If she did not obey her own decision, evil would befall her. In this way she could put herself beyond vacillation. She decided now that when the processional reached the next crossroads, she would speak.

She glanced over at him as they rode through the streets of blazing color. If she blurred her eyes just a bit, she could see him as the people on the streets wished to, as an immortal in his sparkling gown of góld dragons, flaming pearls, and scudding clouds, the hem decorated with the beautiful deep-sea *li-shui* patterns. She could see the glittering reflections of her hair ornaments in the polished mirrors of his belt. The images moved as he breathed. She watched a "god's" vapored breath, the small involuntary twitches at the corners of his mouth and the beads of moisture in the sparse, gray-flecked beard. They sat in silence as their carriage lumbered forward; his only utterances were occasional grunts of approval at the displays surging around them. She turned her attention to the luminous offerings. There was time yet before they would reach the crossroads.

The orchestral float preceded them in the avenue ahead. From its gilded heights spun melodies rhapsodic and lilting—"Music for Releasing the Goshawk," and "Crushing the Northern Barbarians"; strings against flute, clapper, and chimes reaching a crescendo. She had never seen anything that compared with being in the midst of the spectacle of the night's city of lights. For the two preceding evenings she had watched the rivers of brilliant light from her vantage point high above in the palace city; now she moved among them and could examine the miraculous structures that constituted those strange glowing rivers. It was the first time in several years that the Emperor had chosen to ride the imperial float down into the city during the festival.

Tiny lanterns of mica and jade, silk and paper bobbed like little stars. There were enormous lanterns shaped like slender boats with ornate dragon prows; huge, multisegmented creatures—serpents, caterpillars, and dragons—moved rhythmically above the heads of the crowd, their undulating torsos illuminated brilliantly from inside and supported on nearly invisible slender rods. The awestruck consort saw occasional great double lanterns set with beads and pearls and inlaid with jade and gold characters. Brave and daring figures, heroes and heroines of ancient legend, were projected from huge revolving picture-tents; atop the largest lanterns, wooden figures of handsome horsemen, falconers, and beautiful dancing girls turned slowly in the blasts of incandescent heat.

But, as if by the dictate of some unbreakable law in this overwhelming dream of light and color that now consumed her, every sight she beheld ahead seemed greater than the one before. And as she entered deeper into the dream, the frenzy of beauty burst upon her in shimmering, nearly frightening torrents. What her eyes could not understand in the rush of images now became clear; the grand avenue was not only filled with the floating confusion of a million bobbing lanterns, but it was lined with agate-covered lamp trees hung with every conceivable color of embroidery and precious metal. And each "tree" was illuminated in the magnificence of five times ten thousand bowl lamps; and each district's "tree" was tended by a thousand gloriously dressed women and their maidservants, their flowered hairpins reflecting the light as the stars reflected the hidden light of the sun. But the dream kept unfolding relentlessly in its infinite layers. She was hearing music now, and remembered the general's stories of his childhood and the sight of the caravan and how light was sound and sound was light . . . A thousand musicians were playing in her head now, melodies of the "Floating Dragon Boat" and the "The Green-Headed Duck." Could so much rapture choke the senses?

A short distance before the crossing of the first intersection into the Avenue of the Vermilion Sparrow, just when she thought that she had surely seen the ultimate spectacle that the festival had to offer, she saw a pair of lamp towers. How could she have missed their coming? Too much beauty was almost an assault on the senses. The towers must have been one hundred and fifty feet tall. Ten thousand lamps in the shapes of dragons, phoenixes, tigers, leopards, and glowing apparitions illuminated tapestries of gold and silver and gems lit like a universe of stars that seemed to reach right up into the soft velvety underside of the canopy of night . . .

As the float moved past the residential district wards where many wealthy merchants lived, she saw that displays of friendly rivalry abounded around the fine houses. Spectators voiced their approval of entries in the competition: If the Weis strung a thousand lanterns, the Lius would hang two thousand. If one family lit six streaming rockets, another would light twenty screaming squibs. And through it all marched the grand processions of solemn Buddhist clergy.

Children wove through the lights waving sparklers and tiny candle lanterns on lacquered sticks. They screamed and laughed at the antics of dancers, acrobats, marionettes, animated silhouette projections, and raucous shadow plays. Around them painted banners advertised the many sponsors of the streetside merriments: "The Clan of Lo Brings Dancers!" "Puppet Tales for the Children Brought by the Munificent Inn of the Happy Pheasant!" This was the world of the city where, she had learned, life is a literal and constant exchange of strings of cash, barter, and credit, where one need sell one's name as often as one's wares to survive.

From her lurching balcony she watched the vast crowds, waves of light and motion, the infinite sea of upturned faces wanting a glimpse of the personage of the Son of Heaven and . . . her. They perched on rooftops, balconies, and graceful arched bridges. The imperial floats passed under banners reading, "Ten Thousand Years to Our August Emperor!"

They were approaching the crossroads, their destination the southern suburbs, where he would ascend the scaffolds waiting there, don the robes of purity and, in the rituals of Heaven and Earth, address himself to the people's hopes for everlasting peace, agrarian abundance, and orderly civil justice. To the people, he was a god and a man at the same time. He was theirs. And tonight, she rode beside him. Her heart quickened as the long line of attendants, drummers, pipers, and lanced horsemen ahead moved into the brightly lit intersection of the crossroads. The Emperor's hand rested on her knee, though he had scarcely spoken. He turned to her.

"It is always preferable to be seen by candlelight, don't you agree?" he asked her. "I fear that if they were to see me in the light of morning, they'd see the tired old man who masquerades as their Son of Heaven—certainly not the vigorous man of years past on whom the Mandate of Heaven was 'bestowed.' " He smiled at her.

"Speaking as one who has seen your face before you have even opened your eyes in the morning, I can assure you that I have glimpsed more than once the boy that you once were," she told him, pressing his hand between her knees. His other hand slid up to her smooth neck and caressed the ivory line of jaw for a moment.

"Perfection and youth," he remarked. "I doubt that I shall have the privilege of seeing even the earliest flaw in this skin or a single touch of autumn to this hair."

The noise of the crowd was increasing as the imperial float drew nearer to the intersection. They were passing into the crossroads. The moment had arrived.

"If you are tired," she began, "perhaps you are expending yourself unwisely." She took a breath. "The one from Loyang does not know, perhaps, the way to turn a man's vital force back to him and not keep it for herself," she said.

He turned to look at her, his smile gone. His hand dropped from her knee. He rubbed his brow wearily, then looked at her again. She waited.

"Perhaps," he said coldly, "you would do me the service of teaching her. It could be arranged."

"I meant no impudence, but I have certain knowledge which—"

He interrupted her. "The extent of your knowledge is truly awesome. It extends everywhere, does it not? And now it is intruding itself into my bedchambers. I imagined that you were a bit more subtle." He raised his clenched hands. "My uncle told me to watch for whores in my politics. It seems that it is my lifelong task to be vigilant for them. I regret that I could not save Uncle from Aunt Wei and the Princess T'ai-P'ing, but I did save myself and my father from those whores. I am not quite so wary lately. Perhaps I have let down my guard too much, but I should have paid heed to Uncle's advice." His voice was quiet and fierce. "Refinement only seems to make them more cunning," he continued. " 'Do not teach a whore to read,' he said. 'It only gives them ideas.' You must teach them instead to dance and play the flute." He nodded to her. "It makes them entertaining, at least, and keeps their hands away from doors, and books, and daggers! 'The swirling will make them dizzy, lightheaded, giddy, unable to fashion ideas of which they should have no part,' he told me. They are less likely, then, to be dangerous. But a whore with ideas—"

She interrupted, speaking between clenched teeth. "If I am a whore, Celestial Husband, then you are the *whoremaster*." She paused before continuing. "But I feel compelled to correct you. It is something of a Yang family tradition, you see. It was my uncle who taught me to read, not your tutors. You mustn't blame yourself for so dangerous an oversight."

He stared hard at her.

"Then your most noble and learned uncle," Minghuang returned, "has done us all a great injustice."

She glared back. With a sudden shout, he ordered the float to a halt. They lurched forward for a moment, her high headdress nearly toppling. The attendants stood waiting, puzzled. Processional floats behind them began to bump into one another, not expecting to stop. Ahead, the music drifted away as the orchestral float gained distance on the other side of the intersection.

"You, my girl," he said quietly, "are going back to the harem. Perhaps someone there can teach you how to comport yourself. And the lesson begins now."

"Thank you, my master, and just in time. It is unusual for such an open fretwork design, but it seems the air has become almost unbreathable in here. How would you explain it?"

He shouted to the attendants to bring a litter immediately.

"And thank you for your kind offer," she said as she stood, "but I will not be going to the harem. My brother's house in the city is much more to my liking. Perhaps you could be so kind as to have my clothing and effects sent there."

With a rustle of silk and tinkling of ornaments, she was helped down from the imperial float while the Son of Heaven glared straight ahead in silence. The door shut behind her, and he gave the order to continue the procession on to the southern suburbs and to the Altar of Heaven and to the ceremonies of the New Year.

::

When she appeared at his door, Brother, to his eternal credit, had asked no questions. Though he wore his maddening Buddha smile on his lips, he had listened politely and passed no judgment, telling her that his home was her home for as long as she liked. That night, she was unable to sleep at all as her imagination seethed. She tormented herself with an image of the demure little smile of triumph which she was quite sure the despicable Plum Blossom wore on *her* lips as she entered the Emperor's bedchamber. Without a doubt, she thought, pacing the floor of her rooms late into the night, she is in his bed at this very moment.

She had not returned to the palace at all, but had come directly here. Her brother's house was far removed from the center of the city and the noise of the final night of festivities, but she could see from her window the horizon glowing with the light of millions of lanterns. An occasional rocket ascended to the sky and bloomed into a fiery flower.

If it is Plum Blossom he wants, she thought bitterly, then it is Plum Blossom he shall have. If he wants her so badly that he breaks promises to me, then by all means, let him be unobstructed. Let him play music with her and create dances for her. Let him take her to the hot springs and inspire in her a love of antiquity. Let *her* carry the title of Precious Consort. Let *her* ride through the city with him. For that matter, let her be empress! Oh, she will make a fine empress indeed. She saw in her mind a grimly satisfying picture of herself growing old, alone, as the woman who nearly became the empress, but who was deposed by an upstart. A pudgy upstart.

She looked toward the center of the vast city. Somewhere out there were her sisters and their cousin Yang Kuo-chung; they had told her that they were going adventuring that night in the streets of Ch'ang-an. It would not take long for them to find out what happened. She watched a steeply climbing rocket shoot into the sky and rain spirals of fire down on the city, and reflected that as sure as the sun would rise tomorrow morning, she would be receiving a visit from her sisters. She had been unable to fit the sisters into her picture of the Emperor with his new empress Plum Blossom; neither, she was sure, would they. But they would simply have to accept what she had done, for there was no undoing it. Did they think that she lived only so that they could play at being queens?

She lay in the dark and repeated in her mind, with occasional embellishments, her conversation with the Emperor that had led to her exit from the imperial float. She had not looked back at all as she climbed down, and now she watched herself, as if with the Emperor's eyes, turning and descending without so much as a glance in his direction. She was filled with angry satisfaction as she relived the episode again and again.

When she opened her eyes to the early morning light, her first feeling was that she had destroyed it all. Miserably, she sat up and looked around her. Daylight changed everything. It was as if she were a different person entirely last night than the one who woke up now. She felt impossibly distant from the palace, the Emperor, the life she had known. She thought of the city, the streets strewn with rubble and people still lying where they had passed out the night before, the sun's rays exposing mercilessly what had seemed glorious by night, by the light of candles, rockets, and lanterns. It was the same for her. She had spoken words last night, and had defied the Emperor in ways that seemed incredible to her now, exposed to the light of day. Without a doubt, she would never see the Emperor or the inside of the palace again. What had she done?

Then she remembered Plum Blossom. It was not difficult to recall the sound of her rival's voice whispering, crying, or giggling behind the Emperor's door; nor was it difficult to recall the Emperor's fond gaze as the woman grunted and sweated her way through a dance. By the time Precious Consort was up and looking at her own face in the mirror, her feelings of righteous wrath and the certainty that she had done exactly the right thing were mostly, if not quite completely, restored.

And she had been right, too, in expecting a visit from the ladies of Kuo, Han, and Chin.

: :

"You can write him a letter, and we will take it back to him," said the Lady of Kuo firmly, standing over Precious Consort.

"If you do it immediately," the Lady of Han said, "we are fairly certain that the damage can be repaired, with our help."

Precious Consort stared out the window and said nothing.

"Such a willful child!" said the Lady of Chin. "She tells an Emperor whom he may sleep with!"

"And then she is surprised when he tells her that it is none of her business!" the Lady of Kuo declared. Precious Consort turned toward her sisters.

"I cannot believe that I am hearing this from you," she said, making an effort to speak calmly. "You care nothing for my feelings, it is obvious."

"Nothing for your feelings!" cried the Lady of Han, incredulous. "Do you think we are going to allow you to disgrace yourself and ruin everything in your life because of your fits of jealousy?"

"You mean ruin everything in *your* lives," Precious Consort said sharply, turning back to the window. "I know where your concern lies. And how dare you call my hurt 'fits of jealousy'! He has broken promises to me, and embarrassed me in front of everyone with his carrying on. He has thrown that little bitch in my face, again and again. I will not have it!"

"She will not have it," the Lady of Kuo repeated to her sisters. "Who is this speaking? An emperor's consort or the wife of a shopkeeper?"

"There!" Precious Consort said vehemently. "You have uttered the important word yourself. Wife! That is what I am. That is what *he* has called me himself. I am his wife, but I am being treated as if I am merely another of his harem women. Another woman in a long succession of women!"

"But he has never treated you as if you were just another female!" the Lady of Kuo said. "You were always treated differently. He has given you nearly his full attention. You were practically an empress. I cannot understand why you should care at all about this Plum Blossom, this insignificant pastime. She is not worthy of your attention!"

"If she is so insignificant, then why doesn't he get rid of her? He would do it if he really wanted to please me. He says he will get rid of her, and then does not. It is quite clear to me that I am no more important to him than the hundreds of nameless women who have passed through his hands over the years."

Her sisters looked at each other with expressions of exasperation.

"Think of what you are throwing away," said the Lady of Kuo quietly, her tone patient. "We confess that we are very happy with our lives now. And so should you be. He has treated us well, and all because of you, and we are grateful. Please tell me what is to be gained by your insolence, your unbecoming displays of possessiveness, your temper tantrums."

Precious Consort looked hard at her sister. "Is this my sister speaking, or am I hearing words from the Admonitions of the Instructress? It seems to me that I remember you, Dear Sister, telling me that the rules were for other women, ordinary women. Not for the likes of you and me. My ears are having a difficult time making me believe that now I am receiving from you a lecture on female decorum! You speak of what is unbecoming! I wish you could see yourself!"

"We are not speaking of rules here, Little Sister," said the Lady of Kuo, eyes flashing with anger. "We are speaking of good sense, reasonable behavior! You have been acting like a fool, like a child! Perhaps you do need a good set of rules on your hot little head!"

The two sisters glared at each other for a moment before Precious Consort began to cry. She covered her face and sobbed, holding nothing back. Maybe now they would see. Maybe now they would understand the depth of her outrage. They were treating her as if she were merely playing a feminine game, some coy strategy.

She knew that her sisters could not stand to see her cry. The Lady of Kuo held out for only a moment before she softened, putting her arms around Precious Consort. The Lady of Han and the Lady of Chin both sighed, then stood and came to where she was sitting. One sister stroked her head while the other held her hand.

"I will not go back," she declared between sobs. "Not as long as that creature is there. It is unbearable to me."

"Will you at least send him a message?" the Lady of Han asked gently. "We will deliver it to him. If you won't apologize for *what* you said, at least apologize for the time, place, and manner that you chose."

"We know that you really want to go back," said the Lady of Chin. "We know that you wish you were there right now."

Precious Consort raised her head and looked at her sisters.

"I will apologize for nothing," she said. "And he knows what he must do if he wants me to come back. That is the message you can take to him. If he wants me, he will send for me."

The Lady of Kuo sighed and dropped her hands. She turned to her sisters and shook her head.

"The child is not in her right mind," the Lady of Kuo said. "There is nothing to be gained by talking to her now. Let us leave her to contemplate what she has created."

They left, clothes rustling, ornaments tinkling, faces set with reproval.

Alone again, she thought. A month. He will send for me inside of a month. I will do nothing at all. He *will* send for me.

: :

Kao Li-shih put his ear to the Emperor's bedchamber door and knocked softly. There was no response. He knocked again, louder, and listened. Nothing. It was early afternoon. He had waited as long as he could, but now concern and curiosity had got the best of him. Last night, the Emperor had not wanted to talk at all and the eunuch had obliged him.

The Emperor had returned from the imperial procession alone. Kao Li-shih had been on hand to meet the float when it arrived back at the palace and was shocked at the sight of the Emperor's grim, angry face as he emerged. It took a moment for Kao Li-shih to realize that the consort was not with him; she had vanished, it appeared, somewhere, somehow, during the ride through the city. The eunuch's first thought was that she had been abducted. He had rushed over to where the Emperor was standing, in the light of lanterns held by servants. The Son of Heaven was ripping off his ceremonial robe and headgear, flinging them heedlessly to the ground. Oh, no, Kao Li-shih thought. Something truly dreadful has transpired. Kidnappers? Brigands? How could they have done it in a crowd like that, with the imperial couple surrounded on all sides?

"What has happened?" he said, thoroughly alarmed. "Where is she?"

The Emperor looked at Kao Li-shih with an expression of pure fury on his face that made the eunuch take a step back.

"Perhaps," he said after a moment, in a cold voice, "she is where she belongs, in some high-priced whorehouse at the other end of the city. I don't really know, Kao Li-shih. Nor do I care." With that, he stalked away, leaving Kao Li-shih where he stood.

Kao Li-shih had questioned the bearers and attendants, and from them learned what had happened. Just like that, they said, the Son of Heaven ordered us to stop. She climbed out. She looked just as angry as he did just now. She didn't turn around, not once. And a sedan chair carrying somebody else, a magistrate or someone, was commandeered. She got in and was taken away.

Where? We don't know exactly. But we heard her say something about her brother's house.

Kao Li-shih had deemed it prudent to leave the Emperor alone, at least until the next day. When morning had given way to afternoon, and the Emperor had not emerged, the eunuch summoned the courage to go and knock on his door. After the third knock, when he started to push the door open but found it bolted from within, the Emperor spoke:

"Go away, Kao Li-shih."

"Is there nothing I can do to help you?" asked the eunuch solicitously through the heavy wood.

There was a short silence.

"Give me one month of solitude, Kao Li-shih. No questions. No kind offers of assistance or sympathy. No tempting delicacies, no invitations, no beautiful harem women, no stern confrontations, and no concerned and non-chalant little visits in the afternoon. I beg you."

Kao Li-shih stood silent outside the door. He knows me as well as I know him, he thought.

"Especially," the Emperor added, "no women."

A longer silence followed. Kao Li-shih could feel the Emperor's unspoken words: It was you, Kao Li-shih, who brought her into my life, but I am too fond of you and too much a gentleman to say it out loud.

"As you wish," Kao Li-shih said, and quietly turned and left.

His heart, as he walked away from the Emperor's rooms, was heavier than it had been for a long, long time. What had happened, he sensed, was no mere lovers' quarrel. The Emperor's refusal to talk, his behavior, the tone of his voice when he spoke his desultory words—all of it reminded Kao Li-shih of that painful time before the Precious Consort came to the palace. Something had gone very wrong, and Kao Li-shih had a foreboding sense that the palace might never see the Precious Consort again. It made him sorry, because he was fond of her and knew that no matter how angry the Emperor was, he would grieve over her nonetheless.

But Kao Li-shih's mind was divided. Perhaps it would be best, ultimately, if she did not return. Another part of him had been worried for a long time about the sheer amount of life-force the Emperor expended on his love affair. Yes, he had been happy, no longer lying in bed with the curtains drawn mourning Prince Ying and the Empress and pondering the dilemma of being born an emperor. But was he not, in fact, just as far from meeting his responsibilities as a ruler as he had been during that dreadful time? And was Li Lin-fu not, more than ever before, offering his services in the void? Were there not ominous rumors of dissatisfied factions unhappy about a weak emperor allowing his chief minister to do his job?

And soon now, very soon, the entire city would witness a most graphic demonstration of Li Lin-fu's growing power and an emperor's default. The message had arrived just that morning. An Lu-shan was only a few weeks away from Ch'ang-an. He had kept his end of the bargain with Li Lin-fu: He would be delivering, after a forced march of many hundreds of li from the north and through the streets of the city right to the very doors of the Chancellery, eight thousand captured Hsi and Khitan warriors. Eight thousand living symbols of Li Lin-fu's will.

Well, thought Kao Li-shih, I will certainly give the Emperor his month. But it is difficult to picture Master An Lu-shan exercising such restraint.

BOOK THREE

PING CH'E HSING*

A SONG OF WAR CHARIOTS

*Title of a poem by Tu Fu. So powerful and evocative is this piece that the rumbling of the carts, the sounds of marching feet, and the pitiful wail of parents as their sons are taken off to war are conjured up in the original Chinese.

~ 16 ~

The Gift

In 750 hostilities again broke out. Some sources accuse [An Lu-shan] of deliberately provoking them. . . . He presented 8,000 Hsi prisoners at court. His arrival was the signal for still greater rewards and honours. . . .

—*Edwin Pulleyblank*

It was at the Li-shan hot springs that An Lu-shan once presented the emperor with jade and stone fish, dragons, ducks and geese, in addition to a stone bridge. . . . These objects were skillfully carved and realistic in appearance. [They were] placed in the waters of the hot springs. And when [Minghuang] went there to bathe, possibly after an evening of inebriation, it seemed to him that the animals had come to life. He thought that the fish were moving their scales and that the birds were about to fly away.

—*Howard S. Levy*

NOMADS, shepherds, horsemen, herdsmen, proud falconers and hunters, clansmen and warriors, Khitan and Hsi alike, all were reduced to the brutal ignominy of a forced march deeper and deeper into a strange, alien world. They had been walking for well over a month by the time they reached the fertile wetlands of the Wei River outside of Ch'ang-an. If there had been defiance on their faces when the march began, it was long gone now, replaced by utter fatigue and despair. Each man walked as the ones behind him, in front of him, and next to him did: as if he could no longer remember who he was or the names of the members of his family whom he had been forced to abandon.

The Chinese peasants inhabiting the flat farming suburbs around Ch'ang-an did not cheer, wave their arms, or shout in triumph at the spectacle that passed by. They watched because they could not help it; the line of men and boys extended past the limits of their sight in either direction. And as they watched, leaning on hoes, rakes, scythes, shovels, and plows, they were quicker to empathize with the pain and suffering before them than to jeer in triumph.

The prisoners were uncountable. It was as if the male population of an entire province were being marched before their eyes. Men and boys, ragged, filthy, broken; many were only children who could no longer lift their feet and had to be carried on someone's back. To the people witnessing this passing sea of human misery, there was little worth praising; the farmers' own sons had been tithed in meaningless wars, too.

The tired procession passed all that day along the high narrow ramparts that wound between the wet, muddy, fields, heading southward toward the great forested imperial parks and the eastern walls of the capital beyond. The sound of men's feet, horses' hooves, and the shouts of soldiers closing the gaps in a parade that straggled out in weariness carried by the farms well past the middle of the night and into the Hour of the Hare. In the humble houses along the route, farmers and their families lay sleepless in their beds and listened . . .

: :

Military Governor-General An Lu-shan forced his march the final sixty li around the northern perimeter of the city, past the forests of the Forbidden Park and the ancient ruins of Han, along the southern banks of the Wei River and south again down Ch'ang-an's walled eastern boundary. He would ride over the Pa Bridge and through the P'ing Kang Gate, just as he had the very first time he entered Ch'ang-an, with General Feng at his side, on that morning that seemed so long ago now. And he would follow the same route he had on that strange morning, after he had been separated from Feng and had traveled the alleys and boulevards of the eastern wards as if the city were a great river he had been thrown into, his head hot, feverish, confused, and beguiled.

But it would be different this time. The bridge was just coming into view, and he noted with satisfaction that a commamd he had sent ahead by messenger had been carried out. Waiting for him at the guard station was a luxurious shuttered carriage drawn by a matched team of horses. He called out to the small detachment riding with him ahead of the processional of prisoners. They halted, and An Lu-shan climbed down off his dusty, sweaty horse. Today he would ride into the city in a style more appropriate to a well-heeled, successful suitor.

This was how he saw himself. The woman, Ch'ang-an, who had seemed coy, teasing, contrary, and resistant to his advances when he first knew her, was now gracious, open, and receptive. He climbed into the carriage, settled on the silk-cushioned bench, and shouted the order: Proceed. We enter the city now.

As they approached the P'ing Kang Gate, the appreciative crowd along the route grew larger and more vocal. The taciturnity of the peasants in the countryside had given way: he heard cheers and insults shouted to the wretched prisoners, and occasionally, his own name being called. He laughed, thinking of what Feng had said to him once when they were both drunk: the beauty of the city, he had declared, was so much like a woman; the closer you get to her gates, the more sensitive she becomes. It was Feng who had told him of the strange ways of Chinese nuptial formalities—the "six rites of welcome," the letters of introduction, the gifts, and all the rest of the horrendous and nonsensical formalities and rules. And though An Lu-shan remembered thinking at the time that all of it was preposterous—you simply took the woman you wanted—it made sense now. And hadn't Feng been his go-between? And weren't these prisoners his tribute offerings to her? Ch'ang-an. He could still roll that name around on his tongue the way a fisherman rolled the lustrous surface of a pearl between his calloused fingers.

Feng. Where was he now? There were two people he keenly wanted present to witness his splendid return to the city with the captured prisoners: Chief Minister Li Lin-fu and General Feng. But the eunuch general had, he knew, been sent far into the northwest to the Talus River to battle the Muslims. Dangerous foes they were, with their turbaned heads and their strange singing invocations to their damnable ar-Rahman. It worried him. Even the great General Feng might not be able to escape them. Muslim warriors, he knew, were as fierce as cornered leopards, swinging their sacred scimitars against the infidel. Sacred! That was their delusion, and the source of their fearlessness: A Muslim killed in battle against the unbeliever went directly to Paradise, so they fought with all the more fury. He fervently hoped that Feng had dispatched a good many of them to their Paradise and that it would not be the other way around. He worried that Feng would die without returning to see what he, An Lu-shan, had become.

General An Lu-shan's prisoners trailed behind his coach for nearly one and one-half li, his own well-armed soldiers flanking them and spread out behind. An Lu-shan heard approaching hoofbeats and put his head out the window. What he saw was most gratifying: Several hundred of the city's militia were converging on the forward vanguard of the entourage as it entered the urban boundaries of the eastern wards. An Lu-shan smiled. Ch'ang-an's "handmaidens" had come to receive her gifts.

: :

From a third-floor balcony of one of the larger wine houses in the eastern wards of Ch'ang-an—the Munificent Inn of the Happy Pheasant—two young scholars looked down upon the extraordinary spectacle passing below them. The younger, about twenty-two, gazed somberly at the sight of thousands of bewildered, exhausted, tattered men and boys and the clouds of dust that wafted up from their shuffling feet like winter cooking smoke. He cradled his chin pensively in two slender hands at the ends of long twiglike stalks of arms, his bony elbows resting on a table.

The older student, who was standing near the railing, shifted his own gaze from the strange parade to his companion. It seemed to him that his friend wore a rueful expression on his face. The older student knew the portent of such a look; it was more than likely that if he was patient and said nothing, he would be treated before long to some insightful profundity pertaining to the phenomenon in the street below. He took another long sip of thick sweet wine from the cool porcelain cup in his hand and looked back down at the prisoners.

The two remained in silence this way for a long time, the older student occasionally flicking his eyes surreptitiously back to his friend's face. Once, the younger student glanced up and nearly caught his friend looking at him; the other had to quickly dissemble by pretending to be summoning the wine steward.

The two young men knew each other well: they had attended the same village academies and had successfully traveled the upward routes of the provincial exams together, now to face the ultimate ordeal in the life of a student aspiring to a good position in civil office: the Palace Triennial Exams. Ch'ang-an was certainly receiving her share of men this spring, the older student reflected. Her gates had been receiving, in the last two weeks or so, thousands of scholarly aspirants like himself, from all over the empire. And today, he thought, she receives our counterparts: the thousands of wretches marching below us here.

What, he wondered, could the city and its people look like to these barbarians? He studied them. Strange men they were, wild and fierce-looking. Even from this distance he could see that their eyes held a language utterly different from his own. An interesting thought occurred to him then: not a single one of these prisoners from the distant north, from the windswept lands beyond the empire's northernmost borders, knew how to read or write, he was sure. But among them, without a doubt, were individuals who, had they been educated, possessed the intelligence to place much higher than himself in the Triennial Exams.

His mind began to wander down familiar paths of philosophical speculation, paths that tended to lead nowhere or in circles: why was it not the other way around? Why was it not *himself* marching down there, half dead, in a strange land hundreds of li from his home and with no idea of whether he was to live or die? And why wasn't one of those men down there the one watching from a balcony, a wine cup in his hand and his head full of lofty ambitions and clever introspection? That fellow, for instance, he thought, picking out a large man with broad shoulders and a bald head and wearing a tattered leather garment.

At the moment that he thought this, the man bent his neck upward and looked directly at the student leaning on the railing. The student stared back, shocked by the contact. The man's face was square and flat, the eyes opaque; in the next moment, he lowered his head again and moved on. Feeling strangely flustered by the encounter, the older student looked back at his friend and saw that he was about to speak. He held himself quite still, fearing that any distraction from himself might send whatever the other was about to say back into the pure realm of ideas. The younger boy had always been like that; one waited patiently for a few very significant words from him. Usually, they were worth the wait.

"You know," the younger man said at last, "I have been thinking about those prisoners down there and gauging what I see against what I have heard of their 'illustrious' captor. Although they are probably very tired—and they do appear quite exhausted—they do not appear to be at all hungry. Don't you agree?"

"I had not noticed," the older student responded truthfully.

"You can see the exhaustion in the eyes, but the fullness in their faces tells me they have eaten well . . . far better, in fact, than the average soldier. They have been fed more than mere rations. It is obvious to me what has happened: no doubt 'he' has commandeered food from every poor villager along the way, perhaps taken the last of many a farmer's meager chickens or his single breeding sow . . . I don't know . . ." The younger boy's voice trailed off.

"And what does it mean?" the older one said quickly. I must keep him talking, he thought, if I am to learn what else he sees behind those faces.

"Isn't it evident? Like everything the Fat One does, appearance is of prime importance. I have been thinking about him a great deal lately since we first came to the capital; I have been listening carefully to everyone and to the rumors and stories. He is on everyone's lips. Everything he does is carefully calculated for its effect, for how it will help to make him look extraordinary. I would not imagine that he orders supplies packed and then wastes time with slow ox-drawn carts. He merely takes what he wants from anyone along the way. This is how he saves time. Like the delivery of a herd of fat horses far ahead of his appointed time, he delivers fat prisoners. He pushes them way beyond their limits, but compensates for the strain by overfeeding them. So he is hailed as a miracle worker—but the irony is that he has certainly left behind him greater hardship and poverty the further south he has moved. He will deliver this prize herd; some will be sent to dredge the canals and build roads, others will go to the military agricultural colonies. All of them in prime condition—except that no one notices their eyes. It is in their eyes, you see. But I must be still now; the wagging tongue eventually cuts itself."

The older student shook his head in amazement at his friend's incisive thinking, and raised his cup in an appreciative toast.

"You are right, of course; though it is not quite everyone who fails to notice their eyes," he said.

They leaned their elbows on the rail and looked down again on the prisoners and soldiers passing forever below, and on the dark sea of heads, watchers like themselves, protruding from the lower balconies of the Munificent Inn of the Happy Pheasant. Dust was settling everywhere on the tiles and railings.

The older student thought of the flat black eyes of the prisoner who had looked up at him. Where, he wondered, would that man be sent when An Lu-shan's great march through the city was over? What would happen to him?

: :

An Lu-shan was angry and disappointed. During the long trip from the north, he had anticipated with every step that took him closer to Ch'ang-an the reception he would surely receive when he arrived. The march through the city had met his expectations; the throngs of people lining the streets all the way to the Chancellery gates had vociferously shown their appreciation. But he had wanted more than that.

The first disappointment came when he was informed that Chief Minister Li Lin-fu was out of the city, gone somewhere for his health. An Lu-shan felt robbed. Yes, Li Lin-fu would receive the message that the prisoners had been delivered, and many months earlier than the date they had agreed upon; but by the time the chief minister returned, the eight thousand men and boys would be dispersed to their various fates, scattered throughout the empire. He would not see the amazing spectacle with his own eyes, and that fact infuriated An Lu-shan. Without a doubt, he thought with vexation, Li Lin-fu had planned it this way. Had purposely, premeditatively, cheated An Lu-shan. His "health," indeed! He never meant to be here at all. No doubt he left the city as soon as the runners arrived with the message that An Lu-shan was on his way.

Or maybe, An Lu-shan had thought with disgust, he really is here, pretending not to be, watching through a crack in a wall. He had looked around, imagining for a moment that he could feel the chief minister's eyes watching him from some hiding place. There had been nothing to do but make his report at the Chancellery and leave. At least he could be sure that they were all waiting eagerly for him at the palace.

Or so he thought.

Arriving at his quarters, he had wanted a message sent to the sisters and the Emperor: he was here, he was triumphant, he was ready for pleasure and relaxation, and he dearly wanted to see them that evening—to dine, drink, and tell them about his adventures. Instead, he was met with the stupidly discouraging news that the consort was exiled from the palace and the Emperor's affections; that her sisters, though not officially exiled themselves, had discreetly taken leave and gone on a journey to visit relatives; and that the Emperor was sunk in bleak depression and despair behind locked doors, seeing no one, speaking to no one.

A fine welcome.

What, he wondered, could have happened between the Emperor and the consort? They had been like two turtledoves when he had last set out for the north over a year ago. Whatever it was, he was sure it was damned foolish. One thing was certain: he had no intention of waiting about until the Emperor decided to crack his door. He was going there first thing in the morning. A man capable of attacking the Khitan in their own territory and forcing several thousand of them to march like obedient children should have no fear of a closed door with an old man behind it. Besides, An Lu-shan thought, he cannot be allowed to fester in his loneliness and sorrow. Someone must, in spite of him, offer aid and comfort.

: :

"If you do not let me in through the door," An Lu-shan shouted, "then I shall be forced to climb the wall and enter through the window."

He gave the latch a shake to show that he meant what he said. He listened. He thought he could hear the Emperor muttering to himself, slippered feet moving across the floor. He listened intently. Then he heard the Emperor's voice, directly on the other side of the door, so near that it startled him.

"You are alive and well, An Lu-shan?"

"Of course I am!" he answered. "What did you expect? I am back, and I wish to see my Father!"

There was a short silence. Then An Lu-shan heard the bolt slide back. The Emperor pulled the door open.

An Lu-shan was shocked. The Emperor was, if it was possible, thinner than he had been before; his hair was unkempt, his robe old and wrinkled. The rooms behind him were dark, the curtains tightly closed against the daylight. The smell of musty clothes and lamp oil hung in the stale air. There were papers, brushes, and eating utensils sitting carelessly here and there, on tables, chairs, the floor, the daybed. A bell tinkled. One of the huge gray cats rubbed at the Emperor's bony ankles and looked up at An Lu-shan. The Emperor ran a hand through his hair and attempted to straighten his robe so that it would cover his thin chest.

"Welcome, An Lu-shan," the Emperor said, subdued but pleasant. "Welcome."

An Lu-shan stared, incredulous, before he found his tongue.

"Father!" he said. "What is all of this about? What has happened while I was gone? Does everything fall apart as soon as I leave? I will never leave again!"

The Emperor shook his head and ran his hand through his hair again.

"I am almost ready to talk about it," he said. "But who would be willing to listen to a long, boring story told by an old fool?" He smiled ruefully at An Lu-shan.

"Why, another fool, of course. Another fool would gladly listen," An Lu-shan declared.

The Emperor looked thoughtfully at the floor, then looked up again.

"In that case," he said, "would you care to dine with me, An Lu-shan?"

"There is nothing I would like better."

"Ten days from now. Give me ten days, and we will have dinner together and I will bore you with every tedious detail. But for now, you must leave me be."

An Lu-shan stepped back deferentially. The Emperor's manner, his strange, sad, remote mood, left little room for anything but acquiescence. An Lu-shan had come here this morning determined to be bluff and jolly, to cut through the Emperor's resistance with humor and sheer will. But his determination had retreated as soon as he saw the sad face in the doorway.

"Very well," he said quietly. "Ten days."

The Emperor nodded, smiled faintly, and softly closed the door.

Ten days. An Lu-shan had an idea. He was thinking intently as he walked away from the Emperor's quarters; ten days, he decided, might possibly be just enough time to do what he wanted to do.

: :

"You see, An Lu-shan, it is not my curse exclusively. My entire house is cursed—more, it seems, than any previous dynastic house—by the influence of women. You have only to look at the tales of my grandmother, and of my uncle and father."

The Emperor's tone was sad and reflective; he and An Lu-shan were well on their way to being drunk, and An Lu-shan's face empathetically mirrored every expression on the Son of Heaven's. They had come, at An Lu-shan's insistence, out to the hot springs for their dinner together. They had eaten their food, and sat in the fading light of late afternoon on the Emperor's veranda by the Nine Dragon Lake pouring themselves cups of wine. An Lu-shan had listened gravely to the Emperor's account of the consort's growing jealousy, culminating in the fateful ride through the city on the last night of the Festival of Lanterns.

"But she is different. You have said so many times yourself," An Lu-shan said imploringly.

"Indeed she is. Then you see right through me. I thought I could cover up my distress by blaming it on the nature of women in general, by talking to you about their natural deficiencies and how they are best kept out of my life. It is a rather thin, unconvincing line of argument, is it not? And one that is not working well at all. I fear I am not deceiving anyone."

"Not even this slow-witted but loyal general."

"She is indeed different," the Emperor said. "And I see in your eyes, my fat friend, what you are thinking. Tell me if I am not right. You are thinking that I am both stupid and crazy." He held up his hand, silencing An Lu-shan's protest. "You are thinking, 'What problem is there? Why does he not simply order her to return?' But that would be futile, An Lu-shan. Nothing worth having can ever be possessed. You only really learn that, if you learn it at all, when it is too late." The Emperor gazed out over the water like an old sage. "She is different," he said then. "I want her to return only of her own free will. I don't want her any other way." They sat in silence. Then the Emperor leaned toward An Lu-shan. "But I am also adamant that she apologize," he said, his tone hardening, "for her most unseemly, unfilial behavior on that night."

But An Lu-shan thought that the Emperor did not sound adamant at all. His voice was unsure, testing; the words "unseemly" and "unfilial" sounded especially insincere in his mouth, as if he felt obligated to say them, for the sake of decorum, but did not believe them in his heart.

"Women!" An Lu-shan said, trying to put as much disdain into his voice as he could. "They are not happy unless they are making trouble out of nothing," he added, though he was not altogether sure that he knew what he meant by it.

"So you see my problem," the Emperor said. "You see how I am torn." He shook his head sadly. "It is *that* one, An Lu-shan. Until she left, I did not realize what she was. She lightened my world. With her, it was as if I were exempted from the physical laws that embrace and crush other men. Now that she is gone, the crushing weight pours down on me as if an earthen dam had burst. With her, I have felt that it was almost possible to fly—to feel what immortals feel. Do you understand me?" the Emperor asked An Lu-shan, looking candidly into his eyes.

Embarrassed by the pain he saw on his friend's face, and feeling helpless to assuage it or fully comprehend it, An Lu-shan grabbed the leather wineskin filled with koomiss that he had brought with him from the north, and squeezed the milky liquid into his mouth, letting white froth dribble down into his beard for the Emperor's entertainment. Grinning, he offered the skin to the Emperor, who contorted his features into an expression of consummate disgust, exactly as An Lu-shan knew he would.

"Try it!" he joked. "It's just like a wetnurse's fat, full dug!" He wiped his mouth then and spoke seriously. "I barely understand half of what you say, if that much. You are far too poetic and learned for a crude peasant like me. That is why the Mandate of Heaven sits upon your shoulders, while I am just your fat, stupid servant, your fearless warrior . . ." This made the Emperor laugh, causing An Lu-shan to glow with pleasure. Whatever it took to cut through his gloom and despair, he would do, and gladly.

"Very clever, An Lu-shan. But you shall never convince me that you are stupid," the Emperor responded, still laughing, his eyes bright and alive at last.

Now is the time, An Lu-shan thought. While he is in a receptive mood, and before the light fades much more. He looked outside. The light was perfect—enough for visibility, but diminished sufficiently to make good shadows. There was no one around; the servants had withdrawn for now. In order for his present to be successful, they would have to go alone down to the water.

"I am stupid," said An Lu-shan, getting to his feet, "but loyal. You must never forget that, my Imperial Father." He squeezed more koomis down his throat and wiped his beard with his sleeve.

"So you tell me all the time, Lu-shan. You have so much loyalty that the only place large enough for you to keep it is in your huge belly—am I right?" the Emperor said, pointing at the ponderous rolls hanging out of the front of the general's open robe.

An Lu-shan roared with blissful, drunken laughter, causing the flesh to ripple comically.

"You are right," he said, cradling his stomach fondly. "There is nothing at all in here but loyalty to you. And now! We must partake of the soothing medicinal properties of a bath in these hot spring pools. The perfect end to our fine meal." He started toward the stairs. "Let us go to your personal pools. If we go to any of the others, we are bound to encounter servants and attendants. I am in no mood for anything but peace and solitude this evening. There are times when I wonder how it is that you can tolerate the army that surrounds you most of the time. All the fussing and primping."

"I suppose I am accustomed to it, An Lu-shan. Though I do appreciate solitude. Probably more than you do, because it is rarer for me." They descended the stairs, An Lu-shan leading.

"It is easy for me to forget that you are not just a man," he said to the Emperor. But as he said it, he thought to himself that, more often, the difficulty lay in remembering that he *was* flesh and blood. In An Lu-shan was the constant awareness, the weight, of this man's semidivinity; it was always there, no matter how close their friendship became. It was not a feeling that An Lu-shan could quite put into words; it frustrated him. He was not at all like General Feng, who could express such abstract ideas with ease. But he knew that the differences between himself and the Emperor were profound. He was sure that the Emperor felt pain more intensely, that he saw the world in a way he never could. And although An Lu-shan was disturbed by the Emperor's sadness over the Precious Consort, he could not understand the old man's passivity. That angered him. Take what you want, you old fool!

"We shall sneak out by the rear door, General. That way we will elude the household staff of the inner chambers. They think the old man can't even take a bath by himself."

Although the pale blue sky was still light, the sun had already gone below the forested camel-hump of Mount Li Shan when they entered the covered walkway below. On the summit of the hill stood the king of Chou's ancient stone beacon tower, silhouetted like a great tope in the slanting light.

They followed the walkway toward the largest of the Emperor's outdoor pools. The air was still and warm, sweet with the perfume of spring blossoms. The grounds were peaceful and motionless in a way that was different from the heavy, stifling quiet of late afternoon in the hot summer, many weeks away yet.

One of the reasons it was so quiet at the hot springs was the cessation of restoration activity. If this were a year ago, An Lu-shan thought as they walked, the artisans and workers would have been still at it, the Emperor presiding, until the light was completely gone and they were forced to quit. It saddened An Lu-shan to know that the Emperor had let his beloved project go by. He began to walk more quickly, pleasurably anticipating his surprise for the Emperor—a gift that would, An Lu-shan fondly hoped, revive his interest. As they neared the tiled gate of the large pool, they passed some forlorn, abandoned scaffolding. An Lu-shan seized the advantage.

"There is not so much work happening here anymore, I see. The scaffolding is exactly where I remember it. It seems that nothing has changed."

An Lu-shan looked about, then turned around to face his companion. The Son of Heaven was a few paces behind him. They both stood outside the pool's moon gate for a moment.

"You are quite right, An Lu-shan. Not only has my Precious Consort's absence caused my enthusiasm to wither, but her cousin, our good minister of finance Yang Kuo-chung"—An Lu-shan suppressed any reaction to the sound of that name—"has made me feel a bit ashamed that so much money has slipped from the public coffers into these restoration projects. For now, at least, things remain as they are."

"And how long has it been since you bathed in the large pool, my Emperor? I have heard that it has been some time indeed," An Lu-shan said, stepping back with a smile and letting the Emperor go first through the gate. "It will do you good," he went on as he followed. "This pool is the most 'auspicious,' is it not? You have said so yourself. It is nearest to the center of the hot springs' source of magic and power and all. It was the ancient king of Chou's favorite, too, am I right?"

"Its location is most favored geomantically," the Emperor corrected in a formal tone, making An Lu-shan laugh.

"Well, then, I don't suppose that the Old Man would care to immerse himself in that clear sweet geomantic water with me and swim under the surface while there is still plenty of light," An Lu-shan suggested. He knew that the Emperor enjoyed, exactly the way a young boy might, swimming underwater and looking at the multicolored textures of pebbles and sand.

The Emperor had told An Lu-shan more than once that this was the closest one could come to achieving the state of the immortals, who rode the clouds and winds. It was like flying, he had said. And like that strange metaphysical state that the poets described, it involved neither the body nor the soul completely, but in some mysterious way, both. Swimming underwater was like flying entranced, half in a dream and half in the waking world— grasses and reeds waving beneath you in the gentle currents like the feathery crowns of trees on rolling slopes of hills seen from the clouds. It was a time when you could forget you were a man, he had said. An Lu-shan knew of the Emperor's fascination with this state: He had seen his elaborate worlds of miniature cork carving, and he had swum underwater with him many times.

"You are getting old," An Lu-shan said as they approached the water. "I doubt that you can hold your breath underwater long enough to get to the other end of the pool."

The Emperor had always bragged that he could hold his breath like a young coastal pearl diver. An Lu-shan knew that he would find the challenge irresistible.

"I will show you how 'old' I am," said the Emperor, dropping his robe and starting down the tiled stairs into the warm water. An Lu-shan followed, but held back a bit. Looking at the Emperor's thin back with the shoulder blades protruding, he thought what an odd sight the two of them must present: like two wineskins—one taut, round, filled near to the point of bursting; the other squeezed dry, shrunken and empty.

The Emperor took a deep lungful of air and pushed himself off the step, splashing and kicking, then slid under the water. An Lu-shan watched the Emperor's form become hazy and indistinct and then disappear altogether out toward the center of the pool where the bottom was still in a natural state: a world of plants, fish, and algae-covered logs and branches. The pool was not one of the very hot ones; it was fed by cold streams so that its temperature was ideal and life still thrived in it.

By the time the Emperor reached there, An Lu-shan knew his eyes would be adjusted to the crystal-green depths. At any moment, he would be moving, through thick slanting shafts of sunlight, over the landscape of the deepest part of the pool. He waited, knee-deep, intently watching the smooth surface. Any moment now . . .

The Emperor burst through in a silvery explosion of water and began swimming violently toward the shore as if some horrible predatory creature were right behind him. An Lu-shan laughed and shook his head with admiration. He looks truly frightened, afraid for his life, he thought. He is better at my own joke than I am.

"My heavens, man, what is it?" An Lu-shan shouted in an alarmed, serious voice. "I will kill it with my bare hands!" He rushed waist deep into the water, ready to pull the Emperor out.

"There are things down there, An Lu-shan!" the Emperor gasped, climbing the stairs, his narrow chest heaving with exertion.

"Things?"

"Yes. Things! Hideous creatures, the likes of which I have only seen in my worst dreams." A faint smile appeared on the Emperor's face, though he held his eyes wide with fright. "They must have come through the fissures in the earth that feed the pools . . . There is no other way in!"

"Yes!" An Lu-shan could no longer suppress a broad smile. "Yes! there is *no* other way! They *are* monsters, Old Man. Dreams come to life to pay you back for your whoring indulgences!"

"Or else," the Emperor said, fixing An Lu-shan with narrow, suspicious eyes, "they got in another way. Born of a perverse imagination." He seized a stick from the ground. "For that, I shall revive the barbarous practice of my ancestors and execute you!" he cried, thrusting the stick at An Lu-shan's belly. Then he shook his head sadly. "But no weapon exists that is long enough to penetrate your thick hide and get to your vitals. To get through that great sack of . . . of . . ." He pretended to search for a word.

"Sack of loyalty!" An Lu-shan cried, hoisting the flesh in his hands and giving it a mighty shake. "Sack of loyalty, Imperial Father!" They were both laughing now. Tears rose in the Emperor's eyes as he laughed the way a man does when he has not laughed for a long, long time.

"That was not the exact word I was going to choose, An Lu-shan," he said, weak with hilarity. "But it will do, because I am certain, General, that in your case, a sack of loyalty and a sack of shit amount to one and the same."

"Then I shall drown myself," An Lu-shan declared. He walked to the water and heaved himself in with an enormous splash.

"No, An Lu-shan! I beg you! You are the most noble and talented bag of shit in the empire!"

"Then I shall not," An Lu-shan said, kicking his feet up and floating on his back in the water.

"Please. At least, not in my favorite pool," the Emperor said. "It will take the fish a year to dispose of the corpse!" He put on his robe and sat on a stone bench, letting his laughter subside. "Tell me though, how did you do it?"

An Lu-shan lay peacefully in the water, arms and legs moving just enough to keep him afloat, and spoke to the early evening sky.

"It was not so difficult. After I delivered the prisoners and came to see you and you would not even open the door, I knew that something had to be done. I found out that you had even neglected your work out here. I knew that I could not bring the consort back, but I thought that I might perhaps be able to bring you a bit of pleasure by contributing something to the hot springs. I had an idea, but being only a poor illiterate fool, I needed assistance. I commanded my eunuch Chu-erh to seek out the imperial archivists to find for me sketches and woodblocks in the libraries of all manner of strange sea creatures from the dragon's domain. I made my selections and then bribed the artisans, stonecutters, and sculptors with many times their usual salaries. They finished them, working night and day, and I had them installed at the bottom of the pool just last night."

"You created such bizarre and exquisite statuary in only ten days' time?" the Emperor asked, incredulous. An Lu-shan moved toward the steps, then stood and began to climb out.

"Nine days," he said. "Of course, I had to threaten them, too. I told them that if they revealed my secret or failed to finish on time, I would make shameful 'bobtails' out of them." He rubbed himself briskly with his robe. "I think that had more effect than the promise of extra pay."

They looked at each other and began to laugh again.

"Come back to my apartments with me, Master An," the Emperor said, standing. "I am most grateful and thankful for your gift. I shall drink a toast to you . . . with decent grape wine, not that rank mare's urine that you barbarians drink. And then, perhaps, after you are warm, dry, and comfortable, I will have you killed for nearly frightening me to death. A man should not die cold and wet."

::

About three weeks after An Lu-shan's return, Kao Li-shih was lured from a deep sleep one night by a note from a single flute. The sound hung like a thin, straight, translucent ribbon over the Nine Dragon Lake; before the echo from the first note had died, a second one took its place. Then came another note, deeper, as if reverberating from the bottom of a well. A rush of notes followed, fragments of an unfamiliar melody. Not asleep anymore, but not awake either, Kao Li-shih let himself imagine that he was hearing the perfect, harmonious song of some idealized bird. The music took hold of him, and he let himself be carried wherever it cared to take him.

Now the musician was playing the theme. The notes trilled in flourishes and embellishments, raced in sunlit flashes like the ascent of a swallow, then dropped down into leafy green darkness: the voice of nightingales, whip-poorwills.

Every note was crystal, distinct. Kao Li-shih thought that this was what notes would sound like from the flute of a spirit, a god, or . . . something was rising in his memory, something he hadn't thought of for a long, long time: the songs. Taught to him by his adoptive eunuch father. Poetic descriptions over a thousand years old of music so perfect, played by shamans at the behest of the bereaved, that it would lure the souls of the dead back to this world, promising that more such splendid music awaited them if they returned. Eyes still closed, he recited a verse:

> "In the perfect cadence of well-practiced elegance, the musicians of
> Tai ready their pipes . . .
> They sound the four trebles in force as they enjoin the final
> modulations . . .
> Oh Spirit-Soul, return! Listen to these songs of otherworldly
> beauty and be calmed."

There was a brief pause, and then the flute wandered aimlessly and effortlessly up and down the scales, testing its powers. Kao Li-shih drifted again, the silvery traces of music beginning to shape his sleep.

He was jolted awake when the music leapt to life again, this time with other musicians joining in: weir drums, clappers, stone chimes, and porcelain pipes danced a wild, frenetic rhythm with the flute. Kao Li-shih opened his eyes, the spell broken. He recognized the melody. It was a northern folk tune, from Kucha, the place of An Lu-shan's birth. What he was hearing was the Emperor rehearsing with the Pear Garden Orchestra a series of new compositions based on many such tunes, recently gathered by the Yueh-fu Music Bureau, to be played in an upcoming ceremony in the barbarian's honor. The Emperor was applying his special genius to the arrangements of the pieces, his gift to the general. His gift in return for what An Lu-shan had given to him.

The music Kao Li-shih had heard that had inspired thoughts of magic in him had issued, he knew, from a flute carved from solid jade, translucent and milky white, fitted with reeds of gold and silver. The Emperor had proudly shown it to Kao Li-shih that afternoon, exclaiming over its beauty and blowing a few notes on it to demonstrate its uniqueness. See, he had said, it lacks the breathiness, the tonal uncertainty, the reediness of a flute fashioned from bamboo. It will never warp or lose its pitch. It was modeled, he explained, from a temple instrument used to call the monks to prayer; the general had commissioned it from a master artisan somewhere west of Tunhuang. Kao Li-shih had wondered what An Lu-shan had been doing that far west, but had said nothing, deciding that such questions were best left to military minds better than his own. And as the Emperor marveled over the exquisite gift from An Lu-shan, his eyes were bright and happy. It was plain to Kao Li-shih that it was the barbarian's influence that had worked this magic on the Emperor, and nothing else, accomplishing what Kao Li-shih himself had been powerless to do. Kao Li-shih had conceded that the instrument had a remarkably fine tone, but it wasn't until he heard it played in the middle of the night just now, carrying over the water, that he realized how fine it really was and what pleasure, what rapture, it was giving to the Emperor.

Kao Li-shih lay awake, listening to the exotic strains of the Emperor's new music pouring forth with such vigor and joy from the oriel at the rear of his hot springs apartments. It was An Lu-shan who had made this music happen. And who, Kao Li-shih wondered for perhaps the thousandth time, was An Lu-shan? He was a man about whom rumors and dark stories flew. Among the eunuchs of the Flying Dragon Elite, tales circulated of beatings, murder, and lies. He flaunted his power, which seemed to grow every day. He was uncouth and boorish, and treated Kao Li-shih with disdain, as if he found the eunuch odious. And yet, Kao Li-shih reflected, look what he could do, and did do . . . He treated that old man with such tenderness, such selfless concern that you would think they were mother and child.

He sat up. The music was not going to end soon, that was plain. It would probably go on until dawn if An Lu-shan and the Emperor were drinking, which he was sure they were. There would be no sleep tonight. He rose in the dark and found his robe. A walk in the night air would do him good.

Outside, he descended a stone staircase and walked toward a curved footbridge that would take him in the direction of the open fields and woods. The Emperor's concert faded in the distance, though he could still hear it. He thought about the shaman-musicians who played to the dead to try to call them back to the world. They weren't completely deluded; at least they understood that music was more than mere ritual. They knew it had real power, as did all art. If there was anything that could call back the dead, Kao Li-shih thought, it would be music. But Kao Li-shih had seen death and harbored no illusions about it. Not even the sweetest music, played from the most sincere heart, could change the fact of death.

With these thoughts in his mind, he started up the ascending curve of the bridge and was startled to see a ghostly figure in the darkness standing at the bridge's highest point looking out over the water. He hesitated, not wishing to disturb someone's meditations.

"Master Kao?" came a tentative voice.

Kao Li-shih smiled in the dark. "It is I, Lu Pei," he answered, and walked to the top of the bridge. "You can't sleep either, eh?"

"I was awakened by the most beautiful music," said Lu Pei dreamily.

"That was the Emperor playing his jade flute," Kao Li-shih said. "I was awakened by it, too."

"Oh," Lu Pei said. The disappointment was obvious in his voice. "It never occurred to me that it was just a *flute*. I was hoping that I was the only one who had heard it." He turned toward Kao Li-shih. "That is very selfish of me, isn't it? I shouldn't think that way."

"I don't think it is particularly selfish, Lu Pei. I entertained the same fantasy myself. And if it is selfish to hope for some evidence of another world . . . well, who could blame us?"

They stood and looked out over the water. The distant music stopped. A few stray notes were blown on the flute, and then another tune commenced, slower than the last, heavily rhythmic.

"Do you really believe that we are being tested all the time?" Kao Li-shih asked. "Surely there is no one and nothing standing over us, looking into our hearts and minds and judging every thought. No gods, no omniscient spirits, no one from beyond the grave. No ancestors." Kao Li-shih smiled at the startling clarity of his own heresy.

"Well," said Lu Pei hesitantly, "I don't know. There is always someone watching, even if it is only ourselves."

"And that is more than sufficient for me, Lu Pei."

He left Lu Pei on the bridge thinking on these profundities and walked in the direction of a pavilion he knew of, far from where the music was being made, where there was a comfortable couch on which he might find some sleep for the rest of the night. He tried to imagine what it would be like to believe that someone, something, was watching him, listening to his thoughts. But he could not. He knew he was quite alone.

: :

Late the following morning, Kao Li-shih returned to his apartments to find that a messenger had called. The old servant said that he did not recognize the man, but Kao Li-shih did not regard that as anything unusual. The elderly retainer recognized few people anymore. Kao Li-shih would have been surprised if he *had* recognized the messenger. It was only a matter of time, Kao Li-shih reflected, before the old man would no longer recognize *him,* either. The rate of decline had been especially noticeable this last year; but that was as it must be, he thought. What was it the poet had said? ". . . from child to child."

The old man announced to Kao Li-shih that the messenger had left a magnificent lacquer box, a gift to be delivered to the Emperor. The box was on the breakfast table; Kao Li-shih called for some tea and sat down to inspect the gift.

It was nearly a foot square, its many carved layers of resin meticulously worked and set about with the most delicate mother-of-pearl and gold flowers, curling leaves, fruit, and animals, and emblazoned in the center with an over-sized, ornate seal of the Hung Nung branch of the Yang family. And the messenger had stated the Emperor's "discreet and secretive" lover's wish that the eunuch should act as go-between. Kao Li-shih felt a surge of pleasure. The Precious Consort was breaking the silence, making a conciliatory offering. It was as if the "six rites of welcome" must be started all over again.

She had been gone for the better part of two months now, and Kao Li-shih had reevaluated his original notion that perhaps the Emperor was better off without her. He was certainly not getting over her. An Lu-shan had helped him, had brought him back from his bleak, lonely solitude; they drank together nearly every night. But the conversation always came around eventually to the consort. He was a man possessed, obsessed—and unable to face even the most minor legislative task. At least before, when she was present, there had been some progress. Kao Li-shih had been able to prevail upon the Emperor to act upon the problem of the Censorate, for example. But now, drinking wine and playing music were the only things that he could find time for.

He lifted the box and turned it over. It was fragrant and fairly heavy. Attached to the underside was a small slip of silk carrying what seemed to be instructions in the form of a prosodic riddle for opening the box. Indeed, the box appeared to be solid; he could see no obvious way to open it. He had seen smaller, less elaborate versions of such boxes before. A series of hidden panels and latches must be slid, clicked, snapped, and twisted in just the right order for it to open. And on the same piece of silk was another very determined bit of information: "The Emperor's nose," he read, "must be the first to the opened box in order that its heavenly fragrance might assail the Son of Heaven's nostrils before it is defiled by another's." Kao Li-shih laughed out loud with delight.

Good! Excellent! Someone had chosen to move the first stick on the gaming board, and in a playful, clever, irresistible way. The Emperor would, he knew, work all day and into the night at the puzzle if necessary. Kao Li-shih thought it likely that Precious Consort's sisters had been instrumental in this. No doubt they thought the foolishness had gone on long enough . . . though how they had got through the consort's stubbornness, which was easily the equal of the Emperor's, he could not imagine. He was grateful. Without them, there might be no thaw in this winter . . . and now that the Emperor, thanks to the barbarian, was in a better mood . . . well, he would waste no time. She was a smart woman. She was making it possible, by initiating a first move, for the Emperor to relent from his position.

: :

As Kao Li-shih made his way toward the Emperor's apartments it occurred to him that perhaps it was An Lu-shan who had put the sisters up to this. The sisters and An Lu-shan were fond of each other, and he no doubt missed them—especially the Lady of Kuo. He studied the etched beauty of the box in the bright morning light. Yes, he could imagine An Lu-shan making a diplomatic mission to the suburbs to plead with the Precious Consort.

The odors that wafted from the box to his nostrils were familiar and unfamiliar at the same time. He smelled something that reminded him of rose petals; also citronella, and peach blossoms. But there was another that he couldn't place. A spicy, hypnotic sweetness that made him think of the tropics, of an exotic world impossibly distant from the familiarity of here and now. The eunuch thought that the box was like a wonderful puzzle from some obscure little magician's shop: something that, seen when one was a child, one could never forget. Radiating mystery and strange beauty, the image of it would haunt you for the rest of your days, turning up in your memories, your dreams. He could imagine years going by, and one day being very old and smelling roses, peaches, or citronella, or that other smell, the one he couldn't put a name to, and having the memory of the box, and the time and place of it in one's life, and the emotions it aroused once, come vividly to life in the mind. Or you might see the box once, and then years later wonder if you had really seen it at all, or dreamt it.

But who could expect anything less of the Yangs?

By the time he placed his right foot on the first stair step leading to the Emperor's outside terrace, his mind was alive with visions engendered by the box's smells. He felt elated and consumed with curiosity to know what was inside—what rare, enticing gift the sisters had selected to soothe an emperor's feelings.

Members of the imperial household and kitchen staffs moved silently through the halls and into the inner imperial bedchambers with trays of covered dishes, bowls, and moist steaming towels wrapped around fragrant sachets, and the silks of the Emperor's morning wardrobe. Kao Li-shih decided that even if he were not coming this morning bearing gifts of reconciliation, it was nevertheless a good time for a visit. It had been a long time since Kao Li-shih had taken his customary morning repast with the Emperor. The chances were good that the barbarian, though he undoubtedly spent the night in the Emperor's adjoining rooms after last night's revelry, would stay asleep for several hours yet, giving them some rare time alone.

::

"So," the Emperor said, his words muffled by a mouthful of jellied fruit, "I am sure you are right that An Lu-shan got to her. He can be most persuasive. She has given in. She has seen where her obstinacy gets her and is trying another tactic. Now she wishes to come back like a wounded dog, tail tucked between her legs. A little humility will be good for her. Stubbornness is the worst failing of these Yangs, Kao Li-shih." He reached for more food.

Look at who is talking, thought Kao Li-shih. A man who would burst before pissing or turn blue before breathing simply to win a contest. In other days he would have spoken these words out loud, but he had no wish to say or do anything that might jeopardize a possible reconciliation. Besides, he knew the game the Emperor was playing now. Feigning nonchalance, as if the box and what was inside it and what it meant were only of passing interest, the Son of Heaven continued to eat, delaying his reward. Kao Li-shih helped himself to more food, poured another bowl of tea, and regarded the Emperor with bemused interest.

Casually, as if he were idly reading some stray scrap of writing he happened to find, the Emperor reached for the slip of silk bearing the instructions. He looked at the box, back at the instructions, and then at the box again. He reached out and turned the box around slowly, studying the elaborate design work.

" 'With each turn of the ox head,' " he read aloud, " 'one bale of wheat to sow.' Heavens! What is this? 'With each three beats of the osprey's wings a pearly carp must go . . .' and there is more!" The Emperor's tone was pleasantly exasperated as he experimented with small recessed knobs and plucked at little hinged arms, levers, and swiveling clasps. His eyes narrowed with interest as he commenced the task of matching the abstraction of the written word to the enigma before him.

Kao Li-shih knew the pretense was over, and that now the challenge would begin in earnest.

" 'In the halcyon days of autumn, golden leaves are just for show; it is the seeds that must be cast before the millets grow.' " He poked at the box for a bit, then shoved it toward Kao Li-shih. "Does she think I am a damned *magician*? Help me with this, Eunuch—don't just sit there like a contented gelding fattening yourself on my food. Earn your keep."

Kao Li-shih thought of the puzzles he had had to face and leave unsolved. Puzzles he had never brought to the Emperor. If you only knew, he thought.

"I remember a noble young prince and an earnest ruler who once had a great deal more patience than this," Kao Li-shih replied and pushed the box back toward the Emperor.

"It is age, Kao Li-shih, and worry. Worries about women."

"It is certainly not worries of affairs of state."

"I do not need the lectures. Just open the damned box." The box was shoved back across the table toward Kao Li-shih along with the slip of silk.

Kao Li-shih looked disdainfully at the box, but made no move to touch it or study the verse. Instead, he reached for a round sesame and anise cake and dropped it on his plate. He placed his bowl back on the table and very slowly poured tea into it again.

"And I suppose that I do not suffer the same afflictions of age that you do?" he said.

"You do not suffer from *women*, Master Kao . . ."

"No . . . just from tiresome despots and their rotund drunken friends."

Kao Li-shih and the Emperor were smiling at one another now. This was the way they used to talk to each other—friendly insults that they both enjoyed, that came dangerously close to the truth.

"He's asleep in the other room," said the Emperor. "He won't even be up to insult you this morning. Now help me!"

"You leave me no choice. You nag worse than an old scullery maid. And much more persistently." Kao Li-shih lifted the instruction slip closer to his eyes. "My first suggestion would be to repeat the poem with all lines together. To find an order in it."

"See? You can be helpful."

"Now listen to the poem." Kao Li-shih chanted the first of two couplets: " 'With each turn of the ox head, one bale of wheat to sow . . . With each three beats of the osprey's wings, a pearly carp must go' . . ."

Kao Li-shih mused over the lines for a few seconds. "Oxen, bales of wheat, osprey . . ." he said, thinking out loud.

"The words are clear descriptions of things, objects," the Emperor exclaimed. "Look at the box, Kao Li-shih! Look at the tiny embellishments on the buttons and levers . . . birds, fish and . . ."

"That's right!" said Kao Li-shih. "What do you need me for?"

"To offer me incentive by insulting me," answered the Emperor cheerfully, excited by his discovery. "Now read me that last couplet."

"Ah . . . yes . . . 'In the halcyon days of autumn, golden leaves are just for show; it is the seeds that must be cast before the millets grow.' That's all of it." Kao Li-shih put the slip back down on the table.

The Emperor picked up the box.

" 'With each turn of the ox head, one bale of wheat to sow,' " he said, and tentatively turned the ox-head screw on the side of the box and pulled down one small lever shaped like a sheaf of wheat. The ox-head button dropped off, hit the table top and rolled to the floor. The Emperor smiled triumphantly. " 'With each three beats of the osprey's wings, a pearly carp must go.' " He pushed a small set of hinged wings in ivory relief. At first they did not move. He pushed down on them harder; they gave slightly. He pulled them out a hair and pushed down again. They moved easily now, clicking down three notches. They stopped. The fish? The pearly fish? He turned the box around. It was Kao Li-shih who spotted the mother-of-pearl carp first. There were two, perfectly matched, tail to tail, on the opposite side of the box.

Kao Li-shih tried to pluck the two inlaid fish. That failing, he pushed both of them. He felt a tiny movement in one of the fish.

"Kao Li-shih, remember," the Emperor said. " 'A pearly carp must go.' A *single* pearly carp must go; that's clear from the poem. Maybe one locks the other. Try one alone."

Kao Li-shih worked at the right-hand fish. Nothing. Then the other. The left-hand fish rotated as if mounted on a minute pin. He pulled it again, prying the delicate carving with his fingernails. It slipped out, and he held it up with a smile. Now the right-hand fish moved easily, too.

Now Kao Li-shih was in the game as fully as the Emperor. Before the latter could open his mouth, the eunuch recited the next couplet.

" 'In the halcyon days of autumn, golden leaves are just for show; it is the seeds that must be cast before the millets grow.' This is confusing. There are golden leaves about here and there, but the riddle seems to be telling us to ignore them." Kao Li-shih studied the box closely.

"But if we ignore these gilded leaves, we have nothing, Kao Li-shih. There is nothing resembling seeds or millet anywhere on this box."

"Have you thought that perhaps the clue rests with the word 'autumn'?" Kao Li-shih asked, suddenly inspired. "After all, the fact that seeds are not sown or 'cast' in autumn may be very significant to this puzzle." Kao Li-shih again turned the box upside down.

"We are missing something, Eunuch . . . We are, indeed, missing something . . ."

"We all know what eunuchs are missing!" came a gravelly voice from the other end of the room. Kao Li-shih and the Emperor looked up and saw the enormous naked figure of An Lu-shan standing in the doorway groggily rubbing the sleep from his eyes.

"I thought you assured me that your friend would not wake up while I was here," Kao Li-shih remarked to the Emperor, and returned his attention to the box. The Emperor shrugged apologetically.

"He is nothing if not unpredictable. His capacity for wine never ceases to amaze me. Like a Bactrian camel storing water. And his capacity for recovery never ceases to impress me, either. We are hard at work, An Lu-shan, trying to penetrate the mystery of the puzzle you and the consort have inflicted on me."

"The *what?*" An Lu-shan said vaguely, and sat down on a couch in the corner and pulled one of the Emperor's fresh robes around himself. "What is there for this underfed warrior to eat this morning, my '*majesties*'?"

With those last words, Kao Li-shih could feel An Lu-shan looking at him and could sense the mocking smile on the general's face. But Kao Li-shih kept his attention impassively averted.

"I am nearly starving," An Lu-shan said. "I believe that I must have given everything up last night, and my poor stomach groans for food."

The Emperor laughed. "You did, An Lu-shan," he said. "And the fish were most grateful. They look forward to the feasts you serve them."

Kao Li-shih was disgusted but said nothing. The fish are not half so grateful as I am, he thought, to have missed the general's vulgar ritual.

"Cakes, fruit, tea . . . all here," the Emperor said, indicating the silver and milk jade trays on the rosewood tea table, piled high with the morning's delicacies. The Emperor's eyes returned to the puzzle box. Kao Li-shih continued to study the poem on the silk slip.

"Meat . . . I need meat," An Lu-shan said hungrily. "That crap is fine for you, my Imperial Father; fine indeed for a skinny bag of bones, but this fat peasant needs food. Get me meat, Servant!" he yelled to the steward of the inner chambers.

"You know, General, I am apt to believe that you do not know anything about this box," the Emperor said without looking up. "It was evident on your face when you stumbled in here, and is becoming more evident by the minute. You would be quite unable to hide your curiosity and interest. His thoughts are especially transparent, Kao Li-shih, before he has eaten in the morning."

"I am delighted to know that, I am sure," Kao Li-shih answered without looking up.

"I don't even know what you're talking about," An Lu-shan assured them, picking up a half-full ewer of wine that still remained where they had left it the night before.

"Then the sisters initiated it themselves. All the better," Kao Li-shih said. "But I have figured it out, I believe . . . We don't cast seeds because it is not the time of sowing—autumn. This last clue is a trick of sorts. We *do* cast away these leaves that are 'just for show,' however. That is, we ignore them, or . . . push them aside . . . away . . . These two large gilt ones definitely move, ever so slightly. See . . . there!" He demonstrated the movement of the leaves to the Emperor, then pushed them harder. "There." The leaves opened out, unfolding like the wings of a butterfly. A faint click came from inside the box, and a lid, the irregular edges of which had been invisibly incorporated into the elaborate design, revealed itself by opening ever so slightly.

The fragrance that had been a subtle suggestion before, the exotic, tropical smell that Kao Li-shih had not been able to identify, was much stronger now, overpowering the peach and citronella, and even the tea and the fragrent sachets that accompanied the Emperor's morning silks. Then he remembered the admonition.

" 'The Emperor's nose must be the first to the opened box in order that its heavenly fragrance might assail the Son of Heaven's nostrils before it is defiled by another's,' " Kao Li-shih said deferentially and pushed the box toward the Emperor. "I have no wish to defile the consort's gift with my lowly nose."

In the corner, An Lu-shan sat hunched over, chin on his chest and elbows on his knees, massaging his temples and groaning and muttering to himself. The Emperor lifted the box to his face, closed his eyes, and inhaled deeply. With his thumbs, he attempted to push the lid further open.

The pressure of his thumbs caused a faint whirring sound from within, as of a spring mechanism. The Emperor looked questioningly at Kao Li-shih over the top of the box; in the corner, An Lu-shan abruptly ceased the circular motion of his hands on his temples and raised his eyes, fierce and alert as a predatory animal's.

"The box!" he shouted, lunging up from the couch and hurling himself across the room.

The Emperor rose to his feet in alarm, spreading his hands wide apart and stepping backward. The box dropped to the floor and landed heavily. The spring mechanism released, the lid flew back completely on its hinges, and a shower of red and black fragments shot forward at an angle calculated precisely to hit an inquisitive face. Flower petals? wondered Kao Li-shih for an instant. In the next instant he saw motion.

Spiders. Hundreds of them, furious and agitated, separating from the scattered petals and spreading in every direction on the floor. And An Lu-shan, bellowing like a wounded ox, running right through them and lifting the Emperor bodily from the floor, raising him high over his head with both arms. And a wail of fear from the Emperor, long and sustained. The same wail that Kao Li-shih had heard echoing down long, empty corridors four decades earlier, the cry of a young crown prince fighting for his life, cornered by assassins, partisans of the Princess T'ai Ping . . .

Spiders, black and shiny, swarmed up the naked legs of An Lu-shan and onto his belly and backside. Still holding the Emperor high, he kicked and stamped in a frenzy to shake them off. Guards and servants rushed in and stood aghast.

"Take him!" An Lu-shan shouted. A guard came forward, saw the spiders, and hesitated. "Take him, Fool!" An Lu-shan roared again, enraged. The
guard stepped forward, held his arms out, and An Lu-shan heaved the Emperor
like a sack of grain. The guard caught the Emperor at an awkward angle,
staggered under the impact, recovered his balance, then turned and ran from
the room with his precious burden.

The other guards and the servants sprang into action then, running and
shouting, beating the floor, the walls, and An Lu-shan's legs and body with
brooms, pillows, bedclothing. Kao Li-shih violently shook the hems of his
robes and tore at his sleeves, convinced he felt spikey legs running everywhere
in the folds and on his skin. A hot needle pierced the flesh of his ankle; furiously,
he wiped the spider off and squashed it under his foot. Then blows, hard and
heavy, rained down on his back and shoulders. Confused, he turned. An Lu-
shan stood over him, eyes crazed, hand raised, ready to strike again. Kao Li-
shih raised his own arms to defend himself.

Then he saw and understood.

An Lu-shan's hand glistened with the pulp of mashed spiders that he had
killed before they could get to the flesh of Kao Li-shih's neck. Eunuch and
general stared at each other for an incredulous moment before An Lu-shan fell
to his knees, causing a tremor like a small earthquake in the floorboards.
Servants and guards jumped back.

"You too, Eunuch . . ." said An Lu-shan in a weak voice, then collapsed
face down on the carpet.

"The physician!" Kao Li-shih heard himself shouting. "Get him to the
physician, now!"

An Lu-shan rolled onto his side and groaned, mashed and flattened dead
spiders from the floor clinging to his flesh.

"Hurry!" Kao Li-shih shouted, wondering at the strange echo of his own
voice.

Two servants, obeying the order, ran from the room. There was no
more motion; every spider, it seemed, had been killed.

Kao Li-shih trembled with exertion as he bent over An Lu-shan. His
ankle throbbed where he had been bitten, and his head swam with nausea. An
Lu-shan, who despised him, had saved his life; and now he, Kao Li-shih, who
despised An Lu-shan, was trying to save *his* life—and it was happening spontaneously, before he even willed it, like the righteous man's intrinsic goodness.
Who would have believed it?

The servants brought hot towels and covered An Lu-shan's bitten flesh
with them, then the guards, with a tremendous effort, lifted his inert weight
onto a palanquin.

"The Emperor!" Kao Li-shih said to one of the guards. "Was he bitten
at all? Where is he?"

"No, Master Kao. He is untouched and completely out of harm's way."

Kao Li-shih stood, but a wave of vertigo nearly toppled him. He steadied himself on the edge of the table and watched the guards carry An Lu-shan away.

"Hurry!" he called after them.

Servants whispered and scurried about, trying to restore some order to the room.

"Don't touch the box," he ordered. It would be needed, he knew, for the investigation. His mind seethed. The consort? Had *she* done this? And the sisters? He could not think at all.

He looked at the floor. The beautiful box, the magic box from a magician's shop, sat like a viper with its mouth wide open, its poison spent. Flower petals and dead spiders were ground into the carpet. Carefully, afraid of falling, he bent over and picked up some of the petals and sniffed them. They were the source of the smell that had made him think of the tropics and places he had never been to. He let them fall from his hand back to the floor, and slowly, painfully, straightened up.

He felt not at all well. His ankle was beginning to swell, his chest was constricted, and his heart raced. The place where the spider had driven its fangs in was like fire spreading up his leg. An Lu-shan, he knew, had been bitten hundreds of times. He felt a premonitory stab of the Emperor's terrible grief.

Surely, the warrior An Lu-shan was a dead man.

: :

The limestone cliffs stood like immense jagged stele above the low brush of the river bank. The village could not be far; they had been walking for days. Where the path came close to the water, the brush grew thicker, obscuring the way, and the old monk hacked at it with his cane as he went. High on the cliffs above, and visible now in the limpid washed light of early dawn were the black holes of caves and the fragmented carvings of a hundred thousand holy figures in the cliff sides—Kshitigarbha, Mahasthamaprapta, Avalokitesvara, Bodhidharma, Amitabha, Sakyamuni, Vairocana the Creator—their faces gone, blasted by countless eons of wind-driven gravel. Their bodies, too, were crumbling: the lighter color of the shattered folds of limestone raiments and broken toes, fingers, noses, and ears stood out among the weathered piles of dark, lichen-covered rock at the base of the cliff wall.

The bald monk walked in front without speaking, singing softly to himself the incomprehensible gibberish that old monks often did. And the boy, Rokshan, hoped that the old man would not turn around to face him again. But Rokshan knew that sooner or later the monk would have to turn around, and that thought made the child sick with fear and disgust. The boy maintained a constant distance behind as the old man cut through the over-grown path.

"You know, boy," the old monk broke the silence without turning his head but still causing Rokshan's heart, sunk in dread, to beat faster in horrid anticipation, "it is not everyone who can understand such a trick as you will experience today . . . No! Not everyone! 'Out of the many are chosen a few.' Perhaps you may be able to understand, and perhaps you may not."

The boy could see from behind that the bald tattooed head of the monk shook with silent laughter. He was relieved that the old man had not turned around. Instead, the monk began to sing and chant again in that strange voice that seemed to come from nowhere and everywhere at the same time.

They must have walked several more li, but Rokshan wasn't aware of doing it. Only now, when the sound first echoed inside his head, they appeared to be much further downriver. It seemed as if he heard it and felt it before any noise was actually made: a deep rumbling that gathered strength as if the earth were about to crack and a great dragon vein open and issue from its fissure a fiery breath of searing steam and molten rock. He was frightened and wanted to cry out to the old monk, but he didn't dare; the man would most certainly turn around, and that was too terrible; it made him sick with fear.

The noise became louder, real, and more immediate, outside his head now, a sound like thunder, only many times worse—deafening. The earth trembled. Ahead and high above, an enormous protruding yellow portion of the limestone cliff face began to split away. At first only a thin, irregular black line accompanied by a raining mist of dust defined the rift. Then it widened all at once to a gaping black rent and a hail of showering stone, and the severed cliff face, a gigantic carved figure of the reclining bodhisattva, slid down the hillside and splintered into jagged staffs of rock that drove themselves into the earth around the two travelers.

But the old monk kept pushing down the path, singing and chanting and humming, swatting and cutting through the undergrowth, ignoring the storm of rocks and boulders, the falling ruins of toes and arms of the merciful patron saint dislodged from their centuries-old posture of royal ease. He continued to sing and chant, and chant and sing. The young Rokshan now moved closer to him, still fearful that the monk would turn around but more afraid, for the moment, of the terrible quake.

The rocks fell close on all sides, slamming to the ground and rolling through the brush. The old man, never turning his head, never deviating from the path ahead, began waving his cane and laughing wildly—a deep, coarse, resonant laughter that rose now and then to high, delighted squeals. He laughed for some time before returning to his incomprehensible song. The boy watched him, uneasy. Don't turn around, he implored silently.

As they rounded the next bend, Rokshan saw the first sign of the settlement. Strands of cooking smoke hung in the early morning air above the village like enormous aquatic weeds in the quiet water of a lake, swaying gently as they disappeared into the hazy sky. The vertical lines of smoke and some crumbling brick walls were all Rokshan could see of the unnamed place from where he was on the path. He heard animals—sheep, horses, roosters —above the sounds the old monk made. But he heard no human voices.

Why? Was it possible that they still slept? It did not seem to him to be that early. How could peasants make their livelihood if they all slept as late as princes? Behind them now and far above, the rocks continued to roar and crash as more of the cliff fell down into rubble, but he no longer felt any concern. They were in the open, far away from the commotion, the river no longer following the base of the cliffs.

"We are at the village, are we not?" the old man said, and slowly, deliberately, began to turn his head. Panic gripped the boy, and at the same time, an irresistible compulsion to look. What he could not bear to see, but could not stop himself from looking at, was that where the monk's face should be, there was none. No ears, no nose or eyes: just a mouth and a big fleshy flap of skin—like the great pendulous earlobe of a carved icon—that hung down from his shiny tattooed head to the place where his nostrils should have been. Below it, the mouth talked and smiled.

The monk had one arm. The other was a short stump closed at the end like a sack of rice, the flesh all twisted and knotted in red and purple lumps. And when he spoke, he waved his stump about like the wing of a flightless bird. Although the boy hated to look at the old man, he was also powerless to leave him. He was not sure whether he actually wanted to leave the monk and merely lacked the will to do it, or whether the old man had woven some invisible spell that made it impossible to even consider that course. It had never been clear, and try as he might to figure out what it was that held him to this man, each day would pass as the one before it and each morning would see him waking in the old monk's company. Sometimes, the old man seemed a repulsive, sightless freak to the boy, and at other times, he was a comforting old presence . . . as long as he did not have to look at him.

"Yes," Rokshan managed, averting his eyes from the frightful visage, "we have come to the path just before the gate."

"That is good! I thought that the rocks beneath my feet felt familiar. See! There are always clues if we listen." The monk waved his staff above his head, his mouth smiling a sighted smile. He laughed silently and turned quickly back around to face the village, causing the bluish fold of skin to sway heavily, pendulously. A strange caution possessed Rokshan. He fell further back than usual as he followed the old man through the gate in the low grimy wall. The old man, he was sure, sensed his hesitancy, but said nothing.

What the boy saw inside the wall was not at all what he had expected.

There were no hovels of straw, mud, and stone, and no villagers—just animals. Goats, horses, chickens, sheep, and pigs wandered through rows and rows of statues of the blessed Buddha and his myriad forms: the Buddha of no toes, the Buddha of no face, the Buddha of no hands, the Buddha of no feet, the Buddha of no ears, the Buddha of no eyes, and the Buddha of the third eye; the Buddha of upraised hands, the Buddha of castigating glances, the Buddha of all language, and the Buddha of no language; the Buddha of the sutra of infinite wisdom, and the Buddha of the sutra of infinite gibberish. The Buddha of silence, the Buddha of noise, the mirthless Buddha and the laughing Buddha of boundless humor; the Buddha of punishment and recrimination and the Buddha of absolute mercy; the Buddha of infinite patience and tolerance, and the fearful screaming-mouth Buddha of none; the selfless Buddha of complete transparence and the heavy, opaque Buddha of greed.

They were everywhere in even rows, frozen in stony silence, except that the the the Buddha of mantras chanted and the Buddha of music, as the boy passed by, hummed high heavenly tunes that changed to low, inaudible vibrations as the boy moved away. When Rokshan finally took his eyes off the statues, he found that the old monk had gone. He must have disappeared in the maze down one of the rows, the boy thought.

He ran down one dry, dung-strewn Buddha-alley after the other, but he found only animals. He found no one, and he found no evidence of the source of the cooking smoke he had first seen. But there was dust and it had begun to rise up off the ground . . .

Rokshan came to an open courtyard where a frail arid breeze rattled the branches and leaves of a small huddle of brittle, barkless trees. As quickly as it had come, the breeze died again; there was no movement or sound at all. The boy went to the small grove of trees and placed himself on one of the stools sitting here and there beneath the limbs. He resolved to sit there until the old monk, or someone, came. As much as he did not want to see the old man's face again, he had no idea where to go.

A low breeze raked along the ground and fluttered at his leggings, pushing dust and pebbles into five tiny whirlwinds that moved out from the center and danced along the fringes of the maze of alleys. Rokshan followed them with his eyes as they darted into the narrow corridors between the statues and out into the courtyard again, hissing louder as they picked up more debris. Tucking his legs up under him on the bench the boy drew himself into a ball and sat perfectly still, enchanted by the gritty specter of the whirlwinds. They came closer.

"So you have found your way to the center," a voice startled him, so close to the Buddha of infinite infinites that, for an instant, he thought that the statue had spoken. Then he recognized the voice of his old guide. The monk moved into the open where Rokshan could see him clearly. The boy stared at the single arm and the fleshy mask of his face. "I felt your breath," the monk explained, and walked toward the cluster of trees under which the boy sat. "I felt your presence here. You have been waiting for some time, my son. I knew that it was you when I came to the courtyard. I could feel you when I reached the Buddha of infinite infinites . . . I can always tell when I am there because the silence becomes heavier, weightier . . . you see, it is not that the Buddha of infinite infinites does not make noise . . . does not speak . . . it is simply that there are lapses of infinite time between the resonant utterances of his voice."

"I thought you had left me . . . and there is no one . . . ," Rokshan began.

"I am good to my word, boy. Never let it be said that the old monk is not good to his word . . . but you are wrong; there are others here." The old man pointed to the right of the boy with his cane. Rokshan turned around and saw five figures seated on the stools opposite him under the trees. The wind was quiet, the dust devils gone.

Had he known this was where he was going, he would have refused. If he could have. Their appearance was as shocking as that of the old man. And now he remembered the rhyme he had heard about this place and these people:

> Their faces were eyed and were nosed and were eared
> But where their mouths should have been
> Just a loose flag of skin
> Hung down past their chins like a beard.

Was it the old monk that had recited it, or someone else? He thought hard. No. It was a simple children's rhyme recited once by an old storyteller, the boy remembered now. That was it! First there was the old monk with just a mouth but no ears or eyes or nose. And now, these hideous creatures who sat across from him, perfectly still, were much the opposite. It was maddening the way he could not completely read their faces. The old one smiled with his mouth but you could not read that smile in his eyes; the others smiled only with their eyes, revealing nothing else.

The five mouthless beings stared at him from their perches on the stools opposite and Rokshan experienced a strange sensation that came on him very suddenly. He felt as if his entire body were swelling and, at the same time, as if his conscious will were being pushed outside of it. Now he was being pushed back into a body, a huge, heavy body that seemed about to burst with painful throbbing . . .

An Lu-shan's face was covered in a thick beard. He was large and very strong and magnificently fat—and now he remembered who he was. Loud, arrogant, boastful, and proud; powerful, grand, and respected . . . General and Commissioner and Military Governor An Lu-shan . . . I am General An Lu-shan, and they all have to respect me now. He was in Emperor Minghuang's apartments at the springs; they talked of women and horses and . . .

The five mouthless beings stared at him, eyes smiling unreadably. A wave of intense disappointment and anxiety broke over him when he saw that he was still under the barkless trees in the middle of the Buddha maze courtyard.

"So now you will know the trick, General An Lu-shan: 'How do you hold all men captive without force?' Yin over yang, if you will, General," the old monk said from behind him. But his voice was different this time. Soft, dangerous . . .

An Lu-shan turned to look at the old monk. I know that voice! That voice is not *his* . . .

"Yes," he continued. "How to hold all men captive without force is a matter of yin over yang, General . . . of water over fire, but unfortunately, I do not know how to tell you. You see, although I know it is done, I have never seen it performed. And these five, as you can well see, General . . ." He waved his stump toward the beings.

An Lu-shan *knew* that voice, that taunting, teasing voice . . . but from where . . . ?

"Alas, although they have seen it and heard it, they cannot tell it." And the monk's mouth, suddenly recognizable, smiled beneath the flap of skin.

Then he knew. That voice! That damnable voice! And as An Lu-shan stared bitterly at the old monk, he changed. A face appeared, replacing the hideous pouch. It was Chief Minister Li Lin-fu.

He could feel the others moving closer to him now. He turned to face them. They circled slowly around, each armed with a wicked dagger in one hand and a long sword in the other. Then they lowered their weapons in ritual unison until they were evenly pointed at the great mound of his belly. The sunlight flashed on the polished metal.

"Since they cannot tell you, either," Li Lin-fu said, "they are going to slice open your belly and put the knowledge inside . . ."

I'll crush these ugly bastards, An Lu-shan thought. He tried to throw himself to his feet, but he couldn't move. With all his will and strength he struggled to raise his arms, but he couldn't move them either. He shouted and fought against the invisible force that held him. The five pushed their swords toward his belly. He screamed in rage, his right hand breaking free, his eyes springing open . . .

::

"His arm! Hold him down! He is breaking the restraints!" the diminutive brown-skinned physician yelled to his assistants. He raced to remove the glinting golden needles marching in a single quivering line from the middle of An Lu-shan's head up and over the great mound of his belly to the bottom joint of his little toe along the Shao-Yang foot meridian. The leather strap that bound the general's right arm had snapped, and the arm flailed about dangerously.

Instantly four eunuch assistants leapt onto the howling An Lu-shan, pinning his right arm and shoulder while the physician tied the limb down again with a piece of rope.

"The fever may have broken," the small man said, his voice raspy with fatigue.

An Lu-shan strained to lift his head. His vision was blurred and his eyes stung with sweat. A circle of strange faces looked down on him. Although he could not bring them into clear focus, he was relieved to see that they had mouths, eyes, and noses. Every joint in his body ached, and his skin was hot and stretched tight. And he was thirsty—thirstier than he had ever been in his life.

He struggled to free his hands and he tried to break the restraints that held his feet. He wanted to stand up, to clear his eyes to see. He wanted water. He wanted to know why he was tied down, and who all these fools were . . . and then he remembered.

The lacquer box. The whirring sound that had cut through his torpor like the buzz of a serpent, warning him that the Emperor's life was in danger. The spiders. And as he looked around, his eyes cleared a little, and he realized where he was: his apartments at the hot springs.

So, An Lu-shan, he said to himself, you didn't die.

He stopped struggling and lay still, fixing on the anxious faces above him.

"Wipe my eyes, Servant," he said. "They are burning. And bring me some damned water." His voice had an immediate effect on the faces above him. Tense expressions relaxed into relief; the physician actually smiled. A damp cloth was brought to his forehead, but An Lu-shan shook his head violently. "My eyes, you fool," he said. "Get this stinking sweat out of my eyes so I can see who you *bastards* are."

One of the attendants raised a bowl of water to his lips. An Lu-shan grabbed the bowl in his teeth, tilted his head back, and let the water flow down his throat. The attendant looked on helplessly, unwilling to challenge the general for the bowl; An Lu-shan drank his fill and let the bowl roll from his teeth and shatter on the floor. The physician leapt forward, full of admonishments.

"You must drink slowly, General! Such a sudden introduction of fluid into your system could have serious effects upon the internal balance of yin and yang!" he pleaded. "The yang must continue its outward push in the form of this perspiration. And since I have administered such a strong sudorific to induce the sweating, and powerful intestinal cathartics as a purgative against the toxins, the auras of the five *ts'ang* viscera have already been thrown into disorder, so I *must* advise you against drinking so much so rapidly . . ." He trailed off, seeing the general's dangerous expression.

"Why am I tied down like an animal, Physician?" An Lu-shan said quietly.

"General, your convulsions and fevered delusions were quite powerful. We were afraid you would hurt yourself, or—," the physician paused— "one of us. Free his limbs," he said to the attendants, "and prop him against some pillows. I don't think there is any more danger, to the general or ourselves."

"Don't be entirely sure, Physician," An Lu-shan said, painfully raising himself to a leaning position.

The physician laughed nervously. "That is what we like to see. A return of the spirit. Humor! Very good, General. Very good indeed!"

Convulsions and delirium . . . An Lu-shan remembered his dream of the monk, the buddhas, the mouthless monsters and their gleaming swords. It had seemed to go on forever, as if his whole existence had never been anywhere but in that place, that time. He had been far, far away, he knew. So far that he almost didn't find his way back.

"How long . . . ," he started to ask.

"Nearly four days and nights, General. You received enough poisonous bites to kill ten men. Such terrible nightmares as you no doubt experienced were a result of the venom—an excess of *chi* in the liver and spleen, you see. You will rest far better, now. The worst has passed."

"And the Emperor . . . ?" An Lu-shan asked, feeling weak and tired as he spoke.

"Our August Son of Heaven spent two full days and nights by your bedside consulting with the imperial physicians and pharmacologists until he nearly collapsed from the strain and exhaustion. Master Kao Li-shih finally convinced him to rest. But he did not receive any bites, and the chief eunuch received only one, from which he has recovered nicely. All of it thanks to your valiant sacrifice. The nation owes you much, General An. The Son of Heaven gave me strict orders to summon him at the first signs of your recovery or"—he shrugged—"your imminent demise." The physician clasped his fine hands together obsequiously.

"And which one was he waiting to hear, eh? Tell the old fool that I am alive and awake and ready to take him on in his pools or in his harem or at a game of . . ."

An Lu-shan tried to raise himself, to swing his feet to the floor and stand. But he found himself utterly weak, his limbs rubbery and boneless. Spent by the effort, he fell back onto the damp pillows. The physician, alarmed, had leapt forward and easily pushed him back down; An Lu-shan found that he did not even have the strength now to resist this puny little man.

A greenish wave of nausea engulfed him, and the room swam so that he had to hold on to the edges of the bed. He lay perfectly still and stared at the ceiling, steadying himself by tracing over and over again the lines of the beams and the strange painted scenes on the lintels, as he often did when he was drunk and the bed was spinning. He had never felt so powerless. At least the nightmare was over; he was happy to trade it for his present state of weakness and misery.

And he had saved the Emperor. One bite would have killed that skinny old man. An Lu-shan had life-force to spare; the Emperor barely had enough for himself. Not enough meat, in his stomach or on his bones. He laughed weakly at the thought. The physician put a steadying hand on his forehead.

"General, I must implore you not to try to move just yet."

An Lu-shan detected relief of another kind in the man's voice. The Emperor had no doubt threatened the physician and all the assistants with something dire in the event of An Lu-shan's death. That thought made him laugh, too. The physician smiled. "Your eunuch has been sent to summon the Imperial Father."

: :

Kao Li-shih had decided that the time had come to act. It was time to call her back. It was the only thing to do now. A lovers' quarrel had got out of hand, and it had nearly cost the Emperor his life—but not for the reasons that some people at court thought. There had been those advisors to the Emperor who accepted the prima facie evidence of the box as proof that the Precious Consort or her family had attempted to kill the Emperor. After all, the Yang family seal was prominently displayed on it, was it not? And did not she, or her family, have good reason to want revenge?

But the Emperor had rejected the notion as absurd. What assassin sets out to murder an Emperor, he asked, and sends the deadly weapon wrapped in the family seal? Only a suicidal one. If it had been discovered that the consort had put a little dagger into her heart or had drowned herself on the same day the box was delivered, then the theory would be worth considering.

But an investigation had revealed that she was perfectly healthy and had in fact gone on a ride through the city to shop for tropical bird feathers on the morning in question. And the Emperor steadfastly maintained that no matter what her quarrel with him, she was incapable of murder. At any rate, he refused to believe it, and though most of his advisors had to concede to his logic, they still wanted her arrested and put to death simply because the possibility existed that she *had* done it. But the Emperor had forbidden it, so there was no more to be said.

Kao Li-shih believed in her innocence too, partly for those reasons, but mostly because of something that he had remembered, almost by accident, during his convalescence, when his grotesquely swollen leg was propped on cushions and he had nothing but time on his hands.

Kao Li-shih had intercepted a memorial a week or so before the arrival of the box. Titled "Expressing Great Displeasure with the Throne," it had been a formal complaint from an anonymous writer about the Emperor's inattention to his job. Kao Li-shih had read it with care, but had not noticed anything about it that set it apart from other memorials like it. Typical in its form and content, it had confirmed many of Kao Li-shih's worries, but he had not thought it particularly ominous . . . until one day when he sat examining his swollen, purplish leg and wondering at the power of the venom from such a small creature as a spider. At that moment, something jumped out of his memory, and he had sat stunned for a moment before he hobbled over to his desk and removed the memorial from a drawer where he had put it with some others.

As Kao Li-shih's eyes moved over the text, he noted again the usual formalities, literary conceits, obeisances, homages to past kings and to the glory and wisdom of the present ruling house that marked the style of a formal address to the throne of the Divine Son of Heaven, from below to above. Carefully, he read the text again:

> . . . Your subject has frequently heard that from ancient times down to the present, there have been those men who, certainly wishing to exercise rule over a nation, a rule of peace and wisdom, have often, quite unwittingly, thrown things into utter chaos. What explanation can there be for this? And what must be done to defer the inevitable outcome, that all men under Heaven shall suffer from the negligence of the Divine Son of Heaven, and that every event in the world of men shall be reflected in an imbalance in the natural order of things? Shall a failure to assume with strength, fortitude, wisdom and integrity the Mandate of Heaven throw Heaven and Earth into an upheaval? Just as the factions at court multiply in the absence of wise rule and conscientious legislation, just as we are now beseiged by a multiplicity of scandals, blacklists, and dangerous uncertainty while around us military governors and generals arm themselves, weaponry and soldiers everywhere at the expense of the people, and just as evil multiplies, so will even the tiniest of Heaven's creatures. . . . As evil men spread their wrongdoing, so shall the tiniest of creatures multiply and spread their potent venoms. . . .

There it was—the word that, just below the conscious level, had been bothering Kao Li-shih, and now presented itself for consideration: "venoms."

Why had the memorial's author or authors chosen that word? The more common word would be "poisons." But chosen, instead, was another word, slightly awkward in this context due to its very specific application—"venoms," the left-side radical of which literally meant "arachnid." From a strictly literary standpoint, "poison" would have been a much more appropriate choice. The rest of the memorial in no way indicated that the author was prone to making awkward choices; every other word fit neatly and predictably into place.

Now, of course, since the incident of the spider box, the meaning was all too clear. What had seemed to be only an expression of displeasure became, in retrospect, a declaration of intent to murder. Kao Li-shih had little doubt that the author of the memorial and the sender of the gift were one and the same, and that the source of the displeasure was not a jealous, angry woman, but someone so perturbed over the growing power of Chief Minister Li Lin-fu and his general, An Lu-shan, that he was willing to kill the Emperor who had let it happen.

One jealous woman could be dealt with. But where there was one man angered over politics and government, there were bound to be a hundred more just like him. A hundred . . . or a thousand, Kao Li-shih thought unhappily. And the Emperor had never been worse, never more inattentive, never more willing to hand the reins of government over to Li Lin-fu than during these many weeks that the consort had been gone.

That was why her absence had nearly cost him his life, and why she must come back.

: :

"You are right, of course, Kao Li-shih. A flirtation with death has a way of giving one perspective. My execrable stubbornness has been exposed to the light of day, and I am ashamed. And I see myself weakened, unable to concentrate, unable even to read what is put before me. Life offers us gifts, and we contrive reasons to push them away. But Death has a way of walking in the door unannounced and taking you just as you are." The Emperor brought his head down close to the neck of his horse to avoid a low branch. "Death almost took me in the midst of what can only be called a childish tantrum. I am ashamed. My mind has been on her all the time. I can think of very little else. I am not happy without her, I do not function without her . . . and yet, out of pure recalcitrance, I would not do the simple thing . . ."

"It is not too late," Kao Li-shih said.

The Emperor laughed. "Those were exactly An Lu-shan's words to me, Kao Li-shih. You and he are of one mind, for once."

Kao Li-shih rode close by the Emperor's side as their gentle mares ascended the forest trails of the guarded hunting preserve of the hot spring palaces. They were in the midst of a wide, dense march of trees that rose from the edge of the fields to halfway up to the summit of Mount Li Shan. Only an occasional bird song and the muffled sounds of hooves on pine needles interrupted the absolute silence of the woods. The morning sun warmed their backs and lit the tangle of branches around them.

"Then it is settled?" asked Kao Li-shih, reining in his horse and drawing his bow from its ornamental quiver.

"I would be insulting the man who saved my life if I did not ask her to return." The Emperor followed the line of Kao Li-shih's gaze into the dense underbrush. "Besides, I want her back," he added simply.

Kao Li-shih whispered now as he guided an arrow onto the taught cord and drew it solemnly back to his ear.

"Do you see that healthy looking pheasant? A good meal in the hands of the imperial kitchen staff, right?"

"It is too far . . . You will never . . . ," the Emperor began.

"*For her!*" Kao Li-shih exclaimed the moment before he released the bowstring with a clean musical resonance. The arrow flew slightly high; the bird, disturbed by the eunuch's voice, rose to meet it a few feet off the ground. The arrow lodged in the back just between the wings. The pheasant dropped, fluttering in its small tragedy. The outriders were dispatched to end it humanely.

"Don't disturb that beautiful head!" Kao Li-shih called after them. "Just break the neck neatly. I have plans for that bird!" Kao Li-shih turned around in the saddle and smiled at the Emperor. "That is, *you* have plans for the bird."

"I have? You amaze me, Kao Li-shih. You know my mind before I do." They rode out of the forest and into an open field that bordered it. The climbing sun grew warmer as the trees thinned. Kao Li-shih shielded his eyes.

"Have you not heard the theory that ideas float as purest *chi* in the ether? It is only when they cross our paths that they come to mind. I have merely intercepted one that was surely floating toward you."

"And what," asked the Emperor, "has the bird to do with all of this? It has been twenty years since you and I have gone hunting in the morning."

"By special imperial envoy, in a cart with a heated bed of charcoal," Kao Li-shih said, as if he had thought it all through extensively, "you will send the most magnificent dinner to your Precious Consort's place of 'exile.' Those things which should not be prepared beforehand will be prepared on site by cooks who will accompany the retinue. And at the center of the banquet, the dish that will bring her back to you: 'candied pheasant,' with head and tail in full feathered array as a reminder of one of her most notable dance performances. Do you remember the feathers? And in an accompanying letter, you shall tell her that you can no longer eat without her; that you pine for her and hunted the bird in her honor." They trotted in the deep grass out toward the path between the ruins. "I have given this a great deal of thought."

"You are a genius, Kao Li-shih. I will do exactly as you say."

They rode in silence for a few moments, and Kao Li-shih had a premonition of what the Emperor would say next. He had not been looking forward to it, but it was inevitable, and he decided that the time for joking was past. The Emperor, who had moved ahead of Kao Li-shih, turned in his saddle.

"What do you think of the general now, Kao Li-shih?"

The words struck Kao Li-shih with the same intensity as the midmorning sun that now fell full on his face.

"I will be honest. I have never known what to think of your An Lu-shan, but it seems that I owe him my life as well as yours. Certainly yours. It is plain that his loyalty to you cannot be questioned."

"*I* have never doubted his loyalty to me," the Emperor retorted. "He is thoroughly a part of this great House of Li. He is a T'ang. Deep inside, he is Chinese, totally devoted to this empire and its welfare. His sacrifice has proven that to me."

They were interrupted by the sound of hoofbeats. Yang Kuo-chung rode swiftly toward them on the path.

It is about time, Kao Li-shih thought. He had arranged for the Fox to meet them by "accident" in the privacy provided by the vast isolation of the fields. He wanted Yang Kuo-chung there as a witness; his plan was to tell the Emperor what he had learned about the assassination attempt.

"So your hunt for a pheasant has been successful," Yang Kuo-chung called to them. "I saw your outriders go past me with a magnificent bird!" Smiling, he reined in his horse a few feet from the Emperor and the chief eunuch. "Kao Li-shih told me of the clever plan. I am happy to see it coming to life."

"The gift dinner is *his* plan, Master Yang. I am quite relieved to have such a counsel as Kao Li-shih." He looked from Yang Kuo-chung to the eunuch. "But I was about to tell Kao Li-shih of *my* plan. Your morning ride is propitious, Master Yang. No one has heard this news yet—only General An Lu-shan. Because my chief minister has been out of Ch'ang-an this past month, not even *he* knows."

The Emperor nudged his horse forward. Yang Kuo-chung and Kao Li-shih followed, exchanging questioning glances.

"To say that An Lu-shan has proven his loyalty to the empire would be a gross understatement," the Emperor continued. "Last night as I sat by his bed, I saw his loyalty to me, unsullied, pure."

Again, Kao Li-shih and Yang Kuo-chung looked at each other. The Emperor spoke as if he were addressing the trees, the sky, the birds.

"I have asked An Lu-shan to take on even more responsibility, and he has graciously assented. I have promoted him to the military governorships of Fanyang, Hotung, and much of Shuofang—as well as that of P'inglu, which he already holds. I have consolidated, and entrusted to his hands, the safety and preservation of the entire eastern half of China's northern borders."

For a long moment both Kao Li-shih and Yang Kuo-chung were too stunned to respond. They rode in silence; Yang Kuo-chung's horse had begun to prance nervously, shying at every rustle in the grass. Yang Kuo-chung busied himself with the reins, deciding to let Kao Li-shih speak first. He knew what Kao Li-shih had wanted to talk about today; now he wondered exactly what words the eunuch would choose in the face of the Emperor's completely unexpected, shocking revelation.

"Someone has tried to *murder* you, Minghuang," Kao Li-shih said at last in a level voice. He paused as if choosing his next words with care. "This was the first such attempt in many decades. The first since you were a crown prince fighting for your father's honor and for your own legitimacy. And ever since that morning last week when your poor barbarian general dropped to the floor with the bites that were meant for us, I have been thinking. I have not been sleeping well; I have been trapped, alone, late into the night with these thoughts—but I am going to let my thoughts out now.

"I do not know what to think of your promotion of General An Lu-shan. On the one hand, I am distrustful of him and do not like him; on the other, I see his loyalty, and I am personally indebted. My attitude toward him is . . . disturbingly unresolved. But I *do* know what to think about your near death."

A flock of birds burst from the tops of the trees bordering the field. The horses walked quietly now, switching flies from their backs with their long tails. Here it comes, thought Yang Kuo-chung.

"At first I struggled with these thoughts. I wanted to think that the attempt on your life was purely a greedy push by some faction that wanted power—just as it was when they nearly murdered you as a crown prince. But I cannot delude myself any longer. It is worse than that."

Kao Li-shih's candor had Yang Kuo-chung almost holding his breath. The eunuch was walking on painfully sensitive ground; when speaking to the Emperor, he always, until this moment, religiously avoided uttering the words "murder" and "crown prince" in the same context. The Emperor gave no visible reaction; he rode quietly and appeared to be listening.

"Whoever wished you dead," Kao Li-shih continued carefully, "did not wish it because of what you have done, but because of what you have not done. I believe that whoever wanted you dead, and who no doubt still wants you dead, wants it because they fear you are handing this government to . . . *others*. They fear that in so doing, you are negligent, and that you will forfeit everything we have. For these unknown assassins, removing you is but a first step."

The Emperor spurred his horse gently but insistently, so that the animal began to move in a trot. Kao Li-shih and Yang Kuo-chung had to urge their own horses forward in order to keep pace with him.

"So you see," Kao Li-shih continued, "as I listen to the news of your promotion of An Lu-shan, I am torn by ambivalence. You are acting again on matters of state. You are making decisions again. That is good! But you are, at the same time, relinquishing power even faster than your chief minister would wish, and I can feel the eyes of the assassins trained on you with more determination than ever. As to their identities, we have no solid clues. But I have learned something that you will probably dismiss as trivial, but that does nothing at all to help me sleep at night."

"I am listening, Kao Li-shih," the Emperor said over his shoulder as they trotted swiftly along the path in single file.

"The flower petals," Kao Li-shih said, raising his voice so that he would be heard, "that accompanied the spiders. They have been identified for me."

Yang Kuo-chung noticed that they were approaching the same ruin where he had caught his sandal-strap on a pipe one day and nearly broken his neck. And he remembered the conversation that he and the Lady of Kuo had had about An Lu-shan, that had ended in a quarrel and had sent him out roaming to that spot. He looked at the sky now and noticed that gloomy rain clouds had begun to gather.

"The flowers are rare and from those jungled lands far south of the Persian Empire," said Kao Li-shih. "There are some very specific myths attached to these particular flowers, and I can't help but see a highly ominous symbolism in connection with the attempt to murder you. Those sweet-smelling red petals that leapt out of the box along with the spiders that morning are from a flower called 'flame-of-the forest' or 'Nandi flame.' It is used, traditionally, in shamanism. The blossoms are placed before the imprisoning huts of those who break tribal laws. According to the legends, when the unfortunate inmate dies, or more likely, is executed, the flowers are buried with him. This action is intended to prevent his spirit from ever returning to *this world*. Superstitious nonsense, of course—but as a message of intent from your would-be killers, I find it rather too specific and altogether . . . inauspicious," he finished.

The three were now cantering along the pathway. A thick high-piled thunderhead had completely obscured the sun, and rain began to patter on the ground around them.

"Damn you, Eunuch!" the Emperor said, riding faster. "You cast such clouds over a sunny day!"

They rode at a full gallop now, no longer speaking. Both Kao Li-shih and Yang Kuo-chung could feel the Emperor's intent and impatience as they followed, hooves pounding, after the beautiful pheasant that would bring the consort back to the palace.

17

A Lucky Baby Is Born

On his birthday . . . [An Lu-shan] received rich gifts and also favours of a more personal kind, for he was adopted as a son by Yang Kuei-fei. On the third day afterwards she and her ladies, to their own and the emperor's great amusement but to the scandal of future historians, wrapped his huge hulk in baby clothes and went through a burlesque of the ceremony of washing the new-born infant. This incident and vaguer allegations concerning the freedom with which he entered the women's quarters of the palace have led the romantically minded to assume that a love affair grew up between Yang Kuei-fei and her "son." To disprove this idea is of course impossible, but it is too grotesque.

—Edwin Pulleyblank

An Lu-shan once entered the palace to see the emperor and his consort, but bowed first to the mistress. The annoyed monarch asked the reason. . . . [An Lu-shan responded,] "Your subject is a barbarian. A barbarian puts his mother first and his father afterwards. . . . A barbarian only knows that he has a mother, but does not know that he has a father." . . . He further asked to be adopted by [Precious Consort Yang Kuei-fei] as a foster son. . . . This request was granted. . . .

Precious Consort Yang had a huge diaper made out of elegant brocaded material . . . and his "mother" had him washed, dressed in the diaper and promenaded about the Forbidden Palace grounds in a gaily-colored sedan carriage.

—Howard S. Levy

"THERE is nothing you can say that will convince me that you were not responsible for the box of spiders, Little Sister," the Lady of Kuo said cheerfully. "It is an idea that has your mark all over it."

"Oh, no," Precious Consort replied. "It is much more like something that *you* would think of. When I first heard about it, I knew right away."

"Whoever did it," said the Lady of Han, "had to be a woman. I am quite sure of it. It is the most utterly devious thing I have ever heard of."

"Don't be so sure," said the Lady of Chin. "It may have been female in quality, but we should not necessarily conclude that a woman did it. Men are quite capable of assuming female ways of thought and action, just as women are conversely capable."

"Then let us say that it was a female thing to do that may have been done by a man," said the Lady of Kuo. "That is, of course, if we can believe our little sister, who swears that it was not she who did it, as a means of either dispatching the Emperor or, failing that, causing him to call her back to the palace."

Precious Consort did not answer, but listened thoughtfully to the sound of the carriage wheels making their slow progress through the crowded streets, carrying her, escorted by her sisters, back to the Palace of Grand Enlightenment.

Though their talk was all in fun, her sisters could not possibly know the effect their words were having on her. She had not, in fact, been the perpetrator of the fearsome spider box, but when the news reached her at Brother's house, she had been profoundly disturbed and impressed by how much the incident resembled her own recent fantasies. It gave her the uncomfortable feeling that by merely thinking of something, she had made it real. She had no wish at all to harm the Emperor. But her mind, as it had since childhood, tended to run to extremes in fantasies of retribution.

How many times had she imagined her sisters beheaded, exiled, or married to farmers? Or her relatives in rags, with neither money nor teeth, begging for a few grains of rice or a place to squat out of the rain? It was not that she did not love them, and she would be horrified if any of them ever actually suffered. But she had long ago become accustomed to the workings of her mind and was not shocked or disturbed by the dreadful pictures it painted. She rather enjoyed them, in fact, and indulging in them at her leisure was one of her secret, private pleasures. During her time away from the palace, she had often allowed her imagination to run free, envisioning unpleasant fates for the Emperor and Plum Blossom. She had had them caught in a fire more than once. Sometimes they burned up completely; sometimes they survived, but had to go into hiding because they were so ghastly to look at. She also liked to give them a mysterious fever which caused their hair to fall out. On the Emperor, the effect had not been so terrible—without his hair, he was still striking and virile; but on poor Plum Blossom, alas, the effect was purely grotesque. And Precious Consort had entertained herself with thoughts of an ornate box, a "gift" for Plum Blossom, something so beautiful on the outside that the recipient would be flattered into opening it hastily and heedlessly. Inside, Precious Consort placed, in her imagination, something small, swift, and deadly: a tiny, poisonous viper, perhaps, or . . . spiders.

Who had looked into her mind and carried out what was only a private game played with herself? She might never know, but the coincidence left her with an odd feeling. She had best be careful, she thought, of what she allowed to run around in her head, lest it become real—and real in a distorted way: In her fantasy, the box, and therefore the poisonous bites of the creatures within, had always been meant strictly for Plum Blossom, not the Emperor. She shuddered to contemplate how close he had come to dying a painful, hideous death. Were it not for An Lu-shan . . .

What if the Emperor had died that day? What if the news had been brought to her, in the midst of her stubborn silence, that the Emperor was dead of spider bites, the work of an unknown assassin? How would you have liked that, she asked herself? What would all your anger, jealousy, pride, and determination to teach him a lesson have meant then? Less than nothing.

She looked at her sisters. They were vibrant, talkative, bright-eyed; relieved, obviously, that the "siege" was over. What would her life have been if the Emperor had died, and there had been a rift of bitterness between her and her sisters? Both of these things had nearly happened. I'll tell you what your life would have been, my girl, she told herself. It would have been bleak, gray, and desolate as a bad dream at dawn. You think you know how sorry you would have been, but you can't even imagine that, I assure you. Look at you, riding back to the palace, your life intact, the sun still shining. Do you know, do you have any notion of how fortunate you are?

She could scarcely contain her impatience. She wanted to be at the palace, with the Emperor, telling him everything that was in her heart and mind. She lifted the curtain and peered out the window. The carriage was drawing near to where it would begin its climb toward the palace city; outriders pushed back the curious throngs who were always eager to touch an imperial carriage or just get as close to it as possible. The Lady of Kuo looked at the Precious Consort.

"There is someone else who wishes to see you," she said quietly.

"I know," said Precious Consort, lowering the curtain. "An Lu-shan."

: :

She was a crocodile, parting the dark water with only her eyes and the top of her head above the surface. She glided in a straight line down the silvery path made by the moon. Her senses were alert for prey; she seemed to be alone until a ripple off to the left alerted her that something had entered the water. Soundlessly, she slipped under and swam toward her quarry. The ghostly moonlight coming down into the world beneath the water revealed a whitish shape ahead of her, limbs kicking. Such foolish creatures, she thought. Don't they know how dangerous these waters can be? They simply don't think. They just plunge in, and splash around, as if nothing in the world could hurt them. Look at this one, cavorting innocently, heedlessly. For a moment she considered sparing the creature; it seemed a shame to take it when it was in the midst of playing. But she was hungry. Perhaps some other time she would be merciful. She struck, sinking her teeth into one of the white limbs.

Together, the Precious Consort and the Emperor burst up through the water and broke into the cold night air, laughing and gasping.

"I had you," she cried. "You would be dead now, chewed to pieces and in my stomach."

"No, I let you catch me," he laughed. "I was luring you to me." He lunged, picked her up, and pulled her down under the water again. She placed one foot on his belly and shoved hard, disengaging herself. He let her swim a short distance before he went after her, but she dove just as he was about to grab her leg. She swam underwater as hard and fast as she could until she had to go up for air; when she did, he was nowhere to be seen. She stood still for a moment, waiting. Her pounding heart slowed a little, and still he had not appeared. A flicker of alarm crossed her mind then. Had she kicked him too hard? She turned in one direction and then the other, calling his name.

He broke the surface just behind her, taking her completely by surprise, and embraced her around the middle.

"Here I am," he said in her ear. "You called me back from the dead."

She looked down at the arms grasping her firmly about the waist. She lifted one of them to her mouth as if to kiss it, but instead bit it gently, on top, between the elbow and the wrist, and held fast with her teeth, not letting go.

"Harder," he said. "If you're going to do it, then do it."

Tentatively, she tightened her jaws.

"I said harder," he repeated.

She tightened them more. She knew that it must hurt by now, and began to let go.

"No!" he stopped her. "I want to feel it. I want to feel your anger, your hurt, all the bad things you thought about me while you were away."

Slowly, she squeezed her jaws together, by degrees, harder and harder. She heard him suck his breath in. It had to be really hurting him now.

"Don't stop until you taste my blood," he urged. "Don't be afraid. Pretend that I am dangerous and trying to kill you. Think of the worst thing you can about me. Think of me . . . ." He paused for a moment, then whispered in her ear, "Think of me making love to Consort Plum Blossom."

Resolutely, she sank her teeth together. She felt the skin break, he howled with pain, and she let go in the next instant. He sank back onto the water with a splash. She was seized with remorse and tried to hold the bitten arm, to soothe it, but he only laughed.

"Thank you," he said. "Now I am properly punished. Now I know exactly the extent of your anger, and if I ever forget, all I need do is look at the scar. Your mark, my love."

"You made me do it," she said, though she felt a creeping delight at what he had just done for her. He had allowed her to brand him. The imprint of her small, white teeth would be plainly visible there on his arm forever, for all the world to see. She could already see it in her imagination: little purplish dents, forming a fine, delicate arch, that would change color in cold weather, peeking out from under the silk sleeves of his robes. She would make sure her sisters saw it; they would be, she knew, greatly impressed. Then inspiration struck. She held out her own arm to him.

"I deserve no less," she said.

He took her arm, stretched it out, ran his hand and then his mouth along it appraisingly. He nibbled along the tender white skin of her inner elbow, then up to her armpit, then all the way down to her wrist, biting a little here and there, as if seeking just the right spot, the tenderest, juiciest place. She held her breath, shivering a little with anticipation in the night air, his lips tickling her arm. She closed her eyes and waited.

Nothing happened. She opened her eyes. He was standing there in the water, holding her arm, gazing at her.

"Go on! I am waiting!" she said impatiently.

But he shook his head.

"I can't," he said.

"But I did it to you!" she protested.

He continued to shake his head.

"I can't do it. A woman can bite a man, but a man cannot bite a woman."

"Why not?"

"It would just be . . . unseemly," he said. "Besides, I deserve it. You do not."

"I deserve it as much as you do!" she said, knowing that what she said was not quite logical, for what right would she have to inflict such a wound on him if she were just as deserving of punishment as he? But she *wanted* him to do it to her; she wanted each to leave this mysterious, terrible, permanent mark on the other; it would be a bond between them that could never be changed, never be intruded upon by anyone else, and which would always remind them of this moment.

But she could see that he meant it. He was not going to bite her. She would have to be satisfied with leaving her mark on him. They were both shivering now, standing naked in the waist-deep water.

"No, you don't deserve it," he said, pulling her down so that only their heads and necks were above the warm water of the small lake that was fed by the underground warm springs all around them. They tangled their weightless limbs together languidly.

"Why do you say that? Why don't I deserve it?" she asked. She was pressing him, she knew, but if he wasn't going to let her have the privilege of being bitten by him, then he would have to give her something in its place.

"It was heedless and unkind of me to do what I did," he said, and she knew that he was talking about Plum Blossom. "And most of all, unnecessary. I was using my position to indulge my careless lust." He shook his head. "If you only knew how often I have pondered the predicament of being an emperor. Am I a man who is an emperor, or an emperor who is a man? Trying to disentangle the two has caused me much grief and wasted more of my time than I care to tell. What things do I do, or are done to me, because I am an emperor? What things are done by the mere man?"

Her legs were around his waist now, her hands resting on his shoulders, while his hands wandered over her body.

"I know now," he continued, "which part of me was acting when I took Plum Blossom as a consort."

"It was the emperor," she said.

"No. It was the man, hiding behind the emperor. As an emperor, it is my prerogative to do as I please, responsible to no one, least of all to a woman. As a man, as your lover, I am responsible to you. I was avoiding that responsibility," he said simply. "And it was ironic and to my great detriment, because when all is said and done, it is the man, not the emperor, who loves, and feels, and wishes to be loved in return. So it is he who must act and he who must suffer. From now on, my love, I will do my best to see to it that when you encounter the man, he will not be hiding in the emperor's robes."

As he spoke, he gathered her hair, trailing in the water behind her, into a horse's tail. She let her head relax backward and enjoyed the gentle tugging.

"Coming close to death as I did, and seeing An Lu-shan almost die, made me see with the eyes of the man. And now I want to know," he said, "why you think that *you* deserve punishment."

He let go of her hair, and she brought her head back up so that their eyes were level again.

"You could easily have died while I was gone. It would have been unforgivable if we had parted forever with silence and hostility hanging between us. I saw with different eyes, too. I saw myself in a bleak, dead landscape, victorious, avenged, and completely alone. We think that we will be here forever and that we are made of stone, but our lives are really so fragile. Like a silk thread. Like a drop of water clinging to the side of a vase. I saw it, I saw it!"

The Emperor smiled. "And what of the one who really did nearly die?" he asked. "Is he not the one who opened our eyes? How do we show him our appreciation?"

"We make a vow," she answered seriously. "That we will put aside quarreling. That we will never again let anything separate us. That we will not act as if we have another thousand years to live. That we will not let Death sneak up on us and capture us in a snit or a bad temper."

The Emperor laughed appreciatively at this.

"I could not have put it better myself. And I think that An Lu-shan would like to hear it with his own ears. We cannot let him find out that his sacrifice was nearly wasted on a pair of irritable ingrates, can we? We may not be able to hide our true selves from each other, but let us at least keep *him* from knowing. He will be awake soon," he added.

An Lu-shan, recovering from the poisoning, had at first slept all day and all night; now, as he improved, he slept during the day and was awake at night. When he awoke tonight, they meant to be in his room, with Precious Consort's face the first thing he would see when his eyes opened; it would be the first time he had seen her at all since her return.

An Lu-shan was tended to lavishly in his private quarters at the hot springs. A physician was never more than a few steps away from his bed, night or day, and any food or drink he might desire was rushed to him no sooner than the words had fallen from his lips. The physicians had recommended that he receive massage treatments in order to work the poison from his system, so the Emperor had seen to it that not one, but eight women were available to pummel, squeeze, and stretch the barbarian's limbs and body. And there were six large, strong eunuchs whose job it was to carry him, if he desired it, into the hot, healing waters as often and for as long a time as he desired, and to carry him out again and back to his quarters. There were musicians if he was in the mood for entertainment, and he was given clean bed linens several times each day, necessary because of his copious sweating. The physicians, watching the droplets gather and roll in rivulets off the barbarian's body and soak the bed quilts, had nodded their heads in agreement that the sweating was a good thing, and probably, along with his unusual size and tremendous vitality, what had saved him.

It was time for them to go. The Emperor and the Precious Consort climbed onto the rocks and wrapped themselves in soft robes. They stood for a moment looking out at the silvery black water, steam rising in wisps here and there. Precious Consort stared hard at the unearthly beauty of the hot springs lake in the moonlight, at the shadowy stones, at silhouettes of graceful pavilions. Water bubbled up from the earth, wavelets lapped, frogs sang, and nightbirds called to one another in the woods. All of it as it had been for centuries. She tried to comprehend the vast sea of time stretching behind her and in front of her; this place, here, just as it was now, existing long before her eyes and ears came into existence, and continuing to exist when she and anybody carrying the memory of her were dust.

Thinking of the future made her feel cold and small. She strained her senses, trying to take in what was coming to her through her eyes, ears, nose, and skin, but she could not shake the feeling that she was cut off somehow, obstructed, insulated, and that time passed only because humans failed to fully comprehend the world. She stood very still, concentrating, willing time to stop. Let this moment last forever, she implored the woods, the stones, the dark water.

The Emperor stood next to her, his arm around her; she could hear and feel his breathing and heartbeat. She shivered.

"Your arm!" she said then, remembering. "We must tend to it!"

"We will. But first, we must let An Lu-shan see what you have done, don't you think?"

She could see him smiling in the dim light. She smiled back, pride, delight, love, and devilish playfulness moving through her, displacing the cold, strange mood of a few moments ago.

"Yes, of course. He must absolutely see," she said, and they started up the stone steps.

: :

"An Lu-shan . . . An Lu-shan!" she whispered in his ear as she held his great hairy hand. "An Lu-shan!"

He was propped against a small mountain of cushions, his head to one side, frowning in his sleep as if he were having an unpleasant dream. His breathing was thick and harsh, and in the lamplight she could see on his face and body traces of the swelling which, the Emperor told her, had sealed his eyes shut for many days. She wiped his sweaty brow.

"An Lu-shan!" she said again.

He sighed, and with a great effort opened his eyes and looked at her; as he did, the troubled frown turned into a radiant smile. "Mother!" said An Lu-shan to Precious Consort.

They laughed. This was a good joke, when one considered that An Lu-shan was at least twenty years older than the Precious Consort. She was relieved to see the old light in his eyes, unaffected by the illness.

"Yes, my little baby," she answered, putting a stern expression on her face. "Mother has returned. And she is very cross with you. How many times has she told you not to play with spiders?"

"I never want to make you angry, Mother," he said. "I have too much love for you."

"And what of your father?" asked the Emperor. "Have you any love for him?"

An Lu-shan gave him a sly look. "Though I love you well enough, I am a barbarian. And as you surely know, a barbarian can never be completely certain who is his father!"

The Emperor laughed with wild delight at this.

"Nor can any man, eh?" he exclaimed.

An Lu-shan's eyes fixed on a bloody bit of silk tied around the Emperor's forearm. The Emperor and Precious Consort looked at one another, and the Emperor began to unwind the silk.

"She loves me, An Lu-shan. She showed me how much. I finally understand." He exposed the wound; the small red circle of toothmarks looked like a flower tattooed on his arm.

They sat before An Lu-shan, smiling absurdly, their hair wet and disheveled. The barbarian shook his head admiringly.

"I am a happy little baby," he said, "because my mother and father love each other and are back together again."

Precious Consort was glowing with satisfaction and pleasure. She loved hearing herself and the Emperor called "mother" and "father"; it made her feel securely and intimately bound to her imperial husband. And she loved the ludicrous image of An Lu-shan as a "baby." Inspiration came to her then.

"I have an idea!" she cried. "You *will* be our baby. It would be most appropriate! A new era, a new life, and we owe it all to you!"

An Lu-shan waved away her thankful declarations and lowered his eyes modestly.

"I have no special courage," he said. "Just deep love for my father."

"What nonsense! No special courage! Tell that to the man whose life you saved," she said, turning toward the Emperor. "We will have a ceremony of adoption. We will make him ours! And there will be an announcement of an imperial 'birth.' Food, drink, and presents will be given to every citizen of Ch'ang-an!"

Both the Emperor and An Lu-shan were smiling now; it was plain that they liked the idea.

"But before I agree to be born," An Lu-shan said, "my mother and father must make a promise. Otherwise I cannot come into the world a happy baby! They must promise me that my little ears will never hear a harsh or discordant word between them and that my little eyes will never cry any tears because my parents have quarreled or turned away from each other." He looked at them imploringly.

"We promise, An Lu-shan," said the Precious Consort.

"In any case, I have no wish to be bitten again," the Emperor joked. "The next time, all that will be left of me will be gristle and pieces of skin. Yes, we promise."

"Then I will be the happiest, luckiest baby that was ever born," said An Lu-shan. He looked at the Precious Consort. "I will be very hungry after I have been born," he said with a rascal's smile. "Will my mother suckle me at her breast?"

"A baby born with such a full set of large, yellow teeth as yours does not need mother's milk. He will be given a bone to gnaw on instead," Precious Consort retorted. "Obviously, any fears we may have had as to the completeness of his recovery were groundless," she said to the Emperor.

"Indeed. He is probably completely well already, and has been for some time, but is content to spend his days sleeping and being waited on." The Emperor leaned forward and spoke in a confidential tone. "When you are well enough to need a woman, An Lu-shan, be sure to tell me. Let me select just the right one for you."

A slow smile spread across An Lu-shan's face. "I think that that may be just what your little baby needs," he said. "I am still a bit weak, perhaps, but I have strength where it counts! I accept your gracious offer, Father. I am ready."

The Emperor and Precious Consort stayed for several more hours. Food was brought to them, and wine. It was a beautiful, soft night, and they partook freely and became drunk. An Lu-shan drank, too, and his ashen complexion took on a rosy hue. Precious Consort felt that the world was quite perfect. One moment, she thought, looking at the Emperor and An Lu-shan talking and laughing in the golden lamplight, and feeling her own body tingling with a strange weightlessness and joy; one moment everything is pain and doubt, and then in the next moment everything is transformed: perfect, transcendent, luminous. The wine filled her head and ears with a roaring sound; she laughed and laughed, unable to stop, and heard her own laughter coming from far, far away. The Emperor and An Lu-shan laughed with her. They didn't even know what was so funny, but they could not help themselves. Precious Consort could imagine the sound carrying, out into the dark of the hot springs, across the lake, startling little animals and making them run for their burrows, bouncing and echoing around the still, dark walls of stone that had stood silently for all those centuries, and the thought of it made her laugh harder still.

: :

An Lu-shan awoke to hands caressing his body. It was early dawn, and he could see just well enough to discern the figure of a woman seated next to him on the bed. He was surprised to find that he had slept after the Emperor and consort had left him. It must have been the wine, he thought, rubbing his eyes and trying to focus them.

And who was this? Though there was not enough light for him to see her face clearly, he did not think that she was one of the women who had been massaging him. Certainly, none of them ever touched him the way this one was doing. He had begun to reach for the lamp to turn it up, but his hand dropped slowly back to the bedclothes, his eyes closed, and his head sank to the pillow when he felt one of her small, cool hands pushing back his belly while the other closed around his "old man" and exerted an exquisite pressure. He remembered the Emperor's offer. Well, he had certainly wasted no time in carrying out his promise. An Lu-shan sucked his breath in with pleasure. There's life in you yet, he told himself, relaxing and giving himself over to this woman, whoever she was, who had materialized out of the dawn and his obscure dreams.

She knew just what to do. He barely had to move a muscle; all that was required of him was that he lie still and cooperate. Oh, he would get completely well with this kind of treatment, without a doubt, he thought, unable to believe his good fortune as he felt her mouth, warm and wet, closing over him. He had heard that there were women willing to do this, but so far in his life the experience had not come his way. She moved her mouth slowly up and down, up and down, occasionally allowing her teeth just the slightest contact with his flesh. The sensation was dangerous and thrilling, and he could scarcely believe that he was allowing it. This utter stranger, this woman without a face, could, if she chose, inflict the most dreadful pain and damage on him at any moment. But he was powerless. The danger and the pleasure mixed, like some dark magic potion, and like a drunk who has to finish the last drop of wine, he knew nothing could stop him now. There was nothing in the world but her mouth, warm and slippery, and his blood, hot and pulsing. He felt a small fist tightening in his groin.

Abruptly, she withdrew her mouth. His "old man" stood stiff and abandoned in the cool air for an agonizing moment while the woman deftly pulled up her dress and climbed on top of him. The next thing he felt was her body, warm and wet like her mouth, closing around him. She rode him like a horse, her knees straddling his great belly hanging down on either side. She leaned forward on her arms then, and delicately took his ear between her teeth, her hair falling all over his face. The smell of her surprised him: damp earth; wet leaves. With his ear in her teeth, she emitted a soft, low growl that sent unbearable erotic tingling sensations through him; her knees gripped hard as she moved up and down on him, rhythmically, smoothly, making the fist in his groin tighten and tighten; her smell made him think of roots pulled from black dirt, cool moss, the underside of a log decaying on a forest floor. He took a handful of her hair and pulled it off his face so that he could breathe, then bunched it and held it to his nose and inhaled the earthy perfume. The growl in his ear rose in pitch to an urgent whine, carrying him with it; he rose on that sound, until the fist in his groin sprang open and he felt all the poison and sickness left in his body spurting out of him. She gripped him harder with her legs, as if he were a runaway horse that was going to pitch her off.

She let his earlobe go, but he still held loosely onto her hair. He opened his eyes. It was lighter now; the room was bathed in faint gray. Moving his fingers in her hair as their breathing returned to normal, he felt odd little bits of debris; twigs and leaves. There were tangles, too, as if she had not combed it for many days. He found it remotely curious, but was too relaxed and pleasantly groggy now, and sinking fast back down into sleep, to worry or care about it. It was funny. He laughed a little. She smells like earth and has twigs in her hair.

He was vaguely aware of her rising up off his body, but all he wanted to do was sleep. He felt infinitely relaxed and comfortable, and well for the first time in weeks. He closed his eyes. When he saw the Emperor later, he would thank him for a most excellent, perfect choice. Most perfect. He slept.

: :

Kao Li-shih's face was a study in carefully contained reproval as he approached the outdoor pavilion where Lu Pei sat. Lu Pei had seen the look before; he knew without having to ask that Kao Li-shih had been talking to the Emperor. He also knew that it would take very little coaxing to get the chief eunuch to talk about whatever had passed between them. When Kao Li-shih was vexed, as he often was these days, it was usually over An Lu-shan or Li Lin-fu, and he seemed to find relief in ranting about it to Lu Pei. He knows, the younger eunuch thought, that my curiosity is insatiable, that I enjoy hearing everything he cares to tell me—but he also knows that I will be utterly discreet. What a privileged fellow I am indeed!

Lu Pei knew, too, that hungry for details though he might be, a certain amount of restraint would bring about the best results. When Kao Li-shih sat down without a word on the stone bench adjacent to where Lu Pei sat, the younger eunuch kept his attention on the very poor ink painting on which he was at work.

He was trying to sketch a pavilion across the way that was magically reflected in the smooth surface of the lake. The picture that he had in his mind, that he wanted to get onto the parchment, was so simple and beautiful—and bore so little resemblance to the flat, clumsy facsimile appearing under his brush. When he had first seen Kao Li-shih approaching, he had been embarrassed and was about to put the painting away under the bench, but realized as soon as he saw the older eunuch's face that he would not be even remotely interested in Lu Pei's artistic endeavors.

Lu Pei waited. Kao Li-shih was silent, but his fingers drummed on the side of the stone bench and he stared out over the water; presently he let his breath out in a long sigh that eloquently suggested fatigue and incredulity. Lu Pei knew that he would soon speak.

"The Emperor and the Precious Consort are expecting a child," Kao Li-shih said presently in a matter-of-fact tone. Lu Pei looked up in astonishment.

"A child? So soon? But . . . she has been back for less than two weeks! How could they know . . . ?"

"Yes," Kao Li-shih replied. "It is astounding, isn't it? And not only that, they know that the baby will be male, that he will be a brave and fearless leader, and that he will save the empire."

"What have they done? Consulted a soothsayer?" Lu Pei asked.

"I wish they would," Kao Li-shih said gloomily. "I am tempted to consult one myself." He looked at the apprentice. "And there is more. This amazing infant will be born weighing as much as four men. He will have a full set of teeth, and as soon as he is born, he will drink a pitcher of wine and eat meat and throw the bones over his shoulder. And the birth, Lu Pei, will take place ten days from now."

Lu Pei smiled.

"Well, Master Kao, you have dropped a riddle in my lap. I will think about it, and maybe I will be able to grasp your meaning."

"I will give you two more clues," said Kao Li-shih. "He will also be born, in all likelihood, with an erection, and will grab the first female creature he sets eyes on. And he will have a nickname, one most appropriate for a child born to such illustrious parents. They will call him 'Lucky Baby.' "

Lu Pei had heard the name before. Li Chu-erh, An Lu-shan's eunuch, had told him and Kao Li-shih once that when the barbarian got drunk, he would sometimes sing maudlin, sentimental songs in the Kushan tongue. These songs, Chu-erh had told them, were invariably about the infant An Lu-shan being suckled, fondled, caressed, bathed, and doted on by his mother—and he had a secret name for himself that he used in these songs about the fat, contented baby full of warm milk who waved his little arms and legs under his mother's adoring gaze: Lucky Baby. The eunuchs had laughed incredulously at the grotesque contrast between the huge, hairy barbarian and the little pink baby he saw in his songs, and they often joked about it, privately, and always well out of An Lu-shan's range of hearing.

So An Lu-shan was to become the Emperor and his consort's "Lucky Baby." What did it mean? Lu Pei was not at all sure he understood.

"Well, Master Kao, I am afraid my imagination is too dull to reveal this thing to me. You are going to have to tell me."

"I have a better idea, Lu Pei," said Kao Li-shih, rising from the bench. "You shall see for yourself. Ten days hence. You will accompany me, as my assistant, and you will see how such a creature is born. I think the experience will be valuable to your education," he added darkly.

Kao Li-shih turned then and walked down the small stone staircase leading out of the pavilion, leaving Lu Pei with his painting and a feeling that he was going to see some things that he had probably never seen before in his life and might never see again. He watched Kao Li-shih, who was walking away with a thoughtful, pensive air. Whatever this thing was, this mystery involving the consort, the Emperor, and the "Lucky Baby," it was clearly something completely outside of Lu Pei's experience. But Kao Li-shih's stunned and exasperated demeanor suggested all manner of lewd, strange, and enticing things to the boy. Though he had a strong desire to run after Kao Li-shih and ask more questions, he found it in himself to restrain the urge. Lu Pei couldn't help the feeling that a little patience—ten days' worth, to be exact—would reward him richly.

He forced his reluctant attention back to his work, then looked at the graceful pavilion opposite. He sighed, picked up the parchment, and crumpled it. He took out a new sheet and tacked it to his board. He would give it one more try.

: :

She came to An Lu-shan again very early one morning. Nearly two weeks had passed since her first visit, and he had given up hope that she would pay him another. And there had been no way of finding her, because no one knew who she was. When he thanked the Emperor for sending him a woman so promptly, the Emperor had smiled and shaken his head, saying that he had done no such thing. Whoever she was, the Emperor told him, she came to you entirely of her own volition. She chose you herself. Twigs and tangles in her hair? I'm afraid I can shed no light on the mystery.

None of the women who attended An Lu-shan knew who she might have been either. You are quite sure, he had persisted, that none of your sisters confided in you or bragged just a little bit that she had paid me a visit? No, they had said, looking at each other and giggling; and we would certainly know about it if anyone had said such a thing. He had carried the frustrating question about with him for days. He had only to think of the strange woman on top of him in the dark and he was instantly aroused; he thought about her mouth and her sharp teeth caressing the tender skin of his organ. He yearned to feel those teeth again. He even sent for one of the harem women and tried to re-create the experience; she had done her best to oblige him, but her teeth had raked him so that he howled with pain and he had been afraid for days afterward that he was permanently injured. And still his obsession grew; at night, he would caress himself to arousal, stretching out the sore spots on his skin so that he was in a maddening state of swollen, painful desire.

And he waited. He did not like it, this passivity; it annoyed him that he should have to wait for her to decide to come to him; he liked even less not knowing if she intended to come at all. After a week, when she still had not come, his hope had begun to fade; after nearly two weeks, he had given up, though he continued to have dreams about her.

He was in the middle of a dream about her when he awakened to find a weight pressing on his body. He knew instantly that it was she; he had been asleep on his back and she was lying stretched out on top of him. He smelled earth and leaves, felt the tangle of her hair on his face. His dream and what was actually happening to him merged perfectly. In the dream, she had been lying on top of him and he had been fucking her slowly, luxuriously. He woke to find himself doing exactly that. He seized her as if afraid she would leap off him and escape, and thrust himself into her with ardent force. I was still weak and ill that first time, he muttered into her hair; but now, I am strong again. I have been waiting to show you what I can really do. You will not stay away so long after this. You will come to me every night. Every night.

He meant to last longer. He meant to show her that he could keep her pinned and at his mercy, but he was helpless. Before he knew what was happening, she was whining in his ear, just as she had the first time, and he knew he would soon be finished. He gave himself up, riding the rising pitch of her voice until he was spending himself violently, powerfully, feeling her drawing his life-force right out of him.

When he opened his eyes, he found himself looking through the tangled mass of her hair as if he were looking out from inside a bramble thicket. He saw that the gray of early dawn had given way to ghostly daylight. The last time she had come, he had never even seen her face; he would not have known her at all if he had encountered her in the daytime. Her head was turned away from him now as she lay on top of him. He grasped her by her shoulders and pushed her up and away from him. The curtain of hair across his eyes lifted, and he was looking directly into her face. It was not the first time he had seen that face, and the recognition sent a shock through him like the bite of the assassin spiders.

She was the woman he had seen in the ruins that day long ago when Feng had first brought him to the hot springs. The woman who had looked up from the carcass of a gazelle and smiled at him with blood on her teeth.

She smiled that same smile now, but this time her teeth were white and clean. Without the blood, the smile had a different meaning; before, he had felt himself drawn into solemn, unspeakable mysteries while being invited, at the same time, to laugh ludicrously at them. Now, the smile was pure mystery, and the invitation in it was to delicious conspiracy. His heart pounded with excitement, shock, and exquisite pleasure. He stared at her face, so utterly beautiful and strange. She disengaged her body from his and rolled deftly off him, landing on her feet and pulling down her ragged black dress. Don't leave, he started to say, but she raised a silencing finger to her mouth. She turned then, and he could only lie there and watch, astonished, as she climbed out the window and dropped to the ground below. He heaved himself up from the bed and went to the window. It was a long way down—at least the height of a tall man. And she was gone. Completely vanished.

: :

Lu Pei found that he could go where he wanted, for nobody seemed to notice his presence. He had been fed well this evening, sitting by Kao Li-shih's side, and had drunk enough wine so that his head felt light and his feet very far away. The more he drank, the more he felt like a substanceless phantom. And what is a eunuch anyway, he thought, but the ghost of a man? That is why they ignore us; because we are not actually men. We are not quite real. He had heard that ghosts are jealous of the living just for being alive; that they watch, with hungry, disembodied eyes, the most commonplace, pedestrian of human activities; that when you blow your nose, light a lamp, or swat a fly, you cause the ghosts that watch you such acute envy that they are practically consumed by it. He liked to think of their invisible hands fruitlessly trying to pick up a comb or lift a latch. Well, tonight he knew a little about what those ghosts must feel.

The party was being held in the Emperor's own private apartments and adjoining bathing rooms at the hot springs. The festivities had begun many hours ago, long before Lu Pei and Kao Li-shih had arrived. It took an effort for Lu Pei to remember back even that far. When the two eunuchs had joined the Emperor for the evening meal, it was late afternoon becoming early evening, the reddish sun growing fat and lazy on the horizon. As they approached, they had heard music floating prettily over the lake in the dying light, and to Lu Pei, the world seemed at that moment to be a most sublimely beautiful place. Kao Li-shih had appeared unimpressed, however, walking gloomily and silently along the rocky path, his face set and his mind plainly preoccupied. Once they had arrived and the Emperor had greeted Kao Li-shih warmly and enthusiastically, the older eunuch put on a friendlier face and even accepted a cup of wine and drank a toast with his imperial master. Lu Pei saw many court ladies and gentlemen that he recognized, including the three Yang sisters, but he saw neither the consort nor An Lu-shan.

The atmosphere was entirely relaxed. The Emperor himself wore only a light robe and his feet were bare—Lu Pei had been embarrassed at first, turning his eyes away. The Emperor's naked feet! But he soon gave up, for there were naked feet everywhere, and naked bodies as well. It was a bathing party, and men and women, at least fifty of them, floated, splashed, and frolicked in the water of the Emperor's finest, largest hot pool. The surface of the water was strewn with fragrant flowers, and the rising steam carried their perfume into the air; in the adjoining pavilion, the Pear Garden Orchestra played light, airy tunes that made Lu Pei think of sparkling water dancing over rocks in the sun. If he wanted wine, he had only to raise his cup and it was filled by one of the scores of servants circulating among the guests. If he wanted food, he had only to take it from one of the trays moving by every minute or so. As the sun sank lower and lamps were lit, Lu Pei, who had been drunk only two or three times before in his life, drank cup after cup. Some of the wine was sweet, some was hot and peppery, and all of it slid down his throat with ease.

While Kao Li-shih and the Emperor talked, Lu Pei moved about. The bathing pool was joined by a gradual staircase to an open-air party pavilion of many rooms with balconies overlooking the lake and grounds. It was here that the orchestra played, and everything he saw spoke of comfort, pleasure, and the contemplation of beauty; every door framed a view that might have been composed by a master painter. The manmade structures, the walkways and buildings visible from the pavilion in the twilight, blended so subtly with the structures of nature—the rocks, water, and trees—that it was difficult to know where one left off and the other began. And on the covered balconies were comfortable couches with gauzy silk netting around them, through which Lu Pei could see men and women, their robes open, fondling each other's bodies. Nearby, other people ate, talked, and drank wine, ignoring the love-making plainly visible through the netting.

It was then that he had felt a kinship with those watchful spirits jealous of the ability to lift a cup or shut a door. He stood in the soft light a few feet from a couch where a man and woman talked and laughed and gazed fondly into one another's eyes. The woman was sitting on the man's lap, facing him, her legs clasped around his waist while he moved in a slow, meditative rhythm, one of her small breasts cupped in his hand. I am truly a ghost, Lu Pei thought, moving back into the shadows.

He moved about for a long time, satisfying his curiosity until he was sure there were no mysteries left in the universe. On another bed, he saw two women and one man, joined in an unbroken chain of sensuality that made him think of a snake eating its own tail.

Presently he became aware that guests were gathering in the main room of the pavilion and settling down on cushions and chaises. The air was charged with anticipation, as if all the people in the room shared a secret knowledge of something that was about to happen. Lu Pei suspected that his "education," as Kao Li-shih had put it, was about to be furthered, and chose a discreet position off to the side that afforded him a good view while allowing him to feel inconspicuous. The Emperor and the three Yang sisters came into the room and settled down near the front; he looked for Kao Li-shih, but did not see him.

The music stopped, and the murmuring and laughter of the crowd swelled in his ears. He felt dizzy and closed his eyes for a moment. The orchestra began again, a slow, ponderous, ceremonial tune that quieted the talk and noise immediately. Lu Pei looked at the Emperor, who wore a satisfied smile on his face as he directed his attention to the wide doorway that led in from the bathing area. In the next moment, the crowd gasped and then applauded; Lu Pei thought that he could only be dreaming or suffering from some derangement of his senses.

The Precious Consort had entered the room, but she was so tall that she had to duck her head in order to avoid hitting it on the doorjamb, which was half again the height of a normal man. She wore a long, long robe that trailed along the floor as she walked, with a strange swaying gait, to the center of the room, where she stood, hands clasping her belly, which appeared to be swollen as if she were about to give birth to something very large. Her features, fixed in a faraway, bemused expression, were those of a woman who has just felt the first faint pangs of labor.

Lu Pei stared, not trusting his eyes, at the fantastic elongated figure of the Precious Consort in the lamplight. She began to move in a circle, swaying and dipping, as the tempo of the music increased; she clutched her belly harder, grimacing with pain, eyes still fixed straight ahead. Sympathetic cries and groans rose from the audience; the Emperor himself stood, clutching his own lean belly and moaning pathetically. Laughing, the sisters pulled him back down as the guests howled and screamed with amusement.

Now the consort was bending backward at an impossible angle, then forward again while slowly sinking to the ground. Lu Pei was not at all sure what he was seeing. He thought that he must be very, very drunk or was witnessing, perhaps, some sort of secret magic that the court aristocrats reserved for themselves. The music was whining and wailing now; the consort ground her teeth and writhed her shoulders, and her huge belly undulated beneath her robe. The room held its breath, waiting to see whatever it was that was about to be born.

Her hem was lifted, and a round pink face peeked out. The crowd broke into shouts and applause, daring and exhorting the "baby" to come out and show itself to the world. Lu Pei had to look twice before he recognized that face: it was An Lu-shan, with his beard and hair entirely shaved off, crawling out from under the Precious Consort's dress. In an instant Lu Pei understood what should have been obvious, but which had completely bewildered him: An Lu-shan had been carrying the consort on his shoulders underneath her voluminous, trailing skirt; the bulge of her "belly" had been his head. When she had sunk to the ground, he was merely lowering her to her own feet. And now he was being born.

The room was in pandemonium as the infant An Lu-shan came forth into the world. He was naked, as naked as the day his real mother had pushed him out of her body. Every bit of hair that had been on him was shaved off. Hugely fat and pink, his belly hanging down like a sack of rice, he perfectly resembled a grotesque giant baby. He sat on the floor and looked around perplexedly at the guests, then crumpled his face exactly as a baby would who is about to cry, and let out a wail that would pierce the heart of even the coldest, cruelest mother. The Precious Consort held out her arms to him, and he crawled over to her and cradled his head against her bosom. The crowd, it was plain, wanted more. They shouted encouragement. The huge "baby" looked up at his mother imploringly; she gazed into his eyes while opening the front of her robe and brought out one perfect, round white breast, the nipple painted bright red. She offered it to her newborn. He began to suckle, eyes closed in rapture, as the people in the room applauded and voiced their enthusiastic approval so that Lu Pei thought the very roof of the building would rise. The Emperor was smiling broadly, and the three sisters were exultant.

When the "baby" had sated himself at the breast, he rolled off the consort's lap and lay on the floor, arms and legs waving in the air. The consort raised her hand in a discreet signal, and a dozen women, beautiful harem ladies in loose robes, some with their hair streaming and still damp from the hot pool, descended on An Lu-shan, tickling, rubbing, and kissing him. He put himself completely at their mercy, a helpless baby suffering the ministrations of women. One of them produced a huge square of soft white cloth then, and she and another lady held the cloth up for the guests to inspect. They roared, whistled, and stamped their feet, giving Lu Pei the certain knowledge that something was about to happen, something so strange and memorable that he would be telling the story of it for the rest of his life.

The women laid the square of cloth onto the floor, and folded it in half diagonally so that it made a large triangle. Then, giggling, their hair falling over their faces and arms, their robes falling open here and there to reveal a breast or a glimpse of thigh or belly, they all got on one side of An Lu-shan and struggled to roll him over onto his stomach; Lu Pei could only think of ants striving with a great pale beetle grub. They moved the triangle of cloth so that it was alongside An Lu-shan on the floor, and then, faces red with effort and mirth, rolled him back to his original position so that the cloth was now under him.

The huge infant lay passive, legs bent at the knees and spread wide. Lu Pei stared in rapt fascination at the spectacle of the military governor of Fanyang and Hotung Provinces lying naked and hairless, big sagging belly and genitals exposed as unselfconsciously as a newborn baby's.

The women, with much laughter and merriment, began rubbing him between his legs with oil, giving him an erection; the "baby" tried to pull first one woman, and then another, onto him. They wrestled, struggled, teased, and shrieked while he pulled at their robes, exposing breasts, shoulders, buttocks, until they overpowered him and pinned his arms to the floor, four or five women on each side.

Around Lu Pei, the guests were doubled over with laughter. The orchestra played, wine cups flew through the air and smashed to the floor, people shouted suggestions and obscenities. Several harem women, some completely naked now and others with their clothing hanging off them in disarray, weak and panting with the hilarity, held the huge baby down while two others pulled one corner of the cloth triangle up between his legs and pulled the other two corners across his mountainous stomach and tied the three together. They had diapered the newborn "son" of the Emperor and Precious Consort.

The Precious Consort pulled An Lu-shan's head into her lap and patted his face lovingly. The Emperor walked over to them, knelt and embraced the mother and child, then stood and applauded while the guests cheered and pelted the "family" with flowers. He held up his arms for silence; the orchestra stopped immediately, but it took two or three minutes for the room to quiet down. Lu Pei looked around again, searching for Kao Li-shih, and saw him standing quietly, all the way to the rear of the crowd, face expressionless, hands hidden in his sleeves. Lu Pei snapped his attention forward again. The Emperor was about to speak.

"My friends," he said, when his guests finally allowed his voice to be heard. "The birth of a son is always an occasion for joy and celebration. Tonight we have special reason to celebrate. The son that has been born to me is also born to you; he is like four hundred sons born in one man. He belongs not only to my consort and me, but to the empire, to the T'ang itself. His name is Lu-erh. He is 'Lucky Baby'! He is mine, he is yours!"

There was no possibility of the Emperor saying anything else that would be heard; his guests drowned him out completely. The music began anew, and Lu Pei squeezed his eyes shut to fight off a wave of dizzy nausea from the wine. When he opened his eyes again, he looked toward where Kao Li-shih had been standing.

He was gone.

: :

It was a perfect ending to the night of celebration. They had not slept at all, and now the sun was high in the sky. The consort and the Emperor were going to spend the day sleeping—not in the imperial bedchamber, but in a large, cool, shady tent the Emperor had had prepared. They went there together after the last of the guests had fallen asleep or departed. The tent waited for them in a grove of trees on the other side of an open meadow. It was the most inviting sight the consort had ever seen, she thought, walking slowly arm-in-arm with the Emperor through the dry, golden grass, the hot morning sun on their shoulders and delicious fatigue in their limbs.

The sides of the tent billowed softly in the breeze, and banners adorning the poles rippled colorfully. Spreading branches of tall trees shielded the roof of the tent from the sun. The entry flap was fastened open, with a gauze netting in place against bothersome insects. Inside were carpets, pillows, quilts, tinkling wind chimes, fresh silk robes, and a table spread with tea, cool drinks, and pastries.

They lay down. She rested her head on his shoulder and gazed at the light filtering through the fabric walls. The Emperor's breathing grew slow and regular almost immediately; soon she heard him snoring lightly. She was deeply content.

They were truly a family at last, she felt. Not only were they a "mother" and "father" now, but the filial ties were further deepened by the marriage of one of the Emperor's daughters, a comely fourteen-year-old princess, to An Lu-shan's younger son, An Ching-tsung, who had come down from the north with his father this last time. Perhaps in a year or two there would be a child from that union, and An Lu-shan and the Emperor would be bound by blood.

Thank the gods, the fates, the powers, or whatever ruled people's lives for sending An Lu-shan, she thought, closing her eyes. Because of him, the Emperor was alive and he and she were together again; because of him, they were given a glimpse of what their folly could have been without having to actually suffer it. How close they had come. Instead of the two of us lying here in this tent, with the sweet, glorious perfumed air blowing all around us, and our hearts light and glad, the Emperor could be lying cold, stiff, and dead in his mausoleum, and I could be tearing my hair out by the roots, a broken, bitter, ruined woman.

She held the Emperor tighter for a moment in an effort to banish the dreadful picture. She listened to the slow, steady thumping of his heart, and with this reassuring sound in her ear, prepared to sleep. She smiled to herself. Best of all was the promise he made to her last night: You are the only one, he had said; you are all I need. There will be no other women.

18

A General Stumbles

In the Selection Examinations [for high imperial offices] . . . there was a case of gross favouritism. Chang Shih, the son of Chang I, who was Vice-President of the Censorate . . . was given first place although he was known to be illiterate (*pu tu shu*). Although that caused a good deal of resentment, no one dared to say anything about it because Li Lin-fu himself was President of the Ministry of Civil Office and so responsible for the Selections.

—*Edwin Pulleyblank*

Li Lin-fu was a patient man, a tolerant man, but things had reached an impasse, and something had to be done. There was not going to be any more pounding on furniture, or books and vases hurled to the floor; he was past that sort of impotent and detrimental display of temper. Indulgence in intemperate tantrums was, he was sure, a large part of what had set his health back recently.

He had been forced to travel many hundreds of li south of Ch'ang-an, to the caves that lay deep in the huge rock formations along the Li River. His physician had recommended the treatment, saying that the air in the caves came from the center of the earth and had never before been breathed by any lungs, animal or human. For this reason, he said, it would be beneficial in driving out the deep congestion, because it was "pure" air, uncontaminated by moisture or "particles." The journey had been a long one, and Li Lin-fu had not liked traveling in the opposite direction from where he considered that his responsibilities lay. And every day since he had been here, which was more than three weeks now, he was obliged to allow himself to be carried deep, deep into the earth, to lie for most of the day in nearly complete darkness with a poultice on his chest. The only form of light allowed down into the caves were lanterns filled with glowing worms. There could be no lamplight because their smoke, the physician said, would compromise the purity of the air. Li Lin-fu had wondered if the worms breathed air themselves, but had been assured that the worms were sealed into their lamps and that the air inside was sufficient to keep them alive for days. The light they gave off was feeble at best and cast a greenish illumination for only a few inches around them—until one's eyes adjusted after an hour or so. Li Lin-fu had presently become aware of ghostly, rocky walls around him and felt that he was seeing with the eyes of an underground creature who dwelled eternally in the dark, unaware that there was a world of light above the ground.

He had expected the caves to be cold, but they were not. As one went deeper into them, one found the walls becoming warm to the touch. Lying in the dark, scarcely moving, for endless hours, Li Lin-fu began to fancy that he could hear the heartbeat of the earth deep in the rock around him. The monotony and isolation had got to him quickly, and after the first two days he had sent for musicians, who followed his litter down into the darkness and played for him. They could not be close to him, but had to remain about one hundred paces up the tunnel he had traveled down so as not to put "particles" from their own bodies into the "pure" air breathed by Li Lin-fu. The last hundred paces he had to walk alone, unassisted, to the bed set up for him by servants who breathed only once every sixty heartbeats and then exhaled their breath into bottles.

The musicians were playing now, a tune he recognized as having been written about springtime and greenery and birds on the wing and all of that. He was enjoying the incongruity of listening to this musical image while lying in a dark cave. Bird songs bounced around the walls of dark stone.

He blamed Yang Kuo-chung, the lieutenant chief minister, for this most recent steep decline his health had taken. He had had to expend far too much precious energy in disciplining the Censorate officials, energy that he could scarcely afford to waste, and which would have been far better spent on the vital business of seeing to the defense of the empire. He sighed in the near total darkness. There was always someone eager to waste his time and strength. Not long after the "farewell party" for the eunuchs, the unforgettable "Flowers of Hainan Banquet," he had awakened from his sleep with a coughing spell that had left him dizzy, shaking, and unable to catch his breath for many agonizing minutes. Up until then, the sickness had at least left him alone while he slept; now it was attacking and ripping him from his dreams, robbing him of his rest.

That was when the physician had told him about the caves. Dubious, the chief minister had at first rejected the idea as a waste of precious time and effort. For the better part of a year he had held out, conserving his energy and doubling the regular treatments, enduring a new and ever more nauseating array of noxious substances held under his nose by the anxious physician. But one night he awoke from a nightmare with fire in his lungs. He coughed until he thought his chest would split open, and brought up blood—dark red blood that glistened on the white of his silk handkerchief, looking at him like an eye.

He had called for the physician, who examined the discharge, shaking his head and muttering. The disease, he said to Li Lin-fu ominously, has advanced to the next stage. Drastic measures must be taken. The caves, Your Excellency. I am aware of your reluctance to go, but I feel that they are your only hope now. And he had gone on to explain again in detail the purported curative powers of going underground in the dark for weeks on end. He had discoursed eloquently and convincingly about caverns winding their tortuous way up from the very core of the earth, carrying air of such purity that its life-giving properties were concentrated to approximately thirty to forty times that of the air above. Indeed, by the time the physician had finished, it seemed to Li Lin-fu that the air around him, that he had been breathing all of his life, was stale, overused, depleted, and swarming with contamination and filth, having been in and out of the bodies of every sort of creature, clean or foul, from human beings to frogs. It was a singularly unappetizing thought—particularly the idea of human beings. He thought of the fly-encrusted beggars he often saw on the streets, breathing through mouths black and yellow with decaying teeth, contributing their unwholesome effluvium to the air—*his* air —that he, Li Lin-fu, must breathe. Though he had no wish to travel and resented mightily the loss of time and the distraction from his work, he decided that he would go to the caves.

He had ridden in a closed carriage for the entire distance, trying to move as little as possible; movement brought fatigue and sometimes the dreaded deep tickle that warned him that another bout was gathering strength inside him. He would do nearly anything to avoid the coughing; it made him feel that he was tearing himself to pieces inside. His body, once wiry, sturdy, and dependable, seemed now to be a frail thing made of bird bones and paper. But it was all he had. And there was still so much work to be done. So much work.

After several weeks in the caves, he allowed himself to feel a very cautious hope. He had not coughed for at least ten days and, now that he was accustomed to the strange environment, was beginning to find the soothing isolation almost pleasant. For one thing, he had discovered that the darkness and enforced lack of activity allowed him to concentrate his thoughts in a very effective way. He found that he could create clear, concise pictures in his mind of any given situation or problem, and the solutions would follow naturally, easily, logically, the false pictures quickly dropping away, leaving only what was true, practical, and feasible.

When he had received the news about An Lu-shan's promotion, he felt, at first, the familiar anger which in earlier days might have led to an outburst. But the calm, dark solidity of the rock he had been dwelling in for weeks had seemed to become part of him, and he was able to think things through without taxing his strength or experiencing the urge to destroy inanimate objects. He lay in the greenish darkness now, the music drifting down the tunnel to him, and thought about this latest outrage, this new affront to himself and all the careful work he had done.

The Emperor had not consulted him when he promoted the barbarian to the military governorships of Fanyang and Hotung. This was the second time recently that Minghuang had put someone in a vitally important position without asking the chief minister's advice. The Emperor was, he knew, rewarding An Lu-shan for saving his life; the incident of the box of spiders and the Emperor's subsequent gratitude had been reported to Li Lin-fu within days of its occurrence.

The first thing the chief minister had done was to dispatch instructions that his agents should trace the box of spiders to its source. The perpetrators were to be executed immediately, and word was to be put out through the various court networks that Li Lin-fu was aware of all opposition to the Emperor, which was tantamount to opposition to himself. The word would be this: harm a hair on the Emperor's head or the head of any member of his family, and you will answer to Li Lin-fu.

That the box of spiders got into the Emperor's hands at all was a grave oversight that would not have happened had he, Li Lin-fu, not been far away, lying in a dark cave resembling a tomb; he would not have been in this "tomb" had he not sapped his strength tending to the matter of the Censorate eunuchs and the upstart Yang Kuo-chung, foolishly put into important offices by the Emperor.

Li Lin-fu imagined that there were those who credited *him* with the attempt on the Emperor's life. He had to admit that a box of deadly spiders was almost worthy of him—though had it been his invention, his plan, he would have seen to it that the Emperor was quite alone at the moment when he received it and opened it. There would have been no foolish errors resulting in failure and the further glorification of An Lu-shan.

But it had never been his plan to do away with the Emperor. Irritated as he was with him, he did not want him dead. Aside from the fact that he bore him a certain filial fondness, Li Lin-fu found the tacit mutual arrangement between the two of them to be quite satisfactory: that he, Li Lin-fu would carry the serious work of governing while the Son of Heaven occupied the public, ceremonial position of Emperor, satisfying the appetite of the people for an object of worship and glory. No doubt whoever it was who had wanted the Emperor dead was fully aware of this special relationship; Li Lin-fu was certain that the attempt to eliminate Minghuang was an attempt to eliminate himself.

He doubted that Minghuang knew the difference anymore between ceremony and shrewd government; giving key positions to the playboy Yang Kuo-chung and then promoting An Lu-shan proved it. To the Emperor, it was all just a grand and glorious game, and jobs like lieutenant chief minister or military governor were fancy baubles to be frivolously bestowed on favorites without a thought as to whether the recipient was any more suited for the job than, say, a favored concubine or a horse. All of this not only endangered Li Lin-fu's careful work and planning, but added to his already considerable burden; it was to him, naturally, that the task fell of disciplining the recipients of these "honors," letting them know that they were not to think of themselves as unduly important or influential. His work with Yang Kuo-chung and the Censorate officials had been, he felt, satisfactory. In the year since the banquet, there had been very little Censorate activity of any consequence; they had wisely confined themselves to routine reports, refraining from too much inquisitiveness. And Li Lin-fu was pleased that during that year, there had been no face-to-face meeting between the chief minister and his assistant. He smiled. Yang Kuo-chung has never seen my face, he thought, though I, of course, have seen his. And the lieutenant chief minister had not interfered with Li Lin-fu's decisions concerning military movements and expenditures in the north; when An Lu-shan had marched into Ch'ang-an with eight thousand captured Khitan warriors, there had been nothing more than a short memorial from Yang Kuo-chung to Li Lin-fu, questioning the necessity for such a policy of aggression and expressing concern for the expense. Li Lin-fu had not answered.

Yes, An Lu-shan had done well. Very well. He had kept the first part of the bargain he and Li Lin-fu had struck concerning the ten-year program of methodical expansion of the northern borders. For delivering the eight thousand warriors, An Lu-shan would receive further requisitions of men and supplies; with the next eight thousand warriors delivered, representing so many li of Khitan territory conquered, he would receive more men and supplies, and so on. A simple system of incentive and reward. It was plain that An Lu-shan was made for the job; the problem that presented itself now was maintaining the barbarian's appreciation of how the job came to be his in the first place.

His frolicking with the court gentry had irritated Li Lin-fu, but seemed harmless enough. But things had gone far beyond that. Much too far beyond that. The Emperor now owed his life to the barbarian and had taken the drastic step of making him a member of his family, both through the grotesque "adoption"—Li Lin-fu shuddered to contemplate the spectacle—and through the marriage of An Lu-shan's younger son to one of the Emperor's countless daughters.

These things were extreme, absurd, preposterous; but Li Lin-fu could have tolerated it all were it not for one further development: the promotion. That was the final blow. The Emperor had no business giving the military governorship of Hotung to An Lu-shan, for the simple reason that the job was already taken—by Li Lin-fu himself. He had held the position *in absentia* for years, to his own and everybody else's satisfaction. And there was one more aspect to it that made his blood boil and stirred his resentment: it was in Hotung that the great Silk Road crossed the border into China; the unofficial custom among the traders entering there was to make generous tribute offerings to the military governor. For years, Li Lin-fu had had his choice of the finest rare and exotic goods brought in from the west. The thought of the fat, hairy hands of An Lu-shan picking over treasures that rightfully belonged to Li Lin-fu . . . he felt the familiar anger rising, and pushed it back. He shut his eyes and breathed deeply the pure air from the center of the earth. No more of that, he told himself. You cannot afford it. Instead, you will direct your energy toward teaching the Fat One a good lesson. Remind him, as only you are capable of doing, that his importance is limited to his ability to serve the empire—which means serving me, Li Lin-fu—and that were it not for me, he would not have that opportunity at all. And certainly, he would never have had the opportunity to cavort with the Yang females, eat the Emperor's food and drink his wine, put his paws on the Emperor's harem women, or prance about in silly costumes to the titters of the court effete. Military governor of Fanyang and Hotung, indeed.

It had been a good long time since An Lu-shan had been in the physical presence of Li Lin-fu. Too long, now that he thought of it. It was no wonder that An Lu-shan had grown independent. Gazing upon Li Lin-fu's face was something that always had a salutary effect on the barbarian's sense of priorities. He remembered the rivers of sweat rolling off An Lu-shan's brow, the barely controlled tremor in his limbs, the whites of his small eyes. Perhaps it is time for us to meet again, thought Li Lin-fu.

As usual, no sooner had he decided that action needed to be taken than an idea began to form. The wasting illness may have turned his lungs into paper, but his mind still functioned like the greased gears of one of his own machines.

He had remembered something. Something he hadn't thought of for a long time: the cartographer's *bao-tse*. He recalled the mysterious premonitory instinct that had prompted him to purchase these bits of flesh after they had been severed from their owner, the unfortunate man who provided the map to An Lu-shan at the time of the barbarian's fateful and famous river crossing. And they had lain, carefully wrapped and stored, in a locked chest in Li Lin-fu's house for all these years. Waiting. He had always known that he had obtained them for a purpose; on three or four occasions over the years he had actually taken them out and looked at them, wondering what that purpose could be. Shriveled scraps of leather, pathetic remnants of a man's honor and virility. At last, that purpose had revealed itself. Li Lin-fu shook his head and laughed softly. "You are a devil," he said out loud in the dark.

There would be, naturally, a bit of risk to himself. Perhaps a bit more this time than at other times. The key to success lay in his ability to predict the behavior of the major players in the little drama he was composing in his mind. He felt confident that he knew An Lu-shan well enough. But what about the officials in the Ministry of Examinations and Civil Appointments? Surely they were aware of Li Lin-fu's displeasure with the Censorate and his subsequent disciplinary action. Surely they knew better than to interfere with anything that had the name of Li Lin-fu even remotely connected with it. Surely they were wise men who wished only to keep their positions and whatever they had between their legs and to go home in the evenings to their families and sit down to a good meal with minds unclouded by dread. He thought about it. Yes, he decided. Surely that is the sort of men they are.

And what sort of man was An Lu-shan? Li Lin-fu laid it all out very carefully in his mind. A man enjoying his new prestige. A man eager to prove himself important. Eager enough to ignore the first tenet of discreet gentlemanliness—minding one's own business and allowing others to mind theirs—and run to the Emperor with a bit of news that might serve to advance his prestige even further? Li Lin-fu smiled again. Definitely that sort of man.

The music had stopped. The springtime piece was finished. Li Lin-fu could hear the musicians' voices softly conferring over what they would play next. The musicians could never know how appropriate their last choice had been. It so happened that the Chin-shih examinations were a springtime event, when the city was thronged with hopeful applicants trying to win positions in government and civil service. They choked the streets, teahouses, and wine-shops, just as the winners among them would eventually choke the offices of government as they took their places in the vast, lumbering bureaucracy that was growing larger year by year. The Chin-shih examinations meant the difference between success in life and total disgrace for most of the young men who came to try their hands. Most had to rely purely on their knowledge of history, government, and literature; others, not so well equipped, found other ways. Cheating was difficult and very risky, but it did, of course, happen. And it was along these lines that his idea, his glorious idea which would serve to discipline An Lu-shan, bloomed like a flower in spring.

Spring! There it was again. He thought about the curious nature of the human mind. Had he got his idea from the music and the subtle associations it carried? Quite possibly. The music started again. This time it was a song about the joys of an old man rediscovering love late in life. At first Li Lin-fu thought of the Emperor, but then a stronger picture took over: that of himself renewed, rejuvenated. He shifted comfortably on his couch and contemplated happily the details he would have to attend to in implementing his plan, part of which entailed his temporary absence from Ch'ang-an. Well, that was fine. He would stay right where he was and breathe pure air from the center of the earth for just a while longer.

: :

"How our baby has grown, Father," said the Precious Consort fondly to the Emperor as An Lu-shan entered the elegant little sitting room where the three of them were to dine that evening. An Lu-shan bowed deeply, then kneeled and took the consort's hand.

"But I am full of sorrow, Mother," he said, resting his head on her lap. The Emperor and the consort smiled at each other; they could see that An Lu-shan was in fine form this evening.

"And why is my little Lu-erh full of sorrow?" asked the consort solicitously, stroking his bristly head. The hair was growing back quickly, thick and black, but with touches of gray she had not noticed when his hair was profuse.

"It is nothing," he replied, raising his head. "Nothing at all. You should not even have to think about it."

"Tell me," she coaxed. He shrugged and hid his face in her lap again.

"It is only the sorrow a baby feels," he said, his voice muffled in the silk of her gown, "when he is no longer allowed to drink at his mother's breast."

She shoved him away playfully, but hard. "I might have known," she said, laughing. "You and your 'mother's milk.' Didn't you get any when you were an infant?"

"I did," he said, rising to his feet. "But not enough. I was taken from my mother's breast before I was ready to relinquish it."

"Would you ever have relinquished it?" asked the Emperor as An Lu-shan made himself comfortable on the cushions. "Might you still be at the breast today if you could be?"

An Lu-shan looked surprised at the question. "Wouldn't you? Wouldn't everybody?"

"Please, An Lu-shan," said the Precious Consort. "Have some consideration for the ladies. Forty years is a long time."

"An Lu-shan," said the Emperor thoughtfully, "if you are truly thirsty for this drink, I could see to it that you get some. It is not exactly . . . unobtainable," he added with a smile.

An Lu-shan looked at the Emperor with astonished pleasure. "Do you mean it?"

"I should hope that I can do at least that." The Emperor shrugged. "What would it mean to be an emperor if I couldn't get you some mother's milk to drink?"

"From the source?" asked An Lu-shan with a lascivious smile.

"If not from the source, then at least still warm," the Emperor answered.

"And he calls himself an emperor!" said An Lu-shan to the consort.

"All right, then," said the Emperor, laughing. "I promise that you shall have it from the source, my spoiled little princeling. It is not enough that we heap honors and privileges on him. He must have mother's milk as well. What would the soldiers serving under you in the north think if they found out that their grand and glorious leader, their commander, the military governor of the entire north, nurses at the breast?"

"They would be jealous," said An Lu-shan, taking a tiny roasted bird from a tray carried by a servant before it was even put onto the table. "They would all want some, too," he added, speaking through a mouthful of meat.

"Tell him about the additional honor and privilege that has been bestowed on him," said the consort.

"Oh, yes," said the Emperor. "You are now, in addition to everything else, the Vigilant Overseer of Truth and Honesty for this year's Triennial Examinations."

"Triennial what?" asked An Lu-shan, looking up from his food.

"Examinations, An Lu-shan. Surely you have noticed the unusual number of scholarly-looking young gentlemen on the streets of the city this spring. Drinking and arguing in the wineshops. Pontificating in the public gardens."

An Lu-shan chewed and looked thoughtful for a moment before he answered.

"I have seen them," he said. "But I thought they were next year's crop of eunuchs, come to the city looking for surgeons."

"An Lu-shan, you are incorrigible," the Emperor replied. "No. They are here to prove their proficiency at everything from history to philosophy to composition to calligraphy. The tests are the entire world to them. Life and death. Disgrace or success. Some come back in three years to try again if they fail; others simply kill themselves. A passing grade becomes the most important thing in each candidate's universe. Cheating is difficult—but they do, on occasion, find a way."

"And I am supposed to stop them?" An Lu-shan asked, puzzled.

"A better way to put it," said the Emperor, "would be to say that the office of the board of civil office under the auspices of the Ministry of Examinations and Civil Appointments wishes to honor you by evoking your name as an example, an incentive, and a reminder to the candidates to not even think about succumbing to temptation."

"A wonderful honor, when you consider that I neither read nor write," said An Lu-shan.

"The members of the ministry know that," the Emperor said. "I suppose that it is their way of bestowing a sort of honorary literacy on you. In any case, it is most definitely meant as a tribute. I received the request yesterday. They asked that I confer the title on you myself, which I am now doing. Congratulations."

"Well, then, I accept," An Lu-shan said with a shrug. "If using my name scares some silk-trousers out of his plan to cheat, then it will be well worth it. Tell them that anyone caught being dishonest will have to march to the northern provinces with me to fight the Khitan. And they will be forced to drink horse urine along the way to build up their manhood. That should do it!" he said, pouring a cup of wine each for himself, the Emperor, and Precious Consort. "And I sincerely hope they catch someone at it," he added. "Nothing would give me greater pleasure than disciplining some smart dandy."

"I will tell them," said the Emperor, laughing.

"An Lu-shan," said the Precious Consort coyly, "your Imperial Father and I have been wondering about the strange wanton woman who has been compromising our baby's virtue. Has she been back to see you?"

An Lu-shan felt his face flush pink. She had, in fact, visited him that morning, after a long absence during which he had given up hope that he would ever see her again. She had come at dawn and inflicted such excruciating pleasure on him that he thought he might die from it. And when she put her mouth on his, he had thought that he tasted blood. He didn't want to tell the Emperor and the consort about that; he was, he realized, reluctant to discuss her at all. He felt strangely secretive about the woman's visits, as if talking about her caused her to stay away longer. But his red face, he knew, was telling the whole story. He smiled at the consort.

"Your little baby is perfectly happy, Mother; don't worry."

"And what about her hair? Does she still not comb it?" The consort leaned forward as she spoke. "Has she talked at all?"

Damn. This was going to be difficult. He could see that the consort's curiosity was going to be hard to satisfy.

"How motherly of you," he said, "to worry so about me."

"An Lu-shan, I want to know," the consort persisted. "Has she spoken to you at all? Ever?"

"Not in words," he said after a moment.

The consort looked at the Emperor. "Think of it," she said. "There is a wild woman at the hot springs. She doesn't talk. She doesn't comb her hair. She sleeps outside, in the woods, curled up like an animal. Who could she be?" she asked the Emperor, then looked at An Lu-shan. "And she comes and makes love to this one here. And he's not telling us everything," she added, giving him a penetrating look.

"And why should he?" said the Emperor. "He doesn't have to talk about it if he doesn't want to. Ignore her questions, An Lu-shan, unless you want to end up revealing everything, because she *will* get it out of you, I promise."

"Maybe she'll take you to her den, An Lu-shan," the consort said. "You will sleep with her on her nest of branches and hair. And there will be bones all over the floor."

Bones all over the floor. An Lu-shan saw the woman again in his mind, sitting over the carcass of the gazelle. The consort's jokes were uncomfortably close to the truth.

"I should correct myself. She did speak to me once," he lied. He looked significantly at the consort, then the Emperor. "She told me that if I ever try to follow her or to find out who she is, or if I talk about her too much to anyone, that she will know, and she would stop coming to me. So you see"—he gestured supplicatingly—"I am bound."

The consort looked at him for a moment, then smiled. "All right," she said. "You have won. We will not talk about her anymore. But I will say one more thing." She leaned close to An Lu-shan and spoke in a playfully ominous, low voice. "The next time she comes to you, ask her if her name is Li Shan Lao Ma."

This was the third time An Lu-shan had heard that name. The first person to speak it was General Feng, when An Lu-shan told him about the leopard at the hot springs and the woman eating the flesh of the gazelle. Since the morning he recognized his mystery lover as that same woman, he had, of course, relived that strange experience a thousand times in his mind in great detail: the shock of finding himself looking into the cold yellow eyes of the big cat, the way it leapt to the top of the wall with such fluid power; but most of all, the woman smiling at him with blood on her teeth. But he had forgotten Feng's joke about the woman being this Li Shan Lao Ma.

And the second time the name was spoken to him was when he stood in the grassy park that day with the Yang sisters, demonstrating his screaming arrows. It was the Lady of Kuo who had said it: it sounds as if you have caught a glimpse of Li Shan Lao Ma. Don't let any young women without credentials seduce you at the hot springs . . . he had not thought of those words at all since she had spoken them. And now the consort had evoked the name again.

"I don't care who she is or what her name is," he said at last. "Just so she keeps coming."

"It is that good, eh, An Lu-shan?" asked the Emperor.

An Lu-shan did not answer in words, but picked up his cup, looked into it, then raised his eyes to the Emperor's and looked at him steadily before dropping eyes again. He was aware that his uncharacteristic reticence was only serving to increase their curiosity; a better way to dissemble would be, he knew, to brag and carry on in his usual manner. But he could not help himself. He realized now that he believed his own words of a moment ago, hastily contrived for the purpose of throwing the consort off the trail: that if he talked about the mystery woman, she would know, and he would never see her again. He knew now, was absolutely certain, that those words were true. And a terrible thought gripped him now: perhaps he had already gone too far, said too much. Maybe he would never see her again.

But the Emperor, ever gracious, seemed cognizant of An Lu-shan's discomfort and abruptly changed the subject.

"You will be happy to know, An Lu-shan, that I have received a new shipment of glazed tiles from the kilns at Kaolin. Tomorrow, you and I can inspect them, though I have already looked at the top layer in the crate, and I can assure you, they are superb. I am very happy with the progress of my restoration work. Quite possibly, we will be ready by spring for the revival of an historic festival that the consort and I have been planning for some time. But we cannot do it without you!"

"Without me?" said An Lu-shan, surprised.

"Yes. We need you to play the role of Kao Mei. He was a god of fertility."

An Lu-shan smiled broadly at this, then threw his head back and laughed. "I will be only too happy," he said.

They all laughed then, the serious mood dispelled. They spent the rest of the evening talking and planning happily for the projected event. He listened as the consort spoke of re-creating a golden age, bringing back a time when life was a dream of magic, beauty, fulfillment, and high symbolism. He watched the Emperor watching the consort, and saw the undisguised love and admiration in his eyes. He drank, and thought of his own lover.

He had always known that Ch'ang-an was a woman, but he had thought that she would be all rustling, perfumed silk like Purple Gown. Like the Lady of Kuo; like the consort. Instead, she smelled of earth and moss, growled like an animal, and climbed through his window in the night. And he didn't even know her name. Or did he?

His attention wandered in and out of focus as the evening wore on. He kept thinking of that strange name: Li Shan Lao Ma. Who was she? How could he find out without asking the Emperor, the consort, or the sisters?

He took another drink. Well, old fellow, he told himself, it looks as though you are being reminded once again that life is a mystery. He poured himself more wine. He had decided a while ago that he was going to get very, very drunk tonight.

:: :

The candidate's head rested on a small cleared space on the desk which took up the entire width of the examination stall. He had drooled in his sleep, causing a little pool of spit to form next to his slightly open mouth. Even asleep, he was aware that soon he would have to wake, that he could allow himself only so much time and could not give himself up completely. Though bright daylight showed through the cracks around the door, it may as well have been night inside. An oil lamp burned over the desk; brushes, paper, booklets, and ink were arranged to one side of the sleeper's head. A crockery jar nearly filled with urine stood in a corner of the stall.

A long, loud wail jerked him awake. He sat disoriented and terrified for a moment, the reverberation hanging in the air around him. The cry had seemed to be in the tiny room with him; he thought it was his. But the cry came again, to his relief, from somewhere outside the stall, not from his own throat. Sobs and unintelligible speech followed. Swift footsteps passed his own door, and he heard another door being opened. The sobbing, out in the open air now, became momentarily louder, but faded as the perpetrator of the disturbance was hauled away. Peace was restored.

Inside the stall, the young man experimented. He took a deep lungful of air as if he were about to scream out. That is all I need to do, he thought, and I will find myself out in the sunshine again, and in a teahouse within an hour. He held his breath, then let it out gently. Not I. He picked up his writing brush. With his sleeve he carefully wiped up the little puddle of drool. Others may crack under the pressure, give it up, cry like children, and plunge themselves into ignominy. He addressed himself to his work. Not I.

The hairs of the smaller writing brush were splitting at the tip. The extra hairs were confusing the lines of his radicals as he wrote. The small characters of the margin notes would be imperfect. He would have to ring for the attendant to bring a new brush; it would also be an excuse to catch a glimpse of the blue sky. The blue sky, he thought, that waits for me out there, and which will be that much sweeter after my several days' imprisonment. The sky under which I will live the rest of my life, if I do well here, as a man of rank and position.

He glanced at the candle. He had timed himself well with its markings; his pace was good. He had polished the poetry sections in perfect regulated meter: first, four characters to a line; then five; then seven with caesura and parallel couplets. He decided that he would save the request for the brush for later; his sleep had refreshed him. By carefully allowing himself short intervals of rest, he had avoided the mental fatigue he had been warned about. He would complete another section of the exam, with the bit of sky being his reward after. He turned to the essay question he'd chosen:

I. In terse, ancient prose style, cite major contributions of the Han Lin Academy of Letters to the literary thought of the nation.

IV. Argue the new laws regarding primogeniture and the land inheritance provisions from the point of view of classical thinkers Mencius, Hsun-tzu, Mo-tzu, and Han Fei-tzu, paying particularly close attention to the essential nature of man as good or evil. For purposes of consistency, cite all classical quotes from the Stone Tablet Recensions only.

He felt especially confident about question IV. When he was a child, his uncle was with the office of the census and had spoken intelligently about the new land laws. The boy had always listened attentively; now it would pay off. He would impress the Selection Board's exam readers without benefit of a father in high office. His own father was only a minor district magistrate.

Some, he knew, found ways to cheat. There were bribes, and there were readers who were not immune to the effect of certain family names. There had been talk of reform in the exam procedures, where each candidate's papers would be anonymous to the readers, perhaps even copied so as to disguise an individual's brushstrokes. But these reforms were still just talk, and it still happened that occasional undeserving candidates obtained good grades and a resultant position. But it was not the rule. Most, like himself, had only the brilliance of their words, the cogency of their thought, and their thorough knowledge of the classics to see them through.

He quickly wrote the major provisions of the new primogeniture laws in the margins. He inscribed the cardinal numbers inches apart in the clear, precise strokes of his best formal calligraphy—a good hand, sure and clear, if not quite as artistic as some. Light seeped in as the afternoon sun aligned itself with the small spaces beneath the eaves. The western row of four hundred exam stalls was bathed in the late afternoon sunlight of the candidates' second day of confinement. One more day to go.

He had come to Ch'ang-an with a friend from Ching Chou prefect several weeks before. The two had high hopes of doing well on the exams and joining the ranks of the nearly eighteen thousand upper-grade officials who made up the T'ang bureaucracy. Barring admission to the upper ranks, there would be, perhaps, places for them among the tens of thousands of minor officials. He and his friend had traveled to the capital together, joining the hundreds and hundreds of other candidates who carried with them the hopes of their sponsors; some were sent by their families, some by entire villages. It was a great adventure for the young men. Serious and fraught with responsibility though their purpose was, the capital city in springtime offered itself to them like a jewel.

Ch'ang-an was in bloom. Sweet air swept over the cool waters of the wide Wei. The fertile elbow of the river where the city lay was buoyant with hazy green. It had been a long, dreary winter of paralysis and confinement, but the snow and ice were finally gone and the avenues flowed freely as the inhabitants went about their business of commerce or pleasure. It was the ninth year of the compassionate Brilliant Emperor's Tien Pao reign period, and Ch'ang-an seemed now to be the material realization of that name. Here was the center of humane earthly government, the locus of Heaven's divine ruler.

Once every three years the candidates turned out, ready to submit themselves to three days of testing designed not only to measure a man's knowledge, literacy, and creativity, but his physical and mental endurance as well. Refuge was the reward they sought—refuge in the celestial ranks of the ordered kingdom of officialdom. These were the highest levels of national exams—the Imperial Palace Triennials.

Young men roamed the streets, their clothing either in or out of fashion depending on the wealth of their families and their relative proximity to the opulent centers of fad and eccentricity. Some were boys in their early twenties whose brilliance merited an early chance to qualify for civil office; others were men, older by many years, their faces slightly weary, back for another try. The older men returned each time hoping to correct the mistakes that had brought them back: the gaps in their education, the lack in language or style.

The young man in the stall and his friend had spent their two weeks in the city prior to being locked in their stalls cultivating certain illustrious acquaintances at court of the friend's father—high officials, scholars, men of letters whose writings were influential and widely read. Ostensibly, the youths went to them for instruction. But there was another aspect to the visits, tacitly understood by all: it was a way of gathering support. There was no harm in telling the world of rank that you had arrived, that you had made candidacy, and that you were to be reckoned with after you had passed. His friend had been better at this than he had, being naturally more audacious as well as born to the game.

In teahouses and restaurants around the city the constant topic of conversation was the exams and the questions one might be asked. Likely subjects were discoursed upon, dissected, shouted about. It was important to expose oneself to these discussions, but it was possible also to become confused by the disparity of opinion. One man's thoughts on water conservancy problems of the Wei River might sound sensible and incisive, until someone else rose to his feet to challenge him. Perhaps the challenger's knowledge of locks and levies on the river and their use in barge traffic for the crucial grain supply to Ch'ang-an superseded the other's. The young man had listened carefully to hundreds of conversations on social and political administration, the maintenance of post roads, imperial grants for public works versus tax revenue, state monopolies versus private initiative, problems of military finance and execution in the troubled northern provinces, and colonial grants. And always the conversations spilled over into the philosophical, the ethical, and the metaphysical, for one was expected to formulate one's answers to these practical questions of commerce and government out of a thorough knowledge of the mind and soul of mankind. One was also required in the bargain to be a poet and calligrapher. It was not enough to simply know the answers: One's artistry in expression was also measured.

Though the discussions were usually polite, with participants according one another respect and not raising their voices unduly, there were times when decorum did break down. The young man and his friend had got into a debate in a teahouse with an older fellow; the subject in question was the taxation of the common people. They had argued, the older man taking the position that the common people had the most to gain from taxation, because taxation allowed public works. The young men maintained that the wealthy should be taxed more heavily; it caused less difficulty in their lives. The wine flowed freely, and, at a certain point in the discussion, the young man had felt the connection between his brain and tongue suddenly smooth out and had astonished himself with his own eloquence.

The older man had listened, looking, it seemed to the young man, attentive and appreciative, right up to the moment when he overturned the table onto the two candidates, soaking them with sticky wine. Though the young man's head had throbbed the next day, his own words still sounded, in retrospect, like the truth.

Inside the stall, the candidate stood up to stretch. His legs felt like blocks of wood. He urinated, filling his jar to the brim. He picked up the water bottle sitting on the deck and drank deeply, splashing some onto his face and neck. It was time to ask for the brush. He pulled the string that rang a bell to summon the attendant. He sat, thinking about what he would write next, until the door opened. The light from the outside hurt his eyes for a moment; the air that rushed in was sweet and fresh. Time for all of that later, he thought. He signaled to the attendant, pointing to the crockery jar about to overflow and handing him the worn brush. The attendant had looked apprehensive when he opened the door; I can imagine, the young man thought, that we must begin looking like crazed animals in cages after the second day. He smiled at the man to reassure him that he was not in any particular anguish, that he was not about to leap for his throat, or cry or scream.

After the attendant had gone and he was in his solitude again, he contemplated the many ways to fail. There was the usual way, which was to simply not do fine enough work. But some feared the irony of doing too well;

it was said that occasionally, the richness of one's poetry and prose, the brilliance of one's metaphors and allusions drawing on history and the classics, or the antithetical polish of one's syntax aroused jealousy rather than admiration on the part of a reader. Instead of an appointment or the Academy of Talents being one's destination in such a case, it was a ride back to one's village in a donkey cart, a ride to oblivion and ignominy for some. There were suicides, too. Some couldn't face returning to their families or, worse, the entire villages who had sponsored them with hopes of betterment for everyone. Some were dogged, returning time after time to face the ordeal. And of course, there were the ones who broke, who begged to be let out of the stalls halfway through.

He personally felt that he had some degree of immunity to that. He resembled his grandfather in temperament as well as appearance, so the family said. His grandfather had told him a story years ago which, if true, would indicate that the old man's descendants were well equipped for the test of courage and confinement. As Grandfather told the story, he had, as a youth, hidden in the house of a neighbor to spy on the neighbor's pretty daughters. He had secreted himself in a closet, only to find himself trapped there amidst the sweet smells of sachets and perfumed silks. It happened that the eldest daughter was to be married, and the nuptial preparations went on for two days. Grandfather had crouched in the dark closet for a full day and a night until his knees burned, looking out from the darkness through a narrow slit between the shutters until the beauty was finally sent on her journey to the house of her new husband's family, unaware of her rapt admirer holding his breath, and his bladder as well, a few feet away from her in the closet. And he remained, he said, for another hour or two until he was sure he could safely slip away.

With the example of Grandfather's youthful endurance before him, he knew he could last through the three days. He had written, he guessed, nearly three thousand characters. He could write many more, and would do so until there was nothing left to write. His work would be held up as exemplary. Some, he knew, would break and run away, like the poor devil who had awakened him from his nap; others would find a way to cheat. But *he* would turn in perfect work.

: :

He had said too much. He was sure of it. He had opened his big mouth, and talked about her, and she knew it. Why had he ever said anything at all? Why hadn't he just kept it to himself? He wanted to light the lamp, to get up and walk around, but he didn't dare. If she were approaching his window and saw a light, then she would turn and go away. There was no hope of any sleep at all tonight, but he had no choice except to lie there in his bed—restless, sweating, seething with frustration and urgent need.

He had lied, and she had heard his lie and made it the truth. She will not come if I talk about her, he had said to the Emperor. Well, he castigated himself, you've really done it, haven't you, Fool? An Lu-shan shut his eyes and tried to calm his mind, which was swirling like a muddy, debris-filled stream.

Someone had told him a long time ago that a lie, once told, once set free, would strive to form itself into truth. He had never believed it until now. He had always lied when it was necessary; lies rolled off his tongue as easily as notes from a musician's flute. He thought now, for the first time in his life, about the nature of telling a lie. He knew that the success of a lie depended on how much you believed the lie while it was being told. And he always believed his lies. What a strange thing. You believe it, but you know it's a lie.

He couldn't stand it any longer. He got up, went to the window, and leaned outside. He listened to the noises of the night at the hot springs. Frogs and a lone owl. An intermittent high whistling sound which he could not identify. The faint gurgling of water. The wind moving the great branches of tall pine trees. Nothing else. He stared into the woods, trying to force the dark, indistinct shadows to take the shape of a woman standing between the trees. She would stand right there, looking at my window. Right there. He watched a black shape near the base of a big tree, looking at it steadily until it seemed to shift and move toward him. A shock ran through him. She was there! He held his breath, his heart pounded. He stared until his eyeballs were dry, then let his breath out again gently.

He was wrong. She was not there at all. Shadows were tricking him, taunting him in his abject state of desire. The shadow he had thought was a woman moving toward him had reverted now to its amorphous shape. He was incredulous. There was nothing there, but he had seen her.

He knew what he would have to do if he was going to get any sleep. He returned to the bed and sat down heavily. He groped in the dark for his ever-present pitcher of wine, drank deeply, and lay down again.

What would he have her do if she came tonight? He began to stroke and fondle himself and tried to concentrate on images in his mind. *I'd like her to remove all her clothes and stand before me in the lamplight. I'd like her to raise her arms and turn slowly in a circle.* He felt a small stir of response and strove to keep the picture in his mind intact while he rubbed harder on his flesh. *I would lie on the bed, and order her to come to me. I would tell her to climb up onto the bed and stand over me with her legs spread apart.* At this, his "old man" reluctantly stiffened, and he fought to keep the picture intact. *She stands over me on the bed. She bends her legs slowly, slowly, lowering herself onto me. Lowering herself, slowly. She gasps with pain and pleasure at the huge size of my organ.* He clenched his teeth and worked at his flesh, but he could feel it growing obstinately soft in his hand. Damn! It was like trying to coax a thin little flame into a fire, and then the wind comes along and blows it out. He tried again, summoning the picture, screwing his eyes shut, rubbing and squeezing himself.

But it was no use. His "old man" flopped uselessly in his hand, and the picture in his mind faded into fragments. He opened his eyes. He could feel the sweat on his forehead. That cursed witch, he said to himself. She has come to possess me so thoroughly that I pace the floor at night, willing her to climb through that window. I look at shadows and see her creeping toward me. But she doesn't come. She condemns me to flailing vainly away at my own flesh, but there's no relief, no satisfaction, nothing but thinking about her until my mind is weary, disgusted, and sick.

Enough of this. He *would* sleep, and forget about the female. He seized the wine pitcher and drank the rest of its contents without stopping. He sat still for a few moments, feeling the alcohol move from his stomach out into his limbs and up into his head. Damn her. He put his head down on the pillow, closed his eyes, and lay completely still, emptying his mind. He began to drift, started awake, then drifted again. Pictures of the north moved through his mind. Barren landscapes, starry skies, the comfortable solitude of a tent, the hard ground, and the wind. Up there, he would never have to think of her at all. Never at all.

Why was he awake again and sitting up in the dark? There had been a noise. He sat tense and unmoving, but heard nothing. Just when he decided that he had dreamed it and started to put his head down again, he heard a sound that he knew was no dream.

Someone was knocking softly but insistently on his door. He was on his feet instantly. She had never used the door; for her, apparently, doors didn't even exist. But he would put nothing past her. She was completely unpredictable. He pulled the door open and peered into the darkness of the hallway.

"I have been waiting for you," he said in a low voice.

"You have been waiting for me?" answered an unfamiliar male voice, confused.

An Lu-shan started. "Who is there?" he demanded. He saw the figure step back at his abruptly different tone.

"I am only a messenger. Only a messenger. My name, my identity, everything else about me is unimportant," the man said in a none too confident voice.

"A messenger? Who from? State your business," he said gruffly.

"Are you An Lu-shan?"

"Yes, I am An Lu-shan." He had sensed immediately that the man was not armed or physically dangerous. The poorly concealed fear in his voice and the way he stood made that plain.

"You, then, are the Vigilant Overseer of Truth and Honesty, are you not?"

"The vigilant what?" An Lu-shan said irritably.

"For the Palace Triennial Examinations. The Vigilant Overseer . . . of Truth and Honesty," the man said, and waited.

An Lu-shan tried to think where he had heard that silly-sounding title before. Of course. The Emperor had conferred it on him. They had all laughed, and he had not thought of it since.

"Yes, I suppose I am," he said at last. "I suppose I am. What do you want?"

"To report a breach. A grievous insult to the empire. My conscience has driven me. I could not keep it to myself for another day."

"Go on," said An Lu-shan, interested now.

"His name is Chang Shih, Your Excellency. He has cheated. He has made a mockery of everyone else, all the others who studied until they sweated blood and who struggled to hand in honest work, real work. Who, Your Excellency, deserve the positions! Who have families with their hearts set on them!"

"He has cheated on the Triennial Exams?" An Lu-shan said authoritatively.

"That is exactly correct, Your Excellency. He never even wrote anything. But he has a father in high places."

"And how did you come by this information? Are you a student, too?"

There was only the smallest hesitation before the other answered. "Yes, I am. Armed only with my hard work. No money, no family name. I found out from his own brother. The usual way. He bragged."

"What was the cheater's name again?" asked An Lu-shan.

"Chang Shih," said the man. "And his father is Chang I. You must tell the Emperor, Your Excellency. He must know. And soon, before the awards are presented, before irreversible damage is done."

"Of course," said An Lu-shan, memorizing the two names. "Is that everything?"

"That is everything." The man sighed. "I am vastly relieved, because I know that you will not let a cheater escape justice."

"Don't worry. He will not escape," said An Lu-shan, and shut the door. He opened it again hastily, remembering something. "Tell me your name!" he called after the man.

"I told you it is of no importance," he called back, his feet picking up speed. He was practically running now.

An Lu-shan listened until the footsteps disappeared down the open hallway.

Well. Tomorrow, he would see the Emperor, and report this Chang

Shih, who sounded like a fool. It would be like giving the Emperor a little present. Probably the Emperor had forgotten all about the Vigilant Overseer business, just as he had, but it would please him to see that An Lu-shan could carry out any job given to him, no matter how trivial, no matter what it was. It would be another small feather in An Lu-shan's cap.

Not that he gave a damn about some fool's chosen method of getting himself a job and an award, he thought, stumbling back toward the bed. Give him ten awards. Make him grand chancellor of the universe, for all I care. He fell heavily onto the bed.

Damn. He was thoroughly, hopelessly awake again. He sighed, exasperated, as his hand moved of its own volition down to his groin to begin again its weary coaxing of his unresponsive flesh. Damn her, he said to himself for the thousandth time that night, while he shut his eyes and summoned once more the image of her, naked, turning slowly before him in the lamplight.

Damn her.

::

Blank sheets of paper, it seemed, had procured for one Chang Shih first place in the Imperial Palace Triennial Examinations. The paper was magnificent, the finest of Suchow's commercial handiwork—the fibers beautifully and delicately interwoven, and so translucent that shadows of the examiner's fingers showed through its silken surface, unsullied by any traces of ink. It was on just such paper as this, the textured one-dimensional plane ready to receive the brush, that a bureaucracy was built. Edicts, promulgations, litigations, assessments, proclamations, lists and inventories, census accounts, drafts, notices, provisions, service appointments, discharges, sinecures, suggestions, remissions, records, promotions, rebuttals, and, finally, literature: all found reality on paper. And this paper was simply beautiful. The examiner turned one of the sheets over slowly, the lambent light of the lamp diffusing through it.

An order had come down from the Emperor. The vice president and the secretary of the Ministry of Civil Appointments were to conduct an investigation; the newly appointed and highly unlikely Overseer of Truth and Honesty had reported to the Emperor that Chang Shih had come by his honor through other than legitimate means: he was, in short, a cheat. The world of scholarship, degrees, awards, and civil service would not seem to be areas of concern to the barbarian General An Lu-shan, but evidently he took his duties, whatever they might be, seriously. Now the two officials had before them the "work" of Chang Shih.

The vice president of the Ministry of Civil Appointments was the first to break the dismayed silence. He had been considering the possibilities, and now voiced a possible explanation, preposterous though he knew it to be.

"Have we a joke on our hands?"

The Triennial Examinations seemed an unlikely arena for the expression of humor, though one never knew. His colleague, the secretary of the Ministry of Civil Appointments, did not answer immediately, but continued to peruse a sheaf of papers in his hand.

"The records indicate that he left the exam stall on the second day," the secretary finally said. "But there is no indication of who was the first to pass on his empty exam booklet. Nor do we know how it bypassed or got through the readers, or why he was never asked to appear before the Selection Board of this office. There are no reports on his character, oratory talents, or reasoning ability, either. Nothing."

"Is there a report from the Ta Li Shih?" asked the vice president, referring to the office in charge of investigations.

The secretary dropped a small sheaf on the desk in front of him. As his superior leafed through the pages stamped with the official seal, the secretary spoke.

"As you will see, there are serious gaps in the information. Other things are there—the names of the gatekeepers, the attendants seeing to the food, water, and lavatory needs, and the dates and times the candidates turned in their booklets. It shows who became sick and who reelected to the next triennals. Yet somehow Chang Shih's booklet continued on its way."

"Yes," said the vice president. "To be 'read' and 'graded' and given the highest *chia* honors, which the work so obviously deserves."

The secretary looked again at the name on the booklet before speaking.

"Chang Shih. Who is his father?"

"I believe his father is Chang I, a fairly high official. Let us look up his name in the *Records of the Redactor and Compiler for the Commissioner of Promotions*," the vice president suggested, getting up from his desk and approaching the west wall of the office, which had shelves from floor to ceiling solidly packed with bound sheafs. He searched for a few minutes, running his finger down the rows of inscriptions until he found the volume he was looking for. He pulled it down and carried it to his desk. He opened it and began leafing through the pages. "Here he is. Chang I . . . has been a high third-grade official for twenty-seven years . . . holds neither the Ming-ching nor Chin-shih degrees . . . It would appear that he secured his position through exercise of family privilege rather than through knowledge of letters or politics. That," he said, looking up at his colleague, "is known as choosing one's ancestors with care. The son could have followed the same path as his father, if he had chosen. There was no need for him to enter the exam stalls at all."

"What information we have on the boy," the secretary said thoughtfully, "indicates that he is, to put it bluntly, something of a dullard. Not completely illiterate; apparently he can read well enough to find his way to the brothels and drinking houses of the city. But this blank booklet we have before us is a good representation of his literary abilities and his knowledge of government. Not a well-lettered family; the boy is clearly from 'outside the current' of the literati."

"And that is putting it kindly. Though obviously, someone intended for the son of Chang I to change that tradition. The oriole indeed flies to a tall tree," said the vice president, still skimming the information on Chang I. "Why such a family would develop a sudden interest in position through scholarly excellence, even through pretense, I cannot imagine." His eyes, which had been moving along the rows of characters he was reading, stopped short. He stared, incredulous, at the entry above his fingertip. "What have we here?" he exclaimed.

The secretary hurried around to see. He looked over the vice president's shoulder and read aloud: ". . . Promoted in autumn of the ninth year of the Tien Pao reign period to the position of vice secretary of the Chancellery of the Ssu-k'ung office . . ." He paused. "That would be last autumn! But this is not an official entry. The characters are jammed into the margins. The ink is a different color . . ." He stopped when he realized what he had said, and raised his eyes from the page to the vice president's face. The two men looked at each other.

The vice president shook his head. "I had a suspicion," he said at last, "that neither the father nor the son had the nerve, cunning, or ambition to pull off such a thing."

"No," the secretary replied. "It is obvious that there is a far more audacious personality behind all this."

Both men stood silently in the small office. Dusk had turned to evening; insects flew erratically around the oil lamps. Each man knew the other was beginning to see the same idea, and neither wanted to be the first to voice it. It was common knowledge that the Ssu-k'ung office was the exclusive domain of Chief Minister Li Lin-fu.

The vice president sat down, picked up a sheaf of papers, and riffled through them absently.

"Let us think it through carefully," he said. "Hasn't An Lu-shan received other promotions recently?"

"The Emperor promoted him to the military governorships of several nothern provinces, including Hotung."

"He was not appointed by . . ."—he hesitated—"the chief minister?"

"No. I understand that the Emperor promoted him after the general saved his life," the secretary said with a shrug.

"So An Lu-shan and the Emperor are close friends."

"More than that. The general is his adopted 'son.' "

"But An Lu-shan was originally sponsored by the chief minister, was he not?" asked the vice president. "He arrived a rustic with horse sweat on his backside and grit still in his eyes, and now he is one with the Emperor and the Yangs, is adopted into the imperial family, and receives promotions without benefit of the chief minister." He shook his head sadly. "I think I understand. There is one last piece to this puzzle. If it fits, well . . ."

"I think that the same question is occurring to you and to me," said the secretary. "What we are both wondering is how An Lu-shan came to be appointed Vigilant Overseer of Truth and Honesty. The order came from the Emperor, but the wording of his memorial to us sounded as if he was responding to a request from this office that An Lu-shan be appointed. I know of no such request, do you?"

"I did not even know that there was such a thing as a Vigilant Overseer," the vice president said candidly.

His colleague looked at him, surprised. "Neither did I," he admitted. "I wasn't going to say anything, but now that you have said it . . ." He stopped. "Do you realize that we don't even have the name of the person who informed on Chang Shih?"

"Say no more," the vice president interjected, holding up his hand. "I believe I see it now. An Lu-shan is being disciplined, somehow, by the chief minister, and you and I, this office, and even the Emperor himself are unwitting participants. As for Chang Shih, well . . . whether the chief minister has any real plans for him or not we will never know. But the fellow is going to find himself with a high government position, whether he wants one or not." He sighed. "Now I know what it feels like."

"What it feels like?" the secretary asked, puzzled.

"I have been in government for twenty years. I have heard men talk about the chief minister—their fear of ever attracting his attention, or getting in his way, or being a victim of his. They always said that there was nothing one could do to prevent it, that you could mind your own business completely and keep entirely to yourself, and then one morning wake up and find that Li Lin-fu has changed your life forever. I never really believed it. I thought that by doing my job with integrity and tending to my own affairs that I would never have to worry about such things. But now . . . I know what they were saying. You and I are of no importance whatever to Li Lin-fu beyond a certain fact of which he has sure knowledge."

"I know," said the secretary glumly. "We are not going to report our findings to the Emperor."

"Do you have any wish to make out a report indicting Li Lin-fu?" the vice president asked simply.

"Do I *look* like a fool or a hero?" the secretary answered with equal simplicity, then shook his head in wonderment. "Think of it. He also knew that we would look up Chang I's name and find the entry about his 'promotion.' He sent somebody in here to tamper with official records and then purposely left it looking hasty and contrived. He didn't even try to deceive us, to cover it up! He knew he didn't have to!" He stared at the wall of books. "It was his way of giving us a message! That *he* was behind it all, and that we should behave accordingly! And he *knew* we would! He *knew* it!"

"That's what I meant," said the vice president quietly, "when I said that now I know what it feels like." He picked up a writing brush and smoothed the bristles thoughtfully to a point. The two men looked at one another. "Well, my friend," he said. "Are you fond of travel?"

"That depends entirely on who is to be my guide," the secretary replied, staring at Chang Shih's exam booklet. "This fateful turn of events does, at least, allow you and me that much choice: whose wrath do we choose to face? The Emperor's, or Li Lin-fu's?"

"Need I tell you?" the vice president replied, putting down the writing brush and picking up the exam booklet. He stood and went to one of the oil lamps on the wall. He touched the crisp parchment to the flame, then dropped it onto a brass tray; they watched Chang Shih's booklet curl up and turn black. The vice president stirred the ashes and fanned the smoke from the air with his hand. "So be it. We are agreed. We are not heroes or warriors. We will make no report."

"So be it," the secretary said.

The vice president turned resolutely toward a pile of documents on his desk and picked them up.

"We have much other business to attend to. Let us not waste any more time."

: :

On the other side of the city, at the Big Wild Goose Temple, the successful candidates celebrated. There were debates, poetry competitions, music, and most of all, drinking. They drank as much wine as they could hold, but no amount of drunkenness could match the exultance they felt. It was over. The years of preparation, the months of intensive anticipation, the doubt, the confinement, the sheer arduous work of it were over, and they were wild with triumph. In other parts of Ch'ang-an, those who had failed—whose names had not appeared on the long lists posted on a wall near the Orchid Terrace —also drank. But there was no laughing, and certainly no poetry.

In the bureaucratic city, lights burned late into the night, too. At the board of civil office the secretary and vice president busied themselves with the list of names to be sent to the Bureau of Appointments within the Ministry of Examinations and with the vast preparations to be made for the fortunate candidates, including one Chang Shih. Though these two men were not, as they themselves had put it, heroes or warriors, but men who worked indoors in a world of words and abstractions, they had courage enough. They did their work competently and thoroughly, despite the knowledge that very soon there would most likely be two vacancies in the Ministry of Civil Appointments. They worked and spoke no more of An Lu-shan, the blank booklet, or Chief Minister Li Lin-fu.

: :

An Lu-shan paced back and forth in the Lady of Kuo's garden while she sat, deep in thought, on a stone bench. In her hand was a piece of parchment with a message written on it in a concise, delicate, feminine hand.

When he had received the letter, An Lu-shan had recognized immediately the seal of Li Lin-fu's Ssu-k'ung office. And though he couldn't read a single character, the letter, when he held it in his hands, had sent instinctive needles of fear up his arms while little droplets of sweat popped out on his forehead.

There had been only one person to whom he cared to take the letter to have it read. The Emperor had been out of the question; An Lu-shan had no wish for Minghuang to know the extent of his dread of the chief minister. And he had had to wait, in an agony of suspense, for an entire night and most of the next day until he could get the Lady of Kuo alone, without the seemingly constant presence by her side of the sullen and arrogant Yang Kuo-chung. And now that he had heard the message, he felt that he knew even less than he did before.

"Read it again," he said to her.

"I will be glad to, but I suggest that you stop marching up and down and sit calmly and listen," she said, indicating the bench opposite her. He did as she told him to, sitting down heavily and sadly, and she began to read:

> "To the Grand and Glorious General, Commander for Foot and Horse of P'inglu Province, Military Governor of Fanyang, Hotung, and P'inglu Provinces, Imperial Son of the Emperor T'ang Minghuang, and Vigilant Overseer of Truth and Honesty An Lu-shan:
>
> In recognition of your outstanding service to the empire in all of your endeavors, the office of the Ssu-k'ung and Chief Minister Li Lin-fu in particular extend to you an invitation. A banquet will be held in honor of the successful candidates who passed the Palace Triennial Examinations and who are to receive appointments; the chief minister wishes to honor An Lu-shan by inviting him to attend in place of a favored protégé of the chief minister, Chang Shih, unable to attend or accept the honors due him because of an unfortunate upheaval in his family. The chief minister feels that it would be most appropriate for An Lu-shan, himself a favored 'son,' to sit in Chang Shih's chair in his stead, and begs the brave general to accept the invitation."

The Lady of Kuo finished reading and looked at An Lu-shan. He stood and began pacing again; she waited a few moments before speaking. She studied the script, the youthful feminine hand all too familiar to her.

"Unless you tell me everything, I cannot help you," she said. "To me, not knowing the details, this letter seems entirely innocuous. Yet you are pacing and sweating like a madman. What is it, An Lu-shan?"

"I turned him in," he answered.

"Turned *who* in, An Lu-shan?"

"Chang Shih. For cheating. I reported to the Emperor that he had been cheating, and turned him in."

"I don't understand. Why? How did you know? Do you know this man?"

"No, I don't know him," he said with exasperation. "I didn't even know the damned fool existed until somebody came to my door at the hot springs in the middle of the night to tell me he had cheated on the exams. I didn't know, and I certainly didn't care. Why couldn't it have stayed that way?" he asked despairingly.

"And why did this 'somebody' come to *you*?" the Lady of Kuo persisted.

An Lu-shan heaved a heavy sigh. "Because I was appointed, by the Emperor, to be the Vigilant Overseer of Truth and Honesty for the Palace Triennial Exams," he said. "And the next thing I knew, an infraction was being reported to me, so I reported it to the Emperor."

"And the cheater's name was Chang Shih."

"That is correct, madam. And my name is Fat Blundering Fool. Fat Blundering *Dead* Fool," he said, yanking a flower up by the roots and hurling it across the garden.

"And you are upset because you have received a letter from the chief minister informing you that Chang Shih was a favorite of his, but will not be receiving an award or an appointment."

"What does he mean?" An Lu-shan asked desperately. "What is he saying? He must know that it was *I* who turned the idiot in. Madam, you must help me!" he said, wheeling about and flinging his arms wide.

"Let me think for a moment, An Lu-shan," she said. "But sit down, please, and kindly desist from tearing up my garden."

An Lu-shan sat and glared into the small reflecting pool where three red-gold carp lazily wafted their fins. He had not felt this way since the chief minister invited him to play with the Pear Garden Orchestra when he had first arrived at court. He remembered the feeling well now, though he had forgotten it quite thoroughly these last few years: lost, ignorant, foolish; the feeling—infinitely infuriating—that he was being toyed with, played for a fool, manipulated. But it was far worse this time, for the feeling was compounded by deadly fear—fear that he had transgressed against Li Lin-fu himself. People paid for that. He had heard the stories. Thinking of it, he felt cold, isolated, exposed to mortal danger, and unable to defend himself. Perhaps he should get on his horse and just leave. Go back to where he came from and forget everything! What was to stop him? He wiped the sweat from his forehead and looked anxiously at the Lady of Kuo's face. She was reading the letter again, this time to herself, pensively. He waited. Finally she looked up at him.

"Go to the banquet, An Lu-shan. Behave as if nothing is amiss. It is my guess that this letter is meant to do exactly what it has already accomplished, and nothing more: to fill you with apprehension, loathing, and uncertainty. You are far too valuable for him to be planning to kill you, or demote you, or inflict any real punishment on you." Her eyes, steady and full of penetrating intelligence, had a calming effect on his blood as she spoke. He let his breath out. "There are designs and strategies behind this letter that we will never know," she continued. "Things known only to him. For instance, do you know the identity of the person who gave you the information?"

"No," he said, feeling stupid. "But he told me he was a student as well. I had no reason to doubt it," he added, somewhat defensively.

"Of course you didn't. And what would it matter, anyway, who this person was? But now, in light of this letter, we can only wonder." She tapped the stone bench with a long fingernail. "We can only wonder," she repeated, then folded the paper up and handed it back to him. "Just remember how valuable you are, An Lu-shan. That is the best advice I can give you."

"Come to the banquet with me," he said impulsively. She laughed.

"Do you think you need me to protect you?" She shook her head. "No. It would be ludicrous. You certainly don't need me. And besides, I wasn't invited."

"*I* am inviting you," he said quickly.

"No, An Lu-shan. Go by yourself. Know who you are, and no harm can come to you. And don't jump onto your horse and disappear, either. If you do, you will be acknowledging that he has frightened you. You don't want that, I am sure."

He cast her a surprised glance. How had she known that he was thinking of doing just that?

"Madam, I never considered it for a moment," he said, tucking the letter into his sleeve.

She smiled. "I'm sure you didn't," she said. "I just thought I would mention it."

Looking at her, he felt a small surge of the desire that he used to feel for her almost constantly. He had an impulse to tell her about the strange, dank-smelling woman who climbed through his window to inflict exotic pleasures on him in the dark. The woman, he thought bitterly, who had not been to see him for nearly two months now. The Lady of Kuo watched him, as if waiting for him to speak. He opened his mouth, then shut it again. No. He had been talking far too much lately, a fact that had been made abundantly clear to him.

"Some music, An Lu-shan?" she said then, rising from the bench. "It has been a long time since we have played together."

"What about . . . your cousin?" he said. He had no wish to be here when Yang Kuo-chung returned.

She sighed. "You still resent each other, don't you? Well, don't worry. I don't expect him until the evening meal. Stay. Relax. We will play music, and your mind will be soothed," she said, leading him onto the covered porch overlooking the garden.

Her musical instruments leaned against the walls here, waiting for their mistress. He lowered himself onto the cushions and picked up the stone chimes that she had taught him to play when they first met. They looked absurdly small and silly now, and when he held them up and struck them, the sound was so tiny and insignificant that it made him smile.

::

An Lu-shan's eyes adjusted to the dim light of the banquet hall. He had been seated at one of the long central tables and could do nothing now but wait, rubbing his wet palms back and forth over his knees. His eyes traveled warily over the faces gathering at nearby tables. None but a few out of the hundreds present and entering the hall were familiar to him. Inside his clothing, sweat rolled down his sides; he was acutely conscious of it glistening on his face. He nodded occasionally to various dignitaries as they were seated in his vicinity.

The huge room was gradually filling. There was bowing, soft words, the scrape of stools being politely pulled back. An Lu-shan felt grotesque and foolish, an unlettered boor unable to utter a word amidst the educated banter he heard around him. No doubt Li Lin-fu had calculated this effect as well, he thought. It had been a very long time since he had felt so uneasy, so out of place. All around him was polite talk, the impeccable manners of urbane men in rich rooms. *What was he doing here?* Seated at the central table, in full view of all the guests, he felt like some huge dressed monkey, a mockery of the splendidly attired ministers in their caps and robes. A distorted image of his vast, stupid round head presented itself to him in the curved surface of a silver tureen. And underneath the table, his wet hands rubbed and rubbed his knees.

He stared through the filing attendants bearing trays of food; aromas of spiced, peppered lamb, deer tail, nutmeg, and roasted ginger entered his nostrils, but his appetite was dead, his mouth dry. He was looking for one face in the crowd, without even knowing if he would find it; the letter had not said whether the chief minister would actually appear. The tables were nearly filled now, occupied with nameless officials whose robes indicated that they were from the Chancellery, the ministries, and the Secretariat—but nowhere was that one face he dreaded to see. He flexed his agitated hands under the table. I could crush Li Lin-fu, he thought, with one blow from this jade chafing dish. He was unarmed; the Khitan dagger he always carried in his boot had been taken away from him by the attendants at the door when the lodestone had triggered the warning bells. He repeated in his mind the Lady of Kuo's words in an effort to calm his jumping heart and churning gut: You are too valuable to him. He would not dare harm you in any way. As he was intoning these words to himself, a flurry of motion at the door drew his eyes sharply in that direction.

An Lu-shan's heart palpitated as Chief Minister Li Lin-fu entered the great hall. He looked shrunken, even smaller and punier than the last time An Lu-shan had actually set eyes on him at least two years earlier. Around him were his ever-present guards, big stupid-looking thugs with expressionless faces. The chief minister had become the focus of attention as soon as he was through the door; conversation dropped to whispers and murmurs as he moved into the room, a slightly stooped figure in a bright turquoise robe nodding and saying a word here and there to those he encountered. He was moving in An Lu-shan's direction, though nothing in his manner indicated that he even saw him. It became quickly evident that he was going to sit at the same table with An Lu-shan; cursing softly under his breath, the barbarian rose from his chair, legs weak and shaky under him. His eyes stung as rivulets of sweat ran down into the creases around them. Unable to resist the impulse, he brought his hand up and wiped his face.

Li Lin-fu, behaving as if he had not yet noticed the enormous man in his abject state on the other side of the table, settled into a seat directly opposite An Lu-shan. I am a dead man, An Lu-shan thought, lowering himself back into his seat; fat, sweating, eating, drinking, and talking—but dead. He looked at Li Lin-fu, now only a few feet away from him.

His skin was yellowish and stretched tight across his bony face. He glanced at An Lu-shan for a brief moment with hooded eyes that were bright and black; the look revealed nothing. The eyes moved quickly on to a court official seated nearby; the mouth uttered polite greetings all around the table. Then Li Lin-fu, his expression still blank, looked An Lu-shan full in the face. He smiled, displaying short teeth under a sparse mustache.

Hot blood rushed to An Lu-shan's head. His eyes watered. He had never seen Li Lin-fu smile, and the sight of it shocked him. Confounded, he smiled back as the chief minister raised his cup in An Lu-shan's direction.

::

Many hours later he was blind drunk, unable even to stand. Attendants had loaded him onto a palanquin and carried him roaring and laughing from the banquet hall. Now he lay immobile on the canopied bed, his clothing and the silk cushions he lay on stained with vomit. His eyes, the lids weighted with drowsy sickness, blurred the gold coffered ceiling. When he shut his eyes, the bed spun in a vortex of nausea. He shouted for the eunuch Li Chu-erh as another river of vomit welled up; there was the sound of running footsteps. He lunged at the bucket in the eunuch's hands, pulling at his clothing, and heaved. Pushing the bucket away when he was through, he wiped his face and mouth with a fistful of Chu-erh's brocade robe. He raised his eyes soddenly to the eunuch's face.

"You," he said. "You stink, Old Woman. Don't you ever change your clothes? You make me want to puke again!" He roared with laughter at his joke, then began to retch again.

Holding his anger and disgust behind an impassive mask, Chu-erh lifted An Lu-shan's heavy, stinking head over the bucket. The general's massive hands reached for the eunuch's shoulders; Chu-erh staggered backward in dismay as his master lunged forward off the bed, his hands sliding down the front of the servant's waistcoat and catching in the pockets. For a fraction of a second An Lu-shan's body was suspended between bed and eunuch like a great fat bridge before crashing to the floor as the pockets tore from the jacket. He passed into oblivion.

:: :

Cold water pouring onto his head brought him back to consciousness after the late morning watch. Li Chu-erh, unable to move his master, had left him as he had fallen, sprawled face down on the floor, knees bent, the tips of his booted toes still resting on the edge of the bed. He groaned. His neck was stiff and twisted and his head throbbed.

The eunuch had awakened him for a reason. There was a message, it seemed, that had just come from the Chancellery; Chief Minister Li Lin-fu wished further audience with the general in order to bestow on him a small gift, a token of esteem and a memento of his military prowess.

An Lu-shan was stripped, washed, perfumed with scented oils, and dressed in handsome brocades. He leaned heavily against the wall with one outstretched arm as the eunuch worked. He studied Chu-erh's face, which remained expressionless as he prepared his master, as if nothing at all had happened the night before. An Lu-shan remembered little from the time he had been carried out of the hall, but the one thing he did remember was puking, and the eunuch's disapproving face floating above the porcelain bucket. He looked around. The floor and the bed were clean, though his own clothing had been stained and sodden when he awoke. Somehow, the eunuch had cleaned around him while he lay unconscious on the floor. He shook his head and smiled. What a luxury to puke your guts out, he thought, over and over in one night. How different from his starved, sparse boyhood, when he was always, it seemed in retrospect, looking for something to eat. My capacity is endless, he thought. I put them all to shame last night. That skinny little lizard Li Lin-fu looks as though he's never had a decent meal in his life. And after I had eaten all my own food, he fed me from his own plate!

There was a hazy memory of the chief minister's smile—no longer sinister, but laughing and friendly—encouraging him to eat, eat, eat, and his bony hand thrusting morsels into An Lu-shan's face. With each bite came an explanatory lecture: these are roasted baby owls, he had said, and this is the breast of a dragon unhatched from its egg. These are mushrooms from the bottom of the sea, seasoned with pollen gathered from flowers that grow only at the top of Mount Li Shan. And these, he had hissed, are the tongues of talking swans!

There had been much laughter and hilarity around the table as the chief minister improvised, and the amber rice wine had poured in torrents down An Lu-shan's gullet as Li Lin-fu went on to dedicate these exotic dishes of his imagination to the barbarian, extolling his achievements to everyone at the table, calling him "hero" and "savior of the empire" and so forth. Not a word had been spoken at any time about the Palace Triennial Exams, or any Chang Shih, or the Vigilant Overseer of Truth and Honesty. An Lu-shan looked at the gold and silver threads of the jacket Li Chu-erh had put on him, glittering in the morning sunlight. He tried to recall the fear with which he had been struggling just a day before. It was a wraith to him now; he could scarcely conjure up even its memory. He contemplated with pleasure the coming meeting with Li Lin-fu. The Lady of Kuo had been right. He was a fool to be afraid of anyone, especially the chief minister, who depended on him.

A chair had been sent to carry him from his apartments to the chief minister's basilica complex in the extreme west end of the palace city. The four men who carried it grimaced with the strain as they lifted the chair and set out. He felt empty, and his head still throbbed as he laid it gently on the silk cushions and dozed as he was carried along.

He was jolted awake as the litter was lowered to the ground. They had arrived. The bearers waited silently for their passenger to climb out; he impatiently ordered them to assist him in standing. They pulled him up by the arms and left him, swaying slightly, at the entrance to Li Lin-fu's Chancellery quarters. The new upright position caused the blood to pound painfully in his head for a few moments; he shut his eyes and felt his heart clenching and unclenching like a fist. The pain in his head subsided and he began walking.

The door was standing open. He put his head in cautiously, saw no one, and went in. He walked through the first room, and found the next to be empty as well. He proceeded, mildly surprised that there was no one about. The Lizard is hiding under a rock, he thought, while he enjoyed the strangeness of walking unattended through the private quarters of the man second only to the Emperor. It was like dreaming. The sun slanted through the windows as he walked through room after room, encountering no one. The library, the usual place for a meeting, was empty. So was the sitting room. He found the dining room, where a faint trace of the odor of food lingered, causing him a small ripple of nausea. On the table was a covered teapot and a bowl. He touched the teapot; it was hot, and full of tea. He considered. A lone bowl and a pot of tea seemed to him a definite invitation. He sat down and poured. He would sit here and wait.

The hot tea was delicious and soothing to his head and stomach. He sipped it, gazed out the window at the drifting clouds, and pleasantly contemplated the nature of the "gift" the chief minister wished to bestow on him. After the honors heaped on him the night before, the endless rounds of toasts to his health and continuing success, a gift seemed superfluous. But apparently, that is the way it's done, he mused. You feast and drink all night, and then, the next day, they give you presents. Never mind that you would prefer to stay under the covers until the sun sinks again. After all this time, and just when he thought he knew everything about court life, there was still something to learn. His large calloused hands lay on the shining surface of the table, rings glinting on the fingers. He smiled. I don't have room for very much more jewelry, he thought, and wondered remotely when the chief minister would reveal himself. He drowsed in the warm sunshine.

"My father sends his regrets," came a child's voice behind him, "but he is indisposed. He wishes you to have this."

An Lu-shan whirled in his seat. A young girl stood in the doorway to his left, holding in her delicate hands a small carved box. He had heard nothing—no footsteps, no rustle of clothing, nothing. He stared at her, speechless with surprise. She walked to the table, put the box in front of him, took a few polite steps backward, and stood and waited. She was a pretty child, perhaps fourteen or fifteen, he could not tell—but it was her eyes that made him sit and stare wordlessly. They were bright, black, and hooded; they were the eyes of Li Lin-fu. To see the eyes of that ugly man in the face of such a pretty female child was profoundly disturbing. My father, she had said.

She moved her gaze from his face to the box on the table. Clearly, she wanted him to open it. Regaining his composure, he gave her a conspiratorial smile which she did not return. He picked up the box.

"A present from Father, eh?" he said, attempting to sound jolly and hearty, but his voice came out strangely flat and drew no response from the sullen, exquisite face of the girl. Very well. If she did not want to talk, then neither did he. He looked at the box in his hand. It was attractive, but not exceptionally beautiful. He hesitated for a fraction of a moment, thinking of the spider box. But he could feel the girl's eyes on him, and he would be damned if he would let her see even the smallest flicker of apprehension. He slid the top back and found a folded piece of parchment. He took it from the box, which was otherwise empty. No jewelry, he thought, unfolding the paper.

As he opened it, something slid out and plopped onto the polished tabletop. It looked like a scrap of leather with sparse hairs. He picked the curious object up to look at it; no sooner had he touched it than he dropped it in horror and disgust. *Bao-tse!*

He looked at the yellowing paper in his hand and saw that it was part of a map.

A map of a river.

And there were reddish lines, drawn in ink made from his own blood, indicating a crossing point on that river.

He stood, knocking over the chair he had been sitting in. The girl had not moved, but studied him with her hooded eyes.

Something had been written on the map. She held out her hand.

"I will read it for you," she said, and took the paper from his unresisting fingers. " 'You shall be allowed to keep yours for the time being,' " she read in an expressionless voice. " 'Others were not so lucky.' "

: :

The carriage driver pushed the swift four-horse team to its limit along the narrow unpaved ribbon of road that ran from Ch'ang-an to the hot springs and north to the village of Lin-tong beyond. The carriage drove headlong into the heavy current of the morning traffic of ox carts, donkeys, and pedestrians making their way toward the markets of the city. From the shuttered confines of the passenger compartment, An Lu-shan bellowed at the nervous driver to push the unstable vehicle still faster against the flow. The two high-spoked wheels skipped and bounced over ruts and gravel while the top-heavy canopy swayed precariously.

In the carriage's satin interior, An Lu-shan braced himself with his legs and gripped a leather hand-strap affixed to the frame. Opposite An Lu-shan, the eunuch Li Chu-erh, wordless and white-faced, hung on as best he could while his master raged at the driver and the outriders to show no mercy to anyone in the way. The whip cracked over the backs of the tortured team; white patches of foam loosened from the animals' mouths as the carriage rumbled faster and faster. An Lu-shan was only peripherally aware of angry shouts and cries in the carriage's wake, the clatter of spilled freight and the bellows of oxen as carts overturned and collided. The damned fools should know to stay out of his way.

He was leaving Ch'ang-an now, today. He had stormed out of Li Lin-fu's quarters, but not without first snatching the bit of paper from the accursed child's hand and the odious and detestable piece of dried flesh from the table. Without looking back at the little witch, he had left the dining room, knocking over chairs and tables as he went. Back at his own apartments, he had barked his orders to Li Chu-erh: pack what we can carry. Have a messenger dispatched immediately that we are to be met at the hot springs, at my apartments, by carts and oxen and a traveling regiment. We leave today for the north.

Now Li Chu-erh was doing his best to keep from being tossed against An Lu-shan as the carriage hurtled along. An Lu-shan, absorbed in his bitter thoughts, ignored the eunuch and grimly watched the countryside rushing by outside the window. The farther from Ch'ang-an I am, the gladder I will be, he thought. And the faster I get away, the better, too.

Oh, yes, Ch'ang-an was a most magnificent woman in springtime; a beauty—fragrant, tantalizing, and bewitching, and well aware of it. She was also the woman that had rebuked him. Slapped him. Not a coy lover's slap, not a playful slap that said an amorous hand had gone too far along a thigh too soon; not the gentle courting slap that held promises of later, forever. She had slapped him full and hard across his face, a stinging, impudent slap, delivered when he was at his most ardent, most tender. It was a slap that left its raw red mark on him that everyone would see. A slap that said he had gone too far, had assumed too much. A slap that had rejected his advances, had put an end to them. Go no further, she said. You have no chance with me! And she would pay for that. She would find out quickly that An Lu-shan does not crawl back on his knees after a woman has insulted him.

Even his own dreams had insulted him. If he were some superstitious fool, he would be forced to conclude that the city of Ch'ang-an, and even the hot springs themselves, had gathered their spirit in some insidious way to mock him. Against it, even his father the Emperor and his mother the Precious Consort were powerless to do anything. And Li Lin-fu was the embodiment, if anyone was, of that spirit that mocked, humiliated, and scorned him. That made him sweat, made him feel like a laughable monkey in a damned cage. And the chief minister enjoyed his role, that much was obvious. Make the Fat One beg; make him blubber like a moron whose tongue has swollen until it fills his mouth and then make him speak so everyone can laugh. Above all, make certain that the general knows he is only a savage, a barbarian, that he can never understand their world—their pompous, fragrant, complex world of layer upon layer of manners, propriety, and protocol. Let him know his place.

His place! An Lu-shan seethed with fury to think of Li Lin-fu setting him up. Laughing and smiling at the dinner. Feeding him from his plate, calling him "hero" and "savior" while simultaneously, behind that ugly, smiling countenance, he was anticipating tomorrow morning's pleasure—putting in the general's hand the dried balls of a man An Lu-shan should have had killed long ago. And wrapping the balls in the map. His map! Where in the name of all the gods had Li Lin-fu got the map? The last time An Lu-shan had seen it, it was in the hands of the investigating eunuchs, who said they were next going to interview the cartographer. Had they turned it over to the mapmaker? They might have, as part of the punishment. Cut off his balls and give him the map to remind him of why he was being punished. Li Lin-fu must have obtained the map at the same time he obtained the balls. But when had he done it? Why? How did he know? How did he always know everything? An Lu-shan was helpless in the face of these infuriating riddles. He could only focus on the hazy memory of the cartographer, a shadowy figure bent over a table in a tent years ago. An Lu-shan wondered if the man were still alive somewhere. If Li Lin-fu thinks he has taught me a lesson, An Lu-shan thought, he is right. He has taught me the futility of being kind and merciful.

One of the first things he would do when he arrived in the north would be to instigate a search for the cartographer. If the ball-less traitor is still alive, I will find him and kill him once and for all, An Lu-shan thought. Then I will make a gift of his head, pickled in brine, to the chief minister. A gift in kind, to match Li Lin-fu's own.

He turned from the window of the careening carriage just in time to catch Li Chu-erh's eyes upon him, his face blank and sullen. The eunuch's eyes darted away the instant An Lu-shan's met his. An Lu-shan stared at him, knowing the youth would be unable to resist the compulsion to sneak another look at his master, which he did after a few moments. And *you* had better watch yourself, too, he said with his eyes to the eunuch. You had better just watch yourself too.

They were only a few minutes' ride from the hot springs now. He had made his plans. He was expected to attend a private dinner with the Emperor and the Precious Consort tonight, but he would not be there. Nor would he leave word. He would take what he wanted from his hot springs apartments and join his travel regiment in the nearby village of Lin-tong. It was not that he wished to punish his imperial mother and father in any way or make them suffer; it was just that there was no pleasure left in the intimacy of those private dinners anymore. There was simply no pleasure left in any of it for him now. Master Li Lin-fu had seen to that.

The carriage sped onto the cobblestone terrace at the entrance to the hot springs and threw up a spray of rocks and gravel. Gatekeepers and grounds-keepers leapt into the hedges bordering the drive as one of the high wheels separated from the axle and rolled into the brush. The carriage dropped to its hub on one side, throwing the driver onto the ground. Breaking free from the frightened team, the carriage slid sidelong and slammed into the embankment of a small cultivated hill garden. The frenzied horses ran out of control into the grounds, dragging the splintered remains of the yoke behind them. Three men ran in pursuit.

An Lu-shan emerged and pushed his way through the horde of grooms and attending servants that surrounded the remains of the carriage. They pulled a dazed Li Chu-erh out of the wreckage and dusted him off. The eunuch was bruised and had a cut on his head, but that was all. He stared after his master, who was striding away across the grounds, unaffected by the accident, too angry to be injured.

An Lu-shan charged across the bridge over the Nine Dragons Lake to the terraced garden of his apartments. Beneath his balcony waited the three heavy ox-drawn military carts he had ordered, plus a small regiment of soldiers.

At his command, the soldiers began emptying the rooms. They removed carpets, tables, day couches, stools, desks, scrolls, screens, bedclothes, and quilts. They tore down the curtains, exposing to the full light of day the bed where An Lu-shan had received the strange favors of the woman with tangled hair who climbed through his window. He paused in the midst of the activity, his men swarming around him, and stood and looked at the bed, remembering. The bed where he had also waited in vain, filled with urgent, burning, foolish need.

He could scarcely believe that he had ever let himself get into such an abject state. It was as if his head had been filled with clouds and smoke, and his anger was like a strong, clear gust of wind that blew it all away so that he could see clearly again. He had been seduced, blinded, enslaved. But it was over now. An Lu-shan waited for no woman, be she perfumed and clad in silk, or smelling of earth and moss and exhaling voluptuous sensuality with every breath. He thought for a moment of the feel of her mouth on his "old man." He angrily pushed the memory away. You, too, he said to her, just as much as Purple Gown, are Ch'ang-an.

He ordered the bed dismantled and carried out to the carts. One of these nights, he muttered, you will climb through that window and find nothing. You will know I am gone, and you will wait for me the way I waited for you. He looked with satisfaction at the empty place where the bed had been. There were dents in the carpet and a few dust balls, and that was all. He turned and went outside to supervise the work.

He shouted at the men to be careful, but it was unnecessary. They were packing the carts as gently as if they were handling the treasures of a royal bridal dowry. Each piece had been handpicked to fill his rooms here, but he had other plans for them now. He thought of the eunuchs gathering in his tent for the investigation of the river crossing years ago and ignoring the furnishings he had been so proud of, as if they were nothing and he was only a boor crudely imitating refinement. But soon, very soon, they would all know just who he was.

He was An Lu-shan, Commissioner of Foot and Horse for eastern Shuo-fang, for Hotung, Fanyang, and P'inglu. He was a member of the royal House of Li now, a prince by adoption; his youngest son, An Ching-tsung, a prince too by marriage into the royal Residence of the Ten Princes. He was An Lu-shan, Grand Commissioner of Foot and Horse for the northern border of the greatest empire between Heaven and Hell. They should not forget that, and they would not. He left the men to their work and went back over the bridge to where the others waited.

He shouted for his mount and the five or six soldiers and Li Chu-erh who were to ride with him. The packing was well under way; the carts could follow at their own pace. He would wait no longer. Li Chu-erh held the reins of his horse while he got on, then climbed onto his own animal. The eunuch had not spoken a single word since they left the city, and the look on his face made it plain that he was not going to speak at all on the journey either. Good, An Lu-shan thought, wheeling his horse toward the gate and the road to Lin-tong. I have no need for the chattering of females, anyway. I have heard enough.

The grooms fell back as the riders spurred their horses and clattered out through the gate. As he passed through, An Lu-shan muttered an apology under his breath to the Emperor for breaking their dinner engagement. I am sorry, Father, he said; but it cannot be helped.

: :

At the seat of the military governor at Yu in the center of Shuofang Province five hundred li directly north of Ch'ang-an, An Lu-shan had ordered built what he liked to think might be the tallest tower in all of China. Construction had begun while An Lu-shan was still in Ch'ang-an. Shortly after the general's recovery from the spider bites, envoys had carried north word of Minghuang's consolidation of four military government commands under General An Lu-shan. They also carried orders and plans for a tower to commemorate this historic unification of China's northern defenses.

The tower had been built atop the level summit of a steep rise. From the base of the hill it sat on to its top, the tower reached a height of nearly two hundred feet. Narrowing gradually from its wide stone base, the structure rose through six tiers to a crenellated platform protected by a peaked roof. The tower had not yet been entirely completed when An Lu-shan and his small band of riders had arrived from the south, exhausted and filthy; he had not been expected for at least another month or two. With the general present to oversee the work, it progressed rapidly. By the time the ox carts from

Ch'ang-an and the regiment of men guarding them finally made their way into the camp, the tower was finished. But the workers had one more task.

Under An Lu-shan's direction, they were to carry selected pieces of furniture and fittings to the highest platform of the tower. Some pieces were carried up the stairs on their backs; others, too large or awkward to go up the staircase, were hoisted by means of ropes and pulleys. The men and their families had never seen such treasures before. A large crowd of wives, children, old men and women, and soldiers not working gathered to watch the proceedings. One by one, the tarpaulins came off the ox carts, revealing An Lu-shan's bounty wrapped in carpets and tied with heavy twine. As each piece was unloaded and unwrapped, cries of admiration went up from the spectators.

And in the midst of it all, General An Lu-shan strutted about, shouting orders, making jokes, and looking, everyone agreed, altogether splendid in his embroidered finery and ornamental armor. And wasn't he even fatter and grander than he had been when they had seen him last, they asked one another? Indeed, he was a colossal, majestic figure, they agreed. They had all heard the stories, of course, about how he had almost died protecting the Emperor. Looking at him now, manifestly alive and robust, they could scarcely believe that he had been near death not so long ago. Hadn't he been covered from head to toe with deadly spiders? He had the strength of ten men to have survived that. And wasn't the tower a grand thing, too, they asked one another? Wasn't it his gift to them, a thing they could all be proud of? He had told them that it was his tribute to them, the people of the northern provinces, the most important people in the defense of the empire. All they had to do was look at it, he had said, and they would be reminded of who they were. A shout went up from the crowd now as a gleaming black table was hoisted into the air, the men straining at the ropes while the workers above on the platform yelled encouragement, their red, grinning faces visible over the railing.

On the ground, An Lu-shan watched the table rising, heard the enthusiastic cheers of the people filling his ears, and felt a deep satisfaction. This was fine, and impressive, but it was mere preparation for another event. He had been making plans during the hard ride north. Soon, they would have something to talk about not only in the length and breadth of the northern provinces, but in Ch'ang-an, as well—in the streets, the wineshops, and at court. The talk would be everywhere. And without fail, it would, he knew, reach a certain set of ears. Chief Minister Li Lin-fu would hear and would know that An Lu-shan was no plaything, no trained monkey needing reprimands. And though he was sure that everyone at court had been amused by his buffoonish antics, they, too, must be reminded of who An Lu-shan was.

:::

Three days later, colorful silks festooning the pavilion atop the tower flapped in the breeze. The gleaming table of teak and rosewood sat surrounded by stools cushioned in icy, iridescent silks; a thick carpet of deepest blue with scudding white clouds covered the rough floorboards. Small, elegant lacquered tables with intricate pearl inlays held, atop polished brass trays, delicate ceramic vases and horses, their multicolored glazes dripping down sumptuously. An elaborately painted screen depicting a mythical hunt scene formed the rear wall of the pavilion; in front of it, a comfortable couch with heavy silk embroidered cushions reclined invitingly. In the center of the table sat a silver and jade imperial five-clawed dragon wine ewer from which General Commissioner An Lu-shan poured a cup of sweet amber rice wine for himself, his son An Ching-hsu, and for each of the five officers he had invited to sit with him atop his tower on this day. He lifted his eyes from the solemn faces around him to the horizon. A dust cloud was rising; at the same time that he saw it, a roar went up from the assembled throng of people below. It was about to begin. He rose and went to the railing.

:: :

The great cloud of dust had become a river, flowing from horizon to horizon past the tower where An Lu-shan stood. Glinting through the haze were the armor, swords, and lances of the soldiers, some on foot, some on horseback, comprising this mighty river that would take a full day and a night to pass by. The delirious noise of the spectators, the thunder of hooves, the creaks and groans of ten thousand axles of chariots, and the rumble of iron-rimmed wheels rose to his ears like music. But it was the sound of the marching feet of the soldiers—fully two hundred and fifty thousand strong—that was the sweetest music of all to An Lu-shan.

From the prefectures, superior prefectures, the military and agricultural colonies in the provinces of P'inglu, Fanyang, Hotung, and eastern Shuofang, An Lu-shan had assembled the largest single display of men and armaments, horses, military carts and chariots in the empire. And these vast armies were united for one reason only: their loyalty to him. A huge contingent was from Hopei Province, where the threat of angry secession had always been strong and where the distant T'ang court and the House of Li was traditionally regarded with suspicion and hatred. But around the person of An Lu-shan, whom they called brother as well as leader, they could unite in loyalty. And through their leader's own fierce loyalty to the empire, they became part of the powerful northern defense essential to the survival of the T'ang.

He imagined that he could feel the earth shaking under the thousands of marching feet, the reverberations traveling to the top of the tower where he stood and up the bones of his legs, soothing out of him, once and for all, the sharp sting of humiliation. The feeling that had been eating and gnawing at him since the moment he had walked in fury out of Li Lin-fu's apartments, that had diminished only slightly during the journey north as Ch'ang-an receded behind him, and had faded a bit further when he rode into the camp to the wild cheers of welcome of his subjects. The feeling that he had allowed himself to become a laughable monkey, a puppet, at court. Seduced by pleasure. Manipulated. A slave to females.

He could scarcely admit these last two to himself. He did not know which was worse: the knowledge that his sweating, abject fear of Li Lin-fu was so obviously transparent that the chief minister was able to easily use it against him, as if he were a child or an animal; or the knowledge that he, An Lu-shan, had waited, sick with lustful desire, for a nameless female who ate raw meat in the Emperor's gardens to climb through his window when it suited her to do so. A slave. That is what you were, he told himself now. The worst sort of fool. He cringed as the two humiliations intertwined, indistinguishable from each other, one magnifying the other.

But the feeling did not last. He looked at his officers, their faces solemn with awe and respect. He heard the steady rhythmic chant of his name rising from thousands of throats. He looked down at the column of armies, marching ten abreast. His humiliation, that he had carried with him all the way from Ch'ang-an, was dying, trampled into the dust under a quarter of a million marching feet.

19

Unnamed Daughters

The presence of a new factor [now became apparent] in the military picture, a small force commanded by eunuchs. It is referred to as the *Flying Dragon Palace Army*, and four hundred of its men under the direction of Kao Li-shih captured the rebel leaders.

—*Edwin Pulleyblank*

By now [Yang Kuo-chung] had become bolder in his opposition to the dictator [Li Lin-fu] and more open in his ostentation of the favour he received from the emperor.

—*Edwin Pulleyblank*

". . . a display of men and arms such as the world has rarely seen . . . stretching between the two horizons, shaking the earth, and all throats speaking . . . with one voice . . . the name of An Lu-shan . . ."

Yang Kuo-Chung strained his tired eyes in the lantern-light, trying to make out the difficult characters of the letter on the desk in front of him. He understood significant phrases, but knew that much of it was escaping him. He sighed. His skills were improving all the time, but a literary mind such as Li Shih-chih's did not easily lend itself to his incomplete abilities. He wished the Lady of Kuo had accepted his invitation to spend the evening with him; she would be able to translate every word and subtle nuance. He considered going and waking her up, but decided that he would be wise to wait until the morning.

He understood the first part of the letter well enough. It was evident that An Lu-shan had staged some sort of huge parade in his own honor, and Li Shih-chih had found it disturbing, and rightly so. But he neglected to mention anywhere in the letter, at least as far as Yang Kuo-chung could decipher, where he had been and what had happened to him since his last letter—the one that Yang Kuo-chung had received with the seals broken and the lies about An Lu-shan inserted at the end in a child's handwriting.

It was intensely frustrating to hear from his missing friend and not know where he was now. At least he is alive, Yang Kuo-chung thought. He turned his attention to the last part of the letter. It appeared to be in verse, and it made no sense to Yang Kuo-chung at all. He could not understand why his friend had included it in the letter:

> Heaving a great sigh, what can be done?
> Heaven's decrees are set against me.
> What good to think of my mother's son?
>
> Man passes through his single lifetime,
> Gone like morning dew that dries upon the leaves.
> The year is exhausting between the mulberry and the elm.
>
> A shadow, an echo, that cannot be traced.
> To think of not being impervious as metal and stone,
> And suddenly it grieves my heart.
> Grieves my heart and moves my soul—
> Put it from your mind and speak no more!
>
> Can I help my painful, bitter brooding?
> What are these thoughts?
> I wipe back the tears and take my endless trek;
> This brush, its wealth concealed, bids farewell.

He straightened his aching back. He realized that he had been sitting hunched over the letter for hours now, ever since it had been brought to him earlier that evening by a eunuch he did not know. This time, Li Shih-chih had not chosen the regular postal routes. Instead, the letter had made its way to the capital and into Yang Kuo-chung's hands through the Flying Dragons. Which meant that it would have to be, he realized, through the Flying Dragons that he would find out where his friend was and what had happened.

He stood and stretched his legs. He put his hand on the teapot standing nearby, which he had entirely forgotten, and found that it had gone cold. Cold tea was better than no tea, he thought, pouring it into a bowl.

Overhead, he heard the running footsteps of an animal. Cats on the roof, he speculated. The Emperor's cats often roamed at night, and one of their favorite games was to chase one another up trees and onto rooftops. He drank his cold tea and thought about animals' lives. What would it be like, he wondered, to own nothing but one's fur and to think only about the present moment? Why did nature make an animal such as man, who, because of the way he was put together, had to think about the past and the future as well as the present and had to live with the daily knowledge of his own death?

A yowl from outside interrupted his ruminations. Damn. The cats were fighting again, probably with one of the many wild cats that lived on the grounds and in the woods. It was the mating season, and Yang Kuo-chung had been hearing their serenades for the past few nights here at the hot springs. A fearful snarling and screaming now followed the first yowl. Exasperated, Yang Kuo-chung jumped to his feet and grabbed the pot of tea. A good dousing would get the beasts' minds off their altercation.

He went quickly outside and down the short flight of stone steps that led into the garden. He stood, trying to adjust his eyes to the dark, and listened. Moans issued from the inside of a stand of ornamental shrubbery. He knew what those moans meant—they were the precursors to the imminent engagement of claws and teeth. Now the cats would be glaring at each other through narrowed eyes, ears flattened and tails lashing while they sang their ear-grating duet. Then, at some signal exchanged between them, some moment of perfect agreement, they would fly at each other and become one ball of fury. He had to smile. Unlike men, animals always behaved like perfect gentlemen. They fought, but they never failed to obey the rules. Their protocol was impeccable and inviolable.

Well, gentlemen, he thought, tiptoeing closer and taking aim at where he ascertained the cats to be, I have enjoyed your singing very much. Perhaps I could persuade you to come and perform at the next party of the Emperor's. He is always ready to hear new folk tunes.

He flung the cold tea into the dark bushes, hoping for the best. The yowling ceased abruptly as the tea hit. The startled cats fled, one breaking through the rear of the shrubbery and the other darting toward Yang Kuo-chung, grazing his leg as it passed. He was sure it was one of the Emperor's big Persians. Maybe he had saved it from getting a nasty wound—though the Emperor's cats, of course, had their own personal physician.

He listened. Everything was quiet. Minister of Finance and Lieutenant Chief Minister Yang Kuo-chung has restored peace to the empire, he thought, and he turned back toward the stairs. As he neared the top step, he realized that he was still in the dark. When he left his apartments, the lights had been burning brightly—but in the few minutes that he had been outside, they had all been extinguished.

Cautiously, he felt his way to the door and listened. Only a fool would walk into a darkened room. An excellent way to receive a blow to the back of the skull.

"Just hurry up and come in," said an impatient female voice from the direction of the bed. "I am waiting for you." He let his breath out in a rush of relief and delight. So Kuo had changed her mind, and come to him tonight after all.

"You cannot know how happy I am that you have come, my love," he said, shutting the door behind him and moving toward the bed. "I need your help." His groping hands found the brocade cover. He climbed onto the bed and moved about, expecting to touch her warm flesh at any moment. He hoped that she would be naked.

"Where are you?" he said, his hands encountering only empty air. There was no answer. Instead, there came from the other side of the room a sound that caused him to freeze, hands stretched out before him in the darkness. A soft, almost inaudible sybillant hiss, like the sound of dry leaves skittering on stones.

He reached for the oil lantern on the writing stand by his bed, but he could find only the flint. Objects clattered to the floor. He leaned over the side of the bed, hands sweeping blindly, then groped back up to the desk and shelves nearby. The lantern, always by the bed, was not there.

"Kuo!" he called out, his voice sounding hollow and thin in his ears. The only reply was the steady hissing, rising and falling slightly in pitch.

The sound was moving now. One of the things that had clattered to the floor was his long dagger; he had heard where it had hit the floor near the bed. He found it and brought it up, drawing it slowly from the sheath and holding it out in front of him. He rose cautiously to his feet and stood on the bed with his back wedged into the corner of the room against the window shutters.

The hissing seemed to move in circles, and the circles were moving gradually closer to the bed. He knew now that this was definitely not the Lady of Kuo playing a trick, or anything like that. Because as it got closer, he could smell whatever it was that moved around in the dark in front of him. A damp smell. He thought of an animal's wet fur. Faint lantern-light from outside came through a crack at the bottom of the blinds. With his free hand he reached behind him. If he could just push the blinds up a bit, get some light into the room. But as he pushed up, the blind became unbound and dropped, unrolling its full length to the floor, extinguishing the narrow leak of light. The room was even darker than before.

The hissing stopped, ten or twelve paces from the far edge of the bed.

"Why do men always want light in the bedroom?" asked a female voice, sounding not even remotely like the Lady of Kuo now, but like the voice of an elderly woman. "I am not at all presentable, and even a woman of my advanced years has her vanities. Necessary, though, to carry us through every age, don't you think? First narrow shoulders and broad hips are the fashion, and then suddenly they are no longer attractive . . . then it is wide shoulders

and the tiniest of waists, and women must be mere wisps of things once again
. . . Ahhh!" The speaker snorted disdainfully.

Yang Kuo-chung tightened his grip on the dagger and listened carefully
to the strange voice.

"You see, Master Yang," the voice continued, "I had so little time this
evening to reach you, so little time to prepare myself . . ."

He stared into the darkness, his heartbeat racing uncomfortably. Now
he thought he smelled rotting wood, damp leaves, smoke.

"I am not the one you should be afraid of, Master Yang," the voice said
in a new tone, firm and imperative. "Those who attempted to take the life of
the Emperor are with us at the hot springs' palaces tonight. Even now they
are moving toward the Emperor's sleeping quarters." She spoke rapidly, urgently now. "This time they will not miss; they mean to do the job themselves.
Summon Master Kao and a small armed contingent of his eunuch elite and
rouse the Son of Heaven, put him under protection, and wait quietly for them
in his room. Be patient, and they will come. I have seen a thousand palace
coups . . . patience is the key! Be silent lest they sense your presence and you
lose the winning element of surprise." There followed a swishing noise along
the floor, moving away from him, then silence.

He stood on the bed for some time, listening, until he thought that his
visitor was gone. He leapt down and groped his way toward the door. Weapons! He needed a sword, his bow. He felt his way toward the chest, right near
the door, where he kept them. Then he would proceed straight to the Emperor's bedchamber. There might not be time to rouse Kao Li-shih and gather
the eunuchs together if all of this was true. And he could scarcely afford to
believe that it wasn't, could he? Light! He needed light! Where were the damned
lanterns? He knocked over a small table. What was that doing there?

"I would not go to the Emperor's bedchamber alone."

The voice behind him and to his right made him stand up abruptly in
shock. She . . . it . . . was between him and the bed now! While he was
stumbling around blindly in the dark, this creature moved nimbly about. He
had the unpleasant certainty then that she could see him in the blackness as if
it were daylight. Like a cat.

"I tell you, Master Yang, that to go there alone would be a dangerously
daring and most foolish thing to do. There is still time to enlist Master Kao,
if you move quickly and purposefully." The voice was moving again.

He turned slowly where he stood, so that his back would not be to her.

"These are not foolish amateurs or outsiders we are dealing with. They
are high officials from inside the Celestial Gates. The worst danger is always
from our own!"

The words entered his mind like arrows shot cleanly from a bow, and he knew in an instant that they were true. He had turned, following the voice, in nearly a complete circle.

"They are brothers . . . clever and dangerous men, who, like yourself, have seen much military training. Men of your same abilities. Do not underestimate them—they are especially displeased now. They did not like the Fat One's splendid parade very much at all!"

This time she was gone, he was certain. Even the damp smell had vanished. His thoughts raced and tumbled over one another as he rummaged blindly through the chest and found his long Persian sword and sheath. Brothers, high officials . . . the Fat One's parade . . . the Emperor's life! He fastened the sword to his waist, found the door, and ran down the outside steps.

: :

It could only have been the knowledge that twenty others—eunuchs armed with crossbows, broadswords, daggers, wicked halberds, and the brutal, resolute skill to use them—moved silently and invisibly in the darkness behind them that spurred Yang Kuo-chung and Kao Li-shih out into the hostile night on the word of a phantom, a dream, a . . . Yang Kuo-chung did not know what. He could only be supremely grateful to Kao Li-shih for reacting the way he did when Yang Kuo-chung woke him with his strange account: with alacrity, obvious faith in Yang Kuo-chung, and without time-wasting questions. Questions to which he had no answer, in any case.

They halted at Yang Kuo-chung's soft whistled command in a clearing near the Emperor's apartments to listen to his final instructions. The object, he told them, was to surprise the assassins and catch them in the act of trespassing in the Emperor's private quarters; therefore, the would-be murderers must not be stopped on their way in.

"You will keep yourselves hidden and allow them to pass," he whispered. "Master Kao and I will go first now, dispatch the guards and servants, wake the Emperor and remove him to safety, and then place ourselves, along with three Flying Dragons to assist us, inside the bedchamber. Fifteen of you are to follow when you hear me whistle, and place yourselves behind the silk screens in the reception gallery leading to the bedchamber. Those of you with crossbows should have them loaded, springs cocked back and ready. The rest of you should be ready to back them hand to hand with swords. Place yourselves further from the entrance to the bedroom. When something happens, you will be aware. You will know when you are needed."

Kao Li-shih and Yang Kuo-chung, accompanied by five Flying Dragons, passed easily and quietly through the row of imperial standards and the guards outside the Emperor's chambers. They wore heavy breastplates of lacquered leather and chain mail under their outer jackets. Kao Li-shih wore a small Ordos dagger at his waist and carried, as did Yang Kuo-chung, a dim lantern in front of him. The guards immediately obeyed Yang Kuo-chung's order to put down their weapons, remove themselves quietly, and to go with two of the Flying Dragons to where they would wait out, under the watchful eyes of the two armed eunuchs, whatever lay ahead tonight. He did not want them involved in the delicate maneuver they had planned, nor did he want to risk the possibility that they were part of any plan to kill the Emperor.

And the same went for members of the household staff. Kao Li-shih woke the sleeping servants and told them to leave the premises at once along with the guards unless they wished to be caught up in something they might rather not. Yang Kuo-chung, short-tempered and abrupt, sent one slow-moving and questioning young member of the inner household staff on his way with a jab between the shoulder blades with the haft of his Persian long sword. The servant yelped and ran. There is far too little time, Yang Kuo-chung thought with irritable impatience, for civilities.

Once the guards and servants were removed, another whistled signal brought in the fifteen eunuchs waiting outside to assume their positions. Two of them, posing as servants, weapons concealed, were posted directly outside the Emperor's door. Kao Li-shih and Yang Kuo-chung turned their lanterns down as low as they would go without extinguishing them and, in the company of the three remaining Flying Dragons, entered the outer rooms of the Emperor's apartments.

Kao Li-shih was happy that Yang Kuo-chung was assuming command so easily and naturally. He felt that his own military instincts had grown weak and flabby, succumbing, like everything else about himself, to lethargy and disuse. But he was not completely useless, he thought. Had he not, on a moment's notice, assembled this small but highly responsive contingent of the Flying Dragons?

When Yang Kuo-chung had come to him with the story of the bizarre visitation and warning, he had not hesitated. He had come to trust the other's instincts; if Yang Kuo-chung believed that there was danger, then the source of the information was irrelevant. One look at the intent and urgency in his eyes had told Kao Li-shih that there was not a moment to waste in equivocation. Whoever had taken the trouble to present the elaborately lethal "gift" to the Emperor would not be easily discouraged. Something was upon them. Only a fool would sit and argue about it. A trick? Possibly. But they had made their choice. Unpleasant memories of palace coups returned to him. To think that he had once been nearly complacent enough to believe that such things were gone forever!

"We will go in and I will wake him," Kao Li-shih whispered, "and remove him to safety." He paused and listened. "You three," he addressed the armed eunuchs, "will occupy the narrow rear entrance alcove of the bedchamber. Be ready for anyone who tries to escape that way. The door will be bolted from within, so no one will be able to enter there. That leaves only one way for them to come in."

They were just outside the doors to the Emperor's bedchamber. Yang Kuo-chung removed his long sword, an enormous Muslim yataghan, from its sheath beneath his outer jacket and ran his hand lovingly along the curved surface of the blade, its hard bluish metal touched coldly by the lantern-light. Though his visitor had told him there was enough time to get to the Emperor before the assassins did, he wanted to have his weapon ready when they opened the door. There was always the possibility that someone was inside waiting for them.

Cautiously, they pushed open the heavy door to the Emperor's bed-chamber and saw by the lantern's feeble glow that nothing was amiss. They also saw that he was not alone: the Precious Consort's long black hair was spread out on the pillow like a fan.

She awoke immediately, completely alert as soon as her eyes opened; seeing her cousin and Kao Li-shih, she seemed to assess the situation instantly.

"Help us get him to safety, Little Cousin," Yang Kuo-chung whispered.

She was on her feet in the next instant and did not ask questions. She and Kao Li-shih then easily roused the Emperor and walked him, docile and still half-asleep, from the bed. Kao Li-shih peeled back the carpet in the center of the floor, slid back two heavy iron bolts, lifted a trapdoor, and guided the consort and the Emperor down a ladder. Then, with the admonition to stay very quiet and to bolt the trapdoor from the inside, he tossed a pile of warm bedclothes down after them, closed the hatch, and rolled the carpet back into place.

"The Emperor will be quiet, in any case," Kao Li-shih said, going to the bedside table and raising a vial of powder to his nose and wrinkling it in disgust. "No doubt he will sleep through whatever happens." Neither of them had any concern that the consort would make a sound—not where the Em-peror's life was at stake. Kao Li-shih had the feeling that she would put herself between him and an assassin's sword, if it ever came to that. "And now, we will use a skill we both no doubt perfected in our childhoods," he said, and removed a quilt from a chest. He pulled back the bedclothes and began to swiftly shape the quilt to resemble a sleeping body.

Yang Kuo-chung watched with admiration. "I commend you, Master Kao," he whispered. "And the trapdoor?"

"The Flying Dragons have equipped all of his quarters with at least one or two such hiding places," Kao Li-shih replied, putting the finishing touches on the "Emperor" and yanking the bedclothes back into place. "Each contains a bed, water, dried bread, a chamberpot and a tunnel leading into a hollow bit of masonry some distance away in a garden, so that he may get himself out should his own allies be . . . how shall I put it? Should we be unable to retrieve him. The door at the end of the tunnel is always securely bolted from the inside, and the trapdoor into the room is bolted from above so that it cannot be used as a route into the Emperor's quarters. But it is unlikely that anyone would try; no one, not even the servants or guards, knows about the rooms. Only the Flying Dragons . . . and you, Master Yang. And now, of course, the consort."

"Well, Master Kao, we Yangs are honored to be in such distinguished company. And we have much to thank your eunuchs for," Yang Kuo-chung said. "Now we will wait. I will take a place behind this screen, and you . . . across the room. There," he indicated a tall heavy dressing chest. "There is a space between that tall chest and the adjoining wall. And you," he spoke to the three silent Flying Dragons, "take your places at the other end of the room. Crouch low in that alcove and you will not be seen. Try to put yourselves in a comfortable position. We may have a long time to wait, and you don't want to find that your legs have gone numb when you need them most." When everyone was hidden and settled, he extinguished the lantern.

:: :

Yang Kuo-chung had never been good at waiting, and he found it almost impossible tonight. Ever since the voice in his chamber had spoken its ominous words, he had been in motion, seething with purpose, every sense heightened, every muscle and tendon in his body ready for action, ready to fight, run, kill. And now he had to sit as if he were carved of stone, and wait. His legs were cramping painfully. He shifted his weight, knocking against the screen and nearly toppling it. Had he not known that there were three other men in the same room with him, he would have sworn he was utterly alone. What stoic patience these eunuchs have, he thought. I have not heard so much as a sneeze or a shuffle out of them, while I crash around here like a buffalo in a thicket.

And what was that? The first light of dawn? Impossible. He willed the darkness to retain its opacity, straining his eyes toward the window. He realized then that the emotion he was feeling was nothing other than disappointment. He *wanted* someone to come. After what he and Kao Li-shih had done tonight, he wished keenly for something to happen. *Wanted* someone to come and threaten the life of the Emperor! He reminded himself then of Kao Li-shih's words: "Should the Emperor's allies be unable to retrieve him . . ." The only way we will be unable to is if we are dead, he told himself. Do you think that you are playing a game?

He listened to the silence around him. Impatience was his worst flaw, he knew. But he had always felt that patience wouldn't do him any good, that it was too closely related to hesitancy, procrastination. That it could cost him by stifling the inception of an idea, the power of the moment. It was very different, he knew, for Kao Li-shih. The eunuch's patience was something like that of a monk vowed to silence. It was on another level altogether; he seemed to draw strength from it. It was the same with the other eunuchs, too, he thought. There must be something about being what they are . . . some strength of control that they gain, some compensation for their loss. Yang Kuo-chung yawned and shifted his weight again, this time with much more care.

He satisfied himself that the "dawn" he thought he had seen was only a dim light from a nearby pavilion. Occasionally he thought he heard something in the outer reception hall; he held his breath and strained his ears. Once he was almost tempted to whisper across the bedroom to Kao Li-shih that this was *it*! But it was nothing. The cats, maybe, at their nighttime duties.

One of his legs, he feared, was completely dead, simply from holding it still. Soon, he would stand up, walk about, call the whole thing off, and return to his quarters to get some sleep. When the dawn came, they would leave. No one would attack except in the night. And what had made him give credence to words spoken by a voice in the dark? Nothing other than the fact that this was the damnable hot springs, and he was finding himself under its damp, dark, living, primordial spell again.

Before his mind had even interpreted the message sent by his ears, his body had stiffened. A scraping sound, soft and gentle. Then silence. The cats? No. Kao Li-shih moving? No. wrong direction. Then where was it coming from? He was confused for a moment. Neither from the outer reception hall nor the back alcove. But there it was again. Wood sliding over wood. A light thumping sound, then the definite sound of panels being moved. He was sure that Kao Li-shih had heard it too. He heard the faintest movement from the eunuch's direction, a stiffening to attention, the first thing he had heard from him all night. There was another bump of wood—soft, then bolder. The dry rattle of parchment. Parchment? Then he knew. Gods! The ceiling! The roof! They were coming through the skylight! What fools we have been, waiting all night, looking only at the doors!

His scalp tightened as he made out shadowy forms swinging soundlessly and acrobatically along the ceiling rafters, then dropping to the floor in the far corner of the room like big cats. In the faint light he saw darkly clothed figures—six? ten? he could not be sure—moving across the floor on silent, slippered feet. Trained assassins? From where? Somehow, they knew where the Emperor was, that he had come for one night only to the hot springs. If this were tomorrow night, he would be in Ch'ang-an, inside the palace, inaccessible. How had they known? Insiders, the voice had told him. She had been right. How else could they have known? But then, he thought, how had he himself known to be here?

He held himself still, though his heart pounded. It would be foolhardy to rush them. There would be no advantage. Yang Kuo-chung knew that if he and the eunuchs were to move now, they would more than likely not emerge from the bedchamber alive. The assassins must be allowed to proceed toward the bed and the sleeping figure of the "Emperor." He wondered how they planned to exit. The same way they had entered?

Then from the opposite side of the room near the massive dressing chest came a sound that nearly made Yang Kuo-chung jump out from his hiding place: metal sliding against metal, the sound of scores of swords being drawn. If he did not know better, Yang Kuo-chung would have thought Kao Li-shih had two dozen armed men concealed in the dark with him.

Then a dreadful shuddering noise. The dressing chest toppling forward, its massive weight shaking the room as it hit the floor. A mighty yell from Kao Li-shih, and one of the assassins bellowing a command that the others were to leave any way they could while he stayed to finish the job they had come to do. Some of them rushed the door to the hallway; others sprang up toward the rafters to try to leave the way they had come. The deadly snap and zing of crossbow springs releasing reverberated from the alcove where the three Flying Dragons were hidden; with howls of agony, bodies thudded to the floor, some shot down from the rafters like treed animals, others as they fought one another to get through the door to the hallway. The one who had given the command ran to the bed and lifted his hands up over his head, his long sword pointing straight down.

"Ten thousand years to our August Imperial Father! And death to Li Lin-fu and An Lu-shan as well!" the man shouted at the top of his voice and plunged the sword with fearsome force, his full weight upon it, into the effigy of the sleeping Emperor. Though he knew it was only a rolled-up quilt receiving the murderous blade, a violent spasm of revulsion and shock went through Yang Kuo-chung's body. The assassin, realizing that it had not been bone and muscle that his sword had plunged into, ripped back the bedclothes and uttered a disgusted curse at what he saw.

Yang Kuo-chung sensed his chance as those left alive pushed out into the hallway, the open door casting a shaft of light into the room. He leapt from behind the screen at the assassin, howling and swinging the enormous Persian blade above his head with both hands. The assassin wheeled about and received Yang Kuo-chung's blade through his neck, front to back. The man's long sword clattered from his hand to the floor. Yang Kuo-chung held his blade in place for just a moment while he and the assassin looked into one another's eyes in the dim light. Yang Kuo-chung had seen this face before, but he did not know where.

"Ten thousand years to our August Imperial Father," Yang Kuo-chung said in an even voice to the doomed man and withdrew the knife from his neck with a sudden, brutal pull. Before the body even had time to collapse to the floor, Yang Kuo-chung pushed the blade of the yataghan between the man's ribs and into his heart.

Out in the reception hall, the Flying Dragons had closed in. There were screams of pain and surprise and the sounds of running feet and furniture splintering; Yang Kuo-chung knew that the eunuch elite would finish off each and every one of the assassins with deadly precision before the intruders had a chance to draw even a single weapon.

"Leave at least one alive!" he shouted into the hallway. "To answer questions!" For the rest, crime, inquisition, trial and punishment would all begin and end in one small furious circle of time.

Presently, one of the Flying Dragons pushed a man, arms tied securely behind his back, through the doorway and onto the floor. The eunuch stood with one foot resting on the man's head.

"Here he is, Master Yang. The only one left alive."

With a hand that trembled only slightly, Yang Kuo-chung struck a flint and lit the bedside lamp. With a corner of the ruined quilt that had received the death thrust meant for its master the Emperor, he wiped the blood from the long, curved blade of his weapon. Kao Li-shih came across the room, stepping carefully over corpses, and stood over the man Yang Kuo-chung had killed.

"I remember you telling me, Master Kao," Yang Kuo-chung said as he cleaned the yataghan, "that our beloved and astute chief minister has been credited with saying that a Persian is good for only three things: the firm management of his seraglio, his knowledge of the heavens . . . and his weapons. He was right on that last count, I can say without hesitation."

Kao Li-shih moved around the corpse, put his head out into the hall, and then came over to the bed and sat down.

"Six dead in the hall. Four in here. One who is not yet dead," he said significantly, looking down at the frightened eyes of the man under the Flying Dragon's foot. "Eleven assassins."

"Master Kao, I thought that you had hidden two dozen men behind that dressing chest with you. I swear I heard them draw their swords," Yang Kuo-chung said, poking with his toe at the bloody corpse of the assassin, which lay crumpled, face down, one arm folded beneath it. "How did you do it?"

"The 'Invisible Army,' " Kao Li-shih said. "A trick demonstrated to me once. One of those things that is only effective because of its unexpectedness. The corner where you put me happens to be where the Emperor keeps a small chest full of antique weapons. Mostly useless for anything but show; some of the blades have not been sharpened for a hundred years. I sensed that we had a long time to wait, so I busied myself. I removed about twenty of them, one at a time, and wrapped them two by two in the heavy fabric of my outer jacket. Let me show you. Perhaps someday you can use it yourself." He went over to where his long jacket, swords and daggers glinting from its folds, lay in a heap on the floor in the space next to the dressing chest. In a few moments he had deftly rolled the weapons up in the cloth. "Now watch closely." He pulled on the fabric, causing it to unroll slowly. Swords and knives slid metallically over one another. "In the confusion of a moment," Kao Li-shih said, "one could believe that one's enemies had multiplied . . ."

Yang Kuo-chung was laughing now, incredulous, the hours of tension and apprehension discharging. "And when you pushed that massive chest over onto its side and screamed to scare the 'kings of Hell' . . ." He shook his head, then looked up quickly. "You rolled those weapons up while you waited behind the chest, and I never heard so much as a clink of metal. How did you do it? How?"

"Patience, Master Yang," Kao Li-shih said with a shrug.

"And now we have the face of our assassin before us." Yang Kuo-chung rolled the corpse onto its back with his foot. "I have seen this man before, but I cannot place him. Can you?"

Kao Li-shih studied the dead face, the eyes reflecting the lamplight, the mouth slightly open and trickling blood from one corner.

"I have seen him before, I am sure. But I do not know him either," Kao Li-shih agreed. "But our guest here will no doubt make a formal introduction," he said to the man under the eunuch's foot. "Get him out of here," he ordered. "He has already spent far too much time in the Emperor's private quarters. There is a cellar room beneath my own apartments. Lock him in there until morning."

At that moment, the commander of the Flying Dragons entered the room and spoke to Kao Li-shih and Yang Kuo-chung. "We have removed all the corpses to the outside. We have picked up the broken furniture as best we could. But there is, I regret to say, still much blood on the floors and carpets," he said, seriously and apologetically.

Kao Li-shih laughed and patted the man's shoulder affectionately. "How dare you spill blood on the Emperor's carpets?" he joked. "He will have your head for this!"

The commander laughed too, and Yang Kuo-chung and Kao Li-shih joined in. The relief was tremendous. Yang Kuo-chung sank down onto the bed and felt the tears starting from the corners of his eyes. Some of the other Flying Dragons stood in the doorway and laughed along with them. The only one not laughing, Yang Kuo-chung thought, is you, my friend. He poked the dead man with his toe.

Their laughter was interrupted by loud, insistent knocking from beneath their feet, and the muffled sound of the Precious Consort's voice. Yang Kuo-chung jumped up. They had completely forgotten their "prisoners." He rolled back the carpet, unbolted the trapdoor, and yanked it up. The consort's head

appeared, eyes wide. Yang Kuo-chung pulled her up the ladder and hugged
her.

"And where is our Imperial Father, brave Little Cousin?" he asked.

"Asleep," she said, tilting her head toward the trapdoor. "He missed it
all."

::

> . . . Heaven's decrees are set against me!
> What good to think of my mother's son?
> . . . Gone like morning dew that dries upon the leaves.
> The year is exhausting between the mulberry and the elm.
>
> A shadow, an echo, that cannot be traced.
> To think of not being impervious as metal and stone,
> And suddenly it grieves my heart.
> Grieves my heart and moves my soul—
> Put it from your mind and speak no more!
>
> . . . Bitterness and pain?
> What are these thoughts?
> I wipe back the tears and take my endless trek;
> This brush, its wealth concealed, bids farewell.

The Lady of Kuo put down the narrow sheet of writing silk. She delib-
erated for a while before lifting her eyes and looking into her cousin's face.
He knew what she was going to say.

"Your friend Li Shih-chih is dead." She spoke with deep regret, though
she had not known Li Shih-chih.

Yang Kuo-chung knew that it cost her dearly to bring him bad news of
any sort. A part of him had known that this was what she would find hidden
in the mysterious verse at the end of the letter. Though the literary allusions
had been beyond him, he had intuited his old friend's message. But he had to
be sure—so he had brought her the letter. She had spent the previous day
studying it; today, they had ridden their horses to a secluded grove, dismounted, and rested.

Yang Kuo-chung, weary from lack of sleep, lay stretched out on the
grass. Three days had elapsed since he and the Flying Dragons had mobilized
against the assassins, and Yang Kuo-chung doubted that he had got more than
a few hours' sleep each night. He was worried. He felt as if he were in a maze,
and had a vaguely foreboding sense of time running out.

"At least his son will no longer have to wonder at the truth about his
father," he said, eyes closed. "He is somewhere in the city. I will find him

and tell him myself. I suspected this, but I wanted to believe differently, you understand. I hoped that if the poetry contained a clue, that it would be . . . ambiguous," he said with only the faintest hope, opening one eye and looking up at her.

She shook her head firmly. "There is a clue, but it is not in the least ambiguous. At least, it lost any ambiguity it may have had once I understood. Knowing what I do of Li Shih-chih from what you have told me of his poetry and scholarship, it is plain that he would be unlikely to misquote, use the wrong allusion, or take something out of context without a purpose."

"No, he wouldn't," Yang Kuo-chung assured her, feeling as he did so that he was putting an end to his friend's life once and for all.

"I didn't see it at first," she said, picking up the letter again. "But I knew for certain that the poem—the part of a poem—that he used at the end of his letter was something very old and not something that he composed himself . . . It was the style and the archaic language. Though I suppose he was capable of imitating anything. But I decided that the fragment must be part of a fairly well-known poem." She turned the page sideways and placed her thumbs evenly across the final couplet.

"Why?" he asked.

"Because I imagined that his circumstances—hiding, on the run from Li Lin-fu and his agents and perhaps even An Lu-shan—would not have allowed him the luxury of taking many books. Besides, he would not want to make his meaning too obscure. I decided that whatever piece the poetry had come from would be among the most quoted works in the *Wen Hsuan* anthology. And it was. I found it. It came from a poem by Ts'ao Chih, written some five hundred and fifty years ago, under what may have been similar circumstances."

Yang Kuo-chung said nothing, but looked at her with admiration, wondering how many other women had such unrecognized brilliance. She looked back at him for a moment, as if tacitly acknowledging his compliment, and perhaps wondering the same thing herself.

"You do amaze me," Yang Kuo-chung said. "It should be you grappling with our chief minister, not I. You are infinitely more qualified."

"It seems that I am involved, in any case," she said, and returned her attention to the page. "As I was saying . . . I found the poem, but I did not, at first, see anything unusual. Li Shih-chih used Ts'ao Chih's phrase 'my mother's son,' of course, to refer to himself, just as Ts'ao Chih had. But then I began to notice that Li Shih-chih had made some subtle changes in the poem . . . things that were not in the original. For instance, the line about 'the mulberry and the elm.' "

"I'm afraid that you'll have to explain the allusion to me," Yang Kuo-chung said.

"It signifies constellations and denotes the passage of the seasons, of time itself. But Li Shih-chih spoke of the year ending or 'exhausting' between 'the mulberry and the elm.' That is not how it was expressed in the original."

"Constellations," Yang Kuo-chung muttered. "I have never enjoyed the stars. Now I have another reason not to."

The Lady of Kuo glanced down at him sympathetically. "It was with the last line, though, that Li Shih-chih finally spoke directly to me," she said, lifting her thumbs from the page, revealing the final vertical line of the poem.

"Before you tell me what you found," Yang Kuo-chung interrupted. "Just reassure me. Did he . . . die with some dignity?"

She sighed. "If we can trust the accuracy of his last allusion, then the answer is definitely yes. By his own hand, in solitude and quiet. That is what he says to me. The original poem of Ts'ao Chih states simply, 'With this brush I bid you farewell.' But your friend Li Shih-chih wrote, 'This brush, *its wealth concealed,* bids farewell.' 'Wealth concealed' is not a part of the original poem."

Yang Kuo-chung rose up on one elbow, recognition dawning on him. " 'Its wealth concealed . . .' Of course. If I had the skill at reading that you do, I would indeed have understood," he said sadly. "Li Shih-chih once told me the tale of the Righteous Prince whose writings could not effect changes in a corrupt government . . ." Yang Kuo-chung searched his memory. "But his writing brush, though it could do no good against all the corruption, contained a hidden treasure . . . how did he put it?"

" '. . . Its wealth concealed,' " she quoted.

"That was it! It was the promise that if all else failed, he had a blade hidden in the handle of his brush . . . that is the 'concealed wealth,' isn't it? Li Shih-chih is telling us that he intended to push a blade through his heart immediately after finishing the letter."

"I am afraid so, my cousin. But there is some comfort in the fact that neither Li Lin-fu nor An Lu-shan got to him. We know they didn't, because he was able to make his report about An Lu-shan's military parade and to include the poem in his letter. No one was standing over him. The Righteous Prince was alone, his hand unforced."

"Perhaps not directly," Yang Kuo-chung said with bitterness. "But they are responsible for his death, nonetheless."

The Lady of Kuo said nothing. He looked at her.

"No words of defense for your friend An Lu-shan?" he asked.

She glanced down at the letter. He continued to look at her.

"An Lu-shan has been my friend," she said at last. "And he has been the Emperor's friend, too. I don't think anyone could require further proof than what he has furnished."

"I will grant you that," said Yang Kuo-chung, and waited.

"However, it seems that there is another An Lu-shan who is a stranger," she said carefully. "I do not know him and neither, I think, does the Emperor."

Yang Kuo-chung was astounded, though he carefully concealed it. He lay calmly back down on the ground and shut his eyes, as if their conversation were perfectly commonplace. This was the first time he had heard anything from her lips that conceded that An Lu-shan might possibly be something other than a big, harmless heroic "baby."

"I do not think that he is quite the same man when he is up north that he is when he is here," she added. "At least, there seems to be some very strong sentiment against him. Little Sister heard what the assassin said: 'Death to An Lu-shan.' She told me that it chilled her very bones."

"It chilled mine, I can assure you," Yang Kuo-chung said, recalling the sword being pushed down into the bed with the man's full force behind it. This was one of the things that had kept him from sleeping these past few nights: time after time, just as he began to drift off, the dark shape of an assassin would materialize over his own bed; and just as the cold blade came down toward him, he would jerk back into wakefulness. "We tried to tell the Emperor," he said, "but since he managed to sleep through the entire attack, he did not hear it with his own ears . . ."

"Surely he does not think that you, Kao Li-shih, and Little Sister are lying!"

"No. Of course not. But he thinks that perhaps we misjudged, that the assassin was merely repeating some sort of ritual phrase. He does not know. He did not *hear* it the way we did! He did not hear what was in the man's voice! It is a cursed, rotten piece of luck that he had drugged himself that night."

"Little Sister tells us that real sleep is a rare thing for him."

"Well, he nearly went to sleep forever," he said, moving over to her and putting his head in her lap. "It is all so strange. The way I was warned. She . . . it . . . whoever it was who visited me that night put out all the lights and spoke in your voice! Who was that? How did she know? I tell you, my skin still crawls to think of it."

"It could only have been Li Shan Lao Ma."

"Who is that?"

"An immortal. A witch. The spirit of the hot springs in human form, if you will."

She was smiling as she said it. She was playing, trying to lighten the mood, he knew. But her words gave him an uncomfortable feeling. It was as if his own amorphous uneasiness about the hot springs, his vague feeling that it was a living being, and a not altogether benign one, were being expressed perfectly.

"I don't believe in witches," he said, thinking of something else the voice had said when warning him of the approach of assassins: They are especially displeased. They did not like the Fat One's parade, either . . . he sat up and looked into the Lady of Kuo's eyes. "We cannot let Li Shih-chih die in vain," he said. "The very least that your friend An Lu-shan is guilty of is excess. Li Shih-chih was worried enough that he took the risk of writing to tell me about it. And twice, attempts have been made on the Emperor's life; now we know why. We have heard it with our own ears. *Death to Li Lin-fu and An Lu-shan!* They are trying to kill an Emperor who allows the steady, unchecked growth of power of those two! And my visitor was right about another thing. She said they were not outsiders. We found out from the prisoner we took that night that the perpetrator was a high official."

"Who?"

"His name is Wang Hung. None other than the governor of this province. He was not there in person that night, but he sent someone to do the ghastly deed for him—his own brother, Wang Han. That was the man who pushed the sword into the bedclothes. Agents were sent to arrest Wang Hung, but of course, he had vanished. Wang Han and the others we killed that night lie in their ignominious unmarked graves, but Wang Hung still lives. Think of it: a respected official turned assassin because of his disgust and alarm over Li Lin-fu and An Lu-shan. It is a very bad situation indeed." Yang Kuo-chung rubbed his tired eyes. "And still, the Emperor will hear nothing against either one of them. Kao Li-shih has been trying for years to make him listen. And now, of course, An Lu-shan can do no wrong in the Emperor's eyes. An Lu-shan saves his life, so the Emperor rewards him with promotions, armies, territories! And now they are trying to kill the Emperor because of it! It is altogether too ironic," he lamented.

"When the Emperor promoted An Lu-shan," the Lady of Kuo said thoughtfully, "he did it without Li Lin-fu's consent, I seem to recall."

"That is true," Yang Kuo-chung replied, watching her. He could see that she was considering her next words with great care.

"I have something to offer which may be helpful to you," she said. "Not so long before An Lu-shan left for the north, he came to me," she said. "He had a letter to him from Li Lin-fu. He could not read it, of course, but he knew that it was from the chief minister. Even without knowing what the letter said, he was agitated, to say the least. Frightened would be a more accurate description."

Yang Kuo-chung was fully attentive now. This was an interesting piece of news indeed.

"He had me read the letter. It seemed, on the surface, innocuous enough, but it unnerved him completely. He was ready to bolt then and there. Had I not stopped him, he would have been on his horse and through the gates of the city that afternoon."

"What did the letter say?" Yang Kuo-chung asked, excited.

"It was an invitation to a party. A dinner at the Big Wild Goose Temple in honor of the successful candidates of the Palace Triennial Examinations. It seemed that Li Lin-fu was inviting him to attend in the place of a candidate, a personal favorite of his, who could not attend."

"I do not understand," said Yang Kuo-chung, shaking his head.

"Neither did I. But I told him that he would have to tell me everything if he expected me to be of help. He was reluctant, but he told me. It was too strange." She paused, remembering.

"Go on!" he urged.

"Among the candidates who could not attend," she said, "was one whom An Lu-shan had turned in for cheating. I tell you, when he found out that this person was a favorite of Li Lin-fu's, he turned white with terror. And the whole tone of the letter—so genial, so completely devoid of any mention that the youth had been caught cheating or that An Lu-shan had anything to do with it—was purely ominous to poor An Lu-shan. He understood nothing, but he smelled trouble. He was floundering—like a man who cannot swim being tossed into the ocean." She thought for a moment, then added: "All of this happened very soon after his recovery and promotion. And his 'adoption.' And he departed for the north, without a word to anyone, the day after the dinner."

"I think I understand," Yang Kuo-chung said. "It sounds too familiar. The chief minister does not like it when he is not consulted. The Censorate eunuchs who disappeared after my own promotion by the Emperor were 'invited' to a 'party,' too. The whole city talked about it for months afterward."

"I remember," the Lady of Kuo remarked. She put her hand on his arm. "It is plain to me. There is enmity between Li Lin-fu and An Lu-shan. The chief minister was punishing the general in some way. And An Lu-shan loathes and fears him, the way a dog fears its cruel master. And I would be willing to wager almost anything that Li Lin-fu has heard all about An Lu-shan's mighty parade and is not happy about it. Not happy in the least. Things are far from perfect between them. And that, my love, is your opportunity."

He looked at her, not understanding at all what she could have in her mind. "My opportunity?"

"Seize the initiative!" she said, pressing his arm. She held the arm for a moment, waiting for his reaction. She let go and sat back, watching him intently. "Yes, I can see it. You have a destiny to fulfill. You must go to Li Lin-fu."

"You are mad," he said, though the truth of what she was saying had already begun to dawn on him. "Mad!"

"You are the one," she said. "Who was it who said that Li Shih-chih must not die in vain? Go to him. Cut through all of this, like a knife. Tell Li

Lin-fu your reservations about An Lu-shan. Tell him that you and he would do well to put aside your enmity and unite on this one thing. I think you will find that the two of you are in accord to a degree you would not have expected."

"You would send me into the jaws of the lion?" he asked, amazed. "I remember the morning when I told you that I had been appointed lieutenant chief minister. You told me that Li Lin-fu was far too dangerous, that I would be killed, and that it would be your fault."

"I am still trying to save your life," she declared. "I am still filled with fear for your safety. I am telling you these things because I *am* afraid! I said that he was a dangerous *opponent*. That is why I want you to take this opportunity while it is before you, begging to be taken. You have a reason now to become his ally and cease being his opponent," she said with finality.

Li Lin-fu's ally! This was indeed the most bizarre concept he had ever had to consider.

"Your theory is impeccable," he said, shaking his head. "But don't you think that in practice he would just have me killed on the spot?"

"You don't give him enough credit, my love," she replied. "He is no ordinary thug. I think that he would find your audacity in approaching him sufficiently astonishing that he would be intrigued. I know that he would hear you out. Then all you would need to do is show him that you are valuable to him."

He put his head down into her silky lap again. She stroked his face, and tugged gently at his topknot.

"And what have you heard about his health lately?" she asked.

He looked up at her.

"That it is poor. Kao Li-shih tells me what the eunuchs tell him. The reason he was out of the city recently was that he went to the caves on the Li River."

"If he is dying, he is aware of it," the Lady of Kuo said.

"Maybe he will do us a great service and go soon to his death."

"Do you think that things are going to get better when he dies? He will have to have a successor. Who do you suppose that successor will be?" she asked.

He thought for a moment. "You are mad," he said again. "How can I possibly do what you have suggested? It is far too dangerous." He rolled off her lap and pulled her down to the ground with him. "What would An Lu-shan think if he heard what you have said to me today?"

"What I say is for his good, too," she said seriously. "I have not betrayed him. I am afraid for him, too. Besides, he cannot hear me. No one can. Only you."

He tightened his arms around her. They lay that way in the afternoon sunlight, not speaking, for a long time.

:: ::

The next morning, before Yang Kuo-chung was fully awake, a servant brought a message to his door. It was a letter bearing the official seal of the military governor of Szechuan. He was delighted. He had not heard from his old friend Hsien-yu for several years. He wrapped himself in a quilt, taking care not to disturb the Lady of Kuo, and broke the seal.

He became perplexed as he read. It appeared to be a request for his presence in Szechuan. He tried to focus his still bleary eyes on the characters on the page. They said something about conscription procedures and something about a military installation. He sighed and looked at the sleeping Lady of Kuo. Perhaps I should wait until she awakes, he thought. I am almost embarrassed to ask her to read yet another letter. But she is so good at the subtleties of prose, while I can only grasp the basic rudiments of meaning. He looked at the letter again, and curiosity got the better of him. He reached over and gently shook her. She opened her eyes, and he held the letter for her to see.

"I need your help again, Cousin," he said apologetically.

She sat up, pushed the hair from her face, and took the letter. Her eyes moved quickly up and down the rows of characters. She looked at him questioningly.

"He wants you to come to Szechuan immediately. Your services, in your official capacity as lieutenant chief minister, are required. They wish to consult your expertise in the field of conscription, as it is applicable in the territory surrounding a new military outpost in a remote region of Szechuan. It is signed Hsien-yu, military governor of Szechuan.

"That is all?" he said.

"That is all."

"No greeting? No personal words?"

"Nothing else. It is completely official. What is this, Cousin?" she asked apprehensively. "I don't like it. I don't want you to go to Szechuan."

He took the letter from her hand and examined it, shaking his head.

"Don't worry. I will not be going to Szechuan," he said, and put the paper on the table. "He has made a mistake."

"Who has?"

"Li Lin-fu. He doesn't know that Hsien-yu is a friend of mine. And if he did know, I am certain he would have had him deposed already. You will remember that I worked with Hsien-yu many years ago when I was involved in the military horse trade there. We became quite close. This letter could not have been written by him. He would never be so cold, so dry, so impersonal with me. He would not speak to me like a stranger, even in an official letter. This is simply not his voice," he said, gesturing toward the paper on the table.

Now the Lady of Kuo looked genuinely alarmed.

"How does he always seem to know? We did nothing more than talk about him!"

"His instinct is uncanny, my love. We spoke about him, and he felt it. Probably the very air around him changed temperature. I don't know how he knows. It is because he is Li Lin-fu. But his instinct is not infallible. The night that Niu Hsien-ko died, Kao Li-shih and I knew about it before he did, and we got to the Emperor before the body was found. We ran every step of the way, but we got to the Emperor before Li Lin-fu even knew that his first-in-command was dead."

"Why does he want you in Szechuan?" she asked, pulling her robe around her shoulders.

"At the very worst, he wants to get me out there and have me killed where I would have no protection and he would have no witnesses. But I have not been a particular bother to him lately. Perhaps he just wants me occupied, indisposed, far out of the way while he executes some sort of plan having to do with military expenditures, the Censorate, or An Lu-shan. I don't know." He put his hand on hers. "Don't look so unhappy, Cousin. I am not going. And Li Lin-fu has made a decision for me. He is going to receive a surprise. One for which not even his superb intuition could have prepared him." He got back under the bedclothes with her and took both her hands. "I am going to take your advice and go to him, just as you suggested."

The Lady of Kuo looked relieved and frightened at the same time.

"First, I was afraid you wouldn't listen to me. Now that you intend to, I am afraid," she said unhappily.

"But how to do it? I would not imagine that one simply turns up un-announced at Li Lin-fu's door and obtains admittance," he said. "Nor does one send a mere letter asking for an audience. No. I think that in order to get his attention, one must show oneself worthy. Present the proper calling card, so to speak. One must do something that he himself might do." He ran his hands up and down her arms under the warm bedclothes. "My dear Lady of Kuo, I need your wicked imagination. I want you to pretend for a moment that you are Li Lin-fu and that you want to arrange a meeting with an ad-versary. What would you do?"

"You want me to pretend I am Li Lin-fu?" she said. "Very well. Let me think."

He waited patiently, gently running his hands over her smooth skin, confident that she would provide him with the answer to his question. It did not take her long.

"I have an idea," she said. "The corpses of the assassins. Where are they buried?"

: :

Yang Kuo-chung held a silk cloth over his nose and mouth against the fetid breeze blowing off the harbor of the busy Kuan-yun Transport Canal at the edge of the city. Crows cawed and circled overhead, and flapped with ponderous dignity down to the bountiful offal heaps of bones, rotten vegetables and fruit, fish heads, and animal innards, where they strutted and argued with one another over choice morsels. Rancid black smoke rose from refuse incinerators; from the direction of a slaughterhouse on the water's edge, where animals were unloaded from barges and met their fates directly, the frightened squeals of pigs carried on the same unclean wind. There were men's voices, too; merchants and buyers haggling with suppliers, workers singing, shouts, coarse laughter and jokes.

In a field on a slight rise about a hundred paces up from the water, Yang Kuo-chung stood among the low unmarked mounds that were the graves of murderers and criminals. Two men, prisoners on a corvée labor detail, dug the earth in front of him, throwing shovelfuls of dirt over their shoulders, faces grim and expressionless. A guard in charge of the prisoners stood on the other side of the grave. Nearby, but keeping a respectful distance, an interested group of slaughterhouse workers with blood spattered on their bare chests and arms stood and watched the proceedings.

When the shovel of one of the prisoners struck something soft only a few feet down, he spoke to his fellow in the Khitan tongue, telling him to stop digging. Carefully, they cleared the remaining earth from around the corpse's head, and unwrapped the shroud from the face. They looked up at Yang Kuo-chung.

"That is he," Yang Kuo-chung said in their own tongue.

If they were surprised that this Chinese high official spoke their language, they did not show it.

"There is no need to bring the body up," he told them. "Just uncover the right arm."

Kneeling down, Yang Kuo-chung leaned into the hole, and with his Persian sword, the same one he had used to kill the man in the grave, cut the right hand off at the wrist, slicing easily between the bones and through the tendons. A small quantity of dark blood oozed out.

Picking the hand up with the cloth he had been holding to his nose, he noted with satisfaction that a distinctive copper ring still adorned the index finger. The two men who had done the digging watched, their flat eyes revealing nothing of their thoughts, as Yang Kuo-chung wrapped the hand in a piece of leather and put it in a small wooden box. Feeling the prisoners' eyes on him, he looked at them.

"He deserves this," he assured them. "He was a murderer." He rose to his feet and turned to leave.

The guard harshly ordered the men to fill the hole in again.

Yang Kuo-chung turned back to the prisoners then. "Were you among the prisoners who came from the north with An Lu-shan?" he asked them.

Their eyes betrayed emotion then for the first time. "Yes," said the older of the two. "And we wish to go home. We do not want to die here."

Yang Kuo-chung looked at the guard.

"I am setting these prisoners free as payment for the work they have done today. They will be accompanying me." He looked back at the men. "I will see that you get home."

: :

Yang Kuo-chung had thought that he would have to distract Kao Li-shih's attention during the ride back from the morning audience, but it quickly became evident that the eunuch's mind was already so occupied that he would not have noticed if it had suddenly turned into the dead of winter outside of their carriage.

They had ridden in silence for a long time, the Emperor's carriage preceding them in the entourage, before Kao Li-shih began to talk about the matter that occupied his mind. They were coming from the morning audience, which the Emperor had attended today for the first time in years. But what should have been an occasion for rejoicing—the Emperor occupying his rightful place before the petitioning ministers and officials—found Kao Li-shih glum and pensive.

Had they not known better, the Emperor's reappearance at the official function this morning might have indicated an end to, or at least a weakening of, the chief minister's rule by proxy. But Kao Li-shih knew better. The Emperor's decision to attend had been arrived at not because of Kao Li-shih's persuasiveness, or because the Emperor had awakened to the gravity of the situation, or even because he was curious. He had gone because of the way the fortune-teller's sticks had landed, or perhaps because there had been a certain pattern in the clouds. Or was it because of the random premonitory fissures in a diviner's tortoiseshell? For the infuriating, baffling, absurd, and ludicrous fact was that the Emperor had taken to consulting soothsayers.

So far, Kao Li-shih had desisted from discussing this strange new development with the Emperor. He told himself that it was merely ridiculous and probably harmless enough.

"But what bothers me," Kao Li-shih was saying to Yang Kuo-chung as they rode, "is the hypocrisy of it. Magicians and diviners at court. Not so very long ago, even the rumor of any of them around the palace or the royal households was a matter of utmost seriousness. Their mere presence was still a crime punishable by banishment, or worse." He thought of the Empress Wang, and the Emperor agonizing over the necessity to punish her for employing the witch-woman to help her conceive an heir. Silently, in case she was watching the Emperor over his shoulder at his new game, Kao Li-shih apologized to her ghost. I am sorry, my lady. I have no excuses to offer you. Just the hope that it will pass. He shifted uncomfortably in the cramped quarters of the carriage. "But it is not as if the history of China weren't strewn with examples of superstitious rulers that some righteous Confucian prince had always to put straight," he added.

"I trust you are not referring to me, Master Kao," Yang Kuo-chung laughed. "I am hardly the righteous prince you are looking for."

They both laughed then, but Yang Kuo-chung did not think that Kao Li-shih laughed very convincingly.

"It seems that the definition of 'dangerous heterodox' magic is clearly an imperial prerogative. Of course, when these charlatans are in the services of the Emperor, they are not soothsayers, diviners, or practitioners of Dark Taoism. Listening to him speak, one would have to conclude that he consults counselors of state. Advisors of a 'non-Confucian' persuasion," Kao Li-shih said drily. "Just this very morning when I arrived at his palace apartments for morning tea, I found one of these 'advisors' already in attendance. Imagine, if you will, a strange, foul-smelling, gibbering little fool defiling the air in the Emperor's rooms. Far worse even than the filthy, unkempt rustic poet Li Po," he said, pronouncing the name with disdain. "But this creature was unique. He was strung from head to toe with a multitude of tiny glass and silver bells, brass cymbals, wind chimes, and miniature clappers. In short, he wore on his person every noisemaker ever found in the stocks of all the peripatetic toy vendors of the world."

Yang Kuo-chung listened, amused, encouraging Kao Li-shih by his attentiveness to continue. He hoped that he would keep talking and not take notice of the distance they had already gone. It seemed that there would be little problem; Kao Li-shih had spent nearly a week with the Emperor since the second assassination attempt, and he was full of tales.

"And the Emperor welcomed this odious creature with open arms, as if they had been long lost brothers," Kao Li-shih continued. "The Emperor prevailed upon me to listen out of politeness to the man's explanation of why he was adorned to resemble something a farmer puts in his field to scare away the crows. Of course, when he told me, it made perfect sense, and I was ashamed of my peevishness. Ultimately," he declared, holding up his finger pedantically, "with the incessant tinkling and clanging of the paraphernalia on his body, a magic confluent moment will inevitably occur, he explained.

Eventually, the proper sequence and combination of noises will vibrate in exact harmony with the secret ineffable musical notes of Taoist lore. And the little oaf, at that moment, will be whisked, smelly robes and all, right out of this gross and vulgar plane of existence, to his divine nirvana. Or to wherever it is he wishes to be whisked. It is simply a matter of time, patience, and infinite possibilities." Kao Li-shih shrugged. "What right do we have to be cynics in the face of faith such as that?"

They both laughed.

"So these are the 'advisors' who tell Minghuang which days are auspicious to attend the morning audience and which are not," Yang Kuo-chung mused.

"Not only that," said Kao Li-shih, "But he consults them in the selection of clothing every morning. Auspicious combinations of colors, and so forth." He shook his head. "It is plain to me that he once banned these things not simply because of his fear of their effect on other men. It was because of his fear of their effect on himself. And now, his frailties are drawing him inexorably toward those very things he held in such awe."

What Kao Li-shih did not tell Yang Kuo-chung, and which he barely admitted to himself, was that he was fairly certain that the Emperor was studying the canonical heresies of the *Tao Tsang,* the endless volumes of ancient Taoist lore, wherein lay the secrets of necromancy, alchemy, divination, and the preparation of dangerous elixirs of immortality. This last was the one that bothered him. He had no particular reason to think that the Emperor had taken that step and was dabbling with the notion of foiling death, but he knew that Taoist writings were as full of references to it as the earth was full of stones. The forbidden lure of the arcane, he feared, was drawing him in.

Yang Kuo-chung looked at Kao Li-shih's silent, thoughtful profile. He thought about telling the eunuch what the Lady of Kuo had said, apropos of the Emperor's pastime. Little Cousin, of course, told her sister everything. To the consort, it was a game, part of the exploration of the mysterious past. But the Lady of Kuo took it much more seriously. She had told Yang Kuo-chung that she herself found it more than a little disconcerting.

Discreetly, Yang Kuo-chung moved the curtain aside to check their progress. They were no longer behind the imperial livery, moving toward an ostensible meeting with the Emperor, but had detoured and were moving alone with only their outriders. Kao Li-shih had noticed nothing. Yang Kuo-chung replaced the curtain and returned his attention to their conversation.

"And what is Taoism but a mirror of the dark, obtuse side of human nature?" Kao Li-shih said. "The land abounds with incantations. We try to impose our own wills on a universe that will, in any case, make its own decisons or none at all in the face of our pleadings. Every other moment, some peasant woman drowns a firstborn child because it is a girl—unable to carry on the family name and support the parents in their later years. Everywhere, rivers bob with the tiny bodies of infants given no chance for life merely because their births were untimely. And everywhere peasants burn the joss sticks and offer up prayers and make pilgrimages to magical sites so that they should be spared this ignominious event."

Yang Kuo-chung tried in vain to ease his cramped legs into a more comfortable position. He wondered how Kao Li-shih, a head taller than he, could stand it; but he seemed oblivious.

"But the actions of the common man are not a reflection of the purity of real Taoism," Yang Kuo-chung offered. "Let us not assume that the Emperor will sink down into such a mire."

"That is true," Kao Li-shih said. "We are talking of superstition, ignorance, folly—the lowest end of human nature. It is comparable to what happens to a fine meal. No matter how superb the food—how subtle the spices, how fresh the ingredients, how great the variety, rarity, and juxtaposition of textures—no matter how masterful the sauces or the preparations, the most harmonious blending of the fives tastes are reduced to the lowest and meanest of substances in their journey through the human organism: all of the work of the greatest culinary artists becomes, simply, *shit*. And the same is true, I suspect, with philosophy. Indeed, the *hundred names** make all great ideas vulgar, passing them through unclean minds as the body passes the food through unclean organs. And it is very distressing to the rational mind."

"But isn't dung the substance from which all food is nourished and grows?" Yang Kuo-chung said, causing Kao Li-shih to smile appreciatively. "Is that not the order of the universe—the endless cycle of opposites?"

Now both Yang Kuo-chung and Kao Li-shih tried to rearrange their limbs. The feeling of cramped confinement was perfectly symbolic of the feelings of frustration and irritation both of them felt after the events of recent weeks.

"This carriage must have been designed with small children in mind," Kao Li-shih said testily.

"Or dwarfs," offered Yang Kuo-chung.

The carriage slowed to a a stop. A covered palanquin was waiting right outside the door. Kao Li-shih looked around him and noticed that they were not where he had expected to be: in the side alley that ran the length of the palace toward the Emperor's secluded rear apartments. He cast a questioning look toward Yang Kuo-chung, who simply nodded his head.

"Trust me," he said to the eunuch, who shrugged and climbed into the palanquin.

*Common men (i.e., the masses).

Inside, their quarters were even more cramped than they had been before, if such a thing was possible. The bearers, two at each corner, hoisted them aloft and began walking. Kao Li-shih turned to Yang Kuo-chung.

"I take it we are not going to see the Emperor in his quarters this morning?"

Yang Kuo-chung shook his head.

"You will see. You and I are going to accomplish much today."

The eunuch raised his eyebrows and then settled back into the cushions without another word.

Yang Kuo-chung had got Kao Li-shih to ride with him today on a pretext. Several days earlier, he had prevailed upon the eunuch to obtain a private audience with the Emperor for that morning. The Emperor, increasingly obsessed with his hobbies, had become almost as elusive and inaccessible as his chief minister, necessitating the arrangement of an appointment days in advance.

In truth, they were not going to see the Emperor at all. Yang Kuo-chung had kept their real destination a secret from Kao Li-shih, partly because he was afraid that the eunuch would not agree to go with him—and he very much wanted him along—and partly because he was afraid that Kao Li-shih might try, successfully, to dissuade him, to somehow change his mind. He himself could scarcely believe where they were going today, and he felt that he had best refrain from anything that might interfere with his dearly bought courage. And so he had determined to say nothing until it was too late to turn back. What had made him reticent this morning, and caused him to shiver in anticipation, and which he did not yet want to put into words to Kao Li-shih, was that Li Lin-fu had consented to a meeting. His macabre "calling card," suggested by the Lady of Kuo, had been effective. It would seem that she had also been right about what the chief minister was feeling—about An Lu-shan, and about his own mortality. What a fortunate thing for all of us, he thought, that the Lady of Kuo is not the sort to misuse her remarkable powers.

The palanquin rocked gently with the rhythm of the bearers' steps as they moved toward their destination. Yang Kuo-chung was supremely grateful to Kao Li-shih for his equanimity and forebearance; the eunuch did trust him and did not ask questions. And soon, any moment now, something would happen. He glanced at Kao Li-shih's profile, and in the same instant heard the clatter of hoofbeats on the cobblestones outside. He braced himself as the palanquin came to an abrupt halt.

The sound of large wheels rumbled over the stones alongside them. Orders were shouted. Kao Li-shih still said nothing, but only looked at Yang Kuo-chung. Then the palanquin was jarred violently and lifted at an awkward angle; another shout, at very close range, protested the clumsy handling of the palanquin by such morons. The angle leveled out, and they felt themselves being dropped heavily. Be careful, the voice growled; he would not be pleased to hear of your brutish handling of his guests.

Then the noises outside became muffled; at the same time, the bright morning sunlight that leaked through the spaces between the shutters was blotted out. The palanquin, Yang Kuo-chung guessed, had been covered by a heavy tarpaulin. They felt the jolt of forward motion and began to move— this time without the swaying gait of human bearers, but with the smooth rumble of wagon wheels beneath them.

Yang Kuo-chung released his breath in the stuffy darkness. The action had been quick, studied, frighteningly precise. Practiced. That was the only word to describe it. They were surrounded by the noise of clattering hooves and voices closing ranks around them. They picked up speed. The hooves of their invisible outriders pounding out a fast trot increased to a canter over the stones.

The wagon seemed to be taking a broad, gentle curve. They heard unintelligible orders being shouted far ahead now. Yang Kuo-chung braced himself again, expecting to be thrown against Kao Li-shih, but found it unnecessary. Except for an occasional rut in the road, their ride was smooth now. The commander's orders, it would seem, had been heard.

The carriage made another turn, this time off the pavement onto the rougher surface of a dirt road. They rose up the steep grade of a hill and felt their own weight pressing back on them.

"Well, Master Yang," Kao Li-shih said at last in the muffled darkness, "should I still trust you? I fear that I know who is behind this, unless there is another with his style."

"You are quite right. We are going to meet Li Lin-fu. At my suggestion, and on his terms. But one of the conditions was imposed by me."

"And what was that condition?" Kao Li-shih asked calmly, as if visiting the chief minister were an everyday event.

"That you be permitted to accompany me, so that there would be no misunderstandings."

"Thank you so much," Kao Li-shih said in a flat voice.

"His conditions," Yang Kuo-chung continued, "were that no one else come with us, and that the location of the meeting be a secret, even from us. I apologize, Master Kao, for my omission in not informing you of where you were going today. But I had a feeling that you might possibly be less than enthusiastic."

"You are quite right, Master Yang," Kao Li-shih said, putting out a steadying hand as one of the wagon wheels hit a deep rut. "I can only hope that this conveyance that we are riding on stops before we reach the South China Sea."

Yang Kuo-chung laughed nervously. "I think we can be fairly confident that it will. The readiness with which he accepted my proposal to meet indicates that he and I share a common concern."

"Which is . . . ?"

"An Lu-shan," Yang Kuo-chung said as the wagon once again picked up speed.

: :

When the silk cloth was removed from Yang Kuo-chung's eyes, he found himself in an enormous, hollow room virtually bare of furniture or decoration. In the center of the floor was a raised and carpeted dais like a small island; a couch on the dais bore a diminutive, semiprone figure in heavy robes. Even from the distance of thirty or so paces between Yang Kuo-chung and the figure on the dais, he could feel the intensity of the eyes. Set in a narrow, skeletal, sparsely whiskered face, they burned like dark, cold fire. He remembered what Kao Li-shih had said to him once: There is no warmth of mercy in those eyes, Master Yang. They burn without the heat of compassion. Cold, deep, icy wells of intellect and reason. That is all you will find.

As he walked closer to the dais, Yang Kuo-chung became aware of how small, thin, and frail was the man before them. The facial skin was nearly translucent, like oily parchment. What he saw in no way matched the mental picture of Li Lin-fu that he had carried in his imagination for so long. And how much more profoundly disturbing it was to find that the legendary omniscience of Li Lin-fu emanated from such a shrunken vessel. This was the man feared by everyone, the one who cast the shadow felt across the back of men's necks. This, Yang Kuo-chung thought, was the man who caused An Lu-shan to shake with trepidation. And Yang Kuo-chung saw something else, too: the rumors were true. It was plain that the man before them was dying. Only the eyes showed no age or loss of strength.

Looking steadily into those eyes as he approached, Yang Kuo-chung thought: I am here, Chief Minister, and not where you would have me, in the remoteness of Szechuan. And you allowed me to come because you need me. I have won this round on the gaming board.

Kao Li-shih stood, arms crossed, twenty paces behind Yang Kuo-chung, shoulders hunched slightly forward to remedy the pain in his back. It had been a long, uncomfortable ride here, and either Master Yang would get them killed today or he would make history. He had told Kao Li-shih once that he was not afraid of Li Lin-fu; the eunuch watched as Yang Kuo-chung walked steadily toward the dais. Well, Kao Li-shih thought, he does not give the impression of a man who is afraid.

But overshadowing even the strangeness of being where they were was his astonishment at Li Lin-fu's appearance. How drastically the man who wished to be called simply "Councillor" had changed in the decade since Kao

Li-shih had last set eyes on him! And what irony that his appearance of ten years ago seemed positively robust by comparison. Now, in the room's filtered morning light, in the patterned shadow of a window shutter, Kao Li-shih saw with his own eyes the ravages of the chief minister's mysterious wasting disease: the man had been fighting a desperate battle with an invisible enemy that had left its very visible mark on a decayed face and dessicated frame.

Across the room Li Lin-fu partially reclined, his upper back and head supported by the arm of the couch. One foot was planted firmly on the floor; the other leg was stretched out straight on the cushions in front of him. He is quite relaxed for such an historic meeting, Kao Li-shih thought. But to this one, nothing is new; the world repeats itself in endless cycles. He is the Minister of Iron, living again, willing an empire to his bidding.

While the chief minister and Yang Kuo-chung fixed one another with their eyes, Kao Li-shih removed his own eyes from the spectacle and turned his attention to the details of the room they occupied. Huge and cavernous, it was strangely plain—devoid of any symbols of wealth or power. But it must have been a very grand hall in its day. From its plan, Kao Li-shih guessed that once upon a time it had been used for solemn rituals of some sort. But what, exactly? Affairs of state? State worship? That was it, without a doubt. This had been a Confucian temple, built on a scale of enormous wealth. But where were they exactly? They had traveled a good distance from the audience hall, and he had not been paying attention to the route in the first part of the trip, before they switched to the palanquin. And then they had taken so many twists and turns that he had lost all sense of direction. But his instincts, and the hilly terrain and rutted roads, told him that probably they had gone north through the forested wilds of Tungchien and Tung Yuan parks. But where?

And it was not just the furnishings that had been removed. This hall had been stripped of all its ornament—even the decorative panels that had un-doubtedly once covered the walls and spanned the distances between the in-terior pillars had been removed. But not merely removed. No, Kao Li-shih thought. All the decorative elements had been purposely—viciously—pried away, revealing structural timbers here and there. And why had the word "vicious" come to his mind? Because his feeling was that it was not a ruin as a result of time and neglect: this building had been purposely desecrated—reduced with cruel, methodical efficiency.

In the center, on the island dais, a few desks and stools and low tables were grouped closely around Li Lin-fu's couch.

"I am pleased that you could join us, Master Kao." The chief minister's voice, like his eyes, was still strong.

"It has been a long time, Councillor, since I have had the honor of your presence," Kao Li-shih responded with perfect equanimity.

"Nearly ten years, Master Kao . . . a decade during which the burdens of my work have resigned me to a reclusive existence. So much to do . . ."

And so little time to do it, Kao Li-shih thought. You nearly said it. The reason the three of us are together in this room today.

"So much to do, Master Kao," Li Lin-fu repeated with finality. "A man of your position understands, surely."

Kao Li-shih did not respond, but Li Lin-fu did not allow the pause to be noticed.

"But I am flattered," he continued. "There are fewer and fewer who would be 'honored' to be in my presence."

He stretched a hand out in front of him and took in the vastness of the hall. Great shafts of late morning sunlight slanted through high windows. "Perhaps you have guessed where you are," he said. "I apologize for the secrecy, but surely you understand the precautions I must take. The unfortunate events of recent months—the clumsy attempts to replace our wise and August Imperial Father and his humble councillor with the young and inexperienced crown prince—necessitate it. Once again, after so many years, the family name of Wang appears in scandal. And we are grateful to you, Kao Li-shih, and your cohorts, for aiding Master Yang in their capture; and we are thankful, Master Yang, for your investigations through the Censorate that revealed their identities. So perhaps I must begin to think that we can work together." He smiled amiably at Yang Kuo-chung.

What irony, Kao Li-shih thought. Gratitude to the Censorate, which he nearly destroyed, and to Yang Kuo-chung, its leader. This is a strange man, indeed.

Li Lin-fu was now smiling in Kao Li-shih's direction. "But do you know where you are now?" he asked him. "Where I brought you?"

"Of course I have no idea," Kao Li-shih began. "But my conjecture is that we have come about ten li north of the palace. That is, if my poor instincts serve me correctly, Councillor." Kao Li-shih paused and returned the smile, reading the astuteness of his guess in the chief minister's eyes. I was right, he thought. "Specifically, we are near the ruins of the palaces of Han at the center of the Chin Yuan woods," he finished triumphantly.

"Commendable, Master Kao," Li Lin-fu said curtly, and swung his other foot to the floor, pushing himself into an upright position on the day couch. "Then, as my honored guests, you deserve the rest of the truth. You are standing in the hall of my ancestors. The ancestral shrine of my father and my father's father. And it is empty, stripped of its ornament, of the wasteful altars of icons and symbols of ill-spent time, because I do not honor *it* . . . or *them*! I do not attribute any importance to this hall or to any memory of them. We meet in a place that is deserving of no honor of its own nor of any artifice of dignity. And in any case, Master Kao, historians will demand that the dignity come from our meeting and from nothing else." Li Lin-fu said all of this without moving his eyes and with a face carefully devoid of expression.

Kao Li-shih responded in kind, keeping his own expression unresponsive. Li Lin-fu, in speaking with such detached calm of desecrating an ancestral shrine, was challenging him and Yang Kuo-chung to react. He himself was quite determined not to, and he trusted Yang Kuo-chung to take his cue from him. And what exactly was the meaning of his strange words? Were these the rantings of a madman, or were they carefully calculated to throw his listeners off guard in some way? He looked at Li Lin-fu. No, he thought, no one could call him mad. He is the paragon of control. It is what he has built his life on over the years.

And yet, looking at the diminutive figure of the dictator sitting up straight on the couch, Kao Li-shih had a momentary impression of a man capable of raving out of control in solitude. He would never know if this were true, but somehow it was not at all difficult to see that wasted body, that studied demeanor of placid calm twisted in rage and anguish. Possessed by inner demons. And just who were the ghosts locked inside the chief minister, he wondered?

Kao Li-shih's speculations were interrupted when Li Lin-fu lifted a small silver bell from the desk near his couch and gently rang it three times. A man entered from a side hallway carrying a bundle of writing instruments and paper under his arm; he ascended the stairs to the dais and sat down at a small table. He unrolled the parchment, filled the stone reservoir with water, and began to prepare the brushes and inks. Kao Li-shih breathed a secret sigh of relief. Probably Li Lin-fu did not intend to kill them in the presence of a scribe.

"Historians will demand an account of such an important meeting as ours, don't you agree?" Li Lin-fu said to both of them. "Most metaphysicians agree that the world is eternal—has always been here and always will be. But can historians speak with comparable certainty of the dynasty?" He took his eyes off the scribe and looked quickly from Kao Li-shih to Yang Kuo-chung. "And if there is anything that you should require stricken from our record, do not hesitate to request it! We stand, so to speak, already too vulnerable, too naked, before our inheritors."

Li Lin-fu paused and leaned back. The scribe held his brush poised above the parchment, signaling that he was ready.

"Master Yang," Li Lin-fu said, "we begin this historical meeting and . . . truce . . . at a great disadvantage. We struggle against each other. We expend great energies in this effort." From a drawer in the desk, Li Lin-fu took a small wooden box, the sort used to store fine writing brushes. "But then," he said, sliding the top back and removing a roll of heavy silk, "we also begin at a great advantage, do we not?"

He let the silk unroll; a severed hand fell to the desk with a thud. The ring carrying the Wang family seal was still in place below the knuckle of the first finger.

"It seems that the three of us are brought together," Li Lin-fu said, looking down at his guests. "Because we faced the same enemy. Had this man succeeded at his task," he said, picking the hand up by one finger, "then do you believe that I would have been spared? It was, of course, ultimately, an attempt to get *me*. And do you think for one moment that you, Master Yang, or you, Master Kao, would have been spared either?" He turned the hand around slowly, examining it. It was purplish in color, the fingers frozen in the spikey attitude of a crab's legs as if still grabbing after something. "This hand would have tried to kill us all, I assure you," he said, letting it drop once more to the desk.

Little remained of the casual graciousness that they had first heard in Li Lin-fu's voice. His tone had become, by gradual degrees, harder and more serious.

"But now that we are through with talk of plans of assassinations and palace coups, Master Yang, we must turn to the real reason for your being here. I will judge your intent only by your first words." Li Lin-fu gathered up the hand, the perfumed shroud of silk, and the box, and dropped them into the opened drawer. He slammed it shut with his knee. "Choose these words wisely. Very wisely. That is my recommendation to you. Answer me, now! Why have you come to me, Yang Kuo-chung?"

The Fox stood perfectly still in the center of the room, his arms folded behind his back. He did not look at Li Lin-fu. As Kao Li-shih studied his companion, he thought that nothing in the man's posture indicated any position of inferiority to the dictator on the dais. His equanimity, the eunuch thought, must be more than a little bit vexing to the chief minister.

Li Lin-fu waited while Yang Kuo-chung stood as if sunk in thought. Finally, Yang Kuo-chung raised his eyes to Li Lin-fu's and walked slowly toward the carpeted steps of the dais.

"I am here, Councillor, because I believe that we have something else in common. Something wholly pertinent to what we have been discussing." Yang Kuo-chung put his right foot on the first step. "We could continue to chop off hands until there was a pile reaching to the ceiling of this great room, but until we acknowledge our true enemy, the danger will continue. What you and I have in common, Councillor, is a profound concern about an ambitious and unscrupulous 'Lucky Baby.'" He brought his other foot up then so that he stood fully on the first step. His gaze was steady and impassive, matching the chief minister's. "But it is not his father that I approach. His father is deaf and blind. Instead, I choose to approach his creator."

Good! Kao Li-shih thought. Impressive! You have made your point well, my friend—that is, if we are not both executed where we stand. How many other men had audacity like this? He thought uneasily of his own reassuring words to Yang Kuo-chung when he had told him that the Flying Dragons would be watching out for him. Had he been right to speak so confidently? Would they really be a match for the chief minister's palace armies? Would it ever come to that?

There was a tense silence. The chief minister, his expression unreadable, looked down from the vantage of his day couch, resembling a mad king on his throne, his black eyes fastened on Yang Kuo-chung. But the Fox never flinched. And Kao Li-shih, his own eyes locked on the spectacle, saw something so strange that he wondered if he could trust his senses.

The chief minister had become larger, more powerful; his actual physical presence had expanded, the dissipations of his disease falling away as if they had been merely a trick of light and shadow. Like a demon, Kao Li-shih thought, that plants in the mind any image that it pleases to conjure, so Li Lin-fu had altered his own appearance. No longer was he the decaying, moribund shell they had perceived when they entered the room. He was, for the moment, restored; the dictator in his prime had reemerged, and gazed down at them. Kao Li-shih wondered if Yang Kuo-chung saw the same thing. He issued a mental warning: Do not let him have you, Fox!

"You created him, Councillor, and he grows too fast. None of us is safe," Yang Kuo-chung said to the apparition, as if he had not seen the effect at all.

So, Kao Li-shih thought; you only see it if you believe it. Evidently, the Fox does not believe!

Li Lin-fu moved uncomfortably on the couch. Kao Li-shih blinked. He had shrunk again! It was as if the illusion had been a desperate measure that he had lacked the vitality to sustain for more than a few moments. And it seemed to have cost him. The composure left his face as he shifted his body as if he intended to stand. His mouth twitched as if he were going to speak. But the Fox had not finished. He climbed up one more step.

"And who will keep a restraining, watchful eye on him, now that the Censorate has been struck dumb and blind?" Yang Kuo-chung said quietly. "Now that all other military governors in his territory have been reduced, to his advantage?"

"It is the Emperor who has foolishly promoted him! Behind my back and without my permission!" Li Lin-fu blurted out angrily.

"But who was it who set the precedent?" Yang Kuo-chung countered. "You, who have kept An Lu-shan supplied with unlimited arms and money! You, who have set him in gratuitous campaigns against enemy nations so torn from within by their own internecine struggles that they are already nearly on their knees! And do not blame the Emperor. What he has done has been only a result of his uncompromising faith in you. He follows your lead like a blind man hanging onto the arm of his friend in the wilderness."

Yang Kuo-chung was now on the dais no more than fifteen paces from the chief minister's couch. Kao Li-shih's pulse raced with excitement. If he has us killed now, right here, he thought, it will have been worth it! Li Lin-fu leaned forward away from the backrest toward Yang Kuo-chung. A twitch, a tiny flicker of motion rippled under the mottled skin of his temples and the loose fleshy folds around his left eye as he stared at the brazen young man before him.

"And with all respect, Councillor," Yang Kuo-chung continued, his voice still calm and controlled, "I do not think that you will find the answer in the pure ether of a cave." He folded his arms then. He was finished.

Kao Li-shih held his breath, the beat of his heart pounding in his ears, filling, it seemed to him, the great empty desecrated hall with its sound. He thought how little his title and position meant. Here, in Li Lin-fu's domain, they were meaningless. There was no immunity from danger, no charmed invulnerability in the fact that he was the Emperor's chief eunuch, advisor, and best friend. What of it? There were no sacrileges that had not already been committed in the name of power. This was the man who arranged the death of the Emperor's favorite son, was he not? And if I die at Li Lin-fu's hands, he mused, historians will undoubtedly find a justification. "So horrible a death," they will say, "is simply proof of so monstrous a life." They will assume that my life was one marked by plots, palace coups, intrigues, and assassination attempts, and they will find a way to demonstrate that the eunuch Kao Li-shih got what he deserved. What would they know of a man whose greatest joy was the solitude of his garden? Historians will have little trouble dealing with the death of the fiery Master Yang. They will call him the mighty Li Lin-fu's arch opponent, and cite his temper and his brashness. That will be the cause of *his* death; mine will simply be by association.

Yang Kuo-chung's amazing words reverberated in the cavernous air. The two men stared at one another until Li Lin-fu, the skin around one eye twitching and fluttering like a dying bug's wing, slowly leaned back onto his cushions and turned toward the scribe, who was finishing a page with a flurry of strokes.

"Have we gone too fast for you?" he asked the man.

The scribe shook his head.

"You see," Li Lin-fu brought his gaze to Kao Li-shih's face now, "I must rely totally upon my scribes." He raised his hands in supplication, then looked back at Yang Kuo-chung. "I cannot read or write a word of this language. It simply will not hold still for me. In certain less-than-lucid moments I have thought of my condition as a plague, a curse, bestowed upon me by my father who hated me. You see"—he smiled—"I was ugly, and that was an embarrassment to him. Much as he wanted to do it, I could not simply be tossed into the river like the firstborn daughter of an impoverished family—at least not without considerable scandal to one of the leading clans of the Kuanchung aristocracies. There would have been such talk among the houses of the Hsuan-yang capital district, you understand—not to mention the name of the royal House of Li which we are so heavily burdened with. This ugly, sickly, small, diminutive child—an insulting product of his own defective life-force and the only male offspring he would ever produce . . ." His voice trailed off, as if he were lost in contemplation.

Yang Kuo-chung and Kao Li-shih waited, somewhat stupefied by the chief minister's digression.

He looked up again. "As I have said, I was not worth a scandal among the leading province's most powerful family. A serving maid once told me that my father crept into the nursery late one night when I was already three—not counting the year in the womb—and it was obvious that he had meant to leave no trace. His hands were already around my tiny neck. He was very close to strangling me, had her entrance not interrupted him. And even at so young an age, she said, I did not cry. But my eyes frightened him." He laughed, his manner easy and gracious again now as if he were entertaining Yang Kuo-chung and Kao Li-shih at a dinner party.

"And here I am now, before you, illiterate and inextinguishable . . . I have often thought how good a thing it is that I am illiterate. Reading and writing are acts that merely disguise the beast in man. Chuang-tzu was right: the real is inexpressible. My knowledge of the beast is intimate. This beast that is 'human nature' is disguised—no, inadequately defined—by the limited essence, the narrowing parameters of the written word. There is none among all the poets, the literati, whose words are sufficient to describe the evil that is present in us! But I fear that this realization would put dear, naive Mencius in a state of shock. And even the others, the ones who believed in innate evil, were only partly correct. It is much worse than even they imagined."

The scribe, with a perplexed expression, lifted his head up from the page and looked questioningly to the chief minister.

"Do not strike any of this from our records," he admonished the man. "Our progeny must know that it is the illiterate as well as the evil who will inherit this world. And if it is not to be myself . . ." He shrugged. "In my own case, I must be satisfied with the immediate satisfactions of the gift of illiteracy." He leaned forward again, fired by his own words. "It has allowed me, gentlemen, to hone my other sensibilities. The instruments of reason and comprehension, pure and uncompromised. Leaving writing and reading to others frees fundamental and far more profound capacities of insight and introspection . . ."

Li Lin-fu paused and looked from Yang Kuo-chung down to his own thin, veined hands which he now rested on the edge of the desk. "If you will allow me another short digression, Master Yang Kuo-chung?"

Li Lin-fu seemed to be rambling, Kao Li-shih thought. It was not at all the way the eunuch remembered him—a man whose words and ideas had always flowed, logical and cogent, as smoothly as warm honey from a hive. The realization came now to Kao Li-shih: Li Lin-fu was failing, had been failing for some time now. He was not the man he once was.

"Our forces in the far northwest have begun to crumble, as you well know," Li Lin-fu continued, lifting his hands slightly above the desktop and bringing them down again with an emphatic slap, ". . . with dreadful and ominous regularity, to the Muslims. And their prophet Mohammed was quite unable to write down his own divine rules. He, too, was illiterate! I make a point of knowing my enemies well; I have even studied his book. My scholars have translated much of it for me. According to the legends of the Muslim people, it was Mohammed's archangel who recorded his 'blessed' Koran on the shoulder blades of sheep, as the prophet recited it . . . and now, millions do his bidding. But as you speak of An Lu-shan, I also think of his raw, illiterate power. But you may be correct, Yang Kuo-chung. Illiteracy is, perhaps, far more dangerous in such a man than I had at first assessed. He is untempered by even the most rudimentary restraints of civilization. And those restraints are, perhaps, more due to the power of 'written words' than I may have previously thought. But An Lu-shan was an illiterate, and his naive ruthlessness served us well. That was his advantage over other men; that was how I saw the phenomenon of our good general."

Li Lin-fu pushed away from the desk and laid his head back on the cushions, his eyes drifting to the far lintels of the ceiling, his breathing labored. The scribe's brush halted at the same moment and sat poised in his fingers, waiting for the next words of the historic meeting. The Fox had uncrossed his arms and stood leaning with one hand on a nearby desk. Was he relaxing his guard, Kao Li-shih wondered, or was the pose a signal of some sort to Li Lin-fu, a subtle way of telling him that the long war of attrition between them could be ended? Must be ended? Li Lin-fu raised his head from the cushions and directed his gaze at Kao Li-shih. After a long while, the chief minister spoke again.

"We have heard nothing from you, Master Kao. Am I to take this as a sign that you have nothing to add as our August Imperial Father's servant?"

Kao Li-shih was fairly certain that his impression of a few moments ago was correct, that Li Lin-fu was no longer in control of this meeting. But he was a clever man, to say the least. The appearance of uncertainty could be an effect, carefully calculated.

"As my Emperor's servant," Kao Li-shih replied, moving toward the dais, "I have nothing to add. I cannot speak for a man who now seeks after magic—the convolutions of the Dark Tao—for his answers, Councillor. Surely, you, of all people, understand Minghuang's inattention to affairs of state." Kao Li-shih followed Yang Kuo-chung's example, walking slowly to the foot of the chief minister's stairs. He placed one hand on the ornate banister, the lone concession to decoration in the room. His heart pounded painfully against his ribs now. Move slowly, he told himself. Move slowly and speak deliberately.

"But I can and will speak for myself. Your existence alone, and the power you hold, are proof of the fragility of his link to reality, Councillor." He took a step up. "And, if you will excuse me, Councillor, your own link grows weaker."

"And what link is that, Master Kao?" Li Lin-fu said, fixing his eyes on the eunuch.

"It has been ten years since I saw you last, Councillor. I know what ten years can do to a man. I know what it has done to myself and to the Emperor. But you"—he shook his head—"have not aged ten years. You have aged thirty."

"Then what do you tell me?" Li Lin-fu defied him.

"I see Death, Councillor," Kao Li-shih said, not quite believing that the words were issuing from his own mouth. "It is looking over your right shoulder."

"But Death is always with us from the moment of our inception," Li Lin-fu said with a smile. "From the moment before our consciousness enters the world, it is an imminent parameter of our being. An inevitable limit that we face, Master Kao, that gives meaning to the rest. Nothing exists without its borders defined."

"I am not speaking of death as an abstract concept, Councillor. I am speaking of its palpable presence. As a visitor in your house. I too know that I will die some day, but as yet, I have not felt Death's arm draped over my shoulder or heard it whisper in my ear." He took another step up. "I am speaking of your own death, Councillor, which you seek to avoid. At terrible expense."

"At *what* expense, Kao Li-shih? What expense do you speak of?" Li Lin-fu said in an ominous voice, his facade of cheery fellowship evaporated.

Kao Li-shih ascended the final few stairs and stood next to Yang Kuo-chung. Now he too looked directly down into the ruined face and the small cold eyes.

"Certainly it is not at my expense. That alone would matter little. No, it is at *our* expense. Everyone's. And the peace and prosperity that our Imperial Father once worked so hard at, and for which we have him to thank."

"Eunuch," Li Lin-fu said, addressing him that way for the first time, his voice filled with disdain, "our Emperor is a fool. Let us not play at word games any longer. He may have been a great Emperor once, but he is as useful now as one of his five-year-old princelings in the imperial nursery. He is lost in irresponsible pleasure dreams, fantasies." He turned his eyes to Yang Kuo-chung. "Fantasies nurtured by these Yangs." He pronounced the name contemptuously. "If there is peace, it is because I have worked to maintain it. There is no peace except peace through strength!"

"And will you lose it for all of us, Master Li Lin-fu? Will we lose it because you cannot reconcile yourself to your imminent mortality?" Kao Li-shih said, placing his hands on the other side of the chief minister's desk and leaning toward him.

He felt exhilarated. An energy was rising, flowing through him, that he had not felt in years—not even on the night when he had crouched behind the Emperor's dressing chest awaiting the assassins. Maybe he had never felt this: he was drawing on some great, untapped reserve of strength. This, his instincts told him, was the real battle. Everything else had been play, a child's practice for real life, games of mock combat played with false mustaches, wooden swords, and hobbyhorses while safely within the walled enclosure of a garden compound. But this was real.

"Councillor," Kao Li-shih said. "Something has been set in motion, by you. Something that grows more difficult for you to control with each passing day. You speak of games and fantasies. The Emperor's delusions are as nothing compared to those of a man who tries to elude his own death." He straightened up. "Do not lie to yourself, Chief Minister. Do not lie with your stars and your numbers. Do not deceive yourself. You are dying. Your informers have told you what is already happening in the north. He is barely under your control now. What will happen when you die?"

"An Lu-shan garrisons a display of force, a military maneuver, a simple and highly effective parade of the T'ang's northern border solidarity," Li Lin-fu countered, ". . . a singular, clear message stating our resolve and intent to the Mongolian Khitan and Hsi and, yes, even to Mohammed's scourge . . . and this frightens you?"

"I grant you that it is a message of solidarity and arrogant strength," Yang Kuo-chung said. "But I fear that the message is to *himself* only, Councillor. I have seen it in his eyes, and so has Kao Li-shih. He does not kowtow to us as he does to you. You have never seen the anger of the caged animal, the murderer in his eyes. You have never seen him seethe with resentment. He parades his solidarity—two hundred and fifty thousand strong and growing—to appease only himself. And he has found in the secessionists of Hopei Province, among those who hate this House of T'ang, a brotherhood. People who allow him to be a king, an emperor, call it what you will."

"And who tells you this, Master Yang?" Li Lin-fu leaned forward onto the desk, his temple twitching violently.

"One that you would have liked to have seen dead long ago."

Kao Li-shih looked sharply in the Fox's direction.

"Someone who is beyond your reach now, and beyond the reach of An Lu-shan as well. You remember Li Shih-chih, I am sure. A man you deposed in favor of our 'Lucky Baby.' "

Kao Li-shih was startled by Yang Kuo-chung's bluff. He spoke as if Li Shih-chih still lived. Was it possible that his death was not known to Li Lin-fu yet? Evidently Master Yang thought so and sought to use the possibility to gain some subtle advantage. Just as he had earlier when he revealed that he knew about Li Lin-fu's desperate journey to the caves. Kao Li-shih was impressed. Master Yang portioned it out slowly to Li Lin-fu, like a chef adding ever stronger condiments to a delicate broth.

"A man who would have been dead but for the fact that your machinery of reprisal is losing its efficiency," Yang Kuo-chung said.

Now Kao Li-shih understood.

Li Lin-fu seized the corners of the desk for a moment, then let go and raised his bony hands, clenching them into fists. It looked as though he meant to strike either his own face or the surface of the desk. But he didn't. Slowly, he lowered them. Then he pushed himself up from the couch to his feet, one steadying hand firmly on the desk.

"Yes, gentlemen. Kao Li-shih; *Duke* Yang Kuo-chung—that is what they call you now? Duke! So many titles and favors from our Emperor . . . so many . . . Your rise so much like my own so many years ago." He gave a dry half-smile. "Kao Li-shih will tell you of those precious days when I played my music and supped with an already foolish Emperor. Yes, gentlemen, you are right. I am dying. What time I have I do not know. The physicians argue and debate over the merits of this and that cure . . . they pore over books and come up with all manner of foul-smelling concoctions, and force me to swallow them. And indeed, there are times when I do not cough all night . . . long periods when I do not bleed from the mouth and nose. Times when I can eat again, when I can convince myself that the shadow is passing, that there may yet be harmony between my *hun* and *p'o* vital spirits." He sat down heavily and gently massaged the sides of his head. "But I am not deluded. I realize, now, that the absence of the shadow is only a hole in the clouds, and a small one at that. It does not last. The clouds quickly move in to cover that small, warm, bright rift. The fits of coughing return; the fire burns my lungs like paper; the foul discharges colored with blood again pass the breathing gates." He looked up at his visitors. "Truly, I am not the 'glistening and splendid lion' that I once was, not the 'executor and accomplisher' anymore." He fell silent for a few moments, lowering his head into his hands on the desk.

Kao Li-shih and Yang Kuo-chung exchanged looks. Was it almost possible to feel compassion for the man in front of them? If Li Lin-fu ever aroused that emotion, Kao Li-shih thought, and he was almost doing it now, it would be the greatest feat of deception of his life.

Li Lin-fu looked up suddenly as if he had intercepted an idea. "Perhaps, Master Yang, *you* are that 'Lion.' 'Fox' hardly seems to be a worthy epithet for you anymore. Indeed, you have outgrown it. You may not be able to see it, but it is plain to me. What do you think, Kao Li-shih? Does he look like a fox to you anymore? Or has he grown into some other, more splendid, beast? 'A great soul in so small a destiny,' a poet once said. Yes. And we shall change that. We shall change that. Scribe," he said, without looking at the man whose brush flew down the page. "Make a note of this, in particular. There are to be two military governorships in absentia established—the first in Shuofang. Let it be known that I, Li Lin-fu, am reviving my own in absentia military governorship of that province, dormant for fifteen years now, and that such a governorship supersedes any recent appointments to that position, which are to be considered to have been temporary in nature only. And upon my death"—he looked steadily now at Yang Kuo-chung—"that governorship is to pass directly to my lieutenant chief minister, Yang Kuo-chung."

Kao Li-shih wondered at the impassiveness of the scribe. Did he take down such history every day, that he could sit and write as if he were making a list for the kitchens? Shuofang Province had been the Emperor's reward to An Lu-shan for saving his life, the promotion he had bestowed upon An Lu-shan without consulting Li Lin-fu. And Li Lin-fu was neatly taking it back now, on a technicality, so that he could pass that key control of a huge border province on to Yang Kuo-chung, whom it would not have been possible to appoint directly. But by reactivating his own old position, Li Lin-fu was, in effect, finding a way to give it to Yang Kuo-chung and put An Lu-shan, his own protégé, out of the running. I am dying, gentlemen, he had said. And look at how calmly this man works contrary to an emperor's will, Kao Li-shih thought. At that moment, looking down at the wizened chief minister calmly rearranging history and shuffling imperial appointments to his own specifications, Kao Li-shih understood that he was looking at the true ruler of China, the one hidden behind the jade screen. The one who preferred to be called "Councillor" only.

"The second military governorship in absentia to be established," Li Lin-fu continued, "is to be effective immediately. Master Yang Kuo-chung, I believe Szechuan is familiar territory to you. I think you are eminently qualified to oversee the military concerns of that province. Do you accept the position?"

"I accept it, Councillor," Yang Kuo-chung said quietly.

"You are, I believe, the head of the Censorate already."

Yang Kuo-chung almost had to smile at the ironic humor of Li Lin-fu's question. But he did not. "I am," he replied.

"Then you are to use the vested powers of the Censorate, as you see fit, to monitor any military activities in the empire or near its borders which, in your opinion, merit scrutiny. There will be no . . . interference," he said succinctly. "Did you get all of it?" he asked the scribe, who nodded, eyes still on the page as he filled in the last few characters.

A long quiet followed. No one spoke or moved as the significance of the chief minister's pronouncements settled into their minds; the vast empty hall around Yang Kuo-chung made him feel that he was standing alone in a great sea of time and history. The silence grew to a din that raged like the sunlight's fire across the wide polished boards of the floor.

"Do you know, my good guests," the chief minister said at last, "that I am buying time for myself and for the empire? I had tried every cure, until recently, but one. I find it interesting and significant that the most potent cure, the one that has, I can assure you, lengthened my life already and without which I would have been grinning in my mausoleum for many weeks now, is the one that others call shocking, heretical. But one should not unqualifiedly trust the words of others. Each physician seeks to guard the cures that he passes to his sons and denies the effectiveness of others' cures. Jealousy of the trade, I suppose: this one concentrating on the lungs, another upon the spleen, another upon the bowel . . . my own good physician would be appalled at my actions, so I have not told him." He lowered his voice. "It is *our* secret. Scribe, you may leave now. Your services are no longer required."

He sat back with a sly smile as the scribe hastily scrambled to gather up his papers, ink pots, and brushes with as much alacrity as he could muster. When the man had backed up twenty paces or so and then scurried from the room, Li Lin-fu turned back to his guests.

"My physician is a good and faithful servant. And no doubt, many of his breathing exercises have maintained me far longer than cruel nature would have intended. Therefore, I do him the service, the genteel kindness of recip-rocation, of saving his delicate sensibilities. My cure is one that would be considered strange, even outrageous by the squeamish among you. You have heard, I assume, of 'two-legged mutton'? Personally, I find the taste to be more like sweet, young pork. It is really quite delicious when properly dressed and prepared. And of course, it must be fresh; otherwise the essential *chi* is ineffective—dispelled."

He looked at Yang Kuo-chung and Kao Li-shih, who stood listening to the chief minister's words with closed faces.

"Some would call it . . . uncivilized. But then what is civilization? What is heresy? It is all so relative, is it not? How many female infants are drowned or buried alive every day, their flesh going to no better use than to feed the fish and the worms? Better that their flesh give me the strength I need to keep a vigilant eye on our own 'Lucky Baby.' What I do, I do for the empire." He paused conspiratorially. "Besides, what is one child *more* or *less*?"

20

Father Springtime Returns

[An Lu-shan] appealed to [the Emperor and his favorite] as a grotesque clown. He had become enormously fat and with his gaucherie in matters of court etiquette provided much amusement. Later, people saw in this a mask deliberately adopted to hide his treacherous intentions. . . . No doubt he learned quickly and in later years capitalized on the effect of his buffooneries to secure in the emperor's personal favour a refuge.

—*Edwin Pulleyblank*

Spring, A.D. 754

He had forgiven her. How could he stay angry forever? With the first whiff of her perfume carrying on the spring breeze, he knew that his anger was gone, like snow that vanishes in the heat of the sun.

The rolling, gentle gait of the horse beneath him was nearly putting him to sleep. It had been an easy trip down from the north, the landscape turning softer and greener and the air warmer and sweeter as he traveled; today, with less than one li to go until he was at the gate of the city, An Lu-shan felt the warmth on his back as if it were already full summer. He had an overpowering desire to get rid of some of his clothes. He had spent the entire bitterly cold, interminable winter wrapped in heavy, stinking clothes, his body sweating and unwashed beneath.

He jerked his tunic up and over his head, setting free his own rank perfume as he did. In only a few hours, he would be sitting in a hot, flower-scented pool, steam rising around him, soothing water penetrating every fold and crevice of his skin. He had never wanted anything so keenly in his life, it seemed to him at this moment, as a bath. He rubbed his fat chest in the soft air. After the bath, the very next thing he wanted was some female flesh.

Something tender and dainty, sweet and smooth. Something that would giggle and squeal, and squirm a little in resistance, then yield to him prettily.

And of course, he wanted to see his mother and father, who had called him down this spring to help them celebrate. The Emperor had said to him, the first time they ever met, that An Lu-shan would be perfect in the role of Kao Mei, an ancient god of fertility in some festival or other that they wanted to revive. He remembered how the Emperor had shrugged and smiled apologetically, and told him that playing the part would mean that he would have to wear flowers in his hair and make love to a lot of beautiful young women, so probably he would not be interested. Thinking of it now, he laughed aloud. Gods, but he wanted to see his friend and father the Emperor again, too! And he was ready for some fun, that was certain. Already he could picture laughing, happy faces delighting in the antics of Kao Mei, their earthy, rotund god of lust. If it is Kao Mei they want, he thought, then it is Kao Mei they will get.

Ch'ang-an. She was waiting for him. And when a woman waits for a man she knows she has mistreated, she becomes yearning and contrite, sweet and conciliatory. And he was feeling magnanimous. Had he not spent the winter working hard, on her behalf? Making the northern borders secure as iron so that not even a mouse could get through? Had he not sacrificed, riding hundreds of li month after month until his butt was rubbed raw, sleeping in tents with the bitter wind howling in his ears, doing a man's work so that his lady could rest easy, and wear her finery, and luxuriate in her being? This was how it was between men and women, he knew. And he had been angry, but it had passed. The manly thing to do was to forgive. He consented, now, to return and to accept her offerings of reconciliation.

: :

It seemed as if the entire city were dressed in flowers. Looking out over the vast crowd of people in the street, An Lu-shan saw flowers everywhere. They hung in festoons from balconies and windows, spiraled around doorframes, threaded through the spokes of wheels on everything from ox carts to carriages, were braided into the manes and tails of horses, and sat gaily atop the heads and wound around the horns of oxen. The pavement was solid with blossoms, so that the wheels of vehicles passing in slow procession left mashed tracks through them. And every head that An Lu-shan saw wore flowers, from babies in their mothers' arms to old men with no teeth.

And he was lord of all the flowers, lord of the Royal Spring Festival of Kao Mei, last celebrated over a millennium ago and brought back to life now by the consort and the Emperor. He sat on his garlanded litter, being carried toward the Serpentine Park at the far southern edge of Ch'ang-an. As they drew close, the sound of singing reached his ears. First the high, clear voices of girls, then the lower voices of boys answering. As his litter was carried into the park, the crowd parted and the singing surrounded him. On one side of the roadway stood hundreds of young girls; on the opposite side stood the boys. All were dressed in their best and carried armloads of blossoms. They sang back and forth to one another; when they saw Kao Mei approaching, his face painted in all the festive colors of spring and a crown of blossoms on his head, they raised their voices with renewed enthusiasm and hurled flowers through the air as he passed down their ranks. An Lu-shan raised his arms in greeting; the young voices swelled, engulfing him in the antiphonal refrains of a sweet love song: will you follow me to the river, the boys asked. I will go if you give me a good reason, the girls answered. I want to show you something so beautiful there, said the boys. And what could be so beautiful? asked the girls. I want to show you the face of the girl I love; she lives under the water. Just come and look down into the river and you will see her, answered the boys.

On and on the song went, celebrating the sweet absurdities of shy, chaste, circumspect, youthful courtship. As he passed through them, they came toward each other, closed ranks, and joined hands so that they formed a long, long line, with every girl between two boys and every boy between two girls. When he was finally up on his flower-decked throne overlooking the entire green, rolling park and the Serpentine River, he saw that they had turned themselves into a beautiful, undulating dragon. The twenty or so at the head of the line, ones he recognized as being royal children from the Ten Mansions—imperial sons, daughters, grandchildren, nieces, nephews, and cousins—now carried a beautiful, elaborate dragon head made of wood and painted silk, with fearsome, rolling eyes and terrible white fangs. At the other end of the line, they carried his spiked, lashing tail.

Still singing its love song, the "dragon" snaked toward the water on its hundreds of feet and waded in among the river orchids that grew in profusion on the banks. And as it entered the water, the dragon dissolved into its component parts; the girls and boys scattered playfully, laughed, splashed water at one another, and began to pick handfuls of orchids.

While the singing tail of the dragon was still wending its way into the river, the others emerged, dripping and happy, and laid the orchids before the raised dais where Kao Mei sat on his throne. As the boys and girls—from imperial progeny to the offspring of wealthy, titled Ch'ang-an families to the children of ordinary citizens—passed in front of him, An Lu-shan, in his role of the overseer of love, gave his blessings. A pitcher of wine had been put in his hand, and for each blessing he bestowed on a young couple shyly standing before him for a moment after laying down the orchids on the growing pile, he took a long drink. The wine was delicious, sweet and peppery all at once, and it tasted to him as if it had been made from flowers, too.

It was late afternoon, warm and glorious, on this day of the spring equinox. The Serpentine Park was filled as far as the eye could see with celebrants. Little children, heads bright with colorful blooms, rode the shoulders of their fathers. Groups of musicians wandered through the throngs, and food vendors sang out their offerings. Wealthy families, full household staffs in attendance, had staked out the choicest knolls and glens in the park and set themselves up with carpets, pillows, canopies, and elaborate picnics. Groups of boys and girls joined hands in imitation of the "dragon" and threaded their way through the crowds, singing, their numbers growing as others joined the processional. Everywhere, the mood was one of play and lighthearted flirtatiousness. People held up children and tiny baby boys and girls in mock "betrothals," asking for Kao Mei's blessing, which he bestowed lavishly. When his wine pitcher was empty, another one appeared in his hand. His wine-warmed blood moved freely in his veins, like an ice-bound river melting and breaking up when winter is over.

The air over the people's heads turned hazy and golden as the shadows lengthened. Clouds of swirling insects hung in shafts of afternoon sunlight. They, too, knew that it was spring and time for love! An Lu-shan raised his pitcher to them. Kao Mei blesses you as well, he said, laughing and pouring more wine down his throat. He marveled at the air. It was alive: thick, warm and green. He wiped his mouth and beard with the back of his arm and filled his lungs, closing his eyes for a moment. Where had he been? In the north, where the winter air cut him like a knife? Where the ground was hard, gray, and frozen? Where all he saw were grim-faced men in their dark, dreary, heavy clothing, and all he smelled was rancid cooking fat and his own weary flesh?

He had vague memories of being in such a place, but he thought now that he must have dreamed it. He opened his eyes again on the glorious spring day in front of him and Ch'ang-an dressed in her brilliant robes of flowers, and smiled, and raised his pitcher again. A dream. A memory of another life. No such place could possibly exist.

::

"He was splendid today, was he not?" the Precious Consort asked her sisters. "He *was* Kao Mei, in the flesh!"

" 'In the flesh,' indeed, laughed the Lady of Han. "He has sufficient flesh to accommodate three or four gods."

"It was distinctly obvious to *me* that he has less flesh than when he departed last year," said the Lady of Chin. "Our 'Lucky Baby' does not get sufficient food when he is in his northern wasteland, I fear."

"Nonsense," said the Lady of Han. "He is quite as enormous as he ever was. More so, in fact."

"What do *you* think, Sister?" the Lady of Chin asked the Lady of Kuo. "Is he larger or smaller than when we saw him last?"

Lanterns were lit everywhere on the hot springs grounds as night descended. Carriages were still arriving from the city, bringing important guests to the Emperor's private celebration of the Festival of Kao Mei. Laughter and music drifted up to where the Lady of Han, the Lady of Chin, the Precious Consort, and the Lady of Kuo stood on the front balcony of the Lady of Kuo's private apartments high atop a rise overlooking the lakes and pavilions.

The Lady of Kuo was pensive for a moment before responding to her sister's question.

"The only certain difference in his appearance is that he looks happier," she said at last. "I think it does him good to go back up north and live a rough sort of existence for part of the year. I do not think that he could tolerate being here at court all of the time."

"Well, he certainly seems glad to be here now, doesn't he?" the Precious Consort asked happily. "And I am glad that he is here. I am glad that it is spring, that all of us are alive at the same time, and that the world is so beautiful! Do you know what we have done today?" she asked, eyes shining in the soft lantern-light as she looked at each of her sisters in turn. "We have brought back the Golden Age. And the four of us—and the Emperor—are part of it. We *are* it! When we were children, we played at living in magic worlds. Now we truly live in one. Look at where we are," she said, lowering her voice compellingly and conspiratorially. "Is this not magic?"

The Lady of Kuo pondered the question. It was hard not to believe in magic tonight. And what, after all, was magic? Did it have to be something imaginary, unobtainable? If I achieved it, she wondered, would I even recognize it? Perhaps "magic" was such a subtle state that one could miss it. Perhaps, at some time in the future, people would be looking back on this time that she lived in, and she and her sisters and An Lu-shan would appear as magical, mythical figures. If her life looked like magic to those unborn people, then why couldn't it be magic now, while she was living it?

She thought about An Lu-shan. For a while, she had worried that perhaps she had betrayed him by revealing to Cousin the barbarian's fears and unease about Li Lin-fu. But with the passing of the winter, she had come to think that her instincts had been sound. All appeared to be well. Yang Kuo-chung had met with Li Lin-fu, and the Censorate had been watching An Lu-shan— and he had been doing his job and behaving himself. And now he was here —cheerful, ebullient, his old self, the way he had been when she first knew him. It would seem that a little discipline was all that he had needed, and it had not hurt him.

She smiled at her sisters.

"Maybe it *is* magic," she said to them. "In a magic world, one is safe from all danger. And if we feel safe, perhaps we have An Lu-shan to thank."

"Kao Mei," corrected the Precious Consort. Hooves clattered on the drive far below. She rose expectantly and went to the railing.

A carriage solidly decked with flowers had pulled into the long, sweeping drive. A drunken voice sang blissfully from inside, the sound carrying clearly up the rise and through the trees to where they stood; the sisters recognized An Lu-shan's Kushan lullaby. The Emperor, they knew, had been waiting for his 'Lucky Baby' to arrive before holding the grand event of the evening. It was not one the sisters wanted to miss.

"Let us go join the Emperor," the consort said. "Kao Mei has arrived."

: :

An Lu-shan rolled like a river horse in the steaming pool, diving under and rising again and again, letting the water run off him in great rivulets. When he brought his ears up into the air, they were filled with the sweet sounds of the Pear Garden Orchestra, laughter, and singing; when he submerged himself again, the sounds echoing around the Emperor's bathing pavilion became muted, muffled, a hundred li away. He rolled onto his back, held his breath, sank down again, and looked up through the water's surface; lantern-light and blurred forms danced and shimmered before his eyes. He stayed that way for as long as he could, letting a thin stream of bubbles escape from his nose and rise in two little silvery chains toward the light.

When he finally brought his head up for air, the Emperor was standing at the edge of the pool looking down at him.

"Are you drowning, An Lu-shan?" he asked pleasantly. He held an ornate silver urn and wore nothing but a damp silk cloth draped around his middle. "I hope not, because this piece of paper has your name written on it." He held up a folded scrap which he dropped into the urn.

"I am only drowning in bliss, Father," An Lu-shan said, doing a languid breaststroke toward the edge of the pool.

"You have earned it, 'Lucky Baby,' " the Emperor said.

"Please! Tonight my name is Kao Mei! I am the overseer of love and sweet dalliance!"

The Emperor laughed and moved on to another guest.

An Lu-shan pulled himself up out of the water and sat, legs dangling, on the tiled ledge. One of the women approached him immediately, put a pitcher of wine in his hand, and began to dry him with a coarse towel, massaging his flesh as she did. She rubbed him vigorously and dug her little hands deliciously into the meat of his shoulders and back. He took a deep swallow from the pitcher, let his head roll back, and closed his eyes. Wine ran down his chin and neck.

She moved around to the front and began to work on his chest. Eyes still closed, he breathed her fragrance, then brought his head down as she started rubbing his hair and neck. He opened his eyes, focused them with some effort, and found that her breasts under her loose silk robe were on a level with his face. His free hand came up as if it were an independent entity from his brain and pulled aside the front of the robe, exposing a very pretty round breast. She giggled pleasantly and covered herself; he pushed her hand away and pulled the robe free again. He hefted the breast in his cupped hand, feeling the soft weight of it; she giggled again, pushed him away firmly, covered herself, and resumed her rubbing and massaging of his shoulders. He smiled, shut his eyes once more, and dropped his hands acquiescently.

When she finished drying him, she placed a fresh crown of flowers on his head, smiled prettily, and took her leave. He returned the smile, but did not detain her. There was no hurry. The Emperor would be taking care of him tonight.

"Somebody help me stand," he said loudly, raising his arms. Several of the women surrounded him and playfully pushed and pulled as he heaved himself to his feet. His robe was thrown over his shoulders. He swayed for a moment, steadied himself, and made his way toward the stairs leading up to the pavilion where the Emperor and the sisters awaited him. One hand firmly gripping the ornate banister, he climbed.

Music poured down the stairs toward him. The Pear Garden Orchestra was playing a lively dance tune now, and soon he could hear the swirling of the women's dresses and the scuffle of their little bare feet on the floor. When he got to the top of the stairs, he went and stood in the doorway. A great benevolent smile spread across his face.

The room was filled with the Emperor's guests. Some were high court officials, some he recognized as wealthy Ch'ang-an businessmen. Tonight, the barriers between merchant and aristocrat were let down. Others were relatives of the Emperor—sons, cousins, and uncles of the royal family. All, with the exception of the Yang sisters and the harem women, were male. They ranged in age from youths of no more than twenty to men older than the Emperor. They talked and laughed, watching the dancers in the way that men do when they are among themselves. The Emperor stood when he saw "Father Spring-time" in the doorway and beckoned him with a smile to join him and the sisters.

People applauded and smiled as An Lu-shan crossed the room. He felt a warm, satisfied glow of fellowship and goodwill toward them all. They appreciated him, were cognizant of his sacrifices, and knew how to reward him and make him feel welcome. As he passed by them, he jokingly raised his arms to bestow his blessings on them, just as he had been doing all day in his role as Kao Mei.

"Don't waste your blessing on me," said the Emperor when An Lu-shan reached him. "There is only one woman I am allowed to touch." As he spoke, he fondly caressed the consort's hand.

"Oh, you are free to do as you please," said the consort.

"I know that," he said, gazing at her.

"Stop," said the Lady of Kuo. "You are making us ill. Not even Kao Mei himself can tolerate such sickening displays of true love!"

"Kao Mei is in an excellent and most tolerant mood tonight, madam," An Lu-shan said to the Lady of Kuo as he joined them. He looked around then. "I do not see your . . . companion this evening. Does this mean that I dare entertain a hope . . . ?"

"Why would you want a worn-out old hag like me?" she replied. Then she lowered her voice and spoke suggestively into his ear. "Aren't you even curious to know what the Emperor has planned for you?" An Lu-shan licked his lips. Indeed, he burned with curiosity. He had seen the Emperor put the scrap of paper with his name on it into the urn. What did it mean? All these men in the room seemed to know. He flicked his eyes about, from the dancing women to the men and back again. The Lady of Kuo smiled knowingly, and so did the Lady of Han and the Lady of Chin. Drunk though he was, An Lu-shan felt a dark prurient thrill deep in his gut.

The Emperor dipped his hand into the urn and rustled the pile of papers around in a way that An Lu-shan found infinitely enticing.

"My fate is in your hands, Father," he said.

The Emperor looked around the room at his guests, then whispered something to the Precious Consort. Her sisters leaned close to her while she whispered something to them in turn. They nodded at the Emperor, who then stood and raised his hand, signaling the orchestra. They continued to play, but softly now. The women slowed their dance down; their movements became languid, measured, sensual. The men in the room fell silent in attitudes of comfortable contemplation, their eyes following the dancers.

The Emperor, holding the urn, walked to the center of the floor. The watching men applauded as he raised the vessel and then put his hand in again to swirl the contents about. With his arm still inside the urn, the Emperor looked all around the room, catching the eyes of nearly every guest, it seemed to An Lu-shan, and exchanging a secret confidence. His face went through a range of expressions, from perplexity to surprise to sly determination, as he felt around inside the urn. Then his eyes lit up as if he had found something he was looking for, and his hand came slowly out, holding one of the scraps of paper.

With elaborate, exaggerated slowness, he turned the paper around, unfolded it, and turned it around and around again while squinting at it as if it were upside down, illegible, or written in a language he did not quite understand. The watching men laughed and shouted their encouragement. Then the Emperor raised his eyes and directed his gaze toward a group of men to his left. Great smiles spread across their faces. When the Emperor finally read aloud a name, one of the men in the group, a man well into his sixties, An Lu-shan thought, stood triumphantly for a moment before his friends pulled him back down and filled his cup again.

One of the women had come forward with another urn. The Emperor dropped the scrap of paper into it, then returned his attention to the first urn.

There were at least fifty men in the room, and the Emperor selected the names of fifteen of them in all from the urn, never letting up on the elaborate, suspenseful charade. Each time a man's name was read aloud, that man would stand while his fellows cheered, groaned in mock despair, implored the Emperor to make a better choice next time, laughed, and poured themselves more wine. An Lu-shan watched in amazement as the men, some old and fat, some in their prime, and some barely beyond boyhood, saw their names go into the urn held by the woman. He waited in vain for his own name to be called.

Now the woman began to move among the dancers, stopping in front of each one to allow her to pull a name from the urn. The women continued to dance; each man whose name had been chosen now knew that one of the beautiful dancers before them—which one, he could not know yet—held a piece of paper with his name on it. The women whirled and smiled, holding the brightly colored little scraps over their heads enticingly as the music picked up its tempo.

Presently, one by one, each of the dancers went to the Emperor and presented her piece of paper to him. He looked at it and then led the woman by the hand to deliver her to the man who had won her in the lottery. Each man was embraced prettily by his consort of the evening and then led from the room while his fellows roared and applauded. An Lu-shan leaned toward the Lady of Kuo. Before he could even speak, she put her hand on his arm reassuringly.

"Don't worry, An Lu-shan. The Emperor has not forgotten you," she whispered. "Be patient."

Smiling, An Lu-shan leaned back again. Of course, the Emperor would not forget him.

When the Emperor returned, he shrugged apologetically to An Lu-shan. An Lu-shan made a magnanimous gesture in return. They smiled at one another in tacit collusion and settled back to listen to the music, drink more wine, and eat the dainty delicacies proffered by the servants.

After some time, the Emperor and the consort rose from their seats.

"We are going to make certain that our guests are happy, An Lu-shan," said the Emperor. "You are welcome to do the same."

: :

Kao Mei, Father Springtime, god of love and fecundity, wine pitcher in hand, wandered down the long, covered balcony that surrounded the pavilion on four sides. On the balcony and in open-air rooms upstairs and downstairs from the pavilion were silky gauze tents sheltering wide, comfortable couches on which the winners of the Emperor's lottery enjoyed their prizes. Some of the tents were dark, and some were lit from within by soft lantern-light. Inside, entwined bodies moved. Like worms in cocoons, An Lu-shan thought, raising his pitcher to his lips.

This was new for him. He had never before in his life moved calmly among men and women making love by mutual consent. He moved near to one of the couches. He watched an older man with a large stomach sitting propped against a pile of cushions while a woman squatted over him. The man, whose eyes were closed in rapturous bliss, had nothing to do but sit there. The woman supplied all the motion, rising up and down, making the man's fat belly quiver with each downward thrust. A memory rose in An Lu-shan's mind of the nocturnal visitor to his hot springs apartments. He had put her out of his thoughts these many months, but she came back sharply and clearly now. She had done the same thing to him, riding him like a horse until he thought he would expire from the pleasure. He watched the man's face for a while. The mouth moved, but the eyes never opened. Kao Mei bestows his blessings on you, he said silently to the couple and took a drink of wine. And may your "old man" stay up all night, Your Eminence, he said to the woman's partner, whose eyes were still closed while the rest of his face contorted in a grimace. An Lu-shan took another swallow. He laid a fond hand between his own legs and moved unsteadily down a short staircase.

He followed the sounds of music and voices. Poetry. Someone was reading poetry while someone else played an accompaniment on a flute. He soon found the poet and the musician in a comfortable alcove room at the bottom of the stairs, along with a few other guests, and he was surprised to see that the poetry was not being read. The poet, one of the men whose name had not been drawn from the urn, was, it seemed, inventing the verse right then—for it was a metaphorical description, in perfect meter and rhyme, of what was going on behind the gauze curtain in the corner of the room. And from what An Lu-shan could see, it was the poet who was taking his cue from the lovers, and not the other way around. He went closer.

The man on the couch was much younger than the one upstairs and played a far more active role. He was taking the woman from behind, both of them lying on their sides, her leg draped over his; he leaned on one elbow, with his free hand reaching round her to clasp her breast. An Lu-shan positioned himself so that he could see the man's organ sliding like a snake slowly in and out of the woman's gate. The musician played an innocent tune while the poet spoke amusingly of young horses, a mare and a stallion, meeting in a field in springtime. Unconsciously, An Lu-shan's hand returned to his own "old man," which grew hard as he watched the joined bodies before him.

What control this man on the couch had! He seemed to be able to hold himself back forever, remaining calm and apparently disinterested. An Lu-shan fondled himself and watched the man's hand gently squeeze the nipple of the woman's breast and roll it between his fingers while he thrust himself into her with measured strokes, first slow, then faster, then slow again, all the while leaning his head on his other hand in an attitude of casual repose.

An Lu-shan found himself becoming profoundly aroused. So this is what they were always singing about and writing poems about, this "artful" love-making. This must be what the women talked about among themselves, the thing that they admired most in a man. This control, this calm detachment, this applied knowledge of the female body. He was excited in a way that he had never experienced before. This was a revelation. He could scarcely wait to try it himself. He knew that he would excel at it—all he needed was a chance to try. All these other men in the room—were they experts, too, like the man on the couch? An Lu-shan felt a powerful urgency gathering in his groin. He smiled and drank some more wine. Save it up, An Lu-shan, he told himself. That's what the Emperor had always said to him. Save it up. He wondered what else there was for him to see, and moved on.

He soon found the Emperor and the consort at the spacious end of a verandah overlooking the water. The Emperor was playing his jade flute while the consort danced for him. A couple on a nearby couch, finished with their lovemaking, their clothes still in disarray, fed pastries and wine to one another. The Emperor lowered his flute with a smile when he saw An Lu-shan approaching.

"Father Springtime," he called out. "Look at what you have done. The whole world is making love." When An Lu-shan had come and sat next to the Emperor on the cushions, the Emperor leaned close and spoke in a personal tone. "It is pleasant to watch, is it not? The consort and I find it most stimulating." His eyes followed the consort's movements as she crossed the floor toward them.

An Lu-shan could feel, even through the drunken haze surrounding his brain, the palpable anticipation between the two. This is what the Emperor had meant when he had told him to save it up.

"I find it most stimulating, too," he said to the Emperor. "But since my name was not drawn from the urn . . ." He shrugged.

"An Lu-shan," the Emperor said, "it occurred to both the consort and me that perhaps you had grown tired of your old apartments at the hot springs. We know that they contain certain . . . memories for you. Things you may want to forget. We have no wish to pry, but that was the conclusion we came to after your last rather hasty—and thorough—departure."

"How well you know me, Father," An Lu-shan said.

The Emperor was far too much a gentleman to mention the woman who used to visit him there, but he was quite right. The bitch had caused him a lot of trouble. She'd made a fool of him. Against his will, he recalled the feel of her mouth; her teeth raking his flesh, driving him to painful ecstasy; the way she breathed and snarled in his ear like an animal. He felt an uncomfortable deep stir of arousal. The damned bitch. She wasn't going to get him again.

"We hope that you will consent, then, to accepting new quarters from us. We think you will be very pleased. They have been completely restored —the consort and I have personally selected the furnishings for you. They are beautiful rooms, raised up high, airy and spacious, with balconies overlooking the lake."

"My father," An Lu-shan said, sloppily kissing the Emperor's hand. "You take care of me so well. Your little baby is supremely grateful."

The Emperor smiled. "And An Lu-shan—the piece of paper with your name on it awaits you there. It is in someone's hand."

An Lu-shan raised his head and looked at the Emperor. A slow smile spread across his own face, a smile that matched the Emperor's.

"We had no intention of leaving the selection of our gift to you this evening to mere chance," the Emperor continued. "She is new, An Lu-shan. Talented and beautiful. A rare flower. Sixteen years old." He smiled significantly. "And untouched," he added. "Our gift to you. Symbolic of everything new. We wanted you to enjoy yourself, to watch the lovemaking, before you went to her."

"My father!" An Lu-shan said, seizing the Emperor's hand and kissing it again. "I wish to see my new apartments right away," he said eagerly, forgetting all about restraint.

: :

She weighed absolutely nothing. She sat on his lap sweetly, like a child. He could scarcely believe his good fortune. She had a child's translucent skin, guileless smile and innocent manner, and a woman's body. He smiled back at her. He had always been good with children.

"Do you know how to read?" he asked her, putting down the pitcher of wine, wiping his mouth, and taking the little scrap of paper from her hand.

She shook her head, still smiling.

"See, this is my name," he said, pointing to the only three characters in Chinese that he himself knew how to read. "An . . ." He pointed a meaty finger at the first character and raised his eyes to hers.

"An," she repeated after him.

"Lu-shan," he said, pointing to the next two, like a teacher instructing his pupil.

"Lu-shan," said the girl, beginning to dissolve in giggles.

"An Lu-shan," he said, laughing along with her.

"An Lu-shan," she repeated, giggling helplessly, and put her arms around his neck. He picked up the wine pitcher, put it to his mouth and drank. Then he offered it to her. He held it for her while she drank, and the wine ran down her chin and neck. He liked that. And after she had swallowed a big mouthful, laughing and spluttering, he held the pitcher to her lips again, this time tilting it at a sharper angle so that nearly as much wine went down the front of her robe as into her mouth. He took another drink himself, then offered another to her, repeating the ritual until the pitcher was empty, the front of her robe and his own as well were saturated, and she was giddy and sweetly drunk.

Through his own heavy alcoholic haze, An Lu-shan saw in his peripheral vision a slight motion in the corner of the bedchamber in the dim lamplight and remembered Li Chu-erh. The eunuch had been in the room the entire time, keeping unobtrusively to the shadows. Now, it seemed, he was trying to sneak out without being noticed.

"And where do you think you are going, my tailless dog?" he said sharply over his shoulder.

Chu-erh stopped and stood sullenly where he was.

"Bring us more wine," An Lu-shan ordered. "And then return to where you were." He smiled suggestively at the girl's flushed, lovely little face while he addressed the eunuch. "It is time for you to be educated. To learn how a refined court gentlemen makes love to such a beautiful, sensitive creature as this. Not that it will be of any use to you," he added, laughing at his own joke.

When Li Chu-erh returned with a set, expressionless face and handed his master the pitcher of wine, An Lu-shan grabbed for him with his free hand.

"Come here," An Lu-shan growled. "Come here and lift your robes. Our little lady here wants to see what you've got under there!"

Chu-erh stepped nimbly back out of his master's reach. He still said nothing, but looked back with eyes that burned with wordless hatred.

The girl giggled. When An Lu-shan made another ineffectual lunge at the eunuch, she caught his hand, playfully restraining him. An Lu-shan looked at her.

"I am only trying to have some fun with him," he said to her apologetically. "I am only playing!" He glanced back at Chu-erh. "He doesn't like to have fun. But I do!"

Again, Chu-erh moved as if he were trying to sneak out of the room.

"I said stay!" An Lu-shan roared.

Chu-erh froze, then retreated to his place on the cushions in the shadows.

An Lu-shan turned his attention to the girl in his lap. He smelled her sweet breath, made slightly pungent from the wine. Her cheeks were pink and damp; her head lolled on his shoulder. His eyes dropped to the soaked front of her robe. Slowly, fingers clumsy, fumbling, he opened the little silk ties that held the robe shut. He felt her child's breath on his neck. She didn't resist. His own breathing grew harsh with anticipation. He had been saving it up all day, hadn't he? All winter! He pushed her robe open and stared, inhaling sharply.

Her little exposed breasts were the sweetest, tenderest sight he had ever seen. Round, with pink buds for nipples, they lacked even the slightest hint of pendulousness. Child's breasts. Little girl-woman's breasts. He tested the flesh with his hand, giving it a small squeeze and rolling the tiny nipple around between his fingers the way he had seen the man on the couch do with the harem woman. His "old man" stiffened urgently and his ragged breath sounded through his open, salivating mouth. He had waited long enough. In a single motion, he pulled the girl's robe down from her shoulders and arms and off her body completely so that she sat naked upon his lap. He lowered his eyes and felt the blood rush to his head and groin: between her legs was no womanly thatch of thick black hair—just the lightest, downiest fuzz was visible in the lamplight. With one hand he pushed her thighs apart. Yes, he had certainly waited long enough.

: :

This would be a good time to kill him. With his own sword. It would be easy. The weapon was lying across a chair not ten paces from where Li Chu-erh lay in his dark corner, hands pressed to his ears. How many times was he going to force himself into the child? Chu-erh could hardly stand the whimpering and moaning. It had been going on for hours now. When was the sun going to come up and put a stop to it? How long was this night going to last?

I could kill him, and run away. The girl wouldn't tell. She wants him dead, too, I know. Anything to get him off her. Though she had liked it at first, when he was still laughing and playing with her.

Chu-erh had watched with reluctant fascination by the light of the single lamp as the huge man had leaned back on the couch so that his pendulous belly was out of the way, and then, holding the girl under her armpits, brought her down slowly onto his organ. It doesn't hurt, he kept telling her. It feels good. It doesn't hurt at all. And she had laughed, and caught her breath, and let him move her up and down, up and down, while she uttered small sounds of pleasure and surprise.

And Chu-erh had listened to the general's breathing. It seemed to change. It didn't just get faster; it began to sound . . . not even human. Like the breathing of an animal. Rasping, unconscious. And when the girl's cries changed gradually but surely from pleasure to pain, the breathing got louder, harsher, more grating. And less and less conscious.

And so it had gone for hours now. The girl had become prey in the possession of a great, deliberate, slow-moving, brutish animal. Whenever she thought he was finally asleep and tried to move away, it would begin all over again. Ponderously, heavily, slowly, he would be on top of her, or holding her down, or pulling her down onto him, always pushing, thrusting, forcing himself into her while her cries grew weaker, more childlike, with exhaustion.

Lie still, Chu-erh thought desperately. *Stop moving, don't cry out anymore. He will pass out, and then you can get away.*

But she wouldn't stop making noise. And every noise she made only provoked the general's ardor further. That breathing. That horrible, slavering, slobbering breathing. Everything Chu-erh hated about his master was concentrated in that sound. His eyes moved again toward where the sword lay across the chair. He raised himself up on an elbow, heart pounding in his throat.

Kill him.

He lay back down again, pressing his hands to his ears with all his strength. He was a coward. He couldn't do it. He didn't even have the courage to leave the room, let alone push a sword into the general's heaving back. He shut his eyes, willing the girl to stop her crying and struggling, willing the sun to rise, willing the night to be over. At that moment, he felt gratitude, for the only time in his life, for what he was. *I am glad I am not a man. I am glad I can never inflict that kind of pain.*

::

An Lu-shan rose almost to the surface. His swollen bladder had been chasing him through his deep, obscure dreams, demanding his attention. He would ignore it. If he stayed still, did not open his eyes, he could put it off a while longer. Something moved under him. He remembered the girl. Reflexively, he tightened his grip on her and thrust his groin against her two or three times until the tenderness in his lower belly made him stop. He sank back down into sleep, distantly aware of the faint movements of the girl's limbs beneath him, far, far away.

The overpowering need to urinate brought him completely awake in the first faint light of dawn. The room was still very dark; sometime during the night, the lamp had gone out. This is it, old fellow, he said to himself. You can't put it off any longer. He raised his heavy head, wincing at the pain, then heaved himself to the edge of the couch and into a sitting position. He sat for a moment with his eyes shut, gathering strength for the mighty effort of standing up.

Once on his feet in the unfamiliar room, he blundered into furniture and objects in the dim light, cursing with each throb in his head. Unable to recall exactly where the chamberpot might be, he made his way to the doors that led to the balcony, found his way out into the cool morning air, and relieved himself over the railing. He listened with satisfaction to the sound of urine spattering onto the stone terrace a story below. The skin of his organ was chafed and slightly sticky; he smiled, recalling the girl's tight little body. He sucked the air sharply through his teeth, remembering how it felt to push himself into virgin flesh. He would have to arrange it with the Emperor, he thought, to have a virgin brought to him every night. One could develop a taste for it.

Carefully this time, without hitting anything, he found his way back to the couch. Already the faint morning light was growing stronger. His eyes took in the still form of the girl, her skin glowing white against the dark, indistinct background of couch, pillows, and discarded clothing. He swayed slightly, and steadied himself with a hand on a nearby table. Maybe it was time to wake her. He considered.

Yes. It was definitely time to wake her. He wanted one more taste before the sun was up and the spell broken.

: :

Li Chu-erh woke to the sound of An Lu-shan stumbling over a piece of furniture. The eunuch opened his eyes, but did not move. He listened with disgust to the sound of his master urinating off the balcony, and lay as he was, feigning sleep, when he heard him making his way back into the room. He prayed that the general's appetite was sated. He did not know if he could bear it if An Lu-shan started in again on the girl.

The shuffling footsteps stopped at the couch. The general was breathing in a labored way from the effort of moving; Li Chu-erh guessed that his head was hurting him. That meant hardship for himself later. He was always testier when his head hurt after one of his all-night drinking bouts, and the eunuch was the first one he took his foul temper out on. But at least there was no odor of vomit in the room. By some miracle, Chu-erh had escaped having to tend to that loathsome task later in the morning. He shut his eyes.

The next few moments were quiet but for rustlings and creakings as the general lowered himself back onto the couch. Chu-erh waited. He willed his master to just go back to sleep.

Leave her alone.

More rustling, then silence.

"Bloody hell!" An Lu-shan's voice was softly incredulous.

Chu-erh's body tensed in involuntary response. He opened a surreptitious eye. He saw, in the gray dawn light, An Lu-shan standing over the couch staring down at the girl, holding her arm straight up from her shoulder. He let it go. It fell back down limply, heavily, like a thick rope that has been cut. He stooped and put an ear to her chest, then straightened up again slowly.

"Bloody hell," he repeated, his voice even softer this time, almost a whisper.

Chu-erh still did not move, though he understood.

Chu-erh watched his master stand stupidly for a few moments looking at the dead girl. Then An Lu-shan appeared to shake off his torpor. He began to move swiftly, purposefully. He pulled her up to a sitting position, the head hanging heavily to one side. Clumsily, cursing in a soft, steady stream, his breath whistling in his nose, he dressed the corpse in the robe he had flung aside the night before, pulling one arm into a sleeve, then the other, the head rolling about. It was not easy, tying the delicate little ribbons with his fat, agitated fingers. He tied two or three, enough to keep the robe closed, then picked her up and turned toward the balcony.

Astonished, Chu-erh raised himself up on one arm. What in the name of all the gods was he going to do? The light was still too dim for him to see clearly out onto the balcony where An Lu-shan had gone.

The sound of splintering wood made him spring, against his will, into a crouching position; the sound of something heavy hitting the ground below the balcony immediately followed. He was ready to run when An Lu-shan came back into the room.

The general stopped, looking straight at the boy as if just now remembering his existence. Chu-erh held perfectly still, hoping that in the poor light the general might mistake his crouching figure for a piece of furniture.

An Lu-shan's foot came out of the shadows with swift fury, catching Chu-erh under the chin and knocking him back against the wall.

"She fell off the balcony while she was dancing," An Lu-shan said in a flat, dangerous voice. "Do you understand?"

But Chu-erh did not answer. The very next thing he knew, he was up and running, so fast that no one could have caught him. An Lu-shan had lunged as he went by, but grabbed only empty air. Out the door, down the hall, down the stairs, and out into the chill morning air Li Chu-erh ran, the ground flying under his feet.

:: :

Kao Li-shih, taking a pre-dawn walk after a poor night's sleep, was not surprised to see that the party was still going on. People had slept for a few hours here and there, or had not slept at all, and laughter and music still carried across the water in the dawning light along with the twittering of awakening birds. He wondered vaguely what it would be like to be part of festivities like these. He was accustomed to feeling somewhat removed from social frivolity, but the nature of this gathering, the overt celebration of love and fecundity, had made him feel as insubstantial as a phantom.

Like a phantom, he had kept to the periphery of the complex of lakes and pavilions during his walk. He had not given up hope that he might still get some sleep, and when he felt a tempting fatigue come over him after walking for an hour or so, and when he saw the sky turning gray-pink in the east, he decided to return to his bed. He would have the servants shut the blinds, and he would instruct them to admit no one. Not even the Emperor himself, he thought wryly, and started up the pathway that would take him to his apartments.

He looked at the sky. The great Festival of Kao Mei now entered its second day. The consort's dream, years in the planning, a dream from China's past, was being realized. He supposed it was harmless enough. The people, especially, seemed to love it. He recalled the throngs in the Serpentine Park yesterday. For once, An Lu-shan's buffoonish antics were more or less appropriate. More or less. He had resolved to keep his opinions to himself, to say nothing that might compromise the consort's and the Emperor's pleasure in the success of their grand holiday, and he meant to keep that resolve. Then go to sleep, Kao Li-shih, he chided himself. You can't do much talking while you are asleep. He yawned, and climbed the path, thinking now of nothing except a warm bed.

Running, stumbling footsteps behind him made him turn sharply, alarm displacing his quiet thoughts. And a voice, so distorted that he did not recognize it.

"Master Kao . . . Master Kao . . ." the voice sobbed. "She is dead, Master Kao!"

"Who is dead?" Kao Li-shih demanded, though he did not know, in the dim light, who it was that he asked.

Someone collapsed at his feet, crying and gasping for breath.

"She was only a baby, and now she is dead!"

"Li Chu-erh!" Kao Li-shih said, astonished, and knelt to help him up. "Who is dead? What has happened?"

Chu-erh looked up at him. Kao Li-shih made out something dark on the boy's face. Blood?

"He killed her," he said, his voice quieter, more controlled now. "That bastard *killed* her!"

A deep, intuitive dread filled Kao Li-shih. He put his hands under the boy's arms and hauled him to his feet.

"Come. Up the stairs. We must get inside."

: :

Once in his apartments with the door safely bolted, Kao Li-shih turned up a lamp and looked at the younger eunuch's face. One of his cheeks was bruised and swollen. His nose was bleeding. He ordered a servant to bring towels, water, and ice.

"An Lu-shan?" he asked quietly.

The youth did not have to answer. His eyes answered for him.

"Tell me everything," Kao Li-shih said.

"The girl," Chu-erh said, his voice shaking again. "The one given to him for the night by the Emperor. She was only fourteen."

"Fourteen? I was given to understand that she was sixteen," Kao Li-shih said, taken aback.

The other shook his head, taking a wet towel brought by the servant and wiping his face with a trembling hand. "Fourteen. She told me herself. Before he came back last night. We talked for a long time while she waited for him. And when he came, he was already stinking drunk. And he drank more when he got there, and made her drink, too." He looked up at Kao Li-shih, who had never seen such a hard look in the young eunuch's eyes before. "It was horrible. It made me glad to be what you and I are." He dropped his head into his hands then. "But I am a coward. It is my fault she is dead."

"I do not understand," Kao Li-shih said.

"She was crying out for help most of the night. I could have killed him. I wanted to. I almost took his own sword and did it—but I didn't. I just covered my ears and prayed that it would be quiet soon. And when I woke up . . ."

"Go on," Kao Li-shih urged him gently.

"I don't know," he said, his eyes filling with tears again. "She was already dead. I think he just . . . crushed her. Smothered her. He wouldn't let her get away. He forced himself on her over and over and over, and then he passed out on top of her and just crushed the life out of her. She was so small. He has the weight of three men. She couldn't breathe, Master Kao, and she died underneath that bastard while he lay dead drunk top of her! I could have saved her, and I didn't," he cried miserably, his voice strangled with grief and remorse. "But Master Kao," he said, seizing Kao Li-shih's sleeve. "He is going to say it was an accident. There was no accident! Don't believe what he says! He dressed her and threw her body off the balcony. Right through the railing. He's going to tell them she was dancing . . . and drinking . . ." Chu-erh could not finish. He looked as if he were about to vomit. He put his head down and pressed his fists into his neck as if to stop the rising nausea.

"Never mind," Kao Li-shih said. "I understand perfectly. And then he hit you. Very hard, I think."

After a few moments, the youth pulled himself together and looked at the bloody towel in his hand and shook his head. "He kicked me. But it is nothing, Master Kao. I'm quite used to his violences against me. Just a bit of blood from my nose, that's all. But the girl . . ."

"The entire right side of your face is swollen. Allow my servants to apply ice to it. It will help to relieve the pain."

Kao Li-shih stood and went to the door. He put his hand on the latch and turned around again. Chu-erh accepted a silk-wrapped block of ice and pressed it to his face.

"Bring him more ice if he needs it. And another thing," Kao Li-shih said to the servants. "You are to keep the outer doors to my rooms bolted and post a sentry under my direct orders against further . . . disturbances. Keep Master Li Chu-erh safely inside until I return. Even if he should want to leave . . ." He looked directly at him. "Have him put under house arrest, confined to *these* quarters."

"Master Kao?" Chu-erh pleaded, the ice still pressed to his face. "What is this?"

Kao Li-shih ignored the question and turned to his old retainer. "Call the Flying Dragons in, if you must."

"The Flying Dragons? Why, Master Kao? Are we not on the same side?" the frightened young eunuch implored.

Kao Li-shih continued to ignore Li Chu-erh, looking past him and speaking to the old man.

"Call them in if you need them for his detention. The charges against him are contemplating murder against a high military governor of the realm . . ." He pulled the door open. ". . . and conspiracy to undermine the security of the northern defenses. And there is one other thing . . . he is to see no one and speak to nobody in my absence. And anyone demanding entrance to this room should be seized."

Chu-erh stood speechless and uncomprehending in the middle of the room, his eyes pleading for a sign from Kao Li-shih.

"After you have dismissed the servants, should he attempt to escape or to talk to anyone . . ." Kao Li-shih carefully avoided the beseeching eyes and continued to speak directly to the old man. ". . . order the guards to kill him."

He left the room, then waited momentarily in the hall as the doors were barred securely behind him. He listened for the reassuring sound of the heavy bolts being thrown into place. Satisfied that An Lu-shan's eunuch was safe for now, Kao Li-shih went out into the half light of the early hot springs morning.

: :

The lights of Kao Mei, still burning from the night before, sparkled in the thin, shadowy morning light in a hundred different halls and towers throughout the hot springs pleasure palaces. The dark water of the Nine Dragon Lake shimmered in an opalescence of colored lantern lights. Men and women came and went through open pavilions and halls, across gaily festooned terraces, up stairs and bridges; drunken, rowdy, lusty, shouting from balconies and calling to each other down gently curving corridors in teasing playful groups. He knew how it would be: hands caressing hands, exploring under robes;

bodies pressed together, faces revealed in pools of flickering light, tongues and lips touching, testing.

Shadows distorted—elongated, shifting, bending—in the swaying lantern lights, glimmering patterns of gold and red architecture. People—idle, insolent, loud—buzzing like summer insects. None of this had anything to do with Kao Li-shih.

Precious Consort's fairy dreams! He stood for a moment near the apex of the gracefully arched bridge that spanned the narrowest part of the carp-filled lake. He was impaled, as usual, on indecision. This was how it always was when it came down to the perennial struggle: to tell Minghuang the truth, to break the delusions that kept him happy—indeed, that allowed him to live—or to continue to shield him.

He stared down at the water, watching the patterns of reflected light. He had been so decisive a moment ago, in the room. It had been simple: protect the youth at all costs, so that even the servants would not know his intentions. Nor even Chu-erh himself. He moved to the highest point on the bridge and looked in the other direction. As he stared, the colors and lights on the water seemed to become oily and stagnant; the voices, laughter, and merriment receded, drifting from the lake, terraces, and pavilions back into the fields and woods at the base of Mount Li Shan. He turned and resolutely descended the bridge's downward curve. Whatever he decided to do later, he knew what he had to do right now. And there was no more time to waste.

The body had been discovered. Two people, a man and a woman, kneeled next to the sprawled figure on the stone terrace. Their words were unintelligible, but the shock and disbelief in their voices was plain to Kao Li-shih as he approached. Shards of painted wood lay scattered on the ground; the man looked at Kao Li-shih, then raised his eyes to the balcony above. The splintered railing hung in pieces, the exposed, raw inside wood contrasting sharply with the painted exterior. Kao Li-shih felt his gut contract: the sheer force that the brute must have used.

The woman lifted her horrified white face to Kao Li-shih as he dropped to his knees next to them.

"What could have happened?" she asked him. "A child!"

"I know, I know," he said almost brusquely, and carefully lifted the girl's head.

A voice came from above them. "An unfortunate accident, my friends."

They looked up. An Lu-shan stood on the balcony, hands held supplicatingly up from his sides.

"Who would have thought that she could break the railing? Too much wine, too much joy. I am heartbroken." Then he turned and went inside.

Neither the man nor the woman said anything; they looked at each other and at Kao Li-shih, who still held the girl's head. The scalp was badly cut from the fall. There was a patch of blood where her head had lain on the stones.

It was painful to look at her arms and legs so grotesquely twisted about; though he knew she was dead, he arranged them in a more natural position. He looked at the ties on the front of her robe. An Lu-shan dressed her, Chu-erh had said. Indeed, the ties were knotted crudely, clumsily. It had certainly not been the child's own delicate fingers that had last tied them, of that he was certain. And there was something else; the stones beneath her were wet. Kao Li-shih touched the moisture with his fingers, raised them to his nose, and recoiled in disgust. Not only had he killed her, but he left her lying in piss. His own, no doubt. He looked up at the balcony again. Incipient rage moved into his limbs: his next decision had just been made. He laid the girl's head back down gently and rose to his feet.

He climbed the stairs to the second floor, walked down the outside hallway, found the main entryway, and kicked the door open. He had no idea what to expect, nor did he know what to expect of himself. He could not remember feeling this kind of rage ever before. He entered the room, and what he saw shocked him.

An Lu-shan's apartments were in perfect order. Nothing was out of place. Not a single piece of furniture was askew; not even the most fragile pieces of porcelain or jade had been jarred from their precarious perches on shelves and tall slender stands. Carpets, pillows, curtains, and quilts were neat and orderly.

In the far corner by the balcony screen stood the freshly scrubbed General An Lu-shan. His beard and hair had been meticulously brushed, and he wore a fresh robe. He was in the midst of being dressed in a new brocade jacket by a servant when Kao Li-shih entered the room. Traces of patchouli- and jasmine-scented steam lingered as two more servants, eyes downcast and slippers pattering swiftly past Kao Li-shih, carried a washbowl and towels from the room. An Lu-shan turned.

"Good morning, Master Kao!" The general's face beamed a welcome as he waved the last servant out of the room. He turned his enormous bulk around slowly against the pale morning light, displaying his new sartorial splendor for the chief eunuch. Nothing in his aspect betrayed a hint of fatigue or the unsteadying effects that such a night of indulgence must have had on him.

He is a canny one, Kao Li-shih thought.

"How do I look? Am I fit for an audience before our Imperial Father today?" He extended an arm and gracefully rotated it in the light. "A new jacket. The imperial tailors are really the finest, don't you think, Master Kao? The sleeves are cut full in the latest Sogdian manner. Fitting, don't you agree, for a foreigner like myself? New clothes for Father Springtime!"

"So this is how you mourn the death of a child, An Lu-shan." Kao Li-shih spoke without moving from his spot in the doorway.

"You mistake my actions, Master Kao," An Lu-shan said, smoothing the fabric of his new jacket. "I am a lover of children. Father Springtime and I are really very much alike. Do you know that my first military exploits were carried out with children? None were ever hurt, so great is my love for them and my desire to protect them. But what can I do for the girl? She is already dead. Of course, I will express my condolences to her family and see that they receive a sizable pension to maintain them against their most unfortunate grief. But . . ."

"That is not what I am talking about, General," Kao Li-shih said in a firm voice. "It is not what you can do now, but what you have already done, that appalls me."

"I did nothing, Master Kao!" An Lu-shan turned and threw his arms open in an exaggerated gesture of appeal. "She is gone. Nothing can change that. Today we celebrate the birthing of springtime! I am Kao Mei, bringer of life, lover of babes, the fruitful, fertile, potent one!"

"Your potency has never been in question, General. I am wondering about your heart and your grotesque lack of compassion—that you could kill a child and then leave her pathetic corpse lying on the ground below your apartments while you preen and dress up in costumes. I have always had my misgivings about you. Now I know what you are truly capable of."

"Master Kao, you are quite wrong," An Lu-shan protested, though Kao Li-shih detected a faint crack in the general's composure. "I did not kill her! She was ebullient. Perhaps I am to blame for allowing her too much wine for her delicate constitution. She was a dancer, you know."

"I did not know that, General. Tell me more," Kao Li-shih said in a quiet voice. I should have trusted my own instincts, he thought. I should have killed him years ago. And I should have killed his sponsor as well.

"Quite a fine dancer, too," An Lu-shan went on, assuming a bereaved expression. "Hoping eventually to be apprenticed to the Pear Garden Orchestra." He shrugged. "I told her that the Precious Consort and I would make the proper introductions for her when the time was right. She was delighted with the prospect, Kao Li-shih. So delighted that she drank and danced herself off the balcony . . ." He pointed to the broken railing. "I saw her stumble, but I had no time, you see . . ." He staggered, mimicking drunkenness. "I was seated on the day couch over there." He pointed again. "I should not have let her drink so much of the wine . . . but we were laughing, and she was putting on a considerable performance. It all happened very suddenly, Master Kao. As for leaving her body where it fell, what was I to do? It was plain that she was dead. I was dressing, just now, so that I could go and notify the consort and the Emperor myself."

"I am sure that you were, Master An. And how was the child as a sexual partner?"

The eunuch still had not moved from his place in the doorway. There was no doubt now: his questions had begun to unnerve An Lu-shan. The general smiled uneasily, and with elaborately feigned casualness returned to his toilette.

"She was fine, Master Kao, for a child." The general adjusted his jacket, pretending to study his reflection in the mirror, avoiding Kao Li-shih's eyes. "Most delicate," he continued. "I did not think of demanding too much from her."

Kao Li-shih could hear the general carefully testing each word of his lie for its sound of truth.

"As for myself, I was gentle, and it was quite pleasurable . . . but she was merely a child, you understand!"

"Oh, *indeed,* General. I think that I do understand. Far too well." Kao Li-shih walked slowly into the center of the room. Nerves and rage burned at his center. His pulses were knotted and racing. He felt something he had not felt for many years: he was the warrior nearing the moment of engaging the enemy. He was sure that the warrior in An Lu-shan, so much closer to the surface than in himself, sensed his perturbance—the rising and falling of his chest beneath his clothing, the prickling sweat on his brow. Just don't allow him to see your uncertainty, he told himself. Don't let it show in your eyes. To steady himself, he took a deep breath and held it.

He stopped about six paces from An Lu-shan, who turned to face him with a look, now, of undisguised contempt. So this is what it feels like, some distant part of him reflected. What it feels like to be on the verge of killing a man who is so close that you can feel the warmth of his body and smell him, and even hear the thin rush of breath in his nostrils. A hundred tiny irrelevant details intruded on his senses: the hairs on An Lu-shan's face, the way the collar of his jacket stood up stiffly, the rough texture of the skin around his eyes.

An Lu-shan broke the silence. "What do you want, Eunuch?" he asked through clenched teeth. "What do you want of me, Eunuch? Eh?" He waited for an answer.

Kao Li-shih did not oblige him, but continued to stare.

"What can you know of lust?" He emphasized the last word. "What can you know of how it overpowers a man and burns at his insides like fire? How it tortures him and makes him mad? What could you know? What could you ever know of any of it? It is *lust* that makes us move, Eunuch. *Ghost!* You are not a man, Eunuch. You don't move. None of your hideous race moves. All of you are already withered, dead, part of the grave. Ghosts! Walking corpses!"

He turned away and lifted an outer jacket to his shoulders. "Get out of my way and leave my apartments," he said, not looking at Kao Li-shih.

Kao Li-shih did not respond. He moved forward, narrowing the space between them until he stood only three paces from An Lu-shan. The general turned sharply, making a move for the small sheathed Ordos dagger on the dressing table a few paces to the side of where they stood. But Kao Li-shih had been ready. He moved at the same moment, putting himself between An Lu-shan and the table.

"I would not do that, Master An. How would you explain *my* accidental death?" He seized the dagger and tossed it over An Lu-shan's head and out over the broken railing to the terrace below. It hit the ground with a clatter. "Is that about where she landed, Master An? Or were you not quite able to throw her out that far? She was very light. A child. But you were tired. And drunk."

An Lu-shan's face darkened.

"It must have been quite an effort," Kao Li-shih continued, "to make it look real. To determine where she would have landed had she actually fallen. If she were dancing, whirling about, she might have leapt out a considerable distance from the balcony. Then again, one would have to consider that 'stumbling' against the railing would have slowed down her descent—"

"Do you think my *Father* . . ." An Lu-shan interrupted, his voice hoarse with anger, ". . . my Father, the Son of Heaven, would prefer to believe *you* instead of his son? He is all too aware of your hatred of me, Master Kao. It is all too obvious to him that you hated me from the beginning. If you go to him with these outrageous charges, he will simply *laugh* at you!"

Kao Li-shih shrugged. "I have a certain credibility with the Son of Heaven, too, Master An. It will be interesting to see *whom* he believes."

An Lu-shan lunged for Kao Li-shih's throat. The eunuch stepped backward, causing An Lu-shan's fists to land hard on his chest. Kao Li-shih's weight fell against the edge of a heavy table behind him. He brought his arms up underneath the general's, knocking his hands off to either side, then pushed hard against his chest. An Lu-shan staggered backward a few steps, and before he could lunge again, Kao Li-shih sat on the table, put both hands behind himself, and gripping the edge firmly, kicked out with both legs.

One foot caught An Lu-shan's right knee, the heel of the other landed square on the general's groin. An Lu-shan howled in pain. Hands cupped agonizingly between his legs, he collapsed to the floor, coming down full force on the injured knee.

He must not get up again, Kao Li-shih thought. Move quickly, you old ghost! All you have going for you is surprise. Kao Li-shih picked up a footstool, raised it above his head, and smashed it down across the general's shoulders and the back of his neck. An Lu-shan fell to one side, and with the ungainliness of an elephant trying to rise, struggled to get back on his feet, his mouth a dark circle of pain.

"Servant!" he shouted. But he was cut short. Kao Li-shih's slippered foot hit him in the face. Head bowed forward, he gasped and spat a bloody tooth onto the floor.

"General An," Kao Li-shih said, catching his breath, "I took you for more of a sporting man than that. Shouting for help! After all, there is only one of me, and I am only a *ghost*. Certainly this is a far fairer match than you allowed the child!" He drove his right foot down hard against the back of An Lu-shan's neck, smashing his face against the tiles.

An Lu-shan was sprawled face down on the ground, a small pool of blood collecting under his mouth. He groaned and rolled onto his back, hands still cradling his groin. Kao Li-shih stared down at him.

"I should kill you, you ball-less *pig*," An Lu-shan hissed, his voice faint from pain. "Damned stinking cunt of a eunuch!" He rolled his head to one side and spat. "I *will* kill you, Kao Li-shih. I *will* kill you," he whispered, and rolled his eyes up into his head with a grimace.

"Then you had best do it now, General. This is your last chance. You will not have another. I spare you now only because you once saved my life. The score has been evened."

He considered the wretch on the floor in front of him. Raising his foot, he kicked General An Lu-shan twice in the ribs as hard as he could.

"That," he said, exulting in the impact of flesh and bone against his foot, "is for the child who will not be here to smell the flowers of another spring, General."

An Lu-shan moaned, rolled onto his side facing away from Kao Li-shih, and lay still. But for his ragged breathing, he gave the appearance of being dead. Kao Li-shih raised his foot again, but lowered it back to the floor.

What was stopping him? Why didn't he kill this animal now, while he was down? He would probably never get this chance again. Was it loyalty to the Emperor? But standing there now, his limbs beginning to tremble in the aftermath of his exertion, he realized that he had not thought of the Emperor for even one brief second. It was not just that he hadn't thought of what the Emperor might say, or what he might think if he saw what had happened just now—it was simply that the image of the Emperor had never even entered his mind. Had he been that crazed? His only thought, at first, had been to save himself, hadn't it? Wasn't that what it was? And all the rest was the anger, accumulated over years, that he could no longer control. He had not felt anger like this—intemperate, consuming—since that day, decades before, when the Emperor was only a crown prince, cornered by murderous partisans of the wicked T'ai Ping. He felt the same kind of anger now, but something had stopped him from killing An Lu-shan. It could only be that An Lu-shan had saved his life on that day of the spider box. But more important than that was the fact that An Lu-shan had saved the life of the Emperor. Kao Li-shih knew that even though he had not thought of the Emperor at all, something unconscious in him had prevented him from killing the man who had saved the Emperor from death.

His heart pounded like a forger's hammer in his chest. He grabbed hold of the corner of a desk to keep from collapsing. Only now did Kao Li-shih realize the extent of his exhaustion. Suddenly, he was immersed in a fatigue beyond anything he had ever known. His limbs ached. He could barely move. It was as if he were sinking in a pit of mud that grew thicker around him with each passing moment. And he knew that if he fell down now alongside the barbarian, he would sleep for a hundred years on the cold tile floor.

: :

Although Kao Li-shih could not have known it, the general remained on the floor of his apartments for a long time, until the hour of the snake when the pale rosy dawn light, which had gently illuminated the tops of trees and the king of Chou's old beacon tower high on the rounded summit of Mount Li Shan where the early circling crows laughed, scolded, and held their morning court, gave way to the high, strong light of late morning.

And there on the terrace below the broken railings, like the first raindrops to precede a storm, were a few random spatterings of the child's blood that had escaped the groundskeepers' brooms. The ascending sun shone full on the night's legacy of the revival of the ancient Festival of Kao Mei—of children, fertility, and spring: a few drops of blood, and the debris of lanterns and colored paper streamers which had been sodden and clinging in the heavy morning mists but which dried now in the warmth of the sun and blew aimlessly about in the breeze.

And in a darkened carriage that traveled back toward the city, wrapped hastily in heavy cloth and never to be touched by the sun again, the broken body of a young girl who had taken her first and last lessons in love and death all in the same night. It was the night of joyous festival and abandonment transformed . . .

: :

For Kao Li-shih, though he would have preferred more than anything in the world to lock himself into his quarters with guards placed all around and simply drift off into dreamless sleep, the day held no sweet promise of oblivion. Ahead of him was only the sheer weight of the responsibilities that faced him. Today, he would have to tell the Emperor things he would rather not hear—things that he would undoubtedly choose not to believe, in any case.

Or would it be different this morning? Despite his sickness and exhaustion, he did nurture a faint hope. He resolved that before he went to the Emperor, he would speak first to the Precious Consort. He would find out what she knew, what rumors she had heard from the women since the discovery of the girl's body. If she had heard anything bad, any doubts or suspicions as to An Lu-shan's veracity, then he would tell her what Chu-erh had told him. He would try to convince her that the dreadful things she might have heard about her "son" were indeed true. Then, and only then, would he go to Minghuang, and he would ask her to accompany him. He had no intention of going empty-handed to level these ghastly charges against the Emperor's "Lucky Baby." This time, he would be well armed.

When Kao Li-shih left his quarters, Li Chu-erh was still locked in the inner apartments. He had had the guards see to the young eunuch's breakfast, but he himself had not spoken to him or even set eyes upon him since the forced "imprisonment" early this morning. It was best, he thought, stepping out into the beautiful day, that Chu-erh remain hidden and in the dark. It was not over yet; it had only begun.

Kao Li-shih passed the Delightful Spring Pavilion, crossing over the pond by the same bridge he had this morning on his way to An Lu-shan's apartments. When he reached the center of the bridge, he raised his eyes, without wanting to, toward An Lu-shan's apartments and the broken balcony. He could see no one, no activity at all. Was An Lu-shan still lying there, or had someone come to his aid? Had the general been able to cry out for help, in the condition in which Kao Li-shih had left him?

Could he possibly have died?

If An Lu-shan was dead, then he, Kao Li-shih, would probably have to leave the palace and the Emperor forever. Though he had been defending himself—it was plain that An Lu-shan had meant to kill him when he made a move for his knife—he would still have to leave, and seek a life elsewhere. His long friendship with the Emperor would come to an end.

And if An Lu-shan had killed me, he wondered, would the Emperor mourn my death the way he would surely mourn his "Lucky Baby's"? He put the thought out of his head. Kao Li-shih, he said to himself, you sound just like a jealous wife.

Besides, what sense was there to speculation? He would soon know everything. And he had no intention of returning to An Lu-shan's apartments to inquire about his health—certainly not alone. What if the rumors about the Sogdian were true? Born under the red star, the comet, his mother a shamaness in touch with the dead. Unable to be injured permanently, able to rise from death. Was it possible?

Ridiculous. Nonsense. Your brain, he told himself, is addled from fatigue. Get on with it, old man!

He passed the terrace where the girl had fallen and went through a large moongate. He passed the Tower of Righteousness and Precious Consort's favorite Lotus Flower Baths, and began the ascent up the steep stone stairs that entered into a broadleaf forest where the path wound its way around heavy boulders. He passed an ancient stand of knobby old pines and a faded moss-covered pavilion that still sheltered a few broken, discolored ceramic stools. It was a steep climb, but he refused to feel the exertion. He was too tired. If he felt it at all, he might give in to it. It was simply a matter of essence over form, mind over body.

He reached the top of the first small rise, despite the exhaustion of the night and morning, without his breath becoming labored. It could be done! And so, he resolved, could everything else he had to do that day. Only a bit more to go. The stone stairs were still wet with dew. Though the sun was fairly high, it was cool and damp in the shade of the forest. He smelled the rich essence of forest decay, pine needles, moss, and fungus. He found himself acutely aware of everything around him. His senses seemed sharpened, like an animal's. An old monk had once said that the sight of death—sudden, brutal affirmations of mortality—were apt to do that.

No! It wasn't an old monk at all. It was the crude, detestable poet, Li Po, who had said it. Well, he wasn't all bad. After all, he *was* honored for his poems. He was good. China's greatest poet, some said. Why did that come to his mind now? The last step. The ground leveled, and beyond, in a shady copse opening up into a protected glen was a splendid mansion—hidden in this distant corner of the Li Shan Hot Springs, accessible to only a few.

The Yang sisters' magnificent apartments occupied a secret fairylike grotto of rocks and woods on the top of this secluded little summit. An expanse of two-story buildings and raised terraces were connected by a series of elaborate covered walkways that undulated through the trees as naturally and easily as a garden snake through tall weeds.

He had been certain that he would find the Precious Consort here this morning with her sisters, rather than with the Emperor. How he knew this, he couldn't say. Instinct? And he knew exactly where to go, which one of the scores of terraces or gardens he would find them in. He stopped short of the point where the pathway emerged into the open. Still within the protective cover of the forest, he took in the scene.

All four sisters were together this morning for a late breakfast on a shady terrace beneath tall, spreading trees. There were others present: servants and attendants, some courtesans of the music bureau, and some of the Pear Garden players. Before he recognized her face, he recognized the voice of Hsieh A-man, the Precious Consort's dancing instructor. High and clear, it carried like a bell above the murmur of other voices.

Though he was too far away to understand her words, it was plain that she was nervous, agitated. The other voices joined in from time to time, their tones low and serious. One of the musicians was crying. A man was seated with his back to Kao Li-shih; he did not have to see the man's face to know that it was Yang Kuo-chung. He had not expected to find him there this morning. He had envisioned dealing with Yang Kuo-chung, whom he considered his closest personal ally, alone—but he quickly realized that his presence here this morning could only be an asset. Obviously, they were discussing the child's death. Kao Li-shih's timing was perfect. The others would have to leave, naturally; what he had to say was only for the sisters' ears—and now Yang Kuo-chung's as well.

He was not quite ready to be seen yet. He rested there for a while under the big trees, sorting his thoughts, deciding on his words. Then, wishing to get within range of their conversation so that he could understand it, he moved closer. Sacrificing some of his cover, he moved carefully out into the low bushes. He had gone about thirty paces when the Lady of Kuo, whose eyes were as sharp as a fishhawk's, spotted him.

"Master Kao!" she called to him. "What are you doing?"

"Nothing," he said, walking toward them and attempting a smile. "Merely lurking around the homes of the rich like a common street thief." But the grim faces that turned toward him quickly made it plain that there was to be no relief in humor this morning. He looked at the glorious table set with an elaborate spread of delicate, delicious food and steaming tea and realized that he was hollow, famished. Yang Kuo-chung must have seen the look in his eyes.

"You will join us, then," he said, gesturing graciously. Kao Li-shih stepped onto the terrace. A stool was offered for him. He sat, poured a bowl of tea, filled a plate with food, and began to eat voraciously. People were quiet. The shock of death hung heavily over them.

"You have heard, I presume, Master Kao . . . ?" Yang Kuo-chung asked.

"Indeed, I have, Master Yang," Kao Li-shih said, taking another pastry. He raised his eyes and looked steadily at Yang Kuo-chung, who understood the tacit message.

The Fox remained expressionless as he dismissed the courtesans, the musicians, and the servants. They bowed as they rose from the table and left the outdoor terrace. Now only Yang Kuo-chung and the sisters remained.

"Not only have I heard," Kao Li-shih said to them in a discreet voice, "but I know exactly what happened."

::

The Precious Consort sat and stared at her face in the mirror for a long time. The face that stared back at her did not resemble a mythical queen at all; she saw instead a foolish, vain, and gullible woman. Behind her, the Lady of Kuo stood and looked thoughtfully out a window.

"That monster. That filthy, ungrateful beast," the Precious Consort said quietly, and flung her arm violently out to one side, upsetting a small table holding little ceramic cosmetic jars. They smashed to the floor, the broken pieces skittering wildly across the room. In the mirror, she saw the Lady of Kuo jump.

"Little Sister, please!" the Lady of Kuo said. "We are all overwrought! This sort of thing does not help!"

"How could he do it?" the consort implored. "How could he harm an innocent baby? And how could he fling her dead body to the ground as if it were a piece of garbage?"

Her sister shook her head. "I wish I knew. Some men just become blind. From drink, and from lust."

The consort turned back to the mirror, tears of rage starting in her eyes. She had not wanted to believe, but she was left with little choice. The first news had come to her quickly: that there had been an accident, that a girl was dead. That she had been drunk, and had danced off a balcony. And when she found out that it had been the child, the girl she herself had sent to An Lu-shan after reassuring her over and over . . . she had been shocked, had wondered how he could have been so careless. Why hadn't he been watching out for her? Why had he allowed her to get drunk? He may look like a bear, she had told the child, but he is a gentleman.

It had always seemed to her that you could never face a horrible truth, that the thought of it would be too much, that it would break you as easily as a twig under a horse's hoof. But all her life, even back when she was small, she had always known that eventually, something horrible would happen. That it would find her, the way it found everybody else. And she had dreaded it. It would break her, she knew.

But now it had come, and she found that it was not that way at all. When she had seen Kao Li-shih walking out of the woods, she had known instantly that he was carrying the bad news she had been waiting for all her life. And when he told his story, it had rolled over and through her—but it had not broken her.

She had said nothing at first, but listened, watching the faces of her sisters and cousin around her. Yang Kuo-chung's eyes had flashed knowingly, arrogantly almost, in Eldest Sister's direction; she had returned a stunned, uncomprehending look. Her other sisters had covered their mouths and gasped as the details of what the eunuch Li Chu-erh had seen were revealed, calmly and methodically, by Kao Li-shih.

There had been no "accident," no dancing through a railing in a moment of abandon. An Lu-shan's crime was not merely a moment's negligence and intemperance, but something far worse: all night, Li Chu-erh had told Kao Li-shih, the child had struggled underneath the monstrous "baby." All night. And then he had sought to cover his crime with a terrible lie. And Precious Consort had known she was hearing the truth. I may be a fool, she had thought, but I know the feel of truth when I hear it. And her anger had crystallized. Her "Lucky Baby" was a traitor—to her, and to her Imperial Husband. He had caused her to betray a child. Go to him, she had told the girl, who had been uncertain; he will be tender and gentle. Like a father and a lover at the same time.

A gentleman.

It was too dreadful to contemplate the fear and pain, the betrayal, that the child must have experienced before she died. The betrayal—that was the worst, definitely the worst part of it.

"Fool!" she said aloud now to her reflection in the mirror. Foolish little child. A woman with a child's dreams. Fairy tales and ancient festivals of golden ages that never could have existed because they were fiction born only of human longing and inadequacy.

And she saw it all: her games, her frantic efforts at make-believe. Her stupidity, her useless talk and plans, while her handsome cousin smiled at her as if she were still a child and she pretended not to see him looking at her at all. Just the way it had been when she had been the baby, the youngest of four little sisters tended by nursemaids in a remembered childhood garden. They had always smiled so condescendingly at her when she played with such enthusiasm, such seriousness. Such dedication to her worlds of fantasy. But that was long ago, and had only been play.

But now nothing could be undone. And she was angry, and embarrassed, too. She wished she could be someone else, not be herself at all. She wished she could look out at the world through someone else's eyes. And had her "Lucky Baby" seen her as a foolish little child, too? Her games must have been just what he wanted, serving his purposes exactly.

A picture of the girl pinned beneath him through the night returned relentlessly, repeatedly, to her mind. She wanted to kill An Lu-shan. But even the thought of killing him wasn't enough. It did not begin to touch her feelings.

"I don't know, Little Sister," the Lady of Kuo was saying now, looking at her in the mirror. "It would seem that we didn't really know him at all."

: :

Minghuang sat on a day couch against a lattice window, his hands resting on his knees, his head fixed squarely in the middle of his sunken shoulders. His eyes stared straight ahead into nothing. He had been sitting like this for a long time. The absolute silence was contagious; no one spoke.

Two drab sparrows lit on the sill behind the Precious Consort and picked at seeds from a feeder. They flew off nervously, their shadows flitting across the floral anthemion that decorated the lintel above the consort's head. Kao Li-shih yawned. He was very tired. He stretched, then resolutely resumed his posture of waiting. But the Emperor stared off into space as if, perhaps, he might never utter another word again.

At least, thought Kao Li-shih, he is considering the words they had brought to him. Words they had tried over and over to pound into him like wooden spikes into stone.

The only movement in the room was provided by the cats who, having chittered in frustration moments ago at the sparrows who were out of their reach, now tumbled and rolled across the floor locked in a silly dream of mortal combat. Their silver Tibetan collar bells tinkled as their rolling bodies collided with a slender vase stand, bringing a majestic piece of cobalt blue earthenware down. The vase made an enormous sound as it burst apart on the floor. The startled cats raced in opposite directions, eyes black with alarm. The Emperor spoke at last, waving an imperious hand.

"That's it, Kao Li-shih, toss the beasts out of here."

"Do I look like a servant to you?" Kao Li-shih replied, not moving. "I am, unfortunately, a bearer of bad tidings. Perhaps you would rather that I was a simple member of your household staff. And at this point, perhaps I would prefer it, too. The way you listen to me makes me think that I might consider arranging for a transfer." Kao Li-shih looked at the figure on the couch. "It might suit me and save my vital energies in the process. Throw the cats out *yourself*. I, for one, find them a pleasant distraction, considering the gravity of the circumstances."

"What would you have me say, either of you?" The Emperor looked at the Precious Consort. He was practically pleading while she made no attempt to hide her disgust. "I have told you what I think. What I *know*!" he emphasized. "It was an accident. He intended no harm. He has great respect for the women. Great compassion for the young. He treats them with profound tenderness in his lovemaking. We have talked about it often. The alcohol makes him clumsy, slow-witted, stupid . . . He does not know where he puts his weight. He becomes too jolly, too fun loving, and he dances around the room like one of my great white elephants. This inability to handle alcohol is a problem with all the northerners. It is a matter of the disposition of their temperaments, the makeup of their systems. But that is all it is! Look at our good General Ko-shu Han—a mixture, too, of Sogdian and northern Mongolian blood. He is useless to us as a great leader against the Tibetans anymore. Useless to us in any military capacity. The alcohol has rendered him nearly insane. He can only reside in our great city on a pension—cared for day and night by servants provided him by the Chancellery's Ministry of War.

Watched over like an infant lest he stumble and crack his skull or choke on his own vomit in the middle of the night." He paused, raising his hands, imploring his impassive listeners to give up their stubbornness and understand. "It is a problem with the balance of the liquids—of yin—in these northerners' nature. Our good An Lu-shan will make us safe in the night, as Li Lin-fu has provided. Then he, also, will come stumbling down to us from the north. Drunk and harmless. And quite useless. Hardly one of the great Eight Immortals of the Wine Cups, the drink will only render him dull and slow. And we will owe him—our good imperial son—nothing more than the respect of taking care of him, too, for all of his great services to our security and prosperity . . ."

Kao Li-shih was exasperated. Exhausted. He sighed and slapped his open palms down on his lap. Nothing he had said had made any impression. The Emperor had selected from his words only those he wished to hear, and now leaned back confidently on his day couch, certain that he had made good use of all the facts. He was beyond logic. He could not hear. He would not hear! *I have a certain credibility with the Son of Heaven, too.*

"And my 'encounter' . . . ," Kao Li-shih said. "How do you explain it? I was quite close to killing him, because he almost killed me—and he would have, had I not tossed his dagger off the balcony. You say the alcohol makes him helpless: I saw no evidence of a clumsy man, an impaired man. I saw a man refreshed and washed. Putting on his fresh jackets without a bit of remorse in his actions—eyes bright, awake, ready to be received by you, his Father," Kao Li-shih added sardonically. "I saw a man who quite expected a visitor! Quite!"

"I have told you over and over, Kao Li-shih! He is a warrior. He was drunk. You surprised him. He did not even know who you were. He recognizes no one in that state—except me. He finds himself threatened, and in his imagination he is back in the north under attack."

"He was not drunk," Kao Li-shih said tiredly. "I have already told you. He had been drinking all night. I saw the pitchers on the floor. He had only slept a few hours. Anyone else would still have been drunk or incapacitated. But not An Lu-shan. His control, when he cares to summon it, is perfect! And he knew exactly who I was! He greeted me by name when I came in!"

"But you say you kicked the door open," the Emperor said. "Obviously, he felt threatened."

"He threw a girl's body off the balcony to cover up the truth. Doesn't that make any impression on you?"

"He panicked. The shock of her death made him do it. *If* he did it. Whose word do we believe? His, or that of the eunuch Li Chu-erh, who, it is common knowledge, bears his master nothing but ill-will?"

Kao Li-shih was too exasperated by this to even respond to it.

"And what of the sexual excesses? Did the boy invent those, too?" Kao Li-shih said quietly. "He was in the room with An Lu-shan and the girl. He described what he saw. He was *not* lying."

"Kao Li-shih," the Emperor said gently, "what would a young eunuch like Li Chu-erh know of lovemaking? What basis of comparison would he have to be able to know what is excessive and what is not? He is not like the court eunuchs, who see and hear everything that goes on between men and women. He grew up in the north, isolated, inexperienced. Children, as you surely know, sometimes accidentally come upon adults making love. To them, it looks as if terrible pain is being inflicted. They do not understand it. To an uninitiate such as Li Chu-erh, the gentlest lovemaking might appear to be brutal. Cries of pleasure would be heard as cries of distress."

"Oh, please. You will go to any extent to defend him. And what if he had killed *me,* as he intended to do? What if he had disemboweled me in his rooms? What excuse would he have come to you with, and that you would have accepted? That he was dancing with me, and I accidentally fell on his sword? What would there be between *my* legs that would excuse his passions?" Kao Li-shih looked at the consort, her face contorted with the effort to control her tears of anger. "We will not rest until you call him here. Call him before you!" Kao Li-shih said again. "Let him tell you, himself. Look into the eyes of a liar, of a petty small man and tell me you cannot see it. Look into the eyes of a common murderer. But maybe you will see nothing because you are already blind."

Silence engulfed the room again. Kao Li-shih rose from his seat and stretched.

"I am very tired. I am going to my rooms to rest. When you have summoned your general before you to make an account of himself, fetch me. Until then . . ."

He glanced at the Precious Consort as he left the room. She looked back at him with eyes that seemed to beg him to stay, that asked: what am I to say to my imperial husband after you leave and I am alone with him? He looked at her again. It was not his imagination; she was begging him to stay. But Kao Li-shih had had enough. He turned around and walked toward the decorative dragon screens that shielded the doors from the interior of the apartment. He left quickly by the outer corridor.

::

It would have been a most pitiful sight had it not been, ultimately, so ludicrous. The great hulk of a general on his knees, sobbing, wiping his eyes and nose on the wide hems of his robes. Could this abject creature be the same one who, only a day before, had cavorted as Father Springtime, basking in adulation, pouring food and wine down his gullet?

Kao Li-shih watched with interest as the general blubbered and wallowed in his tears. He was good; the illusion was flawless. As fine a performance of a filial son pleading his innocence as any the eunuch had ever seen in a *p'ou-t'ou* dance pantomime. A fabulously entertaining bit of fantasy but for the fact that the Emperor believed every word of it.

Kao Li-shih found that he was not angry anymore. Curiously, the appalling display in front of him aroused no emotion in him at all. He found himself watching An Lu-shan and his Imperial Father with the same detachment with which he had, over the years, watched the act of copulation in all its infinite variety. It was as if the events of the morning had never happened.

He did not know what the Precious Consort thought or felt at this moment. He knew that she was disenchanted, both with her "Lucky Baby" and with the world of make-believe she and the Emperor had conjured. What words had passed between the two after Kao Li-shih had left them alone, he could not imagine. Had she pleaded? Cried? He doubted it. She sat impassively now by the Emperor's side and stared down at An Lu-shan. What could she be thinking at this moment, Kao Li-shih wondered, as her "Lucky Baby" compounded his crime with lies and dissembling? He could not even guess. For his own part, he felt like the ghost An Lu-shan had accused him of being. He merely observed.

"I am not a murderer of children!" An Lu-shan pleaded again. How many times had this been said? But now he augmented his touching words with action. Approaching the Emperor on his knees, he grasped Minghuang's hand as if he were a supplicating lover. Tears ran from the barbarian's eyes in a torrent; they were the bitter tears of one maligned, misunderstood, unjustly accused.

Kao Li-shih stood in the center of the room, hands folded across his chest, remembering the feeling of An Lu-shan's flesh receiving his blows; the way it had felt when his foot had flown against An Lu-shan's teeth. The general was making a grand effort at hiding the fact that he was missing a tooth; his speech was only slightly slurred. Kao Li-shih realized that one would have to know that the tooth was gone to hear the slight impediment in his speech. And he had carefully reapplied the red and yellow cosmetics that he had worn in the park yesterday as Father Springtime. Not only did the paint disguise the bruises and swelling on his face, but it was having a powerful effect on the Emperor's sympathies as well: who could find it in his heart to believe Father Springtime a murderer?

"And does my Imperial Father know the care I took with my young charges in the north?" An Lu-shan wept. "None were ever hurt. None ever suffered. Could my Father know of the efforts I made to assuage the fears of the littlest ones? And were it not for my love of children, I would never have been in your great and glorious service at all . . ." He sobbed, bringing his massive bearded head down to his own robes to wipe away the tears. "And when I was apprehended for the stealing of military stock animals, it was because I was trying to feed my own young. My own young, whom I have always treated like the princes that they are . . . jealous as a tigress for the safety of her cubs . . ." His entire body now heaved spasmodically with his grief. Tears rolled down his cheeks and splashed to the floor.

"I made only the gentlest love to the child . . . most gentle, kind, delicate . . ." he went on, still clinging to the Emperor's hand. "You understand," he said, looking up earnestly, his makeup streaked and his beard glistening with tears and mucus, "when one is as ample all around as I am, one learns to be most careful . . . Surely, although I joke with my Imperial Father and Mother, I realize that my size demands that I be most careful with women of delicate proportion . . ."

He released the Emperor's hand. He appeared to be composing himself. Kao Li-shih wondered what was coming next.

"But the guilt for the beautiful child's death must rest with me. I am at fault! I and I alone, my Imperial Father, am to blame. I was remiss and foolish and unthinking. Had I not drunk so much, she would not have drunk so much. She was young and small. The wine had a much more potent effect upon her than upon your gluttonous and sodden Father Springtime. She fell quite under its spell as she danced . . . she lost her balance, and I was too stupid with drink to realize what was happening to her. And when she fell against my railing, I was far too slow to . . ." He began to weep again. "If my Father wishes it, I shall resign from my positions and leave the palace. You will never hear of your foolish servant again."

A very fine touch, Kao Li-shih thought begrudgingly. Like the last perfectly placed dot of color in a silk painting.

For some time, there was no sound in the room but An Lu-shan's quiet sobbing.

Then the Emperor spoke. "You are forgiven, An Lu-shan. And I am certain that my Precious Consort feels the same way about this most regrettable accident. You have suffered sufficiently already. No further punishment or censure is necessary."

The Precious Consort said nothing, but Kao Li-shih saw the dismay on her face. She had scrupulously avoided eye contact with An Lu-shan throughout the interview. Now she closed her eyes and leaned her forehead on her hand while An Lu-shan stole a discreet glance in her direction, then looked back at the Emperor.

"And there is another thing," the general said. "I wish to apologize to the good eunuch. I was drunk and lost in grief, as I am now. I did not recognize him when he came in. It was the shock, you must understand, of what had happened. Since the attempt on your life, Father, I have been most wary of the unannounced presence of anyone. I was alone, you must understand. My own eunuch had gone to get help."

What could Kao Li-shih do? He knew he could not bring Li Chu-erh out of hiding to let him give witness before the Emperor. What good would the frightened youth's words do when no one else's had any effect? He was not about to risk Chu-erh's life in a hopeless, pointless testimony against his master. His life would not be worth a scrap of paper once the general had removed him to the north again.

"Surely Master Kao knows I mean him no harm," An Lu-shan said. "Why would I risk my life to save him from the spiders, only to attack him gratuitously?"

The Emperor nodded as if this were unassailable wisdom. But Kao Li-shih did not wait to hear the rest. He had been waiting to see how and when An Lu-shan would work his way around to the subject of the spiders; now that he was hearing it, he found he could not tolerate hearing any more. Without saying anything, and without looking behind him, he rose and walked out of the room.

The transcendent whiskered face of a five-clawed imperial dragon reached toward him from the carved gold screen of the entranceway as he passed by. He glanced at it and saw exactly what it was: sightless, impotent, powerless, a flattened, worthless, lifeless idol, lost, drifting unfixed in a useless embellishment of flaming pearls and spiraling clouds. Later, Kao Li-shih would remember how clear his thoughts were at that moment. He remembered thinking quite calmly as he turned into the outer hall how there was no power in symbols; no power at all!

21

The Tortoise and the Snake

The tortoise entwined with the snake symbolized the north, night, winter and the abyss of Yin.

Midway in his 44-year rule, Li Lung-chi, the greatest of the T'ang emperors, came to believe in the Taoist hopes for a harmonious natural life and for the penetration of nature's secrets. . . .

As Li Lung-chi grew older, the mysteries of Taoism absorbed him more and more. Possibly this intense preoccupation led to visions for he once told his ministers that, while burning incense at a private altar, he had been wafted up to Heaven.

—Edward Schafer

When An Lu-shan returned to his post in the spring of 751, he prepared a great expedition against the Khitan. In the eighth month he set out in personal command of 60,000 men gathered from his three commands. The Hsi, who had been vanquished the previous summer, were compelled to send 2,000 horsemen to act as guides into barbarian territory.

—Edwin Pulleyblank

There is no place for death in the Holy Man.

—*Lao Tzu*

SHEETS of water swept across the stone terraces. Rain pelted the Nine Dragon Lake like a hail of stones from the sky, causing the lake weeds and lotus pads to ride the waves like tiny boats and the grasses of the banks to flatten under the downpour. Mud splattered up onto the foundations of the Flying Rosy Cloud Pavilion and the Hall of Cock Fighting, only to wash down again in the next instant in reddish rivulets. Water flowed from the shining roof tiles into the gutters under the eaves, raced to the downspouts, and gushed out onto the flooded lawns . . .

A lone figure, his outline indistinct in the rain, moved with apparent heedlessness through the swamped field behind the Flying Rosy Cloud Pavilion. Anyone watching would have seen him stoop now and again to examine something down among the sodden, drooping weeds and grasses; occasionally he knelt, scratching in the soggy earth, plucked something, and examined it closely. Sometimes, a find would go immediately into a small brown leather satchel over his shoulder; sometimes, he would hold a plant or root in his teeth while he withdrew a pulpy mass of papers from his sleeve. Then, standing utterly still, rapt with concentration, moving only enough to brush away water that dripped down through the wide straw brim of his fisherman's hat and into his eyes, he would delicately separate the sodden pages and peruse them as if making certain of the identity of the weed in question. He might discard this or that little plant or muddy claw of root; or he might reconsider and dig around in the leather satchel to pull something out again, then drop back down to his knees to search some more. Thus he moved, oblivious to everything else in the world, until he had covered many *mou* of the soggy green landscape.

And the rain continued, until at last the terraces and lawns disappeared, their borders merging into the surface of the lake. Halls and pavilions—their upturned gold roofs and ornate red pillars glistening—were transformed into magic isles adrift in a wide reflective pond.

The whole of Kuanchung Province was inundated. The Wei River had run over its banks; the roads were thick with mud, and everywhere wagons were mired, the oxen struggling futilely under cracking whips. In the lowlands around the city, the fields were sunk, unworkable, water creeping up to the tops of the earthen embankments. And talk ran as freely as water. Talk that something was out of balance: Heaven and Earth were not in harmony.

The reasons for the imbalance were unknown. The question of harmony and balance had become a metaphysical issue, and metaphysics was, ultimately, pure supposition. And supposition was on every tongue. Surely, people said, the duly appointed officials of the capital province of Kuanchung and the capital city itself had given their ancestral shrines proper respect, had paid proper homage to the spirits of Heaven and Earth, the chief star spirits, and the regional spirit overlords of the mountains and the rivers. And certainly, people had sought to reassure themselves, the divine ancestors, the deified patriarchs of the royal House of Li had in no way been ignored, nor had the ancestral halls of the royal House of Li been neglected or defiled. That would not have been possible.

But something *was* wrong, and the heated discussions continued, in rural peasant shacks, in city alleyways and teahouses, and in the halls of government, while the rains, explained and unexplained, continued to fall in Kuanchung. It was the heaviest rain in recent history, the worst that anyone could remember. There were those who had a name for it. Though it was not an explanation, it was, at least, a convenient way to think of the phenomenon, to put it in some sort of useful perspective: they said that it was a time of excessive yin.

: :

The old man shook water from the wide straw brim of his hat. Little pools formed on the polished terrazzo under his feet. His robes were soaked; the household servants brought thick drying linens and fresh clothing. They struggled to undress him and dry him while he, preoccupied, ignoring their ministrations, continued to bend over the table.

He spilled out his collection of roots from the satchel. A soggy mass of paper fell from his sleeve as the servants strove to remove his inner robe from his body. He bent to pick it up again: the esoteric section of the Herbal Concordance of the *Tao Tsang*—the collected works of Dark Taoistical lore. Though it was soaked, it was still readable, the sketches still recognizable. As he stooped, the servants stooped with him, pulling a thick quilted robe over his arms.

The shelves of this hot springs room were lined with more rare volumes, bound with string, in silk and bamboo covers. Books lay open on tables here and there, displaying strange twisting diagrams mapping the ebb and flow of Taoistic magic, diagrams of the human body and the centers of grand heavenly circulation, and the triune forces of the universe—heaven, earth, and man.

Other books lay open to what might look, to the uninitiated eye, like detailed brush drawings of mountains and forests; but just as the universe hides its own secrets in the mysterious formations of nature, a closer examination would reveal inscriptions, recondite and mystic, rendered in coiling, tortuous characters concealed in the calligraphic inked lines of trees and waterfalls. More books were stacked in precarious piles, their pages marked with pieces of silk. Volumes that had, at one time, been banned by the Emperor now lay everywhere in his apartments: on tables, desks, day couches, stools, vernal couches, shelves, and chests, strewn carelessly about like the rumpled clothing and bedding of impassioned lovers.

The Precious Consort had been waiting for Minghuang's return from outside. She had gone over in her head again and again the things she would say to him, carefully selecting and rejecting her words. She knew that if she were to say everything she wanted to say, he would become irritated with her; but she was annoyed—jealous, actually—that this preoccupation was competing with her for his attention.

At first she had found Minghuang's fascination with this rare, dark world amusing, tantalizing, and even seductive. For a while she had actually encouraged him—it was another hobby, like the carving of miniature cork worlds, but this time it was an adventure that she could participate in. She had enjoyed the mystery, abstruseness, abstraction, and secretiveness: she and the Emperor, like two children sharing a private game, were drawn that much closer together. The lore and practice, conjuring as it did the distant past, had appealed to her: stories of ancient golden worlds of Taoist *hsien.** And that was fine. It was more play, and she had loved it—at first.

Her sisters had taken a different view. They said that what she was doing was most foolish and unseemly. But she didn't care. It was the Emperor's pursuit, part of his life. And she was a part of it, too. That was good enough for her, she had told them. Certainly, considering all that she and Minghuang had been through, she thought of this as a pleasant diversion, a relief.

The Lady of Kuo had agreed with her, at least to that extent. Doing something together would help them to stay close, she had said. But she had looked askance at the occult aspect of it, causing Precious Consort to think that her eldest sister had become as humorless and pragmatic as her cousin Yang Kuo-chung. There was a time when the Lady of Kuo would have been the first to appreciate the compelling Taoist mysteries; the consort herself had found them quite irresistible.

There were stories of strange hermits who lived in dark, dank subterranean caverns and partook of exotic and esoteric practices, who collected dew in cups of pure gold under the bright globe of a full moon. There were tales of searches for elixirs, of rare combinations of herbs and elements ground in mortars of rhinoceros horn with pestles of jade. There were the things the Emperor studied in his books: diagrams of change and flux, notations and prescriptions hidden in mystic "cloud script" or Taoist "bird script," arcane tables and formulae pertaining to the distillations of mercuric essences and cinnabar. A careful practitioner, the Emperor had told her, might extract from such a nostrum eternal life; someone else, only slightly less skilled, might acquire instead instant blindness before going to a slow, agonizing death. He had laughed, of course, saying that he could see little difference; she had laughed along with him, enjoying the delicious hint of danger, the manipulation of natural laws.

But it was not all theory and abstraction. In studying the principles of the intermingling of yin and yang, there were specific sexual practices for them

*Immortals.

to explore pertaining to the flow of male and female essences—the consort and the Emperor had passed some rapturous nights in such experimentation and had made some discoveries of their own.

Yes. She had enjoyed this new hobby of the Emperor's. But now her enthusiasm was beginning to sour.

He was beginning to take it too seriously. It was going beyond tales, and lore, and experiments. It was not quite so amusing anymore. With all the other things they had done together—the re-creation of ancient festivals, the revival of dance and music from past eras—there always came a moment when the fun was over for the day, or the night, and they would simply be themselves again. But with this, it was different. He never let it go, never put it aside.

He was going way beyond the admirably simple Taoist hopes for a natural and harmonious existence. He was becoming obsessive, searching for something she didn't understand; gradually, subtly, where she had once felt intimacy and camaraderie with him, she was beginning to feel estrangement. He was leaving her behind, going places where she could not follow.

It had occurred to her that one day he might simply step out the back door of life as an emperor and enter into a different life altogether. Minghuang as a wandering Taoist, a practitioner of the arcane arts, in touch with the dark spirits of earth and nature, his only home a robe and a pair of sandals? Yes. She could see it. She could actually see it.

And there was something else: Li Lin-fu was dying. Everybody knew it. He had moved to his previously unused hot springs apartments to steep himself in the curative vapors and was clinging to life, so they said, by his fingernails. If there were no Emperor Minghuang and no Li Lin-fu, who would control their "Lucky Baby"? The thought was a disturbing one.

She studied the figure of her husband warming himself over the small charcoal brazier in the far corner of the room. He was no longer familiar to her: He was distant, removed. She had to say something to him while she still could, before he slipped away completely.

She walked over and stood near him. Deep in thought, he barely acknowledged her. She took a breath.

"I will not hide the truth from you any longer," she said, her own words startling her with their bluntness. "I am worried about you, and unhappy." She grew bolder. "It is simply not fun anymore."

"What is no longer fun? And for whom?" he asked, challenging her with his eyes, as if he had no idea what she meant.

"It is changing you," she said firmly. "It is becoming tedious and worrisome. Everybody has noticed it. I am not the only one." She wondered whether she should have said it. But now that she had, she was relieved. It was out at last!

He avoided her eyes and looked toward the slender phoenix-shaped brazier. He rubbed his hands together, pretending to concentrate on the heat, making time for himself. His profile was sullen.

"So now *everyone* is gossiping about my private pursuits," he said at last. "Is that what you're trying to tell me? And *everyone* doesn't care for it." He paused. "And what is it that disturbs *you*?"

His attitude provoked her. She decided to hold nothing back.

"You've become careless. Obsessed. You have become a silly, vain, stupid, and arrogant old man, and it is because of me. I have distracted you and encouraged you in all of these selfish pursuits!" She made a wide, exhausted gesture that took in the charts and Dark Taoist incunabula scattered about the room. She hesitated, then spoke. "*Please* don't see that crazy old woman again! Please!" She was surprised to hear herself practically pleading. He hated it when she spoke like that. "If you won't listen to me," she added quickly, "then listen to your councillors of state. Listen to Kao Li-shih. Listen to my cousin Yang Kuo-chung!"

"I *listen* to them. I *listened* to them. And I review the memorials that are sent up to the throne. But their advice is only good for the things of this earth. Of late, I find that that is not enough. It simply does not satisfy me anymore. There are other things. Higher realms. Master Kao and your cousin and the rest of them are afraid to deal with those things. But the old kings understood them. They did not question the fact that an emperor was the leader of his people . . . and that it meant both temporally and spiritually. And"—he appeared to search for a word—"and *metaphysically*. You are always talking about mythical harmonious golden ages, and trying to re-create them with festivals and such. Well, I am going beyond mere festivals. I am seeking the actual higher truths that the ancient kings and princes sought!"

"Yes, and look what has happened because of my 'mere festivals'!" she said impetuously. "Look where they have got me!"

He lifted his eyes, warning her not to continue. She knew that she had let her tongue slip. She had almost said it: Kao Mei. It was still a sore subject between them. Quickly, she dissembled, moving to generalizations. "*None* of it has been successful. I have not been much of a *mother* to anyone."

"The crazy old woman," he said, ignoring her last words, "has requested that you come with me tonight."

Precious Consort did not understand. Why had he said "come with me tonight"? Hadn't the old woman always come to *his* chambers to consult?

"She told me that whatever harmony we will reach, we must reach together," he said. The statement sounded contrived and flimsy to the consort. "Because no one but yourself has sat so close to the position of empress since the Consort Wang," he finished.

"How can you tolerate the sight of that old woman after what happened to the Empress?"

"What happened to the Empress occurred a long time ago. Ming Wu was not to blame. She merely provided Wang with what she had asked for —charms, spells, talismans. The Empress called her to her rooms of her own volition, and against my wishes. It was certainly not the old woman's fault."

"Well, I do not want to see her. She is hideous," Precious Consort said, turning away.

"How do you know she is hideous? Have you ever seen her?" he asked.

"She is old, that is all."

"She was old and repulsive then, too, from what I hear. She must be quite ancient by now and a great deal uglier," the consort retorted, and went to the couch and sat. She sounded to herself like a child, but she couldn't think of anything else to say.

"I don't know how old she was then," the Emperor said thoughtfully. "We—that is, I and members of the household staff—would see her from time to time skulking about the corridors of the palace. We had become quite accustomed to having her around. She came and went as she saw fit. No one cared, until the incident with the Empress . . ." He paused for a moment, remembering. "I never really paid her much attention, my dear, to tell you the truth. But now that I think about it, it does seem that she has always been old. Certainly, she is old now. A toothless and wrinkled hag, without a doubt. Does that bother you? Do you dislike looking upon old age? You never stay when she comes to visit me."

"If I were bothered by age, then I would not be able to look at *your* face," she said.

He smiled at this.

Good! At least she could still joke with him. "But why are you going to see her? Why isn't she coming here as she usually does?"

"I usually summon her through the network—groundskeepers, gate-keepers, guards—anyone who will spread the word that I am looking for her. Sometimes she comes very soon. Other times, I wait in vain. She is quite independent, you know. We don't always know where she is. When she is not in the imperial city, then she's probably somewhere in the hills of Li Shan right here at the hot springs or wherever else it is that she goes. I do not wish to miss an opportunity to see her. If she tells me that I am to come to her, then I go, because I do not always know when I will see her again."

"And why tonight?" the consort persisted impatiently. "Haven't you had enough of all this lately? Have you not had your fill?"

"Certainly not. I am just beginning to get somewhere. My dreams of this last week have been most significant. She told me that this is a crucial time in the travels of my soul. She gave me herbs and told me that they would bring about revelations. Which they have. She told me to go to the woods tonight when the rains have stopped."

"When the rains have stopped? Is that what she said? Do you mean to tell me that she made a prediction that the rains would stop tonight? Were those her words?" the consort demanded, making no effort to hide the scorn in her voice. "And did she also know *when* you would have these 'significant' dreams?"

"She knew that I would be consuming the herbs according to her directions and that such herbs would induce dreams," the Emperor countered firmly. Then his expression softened, and he went over to her couch and sat beside her, covering her hand with his as if to comfort her.

"I am beginning to hate all of it," the consort said, pulling her hand out from under his. She looked away and made a movement as if to get up. Then she stopped and looked back at him. "Especially that old woman. I find it all most tedious. I do not want to go with you, and I do not want to hear what she has to tell you about your dreams."

She moved away from him, rose disdainfully from the couch, and stood with her back to him.

"Listen to me." He tried to take hold of her hand again, but she pulled away. "My dreams were most beatific. I do not know why you are so worried!" He rose from the couch and stood near her. "They were harmonious visions. Taoist sojourns. There are answers buried in them. Answers that neither Kao Li-shih, your cousin, nor any of my good councillors can offer. There are answers in our dreams to everything that we face! History, literature, poetry. They are all full of tales of dreams. *Dreams!*" He said the word with fond reverence.

He approached her again. This time, she reluctantly let him take her hand. Nothing had been conceded, and he continued to ply her. "And it is not horrible. The nation is strong and prosperous. There is no reason for dread. None at all! You *will* come with me tonight. That is final! We will go to the woods behind the hot springs. Ming Wu has told me how we will find her. She told me what paths to follow from the fields."

She looked at him. His eyes were shining with anticipation of the adventure. She could refuse, of course. He could never order her to anything she did not wish to do. She could refuse to go, but she saw that she was absolutely powerless to stop him from going. If she did not go with him, he would go alone. Without her.

"I will go," she finally assented reluctantly.

"Good!" he cried. "But we must go by ourselves. No servants, no entourage. Ming Wu will be pleased," he said, smiling at her. "She was quite adamant that you come with me this time. Most adamant!"

"So," she said, smiling a little, trying to lighten the mood, "now my Imperial Husband's chief councillor is a witch."

: :

The rain ended that evening, just as the old woman had said it would. The air was fluid and cool with excitement as they walked through the wet grass to the far perimeters of the field, toward the dark border of the woods at the base of Li Shan. A pale crescent moon shone through the thinning clouds. The hems of their robes brushed against the weighted grasses that hung over the path. The Emperor carried a long pole lantern that illuminated a silvery elliptical patch in front of them.

The heavy rains had driven all the animals deep into the canopied shelter of the forest. As the consort and the Emperor entered the trees, there were no sounds but their own footsteps, muffled and dampened on the soft, mossy forest floor. It was cooler here, the air rich with the enticing odors of pine and decay. The path they followed wound through a dense copse of tangled evergreens; low resiny twigs snapped at their faces and shoulders as they pushed their way through. They paused while the Emperor turned up the wick in the lantern to give them more light.

This was virgin forest, uncut by the charcoal vendors of previous centuries. The lantern revealed lofty cavernous spaces between the giant trees, the crisscrossing branches silhouetted against pale patches of moonlight. The path through the quiet woods rose gradually until they found themselves climbing.

The Precious Consort felt a strange fluttering just above her stomach; her throat was as dry as paper. She doubted that she would be able to speak, so she didn't; she trudged wordlessly behind Minghuang, twigs cracking under their feet, wondering what he was feeling. He seemed to know exactly where he was going. But then, these had been his woods since he was a boy. Of course he knew where he was going.

The higher they climbed, the larger the stars seemed to be against the deep black of the sky showing through the clouds. She wondered if they were larger because she and the Emperor had climbed that much closer to Heaven or if it was just that she had not seen stars for so long and had forgotten what they looked like. If they kept climbing they would reach the ruins of the ancient king of Chou's beacon tower. That must be where he was taking her, she thought. She was nearly out of breath.

"Please . . . I need to rest!" she said at last. She was exhausted by the steepness of the path.

"I am three times your age," the Emperor said, though he obligingly stopped walking.

"That is a bit of an exaggeration," she said, leaning against a tree for a moment, catching her breath. "A woman does not have brute strength, my husband, but she *is* endowed with longevity."

"You are winded, then? We will sit down here for a bit." He lowered the lantern to the ground near a huge fallen tree trunk. They sat. "We are almost there, in any case," he said.

"I take it we are going all the way to the top?" she asked.

"That is right, my dear. To the ruins."

"Why is she way up here?" She sighed. "How does she do it?"

"She prefers the old to the new. I suspect that she has built her strength over the years. Old people are quite resilient."

Precious Consort could see him looking up the path. He was impatient to be on his way, but he was waiting, for her sake.

"Ming Wu is more comfortable living among the ruins. She tells me that she finds the restorations despicable—we have been true to the ancient plan of the springs, she says, but not to its spirit. I have asked her how I might remedy the deficiency, but she just laughs at me. So I continue, doing the best I can."

"You didn't tell me that we would be climbing the mountain," she said peevishly.

"If I had, you would have refused to come. Am I right? And I am sure that your attendant Hung-t'ao would have told you that such a climb would be detrimental to your delicate female constitution. As if she were a physician!"

"She is very knowledgeable. She certainly would have known to advise me to stay away from this damp night air, this treacherous climb, and that old witch-woman of yours. Hung-t'ao tells me that sometimes, when she throws the shutters open early in the morning to prepare my baths, she spies the old woman on the grounds. She does not like her at all. I trust her instincts."

"And *I* do not trust her little handmaiden hysterics, girl! Are you ready?" He stood and picked up the lantern pole. She rose, and they started walking again. "You should be honored that you have been invited to come up here with me. There is a story I will tell you about this very place. Over two millennia ago, the king of Chou's chief concubine thought it a grand joke to make her imperial husband light the beacon tower fire, thereby summoning the elite forces from the capital. Each time he did it, they would have an enormous laugh. But the soldiers—the capital's finest—became very tired of the joke at their expense. The commander of the garrison, himself a man of noble lineage, became distrustful and disgusted with this foolish emperor. But still the monarch kept playing the same joke—nearly five times within a month—and the loyal troops still came, each time feeling more humiliated and used. And, you can imagine, very, very angry."

"I think I know what happened the sixth time," she said.

"Yes. Still joking, they sent a servant up the hill with an order to light the tower. By that time, I am sure that the keeper of the flame was also growing weary of the game. It was very clear that night. And that time, from the top of the tower, they could see fires burning many li north of the capital. The outlying villages were engulfed in flame . . . evidently, the prince of the neighboring city-state had finally made good a perennial threat against the foolish old jokester. Perhaps the garrison commander, out of insult or anger, had leaked word of the game to the prince. I don't know. In any case, they lit the village beacon towers, making the flames bigger than usual, desperately trying to summon help. But the commander was fed up. He refused to muster his forces that night, and, well . . ."

"How can you talk and climb this ridiculous hill at the same time?" she said, interrupting his tale of morality. "It is quite sufficient for me to just climb."

They were emerging from the trees. Ahead lay the final stretch of the path, steep and rocky. The air was pure and sweet, the stars huge.

"I feel strong," he said. "Perhaps the witch's herbal prescriptions have already begun to have their effects. Surely you yourself have noticed a change in me, have you not, my love?"

She knew what he was referring to. And it was true, she was forced to admit. Her aging husband had the sexual vitality lately of a much younger man—though she had attributed it to her own attentions, and not to the old hag's.

"And she says that if I need it," he continued, laughing, "she has a special mixture for me. *Hung* pills, she called them. Made of moon's blood discharge of thirteen- and fourteen-year-old maidens. My 'old man' will be standing stiff day and night like an adolescent boy's."

They were both laughing now. The exertion and the laughter were finally affecting Minghuang; he, too, was growing short of breath as they climbed the final steps to the summit.

"If it is her doing, then I will thank her for it," the consort said, gasping for breath.

"You should sample these elixirs with me."

"I am in need of nothing. Besides, I have no desire to touch the old witch's poisons." The consort stopped, placed her hands on her knees, and tried to catch her breath.

"The top!" Minghuang exclaimed triumphantly. "You see how simple that was!"

Ahead of them, beyond the feeble light of their pole lantern, an enormous black shape loomed against the sky.

"What is that?" the Precious Consort whispered, wondering at the huge shape that blotted out the stars.

"Why, it is the beacon tower, of course," the Emperor replied. "You have never been up here before. You have simply never seen it up close."

"It is quite enormous," she said with awe. "It does not look anything like this from down below."

"It never fails to overwhelm you the first time," he told her. "Especially at night, because there is no warning until it is practically upon you. Then suddenly, there it is. It still startles me, if I am not ready for it. Yes, the appearance from below is deceptive, is it not? It seems so much smaller from there. Our forefathers seem to have built things on a far different scale. And wait until you see the view from the top!"

"By all means, show her the view from the top," a woman's voice said from the darkness to their left just beyond the circle of light cast by their lantern.

They both jumped, the consort grabbing Minghuang's arm, causing him to nearly drop the lantern pole.

"Ming Wu!" he said. "You startled us!" He moved the lantern forward, trying to find her. The light revealed nothing except lazy clouds of sweet-smelling smoke drifting out of the darkness and hanging in the air.

"What else can a decrepit old woman do?" the voice said, still in the shadows. "She cannot assault you and steal your jewels, can she?"

"Though she would if she could, I have no doubt," Minghuang replied.

"Yes, she would. You are right!" the woman said, laughing.

The consort was having some difficulty reconciling what she was hearing with what she had been expecting. The voice had startled her not just because of its suddenness, but also because of its sound: this was not the voice of an old woman at all; hearing it, the consort saw in her mind the image of a young, vital, beautiful woman.

Minghuang moved forward, extending the lantern pole, the consort following close behind him. If the consort was startled a few moments ago, she was shocked now by the incongruity of the youthful, virile voice and Ming Wu's appearance.

The old woman sat on a rock. She was dressed entirely in black, though draped about her neck and waist were what appeared to be a collection of bones, pieces of glass, and bright bits of metal. A black cloth was tied tight on her skull. In her hand she held what looked like a carved root with a hollowed bowl at one end; she raised the root to her shriveled, obviously toothless mouth and sucked on it, causing a ball of ash in the bowl to glow brightly, then allowed a languid stream of smoke to pour from her nose and lips while she grinned and squinted, her face a net of crisscrossing wrinkles. The consort had never before seen anything that resembled this performance. It was as if the old woman were on fire inside.

Now, grinning directly at the consort, she passed the smoke up from her mouth and sucked it into her nostrils before blowing it out again.

It was a strange moment for the consort. She had heard a lot about this old woman, had even caught glimpses of her from a distance, but had certainly never been face to face with her or spoken to her; nor had she wanted to. Earlier this evening, the thought of such an encounter had filled her with disgust.

But now, she found herself curious and intrigued. Ming Wu's smoke had a sweetish, compelling smell, and the sight of her framed against the inky black immensity of the tower wall had the effect of diminishing her so that she seemed to be nothing more than a harmless, benighted old eccentric, with her strange smoking stick, her black clothes, and her charms.

"Is this where you live?" the consort heard herself asking, her own voice sounding small and foolish.

"Sometimes, my girl. Sometimes," Ming Wu answered in her low, young woman's voice. "But why does she ask such impertinent questions, my Emperor?" she said, turning her smile toward Minghuang.

"I must apologize for my Precious Consort, Ming Wu. She is at times the same fresh and overly inquisitive child that she was when I first met her."

"Do not apologize to old Wu," she said. "I *like* her. She is a very smart girl, and very pretty." She drew thoughtfully on her smoking stick. "And I would guess that she did not want to come with you tonight to visit me. Am I right?"

"You are right," the Emperor answered simply.

"I shall answer your question, girl. I live here some of the time. I like the ancientness. It makes me feel young," she said, poking the bowl of her smoking stick with a bony finger. "Here, I have no other landlord but Time—and his demands are always perfectly predictable. I do not register on the provincial census roles. I cannot be pushed off my land like a poor farmer. And our good Son of Heaven does not demand taxes of me," she said, casting a sidelong glance and an insolent smile toward the Emperor. "Taxes that would only go to feeding armies and carpeting the cold floors of the rich!"

The Emperor laughed. He and Ming Wu seemed to know each other well, the consort thought, feeling the smallest pang of jealousy.

"Ming Wu does not have carpets, nor even floors," the old woman said. "She is too poor!"

She and the Emperor laughed together now. Then Ming Wu rose from her rock.

"But come." She motioned for them to follow her. She took them around to the north-facing wall of the tower to an arched doorway. "Come inside! Old Wu would be a most ungracious host if she did not properly receive our August Emperor and his beautiful queen!" she exclaimed.

It was the first time the Precious Consort had ever heard that word— queen—applied to her. It had been one of her private yearnings, of course, one she kept to herself. Hearing it from the old woman, who spoke the word as if she had plucked it from the consort's own mind, made her feel embarrassed.

Inside, the ancient stones gave off a dank, earthy smell. The Emperor's lantern revealed precarious, unprotected steps hugging the circular wall and spiraling up into the blackness. The consort hesitated. She had not expected anything so terrifying as those steps. But Ming Wu bounded up, talking as she went, and the Emperor followed, pulling the consort after him.

"It is a rare pleasure to have such noble guests," she said. "Usually, it is *I* who must pay calls. And the girl has never been to the top of the tower, has she? I apologize. It is dusty and full of spiders, but old Wu is too feeble to clean the webs," she said, climbing with no trace of feebleness, her voice echoing, amplified by the vast vault of stone. "Besides, they are my only company. They never say that old Wu is tiresome. They make no judgments." The wooden staff of Minghuang's pole lantern scraped noisily against the damp mossy wall as they ascended the dizzying tower steps. He held the consort's hand tightly as she climbed behind him.

"Do you know that I know what the little spider thinks?" the old woman said over her shoulder. "It thinks only of the moment in its most indivisible form. It is the most present-minded of creatures. Pinpricks of light in the infinite consciousness. Tiny little eyes through which tiny little worlds are seen. Spiders are unassuming and comforting. Even the bats and squirrels and rats are far too quarrelsome and assuming. But the spider does not assume. He cannot. Each moment escapes at the same moment it arrives into the emptiness behind. Each new moment seeks him out and just as quickly passes out of reach. No memory. No reflection. That is a blessing few of us can ever know!"

She was far ahead of them by now, her voice and her quick, light footsteps carrying down to them out of the darkness above.

"But you have dreamed, Minghuang, as I said you would, and you came to see me when the rain ended."

The higher they climbed, the more the consort could feel the great empty height to the side of her. She was grateful that it was not daytime and that she could not actually see down to the floor of the tower. Pressing herself against the wall, her stomach light and tingling with fear, she climbed behind the Emperor toward the top, expecting at any moment to plunge to her death.

"And what about these rains, eh?" Ming Wu said cheerfully. "They have ceased for the time being in Kuanchung Province, but they are traveling north right now, searching for our 'Lucky Baby,' An Lu-shan. They are following him, plaguing him like a lovesick woman," she laughed. "But the rains should be more at home up there," she said as she reached a trapdoor, pushed it up, and stepped onto the circular platform at the top of the tower. The Emperor's lantern revealed her face grinning down at them through the opening. "The dark abyss of the yin is dominant in the north. The tortoise that couples with the snake may feel more comfortable there—the 'dark warrior' more at peace with our own General An. Though *he* may not be so comfortable with them."

"Ming Wu," the Emperor said, "I am afraid that I have no idea at all what you are talking about. Please remember that we are nowhere near as learned as you are."

The old woman laughed appreciatively. "I simply mean that the deluge may cause our Fat One considerable hardship. That is all, my good Imperial Father."

"It has caused us all hardship," the Emperor said, helping the consort up the final steps onto the platform.

In the center of the windswept platform was a great copper bowl as wide across as a man's height. It rose into the night sky, sitting on a massive, unornamented frame of iron and brick. The consort put her hand on the cold metal.

"How do you know all of this, Ming Wu?" she asked, pulling her jacket up around her neck against the gusting winds.

"Pretty, smart, and curious, too!" Ming Wu said, looking appraisingly at the consort.

The Emperor laughed. "There are no answers to some questions," he said.

"There are always answers, my Emperor," Ming Wu corrected. "There are simply not always explanations." She paused. The wind was driving the clouds to the north, clearing the sky. "But old Wu listens. She doesn't talk much. She listens. She learns a great deal that way. She even listens to the crows and ravens—although they are far too assuming for this old woman's tastes. Still, they tell me much."

So, you don't talk much, the consort thought, and smiled. Until now, you have done nothing but talk. She was bemused and ever so slightly irritated by the old woman's obliqueness, but had accepted it as part of the game. And it was as though Ming Wu were doing it on purpose, certain of the reaction it evoked in the consort, and enjoying the joke. And at the same time, the consort was beginning to feel comfortable with her. The old witch was not so terrible, not so disgusting, strange, or repulsive at all. The Emperor had been right. She was just old. And beneath her veiled, often sardonic and teasing conversation, the consort sensed infinite passivity and patience.

The consort said nothing. Instead, she walked to the rail between the high brick crenellations and put her head out into the night.

The view was extraordinary and strangely disquieting; the world lay revealed and vulnerable beneath them. To the southwest, in rigid geometrics, spread the enormous blanket of light that was Ch'ang-an, and far beyond, past the scattered specks of lights of outlying villages, was the dark line of the mountains. To the north, the meandering serpent of the Wei River reflected the pale light of the moon and stars, and to the east, the bright beacon fires of the T'ung-kuan Pass burned, protecting the capital's eastern flank. The first three lights were visible; the other seven were lost behind the hills of the pass. Since the days of the king of Chou and his foolish empress, the principle had changed: now, a lit tower was reassurance that the path to Ch'ang-an was secure and unthreatened.

She lingered for only a few moments. The wind and the vastness caused her an uncomfortable chill. Wrapping her arms tightly about her chest, she turned back toward her husband and the old woman. Ming Wu was making a small fire on the corbeled brick platform beneath the overhang of the king of Chou's ancient copper firepot. Already, the two were deep in discussion.

"But you did say that I would have dreams," the Emperor was saying, "and that the herbs would induce them."

"I told you that you would have dreams. But you had them only because I told you that you would have them," Ming Wu said, blowing on a pile of twigs, encouraging a small tongue of flame. "It was not the herbs, but my suggestions that induced your heart to search for the truth. The herbs are nothing. Harmless and useless. Except, perhaps, as cleansers of the blood or as minor restoratives for the lungs. But that is all."

"These were dreams of Taoist immortality," the Emperor said. "I know it. They were not mere creations of my own mind."

"Mere creations of the mind, you say?" The old woman laughed. "The mind is our gate to everything. I have traveled through the stars, seen them spin and whirl, explode and change colors. Red, blue, yellow. I have seen them diminish into black vortices that suck into them all time, all memory. Islands of stars adrift in clouds of glowing dust. Hah!" she snorted. "Mere creations of your mind. Is that what you believe? If so, then old Wu can take you nowhere." She shook her head as she stirred the fire, her charms tinkling and jangling her reproval.

"When you hear these dreams, Old Woman, you will know what I am saying," the Emperor insisted. "There were two, this last week, of extraordinary vividness. Induced, I am certain, by the potent herbs that I had consumed before retiring."

"You are more assuming even than the ravens!" Ming Wu said, and clucked her tongue in mock rebuke. But she was settling herself into a comfortable, listening attitude. She lit her smoking stick again, released a cloud of smoke, and stirred the fire in front of them. "But, please, tell your dreams to old Wu. You came here tonight for that purpose. Perhaps, if they are of any interest, she can add them to her collection."

"The first was not even three nights ago," the Emperor said eagerly, closing his eyes in concentration. "I would have sworn that I was awake, offering my daily respects to the shrine of the imperial house, burning incense at the Li family altar. Every detail of the hall—the smells, the sounds, the bells, the attendants, the rustle of the ritual silks, the inscriptions above the altar—was absolutely real. And then a cloud rose from the floor . . ."

"A cloud?" the Precious Consort asked. "You didn't tell me that part."

"Yes. I remember now that it was a cloud," he said. "It was not smoke or incense. It was a cloud!"

"And what did this cloud do?" Ming Wu asked, poking the fire with a stick so that orange sparks danced upward.

The consort moved closer. The warmth of the fire was most welcome.

"It was solid and insubstantial at the same time," Minghuang continued. "But I did not remember thinking it was at all strange the way it wafted me . . . carried, lifted me . . . toward Heaven, because a Taoist immortal can maintain the solidity of transient substances such as smoke and mist . . ."

"Because you were dead!" the witch said flatly. "Because you were dead, the cloud appeared to have weight and solidity. Because you had none. It is a simple dream of death, Imperial Father."

"It was the dream of a *hsien*—an immortal floating. A pure dream of Taoist transcendence, Witch," the Emperor insisted.

"You don't consider death to be transcendent?" she asked, suddenly serious, startling the consort with her tone. But the Emperor merely looked annoyed that he was not being taken seriously.

"All right, all right," Ming Wu said, her face relaxing into a smile again. "Tell me the other one. Each yin dream must be matched by a yang dream."

She winked at the Precious Consort as if the two of them were sharing a joke at the expense of the Emperor, though the consort was not at all sure what the joke was.

"You see, in the first dream, nothing happened," Ming Wu said. "It was passive. Now I want to hear the second one."

"The second dream was only last night," the Emperor began. "Again, it was vivid. Not at all like a dream. I thought I was awake, traveling down the familiar corridors of the palace. I had been summoned by the painting master Wu Tao-tzu to view his progress on the landscape mural in the waiting halls of the Han-yuan Hall throne room. So real was this dream that I could even feel the cold of the polished stone floors beneath my feet. In reality, Wu Tao-tzu has been working patiently and in great solitude on the fresco painting for some time, keeping it covered so that even I should not look upon it until he is ready to reveal it, piece by piece. So I did not suspect that this was a dream at all. I believed that he had finally decided to let me see it.

"When we had reached the hall and he drew the cover from the painting, it was magnificent. And it was, truly, a painting by Wu Tao-tzu in every detail. Every stroke of the brush executed with his peculiar dignity, vigor, and purpose, each line with the same powerful elegance possessed in his paintings of Buddhist holy scenes and disciples. There were twisting trees, and waterfalls, and rocks, and cloudy pinnacles against empty expanses of sky; birds, and thatched cottages, and tiny figures of men far off in the hills along rocky paths.

"But then Wu Tao-tzu told me that there was a spirit dwelling in a cave in one of the mountains in the painting. A recluse, an immortal. And then he clapped his hands, and far away in the mountain scene, a tiny cave opened." Minghuang threw his hands apart to illustrate the suddenness and speed with which the painted rocks, which had become real rocks, had split apart. "And then, pointing to the far-off cave in the painting, the artist told me that the inside of the cave was magnificent, beautiful, magical beyond any means to describe it, and I was to follow him. 'Let me lead the way,' he said, and in an instant he had become tiny, like the figures in the painting, and was climbing the path. I watched as he disappeared into the cave. And before I could even begin to follow . . ."

". . . the mountains, the trees, the cave," Ming Wu interrupted, "and then the entire painting faded. Not a single brushstroke remained on the old palace wall." She took a deep draw on her pipe and leaned comfortably back, sheltered from the wind, against the brick base of the firepot. The Emperor looked at her in a way that made it clear that she had stated it exactly as it had happened.

"Why do I even bother to tell you, if you know it already?" he asked her.

Ming Wu leaned forward, her face serious again.

"If you come to Ming Wu, then you ought to listen to Ming Wu. That was not a Taoist dream, not a dream of inaction, not a dream of yin. That was a yang dream of action. Of escape. Wu Tao-tzu escapes. He hides. But there is no place for our Emperor to hide." She paused. "No place to go," she said, as if to herself, shaking her head sadly, the smoke drifting from her lips as she spoke.

"Old Woman, you are an arrogant, insolent old crone and a very poor host!" The Precious Consort was angry.

"Hush, girl!" Minghuang said sharply.

"You cannot insult Ming Wu," the old woman said pleasantly, looking at the consort. "But if you do not like what old Wu tells you, then you ought not to waste your time coming to see her. And you shouldn't let the old man come, either."

The consort sat back down with a sharp feeling of having been reprimanded by an elder for impertinence. Her cheeks burned the way they had when she was a little girl being scolded for some childish transgression.

Then Ming Wu smiled at her. "You are very pretty, and very smart," she said. "You are right to defend him, to try to protect him. It is your duty. And it is true, old Wu is certainly an arrogant, insolent old crone." Then she turned to the Emperor. "The trouble is, my Imperial Father," she said to him almost apologetically, "that you do not really want the Taoist magic of immortality. In the face of what is to come, *immortality* may not be what you want at all!"

"We are leaving, Old Woman," the Precious Consort said curtly. "This is nonsense. And he is listening to it. I am afraid I cannot permit it to go on." She felt very sure of herself all of a sudden. Guarding the Emperor, protecting him, was indeed her responsibility, and this had gone quite far enough. She stood, pulling on his arm. Obediently, he rose to his feet, and she pushed him toward the trapdoor.

"Must you leave?" the old woman said, as though she were genuinely disappointed.

"We must," the consort answered.

The Emperor started down the stairs. She let him go ahead a few steps, then started down after him. Before her head descended below the level of the platform, Ming Wu spoke again.

"Wait, Beautiful Queen."

The consort turned. She felt sure that Ming Wu was about to apologize. She would accept the apology and they would be on their way. She waited. The old woman leaned close.

"You know, my dear," she whispered very softly, so that only the Precious Consort could hear her now. "The more you spread your legs for that old self-centered reprobate, the wider your hole becomes."

The consort drew back, shocked and speechless.

Ming Wu put her smoking stick back in her mouth. "And," she said, taking it out again, little puffs of smoke accompanying her words, "the wider the regal old cock reams your sweet cunt, the easier it is for your brains to fall through. Remember that, girl. You could end up as stupid as he is!"

She leaned back then and looked at the consort with a broad, toothless, lascivious smile that the consort thought was the most revoltingly obscene thing she had ever looked at. The old woman began to rock back and forth, convulsed with silent, delighted laughter, while hot shame rushed to the consort's face.

She scrambled down the stairs, bringing the thick wooden hatch down hard above her head. Guiding herself with her hands against the curving stone wall, she took the steps two at a time, heedless of the unprotected drop, until she had caught up with the Emperor. Her heart beat wildly and she was out of breath, her confusion and anger racing through her. She said nothing to the Emperor, but urged him along faster toward the bottom of the stairs.

"What did she say to you?" the Emperor asked.

"Nothing at all," the consort answered quickly, striving to keep her voice steady. "She wished us a good night and many interesting dreams."

When they reached the base of the tower and stepped out onto the path, the Precious Consort looked up and saw the flickering glow of Ming Wu's fire atop the tower. She imagined for a moment that the old woman was looking down on them from the crenellations. Looking down on *her*. But she saw that she was mistaken. There was nobody. The old woman had probably not moved at all.

: :

Li Chu-erh stayed close to An Lu-shan's son An Ching-hsu, keeping him between himself and An Lu-shan whenever he could on the long ride deep into Khitan territory. The two youths had made a pact that they would try to protect one another from the general. If possible, they agreed, neither one of them would ever be left alone with him, and each would be observant of the vagaries of his moods. They both knew An Lu-shan well, and knew of a hundred different ways to distract him.

Fortunately, he was paying little attention to either of them on this ride, so thoroughly obsessed was he with penetrating deep into enemy country and making his strike. They had been riding for two and a half weeks now, not making camp until well after dark and rising again to move on before the sun was up. For the past three days of the ride, it had been raining steadily, and tempers were foul and morale low. Behind the general rode almost sixty thousand men; riding with them were two thousand Hsi horsemen—conquered enemy, now compelled to guide the Chinese into the barbarian lands. With so many thousands of men around them, and with An Lu-shan responsible for the vast army and anxious for the success of his mission, An Ching-hsu and Li Chu-erh felt blessedly insignificant.

An Lu-shan had been uncharacteristically taciturn since leaving Ch'ang-an soon after the disastrous Festival of Kao Mei. Li Chu-erh could have stayed behind if he had wanted to and never again suffered An Lu-shan's domination. He had been under the protection of Kao Li-shih from the moment he ran to him on that terrible morning at the hot springs. And Kao Li-shih had offered to make arrangements for him, to set him free forever. He could have gone to the house of the head of the Flying Dragons and never set eyes on An Lu-shan for the rest of his days.

And he had gone to that secret house in the city for a while, thinking that he was, at last, free. But he had not been able to forget the pitiful moans and cries of the dying girl and had castigated himself over and over for not having had the courage to even try to save her. One night about a week after he arrived, he asked to be sent back to the palace.

The dead girl's ghost had come to him in a dream, he explained to Kao Li-shih when he got there, and he had promised her that he would at least try to avenge her death. I have no particular courage, he had told the ghost, and I may fail. I wish I could be more of a warrior for you. But I will try. He expressed to Kao Li-shih that he wished to be officially reaffirmed as a Flying Dragon, to continue to be a discreet and observant set of eyes and ears, and to accompany An Lu-shan back to the north. If he did not do this, he said, his life would be worthless. Kao Li-shih had looked at him for a long time, then agreed.

And so he had returned to his master. An Lu-shan subsequently punished him for running away that morning, but not for anything else. He had no knowledge that the youth had told Kao Li-shih everything about the girl's death. The Emperor had, in any case, excused his "Lucky Baby," and Kao Li-shih had taken full responsibility for casting doubts on the barbarian's veracity. They had returned to the north, with An Lu-shan moody and silent during the trip. And when they reached his headquarters in Lu-lung in southern P'inglu Province, he had retreated into his tent for several days. Soon the word was spreading through the camp: A great expedition against the Khitan would be mobilized. Preparations were to begin immediately.

And An Ching-hsu and Li Chu-erh had watched in awe as the great war machine smoothly and efficiently formed itself. Three regiments of twenty thousand men each, the best fighters from An Lu-shan's three commands in the northernmost provinces of Fanyang, Hotung, and Shuofang, assembled at the Lu-lung camp. Every day more of them poured in until the entire camp was filled. Each man was given his own supply of food to carry, and a forward regiment of twenty thousand archers was heavily armed. Then, with An Lu-shan at the head, they began their long journey. When they passed through Hsi territory, the two thousand horsemen joined them and the expedition was officially under way.

Both Li Chu-erh and An Ching-hsu knew it was during the trip up from Ch'ang-an that An Lu-shan had made the decision to wage this campaign. It was why he had hardly spoken and had stayed alone in his tent at night with the oil lamp burning. It was why he had hardly paid any attention to either of them. And now, because of just a few words from him, an army was moving north. What must it be like, they asked each other, to be able to assuage one's smarting sense of dignity, to soothe one's angry sense of having been doubted, with the obedient response and mobilization of an army of fierce warriors? Lying in their tent at night in enemy territory, they had whispered these questions to each other. And they could not imagine it. They themselves were the most inconsequential of creatures, alone and small, whereas An Lu-shan was incalculably huge, a creature with thousands upon thousands of arms and legs responsive to his will.

Two weeks after the expedition began, An Lu-shan's army had come to the T'u Hu-chen River. While they were fording the broad, flat, shallow waters, it began to rain from the low gray sky; lightly at first, scarcely noticeable. During the several hours that it took to get the entire army across, the pattering on the water around them had grown more insistent. By the time they reassembled on the other side, the rain had become so heavy that they could no longer make out the hills on the horizon, and men and horses were as soaked from the downpour as they were from the river.

But there was to be no stopping, An Lu-shan had declared. They were only about five days' march from where he believed the Khitan were camped, and he did not intend to lose the advantage he had already gained merely because of some rain. A few of his officers had attempted to reason with him, but he would not hear them. And it was plain that their entreaties were only reinforcing his determination. An Lu-shan's army moved on, and the rain continued.

Three days later it was still raining. The officers, A Pu-ssu in particular, had tried to reason with An Lu-shan again. Had they not gone far enough? Perhaps there was no Khitan encampment. Why not wait until the rains stopped and send out scouts before going any further? The men were soaked, demoralized. They had not been able to rest properly or start fires to cook hot food. How could they be expected to do battle under such conditions?

And An Lu-shan had asked them in a quiet voice if they thought that they were ladies on a royal picnic. Both Li Chu-erh and An Ching-hsu had instinctively cringed at the familiar, dangerous tone of the general's words and had moved carefully out of his line of vision while he conversed with the officers, the rain pouring down on their heads without mercy, the bleak landscape stretching to infinity on all sides.

What do you think soldiers are, An Lu-shan? A Pu-ssu had asked him then. Cattle? Slaves? Yes, they are supposed to be adaptable to hardship, to do without luxuries or pampering, to sleep on the bare earth and be prepared to die at your command. But remember, they are serving you, and you owe them fair treatment. Fair treatment! An Lu-shan had glared at his officer. When your rank equals mine, he said, when you have proven that you know as much as I do about military affairs and the handling of soldiers, then perhaps I will listen to you. Perhaps!

And the army had moved on.

Li Chu-erh and An Ching-hsu rode side by side. It was the afternoon of the fifth day of traveling since they had crossed the river and the rains had begun; the men rode with their soaked saddle blankets over their bowed heads. An Lu-shan had not spoken to anyone all day. The youths could see the officers conversing quietly, out of An Lu-shan's earshot, discussing, no doubt, their commander's insanity.

Someone shouted that the clouds were breaking up ahead. They lifted their faces and saw that it was true: on the horizon, over some low hills, they saw patches of blue sky and shafts of sunlight. Though the clouds were still thick over their heads and the rain still fell on them, a great cheer went up from the ranks.

Li Chu-erh asked himself how An Lu-shan did it. Now the mood around him was one of gratitude, as if the general himself had parted the clouds as a gift to the soldiers. First, they had been driven almost to despair by the rain, and now they were ready to do anything for An Lu-shan because he had stopped it. Even though An Lu-shan rode a considerable distance ahead of Li Chu-erh, the eunuch could clearly see by a slight change in the general's posture in the saddle that he took full credit for the miracle.

When they reached the low hills, the rain had virtually stopped, though the holes in the clouds had closed up again, taking away those enticingly beautiful shafts of light. An Lu-shan raised his arm, the signal to stop.

"The men will wait here," he said to his officers. "Two of you and ten scouts will accompany me."

Li Chu-erh and An Ching-hsu shrank down, positioning themselves, out of habit, so that several mounted soldiers were between them and the general. They had no wish to be noticed and compelled to accompany An Lu-shan. They knew that his instinct for sniffing out the enemy was uncanny. The encampment was undoubtedly somewhere very close; he was rarely wrong. As An Lu-shan and his small group rode off to the northwest, a feeling of sick apprehension crawled up Li Chu-erh's limbs. Why was he here? Why wasn't he in that beautiful, comfortable house in Ch'ang-an? He was no soldier, no hero. He was a young fool trying to assuage his guilty conscience.

The rain started again, lightly, a mere sprinkle. It was nothing compared to what they had endured for the last five days.

"Remember," An Ching-hsu said to Li Chu-erh. "We stay together, no matter what."

An Lu-shan and his scouts and officers returned after three hours. The look on the general's face as he reined his horse in told the waiting officers and men that they had found their target: the enemy encampment.

: :

They rode harder now, but still restrained, cantering steadily forward in formation over the rolling grasslands, prepared to break into a full gallop when the general gave the signal. There were still a few hours of daylight left, and An Lu-shan intended to sweep down onto the enemy with furious speed, cut them to the ground, and rout them into the night as it fell. The Khitan, hearing the approaching hoofbeats of the advance regiment, would undoubtedly mistake the sound for thunder at first; by the time they realized their error and scrambled for their horses, their weapons, it would be too late.

A regiment of archers had been sent well ahead of the rest of the army to deal the first blow to the enemy in their valley encampment. They had ridden forward in row upon row of orderly ranks, each man ready to replace the man in front of him if he fell. When they had disappeared from view, An Lu-shan gave the order for the rest to follow: himself, his officers, the remaining soldiers, and the Hsi horsemen bringing up the rear. Now An Ching-hsu and Li Chu-erh rode as close to An Lu-shan as they could: when it came to staying alive, the general seemed to be charmed, and they strove to stay within his protective aura.

Li Chu-erh bent low over his horse, the chill wind cutting through his wet clothing, his senses engulfed by the sound of thousands of hooves pounding the earth. He was a creature without feelings, fear, or memory, swept along by the vast army of men and horses.

He heard battle cries in the distance: the enemy had been engaged. The archers would be pouring down from the hills, scattering the Khitan, cutting through them, creating chaos and terror, preparing the way for the rest of the army to finish the job. Soon An Lu-shan would give the signal, and they would whip their horses to full speed.

But someone was coming back. They could see on the horizon a long ragged line of riders, retreating, it seemed, from the rear of the regiment of archers. Seeing the broad front of their own approaching army ahead of them, the retreating archers began to scatter to the sides. And behind them were more. Wave after wave of archers were turning back, dispersing, fleeing. Li Chu-erh heard An Lu-shan cursing at the sight.

But there was one lone man who did not veer to the side. Shouting unintelligibly, he headed straight toward them, seeking out An Lu-shan who was riding in the forward row. He will be trampled, Li Chu-erh thought, but the man turned his mount around and moved forward again so that when the the army caught up to him, he was riding along with them. He was still shouting as he worked his way in among the officers with great skill so that he was directly beside An Lu-shan. The general turned his furious face toward the man.

"The bowstrings!" the archer screamed over the wind. "They are soaked! Useless! The men cannot shoot! They are dying by the hundreds! By the thousands!"

"They are cowards!" An Lu-shan screamed back.

"You must order a retreat!" A Pu-Ssu, riding on his other flank, shouted to An Lu-shan. "It is suicide! Murder!"

"Cowards!" An Lu-shan shouted, then pulled his sword and brutally cut the archer from his saddle. "We will attack!" He lashed his horse.

The order traveled fast, the well-trained army of horses and men reflexively obeying their general's command. But Li Chu-erh could hear the shouted words spreading from man to man, down the ranks, even as the horses broke into a full gallop: the bowstrings. The rains have ruined the bowstrings. He cast a frightened look in An Ching-hsu's direction; his friend looked back at him with the same fear in his eyes.

As they got closer, they could see archers trying vainly to shoot, then throwing their useless weapons to the ground and fleeing. By now the Khitan were moving up out of their valley, an invincible fighting front, cutting the defenseless Chinese down, driving them back toward their own army. Now An Lu-shan and his men were riding over hundreds of dead and dying soldiers, the bodies bristling with Khitan arrows, as the survivors set out to the sides in both directions, seeking the safety of the hills, most of them falling from their saddles as they fled. There were hardly any archers left between An Lu-shan's army and the enemy now, and the Khitan arrows were beginning to find them.

One of An Lu-shan's officers fell, an arrow impaling his chest; three other men riding near him took arrows in their necks and bodies. Two fell immediately; the other slouched down over his horse's mane but hung on for a while before sliding to the ground and being trampled. Li Chu-erh and An Ching-hsu put their heads as far down as they could, riding blindly.

"Drop back!" someone was shouting close by.

Li Chu-erh looked up to see A Pu-ssu riding alongside him.

"Let him go!" A Pu-ssu shouted.

Just ahead, they could see An Lu-shan, an arrow in his leg, still whipping his mount forward, disappearing into the ranks of men and horses.

"Follow me!" A Pu-ssu called, reining in his horse, allowing the other riders to flow around him. Li Chu-erh and An Ching-hsu did the same, pulling their animals back, urging them over, pulling them back again, while straining to keep A Pu-ssu in sight. By now hundreds of other riders, seeing the futile carnage ahead of them, were giving up as well; the two youths soon found themselves part of a large body of men and horses veering sharply to the north. Li Chu-erh kept his eyes fixed on A Pu-ssu's distinctive helmet. Don't lose him, he told himself desperately; he is your only chance to make it out of this alive.

A Pu-ssu veered again, to the northwest now, so that they were almost doubling back in the direction they had come from. They rode hard, heads down, not looking behind them, Li Chu-erh expecting an arrow in his back at any moment. The hills were getting closer, but were still maddeningly distant. Battle cries to their left made them raise their heads. They looked over to see a pack of hundreds of Hsi horsemen heading right for them. It was a revolt! The Hsi, hearing the word that the battle was a hopeless one, that the Chinese archers were riding virtually unarmed toward the Khitan, must have been breaking into lethal bands, attacking the Chinese from the rear, but outnumbered, were going for the smaller fleeing groups—like themsleves.

The Hsi arrows were flying. Li Chu-erh wondered fleetingly how it was that their bows would shoot when the Chinese ones would not, but, in any case, he knew that A Pu-ssu would not choose to stay and fight. Not with the Hsi on one side and the Khitan rapidly closing in on the other. There was nothing to do but ride for their lives toward the hills, and let other Chinese soldiers fleeing behind them absorb the fury of the Hsi.

: :

They had ridden hard for a long time until the pursuing riders finally dropped away, their cries fading, and night had fallen. Though it was impossible to count them in the dark, there seemed to be about fifty men in the group led by A Pu-ssu. Li Chu-erh and An Ching-hsu had stayed together, as they had promised each other they would.

They rested now, having made a crude camp. A Pu-ssu had ordered that no fire be lit, so they lay in the dark, wrapped in their damp blankets talking while the exhausted horses cropped grass in a circle around them. There were two questions on everyone's mind: the bowstrings, and whether An Lu-shan was dead or alive.

"Why were the Hsi rebels able to shoot their arrows while our men could not? Did it not rain just as hard on them?" An Ching-hsu asked. "What was that? Magic?"

"No magic," A Pu-ssu replied, his voice tired. "The rain fell on them just as hard. They were just as wet. But the bows they carried were their own. They were not issued to them by the Chinese military."

"I don't understand," Li Chu-erh said.

"Nor do I," A Pu-ssu said. "Not fully. Not yet. But I do know this: if hide is not cured properly, it can lose its strength when it gets very wet—if it gets soaked, for example, by heavy rains."

"Improperly cured?" An Ching-hsu asked.

"Improperly or . . . incompletely cured."

There was silence for a few moments as these words were contemplated. Li Chu-erh could hear A Pu-ssu rolling over, trying to make himself more comfortable on the hard ground.

"General An Lu-shan was, shall we say, in a great hurry," A Pu-ssu continued. "And his terrible impatience marked every stage of the expedition. It was hastily planned, hastily executed. From the arming and mobilization of the men, to the way he pushed and drove them, with barely enough time to eat or sleep, not stopping even for the rains, and, finally, the attack itself. What we have just witnessed, and which almost cost us our lives, is the price that this sort of impatience can exact. As for the bows . . . I know only that they were new. Recently commissioned. Obviously, An Lu-shan did not have the patience to wait until they were properly seasoned."

"And even when he knew that the bows were failing," An Ching-hsu said, "he ordered the attack. The soldier who came back and tried to tell him . . ."

"Yes. He was very brave, whoever he was. And you saw how your father rewarded his bravery." There was another short silence. "But I can tell you this, as another military man: the expedition could have been a brilliant success. The strategy was almost perfect. And had he succeeded, he would have dealt the Khitan a disabling blow indeed. The camp that he tried to attack represented a major part of their forces. Why, within a week Ch'ang-an would have been celebrating another stunning victory for the great General An Lu-shan, the protector and savior of the T'ang." A Pu-ssu snorted in disgust. "But he ruined it. He was in a big hurry, and he ruined it."

They lay and looked up at the blank night sky, opaque with clouds. Li Chu-erh knew what An Ching-hsu was thinking.

"I hope he is dead," the young eunuch said in a soft voice.

"So do I," An Ching-hsu replied.

A Pu-ssu did not speak immediately. They understood his tacit assent, but knew that, as a high-ranking Chinese general, he was bound by honor not to put his feelings into words. But they had all seen An Lu-shan riding toward the welcoming arms of the Khitan with an arrow in his leg. And then they had seen him no more.

"An Lu-shan dead? It is not a wager that I would make," A Pu-ssu said finally. "Not if I couldn't afford to lose a great deal of money."

∷

Never travel anywhere without taking some alcohol. Not even into battle. That's what he had always told himself—wise words that were now paying off. An Lu-shan squeezed his wineskin, filling his mouth. He swallowed and opened his eyes. The throbbing in his leg and shoulder was beginning to dull. He gripped his upper thigh with both hands and looked at the wicked shaft buried all the way into the bone just above the knee. When he got drunk enough, he would pull it out. One clean pull.

He experimented, putting his hand on the arrow and tugging a little. The pain nearly made him pass out. Not yet. More wine first.

It was dawn. He had ridden all night, galloping and then walking when his horse was too weary to go any faster. But he had kept moving, deeper into the hills, until he was sure that no one pursued him and he was completely alone. Then he had started drinking wine, staving off the agony that he knew was lying in wait for him.

He would leave the arrow in his shoulder until he got back to camp.

Too many times he had seen men die after pulling them out when they were so close to the vital organs. The blood fairly flowed from their bodies, like wine from a barrel when the cork is removed. He put his head back down on the grass, his blanket under him, his horse's reins twined tightly around one wrist. He would be damned if he was going to bleed to death out here or be left behind if the horse decided to run away. He raised the skin to his mouth and squeezed.

It was going to be bad for him. He knew it. Word of his disastrous defeat was probably already on its way to the capital. And he knew what that would mean: eunuchs. Sniffing, meddling, prying Censorate eunuchs, inflicted on him by the insufferable Yang Kuo-chung. Certainly not by Li Lin-fu—the chief minister cared little for their interference. But they would be on him, as surely as dogs follow a scent. The dull pain in his leg and shoulder were already talking to him: the eunuchs would be coming.

But the wine was beginning to talk to him, too. It was telling him that the universe would work for him and not against him, if he would use his intelligence. The forces that had opposed him would befriend him. He thought of the soldier who had ridden back toward the charging army of horsemen, turning his horse around so that he was not trampled, but rode with them when they overtook him. There is a lesson to be learned there, old fellow, he told himself.

If investigators came, then they would not be permitted to return to the capital to deliver their report. The rain that had plagued him in his mighty effort against the Khitan would be his ally.

The rivers and streams south of Lu-lung would be nearly impassable by now. Dangerous and swift. If word arrived at the capital that the investigators had drowned in an unfortunate accident, never making it to the military commandery headquarters at Yu, much less to Ch'ang-an itself, who could dispute it? Then the whole unfortunate thing would become only a minor defeat, and everyone would soon forget it. He would go on to even greater victories than before.

Grimacing, he eased a hand under his leg to support it. There would have to be some executions, of course, to set an example to the survivors of the battle, to remind them to keep their mouths shut. He did not enjoy the prospect, but the stinking eunuchs would, he was sure, leave him little choice.

He thought of another time when they had come sniffing around. A long time ago, when he was a general who had yet to prove himself. He remembered a swollen river, a mass of earth and trees blotting out the night sky, and soldiers drowning. And it was not long afterward that he had had to face the eunuchs, while they judged him, discussed him, inspected him. But the joke had been on them: he had them believing that he, An Lu-shan, didn't understand a word of what they said.

He remembered sweet perfume mingled with their pissy, sweaty smell. And he remembered himself sweating like an animal in front of them, and the smug satisfaction on their faces.

Their faces. He would not soon forget their faces. Even now, he could shut his eyes and see those faces in detail. Particularly the Toad. The short, flat-faced, bulging-eyed creature who had said nothing, but had sat blandly staring at him, sizing him up in his ugly little heart.

He filled his mouth with wine. He had very nearly lost control that day, sweating inside his lacquered breastplate, the smell of the eunuchs nauseating him, the water running down from the pits of his arms to his belly. What he had wanted to do was to impale little bastard Toad-Face on his sword and let him writhe and shriek. He imagined himself shouting at them triumphantly: do not overturn the rock, ladies, unless you are prepared to deal with what is under it!

Was he drunk enough yet? Still prone, and without looking down at his leg, he put his hand on the arrow and moved it tentatively. He was almost drunk enough, but not quite. He felt the wineskin, inspecting its weight and fullness. This would be a very bad time to run out. He would like to stay drunk for the rest of the day.

He smiled. Was it possible that the little brooding Toad would be among the investigating eunuchs? Oh, yes, he thought. I would surely like to see you again. And Tall Girl-Face. Would Girl-Face do me the honor as well? I would listen most compassionately to Girl-Face whining and sobbing for his life. Yes. I would listen to all the reasons why he should be spared, and then I would take his filthy little neck in my hands . . .

He gripped the arrow and jerked with all his strength. The pain was like a pure white light washing through him; he lay gasping, looking up at the pale empty sky. But the wine had protected him. It had removed him just enough from the pain so that he did not faint.

What did those useless, ugly she-men know about pain? Had any of them ever fought in a battle? Eunuchs. Grotesque, vile creatures. He hated them all. I'd like to see one of them pulling an arrow from his body with his own hands, he thought, cradling the wounded leg tenderly, rocking his entire body gently back and forth while Toad-Face, Girl-Face, and Kao Li-shih merged in his mind into one loathsome creature.

What right did they have to judge him?

: :

A few hours later An Lu-shan was back on his horse, bent forward over the animal's neck while he clung to its mane. He emptied the wineskin, nursing it dry like a baby at the breast until the pain was so far away that it might as well have belonged to someone else. He drank until he saw everything that had happened in his life and everything that he had ever done. And inspiration was coming to him.

He was remembering stories that old General Feng had told him years ago: tales of the Persian satraps and Arab princes who had developed the fine art of the elimination of one's rivals—leaving no clues, no traces—to perfection. An Lu-shan had listened to Feng's stories, filled with secret admiration for these ruthless, ingenious people. He remembered thinking that he himself would have made a good Arab.

His cheek rested against his horse's neck. Lulled by the rhythm of its walking, the smooth, steady roll of bones and muscles beneath him, he thought that he was really quite comfortable just like this: drunk, hanging on to his animal, an arrow embedded in his shoulder, soaked to the skin, and so tired that his body was a numb rock, beyond pain and fatigue.

And his mind was perfectly lucid. He marveled at the purity and clarity of his thoughts. It was the wine, of course. Wine debilitated some men—like the generals, old broken-down war-horses, who were forced to retire on government pensions in the capital. Alcohol had made them useless, stupid and fumbling, dangerous to their mission and their men and therefore dangerous to themselves. But it was not so with him. The more he drank, the clearer his thoughts became. The world did not spin in front of his eyes; it stayed perfectly still. It did not soften with drink or become blurred and unreal; it became more substantial, its borders and limitations more clearly defined.

Not only could he remember his particular favorite stories of Feng's, but he could remember the time and place of the telling. It had been in a garden in the imperial city. It had been autumn, one of those days so beautiful that you thought that you were receiving a glimpse of the weather in Paradise. A perfect day, and two stories of murder refined to perfection. Stories, he remembered thinking, that were most instructive and which might someday serve An Lu-shan himself.

The first story concerned a Persian prince who had killed all his enemies with great efficiency by gathering them together under one roof; the subject of the other was more subtle, a bit more complicated perhaps, but one that An Lu-shan had found most enticing: a prince who made his rival into his ally by compelling him to commit the prince's crime for him. He imagined a slight variation on this theme, whereby he could use the same principle to forge the bonds of filial submission. His son An Ching-hsu, the sullen, rebellious one who caused An Lu-shan constant grief, would help An Lu-shan carry out his plan of eliminating the Censorate eunuchs—without knowing it, of course. The boy would not find out, or even suspect, that he was an accomplice to murder until the deed was done. And if he planned things carefully, he could rid himself of the sullen and resentful Li Chu-erh at the same time. Provided, of course, that his son and the eunuch had survived the battle. Perhaps the Khitan had taken care of them both for him.

The slow, steady thumping of his heart reassured him: he was alive. He had only to stay alive, now, for the rest of the long ride to the camp at Lu-lung, far south of the scene of the lost battle in P'inglu Province. He was quite sure that wagers were being made right at that moment as to whether General An Lu-shan was going to ride into camp or whether he lay dead on a Khitan battlefield while crows hopped about on his rib cage and pecked at his empty eye sockets.

He would see to it that some bets were lost. They would soon learn just how strong was An Lu-shan's life-force.

:: :

"I don't like it at all," A Pu-ssu said, pushing his wine away from him across the table. He always refused to drink before the sun went down. "It is dangerous. And stupid. There is too much that can go wrong. Let it go. As it is, you will probably receive nothing more than a censure for the defeat. A minor censure, at that. They will simply put it down to the unpredictability of the rains that far north. You are such an imperial favorite, my noble commissioner, such a favored son of our August Emperor, that you will not even be diminished. Not in the singular number of your titles, not in any way." He glanced toward the other officer present, General Sun, looking for support. "My advice is to leave this whole investigation alone. The rains . . . the rebellion of the Hsi horsemen . . . the damaged bows . . . incomplete information on the strength of the Khitan . . . it will all be understood as the unforeseen conditions of Heaven. Why you undertake something so extreme, why you take such a terrible risk, I cannot understand. There is no reason for it."

"And I, for one, do not approve of including your son in the plan," General Sun added. "He could ruin everything. The role you have given him to play is pivotal to the success of this thing. You have put too much emphasis on his actions, and I do not believe that it is possible to truly anticipate his behavior when the crucial moment arrives. Especially since he knows nothing, has not agreed to participate, and does not even know that you will be using him. He is not *with* you. He never has been. And it is the same with the eunuch Li Chu-erh. Why use them at all? That is what *I* do not understand." He shrugged and looked uncertainly from An Lu-shan to A Pu-ssu. "The plan is already a very elaborate one, dependent on a chain of events that you cannot really predict. And now you add two very weak links . . ." He gestured futilely.

An Lu-shan, his wounded shoulder and leg heavily bandaged, took another drink of wine from the silver ewer and looked at his two officers. A

Pu-ssu looked back at him. Since An Lu-shan's return to camp ten days before, more dead than alive and tied to his own horse, he enjoyed catching A Pu-ssu's eye from time to time. The officer's disappointment had been plain when he came out of his tent that day to see An Lu-shan being helped down from his horse, and now An Lu-shan enjoyed the guilty look he saw on his face whenever their eyes met, and enjoyed the silent messages that passed between the two of them. Yes, you dog, I am alive, An Lu-shan's eyes said; you have been deprived of your fond wish. And A Pu-ssu's gaze spoke in return: why didn't you do the empire and yourself a favor, and die a hero when you had the opportunity?

"You two are no better than the eunuchs who are on their way here," An Lu-shan said evenly, bringing the ewer down with just enough force to make the officers' cups rattle. "Nothing will go wrong. It is a perfect plan. The presence of the boy and the eunuch Li Chu-erh will be reassuring to the Censorate officials. And there is no other way to use the two of them; they would certainly never cooperate. And by the time young Master An discovers what he has done, he will be trapped into complicity with us. Only the innocent talk. And he will not appear to be innocent, so he will keep his mouth shut. I know him. He will not dare say a word to anyone. And Li Chu-erh will not be speaking, ever again," he said with a meaningful grin. He looked out the door of the tent toward the hills. "Then, we will prepare a false report. But the Censorate eunuchs will not deliver it themselves; word will be sent that they met with an unfortunate accident. The rivers are high and swollen. It would be easy, and perfectly believable, to say that they drowned. Or that they could not cross because the waters were too swift, and were attacked by a band of Hsi or Khitan. Then I will see to it that the false report is delivered to the capital, and that will be the end of it."

"Perhaps it will work, Commissioner, though I scarcely believe that it will," A Pu-ssu said. "But why do it at all? Your position is not so insecure, so tenuous, that you need to even contemplate such a thing. I cannot grasp it!"

An Lu-shan leaned forward, ignoring the pain in his shoulder, and spoke with deliberate emphasis.

"I am not satisfied with receiving a 'minor censure,' as you put it," he said. "Nor am I interested in a reprimand, however mild or slight or cere-monial, from the Censorate. I do not wish to be discussed by them *at all*. Do you understand? I do not wish for my name to be even *on their tongues*. I do not wish the name of An Lu-shan to be even slightly compromised. There has been quite enough talk already." He leaned back in his chair. A Pu-ssu said nothing, but An Lu-shan knew that his officer was aware of the incident he referred to: the traitorous child who had caused him such trouble by dying beneath him, and the subsequent questioning before the Emperor, when he had had to grovel on his knees, thanks to the stinking, damnable Kao Li-shih. There was to be no more of that, ever again.

"If it is what you want, Master An, then we will certainly be unable to talk you out of it," General Sun said.

"It is not what I want that matters," An Lu-shan said slowly. "It is not what *I* want that is important. It is what we *must* do to preserve ourselves against the decisions of 'others' at the court. We are military men. We must support one another."

A Pu-ssu shook his head.

"I tell you, you will be caught. And your name will be more than compromised. You are asking for real trouble with this, General."

"And who will inform on me, Master A Pu-ssu?" An Lu-shan said, taking a drink from the ewer and wiping his mouth with the back of his hand. "Neither the eunuch investigators nor their escorts will be alive. The villagers will not speak. My general will see to that!" An Lu-shan looked briefly at Sun. "The dead cannot speak. An Ching-hsu will say nothing, and Li Chu-erh will be dead. If young An is even in the slightest way implicated in so heinous a crime, he will be put to death. Or perhaps I will betray him *myself.* General Sun, though he sits here arguing feebly about whether or not I should use the two worthless pups, is with me. He has agreed to give me his help in carrying out certain parts of the plan." He looked at Sun, who lowered his eyes and toyed with his cup. "That leaves only you, A Pu-ssu. Are you planning to tell them? Perhaps *you* are the one I should not trust."

A Pu-ssu shook his head.

"No, General," he said, looking at An Lu-shan with the same look that he had bestowed on him when he had ridden back into camp ten days ago. "I have no intention of saying anything to anybody."

An Lu-shan leaned back with a broad, satisfied smile. He poured more wine for General Sun and pushed A Pu-ssu's untouched cup back toward him.

"I insist that you drink with me. We have had our differences, and we have settled them."

But A Pu-ssu did not drink. He stood up from the table.

"I am not in the mood, General," he said, and turned and ducked out the door. An Lu-shan smiled, raising the ewer to General Sun, who still sat at the table. The silver gleamed in the afternoon sunlight streaming into the tent.

"Have you ever seen anything so beautiful?" he asked Sun. "I had this commissioned personally from a master silversmith in Kokand. I believe that it suits me quite well." He raised it, then lowered it slowly, watching the light play on the repoussé Ferghanian stallions. "Horses of Iron," he said admiringly while Sun did his best to look interested. "See how they seem to come alive when the light moves over them. You can almost see the muscles in their flanks and shoulders sliding over one another. And the eyes! Eyes of flame! I told the silversmith that nothing would do except rubies for the eyes."

The silversmith had truly been a master. The horses, uncompromising embodiment of purpose and power, spoke to him now as the wine warmed him. He gazed at the ruby eyes of the "Horses of Iron": blood-red eyes that made him think of murder.

: :

In the middle of a great open plain not far from the steep grassy banks of the T'u Hu-chen River, an agreeable and comfortable settlement of colorful ban-nered tents and corrals was set up to receive the Censorate entourage. A feast was being prepared, after which, it had been announced, the commissioner would give an open review of the facts that culminated in the disastrous defeat.

It seemed more like a Mongolian village festival than preparation for the reception of the eunuch military investigators from the imperial Censorate. The people making the preparations knew only that their visitors would be important men from a mythical world they heard about often enough, but would never see.

Lambs and pigs went about, wandering peacefully among the horses, oxen, wagons, and gaily decorated carriages, innocent of the knowledge that these were their final moments—that in a few hours they would be in the two huge cauldrons that steamed over smoky fires, part of an oily, spicy stew being made for the delectation of the distinguished guests.

In the middle of the compound of tents and yurts, old leather-skinned women fried doughy cakes in sizzling pots of lard and baked intoxicating puddings of sweet, almond-flavored curdled mare's milk in the mud-brick ovens. Their husbands began to gather the feast animals for slaughter, while children ran back and forth performing a hundred small tasks for the old people. Great iron pots of mutton fat sat ready atop the brick furnaces, while bundles of vegetables went under the cleavers of a score of choppers, and earthen jars of spices were unpacked from wooden crates.

Although the day was warm and gently breezy, the clouds high and few, and the sky a deep cobalt, there were still occasional moments when a sudden and oddly chilly blast of air blew across the steppes from the north, a reminder of the tenuousness and instability of the Mongolian spring. And although the rains had abated at last, the meadows were damp and spongy, and even the light breezes brought with them fine frigid hints of moisture.

The eunuch investigators and the envoys had traveled the great distance from Ch'ang-an north to the military administrative center of Yu in Shuofang Province. From there, the retinue had continued on in gradual steps north-eastward to what had been the farthest line of the Khitan's southern advance after An Lu-shan's defeat and before the barbarians were routed again by

Chinese reinforcements. There, deep in P'inglu Province at the camp at Lu-lung, many li below the southernmost bend of the T'u Hu-chen River, An Lu-shan had arranged to receive and accommodate them for the duration of their fact-finding mission.

Not more than a third of a li up from the colorful row of yurts at the center of the festive preparations, on a dry, grassy knoll, a special tent had been erected for the grand dinner that was to be served in honor of the guests. In the shape of an enormous oblong yurt, the tent was high and long, its ceiling supported by a row of slender springy saplings bent into delicate arches; floors, sides, and ceiling were stitched together into a single unit with small slits for ventilation and narrow overhead openings to conduct the smoke of the naphtha-filled burners placed inside to heat the air and keep the food warm.

The floor of the long tent was especially thick, lined with extra layers of felt and raw silk against the cold wet of the grassy plain beneath, and covered with richly patterned blue and yellow carpets. Low tables and pleasing or-namental satin cushions were the only furnishings. The entryway was designed like the drawstring opening of a purse, capable of being quickly sealed, by a pull of the ropes, against rain and chilling winds. At the entrance to the Censorate banquet tent, two large *naccara*—Mongolian kettledrums, captured in a recent raid on a Khitan *noyan*'s military camp—were proudly displayed.

When the great drums rolled late that afternoon, it was to announce the arrival of the long-awaited investigating party. The deep thunder sounded across the low grassy plains of the river valley and into the hills. Preparations were nearly complete; Li Chu-erh was inside the banquet "hall" overseeing the placing of cushions and utensils, and outside, in front and slightly to the right of the entryway, An Ching-hsu stood near a magnificent eight-horse team hitched to a grand and exceedingly comfortable coach, a touring con-veyance that was to be put at the disposal of the Censorate officials for their work. Indeed, An Lu-shan was being most cooperative, showing every con-sideration to his visitors for their well-being and convenience.

Following his father's instructions, An Ching-hsu stood obediently by. He had been told that it was his job to see that the horses remained calm and under control, and to assist the grooms if he was needed. There are to be no clumsy mishaps today, An Lu-shan had warned An Ching-hsu and the grooms, not in front of the honored guests. Everything must be perfect.

The carriage was so elaborately decorated as to be almost ridiculous, with colorful silk streamers and flags, and festoons of tiny blue flowers gathered painstakingly by the women and girls all the day before and this morning. The grooms had joked with one another, but they, like everyone who knew An Lu-shan, were accustomed to his indulgences, especially when he was making an effort to impress.

An Ching-hsu had obeyed wordlessly. He never talked to his father at all if he could avoid it. He had barely spoken with him since the ill-fated campaign. He remembered how Li Chu-erh, with a look of utter disgust and fury, had come to find him the day An Lu-shan, severely wounded, had returned to the camp days after the battle, during which time they had come to believe, to hope, that the general was dead, that they were free of him at last. The two had commiserated after An Lu-shan's return. They asked each other how he did it. Was he charmed? Couldn't the arrow just as easily have entered his heart as his leg?

The youths stayed close together, doing what they were told, keeping a wary eye on the general. They were determined to survive, and the two of them had formed an alliance to that end. The last few days preceding the arrival of the investigators had been relatively easy. An Lu-shan seemed to have forgotten that the two existed . . . until today, when they were given their orders.

: :

The Censorate entourage from Yu consisted of approximately twenty horsemen and the fifteen Censorate officials who rode in two sturdy canopied wagons drawn by swift but temperamental Bactrian camels. General Sun and a handful of outriders galloped out onto the open plain to meet the commissioner's guests.

The final preparations, now involving the entire camp, seemed like the precision movements of a well-choreographed dance pantomime. No one spoke: people passed one another in silence as each went about his assigned tasks. But all heads turned to follow as these most unusual guests were ushered past the bright Khitan banners that served as royal "doorposts."

An Ching-hsu looked at the fatigued surprised faces of the eunuch officials as they climbed down from their wagons. Evidently, they had expected their presence to be only grudgingly tolerated; such flattery, pomp, and festiveness as they found here were hardly what they had anticipated. An Ching-hsu studied the officials: they conversed quietly and unsmilingly with one another, taking in the tent, the banners, the pots of food, the festooned and streamered carriage, and the crowd of villagers who stood to either side staring at them with unabashed curiosity.

General Sun welcomed the officials almost obsequiously and informed them that An Lu-shan would be joining them shortly after he returned to camp and had a chance to wash the grime and stink of the trail from his person. In the meantime, they were to rest and partake of the feast that had been prepared for them. Master An Lu-shan was still a good many li north of the encampment, General Sun explained, scouting the borders that had only recently been recovered since the disastrous military "setback." What sounded like an acceptable reason to everyone else for An Lu-shan's absence seemed a strange and unnecessary piece of dissembling to Li Chu-erh, standing in the entryway listening. An Lu-shan was not out scouting the borders; he had seen the general just that morning, issuing orders in his tent. He wished that he could speak to An Ching-hsu, but his friend was a good thirty paces from the entryway, staying obediently at his post next to the team of horses. But he did turn and look at Li Chu-erh, exchanging a questioning look with him.

Li Chu-erh averted his eyes from An Ching-hsu's in the next moment and bowed deeply as the first of the Censorate eunuchs filed into the long reception tent. The naphtha braziers had been lit, and the air inside was comfortingly warm and inviting, in contrast to that outside, which had grown cold and cloudy as the afternoon wore on. That was how it was at this time of year—all the advances of spring could be lost in an hour's time.

The eunuchs were seated on the low cushions and were brought bowls of warm, fragrantly spiced water and small felt towels for their hands and faces. Sun, leaving his men outside, was seated in their midst, joking and talking pleasantly, putting them at their ease. The wine was brought out immediately. It was Li Chu-erh's job to see that the cups stayed filled.

Li Chu-erh stood back after he had gone once around the table with the pitcher, and watched the eunuchs with interest as they began to relax. He was quite sure he had seen at least two of them before: a short, pudgy one with slightly bulging eyes and an irritable expression who looked right at him for a moment, and another with an absurdly small, delicate head atop a long, ungainly body. Then he placed them: these were two of the same Censorate officials who had come to investigate after the doomed river-crossing so many years before, when he had accompanied An Lu-shan to the meeting with the forged map and had acted as "interpreter." He recognized them, but it was obvious that they did not recognize him. He had been much, much younger then, scarcely into his teens, and had grown considerably. Enjoying his anonymity, he watched them while he continued to keep his eyes on the cups around the table.

Outside, An Ching-hsu was wondering what the general had planned for today. It seemed as if he were trying to distract these officials with the elaborate, ostentatiously unsuitable welcome. Sometimes his father's actions were transparent; at other times it was impossible to even guess at the structure of his schemes and reasoning. Did he hope to lull the eunuchs, to win them over with all of this so that they would be less inclined to bear a negative report to the capital? One look at their implacable faces had told An Ching-hsu that such a plan would not work at all. And surely his canny father was not so naive. What, then?

Meanwhile, villagers working as servants began to carry food past An Ching-hsu into the tent. The delicious, spicy odors wafted by under his nose. Perhaps later, he thought, there will be something left over for me.

Inside, Li Chu-erh watched hungrily as food was served to the eunuchs. If they thought that the elaborate welcome was a bit odd, they did not let it affect their appetites. They ate greedily, and drank, and talked with General Sun. Li Chu-erh overheard Sun praising An Lu-shan's courage and abilities as a military leader, including a detailed description of the nearly fatal wounds the general had sustained in this last encounter. The eunuchs on either side of Sun looked very interested in this and began to ask him pointed questions about the ill-fated campaign: its objectives, the number of men lost, the extent of the damage, if any, to the security of the northern borders. Li Chu-erh was surprised to hear Sun answering the questions candidly and accurately. It would seem that An Lu-shan had adopted a new policy of honesty, though Li Chu-erh doubted it.

When Sun excused himself and rose unsteadily to his feet to go outside, explaining that he had to pass his wine, the eunuchs leaned close, talking, nodding, and whispering. It was plain that this was a very serious, high-priority investigation and that they meant to get all the facts.

An Ching-hsu, still at his post with the horses, had sat down on a log to rest, but jumped to his feet when he saw General Sun emerge from the tent. The general hurried past, ignoring him, heading for the row of smaller tents nearby.

A servant carrying a covered pot appeared then from the other side of the banquet tent; just before the man ducked inside, An Ching-hsu was shocked to see that it was A Pu-ssu, his father's officer, scarcely recognizable in the rough clothes of a villager, his head down. He raised his eyes for an instant to An Ching-hsu's. You do not see me, boy, his look said, before he lowered his eyes again. An Ching-hsu glanced furtively about; Sun's men, the only ones who might recognize A Pu-ssu, were posted a good distance away and seemed to have noticed nothing. A Pu-ssu disappeared into the tent.

Confusion and dread gripped An Ching-hsu. Why would A Pu-ssu wish secrecy, unless he knew something and was trying to convey a warning? Something whispered to An Ching-hsu that he should run, that he should get away now while he still could. But Li Chu-erh was inside the tent and had been told to stay inside. He could not abandon his friend. Afraid of catching the attention of Sun's men, he restrained himself from moving at all and stayed miserably where he was, watching the tent.

Li Chu-erh, pouring more wine and trying to remain discreet while eavesdropping on the eunuchs' conversation, did not take particular notice of the servant who ducked into the tent. It was not until he straightened up and looked across the table that he realized that it was General A Pu-ssu looking intently at him, a finger pressed to his lips to warn Li Chu-erh to keep quiet. Then A Pu-ssu moved his eyes toward the entryway in an urgent signal meant only for him. Li Chu-erh was not sure what A Pu-ssu meant. Was he telling him to get out or warning him that someone was about to enter? Helpless, he stared back.

A Pu-ssu now made a gesture with his head as well as his eyes, his movements becoming more exaggerated and emphatic. This time the message in his eyes was clear: go. Get out. Now. Attract no attention. Li Chu-erh put down the pitcher and moved toward the entryway, hoping his slowness in understanding had not cost him his life. The suddenness of his movement caused several of the seated investigators to look at one another questioningly. Then A Pu-ssu was behind him, pushing him through to the outside and shouting back over his shoulder to the Censorate investigators.

"Save yourselves! Run!" Li Chu-erh glanced back in time to see the beginnings of chaos and panic as the eunuchs struggled to rise from their seats, knocking over furniture and plates and pushing one another aside in their haste to be first through the narrow entryway.

As Li Chu-erh ducked through to the outside, he caught a glimpse of An Ching-hsu struggling to keep the horses quiet and looking anxiously in the direction of the tent. Their eyes met, and Li Chu-erh began to run toward him.

"Not that way!" A Pu-ssu screamed behind him. "To the left! To the left and the hills! Run for your life, damn you! Run for your life!"

As he veered, Li Chu-erh felt an arrow drive itself into his chest. He kept running, feeling no pain yet, and saw An Ching-hsu running toward them, away from the animals. They ran blindly, the ground racing beneath them, knowing they would die at any moment. But they were running. They had a chance. For those still inside the tent struggling to get out, there was no time. What had begun was under way in the fury of one brutal hellish instant.

Arrows whistled through the air, striking the rumps of the lead horses of the team. The animals reared and whinnied, alarm spreading among them, then bolted forward, pulling the grand carriage with them. Ropes, hidden beneath the absurd decorations and disappearing into the ground, pulled up from where they had been carefully buried in the earth and snapped taut behind the carriage as it was jerked forward by the horses; at the same moment, the ropes that ran through the grommets at the entryway to the tent pulled the banquet yurt shut as tight as a miser's purse. Inside, the ribbing of saplings snapped and collapsed. The naphtha-filled braziers toppled from their stands, liquid fire soaking the thick carpeted floor and racing up the sides of the tent.

Trapped in their fiery prison, the Censorate officials and servants wailed in futile agony. Pulled up from its anchoring stakes, the tent was now a ball of flame bouncing behind the festive carriage with its banners and flowers; the crazed horses, shackled to the unholy conveyance, dragged it through the settlement gates, tearing up flags and banners as they went. And it must have seemed to the villagers as they ran screaming that some demonic spirit drove his fiery meteor across the plain, the grass blackening and smoking in its wake.

Now Sun's horsemen surrounded the scattering peasants who had prepared the feast. They pulled their arrows from their quivers: no one from the "festival" at Lu-lung would live to report anything.

::

A Pu-ssu pushed An Ching-hsu and Li Chu-erh behind the cover of a cluster of small boulders and placed his hands over the eunuch's mouth.

"Scream now, Eunuch," A Pu-ssu said to Chu-erh, "and the loss of your precious balls will seem like nothing in comparison to what An Lu-shan will do to us."

The eunuch shook his head, tears welling in the corners of his eyes, his face set against the pain.

"No screams, boy. Promise me, or I will have to kill you myself!" A Pu-ssu cautiously removed his hand from the eunuch's mouth.

Li Chu-erh sucked dryly at the air, the tears rolling down his cheeks, his shoulder and chest glistening with the purple drench of his blood. The feathered dart—for that was all that was used on the horses—protruded from just beneath his right collarbone.

"I am all right, am I not?" Li Chu-erh asked, whispering painfully to An Ching-hsu who grasped his hand firmly. Then the eunuch turned his head. "I am all right, Master A Pu-ssu? Tell me I am not going to die!" he demanded. He looked at An Ching-hsu again, who gave a frightened and unconvincing nod. The eunuch's head swayed from side to side before dropping back into the advisor's lap.

An Ching-hsu looked up, terrified.

"He *will* be all right. The bolt did not go very deep," A Pu-ssu assured young An. "It was designed merely to sting and startle a horse without injuring it. See!" He pulled on the small, thick dart; it puckered the skin before giving up its hold. "Much blood, but little actual damage. The barb is no longer than the joint of a man's finger, if that. He has simply fainted. We shall wash the wound, cauterize it, and wrap it. But we are most fortunate. Our only injury from your father's insanity will be to our ears when this one wakes." A Pu-Ssu smiled. "It is a small sacrifice. He has stood between you and your father for so many years. This Chu-erh is a good friend to you, is he not?"

An Ching-hsu was relieved.

"But how do we get out of here alive?" he whispered urgently.

"There has been another revolt against your father. One that he has not even heard of yet. In Shuofang, fifteen thousand of my tribesmen will already have abandoned him, if I have counted the days correctly. They do not wish to be a part of another of the madman's campaigns. Four thousand of their brothers vanished without a fight in the last battle. You see, my first duties are to them . . . they serve An Lu-shan only as long as I do. And I no longer choose to serve him.

"Your father had planned another campaign in the regions north of Shuofang. It was to be a forced campaign to redeem himself in the face of this disaster. But my men merely awaited my orders to burn the granaries and military storehouses in Shuofang before he could mobilize. They received the orders. I have confirmation of that. They have destroyed An Lu-shan's stores. They are, no doubt, already far north into the desert by now; they have inflicted a serious setback on your father's plans . . . we can only hope that two disastrous failures in a row will be enough to slow him down.

"When he hears about the revolt and discovers that his loyal advisor A Pu-ssu has failed to arrive to join his expedition, well . . ." He shifted the eunuch's head resting in his lap. "I am now as much a fugitive as *you* are, Master An Ching-hsu. We are to be met tonight. We can only hope that my good lieutenant and our escort have not already been found out . . . if they have, then we can be quite certain that we will be hunted down before we move ten paces from these rocks, before we take our first step toward the capital."

"Do you mean Ch'ang-an?" An Ching-hsu said incredulously. "Is that where we are going?"

"Somebody must carry the news of what has happened here. If we do not do it, no one will. Do you want him to get away with it, as he always does?" A Pu-ssu asked fiercely.

Until that moment An Ching-hsu had not the slightest notion of his own fate. There had not been time to think about it. Now he was running once more, just as they had from the Khitan. But this time he was running from his father's own men. And although he understood that it had not been his father's intent to kill him in the banquet yurt with the eunuchs, he doubted that Sun's men would differentiate. They would simply cut down anyone who fled from the camp. Anyone!

A Pu-ssu shifted Li Chu-erh gently to the damp ground and looked out past the rocks toward the low blue hills. An Ching-hsu followed the officer's gaze across the grassy plain. Far in the distance rose a plume of thick naphtha smoke, all that remained of the burning tent and the men trapped inside. And he realized that his father had meant for Li Chu-erh to be among them, just another corpse charred beyond recognition. And though he, An Ching-hsu, had been ordered to stay outside and tend to the horses, what An Lu-shan had intended for him was a far greater torture than burning to death in a tent being dragged by a team of maddened horses: if An Lu-shan had had his way, then An Ching-hsu would have participated in the murder of his friend Li

699 :: THE·TORTOISE·AND·THE·SNAKE

Chu-erh. That would have been his father's gift to him: he was to have killed his own best friend.

They grew quiet for a long while, the screams of the villagers growing less frequent. The arrows were flying efficiently, silencing every old man and woman who had prepared the feast. Crouched behind the rocks, An Ching-hsu witnessed his father's brutal, cold-blooded thoroughness. "Old people talk too much," he now remembered An Lu-shan saying.

They remained hidden, waiting for darkness and General Sun's men to withdraw from the massacre. He turned to A Pu-ssu.

"I never want to see my father again. Never. I want to kill him. I want to cut his heart out. I want to tell everyone who he really is. Take me to Ch'ang-an, A Pu-ssu." There were tears in his eyes. "Please take me! Please keep me alive that long. That is all I ask."

: :

For the last hour of their journey, Lu Pei had not spoken. Kao Li-shih could see that the boy had, for the moment, given up trying to find out where they were going or why they traveled like peasant farmers in a rustic ox cart. It seemed that, for the moment, Lu Pei's curiosity was appeased by the strange sights around him; he sat placidly transfixed, absorbed by the dreamlike summer landscape.

They had left the grand Avenue of the Vermilion Sparrow some six li south of the palace and bureaucratic cities. They had turned off the main boulevard, their thick wooden wheels rumbling onto the cobblestones of a wide tree-lined lane that rose and fell and twisted and turned, defying the strict grid pattern of the rest of the streets of Ch'ang-an, through beautiful, man-made hillocks where wooded groves were reflected in exquisite little ponds. And although they had not traveled more than a half li from the noisy, crowded thoroughfare that was the Vermilion Sparrow, it seemed as though they were in the middle of the quiet countryside.

Long arcs of birds peppered the skies above giant old cedars. Vast estates climbed the hillsides behind high stone walls, their halls, galleries, towers, and concourses wending fluidly over green meadows and between dark blue-green groves of conifers and mirror-still ponds of rock and orchid.

When they had gone another quarter li, they came upon a very high wall topped with ornamental tiles and brightly painted porcelains of mythical beasts and gods and goddesses of popular Buddhism. Far back behind the wall they could see a row of four- and five-story chambered towers rising against the shadowy green backdrop of an elm-dappled hillside. The blue-tiled roofs with colorful supporting brackets and lintels made the whole structure resemble a bouquet of gigantic flowers. Deer, gazelle, and zebras wandered in the open grasslands on the hillside, and graceful long-necked birds on stiltlike legs delicately trod the cool lawns. The grounds around the enormous house complex had obviously been designated as a refuge for exotic, imported wildlife.

Kao Li-shih stopped the humble cart they rode in and waited for the inevitable question. He knew that the boy could not hold out under such suspense much longer. Thus far, Kao Li-shih had kept him in the dark, and the younger eunuch's patience had been laudable; Lu Pei had barely spoken a word since Kao Li-shih had invited him to come along on this mysterious journey.

He had sat on the wooden bench next to Kao Li-shih, silent for li after li, asking no questions, knowing that Kao Li-shih would reveal everything when the time was appropriate. Kao Li-shih was pleased: he had managed to instill something in the boy over the years. Of course, his seeming patience and forbearance could be accounted for by the fact that he was spellbound by the sights of a part of the city that he never dreamed existed. Still, it was a good sign: he had learned to wait for an answer. Keep still and wait, Kao Li-shih had told him time and again; when the answer does come, you will have learned much more than by prodding and digging for an answer. But now that they had stopped the wagon and sat looking at the high, ornamented wall, Kao Li-shih knew what the boy was going to ask.

"Master Kao," Lu Pei said at last, almost whispering. "Where are we? Is this a house or a palace? Who lives here?"

Kao Li-shih had already climbed down from the wagon and was nearly to the high circular slate door in the gate when he stopped and carefully looked up and down the empty lane to reassure himself that they had not been followed. He walked to the door and placed his right hand on a red lacquer knob that protruded through the slate slightly above the level of his waist. But before pulling on it he turned to Lu Pei, who still sat patiently on the wagon bench.

"It belongs to a very wealthy eunuch and his wife," Kao Li-shih answered matter-of-factly. Lu Pei looked more confused than ever, Kao Li-shih thought with amusement. He looks as though he is about to expire from curiosity. "This is the home of the inner official of the Flying Dragons," he went on. "But no one knows that about him. To everyone else, he is merely a shipping merchant. Embarrassingly rich, it would seem. Unseen. Virtually invisible. But then, this district of the city affords that kind of privacy." Kao Li-shih gestured, taking in the whole of the house and grounds. "You see the house and its pavilions. He seems to have escaped all the sumptuary laws regarding the size of his estate, has he not?" Kao Li-shih cast a conspiratorial look at Lu Pei. "There is even more beneath the earth than above."

He pulled the red knob twice and waited.

"When the grate at the top opens, Master Lu Pei, say nothing."

The boy's eyes followed his to a narrow rectangle at the top of the door. The panel slid open with a scraping sound, making Lu Pei jump. Kao Li-shih composed himself before speaking, then began carefully.

"I am Kao Li-shih. From the family of Feng. From the *Chou* of P'an. From the Province of Kuangtung. Presented to the court by the *T'ao Chi Shih* for Lingnan, Li Ch'ien-li, in the first year of the Sheng Li reign period. The adopted son of the eunuch Kao Yen-fu and his wife," Kao Li-shih finished, listening to the echo of his words for any errors. He knew that if he misplaced a single syllable in this elaborate litany of identification, the grate would slide shut with finality.

But the grate remained open.

"I have come to speak with the guests of your household," Kao Li-shih went on, "the young man An Ching-hsu and his companion, the eunuch Li Chu-erh, and the general A Pu-ssu." There was another wait; then the massive door opened slowly. He turned and hastily motioned Lu Pei down from the wagon.

22

The Inheritor

Li Lin-fu [had come in his final days] to reside at the Hua-ching [hot springs] palaces. He was severely ill and considerably wasted. [Yang Kuo-chung] entered his room and saw the chief minister on his couch.

Li Lin-fu said, "Yes, it is true. I am dying, and, moreover, you, young Duke Yang, will be [forced] to take over my duties as minister of state. And after you do, you will find that these duties will be intensely troublesome. . . ."

Yang Kuo-chung dreaded the chief minister's power and deceit [but feared his death even more] and did not dare to look into the chief minister's eyes, [but knowing at that moment what he faced] was seized with great anxiety and trepidation. . . . Li Lin-fu died shortly thereafter.

—from Hsin T'ang Shu (New T'ang History),
translated by Daniel Altieri

THE steam that rose through the wide stone grates carried strange, astringent odors. Aromatic essences of camphor, myrrh, and labdanum hissed on the heated rocks below, sending up powerful medicinal vapors—cleansers, purgatives, emetics—that stung the eyes of the physician and the attendants. They moved back and forth through the hot, moist fog, carrying towels, liniments, and oils for the frail figure reclined on a couch in the center of the cell.

Li Lin-fu sucked the pungent air into his lungs and held it. He let it go, then took another long deep draught so that the vapors could fully circulate the channels and cavities of the upper vessels. Slowly, and with great effort, and despite the growing intensity of the pain in his chest, the chief minister drew the air in deeper, held it, then released the spent vapors in short, rhythmic puffs.

The physician, standing nearby, timed this breathing ritual by beating a pair of wooden clappers. With each beat, the strain of the effort grew more intense; the procedure had practically become a torture. Three times the physician had sought to cut the session short, and three times the chief minister had impatiently gestured to the physician to keep going.

"Too much and you will damage yourself further, Grand Councillor," the physician entreated, his eyes watering.

"Too little," Li Lin-fu retorted, "and I am a dead man sooner."

"Councillor!" a voice called tentatively from beyond the wall of steam.

Gratefully, the physician ceased beating the wooden clappers.

"Councillor, there is a most urgent message from your lieutenant chief minister, the honorable Master Yang Kuo-chung."

From the man's labored breathing, Li Lin-fu guessed that the messenger had expended a lot of energy running and kowtowing. That could only mean one thing—that Yang Kuo-chung was right behind the messenger and was probably already in the cell.

"Come in, Master Yang Kuo-chung," the chief minister called through the heavy vapors. "Do not stand on ceremony."

It had been some time since Li Lin-fu had seen his lieutenant chief minister. He drew the damp linen wraps tightly around his body, had his attendants raise him up to a sitting position, watched with interest as the tall, straight figure approached through the heavy mist, seeming to materialize before his eyes like a ghost, and came into focus near his couch. Neither one of them spoke for a moment, but looked intently at the other. What prevented Li Lin-fu from speaking immediately was the youth and health of the man standing before him; for Yang Kuo-chung, it was plainly the shock of the chief minister's wasted appearance. Life looks at death, and death looks at life, Li Lin-fu thought.

"I was never a handsome man, Master Yang," he said. "And age and ill health have done little to improve my appearance."

"I apologize for staring, Councillor," Yang Kuo-chung said.

"Let me guess what brings you here today. I can think of only one personage whose actions might motivate you to seek me out." He dismissed the attendants and the physician so that they would be alone. When the heavy doors of the steam chamber had closed, he turned back to Yang Kuo-chung. Looking at him more closely now, Li Lin-fu could see that worry and fatigue had left their mark on the younger man's face.

"An Lu-shan's son and his eunuch have arrived in the city," Yang Kuo-chung began. "They have come over fifteen hundred li from the banks of the T'u Hu-chen River. They barely escaped with their own lives, Councillor. They have a story to tell that I think you should hear."

"Yes?" Li Lin-fu waited.

"Do you recall the twenty-three Censorate investigators sent to the north to look into General An Lu-shan's disastrous campaign against the Khitan? Do you recall the news that reached the capital that they had been attacked en route by a band of enemy warriors, driven into a rain-swollen river, and drowned? Do you recall the 'report' that reached us, supposedly a duplicate of the one carried by the Censorate officials and sent by a different route just in case something should happen to the original report?"

"I recall all of it, Master Yang," Li Lin-fu said quietly.

"Well, it seems that it is all a lie, a cover-up for premeditated murder carried out in a particularly gruesome manner. Not that I ever believed any of it. But now we have living witnesses who are ready to tell us the truth. I want you to hear their story, Councillor. And I want you to consider the implications." He paused and took a deep breath, gathering his thoughts, then spoke carefully. "I do not expect you, of all people, to be shocked by murder and deceit, Grand Councillor. I know that what An Lu-shan has done is only a naughty little antic compared to some of your own . . . accomplishments. And I know that the Censorate, in particular, has never been, shall we say, the greatest object of your sympathy. I do not come to you with this story expecting you to be outraged at the obstruction of truth and the deaths of innocent men, government officials in the service of the T'ang. I am not so naive."

"What I do," Li Lin-fu said flatly, "I do for the sake of the empire."

"Perhaps so. I have no doubt that you believe that. That is why I want you to be cognizant of every detail of what your general is doing. He is growing up, Councillor. He has taken his training well. He is learning by example, and you are his mentor. What I want you to consider is this: is An Lu-shan the one you want to carry on your methods? Are An Lu-shan's motivations as pure as yours? Does he have the welfare of the empire foremost in his mind? Or is he driven by some other force?" He leaned forward now and spoke with grave emphasis. "Do you dare to die and leave An Lu-shan behind, unwatched, unchecked?"

"Where are the two youths?" Li Lin-fu asked slowly.

Yang Kuo-chung relaxed visibly at the question.

"They are under the watchful care of Master Kao Li-shih. They can be sent to your chambers at any time, whenever you decide that you are fit to receive them. Their story is a most interesting one." Yang Kuo-chung bowed perfunctorily. "Thank you for giving me this time. If you need me, I shall not be hard to find," he said, and turned, disappearing into the steam.

Li Lin-fu heard the heavy doors open and close, and he was alone. Rising slowly and carefully to his feet, he went to one of the narrow slit windows. He watched the young man, his hair damp from the steam chamber, striding purposefully out into the sunlight.

Time, Li Lin-fu thought. That is what he has that I do not. An abundance of time. He remembered when he, too, enjoyed the luxury of time stretching out before him. When was the exact moment that he had begun to feel cramped? When had he felt the first nagging pressure of time running out? He could not remember. He had lived with the feeling for so many years now that he was accustomed to it.

And what did men with responsibilities do when they ran short of time? He knew the answer to that, though he had thus far avoided it: they chose a successor. He craned his neck, watching Yang Kuo-chung until he disappeared. It was not enough that the younger man simply acquired Li Lin-fu's title upon his death. He would have to become his successor in a much more profound sense—at least where General An Lu-shan was concerned.

He made his way back to his couch, fatigued by the mere effort of walking across the room. He watched a wisp of steam drift through the slit of the window and vanish; that, he told himself, is precisely what is going to happen to you soon. You are becoming as insubstantial as vapor. Everything that you are—your own jealously guarded and carefully cultivated essence—is trapped in your dying form and will soon dissipate.

There is one thing that you cannot allow to die with you, and that is your power over An Lu-shan. Yang Kuo-chung, whom you once regarded as an upstart, a nuisance, and an enemy, but who is now to be your successor, has quite rightly recognized that An Lu-shan is a force that needs to be controlled. Somehow, Yang Kuo-chung must inherit, along with the title of chief minister, your power to govern An Lu-shan. Of course, a balance would have to be struck. Left to his own devices, Yang Kuo-chung, as soon as he is in power after your death, would remove An Lu-shan entirely from his duties. He would strip him of all his rank and power, demote him to slave status, or imprison him. Or, more likely, execute him.

And that would not do, not at all.

Li Lin-fu still believed that the empire needed An Lu-shan. More than ever now, what with the impending fall of the northwest to the Muslims and the secessionists in the northern provinces rumbling their discontent. An Lu-shan's strength and skill, which Li Lin-fu had recognized from the start, must continue to serve the empire, and Yang Kuo-chung must be made to see the necessity of that. He must be made to see that those dangerous traits of An Lu-shan's were the vital essence that made him so valuable—but only when he was properly harnessed, properly imbued with fear and respect. Li Lin-fu could not die without influencing the two men whom he would leave behind—men who loathed one another—to carry out the vital work which he had devoted his life to. Both men must be made to serve the empire. Somehow, he must take the enmity between them and forge it into something useful. Somehow, his will must extend beyond the grave.

How would he do it?

As soon as he had asked himself that question, Li Lin-fu felt old, familiar, pleasurable stirrings. He smiled. You are not quite dead yet, old fellow, he thought.

A plan was forming. It had been a good while since he had used his powers. That part of him, at least, was unaffected by the wasting illness which was robbing him of everything else. He called the physician back into the room. The man came and stood solicitously near.

"Tell me, Physician, . . . what time is left for me?" he asked pointedly.

"Well, Councillor, I would say that you have spent quite long enough in the steam chamber and considerably longer at the exercises . . ."

"How obvious must I be, Fool?" he interrupted irritably. "I mean what time is left for me before I am dumped ignominiously into the same hole as my detestable father?"

"It is not customary for a physician to discuss death with a patient whose life he is trying to extend. We must avoid all negative thought patterns . . ."

"We have avoided the question long enough. And as for negative thought patterns, it is far too late for that game now." He looked the physician square in the eye. "How much time?" he asked again.

"All right," said the physician. "Since you give me no choice, I will detail to you my observations. But observations and instincts do not always match . . ."

"I want your observations only, Physician."

The physician sighed.

"Well," he said, adopting a formal, pedantic tone. "The signs are clear. From your weight, posture, and coordination, it is plain that the bones of your body have become brittle and are already in a state of decomposition. The marrow in the shoulder bones has clearly begun to disintegrate. This would be the cause of the pains you speak of, that have moved from the chest to the shoulders and to the nape of the neck . . ."

Li Lin-fu listened quietly to the litany itemizing his disintegration being read off with all the passion and emphasis of a vending grocer reciting a list of produce.

". . . the pallor and sagging of the skin, the cavities of the chest filling with gases, making your breathing both difficult and painful—a situation that has increased considerably in these last weeks, noticeable today especially— your difficulty in urinating, and the severity of the internal pains in the lower yin organs when you do finally successfully pass your water, all point to one thing."

The physician paused. Li Lin-fu waited. Would he go on? What else was left of him to fall apart? The physician looked as though he were about to continue, but thought better of it and said no more.

"The symptoms are the classic signs of impending death, are they not?" Li Lin-fu asked quietly. "Only a fool would try to evade the truth. Based on these dismal facts, what is my prognosis? Six months? A year? Not discounting, of course, the power of my will." He waited for the physician to reply, but the man merely lowered his eyes. "Are you telling me, then, that it is only a matter of months? That is what you believe, is it not? The pains have advanced to the shoulders and neck, and I have only months left to live."

The physician gave a very slight nod, as if assenting, but barely so.

"No. No," Li Lin-fu said, shaking his head. "I must have more time than that."

"Well, Councillor," the physician said reluctantly, hesitantly. "There is always the possibility that the pain in your shoulders and neck is not a true sign . . . not a true pain of the sort we were discussing, but one that has traversed the meridians from the debilitating conditions of dampness in the joints of your lower extremities. That would explain . . ."

"We could go on and on," Li Lin-fu snapped. "But we shall not. Suffice it to say that I shall live as long as I shall live."

The effort of talking was going to make him cough. He felt the dreaded ticklish spasm approaching. At first he thought that he might get off with just a short spell of dry hacking; but it quickly grew to a grueling, draining convulsion. He clasped his chest with both hands, and with his elbows extended like wings at his sides, doubled over while the demon in his chest stuck its red-hot iron rod deep into his lungs and raked up balls of phlegm laced with dark blood. He spat into a bowl on the table by his couch while the physician, in a futile effort to relieve the pain, massaged between the chief minister's shoulder blades. Li Lin-fu held his head down, with his eyes shut, until he was certain that the spell had passed.

He was left breathless, dizzy. He sat up again, his chin resting on his heaving chest; after a few moments, he recovered the strength to raise his head.

The old physician called for the attendants, who rushed into the steam chamber with heated poultices which they applied to the chief minister's chest. They wrapped him in a warm, heavy quilt. The treatment, a precisely metered daily ritual now, was over for today.

The attendants began to lift him.

"No," he protested. "I can walk. I have been doing it for many years on my own. I do not need help."

He walked to the waiting sedan chair outside the chamber, the quilt trailing along the floor behind him, the physician hovering a step or two behind, ready to assist. Arranging himself comfortably in the seat, the chief minister addressed the steward of his hot springs staff, who stood waiting for his orders for the rest of the afternoon.

"Set three places at the table in the reception hall. I should like a light fish broth and some simple fruits and vegetables in pickled brine. And send a messenger after Master Yang Kuo-chung, inviting him to dine. He is on the grounds somewhere. Probably at the Lady of Kuo's apartments. He cannot have got very far." He turned to the physician, who waited, ready to walk by the chair in case he was needed. "You will join us, my friend. I will be waiting."

: :

The chief minister's hot spring's rooms were located on a unique part of the grounds. In many ways, the arrangement resembled his Chancellery fortress. Both buildings occupied discordant and strangely ungeomantic corners of their respective worlds.

The entire structure grew out of a cliff face at the base of Mount Li Shan. The building could be reached only from the front by a narrow flight of stone stairs carved in the natural rock shelf and rising up out of the pines to wind steeply through a cluster of mossy boulders—the ancient spiky talus at the base of the cliff wall—and onward through an almost perpendicular field of ferns. The building had a remote, rarified, inaccessible quality to it, like the monasteries perched on lattice scaffolds built out from the steep walls of the Yangtze River gorges.

Although the chief minister's retreat was not far from the steam chambers where he took his treatments every morning and his private sulphur pools at the rear of the springs, the steep daily journey was an arduous effort for the bearers, despite the fact that their burden was growing lighter every day.

: :

The table was set on the enclosed balcony which extended out from the cliff face on the upper level of the reception hall. Downstairs, the steward and receiving servants awaited the arrival of the lieutenant chief minister Yang Kuo-chung while the chief minister and the physician reclined on chaises under the balcony's awnings. They sat together in thoughtful silence sipping slowly from cups of thick, sweet ginseng-and-bee-secretion-extract wine. They gazed out on the bluish crowns of conifers and the fields and roofless ruins of the ancient bathing halls beyond the woods. Here and there among the pines, the softly rounded tops of great deciduous trees stood out, their top branches swaying gently, showing the silver undersides of their leaves.

Li Lin-fu found himself curiously, exquisitely contented for one brief moment. Where had the feeling come from? He was sure that it was an echo of another time and place, of a pleasant interval from the past: perhaps with his family a long time ago on some forgotten summer afternoon, when he sat with them listening to music and looking out over a beautiful view like this one but without the deadening weight of so much thought. He did not know. But it passed very quickly, leaving only a shadow of some immense contentment, almost euphoric, that he could not place. The feeling evaporated until only a thin impression of it remained. He returned to his wine.

"Grand Councillor," the physician interrupted their silence, "I thought that you told me that no one ever came up this path but those on official business or those in your employ."

His eyes were following movement below them. Then Li Lin-fu saw something, too.

A figure dressed in dark clothing moved in and out of the forest shadows along the lower portion of the path. A villager gathering wood, no doubt, Li Lin-fu thought.

"Councillor, it is Ming Wu!" the physician exclaimed. "This is the third or fourth time I have seen her in the vicinity. What is she doing, trespassing here?"

"The old woman lives up above this place," Li Lin-fu said. "She often uses the path. She lives alone with the rats and the spiders in the ruins at the top of the hill. No doubt you listen to all the superstitious tales, but she is really perfectly harmless. She is probably going about her daily harvest of herbs, worms, and insects for her brews and poisons." Li Lin-fu was amused to see the physician draw his face into an expression of pained revulsion. "Perhaps it is she I should be consulting. Perhaps she has a remedy for this condition of mine." He smiled at the physician. "Then she could have your job, and you could spend your days picking berries."

Now the physician put a look of offended propriety on his face.

"Well, you may think she is harmless, but it looks to me as though she is watching this place."

"Perhaps she intends to rob me, Physician," Li Lin-fu joked. At the sound of horses and people on the trail below the steps, Li Lin-fu's attention was entirely diverted from the topic of the old woman. He rose slowly and carefully and went to the rail of the balcony. Where the trail emerged from the woods, he could see the figures of Yang Kuo-chung and the Ssu-k'ung's internal securities escort approaching the steep rocky course that wound through the ferns and up to the apartment's terraced steps.

: :

"This morning, Master Yang Kuo-chung, my escorts brought you to my steam chamber. My staff does not bring visitors there unless the matter is urgent. You conveyed your urgency to them quite effectively, obviously. And you were right to do so. For you also imparted to me a sense of the urgency that you are feeling." The steward poured three bowls of hot green tea, bowed, and stepped back from the table like a ghost. "But you did not bring me any news," the chief minister said, placing Yang Kuo-chung's tea in front of him and discreetly watching his expression. "You see, I already knew about the murder of the Censorate investigators. I have other sources that keep me informed of matters in the far north. So, though I will be receiving the two youths this afternoon or tomorrow and hearing their story, they will not be telling me anything I do not know about anyway. Perhaps they might provide some missing details, since they were close witnesses to the event, but that will be all."

The servants brought the food, spicy and fragrant, and placed it before Li Lin-fu and his guests: fruits and vegetables in brine, and a broth thick with diced leeks, spring onions, fish, and river mussels.

"I am sure, Master Yang, that you have heard, in your travels in the northwest, many Arabian tales. No doubt you are familiar with the tale of the djinn, the powerful being released from a bottle to do its master's bidding. The djinn exists for one purpose only: to serve. It is not a complete being. It can have no independent existence, because it does not have powers of discrimination, nor judgment, nor a soul as we think of it. It has tremendous strength and the ability to break down obstructions. But it must always be directed; and in order to be directed, it must remain under the power of its master. And in order to maintain control, the master must know his particular djinn. For they do have idiosyncrasies, rudimentary personalities, if you will." He looked thoughtfully down at his untouched food. "I think we may compare General An Lu-shan to the djinn. And I take full responsibility for having released him from his bottle." He raised his eyes from the food to Yang Kuo-chung's face. "Now, it is my responsibility to teach his new master how to control him so that his great powers may continue to serve."

Yang Kuo-chung looked quietly back at the chief minister. Li Lin-fu could see that the younger man was carefully considering what he had just heard.

It is curious, Yang Kuo-chung thought, that the chief minister looks so much healthier now than he did a few hours ago. He had noticed it as soon as he had walked out onto the balcony. Color had returned to his face, and his voice and gestures had more strength and animation. Was it the light that was creating the illusion?

He had come to think of Li Lin-fu's countenance as the face of death. The feeling had crystallized for him on the day that he and Kao Li-shih visited him in his ruined ancestral shrine. And he had deteriorated a lot since that day. When Yang Kuo-chung had seen him in the steam chamber earlier this morning, he had wondered if the chief minister would live through the afternoon. But now he only looked tired, a bit haggard perhaps. But not like a man about to die. Not at all. Very curious, he thought.

The physician cleared his throat and dipped his head deferentially in Yang Kuo-chung's direction.

"Master Yang Kuo-chung, if I may," the physician began, "I should like to ask you a question." He seemed reticent, embarrassed, as if he did not expect Li Lin-fu to be pleased with what he was about to say. "Did you see anyone as you came along the path through the woods just now?"

Yang Kuo-chung thought for a moment.

"Two children, I believe. Two little boys from the village, I suspect, gathering firewood." Yang Kuo-chung smiled politely at the physician.

"You saw no one else?" the physician pressed him. "You are certain?" He seemed anxious to pry loose some forgotten memory from Yang Kuo-chung.

Yang Kuo-chung thought hard, wishing to oblige the man. Then he remembered something that he had dismissed immediately because it was so commonplace.

"Well . . . there *was* an old man in the field, alone, doing his t'ai chi. I saw him as I was crossing, on my way toward the trail."

"Perhaps," the physician suggested, "it was an old woman? In dark clothes?" He seemed oblivious now to the possibility that the chief minister might reproach him for his persistence.

"That is certainly possible, Physician," Yang Kuo-chung politely conceded, bemused now, "although I must be honest and tell you that I did not pay very much attention. I saw *someone,* an older person, I am fairly certain, going about his—or her—morning exercises. An old man, an old woman. What is the difference?"

"Enough!" Li Lin-fu interjected. "Our good physician indulges himself. He allows his imagination to play tricks on him, and now he seeks to have you corroborate his delusions for him."

The physician merely sat quietly, shaking his head from side to side.

Li Lin-fu turned to Yang Kuo-chung. "You see, he is obsessed with the notion that someone is watching me. I tell him that the only thing stalking me now is Death itself. And Death, as we all know, is dressed in gleaming white robes."

"You do not take me seriously," the physician said, throwing his hands up in disgust.

"You ingest too many of your own mixtures," Li Lin-fu retorted. "Perhaps you are hallucinating on too much thorn apple."

The chief minister laughed in a way that invited Yang Kuo-chung to laugh along with him at the physician. But Yang Kuo-chung merely smiled, wanting neither to hurt the man's feelings nor to contradict the chief minister. Li Lin-fu's face and manner became abruptly serious as he turned back to Yang Kuo-chung.

"I do not know anything about the physician's delusions. But we all know for certain that Death is stalking me, and very closely," he said with grave significance.

Yang Kuo-chung put his chopsticks down on the edge of his plate and waited.

"We cannot predict what time is left for me. Therefore, we must assume that there is very little time for me to teach you how to control the djinn. There is a line from the *Book of Odes:*

> "Neither does he persecute the weak and solitary
> Nor shrink from the fierce and brutal . . ."

An interesting bit of hypocrisy, Yang Kuo-chung thought, to hear that verse coming from you, Chief Minister. Before Li Lin-fu could open his mouth again, Yang Kuo-chung completed the stanza:

> "Inner strength is light as a feather;
> Yet impossible for the common people to lift."

The chief minister lifted his eyebrows in appreciation of Yang Kuo-chung's literary acumen.

"Well done, Master Yang!"

"It is the Lady of Kuo's doing, Councillor. Her family was in favor of a female learning to read, write, and study the classics if so inclined." There are a few things about me that you do not know, Lizard, the Fox thought with satisfaction. And probably, you will not live long enough to find them out. At the same moment that he thought this, Yang Kuo-chung realized that he did not at all enjoy the prospect of the chief minister's death.

"An admirable stance," Li Lin-fu returned. "But there is still more to the ode, Master Yang:

> "When the robe of state is tattered
> Who is there to mend it?"

Li Lin-fu smiled as if reciprocating a clever move on the gaming board.

"That is the pressing question, Master Yang. After my death, who? There is an art to controlling the barbarian. 'Inward power,' 'light as a feather, yet too heavy for common people.' That is the secret. An Lu-shan is a dangerous man; but it was just such danger toward other men that I recognized as being the only thing that could subdue the Mongolian nations, the Hsi and the Khitan. For make no mistake about it: they are dangerous, too. Never underestimate their determination. The struggle has lasted for centuries, as you well know. And in recent months the situation has been growing worse—as bad as it has been for a hundred years, at least." Li Lin-fu let that last piece of information hang in the air for a moment while he took a sip of his broth.

"The power to control men is not well understood, Master Yang," he continued. "It is a delicate balance between *wei* and *wu-wei*—activity and inactivity. I do not know if you fully understand this. It is not always a matter of physical force, nor even quick wits. It is a far more subtle thing.

"With our barbarian general, one must use particular care. If An Lu-shan encounters too much activity in the form of direct force against him, too much obvious interference with his own will, he revolts in one way or another. I believe we have a perfect example before us in the recent unfortunate events up north. If you will remember, An Lu-shan was subjected to heavy censure by the eunuch Kao Li-shih just before the general departed for the north this last time. He was called before the Emperor and the consort and forced to defend his character in a most abject and humiliating way. What followed, from the disastrous battle to the murders of the Censorate officials, was an inevitable and almost perfectly predictable reaction, and a clear illustration of his nature. One does not corner An Lu-shan. One does not reprimand him with force or threats. The secret to controlling him is to direct, so to speak, his own natural endowments so that he may control *himself.* Then, he remains a loyal servant to the empire and to our cause along the northern borders as he has been all these years."

He stopped talking when he thought he felt a coughing spell coming. The physician, as alert to the signs as he himself was, leaned forward uneasily; Li Lin-fu tightened his grip on the arms of his chair and, summoning his will, fought back the teasing little itch in his chest. He did not wish to have Yang Kuo-chung witness the performance of himself coughing blood and fighting for air while his eyes bulged from his head; he also did not think that he could survive another spell so soon after the one earlier that day. He took shallow, cautious breaths, sitting perfectly still, until the demon tiptoed away again. He slowly released his grip on the arms of his chair, took another sip of broth, and turned his attention back to Yang Kuo-chung, who was regarding him with a closed, solemn expression.

"An Lu-shan has a natural . . . shall we say, *respect* for me, which causes him to be almost meek in my presence. Therefore, Master Yang, I must teach you by example, and, at the same time, I must impart to you, in the eyes of An Lu-shan, my personal power over him. We must impress upon him that nothing is going to change with my death: he must fear you exactly as he fears me. He must know that you will be my eyes, my ears, and every aspect of my will after my death. And Master Yang," he said significantly, "it cannot be an act. It must be real, or it will not work. May I say, with all due respect, that it will be an opportunity for you to put your arrogance and stubbornness to good use."

Yang Kuo-chung smiled faintly at this.

"It is not our lives that matter," he continued. "Not anymore—if, indeed, they ever did. They are petty and insignificant if they are not dedicated to the compassionate service of the fifty-three million lives in this empire."

Interesting words, Yang Kuo-chung thought, coming from the chief minister. But it was evident that he meant them absolutely.

"Power over An Lu-shan," Li Lin-fu said, "is the power of compassion—for every life, no matter how mean its existence.

"We will summon our djinn from the north. We will dispatch a message today, this hour. He will stand before both of us at the same time. He will see that there is nothing about him that you do not also know. In his eyes, we will become one," he said, pronouncing the last word with slow emphasis.

Yang Kuo-chung contemplated the prospect of becoming one with Li Lin-fu. It is a strange world, he mused, and becoming stranger at every moment.

"But we must hurry. We have so little time," Li Lin-fu added. He was no longer addressing Yang Kuo-chung directly. His eyes looked out over the empty space above the trees. "So little time," he repeated.

: :

It was midsummer, the air torpid with heat and the sound of a billion whirring wings under an opaque sky. Yang Kuo-chung had just climbed the steep stone staircase to Li Lin-fu's hot springs mansion, and standing now on the threshold of the reception room, he found that he was as wet under his clothes as if he had just immersed himself in one of the pools.

"Welcome, Master Yang," a voice said as he opened the door and stepped into the room. He was careful to conceal his shock at what he saw.

Li Lin-fu had aged a hundred years in the weeks since their last meeting; the figure that reclined on the satin couch had begun its final dissolution into death. Yang Kuo-chung found it impossible now to believe that he had perceived an improvement in Li Lin-fu's health when he had sat on the balcony with him scarcely a month before. The face had the same high color that it had had on that day, the eyes bright and feverish, but now he understood that this was not some small sign of health he was seeing, but the glow of the fire that was burning the man up from within. He imagined Li Lin-fu's lungs and innards like the interior of a burned wooden building: scorched, blackened, and brittle.

Yang Kuo-chung studied Li Lin-fu now with the fascination of the living for the dying. Even the act of raising a bowl of tea to his lips was performed, Yang Kuo-chung observed, with extraordinary care and with an expenditure of energy so delicately controlled as to virtually conceal the chief minister's discomfort and exhaustion. The flesh of his hands and face, all that was visible of him under heavy robes, resembled the paper of a child's kite stretched over a frail wooden frame. It seemed to Yang Kuo-chung that the chief minister was already dead, his soul lingering like the last one to abandon a burning mansion.

Li Lin-fu smiled. Yang Kuo-chung felt that he knew that smile well now, having been guided past its deceptive dangers. There was humor and wit in the smile, even humanity. It was odd that the notion of Li Lin-fu's humanity should have occurred to him, because Yang Kuo-chung knew that there was none in this man. This was the man who had caused immeasurable suffering; this, he reminded himself, was the murderer of the crown prince. Though he told himself these things, he still felt a little pull of compassion, a feeling of sadness for the dying man. But then, wasn't that part of his power? To make you feel what he wanted you to feel, grotesque or inappropriate though such feelings might be? And he wondered: what effect would the sight of a nearly dead Li Lin-fu have on An Lu-shan? Surely, it was not part of the chief minister's design to arouse compassion or pity in the barbarian general.

"Sit, Master Yang," the chief minister invited with a wave of his bony hand. "Tea?" he inquired politely. Despite his appearance, it was plain that Li Lin-fu, propped against the pillows comfortably, was completely composed. He was the brilliant ruler of China, about to receive his subject, General An Lu-shan.

A tea table sat at the foot of the couch, and two tables had been set up at either end of the small room for the recorders. There were writing brushes, ink, and paper ready, but the stools alongside both of the tables were vacant, awaiting the scribes. Alongside the chief minister's couch was a desk, its top folded back to reveal a strange inlaid wheel. The chair that the chief minister invited Yang Kuo-chung to sit in was close to the desk; he sat so that he would have a good view of the device.

The wheel was divided into eight segments, each bearing a recessed jade and mother-of-pearl ideogram, the ancient trigrams of the *I Ching* (the *Book of Changes*), the characters of the diviner. In the center of the wheel, covering the hub, rested a stationary square of cinnabar enamel. Four intersecting lines of gold wire divided the large square into nine small squares of equal size; each square was marked with a red numeral from one to nine.

When Yang Kuo-chung looked up, he found the chief minister watching him with a teasing smile.

"You are curious, but you do not push too hard," Li Lin-fu said. "You choose instead to let the answers be revealed to you. You are a lot like me, Master Yang. We wasted a great deal of time being enemies, I suspect. Essentially, we were turning our energies against ourselves. Do you know the ancient tale of the man who fought his reflection? No? Well, no matter. But I can say that for us to fight each other would be of as much use as my fighting death—no use at all. A far better thing would be for me to place my efforts where they are needed, would it not?"

"An Lu-shan is here," Yang Kuo-chung said, wishing to turn the conversation to more tangible matters.

"Yes. My Chancellery runners tell me that he has been here since early this morning. But I am in no hurry. I have found that it is advantageous to keep him waiting. To let him fret and speculate. You see, when he is apprehensive, unsure, he sweats. Profusely." He paused and clasped his hands together. "I am plagued by water on the inside; An Lu-shan is tormented by that same deceptive element on the outside. That is one of his weaknesses. He cannot control it, and it provides a most visible and accurate gauge of his inner thought processes. I want you to observe the phenomenon today. It will be your first lesson in statecraft where master An Lu-shan is concerned."

"I have never seen him sweat," Yang Kuo-chung said. "But I have watched him do a number of other things."

"Well, you will see it today, I promise. It is a most curious effect."

A welcome bit of air blew in from the balcony. Below, the treetops were swaying in a way that suggested a possible thunderstorm later in the day.

"Are you interested in mathematics, Master Yang?" Li Lin-fu said, giving his mysterious wheel a spin with one hand.

"I am not what you would call erudite on the subject, Councillor," Yang Kuo-chung said, "though you have certainly aroused my curiosity."

The chief minister looked at Yang Kuo-chung with the interest of a teacher evaluating a bright but stubborn student. The wheel was still spinning smoothly and silently from the first spin he had given it; he put his hand down on it and stopped it abruptly.

"It would give me great pleasure to share a small part of what has been a lifelong fascination and love affair with numbers," he said candidly and pleasantly. "The wheel," he began, practically caressing the device, "is divided into eight segments representing the eight sides of the *I Ching* octagon. Each of those segments is inscribed, as you can see, with one of the trigrams. On top of the wheel, this rectangular hub represents the magic square. You may have heard it referred to as the Nine Mansions, the Universal Model, or the Lo Document. Various names for the same thing. It is one of the simplest and yet most formidable mysteries of the universe; one of Heaven's ultimate secrets. It is a glimpse into the inner workings of a perfectly ordered mathematical universe, Master Yang. Each of the square's nine smaller squares is inscribed with a number, one through nine. Each of the rows, horizontal, vertical, or diagonal, will always add up to fifteen. Then . . ." He paused. "There is a complex interaction of the eight trigrams below," he said, indicating the wheel,

"and the nine realms above, which, simply put, applies to celestial motion."
He leaned back into the pillows. "I tell you all of this because I trust you to
distinguish between exact science and superstitious twaddle. We may know
our natures and even predict the courses of our lives by looking at the stars.
But I am not speaking of the methods and principles of the astrologers, those
witches and self-deluders. I am talking of mathematics: prime, indivisible,
perfect!" What you mean, Yang Kuo-chung thought, is that anyone is a fool
who cannot read *your* Mandate of Heaven.

"Our determinations of the course of men's lives," Li Lin-fu went on,
"are as infinite as the mathematical possibilities of the heavens. By the system
of numbers that the octagon of trigrams coupled with the universal Nine
Mansions affords us, our heavenly windows of observation are certain and
nearly infinite. Each finite window is an exact fractal of the eternal, the infinite
window, capable of being divided into smaller and smaller units, each identical
in conformation to the whole. Eight raised to the power of three, raised once
again to the order of nine and to the power of nine, multiplied by fifteen and
raised again by the trigonometric value of pi. You see, the heavens are a globe
. . . not simply a circle or canopy . . . those ancient inventors of the armillary
sphere understood that. They understood the Gauge of the Yellow Road and
the Gauge of the Enveloping Sky—that they surround the *globe* that is our
world."

Yang Kuo-chung felt that the chief minister may have been attempting
to try his credibility with this last statement. Probably he was being tested;
he would simply weather the torrent of obtuse theory, listening and comprehending as well as he could, until Li Lin-fu reached some sort of conclusion.
Where he was being taken, he could not be sure: but he would be patient. He
would listen. He would give the chief minister his full attention, just as if he
were another mathematician fully initiated into the mysterious and the two
of them were on equal footing.

As he listened, it occurred to him that Li Lin-fu was practicing his verbal
swordplay on him, tuning his instrument, so to speak, before using it on An
Lu-shan. Well and good. He would let himself be put to use this way; he
wanted Li Lin-fu to be especially strong and effective today.

"A globe. I am certain, Master Li Lin-fu," he conceded without conviction.

"I do not expect you to fathom it or believe it. You, in your arrogance,
no doubt, consider it a feckless course of study," Li Lin-fu returned. "But I
have determined what the nonsense of the Red Star of the general's birth is
all about. That yang star was a comet, and it was indeed quite real, not simply
hearsay or myth. But Master Yang, it was definitely not in the sky at the time
of An Lu-shan's birth. But astrologers simply did what astrologers have always
done—adjusted the facts to make a rousing tale. The existence of this phe-

nomenon is real, but it preceded him by many years. It has no significance, no portent whatsoever concerning an imbalance of yin and yang. I hold to the theory of Master Chin Fang. Over twelve hundred years before our own time, he understood that the comets are simply extrusions of the planets."

"Then what do we have, Master Li Lin-fu?" Yang Kuo-chung was growing impatient and slightly weary.

"We have the wondrous and frightening weapon of superstition. That is what we have. This heavenly occurrence—this red-tailed comet—will return to the sky to occupy the exact position it is erroneously believed to have occupied at the time of An Lu-shan's birth. It has no significance as a portent. It simply obeys the laws of the heavens. But An Lu-shan does not know that; he is superstitious. And this gives us our advantage. I have given this much thought.

"I will be speaking to him. My words will be simple and effective; but in order to ensure that the lesson in those words becomes part of him, he must be fired like a clay pot in a kiln. And the fire that we will use that will infuse the meaning into him, hardened and permanent, will be the fire of his own highly superstitious nature. And we will do it before he leaves the room today."

Yang Kuo-chung found himself suddenly very interested in the chief minister's words, which were now making a great deal of sense. The man's technique was fascinating. Just when you think that he is rambling in an irrelevant or distracted way, Yang Kuo-chung reflected, he abruptly pulls the tangents together and catches you off guard, like a rabbit out in the open, with the utter clarity of his intent.

"We will approach him first on a more mundane level of superstition. I have always found it both useful and effective to demonstrate knowledge of what he believes are his secrets. There is no magic involved, of course; just vigilance and the ability to logically predict his thought patterns. Deceptively simple, really. But a few words, judiciously chosen and expeditiously inserted into a conversation, that make him believe you possess some uncanny ability to see into his life can be most effective. He has a vivid imagination; I let it do my work for me."

Yang Kuo-chung was nothing short of fascinated now. To hear Li Lin-fu speak of what was a legendary attribute of his, which had held so many in awe and terror aside from poor An Lu-shan, was almost like hearing the confessions of a minor deity.

"Let me give you an example of what we may mention to him today, which I believe might be of use to us. Without a doubt, he believes that both his son and the eunuch Li Chu-erh perished in the burning tent along with the unfortunate eunuchs. Yes, they were seen running from the tent by a few soldiers, who shot arrows at them but failed to bring them down. But do you think that a single one of those soldiers would confess to An Lu-shan that they had let them get away? Of course not. Would you?" he asked, but did not give Yang Kuo-chung time to reply. "He does not know that they are here, alive and safe, and have told us every minute, grisly detail of the incident. We will know things that we could not possibly know. He will believe"—Li Lin-fu leaned forward again—"that we are able to read his mind. *We*, Master Yang. He has believed it about me all these years; now we will subtly transfer that belief to apply to *you* as well. Then he will come to fear and respect you in the same way."

Li Lin-fu stopped talking and sipped his hot tea. Yang Kuo-chung could see his chest heaving under his robes as he composed himself, and could see that he was drawing on some final reserve of strength in order to make this tremendous effort today—but it was costing him.

"Then we will move to the next level of superstition," he resumed. "Do you know what will have made his mind accessible to you like a house with the door left standing open?" He paused, smiling with genuine pleasure at what he was about to say. "The Red Star. You will tell him that its coming, its return to the place in the sky where it was at his birth, has opened his mind for you like a simple book. My advice to you is to devise a dream that you supposedly had, involving the Red Star and General An Lu-shan and some details of what happened on the day that he assassinated the Censorate eunuchs. I will leave it to you. You will have ample time to think, to formulate your plan." He looked at Yang Kuo-chung conspiratorially. "You do understand, I trust?"

"Yes," Yang Kuo-chung said, feeling an almost pleasurable anticipation growing in him. "I understand." You old devil, he thought; you knew that I would enjoy this. You know a few things about the workings of my mind, too, and you are letting me know it at this very moment.

"We must use everything in our power," Li Lin-fu said quietly. "There is something else I hope you understand, and that is the gravity of the military situation along our borders. It grows worse every day. We need him. Despite his excesses, An Lu-shan is the greatest defender of the sanctity of the T'ang that we have, our most formidable weapon. Without him, we may not survive. And now," he said abruptly, "I must rest. He will be here in an hour. My steward has a pleasant meal waiting for you on the balcony. Simple, nourishing foods to fortify you for our session with the barbarian. And," he added as Yang Kuo-chung rose to go, "time for you to think . . . and dream."

: :

Yang Kuo-chung listened to An Lu-shan's distinctive tread on the wooden stairs and thought that the sound was particularly eloquent today. The familiar heavy footsteps were slow and reluctant and spoke rather poignantly of the general's wish that he were somewhere else—anywhere but climbing a staircase for an imminent meeting with Li Lin-fu. His step was almost apologetic as well, as if he had recently understood how things had to suffer under his enormous weight, and he was sorry.

Just as Li Lin-fu had withered and diminished since Yang Kuo-chung had seen him last, so An Lu-shan had expanded, taking up ever more room and life-force. Enormous, hairy, red-faced, black-bearded, he stepped into the room, his breath whistling and the pungent odor of his sweat perfuming the air. He did not notice Yang Kuo-chung sitting discreetly to the side near the scribes; his small, nervous eyes fixed immediately upon Li Lin-fu, arranged serenely on his couch with a silk coverlet over the lower half of his body, wearing the formal purple robes of his Ssu-k'ung office, his head and shoulders propped up on the pillows, looking as if he had risen from the grave to keep the appointment today. Which was not far from the truth, Yang Kuo-chung thought. And the chief minister had obviously chosen not to hide from An Lu-shan the fact that he was dying: he meant to use it to full effect.

An Lu-shan was already shiny with sweat. He moved to within about ten paces of Li Lin-fu's couch and stood waiting for the chief minister to speak. Li Lin-fu nodded pleasantly at him.

"Why did you come here today?" the chief minister said by way of greeting, his voice soft and even.

"Because . . . I was commanded to do so by the Ssu-k'ung office of the Chancellery and the Ministry of War, Chief Minister," An Lu-shan answered deferentially.

"And this request . . ." The chief minister lowered his hand. "By whom was it made?"

"By you, of course, Chief Minister," An Lu-shan answered carefully.

"By me, of course. That is correct, General. I requested that you visit me, didn't I? That you have an audience before me. That is it precisely." The chief minister shook his head slowly as if he had just comprehended a difficult mathematical problem. "Then I am the reason you came here?"

"Yes, uh . . . indeed, that is so, Chief Minister," An Lu-shan stammered uncomfortably.

"Come closer, General, into the light of the balcony. As with everything else, my eyes are failing, too. It has been some time, and I want to have a good look at you."

An Lu-shan moved a step or two closer to Li Lin-fu's couch. The chief minister looked him up and down approvingly. Then he raised his hand and made a twirling motion.

"Please, General, will you turn around slowly for me? Excuse me. It is 'Commissioner' now, is it not?"

The general nodded cautiously.

"You see, the mind is going, too," Li Lin-fu said, rolling his head slowly from side to side in mock disgust with his own pitiful condition.

An Lu-shan turned slowly around. Damp spots of sweat already stained the fresh silks that he wore. Yang Kuo-chung, watching the performance, found his own palms growing moist with apprehension. A quivering droplet of perspiration now hung tenuously from the tip of the general's nose. As he moved, the light sparkled from the droplet in cruel exaggeration. When he had half-completed his rotation, his eyes found Yang Kuo-chung sitting quietly in the corner; Yang Kuo-chung had never before seen such a look of dumb shock on the general's face. They had taken him completely by surprise. He stared for only a moment at his old enemy before recovering his composure and completing the turn.

"Thank you, General," Li Lin-fu said. "Or rather—please excuse me—Commissioner. I notice something about you," he declared.

"I do not know what that could be," An Lu-shan said, hesitating, attempting a smile, "unless it is that I have grown fatter."

"Without a doubt," Li Lin-fu replied. "Since the five elements are constants in the universe, you have probably gained the flesh that I have lost. But that is not what I am seeing." He tapped a front tooth thoughtfully. "I know what it is," he said in a tone that suggested that he was about to pay An Lu-shan a great compliment.

An Lu-shan waited; the suspense was almost as palpable for Yang Kuo-chung.

"It is that you, 'Prince' An Lu-shan," Li Lin-fu continued, "are a bigger fool than you were before."

An Lu-shan opened his mouth to speak but Li Lin-fu cut him off.

"Why did you come here?" he said, the anger rising in his voice. "Because you are a greater fool than anyone but myself could ever imagine. You came simply because a dying chief minister ordered you. And if you had not come, what could this dying chief minister have done? What could this chief minister, this moribund shell of a man sitting in judgment before you, have done? You are a fool, General. A great fat, stupid fool. Because I could have done nothing! Yet you came here simply because I asked it."

"Councillor . . ." An Lu-shan began.

"Shut up, An Lu-shan," Li Lin-fu hissed, leaning forward, all traces of his former gracious manner gone. "There is nothing that you can say that will please me. You are a murderer and a traitor."

"I am a soldier of the T'ang," An Lu-shan asserted valiantly. "I fight only for the T'ang, Chief Minister." An Lu-shan's face grew a furious shade of red as he spoke.

"General, if you speak again, I will have you cut down, on this spot, here and now. And not even you will battle your way out of this one, nor will you lie your way out of this one, nor will you entrap and burn your way out of this one. And I will do with you as I want, General. If you leave and return to the north after today, it will only be because I wish it. And if you lie in those woods beneath us today, writhing hacked and limbless, it will be because I wished that too. I have killed many men in my time. And I am not subject to fits of conscience, nor am I subject to even a moment of indecision. And I know what you are thinking," he said, holding up a warning finger. "Not even your Imperial Father can come to your aid. Because, in truth, General, Minghuang is merely the titulary. *I* am the ruler of China. I bought your skills because I thought they would be useful for the empire. In a bid for strength and stability in the north, I opted for your skills. But it appears that I have also bought your vainglory . . . your monstrous, swaggering, cock-headed, drunken-balled vainglory."

An Lu-shan did not speak. Yang Kuo-chung had to give him credit, though; he did not hang his head abjectly or avert his eyes; he continued to look the chief minister in the eye. Yang Kuo-chung now found himself apprehensive that the terrifying harangue that Li Lin-fu was delivering to An Lu-shan would cause the chief minister to keel over dead at any moment. But he continued, his voice steady and strong.

"Did you ever think that anything you did would escape my notice?" Li Lin-fu asked, his tone almost kind again. "I *gave* you the eunuchs of Master Yang Kuo-chung's Censorate," he said, directing his eyes toward where Yang Kuo-chung sat. "I offered those eunuchs to your bloodthirstiness, An Lu-shan, because I wanted to see what you would do. And you did as I expected. You see, I, too, have little use for them."

Yang Kuo-chung was appalled. Was Li Lin-fu telling the truth? Certainly he was capable of such a thing. Or was he extemporizing for the barbarian's benefit? Steady yourself, Yang Kuo-chung, he thought; never leap to any conclusions where Li Lin-fu is concerned. Just stay quiet and listen.

"I knew that you would jump at the bait," Li Lin-fu said. "I knew that you would fall into my hands by murdering them. You simply cannot avoid your own undoing."

Now An Lu-shan's face went from bright red to deathly pale, and the sweat rolled down his forehead from his scalp, causing him to blink uncomfortably to keep the stinging salt out of his eyes. The day was hot, Yang Kuo-chung thought, but the amount of sweat the general was putting out was far too much even for that. Li Lin-fu sat calmly, his hands clasped together under his chin.

"You are nothing, An Lu-shan, if not predictable," he said. "Extraordinarily, eminently predictable! You sit up in the north, in your grand tents, fat and satisfied, thinking how you have deceived everyone with your cunning.

And yet everything you do writes itself indelibly all over your face. You are not clever enough to conceal anything, General. You cannot conceal it from me, nor will you conceal it from Master Yang. He sits before you, too, having the same knowledge of your treachery as I. He knows the same things that I know. He knows about your maps and your forgeries, your murders, your lies, your battle plans pushed ahead against the better judgment and the protests of your advisors and the well-being of your soldiers. He knows about the gratuitous loss of life that always results from your arrogance and impatience. He knows, just as I know, everything there is to know about your base stupidity and cruelty."

Maps and forgeries? Yang Kuo-chung wondered what Li Lin-fu had meant by that. The words had had a profound effect on An Lu-shan; it was the only time during the excoriation that he had actually lowered his eyes. Obviously, the chief minister was referring to some particularly dark, base secret. And all the while that he spoke, his eyes were speaking, too. *You will sweat*, they said. *You have only begun to know what fear is, General.*

The general remained perfectly still. The only movement was an involuntary twitching of the muscles of his neck and a spasmodic clenching of the fingers as if they were dreaming of closing around the chief minister's neck. Then, reluctantly, it seemed, he brought a cuff to his forehead and wiped at the sweat. It was strange for Yang Kuo-chung to see this fear so close and visible. It would almost have been unbearable to watch but for the fact that it was An Lu-shan who was suffering.

The power that Li Lin-fu wielded over the enormous creature before him was formidable. Until now, Yang Kuo-chung had only heard about it. Now he was seeing it; even once removed, it was frightening. He felt helpless, inadequate. How could he possibly take the chief minister's place as An Lu-shan's master? He did not have that power. He would never have that power. He looked at the dead man propped up on the couch, shrouded in his purple robes, and knew that there was no way out. The office would soon be his, whether he wanted it or not.

Li Lin-fu leaned forward again, resting his chin on one hand, his elbow on the arm of the couch. He was pleased. He had An Lu-shan exactly where he wanted him.

"But perhaps I am being unfair, General," he said then. "Because really, none of it is your fault. You cannot help what you do. You see, you are one of nature's doomed creatures. A creature out of balance with his universe. A pitiful and shameful creature who considers that patience is a weakness and that the rational man is a fool. I see a creature who stumbles through his universe backward. A creature far too fat, of ungainly proportions, sweating absurdly, driven mad by his own delusions, trapped in a world of his own hatreds, forced to blunder dangerously forward under the power of his own childish impulsiveness. A creature with no control of his emotions. A creature who can never escape the excesses of his own tantrums, who cannot bear when things do not go as he wishes. A childish and impetuous creature subject to stormy fits of rage. There are many men like you, General, but few with the power to subject others to the consequences of their natures."

Li Lin-fu stopped for a moment, allowing his gaze to drift toward the ceiling. An Lu-shan, during the brief respite, took another furtive wipe at his forehead with his sleeve. Along his shoulders and the pendulous line of his belly, the silks were saturated and clinging.

"But that is only what is visible to us on the outside. The imbalance I mentioned is on the inside—an invisible deformity, if you will. You see, General, you are a prime example of a creature afflicted by an excess of yin. To some, you might appear to be quite the opposite—all the typical outward signs of yang, all the way back to the Red Star in the sky that heralded your birth. But even the Red Star, that supposed portent of overwhelming yang, is not what it is believed to be. You see, it travels with its tail pointing *away* from that source of all yang power, the sun. The comet's tail points instead toward the vast empty blackness of yin.

"So I'm afraid that the truth is that your dominating influence is yin. The two—yin and yang—must always be held in balance. But in your case, a great, voracious flood of yin has swept you away, and you don't even realize it. It overwhelms you, because there is simply not enough yang to balance it. If you doubt it, please consider the evidence. You struggle against the men-women, against the eunuchs, and yet they still seek you out. You deceive them, you kill them, but they still come after you. You struggle against the excesses of water, the yin element: flooding rivers, torrential rains, the copious sweats that pour from your body. You do not meet them in balance, so instead, they overwhelm you. Everywhere you turn, you encounter their treachery. If it is not a flooding river, then it is soaked bowstrings, useless and lethal, and men going to their deaths before they even see battle," he said, pausing and looking hard at the general, who was unable to keep his mouth from dropping open just a little at these last words. Li Lin-fu shook his head sadly.

"Even your couplings, General. Even the prurient habits of your insatiable lusts are further evidence of the phenomenon I speak of. Your sweaty pummeling is not the delicate interchange of yin and yang. Rather, it is a grotesque and futile effort at compensation for your lack. The result is that Father Kao Mei crushes the young female creature beneath him. Whether it is soldiers, women, or eunuchs that you encounter, your personal battles with the forces of yin often spell doom for them, too, because of the position of power that you occupy."

Li Lin-fu leaned back, resting for a few moments. Yang Kuo-chung could see the heaving of his chest again and knew that he was approaching the limits of whatever reserves he had called upon today. Soon, he would reach the denouement of his "lesson" to An Lu-shan. The chief minister rubbed his upper lip thoughtfully, as if carefully choosing his next words.

"Yin will be your undoing, General, if you hold to your course. It will rage against you and ultimately destroy you in a most ungenerous fashion. This is not a prediction. The laws of the universe are constant, and no man escapes them. It is that simple. No man, no matter how self-important, is exempt. The physicians will tell you that a disharmony of the body can oftentimes be corrected. But such disorders of the soul can rarely be put right. The Buddhists say that such a confused soul can only be clarified through the silence of"—he raised his hands in a futile gesture—"extinction."

Now An Lu-shan's eyes showed their whites like a frightened animal's. He was entranced, enslaved, paralyzed. Yang Kuo-chung wondered nervously how much of this An Lu-shan would take. Would he rush the couch, seize the chief minister's skeletal form, and crush it like a dried leaf before the guards could enter the room? Would he go mad and rush the balcony railing, hurling himself out onto the rocks and trees below? Yang Kuo-chung could imagine the noise. The crashing and snapping of branches, the splintering of wood, the body rolling and rolling down the hill. But An Lu-shan remained where he was, waiting, sweat dripping now into little puddles on the floor around his feet.

"Perhaps, General, I should simply let you run in the forest beneath us and allow my soldiers to hunt you down with bow and arrow like a broad, meaty roebuck," Li Lin-fu said. "The chase would be grand sport, don't you think? You, white and quivering with terror, your great fat legs clumsy and slow as you push your way through the scrub brush and branches and clamber over rocks and logs, pursued from all sides by the horsemen . . ." Li Lin-fu sat, apparently contemplating the pleasant image. Then he smiled, as if it had been nothing but a joke.

"No, General. That is not for you! You are too important to me; far too important to my successor, Master Yang Kuo-chung. You are far too important to China. You are the greatest general, the greatest military mind the T'ang has ever seen, despite the errors of judgment, the imbalances in your nature. There has never been so efficient and deadly a force to hold back the northern tribal nations of Hsi and Khitan. You have proven yourself indispensable.

"And it seems we face many threats at this moment. Too many. The secessionists, the rebels in your own territories in Hopei Province, have long hated their T'ang overlords. But now we are beginning to feel their wrath. The outbreaks in the northeast against our commanderies are becoming more and more frequent, as I am certain you already know. So far they are nothing that we cannot deal with. But each day, this dissatisfaction seduces more of the outlying Hopei populations north of Loyang and Pien Chou. And each day, our military couriers tell us that these secessionist outbreaks become more virulent and, at the same time, more difficult to predict and control. You, General An Lu-shan, are the only one with whom they can identify. You are our emissary from the T'ang. To those peoples you are like a brother, one whom they can understand. They hate the T'ang, General, but they do not hate you. Under you they might even serve the armies of the T'ang for our common good . . .

"And there is another thing. Perhaps you will not understand it. But it is, nevertheless, part of the cosmic plan. The universe, Heaven and Earth and everything wrought by Man, are comprehensible in terms of mathematical fractals. Each larger reality is simply a mirror image of the smaller realities that compose it. And quite the opposite is also true. Each smaller event is simply a tiny copy of the greater truths, one of the many identical shapes that make up the larger whole—a synchronistic duplicate in miniature. Around us now, the world slips back into a dark age of superstition. Our Imperial Father revels in Dark Taoistic lore. Strange sects and secret societies proliferate. All of these things are small building blocks. Irrationalities, General. Small irrationalities composing a larger and now increasingly irrational universe.

"As I speak, General An Lu-shan, our rational and judicious China has already begun to collapse before its greatest threat. In the far northwest, our forces are falling before the very embodiment of perverse fervor, illogic, and superstition. The Muslim armies, General. Our forces are falling before them like wheat before the scythe. Only today, just a short while before your arrival here, I received news."

Yang Kuo-chung sat up sharply. What news?

"The armies of General Kao Hsien-chih and our good friend General Feng have fallen to the Muslims in a major defeat on the fields of the Tarim Basin along the Talus River. Our soldiers, what is left of them, have retreated. It is doubtful that these territories shall ever be recovered. And now, with this final death blow, the T'ang no longer controls central Asia. The Silk Road is gone and, with it, the vitality that it brought. The penetration of Islam is far from over, General An Lu-shan. The House of Li is falling in upon itself. But, though the northwest of China has fallen, the northeast is still ours—P'inglu, Fanyang, Hotung, Shuofang—though our grip is tenuous. And, you, General An Lu-shan, are the one who can hold that together."

Li Lin-fu had taken Yang Kuo-chung completely by surprise. He knew that his own face now held the same stupefied expression that An Lu-shan's had at the moment when he saw Yang Kuo-chung sitting in the corner. He had known nothing at all about the defeat of the two generals along the Talus River. The last report he had heard had been almost a week ago, and it had appeared that the imperial armies were holding their own, that they were

inflicting satisfactory losses on the enemy and not losing ground. If what Li
Lin-fu said was true, then the empire had suffered a devastating, crippling
blow. And he was right: it was a blow from which it might never recover.

And Li Lin-fu had chosen to deliver this news to Yang Kuo-chung at
the same moment that he delivered it to An Lu-shan. Obviously, An Lu-shan
was not the only one it was meant to impress. He wanted to interrupt, to
press the chief minister for details. How had it happened? How much territory
had actually been lost? What plans were being made, if any, for regrouping,
rethinking strategy?

But he said nothing. Li Lin-fu was not quite finished with An Lu-shan.

"General," Li Lin-fu said, "it is obvious that I will not live very much
longer. I must leave this world, reluctantly, at a time when I am sorely needed.
But I have a successor. He has already assumed many of my duties. He thinks
the way I think, and he looks on the world with the same eyes. And those
eyes will be watching you, General, when I am gone.

"You see, he takes a great, great interest in you. He, too, is filled with
admiration for your military prowess. He, too, is anxious that your great
powers continue to serve the empire. In fact, you have become something of
an . . . obsession with him. Isn't that correct, Master Yang?"

Yang Kuo-chung had to forcibly turn his thoughts away from the defeated armies retreating from the Talus River basin and the victorious Muslims
pouring in to claim the territory. Li Lin-fu was addressing him, drawing him
into the strange "lesson"; now he was being called upon to perform. The chief
minister regarded him expectantly.

Yang Kuo-chung rose from his seat and walked over to where An Lu-
shan would be able to see him without turning away from Li Lin-fu. When
he came into the barbarian's line of vision, An Lu-shan looked at him with
frightened, angry eyes. With both of them watching him now, Yang Kuo-
chung walked slowly to within a few paces of the chief minister's couch and
stood for a moment looking thoughtfully at his hands. This had better be
very, very good, he told himself; this is probably the most crucial test you
have faced in your life. He took a breath and raised his eyes to An Lu-shan's.

"I had a most interesting dream recently," he began. "You, General,
were in a tent somewhere in the north. The tent was far from any settlement,
all by itself out on the windswept plains. The night sky over your head was
clear, the stars brilliant. You were quite alone in your tent, which was richly
appointed, comfortable, and luxurious. You were surrounded by treasures:
silver wine pitchers and cups sat on the polished table, beautiful Persian carpets
covered the floor, protecting your feet from the cold, and elaborate tapestries
lined the walls of the tent, keeping out the bitter wind. You yourself were
dressed in heavy embroidered silks. You were drinking wine from a silver
cup and were about to begin eating a delectable meal. The delicious odors

were rising to your nostrils. You were about to take your first mouthful; you had a sense of perfect well-being and calm."

He glanced toward Li Lin-fu, who returned a subtle, approving look of encouragement.

"Over your head, a fiery comet streaked through the night sky, leaving a trail of red behind it. Closer and closer to the earth the comet moved, until its red light bathed the ground below it. It was like a great searching eye moving over the earth, looking for someone or something. Then it saw your tent, alone on the vast plain. It dove then, and entered the earth. It burrowed under the ground, passing beneath the place where your tent stood. Inside the tent, you had raised your chopsticks to your lips; you inhaled the fragrance of the food, and your mouth watered with anticipation. The comet passed under you and came up out of the earth some distance away from your tent. Its fiery tail had solidified into two ropes of fire . . ." Yang Kuo-chung paused, sensing Li Lin-fu's approval of this innovation. ". . . which pulled up taut out of the earth, displacing dirt, grass, and rocks. You had just put the food into your mouth when the two ropes suddenly jerked your tent closed tightly like a sack, then pulled it behind them up into the sky." Now he felt Li Lin-fu fairly beaming at him, and he noted the violent clenching and unclenching of An Lu-shan's jaws, causing his temples to bulge in and out visibly.

"The tent," he continued, "enveloped in flame from the comet's tail, was pulled up above the earth, a ball of fire. Your cries and howls of pain could be heard faintly coming from within, but soon the comet disappeared into the heavens and everything was quiet again." He looked at An Lu-shan, who appeared to be trembling with exasperation.

"It was most vivid. And rather peculiar, don't you agree?" Yang Kuo-chung said. "And the feeling I had from the dream was that the comet's glowing red light, which resembled the light of a thousand great colored lanterns, would always be—how shall I say it?—*looking* for you, General. *Hungry* for you. There really is no other way to describe it, except to say that it is hungry to shine its light on your innermost thoughts, your essence, if you will."

Yang Kuo-chung was gratified to see that An Lu-shan's face still glistened with sweat. But of course, Li Lin-fu had been the primary cause; whether he himself, alone with An Lu-shan, could have provoked the phenomenon, he did not know. But his "dream" had been a good one; it had even sounded impressive to his own ears.

"You may leave now, An Lu-shan," Li Lin-fu said abruptly. "I am weary, and must rest. But you are not to go far. Before you return to your duties in the north, we must wait and see what develops militarily. Your responsibilities may soon be increasing. We have much, much work to do."

Still reluctant to speak, apparently believing that Li Lin-fu meant to make good his threat to cut him down if he did, An Lu-shan turned to leave. As he passed Yang Kuo-chung, he gave him an angry, insolent look that made Yang Kuo-chung doubt that he, Yang Kuo-chung, was any sort of equivalent to Li Lin-fu in the barbarian's eyes. The general left the room and noisily descended the staircase.

Yang Kuo-chung turned to Li Lin-fu. He wanted more details of the defeat at the Talus River basin, and he wanted to discuss the amazing spectacle that had just transpired.

But he was shocked to find Li Lin-fu's face bright red with strain. His body quivered, and he gripped the arms of his couch. Eyes burning, he gesticulated fiercely to Yang Kuo-chung to leave the room immediately. Yang Kuo-chung hesitated, but Li Lin-fu's eyes sent a clear message: get out now, this instant.

Yang Kuo-chung was out the door and on his way down the staircase in the next moment. Behind and above him, he could hear the explosive, spasmodic sound of Li Lin-fu's coughing, a deep, rasping, despairing sound that caused pain in Yang Kuo-chung's own chest just to hear it. Now he understood the burning look and the fierce gestures: the chief minister had fought it off as long as he possibly could, but had, at that moment, reached the end of his reserves.

He moved down the stairs and across the reception hall. Over his head, he heard the chief minister giving in completely to the seizure. He could still hear the dreadful, relentless coughing when he was outside and well down the trail; it was not until he had entered the trees that he could no longer hear the sound over his own footsteps. He paused for a moment and listened: there it was. Faint, distant, a rhythmic, dry hacking. The sound of a man's pain. The sound of his dying.

Keeping a wary eye out so that he would not accidentally catch up to An Lu-shan on the trail, he hurried along to the place where his horse waited for him. He wanted to go and find the Lady of Kuo immediately; he felt that he could not wait even another hour to see her again.

~ 23 ~

Slippers of the Giantess

[A great comet was reported around the time of our story; and another, less than a hundred years later, was reported in the Old T'ang Histories.] On the night of March 22 a broom star appeared in the east. Its length was more than 7 degrees—situated in the first degree of Wei; it pointed west. On the night of March 24, the brightness of its rays was becoming fierce. . . . On the night of April 9 its length was more than 50 degrees. It branched into two tails. One pointing toward Ti, the other hiding Fang. . . . [By May] the broom length was 60 degrees. . . . The Emperor summoned the astronomer royal and asked the reason for this.

—*from the* Chiu T'ang Shu (Old T'ang History) *and* Yuan-shih
Astronomical Treatise, translated by Daniel Altieri

[The poet Li Po] had been brought up in Shu, had roamed about the empire, had committed murder, squandered a fortune, taken wives, acquired concubines, and played with prostitutes; had demonstrated a heroic capacity for loyal friendship; had manifested a devout fondness of Taoist magic and alchemy; had excited people's jealousy and hatred by his drunken haughtiness; had even inspired widespread admiration for his exhilarating prose and even more exhilarating poetry. . . . The fame of this private individual, thought to be the incarnation of some immortal genius, reached the ears of Minghuang. Li Po was called to Ch'ang-an and given a post in the Han-lin Academy, a sort of private secretariat of His Majesty.

—*William Hung*

Then, endlessly, the House of Han blazed the war beacons.
The beacons are always burning—fighting and marching never ends.

Men die in the field, sword to sword;
The horses of the vanquished neigh piteously to Heaven.
Crows and hawks peck for human guts,
Carry them aloft in their beaks, dropping them to hang in the naked
branches of withered trees.
Captains and soldiers are only bloody smears upon the shrubs and
grass;
The general schemed in vain.
Know ye that the sword is a wicked thing
Which the wise man uses only if he must.

—Li Po, translated by Daniel Altieri

IT was not unusual on festival nights for the Yang sisters to glow more brightly than the Son of Heaven. But tonight, the night of the Festival of the Weaving Star, they glowed even brighter than the firmament they honored. And the heavens competed handsomely: Halfway between Ch'ang-an and the hot springs, the lights of the city far behind, the stars wheeled brilliantly in the vast Silver River which flowed across the moonless sky—the river across which the Cowherd star would go that night to join with the Weaving Girl star for the lovers' yearly tryst.

The three carriages that made up the Yangs' processional were followed along the final stretch of road that led to Lin-tong Village and the hot springs by the innumerable children of the royal households. The Residences of the Ten Mansions—the residences of the princes and princesses—had bequeathed on a most prosperous emperor the multitudinous blessing of children, grand-children, great-grandchildren, nephews and nieces; joined by the children of several hundred of the city's families and surrounded by a magnificent escort of palace livery, the entourage must have stretched nearly three li, its sparkling sea of flickering candles trailing light through the leafy elm tunnels of the hot springs' palace road. Carrying their candle lanterns, the children walked side by side, each little "weaving girl" paired with a little "cowherd."

Behind the Precious Consort's blue phoenix carriage, eight horses, their braided manes and tails dyed the variegated colors of the rainbow, pulled Yang Kuo-chung and the Lady of Kuo's splendid high coach. Whether they wanted it or not, they had become, for the people who watched and for the ladies who unrolled their embroidered works along the roadside in the ritual of the Festival of the Weaving Star, the earthly embodiment of the once-yearly ce-lestial lovers. And behind them, followed by the parade of children and can-dlelight, the ladies of Chin and Han rode in an equally elegant carriage, and tossed coins and jeweled hairpins from the rosewood and satin interior to the crowds that lined the way.

Would historians call it the era of the Yang-dominated court? And would they hold the Yangs responsible for everything that was to come? Yang Kuo-chung asked himself these questions as he rode along next to the Lady of Kuo, gazing out over the magical scene.

He was not in a good mood at all, but was doing his best to hide it. He felt gloomy and taciturn, distant and cynical, inured to all the lighthearted beauty flowing around him. He had been feeling this way since the night before, when he had made what he considered now to be a grievous error of judgment.

Yang Kuo-chung had tossed the I Ching sticks, something he had vowed never to do. And the hexagram that had come up had indicated that it had been a mistake to look into the future. Because the oracle had told him that there was no future—not a single changing line that might lift that hexagram up into some semblance of hope or light. Nothing! And he had been irritated with himself for indulging in what he considered to be seductive nonsense and then being unable to dismiss it when it turned out to be inauspicious. Fool, he told himself, you are in quite a bind now, are you not? Your wretched little effort to divine the future did not bring you good news, so now you seek to dismiss it all, to discredit it as rubbish. But you are unhappy and uncomfortable remembering those relentlessly unchanging lines, and now you look around uneasily, watching for signs . . .

As they got closer to the hot springs, disturbing memories that he associated with the place began to rise to the surface: the way the lights in his room had gone out on the night of the attempt on the Emperor's life; the cats yowling in the bushes; the voice that had addressed him out of the darkness, perfectly mimicking the Lady of Kuo. He slouched down into the cushions. And now a celebration underneath a huge sky blazing with stars. He had never been able to explain to anyone just what it was that he loathed and dreaded about the stars. It had to do with their icy, timeless indifference, he supposed, that made the lives of men, his own in particular, seem so puny, futile, and brief. Some people thought they were beautiful. To him, they were a nightly reminder of emptiness, nothingness . . .

"What is wrong with you, Cousin? You do not seem to be having fun tonight," the Lady of Kuo said with light irony.

"I am tired of festivals," he answered, drawing the curtain closed.

"Is it because you hate the stars and they hate you?" she asked. They both laughed then; she had broken through his mood. "May I offer my hand-some cousin the particularly simple solution of not looking upward tonight?"

"You will have to distract me," he said, playing at being a sullen child, teasing her a little, trying to cover his melancholy mood.

She said nothing, but took his hand and brought it down onto the soft satin of her inner thigh. No, he thought at first; not now. I have nothing to offer at this moment. But his body spoke differently. Arousal, sharp and sudden, against his will, pushed aside his gloom and reticence. His "old man" jerked, stiffening slightly, taking his breath. He looked down and watched it move: a life of its own. It jerked again, straightening itself, until it was pinned, hard and painful, pulling against the fabric of his trousers, his heart beginning to pound in his throat. A heavy, unpleasant burning spread from his groin through his chest. He wondered: have I no will of my own?

He wanted her. No, he wanted *it*. The act, separate from himself, separate from her. For one brief moment he tried to resist.

"Why now, Dear Cousin?" he whispered. But it was too late. She was already moving his hand upward along the cool flesh of her thigh until his fingertips caressed the silken hair, the velvet fold of her body.

"Because you are so distracted, my love, and because you will not talk to me about it. You have scarcely talked to me about anything for days. Weeks. You sit and brood. I cannot reach you."

Now she left his hand where she had put it and began to untie the front of her robes. His reluctance evaporated, leaving him consumed with impatience: the anxiety and despondency of recent days transformed itself now into pure desire—hungry, willful, demanding satisfaction.

She opened the silken blouse beneath her jackets. His "old man," as if it could grow any harder, strained between his legs; she leaned over onto him and pressed her breasts against his chest, at the same time forcing the fingers of his right hand to enter her. Now, her face close to his, she reached behind her head and removed the hairpins. Her hair spilled around them both like a curtain, and she moved so that the tip of his "old man" rubbed between her breasts; she changed her motion then so that she moved slowly from side to side, brushing his hardness with her soft flesh. She opened her legs again ever so slightly and with a small rotation allowed his fingers to go deeper into her.

He cupped his left hand behind her neck and brought her face down to his. He traced his tongue along the full red line of her lips and up into the hollows of her eyes, inhaling the child scent of her unrouged skin. She let him linger for a moment before pulling away; then she began to move up and down with a slow, deliberate motion while he kept his fingers still and rigid until her entire body shuddered with gentle paroxysms and she groaned, sucking her breath in, squeezing her eyes tightly shut and baring her teeth. He watched her face, fascinated, and waited for the gentle tremors to subside; then, slowly, gently, drew his fingers out.

She positioned her knees on either side of his lap, and with her eyes fixed on his own and her hair hanging loose around her face and shoulders, challenged him. Quickly, he opened his robes and undid the silk cord of his trousers, struggling awkwardly to bring them down below his knees in the close confines of the moving carriage. She bent down, and bringing the head of his "old man" into her mouth, inflicted a rush of unbearable pleasure on him that made him drop his head backward in surrender. Her tongue glided along the smooth velvet of his stalk, caressing the underside of the head with practiced delicacy. Then, abruptly, she raised herself, and with his fingers stretched nearly around her narrow waist, came down onto him, enveloping him in the warm, soft, moist folds of her gate. He breathed the richness of her hair and sank down, like a stone in dark water . . .

Is it because you hate the stars? How had she known what he was thinking? She had known, but had said nothing until just a few moments ago. But she did that a lot. For long periods of time, she would simply allow him to brood, saying nothing at all to him, almost as if she were being shy and diffident. But that was not it at all. What she did not say to him was as important as what she said. He was always "forgetting" this about her—and relearning it each time.

There was nothing about him, he knew, that could have remained a mystery from her for very long. He was a shallow pool to her. And yet he was always telling himself that she would understand something only if he told her.

But nothing escaped her. She had no opaqueness, no blindness to anything about him. He would go sometimes for days, or weeks, without telling her what was on his mind. And the Lady of Kuo would let him go, would ask no questions. Then, quite suddenly, usually when he was sunk in brooding and feeling quite isolated, she would break the silence in some way that she saw fit. And it would usually begin with her eyes and her touch. Everything that had been closed would open. And then, each time, he was again reminded of her loveliness, perfection, and comprehension—only to forget it again and fall despondently back into himself. Only to forget that she was always able to look directly into him. But never again, he told himself. He would never forget again. Never.

His mind and heart were calm, serene. The carriage rocked gently, reminding him of where he was and the throngs and the hundreds of children following the processional; the tinkling of cowbells and children's laughter brought him back. When he opened his eyes, the Lady of Kuo was gathering her hair back in one sweep and working it into a single braid. Her face was beaded with fine droplets of moisture like the dew on a leaf. She looked at him.

"Something happened to you last night," she said. "You went away for a long time without telling me where you were going. And when you came back . . . I have never seen you looking so bad."

He sighed. As usual, she had seen directly into him. He realized that he would have to confess everything. He looked back at her and ran his hand down the delicate line of her cheek and neck.

"I tossed the sticks last night," he said. He did not bother to cover his nakedness. He preferred it now. He pushed open the carriage shutters and let the cool air waft over his belly, damp with sweat, and his "old man," lying limp and spent against his thigh. It seemed to him that beyond the jolly noise of the processional, the singing, laughing, and tinkling of bells, there was a deep silence reaching into the hills and woods. He waited for her to speak; she said nothing for a long while.

"You?" she asked finally, politely incredulous.

"Yes," he replied. "I consulted the *I Ching*." He resolved now to hold nothing back. It was the passion they had just shared, the intimacy, that had dissolved his reticence.

"But why?"

"It was not entirely my own doing," he said, hearing immediately how absurd those words sounded. "How should I put it? It was a perverse temptation that I gave in to. I wanted to do it and didn't want to do it, all at the same time. So I did it." He looked out the window. "And now I regret it."

"This does not sound like you, Cousin," she said, tying a silk cord around the end of her braid and fussing with the loose strands of hair over her ears. He watched her feeling around among the satin pillows for the hairpins and ornaments she had discarded. He found a clasp and handed it to her.

"I have been thinking too much about the future. Wanting just a look at it. A glimpse. So I consulted the *I Ching,* telling myself that it was harmless, a parlor game, an amusement. That was my mistake. It was as if it were talking back to me, reminding me of the serious forces I toyed with."

"What did it tell you?" she prompted him.

"It confirmed what I already suspected. That we do not have a future."

"And who is *we,* Cousin? Do you mean the Yangs? You, me, and my sisters? Or do you mean just you and me?"

"No one has a future," he said, his words sounding flat and final to his own ears. He took hold of her hand, and in that moment she seemed so fragile. "Tonight, I cannot even bear to look at the eyes of those children that follow us, each one of them full of innocent hope. I feel as if we have betrayed them."

"Which hexagram did you encounter?" she asked quietly.

"It was the Po Hexagram. The 'Coming Apart.' There were no changing lines in the toss. And my intuition told me that I was not looking at some mere random grouping of lines. I *knew* that I was getting the glimpse of the future that I had asked for, that I was looking at the truth." He shook his head. "Five yin lines, supporting the sixth line, a yang line. The symbol of the weight of the roof pressing down on disintegrating walls. Do you see?" he whispered. "The roof. The north. The weight of the north. The House of

T'ang is collapsing, my dear Lady of Kuo." He looked helplessly at her face while he said it, and squeezed her hand tightly.

And she looked back at the intensity in his eyes, perfectly visible even in the dim interior light. And now the carriage wheels began to crunch on the gravel drive: they had arrived at the entrance to the hot springs grounds.

:: :

Peeking discreetly out from the curtains, Yang Kuo-chung saw that the processional carriages, theirs included, sat in the drive in a semicircle. Throngs of people, all holding candles, stood on the hot springs grounds, waiting. And when Precious Consort stepped down from her carriage, Yang Kuo-chung could see that Little Cousin was putting forth her sincerest effort tonight to play the role that they expected of her. To the adoring and worshipful crowds, she was their grand Queen Mother. And tonight everyone struggled for a glimpse of her divine beauty.

This was the Festival of the Weaving Star. Years in the planning, it was the fulfillment of Little Cousin's fondest fantasy: to preside over a festival of her own, to be the matriarch of a new egalitarian golden age—to be, for one night, a goddess. What more could there be for her? The night, the stars, the people, the grounds—everything belonged to her. The Emperor had relinquished the evening. They had talked about it a long time ago, following their reconciliation after the Plum Blossom incident. He was more than willing that she should have her own festival. After all, didn't he have his Thousand Autumns birthday celebrations? He had promised her that the presence of the Son of Heaven would not compete for her brilliance: he would stay away. It would be her night.

They had chosen the Festival of the Weaving Star for its passionate symbolism. Each year at this time, throughout the cities and villages of China, garden banquets were set, candles were lit, and perfumed incense was burned. Each able household rolled out its collective weavings under the night sky, and tiny boxes containing web-spinning spiders were passed among the women. And people, outdoors in the soft summer night, gave special attention to the contemplation of the stars, especially the wide Silver River which the mythical cowherd would have to cross in order to find his weaving girl. Trysts and dalliances, love, light, and magic were on the minds of the people who celebrated the festival.

The Precious Consort, in making the celebration her own, in leaving her mark on it, had ordered the hot springs gates opened to the common people for the night and the day to follow. And Yang Kuo-chung could see that she was making a supreme effort to live up to their expectations: Little Cousin was using all of her skills as a dancer and a pantomime player to make her role convincing. She glided across the lawns almost as if she did not walk, but floated, like a true goddess, like something freed from a fairy tale. And doubtless, she was aware of the splendid effect she was having.

Tonight, it was as if there were a tenth ritual office added to the nine imperial courts of the T'ang. Between the ceremonial functions of the Banqueting Court and the Court of Granaries and Parks, there now existed, because of her, for one night only, the Court of the Celestial Matriarch.

And in keeping with her new title, she wore a silk gown specially commissioned from the palace seamstresses: embroidered with the twelve animals of the duodenary cycle of the zodiac, the entire elegant menagerie set against a field of blue sky with braids of brilliant gold threads woven into the exquisite forms of spiraling and concentric stars. Her attendant, Hung-t'ao, trailed alongside her, awed and dazzled by her mistress's brilliance, willingly and wholeheartedly seduced, a handmaiden to a goddess.

It would all have been quite charming but for the fact that Yang Kuo-chung knew exactly how hard Little Cousin was working. The disaster of the Kao Mei festivities had robbed her. The harsh ugliness that had intruded on her fantasies had stayed with her, like an unwelcome guest who comes to one's home, settles in, puts his muddy feet up on the furniture, and shows no signs of leaving. He felt sad for her; he knew how real it had all been to her once. He knew, because he had shared the fantasy himself for a while. Hadn't he, when he first came to court, been just as susceptible to the notion that the Yangs had been singled out by the universe to live untouched lives as its favored darlings? And wasn't that, after all, the definition of royalty—that the universe craved to express its capacity for magic through a chosen few privileged beings? And they had all believed it: they had been those chosen ones.

But other laws of life were asserting themselves. The "Lucky Baby" had turned into something odious and menacing, and Li Lin-fu, the wily old lizard who kept him in check, was dying. What an exquisite paradox, Yang Kuo-chung reflected. Li Lin-fu, who himself had no use whatever for play and frivolity, was, in fact, the reason that they had been able to play at all. Li Lin-fu had held it all together: one frail, sick elderly man whose will of iron had already extended his life unnaturally. We fear and loathe him, Yang Kuo-chung reflected, but we are terrified at the thought that he will soon be gone. Contemplating the fact that he was to succeed him caused a hollow feeling around Yang Kuo-chung's heart and stomach.

He thought again of the discouraging hexagram and the reports that came in almost daily now about the deteriorating situations in both the northwest and the northeast. The territory lost to the Muslims had not been regained, and Hopei Province, a hotbed of secessionist uprisings, could soon be lost to the empire completely; then it would only be a matter of time until the others around it fell in succession. Li Lin-fu had recently dispatched An Lu-shan to return to his duties. Yang Kuo-chung had never believed that he would feel this way, but he took great comfort—like a little child whose big brother steps in to protect him from bullies—in knowing that General An Lu-shan was on his way back to the north to protect the empire. He reached for the Lady of Kuo's hand and held it tightly. She looked at him, and he saw that she knew his thoughts completely.

"Master Yang," she said, raising his hand to her lips, "there are as many interpretations of any given hexagram as there are people to read it. You are far too superstitious for your own good. As gullible as a peasant." She looked hard into his eyes. "As gullible as a poor illiterate peasant. Aren't those your own words? Your *exact* words?"

"A shallow pool," he said to her enigmatically, and kissed her.

He dared not think beyond tomorrow. Tonight, he would throw himself into Little Cousin's games. He understood the heavy burden of obligation that she carried in trying to recapture her fragile dream—not just for herself, but for the people pouring in through the gates, all hoping for just one look at the queen. He would do his best for her, and for all of them. Tonight, he would be a royal Yang.

The people were still coming, filling the lawns and gardens. No one wanted to miss out on the unique circumstance of a vast amount of free food and wine and a chance to roam the hallowed grounds, to breathe the same rarefied air as the celestial and mighty. This evening, they were released for the moment from the drab dinginess of their own lives, and they swarmed over the gardens east of the Nine Dragon Lake with a vengeance. Like a plague of locusts, Yang Kuo-chung thought ungenerously.

He expected that a few of the braver among them might even attempt a peek at the forbidden and sanctified western grounds, the domain of the Yangs. And those who made it past the guards might even find their way to his own hot springs apartments. And he decided at that moment that he would be more than willing to let them have it. In fact, let them have the whole bloody place: infernal bubbling springs, mountain, and all.

On a long stretch of level grass on the eastern side of the lake an imperial feast was being laid out on endless rows of tables by a thousand servants. And through a break in the crowds of people, Yang Kuo-chung glimpsed lights, moving slowly, close to the ground, over the garden hillock in front of the Nine Dragon Bridge: the simulated Silver River, Precious Consort's pride and joy, and her own invention for the occasion. And he knew that soon the consort's attendant would be coming for them, so that he and the Lady of Kuo could, for a few moments, act out the roles they had consented to play.

Well, he thought, I have promised to be a Yang tonight. I shall do it in grand style—as though it were my last opportunity. The Lady of Kuo looked at him, seeming to notice for the first time that he had not yet put his clothes back on.

"You should get dressed. Little Sister will be so terribly disappointed if you fail to appear. And I can assure you that she would find some way to blame *me*."

"I intend to appear," he said, and smiled at her. "Little Cousin will not be disappointed, and neither will you be!"

The Lady of Kuo raised her eyebrows as a knock sounded on the carriage door. He recognized Hung-t'ao's high little voice calling to them.

"Are the cowherd and the weaving girl ready to appear?" she asked.

Kuo looked at him again, then opened the carriage door and began to climb out. Yang Kuo-chung caught a glimpse of the face of the Precious Consort's attendant, beaming stupidly with earnest enthusiasm. He lunged forward and grabbed the Lady of Kuo around the waist, pulling her back into the carriage so that she fell across his naked lap. The weight of her body and the slippery feel of her silk gown were all he needed: he began to stiffen again.

"So soon, my love?" she asked.

"Since I am forced to play this role, my dear Lady of Kuo," he whispered into her hair, "I shall do it in the proper style of the Yangs. I shall do this poor, frustrated cowherd a bit of justice. I doubt that he goes to his once-yearly tryst with a limp member," he said, shifting her weight and pulling the remaining robes up over his head and kicking off his silk trousers so that he was completely naked. "Behold!" he said. "The cowherd during his last month of waiting!"

She looked down at his lap and laughed. Then she bent and caressed him with her tongue for just a moment, bringing him to full arousal.

"That should complete your costume," she said, and slid off his lap and out the door.

"Your cowherd is ready," he said, following her out the carriage door, naked and fully erect.

Hung-t'ao looked at Yang Kuo-chung and allowed her eyes to rest on his lower belly. She covered her mouth and giggled.

"Be careful, my dear," the Lady of Kuo said to the consort's attendant, "or he may decide to have you right here and now. My cousin takes what he wants when he wants it." Then she took his hand and pulled him across the gardens, through the parting crowd, and toward the Precious Consort's make-believe Silver River: ten thousand ancient, slow-moving tortoises, each carrying a burning candle on its shell.

The people were ecstatic at the sight of the royal couple. Children screamed and giggled, looking at the Very Grand High Minister Yang Kuo-chung naked and rampant; the men cheered and clapped and the women gasped with delight and shock. Hand in hand, the lovers picked their way through the flickering river of celestial light, the dignified tortoises looking like so many disgruntled old grandfathers.

On the far side of the tortoise-star river, Yang Kuo-chung lifted his cousin into his arms and carried her through the gauzy silk curtains at the doorway of a miniature pavilion and put her down onto a pile of soft, thick quilts and cushions.

Through the curtains they could see the Precious Consort atop her dais, the goddess of a celestial court ministering to her subjects—thousands, eating and drinking the great bounty of food and wine provided by the court in a grand act of public munificence, and the grounds open to all to roam freely, as people once did in the grand imperial hunting parks of an earlier age.

From behind the Precious Consort and high above the river of tortoise starlight, there issued the music of the spheres. The heavenly tune originated simultaneously in three parts from three identical pavilion platforms, their number the quintessential mirror of the triumvirate of Heaven, Earth, and Man. This, too, had been the Precious Consort's idea.

She had separated the Pear Garden Orchestra into three groups to perform compositions created especially for this festival night—melodies dedicated to the stars. Those instruments requiring breath—the *hsuan* and *sheng* pipes, and the *hsiao* flutes—were played at one pavilion; those which were plucked by the fingers—the *bi-pa* and the various *chin* lutes, were played at a second pavilion—and the percussive instruments—the weir drums, kettledrums, clappers, cymbals, and stone chimes were sounded from the third. The effect was unique and startling, Yang Kuo-chung thought. The melodies of the Pear Garden Orchestra surrounded them.

The music was rich and solemn, the registers high, the lines replete with embellishments and trills, the rhythmic pacing slow and languid and punctuated with dramatic percussive phrases. Sad, haunting, and evocative, he thought; the hollow vibrato of the flutes and pipes, lugubrious and solemn, repeated the motifs of the strings in the manner of an echo worn by distance and despondency. He imagined that the music was telling the tale of the eternal travels of the stars across the cold, empty dark of the night sky.

On the canopied bed, Yang Kuo-chung and the Lady of Kuo sipped wine and listened to the Pear Garden Orchestra perform. The music played through him. And whether it was the effect of the music or the irony of the frivolity around him, he felt his despondent mood returning. Though he was tempted to sink down into his melancholy, he decided that it would be best to conceal it. He wanted the Lady of Kuo to think that he had taken her advice to heart and gave the matter of the hexagram no more credence. That was the key, of course; if you did not give thoughts credence, they lost their hold.

Then, abruptly, the orchestra stopped playing. Only the drums, cymbals, and clappers continued, filling the night with anticipatory thunder and clamor. Something was about to happen. Resolving to enjoy it, or at least to appear as if he did, Yang Kuo-chung reached for the Lady of Kuo's hand under the quilt and smiled at her.

Now the huge brass gongs were struck. The deep metallic sound reverberated off the hills, causing the crowd to go quiet and turn their faces toward the Precious Consort's throne. The powerful sound must even have penetrated the consciousness of every last tortoise, Yang Kuo-chung imagined; he pushed his head out through the gauzy curtains as a small company of men made their way past them, followed by a line of servants, carts, wheelbarrows, and chests, approaching the Precious Consort's throne.

Yang Kuo-chung recognized some of the men leading the small processional. They were high-ranking but useless ministers, elderly men who had outlived the empty dignity of their titles, who had outlived almost any purpose whatsoever other than to play at these festivals. But then, perhaps, that was more useful than governing. Yang Kuo-chung could not help but think about the meaningless horde of titles that had collected on his own name—gnats on vinegar, the poet always said.

Tonight, these aged councillors, members of the five royal houses, brought offerings to the Queen of the Stars. Each of them was followed by an attending steward overseeing the delivery of his gift to the bottom of the Precious Consort's steps. Some of the gifts were rolled up to the base of the carpeted dais in small high-wheeled barrows, others were brought in chests borne on small litter racks.

The Precious Consort, the perfect attentive matriarch, sat high above the gifts laid at her feet. She smiled at the deferential ancient councillors as they backed away, nodding their heads incessantly to make up for the fact that they could no longer kneel or kowtow. Hung-t'ao, it seemed, was even more excited than her mistress over the prospect of the gifts. A steward stood by to read the inscripted slips of silk that accompanied each of the offerings.

Yang Kuo-chung and the Lady of Kuo did not speak, but the tacit understanding between them was plain enough. He knew that his mood had infected her; now she was trying to hide it from him. They watched in silence, holding hands under the quilt, communicating their thoughts through the pressure of their fingers, as the presentation was made to the Queen of the Stars.

The steward read the list of the offerings made in the name of the Emperor and the four major families—Yang, Hsueh, P'ei, and Su—allied by marriage to the imperial House of Li. Each gift was more exotic, rare, and unusual than the one before it, and with the announcement of each, Yang Kuo-chung noted, Little Cousin's ingenuous joy seemed to double. Her eyes grew wider, her gestures more animated, her joy and gratitude beamed from her face. For the adoring crowds who watched her, her happiness was real; but her cousin, watching from the privacy of the curtained pavilion, could see the subtle presence of sadness and worry around her mouth and eyes. She was a consummate performer; there was no doubting that.

The gifts were rare and exquisite indeed: a set of musical stone chimes made entirely of green *lan-t'ien* jade was assembled before her dais on an intricate stand of gold and silver inlay; a table was set before her with a display of rare Dragon Brains incense shaped into the most detailed forms of cicadas, worms, and delicately fashioned weaving spiders, the bodies supported on legs of finely spun gold wire. It occurred to Yang Kuo-chung that they could have dropped a sack of pig manure at her feet and she would have appeared just as pleased.

Then a ripple of merriment began to spread through the crowd. Heads were turning away from the spectacle of the gifts. Something invisible was moving toward the throne, the people stepping aside to form a clear pathway, laughing and craning their necks. Yang Kuo-chung and the Lady of Kuo stood up on their couch to try to see what was happening. All they could make out was a strange shape, covered in pure white silk, dangling from a pole raised high above the heads of the people. The mysterious object approached the throne.

"Let us through. Let us through!" an arrogant, high-pitched little voice cried. "Do not trample the grand councillor's celestial knight!" A diminutive figure stepped from the crowd into view on the terrace with its row of gift tables. He wore silken trousers, a long elaborate cape embroidered with the images of shooting stars and lunar crescents, and a wide-brimmed horsehair cap adorned with feathers atop his bulbous head. "Now go away! Remove yourselves! Shoo!" he cried, waving his stumpy arms at the old gift bearers and their servants. "You are boring the Queen of the Stars with your silly trinkets. Leave, leave, leave, leave, leave, leave. Make room for my voluptuous lady and her gift. Go now! Go! Go! Shoo!"

He jumped around the terrace, scattering the confused old councillors away from the dais, chasing after them comically, pretending to whip the backs of their legs to hurry them along. Then, with a grand gesture, he swished his great cape to the side, and dropped to one knee on the lowest step beneath the Precious Consort's throne. Behind him, Madame Li, dressed in a gown of pure white silk, pushed her way out of the crowd, followed by a servant who bore the silk-covered shape that dangled aloft from a slender bamboo pole. All eyes now shifted from the dwarf to her. Madame Li had the servant lower the object slowly and set it carefully on the step alongside the dwarf.

"May I join you, Master Yang?" came a voice from just outside the pavilion where Yang Kuo-chung and the Lady of Kuo watched the proceedings, startling them both. "You are with the lovely Lady of Kuo, I see. I am doubly delighted. You seem to occupy the best perch from which to see our little friend's spectacle. I have brought you some excellent mare's teat grape wine."

It took Yang Kuo-chung a moment to recognize the scruffy, ill-kempt figure standing deferentially to one side, waiting for an invitation to enter. Then he smiled and pulled the curtain wide.

"You must join us, Master Li Po. We insist."

The reclusive poet, dusty and bearded, had decided to show himself on this festival evening. Yang Kuo-chung was pleased and instantly cheered. This was an excellent distraction!

"It is always good to see a brilliant old reprobate like yourself," Yang Kuo-chung said as their guest, smelling of wine and sweat, stooped and entered the cozy interior. "I did not even know that you were in Ch'ang-an, Poet!"

The Lady of Kuo took the flask of wine from Li Po and helped him up to the couch, where the poet stretched himself out langorously on the pillows between them.

"My swollen old nose could sense this party two provinces away. Drink up!" he said, gesturing toward the flask. "I am already well down the golden road of pleasant inebriation. You two have a way to go before you catch up to me." He grinned at his host and hostess each in turn, regarding them with the penetrating eyes of the practiced habitual drinker. "Beautiful," he said admiringly. "How can you both stand to be so overpoweringly beautiful? Doesn't it sicken you after a while?"

"One becomes accustomed to it, Poet," Yang Kuo-chung answered, laughing, taking the flask from the Lady of Kuo.

"Watch the little man," the poet said, turning his attention to the scene before the throne. "We don't want to miss anything of his performance. I myself have great faith in any associate of Madame Li."

"I am certain you do, Poet." Yang Kuo-chung mused.

"So she is a friend of yours, too?" the Lady of Kuo asked.

"A most excellent friend," the poet answered. "I count among my finest friends more than a few of the city's brothel-keepers."

"And I am sure that your friendships are all of the higher sort," she joked.

"Some are very high indeed. Some are not so high. Others are what you would call very low. I am a well-rounded poet, eager for every kind of experience," he said, pausing to sip from the flask before passing it along to the Lady of Kuo. "But truly, my lady, I have been meaning to put those lustful urges aside to concentrate on my writings. But I have had about as much luck as a Taoist alchemist searching for his philosopher's stone." The poet raised his arms over his head and stretched his back until Yang Kuo-chung could hear the popping of his bones. "And where the pecker rules, wine is sure to follow. You may quote that, Master Yang. Tell my detractors that it comes from the great poet Li Po, that with your own ears you heard him speak those words." He pushed himself to a sitting position against a long straight pillow and stroked his wine-dribbled beard thoughtfully. Outside, in the meantime, the dwarf was doing an absurd ceremonial dance before unveiling his gift, capering and grimacing while the crowd roared its appreciation.

"But as I was saying, Madame Li and I go back a long way. In fact, she no longer charges me for the entertainments of her house. She exacts one cost only, and that is that I bathe before going to her ladies. Everything has its price."

Yang Kuo-chung clucked his tongue sympathetically.

"As a young man," the poet went on, "I was not quite as refined a fellow as I am now. You might think that I was always the gentleman you see before you." Li Po indicated his filthy robes. "But I will tell you," he whispered clandestinely, narrowing his eyes, a wild slyness around his mouth, "I once became quite involved with a certain man for Madame Li's sake. A person of highborn lineage." He looked outside again: the dwarf was still whirling in his dance, performing for the consort and the merry crowd. The poet adjusted his robes and raised himself to his elbows.

"It is a long story, but one that can be made quite simple. Needless to say, the details are a secret and must remain that way. The P'ing-k'ang ward constabulary would still, after so many years, love to solve that one. You see," he said, lowering his voice and bringing his head closer to them, "it is the story of a very high magistrate who had come, like so many, to make a visit to Madame Li's a routine for his bodily well-being. There was a particular girl there who appealed greatly to him. In fact, after a time, he only came to Madame Li's establishment for this one girl. It was some small thing that had captivated him—her eyes, the pouting of her lower lip. Suffice it to say that she excited him tremendously. Just the thought that he would soon see her caused all sorts of warm, delicious lust to burn in his chest. He could think of nothing else. His work suffered. He passed errors on to the clerks below him. He was a scholar, with the imperial Han Lin Academy of Letters. He even drafted words for the Emperor himself, on special occasions, in addition to enormous administrative duties.

"This magistrate began to visit Li's more and more frequently, so enamored was he of this young girl. His 'old man' would stick up, hidden beneath his robes, for hours in his office in sweet anticipation. But he was always secretive and cautious. You see, he was married. In fact, he had several wives. And there were no problems at home. All three women shared his house with great intimacy and good friendship. It was not wife number one who worried him, but wife number three. She was extremely jealous of any woman outside the family. She would have caused a great and very embarrassing disturbance in his household. Not very good for someone with such a high position in government." He accepted the flask from the Lady of Kuo and put it to his lips, then wiped his chin and passed the flask along with a ceremonial bow of his head.

"And then it began to be noticed that a stranger, a very dignified, older gentleman, was hanging about outside Li's mansion at odd hours. He could be seen just before dawn, for example, or perhaps late in the afternoon, sitting in a noble-looking carriage, peeking out from behind the curtains. On other occasions, he would be seen standing at the entrance to the drive with a burning look in his eyes. The inhabitants of the mansion were, needless to say, quite perturbed by their mysterious observer.

"Now, as you know, all the girls who work for Madame Li do so quite voluntarily. In fact, she is so kind and good-hearted that many have escaped their own rigid and overdisciplining families to enjoy the sweet pleasures of a life with Madame Li. They have everything they could ever want: freedom and dignity, and they are taught music and poetries, many acquiring the rare and difficult skills of learning to read—almost as well as you, my dear Lady of Kuo. They dine on the finest food, and dwell in a most beautiful house and garden. And all the girls are very fond of one another. It is an ideal situation. And there is one other thing, probably the most important consideration of all: none of these beauties need ever suffer the tyranny of one husband—the tedious chore and unrewarding predictability of submitting to his peculiar lusts and the nagging bitches of his mother's household.

"It seemed that the presence of the old noble keeping his vigil outside the mansion made one of the girls in particular very nervous. I am sure you can guess which one. Yes, the beauty with the pouting lip who ruled the heart of our other character, the magistrate. The nosy stalker with the angry eyes was, she finally admitted, her father. He had been looking for her for many years, ever since she had vanished from the house of her husband, having been married off conveniently and at a very tender age to another noble house. But she had detested her husband and the other females of the household. Being an independent and determined young thing, she had escaped her matrimony. Father found out, of course, that she had disappeared, but no one had any idea where she had gone off to. Eventually, he had begun to hear rumors: there was, it seemed, a beautiful young woman at Madame Li's whose description fit that of his daughter. But since he was fearful of going into Li's himself, lest he be found out, he could only aggravate his curiosity by wandering back and forth outside the gates."

Yang Kuo-chung and the Lady of Kuo were silent, captivated by the poet's tale. The crowd near the throne were clapping their hands in time to the music while Madame Li's dwarf whirled and strutted; the poet raised the flask to his lips and stared out at the lights, music, and people. Yang Kuo-chung feared that the poet had lost the thread of his story and that they would never learn what happened to the girl, her lover, and her angry father. He looked over at the Lady of Kuo, and the two of them watched the poet's profile anxiously while he took another swallow of wine. Yang Kuo-chung was just about to poke him in the ribs to get him talking again when he broke his silence.

"The young beauty became very frightened that she would be dragged away from her pleasant life and disgraced in the home of her husband—a husband she despised and wished never to see again. Or that she would be returned to her father's home and made a prisoner. So she did the only thing she could do—she poured out her heart to her roguish admirer from the Han Lin Academy. Madame Li was disturbed, too, by the presence of the old noble outside the gates. The man surely had the influence to close her down. Our scholar-magistrate, of course, obsessed with love and lust for the young girl, would do anything to protect her and ensure her happiness. So he told them not to worry, that he would take care of the situation. Can you guess what he did?" the poet said, looking craftily from one to the other of his listeners, who shook their heads eagerly.

"It was very simple," he whispered. "He accosted the meddling old noble on some pretext, killed him, and dragged his body into an alley in a quarter of the city where the residents are not known for their kindness and hospitality. Of course, it was generally believed that the murder was a robbery. The usual. But one member of the investigating tribunal for that ward did not seem to accept that decision. And this shrewd and assiduous old investigator would have found me out if my otherwise bad reputation as something of a carouser had not got me removed from office. I left Ch'ang-an just in time. I was not suspected." He leaned back triumphantly.

"So it was you, Poet," said Yang Kuo-chung. "The love-struck magistrate. Do you realize what you have just done? You have confessed murder to a high-ranking government official. What if I were to turn you in, you old scoundrel?"

The poet laughed and looked Yang Kuo-chung in the eye.

"I told you the story because I know who you are, Yang Kuo-chung. You are a rogue and a romantic, deep in your soul, before you are anything else. You have no intention of turning me in. You are too fond of a good story. And as for the Lady of Kuo," he said, turning and looking at her, "I would trust her with my life. She knows that the man I killed was old. He had already lived a full life and was about to make terrible trouble for a beautiful young creature who was just beginning to enjoy her own life. What choice did I have, eh?"

"None at all," she said. "I would have done the same thing myself.

Besides, there is nothing like a beautiful tale of love to make me weep." She pretended to wipe tears from her eyes.

"Ah, love . . ." Yang Kuo-chung took the flask. "The things we do in its name."

And though the tone of their conversation was one of playful banter, the poet's story, masterfully told and intensely real, had a profound effect on Yang Kuo-chung. He understood now what was at the heart of his melancholia, his vague feelings of dread whenever he thought of the empty stars or the ancient, insidious hot springs. He looked at the Lady of Kuo as she laughed and jested with their guest. It was so simple, but he had never quite been able to articulate it to himself until the poet's words revealed the true source of his own despair: death. But not just death itself; rather, it was the thought that he could not love her from beyond the grave.

On the Precious Consort's terrace, the dwarf had finished his dance and was preparing to unveil the gift. With a deep bow and a flourish, he pulled the silk aside and stood hanging his head humbly. This time the consort's exclamations of delight were real: a beautiful cage of polished white ivory lattice sat revealed on the step below the throne; inside the cage was a magnificent pure white jungle parrot.

The dwarf swept up his sparkling cape of moons and comets, and rushed over to where Madame Li stood.

"Tell the Queen of the Stars what the 'Snow-Clothed Lady' can do, my sweet love-thighs," he cried, reaching his arms around Madame Li, caressing her buttocks with his hands, and pressing the side of his face into her belly, the very tip of his plumed cap standing no higher than her ribs. No sooner had he hugged her than he pushed himself away and looked down at the bulge in his trousers. "For shame," he said, shaking a scolding finger at his errant member. "This is no time to stand up and demand attention. Have you no manners?" The people watching were delighted, and the poet, sitting next to Yang Kuo-chung, threw his head back and guffawed his appreciation.

"Foolish little ogre," Madame Li said. "But you tell the queen yourself what the white-gowned Lady Parrot does."

The dwarf drew himself up with great dignity and addressed the Precious Consort ceremoniously.

"This magnificent bird from the torrid jungles of Annam can speak as clearly as you or I. She can even chant great poetries, my precious Queen of the Stars!" He picked the cage up and ascended the steps, then set it down again directly at the consort's feet. "She knows everything there is to know about the stars," he said. "Ask her a question!" he invited. Then he leaned forward and spoke softly, conspiratorially. "You must mention the word 'stars' when you phrase your question."

The consort, her face glowing, closed her eyes and thought for a moment.

Then she looked at the parrot and spoke, enunciating each word with care while the dwarf gestured for silence.

"Tell me, my sweet White-Clothed Lady. Why are there stars in the sky?"

The parrot turned its head sideways and up, looking at her with one reddish eye. It brought a foot up off the perch and scratched its face and head and nibbled on its toes; then it stretched its wings and, emitting small reptilian croaking noises from deep in its throat, began to preen its glistening white feathers. It looked around at the crowd, then whetted its beak on the perch like sharpening a knife.

Precious Consort looked disappointed. She turned toward the dwarf as if she were about to say something, but he raised a stubby finger to his lips. Not a sound came from the crowd around the throne. The bird turned once, stepping around on its perch, then fluttered its wings and eyed the dwarf with its impertinent sideways glance. Then it opened its beak and screeched:

> "If Heaven itself did not love wine . . .
> Then why would a Wine Star shine from the sky!"

The poet, hearing the verse, was seized by a fit of snorting laughter, his shoulders heaving with mirth inside the tiny pavilion while Yang Kuo-chung and the Lady of Kuo smiled quizzically at one another. Having said her piece, the White-Clothed Lady swung upside down, and hanging from her perch by one foot, mumbled some private words to herself. The consort rose from her seat and extended her arms toward the dwarf and Madame Li.

"Is our Queen of the Stars pleased with her gift?" The dwarf asked, taking hold of the Precious Consort's hand and hopping up and down, making her laugh.

"I am delighted, my little man," The consort said. "I am most grateful."

"And I taught her myself!" the dwarf said. "But it was my sweet love, with such an eye for rare birds, who found her at our favorite aviary." He nodded affectionately toward Madame Li. "Her eye for birds is nearly as good as her eye for men! And the couplet that the Snow-Clothed Lady sings is a gift from our great friend, the master poet Li Po!"

Inside the pavilion, the poet shrugged apologetically at his friends and took another drink.

"I am honored by your presence and the great sacrifice of time and patience that went into your gift," the consort said. "I thank you!"

"Oh, but the Snow-Clothed Lady is hardly the *real* gift, my Queen of the Stars," the dwarf declared. "Tonight she is but my messenger, my runner, my intermediary, my mere drafter of memorials to the throne. The bird," he now stated almost disdainfully, "only serves to *qualify* the stars. I, on the other hand, come to *quantify* them." He paused for effect, putting a dignified expression on his countenance. "I am the grand councillor's emissary to the heavens." He bowed deeply.

"Master Li Lin-fu?" the Precious Consort asked, slightly bewildered. "Our chief minister has sent *you*?"

"Alas, our grand councillor regrets that he could not join this celebration in person, what with the stars being something of a favorite subject with him." The dwarf put on a sad face then. "But he is not well this night. His physician has ordered that he stay in his bed and regain his strength. However," he said, brightening, "he wishes to assure us and all the good people whom he serves that he will soon be up and about! And until then, he has set out for us a splendiferous, strange, and befuddling assortment of devices representative of his great and incomprehensible genius!" He indicated the far corner of the terrace, where eight or so burly servants grunted under the weight of something they carried, something large with an indefinable shape, shrouded in silk. They set the object down with infinite care. "With these devices, we shall be able to observe the stars, those careening strumpets of the sky, with wondrous precision!"

The mention of the chief minister's name quickly changed the mood of the proceedings. Where people had been laughing and cavorting, they were now quiet and attentive.

Yang Kuo-chung turned and looked at the poet. Had he known about this gift from the chief minister? The poet returned a perplexed look that said that he was as surprised as anybody.

But the dwarf, master showman that he was, was not about to let the crowd become too solemn. Sweeping his cape aside and bowing toward the people, he pulled the cord of his little trousers, causing them to drop like the curtain at a puppet show, and presented his naked buttocks to the consort. Wild delight swept through the crowd again. You are indeed a master, Little Man, Yang Kuo-chung thought with admiration.

"I have been honored tonight to be the councillor's noble gauge. On my ass, the rings of the armillary sphere are represented in the form of a painted diagram so that we may better appreciate the councillor's gift. On this cheek," he pointed with one finger behind him, "is the calibrated Gauge of the Yellow Road, helpful in calculating the dark augury of eclipses. On the other," he said, moving his finger over, "the Gauge of the Enveloping Sky. Study them well, my queen!" Then he turned, gave the crowd a brief glimpse of the tattoolike markings, and deftly raised his trousers up again.

He bowed to the consort, turned and bowed again to the people, and strutted comically down the steps; when he was nearly at the bottom, he leapt to the terrace, raced toward Madame Li, and flung himself into her arms.

"Over there," he cried, pointing to the corner of the terrace where servants had removed the cloth covering, revealing a strange apparatus made up of tubes, globes, concentric metal rings, and calibrated rods, all affixed to a wooden platform, the lantern-light playing mysteriously on its parts. "The grand councillor's gift to the Queen of the Stars. Tonight, you shall observe the multitudinous denizens of our crowded heavens. And you shall bear witness to the return of the unfilial son." The dwarf disengaged himself from Madame Li, spun around, and opened his arms to the people in a wide and eloquent gesture of supplication.

"These devices are the grand councillor's invitation to survey the heavens, to witness the mighty celestial dance, and to welcome the wanderer's return. For it is now that the great Red Star comet comes back from its trek through the heavens to grace our sky. We cannot all look through the councillor's sighting tube, but we may observe the heavens vigilantly with our eyes. But it will be necessary to extinguish the lights: the beautiful paper lanterns, the candles in your hands, and the ones that ride the backs of the tortoises. They must all be put out. Poof! It is arrogant for us to compete with the lights of heaven."

Already, a hundred servants were at work extinguishing every last candle and lamp. The people blew out the ones they carried, and the grounds of the hot springs were quickly enveloped in darkness. The Lady of Kuo reached up and turned down the small lantern inside their pavilion.

The utter blackness made the stars overhead seem to blaze with new intensity. The people, their eyes raised to the night sky, grew quiet and contemplative. Yang Kuo-chung, reaching behind the poet between them, again found the Lady of Kuo's hand. The dwarf spoke, a disembodied voice in the dark.

"A beautiful flaming Red Star comet returns to our sky from where, you ask? Only the grand councillor knows. But it has flagged its bushy tail of swarming flames across the constellations: passing over Wu-chu-hou, it then crossed Ho-shu, and since passing through the constellation of Hsuan-yuan and T'ai-wei, it arced in an easterly direction, trespassing against Tz'u-fei, Ch'ang-ch'iu, Pei-tou and Saturn, penetrating, at last, the region of Tzu-wei and Ta-huo. And now, the Red Star comes, in a most timely fashion, to join our Weaving Girl Star and our Cowherd in T'ien-ho, our heavenly Silver River! Come, my queen," he said, the sound of his voice moving toward the consort's throne. "Let me take your hand and lead you to the sighting tube so that you may look upon your royal visitor!"

Royal visitor, indeed, thought Yang Kuo-chung. The poet and the Lady of Kuo were, he knew, enjoying the flight of fancy. But for him, the dwarf's words served only to remind him of the desperate game he had played with An Lu-shan in presenting his "dream" of the red comet, and of the icy, indifferent, infinite nothingness that looked down on the earth and on their lives. He groped for the flask of grape wine that the poet had brought with him.

"To the stars," he muttered, taking a drink.

: :

Music from the festival drifted up through Li Lin-fu's open windows. It had gone on all night and continued into the morning. He was hearing things in it that he, a musician all of his life, had never heard before. The music, he understood, was life receding from him, as indifferent to his existence as if he were already dead. The message it carried was clear: in case you ever doubted it, know that the world will continue after you are gone. When your ears have turned to stone and dust, the music will still play, for other ears.

Li Lin-fu had thought that he understood death. He had seen it in every form and had pondered it as thoroughly as a man possibly could, or so he believed. And for the last several years he had accepted that he was going to die sooner than was convenient. But the distant music rising from the hot springs grounds, plaintive and festive, melancholy and rejoicing all at once, made him grasp the fact of his own imminent death with a new intimacy that forced his startled eyes open.

He had been drifting. Like a man asleep in a boat that approaches the rim of a waterfall, he had very nearly gone over. He kicked the sweat-soaked bedclothes from his body and tried to raise himself up on one arm. The attendants immediately rushed to his side. A damp cloth was pressed to his forehead; supporting hands helped prop him up, and the silk coverlet was quickly pulled back over him. Irritably, he fended off their ministrations and focused on the haggard face of the physician, who stood, clasping and unclasping his fingers, looking down on the chief minister.

"This is wrong," Li Lin-fu said to the anxious little man. "I cannot die yet. There is too much work to do." He tried to rise, to climb out of the bed. To stay in the bed was to lie down in Death's arms. If he could just get away from the bed, he thought, he could get away from Death.

The physician jumped forward.

"Chief Minister, please! I beg of you! You are taxing yourself dreadfully!" He put his hands on his patient's shoulders and pushed him back down. Li Lin-fu found that he had no strength to resist, and collapsed into the rumpled linens. He put his hand onto the physician's arm and gripped it tightly.

"Why am I dying, Physician?" he asked, intently searching the other's face. "Why?"

"We all must die eventually," the physician answered weakly. "A physician is not a god."

"And do physicians die, too?" Li Lin-fu asked.

"Most certainly, Chief Minister," the man answered.

"And you. When will you die? How many years do you give your-self?"

"I do not presume to make such calculations, Chief Minister."

"But what do you *feel*?" Li Lin-fu persisted. "And don't tell me that you could die tomorrow. Tell me what you *intuit*. What you *know*. Fifteen years? Twenty? Twenty-five?" The physician looked almost embarrassed. Li Lin-fu could see that the man enjoyed the luxury of a certain knowledge of many solid years in front of him. "Twenty-five years? Thirty?" he pressed him.

"Well," the physician said reluctantly, "I am fifty-five years old now. My mother is seventy-five, and my father is eighty-seven."

"Thirty years," Li Lin-fu said. "You are seeing a good thirty years between you and death. Why, that is practically like being immortal," he said with envy. He tightened his fingers on the physician's arm. "You must give me a few of those years. I am warning you, Physician. Do not let me die. If you do, your own time will be considerably shortened. You can expect to follow me very, very soon. Do you understand?"

"Chief Minister," the physician said unhappily, "I believe that I have already lengthened your life. If not for my ministrations, you would have been dead five years ago."

Li Lin-fu relaxed his grip on the man's arm.

"That is perfectly true. Therefore, I know that you have the ability to give me more time. Three more years, Physician. Give me three years, and it will seem like one hundred to me. That is a reasonable request, is it not? I am not asking for thirty years. Just three!"

The physician's helpless, frightened expression made it plain that to ask for even three weeks, or three days, was to strain the limits of possibility. Summoning his strength, Li Lin-fu again attempted to throw off the bed-clothes.

"Help me rise," he ordered the physician and the attendants. "I must walk. A man dies lying down. Not when he is walking."

"Chief Minister," the physician begged, as if he were about to burst into tears. "You cannot. You must not!"

"Take my arms," Li Lin-fu said to the attendants, who had no choice but to obey him. "Pull me to the edge of the bed. Help me stand."

While the physician hung back, fluttering his hands in useless gestures of horrified disapproval, the two attendants lifted Li Lin-fu as easily as if he were a child. They suspended him between them, his arms over their shoulders.

"Now walk," Li Lin-fu ordered.

Slowly, they advanced across the room, the chief minister moving his legs beneath him, his feet barely touching the floor.

"The balcony," he said then.

They walked him out into the sweet morning air. He had them stand at the railing so that he could look down on the grounds across the steep woods and the field that separated him from the rest of the complex of hot springs pavilions, pools, and apartments. The graceful, curving roofs showing through the trectops here and there, and the music rising, the notes seeming to converge with the swooping and flitting of a cloud of blackbirds from tree to tree, were to him the tenuous landscape of a dream from which he was about to awake.

Awake to what? What world was he about to open his eyes to? A fine sweat, chilled by the cool breeze, stood on his forehead. The last few nights he had felt himself descending with sleep into dark, terrifying places, where moving, predatory figures, as yet unidentified and undefined, prowled restlessly. And he had known that it was he that they were looking for: They were waiting for him to come and join them in their world.

"Take me back inside," he ordered the attendants.

The physician hovered while Li Lin-fu had himself lowered into a chair.

The Chief Minister raised his eyes. "Physician," he said quietly, imperatively, shaking his head. "Do not let me die. Do not allow it."

"I have done all I can do," the man replied sorrowfully, raising his hands in a gesture of despair and resignation. "I can do no more. I am only a man. I am not a magician."

Not a magician? Li Lin-fu continued to fix the physician with his eyes while an idea, formed of his desperation and his fierce intent, crept into a corner of his mind. Was there one more possibility? Was there?

"My daughter," he said. "Bring my daughter to me, now."

The physician turned to one of the attendants, who was out the door in an instant. The girl was close by; Li Lin-fu had had her brought to the hot springs to be near him, in case he might be in need of her assistance. She was only a few rooms away. The physician, obviously believing that Li Lin-fu was calling for his daughter because he was about to breathe his last breath, fell to his knees before the chair.

"Spare me, Chief Minister," he implored. "I have served you as well as I could. No one could have served you better. I gave you years! Please leave me with my life!"

But Li Lin-fu was not listening to the physician. He was looking over the man's abjectly bowed head and into the eyes of his daughter, who stood in the doorway holding her small lap writing desk and her box of brushes and inks. He smiled with pride and pleasure. She always anticipated his needs; he had scarcely to ask.

"Get up. Leave us," he said brusquely to the physician.

"You should return to your bed," the man said, scrambling to his feet. "You should keep your chest covered and warm. You should . . ."

"Leave us," Li Lin-fu said again, his voice weak but still commanding.

The physician backed from the room, then turned and scurried away while the girl looked quizzically at her father. She sat, and arranged her writing desk, paper, and implements before her.

"Father needs you to write a letter for him, my dear." He sat for a moment, gathering his thoughts. His daughter, now a serious young woman, no longer a child, waited with her brush poised over the paper. "The letter is to our August Son of Heaven, Emperor Minghuang."

Her brush touched the page and the characters flowed. As easy as breathing, he thought, watching with admiration.

::

The dwarf rode on the poet's back, clinging to his shoulders, his two stumpy legs supported by the poet's arms. He lashed at the poet with an imaginary whip while the poet whinnied, bucked, snorted, pawed the ground, and galloped in circles in the consort's private gardens to the guests' howls of laughter.

"I am late for the battle," the dwarf cried. "My army has left without me! Oh, woe! Oh, dear! Whatever shall I do? Where is my army? Where is the battle? Tell me, Horse!"

"I know where the battle is, Master," the "horse" replied. "but I have decided not to tell you."

"Bad horse!" the "general" cried, lashing anew with his whip and kicking with his heels into his mount's flanks. "We will be laughed at if we do not go to the battle! We will be disgraced!"

"And we will be killed if we do!" cried the horse. "You may prefer death to being laughed at, because you are a man. But I am a horse. I care nothing for your battles!" With that, he ceased his bucking and galloping and stood still, as if seized by an idea. "I must tell the other horses," he said thoughtfully.

"Tell them what?" the little general cried.

"That the time has come! No more will horses die in men's battles! Let them gallop to their deaths on their own legs! Let them die, if that is what pleases them! But we horses have had quite enough!"

"Impertinent beast!" the general cried. "How dare you disobey me! I am your master!"

Slowly, the horse turned his head around and peered at his rider. An incredulous look came onto his face.

"Why, you are really rather small! How is it that I never noticed it before? And what are you doing on my back?"

The guests shrieked with hilarity.

"I am not small!" the general said with a nervous look, rolling his eyes at his audience and trying to make his voice sound deep and gruff. "I am big. Bigger than you! Now take me to the battle!"

"Let me get a good look at you," the horse said, craning his neck and moving in a tight circle. "Why, you are nothing! Nothing at all!"

"I am your master!" the general cried.

"You are nothing!" the horse cried. "I must share my discovery with the other horses! I am going right now! And I am taking you with me. You will answer to the horses for the crimes of all men!"

"Let me down!" the general howled in terror.

"I will not! We are going!"

And the horse whinnied and bucked, then galloped at top speed down the steps and along the path that led to the woods and fields, the pitiful wails of his rider trailing along behind him. The guests watched them disappear over a small hill. They laughed, the appreciative tears standing in their eyes. This was a fine party indeed!

: :

The poet ran until he was certain that they were out of sight of the guests. He stopped in the tall grass, knelt, and allowed his rider to dismount. Then he leaned against a tree and caught his breath.

"You may be small, my friend, but you are solid. You have the weight of a full-grown man."

"I am a full-grown man, Poet," the dwarf replied, straightening his clothing. "I have the same quantity of flesh and bone as you do. It is merely compressed into a more compact form. But it is all there."

"And I am sure that you believe yourself to be some superior form of man," the poet said, beginning to walk toward the woods with the dwarf behind him.

"We are an ancient and superior race, it is true, Poet," the dwarf said. "But we do not flaunt the fact. We are dedicated to study and service. Therefore, we are careful to allow you large ones to believe in your own superiority. It is rather the converse of the way men control horses. The man, who is small, creates the belief in the horse that he is larger, more powerful than the horse, and through that illusion, gains mastery over the beast. We, as dwarves, allow you, the large ones, to believe that your greater stature is indicative of your general superiority in all things and, through that illusion, we gain mastery over you."

"So that is how you do it," the poet laughed. "You should not be telling me this. Like the horse who discovers that his rider is puny and powerless, if I know the secret of your mastery, you may lose it."

"You will never stop believing in your own superiority, Poet," the dwarf declared. "I have nothing to worry about."

"You have only to demonstrate my inferiority to me, and I will concede," the poet replied.

"I prefer to allow you your illusion."

"You are most generous."

"Not generous, Poet; merely practical."

Talking steadily, they passed from the tall grass of the field into the shade of the woods and followed a trail through the trees. It was the afternoon after the night of the Festival of the Weaving Star, a fine, clear, hot day. The walk in no way compromised their inclination to talk; they were still talking when they approached a clearing where a stream fed a small forest pond. Ming Wu, perched on a rock, was looking down into the water when the poet and the dwarf stepped into the clearing. Without looking up at them, she raised a silencing hand. Politely, they lowered their voices to whispers while they found comfortable places to sit: the poet on a patch of soft moss, the dwarf on the trunk of a fallen tree.

The water where Ming Wu directed her attention was still, unrippled by any breeze or disturbance. Shafts of sunlight penetrated the depths, revealing irregular forms of rocks and sunken branches resting on the floor of the pool, shrouded in an even, velvety covering of brownish-gold silt. Long-legged insects hurried this way and that on the smooth plane of the water's surface.

Ming Wu spoke without looking up.

"A perfect world," she remarked.

"Send me there, Ming Wu," the dwarf said. "I am ready."

"Be sure that you really want what you ask for, because Ming Wu can easily accommodate you!" She raised her eyes from the pool as she spoke and looked at him with a wicked smile.

"He wants it," the poet said. "He has grown weary of cavorting between the thighs of his mistress."

"It is not that I have grown weary of it," he corrected the poet. "It is simply that I have learned all that I can learn there. And of course, as the events of the next several years unfold, I wish to have a different perspective."

"The world through the eyes of one of my friends here," Ming Wu said, looking down again at insects on the surface of the forest pool, "should provide a different enough perspective."

"I have experienced the time of peace and prosperity as a wealthy fool," the dwarf said. "I shall experience the time of pain and upheaval as someone else entirely. I shall descend to the depths of society in the great city; when Ch'ang-an writhes in agony under thousands of marching feet, I, too, shall feel those feet marching across my own back." He paused. "I shall be deaf and dumb, penniless and despised."

"I have a better idea," the poet said. "Rather than deaf and dumb, have instead a laughable impediment in your speech. You will be more despised and reviled that way. Imagine it: a penniless dwarf who drools and stutters."

"Oh, an excellent suggestion," the dwarf said happily. "Not only will I have to endure the ridicule of my own countrymen, the citizens of Ch'ang-an, but think of the disdain and contempt the outlanders will heap on me! The capricious cruelty that they will surely subject me to! The pain, the humiliation, the danger. It will be most instructive, and a most valuable addition to my cyclopedia of knowledge!"

"And you, Poet," Ming Wu said, turning her attention from the tiny world of the denizens of the forest pool. "Where will you go?"

"I will be leaving the city, of course. The dwarf may feel the need to be instructed by human folly, but I am afraid I have seen quite enough. My education is complete. I will be content to situate myself in the mountains and wait for the flotsam, the ragged stray edges of it all, that will find me even there. And as a dutiful poet, I shall try to tell the world what I see and feel, knowing all the while that they do not care, do not listen, do not ever learn." He laughed. "And I intend, naturally, to stay drunk." He looked at the dwarf then. "But before I leave the city, I shall write a poem and deliver it to your mistress, Madame Li. She will be bereft at your sudden departure, drowning in her own tears."

"Yes," the dwarf agreed. "She will be. And she will be taken completely by surprise by the depth and ferocity of her feelings. It has not yet occurred to her that she loves me. What will you say to her, Poet?"

"I will console her. I will tell her one of her own favorite stories, and I will make you the hero of it."

" 'The Slippers of the Giantess'!" the dwarf cried happily. "It is her favorite story. She heard it from her ladyfriends, the Yang sisters. They heard it from a merchant from whom the giantess's father used to buy specially made finery for his daughter. The giantess had died before the slippers could be delivered, and the merchant kept them. He showed them the shoes one day. Graceful, embroidered, silken shoes made for a woman half again as tall as the tallest man! Shoes that would flap on the feet of the most splay-footed, hulking brute of a farm boy! Oh, the exquisite poignancy! Oh, the pathos!"

"Oh, the sentimental rubbish!" Ming Wu snorted.

"Hush, you old cynic," the poet answered. "It is a perfect story, Dwarf. I shall call the poem 'The Pity of Things.' It shall be a poem about a gallant dwarf, a tiny knight, who goes and becomes the lover of the lonely giantess. He is inspired to write the poem to her slippers one day when he sees them sitting empty under her bed. Little does he know that very soon the slippers will be empty forever . . . in his eyes, the giantess becomes the most delicate, fragile, diminutive, and dainty of women. And in her eyes—"

". . . he is a giant of a man!" the dwarf interjected delightedly. "Her lord and master! Her protector! Oh, Poet. You are a genius. 'The Pity of Things.' My Madame Li will read the poem, and she will cry the sweetest tears. She will go into a dream. And when she awakes, she will be sad because I am gone, but perfectly comforted. And *I* will be free to pursue my work."

"I wonder what Ming Wu will do?" the poet asked the dwarf.

The old woman made a contemptuous sound in her nose.

"Don't expect me to leave. They can do as they wish; they cannot disturb me. Come back in one hundred years, and you will find me right here on this rock."

The three sat in contemplative silence for some moments. Sounds of merriment, faint and irrelevant, murmured in the distance.

"Desperate exuberance," the poet remarked.

"Hush, Old Cynic," the dwarf said, causing the poet to smile.

"And yet," Ming Wu continued, "there is one who looks upon our little queen's party with the eyes of a hungry ghost, as if it were life itself—though he is not, strictly speaking, dead. Not quite." She smiled at her friends. "And I have the honor of attending him this evening. Can you imagine it? He thinks old Ming Wu will pull him from the bony embrace of Death at the last moment! Look," she said, taking a folded piece of paper from her sleeve. "A letter written to the Emperor, begging the Imperial Father to send me to him. Listen!" She unfolded the paper and spread it on the rock. " '. . . It is not for myself that I ask,' " she read, her voice quavering, mimicking deadly fear, " 'but for the empire. My good physician has exhausted every means at his disposal. I have never in my life left any work half-completed and simply walked away. For me to die now would be for me to abandon my work, to abandon the empire in the hour of her greatest need . . .' "

"The chief minister looks into the abyss," the poet said, "and finds it not to his liking."

"I am acquainted with the chief minister," the dwarf said. "A most fascinating man. From what I know of him, it is not surprising that he should be . . . shall we say . . . *reluctant* to leave his stronghold. I would imagine that he is quite apprehensive about those whom he believes await him most eagerly on the other side."

While the dwarf spoke, Ming Wu was carefully folding the paper into the shape of a little boat; when she finished, she leaned over the water, set the paper boat on the surface, and blew on it, sending the delicate craft twirling out into the middle of the still forest pool. There was a great commotion among the water striders; they darted back and forth and in and around one another in frantic response to the vibrational disturbance in their midst.

"I will leave it up to you, my friends," Ming Wu said, watching the little boat.

The dwarf sighed. "I think it would be more educational for him to experience death now than to postpone it. He has already put it off too long, I fear."

"I would say let him live forever—but always with the dread and full expectation that he will die tomorrow. But since I know what you have already decided," the poet said to Ming Wu, "and since I have already made my plans to leave the city, then I must agree with our wise dwarf."

"Though I daresay he is going to be surprised," Ming Wu said, rising to her feet, "when he finds out what is actually awaiting him."

: :

I have been looking for you, Li Lin-fu's father said without turning around. Li Lin-fu regarded the odious familiarity of the old man's back; the narrow, sloping shoulders, and the head that wagged as he talked. I always hated you, Li Lin-fu said silently, and I still do.

Thoughts are like words here, the old man said. I hear what you are thinking as plainly as if you were speaking. Then why is it, Li Lin-fu asked, that I cannot hear *your* thoughts? Because I have been here much longer, his father said. A smell of sweetish smoke seemed to permeate the atmosphere. His father turned slightly, so that the outline of his cheek and brow was presented, but no more, and sat in an attitude of supercilious expectation. Well, he said. I am waiting. Waiting for what? Li Lin-fu asked, though he knew perfectly well.

Waiting for your explanation.

Li Lin-fu did not answer, but stood fidgeting and desperate, hearing his father's breath whistling in his nose.

Come, come, boy, the old man said. I am sure you had some good reason for what you did. I am willing to hear your story. I will even help you a bit by stimulating your memory. Do you recall my death? You continued your work, as if nothing at all had happened. No requisite mourning period, no pilgrimages to my tomb. My passing was of no more consequence than that of an obscure servant. Do you know the loneliness and disgrace of being dead and unmourned? Do you know the pain? The living must make a sacrifice to ensure that the dead do not feel that pain, and you did not do it for me, your own father.

You hated me, Li Lin-fu said, his voice weak and barely audible. You tried to kill me when I was an infant because you were ashamed of me. Because I was ugly.

And the family temple, boy, the old man went on, ignoring him. The family temple which you abandoned, boarded up, and allowed to become a habitat of lizards and owls. The altar with my name on it in the shrine, where no candle was lit, no incense burned! That you allowed to become encrusted with the excrement of vermin! I am most eager to hear your story, boy! Most eager!

His father sat, wheezing and whistling in indignation, still not deigning to look at him. The sweet, burning smell was becoming stronger, and now Li Lin-fu saw that smoke was rising from his father's body and clothing as if he smoldered inside from rage and was about to explode into flame. The stoic partial profile remained exactly as it was, but now Li Lin-fu thought he could detect the gleam of the edge of his father's eyeball. Then he knew: the old man was turning toward him, but so slowly that the motion was imperceptible. And he also knew that the moment of his death would be the moment that his father looked him full in the face. He stepped to one side, away from the eye, so that his father's back was to him again. But his father quickly turned the other way so that he again presented the edge of his eye, this time on the other side of his face. And now more of the eye was showing.

If I were you, I would hold still, his father said. You are only losing ground each time you move. You are only bringing it closer. Now Li Lin-fu could see the edge of a terrible smile on his father's face and smoke coming out from between his teeth. He turned and tried to run, and found that he, too, was on fire.

The heat was beginning to penetrate his clothing when Li Lin-fu woke abruptly from the nightmare.

The physician's familiar homely face hovered over him. The soft light of dusk showed at the windows, and the room was shadowy and gray. And he smelled smoke: the same sweet smoke of his bad dream hung in the air.

"Leave us now," a woman's voice said.

"I leave only if *he* orders it, madam," the physician said stiffly. Li Lin-fu turned his head and saw the old woman he had sent for, Ming Wu, sitting on the day couch to the left of the bed. The smoke was emanating from her person, it seemed, drifting out of her nose and mouth as it had from his father's in the dream. He turned his head toward the physician.

"You may leave us, Physician. I *do* request it," he said.

"I cannot leave you alone with her," the man protested.

"Physician," Li Lin-fu said tiredly, and simply looked at him, "leave!"

"Well, I will not be far away," the man said, glaring at Ming Wu for a moment before leaving the room, muttering protests as he went. Li Lin-fu turned to the old woman on the couch and, gathering his thoughts, prepared in his mind what he would say in order to impart to her the knowledge of the urgent necessity of keeping him from death. But she did not give him a chance to speak.

"Tell me," she said, leaning forward, speaking in a low, confidential voice. "Who is looking for you?"

"No one is 'looking' for me, Old Woman," he protested, barely able to raise his head from the pillow. "Do you think I fear ghosts? I am not afraid to die. Death is like dreamless sleep, nothingness, oblivion. No one waits for me. The dead are dead. To believe anything else is superstitious nonsense. It is my work that I cannot leave. Forces are gathering against the empire. I am needed!"

"No one is looking for you? Superstitious nonsense?" she said. "Pardon me. I was under a mistaken impression." She drew back, then rose from the couch as if she were about to leave. "Obviously, you will not be needing me."

"Wait," he said weakly. "Do not be so hard on a dying man." She sat down again and looked at him. He found it very difficult to tell anything but the truth while her small black eyes were on him. He also had a strong feeling that the terrifying worlds he sank into now whenever he slept were familiar territory to her, that she could guide him through those places with the skill of a tracker in a remote mountain forest. She could protect him, he felt. She could, if she pleased, stand between him and the ghastly image of his father. "It is true I am experiencing . . . disturbing visions," he said. "But it is also true that I am needed. I cannot afford to leave this world. Not now. I am not asking for immortality, Old Woman. Just a few more years. A year! A few months!"

"And when those years or months have passed?" she asked, drawing fresh smoke from the apparatus in her hand. "Do you believe that you will go willingly then? Will the time ever come when you will gracefully relinquish your tenacious grip on this world and go to that other one that you are seeing in your dreams now? Will any time be the right time to die?" she asked pointedly, flat ribbons of smoke rising lazily around her head. "Chief Minister," she said then, "I am afraid that I can do nothing to postpone your death. You see, the thing that is devouring you, and which has been for many years now, is your own will. And you know how strong your will is." She shrugged. "Who am I to oppose such a powerful force?"

"But it is my will that I not die. Not yet," he argued.

"It is a bit late for that, Chief Minister." She sat in silence for a few moments. Then she rose and came close, so that he could smell her smoky, musty skin and clothing. "But I will tell you what I will do," she said, dropping her voice to a whisper. "I will accompany you part way."

The room had grown darker while they spoke. Ming Wu, standing over him, was little more than a silhouette now.

"The lamps," he said. "Please have them light the lamps." He lay back, exhausted and sweating, his heart fluttering like a bird behind his ribs. "And do me the honor, madam, of not leaving. Stay in the room tonight, if you would be so kind."

: :

For the next several hours Li Lin-fu fought to stay awake. Once, when he had begun to drift and forced his eyes open again, he thought for a moment that the figure of Ming Wu on the day couch was not the old woman at all, but his father. He had sat up in the bed and was shouting something to the old man, telling him to stay out of this room, to at least have the decency to wait until he was well and truly dead, when the figure rose and came toward him. A hand touched his shoulder, and as it did, he saw that it was not his father after all, but Ming Wu.

So, she said, it is your father who is looking for you. Frankly, Chief Minister, I am surprised that there is but one angry ghost stalking you. I would have expected more.

And she had returned to the couch and sat down again. Then she began to speak in a low, soothing voice that he found quite impossible to resist. Close your eyes, Chief Minister, she said; see in your mind a beautiful, still night in summer. A full white moon floats in the sky. You are in the woods. The silver light bathes the trees, the rocks, your hands in front of your face. You are young, and your body is in perfect health. Your limbs are springy with strength. You begin to run; you know you could run all night without the slightest trace of fatigue. Your feet strike the ground with the precision of a deer's sharp little hooves. The sweet night air nourishes you; with every breath you grow stronger, swifter, more powerful, as your legs carry you through the night forest.

He ran. There was nothing wrong with his lungs after all. The years of illness and fatigue must have been something he had dreamed. And this was real. He stopped in a clearing and tested the air; he reached down and seized a tuft of grass, feeling its crisp dryness; he picked up a rock, felt its tangible weight in his palm, then threw it. He watched it bounce and come to rest against another rock. He flexed his hands and felt the bones of his fingers. There was no doubt: this was real.

He began to run again, leaping exuberantly over fallen logs and dry stream beds, the world a place of sharp shadows and stark relief in the moonlight. He could hear small animals, startled at his approach, scurrying through the underbrush. And each time he disturbed an animal and it scampered away, he could actually feel its little terror, the fear in its tiny animal heart. The mouse, the rabbit, the shrew: he felt their beings with his own.

He did not distinguish at first between their terror and his; not until he found himself running wildly and out of control through the silvery woods, his body twisting as he dodged low branches and jagged pieces of stone. The small animal fear had grown huge until it filled his heart and became his own. Because right behind that fear he felt something else, now, too: the keen arousal of a predator's senses stimulated by the smell and vibrations of prey fleeing for its life. And he knew: the predator was behind him, in the moonlit woods, and he was the prey. Whatever was there had given up its stealth, broken cover, and pursued him now with the intent to run him to earth.

He wanted to look back over his shoulder, to see what sort of creature it was that chased him, but he did not dare slow down long enough to do it. He knew that it was large: he could hear the sound of a heavy body crashing through the brush behind him, and, with his heightened senses, thought he could hear its harsh breathing and smell its fetid carnivore's breath. He ran harder. The terrain grew steeper and more treacherous, and he was beginning to tire. Every breath was pure pain, and, worst of all, a deep, ominous tickle was gathering in his chest.

But he kept running, until his legs were weak and useless and branches raked his face and arms and he fell face down, coughing fire and blood. Unable to move, he heard the creature behind him closing the distance between them. Then it was on him, its heavy, hairy body hitting him with terrible force and pressing him to the earth. He waited for claws to rake the flesh of his back, fangs to pierce his skull.

But there were no fangs, no claws. Just the creature's crushing weight and hairy warmth, and its hot, stinking breath on the back of his neck and head. And the powerful beating of its heart as it pinned him to the sharp rocks while he struggled and fought to draw air into his seared lungs.

Let him up, a woman's voice ordered, and the creature, like an obedient trained dog, immediately raised itself from his back. He heard its retreating footsteps as he lay still, drawing in great draughts of air, still coughing, but not so harshly now. Then he rolled over.

The moonlight had become lamplight, the crisscrossing branches of trees had become shadows cast on the ceiling of his bedchamber. The rocky, painful ground beneath him became his own bed. He knew by the raw feeling in his chest and throat that he had passed through a terrible coughing fit. He looked over toward the couch where Ming Wu had been sitting. She was still there, but appeared to be dozing; he was only mildly surprised to see that her skin was as smooth and her hair as black as a young girl's.

She opened her eyes and looked at him, then smiled with a full set of white teeth. His body quivered with exertion and pain, as if he had truly been running for his life. That hideous creature, he said. It almost had me. No, it did not, Ming Wu replied; it is not capable of really hurting you. It can only frighten you. That is all it can do. Besides, I told you I would stay with you, didn't I?

A marble hallway, she said as she rose and stood over the bed. You are in a marble hallway in a palace on a steep mountainside, high above the world.

He stared up at her beautiful face, her smooth skin and even teeth, and tried to remember if she had ever been the old hag he vaguely remembered. No, he decided; he had been mistaken. This is how she has always looked.

He closed his eyes and went where her low, compelling voice told him to go.

The warm, sweet wind is blowing through the marble corridors, she said. The doors and windows are all open, and outside there is nothing but the pure expanse of blue sky. You go to a balcony and lean over the carved railing, resting your elbows on the cool white stone, and look down. You are so high up that you can barely see the floor of the valley, with a silver river winding through it, far, far below you. You are so high that you are actually above the clouds; as you are looking at the distant floor of the valley, the clouds drift together, obscuring the earth completely, putting you in the sky. You are satisfied to be seeing the last of the earth. You are content to see the clouds close on the earth and all its concerns, because, you now realize, you have been distracted all these years from your true work.

Walking the clean, uncluttered halls of the marble palace, he began to understand where he was. He ran his hand along the stone, admiring minute geometrical patterns that his eye discerned in its surface. This was something that he had never noticed before. There were patterns in the stone, and the stones themselves were arranged in exactly similar geometric patterns that formed the walls, floors, and ceilings of the palace's rooms and hallways, which in turn proliferated like crystals whose every facet fit snugly into the next. He shivered with fierce joy at the prospect: a universe of pure mathematics, infinitely huge in one direction, infinitely tiny in the other, and infinitely complex and beautiful, awaiting his inspection and exploration. And nothing but time, with no more distractions or interruptions, in which to do it.

He started walking down one of the hallways. Where to begin? Anywhere, really. There was no wrong or inappropriate place. He would move into the numbers, the formulae that were already shaping in his mind, each one a beautiful door swinging open, enticing him to enter and explore the mysteries beyond. He could walk through any one of them. The choice was his. And there was music, too. He tilted his head and listened: it came from far down the hallway ahead of him. He started walking again, his eyes closed pleasurably, letting the numbers in the music dance through his mind.

And where do you think you are going, his father's voice said from behind him. You and I have a bit of unfinished business, do we not? He whirled around, enraged at the intrusion on his solitude, but was unable to speak as his throat constricted with horror.

A skeleton, standing in the full light of day that filled the hallway, with shreds of bloody meat hanging from the bones as if they had been gnawed by animals, spoke with his father's voice and pointed a finger at him. You are coming with me, boy, it said through his father's teeth. Music and numbers will have to wait.

He turned to run, but a bony hand caught him from behind by the top of the head, the fingers curving down over his forehead and catching the sockets of his eyes, pulling backward in a hideous grip, bending his neck until he was forced to look up from below at his father's skull-face. He could see the bloody, gristly vertebrae of the neck where they connected with the base of the cranium, and the lower mandible moving as his father spoke.

Running off to play before your responsibilities have been taken care of, eh?

It is not true, Li Lin-fu whispered; I have worked hard all my life. I have always put my responsibilities first, before my own pleasure. Always!

The bony fingers dug deeper into his eye sockets. But what about *me*? the skeleton demanded. What about your responsibilities to *me*? I am sorry, boy, it said, pulling back harshly, causing him to collapse onto the cold marble, but I am scarcely satisfied. You will have to come where I am going.

And the skeleton, fingers still hooked into the sockets of Li Lin-fu's eyes, turned and began to walk in the other direction, dragging him behind along the floor, away from the distant music, the beckoning rooms and hallways, the brilliant light. He twisted and struggled in the horrible grip while his father muttered and cursed. An irresponsible boy you always were, he said. We will teach you some manners, instill some sense of filial duty in you!

He could hear the sound of his father's skeleton-feet clacking on the marble floor; the light faded rapidly, and he felt himself being dragged down a staircase. As they descended, he found that he was losing the incentive and the strength to struggle; soon it was completely dark, and there was nothing at all in the entire universe except the fingers in his eyes and his limp bones bouncing and rattling on the stone steps as they went down, down, down. He raised his hands to his face and found no flesh, just his exposed teeth and jaws and a jagged, sharp-edged hole where his nose should have been. And he knew: he was nothing but a skeleton, too.

After a long time the motion stopped, and his father's fingers withdrew from his eye sockets. Lying in the utter blackness, unable to move, he listened to the sound of bony footsteps retreating into the vast, dark emptiness, echoing on cold stone. So, he thought vaguely, distantly, his consciousness like a guttering candle that is about to go out, this is what it means to be dead.

I can fight it no more, he thought, imagining that he felt tears running from his empty eye holes and streaming down the bones of his face. And he let himself sink into the sleep below sleep, the candle flame of consciousness growing smaller and weaker, until he could scarcely remember the white marble halls and the infinite corridors of light, numbers, and music . . .

: :

How much time had passed? It must have been two or three hundred years. He was waking, rising from the depths. Something was tickling him insistently on the soles of his feet. He was annoyed at first, wanting only to return to his dreamless sleep. Irritated, he kicked his foot. There are mice in my tomb, he thought. The tickling stopped for a moment; but just as he began to sink down, it started again. Leave me alone, he muttered; even a dead man can't get any peace or privacy.

You are not dead, came the message through the soles of his feet. His astonished eyes, heavy with sleep and death, opened minutely on the darkened room, the dim light of a lantern turned down low causing him to wince with pain. How had he understood the words? They had not been spoken, yet he had comprehended them with some other faculty.

Look at me, the words came. He forced his eyes open further and gazed down in the direction of his feet. Ming Wu, wrinkled and toothless once more, stood at the end of the bed. She gave him a conspiratorial grin as she tickled the soles of his feet again. *Do you know my real name?* Unable to hold his head up any longer, he sank back onto the pillows, the realization coming to him at last.

She was writing on the bottoms of his feet. And he, who had been shut out of the mysteries of the written word for his entire life, now comprehended perfectly everything she wrote.

"What is your real name?" he whispered, looking up at the soft shadows playing on the ceiling.

Li Shan Lao Ma.

"So you are the old woman of Li Shan. Am I to believe that you have walked these hills for two millennia?"

Two thousand, one hundred and sixty-three years.

"Not possible," he said weakly. "I don't believe in magic."

I said nothing about magic. You sought immortality yourself.

"Yes. Through science, through logic!"

You simply approached it incorrectly.

"Crazy nonsense," he muttered.

Yes. Crazy old woman.

"Yes," he whispered. "Crazy old woman."

But you are dying, and I am not.

He raised his head slightly and looked down toward Ming Wu. She tilted her head so that it caught the soft light at a certain angle, and he saw that she was not old at all, but young and beautiful. Then she brought her face forward, and the smooth skin seemed to dissolve into wrinkles and collapse inward over toothless jaws; then she moved backward and was young again.

Crazy old woman, she wrote on his feet. And he drifted back toward sleep, thinking that it was a shame that this wondrous comprehension of written words, which had evaded him so infuriatingly during all the years he had lived so that he had had to endure such humiliation and frustration, came to him so late. It was indeed a perverse universe, he decided. Always playing nasty little tricks, always taunting one, always just slipping out of one's grasp.

For the rest of the night, Li Lin-fu rose and sank, always interested to see what appearance Ming Wu, sitting by the bed now, chose to present. Sometimes she was young, sometimes she was old. At one point, he opened his eyes and saw that she was not a woman at all, but a man with a square jaw and a fierce brow; and he was not even slightly surprised when, toward dawn, he looked over at the couch and saw an animal with sleek black fur curled up on the cushions, watching him.

An altogether perverse universe, he thought, and closed his eyes.

: :

Ming Wu rose and stretched in the early morning light. She glanced briefly at the corpse in the bed, then went to the balcony to see what sort of day it was going to be. She sniffed the air. It would be hot, like the day before. Maybe even hotter.

In another part of the hot springs, Yang Kuo-chung awoke in his apartments with the Lady of Kuo's black hair lying across his face and pillow and a sense that his life was about to change forever. He disengaged himself without waking her and sat on the edge of the bed looking down at his bare feet. They looked particularly naked and vulnerable this morning.

Feet, he said, I am sorry for you. You have little choice but to go where I go.

24

The Apostasy

For one last sordid act of vengeance the forces which had combined against the dictator remained united. . . . and all the pent up fury of nearly twenty years of suppression was let loose on the dictator's corpse and his unfortunate relatives.

—Edwin Pulleyblank

Some fifty of [Li Lin-fu's] henchmen in the government were banished.

—William Hung

At the insistence of Yang Kuo-chung, the emperor ordered An to appear at court. Although Yang Kuo-chung warned Hsuan-tsung that this northern renegade would refuse an imperial summons, An came at once. He tearfully reaffirmed his unswerving loyalty. . . . This loyalty oath reassured the sovereign.

—Howard S. Levy

[An Lu-shan] was royally entertained in the Hua-ch'ing Palace. The emperor made up his mind not to doubt An's complete loyalty. . . . [An] then proceeded to order a selection of many thousands of fine horses, . . . to have them sent to his own armies. Moreover, he obtained from the emperor signed certificates of appointments for 500 generals and 2,000 colonels with blank spaces left for the names of the appointees to be filled in by An! An filled in the names of foreign soldiers.

—William Hung

"YOU must think as he did, Master Yang."

Kao Li-shih leaned from the high window of the Chancellery fortress; outside, a cool autumn breeze had cleansed the air to a crystalline blue. He allowed his gaze to take him beyond the steep drop of the wall beneath them and into the quiet green wildness of Tung Yuan Park.

"That does not help me," Yang Kuo-chung, sitting at Li Lin-fu's desk, replied wearily.

"It was not meant to provide the answer. I do not have the answer," Kao Li-shih said absently, still speaking to the sky outside the window. "I simply meant for you to consider how your predecessor might have dealt with this."

"I have been in office for three months. I face the problem of recovering the official faith in a government that has been the exclusive domain of one man . . . a tyrant, a despot for all these years. Surely, the last thing I want to do is emulate the very man from whom I am trying to disassociate myself."

"I am not suggesting that you emulate him so much as I am suggesting that you make a decisive gesture that will leave little room for speculation, just as he would have done in such a situation. Whatever it is you do, you will have to dishonor his memory and make it absolutely clear where you stand as his official successor. It will be necessary for you to separate yourself from him in every way. In everyone's eyes but the general's, of course."

"What about a public proclamation," Yang Kuo-chung began. "A statement of intent . . ."

Kao Li-shih shook his head. "Mere words," he said. "Insubstantial and insufficient. Li Lin-fu's greatest talent, as I remember, was his ability to create a vivid impression that burned itself into the mind and remained there long after words and gestures were forgotten. This is what you must do, somehow."

"Well," Yang Kuo-chung said thoughtfully. "I doubt that I am the first to encounter this problem."

"There is no such thing as a new problem," Kao Li-shih agreed. "Li Lin-fu would have told you that, I am sure. Li Lin-fu was a man of history, always looking to his predecessors for examples."

Yang Kuo-chung thought of the last time he had made a conscious effort to think like Li Lin-fu: it was when he had decided that he needed to send the chief minister some token, something that would get his attention so that Yang Kuo-chung could make his highly audacious request to meet face to face. The Lady of Kuo had supplied both the suggestion and the answer, sending him out to the ignominious burial ground near the garbage dumps and slaughterhouses in pursuit of the hand of the dead assassin . . .

An idea was coming to him. He looked at Kao Li-shih, who was gazing out the window again. Was it too grotesque, too far-fetched?

"Kao Li-shih, you mentioned history a moment ago. Perhaps the answer is there. I remember you telling me once about the events that followed the death of the Empress Wu."

Kao Li-shih turned.

"How appropriate," he said. "She was a great source of inspiration to Li Lin-fu. I am certain that he frequently asked himself what Grandmother would have done in certain situations. And judging by the measured brutality of some of his methods, she was only too happy to whisper in his ear." He left the window and sat in a chair near the desk. "After her death, in order to remove the stigma of their poison from the offices of their successors, all of her henchmen were executed. Several months later their corpses were exhumed and publicly dishonored. It was a most effective gesture." He looked at Yang Kuo-chung, who looked back at him.

"What do you think?" Yang Kuo-chung asked tentatively. "Couldn't we do the same thing?"

"To Li Lin-fu's henchmen?" Kao Li-shih asked.

Yang Kuo-chung shook his head. "No. To Li Lin-fu."

Kao Li-shih rose to his feet and resumed his post at the window.

"The idea is not without merit," he said. "But there is a problem. We don't know where Li Lin-fu's body is interred. It disappeared from his hot springs apartments only hours after his death. The physician found the corpse in the bed; he left momentarily to procure attendants and a funeral litter, but when he returned, the body was gone."

"And nobody saw it being removed?"

"No one. And no one knows where it was taken, or how."

"Here is the real challenge, Kao Li-shih," Yang Kuo-chung declared. "Here is where we must really try to think like Li Lin-fu. Where would they take him? Obviously, they were following instructions left by the chief minister himself. If you were Li Lin-fu, where would you want your body interred?"

Kao Li-shih thought before answering.

"Well, I think I would want someplace very private. Someplace away from the prying eyes of the world at large. Someplace where I would be quite . . . alone. And given the chief minister's penchant for numbers, I have no doubt that the place where his body lies corresponds to some numerical equation of his own devising . . ."

"I have an idea," Yang Kuo-chung interrupted. He rose and went to the small desk that stood in the corner of the office. He lifted the lid, revealing Li Lin-fu's mysterious wheel. He touched it almost reverentially, then gave it a light spin. He was impressed by its instant responsiveness to his touch, by its smoothness, silence, and the speed with which it revolved. "I think I know where he is," he said, looking down at the trigrams of the *I Ching,* whirling in an indistinct blur, the mother-of-pearl flashing.

: :

The corridor stood empty, the latticework's intricate shadows losing their form as they softened in the fading light. The blazing colors of tilework and delicately carved woods, the brilliant hues of the painted lintels with their lifelike scenes of battle, the eaves of blue, the rails and balustrades of purple and vermilion, and the polished gold of the pillars were all dissolving into the soft grayish hues of the evening world.

From far down the lifeless hallway came the indifferent scratching of branches against shutters. Crisp leaves blew about on the stones outside; in the walls, timbers groaned and settled and rodents pattered about on tiny dry feet. The only other sound was the soft brush of Daughter's silk slippers on the cold slate.

She passed under the final painted miniatures of battles on the overhead lintels. Though dusk had robbed them of their color, she knew them by heart: green-gold hills ablaze with flames rendered in burning yellows and reds; brave lancers forever just falling from rearing horses; arrogant bowmen frozen in their timeless warring stance, bowstrings pulled taut against the blue of the sky, their arrows cocked against the foil of swirling clouds. It was always at this point in the hallway that she would begin to hear the enormous yawning and shuddering of Father's machine. She kept walking; she was almost there.

Day and night, the pavilion turned. It was her father's most perfect invention—second only to her, he used to say—paralleling in its fluid, frictionless revolutions not just the perpetual reeling of the constellations through the heavens, but also the opening and closing of infinite mathematical windows. The machinery beneath the great hall had been designed and built to rotate the octagonal building on its bed of liquid mercury for a millennium or more without wear. Its elaborate gears and wheels obeyed the commands of its creator: waterwheels, locks, gates, and intricate escapements eternally regulating and translating waters from the Pa and Serpentine Rivers into the precise mathematical progression of a heavenly clock.

In her first weeks alone in the house, Daughter had had only a general grasp of the theory. She understood that the building at the rear of the house compound turned with profound regularity that corresponded to a formula of her father's, opening and closing massive portals and doors, infinitely re-aligning and redefining the maze of passageways and halls that she must follow to reach her father. And each evening she made her way to where his body rested beneath the central chamber of his great revolving structure, thinking to herself that, through this great, wondrous mechanism, he still talked to her. He had promised that he would explain all of it to her one day, initiate her into its mysteries. And he would have, had his time not run out. But in her weeks alone here, she had become thoroughly acquainted with the great machine's movements. That, together with the little bit that Father had told her before he died, was enough to allow her to arrive at an understanding of it quite on her own. The building moved, she knew, synchronistically not just to the heavens but to his concept of them, focusing universal forces upon itself and its occupants.

She walked quickly now down the final length of corridor. She did not have much time. She had to reach the fourth portal within the next few minutes, it being the only way to the central chamber in the magic square that would be easily manageable this late in the day. She moved with confidence. She had become quite intimately acquainted with the machine's sounds and motions and, from them, knew where to be and when in order to pass through its shifting doors. It spoke to her in its language of vibrations, heaves and shudders; subtle differentiations in the order of groans, clicks, and watery gushes emanating from its innards had become as familiar and readable to her as the body's pulses to a physician.

Although she had never been fully initiated into the infinite complexities of her father's cosmic mathematics, she was *his* daughter. She was most like him. And sometimes, as she roamed the empty galleries, pavilions, and corridors of Father's great house, it seemed that her thoughts were his—that they still shared the same vital essence. When he was alive and she used to sit near him with her writing brush poised just above the paper, she sometimes knew the words he would speak before he even said them. And he used to smile as he watched her work; her brush, so exquisitely wielded, seeming, at times, to outpace his thoughts. He was always delighted and pleased, and ceaselessly amazed. But what she did was no surprise to herself. Even if his mood was angry and distracted when she lifted her brush to take his words down, that act alone seemed to lift him out of himself. The very performance of her writing, he told her, the graceful movement of the wrist and fingers guiding the brush, was as beautiful as the calligraphy itself. He had always been pleased with her, and she had always known it.

Alone in his house now, that thought was a source of infinite comfort to her. She had shared his thoughts when he was alive; now that he was dead, it seemed to her that in understanding his house, his rotating pavilion, and, most important, his motivation in creating it, she shared his insights. The house was alive, and the life-force that inhabited it was his. Listening to the familiar pattern of noises—the rush of water into one of the many containing locks, the click and whirr of gears, the gushing of the spillways opening, the groan of the retaining doors, the metered clicks of volume, the sure build of tensions and pressures, the scrape and clang of the enormous escapements—she understood that her father could not die, that he was still teaching her.

It was time. Another deep groan followed by a tremendous shudder: that was the sign. That was Father speaking. The nearly invisible crack at her feet was widening into an inky black abyss, and she knew what would happen next. The great building was about to turn, about to realign the eight faces of the octagon and to change, in turn, its relation to the nine hidden chambers of the magic square at its center.

With a small, carefully calculated leap she entered the revolving hall; a moment later the entrance closed behind her with the dark muffled finality of stone. When the building had completed its increment of rotation, it grew quiet again but for a soft remnant gurgling of water under her feet.

The passageways were lit with rows of small oil lanterns suspended on delicate bronze armatures, their wicks drawing from a deep-buried reservoir of natural oil. Now, by the third month, Daughter moved with practiced expertise down one dimly lit passageway after another, turning first this way and then that without hesitation, her shadow trailing behind her and in front of her as she moved between lamps. Once she was inside the first chamber of the magic square, her hands slid deftly along the familiar wall to the hidden latch-plates in the latticework. She pushed them in gently; the mechanism in the wall clicked. From behind her came the sound of a gate slamming shut. Ahead, another opened. She stepped into the next chamber.

She passed this way from room to room until she found her way to the center, the stationary pivot around which the entire structure revolved. It was cooler in here, the damp subterranean air announcing the presence of an opening in the floor. A spiral staircase wound deep down into the ground to the crypt where her father's sarcophagus lay. There she had erected a small altar: her father's altar.

Daughter had been down that dark passage over a hundred times. She knew every irregularity in the rough stone steps beneath her feet, and every unevenness in the cold, dank wall where she guided herself with her fingers. It had been very different the first time she had come down here months ago, shortly after Father's death.

At first the death of her father had not seemed at all real. She had not returned to his hot springs apartments after she took his last letter to the Emperor. He had instructed her to return to the house. She guessed now that it was because he knew that he was very close to death, that he would probably die that night and did not want her to see it when it happened. He had said to her so many times in the past that it was necessary for her to see him in every possible light. He had made no attempt to hide from her his struggles with his coughing and his temper. It was good for her, he said, that she understand the sacrifices that he made for his work, for the empire. But it must have become more difficult for him to be so honest with her when he was just about to die. When he did actually die, it seemed to her as if it were something that had happened at a distance.

When the news finally reached their house in the southern part of Ch'ang-an by late morning, she was still asleep, exhausted. She had been up nearly the entire night before his last. When her handmaiden woke her with the news, the words at first did not seem real, as if she had only to awake out of one more level of sleep to find that it was all just a dream.

But it was no dream. She must have been hard to wake that morning because she was so tired. By the time she did finally surface completely, the poor serving girl was frantic and on the verge of hysterics.

The house was in a state of panic and uproar when Most-Prized Daughter finally dragged herself from her bed, her poor frightened servant scurrying about to find her slippers and her morning robe. For Daughter, the news was still not completely real. Father gone? The most powerful man in China gone? Though she had been watching the signs of impending death for years, she found it strangely difficult to comprehend that it had finally happened.

Around her, everyone was leaving in a great hurry. Sisters and brothers, mothers, servants, cooks, nursemaids, groundskeepers, musicians, tutors, scribes, and guards, all rushing out, attendants packing a minimum into bags and crates and tossing them into carriages. And every so often a head would poke into her doorway and startle her and tell her she must hurry. What was all the rush about, she had asked. Don't you know? the excited face would ask. The family has to leave. Why? she had asked.

Because the household—every member of the chief minister's household—every wife, child, servant, and Chancellery soldier of Li Lin-fu would be blacklisted. Everyone connected with him might very well face torture and even death. It was only a matter of time; perhaps only a few days. Her father had been considered a dangerous tyrant by the literati—by many people in government, the excited person said.

Father's hated literati, she remembered thinking—the ones who had always caused him so much trouble, the ones who did not understand how he protected China. And as the head pulled out of the doorway, the person moving quickly down the hall, the frightened voice said that she must get out, must run. It said that her father had caused many people to hate him, had made many enemies. They did not understand him, she called down the hallway. Her father made their China possible. What did they think, she shouted then, that the Emperor or the brash young Yang Kuo-chung would ever have made them safe? She could still hear the hollow plaintive sound of her own voice saying those words and the silence that was the only response to her question.

She had refused to leave. And later that day, as the sounds of running feet, shouts, and crying women gradually receded from the halls, her determination had crystallized: no one would take her father's house from her, ever. She would stay and guard it with her life. She would never give in. She would make him proud of her. She would stay on alone if she had to. She would find stores of food, and she would hide from everyone in the fortress maze of her father's magic pavilion if necessary. She would stay here until she was an old, old lady. She would die here.

And on the evening of that day, when the great compound of rooms, halls, pavilions, and towers that had been her father's home and fortress was completely quiet and every last soul had gone, leaving, so their shouts had informed her, for somewhere in the south, Father came home.

Daughter had heard the clatter of wheels on the cobblestones outside the entranceway beyond the Garden of Supplicating Branches. Cautiously, stealthily, she had made her way down the corridors on her hands and knees and hid behind the pillars of the reception hall. At first she had thought that perhaps it was a member of the household returning for something, maybe even for her. They would not find her. Or, much worse, perhaps it was officials, the enemy, looking for her.

Maybe they had already captured the rest of the household leaving the city. Maybe someone had talked, informed them that she had stayed behind. She had crouched in the shadows behind the pillar and watched.

She soon saw that it was only one wagon that had come through the gates—a rough, simple merchant's cart drawn by a team of two oxen. The thick wheels crunched over the gravel as she crept from pillar to pillar to get a closer look at the driver. She had not been at all frightened—just curious. Still, she prudently remained hidden. The wagon pulled up—so close to where she hid that she could smell the oxen and almost feel the warm air from their nostrils—and a very big man, vaguely familiar even from the back, stepped down and leaned over the back of the wagon, digging his broad arms into what looked like a cloth merchant's pile of fabric bolts.

Before lifting his mysterious freight, he looked up and down the courtyard entrance. Then, lovingly, carefully, he raised something, and she had instantly understood: the roll of fabric the man held was her father's body, disguised. The big man turned around. She had recognized him immediately: it was the one with the talent of many voices. And of all the family, she had been the only one allowed to meet him, a long time ago. With the passing of General Niu, years before, and the death of her father's decrepit chief of internal securities only a short time before Father's own death, there was only one man who remained. And now he was proving his faithfulness. Without any more deliberation, she had stood up from her hiding place.

He smiled at her. His smile conveyed everything. There was no surprise in it. The smile said that he had known that she would be there. She remembered the big eunuch's smile well because it was a gracious, warm smile, without even a trace of urgency behind it. Together, they brought her father down to the elaborate crypt in the caverns beneath the center of the great rotating pavilion at the back of the house. She had known the crypt was there. Father had prepared it along with everything else. But she had never gone down to see that subterranean chamber while he was alive—to do so would have been to admit her father's mortality. But now that deceit was over.

They had prepared him for burial in the stone sarcophagus. Daughter had insisted that he be laid out in a splendid robe, and the big man had acquiesced to her wishes. She was, after all, Li Lin-fu's flesh and blood.

Now, months later, she still felt a thrill of anticipation whenever she went down those stairs, but no sadness. She had not lost him; he was here, and all around her. And even after more than a hundred of these evening visits to her father's chambers, nothing had changed for her. It was all like the first time: the airy fluttering in the hollow of her stomach, the lightness that told her that she was on the final stairs. Then came the narrow corridor that led to the burial chamber.

She walked along its dark, cool length, the walls of stone cold with condensed moisture. As she reached the end of the tunnel, she saw the faint glow of the oil lamps that burned in her father's chamber. She also felt the hint of breeze that came in from an opening somewhere ahead; at other times, when she was in the crypt when the building turned overhead, she noticed that this stream of air became more forceful. Perhaps the wheels that turned the pavilion rotated a giant fan that carried air into the caves below so that the atmosphere was always fresh and pure. She did not know; it was another of her father's mysteries. She contemplated with pleasure the many years that lay ahead of her that she would spend alone in this house, until she was an old, old lady, deciphering all of the riddles, puzzles, and arcane formulae left behind by her father until she understood everything.

"Father," she whispered in the hollow resonance of the cavern. "I have brought an offering for you tonight." She walked over to the tall square granite sarcophagus in the center of the room. On the top of it was a blue, deep-sea-patterned altar cloth on which were candles and sticks of incense set about in small bowls around a gold-and-jade tree hung with hundreds of small silk leaves inscribed with characters.

She burned paper charms for her father every evening, inscribing them first beautifully in her delicate hand with every kind of blessing to see to his needs. This evening, though, she had a special one. Inspiration had come to her while she was working with her brush on this evening's charms. She felt as though she had a gift for him.

With the paper in her left hand, she stepped up to the altar and proceeded with the ritual so familiar to her now that it was almost reflexive. With her right hand, she lit a reddish stick of incense from the small oil flame that burned above. Then she blew out the flame, reducing the tip to a smoldering orange glow, and placed the stick back in its holder so that a delicate curl of perfumed smoke rose in the still air. She opened her left hand, allowing the small folded piece of paper to drop out on the altar cloth.

It was a simple message, but one that she wanted to make sure was offered formally and concisely to her father, so that there would never be any doubt: the message was her written promise that she would never leave him alone.

::

The wagon bearing the coffin of Li Lin-fu rumbled into the Orchid Terrace courtyard of the bureaucratic city. The hundreds of waiting magistrates, officials, and civil servants were quiet and watchful, stepping back deferentially to allow the conveyance to pass to the center of the huge square. Yang Kuo-chung had not been sure what to expect. He would not have been at all surprised to see the crowd become a noisy, spiteful mob, clamoring for vengeance; but instead, the spectators seemed to be absorbed by the strangeness of what they were about to witness. The hush that prevailed was almost reverential, Yang Kuo-chung thought. It was obvious that even after all these months, none of them truly believed that Li Lin-fu was dead.

Riding on the cart with the coffin were two people: a young, very pretty, serious-looking girl, and a large man with a shaved head and broad shoulders. They sat near the coffin in a protective, proprietary way, ignoring the upturned faces that watched their entrance with intense curiosity. As the cart drew near, it became obvious to Yang Kuo-chung that the girl could only be a daughter of Li Lin-fu. It was startling to see the dead chief minister's countenance reflected in a face that was so young and pretty, but there was no mistaking the resemblance. It gave Yang Kuo-chung an odd feeling; it was as though Li Lin-fu himself were looking down at him from the cart.

With Yang Kuo-chung were Kao Li-shih and two men, the Khitan prisoners he had freed some time ago when he had dug up the body of the would-be assassin of the Emperor and cut off the hand to send to Li Lin-fu. He had told the men today that they would be free to return to their homes if they performed one more task for him.

Li Lin-fu's elaborate, polished wooden coffin had been removed from its stone sarcophagus before being put in the wagon. Yang Kuo-chung had the two prisoners lift it now and set it on the ground next to another coffin, plain and made of rough boards, in the midst of the crowd of watching officials. The girl and the bald man climbed down, their serious, watchful expressions making it plain that the purpose of their presence was to maintain a vigil by Li Lin-fu. They said nothing, and they made no attempt to protest or to interfere; they merely stayed close and watched. Yang Kuo-chung was not about to order them away. It was only right, he thought, that somebody represent the deceased, no matter how reprehensible he may have been in life; after all, to be dead was to have the ultimate disadvantage—especially in what was about to occur. He would hope that someone would do the same for him.

Yang Kuo-chung exchanged a look with Kao Li-shih, then motioned for silence, though it was scarcely necessary.

"You are here to bear witness," he said in a loud, clear voice so that everyone would hear him, "that the Ssu-k'ung office officially denounces the policies of its former leader, the late chief minister Li Lin-fu. Those whom he removed from office have all been officially reinstated. The names of those whom he blacklisted, and their families, are hereby washed clean. The present leader of the Ssu-k'ung office—I, Chief Minister Yang Kuo-chung—wish to disassociate this office from all of the characteristics that came to mark the term of my predecessor: subterfuge, terror, reprisal, coercion, and secret machinations. I wish to dispel, like a cleansing wind blowing away foul smoke, the atmosphere of suspicion built up over many long years. Whoever among you who have been hiding, you may now come forth without fear. Those who were banished may return in the full light of day. Whoever among you dared not speak, you may now raise your voice without fear. Whoever among you feels that he has been stripped of possessions or livelihood by the policies of my predecessor may come forth and officially state his case and apply for restitution and reimbursement from the empire. And know that my predecessor's elite guard of agents have, to every last man, been banished ignominiously beyond the borders of this empire and will strike no more anxiety, fear, or uncertainty into the hearts of honest men. And know that I have dispatched a contingent of my own men to the island of Hai-nan for the express purpose of finding and bringing home all the unfortunates banished to that living hell by my predecessor. You will soon, if the Fates grant it to us, be seeing the faces of friends and colleagues you believed to be dead for years. Like the sun rising after a long night, his reign is over!"

There was some polite, restrained applause from the crowd, but still no tumultuous proclamation of acknowledgment. What he was witnessing, Yang Kuo-chung knew, was the measure of Li Lin-fu's hold over them: they simply could not bring themselves to believe that they were beyond his reach. Even dead, he could still make men bite their tongues. Today, Yang Kuo-chung would offer them indisputable proof that Li Lin-fu was well and truly dead.

Yang Kuo-chung stepped back and signaled the two prisoners, who approached the coffin with iron bars in their hands. The girl and the bald man moved to the side to give them room, but kept their eyes on the coffin. The crowd became especially quiet as the two men began prying up the lid, fastened down by wooden pegs. The wood squealed and groaned in protest as the men forced the lid up bit by bit; when it was free, they each grasped an end and lifted it aside.

It surprised Yang Kuo-chung to see how little three months in the grave had changed Li Lin-fu's appearance. The skin lay over the bones like old leather, taut and dry, and the teeth showed between the mummified lips in a sardonic little grin, exactly as if Li Lin-fu had just made a remark or an ironic observation that particularly pleased him.

For a few moments Yang Kuo-chung, Kao Li-shih, the girl, the bald man, the two prisoners, and the officials and magistrates close enough to see stared down at the corpse of the man who had ruled China for so many years. The burial finery glinted in the autumn sun. The prisoners looked to Yang Kuo-chung, who gave them a nod; one of them took his knife and slit the fabric of Li Lin-fu's gold and purple robe from the neck to the knee and down each of the sleeves, leaving the corpse in only a plain muslin undergarment. Peeling the fine robe aside, they lifted the corpse like a piece of old, dry wood from the coffin and put it in the rough-hewn one that waited nearby.

Yang Kuo-chung stole a glance at Li Lin-fu's daughter. She watched the proceedings with her father's own calm detachment; when the lid was pounded into place on the second coffin and the prisoners began to lift it, she turned and climbed back onto the wagon and waited. The bald man did the same. They meant to ride now with the coffin to the burial ground near the refuse dumps of the Kuan-yun Transport Canal, Li Lin-fu's final resting place among the murderers and thieves.

Before the wagon left the courtyard, Yang Kuo-chung spoke to the prisoner who drove the oxen.

"When you have finished, come back to my office. I will give you supplies, horses, and an escort. You will start your journey home."

The man grinned down at him.

"If we meet on the battlefield someday," he said, "I will spare you!"

"I will remember that," Yang Kuo-chung said, and stepped back. The prisoner snapped the reins and the wagon rumbled out of the Orchid Terrace. As he and Kao Li-shih made their way through the crowd and walked in the direction of the Chancellery building, applause broke out, spreading among the ranks, rising in volume until it surrounded them and was the only thing they could hear.

:: :

Daughter, her hand resting on the rough boards of her father's coffin, stared behind her at the receding courtyard and the hundreds of officials milling about, the noise of their jubilation echoing off the great buildings. She looked over at her friend, who gave her a reassuring little smile.

They had done the right thing. She knew that Father would have approved. Yesterday, a contingent of guardsmen had come to Father's house, shown her the seal of the Ssu-k'ung Office, and announced to her that unless she led them to Father's place of interment and relinquished the corpse, a thousand workers would be brought in to dismantle the house, piece by piece, relentlessly, right down to the ground. They had said that she had two hours to make her decision, at which time, if she refused, the workers, who were already assembled and waiting, would appear and begin their labor.

She had retreated into one of the rooms of the revolving pavilion and thought hard about what Father would want her to do. She knew that he would never forgive her if she allowed his house, the living monument to his life, work, and spirit, to be ignominiously reduced to a pile of rubble. His wonderful machine, irreplaceable, meant to last for centuries, ripped apart, its secrets lost forever? His world—an incomparable work of art that surrounded her and spoke to her, that now housed his spirit, and that promised her a lifetime of shelter and inspiration within its walls—violated, murdered?

She had had no recourse. There were only two of them left: she and her friend who had brought Father home. There was no army that she could call forth to defend the sanctity of her father's world. She had only her wits to rely on. Let them have the body, she decided. I will keep my promise to Father and stay with him, wherever they take him. Let them play their little game, if that is what they must do.

The wagon rumbled through the streets of the bureaucratic city. She knew where they were taking Father. She and her friend had made their plan: they would stay with Father and wait patiently. They would live at the burial ground by the canal. They would make a shelter and procure food from the docks. And when some time had gone by, perhaps a month or two, and everything was quiet once more, and the attention of the world had turned elsewhere, as it inevitably would, then they would bring him home again. She ignored the staring faces lining the streets.

::

Yang Kuo-chung poured a cup of wine for Kao Li-shih, and one for himself. He drank his cup down immediately and poured another. He was trying to obliterate the image of Li Lin-fu's dead face from his mind. Why was he feeling as though he had betrayed the chief minister? Hadn't Li Lin-fu himself been, after all, the ultimate murderer and betrayer? It was not as if Yang Kuo-chung had broken his word. Hadn't Li Lin-fu himself been the inspiration for what had taken place today? Wasn't it exactly the sort of thing he would have done? He, Yang Kuo-chung, was thinking like him. He was becoming him.

But the difference was that Li Lin-fu would not have wasted a moment on doubt. Vacillation had been unknown to him. Yang Kuo-chung drained his second cup of wine and poured a third. He felt Kao Li-shih watching him across the table and knew what his friend was thinking about. It was a topic that they had been discussing for months now, ever since Li Lin-fu's death, and which hung between them, unanswered and unanswerable. He smiled ruefully at Kao Li-shih.

"You are thinking that now is the time to confront An Lu-shan."

Kao Li-shih shrugged his acknowledgment. "I don't think you should postpone it any longer. I think it would be most effective for such an encounter to take place very soon after your public disavowal of allegiance to Li Lin-fu. An inquisition carried out by the chief minister himself would be a clear message to An Lu-shan. And for the others watching, it would be a clear rejection of another of Li Lin-fu's policies, which was to let An Lu-shan get away with his crimes and excesses. You can show them, and him, that such behavior will no longer be tolerated."

Yang Kuo-chung sat down heavily and rubbed his eyes. He had, of course, been thinking of little else. It had always been his plan to do exactly what Kao Li-shih suggested, but he had been putting it off because An Lu-shan was far away in the north doing vital work. Or so he had told Kao Li-shih and himself. But there were other reasons for his reluctance that he was only just starting to articulate to himself. How could he make Kao Li-shih understand?

"Master Kao," he began, "what exactly would we be trying to do? Suppose for a moment that we succeed in convincing the Emperor that An Lu-shan has committed murder and instigated a cover-up. Suppose we finally break through the Emperor's blindness toward his 'Lucky Baby.' Suppose the Emperor strips him of his rank and relieves him of his duties. Then what?"

"Then another of the empire's very competent generals takes his place."

"That is exactly the problem, Kao Li-shih," Yang Kuo-chung said, shaking his head. "I fear that there is no one who could take his place. The reports from the north come in almost weekly. Everything they say indicates that the cunning, deceitful, murderous "Lucky Baby" is indispensable to the safety of the empire. Hopei Province was nearly lost to the secessionists, as you probably know. Since An Lu-shan returned to his duties in the north several months ago, the situation has stabilized. His presence has a . . . calming effect on the people of those border provinces. I ask you: who else has that ability? I don't know, Kao Li-shih; I used to believe that any good general could do the job, that An Lu-shan's talents were not particularly unique—or that, in any case, the price we had to pay for them was too high. But the empire is crumbling at the edges. Look what has happened in the northwest. Invaders, foreigners, occupying territory that was once sovereign. I must tell you the truth: I want him exactly where he is, doing exactly what he is doing. I do not like to think of the north without An Lu-shan's strength."

"I do not agree that An Lu-shan is indispensable. His kind of strength is indispensable, yes. But not the man himself," Kao Li-shih argued. "However, if you believe that you need his strength, then it is essential—and urgently so—that you demonstrate to him that you are his master. He must know that such criminal, arbitrary behavior as murders and cover-ups will not be tolerated and will be exposed to the light of day. He must know that he is not his own master. There must be an inquisition into his crimes. It is the only way."

Yang Kuo-chung, listening to Kao Li-shih's words, had an unreal feeling that he was hearing himself arguing with Li Lin-fu. Hadn't that been his own position when he went to the chief minister shortly before his death? He would have been quite ready, at that time, to have An Lu-shan assassinated. Now he could not picture the empire safe without him. You and I will become one, Li Lin-fu had said. Maybe it was already happening.

"We cannot hide these things from the Emperor," Kao Li-shih continued. "Deaf and blind though he may be, it is still our *duty* to make the facts known to him." He was speaking emphatically, leaning on the table now with a fierce, intent expression. "We have an obligation to see to it that everything that we know about the murder and the cover-up is revealed, and that An Lu-shan stands before the Emperor for a hearing of his crimes. If we do not do it," he said slowly, "then we become part of An Lu-shan's lie. And you and I, Master Yang, will be guilty of laying a foundation of lies. History will be built on those lies. We cannot do it. It is wrong." He leaned back again. "Don't you see? What the Emperor does with that knowledge after we have presented it to him is beyond our control. He may ignore it, or we may witness a miracle and he may see who his 'Lucky Baby' really is. What the Emperor does is almost irrelevant. You made a declaration today in front of hundreds of witnesses," he said, pointing a finger at Yang Kuo-chung. "You promised them that this would be a new age, that Li Lin-fu's influence was as dead as his corpse which you displayed in the courtyard today. If you do not order your general to appear before the Emperor and be accountable for a crime of which you have full knowledge, then you are as guilty as the criminal himself. And you will be perpetuating the legacy of Li Lin-fu, which you told the world was dead and buried." He shook his head then and spoke with quiet emphasis. "We do not go about opening coffins and dishonoring corpses unless we mean what we say, Master Yang. Otherwise, what does that make us?"

Yang Kuo-chung looked at his friend. He was right, of course. Every syllable he uttered was as true as a perfectly aimed arrow. He sighed.

"Powerful words, Kao Li-shih."

"But I don't think you need to worry particularly," Kao Li-shih said then with an entirely different tone. "The worst punishment that An Lu-shan might suffer at the Emperor's hands would be a mild reprimand. And I, personally, have little faith in even that eventuality."

He pushed his empty cup across the table. Yang Kuo-chung refilled it.

"But An Lu-shan must never know the source of our information," Yang Kuo-chung said.

Kao Li-shih looked up, pleased at the tacit concession to the argument in the other's words.

"He will not. No mention will ever be made of his son or the eunuch Li Chu-erh. We are obligated to protect them. It is none of An Lu-shan's business *how* we know. It will be quite sufficient for him to simply know that we *do* know. And that the Emperor knows," he added.

"All right, Kao Li-shih," Yang Kuo-chung said. "We will dispatch a messenger today. I believe that things are stable enough in the north for the time being. An Lu-shan may take a few weeks' leave of absence."

They sat in pensive silence for several minutes.

"I wonder if they will find the poor poet-minister Chang Chiu-ling on the island of Hai-nan," Kao Li-shih said then, surprising Yang Kuo-chung with the abrupt change of subject. "I have always felt somewhat responsible for the poor man's fate."

"When did you last receive a letter from him?" Yang Kuo-chung asked.

"It has been years," Kao Li-shih said sadly. "Years."

"It is not your fault," Yang Kuo-chung offered. "I have often felt that if I had done more or had behaved differently, my vanished Censorate eunuchs might have been spared as well. We were all caught, Kao Li-shih, in Li Lin-fu's web. There is nothing any of us could have done."

"But that is all over now, is it not?" Kao Li-shih asked pointedly. "Li Lin-fu is dead."

"He is," Yang Kuo-chung agreed. "Quite dead."

But Li Lin-fu was not completely dead. Though he kept it to himself, Yang Kuo-chung was troubled by the persistence in his memory of certain of the chief minister's words, spoken only a few months ago. Li Lin-fu had been talking about An Lu-shan and the subtle use of power to control such a man. Too much direct force against An Lu-shan, the chief minister had said, will cause him to revolt in one way or another. *I believe we have a perfect example before us in the recent unfortunate events up north,* Li Lin-fu had said. *If you will remember, An Lu-shan was subjected to heavy censure by the eunuch Kao Li-shih just before he departed for the north this last time . . . He was called before the Emperor and forced to defend his character in a most abject and humiliating way . . . what followed was an inevitable and almost perfectly predictable reaction . . .*

But Yang Kuo-chung said nothing to Kao Li-shih about his doubt and discomfort. How could he tell him that Li Lin-fu was whispering in his ear? How, in light of what the eunuch had just told him, and rightly, about building history on lies and deceit, could he explain his feelings? Besides, the decision had already been made. He could not go back on his word; An Lu-shan would be called down.

"I think it would be best," Yang Kuo-chung said thoughtfully, "if the order to appear came not from me, but from the Emperor himself. And that is where I need you, Kao Li-shih."

The eunuch shrugged and put his cup down.

"I think that I can arrange that," he said.

: :

On the day of the hearing before the Emperor, Yang Kuo-chung crossed the Orchid Terrace in the bureaucratic city and thought that he detected a trace of winter in the morning air. For the last two weeks or so, the warm, dry afternoons had given way to cool nights. That was always when you felt it first, he thought; at night, when you woke from your sleep and found yourself reaching for an extra quilt, pulling it over you, keeping the chill from your bones. Now it was morning, the sun shining and the sky clear, but the air was crisp and sharp. As if it had come from the north, Yang Kuo-chung said to himself; as if An Lu-shan had brought it with him.

This would be the first time that An Lu-shan had come to the capital when there was no Li Lin-fu waiting for him. Yang Kuo-chung had caught a glimpse of the general the day before, arriving with his outriders, his face set and grim, his rough clothing dirty and rumpled from the ride. He carried with him the ambience of another world—a world of vast distances, cold winds, and danger; a world of harsh realities unrelated to their own soft life here in the comfort and safety of the capital. When Yang Kuo-chung saw him, he had experienced a feeling very close to chagrin—as if they were imposing on An Lu-shan, interrupting his very serious work, which he performed for their benefit, with their frivolous and time-consuming demand for his presence. Plainly, that was what An Lu-shan himself felt. I have far better things I could be doing, his look had said, than to be here. Yang Kuo-chung doubted that he would have come at all if the order had not come from the Emperor.

Li Chu-erh and An Ching-hsu had met with the Emperor several days ago. He had listened to their story, told with great care, of the long march into Khitan territory in the rain, the soaked bowstrings, and the soldiers falling like broken toys on the battlefield. They had even told him about the man who rode back and tried to warn them, and how An Lu-shan had cut him to the ground and left him to be trampled by the charging army. And they had told every little detail of the murder of the Censorate investigators, the flaming tent being dragged across the plains, and the arrows of the soldiers cutting down old men and women as they tried to run. They had left nothing out.

Yang Kuo-chung and Kao Li-shih had been present for the meeting, and both were impressed by the calm, understated quality of the youths' testimony. No one listening to them could have accused them of exaggerating their story or of fabricating details for effect. The Emperor had listened thoughtfully, thanked them, and dismissed them. Then he had told Yang Kuo-chung and Kao Li-shih that he wished to be alone so that he could assess the information, and dismissed them, too.

Crossing the courtyard this morning, Yang Kuo-chung knew that he was a long way from any sort of resolve. He was not at all sure of what he wanted out of what was to take place today. He pulled his outer jacket tight against the cool air. He had a strong feeling of marching toward an unknowable fate, just like An Lu-shan's soldiers going into battle.

: :

The Emperor had done everything he could, it seemed, to avoid the formal atmosphere of an inquisition. It was more as though he had invited An Lu-shan, Yang Kuo-chung, and Kao Li-shih to have tea and a discussion with him in his private quarters. A few other magistrates were present to ensure that the meeting would be an official one, and there were scribes ready to take down every word.

Yang Kuo-chung entered the room and exchanged a look with Kao Li-shih, who was already there. An Lu-shan had transformed himself since yesterday: he was bathed and combed and dressed in clean, new clothing. He completely ignored Yang Kuo-chung, who crossed the room and sat in a chair to one side of where the Emperor sat, which placed him opposite An Lu-shan, who sat on the Emperor's other side. Kao Li-shih, as was his habit, remained standing to one side with his arms crossed.

"An Lu-shan," the Emperor began, "I have requested your presence here today so that you may . . . shed some light on some unfortunate events that have come to our attention."

"I know what you are going to ask me, Father," An Lu-shan responded immediately, "and I am grateful for the opportunity to unburden my soul before you. I have been deeply, deeply troubled," he said, shaking his head and looking sadly down at the floor.

Yang Kuo-chung and Kao Li-shih looked warily at one another. What sort of performance was An Lu-shan going to put on today?

"Master Yang," the Emperor said. "Why don't you ask the general some questions?"

"Thank you, Father," Yang Kuo-chung said, pointedly using the same form of address as had An Lu-shan. "General," he said then, looking at An Lu-shan, who looked back at him steadily, "we wish to know about a specific campaign that you waged several months ago, in the springtime, against the Khitan."

"Yes," the general said. "Many men were killed. I myself was severely wounded."

"There had been many days of heavy rain during the march, had there not, General?"

"Some of the worst I have ever seen, Chief Minister," An Lu-shan said with a barely detectable trace of sarcasm.

"I will get right to the point, General," Yang Kuo-Chung said, standing up. "What we want to know about is why so many men died. Is it true that their bowstrings, as a result of being soaked through and through by the rain, were as useless as if they had been silk hair ribbons, and that the soldiers found themselves riding forward into the face of the enemy without weapons?"

"The bowstrings were useless, it is true," An Lu-shan said, still looking steadily at him.

"And isn't it true that you were warned? That one of your own soldiers rode back and tried to tell you what was happening, but you slashed the man from his saddle and, ignoring his warning, gave the order to attack anyway?"

"A man rode back shouting something about the bowstrings, yes," An Lu-shan said, and looked toward the Emperor for a moment. "But he was not one of my soldiers."

Yang Kuo-chung was caught completely off guard by this. For a moment he said nothing, but stood there trying to comprehend An Lu-shan's meaning.

"He was sent by the enemy," An Lu-shan went on. "It is a common ploy. And often effective. It serves to unnerve an advancing army, robbing them of their crucial resolve at the last moment. Even if it does not cause the army to turn back, it can take away that edge of courage and purpose needed to win a battle."

"And that is why you killed him?" Yang Kuo-chung asked, incredulous that An Lu-shan would expect even his most loyal admirer to believe such a tale.

"Would I kill one of my own men?" An Lu-shan asked with painful sincerity. "I had to prevent panic from spreading."

"And what did you think when you discovered that what the man said was true? Did you still believe that he had been an enemy in disguise, or did it occur to you then that you had killed one of your own men when he was in the midst of performing a heroic act?"

"Chief Minister," An Lu-shan said, "part of being a military man is the taking of risks and the willingness to make crucial decisions without hesitation. There is always the possibility that you will have to make sacrifices. There will be mistakes. But you do not undertake to lead men, to be a commander, unless you accept beforehand that some of your decisions will inevitably cause some pain and, in certain cases, death. It takes a special courage and sense of purpose to follow your calling when you know that men will die. But it must be measured against the larger purpose, the good that you can do for the greater number. It is a terrible burden. In quiet moments, Chief Minister, it causes me great pain," he said, looking for a moment as if he were going to cry.

Yang Kuo-chung stole a glance at Kao Li-shih. The eunuch raised an eyebrow and shook his head ever so slightly.

"And the bowstrings?" Yang Kuo-chung asked, feeling now as if he were merely supplying cues to An Lu-shan, rather than interrogating him.

"What can I say?" An Lu-shan raised his hands in supplication. "They were no good. They were poorly made. This is a matter to be taken up with those in charge of military supplies. I did not make the bows, Master Yang," he said with a touch of insolence, looking into Yang Kuo-chung's eyes.

Yang Kuo-chung had been watching An Lu-shan closely, looking for the telltale beads of sweat that would indicate that he was slipping into the grip of fear and turmoil, but so far, the general's brow remained quite dry. Yang Kuo-chung turned away, thinking carefully about his next line of questioning.

"General, we received a report from the Censorate officials who traveled to the north. The report, which exonerated you of any wrongdoing, arrived via messenger, but the officials themselves never returned to the capital. Do you know what their fate was?"

Again, An Lu-shan's face reflected his sorrow.

"They were burned to death in a tent while they ate," he said, surprising Yang Kuo-chung even more than he had a moment ago with his story about the enemy rider in disguise.

"We were led to believe that they were attacked and drowned in a river on their way back to the capital," Yang Kuo-chung said, recovering quickly.

Now An Lu-shan's head was resting in his hands. The Emperor leaned forward attentively; An Lu-shan raised his head then and stared toward a window, as if dredging up painful memories.

"There was no drowning," he said. "They burned to death. Trapped in a banquet tent, being dragged by a team of crazed horses."

Yang Kuo-chung waited, on guard. Now what?

"I admit that I fabricated the story about the drowning," An Lu-shan said. "I can only offer my apologies. But I think you will understand when I tell you the reason, and that you will forgive me." He snuffled then and looked down at his lap, as if making a mighty effort to collect himself.

Yang Kuo-chung could see the Emperor's face softening with concern. An Lu-shan heaved a great sigh, as if he were about to confess every sin on his soul.

"I have lived among the Chinese for so long," he said, "that I have begun to think like a Chinese. I have, essentially, *become* Chinese."

Get to the point, Yang Kuo-chung thought impatiently.

"I know that for the Chinese, the most dire insult that can be inflicted on the dead is to be burned rather than to receive a proper burial. And of course, to die by burning is just too hideous to contemplate. To be taken by surprise, as those unfortunate officials were, in the midst of a happy, hospitable occasion . . . the pain and terror must have been dreadful. Dreadful," he repeated, shaking his head.

"And who," Yang Kuo-chung asked, "was responsible for inflicting that pain and terror?" he asked, though by now he had a fair idea of what An Lu-shan was going to say.

"I had ordered a banquet for the officials," An Lu-shan said. "I commissioned an entire village to prepare the food and set up the tent. I wanted it to be pleasant and festive. The officials were done with their work and would be leaving the next day. Naturally, I wanted them to carry the best possible impression back to the capital."

"Naturally," Yang Kuo-chung said, crossing his arms.

"As you no doubt know, the northern provinces are troubled by internal problems. Secessionism is rampant, and there are those among the common people who collaborate with the enemy. I had thought that I had chosen a safe village. As far as I knew, there had been no problems with these particular people. But there were traitors among them, Master Yang. They rigged the tent so that it was a trap of death. They buried ropes, attached to the tent at one end and fastened to the carriage at the other . . ."

"I know about the ropes and the tent, General," Yang Kuo-chung interrupted coldly. "I know about the fire."

"It was a vicious gesture. A bold, hostile gesture against the empire." He paused and looked around the room, resting his sad eyes for a moment on the Emperor. "The trap was meant for me," he said with dramatic emphasis. "It is only a matter of Providence that I had not yet arrived for the banquet. I was gone for most of the day, inspecting border installations."

"And why do you suppose that the traitors among the peasants sprung their trap before you arrived?" Yang Kuo-chung asked, fascinated now by An Lu-shan's inexhaustible inventiveness.

"They grew impatient, I suppose," An Lu-shan said, shrugging. "They thought that perhaps I was not going to appear that day, and so they took their vicious frustration out on the innocent Censorate officials. It was a clear gesture of hostility. My men reacted swiftly, cutting the traitors down as they ran."

"Old people? Children?" Yang Kuo-chung demanded.

"Collaborators often hide among the very young and the very old. That, also, is a common tactic," An Lu-shan said, as though it were something that everyone knew. "There was no time to stop and find out who was guilty and who was not. Alas, it is war. And military men must make decisions, sacrifices." He raised his arms in helpless sorrow, searching Yang Kuo-chung's face for a glimmer of understanding.

Yang Kuo-chung did not have time to express his incredulity or form another question. In the next moment, An Lu-shan turned, lumbered down from his chair, and knelt on the floor before the Emperor, addressing him humbly and earnestly.

"Father, I beg your forgiveness for the lie about the river. But you must understand . . . I knew the pain that it would cause the families of the murdered officials if they were to learn the truth—that death had been by burning and that the bodies had all been reduced to ashes. It just seemed . . . too cruel," he said with heart-wrenching sincerity. "I was only trying to spare them. It was wrong, I know that it was wrong." He bowed his head.

Yang Kuo-chung, seeing two teardrops splash on the polished floor in front of the general, looked with disbelief in Kao Li-shih's direction. The eunuch merely returned a look of great weariness, shutting his eyes and shaking his head slowly from side to side.

"Whatever I do," An Lu-shan went on, the tears flowing freely now, "I do out of loyalty for you. It causes me terrible pain to know that you doubt me." With that, he reached his great, hairy hand forward and seized the hem of the Emperor's robe. He raised his eyes to the Emperor's and spoke through his abject tears. "I have nothing but loyalty for you in my great belly, Father," he said, and buried his streaming nose and eyes in the fabric clutched in his hand.

The Emperor stood, reaching down to An Lu-shan as if he could pull him to his feet.

"I believe you, An Lu-shan. There will be no more questions," the Emperor said, looking fiercely at both Kao Li-shih and Yang Kuo-chung.

An Lu-shan heaved himself to his feet, and stood rubbing his eyes as though he really were some sort of huge baby. And though his tears were streaming, his forehead remained perfectly dry. Yang Kuo-chung understood: An Lu-shan had never had even the smallest doubt about the outcome of the meeting today.

: :

The Emperor gave a dinner that evening and insisted that Yang Kuo-chung and Kao Li-shih attend. An Lu-shan was there, and so was the Precious Consort. The Emperor was attempting to create an atmosphere of reconciliation. The unpleasant little matter of the bowstrings and the dead Censorate officials was not discussed, and it was plain that the Emperor considered that all questions were answered and done with. He raised toast after toast to An Lu-shan, telling him what a splendid job he was doing for the empire, and how grateful they were to him, and may he live for a thousand years.

And An Lu-shan reciprocated, working hard to show the Emperor that he bore him no ill feelings, no hidden resentments for what had transpired today. He laughed and drank and gazed fondly at him, his face and manner eloquently sending a clear message: you are my father. You did what you had to do. But the trust and understanding between us runs so deep that nothing can interfere, nothing can violate it.

Then the Emperor announced to the table that An Lu-shan would be returning to the north very soon, and that from now on, in order to facilitate the excellent and vital work he was performing for the empire, the general would no longer have to go through any official channels in order to procure whatever increases in men and supplies he deemed necessary. The Emperor asked for Yang Kuo-chung to give his own approval to the plan. We must be in complete agreement, he said. We must all show General An that we support him, that we appreciate what he is doing for us. Is there a single one of us here tonight, the Emperor asked, who does not acknowledge that China needs her mighty general more than ever?

Yang Kuo-chung, though his heart and mind were scarcely at peace about it, gave his approval. Perhaps this is the price we must pay, he thought resignedly, for a man of An Lu-shan's unique power. Perhaps we must make terrible sacrifices inversely proportionate to what we expect from him. Even, he asked himself, if it means sacrificing truth and integrity? What did Kao Li-shih say to you about building history on lies?

But he nodded his head in assent to the Emperor's request. Toasts were drunk all around, with the exception of Kao Li-shih, who said that he wished to stay sober this evening. An Lu-shan was hale and jovial—but he could not, Yang Kuo-chung noted, seem to catch the consort's eye or make her smile. She, more than anyone, Yang Kuo-chung knew, had not forgotten Father Springtime. An Lu-shan did not give up; for the next hour, he did his best. He directed little jokes toward her, smiled coyly at her, and tried to get her attention with his stories and antics. When she excused herself early and left the party, his look was one of pure sorrow, and the look was genuine. Yang Kuo-chung could see that it was no ploy.

For the most part, An Lu-shan ignored Yang Kuo-chung, letting his eyes slip over him as if he did not quite exist or else glancing at him with careless insolence as if he were someone An Lu-shan had just met and didn't care for. I am no Li Lin-fu in his eyes, that much is obvious, Yang Kuo-chung thought. But An Lu-shan did not ignore Kao Li-shih, which seemed curious to Yang Kuo-chung; it is I, he thought, who should be the object of An Lu-shan's hatred today.

He watched carefully: whenever the Emperor's attention was diverted for a moment, An Lu-shan's look of joy or sorrow would turn to one of undiluted hostility, directed discreetly in Kao Li-shih's direction. The instant that the Emperor turned his attention back, the look would vanish and An Lu-shan would be smiling, or frowning, once more. The Precious Consort was not the only one who had not forgotten the Father Springtime debacle, Yang Kuo-chung thought uneasily. And plainly, Kao Li-shih was a long, long way from being forgiven for his role in bringing An Lu-shan before the Emperor and the consort. Just as he, Yang Kuo-chung, had done today.

: :

"Maybe we were completely wrong about everything," Yang Kuo-chung said to Kao Li-shih as they crossed an open courtyard in the dark after the "party" had broken up. He was fairly drunk. It had seemed necessary to keep drinking wine this evening; it was the only way any of it made any sense. "Maybe An Lu-shan was telling the truth today."

"Yes," Kao Li-shih replied drily. "And maybe I will get my balls back someday."

A wave of mirth at this remark took Yang Kuo-chung completely by surprise. He had to stop walking while he doubled over with laughter—a strange, helpless, inappropriate, but entirely pleasurable feeling. He had no idea why he was laughing, but it had been at least a hundred years since he had last done so. Kao Li-shih stood patiently by in the dark, waiting for the seizure to run its course.

"Oh, yes, Kao Li-shih," Yang Kuo-chung gasped. "Yes. You will get your balls back, and I will be young and careless again." He wiped his eyes, then rubbed them until he saw flashes of white fire. "It is all true. Every word of it," he said, straightening up and catching his breath. "How could we ever have doubted him?"

"Did I tell you," Kao Li-shih said then, "I have received a message from Chang Chiu-ling?"

Yang Kuo-chung turned to his friend in the darkness, his laughter forgotten.

"When? How?"

"Your contingent has returned from the island of Hai-nan. They brought back about a dozen ragged ghosts, all victims of Li Lin-fu. I was on my way over to the Emperor's apartments when I heard. You were already there, so I told them that I would deliver the news to you. They will want to meet with you first thing tomorrow."

"Chang Chiu-ling is alive, then? Is he here?" Yang Kuo-chung asked, the effects of the wine clearing from his head as he spoke.

"He is alive," Kao Li-shih said. "But he is not here. He did not return with the others. He told them to tell me that the island was his home now, that he loved it, and that he would never leave."

::

An Lu-shan, who had gone to bed after the Emperor's party very drunk with his mind seething, awoke in the dark hours later, his head perfectly clear, with the certain knowledge that someone lay silent and unmoving next to him on the bed. In the next moment, he knew who it was. He would never, even if twenty years were to pass, forget that smell: damp earth, rotting wood. He wondered for a brief moment how she had found him, here, in the palace, in the middle of the city.

He had not thought of her for years; he had not even allowed himself to contemplate the memory of her nighttime visits. Just as he would have used his knife to sever a diseased limb from his own body, so he had brutally cut the disturbing experience from his life. But now, almost before he had time to comprehend, he found himself intensely, painfully aroused. It was as if no time at all had passed.

He rolled over quickly and pinned her with a heavy leg. She was not going to get away. If she had the effrontery to return to his life, then she was going to learn this time who was master. And this time he would make her speak. She was going to tell him who she was.

Her hand came up and caressed his face, slid around to the back of his neck, up to the top of his head, and back down to his neck. As her hand moved down toward his face, she allowed her fingernails to rake the skin of his cheek lightly, dangerously. The hand wandered to his neck again, onto his back and shoulder, and across his face, the nails leaving a little tingling trail that made his heart pound hard and sent a message directly to his groin.

He made a move to roll on top of her. He was going to have her, right now. He was not going to waste any time. He found her legs with his knee and pushed them apart; at the same moment, her caressing nails dug like claws into the flesh of his back. Shocked by the pain, he howled and pulled back. She raked him again, this time across the back of the neck; even more shocking than the sudden pain was the intensification of arousal: his "old man" rose like a warrior's sword, twice as long and twice as hard as it had ever been in his life.

She held on with one hand, nails still embedded in his skin, and pulled him toward her with unexpected strength. He found her knees again, pushed them apart, and heaved himself onto her so that she was pinned. He tried to catch her other hand, but she eluded him. Now both her hands were on him, pulling and clawing, while he drove himself into her with violent fury.

I will make you talk, he said, thrusting with each word. You will tell me your name. You will tell me everything about you. And you will speak my name. Say it, he ordered: An Lu-shan. Say it. She did not say it, but moaned and hissed like an animal, her nails buried in his skin. Say my name, he said, his teeth clenched. Say my name. Say it. Say it. Say it.

Her keening and growling was thinning, rising in pitch. He cursed. He knew what it meant. He had never been able to resist that sound. It would carry him up with it, make him helpless, finish him off before he was ready. He cursed in a loud, steady stream, trying to drown her out, trying to fight the compelling whine that was already vibrating in his ear.

She fought and struggled beneath him with wiry strength. Hot liquid ran down his neck onto his shoulders; he did not know if it was blood or sweat. He imagined that her nails were talons that pierced his body to the bone. He held out as long as he could, but when her voice reached a high, thin pitch of unbearable intensity he had to let go, squeezing his eyes shut as a thousand stars and comets exploded in the center of his brain and shot out across the black night sky of his mind.

It was like rising up out of a dream. He lay limp and spent on top of her, letting his heart slow down and his rasping breath grow quiet again. He wondered vaguely if he dared let her up. Would she try to knee him in the groin or scratch his eyes out? But she was quiet beneath him. Still holding her down, he lifted himself up slightly so that she would be able to breathe. Exhausted and empty, he buried his face in her neck and shut his eyes.

"An Lu-shan," came her low voice right next to his ear.

His head rose up sharply as if someone had jerked it back by the hair. She had spoken! She had said his name!

Still holding her down with one leg, he fumbled in the blackness for the lamp and the flint by the bed. He had to strike the cursed apparatus four or five times before he could get a spark and light the wick of the lamp. He adjusted the flame and turned toward the woman on his bed.

He reared back in shock, crashing against the table and upsetting the lamp, which fell and shattered, extinguishing the flame.

The few seconds of light had revealed an old, old woman, her face like the cracked bottom of a dry riverbed, her toothless mouth stretched in silent, convulsive mirth. Her breasts hung down like shriveled, empty pouches and her bones protruded like a plucked bird's as she lay posing for him audaciously as if she were the ripest, most alluring young beauty in the world.

He was off the bed in the next moment, blundering against furniture, looking for another lamp. He found a vase, mistook it for a lamp, realized his mistake, and hurled it to the floor. He stepped on the broken pieces in the dark, cutting his foot. Cursing, he felt his way toward the door. His fingers closed around a wall lamp; he pulled it from its holder and groped on the floor near the bed for the flint. The first spark failed, but the second one took, and the lamp flared.

She was gone. He looked all around the room, but she had vanished—

whether through the door, out the window, or over the balcony, he did not know.

A trace of musty dampness lingered in the air of the room. Trembling, he reached to the back of his neck, touched his flesh where it stung, and brought his hand forward.

She had been quite real. His fingers were dark with his own blood.

: :

Poets and writers, in their journals, in missives to their friends and relatives, and in short works published in the literary gazettes of the city, claimed to have detected the underlying tenor of the times. Some described it in terms of feelings; others said it was something that they could see. But in the end, it was those who said that they could actually hear it who laid the greatest claim to some sort of valid insight.

Certainly there was no particular noise or clamor that distinguished these final days of autumn from those of any other year. In the country, farmers still worked, shouting to each other and to their hard-working oxen, and children's shrill voices rose in play while their mothers scolded them. In the city, the vast and infinitely diverse populace went about the same activities that it had always gone about. Carriages, wagons, and carts rumbled by the thousands over the paving stones; merchants cajoled and bullied their customers, and the customers, in turn, haggled and insulted the merchants and the quality of their goods, all in the time-honored tradition of commerce. The civil police prodded and kicked the usual drunken, boisterous, and unruly crowds that gathered in various quarters of the great city after the curfew drums had rolled; men laughed at their own crude jokes while women sang, giggled, and gossiped; girls squealed, and boys yelled in exuberance to one another, all of it exactly as it had always been.

And yet the wordsmiths, the poets in particular, spoke and wrote with ever greater frequency of a strange sound that emanated from everywhere and nowhere. They spoke of the air humming with it; they spoke of it rising all around them, they spoke of hearing it at dawn when they were coming up out of their dreams. But no one could quite identify it, or offer a definition, beyond speaking in abstracts—not until the simple lines of one poet solved the mystery and exposed its simplicity:

> And all about me I hear the old folks,
> whose talk lingers more and more in the comfortable
> recollections of a secure and certain past.

That was the sound, everyone agreed: old people, talking in quiet voices about the past. There was nothing unusual about the elderly reminiscing; that was why, at first, the phenomenon escaped notice as the cause of the sound humming underneath all the other sounds of the city. But it was a subtle increase in the steady, constant, and timeless sound that finally caught the attention of that one sharp-eared poet.

They were talking more often and in more vivid detail about the past than they usually did. And their speech conjured images of a world that was safe because it was secure from change: the world of memories. It was as though the very old, who no longer thought of the time in front of them in terms of years, or even months, but in weeks and days, were uncertain of even these small allotted increments and preferred to dwell entirely in the past. And what was the significance of such talk?

Theories abounded, of course. One—which gained a certain popular credence in the wineshops and teahouses—was that old people, with a prescience not unlike the restlessness of geese before an earthquake, tended to escape more and more into the past as they sensed the approaching shadow of war. With the possible exception of children, it was old people who were the most vulnerable, and certainly were the most expendable, in times of war—and so they sought the comfort and inviolability of the past.

But there were no other indications of war. The northwestern territories lost to the invading Arabs had not been regained, but the armies of Mohammed had been unable to penetrate any farther, meeting with a firmly reinforced front line of resistance. And the rumblings of secessionism in Hopei Province actually grew quieter as autumn surrendered to an early winter.

And winter did come early. By the first day of the ninth month,* a thin white blanket covered the ground. By the middle of the month, one of the heaviest snowfalls in recent recorded history fell in Kuanchung Province. Ch'ang-an and the world about it ceased to move. There was no business, no traffic; the world had slowed to a hushed and gleaming standstill. For several days thereafter, few tracks marred the silky surfaces of roads and fields: a motionless white universe, so still and quiet that even death seemed to have no place in it. And just as quickly as it had come, it vanished, melting away in muddy, brachiated streams. By the end of the ninth month, it was warm again, almost like the beginning of autumn.

It was an odd season, some said. But then, hadn't there been much that was strange in the weather in recent times? People had begun to expect the odd imbalances. Scholars and commoners alike conjectured about this; historians, if they had any reason at all to recall these times, would no doubt someday write about the extremes and paradoxes of the weather.

By the second week of the eleventh month, it turned bitter cold and

*Mid-November.

remained that way; the ground froze to the hardness of rock. For weeks there was no snow and not a cloud obscured the brilliant blue sky.

Shortly after the New Year and the Festival of Lanterns, which, it seemed, had been observed with much less enthusiasm these last several years, the Yang family made their ritual outing to the hot springs palace. This year, their gaily festooned caravan was given a greater purpose than the usual one of seeking the springs' steamy warmth. Minghuang traveled with the Precious Consort, while the Lady of Kuo rode with her sisters. Since late that last summer, Yang Kuo-chung had refused to join his cousin at the springs, and she had ceased to pressure him. The outing, the Emperor said, was being made in honor of the Lady of Chin.

One cold morning at the Palace of Grand Enlightenment in Ch'ang-an, while an army of servants struggled to maintain the heat with elaborate arrangements of window quilts, braziers, and much more coal than was usual in their brick *kangs,* Chin had awakened early and forsaken the warmth of her apartments. She went down the long hallway and woke her sisters, who had all abandoned their mansions in the city temporarily because of the cold. She had entered their rooms audaciously, forcing them out of bed by pulling the covers from them as they slept. She gave no explanation, but was laughing merrily and was most insistent that they put on their robes and accompany her to the sitting room. The Lady of Han had protested the loudest, but the Lady of Kuo was far more tolerant, having endured, she told them, her handsome cousin's unpredictable antics. Kuo had told Han to hush, so that they might find out what it was all about and get back to bed.

I had a dream, the Lady of Chin had told her sleepy-eyed sisters. Han responded by saying that if that was all, then she was getting up right now and going back to her warm bed. But she was stopped by a sharp warning look from the Lady of Kuo. Grumbling, she had sat back down, and Chin had resumed her story with enthusiasm. Her dream, she told them, was about a bird. A beautiful songbird. Han had rolled her eyes with impatience and looked as though she were really going to leave this time, but another look from Kuo, even fiercer than the last, conveyed an unmistakable message: sit!

In my dream, it was a glorious day in spring, Chin went on, her eyes shining. It was warm and beautiful. She herself was a bird on a branch, a magnificent songbird of rare beauty, covered with glistening blue and yellow feathers, the brilliant sun warming her back. And she could sing with so much richness, tonality, and originality that she drove the other songbirds nearly out of the province. How, may I ask, does this involve us, the Lady of Han had asked at last, her tone considerably softened. The dream was a message,

Chin said, that she had the ability to be the greatest singer of all. But the dream had made it clear that she could not sing unless she was warm. Therefore, they must wake Little Sister and form their entourage to the hot springs immediately. Little Sister, a musician and dancer herself, would understand the nature of inspiration, Chin said. She would not ask questions. She would pull together a contingent from the Pear Garden Orchestra, and, nurtured by the warm ambience of the springs, Chin could begin her training and meteoric rise into musical legend . . .

And so the coldest months of the year were spent in the warmth and splendor of the hot springs, with the Lady of Kuo making regular trips back to the city to spend time with her cousin, since he was far too busy to travel out to her, and was still refusing to come there anyway; Chin worked diligently on her singing, and, indeed, it looked as though her dream had spoken the truth, for her progress was rapid and her music full of promise. Her sisters accompanied her on their instruments, along with a few select members of the Pear Garden. They decided to plan for a grand performance, to be held in the spring, when the snow and ice had released its grip on the city, and spent their days working toward that.

There were little private performances, of course, and intimate parties and dinners almost every night. The Emperor and the consort, more relaxed and happy with one another than they had been for many years, played music together too; and sometimes, in the evenings, they would sit, up to their shoulders in the hot waters of the Emperor's favorite thermal pool, the steam rising around them, and watch the snow falling gently on the hot springs grounds.

::

Yang Kuo-chung did his best to ignore the cold that continued unabated past the New Year and into the first month. As the winter wore on, he kept a close watch on communiqués from the military commanderies in the north, paying special attention to news that came from the province of Hopei.

But the news came less and less frequently, and he considered that a good sign. It seemed that An Lu-shan was successfully quelling the ambitions of the warlords in that province. Infrequent reports from the Chinese generals meant, to Yang Kuo-chung's mind, a lessening of open provocation and fewer insurgencies along the chain of commanderies that ran north from Huai Chou above Loyang and north beyond Pien Chou. It was a good thing for several reasons, but one stood out in particular: if they had been forced to pour more military strength into a region that had such a long history of enmity with the T'ang, the open display of power could serve to increase the hatred and suspicion already endemic there. For the empire to lose the agricultural wealth of that region would be nothing short of disastrous. And there had always been the worrisome possibility that the people of Hopei, if they continued to remain hostile to being ruled from Ch'ang-an, might very well seek support from the Sillan Peninsula.

But because of An Lu-shan's unique talents, it seemed, none of these dire things were happening. He was the only man, as Li Lin-fu had said, with the ability to bring the loyalties of the troubled province into the sphere of the T'ang, to whatever extent that was possible to do.

As news of outbreaks decreased, Yang Kuo-chung began to allow himself a bit of cautious optimism. For weeks after An Lu-shan's meeting with the Emperor, Yang Kuo-chung had been in a near constant state of doubt and vacillation. Had he done the right thing? Or had he done the thing that Li Lin-fu had warned him against—cornered An Lu-shan, humiliated him? Months later, Yang Kuo-chung allowed himself to consider that, just possibly, it had been the right thing to do. The action of summoning the general before the throne had served Yang Kuo-chung's credibility, but had not, apparently, estranged An Lu-shan any further. It was a precarious balance, but something had been achieved. An Lu-shan was back in the north, had committed no outrageous acts, as far as anyone knew, and was doing his work in an exemplary way. Perhaps the Emperor's final expression of faith had taken hold somewhere in the fat man's belly—perhaps the Emperor had actually touched that great "sack of loyalty," as An Lu-shan himself had so picturesquely put it.

Minghuang had bolstered the general's power in the Hopei commanderies, the *fu-ping* militia units. And by midwinter Yang Kuo-chung knew that his own previous attempts at counterbalancing the growing problems in Hopei by appointing himself military governor in absentia of the neighboring Chien-nan territories had been feeble, and ultimately futile. And Yang Kuo-chung now felt, as his fears of serious outbreaks subsided, that such a position for himself was no longer necessary.

And in the midst of his new and still fragile optimism, it occurred to Yang Kuo-chung that perhaps the Emperor was not quite so blind as they had all thought. Perhaps he knew about something in the fat man that even Li Lin-fu had overlooked—some deep reserve of calm, reason, and loyalty that needed only to be nurtured through faith. Li Lin-fu had always spoken of An Lu-shan as a force that needed to be controlled—but perhaps, after all, he had been wrong.

Perhaps the new peace in Hopei was evidence of something profound that they had never anticipated. Perhaps, Yang Kuo-chung thought, the Emperor had tapped the Tao within An Lu-shan, giving it purpose, definition, direction, legitimacy, and life. Or maybe it was the other way around: by giving credence to an inner reserve of calm and reason in An Lu-shan, Minghuang had brought it into existence. Could it be that, like those legendary rulers of antiquity, Minghuang had subtly altered the course of events and shaped the character of a man in ways hidden to the rest of them? If it was so, then Minghuang, the increasingly aloof and estranged Emperor, was hardly the fool they had believed him to be. What did the Emperor see when he looked into his fat baby's eyes? Yang Kuo-chung would never know.

By the middle of the second month, the iron cold ended. The winds began to blow, and the adamantine blue of the sky gave way to clouds, and then it snowed. It was a light snow, and it actually seemed to warm the air as it fell.

The pace of life picked up again: carts moved through the city streets, and the people, caged for so many months by the bitter cold, turned out and filled the marketplaces. They chattered loudly, gestured with broad animation, and bargained and haggled with the shopkeepers with reborn enthusiasm. The food vendors, rolling their cauldrons of crackling hot oils and dumplings of dough and meat and vegetables along the alleys and roadways called out with clarity and vitality, as if they had, just that day, discovered some great pleasure in the tedium of their work.

Wineshops opened their gates, and here and there, an occasional outdoor table was even set up tentatively in the snow-dusted courtyards. Farmers trod the long distance into town once more, with their preserved, dried, or smoked winter foods. And everywhere people walked briskly, moving lightly over the soft white of the ground as if it were a blessing.

23

Emperor Minghuang's Journey into Shu

The chief minister who had befriended An Lu-shan was dead and the emperor who had protected him was now almost seventy years of age. The swift crumbling of his influence at court may have been an important factor in the decision of An Lu-shan.

—*Howard S. Levy*

Summer

WHEN had she seen him looking so well? She could scarcely remember. He actually looked younger. She had noticed that his face seemed fuller these last few months, but it was not until this morning in the reflected light of the Lotus Pool that she was able to really study him. It was as if a layer of years had been peeled away.

His eyes seemed brighter, too. Although she might attribute that to the presence of the little children in the pool, she could also see that the lines of age and worry were definitely softening. She was certain that the phenomenon was real—it wasn't just an illusion, a trick of light. The skin was firmer; the sagging creases had filled out. From time to time she could plainly see the face of the young man that he once had been.

Was he actually getting younger? Had he, perhaps, found a way, through his Taoist recipes and incantations, to pry loose some small contract from the universe's reluctant and jealous fingers? The thought was exciting to her. She felt some of the old magic returning. Maybe he had found a way to keep them both young forever.

This morning it was a world she would not mind staying in forever. The air was fresh, cleansed by the rains. The morning sky was a pale, delicate blue. Outside the low tiled walls, a soft round copse of leafy trees tilted upward along the lowest ridge of Mount Li Shan. Mist rose, evaporating from the surface of the water. Some forty little children played in the shallows of the Lotus Pool, watched over by ten or twelve female nursery attendants.

The children scrambled over the aquatic statuary. These sculptures had recently been rescued from obscurity; An Lu-shan's gifts to the Emperor—stone dolphins, giant whiskered carp, sea turtles, and a multiheaded dragon —had been dredged from their resting places at the mossy bottom of Ming-huang's pond and brought out to decorate the Lotus Pool. Scrubbed clean of moss and algae, they had been given new life and now gleamed fearsomely in the sunlight.

For the children, they were the source of endless imaginative games. Some of the very little ones were frightened by the ferocious heads of the dragon and refused to approach it. The nursemaids would pick them up, screaming and crying, carry them over to the statue, and make them touch it with their chubby hands so that they would see for themselves that the monster was only carved from stone and could not hurt them. Some of the children were convinced, overcoming their terror and boldly stroking one of the drag-on's snouts while the tears dried on their fat cheeks; others were not so easily diverted from their sure knowledge that the creature before them had a vo-racious appetite for little children. Most of the children came to love An Lu-shan's beast—even if the Precious Consort did not—and having conquered it, climbed on it with impunity.

The Emperor moved down the stone stairs into the pool, splashing warm water on to his shoulders and back, teasing the children hanging on to the carved dolphin. I can do anything a dolphin can do, he told them. Do you want to see? They splashed and giggled, challenging him to dive down like a big fish. He pushed himself from the last underwater step out to the deepest part of the pool, then dove, his feet slapping the surface of the water like a great fish's tail, and disappeared.

The suspense was terrible. Where would he come up? They stared at the rippling water. He was under there somewhere, moving. Then a wave of shrieks and giggles began at one end of the line of children and traveled along the shallow edge where they stood chest-deep in the water. By following the wake of laughter, Kao Li-shih was able to spot a dark, elongated shape traveling beneath the surface. The Emperor had made his way back from the deep part of the pool, swimming underwater to the shallow basin so that he now moved along the wall at the children's feet.

Kao Li-shih was thinking that the Emperor's breath control was quite amazing for an old man, when he suddenly shot straight up through the surface like a sea monster, spouting water from his mouth and snatching two little boys in his arms. They shrieked with delighted terror and beat at him with their fists while the women laughed.

Kao Li-shih closed his eyes, the delicious warm sun on his face, and thought how the children's noise was actually soothing and pleasant, carrying the essence of pure joy and innocence from their little souls.

The Precious Consort stood perfectly still on the sun-baked tiles a few more moments before shrugging her loosened robe from her shoulders and allowing it to drop to the terrace. She joined the Emperor in the water, and together they worked their way playfully through the children who swarmed all around them.

The Emperor was happy at this moment. Truly happy. He was a man without cares. She felt as if she were finally seeing who he really was. She wished that they could live forever, just like this, and that she could protect him from any more trouble. She looked around her, at the sunlight, the water, the laughing children, the beautiful green mountain rising above them, at her own hands in front of her, and tried to encompass the moment with her mind so that time would stop. Why should they go any further than this?

Kao Li-shih sat with his feet in the pool and made ripples on the surface with one hand, thinking that this was as close as he would ever come to frolicking in the hot springs waters. He watched the Emperor and Precious Consort playing with the children. He tried to look at them as if they were people he did not know: two naked strangers splashing about with a swarm of children under a blue sky.

But it was impossible. He knew too much about both of them. And this knowledge made the innocent pleasure of objectivity quite impossible. Just knowing that one word from himself on at least twenty different subjects would be sufficient to destroy the fragile scene of happiness before him made him quite unable to pretend.

Even less able to play the game, he knew, would be Yang Kuo-chung. Not only did he know everything that Kao Li-shih did, but the Fox's life was dedicated to being all those things that the Emperor was not: awake, aware, alert to danger. Yang Kuo-chung had personally assumed responsibility for every problem in the empire, it seemed. He scarcely had his own life anymore. And Kao Li-shih sometimes wondered if those problems, most of them the legacy left by Yang Kuo-chung's predecessor, were now far too overwhelming even for him. In any case, the Fox was not here playing. He never wasted a minute of time anymore, never came out to the hot springs. He had undoubtedly been at work today since before the earliest light of dawn.

The Emperor moved through the water now with a child riding on his shoulders. If the ancient adage is right, Old Man, Kao Li-shih thought, then you are safe, though Master Yang may not be: Praise and blame belong to youth and glory. The praise and blame that are to come are all yours, Fox.

The sun was well over the village of Lin-tong and had burned away the golden morning haze; the sky was a rich blue with a few high white clouds. The Emperor and Precious Consort were alone now in the hot springs Lotus Pool. The children had been taken out of the water and stood in little puddles on the terrace in the hot sun, fidgeting and squirming while the nursemaids dried them.

Kao Li-shih raised his eyes, lazily following the progress of a single moving speck in the blue sky: a lone swallow, darting high above the trees. He followed the bird's erratic path as it climbed directly above the pool and then swooped back down toward the trees on the ridge.

As Kao Li-shih's eyes followed the bird's progress earthward, he spied two figures moving quickly up the path toward the gate. He glanced back toward the consort and the Emperor. From the water, they could not yet see the visitors. Servants? Why would they be moving so quickly? No, not servants, he realized. Imperial messengers. And there was something on their faces that he did not like. All at once, such things as bathing, playing with little children, and whiling away a summer day became irrelevant.

He stood and made his way quickly and discreetly out the gate and down the path to intercept them before they reached the area of the Lotus Pool.

When the messengers came up the final stone steps, they were breathing hard. Now Kao Li-shih was certain that something was not right. Their urgent, fearful expressions gave him a sick feeling.

"Master Kao," the first one said, gasping for air, "we have received news from the beacon tower at the Mount Hua lookout station. A rebel force is approaching the entrance to the T'ung-kuan Pass, seventy-five li east of here. From the length of the column, they have estimated nearly three hundred thousand soldiers, with perhaps an additional ten thousand horsemen . . ."

"And who is in command?" Kao Li-shih demanded.

The messengers' faces were pained and uncomprehending. They seemed afraid to speak the name that was on their tongues.

"Well?" Kao Li-shih said impatiently, looking from one to the other.

"It is General Sun," the second one said, with a pleading look in his eyes, as if he wanted Kao Li-shih to tell him that it was all simply a mistake. General Sun was An Lu-shan's right hand, his second in command.

"They are certain?" Kao Li-shih managed clumsily, although he knew he didn't need to ask.

"They are certain, Master Kao," the first one answered. "The rebel forces must have defeated the remains of the imperial divisions we had sent north.

Then early this morning, without warning, they broke through all the defenses east of the pass. This is our first word. The first that has got through."

"And they are coming here!" the second one added urgently. "The imperial family must prepare to—"

"Where is Master Yang Kuo-chung?" Kao Li-shih interrupted harshly, as the world solidified again.

"He is on his way here now to meet you. He is the one who sent us."

"Leave us now." Kao Li-shih pushed the messengers through the gate and back out to the path.

He stood with his back to the gate. He knew without turning around that the consort was watching him. He desperately wanted a moment to think. His mind tried to assimilate what he had just been told.

Was General Sun leading a rebellion? Had he broken from An Lu-shan and then led an army down from the north? It did not seem possible. Sun would have to command the allegiance of hundreds of thousands of men. He simply was not that ambitious or effectual. It was well-known that Sun, at least, remained faithful to An Lu-shan. There had been no word of a falling-out between the two men. A Pu-ssu had revolted against An Lu-shan—everyone knew that. But Sun?

It was becoming clear. All at once Kao Li-shih understood the lack of communication on the part of the imperial divisions that had been sent up there on peacekeeping missions. When he and Yang Kuo-chung had heard nothing, they had taken it to mean that they were only dealing with localized tribal uprisings. He realized the dreadful implications: if no word at all had reached the capital, then it could only be because each and every imperial soldier, messenger, and Censorate official who had tried to carry the news had met with death.

But they should have known. *He* should have known. The course of rebel outbreaks, the timing, all of it should have told him that something was out of place. He should have smelled it.

With the clarity of hindsight, he realized that the unrest in the northern provinces had seemed, from the beginning, far more virulent than Hopei Province secessionists could have managed. Yang Kuo-chung was aware that something was happening, but even he never suspected anything so sudden, so brutal and final as this. The whole thing was clever. Much cleverer than any of them would ever have suspected.

An invisible hand had been methodically stirring the territories up like the proverbial stick in the hornet's nest. And all the while, that stick had been kept out of sight.

He turned around to see if the Emperor or the Precious Consort had overheard anything. He doubted it: They were too far away, and the gurgling of the water flowing into the pool would have masked the words that he and the messengers had exchanged.

But the consort was looking at him, just as he had known she would be. Her eyes, serious and questioning, met his. She sensed something. But the Emperor sat at the edge of the pool, surrounded once again by the little children, his feet dangling in the water, oblivious.

Reluctantly, Kao Li-shih walked through the gate and across the hot tiles, the consort watching him steadily. Then she turned back to the Emperor. He stopped walking. He didn't have to tell them just yet. He would give them a few more moments of sunlit peace. What difference would a few moments make? None, he knew. The old man could afford just a few more moments of bliss. They were, after all, to be his last.

He knew he was hiding nothing from the consort. In these last moments, she and Kao Li-shih had entered into a tacit agreement to delay the inevitable. But this time she was not indulging in just another idle vanity.

In the warm, luxuriant rays of a benevolent sun, how easily they managed that first realization of their secret knowledge: the world was ending.

: :

The cries and screams carrying to Kao Li-shih's ears from other parts of the hot springs grounds had the same distant quality as the music and the laughter of lovers had on the night of the Festival of Kao Mei. He heard with his ears, but not his mind. Pain and anguish, or joy and celebration—there was little difference for him at this moment. They were just sounds. This must be the way we protect ourselves, he thought, allowing us to do what must be done. Calmly, he confined his attention to the task before him: commanding the household servants who loaded the caravan of ox carts in preparation for the escape of the imperial family.

Kao Li-shih could only think of insects rushing about after the hive has been overturned by a careless foot. At least a hundred servants, it seemed, scurried this way and that, carrying chests, crates, and bundles tied with leather and twine and stacking them haphazardly on the summer lawns for hasty sorting. The recent rains had made the ground soggy, and as bundles were lifted, the grass peeled back like a pelt being skinned from a carcass.

He shouted at the running figures: directions; encouragement; exhortations to hurry, to be careful. There could be no stopping, no time to allow them to think about what was happening—or to allow himself to think about it, either.

He knew that he had never really seen the hot springs until this moment. The intimacy and familiarity that had always cloaked it for him was stripped away; the curves of the rooftops against the sky, and the gardens, lawns, ornamental gates, pools, and bridges, all part of his own interior landscape for so many years, were now alien and transformed. The grounds had become, in a few short hours, ancient, distant, and remote. Yang Kuo-chung was right: it was as if the hot springs had preferred all along to be rid of people. It allowed itself to be possessed for a brief time, tolerating human presence and folly; then, the tenants' lease simply expired. The poets spoke of this: eventually, everything returns to its primal state, the way it was before we presumed ourselves upon it. And what time we waste, grieving over the loss of a place that was never ours. Those had been Yang Kuo-chung's own words. Now Kao Li-shih truly understood them.

The work had put him beyond pain. When the first fleet of wagons that carried the imperial children from the Ten Mansions arrived hours before—some two hundred little nieces, nephews, sons, daughters, and grandchildren, all frightened and crying—he was nearly crippled by his own emotions, as if all of it were his doing. Now he was almost serenely numb.

Someone was running and calling his name. He turned. It was Lu Pei, eyes wild with terror.

"Help me, Master Kao! Help me! The palace guards are taking the infants from their mothers! It is too much for me to manage alone! The women are screaming, throwing themselves on the ground, begging me to intervene!"

"You cannot intervene, Lu Pei. You must let the guardsmen do their job."

"But the babies . . . the women!" he cried, not understanding at all. "The guardsmen are refusing to let the infants into the wagons!"

"And how, Lu Pei, did you expect them to react?" Kao Li-shih said harshly. "There is only room for so many. We cannot take all of them. There are not enough wagons or food, nor are there enough men to protect everyone. Some must stay behind, so that others may live! It is as simple, and as cruel, as that!" He looked at the young, tearful face before him for a moment, then turned resolutely back to his work, making it clear, he thought, that the conversation was ended. But Lu Pei persisted after a moment of stunned silence.

"But what will they do? What will become of them? The babies and the others! The old officials, the eunuchs at the palace, the women . . . what will happen to them?"

Kao Li-shih turned back to the boy and spoke in a gentler voice.

"Some will die," he said. "Others will find a way. But we cannot go back toward the capital to rescue them. Not only is there simply no room, but our only possible route of escape is to go west and then south. We can take only what food and supplies are here, and they are limited. And when we get out into the open country, we cannot assume that there will be food waiting for us there. We have received word from the lookout on top of Mount Hua at the entrance to the pass. Early this morning, the rebels were already within sight of the first of the ten beacon towers to the capital. Word will already have traveled out into the countryside. The villagers . . . the farmers—I know the people too well—they will be long gone. And they will have taken everything, plucked every bit of food from the ground and maybe even burned the land behind them. Just as they always have, for thousands of years, whenever the shadow of war has fallen over them—war that they did not ask for or have any part in making, but for which they must always pay. You can be certain that there will not be anything left for us when we come through. This sort of thing is not new to the people, Lu Pei. They are like the pieces on a gaming board. They don't make history; history is simply done to them. Yes, Lu Pei, people will die. Many, many people will die."

Lu Pei absorbed these words quietly. Kao Li-shih shouted an order over his shoulder to the stablehands who were busy yoking the teams of oxen, then turned back to the young eunuch. There was nothing else to say on the subject. Anything else he might say would seem fatuous and empty. He turned back to the railing and watched the activity on the lawns below.

"Do not waste time with all of those skins," Kao Li-shih called out to a group of men struggling near the forward ox carts. "Load only half of them. There will be sufficient water on the Hsien-yang Post Road to the station at Ma-wei." He pointed to a high pile of stores waiting behind them. "Deal with those things, first. When those carts are loaded gather by the gate and await Master Yang Kuo-chung." He gave these orders in a tone of voice that suggested that he was planning for a day's outing, not a flight from death and destruction. Then he spoke again to Lu Pei.

"You must be my right hand. Now, return to your duties at the Flying Rosy Cloud Pavilion. If it is necessary, you are to order that the mothers and nursemaids be pulled away by force." His voice sounded cold and artificial in his ears. It was not his own voice, but the voice of brutal practicality. He wanted Lu Pei out of his sight; the pain in the youth's eyes had come too close to destroying his own tenuous equanimity.

"That is exactly what they are already doing, Master Kao. And the women are fighting them. It is too much for me," he pleaded. "You must help me!" He looked around at the scurrying servants, the half-loaded carts, the shouting guards, the world being hastily dismantled. He began to cry again. "I do not even know what any of this is about. I do not even know what has happened, or why!"

Kao Li-shih turned back to Lu Pei and saw that it was true. He really didn't know. He knew as much as one of the little imperial grandchildren might know. Lu Pei, involved only in his own small, trivial world, was a true innocent. He owed him at least an explanation. He sighed.

"You do know that there has been trouble for some months now, do you not?"

Lu Pei nodded.

"Some of the northern garrisons were falling. But it did not seem very severe—nothing we had not seen before. And certainly, we thought, there would be little to worry about with An Lu-shan standing guard. No cause for alarm—simply some Hopei secessionists acting up, hating the T'ang as they always have. Some disgruntled Mongolian tribesmen, the legacy of the policy of expansion of our good and zealous Li Lin-fu. It was bound to make enemies for us. But we knew then that these rebels would be no match for our strongest forces, our departments in P'inglu, Fangyang, and Shuofang. Not for Commissioner An Lu-shan. *He* would take care of us."

He looked to see the effect of his words on Lu Pei. Obviously, he still did not understand. He looked back toward the servants, then returned his attention to what he had been saying. He was finding his own words informative. It was, he realized, the first time he had articulated, even for himself, what had really happened. He spoke quickly, trying to compress the order of events so that they would make some sense to Lu Pei *and* to himself.

"One by one the passes were falling and the enemy was advancing south. But we knew nothing. No messages got through, and we continued to believe that we were still dealing with tribal skirmishes, that An Lu-shan would protect us. We sent contingents of our Uighur allies in to assist with putting down the uprisings. They tried desperately, but apparently it was not enough. We could only guess, because after only a few weeks' time, we never heard from them again, either. Without our knowing it, the Tu-men Pass had fallen, then the Tsi Valley. This news did not reach us until very early this morning. We found out because our generals—Kuo Tzu-i and Li Kuang-pi—finally withdrew from Hopei in the north and managed to flee southward with the remnants of their armies. They carried with them the news that had been kept from us all this time. Messengers were sent ahead, but as fate would have it, they arrived at the same time that the lookouts on the beacon tower spotted the enemy.

"General Ko-shu Han and General Feng were dispatched to defend the T'ung-kuan Pass and the valleys east of Ch'ang-an, but it was too late and to no avail. The pass has fallen. Feng and Ko-shu Han have retreated in order to regroup at some further date. And we have only just learned in the past hours that Loyang has already fallen. So now there is nothing between us and the rebels but a small amount of time. And although we had impending signs, Lu Pei, we were blind to them because . . . well, because we never really believed that such a thing was possible. The truth did not find us until just this morning.

"General Feng is not one to panic. He has passed us a few words. He tells us there is no stopping the rebel forces. Not yet. What government could be salvaged in so short a time before Ch'ang-an receives the enemy has already been sent south in advance with the crown prince and one of the six armies of the interior realm to form a provisional government in Szechuan far, we can only hope, from the paths of the advancing battle lines."

Kao Li-shih paused and looked out over the Emperor's hot springs' palace.

"But Minghuang would not abandon the rest of us. He refused to go with them. He sent his son Li Heng, the crown prince, on ahead. But the old man insisted on staying and traveling with his flock, fool that he is."

"But where is An Lu-shan?" Lu Pei begged, holding on to Kao Li-shih's sleeve. "You told me that nearly four hundred thousand men are loyal to him. Where is he? Why isn't he with us? Why doesn't he stop the rebels?"

Kao Li-shih shook his head. "He has never been very far from us. In fact, he is getting closer all the time. He rides at the very front of those four hundred thousand men. Stop the rebels? Lu Pei," he said gently, "they *are* the rebels. An Lu-shan is on his way to take *his* city right now. The 'Lucky Baby' has left his cradle." He looked at the boy's stupefied expression. "Do you understand? *Now* do you understand?"

Kao Li-shih peeled Lu Pei's frozen hand from his sleeve. It was plain that now, at last, he understood.

He turned his head sharply. The screams and cries from the Flying Rosy Cloud Pavilion had grown more urgent and terrible. The noise was causing the servants to stop what they were doing and look over across the lake. The struggle of the women versus the guards had got worse while they stood here talking. The forming of the caravan for the escape of the imperial family had turned into an ugly and violent scene; fear and anger were turning to panic. Kao Li-shih could not send Lu Pei back there alone; it was, truly, far too much for the shattered boy to handle. At any moment the palace guards would have a full-scale insurrection on their hands, and Kao Li-shih would be unable to choose sides. He seized Lu Pei's arm, though the younger eunuch was sobbing now, out of control, and pulled him toward the Nine Dragon Bridge.

: :

Kao Li-shih closed the door of his apartments behind him after gathering up a hasty bundle of possessions. He was glad to be out of those rooms; they had begun to take on the same remote quality that the hot springs grounds had. His desk, the chair he had sat in, the bed, the pieces of clothing scattered about, already had a disused, decaying look, as though they were the belongings of a stranger who had been dead for a hundred years.

He went down the stairs two at a time and took the path through the garden. The caravan was loaded and ready to leave. The imperial guardsmen were holding off the anguished women and others who would be left to see to their own fates. The sisters, the Emperor, the selected children and nurse-maids, Lu Pei, and Yang Kuo-chung awaited him, ready to travel for the rest of the day and most of the night to put themselves well out of range of the advancing enemy.

Passing the Nine Dragon Lake, he was startled to see someone standing at the apex of the curved footbridge: an old woman, leaning on the railing, dropping bits of food down to the carp in the water. He stopped. She must be a peasant woman who had wandered onto the grounds from the country-side. Perhaps she thought that the place was already abandoned and had come to help herself to some imperial wealth. In any event, she was in clear danger.

"Grandmother!" Kao Li-shih shouted. She raised her head and looked at him. "You must leave at once! Soldiers are on their way here! They will kill you and anyone else they find!"

"Soldiers?" she called back, her elbows still resting comfortably on the railing.

"Yes! Rebels! Killers! You must leave immediately!"

"You are right!" she answered, and tossed another handful of scraps down to the fish. "I must leave!" Then she smiled at him. Even from where he stood, a good distance away, he could see that she had no teeth.

"Did you hear me?" he called. "There is terrible danger!"

"Terrible danger!" she said. "I know!" She stood where she was. Still leaning, she spat into the water, then looked back up at him with her broad empty grin.

Crazy old woman, Kao Li-shih thought, suddenly losing patience. Stay here and let An Lu-shan's soldiers feed *you* to the fish. It is not my concern. He turned away from her and walked quickly down the stone path and toward the waiting caravan.

::

They had traveled south of Ch'ang-an and then west, parallel to the course of the Wei River, leaving behind the familiar landscape of fertile plains, villages, and farms that made up the brocade and tapestry of Ch'ang-an's suburbs. Moving out beyond the habitations of men, they also left behind the haze and dust that hung permanently above the city and villages. The anxiety that had been upon them began to fall away as the summer air grew sweet, rare, and hot.

The smokeless sky richened to a deep cobalt blue, and the land began to draw up in great folds: wild, splendid, and indifferent waves of grass and conifer. Here, there was no cultivation, no distinct definitions of paths and irrigation ditches and roads and terraced fields of grains. The farther they traveled, the wilder the world became, the more removed from human concerns, expanding into the rise and fall of the blue-green sea of pointed pines, cresting steeper and steeper, until even the birds that sang in those trees had no knowledge at all of the affairs of men.

It was the second day out from the hot springs. They estimated that they would reach the postal station at Ma-wei sometime late that evening. The imperial cart carrying the silent Emperor and his Precious Consort, with Kao Li-shih on horseback alongside, rolled at the head of the lumbering ten-wagon convoy. Behind them, the imperial children, Lu Pei and the nursemaids, and the ladies of Chin and Han occupied the other carts, along with food and some possessions. Yang Kuo-chung and the Lady of Kuo were on horseback, riding in advance with the guides from time to time, scouting the land. The mounted palace guardsmen fanned out on either side of the entourage, carrying aloft brilliant blue phoenix standards, vestiges of state pomp and circumstance which looked, Kao Li-shih could not help thinking, lost and irrelevant against the primal landscape.

The children cried almost constantly, and Kao Li-shih knew how the sound must be affecting the Emperor. But Minghuang did not speak or react at all, his hands fixed firmly on his knees, his rigid posture defying the swaying motion of the carriage. He kept his eyes straight ahead for hours at a time, not looking at the Precious Consort, even when the wagons halted at rough, steep parts of the road and they all had to climb out and push. Discreetly, Kao Li-shih studied the face of the Emperor of China. Now and again, a merciful breeze raised the wispy yellow hairs over Minghuang's sallow, creased forehead, and Kao Li-shih saw him as he was: once again, a tired old man. And Kao Li-shih could only imagine his hell.

Behind them, the children who had to stand or sit on the floors of the carts because of the lack of room grew sullen and quarrelsome. There were fights with the younger ones for a place. When no adults were looking, some of them were bold enough to pull the little ones from their perches; then there would be another noisy struggle as the little ones attempted to reclaim their positions, cramming themselves onto the already overloaded benches. The bickering and wailing never stopped, but Kao Li-shih found comfort in it. Better the crying and arguing of children than the sad wordlessness of adults. As long as there was still the noise of children . . .

He thought back to the morning before, and the terrible struggle with the women who had to be left behind, and the sound of babies crying. Now, riding in the hot, sweet mountain air under the enormous sky, Kao Li-shih had to fight a vivid, painful memory:

Just as the caravan was about to leave, a woman had tried to smuggle two infants under her robes. Before Chief Minister Yang Kuo-chung and the Lady of Kuo could stop them, the palace guards had pushed her down onto the stones, and the officer of the guards had thought it best to whip her in order to set an example for others who might try the same thing. But Yang Kuo-chung and Kao Li-shih had managed to grab the officer's arm just when he had brought the whip behind his head. They wrestled the cruel leather thongs from his hand before he could strike the pitiful woman.

The officer had cursed them, saying that they did not know what discipline meant, but that they would find out as they traveled. And he told them that it would all break down around them: "Children and women and so little food!" he had snarled. And Kao Li-shih knew that Yang Kuo-chung understood what the officer meant, but they could not admit that it was the truth.

Yang Kuo-chung had sent the officer away. But the man had climbed onto his horse, turned in the saddle, and hurled a poleax at him. And it would have killed Yang Kuo-chung had its tip not first grazed the balustrade of the Flying Rosy Cloud Pavilion, sending it ever so slightly off its deadly course. They could not catch the officer, who galloped away. But he had been right; already, order was collapsing in upon itself like a burning house.

And as he rode over the Nine Dragon Bridge, he had screamed back over his shoulder that the Yangs were filthy leeches, that they had betrayed China and sucked her dry and handed her to a barbarian, and that he would rather die fighting the rebels than aiding their escape.

His men looked on, but they said nothing, and Yang Kuo-chung said nothing. He just stared after the horseman who rode across the lake and out over the lawns screaming "bloody death to the Yangs." And Kao Li-shih knew that those words were more painful to Yang Kuo-chung than the poleax would ever have been.

And now the Yangs, the leeches and betrayers, comforted the children and struggled to push free the high wheels of the carts alongside the contingent of palace footmen. The ground rose steeply, and they had to cut through clusters of young evergreens that had overgrown the road. Yang Kuo-chung rode back to the convoy with the Lady of Kuo.

"The road gets worse," the Lady of Kuo said to Kao Li-shih. "If I were superstitious, I would have to say that those little trees grew there just as we were coming up the post road."

"This is not actually a section of the post road," Kao Li-shih replied. "It is a shortcut, an old firewood trail. Probably unused for years. I thought it would be safer."

"Safer, perhaps. But infinitely slower," she said.

The sound of excited voices and horses crashing heedlessly through the brush toward them caused all heads to turn and Yang Kuo-chung's hand to move to his sword. Men and horses rushed out of the trees into view ahead of them on the trail: their own small advance of outriders had returned, the blue phoenix standard they had been carrying now torn and hanging sorrily. A young guardsman, no more than nineteen or so, galloped up to Yang Kuo-chung and reined in his horse.

"There must be fifty of them!" he said, breathless and agitated, his horse wheeling in a circle, the standard snagging on a branch and falling to the ground.

"Who?" Yang Kuo-chung asked sharply.

"I don't know. Soldiers of some kind. They have crossbows and long swords. They are strangely dressed. I do not think they are Chinese!"

"Not the rebels! Not here!" There was alarm in the Lady of Kuo's voice. "I thought we had escaped them!"

Her words penetrated the Emperor's isolation. He raised his eyes from the floor of the cart and looked toward Yang Kuo-chung. The consort also turned her frightened face toward her cousin.

"Do they have horses?" asked Kao Li-shih.

"No," the boy said. "They seem to be all on foot."

"How far?" Yang Kuo-chung asked.

"Just over the ridge, Chief Minister. Not more than two li from us."

"They could not be any part of An Lu-shan's forces," Yang Kuo-chung said, thinking quickly. "The rebels are coming from the north, and it would be impossible for them to have got this far on foot. They would not do it, anyway. It would be far too dangerous for them to move through this country without horses."

"Who, then?" asked Kao Li-shih.

"I cannot be sure. Did they see you?" he asked the guardsmen.

"I don't think so. We lowered the standard and stayed in the trees."

Some of the mounted soldiers rode to the front of the caravan and flanked the Emperor. The others, nervous and excited, had formed a wide arc around Yang Kuo-chung, straining to catch his words. The unquiet mood seemed to have spread to the horses as well; the animals flinched and stamped. Yang Kuo-chung did not speak, but sat thinking.

"At least allow us the privilege of knowing who our executioners are going to be," the Lady of Kuo said.

Yang Kuo-chung turned to the boy.

"Half of the mounted guardsmen will ride up with me," he said, indicating the crest of the hill ahead of them. "Carry the imperial standards aloft. Raise them high so these soldiers, whoever they may be, will at least know who *we* are."

The men did not respond immediately, but looked at him with uneasy faces.

"I will ride ahead of you," he said reassuringly, and turned his horse.

As they rode up the path, Yang Kuo-chung was peripherally aware of words and glances exchanged between the guardsmen. If he turned to look at any of them, the murmuring abruptly ceased, but their eyes would remain fixed on him. It is their anger and fear, he told himself. Their natural fear, under the circumstances, for they have the responsibility of keeping the Emperor alive, of delivering him safely to the southern capital, of protecting themselves and the entourage from unknown dangers. Of course they are afraid. So am I, he said to himself.

But he knew that there was more to their fear. Something else had been traveling with them since the journey began. He had tried not to acknowledge its existence, but now, riding up the hill in front of the silent, suspicious guardsmen, he could feel its breath on his neck.

Ever since the previous morning and the ugly incident with the young officer of the guards at the hot springs, Yang Kuo-chung had tried to tell himself that the man had been deranged, crazy, isolated in his irrational delusion. But now, he knew, with the plain certainty of the breeze drying the sweat on his forehead as they pushed through the brush and low branches, that the officer's bitter words had expressed what the others also believed, but simply lacked the courage to say. Though they could not speak with that man's directness, what they felt was the same.

And now, those feelings were growing in them, like a poison slowly filling the vessels of the body: resentment, fear, distrust. Something was gradually taking on life and substance, and acquiring the shape and proportion of fact. Somehow, an association had been made in their minds, an imaginary alliance: the Yangs and An Lu-shan.

There had been no direct word or act from any of the young guardsmen to indicate that they believed in some kind of dark collusion between the barbarian and the aristocratic family, but Yang Kuo-chung had been aware of words muttered just beyond the range of his hearing, gestures and looks exchanged just outside his field of vision. Not only did they believe in the alliance, but they believed that it was to be at their expense.

So far, they had not expressed it openly. He was their chief minister, and it would be traitorous to say anything. Their respect for his rank and authority was still intact. Thin and strained, he reflected as they approached the crest of the hill, but still intact.

His attention was drawn to vultures circling in the sky above the ridge. Something had died up there. Something large, he judged from their number; nature was serving up one of her bountiful feasts, and the "guests" were gathering to dine on a "dish" as tempting and delicious to them as a meal from the imperial kitchens would be to himself. He noticed smoke, too—a blackish plume rose from somewhere beyond the trees and into the blue mountain sky.

He signaled for the men to halt then, and listened.

The crystalline resonance of bells and drums came over the top of the hill. Beneath the bells and the soft rush of the breeze another sound carried: a deep, mysterious monotone, like a vibration from the center of the earth; Yang Kuo-chung had to listen for several moments, trying to separate the sound from the wind and the rustling of trees and grass, before he recognized it as the low, droning chant of men's voices.

He let out his breath in gratitude and relief. Yang Kuo-chung had heard such chanting before in his travels in the far, far west. This was not the enemy they were hearing.

"There is nothing to fear," he said to the boy whose horse stood alongside his. He turned and faced his men and saw the dread in their eyes. "It is nothing. It is chanting—very common among mountain people," he explained, irritated at the thin, unconvincing sound of his own voice, disconcerted as he was by their naked suspicion. "It is prayer, that is all. Common practice among such peoples," he repeated. "There is no threat to us at all."

"What people?" one of the men asked.

"What are they chanting?" asked another.

"I do not know exactly," he said, impatience creeping into his voice.

"Then how do you know that they are only 'praying,' Chief Minister?" a third one asked, his voice sharp with distrust.

"And how do you know that these are 'mountain people'? From what mountains?" another persisted.

"I know that they are praying because I have heard it before. And I know that they are mountain people because of *where* I heard it—in the far west. In Tibet. They are obviously conducting a rite of some sort. There is a fire; maybe they are making an offering. Or maybe it is a funeral ceremony," he said, spurring his horse forward up the remainder of the incline. He stopped when he realized that the men were not following. "You will accompany me," he ordered, fixing his eyes firmly on them. "You will see for yourselves that there is nothing to fear."

He waited for them to move, challenging them with his look to defy him. They hesitated. Then one dug his heels into his horse's sides; then another. He urged his own horse forward again. Soon they were all moving up the steep incline; the bells and the voices grew more distinct as they climbed. Yang Kuo-chung expected that the woods grew as far as the crest of the hill, and judged that they would find a clearing just on the other side. He glanced up through the trees. The vultures circled in the haze of smoke, their enormous splayed wings stretched out serenely.

"You," he said to the standard-bearers. "You will ride just behind me. As soon as we are out of the woods, raise the blue phoenix high. The rest of you follow closely."

Leaning into his horse's neck, Yang Kuo-chung was the first to push through the tangle of branches at the edge of the clearing. One standard and then another emerged from the trees and was raised next to him. They had come out on the high side of the clearing, and the view was beyond what Yang Kuo-chung had imagined.

The entourage had climbed for so long that he had not fully realized how high they had come above the valley floor. The hills of the Taibai range rolled out into an eternity of blue-green waves, and, far below where they stood, a layer of humidity hung in the winding valleys like stretched white silk. Yang Kuo-chung guessed that they must be looking all the way into the Chin Ling district and the southern part of the province.

Shifting his focus from the vast majesty of mountains and sky to the gathering of men in the center of the meadow, Yang Kuo-chung was startled to see that the vultures were circling and landing all around the place where the men stood in a loose knot. The drumming and chanting continued, the men ignoring the big black birds dropping from the sky and strutting and squawking around them.

A fire burned in the far corner of the clearing. Two men stood tending it, poking at it occasionally with long sticks, sending fresh black billows of smoke upward. A funeral pyre, Yang Kuo-chung thought, confirming his earlier surmise. One of their fellows has died and they are sending him on his way. It will be good for these ignorant young guardsmen to see that there is nothing here for them to be afraid of. He signaled to them to follow.

He and the bearers moved forward about fifteen or twenty paces, presenting themselves, but maintaining a respectful distance.

It was not until they had moved closer that Yang Kuo-chung noticed that the field around where the chanters and drummers stood was strewn with cut pieces of meat and entrails: a banquet, purposefully laid, it would seem, for the scavenging birds. Deer or wild boar, he guessed, hunted for sacrifice, part of an obscure funeral ritual with its origins in the high, distant land of Tibet, where men held daily communion with the natural world. Very good, he thought with satisfaction; let the young Chinese guardsmen see that unfamiliar or esoteric customs are not to be regarded with suspicion and fear simply because they differ from one's own.

The chanters were lost in their ritual, entranced almost to the point of frenzy, the drone of their voices and the pounding of the small hand-held drum rising and falling. The exotic, foreign sound, incongruous in this piny, flowery meadow, made Yang Kuo-chung think of sparse, high, rock-strewn valleys between tall snowy mountain peaks disappearing into the clouds.

The Tibetans seemed oblivious to everything around them: the vultures working over the chunks of carcasses on the ground, and, now, the Chinese horsemen who gathered in plain view at the other end of the meadow. Yang Kuo-chung signaled to his men to stay still and be quiet; he could feel, without even turning to look at them, their reluctant fascination and rapt attention.

The chanting grew suddenly louder, the steady rhythm fragmenting into a wild, frenetic formlessness. Then, abruptly, it stopped. The echoes vibrated in the silence like ripples on a pond. When the air ceased its phantom humming, the only sounds were the faint sibilance of the wind and the whooshing of wings as more birds dropped from the sky.

The Tibetans, all but four of them, stepped back a few paces, loosening their circle, allowing Yang Kuo-chung to catch a glimpse of what he had expected to see: a shrouded body lying on a low wooden bier on the ground. The four who remained stood close over the corpse: fearsome warriors, *lokapalas*, guarding the dead, their swords and lances glinting in the sunlight.

It was the flicker of blue-silver light reflecting from the weapons that awakened a vague memory in Yang Kuo-chung. He looked over toward the fire in the corner of the meadow and saw what he had failed to notice before: the attendants were feeding it with chunks of flesh, pieces of animal carcasses, causing the flames to hiss and snap and prodigious black smoke to rise. He looked back toward the warriors standing over the corpse.

He was aware of the men stirring behind him, and knew that a ripple of unease was traveling down their ranks as if they shared his mind, as if his uncertainty passed like a contagion from one horseman to another. He sought to reassure himself: what they were witnessing was all part of a typical ritual of sacrifice—an offering to the spirits that would guide the soul. Foreign, strange, disturbing perhaps—but nothing more than a preliminary to the funereal cremation of the body.

But the body was nowhere near the fire, and, though it did not appear that anyone was about to move it, the men in the corner of the field continued to stoke the burning pile of brush. Yang Kuo-chung's eyes followed the plume of rising smoke. Vultures circled in its midst, as if it were sweet incense to them, before beginning their downward spiral; while he watched, his suspicion grew: this was not a funeral pyre being prepared. The purpose of this fire, fed on bones, fat, and entrails, was to make thick, greasy smoke that would entice the scavengers down out of the sky to the mountainside. Once there, they were further tempted by the carcasses strewn about in the flowers: a doubly hospitable invitation.

No, Fox, he told himself; what you are thinking is simply not possible. It is your imagination—the strain and terror of the last two days.

But his earlier vague memory was taking more tangible shape now, and he could not banish it. He was remembering something he had been told once when he and a group of Tibetan traders had been drinking and exchanging tales in a remote way station in Szechuan. He had dismissed most of what they had told him as being simply their efforts to shock and impress a foreigner.

Laughing and pantomiming, they had told him stories of obscure rituals from the lofty Tangkula Mountains in their homeland. Rituals of a people dwelling so high up and close to heaven . . . Apocryphal stories, he had been sure. And with Tibetans, you simply never knew the extent or shape of a joke. A Tibetan might tell you the grimmest, most bizarre and shocking story of human aberrance and wear a merry grin of amusement on his face all the while.

The warriors standing over the corpse raised their swords up toward the sky, and a memory picture leapt up in his mind: the Tibetans in the way station acting something out for his benefit. One of them, laughing, urged on by his fellows, had raised a sword up over his head, and showed the Chinaman how it was done . . .

The flash of the warriors' swords against the blue sky burned away the last mists of forgetfulness in Yang Kuo-chung's mind. He remembered now the exact name of what those laughing Tibetans had been demonstrating for him—a name that, when he heard them pronounce it, had struck him as fiercely poetic and compelling:

Sky Burial.

He felt a terrible surge of alarm. The young guardsmen! This would be far too much for their sensibilities. What had he done? It was too late to force them back into the cover of the trees. And how could he, after ordering them to follow him out into the meadow? His credibility with them, his authority, already strained and tenuous, would be ruined. Most of these palace soldiers had seen no more than sixteen or seventeen harvests. They were displaced and defeated, fleeing from everything they had known to escape the fate of their comrades fallen in the defense of the T'ung-kuan Pass, running south like frightened animals under the command of a chief minister whom they did not trust.

And now this. They were stunned and silent behind him, fixed by dread and curiosity to the scene of utter strangeness before them. Something was about to happen, and he was helpless to prevent them from witnessing it. Still, Fox, he told himself desperately, you could be completely wrong. Your fevered imagination could be whispering things in your ear that are not true.

He watched.

One of the warriors came forward from behind the four who held their weapons aloft, and knelt at the bier alongside the head of the dead soldier. He pulled the shroud from the body, peeling it down slowly from head to toe.

The birds argued and fed on the carcasses, weighted the limbs of the trees bordering the meadow, and cast their gliding shadows on the grass and flowers. Some of those on the ground daringly hopped to within a few paces of the Tibetans and the body; others flapped patiently back into the trees to wait and survey the prospects: quiet attendants of death.

The dead man was completely naked except for what appeared to be a narrow silver anklet on the right leg. They are certainly not Chinese, Yang Kuo-chung thought; to these people, death was absolute nakedness, surrender. And in that instant everything was confirmed in his mind. Death for the Tibetan was not earthly entombment, but the total liberation of body and soul . . . the attainment of selfless Buddha-hood. He fervently wished that the young guardsmen could understand that what was before them was not savagery, but the profoundest respect for the dead.

The one who was acting as the Lamaist priest stood then and stepped back behind the four warriors. He moved around them in a circle, then stopped and touched one of the men on the shoulder and spoke some words into his ear; that one remained motionless as the other three lowered their weapons and broke the circle to join the rest waiting behind. The warrior who had been selected now dropped to his knees near the corpse. He placed his lance carefully on the ground beside him and removed a war ax and a knife from his belt. The ax was not Chinese, either, Yang Kuo-chung noted, his apprehension growing.

The priest spoke to the man once again, and the warrior bowed his head in a way that indicated that he understood. This time, the priest's voice was clear and carried plainly to Yang Kuo-chung's ears; though he could not understand the rest of what he said, one Tibetan word that he did know was plainly discernible, and it obliterated Yang Kuo-chung's last shreds of hope: *dumden*—the word for "butcher."

While the priest chanted and spun his prayer wheel, the warrior raised the ax . . .

Not a single piece of flesh must remain to hinder the soul's upward flight. The vultures, earthly carrion-eaters, become instruments of divine transformation, bearing away every last bit, facilitating the deceased's complete passage into Paradise. Only the bones remain, to be gathered, consigned to the fire, turned into smoke, and carried away by the wind. Thus body and soul disappear together into the vast sky.

The *dumden* brought the ax down with great force into the dead man's shoulder, causing an audible crunch of bone and gristle. Then he knelt, put his ax aside, grasped the loosened arm with one hand, and worked at the joint and tendons with a knife in his other hand. Pulling and twisting, he separated the arm from the body. He stood, raised his ax again, and brought it down on the joint at the elbow, separating the forearm with one clean stroke.

The *dumden* worked quickly and efficiently at the corpse's other limbs, making his way toward the torso and the vile task of funereal evisceration.

That too he did neatly and expertly, slitting the abdomen with his knife and removing the organs in handfuls.

Yang Kuo-chung, unable to take his eyes from the strange dream in front of him, wished fervently that he had come by himself. Behind him, the horses, disturbed by the odor of blood and death, snorted and shied; his own animal pranced about nervously. He worked the reins, fighting to keep control. The young guardsmen were close to panic. He signaled them to be still, feeling their fear thick in the air. Fear, and a sense of betrayal. But they stayed where they were. Their eyes, he knew, were fastened to the scene just as his own were.

With solemn purpose, the other Tibetans gathered the pieces, walked into the crowd of vultures, and spread the offering before the birds as daintily as palace women feeding ducks on a pond. They watched carefully, making certain that nothing was left behind, bending down occasionally to pick up a stray morsel and toss it into the ravenous horde. The birds became very bold, practically seizing the bits right out of their hands; others left their perches in the surrounding trees and flapped in startlingly low over the heads of the Chinese, then soared gracefully, scouting the ground for an opening. Finding one, they dropped to the ground, and stretched their great black wings before folding them neatly and strutting into the jostling feast of human flesh.

When Yang Kuo-chung saw the *dumden* raise his ax over the man's neck for the final dismemberment, he had to close his eyes for a moment. The sight of a man's head parting from his body was too much, even for him. You are, after all, Chinese, he told himself, while he heard, but did not see, the ax fall. But the eyes of the young guardsmen, he was sure, had taken in the sight of this ultimate sacrilege.

After the last pieces of the dead man had been offered to the birds, the priest raised a small horn to his lips. He gave one long note followed by a quick three-note flourish; the sound carried across the valleys and died in a diminishing volley of echoes. The horn's message was plain to Yang Kuo-chung: the dead man's burdens on earth were over and the heavenly journey was under way. The birds had only to finish their work.

The Tibetans now turned their eyes to the Chinese. Yang Kuo-chung saw that there was no surprise; they had been fully aware, while conducting the funeral, of the presence of the watching group on horseback, but had given no acknowledgment at all until this moment. It was as if they had known that no earthly force could disturb them during their ritual.

Slowly, cautiously, twenty or twenty-five of the Tibetans drew their swords and lances. A few cocked the bolts of their crossbows and held the weapons in front of them, ready in case they were needed. Others continued to ignore the Chinese and occupied themselves with seeing to the fire or making sure nothing was overlooked by the birds.

The armed Tibetans were forming themselves into a loose, unconscious battle line. They spoke to each other in subdued tones, their eyes on the Chinese guardsmen.

Yang Kuo-chung heard his own men muttering fearfully. What was wrong? Were the Tibetans preparing to fight? It did not seem that they were openly hostile, but they were plainly uncertain. Surely the Chinese guardsmen could not have appeared to them as dangerous brigands! Could the Tibetans not see the imperial standards? Yang Kuo-chung raised his right hand in a gesture of peace. Then he turned quickly to look at his guardsmen and realized that something was indeed terribly wrong. The standard-bearers were not behind him as they should have been. He looked around then, scanning the ranks, and saw them.

These terrified children doubling as soldiers had retreated to the edge of the treeline and had let the standards fall to the ground. The leader of the Tibetans shouted a command, and the warriors lined up in serious battle stance, weapons aimed. Yang Kuo-chung turned his horse harshly and raced back toward the standard-bearers, calling out to the fools to raise the standards high. They looked at him with frightened, stupid eyes, not comprehending his shouted command.

The Tibetans would be alarmed, too, he knew. They could mistake the intent of his sudden action. At any moment, they might let loose a bolt or an arrow into the Chinese horsemen, and then all would be lost. Desperately, he searched his memory: what was the word for "friend" or "peace"? He could not remember. He spun his horse around again and faced the Tibetans. Keeping one hand on a tight rein he again raised his other hand in what he hoped would look like a friendly gesture. Then he turned back to his men.

The standard-bearers still had not moved; they were paralyzed, the blue phoenix banners dragging limply behind their horses. Glancing over his shoulder, he thought he saw more Tibetan arrows being drawn, cautiously, deliberately. Surely they could not see the Chinese as enemies. Surely dangerous "rebels" would not have waited so patiently . . .

"Raise the standards, fools! Raise them so they can be seen!" he cried, closing the final distance between them. One of the boys galloped off in a panic, letting go of his standard completely as he went. Yang Kuo-chung made for the other youth; he grabbed hold of the standard in the stunned boy's hand, pulled it away from him, and raised it high. Turning his horse, he moved back toward the center of the meadow and the Tibetans.

"Ten thousand years to our August Imperial Father!" he shouted. If there was only one Chinese expression that they understood, it would be that. They could not have served in a Chinese imperial division without knowing those words—without recognizing the standard. Unless they thought that it might have been captured, he thought nervously, facing the row of fierce warriors with drawn weapons aimed directly at him.

But the Tibetans evidently believed what they saw; the leader lowered his own crossbow, and the row of wicked swords and arrows came down.

Two of them left the area around the fire and strode out to meet Yang Kuo-chung as he walked his horse toward them. He could hear the excited voices of his guardsmen behind him, speaking in low tones. But he could not pay them any heed now, though his intuition told him that the tension and fear among his charges had not relaxed particularly. The two Tibetans were nearly upon him, and he wished to give them his full attention.

"Is there one among you who speaks Chinese?" Yang Kuo-chung asked.

The two Tibetans stood only a few paces away. The one who had officiated as priest stepped forward and took hold of Yang Kuo-chung's reins in a relaxed and friendly manner. He soothed the Fox's horse, smoothing a slender hand along the animal's cheek. Yang Kuo-chung noticed that the man's hands did not look as though they were those of a warrior. Perhaps he really was a priest or a monk, a man of some spiritual elevation captured in the Tibetan campaigns and forced to serve the Chinese. He looked up at Yang Kuo-chung and smiled mischeviously.

"I speak your language, Chinaman."

"I am Yang Kuo-chung, holder of the Ssu-k'ung office, chief minister in the government of our Divine Son of Heaven—"

The Tibetan laughed then, interrupting him. "Maybe not so divine, Chinaman," he said, grinning. "The Godhead not need to run from rascals and bandits!" He laughed at his own joke, and turned to his fellows, who laughed along with him. The man shook his head, then stroked the soft velvet of the horse's nose. "Maybe *he* is God," he said seriously.

Yang Kuo-chung smiled; it was all he could do.

"Where have you come from?" he asked.

"Like you, we come from nothing," the man said, and stretched his hands out and brought them above his head in a big circle as if he gestured to encompass the entire universe.

Yang Kuo-chung waited patiently. It was almost obligatory for a Tibetan to make such philosophical jokes, he knew. He had heard them before.

"And we go back to nothing!" the man added. "Yes! But only if we do not keep running." He smiled all around at his friends, then turned a more serious face to Yang Kuo-chung. "We come from T'ung-kuan Pass. Everybody dead. Everybody killed by rebels. No one left, Chinaman. Soldiers go . . . greatest city in whole world go . . ." He threw his hands up again, this time to emphasize total destruction. "Farms go . . . yes!"

"Who did you serve under?" Yang Kuo-chung questioned him.

"Crazy drunk man. General Ko-shu Han. Crazy drunk Chinaman." He turned toward his men and said something in his own language. They agreed with whatever it was he said, gesturing and waving their arms in disgust. "General get very drunk second day . . . come out of tent naked. Laughing. Has two skin of wine under arms. Say no reason to put his armor on . . . we all going to die anyway. So we go. Back to mountains. No rebels can go there."

Yang Kuo-chung had to think quickly. If they were headed back to the Tibetan frontier on the western boundaries of Szechuan, then they would be traveling in the same direction as the imperial entourage. Joining together would be in the best interests of both the Chinese and the Tibetans.

"We are accompanying the Emperor Emeritus and members of the imperial family to the crown prince and the provisional government in Shu-chun," Yang Kuo-chung said. "Will you ask your soldiers if they will join with us? There is greater safety in numbers, and we will be able to afford the Emperor much greater protection." Yang Kuo-chung relied on the assumption that the Tibetans would consider the rightful imperial government of China a far lesser evil than the northern rebels. Still, he expected them to confer before agreeing.

But the leader consulted no one. Instead, he merely nodded and smiled, and tugged lightly at the reins of Yang Kuo-chung's horse, punctuating his decision.

"Sure . . . sure! Good idea!" he said with certainty. He turned to his men and gestured for them to follow.

: :

Kao Li-shih rode on horseback alongside the Emperor, who sat in the lead cart. Around him in the cart rode about fifteen of the little children. The sun had just set, and the wan, crepuscular light made distant objects appear flat against a dull purplish-gray background; trees and hills seemed as thin and lifeless as paper cutouts. Kao Li-shih imagined an eternally twilit world where there was never any more light than this, and thought how fitting it would be.

The children, who had been quiet for several hours, were starting up their crying again. It seemed to spread from one child to another, and Kao Li-shih watched as Minghuang struggled to comfort them: wiping tears, taking hold of their hands, talking to them in soft, subdued tones, in the voice of someone profoundly guilty and ashamed. The children were tired and hungry, and there was very little food left. The supply of rice and millet cakes that they had brought had not been sufficient, and there was nothing left of the fruit. Yang Kuo-chung had been able to hunt some meat, but it had been tough, bitter, and gamey, and the littlest ones had not been able to hold it down, and that had made them weaker. And though the adults ate next to nothing, forfeiting their rations to the children, and though some of the older children stoically followed their example, there was still not enough, and hunger was taking its toll.

But it was the weight that it brought down upon the Emperor that worried Kao Li-shih the most. He was not at all certain that Minghuang could last much longer with the growing knowledge of the lie that he had lived and the consequent suffering brought by that lie. Kao Li-shih knew that it was consuming him more painfully than any disease or the most extreme hunger.

His feelings for the Emperor had turned to intense pity. The anger that he had once felt toward a blind, foolish old man now seemed remote and impossible. Looking at him now, Kao Li-shih wondered how he could ever have felt that way.

It was the eyes in the old man's haggard face. Eyes that could never hide anything to the outside. Even when the Emperor lied to himself, it was only to himself, only to the inside. To Kao Li-shih, and to anyone who understood him, the old man's eyes always told the truth, admitting everything he would not tell himself. Any hidden touch of sadness or disgrace, guilt or abnegation, was obvious and immediate if you knew him. Minghuang's eyes revealed everything.

In fact, Kao Li-shih had always thought that Minghuang's eyes were too candid and readable for an emperor's eyes. And although it may have seemed different many years ago, in truth, Minghuang had never possessed the qualities to rule. Ruling a nation was always a profound lie, carefully maintained. The act of ruling went beyond humanity, compassion, and wise decisions; ruling was an act of abstraction, of pomp and dispassionate play-acting. And although Minghuang had lived the lie of being a ruler for so many years now, he had never really mastered the technique; because, really, in truth, the eunuch reflected, the old man had no innate ability for deceit—no real ability to govern.

Kao Li-shih remembered the day after the Festival of Kao Mei and the effect that An Lu-shan's tearful protestation of innocence had had upon the Emperor. He had appeared to believe every word that came from his blubbering "Lucky Baby's" mouth. He had managed to convince himself one more time of the barbarian's innocence, and defended him to everyone else. But his eyes had told the eunuch differently; they had hidden nothing that day. They had spoken quite candidly and directly to Kao Li-shih.

What they had said was that Minghuang no longer believed in his own tales and fantasies. They told the eunuch that the old ruler was all too aware that his life had devolved into meaningless games, and that his increasing laziness and floundering integrity no longer passed for the distance and abstraction of the esoteric and philosophical man. Nor did it pass, anymore, for the supercilious legitimacy and pomp that marked an emperor's place between Heaven and Earth. In truth, those eyes never lied.

Kao Li-shih studied the old man surrounded, in the carriage, by little crying children. Minghuang's pain and sorrow was all the more acutely evident to Kao Li-shih against this unforgiving emptiness of hills and pines.

Words of the poet Li Po came to Kao Li-shih's mind; the rascal seemed to be following him again. It was strange; he had also thought of the poet on the morning after the brutal death of the child-concubine. What was it that Li Po had said about the landscape, quoting from a piece he had never finished?

> . . . to hear the lonely pines murmuring in the wind, to dream among the immortals and the clouds, to converse alone with the Bright Star spirit, to lose oneself in nature's profound eternity is the ultimate reflection of our own sadness. The branches sighing for the grievousness of our own destruction; the purity of nature is the inexhaustible comment on our wasted life, mocking us with the futility of our foolish journey. Are we not all—even the Son of Heaven—banished officials? It is better to trade all the Golden Tortoise badges of high office for a single skin of wine and the straw sandals of the recluse . . . for old age will come upon us in any case. . . .

No words could have better expressed what Kao Li-shih saw in the faces around him; the weariness, the utter exhaustion he saw in Yang Kuo-chung. A weariness born of futility and bitter defeat. And they were surrounded by the fact of their failure. The crying of these imperial children was simply a small manifestation of that failure; it was a reminder of the crying of thousands. Tens of thousands. The cries of all children. In that moment Minghuang was hearing them, too.

Kao Li-shih knew that Yang Kuo-chung had always anticipated those cries and that he had done everything in his power to prevent them. Though it was almost too sad for him to do it, Kao Li-shih allowed himself to contemplate for a moment the handsome figure riding ahead of them.

History, he suspected, always told a different story from what had really happened. Separated from the truth by time and speculation, it told a fictitious tale. He watched the back of Yang Kuo-chung's head. History will record you, Fox, as a manipulator, a self-server, perhaps even a traitorous plotter, a power-seeker; one who fought and lost. You have failed now, Chief Minister Yang. And you will fail before the historians of the future. If only you weren't so noble, Kao Li-shih thought, then none of this would be half so tragic.

Li Po spoke in his mind again:

Gazing down from the Cloud Terrace I see the Loyang River,
barbarian troops marching in their endless files;
streams of blood spreading over the meadow grasses,
wildcats and wolves in the caps of men!

The poet had written those lines a few days before news of the collapse
of the passes into Ch'ang-an and Loyang had reached them at the hot springs.
As soon as he had shown them to Kao Li-shih, he had torn them up with his
dirty hands. He had never intended for them to be included with the rest of
his work, he said, though he had been uncertain at first. He told Kao Li-shih
that he had thought, before deciding to throw them away, of titling the poem
"A Song of Regret." It was to be a long and tragic poem, a glimpse into the
future.

But then he had abandoned it. It is nothing but self-indulgent rambling,
he had declared, laughing and shredding up the paper after chanting the gloomy,
prophetic couplets at Kao Li-shih with his stinking wine-and-rotting-teeth
breath.

And, of course, his words had been quite correct in their prediction.

Perhaps that was why Li Po was such a debaucher, Kao Li-shih thought.
His filthy habits, his excesses of wine and sex, his constant sojourns from his
official responsibilities. It must have been the only thing that made the painful
burden of his insight bearable. Kao Li-shih was willing to acknowledge that,
at least.

He was brought back to the present by an irregularity in the vast natural
landscape. There was still quite enough light to see, and his eye was caught
by outlines that looked distinctly man-made. It appeared that he was the first
to see it: there was a village ahead, nearly hidden in a black clump of pines.

But something was not right. It was well past the time for the farmers'
evening meal, but there was no evidence of any activity. No smoke rose from
cooking fires, no voices of children carried in the still early evening air. This
was very strange, Kao Li-shih thought. He had expected farms to be abandoned, but not this far west and south of capital. And an entire settlement?
Had these villagers heard something that they themselves had not? Had the
rebels already been here? Or had it been that as the entourage slowly descended
the last ridge to travel the final ten or so li of the post road to Ma-wei, these
villagers had seen them coming and mistaken them for rebels? And then had
they just fled into the hills without any trace? It seemed unlikely.

Kao Li-shih was certain that the entourage could never come upon anyone
by surprise. Wherever they went, they were preceded by the sound of the
imperial children crying and wailing, and other noises as well—the percussive
bells, drums, and discordant voices of the Tibetans. It seemed that these moun-

tain dwellers would take any opportunity to make their strange music, if music it was. Possibly, the sounds had some other purpose, known only to the Tibetans, that escaped him entirely. At least it had provided a welcome distraction from the crying of the children crowding piteously around the Emperor—their father, grandfather, uncle.

Now the Emperor saw the village, too.

"Kao Li-shih, we must stop here. We need food," Minghuang said, breaking his self-imposed silence. "Listen to these children. They are starving. We must find the farmers here and ask them for food that we can buy. Perhaps some cakes of grain or rice for these little ones to eat. If we have to travel a third day before we reach Ma-wei, then I am not so certain about them . . ." His meaning was obvious.

At last Minghuang was speaking, taking some action again. The plight of the children had brought him back to the living. Thus far on the journey, he had barely spoken; he had merely sat and stared.

He lifted two of the littlest ones onto his lap, trying to quiet them, but their crying only grew more urgent, more painful to the ears of the adults. The consort took one of the children and wrapped him in her satin jacket, trying to rock him to sleep. Minghuang turned to Kao Li-shih with helpless desperation in his eyes.

"They have purged themselves too many times. They must have something to bind them. Grain. Bread. Something. Tell these villagers that we will offer them anything we can. And tell them that their food will not be sacrificed to keep a useless old man alive. I do not need to eat. But children simply do not have our reserve, our stamina. They must eat, Kao Li-shih! They must eat!"

Nor do they have our sheer, dumb persistence, Kao Li-shih thought. He turned to Lu Pei.

"Come with me. Everyone else wait here."

They found a trail leading through the copse of pines that sheltered the village. They went alone. They would take their chances, Kao Li-shih thought. He had no sense at all of danger. Besides, reason told him, this could not be a trap set for them. Not this far south. The rebels, he was certain, had already swarmed through the pass and into Ch'ang-an, but he doubted that they had gone any farther. The temptations of a great city had, more than likely, halted their southward progress. And for Kao Li-shih and Lu Pei to bring an armed guard into the village would only invite misunderstanding and trouble.

They came out of the trees and walked to the center of the settlement. Six small mud-brick-and-thatch huts formed a rough circle around a central village hall. Maybe it was a grain warehouse, a storeroom. Or a meeting place. It had a crude wooden gate with a few mismatched colored tiles set in an uneven cement roof—an odd concession to ornament in so rustic and homely a place as this, Kao Li-shih thought.

A small central courtyard was canopied by two big, hoary old pine trees. The village was utterly still, with no breath of life or movement anywhere. It made Kao Li-shih think of a ghost-city, a place of consecrated grounds and empty halls set out for the spirits of the dead. He had heard of such a city in Feng-tu in Szechuan Province, on the banks of the Yangtze, called the Ming Hill—a lifeless maze of buildings and statues, undisturbed even by sacrifices and obeisances by the living. Forever empty and eternally quiet, it existed only as a city for the invisible dead. Standing in the empty village square, he couldn't help but feel that he and Lu Pei had intruded on such a place.

They explored, cautiously poking their heads into the doorways of huts, calling, listening, looking for a shadow moving in the dim light or a shape against the darkened windows. But they found nothing. They decided to investigate the main hall and walked across the central street toward the tiled gate.

They pushed the creaking gate open and stepped into a beaten-earth courtyard. Expecting to find no one, they were both startled to see a whiskered grandfather on his haunches under a giant old cedar tree. He looked up when they entered, then returned his attention to the ground in front of him, where he was playing, it appeared, with a long stick, poking at a hole in the earth.

"Go ahead and look inside," he said, his attention on his stick and his hole. "I think you will find what you need."

The two eunuchs looked at one another. Kao Li-shih went and pulled the massive door open and peered into the gloom.

The roof of the hall had collapsed. The structure stood open to the sky. Here and there a perilously floating lintel or rafter hung against the wan light like the ribs of a dessicated corpse, with bits of thatching clinging here and there like shreds of skin. The interior had been blackened by fire. They went back outside.

The old man made no effort to move or even look up; instead, he muttered to himself and looked down at the ground, carving a trench with his stick.

"You know, if I had some water," he said to his guests, "I could make them a canal. Tomorrow I shall bring a skin of water up from the stream. Ants will swim; they will even use leaves for boats. Tomorrow, I will go into the woods and get them some leaves. These pine needles are no good at all," he said disdainfully, scooping up a small handful and finally looking up at the two imperial eunuchs.

"We have come to ask you if we may buy some food for the imperial children. It is a request from the Emperor. I am Kao Li-shih, chief eunuch of the imperial household. This is my apprentice, Lu Pei. We ask only for enough for the children. Nothing for ourselves. Some millet, some rice. Anything."

"I know who you are," the old man said, looking back toward the ants. "I saw your blue phoenix banners this morning. My legs might not be so good, but my eyes are as good as a hawk's."

He played some more. Kao Li-shih and Lu Pei waited.

"Bring the Son of Heaven to me," he said then. "I would like to talk to someone divine."

Kao Li-shih heard the sarcasm in the old man's voice, but he ignored it; there might be a chance at some food—a bargain to be struck. Certainly there was no danger to the Emperor here. Aware of the irony of appeasing this old peasant as if their roles had been subtly reversed, he sent Lu Pei back to fetch Minghuang. And of course, it is true, he reflected, watching Lu Pei disappear. The old man is the king here, and we are the supplicants.

"I am lonely," the old man said while they waited. "I want to talk to a *god*. At least to a god that answers."

"Did the rebels burn the granary, Old Man?" Kao Li-shih asked.

"What rebels, Eunuch?" He shook his head wryly and continued to carve tiny paths in the dirt. "See how smart these little fellows are? They want to get to me." He waved the stick above his knees to shake the ants free. "No, Eunuch. No rebels. I burned it down *myself*."

"And why did you do that?" Kao Li-shih asked carefully, certain that he was the brunt of the old man's joke. A not wholly inappropriate joke, he was forced to concede.

"Because I had nothing better to do. It was cold and the building was useless. Why do you ask, Eunuch?"

"We were hoping to find a small quantity of rice or millet there . . . some food, as I told you."

"*I* have food. It is not in there, though."

Lu Pei and the Emperor stepped into the courtyard then. They came and stood under the giant cedar next to Kao Li-shih. Though the old man had surely caught sight of the Emperor, he made no attempt to move or even acknowledge Minghuang's presence. He had returned to his engineering. He concentrated his efforts on reinforcing the walls of a miniature canal he had dug.

"You see, it will hold the water better this way. Tomorrow, I test it. I will create a grand flood for the ants."

"You asked for my presence. I am here." Minghuang spoke with a shade of impatience. "Can you help us find food for the children? We will pay, of course. We need your help."

Kao Li-shih knew that this was the wrong thing to say, that the old man would react to the Emperor's question with impertinence.

The old man raised his eyes and regarded the Emperor.

"So you are the Grand Emperor of China, eh? I don't believe it. I think you are an imposter. You are just an old man, like me. A tired-looking old man, just like me. When they had you surrounded with a thousand eunuch servants and a thousand courtiers and clouds of incense smoke, I could never see you clearly. But now I see you and you look just like an old man to me."

"That is what the Son of Heaven is, Farmer. Just an old man. A foolish old man . . ." Minghuang stared vacantly into the splintered remains of the village granary.

"No. The Son of Heaven is a *god*. That is what we have always been told. Prove to me that you are the Emperor!" he said, his voice rising. "If I give you food for your children, will you make me young again? Will you give me back my sons? Will you? Your generals took my sons. By law, one of my sons should have escaped your stupid armies and stayed here to take care of his old father. But the generals took them all. Took them all in the defense of the Son of Heaven. Everyone else fled, too. They said that Prince An Lu-shan was coming; that he meant to kill everybody in his path. I refused to go. I said we are not in his path; he is not coming for our miserable little village. But they didn't believe me. Before they left, they burnt the granary, as you can see. They did not want to feed your *fat* prince's appetite."

"We will take you with us, and . . ."

"I do not go anywhere with traitors," the old man cut in, and spat on the ground between his knees. "I have always wanted a personal audience with the Son of Heaven, so I could do *that*. Yes, I have food. But I do not have any food for your damned children. It is *your* war, Old Ruler. It is *your* turn to die in it."

With surprising suddenness and agility, the aged farmer jumped to his feet and rushed the Emperor with his stick raised above his head. Kao Li-shih stepped between them and took hold of the old man's arms. How wasted and weak they felt. The farmer pulled away with fragile strength and turned and spat on Kao Li-shih's shoulder. He swaggered back in mock victory to his place under the cedar and returned to his position on his haunches. No doubt, Kao Li-shih thought, he had done what he wanted: to attack an evil and frivolous emperor. And in his own mind, perhaps he might even convince himself that he had killed him.

"Let them die, old Son of Heaven. Like my children. I hope that they die on the road. I hope the ravens pick at their bones. And I hope that your own fat prince murders you while you run from him. I hope he eats you and shits divine shit!"

The Emperor did not move or speak, but absorbed the old man's tirade humbly. Kao Li-shih looked at the sparse tufts of white hair on the old peasant's head and noticed for the first time that the scalp was covered with dried scabs and blood. His arms, too, were cut and mottled with bruises and scratches, some fresh. Plainly, these were the marks left by the old peasant's daily struggle to feed himself and haul water from the ravine and up through the woods. He could picture him stumbling and falling on rocks, sharp branches scraping his limbs and head. The old man was at least eighty years old, Kao Li-shih thought. His struggle must be more difficult with each passing day. It was pathetic that an old father had no one left in his final days . . .

: :

They had left the old man and his ants in their solitude. They could have searched the village and seized whatever food he had hidden away for himself, but none of them had the heart for it. When they returned to the entourage and told of their strange experience, the leader of the Tibetans told them that, with the first light of morning, he and his men would find something the children could eat. So they had stopped for the night outside of the ghost village. Eventually, all the crying had stopped as the exhausted children dropped off to sleep.

And the Tibetans had been true to their word. As the sun was rising, several of them had crept off into the dawn. When they returned a few hours later, they had leaves, plant roots, mushrooms, some birds, and armloads of rabbits. Nonchalantly, they skinned and gutted the creatures, and smashed open the skulls to get the brains. Then they fetched water from the stream in the woods and made a crude stew out of everything, using cooking pots retrieved from the village.

The pampered royal children had cried at first, refusing the strange confection, but with some coaxing, had been persuaded to eat. It had quelled their fierce hunger pangs, and there had even been enough left over for the adults to have a few bites, though the Emperor refused any for himself. He would eat later, he had said, speaking the only words he was to utter all day, when they reached the postal station at Ma-wei. And they had traveled the rest of the long, hot summer morning and afternoon and into the evening with the comforting image before them of the postal station's rest and shelter, and real food for themselves and the children.

There, they would most likely find the remnants of an imperial regiment left behind to occupy the station, and a small herd of fresh horses maintained in the conscripted fields of nearby villages. And there would be provisions. With food and additional troops to escort them, the imperial entourage would be able to face the next leg of the arduous journey, including the brutal Chien-menkuan Pass.

As night fell and they came within a few li of the postal station, Yang Kuo-chung keenly anticipated the muted yellow glow of welcoming light that they would soon see in the windows of the old Buddhist oratory. Yang Kuo-chung had enjoyed the hospitality of this way station before in his travels, and he knew it well.

It had been given over by the monks in the final decade of the Sui dynasty as payment for long-overdue land taxes. Only one part of the sprawling oratory had been kept as a hostel for itinerant monastic mendicants; the rest had been converted into a comfortable, if somewhat rustic, travel lodge for the imperial family and traveling dignitaries of the state. Two large floors of graciously appointed rooms surrounded by a cool, screened veranda and a cultured rockery would provide an island of respite from the nightmare of their flight, possibly the last sanctuary in what would be, for several hundred li, an increasingly comfortless, unforgiving, and rocky wilderness.

And though he struggled not to show it, Yang Kuo-chung felt a profound depletion, born of his fatigue and anxiety. He knew that he was near collapse; without several hours' rest, he doubted that he would be able to go any farther. He had felt the eyes of the guardsmen on him all night and all day. If he exchanged a word with any of the Tibetans, he was aware of looks and gestures passing between the young Chinese. And they kept their distance from the Tibetans at all times, making it plain that they regarded the foreigners as their enemies. Yang Kuo-chung thanked the gods that the Tibetans had the sense to behave as if none of this were evident to them; had he been forced to contend with suspicion and wariness from both sides, he might have lost control long ago. He had invited the Tibetans to accompany them because he wanted the extra protection they would afford and because he wanted to show the guardsmen that there was nothing to fear. Plainly, he had made the opposite impression. He felt quite helpless. Any moves that he contemplated with an eye to relieving the terrible strain could, he knew, go very wrong and make things even worse.

But there was one possibility. It had been growing in his mind since yesterday. He had been reluctant to entertain it at first, but now saw that it was absolutely necessary.

He had to get rid of the guardsmen. Now that they had the Tibetans with them to act as escorts, they could get along without them if they had to. Once high and safe on the deserted Chienmenkuan Pass, only a few days from now, he thought, the royal family must have some excuse to separate from the suspicious young Chinese. He would have to arrange a ploy. He would advise Minghuang to order them on some mission away from the entourage, away from the Yangs. Exactly what that mission would be, he did not yet know. He needed to rest, and gather his wits, and think in peace.

The Lady of Kuo rode by his side. What he really needed, he thought, looking at her profile in the dim light from the lanterns carried by the guardsmen in front of them, was a few hours alone with her. He wanted to go to sleep in her arms, then wake and lose himself in her for a while. That was the way to get his strength back. It had never failed before. He reached out in the dark, saying her name. Her hand met his. He took it and held it, feeling her fine bones and dry, soft skin. There were many rooms at the postal station. Enough, surely, so that they could go and be alone together.

When the stone markers told them that they were within two li of Ma-wei, Yang Kuo-chung ordered the guardsmen to light the lamps suspended from the sides of the carriages. Kao Li-shih watched as long strings of paper lanterns came to life and then swayed from side to side in an undulating line as the carriages moved forward—like river barges lit for a festival, he thought remotely. It was their only light. There was no moon at all, and even the stars that had blazed earlier were hidden now behind thick clouds. As the caravan wound along the road, the lanterns made long, moving shadows in the trees on either side.

When they encountered the final stone marker and had but one li to go, Kao Li-shih saw Yang Kuo-chung ride ahead toward the postal station with several guardsmen to announce their arrival. He slumped down in his seat, pressing his weary hands to his eyes. Soon they could all rest. He glanced over to where the Emperor and consort rode. The look of humility that Kao Li-shih had seen on the Emperor's face as he stood before the old peasant absorbing his bitter words had not left his features, which were set and sad in the lantern-light. To think that I spent all those years trying to protect him from words like those, Kao Li-shih thought, only to finally encounter them out here in the wilderness, from a lone old man. An old man that *I* led him to.

He raised his head. He could hear the returning hoofbeats of Yang Kuo-chung and the guardsmen. Too soon. They were returning too soon.

Yang Kuo-chung was the first to reach the carriages. He reined his horse in and looked down from the saddle. Kao Li-shih looked up, and knew full well what the Fox was going to say:

There was nothing in Ma-wei. No one. It was dark and deserted.

"Master Kao"—Yang Kuo-chung had ridden hard, and he collected his horse with a strong rein—"you must have expected this," he said, and smiled a philosophical smile. "I see no surprise at all on your face. None at all."

The two friends looked at one another for a few moments, each searching for some sign of hope or strength in the other's eyes.

"Rebels?" Kao Li-shih whispered.

Yang Kuo-chung shook his head discreetly. "I am certain that there is no one there," he said in a normal voice. "No one."

"What do you mean?" asked the Lady of Han from the carriage behind them. "Do you mean that there is nothing there at all?"

"No food? No soldiers?" asked the Lady of Chin, alarm in her voice. "What are we to do?"

"Hush, foolish Sisters," said the Lady of Kuo sharply. "Do not make it any more difficult. You are not the only ones who are disappointed."

"No matter," said Kao Li-shih brusquely, so that everyone would hear. "At least we have shelter for the night. Possibly there are stores of food."

"Quite right, Master Kao," said Yang Kuo-chung gratefully. "We will proceed." He rode on ahead, and the carriages continued to lumber toward the dark postal station.

Damn, thought Kao Li-shih, observing the news spreading among the guardsmen, the whispering, the uneasy, reticent expressions on their faces. What do the idiots believe? That Yang Kuo-chung planned all of this? That he brought them here for some questionable purpose? Can't they see that he is giving every bit of his being to the safety of everyone around him, themselves included?

Yang Kuo-chung had told him about the unfortunate accident of the guardsmen witnessing the strange Tibetan funeral rite. It was precisely what the ignorant, superstitious youths did not need to see. They simply were not equipped to understand it, and it had excited their imaginations. Something would have to be done. The growing tension was making it impossible for Yang Kuo-chung to function as their leader. Tomorrow, he resolved, he would hold a meeting. Just himself and the guardsmen. He would talk to them in plain language that they could understand, and he would remind them exactly who this Yang Kuo-chung was.

Your enemy? No, you fools. This is the man who has tried, since a time when some of you undoubtedly had not yet seen your first pubic hair, to stop An Lu-shan, to reverse the very destiny of the empire. This is the man who faced Li Lin-fu, unarmed and alone but for a single eunuch. Would any of you have had his courage?

Tomorrow the soldiers would hear Kao Li-shih out. He would make them ashamed.

: :

The postal station was indeed in total darkness. The ancient wooden buildings were only black shapes looming beyond the lantern-light as the entourage came to a halt on the road. Several of the more courageous among the guardsmen, with Yang Kuo-chung leading the way, took lanterns from the carriages and made their way cautiously toward the buildings. Yang Kuo-chung found the oil lamps affixed to the walls of the buildings near the doorways and lit them from the lantern he carried.

Now the entryways of both the postal station and the lodge were revealed in the yellow light, dispelling considerably, Kao Li-shih thought, the sinister air of the place. A group of guardsmen proceeded cautiously down the alley between the two buildings to explore the area to the rear, their lights bobbing in front of them, a few of them holding crossbows cocked and ready.

As more lamps were lit and people began moving about, the atmosphere seemed to relax a bit. There is nothing quite like light to rout the demon of fear, Kao Li-shih thought, climbing down from the carriage. Besides, Yang Kuo-chung had been right. There was no one here. No one at all. He could feel it. No one waited in ambush, no one watched them from the dark windows. And it had been a long time since anyone had been here. He could feel that, too. He stood and stretched his aching body.

The Tibetans dispersed and began to gather firewood and brush to fashion torches. Some of the children awakened and started to whimper; the Emperor and the consort hushed and comforted them, then climbed down from the carriage and stood, their arms about each other, waiting. The sisters stayed where they were, also waiting. The Lady of Kuo sat on her horse, her eyes following Yang Kuo-chung as he moved about giving orders.

Kao Li-shih heard the soft hooting of an owl coming from the woods behind the building. It made him think of idyllic nights at the hot springs, when, from time to time, he encountered a mated pair of owls who nested there year after year. Kao Li-shih used to converse with them. He had practiced until he could mimic their call perfectly. He remembered now the deep, indescribable satisfaction of standing in the dark woods hooting, pretending that he was another owl, and having one of them answer him.

From another place in the trees behind the buildings, a second owl called in response to the first. Probably the mate, Kao Li-shih thought, and turned back toward where the Emperor and consort were standing. He wanted to get the Emperor inside and settled; then he would begin the search for food. Surely there was something—some rice or millet, perhaps. And tomorrow, of course, the Tibetans could go out and procure more game.

A shout from the rear of the oratory brought his head back around sharply. He was just in time to see the shaft of light in the narrow alley between the buildings swing from left to right; at the same moment, there was the distinctive sound of a crossbow bolt spring releasing. A terrible scream of pain stopped his heart for just a moment. Then there were more screams, short and spasmodic, the guardsmen's excited voices shouting, and running footsteps. He saw Yang Kuo-chung leap onto his horse. An animal, Kao Li-shih thought. They have killed an animal. What creature screams like that? In the next moment, he knew.

"You damned fools! You've killed him!" The voice of a guardsman carried clearly from behind the oratory. And he had told himself that the war would not touch them here! It had followed them, had been with them all along. He grabbed hold of Yang Kuo-chung's foot in its stirrup.

"Wait for me!" he cried. "Don't go in there alone!"

About ten of the Tibetans broke from the front of the lodge and began to run through the alley to the back, glowing embers trailing from their torches.

Kao Li-shih yanked a frightened guardsman from his saddle, then kicked his leg up into the stirrup and heaved his weight onto the horse. The animal spooked and began to buck; the eunuch sat deep and pushed the horse forward, reining the thick muscled neck in. He gained control, moving the horse away from the entourage. He and Yang Kuo-chung rode together at a fast trot.

Mounted guardsmen pressed them from behind. Ignoring Yang Kuo-chung's shouted orders to stay back, they flowed around and ahead of them and galloped heedlessly down the alley.

When they were nearly halfway to the back of the oratory and the torchlit chaos behind it, they heard another young guardsman's voice ring out clearly.

"It was Master Yang's Tibetans!" the boy cried. "They were hiding in the trees, calling out like owls! They were calling out to An Lu-shan in the trees!"

Kao Li-shih and Yang Kuo-chung exchanged a single, wordless look as they lashed their horses forward. It had happened. Panic and murder had broken out.

As they got closer, they were better able to discern the direction that the shouts came from: the garden rockery, very near the woods behind the imperial lodge. The Tibetans up ahead flattened themselves against the walls of the buildings to let the mounted guardsmen gallop by. Then they turned to face Yang Kuo-chung and Kao Li-shih, placing themselves in their path and waving their torches. For a moment, Kao Li-shih's mind leapt to a conclusion: an ambush? Yang Kuo-chung, trying to avoid trampling the Tibetans, pulled his horse in; the "priest," the one who spoke some Chinese, seized the reins, an urgent torrent of broken words pouring from him.

"Chinaman governor! Yang Governor! No! No! No go back there!" he implored. "They mad scared! China boys they *hate* Yang Governor! Hate much! Go back! Go back!"

"He is right!" Kao Li-shih said. "Go back, Master Yang!"

Yang Kuo-chung paused for only a heartbeat, staring down into the Tibetan's eyes. Kao Li-shih saw them look at one another in the flickering torchlight; then, strangely, the Tibetan said no more, but dropped his hand from the reins and stepped out of the way. Yang Kuo-chung jabbed his heels into his horse and pushed ahead; Kao Li-shih had no choice but to follow.

The Tibetan's warning had had no effect on Yang Kuo-chung at all. Galloping behind him now, Kao Li-shih saw the same brash, heroic figure who had tried to take on Li Lin-fu single-handedly, storming the halls of the Chancellery. He had to stop him this time . . . if he could.

Kao Li-shih heard the Tibetan shout some final words after them as they rode toward the light at the end of the alley.

"See enough of your deaths for a hundred lives, Chinaman!" His voice was soon drowned out by the noise and chaos ahead of them.

The scene that they came upon was straight out of Kao Li-shih's worst imaginings. Frightened boy-soldiers pushed and shoved at one another; on the ground in their midst, his life-blood soaking the pine needles beneath him, lay one of their fellows, a guardsman who could not have been any older than sixteen. A crossbow bolt in his chest, his eyes stared up at the sky while one hand clutched feebly at the shaft that impaled him. He did not cry out for help anymore. Though he still lived, it was plain that it would not be for very much longer. The young lieutenant of the guards knelt at his side.

The soldiers fell back as Yang Kuo-chung and Kao Li-shih approached.

"What has happened here?" Yang Kuo-chung demanded.

"It was the Tibetans!" one of them cried defiantly.

"They were in the woods hooting like owls! Calling out to the rebels so that they could come and slaughter us! They killed him!" another voice cried.

"Those Yang pigs brought the rebels with them! Then they brought the Tibetans here to help the rebels slaughter us!" somebody shouted. There was a commotion of agreement at this. "To ambush us! They were hiding in the woods!"

One of the braver ones pushed forward and spoke directly to Yang Kuo-chung now:

"You knew this place was abandoned! This is a Buddhist cemetery! But it's not going to be *our* cemetery!"

Agreement spread through the ranks like fire through dry brush, though there were a few among them who shouted for order.

Yang Kuo-chung pushed his horse forward into the middle of the crowd. The guardsmen gave him a wide berth; Kao Li-shih followed close behind. The young lieutenant, the anger and confusion on his face mingling with his fear, rose abruptly to his feet to confront the chief minister. Yang Kuo-chung looked briefly from the lieutenant to the body on the ground, as if trying to recall something about the dead boy. He is no one, Kao Li-shih thought; just another mother's son, lost.

"What happened here?" Yang Kuo-chung demanded again with grave restraint and dignity. "I see a dead soldier, but I see no evidence of an enemy or a battle. Can you explain this to me, Lieutenant?" He looked around at the faces of the boys in the torchlight. "Can any of you explain what has happened here? Why is this man dead? You have blamed the Tibetans. But I can see that this is a Chinese bolt that has pierced him, and from very close range, too. Who fired the bolt? That is what I wish to know first. Or do you *all* wish to be held accountable?"

Kao Li-shih could see that the Fox was struggling to maintain his equanimity; he clenched his jaw and spoke deliberately and clearly, keeping his rage in check. Kao Li-shih wished fervently that he himself had taken action earlier, had spoken to the guardsmen sooner. The confrontation that they had both dreaded, though they had said little about it to each other, was upon them.

The lieutenant turned away from Yang Kuo-chung's unforgiving stare. He directed his eyes at the ground for a second, appeared about to speak, but hesitated. His mouth trembled as he tried again to speak and again faltered. He gazed down at the body. The others stood silently, surrounding him, waiting for a sign. Finally he summoned his courage and lifted his eyes to the chief minister's.

"I will *not* tell you, Master Yang. I do not talk to *traitors*. But I will tell you this, they were fearful of your Tibetans. They heard bird calls in those woods. They panicked. We know that your rebel bandits are in the woods. We know that your An Lu-shan was born under the Red Star and has the voices of all the animals. He is in there, somewhere. It is only a matter of time, is it not? The soldiers know that the Yangs are planning to execute them and to kill the Son of Heaven when the moment is right, when he is unguarded. Do you think your bandits will remember their Yangs when it is all over? Do you think, Master Yang, that An Lu-shan will keep his promises to you?" He spat in Yang Kuo-chung's direction. "Chief Minister," he added disdainfully.

The Fox did not flinch. He took these fantastic words in as if he had been expecting them, as if he had already heard them in his mind. But Kao Li-shih could not believe that he was hearing this. It was a thousand times worse than he had suspected.

"You are an insult to so great a man!" Kao Li-shih shouted. "Every one of you! Fools! Dogs and cowards! Despicable insults! You would honor him if you knew the truth. You would be at his feet! At his feet!" Kao Li-shih was nearly choking with rage. He was too angry to speak in anything but ragged fragments. "He has risked his life! Risked his life to bring An Lu-shan to account . . ."

"It was the Yangs who brought him to court!" another guardsman called out from behind the lieutenant. "That is what we know, Eunuch. They made him a prince and worshiped him!"

To Kao Li-shih's right, one of the guardsmen, drawing courage from these words, put a hand on the hilt of his sword.

"The Yangs gave him everything. All the weapons and men he wanted. Do you support him, too, Eunuch?" The soldier approached him as he spoke, startling Kao Li-shih with his boldness.

"From now on you will address *me*," Yang Kuo-chung said fiercely, his voice bringing silence for a moment. The guardsman's courage failed him, and he backed away from Kao Li-shih. "Master Kao is innocent. Leave him. I will bear you no malice if those responsible will come forth and confess what happened here. I will consider it an act committed out of fear and confusion. The charge will not be one of murder. I give you my assurance . . ."

"You can give us nothing, *Pig* Minister!" one of the soldiers behind the lieutenant cried out.

"You are a bandit!" another one cried.

"A Yang traitor!"

The others joined in now, their shouts growing louder, their strength and boldness multiplying. They jeered and hurled their accusations as they closed in around Yang Kuo-chung. Kao Li-shih caught fragments of their insults flying through the air like deadly arrows.

"Filthy Yang cunts!"

"Killers!"

"Bastard son of a turtle!"

Now the guardsmen were moving toward him, too. Kao Li-shih's horse shied from the crowd, rearing and bucking.

"If any man takes another step toward me, or Master Kao, I will not hesitate to kill him!" Yang Kuo-chung shouted, his voice enraged and hoarse, collecting the reins in one hand and drawing his long yataghan blade with the other. He raised the weapon nearly parallel with his mount's neck. He urged the animal forward a few feet, his eyes fixed on the lieutenant.

"Our chief minister would not hesitate to kill any of us! You heard him say so yourself!" the youth said, turning to the others. He pulled a lance out of one soldier's grip and held it out boldly and conspicuously in front of him, slowly leveling it so that it now pointed at Yang Kuo-chung's waist. His message was clear: he was making a direct challenge.

He began to make quick thrusts with the lance at the flanks of the Fox's horse, plainly trying to panic the creature so that it would throw Yang Kuo-chung to the ground. That would be the end, Kao Li-shih thought. They must not get him down; once they did, they would close in like a pack of hungry dogs. Yang Kuo-chung fought to keep control of his horse, which turned this way and that, its eyes rolling white in their sockets.

One of the thrusts missed the horse and entered the calf of Yang Kuo-chung's leg with a brutal jab, stabbing and withdrawing in nearly the same motion. The Fox grimaced and parried the lieutenant's next thrust, severing the tip of the lance with his Muslim blade. Again the soldier thrust with the broken shaft, but the movement of the panicked horse caused him to miss his mark and strike the animal's wither. The horse turned and reared; as the Fox struggled to keep from falling and tried to rein the animal in, the lieutenant took aim again and buried the splintered tip of the lance into the chief minister's thigh, where it hung, jerked from his hands by the rearing of the horse.

Howling with rage and pain, Yang Kuo-chung reacted with reflexive swiftness. His yataghan sword flashed with deadly speed and precision, coming down full force into the young lieutenant's shoulder. The heavy blade bit down so deep into bone and flesh that for a moment the Fox had to wrestle to retrieve it. The youth dropped to the ground, speechless, his face white with shock. Yang Kuo-chung hacked with his sword at the wooden lance in his leg, dislodging it. Fiercely, he brandished the blade and challenged the crowd of soldiers.

"Who else wishes to commit an act of treason against the law of our Sovereign Son of Heaven and his chief minister? Who? Come forward now!"

The lieutenant had fallen backward, senseless, landing squarely on his buttocks and rolling onto his stomach. Now, trying to rise again, he attempted to brace himself with his injured arm; but the dangling limb folded uselessly beneath him, causing him to topple onto the hacked shoulder, awakening him in an instant of pure agony to the reality of what Yang Kuo-chung had done to him. He screamed the most wicked and terrifying scream that Kao Li-shih had ever heard.

"MY ARM!" he screamed. "MY ARM! HE HAS TAKEN MY ARM!" He rolled onto his back and sat up, cradling the nearly severed arm in his good hand. His comrades looked down on him in horror. "Can't you see what he has done??" he shouted. "Kill him! Kill them all! Or they will slaughter every one of you!"

"STOP!" Kao Li-shih cried as the guardsmen tightened their circle around Yang Kuo-chung. "Stop this insanity! He is the best friend you have! *You* are the traitors!" But his voice was only a futile sound in his own ears. No one heard him at all.

Then Kao Li-shih saw him; he had gone unnoticed, had circled around Yang Kuo-chung to approach him from behind, and now he raised a barbed lance with precision. The Fox was busy pivoting his terrified horse to meet the others in front; with sustained stamina and ferocity, he cut down three young soldiers who rushed at him with swords and daggers. But he did not see the one who stalked him from the rear.

"YANG! Kao Li-shih bellowed. "BEHIND YOU! TURN AROUND!" He tried to ride in, to intercept the lance, but soldiers seized the reins of his horse, turning it, confusing it. They would not let him move. He tried to leap down to the ground, but they restrained him, overpowering him.

"Yes! *Do* turn around, Chief Minister!" the soldier with the lance cried. Too late, Yang Kuo-chung did turn, at the same moment that the soldier hurled the lance with all his strength. Kao Li-shih's eyes followed the lance as, dreamlike, it arced through the air; in the next instant it hung in Yang Kuo-chung's chest, protruding from front to back in perfect symmetry. The Fox held himself upright, fire-gleaming yataghan held out in a rigid arm, maintaining his balance in the high wood and leather saddle.

The soldiers fell back for a moment, staring up at the amazing spectacle of the dying chief minister. Kao Li-shih kicked and fought in his captors' grip, trying to get to his friend; but when Yang Kuo-chung's eyes locked urgently onto his, he ceased his struggling.

"It is over for me, Friend," said the Fox in a clear voice. "Save yourself. And save the Son of Heaven at all costs. We shall have no chance to recover China without him."

Good-bye, Fox, Kao Li-shih said with his eyes.

It took two more soldiers to cut him from his horse, Yang Kuo-chung striking downward with a final effort of will that cost one of the guardsmen his nose. Then, at last, the Fox toppled, a crossbow bolt lodged deep in his neck. The guardsmen dragged him to the ground and severed his head with a massive poleax and in the dying half-light of a wretched Buddhist hell they impaled it on the broken lance, raised it high above them, and cheered.

But Kao Li-shih saw that it was not Yang Kuo-chung on that handsome and noble face; he had already gone.

With one swift motion, while his captors were distracted, the eunuch rammed his dagger into his horse's rump. The horse struck out with its hind legs, catching one soldier fully in the chest, then spun around, dragging four men like weightless paper lanterns and trampling them along the ground, breaking free. Kao Li-shih clung to the animal as it plunged into the darkness of the alley.

When he had nearly reached the entrance to the alley, he saw someone running toward him from across the courtyard, shouting and waving a torch. He lashed his horse; nothing would stop him now. The lone figure jumped aside as he approached. It was then that he heard his name being shouted and recognized the white, terrified face of Lu Pei.

"Master Kao! Heaven defend us! Master Kao!" the boy cried.

Kao Li-shih reined his horse in hard, directing its frenzy into tight, snorting circles.

"The sisters!" Lu Pei sobbed, running to him. "They have killed the Yang sisters! The soldiers left to guard them heard the shouts and the fighting. They turned on them! They killed them as they ran!"

He looked over through the courtyard gate out to the road, where a knot of soldiers, torches in hand, stood over two fallen bodies. Afraid, indecisive, they milled about, staring defiantly in Kao Li-shih's direction, but making no move toward them. Cowards, Kao Li-shih thought. Filthy, craven cowards!

"They were traitors! We executed traitors!" one of them shouted, his voice unsure.

"The Emperor!" Kao Li-shih demanded of Lu Pei. "Where is he? Tell me he is alive!"

"He is. He is," Lu Pei gasped. "He and the consort. They were already inside the oratory. Looking for food. The children and nursemaids are in the imperial lodge." He dropped his voice then. "The lady. She got away. She was too fast."

"The lady?" Kao Li-shih asked sharply, his own voice lowered. "Do you mean Kuo?"

"Yes. The Lady of Kuo. She was on her horse and gone before they even knew it."

Kao Li-shih closed his eyes for a moment in thanks. She lives, Master Yang, he said to his dead friend. They were no match for her. They could not catch her. She lives!

Kao Li-shih jumped down from his horse and put his hands on Lu Pei's shoulders. He looked over at the soldiers, who talked in low voices among themselves, still not making any move. Behind him, he heard the others, the ones who had murdered Yang Kuo-chung, advancing down the alley, shouting and talking excitedly among themselves, some on foot, some on horseback. The Tibetans, he realized, had vanished entirely, wisely melting back into the dark woods, staying out of the trouble that was none of their affair.

"Get hold of yourself, Lu Pei. I will be needing you. You and I must keep the Emperor alive." He gave the boy a firm, gentle shove toward the oratory. "Do not run," he whispered, though the voices of the soldiers coming down the alley told him that they were fast approaching, and the ones in the courtyard were watching them with wary eyes. "Stay calm. Walk."

The flame of Lu Pei's torch that he still held in his trembling hand cast a dancing light around them as they neared the dark building. The impulse to run was powerful, but Kao Li-shih kept a firm hand on Lu Pei's shoulder and forced his own legs to walk slowly. It is running that attracts the hunter to its quarry, he knew; running that awakens the urge to chase and kill.

When he was nearly at the oratory door, he knew without looking back that the soldiers were out of the alley and following them. Not chasing them, but following them, watching them. He could hear their muttering voices. And he could hear something else, too: their uncertainty. And he knew what had happened.

Gazing on the severed head of the chief minister, the moment of glory passed, some among the soldiers must have asked themselves what they had done. And the doubt was now spreading from man to man just as the fear and hatred had. Good, thought Kao Li-shih as he pounded the heavy brass knocker against the thick wood. Good. Ask yourselves what you have done. Ask yourselves what you have really done. I hope you will be spared nothing.

"It is Kao Li-shih," he declared through the door, trying to sound calm, praying that someone was right there, his voice cracking from the strain. Don't make me pound and scream, he begged silently. "Let us in. Now!" He waited, the voices of the soldiers only thirty or so paces behind them. He turned his head briefly in their direction and saw, to his horror, that they had dragged Yang Kuo-chung's body with them into the courtyard, as if to prove to themselves that they had committed an act of heroism. A bolt slid back and the door opened. He pushed Lu Pei through, was through himself in the next moment, pushed the door shut, and slid the bolt back into place.

It was the Emperor himself who had opened the door. The light of the torch revealed his haggard face and the consort in a corner of the room, leaning against a wall. Over their heads, carved in the lintels, the light revealed the incongruous gilded characters of the *Hua-yen* Sutra.

"Yang Kuo-chung . . . ?" the Emperor began. Kao Li-shih shook his head, warning him with his eyes not to ask any more questions in front of the consort. The Emperor did not persist, but a look of terrible pain came across his features. He understood perfectly.

Kao Li-shih held up a warning hand. Heavy footsteps, leather boots on gravel, were approaching the door. Low voices murmured in solemn discussion, their words unintelligible. The Emperor made a move toward the door.

"I will go out," he said.

Kao Li-shih blocked his way. "No. You will not."

"Master Kao," the Emperor said. "Don't you see that it is best that I offer myself to them? That I end this slaughter of innocents once and for all? An Lu-shan is my crime, my blindness. My own loathsome princeling."

"And you think that that will end it? It is clear to me that you are as mad as they are. The extent of your negligence is irrelevant now. It does not matter anymore. It is far too late for that," Kao Li-shih said, standing squarely in front of the door. "There is only one fact that matters: if you die, there will be no hope for unification and peace. No hope at all!" He repeated this slowly and emphatically. "You are the only real, legitimate symbol of this empire. To the people, *you* are still *China*."

"That is not what the old peasant in the village told me," Minghuang said quietly.

"No matter," Kao Li-shih replied. "He would still choose you over An Lu-shan, if he had a choice. But he will have no choice at all if you do not take care to keep yourself alive, Old Fool!" Kao Li-shih declared with passion. He spoke with brutal frankness then, staring hard at the guilt-ridden man in front of him. "Don't compound your crime now by dying. If you die, you will be abandoning those you wronged."

The footsteps had stopped at the door.

"Besides," Kao Li-shih whispered to the Emperor, "I do not think it is you that they want."

At the same moment that the Emperor cast a frightened, questioning look at Kao Li-shih, someone pounded on the door.

"We are here for the Yang consort," a soldier's voice said. "Hand her over to us in order that we may continue to protect the Son of Heaven!" His tone was formal and rehearsed, as if he addressed a memorial before the throne.

Hearing this, the consort said nothing, but sank to a crouching posture against the wall, her eyes on Kao Li-shih. She had heard and understood his words, of course: the Emperor must live, *no matter what the cost.* Kao Li-shih looked back at her, unable to remove his eyes from hers. You can't be thinking it, Eunuch, her eyes said to his. You cannot even be thinking it.

"What do you want with her?" Kao Li-shih called to the man outside the door. "She has done you no harm. Whatever it is, you will take it up with me!"

The soldier did not answer right away. Kao Li-shih heard his footsteps retreating a short distance, and his voice, lowered, conferring with other voices. There were angry shouts, excited arguing, reprimands. Throughout, the consort kept her eyes fixed on Kao Li-shih's.

The footsteps returned.

"She must be executed, Master Kao," the soldier said through the door. A clamor of assenting voices rose behind him. "She is a Yang," he said. "None of the Yangs can be allowed to live. They are all traitors to the sovereign law of the Son of Heaven!"

"And she is the wife of the Son of Heaven!" Kao Li-shih countered. "His Empress! Leave her. Take your men and go. There will be no retribution for what you have done!"

There was another pause.

"No! We cannot leave, and you know it. It is not possible, Master Kao. The Emperor must prove his allegiance to these soldiers and to all the people of the realm by renouncing any ties with the traitorous Yangs. He can do that only by giving her over to us!"

"In the name of Heaven! Why don't they kill me, instead?" cried the Emperor. "I am only a wretched dead man anyway!"

"Quiet him, Lu Pei!" Kao Li-shih ordered. "Quiet him even if you must tie a cloth over his bloody, foolish mouth!"

"Master Kao," the voice continued from outside, the equanimity only a thin disguise, the fear and uncertainty plainer than ever. "The soldiers will not feel their own lives are safe if there is one Yang left alive to influence him . . . to come back for us . . . to avenge these deaths . . . to bend the Son of Heaven's ear against us! Every Yang must be killed!"

He thinks I don't know that the Lady of Kuo eluded them, Kao Li-shih thought.

"Tell the truth, Soldier!" he shouted. "Admit that you know what you have done here is a crime—a ghastly, evil, meaningless crime born of your blindness and stupidity. That is why you want the last Yang killed! We have told you that there will be no retribution. Leave her be! Do not soil your hands with another murder!"

"The Emperor cannot make his journey without us, Master Kao," the soldier said, speaking words that Kao Li-shih knew to be true. "But he must prove his allegiance to us. He must hand her over. If he does, then we offer our absolute protection and allegiance in his war against the usurpers, to the last man among us. And we will not touch any of you." He paused. "And we promise that the execution will be quick and painless."

The consort was rising slowly to her feet, still looking at Kao Li-shih.

Kao Li-shih's thoughts tumbled over one another in his churning mind. A way out. There had to be a way out. He needed time to think, time to plan. Then, almost preceding conscious thought, words came to his lips.

"We agree to your demands," he said through the door.

The consort stiffened, her eyes impaling his.

"But there is one condition."

"What is it, Master Kao?"

"That you and your soldiers leave the final dignity of her death to me!"

"Kao Li-shih!" the Emperor cried.

The consort did not wait to hear any more. She was gone, through the rear doorway and down the dark hallway of the oratory, her swift footsteps echoing.

"Master Kao! Are you mad?" Lu Pei whispered.

"Shut up, both of you. *Shut up!*" Kao Li-shih hissed.

"And how will we know that she is dead?" the voice from behind the door questioned.

"I will kill her, and then I will display her body to you. I will not fail you or the Son of Heaven. I will strangle her with my own hands."

There was talk outside, hushed and serious. There was no more shouting. Then:

"They have agreed to your offer, Master Kao."

"Give me until dawn, and it will be done."

"No, Master Kao," the soldier answered. "I am afraid I cannot. You must kill her now. I cannot hold the men back much longer. If you do not do it now, then we will be forced to find a way in and do it ourselves."

There was a short silence as the soldier waited for a reply. Kao Li-shih said nothing, but stood, his back pressed to the door, thinking desperately, his eyes gazing down at the ancient floor.

"Master Kao?" the soldier called tentatively. "We will retreat to the gate. Only a sentry will be posted outside the door. When you have finished, bring the consort's body into the courtyard."

"Master Kao!" Lu Pei's voice shouted an urgent warning. "Look out!"

Someone hurled himself upon Kao Li-shih. It was the Emperor, striking with both fists at the chief eunuch's chest.

"You foul traitor!" he cried. "Murderer!"

Kao Li-shih seized the old man's wrists and held him at arm's length. Minghuang struggled with wiry strength, while Kao Li-shih, trying not to injure him, turned the Emperor around, pinned his arms behind his back, and shook him hard.

"Listen to me! What else can I do? Refuse them and we may all be dead. And your consort will not die so merciful a death at their hands. It would be an obscenity to let them do it. And they will do it, I can assure you. They will kill her! Let it be me, her friend, who does it."

The Emperor continued to curse and struggle.

"You must live!" Kao Li-shih went on. "Do you think China's generals will rally in the name of your crown prince alone? Do you think that, without you, those same generals will give up their claims on the provincial territories that they hold, even if we should manage to defeat your barbarian? Chaos! That is what it will be! China will be destroyed, and it will be because of you, Old Fool!"

The Emperor went limp, as if all his strength and will had suddenly drained out of him. Kao Li-shih let go of him, and he slunk mournfully back down to the floor.

"You are right, of course, Kao Li-shih. You are always right. Take her. I have made enough mistakes for ten thousand lifetimes. But be quick. Please. Please."

"It is an exchange. One life for millions," Kao Li-shih said, though he saw that any further persuasion was gratuitous. "A lesser evil," he added.

But the Emperor did not look up or acknowledge him anymore. Kao Li-shih stood for another moment looking down on the pathetic figure. Then he went to the entrance to the corridor down which the consort had disappeared. "Lu Pei," he said, "you will come with me."

"Master Kao," the boy pleaded, "I cannot! Please! You must spare me!" The boy began to cry.

"I told you I would need you. I told you that outside. Now that time has come. Light the oil lamp and bring it with you. Come," he said firmly.

Lu Pei knelt on the floor and lit the lamp with a shaking hand. He placed the torch in a holder on the wall so that the Emperor would not be left in darkness, rose obediently to his feet, cast a sorrowful look at the defeated old man on the floor, and followed Kao Li-shih through the dark doorway.

Kao Li-shih moved down the long corridor, revealed now in the light of the lantern. On either side of them were rows of arched doorways, entrances to the numerous small rooms that served sojourning mendicants as hostels and meditation cells. Somewhere, in one of these bare Buddhist prayer cells, the consort hid in the absolute darkness, waiting for death.

There were at least thirty cells. She could be in any of them. How long would the soldiers wait before storming the oratory? They brought the lantern into the first rooms, but of course she was not there. Then Kao Li-shih thought: running for her life, looking for a door to the outside, she would naturally move to the very end of the corridor.

"Stay here, for a moment, Lu Pei," he said. "Watch for the Emperor. Do not let him pass if he tries!" He moved cautiously down the dark hall, away from the odor of burning lamp oil, then stood still and sniffed the air.

There it was: the distinctive fragrance of her perfume, jasmine oil and essence of ginseng. A ghost of more peaceful times, sharp against the dry, dusty odor of old wood and stone. He turned to his left and faced a black doorway. It was strongest here. She was in this cell.

"Precious Consort," he said softly into the blackness.

She did not reply, but he could feel her presence.

"Lu Pei," he called down the corridor, "come here with the light."

He took the lamp from Lu Pei's hands. The boy, looking as if he were in a trance, silently and with measured motions obeyed Kao Li-shih's commands.

Extending the light in front of him, Kao Li-shih stepped into the cell. It was barren but for a single rodent-eaten reed mat on the floor. In the corner between two plain, unornamented wooden pillars, the Precious Consort slumped, head bowed, face hidden in her arms. She is dead, Kao Li-shih thought. She has already taken her own life. How could he have been so stupid as to overlook that possibility? Had she concealed a dagger or some poison? Had she known all along it would come to this? He approached, and bent over to touch her.

Her head came up sharply, startling him, her eyes blazing. He stepped back, placing himself between her and the door.

"Go back down the hall, Lu Pei," he said, not taking his eyes off the consort. "Stand guard. The Emperor must not know what I am going to do."

"I do not understand, Master Kao," the boy said miserably. "He already knows what you are going to do."

"Just do as I say, Lu Pei. Go out in the hall and wait. Be patient. Say nothing." Kao Li-shih listened as Lu Pei's steps receded up to the far end of the corridor.

"Please do not be afraid," Kao Li-shih whispered to the consort, and hung the oil lamp on the wall. She drew her knees in tight with her arms. In contrast to a moment ago, her eyes now looked strangely flat and empty, glazed over with the expectation of death. He knew that he was a stranger to her. A monster. Kao Li-shih had ceased to exist. "I am not here to kill you," he whispered, and took a step toward her.

She was on her feet in the next instant, arms spread out at her sides, palms pressed flat against the wall.

"Please," he begged, "listen to me. I am telling you the truth. You will not die. But you must help me! You are a pantomime player and a dancer. Now you must give us your best performance. You must not move a muscle. You must take breaths so shallow that even you believe that you are really dead. We must bruise the flesh of your neck a bit . . ."

He could see that she was not listening at all, any more than a trapped animal would listen to entreaties of reason. He could feel the impatience of the waiting guardsmen outside. They had already erupted into madness twice tonight, and they had little left to lose. He had to make her understand!

"Consort! Please! The soldiers . . ." He took a step toward her.

It was exactly the wrong thing to say. She sprang for the opposite wall. He took another step, then thought better of it and returned to where he was, his back to the door. She was too quick. If he left the door unguarded for even a moment, she would be through it.

"I am begging you to listen," he pleaded, trying one last time to reach her. This could not go on. If she would not cooperate, then he would have no choice but to force the semblance of death on her. There was a way. He had already thought of it, but had desperately hoped to avoid it. His *ch'i-gong* master of long ago had shown him how to do it, but had warned him that, in the hands of a novice, the results could be violent, uncertain. But she was quickly leaving him no choice. "If you will not play at being dead, then you will have to trust me!"

She sprang for the far corner; he lunged, and she dodged to one side. She made a dash for the door, but he grabbed hold of the tail of her robes; she spun around, kicking and scratching, her nails going for his eyes, her feet raining blows on his shins. Oblivious to the pain, he caught her arms, tripped her, and brought her to the floor. He pinned her wrists and looked down into her face in the posture of an ardent young lover.

"Do you want the soldiers to do it?" he asked her, breathing hard. "Because I assure you that they *will* kill you!"

"And what is the difference, Eunuch?" she screamed at last.

He knew with painful certainty that the sound of her cry had reached the Emperor's ears.

"All the difference," he said urgently. "All the difference."

"You think it is better to die at the hands of a *friend*? Give me to the soldiers! Let *them* kill me instead!" she cried, kicking up hard.

Gently, he pinned both her legs with his knees until she was helpless.

"I am telling you one last time," he whispered. "I am not going to kill you. Do you hear me? But *they* will think that I have."

He moved forward then, so that his knees now pinned her arms, leaving his own hands free. She writhed in vain under his considerable weight. Her legs, no longer restrained, kicked furiously, but he ignored them.

Collecting himself for a moment, desperately trying to remember the instructions as they had been taught him long ago, he put his hands on her neck, her head thrashing from side to side. He worked his thumbs around until they rested over the right and left vessels of her throat.

He concentrated with every bit of his being. It was difficult. Very difficult. Her violent struggling made it almost impossible to judge his force, and to know that his fingers were in the right place on her neck. And then there was the timing, the most crucial factor of all. Misjudge by a heartbeat or two, and she will die. She will die, Kao Li-shih, and what she believes about you at this moment will become truth.

And she will die if you don't do it. That is a certainty. The soldiers will not wait any longer. Do it. Do it now.

The verse rose, after so many years of dormancy in a forgotten part of his mind, to the base of his tongue. He forced her head against the mean stone of the floor and, with a strong deep pressure, pushed his thumbs down onto the pulsing vessels. Her knees pummeled his back with desperate strength, then dropped to the floor.

Her eyes closed against the fear and outrage, against a world gone mad, against the eunuch she believed had betrayed her; her body stiffened, then shook and heaved in rapid, even, rhythmic spasms of lung and heart disharmony. It was frightening and hideous to Kao Li-shih, but it was right. The master had said these tremors would happen.

Hold her still, he told himself, watching the spasms subside. Hold her still. Take a long breath. Release the thumbs for two heartbeats, then reapply them. Keep the pressure even and steady. Begin the count, fool. Now! Chant! Words, unspoken for years, taught to him by the master, verses containing the exact number of syllables for counting the time that the fingers depress the vessels, rasped from his throat:

> "Man's life is but a brief sojourn;
>   his years lack the permanence of metal or stone.
> Ten thousand ages come and go
>   and sages and wise men find no cure."

Pause. Breathe. Heaven help me! Now the final verse:

> "Man—but a pitiful bug,
>   out the gate with fears of death twisted in his heart,
> a corpse fallen in narrow valleys,
>   white bones scattered that no one shall bury."

Now release her!

He lifted his thumbs. He put his hands flat on the floor, willing his heart to slow down. He was having trouble getting air. Hold on to yourself, Eunuch. He forced himself to look at her.

The consort was motionless, her face slack and peaceful, the violent spasms and tremors gone. Her sightless eyes looked back at him, too much like death. Now pray to the all-forgiving Maitreya that you haven't killed her, he whispered. Pray that she is only in a deep sleep. Live, Consort, live, he exhorted, or I am no better than those murderers in the courtyard.

Rising on shaking legs, Kao Li-shih went to the doorway. "Lu Pei," he called into the dark hallway, his voice sounding weak and distant to his own ears. "Come quickly. I need you." He went back inside and knelt by the body of the consort.

Lu Pei was next to him in a few moments, kneeling silently and in awe by his side. Kao Li-shih pulled his knife from his belt and polished it on his sleeve.

"Hold the lamp close," he said softly to the boy, who visibly held back tears. "Take hold of her arm. I am afraid that I am still shaking too much. I doubt I could feel anything other than my own racing, knotted pulse."

"But why, Master Kao?" Lu Pei protested, confused, his tears beginning to flow. "She is dead!"

"I hope not, Lu Pei," Kao Li-shih whispered. The boy's eyes widened; he took hold of the consort's arm while Kao Li-shih held the polished blade under her nostrils. Lu Pei's eyes opened even wider then.

"A pulse!" he said. "Master Kao!"

"Hush!" Kao Li-shih warned him fiercely. A faint fogging appeared on the silver of the blade. There was life. He could only hope that it was enough to sustain her, but not enough to be noticed by the soldiers and not enough to revive her too soon. He put his knife back in his belt and seized Lu Pei's arm. "Lu Pei, you must listen to me now. It is a dangerous game we play. She lives, but she is dead. That is what you know, what you must believe." His quick, soft, forceful words held the boy's astonished attention. "She was strangled by the chief eunuch Kao Li-shih on the sixth month of the fourteenth year of the T'ien Pao. And the Emperor must believe it, too. It is a cruel deceit, but I am depending on you. You will be traveling with him for the rest of the journey. His grief will be terrible. You will want to tell him, to whisper to him that she is not really dead, but you cannot give in to that wish, no matter how much you want to. Not until he is rid of his soldiers. Not until he is with the crown prince at the provisional capital. Then you may tell him. But until then, he *must believe* that she is dead; if he believes in her death, then so will the soldiers, and they will protect him. I warn you now that his grief will wear you down. You will wish to tell him more than anything.

Swear to me now that you will not!" Grunting with the effort, he picked the consort up from the floor. He stood with her in his arms, facing Lu Pei, waiting for an answer.

"I swear, Master Kao," Lu Pei said, his incredulous eyes on the limp body. "But I cannot believe that she is not dead," he whispered. "If I had not felt her pulses myself . . ."

"She *is* dead, Lu Pei," Kao Li-shih repeated softly. "Believe it with all your heart and mind, and the soldiers will believe it." He looked down at her for a moment, then back at Lu Pei. "Besides, she may be as good as dead. I may yet become a murderer. I have no way of knowing if she will revive. I am no master of life and death. She may very well die during the night, or tomorrow, or the next day. Or she may live for years and never wake from her sleep. For all you know, while you and the Emperor are traveling, she may truly have died. That should help you believe, Lu Pei. That should make it more real for you." He moved toward the door. "There is no more time. Carry the lantern. We are going out into the courtyard now."

"But Master Kao," Lu Pei said, his tears starting afresh, "you talk as if you are not going with us."

"I am staying with her. I have no choice. Do you think I would leave her here, to possibly wake alone in this place and see the unburied corpses of her sisters and cousin?"

Unhappily, the boy shook his head.

"You will be taking my place on the journey. In every way. I am depending on you. Now hurry! Take the lantern, and go ahead of me! We have talked too long already!"

They moved down the corridor, the consort's weight heavy in Kao Li-shih's arms. He wondered if her heart, alone in its darkness, had already stopped its feeble beating while they stood and talked. They stepped into the outer room. The Emperor lifted his head.

A shrill hollow wail of grief came from his mouth, filling the small room. But the tragic cry was nothing more than a faint echo in Kao Li-shih's head as Lu Pei pushed open the wooden door and they walked out into the courtyard. The soldiers ceased their talking as soon as they saw him, and stared in awe.

In the light of the torches he raised her to his chest, holding her like a sacrificial offering, her limbs dangling, her head hanging slack from her white neck. The loosened black hair, a bolt of silk unfurled, almost dragged on the ground; the teeth gleamed between her parted lips, and the thin whitish slivers of her blind eyes showed between the heavy lids.

The leader of the soldiers approached slowly, almost reverently. He put out a tentative hand, touched her for an instant, and drew back. Then he looked up at Kao Li-shih's face.

Go on, Coward, Kao Li-shih thought. I dare you to touch her again. Listen to her heart. See if she breathes. Make absolutely certain that she is dead. I dare you, he challenged with his eyes.

But the man did not. He stepped back. "She is dead," he announced.

There was no cheering or tumult; just silence, uneasy faces, and the crackle of the torches.

But Kao Li-shih was not thinking of the soldiers. He was thinking of the Precious Consort's soul and begging its forgiveness. Her soul which, if it had not already left, was drifting uneasily, uncertainly, between this filthy world of men and the pure nephrite halls of imagined Paradise.

:: :

The Lady of Kuo had known the moment when her cousin fell, because he had spoken to her in her mind. It was not inconceivable, he had said as they were decapitating him, that his prophecies of the night of the Weaving Star Festival had all come true. Time was over for the Yangs. Foolishly short, the end coming abruptly and without the dignity of any particular meaning; banal, inane, purposeless . . .

The Lady of Han and the Lady of Chin had been dropped by the soldiers' crossbows before they knew what was upon them. They must have heard the shouted words, death to the Yangs, just as she had; and in the next moment, they were dead. It was all so sudden. She had heard one short scream; whether it had come from Han or Chin she did not know. She barely had time to look, and they were both down. It was far more merciful than what she imagined for her cousin.

Then there came that simple, decisive moment, a relief in its exactness, in which she knew that there was nothing for her to do but save herself. And somehow she had known that she was not fated to die, not then. No young soldier on a horse would ever rival her skill and speed and stamina. She was certain of that. They had pursued her, as she knew they would; but now that it was over and she rode on an empty road with the sun just beginning to rise, the furious chasers seemed no more than old men on tired, sway-backed mules. One by one, they had fallen away.

Now, alone in the piny wilderness, she had nothing to do but think and ride. And although she had loved him with all her soul, she could not grieve. Perhaps she had known all along that it would come to this. Would the tears come later? Or would she somehow be spared, swaddled safely in some icy coldness and distance? Even the thought that she had nothing left but herself was abstract and removed. It was not uncomfortable. It did not even seem odd. Simply nothing!

How often had Yang Kuo-chung said to her that the strangest thing about war, perhaps even the most brutal, though she didn't agree, was that the man who would eventually cut you down was unknown, his face wholly unrecognizable, until the moment that he was upon you? And even then, you might not actually see his face. Her handsome cousin had relished telling her—the way older children tell scary stories to little children—long before he ever considered such a fate possible for her, that the man who cut you down in a war would only meet you by chance on that particular day, at that particular place, and in that exact hour and moment. At any other time, her cousin used to assure her, the unnamed assassin meant for you alone would not be there. And until you met him, no one else's aim would be so true, no one's arm so strong. Fate would not substitute another. Heaven did not work in that way, he always said.

She could see his handsome, square face, the dark eyes chiding her, laughing, just beneath their shining surface, at her feigned naiveté about such weighty matters as death and war . . . and enjoying his role of wise teacher, until she usually hit him for the presumptions of his maleness. Though he had been right about fate, about the one man meant to cut you down, she knew that she had fooled them. She simply had not been there for the one Heaven had decreed for her. She was too fast.

: :

Yang Kuo-chung was with her now. The morning sun was hot on her back as she rode, drowsing, letting the horse find its way.

Death! he said to her. We worry it over and over. He smiled easily in her head. It was really not what I expected it to be; it simply got lost in the exuberance of the moment!

26

Return of the Filial Son

[General] Sun rounded up the remnant officials, eunuchs, palace women, and entertainers and delivered them to Lo-yang, several hundreds at a time. An compelled many of these to enter his service, and in imitation of the Brilliant Emperor's brilliant court, he held feasting parties and gaudy shows with the musicians, dancers, the equipment, the horses, elephants, and rhinoceroses all sent from Ch'ang-an.

. . .

The rebel emperor, An Lu-shan, misbehaved himself so unreasonably that he was implacably hated by his son, An Ch'ing-hsu; his advisor . . . ; and his attendant eunuch, Li [Chu-erh] the Pig [also hated him].

—William Hung

MANY hours after the Emperor and the others had departed for Ch'eng-tu, Kao Li-shih's hands still trembled and the scratches on his face and arms inflicted by the consort's fingernails stung and throbbed as sweat rolled down into the wounds. Using an iron bar he had found, he pried apart the ancient boards comprising the west wall of the Buddhist oratory in order to build coffins: one for Yang Kuo-chung, the parts of whose body he had reunited and which lay under a blood-soaked saddle blanket on the dusty ground; one for the Lady of Han, and another for the Lady of Chin, whose bodies he had moved around to the rear of the building. The Precious Consort lay unconscious inside the darkened, deserted postal station. He had put the sisters behind the building fearing that the consort would awaken and see them before he could get them buried. He had tried to move Yang Kuo-chung, but there had been too much blood, and it had sickened him. So he covered him as best he could and hoped that he could get him into the ground before she opened her eyes. *If* she opened her eyes.

Presently, Kao Li-shih laid his iron bar down and went inside. He stared intently at the consort's face, holding his hand near her nose, feeling for the infinitesimal wisp of warm breath that told him she still lived. Her eyelids had opened minutely; he could see the whites of her eyes twitching slightly. He watched her for a while, then, reassured, stood up and went back outside.

He was surprised to find some of the Tibetans, about fifteen of them, waiting for him in the yard. He had not seen them since they had vanished in the moments preceding Yang Kuo-chung's death the night before. They must have been waiting in the woods, watching, until the soldiers were long gone. They were squatting now in a loose circle around Yang Kuo-chung's body. When Kao Li-shih approached, they looked up at him sympathetically.

"Your friend?" one of the men asked in a thick, strange accent.

"He was," Kao Li-shih said tiredly.

"Very sorry."

"It is not your fault," Kao Li-shih said, and resumed his work on the boards.

"We help you, if you allow it," said the man. "It is not good that you do this work alone."

Kao Li-shih looked at the men. There were many of them. With their help, he could be through with this quickly. He thought of the sisters lying behind the building, and he looked over to where Yang Kuo-chung's body lay, his limbs protruding from under the blanket and the ground beneath dark with his blood, and realized that he could not do without their assistance. And the consort . . . somehow, he had to take care of her and get her away from here. Even though the soldiers were gone, he still feared for her safety. And he did not want her to wake up in this dreadful place. He nodded his head.

"I accept your offer. We need three coffins. And I will need something else."

The man who had first spoken to him looked at him questioningly. Kao Li-shih motioned for him to follow and went back inside the postal station. He took him to where the consort lay. The man looked at her face, then shook his head and uttered small sounds of regret and sorrow.

"Beautiful. A shame," he said admiringly. He continued to look at her, then stiffened, staring intently at her eyes, which danced and twitched under the partly open lids. He looked up at Kao Li-shih, astonished. "She lives!" he whispered.

"Yes," Kao Li-shih said. "Though just barely. I am praying that she will recover. But I need to move her. If she does not wake up soon, we must build a cart of some sort to carry her, something that I can pull. I must get her out of this place.

"Where you take her?" the man asked. "And how?"

"I don't know yet," Kao Li-shih answered absently. "Things have happened very quickly. I am not feeling entirely well. The best place for her would be at her family home in Szechuan. I will have to take her there myself, I suppose."

The Tibetan stood. From outside came the sounds of the men prying boards from the oratory wall.

"We take care of your dead, if you allow us."

Kao Li-shih nodded.

"Yes," he said. "I think I need your help very much. The other two are behind the building."

"Rest here," said the man. "Stay with her. I see to the work." He went to the door, paused, and turned around. "Perhaps no coffins needed," he said. "Maybe your friends like it if we send them into the sky, too." He grinned. "Soul loves it. Sets it free."

Kao Li-shih was not shocked by the suggestion. On the contrary, it seemed a fitting end for the Fox, so intrepid and ostentatious in life. Though he could not have said it to many other Chinese, he rather liked the idea. Sky Burial. To disappear into the great blue sky, rather than be swallowed into the earth.

But the Lady of Kuo still lived, and she would never forgive him if she were to return someday and demand to know where Yang Kuo-chung's body lay and he could not tell her. Vulture dung, my lady. He has become vulture dung. And your sisters, too. No, she would not like it.

"Perhaps we had best just bury them," Kao Li-shih said to the man, who shrugged and went back outside.

Kao Li-shih sat on the floor in the gloom inside the postal station, leaning against the wall with his eyes shut. If he could just sleep for a short while, then perhaps he would be able to think clearly. He would have to find a way to reunite the consort and the Emperor. What was the Emperor thinking about him right now? He believed that the consort was dead and that Kao Li-shih had killed her. What if his grief and despair kills him?

His eyes flew open. This was a very real possibility. What reason would he have to live, now that his "son" had betrayed him and, as he believed, his consort was dead? He traveled alone now with the soldiers. The enormity of his terrible folly would surely be settling on him during the long trip. If only there had been some way to communicate to him that she was not really dead—but it had been impossible. For the soldiers to believe in her death, it was necessary that the Emperor believe in her death.

Kao Li-shih closed his eyes again. A little sleep. Just a little sleep was what he needed. He listened to the noise of the work outside and the murmuring sound of the Tibetans' voices speaking in their incomprehensible tongue, and drifted.

Hoofbeats awakened him. He had no idea how long he had been sleeping.

He glanced over at Precious Consort; she had not moved, but she moaned softly. Someone was talking with the Tibetans. He crept silently to the door and listened, his hand on his knife, the only weapon he had. As he listened, relief spread through his limbs, and he stepped out into the sunlight, blinking his eyes in the brightness.

It was An Ching-hsu, the eldest son of An Lu-shan.

"Master Kao!" the young man said, leaping from his horse, running over to where Kao Li-shih stood, falling to his knees, and seizing his hand in both of his. He wept softly for a few moments. "I didn't think I would find you," he said at last. "What has happened?" he asked, indicating the body of Yang Kuo-chung.

Kao Li-shih shook his head.

"Three of the Yangs are dead. The Lady of Kuo has escaped, and the consort lies between life and death. We are burying Yang Kuo-chung and the other two sisters."

"And the Emperor . . . ?" the boy asked, alarmed.

"He is alive, and on his way to Ch'eng-tu," Kao Li-shih said, "but he may as well be dead. He has suffered very badly."

The boy bowed his head.

"I was very afraid that something like this might happen. And it is not going to help when I tell you what I have heard."

Kao Li-shih looked at him with tired eyes, waiting. The boy stood up and looked around questioningly at the Tibetans, who continued their work.

"They are my friends," Kao Li-shih said. "But let us go inside to talk. You will be more comfortable."

They stepped out of the hot, brilliant sunshine into the cool interior of the building. The boy started visibly when he saw the Precious Consort on the floor. Kao Li-shih bent to examine her face. She breathed more deeply now, her face slightly contorted as if she were having a bad dream. She looked uncomfortable, but he thought she looked more alive than she had before. As if she might soon awaken. He straightened and returned his attention to An Ching-hsu

"My father An Lu-shan has declared himself emperor," he said, his eyes still on the Precious Consort. "He has done many terrible things. However, he issued a decree: that no harm come to the Emperor, the consort, or the sisters. I know that he meant it. I know my father better than anybody. He is a monster, but I know that he would not have allowed anyone to harm the Emperor or the Yang sisters." His eyes filled with tears again. "They were never in any danger."

"So what you are telling me," said Kao Li-shih, "is that their deaths were unnecessary. There was no need to flee."

"They could have gone into the city and been left quite alone. Only Yang Kuo-chung had any reason to fear."

"But what did he expect them to do?" Kao Li-shih said bitterly. "Of course they fled. They had no way of knowing that he didn't mean to have them killed immediately. They could not possibly have known what his intentions were. Was the Emperor still supposed to have infinite faith in his 'son' after receiving word that he rode down from the north with three hundred thousand armed men? His cruelty is even more appalling than I had thought. And Yang Kuo-chung would not be dead now if he had not left the city, if he had not been out in this forsaken place trying to protect the Emperor. He could have hidden. His death had no purpose, no purpose at all."

An Ching-Hsu looked at Kao Li-shih in the dim light. "Would you like to help me kill my father?" he asked quietly.

Kao Li-shih looked back at him sharply.

"That is why I came to find you," the boy said. "There is a plan. Li Chu-erh awaits us."

Kao Li-shih shook his head.

"There is nothing I would rather do. But I cannot. I must see that the consort is taken home. It is the only way that she will be safe and the Emperor will find her again."

"But you must come, Kao Li-shih! We could take her with us."

"No. It would be too dangerous for her. She is nearly dead as it is. And I cannot take her back toward the city. The soldiers blame the Yangs for what has happened. The corpses outside are testimonial to their fear and resentment. It is very likely that there are others also thirsty for Yang blood." He heaved a deep, weary sigh. "Probably you and Li Chu-erh are the only ones who despise An Lu-shan more than I do. So it is quite fitting that the two of you kill him. But I cannot go with you."

They sat in silence. Outside, the Tibetans cracked and splintered the ancient, dry pieces of the oratory wall to the lengths they needed, and pounded pegs to hold the boards together. The sound of wood creaking and splitting made him think of a balcony railing and a young girl's body shattering it with brutal force.

Curious to see the coffins that were to take the royal Yangs down into their graves, Kao Li-shih turned and went back outside, leaving An Ching-hsu to rest out of the sun.

They had taken care of Yang Kuo-chung first. He was grateful for that. The coffin, crude but serviceable, had been carried over to a stand of pine trees a short distance from the buildings. The ground where Yang Kuo-chung had lain had been sprinkled with fresh dirt so that there was no trace of blood to be seen. Kao Li-shih was also grateful for that. A large group of men were at work digging holes near where the coffin rested. They had no shovels, so they used their knives, iron bars, and pieces of wood to excavate the rocky ground, removing the loosened earth with their hands. The other coffins were nearly finished. The men worked steadily, tirelessly.

Kao Li-shih realized now that it would have been impossible for him to do this work alone, and that in trying to do it, he would have collapsed from exhaustion and grief. Tibetans, he had heard, possessed a special knowledge of death and a philosophical mastery of it. He believed it at this moment. Had they not appeared at the precise moment that they were needed, lifting the terrible burden from his shoulders, doing the job with alacrity and efficiency? He turned to go back inside to where An Ching-hsu waited for him.

"Master," a voice said behind him.

Kao Li-shih turned. It was the Tibetan he had spoken to before.

"Young man . . . he wants you to go with him, yes?"

Kao Li-shih nodded.

"We travel through Szechuan on our way back to our country. You say the lady's family is there. We are grateful if you allow us to take her back to her home. Other men and I talk about it. We owe you. These deaths here last night happen because of us."

Kao Li-shih looked at the man. He had a square face and jaw and eyes that looked steadily into his own. I don't even know your name, Kao Li-shih thought, but I believe you.

"She be completely safe," the man said. "Forty-nine of us. We dress her like us and surround her. They have to kill all of us to get to her. We not rest until the lady is in the hands of her family. Only then do we think even a little bit what we owe is paid."

Kao Li-shih thought of An Lu-shan sitting on his mock throne. He thought of the Emperor, a broken old man. He thought of the Fox, whose heroic efforts had been in vain and who was about to go to his ignominious grave, and the sisters, young and beautiful, who would follow him. He thought of the consort's eyes looking into his at the moment she had believed that Kao Li-shih was her executioner; and he thought of An Lu-shan on his knees, weeping into a fistful of the Son of Heaven's robe: *I have nothing in my belly but loyalty to you.*

And it was true that the consort would be far safer with these men than traveling alone with him. Besides, he had a terrible dread: now that she had seen him as her killer, she would never forgive him, never trust him again. It was a long, long journey to Szechuan, and it would be only the two of them. He was not at all sure that he would be capable of protecting her, nor was he sure that she would not be fearful of him every hour of the journey.

But more than anything, he wanted to kill An Lu-shan, to see his death with his own eyes. And inside the postal station waited An Ching-hsu, inviting him to come and help him do the job.

"I accept your offer," he said to the man, and went back into the building.

:: ::

Five days later, Kao Li-shih and An Ching-Hsu were within a li of the southern suburbs of Ch'ang-an. They rode to a place on a hill under some tall trees where An Ching-hsu said they would be met, and dismounted to await night-fall. It was peculiar for Kao Li-shih to see the familiar horizon of the city where he had spent so many years of his life and feel that he was a stranger. Once, Ch'ang-an had been his city. Now, he was the enemy, approaching stealthily and under cover of darkness. An Lu-shan had transformed every-thing.

Kao Li-shih thought about the Precious Consort while he watched the lights of the city begin to shimmer as afternoon faded into evening. By now she and her escorts would be well into the third day of their long journey. She had awakened the day after An Ching-hsu's arrival. She, too, had been transformed, and it was painful for Kao Li-shih to think about it. What he would have done if the Tibetans and An Ching-hsu had not been there, he did not know—for his worst fears had materialized at the moment she opened her eyes.

Though a day and a night had elapsed since he had "strangled" her and she had lost consciousness, for her it was merely the next moment. She had opened her eyes and screamed as soon as she saw his face. It was plain that she thought that he was about to try again to kill her. And she had huddled against the wall, deaf to his entreaties, looking at him through eyes black with fear, a terrified animal. He had had to leave the room and send An Ching-hsu in to talk to her. She knew the youth only by sight, but she grew quieter and listened when he did his best to explain why Master Kao had done what he had.

And Kao Li-shih had crept around to the rear of the building and spoken to her through the thin wooden wall, so that she would not have to see his face. You know that the soldiers killed your cousin Yang Kuo-chung, he said to her, and they killed your sisters, too. They were insane with fear. And they wanted us to hand you over to them as well. You would be with your sisters now under the stones if we had let them have you. And do not blame the Emperor. He was ready to die before allowing anyone to harm you. It was I who insisted that he stay alive, and there was no other way to do it than to pretend that you were dead.

But I may as well be dead, she had sobbed. My sisters are dead. Not all of them, Kao Li-shih had said; the Lady of Kuo lives. Didn't you know? She escaped. She was too fast for the soldiers. Without a doubt she is on her way back to Szechuan now. My sister, Precious Consort had sobbed; I want my sister. I must go to where she is. And so you shall, Kao Li-shih had said. So you shall.

And his friend the Tibetan had gone in and spoken to her for many hours. Listening through the wall, Kao Li-shih had wondered at the Fates that had sent this man. The Tibetan had talked to the Precious Consort about the journey they would make. He talked to her about the joy that her family would experience when they saw her face again. He talked of the beauty of his homeland, his own family awaiting him there, asked her questions about her family, and explained that her two sisters and cousin were not dead at all, that their souls were set free and were, in fact, grateful to the imperial soldiers for assisting them in their journey. But it is our duty to live, he had said, even when we wish we could die, and that during the trip to Szechuan he would do his best to see to it that her appreciation of being alive was at least partially restored. And you will be safe, he had told her. We will evoke the Buddhaform Yamantaka and make an impenetrable circle of protection around you. No one will touch you. Her crying had quieted gradually, and the Tibetan had said that he would get her something to eat and begin preparations for the journey.

And the day they had left, after procuring horses, food, and supplies from a rich farmer who respected the imperial seal Kao Li-shih carried, she could not bring herself to look at the eunuch. She had said that she understood what he had done and why, but she still could not bring herself to look at his face. He could not blame her. He had been her friend, and then she had seen Death in his face. How could she look at him ever again? An Lu-shan had accomplished that transformation, too. And the Precious Consort and her forty-nine Tibetan escorts had ridden from the postal station at Ma-wei, leaving Kao Li-shih with An Ching-hsu and the three Yangs in their graves. And Kao Li-shih and the boy had set out on their own journey in the opposite direction, riding back toward the occupied city of Ch'ang-an.

People they encountered along the way told them that they were crazy, that they were going in the wrong direction. The city, they said, was in a state of siege. Rebel soldiers under the command of An Lu-shan's right-hand general, Sun, were at all the gates, controlling the daily flow of humanity in and out; martial law had been imposed on the populace, with an early curfew and food rationing. The atmosphere in the city was very bad. The rebel soldiers were a dangerous, scruffy, drunken lot who had never seen a grand city with all its wonders before. If they wanted something, they simply took it. Anything at all. And the people were angry and frightened. Some—especially the young men—stayed to fight the soldiers in roving, hastily armed groups; others retreated into their homes, and still others fled the city any way they could.

An Ching-hsu told Kao Li-shih that he had escaped with the assistance of the Flying Dragons, disguising himself as a farmer. Things had been bad when he left, he said, but it sounded, from what people were telling them, as though the situation had degenerated even further. An Ching-hsu was worried. He and Kao Li-shih had been waiting a long time now. Li Chu-erh and a select group of the Flying Dragons were to meet them here tonight. Maybe they had not been able to leave the city. Never mind, Kao Li-shih said; even if they don't come, you and I will get to An Lu-shan ourselves. We will find a way, he said, though he felt a secret despair at the difficulty of their task.

When they had first left the postal station, Kao Li-shih had asked An Ching-hsu where An Lu-shan himself was and where they were going. Was he enthroned in splendor at the hot springs? The boy's answer had shocked him. They faced a much longer journey than Kao Li-shih had thought. My father, he had said, is not anywhere near Ch'ang-an at all. He is in Loyang, the eastern capital, which he has declared the seat of government for the new Yen dynasty. The T'ang, An Lu-shan says, is dead.

We are going to Loyang.

They waited under the trees for many hours, listening to the distant roll of thunder in the summer night sky. Clouds on the horizon were backlit from time to time by silent, faraway lightning. No rain fell as yet where they were; the storm they watched was still well to the northeast. An Ching-hsu grew more restive with every passing hour. Kao Li-shih could see that the boy's thirst for vengeance was nearly consuming him. While Kao Li-shih leaned against a tree, aching with fatigue, An Ching-hsu repeatedly rose to his feet and moved into the woods surrounding the small clearing, whistling softly. Kao Li-shih could feel the youth straining his ears in the darkness for a reply. Eventually, Kao Li-shih could no longer keep his eyes open, though he remained, for a while, aware of An Ching-hsu prowling among the trees: a son whose only desire was to get to his own father and kill him.

He woke to a hand gently shaking his shoulder. He opened his eyes and found An Ching-hsu bending over him in the light of a lantern, his eyes wide and dark; next to him was Li Chu-erh. Standing in the clearing were many more men.

No, he realized, not men—eunuchs. Fifty or sixty of them, and armed. The Flying Dragons had arrived.

::

"The road east to Loyang is out of the question," one of the older eunuchs told Kao Li-shih as the sun was coming up. They had slept for a few hours, but were awakened by rain and now sat wet, cold, and tired discussing their plans. "It is entirely blocked to civilian travel. No one except An Lu-shan's soldiers are allowed to move between the cities. We had thought that we could bypass the eastern gate by moving east below the city, gradually working our way north, and meeting the road somewhere east of Ch'ang-an. But it is impossible. Every li of the road is patrolled, and they are killing at random. We could go the entire distance on farmers' roads and footpaths, but we would have to split up, and the traveling would be slow. We would lose too much time. So we have devised another plan. It is risky, but if it works, it will get all of us to Loyang together, and much more quickly."

"What way is that?" Kao Li-shih asked, seeing the same determination on this man's face that he saw on An Ching-hsu's, and which probably was visible on his own.

"We will still circle around the city, but in the other direction. We are southwest of the city now; we will move north through the countryside west of the city, then to the northeast until we are directly above it. We will find ourselves at the upper edge of the Chin Yuan Woods, where the Wei River flows by on its journey to the east. The river will carry us to Loyang."

"The river!" Kao Li-shih exclaimed. "It is a brilliant idea. But how . . . ?"

"Our new 'emperor' is transporting to his 'capital' everything that he deems necessary for the court of a great new ruler. He is sacking the palace and the offices of government. The barges depart daily."

Kao Li-shih felt a fresh surge of rage. He thanked the gods that the Emperor was far, far away and was spared having to witness the details of his "Baby's" betrayal. What, he wondered, had An Lu-shan intended to do if the Emperor had not left the city? Would An Lu-shan have had in him the cruelty to allow the old man to watch his "Lucky Baby's" desecration?

Kao Li-shih stood, though his stiff, tired body protested.

"Let us not waste any more time. We must get to the river before tomorrow morning."

The other eunuch stood, too.

"Kao Li-shih," he said, "we are of one mind. An Lu-shan must die. But we must be very, very careful. You especially."

"I know that An Lu-shan hates me," Kao Li-shih said. "I am sure that he wants to kill me as much as I want to kill him. I am sure I was not included on the list of those to be spared for the Emperor's sake."

"No," the older eunuch replied. "In fact, there is a reward offered for your death, or even for information leading to your capture. He wants you, Kao Li-shih. And he wanted Yang Kuo-chung as well. He has brutally put to death anyone he could find who was connected to you or Master Yang." He paused for a moment. "It will be very dangerous for you. If you would prefer not to go, we understand and are prepared to carry out the job ourselves."

"No," he said. "I am not a particular hero, and I know that there is no point in my dying needlessly. I do wish to stay alive and go south to where the Emperor is. But I must be there when An Lu-shan dies. I must see it."

The older eunuch looked at him. "Then let us get started."

: :

The rain fell steadily, turning the ground to mud under the horses' hooves as the travelers rode north in the gray morning through rolling farmland outside of the city. Since there were not enough horses for everyone, they moved slowly, taking turns walking and riding. Kao Li-shih, on horseback, held the reins with one hand and a sodden blanket over his head and shoulders with the other. The eunuch he had spoken with earlier rode beside him.

"It was a grotesque and pitiful sight," he said to Kao Li-shih. "Members of the Emperor's family and relatives of court officials who were left behind and tried to follow were simply slaughtered. The soldiers took them by surprise two days after the Emperor's entourage had left. Some had escaped, but others did not appreciate the gravity of the situation until the soldiers were pouring through the gates of the hot springs and the palace city. The imperial guards-men were not of much use. Most of them were mere boys anyway, sixteen and seventeen years old, the only ones left since all the others had been mo-bilized and sent to help defend the T'ung-kuan Pass. They knew they would be overwhelmed, and, seeing no point in dying, many of them had already thrown down their swords and fled. A few stayed and fought, and were killed along with everybody else."

"And where were you?" Kao Li-shih asked. "How did you avoid the danger?"

"I did what any coward does who wants to stay alive," his companion replied. "I pretended that I was dead. While others were trying to flee when they heard that the soldiers were killing everyone in sight, I moved stealthily, found the corpses, and lay down among them. It was better than any hiding place. And I can tell you, Kao Li-shih, that those men were not mere soldiers—they were criminals and murderers set loose on the city. It was not just an act of occupation, a usurpation of the throne. It was an act of vengeance. An Lu-shan wants to tear Ch'ang-an to pieces, and he has sent his general Sun and his army of vicious thugs to do it."

They rode in silence for some time. Kao Li-shih tried to comprehend what the eunuch was telling him. He was quite sure that he was hearing the truth, but it did not make sense. It had always seemed to Kao Li-shih that the barbarian general loved his adopted city. But this was clearly retribution. For what? He could not imagine, but he shuddered. Retribution always had a way of spawning more retribution. Once the cycle was started, it was almost impossible to put an end to it.

"Later," Kao Li-shih's companion said, "when it was dark, and the soldiers were drunk and had sated themselves with looting and celebrating, I crept away and made my way through the city to the home of the leader of the Flying Dragons. The others," he said, indicating the eunuchs around them, "were either there already or appeared over the next day or so."

"And how did you get out of the city?" Kao Li-shih asked.

The other eunuch laughed.

"It was easier than you might think. We became what people often accuse us of being anyway: women. Most of us bony, leathery, and distinctly unattractive women—not the sort that the soldiers would care to detain. People may call us ladies, but there are few among us who would be called beauties. The younger ones, like Li Chu-erh, merely detracted from their comely appearance with a bit of demented behavior and an odor of cow dung. We went to the western gate. We never even tried the eastern gate; we had heard that it was being watched much more closely. To the soldiers, we were ugly peasant women returning to our hovels in the countryside, and they allowed us to pass. We did not leave all at once, of course, but over a period of hours, mingling with the crowds at the western gate. Some of us had horses, some of us didn't. Our weapons were under our clothes. We convened outside the city and came to find you."

Kao Li-shih glanced behind him to where Li Chu-erh walked in the rain beside An Ching-hsu's horse. He thought of the day he had made the young eunuch a member of the Flying Dragons. At the time, he had seen the appointment as little more than ceremonial, something to give the boy heart and help him face the ordeal of returning to the north with his master. What would I have thought, Kao Li-shih asked himself, if I had been able, at that moment, to look into the future and see what it would eventually come to?

The processional moved under the low sky through the wet, green landscape. There were few people working in the fields today in the heavy rain; the ones they saw stopped their work and stared as they went by, without the usual friendly wave of acknowledgment. Some ducked their heads and began to walk rapidly away. Even out here, Kao Li-shih thought, there is fear and suspicion in the air.

They met a farmer coming toward them on the road in an ox cart. When he saw the group of strange men before him, he drove his animal to one side and halted, then sat perfectly still, looking at them with wary eyes.

"Don't worry," Kao Li-shih called out to the man. "We are friends. Sent by the Emperor Minghuang himself."

The man's face relaxed a bit, but Kao Li-shih sensed that he needed more reassurance than mere words. When he was alongside the cart, he showed him the imperial seal that he carried, though he was not sure what it would mean to a poor farmer who surely could not read and had probably never seen an imperial seal before. But it appeared to satisfy him. He looked at Kao Li-shih with an apologetic smile, displaying broken and missing teeth.

"It is not always easy to know who is in front of you," the farmer said. "There are 'tigers and wolves' loose in the woods and fields."

Kao Li-shih understood. The soldiers were not confining themselves to the city, but had spilled out. Unable to resist the lure of the open, unguarded farmland, they roamed in packs, reveling in the pure pleasure of terrorizing the peasants. Undoubtedly, this was their "reward" for the long, hard ride down from the north and all the dangers they had faced.

The man looked at Kao Li-shih and the rest of the eunuchs, some still in women's clothing, some on foot and some on horseback, all of them drenched and weary in the rain.

"Are you the Imperial Army?" he asked with a doubtful look.

Kao Li-shih almost smiled. "No, my friend. The forces of the Emperor have not been reduced quite to that extent. But we are the pledged enemies of the false ruler An Lu-shan." He looked at the vegetables in the man's wagon. "And we are very hungry," he added.

: :

The farmer had fed them generously, and Kao Li-shih had given him the few strings of cash he carried with him for payment. He told the man to come to the palace city when all of this was over and ask for him by name, and he would see to it that he was paid in full. He made the farmer repeat his name several times so that he would remember it.

They continued their laborious journey, the mud growing deeper until it was nearly impossible for those on foot to walk in it, forcing them to double up on the horses. Between the treacherous footing and the extra weight on their backs, the animals had to pick their way slowly and with great care. The rain continued to fall steadily, monotonously, while afternoon thunder rolled in the sky. Miniature brown rivers ran in torrents in the deep ruts left by farmers' wagons, and spilled over, rushing down the embankments in furious little waterfalls.

After many hours, during which barely a word was spoken, the cultivated fields began to give way to trees: they were approaching the southwestern edge of Chin Yuan Park which lay north of the city. Kao Li-shih knew that they would have to stop soon. The trees would afford them some shelter, and there were, he knew, some Han ruins not so far into the park where they would probably be able to find an intact roof under which they could rest for a while out of the rain.

It was a great relief when they finally entered the forest and left the open farmland behind them. The rain did not beat so relentlessly on their heads, and they did not feel so exposed. They also knew that their journey was half over. A few hours' respite, and they would be able to travel for the rest of the night and reach the river by morning. The ruins that he had in mind were a li or so into the park from the northern boundary of the city, and well east of where they were now. If they traveled in a gradual diagonal they might find them. From there, they could proceed directly north.

They made better progress now. There was no mud; the ground here was thick and soft with dead leaves and pine needles. Though the sun would not set for several hours yet, the heavy clouds and the darkness of the forest made it seem much later than it was. After an hour or so, Kao Li-shih looked behind him. Li Chu-erh and An Ching-hsu were not far back in the weary processional; the two had traded places so that An Ching-hsu now rode and Li Chu-erh walked. Kao Li-shih looked at their faces. The rain, the hunger, and the danger were as nothing compared to their intent. Had two minds ever been more in agreement? Kao Li-shih dropped back a bit so that the two would come up alongside him.

"What do you think our chances are?" he said to Li Chu-erh.

"You know how he is," the young eunuch answered. "If he is not drunk every single night celebrating his victory, then I do not know my own name. Though I would prefer to kill him when he is sober, so that he will know what is happening to him."

"No matter how drunk he is," An Ching-hsu said, "he will recognize our faces. He will know. He must see your face, too, Master Kao."

"It is more important that I see him die than that he see me while he dies," Kao Li-shih said. "I only wish that when he breathes his last breath he could be looking on the face of the Emperor."

"That is why he must see your face," An Ching-hsu said. "He will think of the Emperor when he sees your face."

"Perhaps," Kao Li-shih said, "but I doubt it. He never thought of me as anything but a damned stinking eunuch. I am sure that, at the moment of his death, he will look at our faces and that will be all that he sees: stinking, treacherous, murderous, tailless dogs."

"If only," An Ching-hsu said thoughtfully after a moment, head bowed against the rain, "he could look on his own face when he dies."

"No one knows what a man sees at the moment of his death," Kao Li-shih said. "It is possible that we see our own faces looking at us. Let us hope that it is so for Master An Lu-shan."

An Ching-hsu raised his head then.

"Do you hear that?" he said, listening intently and reining in his horse.

"What?" asked Li Chu-erh, stopping too. Now Kao Li-shih heard it as well.

"Singing."

Kao Li-shih stopped and raised an arm to signal those behind him. Men and horses came to a halt, the message spreading down the line. Rain pattered on leaves in the tall trees as they stood still and listened to the only other sound in the quiet forest: male voices. Gruff, drunken voices, singing crudely, unintelligibly. It came from ahead of them; from the direction, if Kao Li-shih's surmise was correct, where the ruins lay.

Wolves and tigers, the farmer had said. Kao Li-shih's instincts told him that they had found some of these roaming brigands. And it was obvious that the presence of the eunuchs in the rainy forest was unknown to the singers, who let their voices carry as if there were nothing whatever to fear in the whole world.

The eunuchs discussed this development in whispers. They could, if they wanted, retreat, circle around the ruins, and continue their journey, avoiding the outlaw soldiers completely. But they would have to search further for a suitable shelter to rest in, and there was always the possibility that they would encounter the soldiers again, under less fortuitious circumstances. And who knew but that these might be some of the very murderers who had helped sack the palace and terrorize the city? In any event, they were the enemy. They were under General Sun's command, who was under An Lu-shan's command. Why should they be spared, left unmolested, singing in the forest, enjoying their victory? No. It was agreed. They would have to die.

Li Chu-erh turned to Kao Li-shih. "I have an idea," he said.

:: ::

Kao Li-shih crouched behind a fallen tree trunk and gazed at the ruined pavilion about fifty paces in front of him in the light of the dying afternoon. Dripping vines nearly covered the graceful curves of large, open arched doorways that had gazed out upon the Chin Yuan forest for nearly five hundred years. Grass and moss adorned the tile roof, and, here and there, trees had grown so close to the structure that they had flattened themselves out upon the stones and grown around them, entwining them, gripping them in a long, lingering embrace.

Inside, about twenty-five rebel soldiers had built a fire in the middle of the stone floor and were cooking a big piece of meat. The aroma of the smoke reached Kao Li-shih's nostrils, making his hungry stomach contract painfully and his mouth water. Another good reason to kill them.

They drank, laughed, and sang round after round of their song. One man in particular seemed to be leading the performance; whenever a verse was finished, he would start up a new one, to great laughter and merriment. Obviously, he was improvising new verses right then and there. Though not a word of the obscure northern dialect was intelligible to Kao Li-shih, the meaning of the song was plain: they were singing of victory and celebration. Kao Li-shih smiled. You are perhaps a trifle hasty, my friends, he thought. Perhaps just a trifle hasty.

The Flying Dragons had spread themselves stealthily, on foot, into a loose circle surrounding the pavilion. Kao Li-shih knew they were there, just as he was, secreted behind rocks, branches, and tree trunks, looking out from behind the foliage; but judging by the stillness around him, he could have sworn he was alone. He waited, and watched the trail that led to the ruin.

Three women appeared on horseback, tattered and travel-weary, blankets protecting their heads from the rain, their robes soaked. As they got closer, Kao Li-shih could see that they were youthful, pretty women, conversing with one another in their high, feminine voices.

One of the soldiers in the pavilion had seen them. He stood, weapon in hand, alert and ready. Some of his fellows noticed his attitude, stopped their singing, and turned their heads. Others, too drunk to be aware of anything, went on with their song. The women, seeing the men in the pavilion looking at them, waved and called out, saying that they were hungry and lost. Whether or not the soldiers spoke Chinese, they would certainly understand that they were being asked for help.

Now all of them had stopped their singing, with the exception of one man, who continued, oblivious, alone, and undaunted. Some men stood, others remained sitting. Astonished faces turned and stared at the spectacle of the approaching women. The face of the man who had first seen them was hard with suspicion until the visitors were within twenty paces of the pavilion and one of the women spoke directly to him. She asked if they might spare some food for herself and her sisters. The lone singer's voice trailed off as he finally became aware that something was happening.

Kao Li-shih watched as the suspicion on the first man's face dissolved into an incredulous grin, which he bestowed, turning slowly, on his fellows behind him. The same grins appeared on their faces. Then he turned back, still smiling, toward the women. Lowering his weapon and gesturing magnanimously as if he were a court gentleman, he bowed and invited them to dismount. His friends called things out in impudent voices, laughing and exchanging suggestive looks. Kao Li-shih did not need to understand their language to know what was being said. The women, meanwhile, came down off their horses and walked toward the pavilion with dainty, mincing steps, every eye upon them. Watching them, Kao Li-shih could only think of the Yang sisters arriving for some royal occasion.

The barbarian soldiers were surprisingly deferential. Though it was plain that their intentions for their guests were anything but honorable, they fell back as the women mounted the stone stairs. The first man took charge. He offered them a flask. The women conferred with each other for a moment, then accepted. They passed it among themselves, coughing delicately after each sip as if they had never drunk wine before, then smiled all around at the men. The soldiers laughed self-consciously and shoved each other while the first man went and cut some meat from the haunch roasting over the fire. Dangling the scrap of flesh from the tip of his knife, he brought it to the women and held it out to them, dripping and greasy. They took it carefully and began to eat, taking sips of wine from the flask in between bites. Kao Li-shih clenched his jaw against the famished rumble of his stomach.

The man who had been singing before by himself started up again. A few of the soldiers joined him, then a few others, until almost all of them were in full song once more. Another flask was produced. The women appeared to be trying to sing, too. Some of the men began to dance while others clapped their hands in rhythm.

It was the first man, the one who had seen them approaching, who finally made a move. He seized one of the women by the arms and pulled her to her feet, danced a few steps with her, then pulled her toward him, thrusting his pelvis against hers. She smiled and pushed him away coquettishly. Kao Li-shih's hand tightened its grip on his weapon. It would be soon now.

One of the other women jumped to her feet then and invited another of the men to dance. A good move, thought Kao Li-shih. The man was reluctant, but his fellows, singing and shouting, pushed him forward. This appeared to distract the first man, who withdrew his attentions from his partner for just a moment and assisted in pulling the second man to his feet. Then the third woman seized a partner from the crowd of men. The rhythmic clapping grew more insistent as the men, three of them now, began to dance in earnest, the women keeping time and encouraging them.

It was growing dark now, but the activities in the pavilion were illuminated by the light of the fire. To the watching eyes in the forest, it was a phantasmal scene, the moving dancers casting long shadows that spilled out the wide doorways and played against the tree trunks in time to the crude, exuberant music of clapping hands and hoarse voices. The dancing was impressive, the tune and rhythm fiery and full of intrigue. For a moment Kao Li-shih thought of how it was just exactly the sort of folk music that the Emperor dearly loved to collect for his Yueh Fu Music Bureau. He would have enjoyed this.

The whistle of a night bird off to his left brought him out of his thoughts. That was the signal: it was time to move.

He began, with infinite care, to creep forward, making sure that he was always in the shadows and never in a beam of light cast by the fire. Now that their wide circle was tightening, he became aware of the others, also moving forward, silently, like so many ghosts. No twig snapped, no leaves crunched underfoot. A few steps, then rest and wait. Then a few more steps and another pause. Imperceptible motion. Anyone glancing out from the pavilion would have seen nothing but the empty woods and impassive trees. But no one was looking. Their guard was completely down. The music swelled. The dancers whirled and stumbled, the men clapped and sang while, out in the darkness, the circle of Flying Dragons grew tighter and tighter.

One of the dancers, the first man, had seized his woman again and pulled her to him, bending her over backward. Then, with a deft, practiced motion, he raised one of his legs, hooked it around hard behind hers, causing her legs to buckle and making her fall backward to the floor. He fell down on top of her, one hand pulling her robe up.

The scream of an angry demon, high, piercing and terrible, came out of the blackness. The men in the pavilion stopped in midmotion, midsong, their mouths still open, their feet and arms still raised. Then there was another scream—this time, from the man lying on top of the woman. He raised himself up on his knees and looked down in horror at the knife in his groin, the handle still in the woman's grip. His eyes moved up to her face for an instant.

That was all he had time for. And the men, coming to their senses and scrambling for their weapons, never even had time to pick them up. The Flying Dragons poured out of the dark from every direction, howling and screaming, vaulting the low sills of the doorways, knocking the soldiers to the floor, impaling them on swords as they tried to run, driving knives into chests, backs, stomachs. The "women" metamorphosed in an instant into killers, knives flashing out from under their robes. Soldiers who tried to run past them fell bleeding to the floor.

It was over quickly. Not a single one of the Flying Dragons was injured even slightly. One soldier escaped, blundering off into the night. Li Chu-erh, no longer a woman, started after him, but Kao Li-shih shot out a hand and stopped him.

"No," he said, holding his arm. "Let him go. Let him tell the story. Perhaps other soldiers will think twice before setting off into the countryside. Let them think that there is an entire army of demon women hidden in the woods and fields, ready to cut them to pieces."

Li Chu-erh stopped, breathing hard. He brought a shaking hand up to his mouth and forehead and wiped the sweat away. The Flying Dragons, when they were sure that every soldier was dead, clustered around him and the other two "women," young eunuchs like himself, and he congratulated them on their performance and their bravery.

"I wanted to kill him as soon as he laid a hand on me," Chu-erh said, looking at the corpse of his would-be lover. "And when he embraced me . . ." He spat and wiped his mouth again.

: :

After they piled the corpses outside the pavilion, they posted sentries and feasted on the meat that the soldiers had been roasting, and drank some of the wine. Kao Li-shih recognized the wine by its taste and knew where the soldiers had got it. Without a doubt, it came from the Emperor's own private stores. It was likely that these soldiers had been among those who had attacked the palace, robbing and murdering.

And the meat? Kao Li-shih knew that it was not lamb, venison, or goat, nor were the bones large enough for the animal to have been a cow or a horse. That left one distinct possibility. The Emperor's gazelle, which wandered the grounds both at the hot springs and at the palace. Beloved pets of the Emperor, each with its own name and a collar with a little bell. Pets that ate from the Emperor's own hand, nuzzling him with their soft noses, enchanting him in the twilight.

Kao Li-shih took another bite and another swallow of wine. The Flying Dragons had killed the right men. He was only sorry that one had escaped retribution.

: :

They arrived well before dawn at the Wei River, upstream from one of the ports that served the city. They abandoned their horses and followed the river east on foot. The rain had abated slightly, though it still drizzled on their heads as they walked in the dark along a farmers' path on the bank of the river.

After they had been walking for an hour or two, a sound came out of the night, carried down to them on the wide river, that made them all stop walking and stand dumbfounded: the trumpeting of a bull elephant. There was no mistaking it; they knew that there was no other sound in the world that remotely resembled it. The first elephant call was echoed as a second animal answered.

Was it possible, they asked each other, that An Lu-shan was even taking the Emperor's elephants to Loyang? And if he was taking the elephants, what else was he taking? They started walking again. Soon, the wind that reached their nostrils carried the rich odor of manure. How many animals were at the port, waiting to begin their journey?

Kao Li-shih saw the advantage that this discovery would give them. Where there were animals, there would be keepers. Especially for the elephants. No one, he knew, handles an elephant but its keeper; the animal will trample or pick up in its trunk and hurl to the ground any other man with the impudence to try to give it orders. And each of the Emperor's trained elephants had its own keeper, who ate and slept with his charge. If the elephants were here, by the river, then so were their keepers—and Kao Li-shih knew each of these men very well.

When they rounded a bend in the river and saw moving lights in the distance, hand-held lanterns, they knew they had arrived. Ahead would be the docks where the barges tied up and were loaded and unloaded, the gang- ways, the granaries, the huge sheds, row upon row of them, where goods of every kind were stored, the pens for animals arriving for slaughter or to be driven onto the barges for shipment. At any other time, all business conducted at these docks would be for the purpose of serving the great city and its infinitely diverse commerce. Morning would always find the port by the river alive with cheerful activity, with farmers, importers, tradesmen, vendors, and workmen carrying on the business that was the lifeblood of Ch'ang-an. The bull elephant trumpeted again. Today, Kao Li-shih suspected, business at the port would be somewhat different.

They advanced with great caution under cover of darkness. They knew the night would not last much longer, so they felt a certain urgency. Getting themselves onto the barges bound for Loyang was the problem they faced this morning, and it had been impossible to plan in advance how to do it, since they had had no idea what to expect upon arrival at the docks. They would have to get a grasp of the situation here and now, then move with alacrity.

Ever since he had heard the elephant, a plan had been formulating in Kao Li-shih's mind. He told the others to wait, then moved in the direction from which the trumpeting had come. It was still dark, so he felt his way along the rail of the animal pens. The elephants, he surmised, would be several pens over. He decided that he would climb the fence and go through the pens, the first few of which seemed to be empty. It was not until he had gone through three pens and climbed into a fourth that he realized it was not empty. His approach had alerted the animals therein, and he could hear hoof- beats and the nervous whinnies of horses as they galloped away from him in the dark. When he reached the next fence, he stood still and listened. He heard the sound of an elephant feeding, the swishing of hay being lifted to the animal's mouth and the grinding of its molars. He could hear also the clinking of the heavy chains around its legs as it shifted its great weight, and the sound of the trunk sweeping the ground. Even if he had not heard these things, he would have known. Though it was still dark, the elephant's looming presence blotted out what little light there was.

Cautiously, he leaned over the fence, and called out a man's name in a low voice. No response. He tried another name then, and waited. He called the name again. A shuffling sound, and then a voice answered, softly, appre- hensively.

"Who is there?"

"It is I, Kao Li-shih."

"Kao Li-shih!" The voice was incredulous. In the next moment, a pair of hands found his in the darkness. "Kao Li-shih!" the man said again. "I thought you were dead. Everyone thinks you are dead."

"Excellent," Kao Li-shih answered in a whisper. "Let them continue to think it. It will serve my purposes well."

"But how did you get here?" the man asked, lowering his own voice to a whisper.

Kao Li-shih sighed. "It is a very, very long story. I will tell you every detail later. Suffice it to say that the Emperor is alive, the consort is alive, two of the Yang sisters are dead, and so is Yang Kuo-chung. But I need your help now. I have sixty eunuchs and the elder son of An Lu-shan with me, waiting. We are going to Loyang to assassinate An Lu-shan. We must get on the barges."

There was a moment's silence as the elephant-keeper thought.

"You may have arrived at the right moment, Kao Li-shih," he said. "For the better part of a week now they have been driving the Emperor's animals here. Some of us have been waiting here for several days. Today is the day that animals and keepers will be shipped to Loyang."

"All of the Emperor's animals?" Kao Li-shih asked in disbelief.

"All of them. An Lu-shan has a particular thirst for the most exotic of them. I think he believes they will make him seem like a real Emperor. And it is not just the animals, Kao Li-shih. It is people, too. Most of the ones who haven't been killed have all been sent. All the musicians and entertainers. All the women. And hundreds of officials and, with them, load after load of government documents. Not to mention furnishings, clothing, art treasures. Everything, Kao Li-shih. Everything. Today it is animals and all the servants and household eunuchs who have not been killed. I think that it will be possible for you and your men to spread yourselves among the eunuchs and stablehands and pass unnoticed. There is not a one among us who would not want to help you. We will give you clothes. Each of us can spare something."

"So An Lu-shan believes that he can make himself into an emperor by surrounding himself with what belongs to the Emperor," Kao Li-shih said, feeling his anger rise anew. "Does he really think that this is all there is to it? Some animals, some women, some stolen treasures?"

"The rumor," said the elephant-keeper, "is that he is planning a huge celebration in Loyang. The establishment of his court. The beginning of a new dynasty."

"When do the barges leave?" Kao Li-shih asked. "How can we get on them?"

"They leave after dawn. They will load with the first light. The eunuchs are in one of the sheds, under guard. The animals are not being watched as closely. They know that those of us in charge of the animals love the beasts too much to leave them and try to escape. And they are right. I would die before I would let any harm come to my elephants. I suggest that you bring half of your men here. They can be 'stablehands.' The rest, while it is still dark, should enter the river and work their way around to the other side of the barges. The ones to the front of the line are to be used to transport people, the rear ones are for the animals. There are ropes to hang onto along the sides. The water is not very cold. Tell them to be patient, to wait for the loading to begin. They will know the right moment to come on board."

: :

Many hours later Kao Li-shih lay on a pile of straw on the deck of a barge being carried on the river's current and thought that if he did not know better, he would have believed that he was dreaming.

All around him were the Emperor's tribute animals, the rare, strange beasts from other lands that the Emperor kept and trained for his own pleasure and to create magic on special state occasions. The barges had been specially reinforced with high wooden railings along the sides so that they had become floating pens. Rails separated one pen from another. Kao Li-shih was in a pen with the two elephants and their keepers. Next to them, a herd of twenty of the Emperor's dancing horses rolled their nervous eyes, showing the whites as they shied here and there on their small, polished hooves. There were twenty more horses in the next pen, and twenty in the next, and ten or so striped zebras in the next, all snorting and whinnying uneasily. You are anxious about your fate, Kao Li-shih thought. You are not the only ones.

Cages of screeching parrots were stacked on the deck. Ostriches, their eyes hooded and their legs tied to prevent them from panicking and leaping overboard or delivering a death blow to someone foolish enough to antagonize them, turned their tiny stupid heads this way and that on their long, ridiculous swaying necks. On the barge in front of them, directly lashed to theirs so that a man could walk from one deck to the next with ease, Kao Li-shih could see the Emperor's two prized black rhinoceroses gazing stolidly out over the water, munching placidly on hay, as if such journeys were commonplace for them. In reinforced iron cages near the rhinoceroses, two enormous white tigers paced and roared with nervous indignation; a huge brown bear, its jaws muzzled with heavy leather straps, sat in its cage in the posture of a buddha. Monkeys of all kinds, large and tiny, some with strange, bulbous blue noses or fearsome ruffs of bristly hair and wild demon eyes, screamed and hurled themselves against the bars of their cages. And everywhere were the animals' keepers, Flying Dragon eunuchs assimilated imperceptibly into their numbers, muttering soothing words, offering food, keeping watchful eyes on their beasts, and on the rebel guards.

Not that they had to worry particularly about the guards. The guards, men who resembled the ones the Flying Dragons had killed in the forest, stayed apprehensively distant at the far end of the barge, clearly uneasy in the presence of the animals—especially the elephants, Kao Li-shih noted with satisfaction. He himself lay stretched out behind the huge animals, resting luxuriously, feeling quite safe with the enormous feet and legs of the elephants, like trees, between him and the guards.

The elephants were feeding peacably. Kao Li-shih watched in fascination as their trunks dextrously and daintily picked up hay and carried it to their mouths. The clouds had partially cleared this morning, and the intermittent sun warmed his tired bones. Nearby, a talking mynah bird asked over and over again the urgent question: am I a man dreaming that I am a bird or am I a bird dreaming that I am a man? Kao Li-shih smiled and drowsed. That had been one of the Emperor's little jokes. He had labored for months to teach the bird to say that.

His friend the elephant-keeper came and sat down next to him on the hay.

"Word has been passed to me from the front barges," he said in a low voice. "Your Dragons are safely aboard. They are no longer fearless warriors. They are now harmless 'household' eunuchs."

"Good," Kao Li-shih answered. "Your help has been invaluable." He shifted his position on the straw.

With everything that had been on his mind, one thing kept rising insistently to the surface, his anger rising with it: An Lu-shan's celebration, the preparations for which this gigantic effort was only a small part. It infuriated him, he realized, more than almost anything else. The image of the general's fat, gloating face savoring his "victory" caused the rage to move down into Kao Li-shih's fingers whenever he thought of it. And he had been giving much thought to what one of the Flying Dragons had said to him: that An Lu-shan was not merely exercising a military coup. He was wreaking vengeance on the city. It was rape, and nothing else. Why?

He looked up at his friend sitting beside him on the straw.

"What do you know about the progress of the imperial forces? I have been in the woods for days. I am completely ignorant."

The keeper shook his head while he swatted affectionately at the leg of the elephant with his long stick. He sighed.

"People are afraid, Kao Li-shih, but they don't know whom to fear most: An Lu-shan's thugs and thieves, or those who would liberate them."

"I don't understand."

"The news that we have heard in the city is that General Kuo Tzu-i has effectively cut off An Lu-shan's northern retreat route and that he is moving closer to Ch'ang-an every day. It is well-known that General Kuo has formed an alliance with a vast fighting force of Uighurs." Kao Li-shih knew that these old allies of the Chinese from the far northwest were fearless and terrible fighters. They loved fighting just as other men loved music and poetry, singing and dancing, and watching the sun rise. "People are afraid," his friend continued, "because they wonder what General Kuo has promised his Uighur soldiers as a reward for liberating the city from the rebels. They are afraid that there is going to be a heavy price to pay, and that they are going to be the ones to have to pay it. There has been so much murder and looting already under General Sun's occupation that the rebel soldiers almost seem to be sated for now. But with a fresh wave of soldiers coming into the city . . . well, Kao Li-shih, I think you understand. The Uighurs are little different from the enemy. It will just be trading one occupying regime for another. There is a lot of fear. It has spread, like a disease." He paused and watched one of the elephants extend its inquisitive trunk over the rail. "Why is it always the people who must pay, Kao Li-shih? And the children?" He turned and looked at Kao Li-shih. "Did you know that the imperial guards killed the infant children of An Ching-tsung?"

Kao Li-shih had been listening to his friend with his eyes shut, lying on his back on the straw. He opened his eyes now and watched the clouds drifting in the sky. An Ching-tsung, An Ching-hsu's brother, was the younger son of An Lu-shan. An innocent boy in his early teens, he had been married ceremonially to one of the Emperor's countless daughters at the time of the "adoption" of the Emperor's "Lucky Baby" An Lu-shan. A gesture heavy with symbolism, the marriage of the two children had forged a familial bond. And when the young princess, no older than sixteen or so, had given birth to twins within the year, the symbolic bond had become real: the Emperor and An Lu-shan were now related by blood through these grandchildren. Sweet children they were, too. Kao Li-shih had often watched them playing and toddling about, innocents with no notion that they owed their very existences to the strange, incongruous union of an emperor and a barbarian.

"How did it happen?" he asked his friend quietly while still watching the clouds.

"Some of the imperial guards. It was after the Emperor's entourage had fled. An Ching-tsung and the princess and the two babies were trying to flee, too, but some of the guards stopped them. There was a terrible argument among the guards. Some wanted to slaughter them all on the spot, simply because he was the son of the traitor An Lu-shan; others argued that they should merely be imprisoned, others wanted to let them go. The ones in favor of death won out. The princess and An Lu-shan's son were sliced to pieces. Their babies were thrown into one of the boiling pools at the hot springs. Children, all of them. Just children."

Kao Li-shih closed his eyes again. It was true, wasn't it? It was always the innocents who paid the price for the folly of those who were supposed to keep them from harm. *Our blindness can be measured in children's tears and in their blood.* Prince Ying, so many years in his grave, had not visited Kao Li-shih for quite some time, but he came back now. The only other person besides himself and poor, lost Chang Chiu-ling who knew the truth—that the boy had been murdered, and murdered by the Emperor's most trusted second in command, Li Lin-fu—was Yang Kuo-chung. And now he, too, was in his grave.

Well, my friend, he thought, addressing his dead comrade, I cannot exactly call you an innocent. You made a man's choice. You could have lived an untouched life. But you abdicated from your birthright and took on adversaries that few men would have dared to face. It is ironic that you, who knew the dangers so well and who parried them with such masterful skill, should have been caught off guard and died the victim of what was really nothing but a misunderstanding. A stupid, ignominious misunderstanding.

But death is usually ignominious, isn't it, Master Yang? Isn't that what it means to be human, to know with certainty that our deaths will very likely be messy, embarrassing, boring affairs that do very poor justice to our vision of ourselves and our lives? Certainly not what we would have chosen ourselves, if nature granted us the choice. It is nothing, though. It is merely nature's perverse little joke on us. Nature fashions us, creatures with grandiose yearnings for immortality and an inexhaustible thirst for order, meaning, glory, and hidden signs, and then kills us like animals. With embarrassing, dirty little diseases, or else blind, toothless and senile. Or with war, or with pointless accidents. Like you, my friend. To be human in this universe simply means to be brave, doesn't it, Master Yang? And you were brave.

Braver than I.

Kao Li-shih looked around himself at the fantastic, improbable scene, the animals from distant parts of the world riding, penned up, caged, or tied down, on a boat on a river in the middle of China, traveling hundreds of li between two cities for the purpose of satisfying one man's thirst for aggrandizement. If I had gone to the Emperor all those years ago when poor Chang Chiu-ling the poet-minister came to me with his terrible knowledge, would I be riding, with these animals, on this river today? Would Yang Kuo-chung be dead, the country at war, and the Emperor a broken old man?

Or would the Emperor have died years ago, of grief that he could not simply have been born an ordinary man and not an emperor? When all is said and done, Kao Li-shih thought, he really would have preferred that. He would have been happy to live a peaceful life as a scholarly artist and musician. But nature played a perverse trick on him: it made him an emperor. It thrust upon him the mandate to rule.

You were trying to protect him, Kao Li-shih, the eunuch told himself. Remember that. You did what you had to do.

Or could you have been braver? Isn't it true that poor Chang Chiu-ling, the peaceful man of letters, the skinny, ugly, undernourished poet whom everyone laughed at, showed more courage than you did?

The mynah bird in its cage squawked out its unanswerable philosophical conundrum. At the same moment, something startled one of the tigers, making it give out with a huge, angry roar, and the terrified monkeys chattered and screamed. The ostriches turned their tiny, blind heads this way and that, while the horses and zebras galloped in a tight, panicked circle within the confines of their corrals, eyes rolling, hooves thundering on the wooden deck. The keepers were on their feet, rushing about, trying to calm the animals, whistling and calling. The bull elephant, interested by the commotion, left off its feeding and raised its trunk into the air and trumpeted.

The mighty sound at this close range went through Kao Li-shih as if his body were made of paper and cloth. The sound, designed by nature to carry over vast distances—mountains, valleys, and plains, deafened Kao Li-shih and reverberated in the air, bouncing off the hills to the north of the river.

And it cleansed him. It cut through his sad, tangled thoughts, shattering them into tiny fragments, clearing them from his aching head.

All your speculation is useless, Kao Li-shih, he told himself sternly. It is time to cease your wallowing. You are here, and An Lu-shan sits on his "throne" in Loyang. And you know what you have to do.

The sun was gone as the gray clouds rolled together again. Rain began to patter softly on the deck.

:: ::

It had been years since Kao Li-shih had been to Loyang. He had almost forgotten what a beautiful city the eastern capital was, even in the rain, with its branching network of rivers wending their way through glorious parks, and graceful, ornate bridges everywhere with boats gliding beneath. After three days of travel on the Wei River and then on the connecting canal, the barges now moved through the heart of the city on the wide and gracious Luo River. People lined up along the banks to stare at the amazing spectacle, but there was no air of festiveness or welcome. Kao Li-shih read fatigue, fear, and suspicion on the watching faces under their streaming umbrellas—the faces of citizens suffering under a tyrant and wondering what was to befall them next.

It had been raining steadily since the sun had disappeared behind the clouds on the first day of the voyage. The animals were thoroughly soaked and dejected, as were the men. Food had been scarce. Kao Li-shih had killed the hunger pangs with handfuls of the horses' feed while he and An Ching-hsu discussed, in discreet tones, what they would do when they reached the city. The elephant-keeper told them that they would be safest among the animals and would be in advantageous proximity to the new "emperor." The others, those among the household eunuchs, would have a similar advantage. Messages were passed from barge to barge, and it was agreed: they would blend subtly and discreetly into the daily activity at the palace, and wait, and be patient.

Above all, they would be patient.

Kao Li-shih found himself vacillating. He would go to sleep, curled up in the wet straw, filled with determination and a certain knowledge that An Lu-shan would soon taste the justice he deserved; then, in the gray, wet morning, he would open his tired eyes and know with the same certainty that there was no justice in the world, that An Lu-shan would reign for the next thirty years and come to believe that the mandate to rule had been his birthright.

The eyes of the people on the banks of the river met the eyes of the men on the barges that moved slowly toward the palace in the southwestern part of the city. The eunuchs and animal-keepers looked back at the citizens of Loyang in silent collusion while the guards looked back with arrogant belligerence. Kao Li-shih wondered if this was how all new dynasties began.

He watched the elephants looking around themselves with mild interest and the horses gazing over the rails of their pens toward the crowded riverbanks, and tried to imagine, for a moment, how the world of men must appear through their eyes—but he could not do it.

An Ching-hsu sat near him.

"I have decided to go to my father and beg his forgiveness," the young man said in a low voice.

Kao Li-shih turned to him, surprised.

"Then we will kill him," An Ching-hsu finished.

"Why go to him?" Kao Li-shih asked. "Why not simply remain hidden in the stables? Why let him know you are even here? How do you know he won't kill you? It seems to me to be a terrible risk."

"Many reasons," the boy answered thoughtfully. "I believe that he will forgive me, if I present myself in the right way. I will humble myself before him, grovel at his feet. He will not be able to resist. Then I can pretend to be his 'filial' son once more. I will know where he is at every moment of every day. Nothing will give me greater pleasure than to betray him."

"What if he is not in the mood to forgive?"

"Maybe he will have me killed. But I doubt it. I am the only one left now."

So An Ching-hsu did know about the death of his brother. This was the first time he had mentioned it. Obviously, he held his father responsible, and he meant to make him pay for that, too.

They were drawing nearer to the imperial city. Kao Li-shih looked toward the high walls that surrounded the palace, their outlines blurred gray and indistinct in the rain, and felt a sharp, unpleasant wave of anticipation ripple through his gut, and an oppressive sense of the obstacles and danger that they faced.

Greetings, "Emperor" An Lu-shan, he said silently. We know that you are behind those great walls somewhere. We don't know where yet, but we have arrived, and we will find you. We wish to help you celebrate the beginning of your new dynasty.

::

The new Emperor of China An Lu-shan raised his cup to the dead chief minister Li Lin-fu.

We can be friends now, he said. Let me pour you some more wine.

He carried the pitcher to the other side of the table where an empty cup rested, and filled it to the top. Then he lifted the cup and drained the wine down his throat. Moving carefully, trying not to upset the furniture, he moved back to the other side of the table where his own cup sat, filled it, and drained it. He giggled absurdly. He put his hand to his forehead. It was dry.

See, Chief Minister? He held out his dry fingers to the empty chair opposite him. It would seem that I have recovered from my affliction with excessive yin. I can sit in your presence now, and we can converse like equals, and I no longer sweat like a hog on its way to market. He laughed again. That's what I always felt like. A fattened hog, ready for the kill.

And you were right, of course. I was afflicted. I was always sliding and slipping in something wet. If it was not mud, it was the moist, slippery gates of women, drawing me into their darkness. Like sliding down into a muddy hole. And my own body, slippery and wet inside my clothes, the sweat running down from my scalp, down my neck and back, or standing in big, stupid droplets on my face for all the world to see. While you, Chief Minister, always remained dry. You told me once that water was killing you, that it had settled inside your lungs and was eating away at you from within. Maybe it was, but to me, you looked as dry as a desiccated corpse. Even your eyeballs looked dry.

But it killed you, didn't it? You held it all inside, and it rotted you. Maybe that's what has saved me: it rolls out of me, pours off of me. It made me look like a fool, but it didn't kill me.

He refilled his own cup and the chief minister's and listened to the monotonous drumming of rain on the roof. Water gushed from ornate rain-spouts and splashed steadily onto the stones below and streamed in long, shimmering ribbons from the roof onto the balcony railings outside and down into puddles and rivulets on the ground. He shut his eyes. He heard music in the sound of the water. It surrounded him, pattering, dripping, tapping, and splashing everywhere: the walls, the windows, the roof. A hundred thousand little notes played at once. Or little voices; varying in pitch from each other only slightly, they sang a strange, tuneless, repetitive melody that went on and on and on.

I will need sons now, he mused, emptying his wine cup. I have none left. One is dead and one is a mangy cur, a coward, if he is not dead too. An Lu-shan was philosophical: the loss of his sons was part of the price he had to pay to be where he was now. He felt a certain sadness when he thought of their faces; the older had shown promise, but had needed discipline all the time and had abandoned him. The younger one seemed to lack some sort of essential manliness. An Lu-shan doubted that he would have amounted to anything much if he had lived. He thought wistfully for just a moment of his two infant grandchildren. A shame. But that, too, was part of the cost of leadership. He took another drink. An emperor has to have sons. I will make a hundred of them in one year.

You can't make sons without women, An Lu-shan, he could imagine the chief minister saying. Yes, he answered; I know. But this time it will be different. He smiled. Things are not quite the same as they were, eh?

Oh, yes. You have done a magnificent job, Li Lin-fu answered. Not only have you lost your sons, but you have lost your father as well.

An Lu-shan felt helpless and desolate whenever he thought about the Emperor. I am sorry, my Father, he apologized for the thousandth time, the tears starting to his eyes. I only hope that you know that none of this was because of you. I truly loved you. You know that, don't you? But you were surrounded. By that stinking, meddling whore of a eunuch and the silk-trousers Yang. Whispering in your ear all the time. Telling you I was a traitor, a thief, a murderer. But you never believed them, and I love you for that. They convinced everybody else, though. I even lost the love of my mother the Precious Consort because of them.

His tears flowed down his cheeks and into his beard. My mother. He saw the consort's face in his mind, smiling radiantly at him. But the smile faded into a terrible look of fear and suspicion. She feared me. They made her fear me! They stole my mother's love from me! The face, the lovely, delicate face, was averted from his and dark with doubt. The eyes would no longer look into his own. And the face was no longer the consort's: it was the face of his own mother, dead so many years. Looking away from him now with doubt and dread. He wept.

Your face isn't so dry anymore, jeered Li Lin-fu. One way or another, the water runs down your face.

Shut up, Old Lizard, An Lu-shan ordered. Shut up. You are where you belong, dead and in your grave. He smiled. I heard that they dug you up. Did you know that? They dug you up, and opened your coffin, and laughed at your pathetic bones. What do you think of that?

Li Lin-fu smiled back.

If they laughed at my bones, then they were only laughing at their own. And everybody's. My bones were always on view, even when I was alive. Wait until they see your bones, so well hidden now under layers of fat. Then they will truly have something to laugh at.

Shut up, Old Lizard, I'm warning you, An Lu-shan growled and took another drink. Just shut up. You are making me angry. And you know what happens when I am angry. Ch'ang-an, the whore city, has felt my wrath. I was sweet to her, but she slapped me in the face one too many times.

Inspiration came to him then, and he leaned toward the empty chair and shook his finger at the invisible chief minister. Do you know what she was? She was a whore with a full set of teeth hidden in her vermilion gates. He laughed at the wicked, grotesque image. That was it!

That was why he would never go back to Ch'ang-an. That was why she had lost him forever. How many times had he offered himself, big-hearted and forgiving, only to have her sink her hidden teeth into him?

And do you know, he said slyly, that I know exactly where her gate is and where those teeth are? He stood. I know that some people regard me as an oaf, an illiterate boor. But I have some poetry in my soul, too. I am not completely incapable of insight. I heard enough poetry from my Father to know that what the so-called "poets" do is not so special. He walked around the room, went to the window and looked out at the sheets of rain.

The part of Ch'ang-an that was her most womanly part, the part that draws men in irresistibly, the part that they want to bury themselves in, the part, he said significantly and with emphasis to the patiently listening Li Lin-fu, where those teeth are hidden—that part of her was the hot springs. Am I a poet, or am I not?

Li Lin-fu had no response to this. He merely waited.

The hot springs: where the water boils out of the dark earth and the steam hangs in the air, heavy with perfume. And so beautiful. Beauty that overpowers a man, makes him stupid. Robs him of his judgment and authority. Beauty that seduces, Chief Minister, do you understand? Seduces. Draws him in and puts him in mortal danger.

Beauty that crawls in through your window at night.

He shut his eyes and allowed himself a moment of remembrance. This time he did not push the image away, but aided by the wine in his veins and the hypnotic sound of the rain on the roof, let it come. He concentrated. He imagined moonlight, and himself lying on a bed, waiting. A woman came through the window and dropped softly onto the quilts, landing on her feet. She straightened up and stood on the bed looking down at him.

But he was having trouble with the face. He was unable to keep it in focus, and it shifted annoyingly. First, it was the Lady of Kuo, then it was the Precious Consort, and then it was his own dead mother. He found himself quite unable to conjure the face of the nameless young woman who had smiled at him with blood on her teeth: she was the only one who refused to appear.

But there was one other who did oblige him: the hag. When he saw her shriveled, mocking face appearing above him, he opened his eyes quickly, abandoning the fantasy in disgust and alarm. He stumbled back to his chair and sat heavily.

I gave special orders that the soldiers clear the hot springs, he said to Li Lin-fu. No one there was to be left alive. No one! They killed everything that moved or crawled. On my orders.

But they were not to touch the Emperor. They all knew. Anyone who harmed him would answer to me and die a hideous death.

Well, said Li Lin-fu with heavy sarcasm, aren't you magnanimous. I'm sure the Emperor appreciated your filial consideration. I am sure he is thanking you from the depths of his soul every day.

Shut up, Lizard! An Lu-shan said sharply. He stood again, abruptly, knocking his chair to the floor behind him.

It was time, and my Father knew it, An Lu-shan declared. The Emperor knew that his time was over. Why do you think he made me his son? His prince? His time as an emperor had passed. He was useless. He was old. He knew that China needed me, his son. He was worn out, Lizard. Worn out. And do you know what wore him out?

Tell me, said Li Lin-fu drily.

Fucking. That is what wore him out. He had been fucking those vermilion gates with the hidden teeth for so many years that he was useless, dried out, depleted. And you, too, Chief Minister. You were fucking them, too. You died out there at the hot springs, all worn out from fucking. You went there hoping for a cure, and what did you find? Only death. Death, Old Lizard! He brought his fist down hard on the table.

Li Lin-fu smiled. Correct me if I am wrong, but do I detect sweat on your brow?

An Lu-shan's hand went to his forehead. His fingers came away hot and moist. Infuriated, he put his hands underneath the heavy wooden table and brought them up hard, sending the table, the wine cups and a full pitcher of wine crashing to the floor. The commotion was terrible, and very satisfying. It also caused Li Lin-fu to evaporate. Good riddance, Lizard, An Lu-shan thought, and booted a chair across the room for emphasis.

He stood there, drunk, swaying, his foot throbbing vaguely, the toneless music of the water penetrating his consciousness again. The roof of the building became the top of his skull, the water dripping and pattering, whispering and gurgling, steadily, relentlessly, unceasingly.

How many days had it been raining? He had lost count. He had had to put off his celebration because of it. But he could not wait very much longer.

Rain or no rain, the Yen dynasty would officially begin, and soon. They told him that the animals had arrived that morning. He would show the city, and the empire, a celebration unlike anything they had ever seen or imagined.

And they would grow to love him, he knew. It would take some time, but they would love him.

:: :

On the third day after their arrival in Loyang, Kao Li-shih had begun to worry that An Ching-hsu had not met with the forgiveness he had expected from his father. Not long after the barges were unloaded, the boy had disappeared from the stables after telling Kao Li-shih and Li Chu-erh that they would be hearing something from him soon but until then, they should do nothing. Unless, of course, they heard that he was dead, in which case they would have to decide for themselves how they would get to An Lu-shan.

And the rain had continued. The rivers were brown and swollen, rising higher every day, the streets of the city deep in mud. But the palace stables were comfortable and dry. For most of the first day after their arrival, Kao Li-shih had slept off his deep exhaustion, ensconced safely in the straw behind the elephants. He began to appreciate the feelings of his friend the elephant-keeper toward the animals; he too began to think of them as his "beloved" elephants. As long as they were between him and any strangers, he knew that he was safe. And the rest of the Flying Dragons, Li Chu-erh included, were quickly becoming expert handlers of the Emperor's exotic menagerie; they were glad, for the most part, to have something to do while they waited.

And they were genuinely needed. Every one of the animals, bedraggled after their long journey, had to be groomed. The horses had to be brushed, their manes and tails combed out, and their hooves polished. The rhinoceroses and elephants had to be washed with big stiff brushes and their hides oiled. The rhinoceroses' horns were painted with bright metallic paint while the elephants' tusks were polished until they gleamed white. And the animals, royal creatures that they were, took the ministrations patiently, with for-bearance. Probably they knew that they would soon be called upon to perform; what they could never know, Kao Li-shih reflected while working the knots from a horse's tail with a large wooden comb, was that they would be per-forming for a false emperor.

An Lu-shan's preparations for his grand party were said to be extrava-gant, and rumors were rife. There was talk of fireworks, to be shot from barges on the rivers, and food and drink for every man, woman, and child in the city. And at the palace, there were to be music and dance performances. What was left of the Pear Garden Orchestra, which had suffered some casualties in the sacking of the palace at Ch'ang-an, had been brought to Loyang to play for the great Emperor An Lu-shan. And for An Lu-shan's generals, the ones who were not still fighting the imperial forces, the munificence of their master apparently knew no bounds: there would be women. The harem that had already resided in Loyang, plus the women brought from Ch'ang-an on the barges, would be offered to these men.

So this was how it was to be, Kao Li-shih thought with disgust when he heard about it. A crude, insulting emulation of the Emperor's own lavish parties. When the Emperor offered women to his high court officials and friends, it was always done delicately and tastefully. Kao Li-shih did not like to think of An Lu-shan's henchmen satisfying their greedy lust, with the example for decorum being set by An Lu-shan himself.

There was a quality of grim parody to everything connected with the upcoming "celebration." Recalling the solemn faces lined up on the banks of the river in the rain, Kao Li-shih wondered how An Lu-shan intended to squeeze the spontaneous expression of joy out of his subjects. He had learned little during his time with the Emperor if he thought that enforced merriment would procure for him the love and loyalty of the people. And in this rain, too, Kao Li-shih thought incredulously. This gray rain that seems to have gone on forever, obliterating the sun completely, and all memory of it.

Do you believe that a city of wet, hungry, terrorized people are going to turn out in the rain, and worship you, and dance in the streets, An Lu-shan? And that musicians and dancers who have been torn from their homes and forced to travel hundreds of li, and who have seen death and chaos at your hands, are going to joyfully perform for you, offering their art for your pleasure and glorification? Is that what you believe? Then you are truly a desperate man.

And there were other rumors, too, which did not bode well for the great celebration. Though An Lu-shan was preparing to celebrate as if victory were already in his hands, it was clear that the fight for the empire was not yet over. There were reports of bitter struggles to the south and east, with heavy losses on both sides. The imperial forces, strengthened now by the addition of provincial armies, were no longer falling back before An Lu-shan's men as they had at the beginning, when the element of surprise was on his side. General Kuo and his Uighur allies were said to be closing in on Ch'ang-an, and, it was also said, General Feng was slowly working his way toward Loyang from the northeast.

General Feng, who had once been a friend of An Lu-shan. Kao Li-shih wondered what each man must be thinking about the other as their forces gained or lost ground to one another. Every few hours, it seemed, brought news: that An Lu-shan's rebel forces had pushed back Feng's army ten li; that Feng had rallied and dealt a blow to the rebels, taking a key defense position; that the rebels had withdrawn, but were preparing for a new push.

The rain continued, and so did the lifeless preparations for celebration.

Men worked, faces tense and grim, and news was passed along as soon as it came in. Sometimes many hours would go by with no news, or an entire day. The men did not talk very much while they were waiting, but dwelled on their private thoughts. If Feng was defeated, if he failed to break An Lu-shan's grip on the capital, then it was possible that China would have a new emperor. It had happened before. Most of them had tried to maintain the belief that they were suffering only a temporary displacement, that order would eventually be restored, that they could go home. But what if it was not to be? What if they had to call the barbarian traitor An Lu-shan "Emperor"?

And if the imperial forces did reach the city, there would still be much death and destruction before it was over. With his northern retreat route cut off behind him, An Lu-shan's back would be to the wall; his retribution, they feared, would be a terrible thing.

The sooner he dies, the better, Kao Li-shih thought, brushing mud from a horse's coat. He wondered if An Lu-shan had a second in command. Had he made any contingency plans in the event of his own death? He doubted it. From what he knew of the "Lucky Baby," he probably held a nearly superstitious belief in his own immortality. He probably believes that he cannot be touched, that he is fulfilling his destiny, Kao Li-shih thought, moving around to the horse's other flank. He tried to conceive the workings of the barbarian's mind: had he thought at all about what would happen if he were to die? Or did he not even think of the possibility of his own death? Or—and this was a disturbing prospect—was it possible that he did not care? Or did he see the rebellion as outliving him, as part of a destiny that exceeded the scope of his own mortal existence?

If he were to die tomorrow, what would befall his great rebellion? Who would take over?

From what Kao Li-shih had seen of the rebel soldiers, a distinct probability emerged in his mind as an answer to the last hypothetical question: no one. No one would take over the role of leader. At least, not effectively. It was Kao Li-shih's instinctive feeling that chaos and anarchy would be the natural result of the death of "Emperor" An Lu-shan, and that Feng's forces would be able to flow into the city unhindered.

Kao Li-shih's anxiety grew almost by the hour. He would have to decide very soon whether An Ching-hsu was going to come back at all, and he would have to take action accordingly. Without a doubt, the young man was absolutely their best possible connection to An Lu-shan, the one who could provide them with intimate knowledge of his father's habits and plans, as well as the physical layout of the palace, the distribution and positioning of guards, etc. But if they had to, they would do without him. They would find another way. They had no choice.

Every new development increased his anxiety: when he heard that Feng's troops had been pushed back, he was consumed with impatience to help the war effort by putting a knife into An Lu-shan's gut; when he heard that Feng had made a significant advance and was closer to the city, he found himself fretting over the possibility that the imperial troops would get to An Lu-shan first and kill him themselves, thus robbing him of the pleasure and privilege of personally seeing to the death of the "Lucky Baby" emperor.

Another possibility, one that he had scarcely allowed himself to consider but which had finally forced its way into his consciousness, maddened Kao Li-shih now as he stood in the stable looking out the wide doors at the rain: that An Lu-shan would, if he heard that his armies were being vanquished and that Feng was practically at his door, take his own life. The thought that An Lu-shan might escape punishment that way, might slip forever out of their grasp, choosing the time, place, and method of his own death, was an irony that he did not think he could bear.

It was now the fifth day since An Ching-hsu had gone. Kao Li-shih, horse brush in hand, stood and looked for a few more moments at the rain and mud, and at the high, gray walls of the palace some distance away, then turned back to his work.

An Lu-shan's son was dead, or imprisoned. He could feel it. He would never see him again. And they had waited long enough; there was no more time to waste. He smoothed a horse's flank with long, thoughtful strokes. He would have to make contact with the Flying Dragons who had mingled with the household staff. He would have to be very, very careful. There were serious risks, but it was the next best thing to contact with An Lu-shan's son.

So far, he and the other Dragons had practiced absolute discretion. The animal handlers and household eunuchs were, of course, aware of them in their midst and knew why they were there, but only a trusted handful had been apprised fully of the details of their intent. And while they waited for An Ching-hsu, barely a word was spoken of their plans. They worked, they discussed in low voices the news of battle losses and victories, and they waited.

Kao Li-shih glanced over to where Li Chu-erh worked nearby, his face closed and sullen. The younger eunuch had remarked to him last night that if something did not happen soon, he was going to do something himself. What, he did not know; but he could not wait very much longer, he had said. Kao Li-shih knew that he would be unable to stop him if he decided to sneak away to find An Lu-shan. Looking at Li Chu-erh now, Kao Li-shih felt certain that something, some plan, was already forming in his mind. Whatever it might be, he knew it would be impetuous, dangerous, and bound to end in disaster.

Desperately, he cast about in his mind for possibilities. Contact between the stables and the palace had not been frequent during the last few days. The only person he had seen from the household staff was a fat eunuch whom he did not even know, who appeared occasionally with a cart bearing the meager provisions of food for the stablehands. He had not seen him since the day before yesterday; before that, he had seen him only once, on their first day at the stables. That meant that the man was due to appear again very soon. Perhaps tomorrow. He tried to recall what he had seen of the eunuch's character on his face. What he could remember did not encourage him: a fat, somewhat insipid countenance, with small weak eyes. Was this the man he would have to take into his confidence? Was this his link with the world behind the palace walls? His heart dropped heavily as he contemplated the prospect of entrusting a message to the nameless eunuch.

Well, he told himself, you could be wrong. You cannot always accurately judge a man's potential by his physiognomy. Please remember the poet-minister Chang Chiu-ling. You were completely wrong about him, were you not?

He approached Li Chu-erh, who was listlessly shoveling horse manure into a barrow. The youth scarcely looked up.

"I have a plan," Kao Li-shih said quietly to him. "The waiting will soon be over."

Li Chu-erh made no reply, but continued working.

"I know that you are coming to the end of your patience," Kao Li-shih continued, "and so am I. But please. I beg you. Do not try to do anything alone. It will end badly. And there will be no second chance!"

Chu-erh still said nothing, but stopped working and stared down at the straw.

"Please!" Kao Li-shih implored. "Do I have your word?"

Reluctantly, Chu-erh nodded his head and lifted another shovelful of manure into the barrow.

Kao Li-shih went back to his own work, thinly reassured. He had spoken to him not a moment too soon. The presence of a scheme in the young eunuch's mind had been all too obvious to Kao Li-shih.

: :

The next morning, Kao Li-shih was awake early and at work. He did not want to risk missing the fat eunuch on whom he had pinned his hopes. As was his habit, he glanced around, looking for Li Chu-erh, but he did not see him. He went over to the brazier where hot bowls of tea were dispensed to the stablehands and did not find him there, either. He went to the door and looked outside. The rain had reduced itself to a scant drizzle. He saw a few people in the yard, going about various tasks, but no Li Chu-erh. Uneasy now, he went back inside. He would work, he told himself, and be patient. Li Chu-erh would appear.

For the next several hours, he watched with increasing desperation for two people—Li Chu-erh and the fat household eunuch—and saw neither of them. His friend the elephant-keeper said that he had no idea when Li Chu-erh had left or where he had gone. Nor did any of the others they discreetly questioned.

And where was the fat fool who brought the food? Kao Li-shih watched the door almost constantly, his worry and anger feeding one another. That stupid boy had broken his word to him and was most likely going to ruin everything for all of them. For all of China, for that matter. Is this how it happens, he asked himself? Does the course of history, the fate of an entire empire, turn on the impulsive actions of one stupid, impatient boy? Even as he asked himself the question, he knew that it was true. Great, purposeful acts, or small, rash, stupid ones: there was no difference.

Roughly, he yanked a comb through a horse's mane. A meeting would have to be called. He must gather all of the Flying Dragons together, the ones in the stable and the ones in the palace. They would have to find Li Chu-erh, and stop him, and lay down a definite plan.

He glanced again toward the door, expecting to be disappointed as he had been a hundred or more times already this morning, and stopped his work abruptly. A squat, robed figure pushing a covered cart moved toward the stable.

Kao Li-shih waited until the fat eunuch had delivered the food and was about to leave before approaching him.

"A thousand pardons, Friend," he said, putting his hand on the eunuch's arm. The other looked at him nervously, questioningly. Kao Li-shih was immediately discouraged, but smiled in a way meant to show him that he intended no harm. "Do you know of a eunuch at the palace named Chin-kang? I would like to get a message to him."

"I have never heard the name," the fat eunuch replied, turning away and beginning to move again.

"Wait," Kao Li-shih said, putting his hand out once more. "He has not been here very long. He arrived only six days ago, from Ch'ang-an."

"So much has happened recently," the other replied. "It is impossible to know who comes from where." The man's eyes darted about, resting for only a moment on Kao Li-shih.

Kao Li-shih fixed his own eyes on the other's face, forcing him to attend to what was being said to him.

"Yes," Kao Li-shih said with grave emphasis, "much has happened recently. That is why it is essential that I get a message to Chin-kang."

The fat eunuch looked at Kao Li-shih with weak, uncertain eyes. He was listening now, but reluctantly.

"Chin-kang," Kao Li-shih repeated the name. "A eunuch from Ch'ang-an. Tall, like me. About five years younger. He would be among the household staff. Tell him that he is wanted in the stables. We need his expert advice, and he should come as quickly as possible. If you do not know who he is, then ask others. Someone is bound to know who he is. You *must* find him," he declared firmly, never letting the man's eyes drift away from his own. "Repeat the name. It will help you to remember it."

The fat eunuch mumbled the name once or twice and hurried away without giving his word that he would deliver the message.

Kao Li-shih watched him leave and felt himself sinking into despair. The encounter had been entirely unsatisfactory. He had seen the fat eunuch's innate weakness while he was talking to him, and had despised him for it. Weakness and fear. What did the fool think he had to lose? Was he content to live under a tyrant, a traitor, merely to keep his own hide intact?

But the poet Chang Chiu-ling came into his mind again. You despised him as well, said a voice in his head. Stood and watched him while he spoke to you of murder, so full of earnest self-importance, and despised him, too, didn't you?

And who turned out to be the weaker, the more fearful, the more indecisive one?

It was beginning to rain hard again. Miserably, Kao Li-shih turned and went back into the stable. He had accomplished nothing.

:: :

Afternoon darkened into evening, and the rain resumed with renewed vigor. Kao Li-shih lay on the straw and listened. Where did it come from? How could the heavens pour forth day after day like this without finally drying up? The respite earlier in the morning and afternoon had been merely a deep breath, it seemed. Now it came down in earnest.

Lanterns flickered here and there in the stable as the men and eunuchs rested. Li Chu-erh had not returned, and no one had come from the palace in response to Kao Li-shih's message. There had been no more news of the fighting; Feng's and An Lu-shan's forces were, for now, at a stand-off many li northeast of the city. Tomorrow would be the seventh day.

He had spoken to the Dragons who were in the stable, about twenty-five in all, and had told them that he and one other would leave that night, rain or not, find their way into the palace, make contact, and return with a plan of some sort for the rest of them. Stealth was a fine art among the Flying Dragons, so there was reason for optimism, however faint. And he had convinced himself that the rain could even be to their advantage; probably there would be fewer guards about. Though they still had their weapons and could quietly dispatch anyone who saw them, they understood the necessity of avoiding being seen at all: leaving corpses behind them as they made their way into the palace would be very poor strategy.

He silently cursed Li Chu-erh for putting them in the position of being forced to act hastily, prematurely, without a solid plan. His mind seethed with visions of what could go wrong, and he maddened himself with imagining An Lu-shan's face, grinning and victorious.

Rest, Kao Li-shih, he told himself. Close your eyes for a few hours. Forget all of it. One way or another, it will be over soon. He stared at a flickering lantern flame, shut his eyes, concentrated on the sound of the rain, and dozed.

He did not descend fully into sleep, but remained aware of the passage of time. After about two hours, murmuring voices brought him to attention. He opened his eyes and saw the glint of rich gold brocade on the jacket of a man approaching him across the floor of the stable. A fine long sword flashed at his side and a regal topknot was silhouetted on his head. He recognized that royal stride. Kao Li-shih was paralyzed and bewitched as the man came closer in the dim light.

It was Yang Kuo-chung.

Kao Li-shih held his breath and forgot everything as the man came to where he lay in the straw, stood for a moment, then dropped to one knee beside him.

He released his breath. It was not Yang Kuo-chung. It was An Ching-hsu, transformed into a prince.

::

"I am sorry it took me so long to return, but you must understand," An Ching-hsu said discreetly, offering Kao Li-shih a flask of wine that he brought out from under his jacket. They had gone to a corner of the stable where they could talk by themselves. "I have been with my father almost constantly."

Kao Li-shih raised the flask and sipped. Again, he recognized the taste: the Emperor's wine.

"I had to show him that I am the perfect filial son," An Ching-hsu said with only a touch of irony.

"So he took you back," Kao Li-shih said. "I was quite sure he had lopped your head off."

"He almost did," An Ching-hsu said, laughing. "But look at me. Instead, he made me a prince."

"You cannot know how relieved I am to see you. But we have a problem. Li Chu-erh has disappeared. We must find him."

An Ching-hsu put a reassuring hand on Kao Li-shih's arm.

"He is safe and will not be taking any action on his own. He is in the eunuchs' quarters, under the watchful eyes of the Flying Dragons. When he left the stables early this morning, before the sun was up, he went to the kitchens. We are fortunate indeed that the first person to see him was one of our own—a Flying Dragon emptying a slop pail outside. He was brought to me. I spoke to him myself. He expressed his own impatience and told me about yours, and I knew that I could not afford even another hour. I told him that the waiting was nearly over and that I would personally come to see you tonight, no matter what. There is a plan, Kao Li-shih.''

Kao Li-shih felt a dark, dangerous thrill in his limbs and stomach. This, he knew, would be real. They leaned closer together, though they knew that no one was listening.

"The celebration begins tomorrow night," An Ching-hsu said in a barely audible whisper. "I have been observing my father closely. I know his little habits well." He smiled. "And there is one in particular that will be his undoing."

∷

An Lu-shan decided that he would dedicate the fireworks to his son, the new crown prince. An Ching-hsu had surprised him—first by turning up alive, then by being audacious enough to beg his father's forgiveness. He had not seen the boy since the disaster of the bowstrings, had decided that he was surely dead, and had also decided that that was a good thing. When word had been brought to him that a young man claiming to be his son had appeared in the palace kitchens and wished to see him, he had nearly ordered them to kill the intruder. But curiosity had got the better of him. He decided that he would have a look at this pretender.

He had been wet and filthy, barely recognizable—but definitely his son An Ching-hsu. But An Lu-shan could see that he was a different person, too. In his memory was the image of a half-grown brat, decidedly on the scrawny side. But An Ching-hsu, in the year or so since An Lu-shan had seen him, had grown and solidified. He almost looked like a man.

His first impulse had been anger. The cowardly, craven pup had deserted him and now came crawling back to beg forgiveness and to share in the spoils of his father's victory. He should have him beaten and sliced into pieces. And he almost did. But the boy had got down on his knees and wept, and implored, and renounced his past. He had grabbed hold of his father's hand and had wiped his eyes on his father's robe. And An Lu-shan had had a strange experience—one that he had heard about from other men, but had not yet known personally: for the first time, An Lu-shan, looking at his son's face, had seen himself looking back.

He had spared him. And he had made him get drunk with him. If you are going to be a man, and be my son, then you are going to drink like a man.

And he had dressed him in finery. This, too, was a rare and completely novel pleasure. He had him scrubbed and combed, and was vastly pleased by the fine figure An Ching-hsu cut in flashing silks and embroidery. Was it possible that this was the sly, insolent creature who had caused him so much trouble? Whom he had been forced to beat and reprimand at every turn? An Lu-shan had obviously done his work well: the cowardly streak that had always irritated him so much was gone. He had looked at his son with drunken, approving eyes. The workings of nature were truly incomprehensible.

He, An Lu-shan, had a crown prince. Now he was a true emperor. And tonight, fireworks on the river and the turning of the great geared orrery-clock in synchronicity with Heaven would commemorate the death of the old dynasty and the birth of the new.

They had tried to argue with him, to tell him that the rain made it impossible. You will find a way, he had ordered. Nothing is impossible. And nature had seemed to be accommodating him: during the night, the rain grew gentler; by morning, it had stopped. His orders were that the fireworks should begin as soon as it was dark.

In the afternoon, he stood on a high balcony that gave him a good view of the main river that ran through the city. He could see the workers setting up the pyrotechnics on a ceremonial barge under the direction of the nervous little expert whom he had imported from Ch'ang-an. He had ordered the best, the cleverest, and the most extravagant display. There would be fire trees, peach blossoms, pinwheels, and flame flowers. Rockets would travel to the sky and explode in a million spiraling, glowing, undulating snakes, dazzling the upturned eyes of the city. And they would be seen beyond the city: the soldiers and generals who were fighting to the northeast would see them too, he fancied.

Perhaps Feng himself would see them. His old friend, now his enemy. He remembered how he used to worry that Feng would die in one of his far-off campaigns. But Feng seemed to be charmed. Nothing ever touched him —no Muslim sword, no Tibetan arrow. And now, even though fate had decreed that they be pitted against each other, he still found himself hoping that Feng would somehow be spared.

He looked at the sky. It was angry and gray, but no rain fell. Below, on the fireworks barge, he saw that the pyrotechnics master was having his men suspend canopies of heavy oiled cloth over the deck. This made him angry. The man was showing poor faith if he thought such protective measures were necessary. He would order him to take them down. How could the people believe in his mandate to rule if they saw that he had to worry about the weather like an ordinary man? His troubles with water were over. The world would know that.

As he turned to go inside, intending to issue the order that the canopies must come down, a single small droplet hit the back of his neck. Another, gentle as a lover's kiss, fell on his hand. Why was it that Li Lin-fu always chose to speak in his mind at such moments? Perhaps you'd best leave the canopies up, Old Fellow, the dead chief minister admonished. A Mandate from Heaven might be more complicated than you suppose. Shut up, Lizard, An Lu-shan growled, and returned to his post on the balcony.

For the rest of the afternoon, An Lu-shan kept a vigilant eye on the heavens. A few drops fell from time to time, and thunder rolled and muttered occasionally in the distance, but evening was approaching and so far he had been spared any real rain. In the kitchens, an imperial feast was being prepared. The dancers and musicians were getting ready for their performance that night, and his guests—generals and some court officials who had been ordered to attend—were preparing to convene.

Military news was brought to him: the two armies had taken advantage of the break in the weather and were moving toward another engagement. At stake was the important Tsi Valley Pass which gave access to the city. By morning, he was sure, the battle would be over, and Feng's army dispersed and decimated. The city and the empire would be his.

Wasn't it always meant to be? Hadn't he served the empire faithfully and hadn't the empire demonstrated her need for him? Hadn't it been destiny at every turn in his life moving him inexorably toward this moment? Hadn't his very own mother died in order to start him on the long journey that put him here, on this balcony, in this city?

He had no intention of postponing his celebration any further. The rain had stopped. Heaven's intent was clear. He looked with satisfaction on the dying afternoon. The sun was nearly down; in a mere hour or so, it would be dark.

: :

Kao Li-shih watched the dancing horses being put through their paces in the large covered corral adjoining the stables. They were rehearsing for their performance tonight at An Lu-shan's private party. Riderless, the animals lifted their hooves gracefully and in unison in time to a lively rhythm beaten out on a small drum by the master trainer. They dipped their beautiful arched necks while they pranced and wove in and out and around one another in practiced precision in response to the master's shouted commands. They were splendid, superb; but Kao Li-shih could scarcely focus his attention on the spectacle.

In only a few hours, he and the others would be leaving the stables along with the animals. And if things went according to plan, T'ang Minghuang's magnificent dancing horses would be spared the ignominy of performing for a false emperor.

Anxiously, Kao Li-shih left the rail and went to where he could peer up beyond the roof of the corral. The late afternoon sky had a threatening aspect, and a few drops fell here and there, but that was all. Please, he silently implored the gray clouds, hold out just a little bit longer. You can do that, can't you?

He returned to his position at the rail. Presently, another eunuch approached and stood next to him.

"Master Kao," he said quietly, "the army of General Feng and An Lu-shan's rebel army have met. The word is that if Feng breaks through, then the city will inevitably fall to him."

"And how does it look?" Kao Li-shih asked.

"They say that the fighting is hard and bloody. But they also say that An Lu-shan's soldiers are perhaps losing their motivation. There are reports of desertions, too."

Kao Li-shih nodded, but said nothing. Striving to contain the anxiety rising in his chest, he returned his gaze to the animals in the ring. He and his companion watched in silence as the horses formed themselves into two circles, one inside the other, and pivoted on their polished hooves.

: :

"Now we will drink in honor of the new crown prince," An Lu-shan said, raising his cup. His generals grinned and raised their cups enthusiastically; the handful of officials sitting with them also raised their cups, though somewhat reticently. An Lu-shan looked at their solemn, ill-at-ease expressions. "You will soon be used to me, my friends," he chided them. "Time will take care of that." An Ching-hsu grinned back at his father. "If you find it difficult to look at *my* ugly face, then look at my son's instead. Look on the comely face of the future Emperor of China. But you *will* drink, whether it is in my honor or his!" He drained his cup and wiped his mouth with his sleeve. They sat at a table in An Lu-shan's private quarters. Soon, when it was dark, they would watch the fireworks from the balcony.

"Father, your cup is empty again. Let me fill it," An Ching-hsu said, bringing the pitcher around to him. After the wine had been poured, An Lu-shan seized the boy's arm possessively and held it.

A low peal of thunder sounded in the sky. He listened for a moment, then went on talking. They had been hearing thunder all day, and it had meant nothing.

"How many of you have sons?" he asked the men at the table. A few of them held up their hands. "Then you know how it is. You are disgusted with your son for years. You despise him. You wonder how such a creature could ever have come from you." He gave An Ching-hsu's arm a shake and gazed up at him. "You think that you should have drowned him like a puppy when he was born—before he had a chance to disappoint you and disgrace you. Eh? Eh?" He laughed and shook the young man's arm some more.

"But then something happens! It is nature, my friends. It is a miracle.

It is like winter turning into summer. It is like . . ." He groped for the image he wanted. "It is like one of those ugly worms that turns into a butterfly. Suddenly, nature gives you a gift. A friend, an equal. An ally. A man! Behold, the ugly worm transformed," he said, giving his son's arm a final shake and shoving him away fondly. He looked around at the faces of his guests. "It is Time, gentlemen. Time and Nature working together." He grinned at the officials with the solemn faces. "Time and Nature," he repeated. "The two things that are going to change the way you look at me."

As he finished speaking these words, thunder sounded again, louder this time, and closer. He cast an anxious eye in An Ching-hsu's direction. The youth jumped to his feet and went out on the balcony.

"It is all right, Father." An Ching-hsu came back in and sat down again.

An Lu-shan relaxed, took another drink, and looked around again at the officials and generals at the table.

"Time, gentlemen. Time has a plan for each and every one of us." His own words sounded impressive to him. The philosopher emperor, he thought. That is what history will call me: the philosopher emperor. Or the warrior-philosopher emperor. He liked it. "In one hundred years," he said wisely, warming to his subject, "not a single one of us will be sitting here at this table. Why? Because Time will have taken care of us."

The officials took this pronouncement without any change of expression; the generals looked at each other, laughed, shook their heads, or gazed admiringly at An Lu-shan.

While he was talking, a soft, gentle pattering had begun overhead. No one spoke at the table now; they sat and listened to the ominous sound. An Lu-shan stood abruptly.

"It is dark enough. We will wait no longer. The display will begin *now*."

An Ching-hsu rose to his feet as well.

"But, Father—"

"It will begin *now*!" An Lu-shan cut him off. "I am sending the order! You!" he said to one of his generals. "Carry the order to the pyrotechnics master personally for me. It is to begin!"

The general hurried from the room. An Lu-shan and the others went out onto the balcony. Light, sparse droplets sprinkled down onto their heads.

"It is nothing," An Lu-shan said. "It will pass."

"Father," said An Ching-hsu, "don't you think it would be wise to wait a bit? It is not fully dark yet and—"

"I have had enough waiting to last me a lifetime," An Lu-shan interrupted harshly. "It is *waiting* that ruins it all. It is *waiting* that turns your resolve to dust. *Waiting* is for women. I am through with it!"

Presently, the general whom he had sent down with the order reappeared, breathless from the exertion of running.

"The pyrotechnics master says we must wait. He says if the rain increases, everything will be ruined."

"Tell him *he* will be ruined if he does not begin immediately," An Lu-shan said angrily.

The general left with haste to deliver the message.

The rain came down steadily, softly. On the fireworks barge, lanterns had been lit as darkness fell. From their vantage point on the balcony, they could see men moving about on the deck and could hear occasional shouted orders, though the words were unintelligible. Now there was arguing: though the figures were indistinct, it was plain that the pyrotechnics master was vigorously protesting An Lu-shan's order. He and the general who delivered the order stood on the deck shouting at one another.

The general, apparently, prevailed. An Lu-shan watched with satisfaction as the workers began to roll back one of the protective canopies.

An Lu-shan watched a flaming torch being carried from one of the lanterns to the vicinity of the flimsy wooden frames in the center of the barge. His eyes followed as fire was touched to a naphtha-soaked wick and then snaked its way toward one of the frames: the frame exploded into a whirling wheel of light that sent sparks shooting out into the night. An Lu-shan and his generals drank a noisy toast. An Lu-shan pulled An Ching-hsu forward.

"I dedicate the firemaster's works tonight to the new crown prince!" Familiar words came to his lips then, though he could not remember where he had heard them before: "He is mine, he is yours!"

As he spoke, the rain began to fall harder. Shouts came from below. Fire was touched to a second wick; it traveled, hissing and sparking, along the coiled length to the next wooden frame. The first fire wheel still spun; now the second one began to move, spinning in the opposite direction. Around and around it went, picking up speed until it matched the first, the sparks from both intermingling like hundreds of shooting stars. An Lu-shan stared at the two wheels: like two great, angry demon eyes, he thought.

By now, the deck of the barge was slick with rain, the fire from the spinning wheels reflected in the wet surface. Men ran to and fro with pieces of the heavy cloth, trying to shield the remaining wooden frames and other apparatus from the steadily increasing downpour. An Lu-shan felt his excitement growing. He was witnessing a battle between the two great forces of nature: fire and water. The two could never coexist; one of them always had to win.

The next wick was lit. The fire traveled a few paces, then went out. It was lit again. It raced along the wick, but before it could reach the wooden frame, it went out. The first two fire wheels were still spinning, but they were fading and beginning to slow. Quickly, while one man tried again to light the wick, several others carrying torches ran to the left of the frames, applied fire to a row of dark shapes, then jumped back out of the way.

One of the rockets shot up into the air trailing stars behind it, but before it reached even a quarter of its full altitude, it arced downward and extinguished itself with a hiss in the dark river. The two spinning wheels had used up their momentum; now they hung skeletally, a few stray tongues of flames burning here and there. The next rocket rose a few feet, then descended to the deck where it writhed like an angry fish hauled from the water, spewing its phosphorescent light in all directions while the men shouted and dodged the sparks. Another rocket did not even rise, but sat on its base spitting and sputtering for several minutes before dying entirely, extinguished by the rain that fell straight down now with remorseless intensity.

The men on the barge gave it up. The ones holding the oiled cloths dropped them and ran. Only two or three lanterns remained lit; An Lu-shan could see the small flames bobbing about and heard the shouts of the pyrotechnics master trying in vain to maintain order. The scene dissolved into chaos. Then the last lanterns went out, and nothing remained but darkness.

An Lu-shan's guests had retreated into the room; only he and An Ching-hsu remained on the balcony, the water streaming down from their heads, their clothing drenched. An Lu-shan shouted into the darkness.

"Fools! Return to your positions! Light the lanterns!"

"Father," An Ching-hsu said, holding his arm, "they cannot hear you. It is impossible. Forget about it. We can have fireworks any time, but not in this rain!"

An Lu-shan turned on him angrily.

"And who is this speaking? Is this the insolent child who required a daily beating? Has he returned? Has he come back to plague me?" For a moment, the two faced each other, and it was as if they had gone back ten years in time. An Lu-shan thought he could see that same look on his son's face, the look that had infuriated him countless times: a passive, reticent hatred, locked away behind the eyes, never put into words, but always there.

"Father," An Ching-hsu said quietly. "We can do this again. We can have a display ten times as grand as this one. We will make them forget completely that this ever happened."

An Lu-shan stared at An Ching-hsu. His rage began to lose its momentum, like the dying fire wheels. He was right. They would make them forget. He and his son together would make them forget all about this. This was no insolent boy standing in front of him. This was no devious child in need of a thrashing. This was a man, his son.

He laughed. He was drunk and his clothing was soaked. He was a fat, wet, drunken fool, standing out in the rain shouting like a madman. He put his hands on An Ching-hsu's shoulders and laughed.

"We have a party to attend, do we not?" he said to his son.

"We do," An Ching-hsu replied, pulling him toward the door. "And they are waiting for us."

: :

When Kao Li-shih heard raindrops on the roof of the stable, he nearly despaired. All day, there had been thunder and thick, gray skies, but nothing worse. Kao Li-shih felt as if it were only the sheer force of his will that had kept the heavens from opening up; but his will was obviously not strong enough. Now night was falling, and nature, in its infinite perversity, chose this moment to send more rain down upon them. Nobody in the stable spoke. they sat and listened as the sound grew from a mere suggestion to a vigorous roar, drowning, it seemed to them, the careful plans they had laid for later that night.

The horses were ready for their gala appearance. They had been brushed until their coats were glossy, and brilliant ribbons of silk had been braided into their manes and tails. They were in fine form. With all the attention they had been receiving, they seemed to know that tonight would not be just another night. The horses, their master trainer, and all the helpers were waiting to be summoned.

Rain or not, the horses would perform. The palace had a huge, covered arena for just such a purpose, with a covered walkway leading there from the stables. And the men in charge of the horses, the eunuchs among them, would accompany the animals. What was crucial was that An Lu-shan not be prevented, because of the rain, from carrying out a certain highly esoteric little ritual, strictly of his own invention, the amazing details of which An Ching-hsu had whispered into Kao Li-shih's ear the night he returned.

Alternate plans presented themselves in Kao Li-shih's weary mind. An Lu-shan will die, he tried to assure himself. If not tonight, then another night. Be patient, Kao Li-shih. Then he thought of Li Chu-erh, somewhere in the palace, and felt a fresh wave of despair.

But Kao Li-shih's introspection was interrupted. He raised his head and looked toward the ceiling, then looked around at the others, who looked at him and each other with slowly spreading smiles.

The rain had stopped. As abruptly as it had begun, it had stopped.

: :

During the walk from the stables, when they had almost reached the arena near the palace, Kao Li-shih and the other eunuchs quietly separated themselves from the men accompanying the horses and fell back into the darkness beyond the covered walkway. The stablehands closed their ranks and kept on walking, lanterns swinging. Following the instructions they had been given by An

Ching-hsu, the eunuchs made their way through dark courtyards and along paths and walkways to a high garden wall. One by one, they scaled it and dropped to the ground on the other side.

Kao Li-shih stood still for a few moments and listened. He could hear the running water of a vigorous stream nearby. At the other end of the walled garden, fifty paces away, light spilled from an arched doorway; strains of music carried from the doorway over the sound of the water. He moved about fifteen paces in the direction of the stream and became aware of a prodigious dark shape in front of him, like a small tower. He put his hand out and touched smooth wood: now he could hear the groaning and sighing of a great moving internal mechanism and could feel the vibrations of slowly turning gears and wheels.

Though An Ching-hsu had told him what he would find here, Kao Li-shih could scarcely believe the reality of it: here was the grand wood and bronze orrery that had belonged to Chief Minister Li Lin-fu—the miraculous, mysterious, infinitely complex mechanism that measured the motions of the stars and planets as well as the hours in the lives of men, that had sat for decades on the Chancellery grounds. Many was the time Kao Li-shih and the Emperor had marveled at the water-driven machine, the invention of a monk and one of Li Lin-fu's most prized possessions. For the dead chief minister, the astronomical clock had been the height of rapture: it translated, so he had said to the Emperor, the pure mathematics of the heavens into a microcosm within the grasp of humankind.

And An Lu-shan had disassembled and transported it from Ch'ang-an to Loyang—along with the technicians in charge of maintaining and adjusting the intricate system of gears, wheels, escapements, linkages, and chain drives—and had set it up again here in this garden: at what effort, Kao Li-shih could scarcely imagine.

He was in the right place. Kao Li-shih gave a low whistle and waited. He heard a rustling sound to his left.

"Master Kao," a voice whispered in the darkness, so softly and so close to his ear that it startled him.

It was Li Chu-erh—an honored guest at this occasion that the Flying Dragons had planned for the new "Emperor" of China.

"You are here," Kao Li-shih whispered thankfully, and clasped the boy's hand for a moment. And Li Chu-erh was not alone. Kao Li-shih discerned other figures moving toward him out of the darkness: the rest of the Flying Dragons, the ones who had joined with the household eunuchs and gone to the palace. He gave a second whistle, higher this time, and moved back toward the wall, pulling Li Chu-erh with him. The Flying Dragons moved into their positions; now they had only to wait.

Sitting on a cold rock, Kao Li-shih listened to the distant, familiar sounds of the Pear Garden Orchestra carrying from the doorway at the far end of the garden. They were playing a tune composed many years ago by the Emperor himself. He closed his eyes, and the music transported him to another time, another life: he was hearing the joyful sounds of one of the Emperor's and consort's parties at the hot springs. He could see them smiling at one another in that way that had seemed to him like a conspiracy. Where was the Emperor now? Where was the consort? He pictured a vast, rocky landscape stretching hundreds, thousands of li, and the two lovers struggling over it, tiny as ants, moving apart from each other, then near, then apart again, and never knowing it.

He wondered about the workings of the barbarian's mind: did An Lu-shan know that what he was playing as a tribute to himself at his sham celebration was from the heart and mind of the man he had betrayed? Did he know it, and derive some sort of perverse satisfaction from it? Or did he think that he was in some way "honoring" his predecessor by playing his music?

Or was he so ignorant and blind that he was not even aware of the irony of his choice?

Whichever it was, Kao Li-shih knew that the musicians of the Pear Garden played through their tears this evening.

He looked up at the sky. There was a break in the dense clouds, the first he had seen for almost two weeks. A patch of glittering stars showed through. He stared, transfixed. He had forgotten about stars, so accustomed had he become to a low, opaque sky. He felt a heavy lid of oppression lifting off him; the hole in the clouds was a window that opened into infinity. His trapped, constricted soul was set free.

: :

An Lu-shan listened to the music of the Pear Garden with tender sentimentality. The tunes they played revived for him the sense of warm camaraderie that he had shared with his father the Emperor and caused a most pleasant, comforting picture to take shape in his mind: he saw the Emperor coming home, coming back to court, and living out his years in serene retirement while his "Lucky Baby" ruled the empire.

An Lu-shan swayed to the music and shut his eyes in pleasant contemplation. Minghuang could devote his last years to his artwork, his histories, and his music. It was all he ever really wanted anyway. He never wanted to be an emperor. Hadn't he told An Lu-shan as much countless times? I will do it for you, Father, An Lu-shan pledged to the hazy image of the Emperor in his mind. When all of this is over. When things have settled down. When they have learned to love me.

He was working hard tonight. With a full pitcher of wine in his hand, he moved among his guests, making sure there was always a smile on his face.

The An Lu-shan who had been so well loved at court was a carefree, fun-loving sort, unburdened by concerns of war and politics. If they were going to love him the way they had before, they must not see any trace of gravity, care, or worry in his face or manner. He must be their "Lucky Baby" again. And he had to show them that nothing had changed; that when it came to merriment, fun, and mirth, he was the master. He had told himself that it would take time—but they *would* learn to love him. Every emperor, he knew, was characterized in history by some outstanding trait. There were scholar emperors, warrior emperors, builder emperors, and humanitarian emperors. He would be the emperor of mirth, the poet emperor of mirth, loved by his people.

Lowering his weight into his chair again, he watched the musicians, letting his fond eyes rest in turn on each woman's face. The ladies of the Pear Garden Orchestra had always been his special friends. They had been with him on his first night at court, when the Lady of Kuo had gently coerced him into playing, dressed in ladies' clothes, before the Emperor. They had been his allies, the ones who had helped him discover the unique talent he had for amusing people and making them laugh. He was grateful to them for that. He had prepared a wonderful surprise for their benefit this evening; he wanted to let them know that he had not forgotten.

His officers were enjoying themselves hugely. Most of them were provincials who had never seen anything but huts and hovels, and had never eaten anything but tough meat and coarse bread. And of course, they had never seen anything at all like the palace, the orchestra, or the harem dancers. An Lu-shan smiled. The men reminded him of himself years ago. He watched their eyes. They were having trouble deciding where to look at each moment—at the dancers whirling in their shimmering silks, or at the fragrant trays of food, each one a work of art, that were being carried into the room.

But he did not like the solemn, constrained expressions on the faces of the dancers. He doubted that his officers took any particular notice, but it was plain to him that the dancers' faces did not match the music or the steps. If the dancers would not smile, then neither would the rest of the guests—the magistrates and ministers who sat quietly as if they were at an official audience. Or a funeral. He looked around. Maybe it was time for his little surprise.

Where was An Ching-hsu? He wanted to make sure his son did not miss anything. He looked around the crowded room, but did not see him. Then he glanced toward the open doorway that led to the Garden of Scented Plums, and saw An Ching-hsu coming through it from outside. He smiled. He was gratified to see that already he and his son had established a royal family tradition. No imperial chamberpots for them! When the wine was flowing, how much pleasanter to go outside to relieve oneself and let the night air cool one's head while the urine flowed.

He caught An Ching-hsu's eye. His son came toward him. An Lu-shan noticed again how splendid he looked in his royal attire—how much like a prince. When An Ching-hsu was standing before him looking down at him where he sat, An Lu-shan said nothing for a few moments, but merely looked back at his son, admiring the vision of royalty that he presented. A questioning look appeared on An Ching-hsu's face. An Lu-shan smiled slyly and raised his pitcher to his mouth to take a drink, but found it empty.

"Let me get you some more, Father," the boy said quickly, taking the empty pitcher from his father's hands and replacing it, almost before An Lu-shan realized what was happening, with a full one that had been on the table nearby.

An Lu-shan took a long drink of wine, then gestured for An Ching-hsu to lean close to him.

"You must take my place for a little while," he breathed into his son's ear. An Ching-hsu drew back and looked at him with an alarmed expression.

"Where are you going?" he asked sharply.

"No, no, no," An Lu-shan said, laughing. "You have the wrong idea. I am only going to leave the room for a bit. Just long enough to . . ." He paused, searching his wine-soaked brain for the right words. He didn't want to reveal too much; the surprise was partly for An Ching-hsu, too. "Just long enough to prepare myself," he concluded enigmatically.

An Ching-hsu looked relieved, though still questioning.

"To prepare yourself for what?" he asked.

An Lu-shan seized his wrist and pulled him close again. "A surprise. A little surprise," he whispered. "Now help me up!" he ordered.

An Ching-hsu beckoned one of the household eunuchs in attendance, who came over to them. The two of them pulled on An Lu-shan's arms, heaving him to his feet. An Lu-shan pushed his son down into the chair.

"Just wait," he said. "Don't go anywhere." He grinned. "And keep your eyes on the dancers," he said meaningfully.

An Ching-hsu sat in his father's chair and tried to contain his nervous agitation. He watched An Lu-shan's form until it disappeared from view; then his eyes moved back in the other direction, to the doorway leading to the garden.

The garden where the eunuchs waited in the dark.

An Ching-hsu had intercepted a bit of military news. The Tsi Valley Pass had virtually fallen to the forces of General Feng. An Lu-shan's army, weakened by desertion and heavy casualties, was being forced back farther every hour. It was almost over. An Ching-hsu had told the messenger to tell no one, that he would see to it personally that his father received the news.

But he had not told An Lu-shan what he knew. Instead, he had gone out to the garden and whispered it into the ear of Kao Li-shih, who had squeezed his arm so hard with excitement and gratitude that he could still feel the eunuch's fingers on his flesh.

Wanting to keep his senses absolutely intact, he had purposely refrained from drinking very much wine tonight; but now, fearing that his heart might burst through his chest, he took a long drink to soothe himself. He let his eyes drift over the strange scene: his father's drunken, boisterous generals; the taciturn, unhappy-looking court officials; and the dancers and musicians performing as if they expected to die tomorrow. They avoided looking at him, just as they avoided looking at his father; he knew that, to them, there was no difference between father and son. He wished he could tell them what he knew—that An Lu-shan's "reign" could end this very night.

But they would know soon enough, he told himself. He hoped fervently that his father did not somehow find out during his absence from the party, while he was "preparing himself," about Feng's major advance toward the city.

Preparing himself? An Ching-hsu tried to guess his father's meaning. Preparing himself for a "little surprise"? Such words, which would sound innocuous coming from anyone else's lips, took on a mysterious and ominous quality coming from his father, the man who had once invited some Censorate eunuchs to dine. He had prepared a "little surprise" for them, too, hadn't he?

He found his rising emotions vying unpleasantly with one another. Something was occuring that he had not anticipated at all, and which surprised and confused him.

When he had approached An Lu-shan from across the room after delivering his news to Kao Li-shih in the garden, he had seen a look of pride and benevolence on his father's face that had made him feel, for a brief, dreadful instant, like a betrayer. And he had known then that however much he hated his father—and he reminded himself now of all the reasons why he hated him, and had hated him for so much of his life—that he could not be the one to actually put a sword into him. He knew that, when the moment came, he would defer to Li Chu-erh. It was not at all what he had expected to feel; a thousand times, from his earliest childhood on, he had imagined himself killing his father, in a thousand different ways. But now that the time was imminent, he found that his hands trembled with clammy dread and that he would be unable to do it.

He would be able, he thought, to lead him to his execution and witness it. But he could not do the deed himself.

He had seen that look of fondness and pride on his father's face, and it had aroused a deep longing in him that he had never known before. A part of him wished painfully that he could be the filial son that his father believed him to be. He wished that his father were someone else. He wished for a different life, a life where he could bask in the pride of a father worthy of his devotion. And he knew that it could never be. Because soon, very soon now, his father must die.

He started to raise the cup to his lips, but put it back down. He was getting too close to feeling drunk. That wouldn't do at all. His nervous eyes moved from doorway to doorway and around the great hall, surveying the crowd, straining to see his father's rotund shape. One of the generals came and put a heavy, comradely arm over his shoulders for a moment, drank a toast to the new Emperor, breathing his pungent breath into An Ching-hsu's face, and staggered on his way. The musicians finished their tune and began another. And still An Lu-shan had not returned.

A sense of foreboding began to steal over An Ching-hsu now. Maybe An Lu-shan had somehow found out what had been planned for tonight, and Kao Li-shih and the rest of the Flying Dragons all lay dead in the garden at this very moment—and perhaps he was next.

Or perhaps his father planned to burn down the palace, with everyone in it. Was that why he had left? Was that the "surprise"? None of these things were too extreme, or too brutal, or beyond An Lu-shan's capabilities. Didn't he, An Ching-hsu, better than anyone except Li Chu-erh, know the depth of his father's cruelty and cunning?

His chest and throat constricted, and he thought for a moment that he actually smelled smoke. He stood up from his chair, ready to run, his eyes on the open doorway. Of course, that could be a trap, too. They would run outside and be slaughtered, or stay inside and be burned. He stood, paralyzed, unable to breathe, move, or act, the music tinkling absurdly in his ears.

A great, explosive guffaw of laughter from the front of the hall turned his head abruptly toward the musicians and dancers. An Ching-hsu stared, not quite believing what his eyes were telling him.

His father had returned. Dressed in a glittering, swirling costume identical to those the dancers wore but specially made to accommodate his pendulous bulk, the enormous, bearded "Emperor" minced, with ludicrous little steps in time to the music, among the pretty young women. He wore on his mouth a coy smile which he bestowed on his generals, who laughed and howled with incredulous delight.

Slowly, An Ching-hsu sat down again. Here was the "surprise" his father had promised. Unable to help himself, he lifted his cup and drank, his hand trembling.

An Ching-hsu knew about his father's legendary antics impersonating the lady musicians and dancers of the court, but had never actually witnessed the phenomenon. Was this, he asked himself, what had made the Emperor love An Lu-shan?

When the dancers moved to the left, An Lu-shan moved to the right. If they whirled in one direction, he whirled in the other. When they undulated their hands and arms with controlled grace, he waggled his own like a chicken trying to fly; when they dipped and rose in perfect fluid harmony, he bobbed like a child's puppet, always a beat or two behind, all the while casting anxious glances around himself at the dancers' faces, feet, and arms, trying to imitate them.

He pretended to trip over the trailing sash of his costume and sat down hard, legs sprawled, forcing the dancers to move around the obstruction. Then he remained there on the floor, eyes and mouth screwed up like a baby getting ready to cry. His generals hooted, whistled, and banged the tables with their hands and wine cups, their faces red and distorted with mirth. An Lu-shan raised his arms imploringly to the dancers moving past him, the way a baby does when it is asking to be helped to its feet.

But the dancers ignored him. None seized his hands and pretended to try to pull him up from the floor, as he seemed to expect them to do. They did not even smile. They moved around him, eyes carefully averted, as if they did not quite see the huge, foolish man in their midst. And the musicians, though they continued to play without interruption, lowered their solemn faces to their instruments. The ministers and officials in the audience also failed to respond, but sat quietly, watching, taking an occasional drink or bite of food.

The generals were ecstatic. One of them jumped up from his chair and onto the dance floor, grabbed An Lu-shan's outstretched hands, and heaved with all his might, in vain. One of his fellows joined him in the effort, then another. Two pulled on one arm, one on the other. A fourth came and pushed from behind. When An Lu-shan finally rose from the floor, the generals cheered, slapped one another with glee, and jumped up from their seats and danced.

An Lu-shan hopped and skipped in little circles, tripped again, and crawled on his hands and knees toward the musicians. He moved around behind the low dais where they sat, clambered onto it, then rose up kneeling in their midst, a set of tiny stone chimes in his enormous hands. He rocked his head from side to side, counting the beats, chimes poised next to his face, eyes wide with exaggerated anticipation, waiting for the exact right place to make his musical contribution. His generals stifled their laughter in the suspenseful moments, fixing their attention on him; when a pause between musical phrases arrived, he flourished and struck with his tiny hammer. The solitary, dainty, silly little sound of his stone chimes ringing out brought a fresh roar of approval and merriment from the officers. Through the din, the Pear Garden continued its song.

An Lu-shan took the applause with demure modesty. Then he looked around at his fellow musicians with an expression that candidly anticipated their profound amusement and their warm, comradely approval.

More than that, An Ching-hsu thought painfully, the look sought their love for him.

The musicians played, but did not lift their eyes. Their pale, exquisite, expressionless faces looked as though they had been carved from ivory. An Lu-shan turned his eager smile from one to the other in turn. Finding nothing, he looked back at his generals and shrugged.

An Ching-hsu had to look away. He knew that the next pair of eyes that his father would seek out would be his own. Even drunk and mad, An Lu-shan could read the thoughts in men's eyes, and An Ching-hsu did not want him to see the pathetic war of emotions that was probably plain on his face: the pity and regret, the anger and sorrow, the love and hate. And the guilt. He could not let him see even a small part of the guilt. He looked down at his hand resting on the table.

Let it be over soon, he thought. And let it be quick.

Presently, An Lu-shan, still in his costume, appeared at An Ching-hsu's side and lowered himself, grunting, into a chair. He was breathing hard from his exertions, and when An Ching-hsu looked up at him, he saw a heavy fatigue on his face. An Lu-shan seized the pitcher of wine and drank. He did not stop until it was empty, and it had been nearly full. Wiping his mouth, he looked at his son.

"I am working hard, and it is all for you," he said. "When you become emperor, they will already love you, and it will be because of me. You will be spared having to work so hard."

Before An Ching-hsu could reply, An Lu-shan started to push himself back up to his feet.

"This wine is moving through me fast," he muttered, turning in the direction of the doorway to the garden. An Ching-hsu leapt up from the chair.

"I will accompany you," he said quickly. He signaled to the eunuch floor attendant who had been nearby all evening, discreetly attentive, waiting for a sign from An Ching-hsu. Instantly, the eunuch was at An Lu-shan's side, supporting him. An Ching-hsu held his father's other arm, and they moved toward the door that led to the Garden of Scented Plums.

: :

It sounded to Kao Li-shih as if the machinery had heaved a gentle sigh. While he waited in the garden, alone with his thoughts, he had grown accustomed to certain rhythmic patterns of sound made by the moving clockwork gears and chains within the tower; now a new sound gently obtruded into his consciousness: a pause, a collective anticipatory rasp, a contraction of the great orrery's mechanical innards as they reached a place in their mathematically appointed progression. Something was about to happen.

On the second floor of the orrery, practically and symbolically placed one level below the bronze rings that re-created the motions of the stars and planets around the earth, a little army of soldiers carved from wood waited at attention, alerted by the vibrations that traveled up through their feet. In the center of the soldiers' circular axis, three poised bronze hammers drew themselves back, then struck, in exact succession, three disparately sized metal gongs. The sound brought the soldiers to life. They marched, in time to the syncopated three-note song, in a tight, prescribed circle, satisfied and fulfilled, happy only to serve.

Kao Li-shih had seen the soldiers many times in the light of day, and his attention had always been drawn to the expressions of fierce joy carved on their faces by the artisan who had made them. And he had always wondered: was it joy at simply being men? Or was it joy at being soldiers? Was it joy at the privilege of marching in time to the movements of the universe? The joy of single-minded unity? Whatever the source of their fixed, unfaltering, defiant joy, it was a secret that the soldiers kept to themselves, and Kao Li-shih had known that he would always be outside it.

Sitting in the dark garden, Kao Li-shih listened to the music of the bronze gongs marking the passage of another hour and pictured the soldiers' wooden faces. He also realized that he and the others had been waiting in the garden for less than an hour, this being the first time the gongs had sounded since they had been here. It seemed like three hours.

He shifted his position and looked up at the sky for the hundredth time. The clouds were drifting farther apart. The stars were spreading. The air was cool and sweet. He glanced again toward the lit doorway and felt something tighten inside himself, coiling for action, just like the water clock getting ready to strike: three figures had appeared in the doorway and were moving slowly toward the garden. One of them, the one in the middle, was An Lu-shan.

: :

Walking between his son and one of the household eunuchs who held his arm on the other side, An Lu-shan felt weary and suddenly very drunk. He had been all right inside, in the light, but now, out in the dark, he was not at all sure he would have been able to stand without help or make his way out into the garden. He felt detached from his legs and feet moving beneath him, as if they belonged to somebody else. He heard his voice humming the tune that the orchestra had just played.

Well, said Li Lin-fu, they certainly proved their love for you tonight. I was most impressed. Every leader should be loved like that.

"Shut up, Lizard," An Lu-shan said aloud. "They are only women. Stupid women."

"What did you say, Father?" An Ching-hsu asked.

"I said I don't care. Women are stupid creatures anyway."

Those ministers and officials as well? Are they also stupid women?

"Go to hell where you belong, Lizard," An Lu-shan muttered.

Your mother must have been the stupidest of them all. A very, very, stupid woman.

An Lu-shan halted abruptly.

"You have no right to even speak of her!" he declared angrily.

"Who, Father?" An Ching-hsu implored. "Who should we not speak of ?"

An Lu-shan stood still, eyes closed, and heard a familiar sound at the far end of the garden. The water clock was gonging. He giggled. A perfect time to make his "offering." The thought appealed to him very much.

"Never mind," he said to his son, and began walking again. "Hurry. We have to get there before it's finished." He stumbled in the darkness, and An Ching-hsu and the servant on his other side grabbed at him and steadied him.

The gongs were still sounding when they got within a few paces of the clock tower. They moved around to its north side, where the rain-swollen stream fed directly into the great water wheel that turned the main drive shaft of the orrery. An Lu-shan positioned himself, with the help of his companions, next to the rushing water, just upstream from the wheel. A cool spray bathed his hot face.

"Hold on to me," he ordered, freeing one hand to hike up the skirt of his dancing costume. He aimed in the dark for the place where he imagined that the rushing water met the wheel.

"This is for you, Lizard," An Lu-shan announced, just as the clock finished its gonging. "I dedicate this to your most revered and esteemed memory. My water helps drive your machine. My piss helps measure the motions of the heavens."

He giggled again. He was unleashing a veritable torrent, the accumulation of an entire evening of wine. It flowed out of him with a sharp, sensual feeling of relief. Almost as good as fucking, he thought, closing his eyes with pleasure. "I saved it up just for you," he said to the dead chief minister, and laughed at his little joke. Save it up, An Lu-shan. That's what the Emperor had always told him. Save it up.

When he was finished, he dropped his skirt. He groped, found the supporting arms again in the darkness, and leaned heavily on them. He moved away from the stream several steps, then stopped.

"What about you?" he said to An Ching-hsu. "Aren't you going to honor our chief minister's ghost? I think he will be insulted if you don't."

"I'd better drink some more wine, Father, if I'm going to make a decent offering. You've put me to shame."

An Lu-shan threw his head back and roared appreciatively. That was good. Very, very good.

"And you," he said, laughing, turning to the anonymous presence on his other side. "Don't you care to honor Li Lin-fu's memory?"

"I would be delighted," a low, familiar contralto voice answered. "But I am afraid it would be somewhat impractical."

The laughter expired in An Lu-shan's throat. The drunkenness vanished from his head and limbs like an abrupt awakening from a dream. The skin of the back of his neck contracted. He turned his face toward the source of the voice: someone very tall stood next to him in the darkness.

It was not possible. It was simply not possible. At that moment, the hands that held his arms tightened in a deadly grip, and he understood everything.

"You," An Lu-shan hissed. "I should have smelled you."

"But you didn't," Kao Li-shih answered.

With a mighty shrug, An Lu-shan jerked both arms free. Someone kicked the backs of his legs hard, toppling him. He hit the ground, knocking the air from his lungs; his head bounced on the rocky earth. He struggled to draw a breath. There was the scratch of a flint being struck. The sudden, brilliant light of a torch flaring to life blinded him painfully for a few seconds.

Then he saw: a tight circle of faces looked down on him. He fought to rise, but heavy feet pushed his limbs back to the ground and held them there. He looked around desperately: An Ching-hsu was nowhere to be seen. He opened his mouth to bellow for help, but a wadded piece of cloth was thrust harshly into it. He stared at the face of Kao Li-shih, his enemy. Vile, stinking, damned, pig-shit whore of a eunuch, he said with his eyes. You and I will meet in Hell.

Then someone knelt down and peered into his face.

It was Li Chu-erh.

: :

Kao Li-shih had known that An Lu-shan possessed the strength of three men, but the force with which he freed his arms took him by surprise and sent one of Kao Li-shih's own hands flying painfully against his mouth. And when An Lu-shan hit the ground, Kao Li-shih felt the earth shake with the impact. He must be brought down immediately, Kao Li-shih had warned the Flying Dragons; it is the only way. He is helpless when he is on the ground. We must bring him down, and keep him down.

The torch was lit, revealing their struggling quarry sprawled on the ground, ludicrously clad in the costume of a court dancer. So that's what you were doing tonight, Kao Li-shih thought as An Lu-shan was gagged and pinned. I am sorry to have missed the performance.

He stood in An Lu-shan's upward gaze of pure hatred and felt the intensity of it.

Li Chu-erh lowered himself so that his face was very close to that of his former master, who shifted his blazing eyes from Kao Li-shih to him.

"We bring you news, An Lu-shan," he said in a firm, quiet voice. "The fight is over, and you have lost. Your army has been defeated. Your old friend General Feng is on his way to the city at this very moment. He will be here with the rising sun. He will be very disappointed when he finds that you are already dead, but when he learns who it was who killed you, he will be glad and satisfied."

An Lu-shan raged and struggled under the grip of his captors, who pinned him, two and three men to each limb, with their full weight. Even so, Kao Li-shih could see that it still took all of their collective strength to hold him down, and he felt the full, frightening power of the life-force that they were about to extinguish, fighting now for its very existence.

Without removing his eyes from An Lu-shan's, Li Chu-erh extended an arm to one side. Somebody put a sword into his hand. He leaned close again.

"Look at my face, An Lu-shan. It is not the face of Li Chu-erh. It is the face of Death." He stood, holding the sword. He moved the blade down from An Lu-shan's heaving belly so that it was pointed directly at his groin. "But before you die, I am going to make you into one of us," he said. "I am going to make you just like me!" An Lu-shan bucked and writhed, the breath rattling in his nostrils, his eyes bulging from his head.

Kao Li-shih had to turn away from the spectacle. He had expected to find exquisite pleasure in every moment leading to An Lu-shan's death, but now, looking down on the doomed man, he found a strange sadness and horror in his heart. And he knew what it was: it was simply the pity of one creature for another.

"No, Li Chu-erh," he heard himself say, putting a hand on the young eunuch's arm. "No. Don't make him one of us. He doesn't deserve the honor."

Li Chu-erh held the blade where it was, stared hard at An Lu-shan for a few moments, then slowly, reluctantly, moved it back up to his belly. An Lu-shan ceased his struggling. His eyes met Kao Li-shih's. The two enemies looked at each other, and Kao Li-shih knew that An Lu-shan understood his unspoken message: that is for saving my life once. That is also for the times you brought pleasure and comfort to the Emperor.

Then Li Chu-erh lunged with his full weight behind the sword.

See, Li Lin-fu said, it is not so terrible. I was surprised at how easy it was. I, who fought it so hard for so many long years, right up until the last breath I drew, scarcely realized it had happened until it was over. And do you know, it suits me very well indeed. I have found myself able, finally, to do some real work. I am free to contemplate numbers, in all their beauty and purity, without distraction. It is more than contemplation. I am no longer several steps removed from them, trying to gain access to their secrets through formulas and calculations. I have actually become the numbers. They have absorbed me. I move within them. I am truly content, at last.

Let it go, "Lucky Baby." That is my advice to you. Let it go.

Epilogue

The old woman stepped nimbly over the splintered wood and shattered stone of broken ornamental rails. Along the gutted tunnel of what had been the outer corridor of the Han-yuan throne room, jagged shards of ruined pillars hung inward; overhead, unsupported lintels sagged precariously low. Farther down, the roof had caved in completely, making the way ahead almost impassible. Blue sky peeked through holes here and there in the fire-blackened walls of chambers off the corridor; forlorn, charred shreds were all that remained of lavishly embroidered window quilts.

Drawing on her pipe, the sweet-smelling smoke drifting around her head, Ming Wu leaned on the rail and scanned the vast courtyard north of the Ch'eng Tien Gate, surveying from her raised vantage point the palace terraces below her and far ahead. She took a small knife from the sack she carried and dug around in the pipe a bit, then tapped the bowl on the railing, letting the embers rain down on the stones below.

Nearly a quarter of a li ahead, a bristling forest of blackened timbers and the great expanse of marble stairs leading up to it were all that remained of the lofty Grand Harmony Audience Hall. Beyond that, the four-story crenellated towers of stone that had flanked the Lin-te Hall stood alone against the sky, keeping guard over nothing but a scorched pit between them nearby; one gray wall of the Vermilion Phoenix Tower that had dominated the heights of the Palace of Grand Enlightenment rose like an enormous lone jagged tooth. But the Flower-Shedding Brilliance Gallery and the Hall of Diligence in Government Affairs stood intact and untouched.

She put her pipe in her bag and turned away from the courtyard view. Wiping soot from the burned railing on the black of her robes, she studied the debris in front of her in the corridor and considered how to get past it and beyond to the stairs that led back down to the level of the courtyard. A piece of filigreed wooden spandrel dangled in front of her eyes; she gave it a light tug and stepped back out of the way as it crashed to the floor. Picking her way through heaps of rubble, she found a space between the fallen timbers and squeezed through; on the other side, the corridor was clear. Ming Wu made her way to the stairs.

The old man on the landing must have been dead for at least a week. Although he was not burned, the heat of the fires that had raged around him had dried and preserved him. He lay there in a most interesting position: like a statue of a running man that had been toppled. His stiff legs were spread in the perfect semblance of a long stride, and his hands and arms were crooked at his sides as if he had been carrying something. Ming Wu poked with her stick, raising flakes of ashes: papers. He had, when the awful moment arrived, chosen his treasures.

He lay on his side, his face turned toward the sky as though he had been looking back over his shoulder while he ran. One eyelid was sealed shut; the other was cracked open, revealing a narrow slit of yellowish eye. Ming Wu looked down as she stepped over him.

"It's all right, old minister," she said, waving her finger. "I agree with you. It is a good joke, isn't it?" She looked around the courtyard below with its piles of blackened timber and scorched brick. "I would have told you to leave a long time ago, but I don't believe you and I are acquainted with one another. Besides, I can see that you are the sort of fellow who does not listen well to advice. Stubborn and complacent, that's you, eh? No one listens to old Wu's advice, anyway. But she tries! What is your name?" she said, rolling him over with her foot so that he stared straight at her now with his cracked eye. "I saw plenty of others like you, just lying around here and there." She removed her foot so that he rolled stiffly back to his original position. "You should get together with the rest of them and talk over the problems of government." She turned, crossed the landing, and continued on her way.

The sack that Ming Wu carried contained some food: bread, a little wine, fruit, a piece of meat. She moved down a long hallway through thin shafts of pale sunlight slanting to the floor from tightly shuttered windows. The carpet beneath her feet was thick with dust and rodent droppings.

She stopped in front of a heavy wooden door. Pulling a key from her pocket, she unlocked the brass padlock that held it shut and passed through. She came to another locked door about twenty paces beyond the first, unlocked it, and passed through.

When she came to a third door, she stood in front of it for a moment as if listening for a sound on the other side. Then she snapped the key in the lock and pushed the door open.

The room beyond the door was stark but for a few pieces of furniture and a bed on which a figure reclined. A feeble movement in response to the sound of the door opening was the only sign that the person on the bed was alive. Ming Wu walked over and looked down on a woman, dirty and ema-

ciated, her tangled black hair spread out on the pillow. Her arms were tied
to her body with heavy bands of cloth. She opened her eyes and looked at
Ming Wu.

"So," Ming Wu said. "They didn't think to set you free when they fled,
and nobody found you."

The woman on the bed tried to speak through cracked, dry lips, but no
sound came out. Ming Wu pulled her to a sitting position and propped her
against the wall behind the bed. With her knife, she slit the bands of cloth
that held the woman's arms.

Ming Wu sat down on the bed, removed the jar of wine from the food
sack, and raised it to the mouth that was still trying to speak.

"Drink," she ordered.

Weakly, the woman sipped the wine. Ming Wu took a piece of bread
from the bag, poured a little wine on it to soften it, and held it under the
woman's nose. The woman responded by seizing the bread and devouring it
all at once. Ming Wu offered the jar again, and the woman drank greedily,
wine running down her chin.

"Hungry, eh?" Ming Wu said, and offered the meat and fruit.

The woman stuffed it into her mouth, then drank the rest of the wine.
Raising her eyes to Ming Wu's, she took a breath and spoke in a weak, scratchy
voice.

"Do you know where my father is?"

"Yes," Ming Wu replied. "I know where he is."

"I must speak to him. It is urgent," the woman said, trying feebly to
rise to her feet. Her legs trembled and gave way. She sat down heavily on the
bed once more and looked at Ming Wu with a face of sorrow and despair.

"He has been away from the city on an extended trip," Ming Wu said,
helping her to stand. "That is why he has been unable to speak to you."

"You see," the woman said, "there has been a terrible misunderstanding.
He blames himself for my death. He believes that I took my own life, but it
is not true." She lowered her voice to an urgent whisper. "I did not kill myself.
I was murdered!"

"Your father will be returning to the city very soon now," Ming Wu
said, walking the woman slowly across the room. "He is most eager to see
you."

The anxious face relaxed into joy at these words. They passed through
the open door and into the dusty, shadowy corridor.

Ming Wu gave her a reassuring squeeze on her bony shoulders. "You
will tell him yourself."

AFTERWORD

EMPEROR Minghuang returned to reclaim the plundered capital of Ch'ang-an in the summer of A.D. 757. The T'ang imperial armies had finally routed the last of An Lu-shan's rebels; the short-lived and illegitimate Yen dynasty was now as dead as its founder. Minghuang, emperor emeritus, returned with his son, the former Crown Prince Li Heng, to a city released from the oppression of a violent and sadistic occupation; and though they were welcomed with the joyful tears of a grateful and weary populace, victory was only a thin veneer.

The people of Ch'ang-an and China, having forgiven him his negligence and blindness, still loved their aged Emperor. For them, he was the symbol of a once just, peaceful, and prosperous nation. But that was only an illusion—one that the Emperor himself no longer accepted. Several times, amidst the exuberant cries of the tens of thousands who turned out to receive them, Li Heng (the Emperor Su-tsung) attempted to return the inherited robes of state to his father. And just as often, his father refused to take them back.

Now in his seventies, Minghuang saw with the unobstructed vision of hindsight that through his neglect and stubbornness China had suffered a disaster, the proportions of which can only be understood when measured against the horrors of our own century. It has been estimated that the Rebellion of An Lu-shan may have cost the lives of nearly one half of China's fifty-two million people. Some estimates are even higher. Historians have never been certain of the figures because the surviving population of China had become too transient to be counted in the official census rolls.

The rebellion also cost China its stable and centralized empire. Despite the fact that Li Heng took up the kingly burden upon his father's refusal, the T'ang never recovered, surviving in name only for another one hundred and fifty years. A once great empire, perhaps the greatest the world has ever seen, was reduced in its final days to a fragmented collection of loosely bound regions—ironically, a much closer approximation of the reality of the "Golden Age" of a millennium before that the Precious Consort had sought to emulate.

But it was a reality that was hardly desirable. Once again China was a decentralized, centrifugal, and feudal world of individual sovereignties—a land divided among warlords and noble families, military governors and ambitious generals who ultimately refused to give up those territories that they had so bravely recaptured for the T'ang.

The tyranny of Li Lin-fu had held China together and had given an empire, already past the vigor of its youth, a true golden age. The dictator had maintained a world of peace and prosperity, bought at a dear price. And with his death, it was over.

: :

Look to your numbers and your stars, Grand Councillor! What do they tell you now?

For the poet, **William James Kovanda III,** in whom the spirit of Li Po lives, raging quietly in the shadows of war:

> And still there is not peace in the world
> Strong soldiers yet surpass the useless pedants.
> But amid the vagaries of winds and dusts,
> What place is there for this old man?

—Tu Fu

(excerpted from the eighth-century poem "The Thatched Hut," translated by Daniel Altieri)